THE DARK SIDE
OF MIDNIGHT

THE
DARK SIDE of MIDNIGHT

FEATURING

THE OTHER SIDE OF MIDNIGHT

RAGE OF ANGELS

BLOODLINE

SIDNEY SHELDON

WILLIAM MORROW

An Imprint of HarperCollins*Publishers*

THE OTHER SIDE OF MIDNIGHT. Copyright © 1973 by The Sheldon Family Limited Partnership. Originally published by William Morrow and Company, Inc.

RAGE OF ANGELS. Copyright © 1980 by The Sheldon Family Limited Partnership. Originally published by William Morrow and Company, Inc.

BLOODLINE. Copyright © 1977 by The Sheldon Family Limited Partnership. Originally published by Warner Books in arrangement with HarperCollins Publishers and The Sheldon Family Limited Partnership.

THE DARK SIDE OF MIDNIGHT: FEATURING THE OTHER SIDE OF MIDNIGHT, RAGE OF ANGELS, AND BLOODLINE. Copyright © 2007 by The Sheldon Family Limited Partnership. All rights reserved. Printed in the United States of America. No part of this book may be used or reproduced in any manner whatsoever without written permission except in the case of brief quotations embodied in critical articles and reviews. For information address HarperCollins Publishers, 10 East 53rd Street, New York, NY 10022.

Designed by Laura Kaeppel

ISBN: 978-0-06-144177-6
ISBN-10: 0-06-144177-5

CONTENTS

THE OTHER SIDE
OF MIDNIGHT

PROLOGUE

ATHENS: 1947

Through the dusty windshield of his car Chief of Police Georgios Skouri watched the office buildings and hotels of downtown Athens collapse in a slow dance of disintegration, one after the other like rows of giant pins in some cosmic bowling alley.

"Twenty minutes," the uniformed policeman at the wheel promised. "No traffic."

Skouri nodded absently and stared at the buildings. It was an illusion that never ceased to fascinate him. The shimmering heat from the pitiless August sun enveloped the buildings in undulating waves that made them seem to be cascading down to the streets in a graceful waterfall of steel and glass.

It was ten minutes past noon, and the streets were almost deserted, but even the few pedestrians abroad were too lethargic to give more than a passing curious glance at the three police cars racing east toward Hellenikon, the airport that lay twenty miles from the center of Athens. Chief Skouri was riding in the first car. Under ordinary circumstances, he would have stayed in his comfortable, cool office while his subordinates went out to work in the blazing noon heat, but these circumstances were far from ordinary and Skouri had a two-fold reason for being here personally. First, in the course of this day planes would be arriving carrying VIPs from various parts of the globe, and it was necessary to see that they were welcomed properly and whisked through Customs with a minimum of bother. Second, and more important the airport would be crowded with foreign newspaper reporters and newsreel cameramen. Chief Skouri was not a fool, and it had occurred to him as he had shaved that morning that it would do no harm to his career if he were shown in newsreels as he took the eminent visitors into his charge. It was an extraordinary stroke of fate that had decreed that a worldwide event as sensational as this one had occurred in his domain, and he would be stupid not to take advantage of it. He had discussed it in great detail with the two people in the world closest to him: his wife and his mistress. Anna, a middle-aged, ugly, bitter woman of peasant stock, had ordered him to keep away from the airport and stay in the background so that he could not be blamed if anything went wrong. Melina, his sweet, beautiful young angel, had advised him to greet the dignitaries. She agreed with him that an event like this could catapult him into instant fame. If Skouri handled this well, at the very least he would get a raise in salary and—God willing—might even be made Commissioner of Police when the present Commissioner retired. For the hundredth time Skouri reflected on the irony that Melina was his wife and Anna was his mistress, and he wondered again where he had gone wrong.

Now Skouri turned his thoughts to what lay ahead. He must make certain that everything went perfectly at the airport. He was bringing with him a dozen of his best men. His main problem, he knew, would be controlling the press. He had been astonished by the number of important newspaper and magazine reporters that had poured into Athens from all over the world. Skouri himself had been interviewed six times—each time in a different language. His answers had been translated into German, English, Japanese, French, Italian and Russian. He had just begun to enjoy his new celebrity when the Commissioner had called to inform him that he felt it was unwise for the Chief of Police to comment publicly on a murder trial that had not yet taken place. Skouri was sure that the Commissioner's real motivation was jealousy, but he had prudently decided not to press the issue and had refused all further interviews. However, the Commissioner certainly could not complain if he, Skouri, happened to be at the airport at the center of activity while the newsreel cameras were photographing the arriving celebrities.

As the car sped down Sygrou Avenue and swung left at the sea toward Phaleron, Skouri felt a tightening in his stomach. They were now only five minutes from the airport. He mentally checked over the list of celebrities who would be arriving in Athens before nightfall.

ARMAND GAUTIER WAS suffering from airsickness. He had a deep-seated fear of flying that stemmed from an excessive love of himself and his life and that, combined with the turbulence usually found off the coast of Greece in summer, had made him violently nauseous. He was a tall, ascetically thin man with scholarly features, a high forehead and a perpetually sardonic mouth. At twenty-two Gautier had helped create *La Nouvelle Vague* in France's struggling movie industry and in the years that followed had gone on to even bigger triumphs in the theater. Now acknowledged as one of the world's greatest directors, Gautier lived his role to the hilt. Until the last twenty minutes it had been a most pleasant flight. The stewardesses recognizing him had catered to his needs and had let him know they were available for other activities. Several passengers had come up to him during the flight to say how much they admired his films and plays, but he was most interested in the pretty English University student who was attending St. Anne's at Oxford. She was writing a thesis on the theater for her master's and had chosen Armand Gautier as her subject. Their conversation had gone well until the girl had brought up the name of Noelle Page.

"You used to be her director, didn't you?" she said. "I hope I can get into her trial. It's going to be a circus."

Gautier found himself gripping the sides of his seat, and the strength of his reaction surprised him. Even after all these years the memory of Noelle evoked a pain in him that was as sharp as ever. No one had ever touched him as she had, and no one ever would again. Since Gautier had read of Noelle's arrest three months earlier, he had been able to think of nothing else. He had cabled her and written her, offering to do whatever he could to help, but he had never received a reply. He had had no intention of attending her trial, but he knew he could not stay away. He told himself that it was because he wanted to see whether she had changed since they had lived together. And yet he admitted to himself there was another reason. The theatrical part of him had to be there to view the drama, to watch Noelle's face as the judge told her whether she was to live or die.

The metallic voice of the pilot came over the intercom to announce that they would be landing in Athens in three minutes, and the excitement of the anticipation of seeing Noelle again made Armand Gautier forget his airsickness.

DR. ISRAEL KATZ was flying to Athens from Capetown, where he was the resident neurosurgeon and chief of staff at Groote Schuur, the large new hospital that had just been built. Israel Katz was recognized as one of the leading neurosurgeons in the world. Medical journals were filled with his innovations. His patients included a prime minister, a president and a king.

He leaned back in the seat of the BOAC plane, a man of medium height, with a strong, intelligent face, deep-set brown eyes and long, slender, restless hands. Dr. Katz was tired, and because of that he began to feel the familiar pain in a right leg that was no longer there, a leg amputated six years earlier by a giant with an ax.

It had been a long day. He had done predawn surgery, visited half a dozen patients and then walked out of a Board of Directors' meeting at the hospital in order to fly to Athens for the trial. His wife, Esther, had tried to dissuade him.

"There is nothing you can do for her now, Israel."

Perhaps she was right, but Noelle Page had once risked her life to save his and he owed her something. He thought of Noelle now, and he felt the same indescribable feeling that he had felt whenever he had been with her. It was as though the mere memory of her could dissipate the years that separated them. It was romantic fantasy, of course. Nothing could ever bring those years back. Dr. Israel Katz felt the plane shudder as the wheels were lowered and it started its descent. He looked out the window and spread out below him was Cairo, where he would transfer to a TAE plane to Athens, and Noelle. Was she guilty of murder? As the plane headed for the runway he thought about the other terrible murder she had committed in Paris.

* * *

PHILIPPE SOREL STOOD at the railing of his yacht watching the harbor of Piraeus moving closer. He had enjoyed the sea voyage because it was one of the rare opportunities he had to escape from his fans. Sorel was one of the few sure box-office attractions in the world, and yet the odds against his ever rising to stardom had been tremendous. He was not a handsome man. On the contrary. He had the face of a boxer who had lost his last dozen matches, his nose had been broken several times, his hair was thin and he walked with a slight limp. None of these things mattered, for Philippe Sorel had sex appeal. He was an educated, soft-spoken man, and the combination of his innate gentleness and truck-driver's face and body drove the women frantic and made men look up to him as a hero. Now as his yacht approached the harbor, Sorel won-dered again what he was doing here. He had postponed a movie that he had wanted to make in order to attend Noelle's trial. He was only too well aware of what an easy target he would be for the press as he sat in the courtroom every day, completely unprotected by his press agents and managers. The reporters were certain to misunderstand his attendance and think that it was a bid to reap publicity from the murder trial of his former mistress. Any way he looked at it, it was going to be an agonizing experience, but Sorel had to see Noelle again, had to find out if there was some way in which he could help her. As the yacht began to slide into the white-stoned breakwater of the harbor, he thought about the Noelle he had known, lived with and loved, and he came to a conclusion: No-elle was perfectly capable of murder.

AS PHILIPPE SOREL'S yacht was approaching the coast of Greece, the Special Assistant to the President of the United States was in a Pan American Clipper, one hundred air miles northwest of the Hellenikon Airport. William Fraser was in his fifties, a handsome gray-haired man with a craggy face and an authoritative manner. He was staring at a brief in his hand, but he had not turned a page or stirred for more than an hour. Fraser had taken a leave of absence to make this journey, even though it had come at a most inconvenient time, in the midst of a con-gressional crisis. He knew how painful the next few weeks were going to be for him, and yet he felt that he had no choice. This was a journey of vengeance, and the thought filled Fraser with a cold satisfaction. Deliberately Fraser forced his thoughts away from the trial that would begin tomorrow and looked out the window of the plane. Far below he could see an excursion boat bobbing its way toward Greece, its coast looming in the distance.

AUGUSTE LANCHON HAD been seasick and terrified for three days. He was seasick because the excursion boat which he had boarded in Marseille had been caught in the tail end of a mistral, and he was terrified because he was afraid that his wife would find out what he was doing. Auguste Lanchon was in his sixties, a fat, bald-headed man with small stumpy legs and a pockmarked face with porcine eyes and thin lips that constantly had a cheap cigar clamped between them. Lanchon owned a dress shop in Marseille and he could not afford—or at least that is what he constantly told his wife—to take a vacation like rich people. Of course, he reminded himself, this was not truly a vacation. He had to see his darling Noelle once again. In the years since she had left him, Lanchon had followed her career avidly in the gossip columns, in newspapers and magazines. When she had starred in her first play, he had taken the train all the way to Paris to see her, but Noelle's stupid secretary had kept them apart. Later he had watched Noelle's movies, seeing them again and again and remembering how she had once made love to him. Yes, this trip would be expensive, but Auguste Lanchon knew that it would be worth every sou of it. His precious Noelle would remember the good times they used to have together, and she would turn to him for protection. He would bribe a judge or some other official—if it did not cost too much—and Noelle would be freed, and he would set her up in a little apartment in Marseille where she would always be available to him when he wanted her.

If only his wife did not find out what he was doing.

IN THE CITY of Athens Frederick Stavros was working in his tiny law office on the second floor of an old run-down building in the poor Monastiraki section of the city. Stavros was an intense young man, eager and ambitious, struggling to make a living from his chosen profession. Because he could not afford an assistant, he was forced to do all the tedious background legal research himself. Ordinarily he hated this part of his work, but this time he did not mind because he knew that if he won this case his services would be in such demand that he would never have to worry again for the rest of his life. He and Elena could be married and begin to raise a family. He would move into a suite of luxurious offices, hire law clerks and join a fashionable club like the Athenee Lesky, where one met affluent potential clients. The metamorphosis had already begun. Every time Frederick Stavros walked out into the streets of Athens, he was recognized and stopped by someone who had seen his picture in the newspaper. In a few short weeks he had jumped from anonymity to the attorney who was defending Larry Douglas. In the privacy of his soul Stavros admitted to himself that he had the wrong client. He would have preferred to be defending the glamorous Noelle Page instead of a nonentity like Larry Douglas, but he himself was a nonentity. It was enough that he, Frederick Stavros, was a major participant in the most sensational murder case of the century. If the accused were acquitted, there would be enough glory for everyone. There was only one thing that plagued Stavros, and he thought about it constantly. Both defendants were charged with the same crime, but another attorney was defending Noelle Page. If Noelle Page was found innocent, and Larry Douglas was convicted . . . Stavros shuddered and tried not to think about it. The reporters kept asking him whether he thought the defendants were guilty. He smiled to himself at their naïveté. What did it matter whether they were guilty or innocent? They were entitled to the best legal defense that money could buy. In his case he admitted that the definition was stretched a bit. But in the case of Noelle Page's lawyer . . . ah, that was something else again. Napoleon Chotas had undertaken her defense, and there was no more brilliant criminal lawyer in the world. Chotas had never lost an important case. As he thought about that, Frederick Stavros smiled to himself. He would not have admitted it to anyone, but he was planning to ride to victory on Napoleon Chotas' talent.

WHILE FREDERICK STAVROS was toiling in his dingy law office, Napoleon Chotas was attending a black-tie dinner party at a luxurious home in the fashionable Kolonaki section of Athens. Chotas was a thin, emaciated-looking man with the large, sad eyes of a bloodhound in a corrugated face. He concealed a brilliant, incisive brain behind a mild, vaguely baffled manner. Now toying with his dessert, Chotas sat, preoccupied, thinking about the trial that would begin tomorrow. Most of the conversation that evening had centered around the forthcoming trial. The discussion had been a general one, for the guests were too discreet to ask him direct questions. But toward the end of the evening as the ouzo and brandy flowed more freely, the hostess asked, "Tell us, do you think they are guilty?"

Chotas replied innocently, "How could they be? One of them is my client." He drew appreciative laughter.

"What is Noelle Page really like?"

Chotas hesitated. "She's a most unusual woman," he replied carefully. "She's beautiful and talented—" To his surprise he found that he was suddenly reluctant to discuss her. Besides, there was no way one could capture Noelle with words. Until a few months ago he had only been dimly aware of her as a glamorous figure flitting through the gossip columns and adorning the covers of movie magazines. He had never laid eyes on her, and if he had thought of her at all, it had been with the kind of indifferent contempt he felt toward all actresses. All body and no brain. But, God, how wrong he had been! Since meeting Noelle he had fallen hopelessly in love with her. Because of Noelle Page he had broken his cardinal rule: Never become emotionally involved with a client. Chotas remembered vividly the afternoon he had been approached to undertake her defense. He had been in the midst of packing for a trip that he and his wife were going to make to New York where their daughter had just had her first baby. Nothing, he had believed, could have stopped him from making that journey. But it had only taken two words. In his mind's eye he saw his butler walk into the bedroom, hand him the telephone and say, "Constantin Demiris."

THE ISLAND WAS inaccessible except by helicopter and yacht, and both the airfield and the private harbor were patrolled twenty-four hours a day by armed guards with trained German shepherds. The island was Constantin Demiris' private domain, and no one intruded without an invitation. Over the years its visitors had included kings and queens, presidents and ex-presidents, movie stars, opera singers and famous writers and painters. They had all come away awed. Constantin Demiris was the third wealthiest, and one of the most powerful men in the world, and he had taste and style and knew how to spend his money to create beauty.

Demiris sat in his richly paneled library now, relaxed in a deep armchair, smoking one of the flat-shaped Egyptian cigarettes especially blended for him, thinking about the trial that would begin in the morning. The press had been trying to get to him for months, but he had simply made himself unavailable. It was enough that his mistress was going to be tried for murder, enough that his name would be dragged into the case, even indirectly. He refused to add to the furor by granting any interviews. He wondered what Noelle was feeling now, at this moment, in her cell in the Nikodemous Street Prison. Was she asleep? Awake? Filled with panic at the ordeal that lay before her? He thought of his last conversation with Napoleon Chotas. He trusted Chotas and knew that the lawyer would not fail him. Demiris had impressed upon the attorney that it did not matter to him whether Noelle was innocent or guilty. Chotas was to see to it that he earned every penny of the stupendous fee that Constantin Demiris was paying him to defend her. No, he had no reason to worry. The trial would go well. Because Constantin Demiris was a man who never forgot anything, he remembered that Catherine Douglas' favorite flowers were Triantafylias, the beautiful roses of Greece. He reached forward and picked up a note pad from his desk. He made a notation. *Triantafylias. Catherine Douglas.*

It was the least he could do for her.

BOOK ONE

I

CATHERINE

CHICAGO: 1919–1939

Every large city has a distinctive image, a personality that gives it its own special cachet. Chicago in the 1920's was a restless, dynamic giant, crude and without manners, one booted foot still in the ruthless era of the tycoons who helped give birth to it: William B. Ogden and John Wentworth, Cyrus McCormick and George M. Pullman. It was a kingdom that belonged to the Philip Armours and Gustavus Swifts and Marshall Fields. It was the domain of cool professional gangsters like Hymie Weiss and Scarface Al Capone.

One of Catherine Alexander's earliest memories was of her father taking her into a bar with a sawdust-covered floor and swinging her up to the dizzyingly high stool. He ordered an enormous glass of beer for himself and a Green River for her. She was five years old, and she remembered how proud her father was as strangers crowded around to admire her. All the men ordered drinks and her father paid for them. She recalled how she had kept pressing her body against his arm to make sure he was still there. He had only returned to town the night before, and Catherine knew that he would soon leave again. He was a traveling salesman, and he had explained to her that his work took him to distant cities and he had to be away from her and her mother for months at a time so that he could bring back nice presents. Catherine had desperately tried to make a deal with him. If he would stay with her, she would give up the presents. Her father had laughed and said what a precocious child she was and then had left town, and it was six months before she saw him again. During those early years her mother whom she saw every day seemed a vague, shapeless personality, while her father, whom she saw only on brief occasions, was vivid and wonderfully clear. Catherine thought of him as a handsome, laughing man, full of sparkling humor and warm, generous gestures. The occasions when he came home were like holidays, full of treats and presents and surprises.

When Catherine was seven, her father was fired from his job, and their life took on a new pattern. They left Chicago and moved to Gary, Indiana, where he went to work as a salesman in a jewelry store. Catherine was enrolled in her first school. She had a wary, arms-length relationship with the other children and was terrified of her teachers, who misinterpreted her lonely standoffishness as conceit. Her father came home to dinner every night, and for the first time in her life Catherine felt that they were a real family, like other families. On Sunday the three of them would go to Miller Beach and rent horses and ride for an hour or two along the sand dunes. Catherine enjoyed living in Gary, but six months after they moved there, her father lost his job again and they moved to Harvey, a suburb of Chicago. School was already in session, and Catherine was the new girl, shut out from the friendships that had already been formed. She became known as a loner. The children, secure in the safety of their own groups, would come up to the gangly newcomer and ridicule her cruelly.

During the next few years Catherine donned an armor of indifference, which she wore as a shield against the attacks of the other children. When the armor was pierced, she struck back with a trenchant, caustic wit. Her intention was to alienate her tormentors so that they would leave her alone, but it had an unexpectedly different effect. She worked on the school paper, and in her first review about a musical that her classmates had staged, she wrote, "Tommy Belden had a trumpet solo in the second act, but he blew it." The line was widely quoted, and—surprise of surprises—Tommy Belden came up to her in the hall the next day and told Catherine that he thought it was funny.

In English the students were assigned *Captain Horatio Hornblower* to read. Catherine hated it. Her book report consisted of one sentence: "His barque was worse than his bight," and her teacher, who was a weekend sailor, gave her an "A." Her classmates began to quote her remarks and in a short time she was known as the school wit.

That year Catherine turned fourteen and her body was beginning to show the promise of a ripening woman. She would examine herself in the mirror for hours on end, brooding about how to change the disaster she saw reflected. Inside she was Myrna Loy, driving men mad with her beauty, but her mirror —which was her bitter enemy—showed hopelessly tangled black hair that was impossible to manage, solemn gray eyes, a mouth that seemed to grow wider by the hour and a nose that was slightly turned up. Maybe she wasn't really *ugly,* she told herself cautiously, but on the other hand no one was going to knock down doors to sign her up as a movie star. Sucking in her cheeks and squinting her eyes sexily she tried to visualize herself as a model. It was depressing. She struck another pose. Eyes open wide, expression eager, a big friendly smile. No use. She wasn't the All-American type either. She wasn't anything. Her body was going to be all right, she dourly supposed, but nothing special. And that, of course, was what she wanted more than anything in the world: to be something special, to be Somebody, to be Remembered, and never, never, never, never, to die.

The summer she was fifteen, Catherine came across *Science and Health* by Mary Baker Eddy and for the next two weeks she spent an hour a day before her mirror, willing her reflection to become beautiful. At the end of that time the only change she could detect was a new patch of acne on her chin and a pimple on her forehead. She gave up sweets, Mary Baker Eddy and looking in the mirror.

Catherine and her family had moved back to Chicago and settled in a small, dreary apartment on the north side, in Rogers Park, where the rent was cheap. The country was moving deeper into an economic depression. Catherine's father was working less and drinking more, and he and her mother were constantly yelling at each other in a never-ending series of recriminations that drove Catherine out of the house. She would go down to the beach half a dozen blocks away and walk along the shore, letting the brisk wind give wings to her thin body. She spent long hours staring at the restless gray lake, filled with some desperate longing to which she could not put a name. She wanted something so much that at times it would engulf her in a sudden wave of unbearable pain.

Catherine had discovered Thomas Wolfe, and his books were like a mirror image of the bittersweet nostalgia that filled her, but it was a nostalgia for a future that had not happened yet, as though somewhere, sometime, she had lived a wonderful life and was restless to live it again. She had begun to have her periods, and while she was physically changing into a woman, she knew that her needs, her longings, this aching-wanting was not physical and had nothing to do with sex. It was a fierce and urgent longing to be recognized, to lift herself above the billions of people who teemed the earth, so everyone would know who she was, so when she walked by, they would say, "There goes Catherine Alexander, the great—" The great *what*? There was the problem. She did not know what she wanted, only that she ached desperately for it. On Saturday afternoons whenever she had enough money, she would go to the State and Lake Theater or to the McVickers or the Chicago, and see movies. She would completely lose herself in the wonderful, sophisticated world of Cary Grant and Jean Arthur, laugh with Wallace Beery and Marie Dressier and agonize over Bette Davis' romantic disasters. She felt closer to Irene Dunne than to her mother.

Catherine was in her senior year at Senn High School and her arch-enemy, the mirror, had finally become her friend. The girl in the mirror had a lively, interesting face. Her hair was raven black and her skin a soft, creamy white. Her features were regular and fine, with a generous, sensitive mouth and intelligent gray eyes. She had a good figure with firm, well-developed breasts, gently curving hips and shapely legs. There was an air of aloofness about her image, a hauteur that Catherine did not feel, as though her reflection possessed a characteristic that she did not. She supposed that it was part of the protective armor she had worn since her early school days.

THE DEPRESSION HAD clutched the nation in a tighter and tighter vise, and Catherine's father was incessantly involved in big deals that never seemed to materialize. He was constantly spinning dreams, inventing things that were going to bring in millions of dollars. He devised a set of jacks that fitted above the wheels of an automobile and could be lowered by the touch of a button on the dashboard. None of the automobile manufacturers was interested. He worked out a continuously rotating electric sign to carry advertisements inside stores. There was a brief flurry of optimistic meetings and then the idea faded away.

He borrowed money from his younger brother, Ralph, in Omaha to outfit a shoe-repair truck to travel around the neighborhood. He spent hours discussing the scheme with Catherine and her mother. "It can't fail," he explained. "Imagine having the shoemaker coming to your door! No one's ever done it before. I have one Shoe-mobile out now, right? If it only makes twenty dollars a day, that's a hundred and twenty dollars a week. Two trucks will bring in two hundred and forty a week. Within a year I'll have twenty trucks. That's two thousand four hundred dollars a week. A hundred and twenty-five thousand a year. And that's only the beginning. . . ." Two months later the shoemaker and the truck disappeared, and that was the end of another dream.

Catherine had hoped to be able to go to Northwestern University. She was the top scholar in her class, but even on a scholarship college would be difficult to manage, and the day was coming, Catherine knew, when she would have to quit school and go to work full time. She would get a job as a secretary, but she was determined that she would never surrender the dream that was going to give such rich, wonderful meaning to her life; and the fact that she did not know what either the dream or the meaning was made it all the more unbearably sad and futile. She told herself that she was probably going through adolescence. Whatever it was, it was hell. *Kids are too young to have to go through adolescence,* she thought bitterly.

There were two boys who thought they were in love with Catherine. One was Tony Korman who was going to join his father's law firm one day and who was a foot shorter than Catherine. He had pasty skin and myopic watery eyes that adored her. The other was Dean McDermott, who was fat and shy and wanted to be a dentist. Then of course, there was Ron Peterson, but he was in a category by himself. Ron was Senn High's football star, and everybody said he was a cinch to go to college on an athletic scholarship. He was tall and broad-shouldered, had the looks of a matinee idol and was easily the most popular boy in school.

The only thing that kept Catherine from instantly getting engaged to Ron was the fact that he was not aware she was alive. Every time she passed him in the school corridor, her heart would begin to pound wildly. She would think up something clever and provocative to say so he would ask her for a date. But when she approached him, her tongue would stiffen, and they would pass each other in silence. Like the *Queen Mary* and a garbage scow, Catherine thought hopelessly.

THE FINANCIAL PROBLEM was becoming acute. The rent was three months overdue, and the only reason they had not been evicted was that the landlady was captivated by Catherine's father and his grandiose plans and inventions. Listening to him, Catherine was filled with a poignant sadness. He was still his cheerful, optimistic self, but she could see behind the frayed facade. The marvelous, careless charm that had always given a patina of gaiety to everything he did had eroded. He reminded Catherine of a small boy in a middle-aged man's body spinning tales of the glorious future to hide the shabby failures of the past. More than once she had seen him give a dinner party for a dozen people at Henrici's and then cheerfully take one of his guests aside and borrow enough to cover the check plus a lavish tip, of course. Always lavish, for he had his reputation to maintain. But in spite of all these things and in spite of the fact that Catherine knew that he had been a casual and indifferent father to her, she loved this man. She loved his enthusiasm and smiling energy in a world of frowning, sullen people. This was his gift, and he had always been generous with it.

In the end, Catherine thought, he was better off with his wonderful dreams that would never materialize, than her mother who was afraid to dream.

In April Catherine's mother died of a heart attack. It was Catherine's first confrontation with death. Friends and neighbors filled the little apartment, offering their condolences, with the false, whispered pieties that tragedy invokes.

Death had diminished Catherine's mother to a tiny shriveled figure without juices or vitality, or perhaps life had done that to her, Catherine thought. She tried to recall memories that she and her mother had shared, laughter that they had had together, moments when their hearts had touched; but it was Catherine's father who kept leaping into her mind, smiling and eager and gay. It was as though her mother's life was a pale shadow that retreated before the sunlight of memory. Catherine stared at the waxen figure of her mother in her casket, dressed in a simple black dress with a white collar, and thought what a wasted life it had been. What had it all been for? The feelings Catherine had had years ago came over her again, the determination to be somebody, leave a mark on the world, so she would not end up in an anonymous grave with the world neither knowing nor caring that Catherine Alexander had ever lived and died and been returned to the earth.

Catherine's Uncle Ralph and his wife, Pauline, flew in from Omaha for the funeral. Ralph was ten years younger than Catherine's father and totally unlike his brother. He was in the vitamin mail-order business and very successful. He was a large, square man, square shoulders, square jaw, square chin, and, Catherine was sure, a square mind. His wife was a bird of a woman, all flutter and twitter. They were decent enough people, and Catherine knew that her uncle had loaned a great deal of money to his brother, but Catherine felt that she had nothing in common with them. Like Catherine's mother, they were people without dreams.

After the funeral, Uncle Ralph said that he wanted to talk to Catherine and her father. They sat in the tiny living room of the apartment, Pauline flitting about with trays of coffee and cookies.

"I know things have been pretty rough for you financially," Uncle Ralph said to his brother. "You're too much of a dreamer, always were. But you're my brother. I can't let you sink. Pauline and I talked it over. I want you to come to work for me."

"In Omaha?"

"You'll make a good, steady living and you and Catherine can live with us. We have a big house."

Catherine's heart sank. Omaha! It was the end of all her dreams.

"Let me think it over," her father was saying.

"We'll be catching the six o'clock train," Uncle Ralph replied. "Let me know before we leave."

When Catherine and her father were alone, he groaned, "Omaha! I'll bet the place doesn't even have a decent barber shop."

But Catherine knew that the act he was putting on was for her benefit. Decent barber shop or no, he had no choice. Life had finally trapped him. She wondered what it would do to his spirit to have to settle down to a steady, dull job with regular hours. He would be like a captured wild bird beating his wings against his cage, dying of captivity. As for herself, she would have to forget about going to Northwestern University. She had applied for a scholarship but had heard nothing. That afternoon her father telephoned his brother to say that he would take the job.

The next morning Catherine went to see the principal to tell him that she was going to transfer to a school in Omaha. He was standing behind his desk and before she could speak, he said, "Congratulations, Catherine, you've just won a full scholarship to Northwestern University."

Catherine and her father discussed it thoroughly that night, and in the end it was decided that he would move to Omaha and Catherine would go to Northwestern and live in one of the dormitories on the campus. And so, ten days later, Catherine took her father down to the La Salle Street station to see him off. She was filled with a deep sense of loneliness at his departure, a sadness at saying good-bye to the person she loved the most; and yet at the same time she was eager for the train to leave, filled with a delicious excitement at the thought that she would be free, living her own life for the first time. She stood on the platform watching the face of her father pressing against the train window for a last look; a shabbily handsome man who still truly believed that one day he would own the world.

On the way back from the station Catherine remembered something and laughed aloud. To take him to Omaha, to a desperately needed job, her father had booked a Drawing Room.

MATRICULATION DAY AT Northwestern was filled with an almost unbearable excitement. For Catherine it held a special significance that she could not put into words: It was the key that would unlock the door to all the dreams and nameless ambitions that had burned so fiercely within her for so long. She looked around the huge assembly hall where hundreds of students were lined up to register, and she thought: *Someday you'll all know who I am. You'll say, "I went to school with Catherine Alexander."* She signed up for the maximum number of allowed courses and was assigned to a dormitory. That same morning she found a job working afternoons as a cashier at the Roost, a popular sandwich and malt shop across from the campus. Her salary was fifteen dollars a week, and while it would not afford her any luxuries, it would take care of her school books and basic necessities.

By the middle of her sophomore year Catherine decided that she was probably the only virgin on the entire campus. During the years she was growing up, she had overheard random snatches of conversations as her elders discussed sex. It sounded wonderful, and her strongest fear was that it would be gone by the time she was old enough to enjoy it. Now it looked as though she had been right. At least as far as *she* was concerned. Sex seemed to be the single topic of conversation at school. It was discussed in the dormitories, in classrooms, in the washrooms and at the Roost. Catherine was shocked by the frankness of the conversations.

"Jerry is unbelievable. He's like King Kong."

"Are you talking about his cock or his brain?"

"He doesn't need a brain, honey. I came six times last night."

"Have you ever gone out with Ernie Robbins? He's small, but he's mighty."

"Alex asked me for a date tonight. What's the dope?"

"The dope is Alex. Save yourself the trouble. He took me out to the beach last week. He pulled down my pants and started to grope me, and I started to grope him, but I couldn't find it." Laughter.

Catherine thought the conversations were vulgar and disgusting and she tried not to miss a word. It was an exercise in masochism. As the girls described their sexual exploits, Catherine visualized herself in bed with a boy, having him make wild and frantic love to her. She would feel a physical ache in her groin and press her fists hard against her thighs, trying to hurt herself, to take her mind off the other pain. *My God,* she thought, *I'm going to die a virgin. The only nineteen-year-old virgin at Northwestern. Northwestern, hell, maybe even the United States! The Virgin Catherine. The Church will make me a Saint and they'll light candles to me once a year. What's the matter with me?* she thought. *I'll tell you,* she answered herself. *Nobody's asked you and it takes two to play. I mean, if you want to do it right, it takes two to play.*

The name that most frequently cropped up in the girls' sexual conversations was Ron Peterson. He had enrolled at Northwestern on an athletic scholarship and was as popular here as he had been at Senn High School. He had been elected freshman class president. Catherine saw him in her Latin class the day the term began. He was even better looking than he had been in high school, his body had filled out, and his face had taken on a rugged devil-may-care maturity. After class, he walked toward her, and her heart began to pound.

Catherine Alexander!

Hello, Ron.

Are you in this class?

Yes.

What a break for me.

Why?

Why? Because I don't know anything about Latin and you're a genius. We're going to make beautiful music. Are you doing anything tonight?

Nothing special. Do you want to study together?

Let's go to the beach where we can be alone. We can study any time.

HE WAS STARING at her.

"Hey! . . . er—?" trying to think of her name.

She swallowed, trying desperately to remember, herself. "Catherine," she said quickly. "Catherine Alexander."

"Yeah. How about this place! It's terrific, isn't it?"

She tried to put eagerness in her voice to please him, agree with him, woo him. "Oh yes," she gushed, "it's the most—"

He was looking at a stunning blond girl waiting at the door for him. "See you," he said, and moved away to join the girl.

And that was the end of the Cinderella and Prince Charming story, she thought. *They lived happily ever after, he in his harem and she in a windswept cave in Tibet.*

From time to time Catherine would see Ron walking along the campus, always with a different girl and sometimes two or three. *My God, doesn't he ever get tired?* she wondered. She still had visions that one day he would come to her for help in Latin, but he never spoke to her again.

At night lying in her lonely bed, Catherine would think about all the other girls making love to their boyfriends, and the boy who would always come to her was Ron Peterson. In her mind he would undress her and then she would slowly undress him, the way they always did it in romantic novels, taking off his shirt and gently running her fingers over his chest, then undoing his trousers and pulling down his shorts. He would pick her up and carry her toward the bed. At that point Catherine's comic sense would get the better of her and he would sprain his back and fall to the floor, moaning and groaning with pain. *Idiot,* she told herself, *you can't even do it right in your fantasies.* Maybe she should enter a nunnery. She wondered if nuns had sexual fantasies and if it was a sin for them to masturbate. She wondered if priests ever had sexual intercourse.

She was sitting in a cool, tree-shaded courtyard in a lovely old abbey outside Rome, trailing her fingers in the sun-warmed water of an ancient fish pond. The gate opened, and a tall priest entered the courtyard. He wore a wide-brimmed hat and a long black cassock and he looked exactly like Ron Peterson.

Ah, scusi, signorina, he murmured, *I did not know I had a visitor.*

Catherine quickly sprang to her feet. *I shouldn't be here,* she apologized. *It was just so beautiful I had to sit here and drink it in.*

You are most welcome. He moved toward her, his eyes dark and blazing. *Mia cara . . . I lied to you.*

Lied to me?

Yes. His eyes were boring into hers. *I knew you were here because I followed you.*

She felt a thrill go through her. *But—but you are a priest.*

Bella signorina, I am a man first and a priest afterward. He lurched forward to take her in his arms, and he stumbled on the hem of his cassock and fell into the fish pond.

Shit!

RON PETERSON CAME into the Roost every day after school and would take a seat at the booth in the far corner. The booth would quickly fill up with his friends and become the center of boisterous conversation. Catherine stood behind the counter near the cash register and when Ron entered, he would give her a pleasant, absent nod and move on. He never addressed her by name. *He's forgotten it,* Catherine mused.

But each day when he walked in, she gave him a big smile and waited for him to say hello, ask her for a date, a glass of water, her virginity, anything. She might as well have been a piece of furniture. Examining the girls in the room with complete objectivity she decided she was prettier than all but one girl, the fantastic looking Jean-Anne, the Southern blonde with whom Ron was most often seen, and she was certainly brighter than all of them put together. What in God's name then was wrong with her? Why was it that not one single boy asked her for a date? She learned the answer the next day.

She was hurrying south along the campus headed for the Roost when she saw Jean-Anne and a brunette whom she did not know, walking across the green lawn toward her.

"Well, it's Miss Big Brain," Jean-Anne said.

And Miss Big Boobs, Catherine thought enviously. Aloud she said, "That was a murderous Lit quiz, wasn't it?"

"Don't be condescending," Jean-Anne said coldly. "You know enough to teach the Lit course. And that's not all you could teach us, is it, honey?"

Something in her tone made Catherine's face begin to redden.

"I—I don't understand."

"Leave her alone," the brunette said.

"Why should I?" Jean-Anne asked. "Who the hell does she think she is?" She turned to Catherine. "Do you want to know what everyone says about you?"

God, no. "Yes."

"You're a lesbo."

Catherine stared at her, unbelievingly. "I'm a *what?*"

"A lesbian, baby. You're not fooling anybody with that holier-than-thou act."

"Th-that's ridiculous," Catherine stammered.

"Did you really think you could fool people?" Jean-Anne asked. "You're doing everything but carrying a sign."

"But I—I never—"

"The boys get it up for you, but you never let them put it in."

"Really—" Catherine blurted.

"Fuck off," Jean-Anne said. "You're not our type."

They walked away, leaving her standing there, numbly staring after them.

That night, Catherine lay in bed, unable to sleep.

How old are you, Miss Alexander?

Nineteen.

Have you ever had sexual intercourse with a man?

Never.

Do you like men?

Doesn't everyone?

Have you ever wanted to make love to a woman?

Catherine thought about it long and hard. She had had crushes on other girls, on women teachers but that had been part of growing up. Now she thought about making love to a woman, their bodies intertwining, her lips on another woman's lips, her body being caressed by soft, feminine hands. She shuddered. *No!* Aloud, she said, "I'm normal." But if she was normal, why was she lying here like this? Why wasn't she out somewhere getting laid like everyone else in the world? Perhaps she was frigid. She might need some kind of operation. A lobotomy, probably.

When the eastern sky began to lighten outside the dormitory window, Catherine's eyes were still open, but she had made a decision. She was going to lose her virginity. And the lucky man was going to be every maiden's bedside companion, Ron Peterson.

2

NOELLE

MARSEILLE—PARIS: 1919–1939

S he was born a Royal Princess.

Her earliest memories were of a white bassinet covered with a lace canopy, decorated with pink ribbons and filled with soft stuffed animals and beautiful dolls and golden rattles. She quickly learned that if she opened her mouth and let out a cry, someone would hurry to hold and comfort her. When she was six months old her father would take her out in the garden in her perambulator and let her touch the flowers and he would say, "They're lovely, Princess, but you're more beautiful than any of them."

At home she enjoyed it when her father lifted her up in his strong arms and carried her to a window where she could look out and see the roofs of the high buildings, and he would say, "That's your Kingdom out there, Princess." He would point to the tall masts of ships bobbing at anchor in the bay. "Do you see those big ships? One day they'll all be yours to command."

Visitors would come to the castle to see her, but only a few special ones were permitted to hold her. The others would stare down at her as she lay in her crib and would exclaim over her unbelievably delicate features, and her lovely blond hair, her soft honey-colored skin, and her father would proudly say, "A stranger could tell she is a Princess!" And he would lean over her crib and whisper, "Someday a beautiful Prince will come and sweep you off your feet." And he would gently tuck the warm pink blanket around her and she would drift off to a contented sleep. Her whole world was a roseate dream of ships, tall masts and castles, and it was not until she was five years old that she understood that she was the daughter of a Marseille fishmonger, and that the castles she saw from the window of her tiny attic room were the warehouses around the stinking fish market where her father worked, and that her navy was the fleet of old fishing ships that set out from Marseille every morning before dawn and returned in the early afternoon to vomit their smelly cargo into the waterfront docks.

This was the kingdom of Noelle Page.

The friends of Noelle's father used to warn him about what he was doing. "You mustn't put fancy ideas in her head, Jacques. She'll think she's better than everybody else." And their prophecies came true.

On the surface Marseille is a city of violence, the kind of primitive violence spawned in any waterfront town crowded with hungering sailors with money to spend and clever predators to relieve them of it. But unlike the rest of the French, the people of Marseille have a sense of solidarity that comes from a common struggle for survival, for the lifeblood of the town comes from the sea, and the fishermen of Marseille belong to the family of fishermen all over the world. They share alike in the storms and the calm days, the sudden disasters and the bountiful harvests.

So it was that Jacques Page's neighbors rejoiced at his good fortune in having such an incredible daughter. They too recognized the miracle of how, out of the dung of the dirty, ribald city, a true Princess had been spawned.

Noelle's parents could not get over the wonder of their daughter's exquisite beauty. Noelle's mother was a heavyset, coarse-featured peasant woman with sagging breasts and thick thighs and hips. Noelle's father was squat, with broad shoulders and the small suspicious eyes of a Breton. His hair was the color of the wet sand along the beaches of Normandy. In the beginning it had seemed to him that nature had made a mistake, that this exquisite blond fairy creature could not really belong to him and his wife, and that as Noelle grew older she would turn into an ordinary, plain-looking girl like all the other daughters of his friends. But the miracle continued to grow and flourish, and Noelle became more beautiful each day.

Noelle's mother was less surprised than her husband by the appearance of a golden-haired beauty in the family. Nine months before Noelle had been born, Noelle's mother had met a strapping Norwegian sailor just off a freighter. He was a giant Viking god with blond hair and a warm, seductive grin. While Jacques was at work, the sailor had spent a busy quarter of an hour in her bed in their tiny apartment.

Noelle's mother had been filled with fear when she saw how blond and beautiful her baby was. She walked around in dread, waiting for the moment that her husband would point an accusing finger at her and demand to know the identity of the real father. But, incredibly, some ego-hunger in him made him accept the child as his own.

"She must be a throwback to some Scandinavian blood in my family," he would boast to his friends, "but you can see that she has my features."

His wife would listen, nodding agreement, and think what fools men were.

Noelle loved being with her father. She adored his clumsy playfulness and the strange, interesting smells that clung to him, and at the same time she was terrified by the fierceness of him. She would watch wide-eyed as he yelled at her mother and slapped her hard across the face, his neck corded with anger. Her mother would scream out in pain, but there was something beyond pain in her cries, something animal and sexual and Noelle would feel pangs of jealousy and wish she were in her mother's place.

But her father was always gentle with Noelle. He liked to take her down to the docks and show her off to the rough, crude men with whom he worked. She was known up and down the docks as The Princess and she was proud of this, as much for her father's sake as for her own.

She wanted to please her father, and because he loved to eat, Noelle began cooking for him, preparing his favorite dishes, gradually displacing her mother in the kitchen.

At seventeen the promise of Noelle's early beauty had been more than fulfilled. She had matured into an exquisite woman. She had fine, delicate features, eyes a vivid violet color and soft ash-blond hair. Her skin was fresh and golden as though she had been dipped in honey. Her figure was stunning, with generous, firm, young breasts, a small waist, rounded hips and long shapely legs, with delicate ankles. Her voice was distinctive, soft and mellifluous. There was a strong, smoldering sensuality about Noelle, but that was not her magic. Her magic lay in the fact that beneath the sensuality seemed to lie an untouched island of innocence, and the combination was irresistible. She could not walk down the streets without receiving propositions from passersby. They were not the casual offers that the prostitutes of Marseille received as their daily currency, for even the most obtuse men perceived something special in Noelle, something that they had never seen before and perhaps would never see again, and each was willing to pay as much as he could afford to try to make it a part of himself, however briefly.

Noelle's father was conscious of her beauty, too. In fact, Jacques Page thought of little else. He was aware of the interest that Noelle aroused in men. Even though neither he nor his wife ever discussed sex with Noelle, he was certain she still had her virginity, a woman's little capital. His shrewd peasant mind gave long and serious thought to how he could best capitalize on the windfall that nature had unexpectedly bestowed upon him. His mission was to see that his daughter's beauty paid off as handsomely as possible for Noelle and for him. After all, he had sired her, fed her, clothed her, educated her—she owed him everything. And now it was time for to be repaid. If he could set her up as some rich man's mistress, it would be good for her, and he would be able to live the life of ease to which he was entitled. Each day it was getting more and more difficult for an honest man to make a living. The shadow of war had begun to spread across Europe. The Nazis had marched into Austria in a lightning coup that had left Europe stunned. A few months later the Nazis had taken over the Sudeten area and then marched into Slovakia. In spite of Hitler's assurances that he was not interested in further conquest, the feeling persisted that there was going to be a major conflict.

The impact of events was felt sharply in France. There were shortages in the stores and markets, as the government began to gear for a massive defense effort. Soon, Jacques feared, they would even stop the fishing and then where would he be? No, the answer to his problem was in finding a suitable lover for his daughter. The trouble was that he knew no wealthy men. All his friends were piss-poor like himself, and he had no intention of letting any man near her who could not pay his price.

The answer to Jacques Page's dilemma was inadvertently supplied by Noelle herself. In recent months Noelle had become increasingly restless. She did well in her classes, but school had begun to bore her. She told her father that she wanted to get a job. He studied her silently, shrewdly weighing the possibilities.

"What kind of job?" he asked.

"I don't know," Noelle replied. "I might be able to work as a model, papa."

It was as simple as that.

Every afternoon for the next week Jacques Page went home after work, carefully bathed to get the smell of fish out of his hands and hair, dressed in his good suit and went down to the Canebière, the main street that led from the old harbor of the city to the richer districts. He walked up and down the street exploring all the dress salons, a clumsy peasant in a world of silk and lace, but he neither knew nor cared that he was out of place. He had but one objective and he found it when he reached the Bon Marché. It was the finest dress shop in Marseille, but that was not why he chose it. He chose it because it was owned by Monsieur Auguste Lanchon. Lanchon was in his fifties, an ugly bald-headed man with small stumpy legs and a greedy, twitching mouth. His wife, a tiny woman with the profile of a finely honed hatchet, worked in the fitting room, loudly supervising the tailors. Jacques Page took one look at Monsieur Lanchon and his wife and knew that he had found the solution to his problem.

Lanchon watched with distaste as the shabbily dressed stranger entered the door of his shop. Lanchon said rudely, "Yes? What can I do for you?"

Jacques Page winked, poked a thick finger in Lanchon's chest and smirked, "It is what I can do for *you*, Monsieur. I am going to let my daughter work for you."

Auguste Lanchon stared at the lout standing before him, an expression of incredulity on his face.

"You are going to *let*—"

"She will be here tomorrow, nine o'clock."

"I do not—"

Jacques Page had left. A few minutes later, Auguste Lanchon had completely dismissed the incident from his mind. At nine o'clock the next morning, Lanchon looked up and saw Jacques Page entering the shop. He was about to tell his manager to throw the man out, when behind him he saw Noelle. They were walking toward him, the father and his unbelievably beautiful daughter, and the old man was grinning, "Here she is, ready to go to work."

Auguste Lanchon stared at the girl and licked his lips.

"Good morning, Monsieur." Noelle smiled. "My father told me that you had a job for me."

Auguste Lanchon nodded his head, unable to trust his voice.

"Yes, I—I think we could arrange something," he managed to stammer. He studied her face and figure and could not believe what he saw. He could already imagine what that naked young body would feel like under him.

Jacques Page was saying, "Well, I will leave you two to get acquainted," and he gave Lanchon a hearty whack on the shoulder and a wink that had a dozen different significances, none of them leaving any doubt in Lanchon's mind about his intentions.

For the first few weeks Noelle felt that she had been transported to another world. The women who came to the shop were dressed in beautiful clothes and had lovely manners, and the men who accompanied them were a far cry from the crude, boisterous fishermen with whom she had grown up. It seemed to Noelle that for the first time in her life the stench of fish was out of her nostrils. She had never really been aware of it before, because it had always been a part of her. But now everything was suddenly changed. And she owed it all to her father. She was proud of the way he got along with Monsieur Lanchon. Her father would come to the shop two or three times a week and he and Monsieur Lanchon would slip out for a cognac or a beer and when they returned there would be an air of camaraderie between them. In the beginning Noelle had disliked Monsieur Lanchon, but his behavior toward her was always circumspect. Noelle heard from one of the girls that Lanchon's wife had once caught him in the stockroom with a model and had picked up a pair of shears and had barely missed castrating him. Noelle was aware that Lanchon's eyes followed her everywhere she went, but he was always scrupulously polite. "Probably," she thought, with satisfaction, "he is afraid of my father."

At home the atmosphere suddenly seemed much brighter. Noelle's father no longer struck her mother and the constant bickering had stopped. There were steaks and roasts to eat, and after dinner Noelle's father would take out a new pipe and fill it with a rich smelling tobacco from a leather pouch. He bought himself a new Sunday suit. The international situation was worsening and Noelle would listen to discussions between her father and his friends. They all seemed to be alarmed by the imminent threat to their livelihood, but Jacques Page appeared singularly unconcerned.

On September 1, 1939, Hitler's troops invaded Poland and two days later Great Britain and France declared war against Germany.

Mobilization was begun and overnight the streets were filled with uniforms. There was an air of resignation about what was happening, a *dèjá vu* feeling of watching an old movie that one had seen before; but there was no fear. Other countries might have reason to tremble before the might of the German armies but France was invincible. It had the Maginot Line, an impenetrable fortress that could protect France against invasion for a thousand years. A curfew was imposed and rationing was started, but none of those things bothered Jacques Page. He seemed to have changed, to have calmed. The only time Noelle saw him fly into a fury was one night when she was in the darkened kitchen kissing a boy whom she dated occasionally. The lights suddenly went on and Jacques Page stood in the doorway trembling with rage.

"Get out," he screamed at the terrified boy. "And keep your hands off my daughter, you filthy pig!"

The boy fled in panic. Noelle tried to explain to her father that they had been doing nothing wrong, but he was too furious to listen.

"I will not have you throw yourself away," he roared. "He is a nobody, he is not good enough for my Princess."

Noelle lay awake that night marveling at how much her father loved her and vowing that she would never do anything to distress him again.

One evening just before closing time a customer came into the shop and Lanchon asked Noelle to model some dresses. By the time Noelle finished, everyone had left the shop except Lanchon and his wife, who was working on the books in the office. Noelle went into the empty dressing room to change. She was in her bra and pants when Lanchon walked into the room. He stared at her and his lips began to twitch. Noelle reached for her dress, but before she could put it on Lanchon swiftly moved toward her and shoved his hand between her legs. Noelle was filled with revulsion, her skin beginning to crawl. She tried to pull away, but Lanchon's grip was strong and he was hurting her.

"You are beautiful," he whispered. "Beautiful. I will see that you have a good time."

At that moment Lanchon's wife called out to him and he reluctantly let go of Noelle and scurried out of the room.

On the way home Noelle debated whether to tell her father what had happened. He would probably kill Lanchon. She detested him and could not bear to be near him, and yet she wanted the job. Besides, her father might be disappointed if she quit. She decided that for the moment she would say nothing and would find a way to handle it herself.

The following Friday Madame Lanchon received a call that her mother was ill in Vichy. Lanchon drove his wife to the railroad station and then raced back to the shop. He called Noelle into his office and told her he was going to take her away for the weekend. Noelle stared at him, thinking at first that it was some kind of joke.

"We will go to Vienne," he babbled. "There is one of the great restaurants of the world there, Le Pyramide. It is expensive, but it doesn't matter, I can be very generous to those who are good to me. How soon can you be ready?"

She stared at him. "Never" was all she could bring herself to say. "Never." And she turned and fled into the front of the shop. Monsieur Lanchon looked after her for a moment, his face mottled with fury, then snatched up the telephone on his desk. An hour later Noelle's father walked into the shop. He made straight for Noelle and her face lit up with relief. He had sensed that something was wrong and had come to rescue her. Lanchon was standing at the door to his office. Noelle's father took her arm and hurried her into Lanchon's office. He swung around to face her.

"I'm so glad you came, Papa," Noelle said. "I—"

"Monsieur Lanchon tells me that he made you a splendid offer and you refused him."

She stared at him, bewildered. "Offer? He asked me to go away with him for the weekend."

"And you said no?"

Before Noelle could answer, her father drew his hand back and slapped her hard across the cheek. She stood there in stunned disbelief, her ears ringing, and through a filmy haze heard her father saying, "Stupid! stupid! It's time you started thinking of someone besides yourself, you selfish little bitch!" And he hit her again.

Thirty minutes later as her father stood at the curb watching them drive off, Noelle and Monsieur Lanchon left for Vienne.

THE HOTEL ROOM consisted of a large double bed, cheap furniture and a washstand and basin in one corner. Monsieur Lanchon was not a man to throw away his money. He gave the bellboy a small tip and the moment the bellboy left, Lanchon turned toward Noelle and began to tear off her clothes. He cupped her breasts in his hot, moist hands and squeezed them hard.

"My God, you are beautiful," he panted. He pulled down her skirt and pants and pushed her onto the bed. Noelle lay there unmoving, uncaring, as though she were suffering from some kind of shock. She had not uttered one word driving down in the car. Lanchon hoped that she was not ill. He could never explain it to the police or, God forbid, his wife. He hastily took off his clothes, throwing them on the floor and then moved onto the bed beside Noelle. Her body was even more splendid than he had anticipated.

"You father tells me you have never been fucked." He grinned. "Well, I am going to show you what a man feels like." He rolled his plump belly on top of her and thrust his organ between her legs. He began to push harder and harder, forcing himself into her. Noelle felt nothing. In her mind she was listening to her father yelling, *You should be grateful to have a kind gentleman like Monsieur Lanchon wanting to take care of you. All you have to do is be nice to him. You will do it for me. And for yourself.* The whole scene had been a nightmare. She was sure that her father had somehow misunderstood, but when she started to explain, he had struck her again and begun screaming, "You will do as you are told. Other girls would be grateful for your chance." *Her chance.* She looked up at Lanchon, the squat ugly body, the panting animal face with its piggish eyes. This was the Prince to whom her father had sold her, her beloved father who cherished her and could not bear to let her waste herself on anyone unworthy. And she remembered the steaks that had suddenly appeared on the table and her father's new pipes and his new suit and she wanted to vomit.

It seemed to Noelle that in the next few hours she died and was born again. She had died a Princess, and she was reborn a slut. Slowly she had become aware of her surroundings and of what was happening to her. She was filled with a hatred such as she had not known could exist. She would never forgive her father for his betrayal. Oddly enough she did not hate Lanchon, for she understood him. He was a man with the one weakness common to all men. From now on, Noelle decided, that weakness was going to be her strength. She would learn to use it. Her father had been right all along. She *was* a Princess and the world did belong to her. And now she knew how to get it. It was so simple. Men ruled the world because they had the strength, the money and the power; therefore it was necessary to rule men, or at least one man. But in order to do that one had to be prepared. She had a great deal to learn. And this was the beginning.

She turned her attention to Monsieur Lanchon. She lay under him, feeling, experiencing how the male organ fit and what it could do to a woman.

In his frenzy at having this beautiful creature under his fat, bucking body, Lanchon did not even notice that Noelle simply lay there, but he would not have cared. Just feasting his eyes on her was enough to rouse him to heights of passion he had not felt in years. He was accustomed to the accordioned, middle-aged body of his wife and the tired merchandise of the whores of Marseille, and to find this fresh, young girl under him was like a miracle come into his life.

But the miracle was just beginning for Lanchon. After he had spent himself making love to Noelle for the second time, she spoke and said, "Lie still." She began to experiment on him with her tongue and her mouth and her hands, trying new things, finding the soft, sensitive areas of his body and working on them until Lanchon cried aloud with pleasure. It was like pressing a series of buttons. When Noelle did *this,* he moaned and when she did *this,* he writhed in ecstasy. It was so easy. This was her school, this was her education. This was the beginning of power.

They spent three days there and never once went to Le Pyramide, and during those days and nights, Lanchon taught her the little that he knew about sex, and Noelle discovered a great deal more.

When they drove back to Marseille, Lanchon was the happiest man in all France. In the past he had had quick affairs with shopgirls in a *cabinet particuliers,* a restaurant that had a private dining room with a couch; he had haggled with prostitutes, been niggardly with presents for his mistresses, and notoriously penurious with his wife and children. Now he found himself saying magnanimously, "I'm going to set you up in an apartment, Noelle. Can you cook?"

"Yes," Noelle replied.

"Good. I will come for lunch every day and we will make love. And two or three nights a week, I will come for dinner." He put his hand on her knee and patted it. "How does that sound?"

"It sounds wonderful," Noelle said.

"I will even give you an allowance. Not a large one," he added quickly, "but enough so you can go out and buy pretty things from time to time. All I ask is that you see no one but me. You belong to me now."

"As you wish, Auguste," she said.

Lanchon sighed contentedly, and when he spoke, his voice was soft. "I've never felt this way about anyone before. And do you know why?"

"No, Auguste."

"Because you make me feel young. You and I are going to have a wonderful life together."

They reached Marseille late that evening, driving in silence, Lanchon with his dreams, Noelle with hers.

"I will see you in the shop tomorrow at nine o'clock," Lanchon said. He thought it over. "If you are tired in the morning, sleep a little longer. Come in at nine-thirty."

"Thank you, Auguste."

He pulled out a fistful of francs and held them out.

"Here. Tomorrow afternoon you will look for an apartment. This will be a deposit to hold it until I can see it."

She stared at the francs in his hand.

"Is something wrong?" Lanchon asked.

"I want us to have a really beautiful place," Noelle said, "where we can enjoy being together."

"I'm not a rich man," he protested.

Noelle smiled understandingly and put her hand on his thigh. Lanchon stared at her a long moment and then nodded.

"You're right," he said. He reached into his wallet and began peeling off francs, watching her face as he did so.

When she seemed satisfied, he stopped, flushed with his own generosity. After all what did it matter? Lanchon was a shrewd businessman, and he knew that this would insure that Noelle would never leave him.

Noelle watched him as he drove happily away, then she went upstairs, packed her things and removed her savings from her hiding place. At ten o'clock that night, she was on a train to Paris.

When the train pulled into Paris early the next morning, the PLM Station was crowded with those travelers who had eagerly just arrived, and those who were just as eagerly fleeing the city. The din in the station was deafening as people shouted cheerful greetings and tearful farewells, rudely pushing and shoving, but Noelle did not mind. The moment she stepped off the train, before she had even had a chance to see the city, she knew that she was home. It was Marseille that seemed like a strange town and Paris the city to which she belonged. It was an odd, heady sensation, and Noelle reveled in it, drinking in the noises, the crowds, the excitement. It all belonged to her. All she had to do now was claim it. She picked up her suitcase and started toward the exit.

Outside in the bright sunlight with the traffic insanely whizzing around, Noelle hesitated, suddenly realizing that she had nowhere to go. Half a dozen taxis were lined up in front of the station. She got into the first one.

"Where to?"

She hesitated. "Could you recommend a nice inexpensive hotel?"

The driver swung around to stare at her appraisingly. "You're new in town?"

"Yes."

He nodded. "You'll be needing a job, I suppose."

"Yes."

"You're in luck," he said. "Have you ever done any modeling?"

Noelle's heart leaped. "As a matter of fact, I have," she said.

"My sister works for one of the big fashion houses," the driver confided. "Just this morning she mentioned that one of the girls quit. Would you like to see if the vacancy is still open?"

"That would be wonderful," Noelle replied.

"If I take you there, it will cost you ten francs."

She frowned.

"It will be worth it," he promised.

"All right." She leaned back in the seat. The driver put the taxi in gear and joined the maniacal traffic heading toward the center of town. The driver chattered as they drove, but Noelle did not hear a word he said. She was drinking in the sights of her city. She supposed that because of the blackout, Paris was more subdued than usual, but to Noelle it seemed a city of pure magic. It had an elegance, a style, even an aroma all its own. They passed Notre Dame and crossed the Pont Neuf to the Right Bank and swung toward Marshall Foch Boulevard. In the distance Noelle could see the Eiffel Tower, dominating the city. Through the rearview mirror, the driver saw the expression on her face.

"Nice, huh?"

"It's beautiful," Noelle answered quietly. She still could not believe she was here. It was a Kingdom fit for a Princess . . . for her.

The taxi pulled up in front of a dark, gray stone building on the rue de Provence.

"We're here," the driver announced. "That's two francs on the meter and ten francs for me."

"How do I know the job will still be open?" Noelle asked.

The driver shrugged. "I told you, the girl just left this morning. If you don't want to go in, I'll take you back to the station."

"No," Noelle said quickly. She opened her purse, took out twelve francs and handed them to the driver. He stared at the money, then looked at her. Embarrassed, she reached into her purse and handed him another franc.

He nodded, unsmiling, and watched her lift her suitcase out of the taxi.

As he started to drive away, Noelle asked, "What's your sister's name?"

"Jeanette."

Noelle stood on the curb watching the taxi disappear, then turned to look at the building. There was no identifying sign in front, but she supposed that a fashionable dress house did not need a sign. Everyone would know where to find it. She picked up her suitcase, went up to the door and rang the bell. A few moments later the door was opened by a maid wearing a black apron. She looked at Noelle blankly.

"Yes?"

"Excuse me," Noelle said. "I understand that there is an opening for a model."

The woman stared at her and blinked.

"Who sent you?"

"Jeanette's brother."

"Come in." She opened the door wider and Noelle stepped into a reception hall done in the style of the 1800's. There was a large Baccarat chandelier hanging from the ceiling, several more scattered around the hall, and through an open door, Noelle could see a sitting room filled with antique furniture and a staircase leading upstairs. On a beautiful inlaid table were copies of *Figaro* and *L'Echo de Paris*. "Wait here. I'll find out if Madame Delys has time to see you now."

"Thank you," Noelle said. She set her suitcase down and walked over to a large mirror on the wall. Her clothes were wrinkled from the train ride, and she suddenly regretted her impulsiveness in coming here before freshening up. It was important to make a good impression. Still, as she examined herself, she knew that she looked beautiful. She knew this without conceit, accepting her beauty as an asset, to be used like any other asset. Noelle turned as she saw a girl in the mirror coming down the stairs. The girl had a good figure and a pretty face, and was dressed in a long brown skirt and a high-necked blouse. Obviously the quality of models here was high. She gave Noelle a brief smile and went into the drawing room. A moment later Madame Delys entered the room. She was in her forties and was short and dumpy with cold, calculating eyes.

She was dressed in a gown that Noelle estimated must have cost at least two thousand francs.

"Regina tells me that you are looking for a job," she said.

"Yes, ma'am," Noelle replied.

"Where are you from?"

"Marseille."

Madame Delys snorted. "The playpen of drunken sailors."

Noelle's face fell.

Madame Delys patted her on the shoulder. "It does not matter, my dear. How old are you?"

"Eighteen."

Madame Delys nodded. "That is good. I think my customers will like you. Do you have any family in Paris?"

"No."

"Excellent. Are you prepared to start work right away?"

"Oh, yes," Noelle assured her eagerly.

From upstairs came the sound of laughter and a moment later a red-headed girl walked down the stairs on the arm of a fat, middle-aged man. The girl was wearing only a thin negligee.

"Finished already?" Madame Delys asked.

"I've worn Angela out," the man grinned. He saw Noelle. "Who's this little beauty?"

"This is Yvette, our new girl," Madame Delys said. And without hesitation added, "She's from Antibes, the daughter of a Prince."

"I've never screwed a Princess," the man exclaimed. "How much?"

"Fifty francs."

"You must be joking. Thirty."

"Forty. And believe me, you'll get your money's worth."

"It's a deal."

They turned to Noelle. She had vanished.

NOELLE WALKED THE streets of Paris, hour after hour. She strolled along the Champs-Élysées, down one side and up the other, wandering through the Lido Arcade and stopping at every shop to gaze at the incredible cornucopia of jewelry and dresses and leather goods and perfumes, and she wondered what Paris was like when there were *no* shortages. The wares displayed in the windows were dazzling, and while one part of her felt like a country bumpkin, another part of her knew that one day these things would belong to her. She walked through the Bois and down the rue du Faubourg-St.-Honoré and along the avenue Victor-Hugo, until she began to feel tired and hungry. She had left her purse and suitcase at Madame Delys', but she had no intention of going back there. She would send for her things.

Noelle was neither shocked nor upset by what had happened. It was simply that she knew the difference between a courtesan and a whore. Whores did not change the course of history: courtesans did. Meanwhile she was without a cent. She had to find a way to survive until she could find a job the next day. Dusk was beginning to brush the sky, and the merchants and hotel doormen were busy putting up blackout curtains against possible air attacks. To solve her immediate problem, Noelle needed to find someone to buy her a good hot dinner. She asked directions from a gendarme and then headed for the Crillon Hotel. Outside, forbidding iron shutters covered the windows, but inside, the lobby was a masterpiece of subdued elegance, soft and understated. Noelle walked in confidently as if she belonged there and took a seat in a chair facing the elevator. She had never done this before, and she was a bit nervous. But she remembered how easy it had been to handle Auguste Lanchon. Men were really very uncomplicated. There was only one lesson a girl had to remember: A man was soft when he was hard and hard when he was soft. So it was only necessary to keep him hard until he gave you what you wanted. Now, looking around the lobby, Noelle decided that it would be a simple matter to catch the eye of an unattached male on his way, perhaps, to a lonely dinner.

"Pardon, mademoiselle."

Noelle turned her head to look up at a large man in a dark suit. She had never seen a detective in her life, but there was no doubt whatever in her mind.

"Is Mademoiselle waiting for someone?"

"Yes," Noelle replied, trying to keep her voice steady. "I'm waiting for a friend."

She was suddenly acutely aware of her wrinkled dress, and the fact that she carried no purse.

"Is your friend a guest of this hotel?"

She felt a surge of panic rising in her. "He—er—not exactly."

He studied Noelle a moment, then said in a hardened tone. "May I see your identification?"

"I—I don't have it with me," she stammered. "I lost it."

The detective said, "Perhaps Mademoiselle will come with me." He put a firm hand on her arm, and she rose to her feet.

And at that moment someone took her other arm and said, "Sorry I'm late, cheri, but you know how those damned cocktail parties are. You have to blast your way out. Been waiting long?"

Noelle swung around in astonishment to look at the speaker. He was a tall man, his body lean and hard-looking, and he wore a strange, unfamiliar uniform. He had blue-black hair with a widow's peak and eyes the color of a dark, stormy sea, with long, thick lashes. His features had the look of an old Florentine coin. It was an irregular face, the two profiles not quite matching, as though the minter's hand had slipped for an instant. It was a face that was extraordinarily alive and mobile so that you felt it was ready to smile, to laugh, to frown. The only thing that saved it from being femininely beautiful was a strong, masculine chin with a deep cleft in it.

He gestured toward the detective. "Is this man bothering you?" His voice was deep, and he spoke French with a very slight accent.

"N-no," Noelle said, in a bewildered voice.

"I beg your pardon, sir," the hotel detective was saying. "I misunderstood. We have been having a problem here lately with . . ." He turned to Noelle. "Please accept my apologies, Mademoiselle."

The stranger turned to Noelle. "Well now, I don't know. What do you think?"

Noelle swallowed and nodded quickly.

The man turned to the detective. "Mademoiselle's being generous. Just watch yourself in the future." He took Noelle's arm and they headed for the door.

When they reached the street, Noelle said, "I—I don't know how to thank you, Monsieur."

"I've always hated policemen." The stranger grinned. "Do you want me to get you a taxi?"

Noelle stared at him, the panic beginning to rise in her again, as she remembered her situation. "No."

"Right. Good night." He walked over to the stand and started to get into a taxi, turned around and saw that she was standing there, rooted, staring after him. In the doorway of the hotel was the detective watching. The stranger hesitated, then walked back to Noelle. "You'd better get out of here," he advised. "Our friend's still interested in you."

"I have nowhere to go," she replied.

He nodded and reached into his pocket.

"I don't want your money," she said quickly.

He looked at her in surprise. "What *do* you want?" he asked.

"To have dinner with you."

He smiled and said, "Sorry. I have a date, and I'm late already."

"Then go ahead," she said. "I'll be fine."

He shoved the bills back into his pocket. "Suit yourself, honey," he said. *"Au 'voir."* He turned and began walking toward the taxi again. Noelle looked after him, wondering what was wrong with her. She knew she had behaved stupidly, but she also knew that she could not have done anything else. From the first moment she had looked at him she had experienced a reaction that she had never felt before, a wave of emotion so strong that she could almost reach out and touch it. She did not even know his name, and would probably never see him again. Noelle glanced toward the hotel and saw the detective moving purposefully toward her. It was her own fault. This time she would not be able to talk her way out of it. She felt a hand on her shoulder, and as she turned to see who it was, the stranger took her arm and propelled her toward the taxi, quickly opened the door and climbed in beside her. He gave the driver an address. The taxi pulled away, leaving the detective at the curb, staring after them. "What about your date?" Noelle asked.

"It's a party," he shrugged. "One more won't make any difference. I'm Larry Douglas. What's your name?"

"Noelle Page."

"Where are you from, Noelle?"

She turned and looked into his brilliant dark eyes and said, "Antibes. I am the daughter of a Prince."

He laughed, showing even, white teeth.

"Good for you, Princess," he said.

"Are you English?"

"American."

She looked at his uniform. "America is not at war."

"I'm in the British RAF," he explained. "They've just formed a group of American flyers. It's called the Eagle Squadron."

"But why should you fight for England?"

"Because England's fighting for us," he said. "Only we don't know it yet."

Noelle shook her head. "I don't believe that. Hitler is a Boche clown."

"Maybe. But he's a clown who knows what the Germans want: to rule the world."

Noelle listened, fascinated, as Larry discussed Hitler's military strategy, the sudden withdrawal from the League of Nations, the mutual defense pact with Japan and Italy, not because of what he was saying but because she enjoyed watching his face as he talked. His dark eyes sparkled with enthusiasm as he spoke, blazing with an overpowering, irresistible vitality.

Noelle had never met anyone like him. He was—that rarity of rarities—a spendthrift with himself. He was open and warm and alive, sharing himself, enjoying life, making sure that everyone around him enjoyed it. He was like a magnet pulling into his orbit everyone who approached.

They arrived at the party, which was being given in a small flat on the rue Chemin Vert. The apartment was filled with a group of laughing, shouting people, most of them young. Larry introduced Noelle to the hostess, a predatory, sexy-looking redhead, and then was swallowed by the crowd. Noelle caught glimpses of him during the evening, surrounded by eager young girls, each trying to capture his attention. And yet there was no ego about him, Noelle thought. It was as though he were totally unaware of how attractive he was. Someone found a drink for Noelle and someone else offered to bring her a plate of food from the buffet, but she was suddenly not hungry. She wanted to be with the American, wanted him away from the girls who crowded around him. Men were coming up to her and trying to start conversations, but

Noelle's mind was elsewhere. From the moment they had walked in, the American had completely ignored her, had acted as though she did not exist. *Why not?* Noelle thought. Why should he bother with her when he could have any girl at the party? Two men were trying to engage her in conversation, but she could not concentrate. The room had suddenly become unbearably hot. She looked around for a means of escape.

A voice said in her ear, "Let's go," and a few moments later she and the American were out on the street, in the cool night air. The city was dark and quiet against the invisible Germans in the sky, and the cars glided through the streets like silent fish in a black sea.

They could not find a taxi, so they walked, had dinner in a little bistro on the place des Victoires and Noelle found that she was starved. She studied the American sitting across from her, and she wondered what it was that had happened to her. It was as though he had touched some wellspring deep within her that she had never even known existed. She had never felt happiness like this before. They talked about everything. She told him about her background, and he told her that he came from South Boston and was Boston Irish. His mother had been born in Kerry County.

"Where did you learn to speak French so well?" Noelle asked.

"I used to spend my summers at Cap D'Antibes when I was a kid. My old man was a stock-market tycoon until the bears got him."

"Bears?"

So Larry had to explain to her about the arcane ways of the stock market in America. Noelle did not care what he talked about, so long as he kept talking.

"Where are you living?"

"Nowhere." She told him about the taxi driver and Madame Delys and the fat man believing she was a Princess and offering to pay forty francs for her, and Larry laughed aloud.

"Do you remember where the house is?"

"Yes."

"Come on, Princess."

When they arrived at the house on the rue de Provence, the door was opened by the same uniformed maid. Her eyes lit up as she saw the handsome young American, then darkened when she saw who was with him.

"We want to see Madame Delys," Larry said. He and Noelle walked into the reception hall. There were several girls in the drawing room beyond. The maid left and a few minutes later Madame Delys entered. "Good evening, Monsieur," she said to Larry. She turned to Noelle, "Ah, I hope you have changed your mind."

"She hasn't," said Larry, pleasantly. "You have something that belongs to the Princess."

Madame Delys looked at him questioningly.

"Her suitcase and purse."

Madame Delys hesitated a moment, then left the room. A few minutes later the maid returned, carrying Noelle's purse and suitcase.

"*Merci,*" Larry said. He turned to Noelle. "Let's go, Princess."

That night Noelle moved in with Larry, to a small, clean hotel on the rue Lafayette. There was no discussion about it, it was inevitable for both of them. When they made love that night, it was more exciting than anything Noelle had ever known, a wild primitive explosion that shook them both. She lay in Larry's arms all night, holding him close, happier than she had ever dreamed possible.

The next morning they awoke, made love, and went out to explore the city. Larry was a wonderful guide, and he made Paris seem a lovely toy for Noelle's amusement. They had lunch in the Tuileries, spent the afternoon at Mal Maison and spent hours wandering around the place des Vosges at the end of Notre Dame, the oldest section of Paris, built by Louis XIII. He showed her places that were off the beaten track of the tourists, the place Maubert with its colorful street market and the quai de la Mégisserie with its cages of brightly hued birds and squeaky animals. He took her through the Marché de Buci and they listened to the din of the hawkers, pitching the merits of their bins of fresh tomatoes, their seaweed-bedded oysters, their neatly labeled cheeses. They went to the Du Pont, on Montparnasse. They had dinner on the Bateau Mouche and finished up by having onion soup at four in the morning at Les Halles with the butchers and truck drivers. Before they were through Larry had collected a large group of friends, and Noelle realized that it was because he had the gift of laughter. He had taught her to laugh and she had not known that laughter was within her. It was like a gift from a god. She was grateful to Larry and very much in love with him. It was dawn when they returned to their hotel room. Noelle was exhausted, but Larry was filled with energy, a restless dynamo. Noelle lay in bed watching him as he stood at the window looking at the sun rise over the rooftops of Paris.

"I love Paris," he said. "It's like a temple to the best things that men have ever done. It's a city of beauty and food and love." He turned to her and grinned, "Not necessarily in that order."

Noelle watched as he took off his clothes and climbed into bed beside her. She held him, loving the feel of him, the male smell of him. She thought of her father and how he had betrayed her. She had been wrong to judge all men by him and Auguste Lanchon. She knew now that there were men like Larry Douglas. And she also knew that there could never be anyone else for her.

"Do you know who the two greatest men who ever lived were, Princess?" he was asking.

"You," she said.

"Wilbur and Orville Wright. They gave man their real freedom. Have you ever flown?" She shook her head. "We had a summer place in Montauk—that's at the end of Long Island—and when I was a kid I used to watch the gulls wheel through the air over the beach, riding the current, and I would have given my soul to be up there with them. I knew I wanted to be a flyer before I could walk. A friend of the family took me up in an old biplane when I was nine, and I took my first flying lesson when I was fourteen. That's when I'm really alive, when I'm in the air."

And later:

"There's going to be a world war. Germany wants to own it all."

"It won't get France, Larry. No one can cross the Maginot Line."

He snorted: "I've crossed it a hundred times." She looked at him puzzled. "In the air, Princess. This is going to be an air war . . . my war."

And later, casually:

"Why don't we get married?"

It was the happiest moment of Noelle's life.

SUNDAY WAS A relaxed, lazy day. They had breakfast at a little outdoor café in Montmartre, went back to the room and spent almost the entire day in bed. Noelle could not believe anyone could be so ecstatic. It was pure magic when they made love, but she was just as content to lie there and listen to Larry talk and watch him as he moved restlessly about the room. Just being near him was enough for her. It was odd, she thought, how things worked out. She had grown up being called Princess by her father, and now, even though it had happened as a joke, Larry was calling her Princess. When she was with Larry, she *was* something. He had restored her faith in men. He was her world, and Noelle knew that she would never need anything more, and it seemed incredible to her that she could be so lucky, that he felt the same way about her.

"I wasn't going to get married until this war was over," he told her. "But to hell with that. Plans are made to be changed, right, Princess?"

She nodded, filled with a happiness that threatened to burst inside her.

"Let's get married by some *maire* in the country," Larry said. "Unless you want a big wedding?"

Noelle shook her head. "The country sounds wonderful."

He nodded. "Deal. I have to report back to my Squadron tonight. I'll meet you here next Friday. How does that sound?"

"I—I don't know if I can stand being away from you that long." Noelle's voice was shaky.

Larry took her in his arms and held her. "Love me?" he asked.

"More than my life," Noelle replied simply.

Two hours later Larry was on his way back to England. He did not let her drive to the airport with him. "I don't like good-byes," he said. He gave her a large fistful of franc notes. "Buy yourself a wedding gown, Princess. I'll see you in it next week." And he was gone.

Noelle spent the next week in a state of euphoria, going back to the places she and Larry had been, spending hours dreaming about their life together. The days seemed to drag by, the minutes stubbornly refusing to move, until Noelle thought she would go out of her mind.

She went to a dozen shops looking for her wedding dress, and finally she found exactly what she wanted, at Madeleine Vionett. It was a beautiful white organza with a high-necked bodice, long sleeves with a row of six pearl buttons, and three crinoline petticoats. It cost much more than Noelle had anticipated, but she did not hesitate. She used all the money that Larry had given her and nearly all her own savings. Her whole being was centered on Larry. She thought about ways to please him, she searched through her mind for memories that might amuse him, anecdotes that would entertain him. She felt like a schoolgirl.

And so it was that Noelle waited for Friday to come, in an agony of impatience, and when it finally arrived she was up at dawn and spent two hours bathing and dressing, changing clothes and changing again, trying to guess which dress would please Larry most. She put on her wedding gown, but quickly took it off again, afraid that it might bring bad luck. She was in a frenzy of excitement.

At ten o'clock Noelle stood in front of the pier glass in the bedroom, and she knew that she had never looked as beautiful. There was no ego in her appraisal; she was simply pleased for Larry, glad that she could bring him this gift. By noon he had not appeared, and Noelle wished that he had told her what time he expected to arrive. She kept phoning the desk for messages every ten minutes and kept picking up the phone to make sure it was working. By six o'clock that evening, there was still no word from him. By midnight he had not called, and Noelle sat huddled in a chair, staring at the phone, willing it to ring. She fell asleep, and when she woke, it was dawn, Saturday. She was still in the chair, stiff and cold. The dress she had so carefully chosen was wrinkled, and there was a run in her stocking.

Noelle changed clothes and stayed in the room all that day, stationing herself in front of the open window, telling herself that if she stayed there, Larry would appear; if she left, something terrible would happen to him. As Saturday morning lengthened into afternoon, she began to be filled with the conviction that there had been an accident. Larry's plane had crashed, and he was lying in a field or in a hospital, wounded or dead. Noelle's mind was filled with ghastly visions. She sat up all night Saturday, sick with worry, afraid to leave the room and not knowing how to reach Larry.

When Noelle had not heard from him by Sunday noon, she could stand it no longer. She had to telephone him. But how? With a war on it was difficult to place an overseas call and she was not even certain where Larry was. She knew only that he flew with the RAF in some American squadron. She picked up the telephone and spoke to the switchboard operator.

"It is impossible," the operator said flatly.

Noelle explained the situation, and whether it was her words or the frantic despair in her voice she never knew, but two hours later she was talking to the War Ministry in London. They could not help her, but they transferred her to the Air Ministry at Whitehall who put her through to Combat Operations, where she was disconnected before she could get any information. It was four more hours before Noelle was reconnected, and by then she was on the verge of hysteria. Air Operations could give her no information and suggested she try the War Ministry.

"I've talked to them!" Noelle screamed into the phone. She began to sob, and the male English voice at the other end of the phone said in embarrassment, "Please, miss, it can't be that bad. Hold on a moment."

Noelle held the receiver in her hand, knowing that it was hopeless, certain that Larry was dead and that she would never know how or where he died. And she was about to replace the receiver when the voice spoke in her ear again and said cheerfully, "What you want, miss, is the Eagle Squadron. They're the Yanks, based in Yorkshire. It's a bit irregular, but I'm going to put you through to Church Fenton, their airfield. Their chaps will be able to help you." And the line went dead.

It was eleven o'clock that night before Noelle could get the call through again. A disembodied voice said, "Church Fenton Air Base," and the connection was so bad that Noelle could barely hear him. It was as though he were speaking from the bottom of the sea. He was obviously having difficulty hearing her. "Speak up, please," he said. By now, Noelle's nerves were so frayed that she could hardly control her voice.

"I'm calling"—she did not even know his rank. Lieutenant? Captain? Major? "I'm calling Larry Douglas. This is his fiancée."

"I can't hear you, miss. Can you speak louder, please?"

On the edge of panic Noelle screamed out the words again, sure that the man at the other end of the phone was trying to conceal from her that Larry was dead. For a miraculous instant the line cleared, and she heard the voice saying as though he were in the next room, "Lieutenant Larry Douglas?"

"Yes," she said, holding on tightly to her emotions.

"Just a moment, please."

Noelle waited for what seemed an eternity and then the voice came back on the line and said, "Lieutenant Douglas is on weekend leave. If it's urgent, he can be reached at the Hotel Savoy ballroom in London, General Davis' party." And the line went dead.

WHEN THE MAID came in to clean the room the next morning, she found Noelle on the floor, semiconscious. The maid stared at her a moment, tempted to mind her own business and leave. Why did these things always have to happen in *her* rooms? She went over and touched Noelle's forehead. It was burning hot. Grumbling, the maid waddled down the hall and asked the porter to send up the manager. One hour later an ambulance pulled up outside the hotel and two young interns carrying a stretcher were directed to Noelle's room. Noelle was unconscious. The young intern in charge raised her eyelid, put a stethoscope to her chest and listened to the rales as she breathed. "Pneumonia," he said to his companion. "Let's get her out of here."

They lifted Noelle onto the stretcher and five minutes later the ambulance was racing toward the hospital. She was rushed into an oxygen tent, and it was four days before she was fully conscious. She dragged herself reluctantly up from the murky green depths of oblivion, subconsciously knowing something terrible had happened and fighting not to remember what it was. As the awful thing floated closer and closer to the surface of her mind, and she struggled to keep it from herself, it suddenly came to her clear and whole. Larry Douglas. Noelle began to weep, racked with sobs until she finally drifted off into a half-sleep. She felt a hand gently holding hers, and she knew that Larry had come back to her, that everything was all right. Noelle opened her eyes and stared at a stranger in a white uniform, taking her pulse. "Well! Welcome back," he announced cheerfully.

"Where am I?" Noelle asked.

"L'Hotel-Dieu, the City Hospital."

"What am I doing here?"

"Getting well. You've had double pneumonia. I'm Israel Katz." He was young, with a strong, intelligent face and deep-set brown eyes.

"Are you my doctor?"

"Intern," he said. "I brought you in." He smiled at her. "I'm glad you made it. We weren't sure."

"How long have I been here?"

"Four days."

"Would you do me a favor?" she asked weakly.

"If I can."

"Call the Hotel Lafayette. Ask them—" she hesitated. "Ask them if there are any messages for me."

"Well, I'm awfully busy—"

Noelle squeezed his hand fiercely. "Please. It's important. My fiancé is trying to get in touch with me."

He grinned. "I don't blame him. All right. I'll take care of it," he promised. "Now you get some sleep."

"Not until I hear from you," she said.

He left, and Noelle lay there waiting. Of course Larry had been trying to get in touch with her. There had been some terrible misunderstanding. He would explain it all to her and everything would be all right again.

It was two hours before Israel Katz returned. He walked up to her bed and set down a suitcase. "I brought your clothes. I went to the hotel myself," he said.

She looked up at him, and he could see her face tense.

"I'm sorry," he said, embarrassed. "No messages."

Noelle stared at him for a long time, then turned her face to the wall, dry-eyed.

NOELLE WAS RELEASED from the hospital two days later. Israel Katz came to say good-bye to her. "Do you have any place to go?" he asked. "Or a job?"

She shook her head.

"What work do you do?"

"I'm a model."

"I might be able to help you."

She remembered the taxi driver and Madame Delys. "I don't need any help," she said.

Israel Katz wrote a name on a piece of paper. "If you change your mind, go there. It's a small fashion house. An aunt of mine owns it. I'll talk to her about you. Do you have any money?"

She did not answer.

"Here." He pulled a few francs out of his pocket and handed them to her. "I'm sorry I don't have more. Interns aren't very well paid."

"Thank you," Noelle said.

She sat at a small street café sipping a coffee and deciding how to pick up the pieces of her life. She knew that she had to survive, for she had a reason to live now. She was filled with a deep and burning hatred that was so all-consuming that it left no room for anything else. She was an avenging Phoenix rising from the ashes of the emotions that Larry Douglas had murdered in her. She would not rest until she had destroyed him. She did not know how, or when, but she knew that one day she would make it happen.

Now she needed a job and a place to sleep. Noelle opened her purse and took out the piece of paper that the young intern had given her. She studied it a moment and made up her mind. That afternoon she went to see Israel Katz's aunt and was given a job modeling in a small, second-rate fashion house on the rue Boursault.

Israel Katz's aunt turned out to be a middle-aged, gray-haired woman with the face of a harpy and the soul of an angel. She mothered all her girls and they adored her. Her name was Madame Rose. She gave Noelle an advance on her salary and found her a tiny apartment near the salon. The first thing Noelle did when she unpacked was to hang up her wedding dress. She put it in the front of the closet so that it was the first thing she saw in the morning and the last thing she saw when she undressed at night.

NOELLE KNEW THAT she was pregnant before there were any visible signs of it, before any tests had been made, before she missed her period. She could sense the new life that had formed in her womb, and at night she lay in bed staring at the ceiling thinking about it, her eyes glowing with wild animal pleasure.

On her first day off Noelle phoned Israel Katz and made a date to meet him for lunch.

"I'm pregnant," she told him.

"How do you know? Have you had any tests?"

"I don't need any tests."

He shook his head. "Noelle, a lot of women think they are going to have babies when they are not. How many periods have you missed?"

She pushed the question aside, impatiently. "I want your help."

He stared at her. "To get rid of the baby? Have you discussed this with the father?"

"He's not here."

"You know abortions are illegal. I could get into terrible trouble."

Noelle studied him a moment. "What's your price?"

His face tightened angrily. "Do you think everything has a price, Noelle?"

"Of course," she said simply. "Anything can be bought and sold."

"Does that include you?"

"Yes, but I'm very expensive. Will you help me?"

There was a long hesitation. "All right. I'll want to make some tests first."

"Very well."

The following week Israel Katz arranged for Noelle to go to the laboratory at the hospital. When the test results were returned two days later, he telephoned her at work. "You were right," he said. "You're pregnant."

"I know."

"I've arranged for you to have a curettage at the hospital. I've told them that your husband was killed in an accident and that you are unable to have the baby. We'll do the operation next Saturday."

"No," she said.

"Is Saturday a bad day for you?"

"I'm not ready for the abortion yet, Israel. I just wanted to know that I could count on you to help me."

Madame Rose noticed the change in Noelle, not merely a physical change, but something that went much deeper, a radiance, an inner glow that seemed to fill her. Noelle walked around with a constant smile, as though hugging some wonderful secret.

"You have found a lover," Madame Rose said. "It shows in your eyes."

Noelle nodded. "Yes, Madame."

"He is good for you. Hold onto him."

"I will," Noelle promised. "As long as I can."

Three weeks later Israel Katz telephoned her. "I haven't heard from you," he said. "I was wondering if you had forgotten?"

"No," Noelle said. "I think of it all the time."

"How do you feel?"

"Wonderful."

"I've been looking at the calendar. I think that we had better go to work."

"I'm not ready yet," Noelle said.

Three weeks passed before Israel Katz telephoned her again.

"How about having dinner with me?" he asked.

"All right."

They arranged to meet at a cheap café on the rue de Chat Qui Peche. Noelle had started to suggest a better restaurant when she remembered what Israel had said about interns not having much money.

He was waiting for her when she arrived. They chatted aimlessly through dinner and it was not until the coffee arrived that Israel discussed what was on his mind.

"Do you still want to have the abortion?" he asked.

Noelle looked at him in surprise. "Of course."

"Then you must have it right away. You're more than two months pregnant."

She shook her head. "No, not yet, Israel."

"Is this your first pregnancy?"

"Yes."

"Then let me tell you something, Noelle. Up until three months, an abortion is usually an easy matter. The embryo has not been fully formed and all you need is a simple curettage, but after three months"—he hesitated—"it's another kind of operation, and it becomes dangerous. The longer you wait, the more dangerous it becomes. I want you to have the operation now."

Noelle leaned forward. "What's the baby like?"

"Now?" He shrugged. "Just a lot of cells. Of course, all the nuclei are there to form a complete human being."

"And after three months?"

"The embryo starts to become a person."

"Can it feel things?"

"It responds to blows and loud noises."

She sat there, her eyes locked onto his. "Can it feel pain?"

"I suppose so. But it is protected with an amniotic sac." He suddenly felt an uneasy stirring. "It would be pretty hard for anything to hurt it."

Noelle lowered her eyes and sat staring at the table, silent and thoughtful.

Israel Katz studied her a moment and then said shyly, "Noelle, if you want to keep this baby and are afraid to because it will have no father . . . well, I would be willing to marry you and give the baby a name."

She looked up in surprise. "I have already told you. I don't want this baby. I want to have an abortion."

"Then, for Christ's sake, have it!" Israel shouted. He lowered his voice as he realized that other patrons were staring at him. "If you wait much longer, there isn't a doctor in France who will do it. Don't you understand? If you wait too long, you could die!"

"I understand," Noelle said quietly. "If I were going to have this baby, what kind of diet would you put me on?"

He ran his fingers through his hair, bewildered. "Lots of milk and fruit, lean meat."

That night on her way home Noelle stopped at the corner market near her apartment and bought two quarts of milk and a large box of fresh fruit.

Ten days later Noelle went into Madame Rose's office and told her that she was pregnant and asked for a leave of absence.

"For how long?" Madame Rose asked, eyeing Noelle's figure.

"Six or seven weeks."

Madame Rose sighed. "Are you sure what you are doing is the best thing?"

"I'm sure," Noelle replied.

"Is there anything I can do?"

"Nothing."

"Very well. Come back to me as soon as you can. I will ask the cashier to give you an advance on your salary."

"Thank you, Madame."

. . .

FOR THE NEXT four weeks Noelle never left her apartment, except to buy groceries. She felt no hunger and ate very little for herself, but she drank enormous quantities of milk for the baby and crammed her body with fruit. She was not alone in the apartment. The baby was with her and she talked to him constantly. She knew it was a boy just as she had known she was pregnant. She had named him Larry.

"I want you to grow to be big and strong," she said as she drank her milk. "I want you to be healthy . . . healthy and strong when you die." She lay in bed every day plotting her vengeance against Larry and his son. What was in her body was not a part of her. It belonged to him and she was going to kill it. It was the only thing of his that he had left her, and she was going to destroy it just as he had tried to destroy her.

How little Israel Katz had understood her! She was not interested in a formless embryo that knew nothing. She wanted Larry's spawn to feel what was going to happen to him, to suffer, as she had suffered. The wedding dress was hanging near her bed now, always in sight, a talisman of evil, a reminder of his betrayal. *First, Larry's son, then Larry.*

The phone rang often, but Noelle lay in bed, lost in her dreams until it stopped. She was sure that it was Israel Katz trying to reach her.

One evening there was a pounding on the door. Noelle lay in bed, ignoring it, but finally when the pounding continued, she dragged herself up and opened the door.

Israel Katz was standing there, his face filled with concern. "My God, Noelle, I've been calling you for days."

He looked at her bulging stomach. "I thought you might have had it done somewhere else."

She shook her head. "No. You're going to do it."

Israel stared at her. "Haven't you understood anything I told you? It's too late! No one's going to do it."

He saw the empty bottles of milk and the fresh fruit on the table, then looked back at her. "You *do* want the baby," he said. "Why won't you admit it?"

"Tell me, Israel, what's he like now?"

"Who?"

"The baby. Does he have eyes and ears? Does he have fingers and toes? Can he feel pain?"

"For Christ's sake, Noelle, stop it. You talk as if . . . as if . . ."

"What?"

"Nothing." He shook his head in despair. "I don't understand you."

She smiled softly. "No. You don't."

He stood there a moment, making up his mind.

"All right, I'm putting my ass in a sling for you, but if you're really determined to have an abortion, let's get it over with. I have a doctor friend who owes me a favor. He'll . . ."

"No."

He stared at her.

"Larry's not ready yet," she said.

THREE WEEKS LATER at four o'clock in the morning, Israel Katz was awakened by a furious concierge pounding on his door. "Telephone, Monsieur Night Owl!" he yelled. "And tell your caller that it is the middle of the night, when respectable people are asleep!"

Israel stumbled out of bed and sleepily made his way down the hall to the telephone, wondering what crisis had arisen. He picked up the receiver.

"Israel?"

He did not recognize the voice at the other end of the phone.

"Yes?"

"Now . . ." It was a whisper, disembodied and anonymous.

"Who is this?"

"Now. Come now, Israel . . ."

There was an eeriness to the voice, an unearthly quality that sent a chill down his spine. "Noelle?"

"Now . . ."

"For Christ's sake," he exploded. "I won't do it. It's too late. You'll die, and I'm not going to be responsible. Get yourself to a hospital."

There was a click in his ear, and he stood there holding the phone. He slammed the receiver and went back to his room, his mind churning. He knew that he could not do any good now, no one could. She was five and a half months pregnant. He had warned her time and time again, but she had refused to listen. Well, it was her responsibility. He wanted to have no part of it.

He began to dress as fast as he could, his bowels cold with fear.

WHEN ISRAEL KATZ walked into her apartment, Noelle was lying on the floor in a pool of blood, hemorrhaging. Her face was dead white, but it showed no sign of the agony that must have been racking her body. She was wearing what appeared to be a wedding dress. Israel knelt at her side. "What happened?" he asked. "How did—?" He stopped, as his eyes fell on a bloody, twisted wire coat hanger near her feet.

"Jesus Christ!" He was filled with a rage and at the same time a terrible frustrating feeling of helplessness. The blood was pouring out faster now, there was not a moment to lose.

"I'll call an ambulance," and he started to rise.

Noelle reached up and grabbed his arm with surprising strength, and pulled him back down to her.

"Larry's baby is dead," she said, and her face was lit with a beautiful smile.

A team of six doctors worked for five hours trying to save Noelle's life. The diagnosis was septic poisoning, perforated womb, blood poisoning and shock. All the doctors agreed that there was little chance that she could live. By six o'clock that night Noelle was out of danger and two days later, she was sitting up in bed able to talk. Israel came to see her.

"All the doctors say that it is a miracle you're alive, Noelle."

She shook her head. It was simply not her time to die. She had taken her first vengeance on Larry, but it was only the beginning. There was more to come. Much more. But first she had to find him. It would take time. But she would do it.

3

CATHERINE

CHICAGO: 1939–1940

The growing winds of war that were blowing across Europe were reduced to no more than gentle, warning zephyrs when they reached the shores of the United States.

On the Northwestern campus, a few more boys joined the ROTC, there were student rallies urging President Roosevelt to declare war on Germany and a few seniors enlisted in the Armed Forces. In general, however, the sea of complacency remained the same, and the underground swell that was soon to sweep over the country was barely perceptible.

As she walked to her cashier's job at the Roost that October afternoon, Catherine Alexander wondered whether the war would change her life, if it came. She knew one change that she had to make, and she was determined to do it as soon as possible. She desperately wanted to know what it was like to have a man hold her in his arms and make love to her, and she knew that she wanted it partly because of her physical needs, but also because she felt she was missing out on an important and wonderful experience. My God, what if she got run over by a car and they did a post mortem on her and discovered she was a virgin! No, she had to do something about it. Now.

Catherine glanced around the Roost carefully, but she did not see the face she was looking for. When Ron Peterson came in an hour later with Jean-Anne, Catherine felt her body tingle and her heart begin to pound. She turned away as they walked past her, and out of the corner of her eye she saw the two make their way to Ron's booth and sit down. Large banners were strung around the room, "TRY OUR DOUBLE HAMBURGER SPECIAL" . . . "TRY OUR LOVER'S DELIGHT" . . . "TRY OUR TRIPLE MALT."

Catherine took a deep breath and walked over to the booth. Ron Peterson was studying the menu, trying to make up his mind. "I don't know what I want," he was saying.

"How hungry are you?" Jean-Anne asked.

"I'm starved."

"Then try this." They both looked up in surprise. It was Catherine standing over the booth. She handed Ron Peterson a folded note, turned around and walked back to the cash register.

Ron opened the note, looked at it and burst into laughter. Jean-Anne watched him coolly.

"Is it a private joke or can anyone get in on it?"

"Private," Ron grinned. He slipped the note into his pocket.

Ron and Jean-Anne left shortly afterward. Ron didn't say anything as he paid his check, but he gave Catherine a long, speculative look, smiled and walked out with Jean-Anne on his arm. Catherine looked after them, feeling like an idiot. She didn't even know how to make a success-ful pass at a boy.

When her shift was up, Catherine got into her coat, said good night to the girl coming in to relieve her and went outside. It was a warm autumn evening with a cooling breeze skipping in off the lake. The sky looked like purple velvet with soft, far-flung stars just out of reach. It was a perfect evening to—what? Catherine made a list in her mind.

I can go home and wash my hair.

I can go to the library and study for the Latin exam tomorrow.

I can go to a movie.

I can hide in the bushes and rape the first sailor who comes along.

I can go get myself committed.

Committed, she decided.

As she started to move along the campus toward the library, a figure stepped out from behind a lamp post.

"Hi, Cathy. Where you headed?"

It was Ron Peterson, smiling down at her, and Catherine's heart started to pound until it began to burst out of her chest. She watched as it took off on its own, beating its way through the air. She became aware that Ron was staring at her. No wonder. How many girls did he know who could do that heart trick? She desperately wanted to comb her hair and fix her makeup and check the seams of her stockings, but she tried to let none of her nervousness show. Rule one: Keep calm.

"Blug," she mumbled.

"Where are you headed?"

Should she give him her list? God, no! He'd think she was insane. This was her big chance and she must not do a single thing to destroy it. She looked up at him, her eyes as warm and inviting as Carole Lombard's in *Nothing Sacred.*

"I didn't have any special plans," she said invitingly.

Ron was studying her, still not sure of her, some primeval instinct making him cautious. "Would you *like* to do something special?" he asked.

This was it. The Proposition. The point of no return. "Name it," she said, "and I'm yours." And cringed inwardly. It sounded so corny. No one said, "Name it and I'm yours" except in bad Fannie Hurst novels. He was going to turn on his heel and walk away in disgust.

But he didn't. Incredibly, he smiled, took her arm and said, "Let's go."

Catherine walked along with him, stunned. It had been as simple as that. She was on her way to getting laid. She began to tremble inside. If he found out she was a virgin, she would be finished. And what was she going to talk about when she was in bed with him? Did people talk when they were actually doing it, or did they wait until it was over? She didn't want to be rude, but she had no idea what the rules were.

"Have you had dinner?" Ron was asking.

"Dinner?" She stared up at him, trying to think. Should she have had dinner? If she said yes, then he could take her right to bed and she could get it over with. "No," she said quickly, "I haven't." *Now why did I say that? I've ruined everything.* But Ron did not seem upset.

"Good. Do you like Chinese food?"

"It's my favorite." She hated it, but the gods certainly weren't going to count a little yellow lie on the biggest night of her life.

"There's a good Chinese joint over on Estes. Lum Fong's. Do you know it?"

No, but she would never forget it as long as she lived.

What did you do the night you lost your cherry?

Oh, I went to Lum Fong's first and had some Chinese food with Ron Peterson.

Was it good?

Sure. But you know Chinese food. An hour later, I was sexy again.

They had reached his car, a maroon Reo convertible. Ron held the door open for Catherine, and she sat in the seat where all the other girls she envied had once sat. Ron was charming, handsome, a top athlete. And a sex maniac. It would make a good title for a movie. *The Sex Maniac and the Virgin.* Maybe she should have held out for a nicer restaurant like Henrici's in the Loop and then Ron would have thought, *This is the kind of girl I want to take home to Mother.*

"A penny for your thoughts," he said.

Oh, great! All right, so he wasn't the most brilliant conversationalist in the world. But that wasn't why she was here, was it? She looked up at him sweetly. "I was just thinking about you." She snuggled against him.

He grinned. "You really had me fooled, Cathy."

"I did?"

"I always thought you were pretty standoffish—I mean, not interested in men."

The word you're jumbling for is lesbian, Catherine thought, but aloud she said, "I just like to pick my time and place."

"I'm glad you picked me."

"So am I." And she was. She really was. She could be certain that Ron was a good lover. He had been factory-tested and approved by every horny coed within a radius of a hundred and fifty miles. It would have been humiliating to have had her first sexual experience with someone as ignorant as she was. With Ron she was getting a master. After tonight she would not be calling herself Saint Catherine any longer. Instead she would probably be known as "Catherine the Great." And this time she would know what the "Great" stood for. She would be fantastic in bed. The trick was not to panic. All the wonderful things she had read about in the little green books she used to keep hidden from her mother and father were about to happen to her. Her body was going to be an organ filled with exquisite music. Oh, she knew it would hurt the first time; it always did. But she would not let Ron know. She would move her behind around a lot because men hated for a woman to just lie there, motionless. And when Ron penetrated her, she would bite her lip to conceal the pain and cover it up with a sexy cry.

"What?"

She turned to Ron, appalled, and realized she had cried aloud. "I—I didn't say anything."

"You gave a kind of funny cry."

"Did I?" She forced a little laugh.

"You're a million miles away."

She analyzed the line and decided it was bad. She must be more like Jean-Anne. Catherine put her hand on his arm and moved closer. "I'm right here," she said.

She tried to make her voice throaty, like Jean Arthur in *Calamity Jane.*

Ron looked down at her, confused, but the only thing he could read in her face was an eager warmth.

Lum Fong's was a dreary-looking, run-of-the-mill Chinese restaurant located under the Elevated. All through dinner they could hear the rumble of the trains as they ran overhead rattling the dishes. The restaurant looked like a thousand other anonymous Chinese restaurants all over America, but Catherine carefully absorbed the details of the booth they were seated in, committing to memory the cheap, spotted wallpaper, the chipped china teapot, the soy-sauce stains on the table.

A little Chinese waiter came up to the table and asked if they wanted a drink. Catherine had tasted whiskey a few times in her life and hated it, but this was New Year's Eve, the Fourth of July, the End of her Maidenhood. It was fitting to celebrate.

"I'll have an old-fashioned with a cherry in it." *Cherry! Oh, God!* It was a dead giveaway.

"Scotch and soda," Ron said.

The waiter bowed himself away from the table. Catherine wondered if it were true that Oriental women were built slantwise.

"I don't know why we never became friends before," Ron was saying. "Everyone says you're the brightest girl in the whole goddamned university."

"You know how people exaggerate."

"And you're damned pretty."

"Thank you." She tried to make her voice sound like Katherine Hepburn in *Alice Adams* and looked meaningfully into his eyes. She was no longer Catherine Alexander. She was a sex machine. She was about to join Mae West, Marlene Dietrich, Cleopatra. They were all going to be sisters under the foreskin.

The waiter brought the drink and she finished it in one quick nervous gulp. Ron watched her in surprise.

"Easy," he warned. "That's pretty potent stuff."

"I can handle it," Catherine assured him, confidently.

"Another round," he told the waiter. Ron reached across the table and caressed her hand. "It's funny. Everybody at school had you wrong."

"Wrong. No one at school's had me."

He stared at her. *Careful, don't be clever.* Men preferred to bed girls who had excessively large mammary glands and gluteus maximus muscles and exceedingly small cerebrums.

"I've had a—thing for you for a long time," she said, hurriedly.

"You sure kept it a secret." Ron pulled out the note she had written and smoothed it out. "Try our Cashier," he read aloud, and laughed. "So far I like it better than the Banana Split." He ran his hands up and down Catherine's arm and his touch sent tiny ripples down her spine, just like the books said it would. Perhaps after tonight she would write a manual on sex to instruct all the poor, dumb virgins who didn't know what life was all about. After the second drink Catherine was beginning to feel sorry for them.

"It's a pity."

"What's a pity?"

She had spoken aloud again. She decided to be bold. "I was feeling sorry for all the virgins in the world," she said.

Ron grinned at Catherine. "I'll drink to that." He lifted his glass. She looked at him sitting across from her obviously enjoying her company. She had nothing to worry about. Everything was going beautifully. He asked if she would like another drink, but Catherine declined. She did not intend to be in an alcoholic stupor when she was deflowered. *Deflowered? Did people still use words like deflowered?* Anyway, she wanted to remember every moment, every sensation. *Oh, my God! She wasn't wearing anything! Would he? Surely a man as experienced as Ron Peterson would have something to put on, some protection so she wouldn't get pregnant. What if he was expecting the same thing? What if he was thinking that a girl as experienced as Catherine Alexander would surely have some protection? Could she come right out and ask him? She decided that she would rather die first, right at the table. They could carry her body away and give her a ceremonial Chinese burial.*

Ron ordered the dollar seventy-five six-course dinner, and Catherine pretended to eat it, but it might as well have been Chinese cardboard. She was beginning to get so tense she couldn't taste anything. Her tongue was suddenly dry and the roof of her mouth felt strangely numb. *What if she had just had a stroke?* If she had sex right after a stroke, it would probably kill her. Perhaps she should warn Ron. It would hurt his reputation if they found a dead girl in his bed. Or maybe it would enhance it.

"What's the matter?" Ron asked. "You look pale."

"I feel great," Catherine said, recklessly. "I'm just excited about being with you."

Ron looked at her approvingly, his brown eyes taking in every detail of her face and moving down to her breasts and lingering there. "I feel the same way," he replied.

The waiter had taken the dishes away, and Ron had paid the check. He looked at her, but Catherine couldn't move.

"Do you want anything else?" Ron asked.

Do I? Oh, yes! I want to be on a slow boat to China. I want to be in a cannibal's kettle being boiled for dinner. I want my mother!

Ron was watching her, waiting. Catherine took a deep breath. "I—I can't think of anything."

"Good." He drew the syllable out, long and lastingly so that it seemed to put a bed on the table between them. "Let's go." He stood up and Catherine followed. The euphoric feeling from the drinks had completely vanished and her legs began to tremble.

They were outside in the warm night air when a sudden thought hit Catherine and filled her with relief. *He's not going to take me to bed tonight. Men never do that with a girl on the first date. He's going to ask me out to dinner again and next time we'll go to Henrici's and we'll get to know each other better. Really know each other. And we'll probably fall in love—madly—and he'll take me to meet his parents and then everything will be all right . . . and I won't feel this stupid panic.*

"Do you have any preference in motels?" Ron asked.

Catherine stared up at him, speechless. Gone were the dreams of a genteel musicale evening with his mother and father. The bastard was planning to take her to bed in a motel! Well, that was what she wanted, wasn't it? Wasn't that the reason she had written that insane note?

Ron's hand was on Catherine's shoulder now, sliding down her arm. She felt a warm sensation in her groin. She swallowed and said, "If you've seen one motel, you've seen them all."

Ron looked at her strangely. But all he said was, "OK. Let's go."

They got into his car and started driving west. Catherine's body had turned into a block of ice, but her mind was racing at a feverish pitch. The last time she had stayed in a motel was when she was eight and was driving across country with her mother and father. Now she was going to one to go to bed with a man who was a total stranger. What did she know about him anyway? Only that he was handsome, popular and knew an easy lay when he saw one.

Ron reached over and took her hand. "Your hands are cold," he said.

"Cold hands, hot legs." *Oh, Christ,* she thought. *There I go again.* For some reason, the lyrics of "Ah, Sweet Mystery of Life" started to go through Catherine's head. Well she was about to solve it. She was on her way to finding out what everything was all about. The books, the sexy advertisements, the thinly veiled love lyrics—"Rock Me in the Cradle of Love," "Do It Again," "Birds Do It." *OK,* she thought. *Now Catherine is going to do it.*

Ron turned south onto Clark Street.

Ahead on both sides of the street were huge blinking red eyes, neon signs that were alive in the night, screaming out their offers of cheap and temporary havens for impatient young lovers. "EASY REST MOTEL," "OVERNIGHT MOTEL," "COME INN," (*Now that had to be Freudian!*) "TRAVELER'S REST." The paucity of imagination was staggering, but on the other hand the owners of these places were probably too busy bustling fornicating young couples in and out of bed to worry about being literary.

"This is about the best of them," Ron said, pointing to a sign ahead. "PARADISE INN—VACANCY."

It was a symbol. There was a vacancy in Paradise, and she, Catherine Alexander, was going to fill it.

Ron swung the car into the courtyard next to a small whitewashed office with a sign that read: RING BELL AND ENTER. The courtyard consisted of about two dozen numbered wooden bungalows.

"How does this look?" Ron asked.

Like Dante's Inferno. Like the Colosseum in Rome when the Christians were about to be thrown to the lions. Like the Temple of Delphi when a Vestal Virgin was about to get hers.

Catherine felt that excited feeling in her groin again. "Terrific," she said. "Just terrific."

Ron smiled knowingly. "I'll be right back." He put his hand on Catherine's knee, sliding it up toward her thigh, gave her a quick, impersonal kiss and swung out of the car and went into the office. She sat there, looking after him, trying to make her mind blank.

She heard the wail of a siren in the distance. *Oh, my God,* she thought wildly, *it's a raid! They're always raiding these places!*

The door to the manager's office opened and Ron came out. He was carrying a key and apparently was deaf to the siren which was coming closer and closer. He walked over to Catherine's side of the car and opened the door.

"All set," he said. The siren was a screaming banshee moving in on them. Could the police arrest them for merely being in the courtyard?

"Come on," Ron said.

"Don't you hear that?"

"Hear what?"

The siren passed them and went ululating down the street away from them, receding into the distance. Damn! "The birds," she said weakly.

There was a look of impatience on Ron's face.

"If there's anything wrong—" he said.

"No, no," Catherine cut in quickly. "I'm coming." She got out of the car and they moved toward one of the bungalows. "I hope you got my lucky number," she said brightly.

"What did you say?"

Catherine looked up at him and suddenly realized no words had come out. Her mouth was completely dry. "Nothing," she croaked.

They reached the door and it said number thirteen. It was exactly what she deserved. It was a sign from heaven that she was going to get pregnant, that God was out to punish Saint Catherine.

Ron unlocked the door and held it open for her. He flicked on the light switch and Catherine stepped inside. She could not believe it. The room seemed to consist of one enormous bed. The only other furniture was an uncomfortable-looking easy chair in a corner, a small dressing table with a mirror over it, and next to the bed, a battered radio with a slot for feeding it quarters. No one would ever walk in here and mistake this room for anything but what it was: a place where a boy brought a girl to screw her. You couldn't say, Well, here we are in the ski lodge, or the war games room, or the bridal suite at the Ambassador. No. What this was was a cheap love nest. Catherine turned to see what Ron was doing and he was throwing the bolt on the door. *Good. If the Vice Squad wanted them, they'd have to break down the door first.* She could see herself being carried out in the nude by two policemen while a photographer snapped her picture for the front page of the *Chicago Daily News*.

Ron moved up to Catherine and put his arms around her. "Are you nervous?" he asked.

She looked up at him and forced a laugh that would have made Margaret Sullavan proud. "Nervous? Ron, don't be silly."

He was still studying her, unsure. "You've done this before, haven't you, Cathy?"

"I don't keep a scorecard."

"I've had a strange feeling about you all evening."

Here it comes. He was going to throw her out on her virgin ass and tell her to get lost in a cold shower. Well, she wasn't going to let that happen. Not tonight. "What kind of feeling?"

"I don't know." Ron's voice was perplexed. "One minute you're kind of sexy and, you know, *with* it, and the next minute your mind is way off somewhere and you're as frigid as ice. It's like you're two people. Which one is the real Catherine Alexander?"

Frigid as ice, she automatically said to herself. Aloud she said, "I'll show you." She put her arms around him and kissed him on the lips and she could smell egg foo young.

He kissed her harder and pulled her close to him. He ran his hands over her breasts, caressing them, pushing his tongue into her mouth. Catherine felt a hot moisture deep down inside her and she could feel her pants dampen. *Here I go,* she thought. *It's really going to happen! It's really going to happen!* She clung to him harder, filled with a growing, almost unbearable excitement.

"Let's get undressed," Ron said hoarsely. He stepped back from her and started to take off his jacket.

"No," she said. "Let me." There was a new confidence in her voice. If this was the night of nights, she was going to do it right. She was going to remember everything she had ever read or heard. Ron wasn't going back to school to snicker to the girls about how he had made love to a dumb little virgin. Catherine might not have Jean-Anne's bust measurement, but she had a brain ten times as useful, and she was going to put it to work to make Ron so happy in bed he wouldn't be able to stand it. She took off his jacket and laid it on the bed, then reached for his tie.

"Hold it," Ron said. "I want to see you undress."

Catherine stared at him, swallowed, slowly reached for her zipper and got out of her dress. She was standing in her bra, slip, pants, shoes and stockings.

"Go on."

She hesitated a moment, then reached down and stepped out of her slip. *Lions, 2—Christians, 0,* she thought.

"Hey, great! Keep going."

Catherine slowly sat down on the bed and carefully removed her shoes and stockings, trying to make it look as sexy as she could. Suddenly she felt Ron behind her, undoing her bra. She let it fall to the bed. He lifted Catherine to her feet and started sliding her pants down. She took a deep breath and closed her eyes, wishing that she were in another place with another man, a human being who loved her, whom she loved, who would father splendid children to bear his name, who would fight for her and kill for her and for whom she would be an adoring helpmate. *A whore in his bed, a great cook in his kitchen, a charming hostess in his living room* . . . a man who would kill a son of a bitch like Ron Peterson for daring to bring her to this tacky, degrading room. Her pants fell to the floor. Catherine opened her eyes.

Ron was staring at her, his face filled with admiration. "My God, Cathy, you're beautiful," he said. "You're really beautiful." He bent down and kissed her breast. She caught a glimpse in the dressing-table mirror. It looked like a French farce, sordid and dirty. Everything inside her except the hot pain in her groin told her that this was dreary and ugly and wrong, but there was no way to stop it now. Ron was whipping off his tie and unbuttoning his shirt, his face flushed. He undid his belt and stripped down to his shorts, then sat down on the bed and started to take off his shoes and socks. "I mean it, Catherine," he said, his voice tight with emotion. "You're the most beautiful goddamn thing I've ever laid eyes on."

His words only increased Catherine's panic. Ron stood up, a broad, anticipatory grin on his face, and let his shorts drop to the floor. His male organ was standing out stiffly, like an enormous, inflated salami with hair around it. It was the largest, most incredible thing Catherine had ever seen in her life.

"How do you like that?" he said, looking down at it proudly.

Without thinking, Catherine said, "Sliced on rye. Hold the mustard and lettuce."

And she stood there, watching it go down.

IN CATHERINE'S SOPHOMORE year there was a change in the atmosphere of the campus.

For the first time there was a growing concern about what was happening in Europe and an increasing feeling that America was going to get involved. Hitler's dream of the thousand-year rule of the Third Reich was on its way to becoming a reality. The Nazis had occupied Denmark and invaded Norway.

Over the past six months the talk on campuses across the country had shifted from sex and clothes and proms to the ROTC and the draft and lend-lease. More and more college boys were appearing in army and navy uniforms.

One day Susie Roberts, a classmate from Senn, stopped Catherine in the corridor. "I want to say good-bye, Cathy. I'm leaving."

"Where are you going?"

"The Klondike."

"The *Klondike?*"

"Washington, D.C. All the girls are striking gold there. They say for every girl there are at least a hundred men. I like those odds." She looked at Catherine. "What do you want to stick around this place for? School's a drag. There's a whole big world waiting out there."

"I can't leave just now," Catherine said. She was not sure why: She had no real ties in Chicago. She corresponded regularly with her father in Omaha and talked to him on the telephone once or twice a month and each time he sounded as though he were in prison.

Catherine was on her own now. The more she thought about Washington, the more exciting it seemed. That evening she phoned her father and told him she wanted to quit school and go to work in Washington. He asked her if she would like to come to Omaha, but Catherine could sense the reluctance in his voice. He did not want her to be trapped, as he had been.

The next morning Catherine went to the dean of women and informed her she was quitting school. Catherine sent a telegram to Susie Roberts and the next day she was on a train to Washington, D.C.

4

NOELLE

PARIS: 1940

On Saturday, June 14, 1940, the German Fifth Army marched into a stunned Paris. The Maginot Line had turned out to be the biggest fiasco in the history of warfare and France lay defenseless before one of the most powerful military machines the world had ever known.

The day had begun with a strange gray pall that lay over the city, a terrifying cloud of unknown origin. For the last forty-eight hours sounds of intermittent gunfire had broken the unnatural, frightened silence of Paris. The roar of the cannons was outside the city, but the echoes reverberated into the heart of Paris. There had been a flood of rumors carried like a tidal wave over the radio, in newspapers and by word of mouth. The Boche were invading the French coast . . . London had been destroyed . . . Hitler had reached an accord with the British government . . . The Germans were going to wipe out Paris with a deadly new bomb. At first each rumor had been taken as gospel, creating its own panic, but constant crises finally exert a soporific effect, as though the mind and body, unable to absorb any further terror, retreat into a protective shell of apathy. Now the rumor mills had ground to a complete halt, newspaper presses had stopped printing and radio stations had stopped broadcasting. Human instinct had taken over from the machines, and the Parisians sensed that this was a day of decision. The gray cloud was an omen.

And then the German locusts began to swarm in.

SUDDENLY PARIS WAS a city filled with foreign uniforms and alien people, speaking a strange, guttural tongue, speeding down the wide, tree-lined avenues in large Mercedes limousines flying Nazi flags or pushing their way along the sidewalks that now belonged to them. They were truly the *über Mensch,* and it was their destiny to conquer and rule the world.

Within two weeks an amazing transformation had taken place. Signs in German appeared everywhere. Statues of French heroes had been knocked down and the swastika flew from all state buildings. German efforts to eradicate everything Gallic reached ridiculous proportions. The markings on hot and cold water taps were changed from *chaud* and *froid* to *heiss* and *kalt.* The place de Broglie in Strasbourg became Adolf Hitler Platz. Statues of Lafayette, Ney and Kleber were dynamited by squadrons of Nazis. Inscriptions on the monuments for the dead were replaced by "GEFALLEN FUR DEUTSCHLAND."

The German occupation troops were enjoying themselves. While French food was too rich and covered with too many sauces, it was still a pleasant change from war rations. The soldiers neither knew nor cared that Paris was the city of Baudelaire, Dumas and Molière. To them Paris was a garish, eager, overpainted whore with her skirts pulled up over her hips and they raped her, each in his own way. The Storm-troopers forced young French girls to go to bed with them, sometimes at the point of a bayonet, while their leaders like Goering and Himmler raped the Louvre and the rich private estates they greedily confiscated from the newly created enemies of the Reich.

If French corruption and opportunism rose to the surface in the time of France's crisis, so did the heroism. One of the underground's secret weapons was the *Pompiers,* the fire department, which in France is under the jurisdiction of the army. The Germans had confiscated dozens of buildings for the use of the army, the Gestapo and various ministries, and the location of these buildings was of course no secret. At an underground resistance headquarters in St. Remy resistance leaders pored over large maps detailing the location of each building. Experts were then assigned their targets, and the following day a speeding car or an innocent-looking bicyclist would pass by one of the buildings and fling a homemade bomb through the window. Up to that point the damage was slight. The ingenuity of the plan lay in what followed next.

The Germans would call in the *Pompiers* to put out the fire. Now it is instinctive in all countries that when there is a conflagration the firemen are in complete charge: And so it was in Paris. The *Pompiers* raced into the building while the Germans stood meekly aside and watched them destroy everything in sight with high-pressure hoses, axes and—when the opportunity presented itself—their own incendiary bombs. In this way the underground managed to destroy priceless German records locked away in the fortresses of the Wehrmacht and the Gestapo. It took almost six months for the German high command to figure out what was happening, and by that time irreparable damage had been done. The Gestapo could prove nothing, but every member of the *Pompiers* was rounded up and sent to the Russian front to fight.

There was a shortage of everything from food to soap. There was no gasoline, no meat, no dairy products. The Germans had confiscated everything. Stores that carried luxury goods stayed open, but their only customers were the soldiers who paid in occupation marks which were identical with the regular marks except that they lacked the white strip at the edge and the printed promise to pay was not signed.

"Who will redeem these?" the French shopkeepers moaned.

And the Germans grinned, "The Bank of England."

Not all Frenchmen suffered, however. For those with money and connections there was always the Black Market.

NOELLE PAGE'S LIFE was changed very little by the occupation. She was working as a model at Chanel's on rue Canbon in a hundred-and-fifty-year-old graystone building that looked ordinary on the outside, but was very smartly decorated within. The war, like all wars, had created overnight millionaires, and there was no shortage of customers. The propositions that came to Noelle were more numerous than ever; the only difference was that most of them were now in German. When she was not working, she would sit for hours at small outdoor cafés on the Champs-Élysées, or on the Left Bank near the Pont Neuf. There were hundreds of men in German uniforms, many of them with young French girls. The French civilian men were either too old or lame, and Noelle supposed that the younger ones had been sent to camps or conscripted for military duty. She could tell the Germans at a glance, even when they were not in uniform. They had a look of arrogance stamped on their faces, the look that conquerors have had since the days of Alexander and Hadrian. Noelle did not hate them, nor did she like them. They simply did not touch her.

She was filled with a busy inner life, carefully planning out each move. She knew exactly what her goal was, and she knew that nothing could stop her. As soon as she was able to afford it, she engaged a private detective who had handled a divorce for a model with whom she worked. The detective's name was Christian Barbet, and he operated out of a small, shabby office on the rue St. Lazare. The sign on the door read:

ENQUÉTES

PRIVÉES ET COMMERCIALES

RECHERCHES
RENSEIGNEMENTS
CONFIDENTIELS
FILATURES
PREUVES

The sign was almost larger than the office. Barbet was short and bald with yellow, broken teeth, narrow squinting eyes and nicotine-stained fingers.

"What can I do for you?" he asked Noelle.

"I want information about someone in England."

He blinked suspiciously. "What kind of information?"

"Anything. Whether he's married, who he sees. Anything at all, I want to start a scrapbook on him."

Barbet gingerly scratched his crotch and stared at her.

"Is he an Englishman?"

"An American. He's a pilot with the Eagle Squadron of the RAF."

Barbet rubbed the top of his bald head, uneasily. "I don't know," he grumbled. "We're at war. If they caught me trying to get information out of England about a flyer—"

His voice trailed off and he shrugged expressively. "The Germans shoot first and ask questions afterward."

"I don't want any military information," Noelle assured him. She opened her purse and took out a wad of franc notes. Barbet studied them hungrily.

"I have connections in England," he said cautiously, "but it will be expensive."

And so it began. It was three months before the little detective telephoned Noelle. She went to his office, and her first words were: "Is he alive?" and when Barbet nodded, her body sagged with relief and Barbet thought, *It must be wonderful to have someone love you that much.*

"Your boyfriend has been transferred," Barbet told her.

"Where?"

He looked down at a pad on his desk. "He was attached to the 609th Squadron of the RAF. He's been transferred to the 121st Squadron at Martlesham East, in East Anglia. He's flying Hurri—"

"I don't care about that."

"You're paying for it," he said. "You might as well get your money's worth." He looked down at his notes again. "He's flying Hurricanes. Before that he was flying American Buffaloes."

He turned over a page and added, "It becomes a little personal here."

"Go on," Noelle said.

Barbet shrugged. "There's a list of girls he is sleeping with. I didn't know whether you wanted—"

"I told you—everything."

There was a strange note in her voice that baffled him. There was something not quite normal here, something that did not ring true. Christian Barbet was a third-rate investigator handling third-rate clients, but because of that he had developed a feral instinct for truth, a nose for smelling out facts. The beautiful girl standing in his office disturbed him.

At first Barbet had thought she might be trying to involve him in some kind of espionage. Then he decided that she was a deserted wife seeking evidence against her husband. He had been wrong about that, he admitted, and now he was at a loss to figure out what his client wanted or why. He handed Noelle the list of Larry Douglas' girl friends and watched her face as she read it. She might have been reading a laundry list.

She finished and looked up. Christian Barbet was totally unprepared for her next words. "I'm very pleased," Noelle said.

He looked at her and blinked rapidly.

"Please call me when you have something more to report."

Long after Noelle Page had gone, Barbet sat in his office staring out the window, trying to puzzle out what his client was really after.

THE THEATERS OF Paris were beginning to boom again. The Germans attended to celebrate the glory of their victories and to show off the beautiful Frenchwomen they wore on their arms like trophies. The French attended to forget for a few hours that they were an unhappy, defeated people.

Noelle had attended the theater in Marseille a few times, but she had seen sleazy amateur plays acted out by fourth-rate performers for indifferent audiences. The theater in Paris was something else again. It was alive and sparkling and filled with the wit and grace of Molière, Racine and Colette. The incomparable Sacha Guitry had opened his theater and Noelle went to see him perform. She attended a revival of Büchner's *La Morte de Danton* and a play called *Asmodée* by a promising new young writer named François Mauriac. She went to the Comédie Française to see Pirandello's *Chacun La Verité* and Rostand's *Cyrano de Bergerac*. Noelle always went alone, oblivious of the admiring stares of those around her, completely lost in the drama taking place on the stage. Something in the magic that went on behind the footlights struck a responsive chord in her. She was playing a part just like the actors on stage, pretending to be something that she wasn't, hiding behind a mask.

One play in particular, *Huis Clos* by Jean Paul Sartre, affected her deeply. It starred Philippe Sorel, one of the idols of Europe. Sorel was ugly, short and beefy, with a broken nose and the face of a boxer. But the moment he spoke, a magic took place. He was transformed into a sensitive handsome man. *It's like the story of the Prince and the Frog,* Noelle thought, watching him perform. *Only he is both.* She went back to watch him again and again, sitting in the front row studying his performance, trying to learn the secret of his magnetism.

One evening during intermission an usher handed Noelle a note. It read, "I have seen you in the audience night after night. Please come backstage this evening and let me meet you. P.S." Noelle read it over, savoring it. Not because she gave a damn about Philippe Sorel, but because she knew that this was the beginning she had been looking for.

She went backstage after the performance. An old man at the stage door ushered her into Sorel's dressing room. He was seated before a makeup mirror, wearing only shorts, wiping off his makeup. He studied Noelle in the mirror. "It's unbelievable," he said finally. "You're even more beautiful up close."

"Thank you, Monsieur Sorel."

"Where are you from?"

"Marseille."

Sorel swung around to look at her more closely. His eyes moved to her feet and slowly worked their way up to the top of her head, missing nothing. Noelle stood there under his scrutiny, not moving. "Looking for a job?" he asked.

"No."

"I never pay for it," Sorel said. "All you'll get from me is a pass to my play. If you want money, fuck a banker."

Noelle stood there quietly watching him. Finally Sorel said, "What *are* you looking for?"

"I think I'm looking for you."

They had supper and afterward went back to Sorel's apartment in the beautiful rue Maurice-Barres, overlooking the corner where it became the Bois de Boulogne. Philippe Sorel was a skillful lover, surprisingly considerate and unselfish. Sorel had expected nothing from Noelle but her beauty, and he was astonished by her versatility in bed.

"Christ!" he said. "You're fantastic. Where did you learn all that?"

Noelle thought about it a moment. It was really not a question of learning. It was a matter of feeling. To her a man's body was an instrument to be played on, to explore to its innermost depths, finding the responsive chords and building upon them, using her own body to help create exquisite harmonies.

"I was born with it," she said simply.

Her fingertips began to lightly play around his lips, quick little butterfly touches, and then moved down to his chest and stomach. She saw him starting to grow hard and erect again. She arose and went into the bathroom and returned a moment later and slid his hard penis into her mouth. Her mouth was hot, filled with warm water.

"Oh, Christ," he said.

They spent the entire night making love, and in the morning, Sorel invited Noelle to move in with him.

NOELLE LIVED WITH Philippe Sorel for six months. She was neither happy nor unhappy. She knew that her being there made Sorel ecstatically happy, but this did not matter in the slightest to Noelle. She regarded herself as simply a student, determined to learn something new every day. He was a school that she was attending, a small part in her large plan. To Noelle there was nothing personal in their relationship, for she gave nothing of herself. She had made that mistake twice, and she would never make it again. There was room for only one man in Noelle's thoughts and that was Larry Douglas. Noelle would pass the place des Victoires or a park or restaurant where Larry had taken her, and she would feel the hatred well up within her, choking her, so it became difficult to breathe, and there was something else mixed in with the hatred, something Noelle could not put a name to.

Two months after moving in with Sorel, Noelle received a call from Christian Barbet.

"I have another report for you," the little detective said.

"Is he all right?" Noelle asked quickly.

Again Barbet was filled with that sense of uneasiness. "Yes," he said.

Noelle's voice was filled with relief. "I'll be right down."

The report was divided into two parts. The first dealt with Larry Douglas' military career. He had shot down five German planes and was the first American to become an Ace in the war. He had been promoted to Captain. The second part of the report interested her more. He had become very popular in London's wartime social life and had become engaged to the daughter of a British Admiral. There followed a list of girls that Larry was sleeping with, ranging from show girls to the wife of an under-secretary in the Ministry.

"Do you want me to keep on with this?" Barbet asked.

"Of course," Noelle replied. She took an envelope from her purse and handed it to Barbet. "Call me when you have anything further."

And she was gone.

Barbet sighed and looked up at the ceiling. *"Folle,"* he said thoughtfully. *"Folle."*

IF PHILIPPE SOREL had had any inkling of what was going on in Noelle's mind, he would have been astonished. Noelle seemed totally devoted to him. She did everything for him: cooked wonderful meals, shopped, supervised the cleaning of his apartment and made love whenever the mood stirred him. And asked for nothing. Sorel congratulated himself on having found the perfect mistress. He took her everywhere, and she met all his friends. They were enchanted with her and thought Sorel a very lucky man.

One night as they were having supper after the show, Noelle said to him, "I want to be an actress, Philippe."

He shook his head. "God knows you're beautiful enough, Noelle, but I've been up to my ass in actresses all my life. You're different, and I want to keep you that way. I don't want to share you with anyone." He patted her hand: "Don't I give you everything you need?"

"Yes, Philippe," Noelle replied.

When they returned to the apartment that night, Sorel wanted to make love. When they finished, he was drained. Noelle had never been as exciting, and Sorel congratulated himself that all she needed was the firm guidance of a man.

The following Sunday was Noelle's birthday, and Philippe Sorel gave a dinner party for her at Maxim's. He had taken over the large private dining room upstairs, decorated with plush red velvet and deep dark wood paneling. Noelle had helped write the guest list, and there was one name she included without mentioning it to Philippe. There were forty people at the party. They toasted Noelle's birthday and gave her lavish gifts. When dinner was over, Sorel rose to his feet. He had drunk a good deal of brandy and champagne and he was a little unsteady, his words a bit slurred.

"My friends," he said, "we've all drunk to the most beautiful girl in the world and we've given her lovely birthday presents, but I have a present for her that's going to be a *big* surprise." Sorel looked down at Noelle and beamed, then turned to the crowd. "Noelle and I are going to be married."

There was an approving cheer and the guests raced up to clap Sorel on the back and wish luck to the bride-to-be. Noelle sat there smiling up at the guests, murmuring her thank-yous. One of the guests had not risen. He was seated at a table at the far end of the room, smoking a cigarette in a long holder and viewing the scene sardonically. Noelle was aware that he had been watching her during dinner. He was a tall, very thin man, with an intense, brooding face. He seemed amused by everything that was happening around him, more an observer at the party than a guest.

Noelle caught his eye and smiled.

Armand Gautier was one of the top directors in France. He was in charge of the French Repertory Theater, and his productions had been acclaimed all over the world. Having Gautier direct a play or a motion picture was an almost certain guarantee of its success. He had the reputation of being particularly good with actresses and had created half a dozen important stars.

Sorel was at Noelle's side, talking to her. "Were you surprised, my darling?" he asked.

"Yes, Philippe," she said.

"I want us to be married right away. We'll have the wedding at my villa."

Over his shoulder Noelle could see Armand Gautier watching her, smiling that enigmatic smile. Some friends came and look Philippe away and when Noelle turned, Gautier was standing there.

"Congratulations," he said. There was a mocking note in his voice. "You hooked a big fish."

"Did I?"

"Philippe Sorel is a great catch."

"For someone perhaps," Noelle said indifferently.

Gautier looked at her in surprise. "Are you trying to tell me you're not interested?"

"I'm not trying to tell you anything."

"Good luck." He turned to go.

"Monsieur Gautier . . ."

He stopped.

"Could I see you tonight?" Noelle asked quietly. "I would like to talk to you alone."

Armand Gautier looked at her for a moment, then shrugged. "If you wish."

"I will come to your place. Will that be satisfactory?"

"Yes, of course. The address is—"

"I know the address. Twelve o'clock?"

"Twelve o'clock."

ARMAND GAUTIER LIVED in a fashionable old apartment building on rue Marbeuf. A doorman escorted Noelle into the lobby and an elevator boy took her to the fourth floor and indicated Gautier's apartment. Noelle rang the bell. A few moments later the door was opened by Gautier. He wore a flowered dressing gown.

"Come in," he said.

Noelle walked into the apartment. Her eye was untrained, but she sensed that it was done in beautiful taste and that the objets d'art were valuable.

"Sorry I'm not dressed," Gautier apologized. "I've been on the telephone."

Noelle's eyes locked onto his. "It will not be necessary for you to be dressed." She moved over to the couch and sat down.

Gautier smiled. "That was the feeling I had, Miss Page. But I'm curious about something. Why me? You're engaged to a man who is famous and wealthy. I am sure that if you are looking for some extracurricular activities, you could find men more attractive than I, and certainly richer and younger. What is it you want from me?"

"I want you to teach me to act," Noelle said.

Armand Gautier looked at her a moment, then sighed. "You disappoint me. I expected something more original."

"Your business is working with actors."

"With actors, not amateurs. Have you ever acted?"

"No. But you will teach me." She took off her hat and her gloves. "Where is your bedroom?" she asked.

Gautier hesitated. His life was full of beautiful women wanting to be in the theater, or wanting a bigger part, or the lead in a new play, or a larger dressing room. They were all a pain. He knew that he would be a fool to get involved with one more. And yet there was no need to get involved. Here was a beautiful girl throwing herself at him. It would be a simple matter to take her to bed and then send her away. "In there," he said, indicating a door.

He watched Noelle as she walked toward the bedroom. He wondered what Philippe Sorel would think if he knew that his bride-to-be was spending the night here. Women. Whores, all of them. Gautier poured himself a brandy and made several phone calls. When he finally went into the bedroom, Noelle was in his bed, naked, waiting for him. Gautier had to admit that she was an exquisite work of nature. Her face was breathtaking, and her body was flawless. Her skin was the color of honey, except for the triangle of soft golden hair between her legs. Gautier had learned from experience that beautiful girls were almost invariably narcissistic, so preoccupied with their own egocentricities that they were lousy lays. They felt their contribution to lovemaking was simply conferring their presence in a man's bed, so that the man ended up making love to an unmoving lump of clay and was expected to be grateful for the experience. Ah, well, perhaps he could teach this one something.

As Noelle watched him, Gautier undressed, leaving his clothes carelessly strewn on the floor, and moved toward the bed. "I'm not going to tell you you are beautiful," he said. "You've heard it too many times already."

"Beauty is wasted," Noelle shrugged, "unless it is used to give pleasure."

Gautier looked at her in quick surprise, then smiled. "I agree. Let's use yours." He sat down beside her.

Like most Frenchmen, Armand Gautier prided himself on being a skilled lover. He was amused by the stories he had heard of Germans and Americans whose idea of making love consisted of jumping on top of a girl, having an instant orgasm, and then putting on their hat and departing. The Americans even had a phrase for it. "Wham, bam, thank you ma'am." When Armand Gautier was emotionally involved with a woman, he used many devices to heighten the enjoyment of lovemaking. There was always a perfect dinner, the right wines. He arranged the setting artistically so that it was pleasing to the senses, the room was delicately scented and soft music was playing. He aroused his women with tender sentiments of love and later the coarse language of the gutter. And Gautier was adept at the manual foreplay that preceded sex.

In Noelle's case he dispensed with all of these. For a one-night stand there was no need for perfume or music or empty endearments. She was here simply to get laid. She was indeed a silly fool if she thought that she could trade what every woman in the world carried between her legs for the great and unique genius that Armand Gautier possessed in his head.

He started to climb on top of her. Noelle stopped him.

"Wait," she whispered.

As he watched, puzzled, she reached for two small tubes that she had placed on the bedside table. She squeezed the contents of one into her hand and began to rub it onto his penis.

"What is this all about?" he asked.

She smiled. "You'll see." She kissed him on the lips, her tongue darting into his mouth in quick birdlike movements. She pulled away and her tongue started moving toward his belly, her hair trailing across his body like light, silky fingers. He felt his organ begin to rise. She moved her tongue down his legs to his feet and began to suck gently on his toes. His organ was stiff and hard now and she mounted him as he lay there. As he felt himself penetrating her, the warmth of her vagina acted on the cream she had put on his penis and the sensation became unbearably exciting. As she rode him, moving up and down, her left hand was caressing his testicles and they began to grow hot. There was menthol in the cream on his penis and the sensation of the cold while inside her warmth, and the heat of his testicles, drove him into an absolute frenzy.

They made love all night long and each time Noelle made love to him differently. It was the most incredibly sensuous experience he had ever had.

In the morning Armand Gautier said, "If I can get up enough energy to move, I'll get dressed and take you out to breakfast."

"Lie there," Noelle said. She walked over to a closet, selected one of his robes and put it on. "You rest. I'll be back."

Thirty-five minutes later Noelle returned with a breakfast tray. On it were freshly squeezed orange juice, a delicious sausage-and-chive omelet, heated, buttered croissants and jam and a pot of black coffee. It tasted extraordinarily good.

"Aren't you having anything?" Gautier asked.

Noelle shook her head. "No." She was seated in an easy chair watching him as he ate. She looked even more beautiful wearing his dressing gown open at the top, revealing the curves of her delicious breasts. Her hair was tousled and carefree.

Armand Gautier had radically revised his earlier estimate of Noelle. She was not any man's quick lay; she was an absolute treasure. However, he had met many treasures in his career in the theater, and he was not about to spend his time and talent as a director on a starry-eyed amateur who wanted to break into the theater, no matter how beautiful she might be, or how skilled in bed. Gautier was a dedicated man who took his art seriously. He had refused to compromise it in the past, and he was not about to start now.

The evening before, he had planned to spend the night with Noelle and send her packing in the morning. Now as he ate his breakfast and studied her, he was trying to figure out a way to hold onto Noelle as a mistress until he got bored with her, without encouraging her as an actress. He knew that he had to hold out some bait. He felt his way cautiously. "Are you planning to marry Philippe Sorel?" he asked.

"Of course not," Noelle replied. "That is not what I want."

Now it was coming. "What do you want?" Gautier asked.

"I told you," Noelle said quietly. "I want to be an actress."

Gautier bit into another croissant, stalling for time. "Of course," he said. Then he added, "There are many fine dramatic coaches I could send you to, Noelle, who would . . ."

"No," she said. Noelle was watching him pleasantly, warmly, as though eager to accede to anything he suggested. And yet Gautier had a feeling that inside her was a core of steel. There were many ways she could have said "no." With anger, reproach, disappointment, sulking, but she had said it with softness. And absolute finality. This was going to be more difficult than he had anticipated. For a moment Armand Gautier was tempted to tell her, as he told dozens of girls every week, to go away, that he had no time to waste on her. But he thought of the incredible sensations he had experienced during the night and he knew he would be a fool to let her go so soon. She was surely worth a slight, a very slight, compromise.

"Very well," Gautier said. "I will give you a play to study. When you have memorized it, you will read it to me and we will see how much talent you have. Then we can decide what to do with you."

"Thank you, Armand," she said. There was no triumph in her words, nor even any pleasure that he could detect. Just a simple acknowledgment of the inevitable. For the first time Gautier felt a small twinge of doubt. But that of course was ridiculous. He was a master at handling women.

While Noelle was getting dressed, Armand Gautier went into his book-lined study and scanned the familiar-looking worn volumes on the shelves. Finally, with a wry smile, he selected Euripides' *Andromache*. It was one of the most difficult classics to act. He went back into the bedroom and handed the play to Noelle.

"Here you are, my dear," he said. "When you have memorized the part, we shall go over it together."

"Thank you, Armand. You will not be sorry."

The more he thought about it, the more pleased Gautier was with his ploy. It would take Noelle a week or two to memorize the part, or what was even more likely, she would come to him and confess that she was unable to memorize it. He would sympathize with her, explain how difficult the art of acting was, and they could assume a relationship untainted by her ambition. Gautier made a date to have dinner with Noelle that evening, and she left.

When Noelle returned to the apartment she shared with Philippe Sorel, she found him waiting for her. He was very drunk.

"You bitch," he yelled. "Where have you been all night?"

It would not matter what she said. Sorel knew that he was going to listen to her apologies, beat her up, then take her to bed and forgive her.

But instead of apologizing Noelle merely said, "With another man, Philippe. I've come to pick up my things."

And as Sorel watched her in stunned disbelief, Noelle walked into the bedroom and began to pack.

"For Christ's sake, Noelle," he pleaded. "Don't do this! We love each other. We're going to get married." He talked to her for the next half hour, arguing, threatening, cajoling, and by that time Noelle had finished packing and had left the apartment and Sorel had no idea why he had lost her, for he did not know that he had never possessed her.

ARMAND GAUTIER WAS in the middle of directing a new play that was to open in two weeks and he spent all day at the theater in rehearsals. As a rule when Gautier was in production, he thought of nothing else. Part of his genius was the intense concentration he was able to bring to his work. Nothing existed for him but the four walls of the theater and the actors he was working with. This day however was different. Gautier found his mind constantly wandering to Noelle and the incredible night they had had together. The actors would go through a scene and then stop and wait for his comments, and Gautier would suddenly realize that he had been paying no attention. Furious with himself he tried to focus his attention on what he was doing, but thoughts of Noelle's naked body and the amazing things it had done to him would keep coming back. In the middle of one dramatic scene he found that he was walking around the stage with an erection, and he had to excuse himself.

Because Gautier had an analytical mind he tried to figure out what it was about this girl that had affected him like this. Noelle was beautiful, but he had slept with some of the most beautiful women in the world. She was consummately skilled at lovemaking but so were other women to whom he had made love. She seemed intelligent but not brilliant; her personality was pleasant but not complex. There was something else, something the director could not quite put his finger on. And then he remembered her soft "no" and he felt that it was a clue. There was some force in her that was irresistible, that would obtain anything she wanted. There was something in her that was untouched. And like other men before him Armand Gautier felt that though Noelle had affected him more deeply than he cared to admit to himself, he had not touched her at all, and this was a challenge that his masculinity could not refuse.

Gautier spent the day in a confused state of mind. He looked forward to the evening with tremendous anticipation, not so much because he wanted to make love to Noelle but because he wanted to prove to himself that he had been building something out of nothing. He wanted Noelle to be a disappointment to him so that he could dismiss her from his life.

As they made love that night, Armand Gautier made himself consciously aware of the tricks and devices and artifices Noelle used so he would realize that it was all mechanical, without emotion. But he was mistaken. She gave herself to him fully and completely, caring only about bringing him pleasure such as he had never known before and reveling in his enjoyment. When morning came Gautier was more firmly bewitched by her than ever.

Noelle prepared breakfast for him again, this time delicate crêpes with bacon and jam, and hot coffee, and it was magnificent.

"All right," Gautier told himself. "You have found a young girl who is beautiful to look at, who can make love and cook. Bravo! But is that enough for an intelligent man? When you are through making love and eating, you must talk. What can she talk to you about?" The answer was that it didn't really matter.

There had been no more mention of the play and Gautier was hoping that Noelle had either forgotten about it or had been unable to cope with memorizing the lines. When she left in the morning, she promised to have dinner with him that evening.

"Can you get away from Philippe?" Gautier asked.

"I've left him," Noelle said simply. She gave Gautier her new address.

He stared at her for a moment. "I see."

But he did not. Not in the least.

THEY SPENT THE night together again. When they were not making love, they talked. Or rather Gautier talked. Noelle seemed so interested in him that he found himself talking about things he had not discussed in years, personal things that he had never revealed to anyone before.

No mention was made of the play he had given her to read, and Gautier congratulated himself on having solved his problem so neatly.

The following night when they had had dinner and were ready to retire, Gautier started toward the bedroom.

"Not yet," Noelle said.

He turned in surprise.

"You said you would listen to me do the play."

"Well, of—of course," Gautier stammered, "whenever you're ready."

"I am ready."

He shook his head. "I don't want you to read it, cherie," he said. "I want to hear it when you have memorized it so that I can really judge you as an actress."

"I have memorized it," Noelle replied.

He stared at her in disbelief. It was impossible that she could have learned the entire part in only three days.

"Are you ready to hear me?" she asked.

Armand Gautier had no choice. "Of course," he said. He gestured toward the center of the room. "That will be your stage. The audience will be here." He sat down on a large comfortable settee.

Noelle began to do the play. Gautier could feel the gooseflesh begin to crawl, his own personal stigmata, the thing that happened to him when he encountered real talent. Not that Noelle was expert. Far from it. Her inexperience shone through every move and gesture. But she had something much more than mere skill: She had a rare honesty, a natural talent that gave every line a fresh meaning and color.

When Noelle finished the soliloquy, Gautier said warmly, "I think that one day you will become an important actress, Noelle. I really mean that. I am going to send you to Georges Faber, who is the best dramatic coach in all of France. Working with him, you will—"

"No."

He looked at her in surprise. It was that same soft "no" again. Positive and final.

" 'No' what?" Gautier asked in some confusion. "Faber does not take on anyone but the biggest actors. He will only take you because I tell him to."

"I am going to work with you," Noelle said.

Gautier could feel the anger mounting in him. "I don't coach any-one," he snapped. "I am not a teacher. I direct professional actors. When you are a professional actor, then I will direct you." He was fighting to check the anger in his voice. "Do you understand?"

Noelle nodded. "Yes, I understand, Armand."

"Very well then."

Mollified, he took Noelle in his arms and received a warm kiss from her. He knew now that he had worried unnecessarily. She was like any other woman, she needed to be dominated. He would have no further problem with her.

Their lovemaking that night surpassed anything that had gone be-fore, possibly, Gautier thought, because of the added excitement of the slight quarrel they had had.

During the night he said to her, "You really can be a wonderful ac-tress, Noelle. I'm going to be very proud of you."

"Thank you, Armand," she whispered.

Noelle fixed breakfast in the morning, and Gautier left for the the-ater. When he telephoned Noelle during the day, she did not answer, and when he arrived home that night she was not there. Gautier waited for her to return, and when she did not appear he lay awake all night won-dering if she could have been in an accident. He tried to phone Noelle at her apartment, but there was no answer. He sent a telegram that went undelivered, and when he stopped at her apartment after rehearsal, no one answered his ring.

During the week that followed, Gautier was frantic. Rehearsals were turning into a shambles. He was screaming at all the actors and upset-ting them so badly that his stage manager suggested they stop for the day and Gautier agreed. After the actors had left, he sat on the stage alone, trying to understand what had happened to him. He told himself that Noelle was just another woman, a cheap ambitious blonde with the heart of a shopgirl who wanted to be a star. He denigrated her in every way he could think of, but in the end he knew it was no use. He had to have her. That night he wandered the streets of Paris, getting drunk in small bars where he was unknown. He tried to think of ways to reach Noelle but to no avail. There was no one he could even talk to about her, except Philippe Sorel, and that, of course, was out of the question.

A week after Noelle had disappeared, Armand Gautier arrived home at four o'clock in the morning, drunk, opened the door and walked into the living room. All the lights were on. Noelle was curled up in an easy chair dressed in one of his robes, reading a book. She looked up as he entered, and smiled.

"Hello, Armand."

Gautier stared at her, his heart lifting, a feeling of infinite relief and happiness flooding through him. He said, "We'll begin working tomorrow."

5

CATHERINE

WASHINGTON: 1940

Washington, D.C., was the most exciting city that Catherine Alexander had ever seen. She had always thought of Chicago as the heartland, but Washington was a revelation. Here was the real core of America, the pulsating center of power. At first, Catherine had been bewildered by the variety of uniforms that filled the streets: Army, Navy Air Corps, Marines. For the first time Catherine began to feel the grim possibility of war as something real.

In Washington the physical presence of war was everywhere. This was the city where war, if it came, would begin. Here it would be declared and mobilized and masterminded. This was the city that held in its hand the fate of the world. And she, Catherine Alexander, was going to be a part of it.

She had moved in with Susie Roberts, who was living in a bright and cheery fourth floor walk-up apartment with a fair-sized living room, two small adjoining bedrooms, a tiny bathroom and a kitchenette built for a midget. Susie had seemed glad to see her. Her first words were:

"Hurry and unpack and get your best dress steamed out. You have a dinner date tonight."

Catherine blinked. "What took you so long?"

"Cathy, in Washington, it's the *girls* who have the little black books. This town is so full of lonely men, it's pitiful."

THEY HAD DINNER that first evening at the Willard Hotel. Susie's date was a congressman from Indiana and Catherine's date was a lobbyist from Oregon, and both men were in town without their wives. After dinner they went dancing at the Washington Country Club. Catherine had hoped that the lobbyist might be able to give her a job. Instead she got the offer of a car and her own apartment, which she declined with thanks.

Susie brought the congressman back to the apartment, and Catherine went to bed. A short time later she heard them go into Susie's bedroom, and the bedsprings began to creak. Catherine pulled a pillow over her head to drown out the sound, but it was impossible. She visualized Susie in bed with her date making wild, passionate love. In the morning when Catherine got up for breakfast, Susie was already up, looking bright and cheerful, ready to go to work. Catherine searched for telltale wrinkles and other signs of dissipation on Susie, but there were none. On the contrary she looked radiant, her skin absolutely flawless. *My God,* Catherine thought, *she's a female Dorian Gray. One day she's going to come in looking great, and I'll look a hundred and ten years old.*

A few days later at breakfast Susie said, "Hey, I heard about a job opening that might interest you. One of the girls at the party last night said she's quitting to go back to Texas. God knows why anyone who ever got away from Texas would want to go back there. I remember I was in Amarillo a few years ago and . . ."

"Where does she work?" Catherine interrupted.

"Who?"

"The girl," Catherine said patiently.

"Oh. She works for Bill Fraser. He's in charge of public relations for the State Department. *Newsweek* did a cover story on him last month. It's supposed to be a cushy job. I just heard about it last night, so if you get over there now, you should beat all the other girls to it."

"Thanks," Catherine said gratefully. "William Fraser, here I come."

Twenty minutes later Catherine was on her way to the State Department. When she arrived, the guard told her where Fraser's office was and she took the elevator upstairs. *Public Relations. It sounded exactly like the sort of job she was looking for.*

Catherine stopped in the corridor outside the office and took out her hand mirror to check her makeup. She would do. It was not yet nine-thirty so she should have the field to herself. She opened the door and walked in.

The outer office was packed with girls standing, sitting, leaning against the wall, all seemingly talking at once. The frantic receptionist behind the beleaguered desk was vainly trying to bring order into the scene. "Mr. Fraser's busy right now," she kept repeating. "I don't know when he can see you."

"Is he interviewing secretaries or isn't he?" one of the girls demanded.

"Yes, but . . ." She looked around desperately at the mob. "My God! This is ridiculous!"

The corridor door opened and three more girls pushed their way in, shoving Catherine to one side.

"Is the job filled yet?" one of them asked.

"Maybe he'd like a harem," another girl suggested. "Then we can all stay."

The door to the inner office opened, and a man came out. He was just a little under six feet, and had the almost-slim body of a nonathlete who keeps in shape at the athletic club three mornings a week. He had curly blond hair graying at the temples, bright blue eyes and a strong, rather forbidding jaw line. "What in hell's going on here, Sally?" His voice was deep and authoritative.

"These girls heard about the vacancy, Mr. Fraser."

"Jesus! I didn't hear about it myself until an hour ago." His eyes swept over the room. "It's like jungle drums." As his eyes moved toward Catherine, she stood up straight and gave him her warmest I'll-be-a-great-secretary smile, but his eyes passed right over her and went back to the receptionist. "I need a copy of *Life*," he told her. "An issue that came out three or four weeks ago. It has a picture of Stalin on the cover."

"I'll order it, Mr. Fraser," the receptionist said.

"I need it now." He started back toward his office.

"I'll call the Time-Life Bureau," the receptionist said, "and see if they can dig up a copy."

Fraser stopped at the door. "Sally, I have Senator Borah on the line. I want to read him a paragraph from that issue. You have two minutes to find a copy for me." He went into his office and closed the door.

The girls in the room looked at one another and shrugged. Catherine stood there, thinking hard. She turned and pushed her way out of the office.

"Good. That's one down," one of the girls said.

The receptionist picked up the telephone and dialed information. "The number for the Time-Life Bureau," she said. The room grew silent as the girls watched her. "Thank you." She replaced the receiver, then picked it up and dialed again. "Hello. This is Mr. William Fraser's office in the State Department. Mr. Fraser needs a back issue of *Life* immediately. It's the one with Stalin on the cover . . . You don't keep any back issues there? Who could I talk to? . . . I see. Thank you." She hung up.

"Tough luck, honey," one of the girls said.

Another added: "They sure come up with some beauties, don't they? If he wants to come over to my place tonight, I'll read to him." There was a laugh.

The intercom buzzed. She flipped down the key.

"Your two minutes are up," Fraser's voice said. "Where's the magazine?"

The receptionist drew a deep breath. "I just talked to the Time-Life Bureau, Mr. Fraser, and they said it would be impossible to get . . ."

The door opened and Catherine hurried in. In her hand was a copy of *Life* with a picture of Stalin on the cover. She pushed her way through to the desk and placed the magazine in the receptionist's hand. The receptionist stared at it incredulously. "I . . . I have a copy of it here, Mr. Fraser. I'll bring it right in." She rose, gave Catherine a grateful smile and hurried into the inner office. The other girls turned to stare at Catherine with suddenly hostile eyes.

Five minutes later the door to Fraser's office opened, and Fraser and the receptionist appeared. The receptionist pointed to Catherine. "That's the girl."

William Fraser turned to regard Catherine speculatively. "Would you come in, please?"

"Yes, sir." Catherine followed Fraser into his office, feeling the eyes of the other girls stabbing into her back. Fraser closed the door.

His office was the typical, bureaucratic Washington office, but he had decorated it in style, stamping it with his personal taste in furniture and art.

"Sit down, Miss . . ."

"Alexander, Catherine Alexander."

"Sally tells me that you came up with the *Life* magazine."

"Yes, sir."

"I assume you didn't just happen to have a three-week-old issue in your purse."

"No, sir."

"How did you find it so quickly?"

"I went down to the barber shop. Barber shops and dentists' offices always have old issues lying around."

"I see." Fraser smiled, and his craggy face seemed less formidable. "I don't think that would have occurred to me," he said. "Are you that bright about everything?"

Catherine thought about Ron Peterson. "No, sir," she replied.

"Are you looking for a job as a secretary?"

"Not really." Catherine saw his look of surprise. "I'll take it," she added hastily. "What I'd really like to be is your assistant."

"Why don't we start you out as a secretary today?" Fraser said dryly. "Tomorrow you can be my assistant."

She looked at him hopefully. "You mean I have the job?"

"On trial." He flicked down the intercom key and leaned toward the box. "Sally, would you please thank the young ladies. Tell them the position is filled."

"Right, Mr. Fraser."

He flicked the button up. "Will thirty dollars a week be satisfactory?"

"Oh yes, sir. Thank you, Mr. Fraser."

"You can start tomorrow morning, nine o'clock. Have Sally give you a personnel form to fill out."

· · ·

WHEN CATHERINE LEFT the office, she walked over to the *Washington Post*. The policeman at the desk in the lobby stopped her.

"I'm William Fraser's personal secretary," she said loftily, "over at the State Department. I need some information from your morgue."

"What kind of information?"

"On William Fraser."

He studied her a moment and said, "That's the weirdest request I've had all week. Has your boss been bothering you, or something?"

"No," she said disarmingly. "I'm planning to write an exposé on him."

Five minutes later, a clerk was showing her into the morgue. He pulled out the file on William Fraser, and Catherine began to read.

One hour later Catherine was one of the world's foremost authorities on William Fraser. He was forty-five years old, had been graduated from Princeton summa cum laude, had started an advertising agency, Fraser Associates, which had become one of the most successful agencies in the business, and had taken a leave of absence a year ago at the request of the President, to work for the government. He had been married to Lydia Campion, a wealthy socialite. They had been divorced for four years. There were no children. Fraser was a millionaire and had a home in Georgetown and a summer place at Bar Harbor, Maine. His hobbies were tennis, boating and polo. Several of the news stories referred to him as "one of America's most eligible bachelors."

When Catherine arrived home and told Susie her good news, Susie insisted that they go out to celebrate. Two rich Annapolis cadets were in town.

Catherine's date turned out to be a pleasant enough boy, but all evening she kept mentally comparing him to William Fraser, and compared to Fraser the boy seemed callow and dull. Catherine wondered whether she was going to fall in love with her new boss. She had not felt any girlish tingly feeling when she had been with him, but there was something else, a liking for him as a person and a feeling of respect. She decided that the tingly feeling probably existed only in French sex novels.

The cadets took the girls to a small Italian restaurant on the outskirts of Washington where they had an excellent dinner, then went to see *Ar-*

senic and Old Lace, which Catherine enjoyed tremendously. At the end of the evening the boys brought them home, and Susie invited them in for a nightcap. When it appeared to Catherine that they were starting to settle down for the night, she excused herself and said she had to go to bed.

Her date protested. "We haven't even gotten started yet," he said. "Look at them."

Susie and her escort were on the couch, locked in a passionate embrace.

Catherine's escort clutched her arm. "There could be a war soon," he said earnestly. Before Catherine could stop him, he took her hand and placed it against the hardness between his legs. "You wouldn't send a man into battle in this condition, would you?"

Catherine withdrew her hand, fighting not to be angry. "I've given it a lot of thought," she said evenly, "and I've decided to sleep only with the walking wounded." She turned and went into her bedroom, locking the door behind her. She found it difficult to go to sleep. She lay in bed thinking about William Fraser, her new job and the male hardness of the boy from Annapolis. An hour after she had gone to bed, she heard Susie's bedsprings creaking wildly. From then on sleep was impossible.

At eight-thirty the next morning Catherine arrived at her new office. The door was unlocked, and the light in the reception office was on. From the inner office she heard the sound of a man's voice and she walked inside.

William Fraser was at his desk, dictating into a machine. He looked up as Catherine entered and snapped off the machine. "You're early," he said.

"I wanted to look around and get my bearings before I began work."

"Sit down." There was something in his tone that puzzled her. He seemed angry. Catherine took a seat. "I don't like snoops, Miss Alexander."

Catherine felt her face redden. "I—I don't understand."

"Washington's a small town. It's not even a town. It's a goddamn village. There's nothing that goes on here that everybody doesn't know about in five minutes."

"I still don't—"

"The publisher of the *Post* phoned me two minutes after you arrived there to ask why my secretary was doing research on me."

Catherine sat there stunned, not knowing what to say.

"Did you find out all the gossip you wanted to know?"

She felt her embarrassment swiftly changing to anger. "I wasn't snooping," Catherine said. She rose to her feet. "The only reason I wanted information on you was so that I would know what kind of man I was working for." Her voice was trembling with indignation. "I think a good secretary should adapt to her employer, and I wanted to know what to adapt to."

Fraser sat there, his expression hostile.

Catherine stared at him, hating him, on the verge of tears. "You don't have to worry about it anymore, Mr. Fraser. I quit." She turned and started toward the door.

"Sit down," Fraser said, his voice like a whiplash. Catherine turned, in shock. "I can't stand goddamn prima donnas."

She glared at him. "I'm not a . . ."

"OK. I'm sorry. Now, will you sit down. Please?" He picked up a pipe from his desk and lit it.

Catherine stood there not knowing what to do, filled with humiliation. "I don't think it's going to work," she began. "I . . ."

Fraser drew on the pipe and flicked out the match. "Of course it'll work, Catherine," he said reasonably. "You can't quit now. Look at all the trouble I'd have breaking in a new girl."

Catherine looked at him and saw the glint of amusement in his bright blue eyes. He smiled, and reluctantly her lips curved into a small smile. She sank into a chair.

"That's better. Did anyone ever tell you you're too sensitive?"

"I suppose so. I'm sorry."

Fraser leaned back in his chair. "Or maybe I'm the one who's oversensitive. It's a pain in the ass being called 'one of America's most eligible bachelors.'"

Catherine wished he would not use words like that. *But what bothered her most?* she wondered. *Ass or bachelor?*

Maybe Fraser was right. Perhaps her interest in him was not as impersonal as she thought. Perhaps subconsciously . . .

". . . a target for every goddamned idiotic unmarried female in the world," Fraser was saying. "You wouldn't believe it if I told you how aggressive women can be."

Wouldn't she? Try our cashier. Catherine blushed as she thought of it.

"It's enough to turn a man into a fairy." Fraser sighed. "Since this seems to be National Research Week, tell me about you. Any boyfriends?"

"No," she said. "That is, no one special," she added quickly.

He looked at her quizzically. "Where do you live?"

"I share an apartment with a girl who was a classmate at college."

"Northwestern."

She looked at him in surprise, then realized he must have seen the personnel form she had filled out.

"Yes, sir."

"I'm going to tell you something about me that you didn't find in the newspaper morgue. I'm a tough sonofabitch to work for. You'll find me fair, but I'm a perfectionist. We're hard to live with. Do you think you can manage?"

"I'll try," Catherine said.

"Good. Sally will fill you in on the routine around here. The most important thing you have to remember is that I'm a chain coffee drinker. I like it black and hot."

"I'll remember." She got to her feet and started toward the door.

"And, Catherine?"

"Yes, Mr. Fraser?"

"When you go home tonight, practice saying some profanity in front of the mirror. If you're going to keep wincing every time I say a four-letter word, it's going to drive me up the wall."

He was doing it to her again, making her feel like a child. "Yes, Mr. Fraser," she said coldly. She stormed out of the office, almost slamming the door behind her.

The meeting had not gone anything like Catherine had expected. She no longer liked William Fraser. She thought he was a smug, dominating, arrogant boor. No wonder his wife had divorced him. Well she was here and she would start, but she made up her mind that she would begin looking for another job, a job working for a human being instead of a despot.

When Catherine walked out of the door, Fraser leaned back in his chair, a smile touching his lips. Were girls still that achingly young, that earnest and dedicated? In her anger with her eyes blazing and her lips trembling Catherine had seemed so defenseless that Fraser had wanted to take her in his arms and protect her. Against himself, he admitted ruefully. There was a kind of old-fashioned shining quality about her that he'd almost forgotten existed in girls. She was lovely and she was bright, and she had a mind of her own. She was going to become the best goddamn secretary that he had ever had. And deep down Fraser had a feeling that she was going to become more than that. How much more, he was not sure yet. He had been burned so often that an automatic warning system took over the moment his emotions were touched by any female. Those moments had come very seldom. His pipe had gone out. He lit it again, and the smile was still on his face. A little later when Fraser called her in for dictation, Catherine was courteous but cool. She waited for Fraser to say something personal so she could show him how aloof she was, but he was distant and businesslike. He had, Catherine thought, obviously wiped the incident of this morning from his mind. How insensitive could a man be?

In spite of herself Catherine found the new job fascinating. The telephone rang constantly, and the names of the callers filled her with excitement. During the first week the Vice-President of the United States called twice, half a dozen senators, the Secretary of State and a famous actress who was in town publicizing her latest picture. The week was climaxed by a telephone call from President Roosevelt, and Catherine was so nervous she dropped the phone and disconnected his secretary.

In addition to the telephone calls Fraser had a constant round of appointments at the office, his country club or at one of the better-known restaurants. After the first few weeks Fraser allowed Catherine to set up his appointments for him and make the reservations. She began to know who Fraser wanted to see and who he wanted to avoid. Her work was so absorbing that by the end of the month she had totally forgotten about looking for another job.

Catherine's relationship with Fraser was still on a very impersonal level, but she knew him well enough now to realize that his aloofness was not unfriendliness. It was a dignity, a wall of reserve that served as a shield against the world. Catherine had a feeling that Fraser was really very lonely. His job called for him to be gregarious, but she sensed that by nature he was a solitary man. She also sensed that William Fraser was out of her league. *For that matter so is most of male America,* she decided.

She double-dated with Susie every now and then but found most of her escorts were married sexual athletes, and she preferred to go to a movie or the theater alone. She saw Gertrude Lawrence and a new comedian named Danny Kaye in *Lady in the Dark,* and *Life with Father,* and *Alice in Arms,* with a young actor named Kirk Douglas. She loved *Kitty Foyle* with Ginger Rogers because it reminded her of herself. One night at a performance of *Hamlet* she saw Fraser sitting in a box with an exquisite girl in an expensive white evening gown that Catherine had seen in *Vogue.* She had no idea who the girl was. Fraser made his own personal dates, and she never knew where he was going or with whom. He looked across the theater and saw her. The next morning he made no reference to it until he had finished the morning's dictation.

"How did you like *Hamlet?*" he asked.

"The play's going to make it, but I didn't care much for the performances."

"I liked the actors," he said. "I thought the girl who played Ophelia was particularly good."

Catherine nodded and started to leave.

"Didn't you like Ophelia?" Fraser persisted.

"If you want my honest opinion," Catherine said carefully, "I didn't think she was able to keep her head above water." She turned and walked out.

When Catherine arrived at the apartment that night, Susie was waiting for her. "You had a visitor," Susie said.

"Who?"

"An FBI man. They're investigating you."

My God, thought Catherine. *They found out I'm a virgin, and there's probably some kind of law against it in Washington.* Aloud she said, "Why would the FBI be investigating me?"

"Because you're working for the government now."

"Oh."

"How's your Mr. Fraser?"

"My Mr. Fraser's just fine," Catherine said.

"How do you think he'd like me?"

Catherine studied her tall, willowy brunette roommate. "For breakfast."

As the weeks went by Catherine became acquainted with the other secretaries working in nearby offices. Several of the girls were having affairs with their bosses, and it did not seem to matter to them whether the men were married or single. They envied Catherine's working for William Fraser.

"What's Golden Boy really like?" one of them asked Catherine one day at lunch. "Has he made a pass at you yet?"

"Oh, he doesn't bother with that," Catherine said earnestly. "I just come in at nine o'clock every morning, we roll around on the couch until one o'clock, then we break for lunch."

"Seriously, how do you find him?"

"Resistible," Catherine lied. Her feelings toward William Fraser had mellowed considerably since their first quarrel. He had told her the truth when he said he was a perfectionist. Whenever she made a mistake, she was reprimanded for it, but she had found him to be fair and understanding. She had watched him take time out from his own problems to help other people, people who could do nothing for him, and he always arranged it so that he never took credit for it. Yes, she liked William Fraser very much indeed, but that was no one's business but her own.

Once when they had had a great deal of work to catch up on, Fraser had asked Catherine to have dinner with him at his home so that they could work late. Talmadge, Fraser's chauffeur, was waiting with the limousine in front of the building. Several secretaries coming out of the building watched with knowing eyes as Fraser ushered Catherine into the back seat of the car and slid in next to her. The limousine glided smoothly into the late afternoon traffic.

"I'm going to ruin your reputation," Catherine said.

Fraser laughed. "I'll give you some advice. If you ever want to have an affair with a public figure, do it out in the open."

"What about catching cold?"

He grinned. "I meant, take your paramour—if they still use that word—out to public places, well-known restaurants, theaters."

"Shakespearean plays?" Catherine asked innocently.

Fraser ignored it. "People are always looking for devious motives. They'll say to themselves, 'Uh-huh, he's taking so-and-so out in public. I wonder who he's seeing secretly.' People never believe the obvious."

"It's an interesting theory."

"Edgar Allan Poe wrote a story based on deceiving people with the obvious," Fraser said. "I don't recall the name of it."

"It was Arthur Conan Doyle. 'The Purloined Letter.'" The moment Catherine said it, she wished she hadn't. Men did not like smart girls. But then what did it matter? She was not his girl, she was his secretary.

They rode the rest of the way in silence.

Fraser's home in Georgetown was something out of a picture book. It was a four-story Georgian house that must have been over two hundred years old. The door was opened by a butler in a white jacket. Fraser said, "Frank, this is Miss Alexander."

"Hello, Frank. We've talked on the phone," Catherine said.

"Yes, ma'am. It's nice to meet you, Miss Alexander."

Catherine looked at the reception hall. It had a beautiful old staircase leading to the second floor, its oak wood burnished to a sheen. The floor was marble, and overhead was a dazzling chandelier.

Fraser studied her face. "Like it?" he asked.

"*Like* it? Oh, yes!"

He smiled, and Catherine wondered if she had sounded too enthusiastic, like a girl who was attracted by wealth, like one of those aggressive females who were always chasing him. "It's . . . it's pleasant," she added lamely.

Fraser was looking at her mockingly, and Catherine had the terrible feeling that he could read her thoughts. "Come into the study."

Catherine followed him into a large book-lined room done in dark paneling. It had an aura of another age, the graciousness of an easier, friendlier way of life.

Fraser was studying her. "Well?" he asked gravely.

Catherine was not going to be caught again. "It's smaller than the Library of Congress," she said, defensively.

He laughed aloud. "You're right."

Frank came into the room carrying a silver ice bucket. He set it on top of the bar in the corner. "What time would you like dinner, Mr. Fraser?"

"Seven-thirty."

"I'll tell the cook." Frank left the room.

"What may I fix you to drink?"

"Nothing, thank you."

He looked over at her. "Don't you drink, Catherine?"

"Not when I'm working," she said. "I get my *p*'s and *o*'s mixed up."

"You mean *p*'s and *q*'s, don't you?"

"*P*'s and *o*'s. They're next to each other on the typewriter."

"I didn't know."

"You're not supposed to. That's why you pay me a king's ransom every week."

"What do I pay you?" Fraser asked.

"Thirty dollars and dinner in the most beautiful house in Washington."

"You're sure you won't change your mind about that drink?"

"No, thank you," Catherine said.

Fraser mixed a martini for himself, and Catherine wandered around the room looking at the books. There were all the traditional classic titles and, in addition, a whole section of books in Italian and another section in Arabic.

Fraser walked over to her side. "You don't really speak Italian and Arabic, do you?" Catherine asked.

"Yes. I lived in the Middle East for a few years and learned Arabic."

"And the Italian?"

"I went with an Italian actress for a while."

Her face flushed. "I'm sorry. I didn't mean to pry."

Fraser looked at her, his eyes filled with amusement, and Catherine felt like a schoolgirl. She was not sure whether she hated William Fraser or loved him. Of one thing she was sure. He was the nicest man she had ever known.

Dinner was superb. All the dishes were French with divine sauces. The dessert was Cherries Jubilee. No wonder Fraser worked out at the club three mornings a week.

"How is it?" Fraser asked her.

"It's not like the food in the commissary," she said and smiled.

Fraser laughed. "I must eat in the commissary one day."

"I wouldn't if I were you."

He looked at her. "Food that bad?"

"It's not the food. It's the girls. They'd mob you."

"What makes you think so?"

"They talk about you all the time."

"You mean they ask questions about me?"

"I'll say," she grinned.

"I imagine when they're through, they must feel frustrated by the lack of information."

She shook her head. "Wrong. I make up all kinds of stories about you."

Fraser was leaning back in his chair, relaxing over a brandy. "What kind of stories?"

"Are you sure you want to hear?"

"Positive."

"Well, I tell them that you're an ogre and that you scream at me all day long."

He grinned. "Not *all* day long."

"I tell them that you're a nut about hunting and that you carry a loaded rifle around the office while you dictate and I'm constantly afraid that it'll go off and kill me."

"That must hold their interest."

"They're having a fine time trying to figure out the real you."

"Have you figured out the real me?" Fraser's tone had become serious.

She looked into his bright blue eyes for a moment, then turned away. "I think so," she said.

"Who am I?"

Catherine felt a sudden tension within her. The bantering was over and a new note had crept into the conversation. An exciting note, a disturbing note. She did not answer.

Fraser looked at her for a moment, then smiled. "I'm a dull subject. More dessert?"

"No, thank you. I won't eat again for a week."

"Let's go to work."

. . .

THEY WORKED UNTIL midnight. Fraser saw Catherine to the door, and Talmadge was waiting outside to drive her back to the apartment.

She thought about Fraser all the way home. His strength, his humor, his compassion. Someone had once said that a man had to be very strong before he could allow himself to be gentle. William Fraser was very strong. This evening had been one of the nicest evenings of Catherine's life and it worried her. She was afraid that she might turn into one of those jealous secretaries who sits around the office all day hating every girl who telephones her boss. Well, she was not going to allow that to happen. Every eligible female in Washington was throwing herself at Fraser's head. She was not going to join the crowd.

When Catherine returned to the apartment, Susie was waiting up for her. She pounced on Catherine the moment she came in.

"Give!" Susie demanded. "What happened?"

"Nothing happened," Catherine replied. "We had dinner."

Susie stared at her incredulously. "Didn't he even make a pass at you?"

"No, of course not."

Susie sighed. "I should have known it. He was afraid to."

"What do you mean by that?"

"What I mean by that, sweetie, is that you come off like the Virgin Mary. He was probably afraid if he laid a finger on you, you'd scream 'rape' and faint dead away."

Catherine felt her cheeks redden. "I'm not interested in him that way," she said stiffly. "And I don't come off like the Virgin Mary." *I come off like the Virgin Catherine. Dear old Saint Catherine.* All she had done was to move her holy headquarters to Washington. Nothing else had changed. She was still doing business at the same old church.

DURING THE NEXT six months Fraser was away a good deal. He made trips to Chicago and San Francisco and to Europe. There was always enough work to keep Catherine busy, and yet the office seemed lonely and empty with Fraser gone.

There was a constant stream of interesting visitors, most of them men, and Catherine found herself barraged with invitations. She had her choice of lunches, dinners, trips to Europe and bed. She accepted none of the invitations, partly because she was not interested in any of the men but mostly because she felt that Fraser would not approve of her mixing business with pleasure. If Fraser was aware of the constant opportunities she declined, he said nothing. The day after she had had dinner with him at his home he had given her a ten-dollar-a-week raise.

IT SEEMED TO Catherine that there was a change in the tempo of the city. People were moving faster, becoming more tense. The headlines screamed of a constant series of invasions and crises in Europe. The fall of France had affected Americans more deeply than the other swift-moving events in Europe, for they felt a sense of personal violation, a loss of liberty in a country that was one of the cradles of Liberty.

Norway had fallen, England was fighting for its life in the battle of Britain and a pact had been signed between Germany, Italy and Japan. There was a growing feeling of inevitability that America was going to get into the war. Catherine asked Fraser about it one day.

"I think it's just a question of time before we get involved," he said thoughtfully. "If England can't stop Hitler, we're going to have to."

"But Senator Borah says . . ."

"The symbol of the America Firsters should be an ostrich," Fraser commented angrily.

"What will you do if there's a war?"

"Be a hero," he said.

Catherine visualized him handsome in an officer's uniform going off to war, and she hated the idea. It seemed stupid to her that in this en-lightened age people should still think they could solve their differences by murdering one another.

"Don't worry, Catherine," Fraser said. "Nothing will happen for a while. And when it does happen, we'll be ready for it."

"What about England?" she asked. "If Hitler decides to invade, will it be able to stand up against him? He has so many tanks and planes and they have nothing."

"They will have," Fraser assured her. "Very soon."

He had changed the subject, and they had gone back to work.

One week later the headlines were filled with the news of Roosevelt's new concept of lend-lease. So Fraser had known about it and had tried to reassure her without revealing any information.

The weeks went by swiftly. Catherine accepted an occasional date, but each time she found herself comparing her escort to William Fraser, and she wondered why she bothered going with anyone. She was aware that she had backed herself into a bad emotional corner, but she did not know how to get out of it. She told herself that she was merely infatuated with Fraser and would get over it, but meanwhile her feelings kept her from enjoying the company of other men because they all fell so far short of him.

Late one evening as Catherine was working, Fraser came back to the office unexpectedly after attending a play. She looked up, startled, as he walked in.

"What in hell are we running here?" he growled. "A slave ship?"

"I wanted to finish this report," she said, "so you could take it with you to San Francisco tomorrow."

"You could have mailed it to me," he replied. He sat down in a chair opposite Catherine and studied her. "Don't you have better things to do with your evenings than get out dull reports?" he asked.

"I happened to be free this evening."

Fraser leaned back in the chair, folded his fingers together and dropped them under his chin, staring at her. "Do you remember what you said the first day you walked into this office?"

"I said a lot of silly things."

"You said you didn't want to be a secretary. You wanted to be my assistant."

She smiled. "I didn't know any better."

"You do now."

She looked up at him. "I don't understand."

"It's very simple, Catherine," he said quietly. "For the past three months, you've really been my assistant. Now I'm going to make it official."

She stared at him, unbelievingly. "Are you sure that you . . . ?"

"I didn't give you the title or a salary raise sooner because I didn't want it to scare you. But now you know you can do it."

"I don't know what to say," Catherine stammered. "I—you won't be sorry, Mr. Fraser."

"I'm sorry already. My assistants always call me Bill."

"Bill."

Later that night as Catherine lay in bed, she remembered how he had looked at her and how it had made her feel, and it was a long time before she was able to go to sleep.

Catherine had written to her father several times asking him when he was coming to Washington to visit her. She was eager to show him around the city and introduce him to her friends and to Bill Fraser. She had received no reply to her last two letters. Worried, she telephoned her uncle's house in Omaha. Her uncle answered the phone.

"Cathy! I—I was just about to call you."

Catherine's heart sank.

"How's father?"

There was a brief pause.

"He's had a stroke. I wanted to call you sooner but your father asked me to wait until he was better."

Catherine gripped the receiver.

"Is he better?"

"I'm afraid not, Cathy," her uncle's voice said. "He's paralyzed."

"I'm on my way," Catherine said.

She went in to Bill Fraser and told him the news.

"I'm sorry," Fraser said. "What can I do to help?"

"I don't know. I want to go to him right away, Bill."

"Of course." And he picked up a telephone and began to make calls. His chauffeur drove Catherine to her apartment, where she threw some clothes into a suitcase, and then took her to the airport, where Fraser had arranged a plane reservation for her.

WHEN THE PLANE landed at the Omaha airport, Catherine's aunt and uncle were there to meet her, and one look at their faces told her that she was too late. They drove in silence to the funeral parlor and as Catherine entered the building she was filled with an ineffable sense of loss, of loneliness. A part of her had died and could never be recovered. She was ushered into the small chapel. Her father's body was lying in a simple coffin wearing his best suit. Time had shrunk him, as though the constant abrasion of living had worn him down and made him smaller. Her uncle had handed Catherine her father's personal effects, the accumulations and treasures of a lifetime, and they consisted of fifty dollars in cash, some old snapshots, a few receipted bills, a wristwatch, a tarnished silver penknife and a collection of her letters to him, neatly tied with a piece of string and dog-eared from constant reading. It was a pitiful legacy for any man to have left, and Catherine's heart broke for her father. His dreams were so big and his successes so small. She remembered how alive and vital he had been when she was a little girl and the excitement when he came home from the road with his pockets full of money and his arms full of presents. She remembered his wonderful inventions that never quite worked. It wasn't much to remember, but it was all there was left of him. There were suddenly so many things Catherine wanted to say to him, so much she wanted to do for him; and it would always be too late.

They buried her father in the small graveyard next to the church. Catherine had planned on spending the night with her aunt and uncle and taking the train back the next day, but suddenly she could not bear to stay a moment longer, and she called the airport and made a reservation on the next plane to Washington. Bill Fraser was at the airport to meet her, and it seemed the most natural thing in the world for him to be there, waiting for her, taking care of her when she needed him.

He took Catherine to an old country inn in Virginia for dinner, and he listened while she talked about her father. In the middle of telling a funny story about him, Catherine began to cry, but strangely she felt no embarrassment in front of Bill Fraser.

He suggested that Catherine take some time off, but she wanted to keep busy, wanted to keep her mind filled with anything but the death of her father. She slipped into the habit of having dinner with Fraser once or twice a week, and Catherine felt closer to him than ever before.

It happened without any planning or forethought. They had been working late at the office. Catherine was checking some papers and sensed Bill Fraser standing in back of her. His fingers touched her neck, slowly and caressingly.

"Catherine . . ."

She turned to look up at him and an instant later she was in his arms. It was as though they had kissed a thousand times before, as though this was her past as well as her future, where she had always belonged.

It's this simple, Catherine thought. *It's always been this simple, but I didn't know it.*

"Get your coat, darling," Bill Fraser said. "We're going home."

In the car driving to Georgetown they sat close together, Fraser's arm around Catherine, gentle and protective. She had never known such happiness. She was sure she was in love with him, and it did not matter if he was not in love with her. He was fond of her, and she would settle for that. When she thought of what she had been willing to settle for before—Ron Peterson—she shuddered.

"Anything wrong?" Fraser asked.

Catherine thought of the motel room with the dirty cracked mirror. She looked at the strong intelligent face of the man with his arm around her. "Not now," she said gratefully. She swallowed. "I have to tell you something. I'm a virgin."

Fraser smiled and shook his head in wonder. "It's incredible," he said. "How did I wind up with the only virgin in the city of Washington?"

"I tried to correct it," Catherine said earnestly, "but it just didn't work out."

"I'm glad it didn't," Fraser said.

"You mean you don't mind?"

He was smiling at her again, a teasing grin that lit up his face. "Do you know your problem?" he asked.

"I'll say!"

"You've been worrying too much about it."

"I'll say!"

"The trick is to relax."

She shook her head gently.

"No, darling. The trick is to be in love."

Half an hour later the car pulled up in front of his house. Fraser led Catherine inside to the library.

"Would you like a drink?"

She looked at him. "Let's go upstairs."

He took her in his arms and kissed her hard. She held him fiercely, wanting to draw him into her. *If anything goes wrong tonight,* Catherine thought, *I'll kill myself. I really will kill myself.*

"Come on," he said. He took Catherine's hand.

Bill Fraser's bedroom was a large masculine-looking room with a Spanish highboy against one wall. At the far end of the room was an alcove with a fireplace and in front of it, a breakfast table. Against one wall was a large double bed. To the left was a dressing room and off that, a bathroom.

"Are you sure you wouldn't care for that drink?" Fraser asked.

"I don't need it."

He took her in his arms again and kissed her. She felt the male hardness of him, and a delicious warmth coursed through her body.

"I'll be back," he said.

Catherine watched him disappear into the dressing room. This was the nicest, most wonderful man she had ever known. She stood there thinking about him, then suddenly realized why he had left the room. He wanted to give her a chance to undress alone, so that she would not be embarrassed. Quickly Catherine began taking off her clothes. She stood there a minute later nude and looked down at her body and thought, *Good-bye, Saint Catherine.* She went over to the bed, pulled back the spread and crawled between the sheets.

Fraser walked in, wearing a cranberry moiré silk dressing gown. He came over to the bed and stared at her. Her black hair was fanned out against the white pillow, framing her beautiful face. It was all the more stirring because he knew that it was totally unplanned.

He slipped the robe off and moved into the bed beside her. She suddenly remembered.

"I'm not wearing anything," Catherine said. "Do you think I'll get pregnant?"

"Let's hope so."

She looked at him, puzzled, and opened her mouth to ask him what he meant, but he put his lips on hers and his hands began to move down her body, gently exploring, and she forgot everything except what was happening to her, her whole consciousness concentrated on one part of her body, feeling him try to enter her, hard and pulsing, forcing, an instant of sharp, unexpected pain, then sliding in, moving faster and faster, an alien body in her body, plunging deep inside her, moving with a rhythm that grew more and more frantic, and he said, "Are you ready?" She was not sure what she was supposed to be ready for, but she said,

"Yes," and suddenly he cried, "Oh, Cathy!" and made one last sporadic thrust and lay still on top of her.

And it was all over, and he was saying, "Was it wonderful for you?" and she said, "Yes, it was wonderful," and he said, "It gets better as it goes along," and she was filled with joy that she was able to bring him this happiness, and she tried not to worry about what a disappointment it had been. Perhaps it was like olives. You had to acquire a taste for it. She lay in his arms, letting the sound of his voice wash over her, comforting her, and she thought *This is what is important, being together as two human beings, loving and sharing each other.* She had read too many lurid novels, heard too many promising love songs. She had been expecting too much. Or perhaps—and if this were true, she must face it—she was frigid. As though reading her thoughts, Fraser pulled her closer and said, "Don't worry if you're disappointed, darling. The first time is always traumatic."

When Catherine did not answer, Fraser raised himself up on an elbow and looked at her, concerned, and said, "How do you feel?"

"Fine," she said quickly. She smiled. "You're the best lover I ever had."

She kissed him and held him close, feeling warm and safe until finally the hard knot inside her began to dissolve, and a feeling of relaxation filled her, and she was content.

"Would you like a brandy?" he asked.

"No, thanks."

"I think I'll fix myself one. It isn't every night a man beds a virgin."

"Did you mind that?" she asked.

He looked at her with that strange, knowing look, started to say something and changed his mind. "No," he said. There was a note in his voice that she did not understand.

"Was I—?" she swallowed. "You know—all right?"

"You were lovely," he said.

"Truth?"

"Truth."

"Do you know why I almost didn't go to bed with you?" she asked.

"Why?"

"I was afraid that you wouldn't want to see me again."

He laughed aloud. "That's an old wives' tale fostered by nervous mothers who want to keep their daughters pure. Sex doesn't drive people apart, Catherine. It brings them closer together." And it was true. She had never felt so close to anyone. Outwardly she might look the same, but Catherine knew that she had changed.

The young girl who had come to this house earlier in the evening had vanished forever and in her place was a woman. William Fraser's woman. She had finally found the mysterious Holy Grail that she had been searching for. The quest was over.

Now even the FBI would be satisfied.

6

NOELLE

PARIS: 1941

To some the Paris of 1941 was a cornucopia of riches and opportunity; to others it was a living hell. Gestapo had become a word of dread, and tales of their activities became a chief—if whispered—topic of conversation. The offenses against the French Jews, which had begun as almost a prankish breaking of a few shop windows, had been organized by the efficient Gestapo into a system of confiscation, segregation and extermination.

On May 29, a new ordinance had been issued. ". . . a six-pointed star with the dimensions of the palm of a hand and a black edge. It is to be made of yellow cloth and bear in black lettering the inscription JUDEN. It must be worn from the age of six visibly on the left side of the chest solidly sewn to the clothing."

Not all Frenchmen were willing to be stepped on by the German boot. The Maquis, the French underground resistance, fought cleverly and hard and when caught were put to death in ingenious ways.

A young Countess whose family owned a chateau outside Chartres was forced to quarter the officers of the local German Command in her downstairs rooms for six months, during which time she had five wanted members of the Maquis hidden on the upper floors of the chateau.

The two groups never met, but in three months the Countess' hair had turned completely white.

The Germans lived as befit the status of conquerors, but for the average Frenchman there was a shortage of everything except cold and misery. Cooking gas was rationed, and there was no heat. Parisians survived the winters by buying sawdust by the ton, storing it in one-half of their apartments and keeping the other half warm by means of special sawdust-burning stoves.

Everything was ersatz, from cigarettes and coffee to leather. The French joked that it did not matter what you ate; the taste was all the same. The French women—traditionally the most smartly dressed women in the world—wore shabby coats of sheepskin instead of wool and platform shoes of wood, so that the sound of women walking the streets of Paris resembled the clip-clop of horses' hooves.

Even baptisms were affected, for there was a shortage of sugar almonds, the traditional sweet for the baptismal ceremony, and candy shops displayed invitations to come in and register for sugar almonds. There were a few Renault taxis on the street, but the most popular form of transportation was the two-seater cabs with tandem bikes.

The theater, as always in times of prolonged crisis, flourished. People found escape from the crushing realities of everyday life in the movie houses and on the stages.

Overnight, Noelle Page had become a star. Jealous associates in the theater said that it was due solely to the power and talent of Armand Gautier, and while it was true that Gautier had launched her career, it is axiomatic among those who work in the theater that no one can make a star except the public, that faceless, fickle, adoring, mercurial arbiter of a performer's destiny. The public adored Noelle.

As for Armand Gautier, he bitterly regretted the part he had played in starting Noelle's career. Her need of him was now gone; all that held her to him was a whim, and he lived in constant dread of the day she would leave him. Gautier had worked in the theater most of his life, but he had never met anyone like Noelle. She was an insatiable sponge, learning everything he had to teach her and demanding more. It had been fantastic to watch the metamorphosis in her as she went from the halting, external beginnings of grasping a part to the self-assured inner mastery of the character. Gautier had known from the very beginning that Noelle was going to be a star—there was never any question about it—but what astonished him as he learned to know her better was that stardom was not her goal. The truth was that Noelle was not even interested in acting.

At first, Gautier simply could not believe it. Being a star was the top of the ladder, the *sine qua non*. But to Noelle acting was simply a stepping stone, and Gautier had not the faintest clue as to what her real goal was. She was a mystery, an enigma, and the deeper Gautier probed, the more the riddle grew, like the Chinese boxes that opened and revealed further boxes inside. Gautier prided himself on understanding people, particularly women, and the fact that he knew absolutely nothing about the woman he lived with and loved drove him frantic. He asked Noelle to marry him, and she said, "Yes, Armand," and he knew that she meant nothing by it, that it meant no more to her than her engagement to Philippe Sorel or God alone knew how many other men in her past life. He realized that the marriage would never take place. When Noelle was ready, she would move on.

Gautier was sure that every man who met her tried to persuade her to go to bed with him. He also knew from his envious friends that none of them had succeeded.

"You lucky son of a bitch," one of his friends had said. "You must be hung like *un taureau*. I offered her a yacht, her own chateau and a staff of servants in Cap d'Antibes, and she laughed at me."

Another friend, a banker, told him, "I have finally found the first thing money cannot buy."

"Noelle?"

The banker nodded. "That's right. I told her to name her price. She was not interested. What is it you have for her, my friend?"

Armand Gautier wished he knew.

GAUTIER REMEMBERED WHEN he had found the first play for her. He had read no more than a dozen pages when he knew it was exactly what he was looking for. It was a tour de force, a drama about a woman whose husband had gone to war. A soldier appeared at her home one day telling her that he was a comrade of her husband with whom he had served on the Russian Front. As the play developed, the woman fell in love with the soldier, unaware that he was a psychopathic killer and that her life was in danger. It was a great acting role for the wife, and Gautier agreed to direct it immediately, on condition that Noelle Page play the lead. The backers were reluctant to star an unknown but agreed to have her audition for them. Gautier hurried home to bring the news to Noelle. She had come to him because she wanted to be a star and now he was going to give her her wish. He told himself this would bring them closer together, would make her really love him. They would get married and he would possess her, always.

But when Gautier had told her the news, Noelle had merely looked up at him and said, "That is wonderful, Armand, thank you." In exactly the same tone of voice in which she might have thanked him for telling her the correct time or lighting her cigarette.

Gautier watched her for a long moment, knowing that in some strange way Noelle was sick, that some emotion in her had either died, or had never been alive and that no one would ever possess her. He knew this and yet he could not really believe it, because what he saw was a beautiful, affectionate girl who happily catered to his every whim and asked for nothing in return. Because he loved her, Gautier put his doubts aside, and they went to work on the play.

Noelle was brilliant at the audition and got the part without question, as Gautier had known she would. When the play opened in Paris two months later, Noelle became, overnight, the biggest star in France. The critics had been prepared to attack the play and Noelle because they were aware that Gautier had put his mistress, an inexperienced actress, in the lead, and it was a situation too delicious for them to pass up. But she had completely captivated them. They searched for new superlatives to describe her performance and her beauty. The play was a complete sellout.

Every night after the performance, Noelle's dressing room was filled with visitors. She saw everyone: shoe clerks, soldiers, millionaires, shop girls, treating them all with the same patient courtesy. Gautier would watch in amazement. *It is almost as though she were a Princess receiving her subjects, he thought.*

Over a period of a year Noelle received three letters from Marseille. She tore them up, unopened, and finally they stopped coming.

In the spring, Noelle starred in a motion picture that Armand Gautier directed, and when it was released, her fame spread. Gautier marveled at Noelle's patience in giving interviews and being photographed. Most stars hated it and did it either to help increase their box office value or for reasons of ego. In Noelle's case, she was indifferent to both motivations. She would change the subject when Gautier questioned her about why she was willing to pass up a chance to rest in the South of France in order to stay in a cold, rainy Paris to do tiresome poses for *Le Matin*, *La Petite Parisienne* or *L'Illustration*. It was just as well, for Gautier would have been stunned if he had known her real reason. Noelle's motivation was very simple.

Everything she did was for Larry Douglas.

When Noelle posed for photographs, she visualized her former lover picking up a magazine and recognizing her picture. When she played a scene in a movie, she saw Larry Douglas sitting in a theater one night in some far-off country, watching her. Her work was a reminder to him, a message from the past, a signal that would one day bring him back to her; and that was all Noelle wanted, for him to come back to her, so that she could destroy him.

Thanks to Christian Barbet, Noelle had an ever-growing scrapbook on Larry Douglas. The little detective had moved from his shabby offices to a large, luxurious suite on the rue Richer, near the Folies-Bergère. The first time Noelle had gone to see him in his new offices, Barbet had grinned at her surprised expression and said, "I got it cheap. These offices were occupied by a Jew."

"You said you had some news for me," Noelle said curtly.

The smirk left Barbet's face, "Ah yes." He did have news. It was difficult getting information from England under the very nose of the Nazis, but Barbet had found ways. He bribed sailors on neutral ships to smuggle in letters from an agency in London. But that was only one of his sources. He appealed to the patriotism of the French underground, the humanity of the International Red Cross and the cupidity of black marketeers with overseas connections. To each of them he told a different story, and the flow of information kept coming in.

He picked up a report on his desk. "Your friend was shot down over the English Channel," he said without preamble. Out of the corner of his eye he watched Noelle's face, waiting for her aloof facade to crumble, taking enjoyment in the pain he was inflicting. But Noelle's expression never changed. She looked at him and said confidently, "He was rescued." Barbet stared at her and swallowed and answered reluctantly, "Well, yes. He was picked up by a British Rescue boat." And wondered how the devil she could have known.

Everything about this woman baffled him, and he hated her as a client and was tempted to drop her, but Barbet knew that that would have been stupid.

He had attempted once to make a pass at her, hinting that his services would be less expensive, but Noelle had rebuffed him in a manner that made him feel like a clumsy lout, and he would never forgive her for that. One day, Barbet promised himself quietly, one day this tight-assed bitch would pay.

Now, as Noelle stood in his office, a look of distaste on her beautiful face, Barbet hurriedly went on with the report, eager to get rid of her.

"His squadron has moved to Kirton, in Lincolnshire. They're flying Hurricanes and—" Noelle was interested in something else.

"His engagement to the Admiral's daughter," she said, "it's off, isn't it?"

Barbet looked up in surprise and mumbled, "Yes. She found out about some of his other women." It was almost as though Noelle had already seen the report. She had not, of course, but it did not matter. The bond of hatred that tied Noelle to Larry Douglas was so strong it seemed that nothing important could ever happen to him without her knowing it. Noelle took the report and left. When she returned home she read it over slowly, then carefully filed it among the other reports and locked it up where it could not be found.

One Friday night after a performance, Noelle was in her dressing room at the theater creaming off her makeup when there was a knock at the door, and Marius, the elderly, crippled stage doorman, entered.

"Pardon, Miss Page, a gentleman asked me to bring these to you."

Noelle glanced up in the mirror and saw that he was carrying an enormous bouquet of red roses in an exquisite vase.

"Set it down there, Marius," Noelle said, and she watched as he carefully placed the vase of roses on a table.

It was late November and no one in Paris had seen roses for more than three months. There must have been four dozen of them, ruby red, long-stemmed, wet with dew. Curious, Noelle walked over and picked up the card. It read: "To the lovely Fräulein Page. Would you have supper with me? General Hans Scheider."

The vase that the flowers rested in was delft, intricately patterned and very expensive. General Scheider had gone to a great deal of trouble.

"He would like an answer," the stage doorman said.

"Tell him I never eat supper and take these home to your wife."

He stared at her in surprise. "But the General . . ."

"That is all."

Marius nodded his head, picked up the vase and hurried out. Noelle knew that he would rush to spread the story of how she had defied a German general. It had happened before with other German officials, and the French people regarded her as some kind of heroine. It was ridiculous. The truth of the matter was that Noelle had nothing against the Nazis, she was merely indifferent to them. They were not a part of her life or her plans, and she simply tolerated them, awaiting the day when they would return home. She knew that if she became involved with any Germans it would hurt her. Not now, perhaps, but it was not the present Noelle was concerned about; it was the future. She thought that the idea of the Third Reich ruling for one thousand years was *merde*. Any student of history knew that eventually all conquerors were conquered. In the meantime she would do nothing that would allow her fellow Frenchmen to turn on her when the Germans were finally ousted. She was totally untouched by the Nazi occupation and when the subject came up—as it constantly did—Noelle avoided any discussion about it.

Fascinated by her attitude, Armand Gautier often tried to draw her out on the subject.

"Don't you care that the Nazis have conquered France?" he would ask her.

"Would it matter if I cared?"

"That's not the point. If everyone felt as you do, we would be damned."

"We are damned anyway, are we not?"

"Not if we believe in free will. Do you think our life is ordained from the time we are born?"

"To some degree. We are given bodies, our birthplace and our station in life, but that does not mean that we cannot change. We can become anything we want to be."

"My point exactly. That is why we must fight the Nazis."

She looked at him. "Because God is on our side?"

"Yes," he replied.

"If there is a God," Noelle answered reasonably, "and He created them, then He must be on their side, also."

In October, the first anniversary of Noelle's play, the backers gave a party for the cast at Tour d'Argent. There was a mixture of actors, bankers and influential businessmen. The guests were mostly French, but there were a dozen Germans at the party, a few of them in uniform, all of them except one with French girls. The exception was a German officer in his forties, with a long, lean intelligent face, deep green eyes and a trim, athletic body. A narrow scar ran from his cheekbone to his chin. Noelle was aware that he had been watching her all evening although he had not come near her.

"Who is that man?" she casually asked one of the hosts.

He glanced over at the officer who was sitting alone at a table sipping champagne, then turned to Noelle in surprise. "It is strange you should ask. I thought he was a friend of yours. That is General Hans Scheider. He is on the General Staff." Noelle remembered the roses and the card. "Why did you think he was a friend of mine?" she asked.

The man appeared flustered. "I naturally assumed . . . I mean, every play and motion picture produced in France must be approved by the Germans. When the censor tried to stop your new movie from being made, the General personally stepped in and gave his approval."

At that moment Armand Gautier brought someone to meet Noelle and the conversation changed.

Noelle paid no further attention to General Scheider.

The next evening when she arrived at her dressing room, there was one rose in a small vase with a little card that said: "Perhaps we should start smaller. May I see you? Hans Scheider."

Noelle tore up the note and threw the flower into the wastebasket.

. . .

AFTER THAT NIGHT Noelle became aware that at almost every party she and Armand Gautier attended, General Scheider was there. He always remained in the background watching her. It happened too often to be a coincidence. Noelle realized that he must be going to a great deal of trouble to keep track of her movements and to get himself invitations to places where she would be.

She wondered why he was so interested, but it was an idle speculation and it did not really bother her. Occasionally Noelle would amuse herself by accepting an invitation and not showing up, then checking with the hostess the next day to see if General Scheider had been there. The answer was always "Yes."

Despite the swift and lethal punishment meted out by the Nazis to anyone who opposed them, sabotage continued to flourish in Paris. In addition to the Maquis there were dozens of small groups of freedom-loving French who risked their lives to fight the enemy with whatever weapons were at hand. They murdered German soldiers when they could catch them off guard, blew up supply trucks and mined bridges and trains. Their activities were denounced in the controlled daily press as deeds of infamy, but to the loyal French the deeds of infamy were glorious exploits. The name of one man kept cropping up in the newspapers—he was nicknamed *Le Cafard,* the cockroach, because he seemed to scurry around everywhere, and the Gestapo was unable to catch him. No one knew who he was. Some believed that he was an Englishman living in Paris; another theory held that he was an agent of General De Gaulle, the leader of the Free French Forces; and some even said that he was a disaffected German. Whoever he was, drawings of cockroaches were beginning to spring up all over Paris, on buildings, sidewalks, and even inside German Army headquarters. The Gestapo was concentrating its efforts on catching him. Of one fact there was no doubt. *Le Cafard* had become an instant folk hero.

ON A RAINY afternoon in December, Noelle attended the opening of an art exhibition of a young artist whom she and Armand knew. The exhibit was held in a gallery on the rue du Faubourg-St.-Honoré. The room was crowded. Many celebrities were in attendance and photographers were everywhere. As Noelle walked around, moving from painting to painting, she felt someone touch her arm. She turned and found herself looking into the face of Madame Rose. It took Noelle a moment to recognize her. The familiar, ugly face was the same, and yet it seemed twenty years older, as though through some alchemy in time she had become her own mother. She wore a big black cape, and somewhere at the back of Noelle's consciousness was the fleeting thought that she was not wearing the prescribed yellow JUDEN star.

Noelle started to speak, but the older woman stopped her by squeezing her arm.

"Could you meet me?" she asked in a barely audible voice. "Les Deux Magots."

Before Noelle could reply, Madame Rose melted into the crowd, and Noelle was surrounded by photographers. As she posed and smiled for them, Noelle was remembering Madame Rose and her nephew, Israel Katz. They had both been kind to her in a time of need. Israel had saved her life twice. Noelle wondered what Madame Rose wanted. Money, probably.

Twenty minutes later Noelle slipped away and took a taxi to the place St. Germain des Prés. It had been raining on and off all day, and now the rain had started to turn into a cold, driving sleet. As her taxi pulled up in front of Les Deux Magots and Noelle stepped out into the biting cold, a man in a raincoat and wide-brimmed hat appeared at her side out of nowhere. It took Noelle a moment to recognize him. Like his aunt, he looked older, but the change went deeper than that. There was an authority, a strength that had not been there before. Israel Katz was thinner than when she had last seen him, and his eyes were hollowed, as though he had not slept in days. Noelle noticed that he was not wearing the yellow six-pointed Jewish star.

"Let's get out of the rain," Israel Katz said.

He took Noelle's arm and led her inside. There were half a dozen customers in the café, all French. Israel led Noelle to a table in a back corner.

"Would you like something to drink?" he asked.

"No, thank you."

He took off his rain-soaked hat, and Noelle studied his face. She knew instantly that he had not called her here to ask for money. He was watching her.

"You're still beautiful, Noelle," he said quietly. "I've seen all of your movies and plays. You're a great actress."

"Why didn't you ever come backstage?"

Israel hesitated, then grinned shyly. "I didn't want to embarrass you."

Noelle stared at him a moment before she realized what he meant. To her, "Juden" was just a word that appeared in newspapers from time to time, and it meant nothing in her life; but what must it be like to *live* that word, to be a Jew in a country sworn to wipe you out, exterminate you, particularly when it was your own motherland.

"I choose my own friends," Noelle replied. "No one tells me whom to see."

Israel smiled wryly. "Don't waste your courage," he advised. "Use it where it can help."

"Tell me about you," she said.

He shrugged. "I live a very unglamorous life. I became a surgeon. I studied under Dr. Angibouste. Have you heard of him?"

"No."

"He's a great heart surgeon. He made me his protégé. Then the Nazis took away my license to practice medicine." He held up his beautifully sculptured hands and examined them as though they belonged to someone else. "So I became a carpenter."

She looked at him for a long moment. "Is that all?" she asked.

Israel studied her in surprise. "Of course," he said. "Why?"

Noelle dismissed the thought at the back of her mind.

"Nothing. Why did you want to see me?"

He leaned closer to her and lowered his voice. "I need a favor. A friend—"

At that moment, the door opened and four German soldiers in gray-green uniforms walked into the bistro, led by a corporal. The corporal called out in a loud voice: "*Achtung!* We wish to see your identity papers."

Israel Katz stiffened, and it was as though a mask fell into place. Noelle saw his right hand slide into the pocket of his overcoat. His eyes flickered toward the narrow passageway that led to an exit in the rear, but one of the soldiers was already moving toward it, blocking it. Israel said in a low urgent voice, "Get away from me. Walk out the front door. Now."

"Why?" Noelle demanded.

The Germans were examining the identification papers of some customers at a table near the entrance.

"Don't ask questions," he commanded. "Just go."

Noelle hesitated a moment, then rose to her feet and started toward the door. The soldiers were moving on to the next table. Israel had pushed his chair back to give himself more freedom. The movement attracted the attention of two of the soldiers. They walked over to him.

"Identity papers."

Somehow Noelle knew that it was Israel the soldiers were looking for and that he was going to try to escape and they would kill him. He had no chance.

She turned and called out to him, "François! We are going to be late for the theater. Pay the check and let's go."

The soldiers looked at her in surprise. Noelle started back toward the table.

Corporal Schultz moved to face her. He was a blond, apple-cheeked boy in his early twenties. "Are you with this man, Fräulein?" he asked.

"Of course I am! Haven't you anything better to do than pester honest French citizens?" Noelle demanded, angrily.

"I am sorry, my good Fräulein, but . . ."

"I am not your good Fräulein!" Noelle snapped. "I am Noelle Page. I am starring at the Variétés Theatre, and this man is my costar. Tonight, when I am having supper with my dear friend, General Hans Scheider, I shall inform him of your behavior this afternoon and he will be furious with you."

Noelle saw the look of recognition come into the corporal's eyes, but whether it was a recognition of her name or General Scheider's, she could not be sure.

"I—I am sorry, Fräulein," he stammered. "Of course I recognize you." He turned to Israel Katz, who sat there silently, his hand in his coat pocket. "I do not recognize this gentleman."

"You would if you barbarians ever went to the theater," said Noelle with stinging contempt. "Are we under arrest or may we leave?"

The young corporal was aware of everyone's eyes on him. He had to make an instant decision. "Of course the Fräulein and her friend are not under arrest," he said. "I apologize if I have inconvenienced you. I—"

Israel Katz looked up at the soldier and said coolly, "It's raining outside, Corporal. I wonder if one of your men could find us a taxi."

"Of course. At once."

Israel got into the taxi with Noelle, and the German corporal stood in the rain watching as they drove away. When the taxi stopped for a traffic light three blocks away, Israel opened the door, squeezed Noelle's hand once and disappeared without a word into the night.

At seven o'clock that evening when Noelle walked into her theater dressing room, there were two men waiting for her. One of them was the young German corporal from the bistro that afternoon. The other was in mufti. He was an albino, completely hairless, with pink eyes, and he somehow reminded Noelle of an unformed baby. He was in his thirties, with a moon face. His voice was high-pitched and almost laughably feminine, but there was an ineffable quality, a deadliness about him that was chilling. "Miss Noelle Page?"

"Yes."

"I am Colonel Kurt Mueller, Gestapo. I believe you have met Corporal Schultz."

Noelle turned to the corporal, indifferently, "No, I don't believe I have."

"At the *kaffehaus* this afternoon," the corporal said helpfully.

Noelle turned to Mueller. "I meet so many people."

The colonel nodded. "It must be difficult to remember everyone when you have so many friends, Fräulein."

She nodded. "Exactly."

"For example, this friend you were with this afternoon." He paused, watching Noelle's eyes. "You told Corporal Schultz that he is starring in the show with you?"

Noelle looked at the Gestapo man in surprise. "The corporal must have misunderstood me."

"Nein, Fräulein," the corporal replied indignantly. "You said . . ."

The colonel turned to give him a freezing look, and the corporal's mouth snapped closed in mid-sentence.

"Perhaps," said Kurt Mueller amiably. "This kind of thing can happen so easily when one is trying to communicate in a foreign language."

"That is true," said Noelle quickly.

Out of the corner of her eye she saw the corporal's face redden with anger, but he kept his mouth shut.

"I'm sorry to have troubled you over nothing," Kurt Mueller said.

Noelle felt her shoulders relax and she suddenly realized how tense she had been.

"That's perfectly all right," she said. "Perhaps I can give you tickets for the play."

"I have seen it," the Gestapo man said, "and Corporal Schultz has already bought his ticket. But thank you."

He started toward the door, then paused. "When you called Corporal Schultz a barbarian, he decided to buy a ticket this evening to see your performance. When he looked at the actors' photographs in the lobby, he did not see the picture of your friend from the *kaffehaus*. That is when he called me."

Noelle's heart began to beat faster.

"Just for the record, Mademoiselle. If he was not your costar, who was he?"

"A—a friend."

"His name?" The high-pitched voice was still soft, but it had become dangerous.

"What difference does it make?" Noelle asked.

"Your friend answers the description of a criminal we are looking for. He was reported seen in the vicinity of the place St. Germain des Prés this afternoon."

Noelle stood watching him, her mind racing.

"What is the name of your friend?" Colonel Mueller's voice was insistent.

"I—I don't know."

"Ah, then he was a stranger?"

"Yes."

He stared at her, his cold pink eyes drilling into hers. "You were sitting with him. You stopped the soldiers from looking at his papers. Why?"

"I felt sorry for him," Noelle said. "He came up to me . . ."

"Where?"

Noelle thought quickly. Someone could have seen them going into the bistro together. "Outside the café. He told me that the soldiers were looking for him because he had stolen some groceries for his wife and children. It seemed such a minor crime that I . . ." She looked up at Mueller appealingly, "I helped him."

Mueller studied her a moment and nodded his head admiringly. "I can understand why you are such a big star." The smile died from his face, and when he spoke again his voice was even softer. "Let me give you some advice, Mademoiselle Page. We wish to be on good terms with you French. We want you to be our friends as well as our allies. But anyone who helps our enemy becomes our enemy. We will catch your friend, Mademoiselle, and when we do, we will question him, and I promise you he will talk."

"I have nothing to be afraid of," Noelle said.

"You are wrong." She could barely hear him. "You have me to be afraid of." Colonel Mueller nodded to the corporal and started toward the door again. He turned once more. "If you hear from your friend, you will report it to me at once. If you fail to do so . . ." He smiled at her. And the two men were gone.

Noelle sank into a chair, drained. She was aware that she had not been convincing, but she had been caught completely off guard. She had been so sure that the incident had been forgotten. She remembered now some of the stories she had heard about the Gestapo, and a small chill went through her. Supposing they caught Israel Katz and he did talk. He could tell them that they were old friends, that Noelle had lied about not knowing him. But surely that could not be important. Unless . . . the name she had thought of in the restaurant popped into her mind again. *Le Cafard.*

HALF AN HOUR later when Noelle went on stage, she managed to put everything out of her mind but the character she was playing. It was an appreciative audience and as she took her curtain calls, she received a tremendous ovation. She could still hear the applause as she walked back to her dressing room and opened the door. Seated in a chair was General Hans Scheider. He rose to his feet as Noelle entered and said politely, "I was informed that we have a supper date this evening."

They had supper at Le Fruit Perdu along the Seine, about twenty miles outside of Paris. They had been driven there by the General's chauffeur in a shiny, black limousine. The rain had stopped, and the night was cool and pleasant. The General had made no reference to the day's incident until they had finished eating. Noelle's first impulse had been not to go with him, but she decided that it was necessary to learn how much the Germans really knew and how much trouble she might be in.

"I received a call from Gestapo headquarters this afternoon," General Scheider was saying. "They informed me that you had told a Corporal Schultz that you were having supper with me this evening." Noelle watched him, saying nothing. He went on. "I decided that it would be most unpleasant for you if I said 'No,' and most pleasant for me if I said 'Yes.'" He smiled. "So here we are."

"This is all so ridiculous," Noelle protested. "Helping a poor man who stole some groc—"

"Don't!" The General's voice was sharp. Noelle looked at him in surprise. "Don't make the mistake of believing that all Germans are fools. And do not underestimate the Gestapo."

Noelle said, "They have nothing to do with me, General."

He toyed with the stem of his wine glass. "Colonel Mueller suspects you of having helped a man he wants very badly. If that is true, you are in a great deal of trouble. Colonel Mueller neither forgives nor forgets." He looked at Noelle. "On the other hand," he said carefully, "if you should not see your friend again, this whole thing could simply blow over. Would you like a cognac?"

"Please," Noelle said.

He ordered two Napoleon brandies. "How long have you been living with Armand Gautier?"

"I am sure you know the answer to that," Noelle replied.

General Scheider smiled. "As a matter of fact, I do. What I really wanted to ask you is why you refused to have dinner with me before. Was it because of Gautier?"

Noelle shook her head. "No."

"I see," he said stiffly. There was a note in his voice that surprised her.

"Paris is full of women," Noelle said. "I am sure you could have your pick."

"You don't know me," the General said quietly, "or you wouldn't have said that." He sounded embarrassed. "I have a wife and child in Berlin. I love them very much, but I have been away from them for more than a year now, and I have no idea when I will see them again."

"Who forced you to come to Paris?" Noelle asked cruelly.

"I was not making a bid for sympathy. I just wanted to explain myself a little. I am not a promiscuous man. The first time I saw you on the stage," he said, "something happened to me. I felt I wanted to know you very much. I would like us to be good friends."

There was a quiet dignity about the way he spoke.

"I can promise nothing," Noelle said.

He nodded. "I understand."

But of course he did not. Because Noelle intended never to see him again. General Scheider tactfully changed the conversation and they talked of acting and the theater, and Noelle found him surprisingly knowledgeable. He had an eclectic mind and a deep intelligence. Casually he ranged from topic to topic, pointing out the mutual interests that the two of them shared. It was a skillful performance and Noelle was amused. He had gone to a great deal of trouble to learn about her background. He looked every inch the German General in his olive-green uniform, strong and authoritative, but there was a gentleness that bespoke another kind of man altogether, an intellectual quality that belonged to the scholar rather than the soldier. And yet there was the scar running across his face.

"How did you get your scar?" Noelle asked.

He ran his finger along the deep incision. "I was in a duel many years ago," he shrugged. "In German, we call this *wild-fleisch*—it means 'proud skin.'"

They discussed the Nazi philosophy.

"We are not monsters," General Scheider stated. "And we have no wish to rule the world. But neither do we intend to sit still and be punished any longer for a war we lost more than twenty years ago. The Treaty of Versailles is a bondage that the German people have finally broken out of."

They spoke of the occupation of Paris. "It was not the fault of your

French soldiers that it was so easy for us," General Scheider said. "A good deal of the responsibility must fall on the shoulders of Napoleon the Third."

"You're joking," Noelle replied.

"I am perfectly serious," he assured her. "In the days of Napoleon, the mobs were constantly using the tangled, twisted streets of Paris for barricades and ambushes against his soldiers. In order to stop them, he commissioned Baron Eugene Georges Haussmann to straighten out the streets and fill the city with nice, wide boulevards." He smiled. "The boulevards down which our troops marched. I am afraid history will not be kind to planner Haussmann."

After dinner, driving back to Paris, he asked, "Are you in love with Armand Gautier?"

His tone was casual, but Noelle had the feeling that her answer was important to him.

"No," she said slowly.

He nodded, satisfied. "I did not think so. I believe I could make you very happy."

"As happy as you make your wife?"

General Scheider stiffened for a moment as though he had been struck and then turned to look at Noelle.

"I can be a good friend," he said quietly. "Let us hope that you and I are never enemies."

When Noelle returned to the apartment, it was almost 3:00 A.M., and Armand Gautier was waiting for her in a state of agitation.

"Where the hell have you been?" he demanded, as she walked in the door.

"I had an engagement." Noelle's eyes moved past him into the room. It looked as though a cyclone had struck. Desk drawers were open and the contents strewn around the room. The closets had been ransacked, a lamp had been overturned and a small table lay on its side, one leg broken.

"What happened?" Noelle asked.

"The Gestapo was here! My God, Noelle, what have you been up to?"

"Nothing."

"Then why would they do this?"

Noelle began to move around the room, straightening the furniture, thinking hard. Gautier grabbed her shoulders and turned her around. "I want to know what's happening."

She took a deep breath. "All right."

She told him of the meeting with Israel Katz, leaving out his name and the conversation later with Colonel Mueller. "I don't know that my friend is *Le Cafard,* but it is possible."

Gautier sank into a chair, stunned. "My God!" he exclaimed. "I don't care *who* he is! I don't want you to have anything more to do with him. We could both be destroyed because of this. I hate the Germans as much as you do . . ." He stopped, not sure whether Noelle hated the Germans or not. He began again, "Cherie, as long as the Germans are making the rules, we must live under them. Neither of us can afford to get involved with the Gestapo. This Jew—what did you say his name was?"

"I didn't say."

He looked at her a moment. "Was he your lover?"

"No, Armand."

"Does he mean anything to you?"

"No."

"Well, then." Gautier sounded relieved. "I don't think we have anything to worry about. They can't blame you if you had one accidental meeting with him. If you don't see him again, they'll forget the whole thing."

"Of course they will," Noelle said.

On the way to the theater the next evening, Noelle was followed by two Gestapo men.

FROM THAT DAY on Noelle was followed everywhere she went. It first began as a feeling, a premonition that she was being stared at. Noelle would turn and see in a crowd a young Teutonic-looking man in civilian clothes who seemed to be paying no attention to her. Later, the feeling would return, and this time it would be another young Teutonic-looking man. It was always someone different and though they were in plain clothes, they wore a uniform that was distinctively theirs: an attitude of contempt, superiority and cruelty, and the emanations were unmistakable.

Noelle said nothing to Gautier about what was happening for she saw no point in alarming him any further. The incident with the Gestapo in the apartment had made him very nervous. He could talk of nothing but what the Germans could do to both his and Noelle's career if they wished to, and Noelle was aware that he was right. One had only to look at the daily newspapers to know that the Nazis showed no mercy to their enemies. There had been several telephone messages from General Scheider, but Noelle had ignored them. If she did not want the Nazis as an enemy, neither did she want them as a friend. She decided that she would remain like Switzerland: neutral. The Israel Katzes of the world would have to take care of themselves. Noelle was mildly curious about what he had wanted from her, but she had no intention of getting involved.

Two weeks after Noelle had seen Israel Katz, the newspapers carried a front-page story that the Gestapo had caught a group of saboteurs headed by *Le Cafard*. Noelle read all the stories carefully, but nothing was mentioned about whether *Le Cafard* himself had been captured. She remembered Israel Katz' face when the Germans had started to close in on him, and she knew that he would never let them take him alive. *Of course,* Noelle told herself, *it could be my fantasy. He is probably a harmless carpenter, as he said.* But if he was harmless, why was the Gestapo so interested in him? Was he *Le Cafard?* And had he been captured, or had he escaped? Noelle walked over to the window of her apartment that faced on the Avenue Martigny. Two black rain-coated figures stood under a streetlamp, waiting. For what? Noelle began to feel the sense of alarm that Gautier felt, but with it came a feeling of anger. She remembered Colonel Mueller's words: *You have me to be afraid of.* It was a challenge. Noelle had the feeling she was going to hear from Israel Katz again.

THE MESSAGE CAME the next morning from—of all the unlikely people—her concierge. He was a small, rheumy-eyed man in his seventies, with a wizened, leathery face and no lower teeth, so that it was difficult to understand him when he spoke. When Noelle rang for the elevator he was waiting inside. They rode down together, and as they neared the lobby, he mumbled, "The birthday cake you ordered is ready at the bakery at rue de Passy."

Noelle stared at him a moment, not sure whether she had heard him correctly, then said, "I didn't order any cake."

"Rue de Passy," he repeated stubbornly.

And Noelle suddenly understood. Even then, she would have done nothing about it if she had not seen the two Gestapo agents waiting for her across the street. To be followed around like a criminal! The two men were in conversation. They had not seen her yet. Angrily Noelle turned to the concierge and said, "Where is the service entrance?"

"This way, Mam'selle."

Noelle followed him through a back corridor, down a flight of stairs to the basement and out to an alley. Three minutes later she was in a taxi, on her way to meet Israel Katz.

THE BAKERY WAS an ordinary-looking shop in a rundown, middle-class neighborhood. The lettering on the window read *B O U L A N G E R I E,* and the letters were flaked and chipped. Noelle opened the door and stepped inside. She was greeted by a small dumpling of a woman in a spotless white apron.

"Yes, Mademoiselle?"

Noelle hesitated. There was still time to leave, still time to turn back and not get involved in something dangerous that was none of her business.

The woman was waiting.

"You—you have a birthday cake for me," Noelle said, feeling foolish at the game-playing, as though somehow the gravity of what was happening was demeaned by the childish artifices that were employed.

The woman nodded. "It is ready, Miss Page." She put a *C L O S E D* sign on the door, locked it and said, "This way."

He was lying on a cot in the small back room of the bakery, his face a mask of pain, bathed in perspiration. The sheet twisted around him was soaked in blood, and there was a large tourniquet around his left knee.

"Israel."

He moved to face the door, and the sheet fell away, revealing a sodden pulp of mashed bone and flesh where his knee had been.

"What happened?" Noelle asked.

He tried to smile but did not quite make it. His voice was hoarse and strained with pain. "They stepped on *Le Cafard,* but we're not easy to kill."

So she had been correct. "I read about it," Noelle said. "Are you going to be all right?"

Israel took a deep painful breath and nodded. His words came in labored gasps.

"The Gestapo is turning Paris upside down looking for me. My only chance is to get out of the city. . . . If I can get to Le Havre, I have friends who will help me get on a boat out of the country."

"Can't you get a friend to drive you out of Paris?" Noelle asked. "You could hide in the back of a truck—"

Israel shook his head weakly. "Road blocks. Not a mouse can get out of Paris."

Not even *un Cafard,* Noelle thought. "Can you travel with that leg?" she asked, stalling for time, trying to come to a decision.

His lips tightened in the rictus of a smile.

"I'm not going to travel with this leg," Israel said.

Noelle looked at him, not understanding, and at that moment the door opened and a large, heavy-shouldered, bearded man entered. In his hand he carried an ax. He walked up to the bed and pulled back the sheet, and Noelle felt the blood drain from her face. She thought of General Scheider and the hairless albino from the Gestapo and what they would do to her if they caught her.

"I will help you," Noelle said.

7

CATHERINE

WASHINGTON—HOLLYWOOD: 1941

I t seemed to Catherine Alexander that her life had entered a new phase, as though somehow she had climbed to some higher emotional level, a heady and exhilarating peak. When Bill Fraser was in town, they had dinner together every night and went to concerts or the theater or the opera. He found a small, charming apartment for her near Arlington. He wanted to pay her rent, but Catherine insisted on paying it herself. He bought her clothes and jewelry. She had resisted at first, embarrassed by some deeply ingrained Protestant ethic, but it had given Fraser such obvious pleasure that finally Catherine had stopped arguing about it.

Whether you like it or not, she thought, *you're a mistress.* It had always been a loaded word for her, filled with connotations of cheap, slinky women in back-street apartments, living out lives of emotional frustration. But now that it was happening to her, Catherine found that it was not really like that at all. It just meant that she was sleeping with the man she loved. It did not feel dirty or sordid, it felt perfectly natural. *It's interesting,* she thought, *how the things that other people do seem so horrible, and yet when you're doing them they seem so right. When you are reading about the sexual experiences of someone else, it's* True Confessions, *but when it's you it's the* Ladies' Home Journal.

Fraser was a thoughtful and understanding companion, and it was as though they had been together always. Catherine could predict his reactions to almost any situation and knew his every mood. Contrary to what Fraser had said, sex with him did not become more exciting, but Catherine told herself that sex was only a small part of a relationship. She was not a schoolgirl who needed constant titillation, she was a mature woman. *Give or take a little,* she thought, wryly.

Fraser's advertising agency was being run in his absence by Wallace Turner, a senior account executive. William Fraser tried to have as little to do with the business as possible, so he could devote himself to his job in Washington, but whenever a major problem arose at the agency and they needed his advice, Fraser got in the habit of discussing it with Catherine, using her as a sounding board. He found that she had a natural flair for the business. Catherine often came up with ideas for campaigns that proved very effective.

"If I weren't so selfish, Catherine," Fraser said one night at dinner, "I'd put you in the agency and turn you loose on some of our accounts." He covered her hand with his. "I'd miss you too much," he added. "I want you here with me."

"I want to be here, Bill. I'm very happy with things the way they are." And it was true. She had thought that if she were ever in a situation like this, she would want desperately to get married, but somehow there seemed no urgency about it. In every important way they were already married.

One afternoon as Catherine was finishing some work, Fraser walked into her office.

"How would you like to take a drive out to the country tonight?" he asked.

"Love it. Where are we going?"

"To Virginia. We're having dinner with my parents."

Catherine looked up at him in surprise. "Do they know about us?" she asked.

"Not everything," he grinned. "Just that I have a fantastic young assistant and I'm bringing her to dinner."

If she felt a pang of disappointment, she did not let it show on her face. "Fine," she said. "I'll stop by the apartment and change."

"I'll pick you up at seven o'clock."

"Date."

THE FRASERS' HOUSE, set in the beautiful rolling hills of Virginia, was a large Colonial farmhouse with sixty acres of vivid green grass and farmland surrounding it. The house dated back to seventeen hundred.

"I've never seen anything like it," Catherine marveled.

"It's one of the best breeding farms in America," Fraser informed her.

The car drove past a corral filled with beautiful horses, past the neatly kept paddocks and the caretaker's cottage.

"It's like another world," Catherine exclaimed. "I envy your growing up here."

"Do you think you'd like living on a farm?"

"This isn't exactly a farm," she said dryly. "It's more like owning your own country."

They had arrived in front of the house.

Fraser turned to her. "My mother and father are a little formal," he warned, "but there's nothing for you to worry about. Just be yourself. Nervous?"

"No," Catherine said. "Panicky." And as she said it, she realized with a sense of astonishment that she was lying. In the classic tradition of all girls about to meet the parents of the man they loved, she should have been petrified. But she felt nothing except curiosity. There was no time to wonder about that now. They were getting out of the car and a butler in full livery was opening the door, greeting them with a welcoming smile.

Colonel Fraser and his lady could have been living out of the pages of an ante-bellum story book. The first thing that struck Catherine was how old and fragile-looking they were. Colonel Fraser was a pale carbon of what had once been a handsome, vital man. He reminded Catherine very strongly of someone, and with a shock, she realized who it was: an old, worn-out version of his son. The colonel had sparse white hair and walked with a painful stoop. His eyes were pale blue and his once-powerful hands were gnarled with arthritis. His wife had the look of an aristocrat and still retained traces of a girlish beauty. She was gracious and warm to Catherine.

In spite of what Fraser had told her, Catherine had the feeling that she was there for their inspection. The colonel and his wife spent the evening questioning her. They were very discreet but thorough. Catherine told them about her parents and her childhood, and when she talked about moving from school to school, she made it sound like adventurous fun, rather than the agony it had been. As she talked she could see Bill Fraser proudly beaming at her. Dinner was superb. They dined by candlelight in a large, old-fashioned dining room with a real marble fireplace and liveried servants. *Old silver, old money and old wine.* She looked at Bill Fraser and a wave of warm gratitude went through her. She had the feeling that this kind of life could be hers if she wanted it. She knew that Fraser loved her, and she loved him. And yet there was something missing: a sense of excitement. *Possibly,* she thought, *I'm expecting too much. I've probably been warped* by *Gary Cooper, Humphrey Bogart and Spencer Tracy! Love isn't a knight in shining armor. It's a gentleman farmer in a gray tweed suit. Damn all those movies and books!* As she looked at the colonel, she could see Fraser twenty years hence, looking exactly the same as his father. She was very quiet during the rest of the evening.

On the way home Fraser asked, "Did you enjoy the evening?"

"Very much. I liked your parents."

"They liked you, too."

"I'm glad." And she was. Except for the vaguely disquieting thought in the back of her mind that somehow she should have been more nervous about meeting them.

The following evening, while Catherine and Fraser were having dinner at the Jockey Club, Fraser told her that he had to go to London for a week. "While I'm gone," he said, "I have an interesting job for you. They've asked our office to supervise an Army Air Corps recruiting film they're shooting at MGM studios in Hollywood. I'd like you to handle the picture while I'm gone."

Catherine stared at him incredulously. "Me? I can't even load a Brownie. What do I know about making a training film?"

"About as much as anyone else." Fraser grinned. "It's all pretty new, but you don't have to worry. They'll have a producer and everything. The Army plans to use actors in the film."

"Why?"

"I guess they feel that soldiers won't be convincing enough to play soldiers."

"That sounds like the Army."

"I had a long talk with General Mathews this afternoon. He must have used the word 'glamour' a hundred times. That's what they want to sell. They're starting a big recruitment drive aimed at the elite young manhood of America. This is one of the opening guns."

"What do I have to do?" Catherine asked.

"Just see that everything runs smoothly. You'll have final approval. You have a reservation to Los Angeles on a nine A.M. plane tomorrow."

Catherine nodded. "All right."

"Will you miss me?"

"You know I will," she replied.

"I'll bring you a present."

"I don't want any presents. Just come back safely." She hesitated. "The situation's getting worse, isn't it, Bill?"

He nodded. "Yes," he said. "I think we're going to be at war soon."

"How horrible."

"It's going to be even more horrible if we *don't* get into it," he said quietly. "England got out of Dunkirk by a miracle. If Hitler decides to cross the Channel now, I don't think the British can stop him." They finished their coffee in silence, and he paid the check.

"Would you like to come to the house and spend the night?" Fraser asked.

"Not tonight," Catherine said. "You have to get up early, and so do I."

"All right."

After he had dropped her off at her apartment and she was getting ready for bed, Catherine asked herself why she had not gone home with Bill on the eve of his departure.

She had no answer.

CATHERINE HAD GROWN up in Hollywood even though she had never been there. She had spent hundreds of hours in darkened theaters, lost in the magic dreams manufactured by the film capital of the world, and she would always be grateful for the joy of those happy hours.

When Catherine's plane landed at the Burbank airport, she was filled with excitement. A limousine was waiting to drive her to her hotel. As they drove down the sunny, broad streets, the first thing Catherine noticed was the palm trees. She had read about them and had seen pictures of them, but the reality was overwhelming. They were everywhere, stretching tall against the sky, the lower part of their graceful trunks bare and the upper part beautiful and verdant. In the center of each tree was a ragged circle of fronds, like a dirty petticoat, Catherine thought, hanging unevenly below a green tutu.

They drove by a huge building that looked like a factory. A large sign over the entrance said "Warner Bros." and under it, "Combining Good Pictures with Good Citizenship." As the car went past the gate, Catherine thought of James Cagney in *The Strawberry Blonde,* and Bette Davis in *Dark Victory* and smiled happily.

They passed the Hollywood Bowl, which looked enormous from the outside, turned off Highland Avenue and went west on Hollywood Boulevard. They passed the Egyptian Theatre and two blocks to the west, Grauman's Chinese, and Catherine's spirits soared. It was like seeing two old friends. The driver swung down Sunset Boulevard and headed for the Beverly Hills Hotel. "You'll enjoy this hotel, miss. It's one of the best in the world."

It was certainly one of the most beautiful that Catherine had ever seen. It was just north of Sunset, in a semicircle of sheltering palm trees surrounded by large gardens. A graceful driveway curved up to the front door of the hotel, painted a delicate pink. An eager young assistant manager escorted Catherine to her room, which turned out to be a lavish bungalow on the grounds behind the main building of the hotel. There was a bouquet of flowers on the table with the compliments of the management and a larger, more beautiful bouquet with a card that read: "Wish I were there or you were here. Love, Bill." The assistant manager had handed Catherine three telephone messages. They were all from Allan Benjamin, whom she had been told was the producer of the training film. As Catherine was reading Bill's card, the phone rang. She ran to it, picked up the receiver and said eagerly, "Bill?" But it turned out to be Allan Benjamin.

"Welcome to California, Miss Alexander," his voice shrilled through the receiver. "Corporal Allan Benjamin, producer of this little clambake."

A corporal. She would have thought that they would have put a captain or a colonel in charge.

"We start shooting tomorrow. Did they tell you that we're using actors instead of soldiers?"

"I heard," Catherine replied.

"We start shooting at nine in the morning. If you could get here by about eight, I'd like to have you take a look at them. You know what the Army Air Corps wants."

"Right," said Catherine briskly. She had not the faintest idea what the Army Air Corps wanted, but she supposed that if one used common sense and picked out types that looked like they might be pilots, that would be sufficient.

"I'll have a car there for you at seven thirty A.M.," the voice was saying. "It'll only take you half an hour to get to Metro. It's in Culver City. I'll meet you on Stage Thirteen."

It was almost four o'clock in the morning before Catherine fell asleep, and it seemed the moment her eyes closed, the phone was ringing and the operator was telling her that a limousine was waiting for her.

Thirty minutes later Catherine was on her way to Metro-Goldwyn-Mayer.

It was the largest motion picture studio in the world. There was a main lot consisting of thirty-two sound stages, the enormous Thalberg Administration Building which housed Louis B. Mayer, twenty-five executives, and some of the most famous directors, producers and writers in show business. Lot two contained the large standing outdoor sets which were constantly re-dressed for various movies. Within a space of three minutes, you could drive past the Swiss Alps, a western town, a tenement block in Manhattan and a beach in Hawaii. Lot three on the far side of Washington Boulevard housed millions of dollars' worth of props and flat sets and was used to shoot outdoor spectacles.

All this was explained to Catherine by her guide, a young girl who was assigned to take her to Stage 13. "It's a city in itself," she was saying proudly. "We produce our own electricity, make enough food in the commissary to feed six thousand people a day and build all our own sets right on the back lot. We're completely self-sufficient. We don't need anybody."

"Except an audience."

As they walked along the street, they passed a castle that consisted of a facade with two by four's propping it up. Across from it was a lake, and down the block was the lobby of a San Francisco theater. No theater, just the lobby.

Catherine laughed aloud, and the girl stared at her.

"Is there anything wrong?" she asked.

"No," Catherine said. "Everything is wonderful."

Dozens of extras walked along the street, cowboys and Indians chatting amiably together as they walked toward the sound stages. A man appeared unexpectedly from around a corner and as Catherine stepped back to avoid him, she saw that he was a knight in armor. Behind him walked a group of girls in bathing suits. Catherine decided that she was going to like her brief fling in show business. She wished her father could have seen this. He would have enjoyed it so much.

"Here we are," the guide said. They were in front of a huge, gray building. A sign on the side of it said "STAGE 13."

"I'll leave you here. Will you be all right?"

"Fine," Catherine said. "Thank you."

The guide nodded and left. Catherine turned back to the sound stage. A sign over the door read: "DO NOT ENTER WHEN RED LIGHT IS ON." The light was off, so Catherine pulled the handle of the door and opened it. Or tried to. The door was unexpectedly heavy, and it took all her strength to get it open.

When she stepped inside, Catherine found herself confronted by a second door as heavy and massive as the first. It was like entering a decompression chamber.

Inside the cavernous sound stage, dozens of people were racing around, each one busy on some mysterious errand. A group of men were in Air Corps uniforms, and Catherine realized that they were the actors who would appear in the film. At a far corner of the sound stage was an office set complete with desk, chairs and a large military map hanging on the wall. Technicians were lighting the set.

"Excuse me," she said to a man passing by. "Is Mister Allan Benjamin here?"

"The little corporal?" He pointed. "Over there."

Catherine turned and saw a slight, frail-looking man in an ill-fitting uniform with corporal's stripes. He was screaming at a man wearing a general's stars.

"Fuck what the casting director said," he yelled. "I'm up to my ass in generals. I need non-coms." He raised his hands in despair. "Everybody wants to be a chief, nobody wants to be an Indian."

"Excuse me," said Catherine, "I'm Catherine Alexander."

"Thank God!" the little man said. He turned to the others, bitterness in his voice. "The fun and games are over, you smart-asses. Washington's here."

Catherine blinked. Before she could speak, the little corporal said, "I don't know what I'm doing here. I had a thirty-five-hundred-dollar-a-year job in Dearborn editing a furniture trade magazine, and I was drafted into the Signal Corps and sent to write training films. What do I know about producing or directing? This is the most disorganized mess I've ever seen." He belched and touched his stomach. "I'm getting an ulcer," he moaned, "and I'm not even in show business. Excuse me."

He turned and hurried toward the exit, leaving Catherine standing there. She looked around, helplessly. Everyone seemed to be staring at her, waiting for her to do something.

A lean, gray-haired man in a sweater moved toward her, an amused smile on his face. "Need any help?" he asked quietly.

"I need a miracle," Catherine said frankly. "I'm in charge of this, and I don't know what I'm supposed to be doing."

He grinned at her. "Welcome to Hollywood. I'm Tom O'Brien, the A.D."

She looked at him, quizzically.

"The assistant director. Your friend, the corporal, was supposed to direct it, but I have a feeling he won't be back." There was a calm assurance about the man which Catherine liked.

"How long have you worked at Metro-Goldwyn-Mayer?" she asked.

"Twenty-five years."

"Do you think you could direct this?"

She saw the corner of his lips twist. "I could try," he said gravely. "I've done six pictures with Willie Wyler." His eyes grew serious. "The situation isn't as bad as it looks," he said. "All it needs is a little organization. The script's written, and the set's ready."

"That's a beginning," Catherine said. She looked around the sound stage at the uniforms. Most of them were badly fitted, and the men wearing them looked ill at ease.

"They look like recruiting ads for the Navy," Catherine commented.

O'Brien laughed appreciatively.

"Where did these uniforms come from?"

"Western Costume. Our Wardrobe Department ran out. We're shooting three war pictures."

Catherine studied the men critically. "There are only half a dozen that are really bad," she decided. "Let's send them back and see if we can't do better."

O'Brien nodded approvingly. "Right."

Catherine and O'Brien walked over to the group of extras. The din of conversation on the enormous stage was deafening.

"Let's hold it down, boys," O'Brien yelled. "This is Miss Alexander. She's going to be in charge here."

There were a few appreciative whistles and cat calls.

"Thanks." Catherine smiled. "Most of you look fine, but a few of you are going to have to go back to Western Costume and get different uniforms. Let's line up, so we can take a good look at you."

"I'd like to take a good look at *you*. What are you doing for dinner tonight?" one of the men called.

"I'm having it with my husband," Catherine said, "right after his match."

O'Brien formed the men into a ragged line. Catherine heard laughter and voices nearby and turned in annoyance. One of the extras was standing next to a piece of scenery, talking to three girls who were hanging on his every word and giggling hysterically at everything he said. Catherine watched a moment, then walked over to the man and said, "Excuse me. Would you mind joining the rest of us?"

The man turned slowly. "Are you talking to me?" he asked lazily.

"Yes," Catherine said. "We'd like to go to work." She walked away.

He whispered something to the girls which drew a loud laugh, then slowly moved after Catherine. He was a tall man, his body lean and hard-looking, and he was very handsome, with blue-black hair and stormy dark eyes. His voice, when he spoke, was deep and filled with insolent amusement. "What can I do for you?" he asked Catherine.

"Do you want to work?" Catherine replied.

"I do, I do," he assured her.

Catherine had once read an article about extras. They were a strange breed of people, spending their anonymous lives on sound stages, lending background atmosphere to crowd scenes in which stars appeared. They were faceless, voiceless people, inherently too ambitionless to seek any kind of meaningful employment. The man in front of her was a perfect example. Because he was outrageously handsome, someone from his hometown had probably told him that he could be a star, and he had come to Hollywood, learned that talent was necessary as well as good looks and had settled for being an extra. The easy way out.

"We're going to have to change some of the uniforms," Catherine said patiently.

"Is there anything wrong with mine?" he asked.

Catherine took a closer look at his uniform. She had to admit that it fitted perfectly, emphasizing his broad shoulders but not exaggerating them, tapering in at his lean waist. She looked at his tunic. On his shoulders were the bars of a captain. Across his breast he had pinned on a splash of brightly colored ribbons.

"Are they impressive enough, Boss?" he asked.

"Who told you you were going to play a captain?"

He looked at her, seriously, "It was my idea. Don't you think I'd make a good captain?"

Catherine shook her head. "No. I don't."

He pursed his lips thoughtfully. "First lieutenant?"

"No."

"How about second lieutenant?"

"I don't really feel you're officer material."

His dark eyes were regarding her quizzically. "Oh? Anything else wrong?" he asked.

"Yes," she said. "The medals. You must be terribly brave."

He laughed. "I thought I'd give this damned film a little color."

"There's only one thing you forgot," Catherine said crisply. "We're not at war yet. You'd have had to win those at a carnival."

The man grinned at her. "You're right," he admitted sheepishly. "I didn't think of that. I'll take some of them off."

"Take them all off," Catherine said.

He gave her that slow, insolent grin again. "Right, Boss."

She almost snapped, "Stop calling me boss," but thought, *the hell with him,* and turned on her heel to talk to O'Brien.

Catherine sent eight of the men back to change their uniforms and spent the next hour discussing the scene with O'Brien. The little corporal had come back briefly and then had disappeared. It was just as well, Catherine thought. All he did was complain and make everyone nervous. O'Brien finished shooting the first scene before lunch, and Catherine felt it had not gone too badly. Only one incident had marred her morning. Catherine had given the infuriating extra several lines to read in order to humiliate him. She had wanted to show him up on the set, to pay him back for his impertinence. He had read his lines perfectly, carrying off the scene with aplomb. When he had finished, he had turned to her and said, "Was that all right, Boss?"

When the company broke for lunch, Catherine walked over to the enormous studio commissary and sat at a small table in the corner. At a large table next to her was a group of soldiers in uniform. Catherine was facing the door, when she saw the extra walk in, the three girls hanging on him, each one pushing to get closer to him. Catherine felt the blood rush to her face. She decided it was merely a chemical reaction. There were some people you hated on sight, just as there were others you liked on sight. Something about his overbearing arrogance rubbed her the wrong way. He would have made a perfect gigolo and that was probably exactly what he was.

He seated the girls at a table, looked up and saw Catherine, then leaned over and said something to the girls. They all looked at her and then there was a burst of laughter. Damn him! She watched as he moved toward her table. He stared down at her, that slow, knowing smile on his face. "Mind if I join you a moment?" he asked.

"I—" but he was already seated, studying her, his eyes probing and amused.

"What is it you want?" Catherine asked stiffly.

His grin widened. "Do you really want to know?"

Her lips tightened with anger. "Listen—"

"I wanted to ask you," he said quickly, "how I did this morning." He leaned forward earnestly. "Was I convincing?"

"You may be convincing to them," Catherine said, nodding toward the girls, "but if you want my opinion, I think you're a phony."

"Have I done something to offend you?"

"Everything you do offends me," she said evenly. "I don't happen to like your type."

"What is my type?"

"You're a fake. You enjoy wearing that uniform and strutting around the girls, but have you thought about enlisting?"

He stared at her incredulously. "And get shot at?" he asked. "That's for suckers." He leaned forward and grinned. "This is a lot more fun."

Catherine's lips were quivering with anger. "Aren't you eligible for the draft?"

"I suppose technically I'm eligible, but a friend of mine knows a guy in Washington and"—he lowered his voice—"I don't think they'll ever get me."

"I think you're contemptible," Catherine exploded.

"Why?"

"If you don't know why, I could never explain it to you."

"Why don't you try? At dinner tonight. Your place. Do you cook?"

Catherine rose to her feet, her cheeks flushed with anger. "Don't bother coming back to the set," she said. "I'll tell Mr. O'Brien to send you your check for this morning's work." She turned to go, then remembered and asked, "What's your name?"

"Douglas," he said. "Larry Douglas."

FRASER TELEPHONED CATHERINE from London the next night to find out how things had gone. She reported to him the day's happenings but made no mention of the incident with Larry Douglas. When Fraser returned to Washington, she would tell him about it, and they would laugh over it together.

Early the next morning as Catherine was getting dressed to go to the studio, the doorbell rang. She opened the bungalow door and a delivery boy stood there holding a large bouquet of roses.

"Catherine Alexander?" he asked.

"Yes."

"Sign here please."

She signed the form that he handed her.

"They're lovely," she said, taking the flowers.

"That'll be fifteen dollars."

"I beg your pardon?"

"Fifteen dollars. They're C.O.D."

"I don't under—" her lips tightened. Catherine reached for the card attached to the flowers and pulled it out of the envelope. The card read: "I would have paid for these myself, but I'm not working. Love, Larry."

She stared at the card unbelievingly.

"Well, do you want 'em or not?" asked the delivery boy.

"Not," she snapped. She thrust the flowers back in his arms.

He looked at her, puzzled. "He said you'd laugh. That it was kind of a private joke."

"I'm not laughing," Catherine said. She slammed the door furiously.

All that day, the incident kept rankling her. She had met egotistical men but never anyone with the outrageous conceit of Mr. Larry Douglas. She was sure that he had had an endless succession of victories with empty-headed blondes and bosomy brunettes who couldn't wait to fling themselves into his bed. But for him to put her in that category made Catherine feel cheap and humiliated. The mere thought of him made her flesh crawl. She determined to put him out of her mind.

At seven o'clock that evening Catherine started to leave the stage. An assistant came up to her, an envelope in his hand.

"Did you charge this, Miss Alexander?" he asked.

It was a charge slip from central casting and it read:

One uniform (captain)
Six service ribbons (assorted)
Six medals (assorted)
Actor's Name: Lawrence Douglas . . . (Personal Charge
    to Catherine Alexander—MGM).

Catherine looked up, her face flushed.

"No!" she said.

He stared. "What shall I tell them?"

"Tell them I'll pay for his medals if they're awarded posthumously."

The picture finished shooting three days later. Catherine looked at the rough-cut the following day and approved it. The film would not win any awards, but it was simple and effective. Tom O'Brien had done a good job.

On Saturday morning Catherine boarded a plane for Washington. She had never been so glad to leave a city. Monday morning she was back in her office trying to catch up on the work that had piled up during her absence.

Just before lunch, her secretary, Annie, buzzed her. "A Mr. Larry Douglas is on the phone from Hollywood, California, collect. Do you want to take the call?"

"No," she snapped. "Tell him that I—never mind, I'll tell him myself." She took a deep breath and pressed the phone button. "Mr. Douglas?"

"Good morning." His voice had the consistency of hot fudge. "I had a hard time tracking you down. Don't you like roses?"

"Mr. Douglas—" Catherine began. Her voice quavered with fury. She took a deep breath and said, "Mr. Douglas, I love roses. I don't like you. I don't like anything about you. Is that clear?"

"You don't know anything about me."

"I know more than I want to know. I think you're cowardly and despicable, and I don't want you ever to call me again." Trembling, she slammed down the receiver, her eyes filled with tears of anger. How dare he! She would be so glad when Bill returned.

Three days later Catherine received a ten by twelve photograph of Lawrence Douglas in the mail. It was inscribed, "To the boss, with love from Larry."

Annie stared at it in awe, and said, "My God! Is he real?"

"Fake," retorted Catherine. "The only real thing is the paper it's printed on." She savagely tore the picture to shreds.

Annie watched, dismayed. "What a waste. I've never seen one like that in the flesh."

"In Hollywood," Catherine said grimly, "they have sets that are all front—no foundation. You've just seen one."

During the next two weeks, Larry Douglas phoned at least a dozen times. Catherine instructed Annie to tell him not to call again and not to bother telling her about his calls. One morning while Annie was taking dictation, she looked up and said apologetically, "I know you told me not to bother you with Mr. Douglas' calls, but he called again, and he sounded so desperate and well . . . kind of lost."

"He *is* lost," Catherine said coldly, "and if you're smart, you won't try to find him."

"He sure sounds charming."

"He invented treacle."

"He asked a lot of questions about you." She saw Catherine's look. "But, of course," she added hastily, "I didn't tell him anything."

"That was very bright of you, Annie."

Catherine began to dictate again, but her mind was not on it. She supposed the world was full of Larry Douglases. It made her appreciate William Fraser all the more.

Bill Fraser returned the following Sunday morning, and Catherine went to the airport to meet him. She watched as he finished with Customs and came toward the exit where she was standing. His face lit up when he saw her.

"Cathy," he said. "What a lovely surprise. I didn't expect you to meet me."

"I couldn't wait," she smiled and gave him a warm hug that made him look at her quizzically.

"You've missed me," he said.

"More than you know."

"How was Hollywood?" he asked. "Did it go well?"

She hesitated. "Fine. They're very pleased with the picture."

"So I hear."

"Bill, next time you go away," she said, "take me with you."

He looked at her, pleased and touched.

"It's a deal," Fraser said. "I missed you. I've been doing a lot of thinking about you."

"Have you?"

"Do you love me?"

"Very much, Mr. Fraser."

"I love you, too," he said. "Why don't we go out tonight and celebrate?"

She smiled. "Wonderful."

"We'll have dinner at the Jefferson Club."

She dropped Fraser at his house.

"I have a few thousand calls to make," he said. "Could you meet me at the club? Eight o'clock."

"Fine," she said.

Catherine went back to her apartment and did some washing and ironing. Each time she passed the telephone, she half-expected it to ring, but it remained silent. She thought of Larry Douglas trying to pump Annie for information about her and she found that she was gritting her teeth. Maybe she would speak to Fraser about turning Douglas' name in to his draft board. *No, I won't bother,* she thought. *They'd probably turn him down. He'd be tried and found wanton.* She washed her hair, took a long luxurious bath and was drying herself when the phone rang. She tensed, went over to it and picked it up. "Yes?" she said coldly.

It was Fraser. "Hi," he said. "Anything wrong?"

"Of course not, Bill," she said quickly. "I—I was just in the bath."

"I'm sorry." His voice took on a teasing tone. "I mean I'm sorry I'm not there with you."

"So am I," she replied.

"I called to tell you I miss you. Don't be late."

Catherine smiled. "I won't."

She hung up, slowly, thinking about Bill. For the first time she felt that he was ready to propose. He was going to ask her to become Mrs. William Fraser. She said the name aloud. "Mrs. William Fraser." It had a nice dignified sound to it. *My God,* she thought. *I'm becoming blasé. Six months ago, I would have been jumping out of my skin, and now all I can say is it has a nice dignified sound to it.* Had she really changed that much? It was not a comforting thought. She looked at the clock and hurriedly began to dress.

. . .

THE JEFFERSON CLUB was on "F" Street, a discreet brick building set back from the street and surrounded by a wrought-iron fence. It was one of the most exclusive clubs in a city full of exclusive clubs. The easiest way to become a member was to have a father who belonged. If one lacked that foresight, then it was necessary to be recommended by three members. Membership proposals were brought up once a year and one blackball was sufficient to keep a person out of the Jefferson Club for the rest of his life, since it was a firm rule that no candidate could ever be proposed twice.

William Fraser's father had been a founding member of the club, and Fraser and Catherine had dinner there at least once a week. The chef had been with the French branch of the Rothschilds for twenty years, the cuisine was superb, and the wine cellar ranked as the third best in America. The club had been decorated by one of the world's leading decorators and careful attention had been paid to the colors and the lighting, so the women were bathed in candlelight glow that enhanced their beauty. On any given night, diners would brush elbows with the Vice-President, members of the Cabinet or Supreme Court, senators and the powerful industrialists who controlled worldwide empires.

Fraser was in the foyer waiting for Catherine when she arrived.

"Am I late?" she asked.

"It wouldn't matter if you were," Fraser said, looking at her with open admiration. "Do you know you're fantastically beautiful?"

"Of course," she replied. "Everybody knows I'm the fantastically beautiful Catherine Alexander."

"I mean it, Cathy." His tone was so serious that she was embarrassed.

"Thank you, Bill," she said awkwardly. "And stop staring at me like that."

"I can't help it," he said. He took her arm.

Louis, the maître d', led them to a corner booth. "There you are, Miss Alexander, Mr. Fraser, enjoy your dinner."

Catherine liked being known by name by the maître d' of the Jefferson Club. She knew that it was childish and naïve of her, but it gave her a feeling of being somebody, of belonging. Now she sat back, relaxed and contented, surveying the room.

"Will you have a drink?" Fraser asked.

"No, thank you," Catherine said.

He shook his head. "I've got to teach you some bad habits."

"You already have," Catherine murmured.

He grinned at her and ordered a scotch and soda.

She studied him, thinking what a dear, sweet man he was. She was sure that she could make him very happy. And she would be happy married to him. *Very happy,* she told herself fiercely. Ask anybody. Ask *Time* magazine. She hated herself for the way her mind was working. What in God's name was wrong with her? "Bill," she began—and froze.

Larry Douglas was walking toward them, a smile of recognition on his lips as he saw Catherine. He was wearing his Army Air Corps uniform from Central Casting. She watched unbelievingly as he came over to their table, grinning happily. "Hello there," he said. But he was not speaking to Catherine. He was speaking to Bill, who was getting up and shaking his hand.

"It's great to see you, Larry."

"It's good to see you, Bill."

Catherine stared at the two of them, her mind paralyzed, refusing to function.

Fraser was saying, "Cathy, this is Captain Lawrence Douglas. Larry, this is Miss Alexander—Catherine."

Larry Douglas was looking down at her, his dark eyes mocking her. "I can't tell you what a pleasure this is, Miss Alexander," he said solemnly.

Catherine opened her mouth to speak, but she suddenly realized there was nothing that she could say. Fraser was watching her, waiting for her to speak. All she could manage was a nod. She did not trust her voice.

"Will you join us, Larry?" Fraser asked.

Larry looked at Catherine and said modestly, "If you're sure I'm not intruding—"

"Certainly not. Sit down."

Larry took a seat next to Catherine.

"What would you like to drink?" Fraser asked.

"Scotch and soda," Larry replied.

"I'll have the same," Catherine said recklessly. "Make it a double."

Fraser looked at her in surprise. "I can't believe it."

"You said you wanted to teach me some bad habits," Catherine said. "I think I'd like to start now."

When Fraser had ordered the drinks, he turned to Larry and said, "I've been hearing about some of your exploits from General Terry—both in the air and on the ground."

Catherine was staring at Larry, her mind spinning, trying to adjust. "Those medals . . ." she said.

He was looking at her innocently.

"Yes?"

She swallowed. "Er—where did you get them?"

"I won them in a carnival," he said gravely.

"Some carnival," Fraser laughed. "Larry's been flying with the RAF. He was the leader of the American Squadron over there. They talked him into heading up a fighter base in Washington to get some of our boys ready for combat."

Catherine turned to stare at Larry. He was smiling at her benevolently, his eyes dancing. Like the rerun of an old movie, Catherine remembered every word of their first meeting. She had ordered him to take off his captain's bars and his medals, and he had cheerfully obliged. She had been smug, overbearing—and she had called him a coward! She wanted to crawl under the table.

"I wish you had let me know you were coming into town," Fraser was saying. "I would have trotted out a fatted calf for you. We should have had a big party to celebrate your return."

"I like this better," Larry said. He looked over at Catherine, and she turned away, unable to meet his eyes. "As a matter of fact," Larry continued innocently, "I looked for you when I was in Hollywood, Bill. I heard you were producing an Air Corps training film."

He stopped to light a cigarette and carefully blew out the match. "I went over to the set, but you weren't there."

"I had to fly to London," Fraser replied. "Catherine was there. I'm surprised you didn't run into each other."

Catherine looked up at Larry, and he was watching her, his eyes amused. Now was the time to mention what had happened. She would tell Fraser, and they would all laugh it off as an amusing anecdote. But somehow the words stuck in her throat.

Larry gave her a moment, then said, "It was a pretty crowded set. I guess we missed each other."

She hated him for helping her out, for making them fellow conspirators against Fraser.

When the drinks arrived, Catherine downed hers quickly and asked for another. This was going to be the most terrible evening of her life. She could not wait to get out of there, to get away from Larry Douglas.

Fraser asked him about his war experiences, and Larry made them sound easy and amusing. He obviously didn't take anything seriously. He was a lightweight. And yet in all fairness, Catherine reluctantly admitted to herself that a lightweight did not volunteer for the RAF and become a hero fighting against the Luftwaffe. Irrationally, she hated him even more because he was a hero. Her attitude didn't make sense to her, and she brooded about it over her third double scotch. What difference did it make whether he was a hero or a bum? And then she realized that as long as he was a bum, he fitted neatly into a pigeonhole that she could deal with. Through the haze of the liquor she sat back and listened to the two men talk. There was an eager enthusiasm about Larry when he spoke, a vitality that was so palpable it reached across and touched her. He seemed to her now like the most alive man she had ever met. Catherine had a feeling that he held nothing back from life, that he gave himself to everything wholeheartedly and that he mocked those who were afraid to give. Who were afraid, period. Like herself.

She hardly touched her food, and she had no idea what she was eating. She met Larry's eyes, and it was as though he were already her lover, as if they had already been together, belonged together, and she knew it was insane. He was like a cyclone, a force of nature, and any woman who got sucked up in the vortex was going to be destroyed.

Larry was smiling at her. "I'm afraid we've been excluding Miss Alexander from the conversation," he said politely. "I'm sure she's more interesting than the both of us put together."

"You're wrong," Catherine said thickly. "I live a very dull life. I work with Bill." The moment she said it she heard how it sounded and turned red. "I didn't mean it like that," she said. "I meant—"

"I know what you meant," Larry said helpfully. And she hated him. He turned to Bill. "Where did you find her?"

"I got lucky," Fraser said warmly. "Very lucky. You're still not married?"

Larry shrugged. "Who'd have me?"

You bastard, Catherine thought. She looked around the room. Half a dozen women were staring at Larry, some covertly, some openly. He was like a sexual magnet. "How were the English girls?" Catherine asked recklessly.

"They were fine," he said, politely. "Of course, I didn't have much time for that sort of thing. I was busy flying."

Like hell you didn't, Catherine thought. *I'll bet there wasn't a virgin left standing within a hundred miles of you.* Aloud, she said, "I feel sorry for those poor girls. Look at all they missed." Her tone was more biting than she had intended.

Fraser was looking at her, puzzled by her rudeness. "Cathy," he said.

"Let's have another drink," Larry cut in quickly.

"I think perhaps Catherine's had enough," Fraser replied.

"Thash not so," Catherine began, and to her horror she realized she was slurring her words. "I think I want to go home," she said.

"All right"—Fraser turned to Larry—"Catherine doesn't drink as a rule," he said apologetically.

"I imagine she's excited about seeing you again," Larry said.

Catherine wanted to pick up a glass of water and throw it at him. She had hated him less when he was a bum. Now she hated him more. And she did not know why.

The next morning Catherine woke up with a hangover that she was convinced would make medical history. She had at least three heads on her shoulders, all of them pounding to the beat of different drummers. Lying still in bed was agony but trying to move was worse. As she lay there fighting nausea, the whole evening flooded back in her memory, and the pain increased. Unreasonably she blamed Larry Douglas for her hangover, for if it had not been for him, she would not have had anything to drink. Painfully Catherine turned her head and looked at the clock beside her bed. She had overslept. She debated whether to stay in bed or call a pulmotor squad. Carefully she pulled herself out of her deathbed and dragged herself into the bathroom. She stumbled into the shower, turned the water on cold and let the icy jets stream against her body. She screamed out loud as the water hit her, but when she came out of the shower, she was feeling better. *Not good,* she thought carefully. *Just better.*

Forty-five minutes later she was at her desk. Her secretary, Annie, came in full of excitement. "Guess what," she said.

"Not this morning," Catherine whispered. "Just be a good girl and speak softly."

"Look!" Annie thrust the morning paper at her. "It's *him.*"

On the front page was a picture of Larry Douglas in uniform, grinning at her insolently. The caption read: "AMERICAN RAF HERO RETURNS TO WASHINGTON TO HEAD UP NEW FIGHTER UNIT." A two-column story followed.

"Isn't that exciting?" Annie cried.

"Terribly," Catherine said. She slammed the paper into the wastebasket. "Can we get on with our work?"

Annie looked at her, surprised. "I'm sorry," she said. "I—I thought since he was a friend of yours, you'd be interested."

"He's not a friend," Catherine corrected her. "He's more of an enemy." She saw the look on Annie's face. "Could we just forget about Mr. Douglas?"

"Certainly," Annie said in a puzzled voice. "I told him I thought you'd be pleased."

Catherine stared at her. "When?"

"When he called this morning. He's called three times."

Catherine steeled herself to make her voice casual. "Why didn't you tell me?"

"You asked me not to tell you when he called." She was watching Catherine, her face filled with confusion.

"Did he leave a number?"

"No."

"Good." Catherine thought of his face, of those large, dark teasing eyes. "Good," she said again, more firmly. She finished dictating some letters and when Annie had left the room, Catherine went over to the wastebasket and retrieved the newspaper. She read the story about Larry word for word. He was an ace with eight German planes to his credit.

He had been shot down twice over the Channel. She buzzed Annie. "If Mr. Douglas calls again, I'll talk to him."

There was only a fractional pause. "Yes, Miss Alexander."

After all, there was no point in being rude to the man. Catherine would simply apologize for her behavior at the studio and ask him to stop calling her. She was going to marry William Fraser.

She waited for another call from him all afternoon. He had not called by six o'clock. *Why should he?* Catherine asked herself. *He's out laying six other girls. You're lucky. Being involved with him would be like going to a butcher shop. You take your number and wait your turn.*

On the way out she said to Annie, "If Mr. Douglas calls tomorrow, tell him I'm not in."

Annie did not even blink. "Yes, Miss Alexander. Good night."

"Good night."

Catherine rode down in the elevator, lost in thought. She was sure that Bill Fraser wanted to marry her. The best thing to do would be to tell him that she wanted to get married right away. She would tell him tonight. They would go away for a honeymoon. By the time they got back, Larry Douglas would have left town. Or something.

The elevator door opened at the lobby, and Larry Douglas was standing there, leaning against the wall. He had taken off his medals and ribbons and was wearing the bars of a second lieutenant. He smiled and walked up to her.

"Is this better?" he asked brightly.

Catherine stared at him, her heart pounding. "Isn't—isn't wearing the wrong insignia against regulations?"

"I don't know," he said earnestly. "I thought you were in charge of all that."

He stood there looking down at her, and she said in a small voice, "Don't do this to me. I want you to leave me alone. I belong to Bill."

"Where's your wedding ring?"

Catherine brushed past him and started toward the street door. When she reached it, he was there ahead of her, holding it open for her.

Outside he took her arm. She felt a shock go through her whole body. There was an electricity that came from him that burned her. "Cathy—" he began.

"For God's sake," she said desperately. "What do you want from me?"

"Everything," he said quietly. "I want you."

"Well, you can't have me," she wailed. "Go torture somebody else." She turned to walk away, and he pulled her back.

"What is that supposed to mean?"

"I don't know," Catherine said, her eyes filling with tears. "I don't know what I'm saying. I—I have a hangover. I want to die."

He grinned sympathetically. "I have a marvelous cure for hangovers." He guided her into the garage of the building.

"Where are we going?" she asked in a panic.

"We're getting my car."

Catherine looked up at him, searching his face for a sign of triumph, but all she saw was his strong, incredibly handsome face filled with warmth and compassion.

The attendant brought up a tan sports convertible with the top down. Larry helped Catherine into the car and slid in behind the wheel. She sat there looking straight ahead, knowing that she was throwing her whole life away and totally unable to stop herself. It was as though all this were happening to someone else. She wanted to tell the silly, lost girl in the car to flee.

"Your place or mine?" Larry asked gently.

She shook her head. "It doesn't matter," she said hopelessly.

"We'll go to my place."

So he was not totally insensitive. Or else he was afraid to compete with the shadow of William Fraser.

She watched him as he deftly tooled the car through the early evening traffic. No, he was not afraid of anything. That was part of his goddamn attraction.

She tried to tell herself that she was free to say no to him, free to walk away. How could she love William Fraser and feel this way about Larry?

"If it helps any," Larry said quietly, "I'm as nervous as you are."

Catherine looked over at him. "Thanks," she said. He was lying, of course. He probably said that to all his victims as he took them up to his bed to seduce them. But at least he wasn't gloating about it. What bothered her most was that she was betraying Bill Fraser. He was too dear a man to hurt, and this was going to hurt him very much. Catherine knew that and knew that what she was doing was wrong and senseless, but it was as though she had no will of her own anymore.

They had reached a pleasant residential area with large, shady trees lining the street. Larry pulled the car up in front of an apartment building. "We're home," he said quietly.

Catherine knew that this was her final chance to say no, to tell him to keep away from her. She watched silently as Larry came around and opened the door. She got out of the car and walked into his apartment building.

Larry's apartment had been decorated for a man. It had strong solid colors, and masculine-looking furniture.

As they walked in, Larry took off Catherine's coat and she shivered.

"Are you cold?" he asked.

"No."

"Would you like a drink?"

"No."

Gently he took her in his arms, and they kissed. It was as though her body were being set aflame. Without a word Larry led her into the bedroom. There was a growing urgency as they both silently undressed. She lay on the bed naked, and he moved beside her.

"Larry—" but his lips were on hers, and his hands began to move down her body, gently exploring, and she forgot everything except the pleasure that was happening to her, and her hands began to grope for him. And she felt him hot and hard and pulsating and his fingers were inside her, opening her up gently and lovingly and he was on top of her and in her, and there was an exquisite joy that she had never dreamed possible and then they were together, moving faster and faster in a fantastic rhythm that rocked the room and the world and the universe until there was an explosion that became a delirious ecstasy an unbelievable shattering journey an arriving and departure an ending and a beginning and Catherine lay there spent and numb holding him tightly never wanting to let him go never wanting this feeling to stop. Nothing she had ever read or heard could have prepared her for this. It was unbelievable that another person's body could bring such joy. She lay there at peace: a woman. And she knew that if she never saw him again, she would be grateful to him for the rest of her life.

"Cathy?"

She turned to look at him, slowly and lazily. "Yes?" Even her voice seemed deeper to her, more mature.

"Could you get your nails out of my back?"

She suddenly realized that she had been digging into his flesh. "Oh, I'm sorry!" she exclaimed. She started to examine his back, but he caught her hands and pulled her close to him.

"It doesn't matter. Are you happy?"

"Happy?" Her lip trembled and to her horror she began to cry. Great sobs that wrenched her body. He held her in his arms, stroking her soothingly, letting the storm spend itself.

"I'm sorry," she said. "I don't know what made me do that."

"Disappointment?"

Catherine looked at him quickly to protest, then saw that he was teasing her. He took her into his arms and made love to her again. It was even more incredible than before. Afterward they lay in bed and he talked, but she didn't listen. All she wanted to hear was the sound of his voice, and it didn't matter to her what he said. She knew there would never be anyone for her but this man. And she knew that this man could never belong to any one woman and that she would probably never see him again, that she was just another conquest to him. She was aware that his voice had stopped and that he was watching her.

"You haven't heard a word I said."

"Sorry," she said. "I was daydreaming."

"I should be hurt," he said reproachfully. "You're only interested in me for my body."

She ran her hands over his lean tanned chest and stomach. "I'm no expert," she said, "but I think this one will do nicely." She smiled. "It *did* nicely." She wanted to ask him whether he had enjoyed her, but she was afraid to.

"You're beautiful, Cathy."

She thrilled to his saying it and at the same time resented it. Anything he said to her he had said a thousand times to other women. She wondered how he was going to say good-bye. *Call me sometime?* Or, *I'll call you sometime?* Perhaps he would even want to see her again once or twice before he went on to someone else. Well, she had no one to blame but herself. She had known what she was getting into. *I walked into this with my eyes and my legs wide open. No matter what happens, I must never blame him.*

He slid his arms around her and held her close.

"Do you know you're a very special girl, Cathy?"

Do you know you're a very special girl—Alice, Susan, Margaret, Peggy, Lana.

"I felt it from the first time I saw you. I've never felt this way about anyone before."

—Janet, Evelyn, Ruth, Georgia, ad infinitum. She buried her head in his chest, not trusting herself to speak, and held him tightly, silently saying good-bye.

"I'm hungry," Larry said. "Do you know what I feel like?"

Catherine smiled. "Yes, I certainly do."

Larry grinned down at her. "You know something?" he asked. "You're a sex maniac."

She looked up. "Thank you."

He led her into the shower and turned it on. He took a shower cap from a hook on the wall and put it on Catherine's head, tucking in her hair. "Come on," he said, and pulled her into the piercing jet water. He took a bar of soap and began to wash her body, starting with her neck and working down to her arms and slowly circling her breasts and moving down to her stomach and her thighs. She began to feel an excitement in her groin and she took the soap from him and began to wash him, lathering his chest and stomach and moving down between his legs. His organ began to grow hard in her hand.

He spread her legs and put his male hardness inside her and Catherine was transported again, drowning in a torrent of water that beat against her body, while inside she was filled with the same unbearable joy, until she screamed aloud in sheer happiness.

Afterward they dressed, got into his car and drove to Maryland, where they found a little restaurant that was still open and they had lobster and champagne.

At five o'clock in the morning, Catherine dialed William Fraser's number at home and stood there listening to the long rings eighty miles away until finally Fraser's sleepy voice came on the phone, and said, "Hello. . . ."

"Hello, Bill. It's Catherine."

"Catherine! I've been trying to call you all evening. Where are you? Are you all right?"

"I'm fine. I'm in Maryland with Larry Douglas. We just got married."

8

NOELLE

PARIS 1941

Christian Barbet was an unhappy man. The bald little detective sat at his desk, a cigarette between his stained, broken teeth and gloomily contemplated the folder in front of him. The information it contained was going to cost him a client. He had been charging Noelle Page outrageous fees for his services, but it was not only the loss of the income that saddened him: He would miss the client herself. He hated Noelle Page and yet she was the most exciting woman he had ever met. Barbet built lurid fantasies around Noelle in which she always ended up in his power. Now the assignment was about to come to an end, and he would never see her again. He had kept her waiting in the reception office while he tried to figure out a way to handle things so that he could squeeze some additional money out of her to prolong the case. But he reluctantly concluded that there was no way. Barbet sighed, snuffed out his cigarette, walked over to the door and opened it. Noelle was sitting on the black imitation leather couch, and as he studied her, his heart caught in his throat for a moment. It was unfair for any woman to be so beautiful. "Good afternoon, Mademoiselle," he said. "Come in."

She entered his office moving with the grace of a model. It was good for Barbet to have a name client like Noelle Page, and he was not above dropping her name frequently. It attracted other clients, and Christian Barbet was not a man to lose any sleep over ethics. "Please sit down," he said, indicating a chair. "Can I get you a brandy, an aperitif?"

Part of his fantasy was getting Noelle drunk so that she would beg him to seduce her.

"No," she replied. "I came for your report."

The bitch could have had a last drink with him! "Yes," Barbet said. "As a matter of fact I have several pieces of news." He reached over to the desk and pretended to study the dossier, which he had already memorized.

"First," he informed her, "your friend was promoted to Captain and transferred to the one hundred thirty-third squadron, where he was put in command. The field is at Coltisall, Duxford, in Cambridgeshire. They flew"—he spoke slowly and deliberately, knowing that she was not interested in the technical part—"Hurricanes and Spitfire II's and then switched to Mark V's. They then flew—"

"Never mind," Noelle interrupted impatiently. "Where is he now?"

Barbet had been waiting for the question. "In the United States." He saw the reaction before she could control it, and he took savage satisfaction in it. "In Washington, D.C.," he continued.

"On leave?"

Barbet shook his head. "No. He's been discharged from the RAF. He's a Captain in the United States Army Air Corps."

He watched Noelle digesting the information, her expression giving no clue to what she was feeling. But Barbet was not finished with her yet. He picked up a newspaper clipping between his stained sausage fingers and handed it to her.

"I think this will interest you," he said.

He saw Noelle stiffen, and it was almost as though she knew what she was going to see. The clipping was from the New York *Daily News*. The caption read "War Ace Weds" and above it was a photograph of Larry Douglas and his bride. Noelle looked at it for a long moment, then held out her hand for the rest of the file. Christian Barbet shrugged, and slid all the papers into a manila envelope and handed it to her. As he opened his mouth to make his farewell speech, Noelle Page said, "If you don't have a correspondent in Washington, get one. I shall expect weekly reports." And she was gone, leaving Christian Barbet staring after her in a state of complete confusion.

When she returned to her apartment, Noelle went into the bedroom, locked the door and took the newspaper clippings out of the envelope. She laid them out on the bed before her and studied them. The photograph of Larry was exactly as she remembered him. If anything the image in her mind was clearer than the image in the newspaper, for Larry was more alive in her mind than he was in reality.

There was not a day that went by that Noelle did not relive the past with him. It was as though they had costarred in a play together long ago, and she was able to recapture scenes at will, playing some on certain days and saving others for other days, so that each memory was always alive and fresh.

Noelle turned her attention to Larry's bride. What she saw was a pretty, young, intelligent face with a smile on its lips.

The face of the enemy. A face that would have to be destroyed as Larry was going to be destroyed.

Noelle remained locked up with the photograph the whole afternoon.

Hours later when Armand Gautier pounded on her bedroom door, Noelle told him to go away. He waited outside in the drawing room, apprehensive about what her mood would be, but when Noelle finally emerged, she seemed unusually bright and gay, as though she had had a piece of good news. She offered no explanation to Gautier, and he knew her well enough not to ask for one.

After the theater that evening she made love to him with a wild passion that reminded him of their early days together. Later Gautier lay in bed trying to understand the beautiful girl who rested beside him but he did not have a clue.

During the night Noelle Page had a dream about Colonel Mueller. The hairless albino Gestapo officer was torturing her with a branding iron, making burning swastikas in her flesh. He kept asking her questions, but his voice was so soft that Noelle could not hear him, and he kept pressing the hot metal into her, and suddenly it was Larry on the table, screaming with pain. Noelle awoke in a cold sweat, her heart pounding, and turned on the bedside lamp. She lit a cigarette with trembling fingers and tried to calm her nerves. She thought about Israel Katz. His leg had been amputated with an ax, and though she had not seen him since that afternoon at the bakery, she had received word from the concierge that he was alive but weak. It was becoming more and more difficult to hide him, and he was helpless on his own. The search for him had intensified. If he was going to be transported out of Paris, it would have to be done quickly. Noelle had really done nothing for which the Gestapo could arrest her: yet. Was the dream a premonition, a warning not to help Israel Katz? She lay in bed remembering. He had aided her when she had the abortion. He had helped her kill Larry's baby. He had given her money and helped her find a job. Dozens of men had done more important things for her than he had, yet Noelle felt no debt to them. Each of them, including her father, had wanted something from her, and she had paid in full for everything she had ever received. Israel Katz had never asked her for anything. She had to help him.

Noelle did not underestimate the problem. Colonel Mueller was already suspicious of her. She remembered her dream and shuddered. She must see to it that Mueller was never able to prove anything against her. Israel Katz had to be smuggled out of Paris, but how? Noelle was sure that all exits were closely watched. They would be watching the roads and the river. The Nazis might be *cochons,* but they were efficient *cochons*. It was a challenge and it could be a deadly one, but she was determined to try it. The problem was that there was no one she could turn to for help. The Nazis had reduced Armand Gautier to a quivering gelatin. No, she would have to do this alone. She thought of Colonel Mueller and General Scheider, and she wondered if a clash ever came, which one would emerge victorious.

The evening following Noelle's dream she and Armand Gautier attended a supper party. The host was Leslie Rocas, a wealthy patron of the arts. It was an eclectic collection of guests—bankers, artists, political leaders and a gathering of beautiful women whom Noelle felt were there mainly for the benefit of the Germans who were present. Gautier had noticed Noelle's preoccupation, but when he asked her what was wrong, she told him that everything was fine.

Fifteen minutes before supper was announced, a new arrival lumbered through the door and the moment that Noelle saw him she knew that her problem was going to be solved. She walked over to the hostess and said, "Darling, be an angel and put me next to Albert Heller."

ALBERT HELLER WAS France's leading playwright. He was a large, shambling bear of a man in his sixties with a shock of white hair and broad, sloped shoulders. He was unusually tall for a Frenchman, but he would have stood out in a crowd in any case, for he had a remarkably ugly face and piercing green eyes that missed nothing. Heller had a vividly inventive imagination and had written more than a score of hit plays and motion pictures. He had been after Noelle to star in a new play of his and had sent her a copy of the manuscript. Now as she sat next to him at dinner, Noelle said, "I just finished reading your new play, Albert. I adored it."

His face lit up. "Will you do it?"

Noelle put a hand on his. "I wish I could, darling. Armand has committed me to another play."

He frowned, then sighed resignedly. "*Merde!* Ah, well, one day we will work together."

"I would enjoy that," Noelle said. "I love the way you write. It fascinates me the way writers create plots. I don't know how you do it."

He shrugged. "The same way you act. It is our trade, the way we make our living."

"No," she replied. "The ability to use your imagination in that way is a miracle to me." She gave an embarrassed laugh. "I know. I've been trying to write."

"Oh?" he said politely.

"Yes, but I'm stuck." Noelle took a deep breath and then looked around the table. All the other guests were engrossed in their own conversations. She leaned toward Albert Heller and lowered her voice. "I have a situation where my heroine is trying to smuggle her lover out of Paris. The Nazis are searching for him."

"Ah." The big man sat there, toying with a salad fork, drumming it against a plate. Then he said, "Easy. Have him put on a German uniform and walk right through them."

Noelle sighed and said, "There is a complication. He's been wounded. He can't walk. He lost a leg."

The drumming suddenly stopped. There was a long pause, then Heller said, "A barge on the Seine?"

"Watched."

"And all transportation out of Paris is being searched?"

"Yes."

"Then you must have the Nazis do the work for you."

"How?"

"Your heroine," he said, without looking at Noelle, "is she attractive?"

"Yes."

"Supposing," he said, "your heroine befriended a German officer. Someone of high rank. Is that possible?" Noelle turned to look at him, but he avoided her eyes.

"Yes."

"All right, then. Have her make a rendezvous with the officer. They drive off to spend a weekend somewhere outside Paris. Friends could arrange for your hero to be hidden in the trunk of the car. The officer must be important enough so that his car would not be searched."

"If the trunk is locked," Noelle asked, "would he not smother?"

Albert Heller took a sip of wine, quietly lost in thought. Finally he said, "Not necessarily." He spoke to Noelle for five minutes, keeping his voice low, and when he had finished, he said, "Good luck." And he still did not look at her.

EARLY THE NEXT morning Noelle telephoned General Scheider. An operator answered the switchboard, and a few moments later Noelle was put through to an aide and finally to the General's secretary.

"Who is calling General Scheider, please?"

"Noelle Page," she said, for the third time.

"I am sorry, but the General is in conference. He cannot be disturbed."

She hesitated. "Could I call him back later?"

"He will be in conference all day. I suggest you write the General a letter stating your business."

Noelle sat there a moment contemplating the idea and an ironic smile touched her lips.

"Never mind," she said. "Just tell him I called."

One hour later her phone rang, and it was General Hans Scheider. "Forgive me," he apologized. "That idiot didn't give me your message until just now. I would have left word for them to put you through, but it never occurred to me that you would telephone."

"I'm the one who should apologize," Noelle said. "I know how busy you are."

"Please. What can I do for you?"

Noelle hesitated, choosing her words. "Do you remember what you said about us at dinner?"

There was a short pause, then "Yes."

"I've been thinking about you a great deal, Hans. I would like very much to see you."

"Will you have supper with me tonight?" There was a sudden eagerness in his voice.

"Not in Paris," Noelle replied. "If we're going to be together, I would like us to be away from here."

"Where?" General Scheider asked.

"I want it to be some place special. Do you know Etratat?"

"No."

"It's a lovely little village about a hundred and fifty kilometers from Paris, near Le Havre. There's a quiet old inn there."

"It sounds wonderful, Noelle. It's not easy for me to get away right now," he added apologetically. "I am in the middle of—"

"I understand," Noelle interrupted icily, "perhaps some other time."

"Wait!" There was a long pause. "When could you get away?"

"Saturday night after the show."

"I will make arrangements," he said. "We can fly down—"

"Why don't we drive?" Noelle asked. "It's so pleasant."

"Whatever you like. I'll pick you up at the theater."

Noelle thought quickly. "I have to come home and change first. Pick me up at my apartment, would you?"

"As you wish, my *liebchen*. Until Saturday night."

Fifteen minutes later Noelle was speaking to the concierge. He listened as she talked, shaking his head in vigorous protest.

"No, no, no! I will tell our friend, Mademoiselle, but he will not do it. He would be a fool to! You might as well ask him to go down and apply for a job at Gestapo headquarters."

"It can't fail," Noelle assured him. "The best brain in France figured it out."

When she walked out of the entrance of her apartment building that afternoon, she saw a man lounging against the wall pretending to be engrossed in a newspaper. As Noelle stepped into the crisp, winter air, the man straightened up and began to follow her at a discreet distance. Noelle strolled the streets slowly and leisurely, stopping to look into all the shop windows.

Five minutes after Noelle left the building, the concierge came out, glanced around to make sure he was not observed, then hailed a taxi and gave the address of a sporting goods shop in Montmartre.

Two hours later the concierge reported to Noelle. "He will be delivered to you Saturday night."

SATURDAY NIGHT WHEN Noelle finished her performance, Colonel Kurt Mueller of the Gestapo was waiting for her backstage. A *frisson* of apprehension went through Noelle. The escape plan had been worked out to a split-second timing, and there was no room for any delays.

"I saw your performance from out front, Fräulein Page," Colonel Mueller said. "You improve each time."

The sound of his soft, high-pitched voice brought her dream back vividly.

"Thank you, Colonel. If you'll excuse me, I have to change."

Noelle started toward her dressing room, and he fell into step beside her.

"I will go with you," Colonel Mueller said.

She walked into her dressing room, the hairless albino Colonel close behind her. He made himself comfortable in an armchair. Noelle hesitated a moment and then began to undress as he watched indifferently. She knew that he was a homosexual, which deprived her of a valuable weapon—her sexuality.

"A little sparrow whispered something in my ear," Colonel Mueller said. "He is going to try to escape tonight."

Noelle's heart skipped a beat, but her face showed nothing. She began removing her makeup, fighting for time as she asked, "Who is going to try to escape tonight?"

"Your friend, Israel Katz."

Noelle swung around, and the movement made her suddenly conscious of the fact that she had removed her brassiere. "I don't know any—" She caught the quick triumphant gleam in his pink eyes and saw the trap just in time. "Wait," she said. "Are you talking about a young intern?"

"Ah, so you *do* remember him!"

"Barely. He treated me for pneumonia some time ago."

"And a self-induced abortion," Colonel Mueller said in that soft, high-pitched voice. The fear flooded back into her. The Gestapo would not have gone to this much trouble if they were not sure that she was involved. She was a fool to have gotten herself into this; but even as Noelle thought it, she knew that it was too late to back out. The wheels had already been set in motion and in a few hours Israel Katz would be either free . . . or dead. And she?

Colonel Mueller was saying, "You said that the last time you saw Katz was at the café a few weeks ago."

Noelle shook her head. "I said no such thing, Colonel."

Colonel Mueller looked steadily into her eyes, then let his gaze drop insolently to her naked breasts and down her belly to her sheer pants. Then he looked up into Noelle's eyes again and sighed. "I love beautiful things," he said softly. "It would be a shame to see beauty like yours destroyed. And all for a man who means nothing to you. How is your friend planning to get away, Fräulein?"

There was a quietness in his voice that sent shivers down her spine. She became Annette, the innocent, helpless character in her play.

"I really don't know what you're talking about, Colonel. I'd like to help you, but I don't know how."

Colonel Mueller looked at Noelle a long time, then stiffly rose to his feet. "I will teach you how, Fräulein," he promised softly, "and I will enjoy it."

He turned at the door to deliver a parting shot. "By the way, I have advised General Scheider not to go away with you for the weekend."

Noelle felt her heart plummet. It was too late to reach Israel Katz. "Do Colonels always interfere in the private lives of Generals?"

"In this case, no," Colonel Mueller said regretfully. "General Scheider intends to keep his rendezvous." He turned and walked out.

Noelle stared after him, her heart racing. She looked at the gold clock on the dressing table and quickly began to dress.

AT ELEVEN FORTY-FIVE the concierge telephoned Noelle to announce that General Scheider was on his way up to her apartment. His voice was trembling.

"Is his chauffeur in the car?" Noelle asked.

"No, Mademoiselle," the concierge replied carefully. "He's on his way up with the General."

"Thank you."

Noelle replaced the receiver and hurried into the bedroom to check her luggage once more. There must be no mistake. The front doorbell rang, and Noelle went into the living room and opened the door.

General Scheider stood in the corridor, his chauffeur, a young captain, behind him. General Scheider was out of uniform and looked very distinguished in a flawlessly cut charcoal-gray suit and a soft blue shirt and black tie. "Good evening," he said formally. He stepped inside, then nodded to his chauffeur.

"My bags are in the bedroom," Noelle said. She indicated the door.

"Thank you, Fräulein." The captain walked into the bedroom. General Scheider came over to Noelle and took her hands. "Do you know what I have been thinking about all day?" he asked. "I was thinking you might not be here, that you might change your mind. Every time the phone rang, I was afraid."

"I keep my promises," Noelle said. She watched as the captain came out of the bedroom carrying her makeup case and overnight bag. "Is there anything else?" he asked.

"No," Noelle said. "That's all."

The captain carried the suitcases out of the apartment.

"Ready?" General Scheider asked.

"Let's have a drink before we go," Noelle replied quickly. She walked over to a bottle of champagne on the bar, resting in a bucket of ice.

"Let me." He moved over to the ice bucket and opened the champagne.

"What shall we drink to?" he asked.

"Etratat."

He studied her a moment and then said, "Etratat."

They touched glasses in a toast and drank. As Noelle set her glass down, she surreptitiously glanced at her wristwatch. General Scheider was talking to her, but Noelle only half-heard the words. Her mind was visualizing what was happening downstairs. She must be very careful. If she moved too quickly or too slowly, it would be fatal. For everyone.

"What are you thinking about?" General Scheider asked.

Noelle turned quickly. "Nothing."

"You were not listening."

"I'm sorry. I suppose I was thinking about us." She turned to him and gave him a quick smile.

"You puzzle me," he said.

"Aren't all women a puzzle?"

"Not like you. I would never believe that you are capricious and yet"—he made a gesture—"first you will not see me at all and now we are suddenly spending a weekend in the country."

"Are you sorry, Hans?"

"Of course not. But still I ask myself—why the country?"

"I told you."

"As yes," General Scheider said. "It is romantic. That is something else that puzzles me. I believe you are a realist, not a romanticist."

"What are you trying to say?" Noelle asked.

"Nothing," the General replied easily. "I am just thinking aloud. I enjoy solving problems, Noelle. In time I will solve you."

She shrugged. "Once you have the solution, the problem might not be interesting."

"We shall see." He set his glass down. "Shall we go?"

Noelle picked up the empty champagne glasses.

"I'll just put these in the sink," she said.

General Scheider watched as she walked into the kitchen. Noelle was one of the most beautiful and desirable women he had ever seen, and he meant to possess her. That did not mean, however, that he was either stupid or blind. She wanted something from him. He intended to find out what it was. Colonel Mueller had alerted him that she was in all probability giving aid to a dangerous enemy of the Reich, and Colonel Mueller made very few mistakes. If he was correct, Noelle Page was probably counting on General Scheider to protect her in some way. If so she knew nothing at all about the German military mind and still less about him. He would turn her over to the Gestapo without a qualm, but first he would have his pleasure. He was looking forward to the weekend.

Noelle came out of the kitchen. There was a worried expression on her face. "How many bags did your chauffeur take down?" she asked.

"Two," he replied. "An overnight bag and a makeup case."

She made a face. "Oh dear, I'm sorry, Hans. He forgot the other case. Do you mind?"

He watched as Noelle walked over to the telephone, picked it up and spoke into it. "Would you please ask the General's driver to come up again?" she said. "There's another bag to go down." She replaced the receiver. "I know we're only going to be there for the weekend," she smiled, "but I want to please you."

"If you want to please me," General Scheider said, "you will not need a lot of clothes." He glanced at a picture of Armand Gautier on the piano. "Does Herr Gautier know that you are going away with me?" he asked.

"Yes," Noelle lied. Armand was in Nice meeting with a producer about a motion picture, and she had seen no reason to alarm him by telling him of her plans. The doorbell rang, and Noelle walked over to the door and opened it. The captain stood there. "I understand there is another bag?" he asked.

"Yes," Noelle apologized. "It's in the bedroom."

The captain nodded and went into the bedroom.

"When must you return to Paris?" General Scheider asked her.

Noelle turned and looked at him. "I'd like to stay as long as I can. We'll come back late Monday afternoon. That will give us two days."

The captain came out of the bedroom. "Excuse me, Fräulein. What does the suitcase look like?"

"It is a large round blue case," Noelle said. She turned to the General. "It has a new gown in it that I haven't worn yet. I saved it for you."

She was babbling now, trying to cover up her nervousness.

The captain had gone back into the bedroom. A few moments later, he came out again. "I am sorry," he said. "I cannot find it."

"Let me," Noelle said. She went into the bedroom and began to search the closets. "That idiot of a maid must have hidden it away somewhere," she said. The three of them looked through every closet in the apartment. It was the General who finally found the bag in the hall closet. He lifted it and said, "It seems to be empty."

Noelle quickly opened the bag and looked inside. There was nothing in it. "Oh, that fool," she said. "She must have crammed that beautiful new dress in the suitcase with my other clothes. I hope she hasn't ruined it." She sighed in exasperation. "Do you have that much trouble with maids in Germany?"

"I think it is the same everywhere," General Scheider replied. He was watching Noelle closely. She was acting strangely, talking too much. She noticed his look.

"You make me feel like a schoolgirl," Noelle said. "I can't remember when I've been so nervous."

General Scheider smiled. So that was it. Or was she playing some kind of game with him? If she was, he would soon find it out. He glanced at his watch. "If we do not leave now, we will get there very late."

"I'm ready," Noelle said.

She prayed the others were.

When they reached the lobby, the concierge was standing there, his face chalk white. Noelle wondered if something had gone wrong. She looked at him for some signal, a sign, but before he could respond, the General had taken Noelle's arm and was leading her out the door.

General Scheider's limousine was parked directly in front of the door. The trunk of the car was closed. The street was deserted. The chauffeur sprang to open the rear door of the car. Noelle turned to look inside the lobby to see the concierge but the General moved in front of her and blocked her view. Deliberately? Noelle glanced at the closed trunk but it told her nothing. It would be hours before she knew whether her plan had succeeded, and the suspense was going to be unbearable.

"Are you all right?" General Scheider was staring at her. She felt that something had gone terribly wrong. She had to find an excuse to go back into the lobby, to be alone with the concierge for a few seconds. She forced a smile to her lips.

"I just remembered," Noelle said. "A friend is going to call me. I must leave a message—"

General Scheider gripped her arm.

"Too late." He smiled. "From this moment on you must think only of me." And he guided her into the car. A moment later they were on their way.

FIVE MINUTES AFTER General Scheider's limousine drove away from the apartment building, a black Mercedes screeched to a stop in front of the building and Colonel Mueller and two other Gestapo men spilled out of the car. Colonel Mueller looked hurriedly up and down the street. "They've gone," he said. The men sprinted into the lobby of Noelle's apartment building and rang the concierge's doorbell. The door opened and the concierge stood in the doorway, a startled expression on his face. "What—?" Colonel Mueller shoved him inside his small apartment.

"Fräulein Page!" he snapped. "Where is she?"

The concierge stared at him, panicky.

"She—she left," he said.

"I know that, you stupid fool! I asked you where she went!" The concierge shook his head helplessly. "I have no idea, Monsieur. I only know she left with an army officer."

"Didn't she tell you where she could be reached?"

"N-*no*, Monsieur. Mademoiselle Page does not confide in me."

Colonel Mueller glared at the old man a moment and then turned on his heel.

"They can't have gotten far," he said to his men. "Contact all the roadblocks as fast as you can. Tell them that when General Scheider's car arrives I want them to hold it and call me at once!"

Because of the hour military traffic was light, which meant that there was virtually no traffic at all. General Scheider's car swung onto the West Road that led out of Paris, passing Versailles. They drove through Mantes, Vernon, and Gaillon and in twenty-five minutes they were approaching the major arterial intersection that branched out into Vichy, Le Havre and the Côte d'Azur.

It seemed to Noelle that a miracle had happened. They were going to get out of Paris without being stopped. She should have known that even the Germans with all their efficiency would not be able to check every single road out of the city. And even as she thought it, out of the darkness ahead of them loomed a roadblock. Flashing red lights blinked from the center of the road, and in back of the lights a German Army lorry blocked the highway. On the side of the road were half a dozen German soldiers and two French police cars. A German Army lieutenant waved down the limousine and, as it came to a stop, he walked over to the driver.

"Get out and show your identification!"

General Scheider opened the rear window, leaned his head out and said, raspingly: "General Scheider. What the hell's going on here?"

The lieutenant snapped to attention.

"Excuse me, General. I did not know it was your car."

The General's eyes nicked over the roadblock. "What's this all about?"

"We have orders to inspect every vehicle leaving Paris, Herr General. Every exit from the city is blocked."

The General turned to Noelle. "The damned Gestapo. I'm sorry, *liebchen.*"

Noelle could feel the color drain from her face, and she was grateful for the darkness of the car. When she spoke, her voice was steady.

"It's not important," she said.

She thought of the cargo in the trunk. If her plan had worked, Israel Katz was in there, and in a moment he would be caught. And so would she.

The German lieutenant turned to the chauffeur.

"Open the luggage compartment, please."

"There's nothing in there but luggage," the captain protested. "I put it in myself."

"I'm sorry, Captain. My orders are clear. Every vehicle out of Paris is to be inspected. Open it."

Muttering under his breath, the driver opened his door and started to get out. Noelle's mind was racing furiously. She had to find a way to stop them, without arousing their suspicions. The driver was out of the car.

Time had run out. Noelle stole a quick look at General Scheider's face. His eyes were narrowed and his lips were tight with anger. She turned to him and said guilelessly, "Shall we get out, Hans? Will they be searching us?" She could feel his body tense with fury.

"Wait!" The General's voice was like the crack of a whip. "Get back in the car," he order his driver. He turned to the lieutenant and his voice was filled with rage. "You tell whoever gave you your orders that they do not apply to generals of the German Army. I do not take orders from lieutenants. Get that roadblock out of my way."

The hapless lieutenant stared at the General's furious face, clicked his heels to attention and said, "Yes, General Scheider." He signaled the driver of the truck blocking the road and the truck lumbered off to the side.

"Drive on," General Scheider commanded.

And the car sped away into the night.

Slowly Noelle let her body relax into the seat, feeling the tension draining out of her. The crisis was past. She wished that she knew whether Israel Katz was in the trunk of the car. And if he was alive.

General Scheider turned to Noelle and she could feel the anger that was still seething in him.

"I apologize," he said, wearily. "This is a strange war. Sometimes it is necessary to remind the Gestapo that wars are run by armies."

Noelle smiled up at him and put her arm through his. "And armies are run by generals."

"Exactly," he agreed. "Armies are run by generals. I am going to have to teach Colonel Mueller a lesson."

TEN MINUTES AFTER General Scheider's car had left the roadblock, a phone call came in from Gestapo Headquarters, alerting them to be on the lookout for the car.

"It has already passed through," the lieutenant reported, a feeling of foreboding flooding through him. A moment later he was speaking with Colonel Mueller.

"How long ago?" the Gestapo officer asked softly.

"Ten minutes."

"Did you search his car?"

The lieutenant felt his bowels turn to water. "No, sir. The General would not permit—"

"*Scheiss!* Which way was he headed?"

The lieutenant swallowed. When he spoke again, it was in the hopeless voice of a man who knew that his future was finished.

"I am not certain," he replied. "This is a large crossroad here. He could have been going inland to Rouen or to the sea, to Le Havre."

"I want you to present yourself to Gestapo Headquarters at nine A.M. tomorrow. My office."

"Yes, sir," the lieutenant responded.

Savagely Colonel Mueller rang off. He turned to the two men at his side and said, "Le Havre. Get my car. We're going cockroach-hunting!"

THE ROAD TO Le Havre winds along the Seine, through the beautiful Seine Valley with its rich hills and fertile farms. It was a clear, starlit night and the farmhouses in the distance were pools of light, like oases in the darkness.

In the comfortable back seat of the limousine Noelle and General Scheider talked. He told her about his wife and his children and how difficult marriage was for an army officer. Noelle listened sympathetically and told him how difficult a romantic life was for an actress. Each was aware that the conversation was a game, both of them keeping the talk on a superficial level that would give away no insights. Noelle did not for a moment underestimate the intelligence of the man sitting beside her, and she fully understood how dangerous was the adventure in which she was engaged. She knew that General Scheider was too clever to believe that she had suddenly found him irresistible, that he must suspect that she was after something. What Noelle was counting on was that she would be able to outmaneuver him in the game they were playing. The General touched only briefly on the war, but he said something that she remembered long afterward.

"The British are a strange race," he said. "In peacetime, they are impossible to manage, but in a crisis they are magnificent. The only time a British sailor is truly happy is when his ship is sulking."

They reached Le Havre in the small hours of the morning on their way to the village of Etratat.

"May we stop for a bite to eat?" Noelle asked. "I'm starved."

General Scheider nodded. "Of course, if you wish." He raised his voice. "Look for an all-night restaurant."

"I'm sure there's one by the pier," Noelle suggested. The captain obediently swung the car toward the waterfront. He stopped the car at the water's edge, where several cargo ships were tied to the pier. A block away a sign said, "Bistro."

The captain opened the door and Noelle got out, followed by General Scheider.

"It's probably open all night for the dock workers," Noelle said. She heard the sound of a motor and turned around. A cargo-loading forklift had driven up and stopped near the limousine. Two men wearing coveralls and long, visored caps that concealed their faces got out of the machine. One of the men looked hard at Noelle, then took out a tool kit and began to tighten the forklift. Noelle felt the muscles in her stomach constrict. She took General Scheider's arm and they started toward the restaurant. Noelle looked back at the chauffeur sitting behind the wheel.

"Wouldn't he like some coffee?" Noelle asked.

"He will stay with the car," the General said.

Noelle stared at him. The chauffeur must *not* stay with the car or everything would be ruined. Yet Noelle dared not insist.

They walked on toward the café over the rough, uneven cobblestones. Suddenly, as she took a step, her ankle turned and Noelle fell, letting out a sharp cry of pain. General Scheider reached out and vainly tried to grab her before her body hit the cobblestones.

"Are you all right?" he asked.

The chauffeur, seeing what had happened, moved from behind the wheel of the car and started hurrying toward them.

"I'm so sorry," Noelle said. "I—I turned my ankle. It feels like it's broken."

General Scheider ran his hand expertly over her ankle. "There is no swelling. It is probably just a sprain. Can you stand on it?"

"I—I don't know," Noelle said.

The chauffeur reached her side and the two men lifted her to her feet. Noelle took a step and the ankle gave way under her.

"I'm sorry," she moaned. "If I could just sit down."

"Help me get her in there," General Scheider said, indicating the café.

With the two men supporting her on either side, they walked into the restaurant. As she walked through the door, Noelle risked a quick look back at the car. The two dock workers were at the trunk of the limousine.

"Are you sure you wouldn't rather go straight on to Etratat?" the General was asking.

"No, believe me, I'll be fine," Noelle replied.

The proprietor led them to a corner table, and the two men eased Noelle into a chair.

"Are you in much pain?" General Scheider asked.

"A bit," Noelle replied. She put her hand on his. "Don't worry. I won't let this spoil anything for you, Hans."

AT THE MOMENT Noelle and General Hans Scheider were sitting in the café, Colonel Mueller and two of his men were speeding into the city limits of Le Havre. The local captain of police had been roused from his sleep and was waiting for the Gestapo men in front of the police station. "A gendarme has located the General's car," he said. "It is parked down by the waterfront."

A gleam of satisfaction came into Colonel Mueller's face. "Take me there," he commanded.

Five minutes later, the Gestapo automobile with Colonel Mueller, his two men and the police captain raced up beside General Scheider's automobile on the pier. The men got out and surrounded the car. At that moment General Scheider, Noelle and the chauffeur were starting to leave the bistro. The chauffeur was the first to notice the men at the car. He started hurrying toward them.

"What's happening?" Noelle asked, and even as she spoke she recognized the figure of Colonel Mueller in the distance and felt a cold chill go through her.

"I don't know," General Scheider said. He started toward the limousine with long strides, Noelle limping after him.

"What are you doing here?" General Scheider asked Colonel Mueller as he reached the car.

"I am sorry to disturb your holiday," Colonel Mueller replied curtly. "I would like to inspect the trunk of your car, General."

"There is nothing but luggage in there."

Noelle reached the group. She noticed that the forklift had gone. The General and the Gestapo men were glaring at each other.

"I must insist, General. I have reason to believe that a wanted enemy of the Third Reich is hiding in there and that your guest is his accomplice."

General Scheider stared at him for a long moment, then turned to study Noelle.

"I don't know what he's talking about," she said firmly.

The General's eyes traveled down to her ankle, then he made a decision and turned to his chauffeur. "Open it."

"Yes, General."

All eyes were riveted on the trunk as the chauffeur reached for the handle and turned it. Noelle felt suddenly faint. Slowly the lid opened.

The trunk was empty.

"Someone has stolen our luggage!" exclaimed the chauffeur.

Colonel Mueller's face was mottled with fury. "He got away!"

"Who got away?" demanded the General.

"Le Cafard," raged Colonel Mueller. "A Jew named Israel Katz. He was smuggled out of Paris in the trunk of this car."

"That's impossible," General Scheider retorted. "That trunk was tightly closed. He would have suffocated."

Colonel Mueller studied the trunk a moment, then turned to one of his men. "Get inside."

"Yes, Colonel."

Obediently the man crawled into the trunk. Colonel Mueller slammed the lid tightly shut and looked at his watch. For the next four minutes, they stood there in silence, each engrossed in his own thoughts. Finally after what seemed an eternity to Noelle, Colonel Mueller opened the lid of the trunk. The man inside was unconscious. General Scheider turned to Colonel Mueller, a contemptuous expression on his face. "If anyone was riding in that trunk," the General declared, "they removed his corpse. Is there anything else I can do for you, Colonel?"

The Gestapo officer shook his head, seething with rage and frustration.

General Scheider turned to his chauffeur. "Let's go." He helped Noelle into the car, and they drove toward Etratat, leaving the knot of men fading away into the distance.

Colonel Kurt Mueller instituted an immediate search of the waterfront, but it was not until late the following afternoon that an empty oxygen tank was found in a barrel in a corner of an unused warehouse. An African freighter had set sail for Capetown out of Le Havre the night before but it was now somewhere on the high seas. The missing luggage turned up a few days later in the lost-and-found department of the Gare du Nord in Paris.

As for Noelle and General Scheider, they spent the weekend in Etratat and returned to Paris late Monday afternoon in time for Noelle to do her evening performance.

9

CATHERINE

WASHINGTON: 1941–1944

atherine had quit her job with William Fraser the morning after
she had married Larry. Fraser asked her to have lunch with him the
day she returned to Washington. He looked drawn and haggard
and suddenly older. Catherine had felt a pang of compassion for him,
but that was all. She was sitting opposite a tall, nice-looking stranger for
whom she felt affection, but it was impossible now to imagine that she
had ever contemplated marrying him. Fraser gave her a wan smile.

"So you're a married lady," he said.

"The most married lady in the world."

"It must have happened rather suddenly. I—I wish I'd had a chance
to compete."

"*I* didn't even have a chance," Catherine said honestly. "It just—
happened."

"Larry's quite a fellow."

"Yes."

"Catherine"—Fraser hesitated—"you don't really know much about
Larry, do you?"

Catherine felt her back stiffening.

"I know I love him, Bill," she said evenly, "and I know that he loves me. That's a pretty good beginning, isn't it?"

He sat there frowning, silent, debating with himself. "Catherine—"

"Yes?"

"Be careful."

"Of what?" she asked.

Fraser spoke slowly, feeling his way carefully over a minefield of words. "Larry's—different."

"How?" she asked, refusing to help him.

"I mean, he's not like most men." He saw the look on her face. "Oh, hell," he said. "Don't pay any attention to me." He managed a faint grin. "You've probably read the biography Aesop did on me. The fox and the sour grapes."

Catherine took his hand affectionately. "I'll never forget you, Bill. I hope we can remain friends."

"I hope so too," Fraser said. "Are you sure you won't stay on at the office?"

"Larry wants me to quit. He's old-fashioned. He believes that husbands should support their wives."

"If you ever change your mind," Fraser said, "let me know." The rest of the luncheon was concerned with office affairs and a discussion of who would take Catherine's place. She knew she would miss Bill Fraser very much. She supposed that the first man to seduce a girl would always hold a special place in that girl's life, but Bill had meant something to her beyond that. He was a dear man and a good friend. Catherine was disturbed by his attitude toward Larry. It was as though Bill had started to warn her about something and then stopped because he was afraid of spoiling her happiness. Or was it as he had said, just a case of sour grapes? Bill Fraser was not a small man or a jealous man. He would surely want her to be happy. And yet Catherine was sure he had tried to tell her something. Somewhere in the back of her mind was a vague foreboding. But an hour later when she met Larry and he smiled at her, everything went out of her head but the ecstasy of being married to this incredible, joyful, human being.

. . .

LARRY WAS MORE fun to be with than anyone Catherine had ever known. Each day was an adventure, a holiday. They drove out to the country every weekend and stayed at small inns and explored county fairs. They went to Lake Placid and rode the huge toboggan slide and to Montauk where they went boating and fishing. Catherine was terrified of the water because she had never learned to swim, but Larry told her not to worry about it, and with him she felt safe.

Larry was loving and attentive and appeared to be remarkably un-aware of the attraction he held for other women. Catherine seemed to be all that he wanted. On their honeymoon Larry had come across a little silver bird in an antique shop and Catherine had liked it so much that he had found a crystal bird for her and it had become the start of a col-lection. On a Saturday night they drove to Maryland to celebrate their third-month anniversary and had dinner at the same little restaurant.

The next day, Sunday, December 7, Pearl Harbor was attacked by the Japanese.

AMERICA'S DECLARATION OF war against Japan came the following day at 1:32 P.M., less than twenty-four hours after the Japanese attack. On Monday while Larry was at Andrews Air Base, Catherine, unable to bear being alone in the apartment, took a taxi to the Capitol Building to see what was happening. Knots of people pressed around a dozen portable radio sets scattered through the crowd that lined the sidewalks of the Capitol Plaza. Catherine watched as the Presidential caravan raced up the drive and stopped at the south entrance to the Capitol. She was close enough to see the limousine door open and President Roosevelt disembark, assisted by two aides. Dozens of policemen stood at every corner, alert for trouble. The mood of the crowd seemed to Catherine to be mainly outrage, like a lynch mob eager to get into action.

Five minutes after President Roosevelt entered the Capitol, his voice came over the radio, as he addressed the Joint Session of Congress. His voice was strong and firm, filled with angry determination.

"America will remember this onslaught . . . Righteous might will win . . . We will gain the inevitable triumph, so help us, God."

Fifteen minutes after Roosevelt had entered the Capitol, House

Joint Resolution 254 was passed, declaring war on Japan. It was passed unanimously except for Representative Jeannette Rankin of Montana, who voted against the declaration of war, so the final vote was 388 to 1. President Roosevelt's speech had taken exactly ten minutes—the shortest war message ever delivered to an American Congress.

The crowd outside cheered, a full-throated roar of approval, anger and a promise of vengeance. America was finally on the move.

Catherine studied the men and women standing near her. The faces of the men were filled with the same look of exhilaration that she had seen on Larry's face the day before, as though they all belonged to the same secret club whose members felt that war was an exciting sport. Even the women seemed caught up by the spontaneous enthusiasm that swept through the crowd. But Catherine wondered how they would feel when their men were gone and the women stood alone waiting for news of their husbands and sons. Slowly Catherine turned and walked back toward the apartment. On the corner she saw soldiers with fixed bayonets.

Soon, she thought, the whole country would be in uniform.

It happened even faster than Catherine had anticipated. Almost overnight Washington was transformed into a world of a citizen army in khaki.

The air was filled with an electric, contagious excitement. It was as though peace were a lethargy, a miasma that filled mankind with a sense of ennui, and it was only war that could stimulate man to the full exhilaration of life.

Larry was spending sixteen to eighteen hours at the Air Base, and he often remained there overnight. He told Catherine that the situation at Pearl Harbor and Hickam Field was much worse than the people had been led to believe. The sneak attack had been devastatingly successful. For all practical purposes America's Navy and a good part of its Air Corps had been destroyed.

"Are you saying that we could lose this war?" Catherine asked, shocked.

Larry looked at her thoughtfully. "It depends on how fast we can get ready," he replied. "Everyone thinks of the Japanese as funny little men with weak eyes. That's horseshit. They're tough, and they're not afraid to die. We're soft."

. . .

IN THE MONTHS that followed it seemed that nothing could stop the Japanese. The daily headlines screamed out their successes: They were attacking Wake . . . softening up the Philippine Islands for invasion . . . landing in Guam . . . in Borneo . . . in Hong Kong. General MacArthur declared Manila an open city, and the trapped American troops in the Philippines surrendered.

One day in April, Larry telephoned Catherine from the Base and asked her to meet him downtown for dinner at the Willard Hotel to celebrate.

"Celebrate what?" Catherine asked.

"I'll tell you tonight," Larry replied. There was a note of high excitement in his voice.

When Catherine hung up, she was filled with a dread premonition. She tried to think of all the possible reasons that Larry would have to celebrate, but it always came back to the same thing arid she did not think she would have the strength to face it.

At five o'clock that afternoon Catherine was fully dressed, sitting on her bed staring into the dressing-room mirror.

I must be wrong, she thought. *Maybe he's been promoted. That's what we're celebrating. Or he's had some good news about the war.* Catherine told herself this but she did not believe it. She studied herself in the mirror, trying to be objective. While she would not give Ingrid Bergman any sleepless nights, she was, she decided dispassionately, attractive. Her figure was good, full of provocative curves. *You're intelligent, cheerful, courteous, kind and a sex pot,* she told herself. *Why would any normal red-blooded male be dying to leave you so that he could go off to war and try to get himself killed?*

At seven o'clock Catherine walked into the dining room of the Willard Hotel. Larry had not arrived yet, and the maître d' escorted her to a table. She said no she would not have a drink, then nervously changed her mind and ordered a martini.

When the waiter brought it and Catherine started to pick it up, she found that her hands were shaking. She looked up and saw Larry moving toward her. He threaded his way between the tables, acknowledging greetings along the way. He carried with him that incredible vitality, that aura that made every eye turn in his direction. Catherine watched him, remembering the day he had come to her table at the MGM commissary in Hollywood. She realized how little she had known him then, and she wondered how well she knew him now. He reached the table and gave her a quick kiss on the cheek.

"Sorry I'm late, Cathy," he apologized. "The Base has been a madhouse all day." He sat down, greeted the captain by name and ordered a martini. If he noticed that Catherine was drinking, he made no comment.

Catherine's mind was screaming out: *Tell me your surprise. Tell me what we're celebrating.* But she said nothing. There was an old Hungarian proverb: "Only a fool rushes bad news." She took another sip of her martini. Well maybe it wasn't an old Hungarian proverb. Maybe it was a new Catherine Douglas proverb designed to be worn over thin skins for protection. Maybe the martini was making her a little drunk. If her premonition was right, before this night was over she was going to get very drunk. But looking at Larry now, his face filled with love, Catherine knew that she had to be wrong. Larry could not bear to leave her any more than she could bear to leave him. She had been building up a nightmare out of whole cloth. From the happy expression on his face she knew that he had some really good news to tell her.

Larry was leaning toward her, smiling his boyish smile, taking her hand in his.

"You'll never guess what's happened, Cathy. I'm going overseas."

It was as though a filmy curtain descended, giving everything an unreal, hazy look. Larry was sitting next to her, his lips moving, but his face was going in and out of focus and Catherine could not hear any words. She looked over his shoulder and the walls of the restaurant were moving together and receding. She watched, fascinated.

"Catherine!" Larry was shaking her arm and slowly her eyes focused on him and everything came back to normal. "Are you all right?"

Catherine nodded, swallowed and said, shakily, "Great. Good news always does that to me."

"You understand that I have to do this, don't you?"

"Yes, I understand." *The truth is, I wouldn't understand if I lived to be a million years old, my darling. But if I told you that, you'd hate me, wouldn't you? Who needs a nagging wife? Heroes' wives should send their men off smiling.*

Larry was watching, concerned. "You're crying."

"I am not," Catherine said indignantly and found to her horror that she was. "I—I just have to get used to the idea."

"They're giving me my own squadron," Larry said.

"Are they really?" Catherine tried to pump pride into her voice. His own squadron. When he was a small boy, he probably had had his own set of trains to play with. And now that he was a tall boy, they had given him his own squadron to play with. And these were real toys, guaranteed to gel shot down and bleed and die. "I'd like another drink," she said.

"Of course."

"When—when will you have to leave?"

"Not until next month."

He made it sound as though he were eager to get away. It was terrifying, feeling the whole fabric of her marriage being torn apart. On the bandstand a singer was crooning, "A trip to the moon on gossamer wings . . ." *Gossamer,* she thought. *That's what my marriage is made of: gossamer.* That Cole Porter knew everything.

"We'll have plenty of time before I leave," Larry was saying.

Plenty of time for what? Catherine wondered bitterly. *Plenty of time to raise a family, to take our children skiing in Vermont, to grow old together?*

"What would you like to do tonight?" Larry asked.

I'd like to go down to the County Hospital and have one of your toes removed. Or have one of your ear drums pierced. Aloud, Catherine said, "Let's go home and make love." And there was a fierce, desperate urgency in her.

THE NEXT FOUR weeks melted away. The clocks raced forward in a Kafka-ish nightmare that turned days into hours and hours into minutes, and then incredibly it was Larry's last day. Catherine drove him to the airport. He was talkative and happy and gay and she was somber and quiet and miserable. The last few minutes became a kaleidoscope of reporting in . . . a hurried good-bye kiss . . . Larry entering the plane that was to take him away from her . . . and a last farewell wave. Catherine stood on the field watching his plane dwindle to a small speck in the sky and finally disappear. She stood there for an hour, and finally when it got dark she turned and drove back into town to her empty apartment.

IN THE FIRST year following the attack on Pearl Harbor, ten great sea and air battles were fought against the Japanese. The Allies won only three, but two of them were decisive: Midway and the Battle of Guadalcanal.

Catherine read word for word the newspaper reports of every battle and then asked William Fraser to get her further details. She wrote to Larry daily, but it was eight weeks before she received his first letter. It was optimistic and full of excitement. The letter had been heavily censored so Catherine had no idea where he had been or what he was doing. Whatever it was she had a feeling that he seemed to be enjoying it, and in the long lonely hours of the night Catherine lay in bed puzzling over that, trying to figure out what it was in Larry that made him respond to the challenge of war and death. It was not that he had a death wish, for Catherine had never known anyone more alive and vital; but perhaps that was simply the other side of the coin, that what made the life-sense so keen was constantly honing it against death.

She had lunch with William Fraser. Catherine knew that he had tried to enlist and had been told by the White House that he could do more good by staying at his post. He had been bitterly disappointed. He had never mentioned it to Catherine, however. Now as Fraser sat across from Catherine at the luncheon table, he asked:

"Have you heard from Larry?"

"I got a letter last week."

"What did he say?"

"Well, according to the letter, the war is a kind of football game. We lost the first scrimmage, but now they've sent the first team in, and we're gaining ground."

He nodded. "That's Larry."

"But that's not the war," Catherine said quietly. "It's not a football game, Bill. Millions of people are going to be killed before this is over."

"If you're in it, Catherine," he said gently, "I imagine it's easier to think of it as a football game."

Catherine had decided that she wanted to go to work. The Army had created a branch for women called the WACs, and Catherine had thought of joining but had felt she might be more useful doing something more than driving cars and answering telephones. Although from what she had heard, the WACs were pretty colorful. There was so much pregnancy among them that there was a rumor that when volunteers went in for their physical examination, the doctors pressed their stomachs with a tiny rubber stamp. The girls tried to read the words but were unable to do so. Finally one of them hit upon the idea of getting a magnifying glass. The words read: "When you can read this with the naked eye, report to me."

Now as she sat lunching with Bill Fraser, she said, "I want to work. I want to do something to help."

He studied her a moment, then nodded. "I may know just the thing for you, Catherine. The Government's trying to sell War Bonds. I think you could help coordinate it."

Two weeks later Catherine went to work organizing the sale of War Bonds by celebrities. It had sounded ridiculously easy in concept, but the execution of it was something else again. She found the stars to be like children, eager and excited about helping the war effort, but difficult to pin down about specific dates. Their schedules had to be constantly juggled. Often it was not their fault, because pictures were delayed or schedules ran over. Catherine found herself commuting from Washington to Hollywood and New York. She got used to leaving on an hour's notice, packing enough clothes to last the length of each trip. She met dozens of celebrities.

"Did you really meet Cary Grant?" her secretary asked her when she returned from a trip to Hollywood.

"We had lunch together."

"Is he as charming as they say?"

"If he could package it," Catherine declared, "he'd be the richest man in the world."

IT HAPPENED SO gradually that Catherine was almost unaware of it. It had been six months earlier, when Bill Fraser told her about a problem that Wallace Turner was having with one of the advertising accounts that Catherine used to handle. Catherine had laid out a new campaign using a humorous approach, and the client had been very pleased. A few weeks later Bill had asked Catherine to help on another account, and before she realized it she was spending more than half her time with the advertising agency. She was in charge of half a dozen accounts, all of them doing well. Fraser had given her a large salary and a percentage. At noon on the day before Christmas Fraser came into her office. The rest of the staff had gone home, and Catherine was finishing up some last minute work.

"Having fun?" he asked.

"It's a living." She smiled and added warmly, "and a generous one. Thanks, Bill."

"Don't thank me. You've earned every penny of it—and then some. It's the 'then some' I want to talk to you about. I'm offering you a partnership."

She looked at him in surprise. "A partnership?"

"Half the new accounts we got in the last six months are because of you." He sat there looking at her thoughtfully, saying nothing more. And she understood how much it meant to him.

"You have a partner," she said.

His face lit up. "I can't tell you how pleased I am." Awkwardly, he held out his hand. She shook her head, walked past his outstretched arm, hugged him and gave him a kiss on the cheek.

"Now that we're partners," she teased, "I can kiss you." She felt him suddenly hold her tighter.

"Cathy," he said, "I . . ."

Catherine put her finger to his lips. "Don't say anything, Bill. Let's leave it the way it is."

"You know I'm in love with you."

"And I love you," she said warmly. *Semantics,* she thought. The difference between "I love you" and "I'm in love with you" was a bridgeless chasm.

Fraser smiled. "I won't bother you, I promise. I respect the way you feel about Larry."

"Thank you, Bill." She hesitated. "I don't know whether this helps any, but if there ever were anyone else, it would be you."

"That's a great help." He grinned. "It's going to keep me awake all night."

10

NOELLE

PARIS: 1944

D uring the past year Armand Gautier had ceased broaching the subject of marriage. In the beginning he had felt himself in a superior position to Noelle. Now, however, the situation was almost reversed. When they gave newspaper interviews, it was Noelle to whom the questions were directed, and wherever they went together, Noelle was the attraction, he was the afterthought.

Noelle was the perfect mistress. She continued to make Gautier comfortable, act as his hostess and in effect make him one of the most envied men in France; but in truth he never had a moment's peace, for he knew that he did not possess Noelle, nor ever could, that there would come a day when she would walk out of his life as capriciously as she had wandered into it and when he remembered what had happened to him the one time that Noelle had left him, Gautier felt sick to his stomach. Against every instinct of his intellect, his experience and his knowledge of women he was wildly, madly in love with Noelle. She was the single most important fact of his life. He would lie awake nights devising elaborate surprises to make her happy and when they succeeded, he was rewarded with a smile or a kiss or an unsolicited night of lovemaking. Whenever she looked at another man, Gautier was filled with jealousy, but he knew better than to speak of it to Noelle. Once after a party when she had spent the entire evening talking to a renowned doctor, Gautier had been furious with her. Noelle had listened to his tirade and then had answered quietly, "If my speaking to other men bothers you, Armand, I will move my things out tonight."

He had never brought up the subject again.

AT THE BEGINNING of February, Noelle began her salon. It had started as a simple Sunday brunch with a few of their friends from the theater, but as word about it got around, it quickly expanded and began to include politicians, scientists, writers—anyone whom the group thought might be interesting or amusing. Noelle was the mistress of the salon and one of the chief attractions. Everyone found himself eager to talk to her, for Noelle asked incisive questions and remembered the answers. She learned about politics from politicians and about finance from bankers. A leading art expert taught her about art, and she soon knew all the great French artists who were living in France. She learned about wine from the chief vintner of Baron Rothschild and about architecture from Corbusier. Noelle had the best tutors in the world and they in turn had a beautiful and fascinating student. She had a quick probing mind and was an intelligent listener.

Armand Gautier had the feeling that he was watching a Princess consorting with her ministers, and had he only been aware of it, it was the closest he would ever come to understanding Noelle's character.

As the months went by Gautier began to feel a little more secure. It seemed to him that Noelle had met everyone who might matter to her and she had shown no interest in any of them.

She had not yet met Constantin Demiris.

CONSTANTIN DEMIRIS WAS the ruler of an empire larger and more powerful than most countries. He had no title or official position, but he regularly bought and sold prime ministers, cardinals, ambassadors and kings. Demiris was one of the two or three wealthiest men in the world and his power was legendary. He owned the largest fleet of cargo ships afloat, an airline, newspapers, banks, steel mills, gold mines—his tentacles were everywhere, inextricably woven throughout the woof and warp of the economic fabric of dozens of countries.

He had one of the most important art collections in the world, a fleet of private planes and a dozen apartments and villas scattered around the globe.

Constantin Demiris was above medium height, with a barrel chest and broad shoulders. His features were swarthy, and he had a broad Greek nose and olive black eyes that blazed with intelligence. He was not interested in clothes, yet he was always on the list of best-dressed men and it was rumored that he owned over five hundred suits. He had his clothes made wherever he happened to be. His suits were tailored by Hawes and Curtis in London, his shirts by Brioni in Rome, shoes by Daliet Grande in Paris and ties from a dozen countries.

Demiris had about him a presence that was magnetic. When he walked into a room, people who did not know who he was would turn to stare. Newspapers and magazines all over the world had written an incessant spate of stories about Constantin Demiris and his activities, both business and social.

The Press found him highly quotable. When asked by a reporter if friends had helped him achieve his success, he had replied, "To be successful, you need friends. To be *very* successful, you need enemies."

When he was asked how many employees he had, Demiris had said, "None. Only acolytes. When this much power and money is involved, business turns into a religion and offices become temples."

He had been reared in the Greek Orthodox Church, but he said of organized religion: "A thousand times more crimes have been committed in the name of love than in the name of hate."

The world knew that he was married to the daughter of an old Greek banking family, that his wife was an attractive, gracious lady and that when Demiris entertained on his yacht or on his private island, his wife seldom went with him. Instead, he would be accompanied by a beautiful actress or ballerina or whoever else struck his current fancy. His romantic escapades were as legendary and as colorful as his financial adventures. He had bedded dozens of motion picture stars, the wives of his best friends, a fifteen-year-old novelist, freshly bereaved widows, and it was even rumored that he had once been propositioned by a group of nuns who needed a new convent.

Half a dozen books had been written about Demiris, but none of them had ever touched on the essence of the man or managed to reveal the wellspring of his success. One of the most public figures in the world, Constantin Demiris was a very private person, and he manipulated his public image as a facade that concealed his real self. He had dozens of intimate friends in every walk of life and yet no one really knew him. The facts were a matter of public record. He had started life in Piraeus as the son of a stevedore, in a family of fourteen brothers and sisters where there was never enough food on the table and if anyone wanted anything extra, he had to fight for it. There was something in Demiris that constantly demanded more, and he fought for it.

Even as a small boy Demiris' mind automatically converted everything into mathematics. He knew the number of steps on the Parthenon, how many minutes it took to walk to school, the number of boats in the harbor on a given day. Time was a number divided into segments, and Demiris learned not to waste it. The result was that without any real effort, he was able to accomplish a tremendous amount. His sense of organization was instinctive, a talent that operated automatically in even the smallest things he did. Everything became a game of matching his wits against those around him.

While Demiris was aware that he was cleverer than most men, he had no excess vanity. When a beautiful woman wanted to go to bed with him, he did not for an instant flatter himself that it was because of his looks or personality, but he never permitted that to bother him. The world was a marketplace, and people were either buyers or sellers. Some women, he knew, were attracted by his money, some by his power and a few—a rare few—by his mind and imagination.

Nearly every person he met wanted something from him: a donation to a charity, financing for a business project or simply the power that his friendship could bestow. Demiris enjoyed the challenge of figuring out exactly what it was that people were really after, for it was seldom what it appeared to be. His analytical mind was skeptical of surface truth, and as a consequence he believed nothing he heard and trusted no one.

The reporters who chronicled his life were permitted to see only his geniality and charm, the sophisticated urbane man of the world. They never suspected that beneath the surface, Demiris was a killer, a gutter-fighter whose instinct was to go for the jugular vein.

To the ancient Greeks the word *thekaeossini,* justice, was often synonymous with *ekthekissis,* vengeance, and Demiris was obsessed with both. He remembered every slight he had ever suffered, and those who were unlucky enough to incur his enmity were paid back a hundredfold. They were never even aware of it, for Demiris' mathematical mind made a game of exacting retribution, patiently working out elaborate traps, spinning complex webs that finally caught and destroyed its victims.

When Demiris was sixteen years old, he had gone into his first business enterprise with an older man named Spyros Nicholas. Demiris had conceived the idea of opening a small stand on the docks to serve hot food to the stevedores on the night shift. He had scraped together half the money for the enterprise, but when it had become successful Nicholas had forced him out of the business and had taken it over himself. Demiris had accepted his fate without protest and had gone ahead to other enterprises.

Over the next twenty years Spyros Nicholas had gone into the meat-packing business and had become rich and successful. He had married, had three children and was one of the most prominent men in Greece. During those years, Demiris patiently sat back and let Nicholas build his little empire. When he decided that Nicholas was as successful and as happy as he was ever going to be, Demiris struck.

Because his business was booming, Nicholas was contemplating buying farms to raise his own meat and opening a chain of retail stores. An enormous amount of money was required. Constantin Demiris owned the bank with which Nicholas did business, and the bank encouraged Nicholas to borrow money for expansion at interest rates that Nicholas could not resist. Nicholas plunged heavily, and in the midst of the expansion his notes were suddenly called in by the bank. When the bewildered man protested that he could not make the payments, the bank immediately began foreclosure proceedings. The newspapers owned by Demiris prominently played up the story on the front pages, and other creditors began foreclosing on Nicholas. He went to other banks and lending institutions, but for reasons he could not fathom, they refused to come to his assistance. The day after he was forced into bankruptcy Nicholas committed suicide.

Demiris' sense of *thekaeossini* was a two-edged sword. Just as he never forgave an injury, neither did he ever forget a favor. A landlady who had fed and clothed the young man when he was too poor to pay her suddenly found herself the owner of an apartment building, without any idea who her benefactor was. A young girl who had taken the penniless young Demiris in to live with her had been given a villa and a lifetime pension anonymously. The people who had had dealings with the ambitious young Greek lad forty years earlier had no idea how the casual relationship with him would affect their lives. The dynamic young Demiris had needed help from bankers and lawyers, ship captains and unions, politicians and financiers. Some had encouraged and helped him, others had snubbed and cheated him. In his head and in his heart the proud Greek had kept an indelible record of every transaction. His wife Melina had once accused him of playing God.

"Every man plays God," Demiris had told her. "Some of us are better equipped for the role than others."

"But it is wrong to destroy the lives of men, Costa."

"It is not wrong. It is justice."

"Vengeance."

"Sometimes it is the same. Most men get away with the evil they do. I am in a position to make them pay for it. That is justice."

He enjoyed the hours he spent devising traps for his adversaries. He would study his victims carefully, analyzing their personalities, assessing their strengths and their weaknesses.

When Demiris had had three small freighters and needed a loan to expand his fleet, he had gone to a Swiss banker in Basel. The banker had not only turned him down but had telephoned other banker friends of his to advise them not to give the young Greek any money. Demiris had finally managed to borrow the money in Turkey.

Demiris had bided his time. He decided that the banker's Achilles' heel lay in his greed. Demiris was in negotiation with Ibn Saud of Arabia to take over leases on a newly discovered oil development there. The leases would be worth several hundred million dollars to Demiris' company.

He instructed one of his agents to leak the news to the Swiss banker about the deal that was about to take place. The banker was offered a 25-percent participation in the new company if he put up five million dollars in cash to buy shares of the stock. When the deal went through, the five million dollars would be worth more than fifty million. The banker quickly checked the deal and confirmed its authenticity. Not having that kind of money available personally, he quietly borrowed it from the bank without notifying anyone, for he had no wish to share his windfall. The transaction was to take place the following week, at which time he would be able to replace the money he had taken.

When Demiris had the banker's check in his hand, he announced to the newspapers that the arrangement with Arabia had been canceled. The stock plummeted. There was no way for the banker to cover his losses, and his embezzlement was discovered. Demiris picked up the banker's shares of stock at a few cents on the dollar and then went ahead with the oil deal. The stock soared. The banker was convicted of embezzlement and given a prison sentence of twenty years.

There were a few players in Demiris' game with whom he had not yet evened the score, but he was in no hurry. He enjoyed the anticipation, the planning and the execution. It was like a chess game, and Demiris was a chess master. These days he made no enemies, for no man could afford to be his enemy, so his quarry was limited to those who had crossed his path in the past.

THIS, THEN, WAS the man who appeared one afternoon at Noelle Page's Sunday salon. He was spending a few hours in Paris on his way to Cairo, and a young sculptress he was seeing suggested that they stop in at the salon. From the moment Demiris saw Noelle, he knew that he wanted her.

Aside from royalty itself which was unavailable to the daughter of a Marseille fishmonger, Constantin Demiris was probably the closest thing there was to a king. Three days after she had met him Noelle quit her play without notice, packed her clothes and joined Constantin Demiris in Greece.

BECAUSE OF THE prominence of their respective positions it was inevitable that the relationship between Noelle Page and Constantin Demiris become an international *cause célèbre*. Photographers and reporters were constantly trying to interview Demiris' wife, but if her composure was ruffled, she never betrayed it. Melina Demiris' only comment to the press was that her husband had many good friends around the world and that she saw nothing wrong with that. Privately she told her outraged parents that Costa had had affairs before and that this would soon wear itself out like all the others. Her husband would leave on extended business trips, and she would see newspaper photographs of him with Noelle in Constantinople or Tokyo or Rome. Melina Demiris was a proud woman, but she was determined to endure the humiliation because she truly loved her husband. She accepted the fact, though she could never fathom the reason, that some men needed more than one woman and that even a man in love with his wife could sleep with another woman. She would have died before she let another man touch her. She never reproached Constantin, because she knew that it would serve no purpose except to alienate him. They had on balance a good marriage. She was aware that she was not a passionate woman, but she let her husband use her in bed whenever he wished, and she tried to give him what pleasure she could. If she had known of the ways that Noelle made love to her husband, she would have been shocked, and if she had known how much her husband enjoyed it, she would have been miserable.

Noelle's chief attraction for Demiris, for whom women no longer held any surprises, was that she was a constant surprise. To him who had a passion for puzzles, she was an enigma, defying solution. He had never met anyone like her. She accepted the beautiful things he gave her, but she was just as happy when he gave her nothing. He bought her a lavish villa at Portofino overlooking the exquisite blue, horseshoe bay, but he knew that it would have made no difference if it had been a tiny apartment in the old Plaka section of Athens.

Demiris had met many women in his life who had tried to use their sex to manipulate him in one way or another. Noelle never asked anything of him. Some women had come to him to bask in his reflected glory, but in Noelle's case *she* was the one who attracted the newspapermen and photographers. She was a star in her own right. For a while Demiris toyed with the idea that perhaps she was in love with him for himself, but he was too honest to maintain the delusion.

In the beginning it was a challenge to try to reach the deep core inside Noelle, to subjugate it and make it his. At first Demiris had tried to do it sexually, but for the first time in his life, he had met a woman who was more than a match for him. Her sensual appetites exceeded his. Anything he could do, she could do better and more often and with more skill, until finally he learned to relax in bed and enjoy her as he had never enjoyed another woman in his life. She was a phenomenon, constantly revealing new facets for him to enjoy. Noelle could cook as well as any of the chefs to whom he paid a king's ransom and knew as much about art as the curators he kept on yearly retainers to seek out paintings and sculpture for him. He enjoyed listening to them discussing art with Noelle and their amazement at the depth of her knowledge.

Demiris had recently purchased a Rembrandt, and Noelle happened to be at his summer island when the painting arrived. There was a young curator there who had found the painting for him.

"It's one of the Master's greatest," the curator had said as he unveiled it.

It was an exquisite painting of a mother and daughter. Noelle was seated in a chair, sipping an ouzo, quietly watching.

"It's a beauty," Demiris agreed. He turned to Noelle. "How do you like it?"

"It's lovely," she said. She turned to the curator. "Where did you find it?"

"I traced it to a private dealer in Brussels," he replied proudly, "and persuaded him to sell it to me."

"How much did you pay for it?" Noelle asked.

"Two hundred and fifty thousand pounds."

"It's a bargain," Demiris declared.

Noelle picked up a cigarette, and the young man rushed to light it for her. "Thank you," she said. She looked at Demiris. "It would have been more of a bargain, Costa, if he had bought it from the man who owned it."

"I don't understand," Demiris said.

The curator was looking at her oddly.

"If this is genuine," Noelle explained, "then it came from the estate of the Duke of Toledo in Spain." She turned to the curator. "Is that not so?" she asked.

His face had turned white. "I—I have no idea," he stammered. "The dealer didn't tell me."

"Oh, come now," Noelle chided him. "You mean you bought a painting for this amount of money without establishing its provenance? That's difficult to believe. The estate priced the painting at one hundred and seventy-five thousand pounds. Someone's been cheated out of seventy-five thousand pounds."

And it had proven to be true. The curator and the art dealer were convicted of collusion and sent to prison. Demiris returned the painting. In thinking it over later he decided that he was less impressed by Noelle's knowledge than by her honesty. If she had wished to, she could simply have called the curator aside, threatened to blackmail him and split the money with him. Instead she had challenged him openly in front of Demiris with no ulterior motive. He had bought her a very expensive emerald necklace in appreciation, and she had accepted it with the same casual appreciation with which she would have accepted a cigarette lighter. Demiris insisted on taking Noelle with him everywhere. He trusted no one in business and therefore was forced to make all his decisions by himself. He found it helpful to discuss business deals with Noelle. She was amazingly knowledgeable about business, and the mere fact of being able to talk with someone sometimes made it easier for Demiris to make a decision. In time Noelle knew more about his business affairs than anyone with the possible exception of his lawyers and accountants. In the past Demiris had always had several mistresses at a time, but now Noelle gave him everything he needed, and one by one he dropped them. They accepted the *congé* without bitterness, for Demiris was a generous man.

He owned a yacht that was a hundred and thirty-five feet long, with four G.M. diesels. It carried a seaplane, a crew of twenty-four, two speed boats and had a freshwater swimming pool. There were twelve beautifully appointed guest suites and a large apartment for himself, crammed with paintings and antiques.

When Demiris entertained on his yacht, it was Noelle who was his hostess. When Demiris flew or sailed to his private island, it was Noelle he took with him while Melina remained at home. He was careful never to bring his wife and Noelle together, but he knew of course that his wife was aware of her.

Noelle was treated like royalty wherever she went. But then it was only her due. The little girl who had looked out at her fleet of ships through the dirty apartment window in Marseille had moved on to the largest fleet in the world. Noelle was not impressed by Demiris' wealth or his reputation: She was impressed by his intelligence and strength. He had the mind and will of a giant and he made other men seem pusillanimous in comparison. She sensed the implacable cruelty in him, but somehow this made him even more exciting, for it was in her also.

Noelle constantly received offers to star in plays and in motion pictures, but she was indifferent. She was playing the lead in her own life story, and it was more fascinating than anything any scriptwriter could concoct. She dined with kings and prime ministers and ambassadors, and they all catered to her because they knew that she had the ear of Demiris. They would drop subtle hints about what their needs were and they promised her the world if she would help them.

But Noelle already had the world. She would lie in bed with Demiris and tell him what each man had asked for, and out of this information Demiris would gauge their needs and their strengths and their weaknesses. Then he would put on appropriate pressures, and from this more money would pour into his already overflowing coffers.

DEMIRIS' PRIVATE ISLAND was one of his great joys. He had purchased an island that was raw land and had transformed it into a paradise. It had a spectacular hilltop villa in which he lived, a dozen charming guest cottages, a hunting preserve, an artificial freshwater lake, a zoo, a harbor where his yacht could anchor and a landing field for his planes. The island was staffed by eighty servants, and armed guards kept out intruders. Noelle liked the solitude of the island, and she enjoyed it most when there were no other guests there. Constantin Demiris was flattered, assuming that it was because Noelle preferred to be alone with him. He would have been astonished if he had known how preoccupied she was with a man of whose existence he was not even aware.

LARRY DOUGLAS WAS half a world away from Noelle, fighting secret battles on secret islands, and yet she knew more about him than his wife, with whom he corresponded fairly regularly. Noelle traveled to Paris to see Christian Barbet at least once a month and the bald, myopic little detective always had an up-to-date report ready for her.

The first time Noelle had returned to France to see Barbet and had tried to leave, there had been trouble about her exit visa. She had been kept waiting in a Customs office for five hours and had finally been allowed to place a call to Constantin Demiris. Ten minutes after she had spoken to Demiris, a German officer had rushed in to offer the profuse apologies of his government. Noelle had been issued a special visa, and she had never been stopped again.

The little detective looked forward to Noelle's visits. He was charging her a fortune, but his trained nose smelled even bigger money. He was very pleased with her new liaison with Constantin Demiris. He had a feeling that in one way or another it was going to be of great financial benefit to him. First he had to make sure that Demiris knew nothing of his mistress' interest in Larry Douglas, then he had to find out how much the information would be worth to Demiris. Or to Noelle Page for him to keep quiet. He was on the verge of an enormous coup, but he had to play his cards carefully. The information Barbet was able to gather on Larry was surprisingly substantial, for Barbet could afford to pay his sources well.

While Larry's wife was reading a letter postmarked from an anonymous APO, Christian Barbet was reporting to Noelle, "He's flying with the Fourteenth Fighter Group, Forty-eighth Fighter Squadron."

Catherine's letter read ". . . all I can tell you is that I'm somewhere in the Pacific, baby . . ."

And Christian Barbet was telling Noelle, "They're on Tarawa. Guam's next."

". . . I really miss you, Cathy. Things are picking up here. I can't give you any details, but we finally have planes that are better than the Jap Zeros . . ."

"Your friend is flying P-Thirty-eights, P-Forties and P-Fifty-ones."

". . . I'm glad you've been keeping busy in Washington. Just stay true to me, baby. Everything's fine here. I'll have a little news for you when I see you . . ."

"Your friend has been awarded the D.F.C. and has been promoted to Lieutenant-Colonel."

While Catherine thought about her husband and prayed for him to come home safely, Noelle followed Larry's every move and she too prayed for Larry's safe return. The war would be over soon and Larry Douglas would be coming home. To both of them.

II

CATHERINE

WASHINGTON: 1945–1946

On the morning of May 7, 1945, at Rheims, France, Germany surrendered unconditionally to the Allies. The thousand-year reign of the Third Reich had come to an end. Those insiders who knew of the crippling devastation at Pearl Harbor, those who had watched Dunkirk narrowly miss going into history as England's Waterloo, those who had commanded the RAF and knew how helpless London's defenses would have been against an all-out attack by the Luftwaffe: All these people were aware of the series of miracles that had brought victory to the Allies—and knew by what a narrow margin it had missed going the other way. The powers of evil had almost emerged triumphant, and the idea was so preposterous, so contrary to the Christian ethic of Right triumphing and Evil succumbing, that they turned away from it in horror, thanking God and burying their blunders from the eyes of posterity in mountains of files marked *TOP SECRET.*

The attention of the free world turned now to the Far East. The Japanese, those short, nearsighted comic figures, were bloodily defending every inch of land they held, and it looked as though it was going to be a long and costly war.

And then on August 6, an atomic bomb was dropped on Hiroshima. The destruction was beyond belief. In a few short minutes, most of the population of a major city lay dead, victims of a pestilence greater than the combined wars and plagues of all the Middle Ages.

On August 9, three days later, a second atomic bomb was dropped, this time on Nagasaki. The results were even more devastating. Civilization had finally reached its finest hour; it was able to achieve genocide that could be calculated at the rate of x number of millions of persons per second. It was too much for the Japanese, and on September 2, 1945, on the battleship *Missouri,* General Douglas MacArthur received the unconditional surrender of the Japanese Government. World War II was ended.

For one long moment when the news was flashed, the world held its breath and then let out a grateful heartfelt cheer. Cities and hamlets around the globe were filled with hysterical parades of people celebrating the end of the war to end all wars to end all wars to end all wars . . .

The following day, through some magic that he would never explain to Catherine, Bill Fraser was able to get a telephone call through to Larry Douglas on an island somewhere in the South Pacific. It was to be a surprise for Catherine. Fraser asked her to wait in her office for him so that they could go to lunch together. At 2:30 in the afternoon, she buzzed Bill on the intercom system.

"When are you going to feed me?" she demanded. "It'll be time for dinner soon."

"Sit tight," Fraser replied. "I'll be with you in a minute."

Five minutes later, he buzzed her and said, "There's a call for you on line one."

Catherine picked up the phone. "Hello?" She heard a crackling and a swell of sound like the waves of a distant ocean. "Hello," she repeated.

A male voice said, "Mrs. Larry Douglas?"

"Yes," Catherine said, puzzled. "Who's this?"

"Just a moment, please."

Through the receiver, she heard a high-pitched whine. Another crackling sound and then a voice saying "Cathy?"

She sat there, her heart pounding, unable to speak. "Larry? Larry?"

"Yes, baby."

"Oh, Larry!" She began to cry and unexpectedly her whole body was trembling.

"How are you, honey?"

She dug her fingernails into her arm, trying to hurt herself enough so that she could stop the hysteria that had suddenly swept over her. "I'm f-fine," she said. "W-where are you?"

"If I tell you, we'll be cut off," he said. "I'm somewhere in the Pacific."

"That's close enough!" She began to get control of her voice. "Are you all right, darling?"

"I'm fine."

"When will you be coming home?"

"Any second," he promised.

Catherine's eyes flooded with tears again. "OK, let's sy-synchronize our watches."

"Are you crying?"

"Of course I'm crying, you idiot! I'm just glad you can't see the mascara running down my face. Oh Larry . . . Larry . . ."

"I've missed you, baby," he said.

Catherine thought of the long, lonely nights that had stretched into weeks and months and years without him, without his arms around her, without his strong, wonderful body next to her, without his comfort and protection and love. And she said, "I've missed you, too."

A man's voice came on the line. "I'm sorry, Colonel, but we're going to have to disconnect."

Colonel!

"You didn't tell me you were promoted."

"I was afraid it would go to your head."

"Oh, darling, I—"

The roar of the ocean grew louder, and suddenly there was a silence and the line was dead. Catherine sat at her desk staring at the telephone. And then she buried her head in her arms and began to cry.

Ten minutes later, Fraser's voice came over the intercom. "I'm ready for lunch when you are, Cathy," he said.

"I'm ready for anything now," she said joyfully. "Give me five minutes." She smiled warmly as she thought of what Fraser had done and how much trouble it must have cost him. He was the dearest man she had ever known. Next to Larry, of course.

CATHERINE HAD VISUALIZED Larry's arrival so often that the arrival itself was almost an anticlimax. Bill Fraser had explained to her that Larry was probably coming home in an Air Transport Command plane or a MATS plane and they didn't run at fixed times like commercial scheduled airlines. You conned a ride on the first flight you could get on—and it didn't matter too much where the plane was headed—just so it was flying in the right general direction.

Catherine stayed home all day waiting for Larry. She tried to read, but she was too nervous. She sat and listened to the news and thought about Larry returning home to her, this time forever. By midnight, he had still not arrived. She decided he probably would not be home until the next day. At two in the morning, when Catherine could keep her eyes open no longer, she went to bed.

She was awakened by a hand on her arm and she opened her eyes and he was standing over her, her Larry was standing there, looking down at her, a grin on his lean, tanned face, and in a flash Catherine was in his arms and all the worry and loneliness and pain of the past four years were washed away in a cleansing flood of joy that seemed to fill every fiber of her being. She hugged him until she was afraid that she was going to break his bones. She wanted to stay like this forever, never letting him go.

"Easy, honey," Larry said finally. He pulled away from her, a smile on his face. "It's going to look funny in the newspapers. 'Flyer comes home safely from the war and gets hugged to death by his wife.'"

Catherine turned on the lights, every one of them, flooding the room so that she could see him, study him, devour him. His face had a new maturity. There were lines around his eyes and mouth that had not been there before. The overall effect was to make him handsomer than ever.

"I wanted to meet you," Catherine babbled, "but I didn't know where. I called the Air Corps and they couldn't give me any information at all, so I just waited here and . . ."

Larry moved toward her and shut her up with a kiss. His kiss was hard and demanding. Catherine had expected to feel the same physical eagerness for him and she was surprised to find that this was not so. She loved him very much and yet she would have been content to just sit with him and talk, instead of making love as he so urgently wanted to do. She had sublimated her sexual feelings for so long that they were deeply buried, and it would take time before they could be aroused and brought to the surface again.

But Larry was giving her no time. He was throwing off his clothes and saying, "God, Cathy, you don't know how I've dreamed about this moment. I was going crazy out there. And look at you. You're even more beautiful than I remembered."

He ripped off his shorts and was standing there naked. And somehow it was a stranger pushing her down on the bed, and she wished that Larry would give her time to get used to his being home, to get used to his nakedness again. But he was getting on top of her without any preliminaries, forcing himself into her and she knew that she was not ready for him. He was tearing into her, hurting her and she bit her hand to keep from crying out as he lay on top of her, making love like a wild animal.

Her husband was home.

FOR THE NEXT month with Fraser's blessing Catherine stayed away from the office and she and Larry spent almost every moment together. She cooked for him all of his favorite dishes, and they listened to records and talked and talked, trying to fill in the gaps of the lost years between them. At night they went to parties or to the theater and when they returned home, they made love. Her body was ready for him now and she found him as exciting a lover as always. Almost.

She did not want to admit it even to herself, but there was something indefinably changed about Larry. He was more demanding, less giving. There was still foreplay before they made love, but he did it mechanically, as though it were a duty to be disposed of before he went on to the sexual attack. And it was an attack, a savage and fierce taking, as though his body were seeking vengeance for something, meting out punishment. Each time they finished making love, Catherine felt bruised and battered, as though she had taken a beating. Perhaps, she defended him, it's just because he's been so long without a woman.

As the days passed, his lovemaking remained the same and it was that fact that finally led Catherine to look for other changes in Larry. She tried to study him dispassionately, tried to forget that this was the husband whom she adored. She saw a tall, well-built, black-haired man with deep dark eyes and a devastatingly beautiful face. Or perhaps "beautiful" no longer applied. The lines around his mouth had added a harshness to his features. Looking at this stranger, Catherine would have thought, *Here is a man who could be selfish and ruthless and cold.* And yet she told herself that she was being ridiculous. This was her Larry, loving and kind and thoughtful.

She proudly introduced him to all her friends and the people she worked with, but they seemed to bore him. At parties he would wander off into a corner and spend the evening drinking. It seemed to Catherine that he made no effort to be sociable. "Why should I?" he snapped at her one evening when she tried to discuss it with him. "Where the fuck were all those fat cats when I was up there getting my ass shot at?"

A few times Catherine broached the subject of what Larry was going to do with his future. She had thought that he would want to remain in the Air Corps, but almost the first thing Larry did when he returned home was to resign his commission.

"The Service is for suckers. There's nowhere to go but down," he had said.

It was almost like a parody of the first conversation Catherine had had with him in Hollywood. Only then, he had been joking.

Catherine had to discuss the problem with someone and she finally decided to talk to Bill Fraser. She told him what was troubling her, leaving out the more personal things.

"If it's any consolation to you," Fraser said sympathetically, "there are millions of women all over the world going through what you're going through now. It's really very simple, Catherine. You're married to a stranger."

Catherine looked at him, saying nothing.

Fraser stopped to fill his pipe and light it. "You can't really expect to pick up where you left off when Larry went away four years ago, can you? That place in time doesn't exist any more. You've moved past it, and so has Larry. Part of what makes a marriage work is that a husband and wife have common experiences. They grow together and their marriage grows. You're going to have to find a common meeting ground again."

"I feel disloyal even discussing it, Bill."

Fraser smiled. "I knew you first," he reminded her. "Remember?"

"I remember."

"I'm sure that Larry's feeling his way, too," Fraser continued. "He's been living with a thousand men for four years and now he has to get used to living with a girl."

She smiled. "You're right about everything you said. I suppose I just had to hear someone say it."

"Everyone's full of helpful advice about how to handle the wounded," Fraser remarked, "but there are some wounds that don't show. Sometimes they go deep." He saw the look on Catherine's face. "I don't mean anything serious," he added quickly. "I'm just talking about the horrors that any combat soldier sees. Unless a man is a complete fool, it's bound to have an enormous effect on his outlook. You see what I mean?"

Catherine nodded. "Yes." The question was: What effect had it had?

WHEN CATHERINE FINALLY went back to work, the men at the agency were overjoyed to see her. For the first three days she did almost nothing but go over campaigns and layouts for new accounts and catch up on old accounts. She worked from early in the morning until late in the evening, trying to make up for the time she had lost, badgering copywriters and sketch artists and reassuring nervous clients. She was very good at her job and she loved it.

Larry would be waiting for Catherine when she returned to the apartment at night. In the beginning she had asked what he did while she was gone, but his answers were always vague and she finally stopped asking him. He had put up a wall, and she did not know how to breach it. He took offense at almost everything Catherine said, and there were constant quarrels over nothing. Occasionally they would dine with Fraser and she went out of her way to make those evenings pleasant and gay so that Fraser would not think there was anything wrong.

But Catherine had to face the fact that something was very wrong.

She felt that it was partly her failure. She still loved Larry. She loved the look of him and the feel of him and the memory of him, but she knew that if he went on this way, it would destroy them both.

SHE WAS HAVING lunch with William Fraser.

"How's Larry?" he asked.

The automatic Pavlovian response of "fine" started to come to her lips and she stopped. "He needs a job," Catherine said bluntly.

Fraser leaned back and nodded. "Is he getting restless about not working?"

She hesitated, not wanting to lie. "He doesn't want to do just anything," she said carefully. "It would have to be the right thing."

Fraser studied her, trying to assess the meaning that lay behind her words.

"How would he like to be a pilot?"

"He doesn't want to go back into the Service again."

"I was thinking about one of the airlines. I have a friend who runs Pan Am. They'd be lucky to get someone with Larry's experience."

Catherine sat there thinking about it, trying to put herself in Larry's mind. He loved flying more than anything in the world. It would be a good job, doing what he loved to do. "It—it sounds wonderful," she said cautiously. "Do you really think you could get it for him, Bill?"

"I'll give it a try," he said. "Why don't you sound Larry out first and see how he feels about it?"

"I will." Catherine took his hand in hers gratefully. "Thanks so much."

"For what?" Fraser asked lightly.

"For always being there when I need you."

He put his hand over hers. "It goes with the territory."

When Catherine told Larry about Bill Fraser's suggestion that night, he said, "That's the best idea I've heard since I came home," and two days later, he had an appointment to see Carl Eastman at Pan Am headquarters in Manhattan. Catherine pressed Larry's suit for him, selected a shirt and tie and shined his shoes until she could see her image in them. "I'll call you as soon as I can and let you know how it went." He kissed her, smiled that quick boyish grin of his and left.

In many ways Larry *was* like a small boy, Catherine thought. He could be petulant and quick-tempered and surly, but he was also loving and generous.

"My luck," sighed Catherine. "I have to be the only perfect person in the whole universe."

She had a busy schedule ahead of her, but she was unable to think of anything but Larry and his meeting. It was more than just a job. She had a feeling that her whole marriage hinged on what was going to happen.

It was going to be the longest day of her life.

PAN AMERICAN HEADQUARTERS was in a modern building at Fifth Avenue and Fifty-third Street. Carl Eastman's office was large and comfortably furnished, and he obviously held a position of importance.

"Come in and sit down," he greeted Larry as Larry entered the office.

Eastman was about thirty-five, a trim, lantern-jawed man with piercing hazel eyes that missed nothing. He motioned Larry to a couch, then sat on a chair across from him.

"Coffee?"

"No thanks," Larry said.

"I understand you'd like to work for us."

"If there's an opening."

"There's an opening," Eastman said, "only a thousand stick jockeys have applied for it." He shook his head ruefully. "It's incredible. The Air Corps trains thousands of bright young men to fly the most complicated pieces of machinery ever made. Then when they do their job and do it damn well, the Air Corps tells 'em to get lost. They have nothing for them." He sighed. "You wouldn't believe the people who come in here all day long. Top pilots, aces like yourself. There's only one job open for every thousand applicants—and all the other airlines are in exactly the same position."

A feeling of disappointment swept over Larry. "Why did you see me?" he asked stiffly.

"Two reasons. Number One, because the man upstairs told me to."

Larry felt an anger rising in him.

"I don't need—"

Eastman leaned forward. "Number Two, you have a damn good flying record."

"Thanks," Larry said, tightly.

Eastman studied him. "You'd have to go through a training program here, you know. It would be like going back to school."

Larry hesitated, not certain where the conversation was leading.

"That sounds all right," he said, cautiously.

"You'll have to take your training in New York out of LaGuardia."

Larry nodded, waiting.

"There are four weeks of ground school and then a month of flight training."

"You flying DC-Fours?" asked Larry.

"Right. When you finish your training, we'll put you on as a navigator. Your training base pay will be three fifty a month."

He had the job! The son-of-a-bitch had needled him about all the thousands of pilots who were after it. But he had the job! What had he been worried about? No one in the whole damned Air Corps had a better record than he did.

Larry grinned. "I don't mind starting as a navigator, Eastman, but I'm a pilot. When does *that* happen?"

Eastman sighed. "The airlines are unionized. The only way anyone moves up is through seniority. There are a lot of men ahead of you. Do you want to give it a try?"

Larry nodded. "What have I got to lose?"

"Right," Eastman said. "I'll arrange all the formalities. You'll have to take a physical, of course. Any problems there?"

Larry grinned. "The Japanese didn't find anything wrong with me."

"How soon can you go to work?"

"Is this afternoon too early?"

"Let's make it Monday." Eastman scribbled a name on a card and handed it to Larry. "Here. They'll be expecting you at nine o'clock Monday morning."

When Larry phoned Catherine to tell her the news, there was an excitement in his voice that Catherine had not heard for a long time. She knew then that everything was going to be all right.

12

NOELLE

ATHENS: 1946

Constantin Demiris owned a fleet of airplanes for his personal use, but his pride was a converted Hawker Siddeley that transported sixteen passengers in luxurious comfort, had a speed of three hundred miles per hour and carried a crew of four. It was a flying palace. The interior had been decorated by Frederick Sawrin and Chagall had done the murals on the walls. Instead of airplane seats, easy chairs and comfortable couches were sprinkled throughout the cabin. The aft compartment had been converted into a luxurious bedroom. Forward behind the cockpit was a modern kitchen. Whenever Demiris or Noelle flew on the plane, there was a chef aboard.

Demiris had chosen as his personal pilots a Greek flyer named Paul Metaxas and an English ex–RAF fighter pilot named Ian Whitestone. Metaxas was a stocky, amiable man with a perpetual smile on his face and a hearty, contagious laugh. He had been a mechanic, had taught himself how to fly and had served with the RAF in the Battle of Britain, where he had met Ian Whitestone. Whitestone was tall, red-haired and painfully thin, with the diffident manner of a schoolmaster on his first day of the term at a second-rate school for incorrigible boys. In the air Whitestone was something else again. He had the rare, natural skill of a born pilot, a feel that can never be taught or learned. Whitestone and Metaxas had flown together for three years against the Luftwaffe and each had a high regard for the other.

Noelle made frequent trips in the large plane, sometimes on business with Demiris, sometimes for pleasure. She had gotten to know the pilots but had paid no particular attention to them.

And then one day she overheard them reminiscing about an experience they had had in the RAF.

From that moment on Noelle either spent some part of each flight in the cockpit talking to the two men or invited one of them to join her back in the cabin. She encouraged them to talk about their war experiences and, without ever asking a direct question, eventually learned that Whitestone had been a liaison officer in Larry Douglas' squadron before Douglas had left the RAF and that Metaxas had joined the squadron too late to meet Larry. Noelle began to concentrate on the English pilot. Encouraged and flattered by the interest of his boss' mistress, Whitestone talked freely about his past life and his future ambitions. He told Noelle he had always been interested in electronics. His brother-in-law in Australia had opened a small electronics firm and wanted Whitestone to go in with him, but Whitestone lacked the capital.

"The way I live," he said to Noelle, grinning, "I'll never make it."

Noelle continued to visit Paris once a month to see Christian Barbet. Barbet had established a liaison with a private detective agency in Washington, and there was a constant stream of reports on Larry Douglas. Cautiously testing Noelle, the little detective had offered to send the reports to her in Athens, but she told him that she preferred picking them up in person. Barbet had nodded his head slyly and said in a conspiratorial tone, "I understand, Miss Page." So she did *not* want Constantin Demiris to know about her interest in Larry Douglas. The possibilities for blackmail staggered Barbet's mind.

"You have been most helpful, Monsieur Barbet," Noelle said, "and most discreet."

He smiled unctuously. "Thank you, Miss Page. My business depends on discretion."

"Exactly," Noelle replied, "I know you are discreet because Constantin Demiris has never mentioned your name to me. The day he does, I will ask him to destroy you." Her tone was pleasant and conversational, but the effect was like a bomb shell.

Monsieur Barbet stared at Noelle for a long, shocked moment, licking his lips. He scratched his crotch nervously and stammered, "I—I assure you, Mademoiselle, that I would n-never . . ."

"I'm sure you won't," Noelle said and departed.

ON THE COMMERCIAL plane taking her back to Greece, Noelle read the confidential report in the sealed manila envelope.

ACME SECURITY AGENCY
1402 "D" Street
Washington, D.C.

Reference: #2-179-210   February 2, 1946

Dear Monsieur Barbet:

One of our operatives spoke to a contact in the personnel office at Pan Am: Subject is regarded as a skilled combat pilot, but they question whether he is disciplined enough to work out satisfactorily within a large, structured organization.

Subject's personal life-style follows the same pattern as in our previous reports. We have followed him to the apartments of various women whom he had picked up, where he remained for periods of from one hour to as long as five hours, and we presume that he is having a series of casual sexual relations with these women. (Names and addresses are on file if you wish them.)

In view of the Subject's new employment, it is possible that this pattern may change. We will follow up on this per your request.

Please find our bill enclosed.

Very truly yours,
R. Ruttenberg,
Managing Supervisor

Noelle returned the report to the folder and leaned back in her seat and closed her eyes. She visualized Larry, restless and tormented, married to a woman he did not love, caught in a trap baited with his own weaknesses.

His new job with the airline might slow Noelle's plan down a bit, but she had patience. In time she would bring Larry to her. Meanwhile there were certain steps she could take to move things along.

IAN WHITESTONE WAS delighted to be invited to lunch with Noelle Page. In the beginning he had flattered himself that she was attracted to him, but all of their encounters had been on a pleasant but formal basis that let him know that he was an employee, and she was an untouchable. He had often puzzled over what Noelle wanted of him, for Whitestone was an intelligent man, and he had the odd feeling that their random conversations meant something more to her than they meant to him.

On this particular day Whitestone and Noelle drove to a small seaside town near Cape Sunion, where they were having lunch. Noelle was dressed in a white summer frock and sandals, with her soft blond hair blowing free, and she had never looked more beautiful. Ian Whitestone was engaged to a model in London and while she was pretty, she could not compare to Noelle. Whitestone had never met anyone who could, and he would have envied Constantin Demiris except that Noelle always seemed more desirable to him in retrospect. When Whitestone was actually with her, he found himself slightly intimidated. Now Noelle had turned the conversation to his plans for the future, and he wondered, not for the first time, whether she was probing on Demiris' orders to find out whether he was loyal to his employer.

"I love my job," the pilot assured Noelle earnestly. "I'd like to keep it until I'm too old to see where I'm flying."

Noelle studied him a moment, aware of his suspicions. "I'm disappointed," she said ruefully. "I was hoping that you had more ambition than that."

Whitestone stared at her. "I don't understand."

"Didn't you tell me that you'd like to have your own electronics company one day?"

He recalled mentioning it to her casually, and it surprised him that she had remembered.

"That was just a pipe dream," he replied. "It would take a lot of money."

"A man with your ability," Noelle said, "shouldn't be stopped by a lack of money."

Whitestone sat there uneasily, not knowing what Noelle Page expected him to say. He did like his job. He was making more money than he had ever made in his life, the hours were good and the work was interesting. On the other hand he was at the beck and call of an eccentric billionaire who expected him to be available at any hour of the day or night. It had raised hell with his personal life, and his fiancée was not happy about what he was doing, good salary or no.

"I've been talking to a friend of mine about you," Noelle said. "He likes to invest in new companies."

Her voice had controlled enthusiasm, as though she were excited about what she was saying and yet was being careful not to push him too hard. Whitestone raised his eyes and met hers.

"He's very interested in you," she said.

Whitestone swallowed. "I—I don't know what to say, Miss Page."

"I don't expect you to say anything now," Noelle assured him. "I just want you to think about it."

He sat there a moment, thinking about it. "Does Mr. Demiris know about this?" he asked finally.

Noelle smiled conspiratorially. "I'm afraid Mr. Demiris would never approve. He doesn't like to lose employees, especially good ones. However—" she paused fractionally, "I think someone like you is entitled to get everything out of life that he can. Unless of course," she added, "you want to go on working for someone else the rest of your life."

"I don't," Whitestone said quickly and suddenly realized that he had committed himself. He studied Noelle's face to see if there was any suggestion that this could be some kind of a trap, but all he saw was a sympathetic understanding. "Any man worth his salt would like to have his own business," he said defensively.

"Of course," Noelle agreed. "Give it some thought, and we'll talk about it again." And then she added warningly, "It will be just between us."

"Fair enough," Whitestone said, "and thank you. If it works out, it will really be exciting."

Noelle nodded. "I have a feeling that it's going to work out."

13

CATHERINE

WASHINGTON—PARIS: 1946

At nine o'clock on Monday morning Larry Douglas reported to the chief pilot, Captain Hal Sakowitz, at the Pan American office at LaGuardia Airport in New York. As Larry walked in the door, Sakowitz picked up the transcript of Larry's service record that he had been studying and shoved it into a desk drawer.

Captain Sakowitz was a compact, rugged-looking man with a seamed, weather-beaten face and the largest hands that Larry had ever seen. Sakowitz was one of the real veterans of aviation. He had started out in the days of traveling air circuses, had flown single-engine airmail planes for the Government and had been an airline pilot for twenty years and Pan American's chief pilot for the past five years.

"Glad to have you with us, Douglas," he said.

"Glad to be here," Larry replied.

"Eager to get into a plane again?"

"Who needs a plane?" Larry grinned. "Just point me into the wind, and I'll take off."

Sakowitz indicated a chair. "Sit down. I like to get acquainted with you boys who come in here to take over my job."

Larry laughed. "You noticed."

"Oh, I don't blame any of you. You're all hotshot pilots, you have great combat records, you come in here and think 'if that schmuck Sakowitz can be Chief Pilot, they oughta make me Chairman of the Board.' None of you guys plan to stay navigators very long. It's just a stepping stone to pilot. Well, that's fine. That's the way it should be."

"I'm glad you feel that way," Larry said.

"But there's one thing you have to know out front. We all belong to a union, Douglas, and promotions are strictly by seniority."

"I understand."

"The only thing you might *not* understand is that these are damn good jobs and there are more people coming in than there are leaving. That slows up the rate of promotion."

"I'll take my chances," Larry replied.

Sakowitz's secretary brought in coffee and Danish pastries and the two men spent the next hour talking and getting acquainted. Sakowitz's manner was friendly and affable, and many of his questions were seemingly irrelevant and trivial, but when Larry left to go to his first class, Sakowitz knew a great deal about Larry Douglas. A few minutes after Larry had departed, Carl Eastman came into the office.

"How did it go?" Eastman asked.

"OK."

Eastman gave him a hard look. "What do you think, Sak?"

"We'll try him."

"I asked you what you thought."

Sakowitz shrugged. "OK. I'll tell you. My hunch is he's a goddamn good pilot. He has to be, with his war record. Put him in a plane with a bunch of enemy fighters shooting at him, and I don't think you'll find anyone better." He hesitated.

"Go on," Eastman said.

"The thing is, there aren't a hell of a lot of enemy fighters around Manhattan. I've known guys like Douglas. For some reason I've never figured out, their lives are geared for danger. They do crazy things like climbing impossible mountains or diving to the bottom of the ocean, or whatever the hell else danger they can find. When a war breaks out, they rise to the top like cream in a cup of scalding coffee." He swerved his chair around and looked out the window. Eastman stood there, saying nothing, waiting.

"I have a hunch about Douglas, Carl. There's something wrong with him. Maybe if he were captain of one of our ships, flying it himself, he could make it. But I don't think he's psychologically geared to take orders from an engineer, a first officer and a pilot, especially when he thinks he could outfly them all." He swung back to face Eastman. "And the funny part is, he probably could."

"You're making me nervous," Eastman said.

"Me, too," Sakowitz confessed. "I don't think he's—" He stopped, searching for the right word, "stable. Talking to him, you get a feeling he has a stick of dynamite up his ass, ready to explode."

"What do you want to do?"

"We're doing it. He'll go to school and we'll keep a close eye on him."

"Maybe he'll wash out," Eastman said.

"You don't know that breed of cat. He'll come out number one man in his class."

Sakowitz's prediction was accurate.

The training course consisted of four weeks of ground school followed by an additional month of flight training. Since the trainees were already experienced pilots with many years of flying behind them, the course was devised to serve two purposes: the first was to run through such subjects as navigation, radio, communication, map reading and instrument flying to refresh the memories of the men and pinpoint their potential weaknesses, and the second was to familiarize them with the new equipment they would be using.

The instrument flying was done in a Link Trainer, a small mock-up of an airplane cockpit that rested on a movable base, enabling the pilot in the cockpit to put the plane through any maneuver, including stalls, loops, spins and rolls. A black hood was put over the top of the cockpit so that the pilot was flying blind, using only the instruments in front of him. The instructor outside the Trainer fed orders to the pilot, giving him directions for takeoffs and landings in the face of strong wind velocity, storms, mountain ranges and every other simulated hazard conceivable. Most inexperienced pilots went into the Link Trainer with a feeling of confidence, but they soon learned that the little Trainers were much more difficult to operate than they appeared to be. It was an eerie sensation to be alone in the tiny cockpit, all senses cut off from the outside world.

Larry was a gifted pupil. He was attentive in class and absorbed everything he was taught. He did all his homework and did it well and carefully. He showed no sign of impatience, restlessness or boredom. On the contrary, he was the most eager pupil in the course and certainly the most outstanding. The only area that was new to Larry was the equipment, the DC-4. The Douglas planes were long, sleek aircraft with some equipment that had not been in existence when the war began. Larry spent hours going over every inch of the plane, studying the way it had been put together and the way it functioned. Evenings he pored over the dozens of service manuals of the plane.

Late one night after all the other trainees had left the hangar Sakowitz had come upon Larry in one of the DC-4s, lying on his back under the cockpit, examining the wiring.

"I tell you, the son-of-a-bitch is gunning for my job," Sakowitz told Carl Eastman the next morning.

"The way he's going, he may get it." Eastman grinned.

At the end of the eight weeks there was a little graduation ceremony. Catherine proudly flew to New York to be there when they presented Larry with his navigator's wings.

He tried to make light of it. "Cathy, it's just a stupid little piece of cloth they give you so you'll remember what your job is when you get into the cockpit."

"Oh, no, you don't," she said. "I talked to Captain Sakowitz and he told me how good you are."

"What does a dumb Polack know?" Larry said. "Let's go celebrate."

That night Catherine and Larry and four of Larry's classmates and their wives went to the Twenty-one Club on East Fifty-second Street for dinner. The foyer was crowded, and the maître d' told them that without reservations there were no tables available.

"To hell with this place," Larry said. "Let's go next door to Toots Shor's."

"Wait a minute," Catherine said. She went over to the captain and asked to see Jerry Berns.

A few moments later a short, thin man with inquisitive gray eyes bustled up.

"I'm Jerry Berns," he said. "May I help you?"

"My husband and I are with some friends," Catherine explained. "There are ten of us."

He started to shake his head. "Unless you have a reservation . . ."

"I'm William Fraser's partner," Catherine said.

Jerry Berns looked at Catherine reproachfully. "Why didn't you tell me? Can you give me fifteen minutes?"

"Thank you," Catherine said gratefully.

She went back to where the group was standing.

"Surprise!" Catherine said. "We have a table."

"How did you manage that?" Larry asked.

"It was easy," Catherine said. "I mentioned Bill Fraser's name." She saw the look that came into Larry's eyes. "He comes in here often," Catherine went on quickly. "And he told me if I ever came in and needed a table, to mention his name."

Larry turned to the others. "Let's get the hell out of here. This is for the birds."

The group started toward the door. Larry turned to Catherine. "Coming?"

"Of course," Catherine said hesitantly, "I just wanted to tell them that we're not . . ."

"Fuck 'em," said Larry loudly. "Are you coming or aren't you?"

People were turning to stare. Catherine felt her face redden.

"Yes," she said. She turned and followed Larry out the door.

They went to an Italian restaurant on Sixth Avenue and had a bad dinner. Outwardly Catherine acted as though nothing had happened, but inwardly she was fuming. She was furious with Larry for his childish behavior and for humiliating her in public.

When they got home, she walked into the bedroom without saying a word, undressed, turned out the light and got into bed. She heard Larry in the living room, mixing a drink.

Ten minutes later he came into the bedroom and turned on the light and walked over to the bed. "You planning to become a martyr?" he asked.

She sat up, furious. "Don't try to put me on the defensive," she said. "Your behavior tonight was inexcusable. What got into you?"

"The same guy that got into you."

She stared at him. "What?"

"I'm talking about Mr. Perfection. Bill Fraser."

She looked at him, not understanding. "Bill's never done anything but help us."

"You bet your ass," he said. "You owe him your business. I owe him my job. Now we can't even sit down in a restaurant without Fraser's permission. Well, I'm sick of having him shoved down my throat every day." It was Larry's tone that shook Catherine even more than what he was saying. It was so filled with frustration and impotence that she realized for the first time how tormented he must be. And why not? He had come back from four years of fighting to find his wife in partnership with her former lover. And to make it worse, he himself had not even been able to get a job without the help of Fraser.

As she looked at Larry, Catherine knew that this was a turning point in their marriage. If she stayed with him, he would have to come first. Before her job, before everything. For the first time Catherine felt that she really understood Larry.

As though reading her mind Larry said contritely, "I'm sorry I acted like a shit-heel this evening. But when we couldn't get a table until you mentioned Fraser's magic name, I—I'd suddenly had it up to *here*."

"I'm sorry, Larry," Catherine said, "I'll never do that to you again."

And they were in each other's arms, and Larry said, "Please don't ever leave me, Cathy," and Catherine thought of how close she had come to it, and she held him tighter and said, "I won't leave you, darling, ever."

LARRY'S FIRST ASSIGNMENT as a navigator was on Flight 147 from Washington to Paris. He stayed over in Paris for forty-eight hours after each flight, then returned home for three days before he flew out again.

One morning Larry called Catherine at her office, his voice excited. "Hey, I've got a great restaurant for us. Can you get away for lunch?"

Catherine looked at the pile of layouts that had to be finished and approved before noon. "Sure," she said, recklessly.

"I'll pick you up in fifteen minutes."

"You're not leaving me!" Lucia, her assistant, wailed. "Stuyvesant will have kittens if we don't get this campaign to him today."

"It will have to wait," Catherine said. "I'm going to have lunch with my husband."

Lucia shrugged. "I don't blame you. If you ever get tired of him, will you let me know?"

Catherine grinned. "You'll be too old."

Larry picked Catherine up in front of the office, and she got into the car.

"Did I screw up your day for you?" he asked mischievously.

"Of course not."

He laughed. "All those executive types are going to have a stroke."

Larry headed the car toward the airport.

"How far is the restaurant?" Catherine asked. She had five appointments in the afternoon, beginning at two o'clock.

"Not far . . . Do you have a busy afternoon?"

"No," she lied. "Nothing special."

"Good."

When they reached the airport turnoff, Larry swung the car into the entrance.

"Is the restaurant at the airport?"

"At the other end," Larry replied. He parked the car, took Catherine's arm and led her inside to the Pan-Am gate. The attractive girl behind the desk greeted Larry by name.

"This is my wife," Larry said proudly. "This is Amy Winston."

They exchanged hellos.

"Come on." Larry took Catherine's arm and they moved toward the departure ramp.

"Larry—" Catherine began. "Where . . . ?"

"Hey, you're the nosiest girl I've ever taken to lunch."

They had reached Gate 37. Two men behind the ticket counter were processing the tickets of emplaning passengers. A sign on the information board read: "Flight 147 to Paris—Departing 1:00 P.M."

Larry walked up to one of the men behind the desk. "Here she is, Tony." He handed the man a plane ticket. "Cathy, this is Tony Lombardi. This is Catherine."

"I've sure heard a lot about you," the man grinned. "Your ticket's all in order." He handed the ticket to Catherine.

Catherine stared at it, dazed. "What's this for?"

"I lied to you." Larry smiled. "I'm not taking you to lunch. I'm taking you to Paris. Maxim's."

Catherine's voice broke. "M-Maxim's? In Paris? *Now?*"

"That's right."

"I can't," Catherine wailed. "I can't go to Paris now."

"Sure you can." He grinned. "I've got your passport in my pocket."

"Larry," she said, "you're mad! I have no clothes. I have a million appointments. I—"

"I'll buy you some clothes in Paris. Cancel your appointments. Fraser can get along without you for a few days."

Catherine stared at him, not knowing what to say. She remembered the resolutions she had made to herself. Larry was her husband. He had to come first. Catherine realized that it wasn't just taking her to Paris that was important to Larry. He was showing off for her, asking her to fly in the plane he was navigating. And she had almost spoiled it. She put her hand in his and smiled up at him.

"What are we waiting for?" Catherine asked. "I'm starved!"

PARIS WAS A whirlwind of fun. Larry had arranged to take a full week off, and it seemed to Catherine that every hour of the day and night was crammed with things to do. They stayed at a charming little hotel on the Left Bank.

Their first morning in Paris Larry took Catherine to a salon on the Champs Élysées where he tried to buy out the entire store for her. She bought only the things she needed and was shocked at how expensive everything was.

"You know your problem?" Larry said. "You worry too much about money. You're on your honeymoon."

"Yes, sir," she said. But she refused to buy an evening dress that she did not need. When she tried to ask Larry where all the money was coming from, he did not want to discuss it, but she finally insisted on knowing.

"I got an advance on my salary," Larry told her. "What's the big deal?"

And Catherine had not the heart to tell him. He was like a child about money, generous and carefree, and that was part of his charm.

Just as it had been part of her father's charm.

Larry took her on the visitor's tour of Paris: to the Louvre, the Tuileries and Les Invalides to see Napoleon's Tomb. He took her to a colorful little restaurant near the Sorbonne. They went to Les Halles, the storied marketplace of Paris, and watched the fresh fruit and meat and vegetables brought in from the farms of France, and spent their last Sunday afternoon at Versailles, and then had dinner in the breathtaking garden at the Coq Hardi outside of Paris. It was a perfect second honeymoon.

HAL SAKOWITZ SAT in his office looking over the weekly personnel reports. In front of him was the report on Larry Douglas. Sakowitz was leaning back in his chair, studying it, pulling thoughtfully at his lower lip. Finally he leaned forward and pressed an intercom switch. "Send him in," he said.

A moment later, Larry walked in, wearing his Pan-Am uniform and carrying his flight bag. He flashed Sakowitz a smile. "Morning, Chief," he said.

"Sit down."

Larry slouched into a chair opposite the desk and lit a cigarette.

Sakowitz said, "I have a report here that last Monday in Paris you checked in for your flight briefing forty-five minutes late."

Larry's expression changed. "I was caught in a parade on the Champs Élysées. The plane took off on time. I didn't know we were running a boy's camp here."

"We're running an airline," Sakowitz said, quietly. "And we're running it by the book."

"OK," Larry said angrily. "I'll keep away from the Champs Élysées. Anything else?"

"Yes. Captain Swift thinks you'd had a drink or two before takeoff on the last couple of flights."

"He's a goddamned liar!" Larry snapped.

"Why would he lie?"

"Because he's afraid I'll take his job away." There was a sharp anger in Larry's voice. "The son-of-a-bitch is a timid old maid who should have been retired ten years ago."

"You've flown with four different captains," Sakowitz said. "Which ones did you like?"

"None of them," retorted Larry. He saw the trap too late. Quickly, he added, "I mean—they're all right. I have nothing against them."

"They don't like flying with you either," Sakowitz said evenly. "You make them nervous."

"What the hell does that mean?"

"It means that if ever there's an emergency, you want to be damn sure about the man in the seat next to you. They're not sure about you."

"For Christ's sake!" Larry exploded. "I lived through four years of emergencies over Germany and in the South Pacific, risking my fucking neck every day, while they were back here sitting on their fat asses, collecting big salaries, and they don't have confidence in *me*? You must be joking!"

"No one says you're not great in a fighter plane," Sakowitz replied quietly. "But we're flying passengers. It's a different ball game."

Larry sat there clenching his fists, trying to control his anger. "OK," he said sullenly. "I get the message. If you're through, I have a flight leaving in a few minutes."

"Someone else is taking it over," Sakowitz said. "You're fired."

Larry stared at him unbelievingly. "I'm *what*?"

"In a way, I suppose it's my fault, Douglas. I shouldn't have hired you in the first place."

Larry got to his feet, his eyes blazing with fury. "Then why the hell did you?" he demanded.

"Because your wife had a friend named Bill Fraser . . ." Sakowitz began.

Larry moved across the desk, his fist crashing into Sakowitz's face. The blow propelled Sakowitz against the wall. He used the momentum to bounce up. He hit Larry twice, then stepped back, fighting for control. "Get out of here," he said. "Now!"

Larry stared at him, his face twisted with hatred. "You son-of-a-bitch," he said. "I wouldn't come near this airline again if you begged me!" He turned and stormed out of the office.

Sakowitz stood there looking after him. His secretary came hurrying in. She saw the overturned chair and Sakowitz's bloody lip.

"Are you all right?" she asked.

"Terrific," he said. "Ask Mr. Eastman if he can see me."

Ten minutes later Sakowitz had finished relating the incident to Carl Eastman.

"What do you think's wrong with Douglas?" Eastman asked.

"Honestly? I think he's a psycho."

Eastman regarded him with his piercing hazel eyes. "That's pretty strong, Sak. He wasn't drunk when he was flying. No one could even prove that he'd had a drink on the ground. And anyone can be late once in a while."

"If that's all it was, I wouldn't have fired him, Carl. Douglas has a low boiling point. To tell you the truth I was trying to provoke him today, and it wasn't hard. If he had stood up under the pressure, I might have taken a chance and kept him on. You know what worries me?"

"What?"

Sakowitz said, "A few days ago I ran into an old buddy who flew with Douglas in the RAF. He told me a crazy story. It seems that when Douglas was in the Eagle Squadron he fell for a little English girl who was engaged to a boy named Clark in Douglas' Squadron. Douglas did everything he could to move in, but the girl wasn't having any. A week before she and Clark were to get married, the Squadron went up to cover some B-Seventeens in a raid over Dieppe. Douglas was flying at the rear of the Squadron. The fortresses dropped their bombs and everyone headed for home. Coming back over the Channel, they were hit by some Messerschmidts, and Clark was shot down." He stopped, lost in some reverie of his own. Eastman waited for him to go on and finally Sakowitz looked up at him. "According to my friend there were no Messerschmidts anywhere near Clark when he got it."

Eastman stared at him unbelievingly. "Jesus! Are you saying that Larry Douglas . . . ?"

"I'm not saying anything. I'm just telling you an interesting story I heard." He put his handkerchief to his lip again. The bleeding had stopped. "It's hard to tell what's happening in the middle of a dogfight. Maybe Clark just ran out of gas. One thing is certain. He sure as hell ran out of luck."

"What happened to his girl?"

"Douglas moved in with her until he came back to the States, then he dumped her." He looked at Eastman thoughtfully. "I'll tell you one thing, for sure. I feel sorry for Douglas' wife."

CATHERINE WAS IN the conference room having a staff meeting when the door opened and Larry walked in.

His eye was bruised and swollen, his cheek was cut. She hurried over to him. "Larry, what happened?"

"I quit my job," he mumbled.

Catherine took him into her office, away from the curious gazes of the others, and put a cold cloth to his eye and his cheek. "Tell me about it," she said, holding in her anger at what they had done to him.

"They've been riding me for a long time, Cathy. I think they were jealous because I was in the war and they weren't. Anyway, today was the topper. Sakowitz called me in and told me the only reason they hired me in the first place was because you were Bill Fraser's sweetheart."

Catherine looked at him, speechless.

"I hit him," Larry said. "I couldn't help it."

"Oh, darling!" Catherine said. "I'm so sorry."

"Sakowitz is sorrier," Larry replied. "I really clobbered him. Job or no job, I wasn't going to let anyone talk about you that way."

She held him close to her, reassuringly. "Don't worry. You can go to work for any airline in the country."

Catherine proved to be a poor prophet. Larry applied to all the airlines and several of them gave him interviews but nothing came of any of them. Bill Fraser had lunch with Catherine and she told him what had happened. Fraser said nothing, but he was very thoughtful all through lunch. Several times she felt he was on the verge of telling her something, but each time he stopped. Finally he said, "I know a lot of people, Cathy. Would you like me to see what I can do for Larry somewhere else?"

"Thanks," Catherine said gratefully. "But I don't think so. We'll work it out ourselves."

Fraser regarded her a moment, then nodded. "Let me know if you change your mind."

"I will," she said appreciatively. "It seems I'm always coming to you with my problems."

ACME SECURITY AGENCY
1402 "D" Street
Washington, D.C.

Reference #2-179-210   April 1, 1946

Dear Monsieur Barbet:

Thank you for your letter of March 15, 1946, and your bank draft.

Since my last report, Subject has secured employment as a pilot with The Flying Wheels Transport Company, a small independent freight company operating out of Long Island. A Dun and Bradstreet check shows that they are capitalized under $750,000. Their equipment consists of a converted B-26 and a converted DC-3. They have bank loans in excess of $400,000. The Vice-President of the Banque de Paris in New York where they have their major account assures me that the company has an excellent growth potential and future. The bank is considering loaning them sufficient money to buy additional airplanes based on their current income of $80,000 per year with projected increases of 30% per year, over the next five years.

If you wish further details on the financial aspects of the company, please let me know.

Subject began work on March 19, 1946. The personnel manager (who is also one of the owners) informed my operative that he felt very fortunate to have Subject flying for him. More details to follow.

Sincerely,
R. Ruttenberg
Managing Supervisor

BANQUE DE PARIS
New York City, New York

Philippe Chardon
President the Board

Chèr Noelle,

Tu es vraiment mauvaise! Je ne sais pas ce que cet homme t'a fait,
mais quoique ce soit, il a payé. Il a été mis à la porte aux Flying
Wheels cie, et mon ami me dit qu'il en a piqué une crise.

Je pense être a Athenes, et je compte te voir.

Mes amitiés à Costa—et ne tien fais pas la petite faveur que je t'ai
faite restera notre secret.

Affectuesement à toi,
Philippe

ACME SECURITY AGENCY
1402 "D" Street
Washington, D.C.

Reference #2-179-210   May 22, 1946

Dear Monseiur Barbet:

This is a follow-up to my report of May 1, 1946.

On May 14, 1946, Subject was fired by The Flying Wheels
Transport Company. I have tried to make discreet inquiries as to
the reason, but each time have run up against a brick wall. No one
there will discuss it, I can only assume that the Subject did something to disgrace himself, and they don't want to talk about it.

Subject is looking for another flying job, but apparently has no
immediate prospects.

I will continue to try to get more information about why he was discharged.

Sincerely,
R. Ruttenberg
Managing Supervisor

CABLEGRAM   MAY 29, 1946
Christian Barbet
Cable Chrisbar
Paris, France

CABLE ACKNOWLEDGED STOP WILL IMMEDIATELY DROP IN-
VESTIGATION OF REASON FOR SUBJECT BEING FIRED STOP
WILL CONTINUE EVERYTHING ELSE AS BEFORE

REGARDS,
R. RUTTENBERG
ACME SECURITY AGENCY

ACME SECURITY AGENCY
1402 "D" Street
Washington, D.C.

Reference #2-179-210   June 16, 1946

Dear Monsieur Barbet:

Thank you for your letter of June 10th and your bank draft.

On June 15th, Subject obtained employment as a copilot with Global Airways, a regional feeder airline operating between Washington, Boston and Philadelphia.

Global Airways is a small new airline with a fleet of three converted war planes, and as far as I have been able to ascertain, they are under-capitalized and in debt. A Vice-President of the firm informed me that they have been promised a loan from the Dallas First National Bank within the next sixty days which will give them enough capital to consolidate their bills and to expand.

Subject is held in high esteem and appears to have a good future there.

Please let me know whether you require any further information about Global Airways.

Sincerely,
R. Ruttenberg,
Managing Supervisor

ACME SECURITY AGENCY
1402 "D" Street
Washington, D.C.

Reference #2-179-210   July 20, 1946

Dear Monsieur Barbet:

Global Airways has unexpectedly filed for bankruptcy and is going out of operation. As far as I can learn, this move was forced by the refusal of the Dallas First National Bank to grant the loan that was promised. Subject is now unemployed again and back to earlier patterns of behavior, as outlined in previous reports.

I will not pursue any investigation into the reason for the bank's refusal of the loan or Global Airways' financial difficulties unless you specifically advise me to do so.

Sincerely,
R. Ruttenberg
Managing Supervisor

Noelle kept all the reports and the clippings in a special leather bag to which she had the only key. The bag was kept inside a locked suitcase and stored at the back of her bedroom closet, not because she thought Demiris would pry into her things, but because she knew how much he loved intrigue. This was Noelle's personal vendetta, and she wanted to be sure that Demiris remained unaware of it.

Constantin Demiris was going to play a part in her plan of vengeance, but he would never know about it. Noelle took a last look at the memorandum and locked it away, satisfied.

She was ready to begin.

IT STARTED WITH a phone call.

Catherine and Larry were having an uneasy silence-filled dinner at home. Larry had been home very little lately, and when he was home he was surly and rude. Catherine understood his unhappiness.

"It's as though some demon is on my back," he had told her when Global Airways had gone bankrupt. And it was true. He had had an incredible run of bad luck. Catherine tried to reassure Larry, to keep reminding him of what a wonderful pilot he was and how lucky anyone would be to have him. But it was like living with a wounded lion. Catherine never knew when he would lash out at her, and because she was afraid of letting him down, she tried to understand his wild rages and overlook them. The phone rang as she was serving dessert. She picked up the receiver.

"Hello."

There was an Englishman's voice on the other end of the line and it said, "Is Larry Douglas in, please? Ian Whitestone here."

"Just a moment." She held the receiver out to Larry. "It's for you. Ian Whitestone."

He frowned, puzzled. "Who?" Then his face cleared. "For Christ's sake!" He walked over and took the receiver from Catherine. "Ian?" He gave a short laugh. "My God, it's been almost seven years. How the hell did you ever track me down?"

Catherine watched Larry nodding and smiling as he listened. At the end of what seemed like five minutes, he said, "Well, that sounds interesting, old buddy. Sure I can. Where?" He listened. "Right. Half an hour. I'll see you then." Thoughtfully, he replaced the receiver.

"Is he a friend of yours?" Catherine asked.

Larry turned to face her. "No, not really. That's what's so funny. He's a guy I flew with in the RAF. We never really got along all that well. But he says he has a proposition for me."

"What kind of proposition?" Catherine asked.

Larry shrugged. "I'll let you know when I get home."

IT WAS ALMOST three o'clock in the morning when Larry returned to the apartment. Catherine was sitting up in bed, reading. Larry appeared at the bedroom door.

"Hi."

Something had happened to him. He radiated an excitement that Catherine had not seen in him for a long time. He walked over to the bed.

"How did your meeting go?"

"I think it went great," Larry said, carefully. "In fact it went so great I still can't believe it. I think I may have a job."

"Working for Ian Whitestone?"

"No. Ian's a pilot—like me. I told you we flew together."

"Yes."

"Well—after the war, a Greek buddy of his got him a job as a private pilot for Demiris."

"The shipping tycoon?"

"Shipping, oil, gold—Demiris owns half the world. Whitestone had a beautiful setup over there."

"What happened?"

Larry looked at her and grinned. "Whitestone's quit his job. He's going to Australia. Someone's setting him up in his own business over there."

"I still don't understand," said Catherine. "What does all this have to do with you?"

"Whitestone spoke to Demiris about my taking his place. He just quit, and Demiris hasn't had a chance to look around for a replacement. Whitestone thinks I'm a cinch for the job." He hesitated. "You don't know what this could mean, Cathy."

Catherine thought of the other times, the other jobs, and she remembered her father and his empty dreams, and she kept her voice noncommittal, not wishing to encourage any false hopes in Larry, and yet not wanting to dampen his enthusiasm.

"Didn't you say you and Whitestone weren't particularly good friends?"

He hesitated. "Yeah." A small frown creased his forehead. The truth of the matter was that he and Ian Whitestone had never liked each other at all. The telephone call tonight had been a big surprise. At the meeting, Whitestone had seemed oddly ill at ease. When he had explained the situation and Larry had said, "I'm surprised that you thought of me," there had been an awkward pause, and then Whitestone had said, "Demiris wants a great pilot, and that's what you are." It was almost as though Whitestone were pressing the job on him and that Larry would be doing him a favor. He had appeared very relieved when Larry said he was interested and then seemed anxious to leave. All in all it had been a strange meeting.

"This could be the chance of a lifetime," Larry told Cathy. "Demiris was paying Whitestone fifteen thousand drachmas a month. That's five hundred dollars and he lived like a king over there."

"But wouldn't that mean you'd be living in Greece?"

"*We'd* be living in Greece," Larry corrected her. "With that kind of money, we could save enough to be independent in a year. I've got to take a shot at it."

Catherine was hesitant, choosing her words carefully. "Larry, it's so far away and you don't even know Constantin Demiris. There must be a flying job here that . . ."

"No!" His tone was savage. "Nobody gives a shit here how good a pilot you are. All they care about is how long you've paid your goddam union dues. Over there, I'd be independent. It's the kind of thing I've been dreaming of, Cathy. Demiris has a fleet of planes you wouldn't believe, and I'll be flying again, baby. The only one I'd have to please would be Demiris, and Whitestone says he'll love me."

She thought again of Larry's job at Pan Am and the hopes he had had for it and his failures with the small airlines. *My God,* she thought. *What am I getting myself into?* It would mean giving up the business she had built, going to live in a strange place with strangers, with a husband who was almost a stranger.

He was watching her. "Are you with me?"

She looked up at his eager face. This was her husband and if she wanted to keep her marriage, she would have to live where he lived. And how lovely it would be if it did work out. He would be the old Larry again. The charming, amusing, wonderful man she had married. She had to give it a chance.

"Of course I'm with you," Catherine said. "Why don't you fly over and see Demiris? If the job works out, then I'll come over and join you."

He smiled, that charming, boyish grin. "I knew I could count on you, baby." He put his arms around her and held her close. "You'd better take off that nightgown," Larry said, "or I'm going to poke holes in it."

But as Catherine slowly took it off, she was thinking about how she was going to tell Bill Fraser.

Early the next morning Larry flew to Athens to meet Constantin Demiris.

During the next few days Catherine heard nothing from her husband. As the week dragged by, she found herself hoping that things had not worked out in Greece and that Larry would be coming home. Even if he got the position with Demiris, there was no way of telling how long it would last. Surely he could find a job in the United States.

Six days after Larry had left, Catherine received an overseas phone call.

"Catherine?"

"Hello, darling."

"Get packed. You're talking to Constantin Demiris' new personal pilot."

Ten days later, Catherine was on her way to Greece.

BOOK TWO

14

NOELLE AND CATHERINE

ATHENS: 1946

Men mold some cities, some cities mold men. Athens is an anvil that has withstood the hammer of centuries. It has been captured and despoiled by the Saracens, the Anglos, the Turks, but each time it patiently survived. Athens lies toward the southern end of the great central plain of Attica, which slopes gently toward the Saronic Gulf on the southwest and is overlooked on the east by the majestic Mount Hymettus. Underneath the shiny patina of the city one still found a village filled with ancient ghosts and steeped in rich tradition of timeless glories, where its citizens lived as much in their past as in the present, a city of constant surprise, full of discovery, and in the end unknowable.

LARRY WAS AT the Hellenikon Airport to meet Catherine's plane. She saw him hurrying toward the ramp, his face eager and excited as he ran toward her. He looked tanner and leaner than when she had last seen him, and he seemed to be free of strain.

"I've missed you, Cathy," he said as he scooped her up in his arms.

"I've missed you too." And as she said it, she realized how much she meant it. She kept forgetting the strong physical impact that Larry had on her until they met after an absence and each time it hit her anew.

"How did Bill Fraser take the news?" Larry asked as he helped her through Customs.

"He was very good about it."

"He had no choice, had he?" Larry said, sardonically.

Catherine remembered her meeting with Bill Fraser. He had looked at her, shocked. "You're going to go off to Greece to *live*? Why, for God's sakes?"

"It's in the fine print of my marriage contract," she had replied lightly.

"I mean, why can't Larry get a job here, Catherine?"

"I don't know why, Bill. Something always seems to go wrong. But he has a job in Greece and he seems to feel that it's going to work out."

After his first impulsive protest Fraser had been wonderful. He had made everything easy for her and insisted that she keep her interest in the firm. "You're not going to stay away forever," he kept saying.

Catherine was thinking of his words now as she watched Larry arrange for a porter to carry her luggage to a limousine.

He spoke to the porter in Greek and Catherine marveled at Larry's facility for language.

"Wait'll you meet Constantin Demiris," Larry said. "He's like a goddamn king. All the moguls in Europe seem to spend their time figuring out what they can do to please him."

"I'm glad you like him."

"And he likes me."

She had never heard him sound so happy and enthusiastic. It was a good omen.

On the way to the hotel Larry described his first meeting with Demiris. Larry had been met at the airport by a liveried chauffeur. Larry had asked to take a look at Demiris' fleet of planes, and the chauffeur had driven him to an enormous hangar at the far end of the field. There were three planes, and Larry inspected each one with a critical eye. The Hawker Siddeley was a beauty, and he longed to get behind the wheel and fly it. The next ship was a six-place Piper in top-notch condition. He estimated that it could easily do three hundred miles per hour. The third plane was a two-seater converted L-5, with a Lycoming engine, a wonderful plane for shorter flights. It was an impressive private fleet. When Larry had finished his inspection, he rejoined the watching chauffeur.

"They'll do," Larry said. "Let's go."

The chauffeur had driven him to a villa in Varkiza, the exclusive suburb twenty-five kilometers from Athens.

"You wouldn't believe Demiris' place," Larry told Catherine.

"What did it look like?" Catherine asked, eagerly.

"It's impossible to describe. It's about ten acres with electric gates, guards, watchdogs, the whole bit. The outside of the villa is a palace, and the inside is a museum. It has an indoor swimming pool, a full stage and a projection room. You'll see it one day."

"Was he nice?" Catherine asked.

"You bet he was," Larry smiled. "I got the red-carpet treatment. I guess my reputation preceded me."

In fact Larry had sat in a small anteroom for three hours waiting to see Constantin Demiris. In ordinary circumstances Larry would have been furious at the slight, but he knew how much depended on this meeting and he was too nervous to be angry. He had told Catherine how important this job was to him. But he had not told her how desperately he needed it. His one superb skill was flying and without it he felt lost. It was as though his life had sunk to some unexplored emotional depth and the pressures on him were too great to be borne. *Everything* depended on this job.

At the end of three hours a butler had come in and announced that Mr. Demiris was ready to see him. He had led Larry through a large reception hall that looked like it belonged at Versailles. The walls were delicate shades of gold, green and blue, and Beauvais tapestries hung on the walls, framed by panels of rosewood. A magnificent oval Savonnerie rug was on the floor, and above it an enormous chandelier of crystal De Roche and bronze Doré.

At the entry to the library were a pair of green onyx columns with capitals of gold bronze. The library itself was exquisite, designed by a master artisan, and the walls were carved, paneled fruitwoods. In the center of one wall stood a white marble mantelpiece with gold gilt ornamentations. On it rested two beautiful bronze Chénets of Philippe Caffieri.

From mantel top to ceiling rose a heavily carved trumeau mirror with a painting by Jean Honoré Fragonard. Through an open French window Larry caught a glimpse of an enormous patio overlooking a private park filled with statues and fountains.

At the far end of the library was a great Bureau Plat desk and behind it a magnificent tall back chair covered in Aubusson tapestry. In front of the desk were two bergères with Gobelin upholstery.

Demiris was standing near the desk, studying a large Mercator map on the wall, dotted with dozens of colored pins. He turned as Larry entered and held out his hand.

"Constantin Demiris," he said, with the faintest trace of an accent. Larry had seen photographs of him in news magazines throughout the years, but nothing had prepared him for the vital force of the man.

"I know," Larry said, shaking his hand. "I'm Larry Douglas."

Demiris saw Larry's eyes go to the map on the wall. "My empire," he said. "Sit down."

Larry took a chair opposite the desk.

"I understand that you and Ian Whitestone flew together in the RAF?"

"Yes."

Demiris leaned back in his chair and studied Larry. "Ian thinks very highly of you."

Larry smiled. "I think highly of him. He's a hell of a pilot."

"That's what he said about you, except he used the word 'great.' "

Larry felt again that sense of surprise he had had when Whitestone had first spelled out the offer. He had obviously given Demiris a big buildup about him, far out of proportion to the relationship that he and Whitestone had had. "I'm good," Larry said. "That's my business."

Demiris nodded. "I like men who are good at their business. Did you know that most of the people in the world are not?"

"I hadn't given it much thought one way or the other," Larry confessed.

"I have." He gave Larry a wintry smile. "That's *my* business—people. The great majority of people hate what they're doing, Mr. Douglas. Instead of devising ways to get into something they like, they remain trapped all their lives, like brainless insects. It's rare to find a man who loves his work. Almost invariably when you find such a man, he is a success."

"I suppose that's true," Larry said modestly.

"You are *not* a success."

Larry looked up at Demiris, suddenly wary. "That depends on what you mean by success, Mr. Demiris," he said carefully.

"What I mean is," Demiris said bluntly, "you did brilliantly in the war, but you are not doing very well in the peace."

Larry felt the muscles of his jaw begin to tighten. He felt that he was being baited, and he tried to hold back his anger. His mind raced frantically, trying to figure out what he could say to salvage this job he needed so desperately. Demiris was watching him, his olive black eyes quietly studying him, missing nothing.

"What happened to your job with Pan American, Mr. Douglas?"

Larry found a grin he didn't feel. "I didn't like the idea of sitting around for fifteen years waiting to become a copilot."

"So you hit the man you worked for."

Larry showed his surprise. "Who told you that?"

"Oh, come, Mr. Douglas," Demiris said impatiently, "if you went to work for me, I would be putting my life in your hands every time I flew with you. My life happens to be worth a great deal to me. Did you really think I would hire you without knowing *everything* about you?"

"I suppose not," Larry said.

"You were fired from two flying jobs after you were fired from Pan Am," Demiris went on. "That's a poor record."

"It had nothing to do with my ability," Larry retorted, anger beginning to rise in him again. "Business was slow with one company, and the other couldn't get a bank loan and went bankrupt. I'm a damned good pilot."

Demiris studied him a moment, then smiled. "I know you are," he said. "You don't respond well to discipline, do you?"

"I don't like being given orders by idiots who know less than I do."

"I trust I will not fall into that category," Demiris said dryly.

"Not unless you're planning to tell me how to fly your planes, Mr. Demiris."

"No, that would be your job. It would also be your job to see that I got where I was going efficiently, comfortably and safely."

Larry nodded. "I'd do my best, Mr. Demiris."

"I believe that," Demiris said. "You've been out to look at my planes."

Larry tried to keep the surprise out of his face. "Yes, sir."

"How did you like them?"

Larry could not conceal his enthusiasm. "They're beauties."

Demiris responded to the look on Larry's face. "Have you ever flown a Hawker Siddeley?"

Larry hesitated a moment, tempted to lie. "No, sir."

Demiris nodded. "Think you could learn?"

Larry grinned. "If you've got someone who can spare ten minutes."

Demiris leaned forward in his chair and pressed his long, slender fingers together. "I could choose a pilot who is familiar with all my planes."

"But you won't," Larry said, "because you'll keep getting new planes, and you want someone who can adapt to anything you buy."

Demiris nodded his head. "You are correct," he said. "What I am looking for is a pilot—a pure pilot—a man who is at his happiest when he is flying."

That was the moment when Larry knew the job was his.

LARRY WAS NEVER aware of how close he had come to not being hired. A great deal of Constantin Demiris' success was due to a highly developed instinct for trouble, and it had served him often enough so that he seldom disregarded it. When Ian Whitestone had come to inform him that he was quitting, a silent alarm went off in Demiris' mind. It was partly because of Whitestone's manner. He was acting unnaturally and seemed uneasy. It wasn't a question of money, he assured Demiris. He had a chance to go into business for himself with his brother-in-law in Sydney and he had to try it. Then he had recommended another pilot.

"He's an American, but we flew together in the RAF. He's not just good, he's great, Mr. Demiris. I don't know a better flyer."

Demiris quietly listened as Ian Whitestone went on extolling the virtues of his friend, trying to find the false note that jarred him. He finally recognized it. Whitestone was overselling, but possibly that was because of his embarrassment at quitting his job so abruptly.

Because Demiris was a man who left not even the smallest detail to chance, he made several phone calls to various countries after Whitestone left. Before the afternoon was over Demiris had ascertained that someone had indeed put up money to finance Whitestone in a small electronics business in Australia, with his brother-in-law. He had spoken to a friend in the British Air Ministry and two hours later had been given a verbal report on Larry Douglas. "He was a bit erratic on the ground," his friend had said, "but he was a superb flyer." Demiris had then made telephone calls to Washington and New York and had been quickly brought up-to-date on Larry Douglas' current status.

Everything on the surface appeared to be just as it ought to be. And yet Constantin Demiris still felt that vague sense of unease, a presentiment of trouble. He had discussed the matter with Noelle, suggesting that perhaps he might offer Ian Whitestone more money to stay on. Noelle had listened attentively and then said, "No. Let him go, Costa. And if he recommends this American flyer so highly, then I would certainly try him."

And that finally had decided him.

FROM THE MOMENT Noelle knew that Larry Douglas was on his way to Athens she was able to think of nothing else. She thought of all the years it had taken, the careful, patient laying of plans, the slow, inexorable tightening of the web, and she was sure that Constantin Demiris would have been proud of her if he had known. It was ironic, Noelle reflected. If she had never met Larry, she could have been happy with Demiris. They complemented each other perfectly. They both loved power and knew how to use it. They were above ordinary people. They were gods, meant to rule. In the end they could never lose, because they had a deep, almost mystic patience. They could wait forever. And now, for Noelle, the waiting was over.

NOELLE SPENT THE day in the garden lying in a hammock, going over her plan; and by the time the sun began to sink toward the western sky, she was satisfied. In a way, she thought, it was a pity that so much of the last six years had been filled with her plans for vengeance. It had motivated almost every waking moment, given her life a vitality and drive and excitement, and now in a few short weeks the quest would have come to an end.

At that moment, lying under the dying Grecian sun with the late afternoon breezes beginning to cool the quiet green garden, Noelle had no idea that it was just beginning.

THE NIGHT BEFORE Larry was to arrive, Noelle was unable to sleep. She lay awake all night, remembering Paris and the man who had given her the gift of laughter and taken it away from her again . . . feeling Larry's baby in her womb, possessing her body as its father had possessed her mind. She remembered that afternoon in the dreary Paris flat and the agony of the pointed metal coat hanger ripping into her flesh deeper and deeper until it tore into the baby with the sweet, unbearable pain driving her into a frenzy of hysteria and the endless river of blood pouring from her. She remembered all these things and relived them again . . . the pain, the agony and the hatred . . .

At five A.M., Noelle was up and dressed, sitting in her room looking out at the huge fireball rising over the Aegean. It reminded her of another morning in Paris when she had arisen early and dressed and waited for Larry—only this time he would be here. Because she had seen to it that he had to be. As Noelle needed him before, so Larry needed her now, even though he was still unaware of it.

Demiris sent a message up to Noelle's suite that he would like her to have breakfast with him, but she was too excited, and she was afraid that her mood might arouse his curiosity. She had long ago learned that Demiris had the sensitivity of a cat: He missed nothing. Again, Noelle reminded herself that she must be careful. She wanted to take care of Larry herself in her own way. She had thought long and hard about the fact that she was using Constantin Demiris as an unwitting tool. If he ever found out, he would not like it.

Noelle had a demitasse of thick Greek coffee and half a freshly baked roll. She had no appetite. Her mind was feverishly dwelling on the meeting that would take place in a few short hours. She had taken unusual care with her makeup and the selection of a dress, and she knew that she looked beautiful.

Shortly after eleven o'clock, Noelle heard the limousine pull up in front of the house. She took a deep breath to control her nervousness, then slowly walked over to the window. Larry Douglas was getting out of the car. Noelle watched as he moved toward the front door and it was as though the march of years had rolled away, and the two of them were back in Paris. Larry was a little more mature, and the fighting and the living had added new lines to his face, but they only served to make him handsomer than he had been. Looking at him through the window ten yards away Noelle could still feel the animal magnetism, still feel the old desire and it welled up in her, mixing with the hatred until she was filled with a sense of exhilaration that was almost like a climax. She took one last quick look at herself in the mirror and then went downstairs to meet the man she was about to destroy.

As she walked down the stairs, Noelle wondered what Larry's reaction would be when he saw her. Had he bragged to his friends and perhaps even his wife that Noelle Page had once been in love with him? She wondered, as she had wondered a hundred times before, whether he ever relived the magic of those days and nights they had together in Paris and whether he regretted what he had done to her. How it must have eaten at his soul that Noelle had become internationally famous and that his own life consisted of a series of small failures! Noelle wanted to see some of that in Larry's eyes now when they came face to face for the first time in almost seven years.

Noelle had reached the reception hall when the front door opened and the butler ushered him in. Larry was staring at the enormous foyer in awe when he turned and saw Noelle. He looked at her for a long moment, his face lighting up in appreciation at the sight of a beautiful woman. "Hello," he said, politely. "I'm Larry Douglas. I have an appointment to see Mr. Demiris."

And there was no sign of recognition on his face.

None at all.

DRIVING THROUGH THE streets of Athens toward their hotel, Catherine was dazed by the succession of ruins and monuments that appeared all around them.

Ahead she saw the breathtaking spectacle of the white-marbled

Parthenon rising high atop the Acropolis. Hotels and office buildings were everywhere, yet in an odd way it seemed to Catherine that the newer buildings appeared temporary and impermanent while the Parthenon loomed immortal and timeless in the chiseled clarity of the air.

"Impressive, isn't it?" Larry grinned. "The whole city is like that. One big beautiful ruin."

They passed a large park in the center of the city with dancing fountains in the middle. Hundreds of tables with green and orange poles lined the park, and the air above them was carpeted with blue awnings.

"That's Constipation Square," Larry said.

"What?"

"Its real name is Constitution Square. People sit at those tables all day drinking Greek coffee and watching the world go by."

On almost every block there were outdoor cafés, and on the corners men were selling freshly caught sponges. Everywhere flowers were sold by vendors, and their booths were a rage of violently colored blossoms.

"The city is so white," Catherine said. "It's dazzling."

The hotel suite was large and charming, overlooking Syntagma Square, the large square in the center of the city. In the room were beautiful flowers and an enormous bowl of fresh fruit.

"I love it, darling," Catherine said, going around the suite.

The bellboy had put her suitcases down and Larry tipped him. "Parapolee," the boy said.

"Parakalo," Larry replied.

The bellboy left, closing the door behind him.

Larry walked over and put his arms around Catherine. "Welcome to Greece." He kissed her hungrily, and she felt the hardness of his body pressing into the softness of hers and she knew how much he had missed her and she was glad. He led her into the bedroom.

On the dressing table was a small package. "Open it," Larry told her.

Her fingers tore the wrapping apart and in a small box inside was a tiny bird carved in jade. As busy as he was, Larry had remembered, and Catherine was touched. Somehow the bird was a talisman, an omen that everything was going to be all right, that the problems of the past were finished.

As they made love, Catherine said a little prayer of gratitude, thankful to be in the arms of the husband whom she loved so much, in one of the most exciting cities in the world, starting out on a new life. This was the old Larry, and all their problems had only made their marriage stronger.

Nothing could hurt them now.

THE NEXT MORNING Larry arranged for a real-estate agent to show Catherine some apartments. The agent turned out to be a short, dark, heavily moustached man named Dimitropolous who spoke in a rapid tongue that he sincerely believed was perfect English but which consisted of Greek words interlaced with an occasional undecipherable English phrase.

By throwing herself on his mercy—a trick that Catherine was to use often in the months to come—she persuaded him to speak very slowly so that she was able to sift out some of the English words and try to make a wild stab at what he was trying to say.

The fourth place he showed her was a bright and sunny four-room apartment in what she later learned was the Kolonaki section, the fashionable suburb of Athens, lined with beautiful residential buildings and smart shops.

When Larry returned to the hotel that evening, Catherine told him about the apartment, and two days later they moved in.

LARRY WAS AWAY during the day but he tried to be home to have dinner with Catherine. Dinner in Athens was any time between nine and twelve o'clock. Between two and five in the afternoon, everyone had a siesta, and the shops opened again until late evening. Catherine found herself completely absorbed in the city. On her third night in Athens Larry brought home a friend, Count George Pappas, an attractive Greek about forty-five, tall and slim with dark hair with a touch of gray at the temples. There was a curious old-fashioned dignity about him that Catherine liked. He took them to dinner at a small taverna in the Plaka, the ancient section of the city. The Plaka comprised a few steep acres carelessly flung together in the heart of downtown Athens, with twisting alleys and crumbling, worn-down staircases that led to tiny houses built under Turkish rule when Athens was a mere village. The Plaka was a place of whitewashed, rambling structures, fresh fruit and flower stalls, the marvelous aroma of coffee roasting in the open, howling cats and vociferous street fights. The effect was enchanting. In any other city, Catherine thought, a section like this would be the slums. Here, it's a monument.

The taverna that Count Pappas took them to was outdoors on top of a roof overlooking the city; the waiters were dressed in colorful costumes.

"What would you like to eat?" the Count asked Catherine.

She studied the alien menu helplessly. "Would you mind ordering for me? I'm afraid I might order the proprietor."

Count Pappas ordered a sumptuous banquet, choosing a variety of dishes so Catherine would get a chance to taste everything. They had *dolmades,* meatballs wrapped in vine leaves; *mousaka,* a succulent meat and eggplant pie; *stiffado,* stewed hare with onions—Catherine wasn't told what it was until she had eaten half of it, and she was unable to eat another bite of it—and *taramosalata,* the Greek salad of caviar with olive oil and lemon. The Count ordered a bottle of retsina.

"This is our national wine," he explained. He watched Catherine with amusement as she tasted it. It had a piney, resonated taste, and Catherine struggled gamely to down it.

"Whatever I had," she gasped, "I think this just cured it."

As they ate, three musicians began to play Bozoukia music. It was lively and gay and infectious and, as the group watched, customers began to get to their feet and move out onto the dance floor to dance to the music. What amazed Catherine was that the dancers were all male, and they were magnificent. She was enjoying herself tremendously.

They did not leave the café until after three A.M. The Count drove them back to their new apartment. "Have you done any sightseeing yet?" he asked Catherine.

"Not really," she confessed. "I'm waiting for Larry to get some time off."

The Count turned to Larry. "Perhaps I could show Catherine some of the sights until you are able to join us."

"That would be great," Larry said. "If you're sure it wouldn't be too much trouble."

"It would be my pleasure," the Count replied. He turned to Catherine. "Would you mind having me as your guide?"

She looked at him and thought of Dimitropolous, the little real-estate man who spoke fluent gibberish.

"I'd love it," she replied sincerely.

THE NEXT FEW weeks were fascinating. Catherine would spend mornings fixing up the apartment, and in the afternoon, if Larry was away, the Count would pick her up and take her sightseeing.

They drove out to Olympia. "This is the site of the first Olympic Games," the Count told her. "They were held here every year for a thousand years in spite of wars, plagues and famines."

Catherine stood looking in awe at the ruins of the great arena, thinking of the grandeur of the contests that had been held there through the centuries, the triumphs, the defeats.

"Talk about the playing fields of Eton," Catherine said. "*This* is where the spirit of sportsmanship really started, isn't it?"

The Count laughed. "I'm afraid not," he said. "The truth is a little embarrassing."

Catherine looked up, interested. "Why?"

"The first chariot race ever held here was fixed."

"Fixed?"

"I'm afraid so," Count Pappas confessed. "You see, there was a rich prince named Pelops who was feuding with a rival. They decided to hold a chariot race here to see who was the better man. The night before the race Pelops tampered with the wheel of his rival's chariot. When the race began, the whole countryside was here to cheer on their favorite. At the first turn the wheel of the rival's chariot flew off, and his chariot overturned. Pelop's rival was entangled in the reins and dragged to his death. Pelops drove on to victory."

"That's terrible," Catherine said. "What did they do to him?"

"That's really the disgraceful part of the story," the Count replied. "By now the whole populace was aware of what Pelops had done. It made him such a big hero that a huge pediment was raised in his honor at Olympia's Temple of Zeus. It is still there." He smiled wryly. "I'm afraid that our villain prospered and lived happily ever after. As a matter of fact," he added, "the whole region south of Corinth is called the Peloponnesus after him."

"Who said crime doesn't pay?" marveled Catherine.

Whenever Larry was free, he and Catherine would explore the city together. They found wonderful shops where they would spend hours haggling over prices, and out-of-the-way little restaurants that they made their own. Larry was a gay and charming companion, and Catherine was grateful that she had given up her job in the States to be with her husband.

LARRY DOUGLAS HAD never been happier in his life. The job with Demiris was the dream of a lifetime.

The money was good, but Larry was not interested in that. He was interested only in the magnificent machines he flew. It took him exactly one hour to learn to fly the Hawker Siddeley and five more flights to master it. Most of the time Larry flew with Paul Metaxas, Demiris' happy-go-lucky little Greek copilot. Metaxas had been surprised by the sudden departure of Ian Whitestone, and he had been apprehensive about Whitestone's replacement. He had heard stories about Larry Douglas, and he was not sure he liked what he heard. Douglas, however, seemed genuinely enthusiastic about his new job and the first time Metaxas flew with him, he knew that Douglas was a superb pilot.

Little by little Metaxas relaxed his guard and the two men became friends.

Whenever he was not flying, Larry spent time learning every idiosyncrasy of Demiris' fleet of planes. Before he was through, he was able to fly them all better than anyone had ever flown them before.

The variety in his job fascinated Larry. He would fly members of Demiris' staff on business trips to Brindisi and Corfu and Rome, or pick up guests and fly them to Demiris' island for a party or to his chalet in Switzerland for skiing. He became used to flying people whose photographs he was constantly seeing on the front pages of newspapers and magazines, and he would regale Catherine with stories about them. He flew the president of a Balkan country, a British prime minister, an Arabian oil chieftain and his entire harem. He flew opera singers and a ballet company and the cast of a Broadway play that was staging a single performance in London for Demiris' birthday. He piloted Justices of the Supreme Court, a congressman and a former President of the United

States. During the flights Larry spent most of the time in the cockpit, but from time to time he would wander back to the cabin to make sure the passengers were comfortable. Sometimes he would hear bits of discussion between tycoons about impending mergers or stock deals. Larry could have made a fortune from the information he gleaned but he was simply not interested. What concerned him was the airplane he flew, powerful and alive and in his control.

It was two months before Larry piloted Demiris himself.

They were in the Piper and Larry was flying his employer from Athens to Dubrovnik. It was a cloudy day and there was a report of wind storms and squalls along the route. Larry had carefully plotted out the least stormy course, but the air was so full of turbulence that it was impossible to avoid it.

An hour out of Athens he flashed on the "seat belt" sign and said to Metaxas, "Hold on, Paul. This may cost us both our jobs."

To Larry's surprise Demiris appeared in the cockpit. "May I join you?" he said.

"Help yourself," Larry said. "It's going to be rough."

Metaxas gave up his seat to Demiris and Demiris strapped himself in. Larry would have preferred to have the copilot sitting next to him, ready to act if anything went wrong, but it was Demiris' airplane.

The storm lasted almost two hours. Larry circled the large mountains of clouds that puffed up ahead of them, lovely white and deadly.

"Beautiful," Demiris commented.

"They're killers," Larry said. "Cumulus. The reason they're so nice and fluffy is that there's wind inside of them puffing them up. The inside of that cloud can tear a plane apart in ten seconds. You can rise and fall thirty thousand feet in less than a minute with no control of your plane."

"I'm sure you won't let that happen," Demiris said calmly.

The winds caught at the plane and tried to fling it across the sky, but Larry fought to keep it under control. He forgot that Demiris was there, focusing his entire attention on the craft he was flying, using every skill he had ever learned. Finally they were out of the storm. Larry turned, drained, and found that Demiris had left the cockpit. Metaxas was in the seat.

"That was a lousy first trip for him, Paul," Larry said. "I may be in trouble."

He was taxiing down the small, mountain-ringed tabletop airport at Dubrovnik when Demiris appeared in the doorway of the cockpit.

"You were right," Demiris said to Larry. "You're very good at what you do. I'm pleased."

And Demiris was gone.

One morning as Larry was getting ready to leave on a flight to Morocco, Count Pappas telephoned to suggest that he take Catherine driving through the countryside. Larry insisted that she go.

"Aren't you jealous?" she asked.

"Of the Count?" Larry laughed.

And Catherine suddenly understood. During the time she and the Count had spent together, he had never made an improper advance toward her or even given her a suggestive look. "He's a homosexual?" she asked.

Larry nodded. "That's why I've left you in his tender care."

The Count picked Catherine up early, and they started driving south toward the broad plain of Thessaly. Peasant women dressed in black walked along the road bent over with heavy loads of wood strapped to their backs.

"Why don't the men do the heavy work?" Catherine asked.

The Count shot her an amused glance.

"The women don't want them to," he replied. "They want their men fresh at night for other things."

There's a lesson there for all of us, Catherine thought wryly.

In the late afternoon they approached the forbidding-looking Pindus Mountains, their rocky crags towering high in the sky. The road was blocked by a flock of sheep being herded by a shepherd and a scrawny sheep dog. Count Pappas stopped the car as they waited for the sheep to clear the road. Catherine watched in wonder as the dog nipped at the heels of the stray sheep, keeping them in line and forcing them in the direction he wanted them to go.

"That dog is almost human," Catherine exclaimed admiringly.

The Count gave her a brief look. There was something in it that she did not understand.

"What's the matter?" she asked.

The Count hesitated. "It's a rather unpleasant story."

"I'm a big girl."

The Count said, "This is a wild area. The land is rocky and inhospitable. At best the crops are meager, and when the weather turns bad, there are no crops at all and a good deal of hunger." His voice trailed off.

"Go on," Catherine prompted.

"A few years ago there was a bad storm here and the crops were ruined. There was little food for anyone. All the sheep dogs in this area revolted. They deserted the farms they worked on and gathered together in a large band." As he continued, he tried to keep the horror out of his voice. "They began attacking the farms."

"And killed the sheep!" Catherine said.

There was a silence before he answered. "No. They killed their masters. And ate them."

Catherine stared at him, shocked.

"They had to send in federal troops from Athens to restore human government here. It took almost a month."

"How horrible."

"Hunger does terrible things," Count Pappas said quietly.

The sheep had crossed the road now. Catherine looked at the sheep dog again and shuddered.

AS THE WEEKS went by, the things that had seemed so foreign and strange to Catherine began to become familiar to her. She found the people open and friendly. She learned where to do her marketing and where to shop for clothes on Voukourestiou Street. Greece was a marvel of organized inefficiency, and one had to relax and enjoy it. No one was in a hurry, and if you asked someone for directions he was likely to take you where you wanted to go. Or he might say, when you asked how far it was: *"Enos cigarou dromos,"* which Catherine learned meant "one cigarette away." She walked the streets and explored the city and drank the warm dark wine of the Greek summer.

Catherine and Larry visited Mykonos with its colorful windmills and Melos, where the Venus de Milo was discovered. But Catherine's favorite place was Paros, a graceful, verdant island capped by a flower-covered mountain. When their boat docked, a guide stood on the quay. He asked if they would like him to guide them to the top of the mountain on mule-back, and they clambered aboard two bony mules.

Catherine was wearing a broad-brimmed straw hat to protect her from the hot sun. As she and Larry rode up the steep path leading toward the mountain top, black-clad women called out, *"Ke-lee meh-ra"* and handed Catherine gifts of fresh herbs, oregano and basil to put in her hat band. After a two-hour ride, they reached a plateau, a beautiful tree-filled plain with millions of flowers in spectacular bloom. The guide stopped the mules and they gazed in wonder at the incredible profusion of colors.

"This named Valley of the Butterflies," the guide said in halting English.

Catherine looked around for a butterfly but saw none. "Why do they call it that?" she asked.

The guide grinned as though he had been waiting for her question. "I show you," he said. He dismounted from his mule and picked up a large fallen limb. He walked over to a tree and hit the limb against it with all his might. In a split second the "flowers" on hundreds of trees suddenly took to the air in a wild rainbow of flight, leaving the trees bare. The air was filled with hundreds of thousands of gaily colored butterflies dancing in the sunlight.

Catherine and Larry gazed in awe. The guide stood watching them, his face filled with a deep pride, as though he felt responsible for the beautiful miracle they were seeing. It was one of the loveliest days of Catherine's life, and she thought that if she could choose one perfect day to relive, it would be the day she spent with Larry on Paros.

"HEY, WE GOT a VIP this morning," Paul Metaxas grinned cheerfully. "Wait till you see her."

"Who is it?"

"Noelle Page, the boss's lady. You can look, but you mustn't touch."

Larry Douglas remembered the brief glimpse he had had of the woman in Demiris' home the morning Douglas had arrived in Athens. She was a beauty and she looked familiar, but that of course was because he had seen her on the screen, in a French picture that Catherine had once dragged him to. No one had to tell Larry the rules of self-preservation. Even if the world were not filled with eager females, he would not have gone anywhere near Constantin Demiris' girl friend. Larry liked his job too much to jeopardize it by doing anything so stupid. Well, maybe he would get her autograph for Catherine.

THE LIMOUSINE TAKING Noelle to the airport was slowed down several times by work gangs repairing the roads, but Noelle welcomed the delays. She was going to see Larry Douglas for the first time since the meeting at Demiris' house. Noelle had been deeply shaken by what had happened. Or, more accurately, what had not happened.

Over the past six years Noelle had imagined their encounter in a hundred different ways. She had played the scene over and over in her mind. The one thing that had never even occurred to her was that Larry would not remember her. The most important event in her life had meant nothing more to him than another little cheap affair, one of hundreds. Well, before she was through with him, he would remember her.

LARRY WAS CROSSING the airfield, flight plan in hand, when a limousine pulled up in front of the big plane, and Noelle Page emerged. Larry walked over to the car and said pleasantly, "Good morning, Miss Page, I'm Larry Douglas. I'll be flying you and your guests to Cannes."

Noelle turned and walked past him as though he had not spoken, as though he did not exist. Larry stood there, looking after her, bewildered.

Thirty minutes later the other passengers, a dozen of them, had boarded the plane, and Larry and Paul Metaxas took off. They were flying the group to the Côte d'Azur where they would be picked up and taken aboard Demiris' yacht. It was an easy flight except for the normal turbulence off the southern coast of France in summer, and Larry landed the plane smoothly and taxied over to where some limousines were waiting for his passengers. As Larry left the plane with his stubby little copilot, Noelle walked up to Metaxas, ignoring Larry, and said in a voice filled with contempt, "The new pilot is an amateur, Paul. You should give him flying lessons." And Noelle got into a car and was driven away, leaving Larry standing there, filled with a stunned, helpless anger.

He told himself that she was a bitch and he had probably happened to catch her on a bad day. But the next incident a week later convinced him that he was facing a serious problem.

On Demiris' orders Larry picked Noelle up in Oslo and flew her to London. Because of what had happened Larry had gone over the flight plan with particular care. There was a high pressure area to the north and some possible thunderheads building up to the east. Larry worked out a route that skirted these areas, and the flight proved to be perfectly smooth. He brought the ship down in a flawless three-point landing, and he and Paul Metaxas strolled back to the cabin. Noelle Page was putting on some lipstick. "I hope you enjoyed your flight, Miss Page," Larry said politely.

Noelle glanced up at him a moment, her face expressionless, then turned to Paul Metaxas. "I'm always nervous when I'm flown by an incompetent."

Larry felt his face redden. He started to speak, and Noelle said to Metaxas, "Please ask him not to address me in the future unless I speak to him first."

Metaxas swallowed and mumbled, "Yes, ma'am."

Larry stared at Noelle, his eyes filled with fury, as she rose and left the plane. His impulse had been to slap her, but he knew that would have been the end of him. He loved this job more than anything he had ever done, and he did not intend to let anything happen to it. He knew that if he were fired, it could be the last flying job he would ever get. No, he would have to be very careful in the future.

When Larry got home, he talked to Catherine about what had happened.

"She's out to get me," Larry said.

"She sounds horrible," Catherine replied. "Could you have offended her in some way, Larry?"

"I haven't spoken a dozen words to her."

Catherine took his hand. "Don't worry," she said, consolingly. "Before you're through, you'll charm her. Wait and see."

The next day when Larry flew Constantin Demiris on a brief business trip to Turkey, Demiris came into the cockpit and took Metaxas' seat. He dismissed the copilot with a wave of his hand, and Larry and

Demiris were alone. They sat there in silence, watching the small stratus clouds slicing the plane into fluffy geometric patterns.

"Miss Page has taken a dislike to you," Demiris said, finally.

Larry felt his hands tighten on the controls and deliberately forced them to relax. He fought to keep his voice calm. "Did—did she say why?"

"She said you were rude to her."

Larry opened his mouth to protest, then thought better of it. He would have to work this out in his own way.

"I'm sorry. I'll try to be more careful, Mr. Demiris," he said evenly.

Demiris got to his feet. "Do that. I would suggest that you not offend Miss Page any further." He left the cockpit.

Any further! Larry racked his brain, trying to think of what he might have done to offend her. Perhaps she just did not like his type. Or she could have been jealous of the fact that Demiris liked and trusted him, but that didn't make sense. Nothing Larry could think of made any sense. And yet Noelle Page was trying to get him fired.

Larry thought about what it was like being out of a job, the indignity of filling out applications like a damned schoolboy, the interviews, the waiting, the endless hours of trying to kill time with cheap bars and amateur whores. He remembered Catherine's patience and tolerance and how he had hated her for it. No, he could not go through all that again. He could not stand another failure.

ON A LAYOVER in Beirut a few days later Larry passed a movie theater and noticed that the picture playing there starred Noelle Page. On an impulse he went to see it, prepared to hate the picture and its star, but Noelle was so brilliant in it that he found himself completely carried away by her performance. Again he had the curious feeling of familiarity. The following Monday, Larry flew Noelle Page and some business associates of Demiris' to Zurich. Larry waited until Noelle Page was alone and then approached her. He had hesitated about talking to her, remembering her last warning to him, but he had decided that the only way he could break through her antagonism was to go out of his way to be pleasant to her. All actresses were egotistical and liked to be told they were good, and so now he came up to her and said, with careful courtesy,

"Excuse me, Miss Page, I just wanted to tell you that I saw you in a movie the other night. *The Third Face.* I think you're one of the greatest actresses I've ever seen."

Noelle stared at him a moment and then replied, "I would like to believe that you are a better critic than you are a pilot, but I doubt very much that you have either the intelligence or the taste." And she walked away.

Larry stood rooted there, feeling as though he had been struck. The goddamned cunt! For an instant he was tempted to follow her and tell her what he thought of her, but he knew it would be playing into her hands. No. From now on he would simply do his job and keep as far away from her as possible.

During the next few weeks Noelle was his passenger on several flights. Larry did not speak to her at all, and he tried desperately hard to arrange it so that she did not see him. He kept out of the cabin and had Metaxas handle any necessary communications with the passengers. There were no further comments from Noelle Page, and Larry congratulated himself on having solved the problem.

As it turned out, he congratulated himself too soon.

One morning Demiris sent for Larry at the villa. "Miss Page is flying to Paris for me on some confidential business. I want you to stay at her side."

"Yes, Mr. Demiris."

Demiris studied him for a moment, started to add something else, then changed his mind. "That's all."

Noelle was the only passenger on the flight to Paris and Larry decided to fly the Piper. He arranged for Paul Metaxas to make Noelle comfortable and stayed in the cockpit, out of sight during the entire flight. When they landed, Larry walked back to her seat and said, "Excuse me, Miss Page. Mr. Demiris asked me to stay with you while you're in Paris."

She looked up at him with contempt and said, "Very well. Just don't let me know that you're around."

He nodded in icy silence.

They rode into the city from Orly in a private limousine. Larry sat up front with the driver and Noelle Page sat in back. She did not speak to him during the journey into the city. Their first stop was Paribas, the

Banque de Paris et des Bas. Larry went into the lobby with Noelle and waited while she was ushered into the office of the president and then down to the basement where the safe-deposit boxes were kept. Noelle was gone about thirty minutes, and when she returned, she swept straight past Larry without a word. He stared after her a moment, then turned and followed her.

Their next stop was the rue du Faubourg-St.-Honoré. Noelle dismissed the car. Larry followed her into a department store and stood nearby while she selected the items she wanted, then handed him the packages to carry. She shopped in half a dozen stores: Hermes for some purses and belts, Guerlain for perfume, Celine for shoes, until Larry was burdened down with packages. If she was aware of his discomfiture, Noelle gave no sign. Larry might have been some pet animal that she was leading around.

As they walked out of Celine's, it began to rain. Pedestrians were scurrying to take shelter. "Wait here for me," Noelle commanded.

Larry stood there and watched her disappear into a restaurant across the street. He waited in the driving rain for two hours, his arms full of packages, cursing her and cursing himself for putting up with her behavior. He was trapped and he did not know how to get out of it.

And he had a terrible foreboding that it was going to get worse.

THE FIRST TIME Catherine met Constantin Demiris was at his villa. Larry had gone there to deliver a package he had flown in from Copenhagen, and Catherine had gone to the house with him. She was standing in the huge reception hall admiring a painting, when a door opened and Demiris came out. He watched her a moment, then said, "Do you like Manet, Mrs. Douglas?"

Catherine swung around and found herself face to face with the legend she had heard so much about. She had two immediate impressions: Constantin Demiris was taller than she had imagined, and there was an overpowering energy in him that was almost frightening. Catherine was amazed that he knew her name and who she was. He seemed to go out of his way to put her at ease. He asked Catherine how she liked Greece, whether her apartment was comfortable, and to let him know if he could do anything to help make her stay pleasant. He even knew—though

God alone knew how!—that she collected miniature birds. "I saw a lovely one," he told her. "I will send it to you."

Larry appeared, and he and Catherine left.

"How did you like Demiris?" Larry asked.

"He's a charmer," she said. "No wonder you enjoy working for him."

"And I'm going to keep working for him." There was a grimness in his voice that Catherine did not understand.

The following day a beautiful porcelain bird was delivered to Catherine.

Catherine saw Constantin Demiris twice after that, once when she went to the races with Larry and once at a Christmas party Demiris gave at his villa. Each time he went out of his way to be charming to her. All in all, Catherine thought, Constantin Demiris was quite a remarkable person.

IN AUGUST THE Athens Festival began. For two months the city presented plays, ballets, operas, concerts—all given in the Herodes Atticus, the ancient open-air theater at the foot of the Acropolis. Catherine saw several of the plays with Larry, and when he was away she went with Count Pappas. It was fascinating to watch ancient plays staged in their original settings by the race that had created them.

One night after Catherine and Count Pappas had gone to see a production of *Medea,* they were talking about Larry.

"He's an interesting man," Count Pappas said. *"Polymechanos."*

"What does that mean?"

"It is difficult to translate." The Count thought for a moment. "It means 'fertile in devices.'"

"You mean 'resourceful'?"

"Yes, but more than that. Someone who is always very ready with a new idea, a new plan."

"Polymechanos," Catherine said. "That's my boy."

Above them there was a beautiful, waxing gibbous moon. The night was balmy and warm. They walked through the Plaka toward Omonia Square. As they started to cross the street, a car raced around the corner, headed straight toward them and the Count pulled Catherine to safety.

"Idiot!" he yelled after the disappearing driver.

"Everyone here seems to drive like that," Catherine said.

Count Pappas smiled ruefully. "Do you know the reason? The Greeks haven't made the transition to automobiles. In their hearts they're still driving donkeys."

"You're joking."

"Unfortunately no. If you want insight into the Greeks, Catherine, don't read the guidebooks; read the old Greek tragedies. The truth is, we still belong to other centuries. Emotionally we're very primitive. We're filled with grand passions, deep joys and great sorrows, and we haven't learned how to cover them up with a civilized veneer."

"I'm not sure that's a bad thing," Catherine replied.

"Perhaps not. But it distorts reality. When outsiders look at us, they are not seeing what they think they see. It is like looking at a distant star. You are not really seeing the star, you are looking at a reflection of light that was there perhaps a million years ago. That is the way it is with us Greeks. In us you are looking at a reflection of the past."

They had reached the square. They passed a row of little stores with signs in the windows that said "Fortune-Telling."

"There are a lot of fortune-tellers here, aren't there?" Catherine asked.

"We are a very superstitious people."

Catherine shook her head. "I'm afraid I don't believe in it."

They had reached a small taverna. A hand-lettered sign in the window read: "MADAME PIRIS, FORTUNE-TELLING."

"Do you believe in witches?" Count Pappas asked.

Catherine looked at him to see if he was teasing. His face was serious. "Only on Halloween."

"By a witch I do not mean broomsticks and black cats and boiling kettles."

"What do you mean?"

He nodded toward the sign. "Madame Piris is a witch. She can read the past and the future."

He saw the skepticism on Catherine's face. "I will tell you a story," Count Pappas said. "Many years ago, the Chief of Police in Athens was a man named Sophocles Vasilly. He was a friend of mine and I used my influence to help him get into office. Vasilly was a very honest man.

There were people who wished to corrupt him and since he would not be corrupted, they decided that he would have to be eliminated." He took Catherine's arm and they crossed the street toward the park.

"One day, Vasilly came to tell me of a threat that had been made on his life. He was a brave man, but this threat disturbed him because it came from a powerful and ruthless racketeer. Detectives were assigned to watch the racketeer and to protect Vasilly, but still he had an uneasy feeling that he did not have long to live. That was when he came to me."

Catherine was listening, fascinated. "What did you do?" she asked.

"I advised him to get a reading from Madame Piris." He was silent, his thoughts prowling restlessly in some dark arena of the past.

"Did he go?" Catherine finally asked.

"What? Oh, yes. She told Vasilly that death was going to come to him unexpectedly and quickly and warned him to beware of a lion at noon. There are no lions in Greece, except for a few old mangy ones at the zoo and the stone ones you have seen on Delos."

Catherine could feel the tension in Pappas' voice as he continued.

"Vasilly went to the zoo personally to check the cages to make sure that the animals were secure, and he made inquiries as to any wild animals that might have recently been brought into Athens. There were none.

"A week went by and nothing happened, and Vasilly decided that the old witch had been wrong and that he had been a superstitious fool for paying any attention to her. On a Saturday morning I dropped by the police station to pick him up. It was his son's fourth birthday, and we were going to take a boat trip to Kyron to celebrate.

"I drove up in front of the station just as the clock in the Town Hall was striking twelve. As I reached the entrance, there was a tremendous explosion from inside the building. I hurried inside to Vasilly's office." His voice sounded stiff and awkward. "There was nothing left of the office—or of Vasilly."

"How horrible," Catherine murmured.

They walked on for a moment in silence. "But the witch was wrong, wasn't she?" Catherine asked. "He wasn't killed by a lion."

"Ah, but he was, you see. The police reconstructed what had happened. As I told you, it was the boy's birthday. Vasilly's desk was piled with gifts that he was going to bring to his son. Someone had brought in a birthday gift, a toy, and laid it on Vasilly's desk."

Catherine felt the blood leaving her face. "A toy lion."

Count Pappas nodded. "Yes. 'Beware of a lion at noon.' "

Catherine shuddered. "That gives me the creeps."

He looked down at her sympathetically. "Madame Piris is not a 'fun' fortune-teller to go to."

They had crossed through the park and reached Piraios Street. An empty taxi was passing by. The Count hailed it, and ten minutes later Catherine was back at her apartment.

As she prepared for bed, she told Larry the story, and as she told it, her flesh began to crawl again. Larry held her tightly and made love to her, but it was a long time before Catherine was able to fall asleep.

15

NOELLE AND CATHERINE

ATHENS: 1946

If it had not been for Noelle Page, Larry Douglas would have had no worries. He was where he wanted to be, doing what he wanted to do. He enjoyed his job, the people he met, and the man for whom he worked. On the ground his life was equally satisfactory. When he was not flying, he spent a good part of his time with Catherine; but because Larry's job was so mobile, Catherine was not always aware of where he was, and Larry found innumerable opportunities to go out on his own. He went to parties with Count Pappas and Paul Metaxas, his copilot, and a satisfying number of them turned into orgies. Greek women were filled with passion and fire. He had found a new one, Helena, a stewardess who worked for Demiris, and when they had a stopover away from Athens, she and Larry shared a hotel room. Helena was a beautiful, slim, dark-eyed girl, and insatiable. Yes, everything considered, Larry Douglas decided that his life was perfect.

Except for Demiris' blond bitch mistress.

Larry had not the slightest clue as to what made Noelle Page despise him, but whatever it was, it was endangering his way of life. Larry had tried being polite, aloof, friendly, and each time Noelle Page succeeded in making him look like a fool. Larry knew that he could go to Demiris, but he had no illusions about what would happen if it came to a choice between him and Noelle. Twice, he had arranged for Paul Metaxas to take over Noelle's flight but shortly before each flight Demiris' secretary had telephoned to tell him that Mr. Demiris would like to have Larry pilot her himself.

On an early morning in late November Larry received a call that he was to fly Noelle Page to Amsterdam that afternoon. Larry checked with the airport and received a negative report on the weather in Amsterdam. A fog was beginning to roll in and by afternoon they expected zero visibility. Larry phoned Demiris' secretary to tell her that it would be impossible to fly to Amsterdam that day. The secretary said she would get back to him. Fifteen minutes later she phoned to say that Miss Page would be at the airport at two o'clock, ready to take off. Larry checked with the airport again, thinking that perhaps there had been a break in the weather, but the report was the same.

"Jesus Christ," Paul Metaxas exclaimed. "She must be in one hell of a hurry to get to Amsterdam."

But Larry had the feeling that Amsterdam was not the issue. This was a contest of wills between the two of them. For all he cared Noelle Page could crash into a mountain peak and good riddance, but Larry was damned if he was going to risk his own neck for the stupid bitch. He tried to phone Demiris to discuss it with him, but he was in a meeting and unavailable. Larry slammed down the phone, seething. He had no choice now but to go to the airport and try to talk his passenger out of making the flight. He arrived at the airport at 1:30. By three o'clock Noelle Page had not appeared. "She probably changed her mind," Metaxas said.

But Larry knew better. As the time wore on, he became more and more furious, until he realized that that was her intention. She was trying to drive him into a rash action that would cost him his job. Larry was in the terminal building talking to the airport manager when Demiris' familiar gray Rolls drove up and Noelle Page emerged. Larry walked outside to meet her.

"I'm afraid the flight's off, Miss Page," he said, making his voice flat. "The airport at Amsterdam is fogged in."

Noelle looked past Larry as though he did not exist and said to Paul Metaxas, "The plane carries automatic landing equipment, does it not?"

"Yes, it does," Metaxas said, awkwardly.

"I'm really surprised," she replied, "that Mr. Demiris would hire a pilot who's a coward. I'll speak to him about it."

Noelle turned and walked toward the plane. Metaxas looked after her and said, "Jesus Christ! I don't know what's gotten into her. She never used to act like this. I'm sorry, Larry."

Larry watched Noelle walk across the field, her blond hair blowing in the wind. He had never hated anyone so much in his life.

Metaxas was watching him. "Are we going?" he asked.

"We're going."

The copilot gave a deep, expressive sigh, and the two men slowly walked toward the plane.

Noelle Page was sitting in the cabin, leisurely thumbing through a fashion magazine when they entered the plane. Larry stared at her a moment, so filled with anger that he was afraid to speak. He went up into the cockpit and began his preflight check.

Ten minutes later he had received clearance from the tower and they were airborne for Amsterdam.

The first half of the flight was uneventful. Switzerland lay below in a mantle of snow. By the time they were over Germany, it was dusk. Larry radioed ahead to Amsterdam for a weather check. They reported that fog was blowing in from the North Sea and getting thicker. He cursed his bad luck. If the winds had changed and the fog had cleared, his problem would have been solved, but now he had to decide whether to risk an instrument landing at Amsterdam or fly to an alternate airport. He was tempted to go back and discuss it with his passenger, but he could visualize the contemptuous look on her face.

"Special Flight one-oh-nine, would you give us your flight plan, please?" It was the tower at Munich. Larry had to make a decision swiftly. He could still land at Brussels, Cologne or Luxembourg.

Or Amsterdam.

The voice crackled over the speaker again. "Special Flight one-oh-nine, would you give us your flight plan, please?"

Larry snapped down the transmitting key. "Special Flight one-oh-nine to Munich Tower. We're going to Amsterdam." He flicked the switch up and was aware of Metaxas watching him.

"Jesus, maybe I should have doubled my life insurance," Metaxas said. "You really think we're going to make it?"

"Do you want to know the truth?" Larry said, bitterly. "I don't give a shit."

"Fantastic! I'm up in a plane with two fucking maniacs!" Metaxas moaned.

For the next hour Larry was wholly absorbed in flying the aircraft, listening to the frequent weather reports without comment. He was still hoping for a wind change, but thirty minutes out of Amsterdam the report was still the same. Heavy fog. The field was closed to all air traffic except for emergencies. Larry made contact with the control tower at Amsterdam. "Special Flight one-oh-nine to Amsterdam Tower. Approaching airport from 75 miles east of Cologne, ETA nineteen hundred hours."

Almost instantly a voice on the radio crackled back, "Amsterdam Tower to Special Flight one-oh-nine. Our field is closed down. We suggest you return to Cologne or land at Brussels."

Larry spoke into the handmike. "Special Flight one-oh-nine to Amsterdam Tower. Negative. We have an emergency."

Metaxas turned to stare at him in surprise.

A new voice came over the speaker. "Special Flight one-oh-nine, this is Chief of Operations at Amsterdam Airport. We are completely fogged in here. Visibility zero. Repeat: visibility zero. What is the nature of your emergency?"

"We're running out of fuel," Larry said. "I have barely enough to reach you."

Metaxas' eyes went to the fuel gauges, which registered half full. "For Christ's sakes," Metaxas exploded. "We could fly to China!"

The radio was silent. Suddenly it exploded into life again.

"Amsterdam Tower to Special Flight one-oh-nine. You have an emergency clearance. We'll bring you in."

"Roger." Larry flicked off the switch and turned to Metaxas. "Jettison the fuel," he ordered.

Metaxas swallowed and said in a choked voice, *"J-jettison the fuel?"*

"You heard me, Paul. Leave just enough to bring us in."

"But, Larry . . ."

"Damn it, don't argue. If we roll in there with a tank half full of gas, they'll jerk our licenses away so fast you won't know what hit you."

Metaxas nodded glumly and reached for the fuel-ejection handle. He began to pump, keeping a close eye on the gauge. Five minutes later they were in the fog, wrapped in a soft white cotton that wiped out everything but the dimly lit cockpit they sat in. It was an eerie sensation, cut off from time and space and the rest of the world. The last time Larry had been through this was in the Link Trainer. But that was a game where there were no risks. Here the stakes were life and death. He wondered what it was doing to his passenger. He hoped it gave her a heart attack. The Amsterdam control tower came on again.

"Amsterdam control tower to Special Flight one-oh-nine. I am going to bring you in on A.L.S. You will please follow my instructions exactly. We have you on our radar. Turn three degrees west and maintain present altitude until further instructions. At your present airspeed, you should be landing in eighteen minutes."

The voice coming over the radio sounded tense. With good reason, thought Larry grimly. One slight mistake and the plane would plough into the sea. Larry made the correction and shut out everything from his mind but the disembodied voice that was his sole link to survival. He flew the plane as though it were a part of himself, flying it with his heart, his soul and his mind. He was dimly aware of Paul Metaxas sweating beside him, calling out a constant instrument check in a low, strained voice, but if they came out of this alive, it would be Larry Douglas who did it. Larry had never seen fog like this. It was a ghostly enemy, charging at him from every side, blinding him, seducing him, trying to lure him into making one fatal mistake. He was hurtling through the sky at two hundred and fifty miles an hour, unable to see beyond the windshield of the cockpit. Pilots hated fog, and the first rule was: Climb over it or dive under it, but get out of it! Now there was no way, because he was locked into an impossible destination by the whim of a spoiled tart. He was helpless, at the mercy of instruments that could go wrong and men on the ground who could make mistakes. The disembodied voice came over the speaker again, and it seemed to Larry that it had a new, nervous quality.

"Amsterdam Tower to Special Flight one-oh-nine. You are coming into the first leg of your landing pattern: Lower your flaps and begin your descent. Descend to two thousand feet . . . fifteen hundred feet . . . one thousand feet . . ."

Still no sign of the airport below. They could have been in the middle of nowhere. He could feel the ground rushing up to meet the plane.

"Decrease your airspeed to one hundred twenty . . . lower your wheels . . . you're at six hundred feet . . . airspeed one hundred . . . you're at four hundred feet . . ." And still no sign of the goddamn airport! The blanket of smothering cotton seemed thicker now.

Metaxas' forehead gleamed with perspiration. "Where in the hell is it?" he whispered.

Larry stole a swift glance at the altimeter. The needle was edging down toward three hundred feet. Then it was below three hundred feet. The ground was rushing up to meet them at one hundred miles per hour. The altimeter showed only one hundred fifty feet. Something was wrong. He should have been able to see the airport lights by now. He strained to see ahead of the plane, but there was only the treacherous, blinding fog whipping across the windshield.

Larry heard Metaxas' voice, tense and hoarse. "We're down to sixty feet." And still nothing.

"Forty feet."

And the ground racing up to meet them in the darkness.

"Twenty feet."

It was no good. In another two seconds, the margin of safety would be gone and they would crash. He had to make an instant decision.

"I'm going to take it back up," Larry said. His hand tightened on the wheel and started to pull back and at that instant, a row of electric arrows blazed out on the ground ahead of them, lighting up the runway below. Ten seconds later, they were on the ground, taxiing toward the Schiphol terminal.

When they had come to a stop, Larry switched off the engines with numb fingers and sat motionless for a long time. Finally he pushed himself to his feet and was surprised to find that his knees were trembling. He noticed a strange odor in the air and turned to Metaxas. Metaxas grinned sheepishly.

"Sorry," he said. "I shat."

Larry looked down at him and nodded. "For both of us," he said. He turned and walked back into the cabin. The bitch was in there, calmly thumbing through a magazine. Larry stood there studying her, aching to tell her off, wishing desperately that he could find the key to what made her tick. Noelle Page must have known how close she had come to death in the past few minutes, and yet she sat there looking serene and undisturbed, not a hair out of place.

"Amsterdam," Larry announced.

THEY DROVE INTO Amsterdam in a heavy silence, Noelle in the back seat of the Mercedes 300 and Larry in front with the chauffeur. Metaxas had stayed at the airport to have the plane serviced. The fog was still thick and they drove slowly until suddenly, when they reached the Lindenplatz, it began to lift.

They rode through the City Square, crossed the Eider Bridge over the Amstel River and stopped in front of the Amstel Hotel. When they reached the lobby, Noelle said to Larry, "You will pick me up at ten sharp tonight," then turned away and walked toward the elevator, the manager of the hotel bowing and scraping at her heels. A bellboy led Larry to a small, uncomfortable single room at the back of the hotel on the first floor. The room was next to the kitchen, and through the wall Larry could hear the clatter of dishes and smell the mixed aromas from the steaming kettles.

Larry took one look at the tiny room and snapped, "I wouldn't put my dog in here."

"I'm sorry," the bellboy said apologetically. "Miss Page requested the cheapest room we had for you."

Okay, Larry thought, *I'll find a way to beat her. Constantin Demiris isn't the only man in the world who uses a private pilot. I'll start checking around tomorrow. I've met a lot of his rich friends. There are half a dozen of them who would be damned glad to hire me.* But then, he thought: *Not if Demiris fires me. If that happens, none of them will touch me. I have to hang in there.* The bathroom was down the hall, and Larry unpacked and took out a robe so that he could go take a bath, then thought: *To hell with it, why should I bathe for her? I hope I smell like a pig.* He went to the hotel bar to have a badly needed drink. He was on his third martini when he looked up at the clock over the bar and saw that it was 10:15. *Ten o'clock sharp,* she had said. Larry was filled with a sudden panic. He hastily slapped some bills on the bar and headed toward the elevator. Noelle was in the Emperor Suite on the fifth floor. He found himself running down the long corridor and cursing himself for letting her do this to him. He knocked at the door to her suite, his mind forming excuses for his tardiness. No one answered his knock and when Larry turned the knob, it was off the latch. He walked into the large, luxuriously furnished living room and stood there a moment, uncertainly, then called out, "Miss Page." There was no answer. So *that* was her plan.

I'm sorry, Costa darling, but I warned you that he was unreliable. I asked him to pick me up at ten o'clock, but he was down in the bar getting drunk. I had to leave without him.

Larry heard a sound from the bathroom and went toward it. The bathroom door was open. He walked inside just as Noelle Page stepped out of the shower. She wore nothing but a turkish towel turbanned around her head.

Noelle turned and saw him standing there. An apology sprang to Larry's lips, trying to head off her indignation, but before he could speak, Noelle said indifferently, "Hand me that towel," as though he were a maid. Or a eunuch. Larry could have coped with her indignation or anger, but her arrogant indifference made something explode inside him.

He moved toward her and grabbed her, knowing as he did it that he was throwing away everything he wanted for the cheap satisfaction of a petty revenge, but there was no way he could have stopped himself. The rage inside him had been building up for months, fed by the indignities he had received from her, the gratuitous insults, the humiliation, the risking of his life. All these things were burning in him as he reached for her naked body. If Noelle had screamed, Larry would have knocked her senseless. But she saw the wild look on his face and made no sound as he picked her up and carried her into the bedroom.

Somewhere in Larry's mind a voice was shouting to him to stop, to apologize, to say that he was drunk, to get out before it was too late to save himself, but he knew it was already too late. There was no going back. He threw her savagely down on the bed and moved toward her.

He concentrated on her body, refusing to let his mind think of what his punishment was going to be for what he was doing. He had no illusions as to what Demiris would do to him for this, for the Greek's honor would not be satisfied with merely firing him. Larry knew enough about the tycoon to know that his vengeance would be far more terrible, and yet knowing this Larry could not stop himself. She lay on the bed looking up at him, her eyes blazing. He moved down on top of her and was entering her, never realizing until that instant how much he had been wanting to do this all along, and somehow the need was all mixed up with the hate, and he felt her arms wrap around his neck, holding him close, as though she would never let him go, and she said, "Welcome back," and it flashed through Larry's mind that she was crazy or she was confusing him with someone else, but he didn't care because her body was twisting and writhing beneath him, and he forgot everything else in the sensation of what was happening to him, and the sudden blinding wonderful knowledge that now everything was going to be all right.

16

NOELLE AND CATHERINE

ATHENS: 1946

Inexplicably, Time had become Catherine's enemy. She was unaware of it at first, and looking back she could not have told the exact moment that Time began to work against her. She was not aware when Larry's love had gone or why or how, but one day it had simply disappeared somewhere down the endless corridor of time and all that was left was a cold hollow echo. She sat in the apartment alone day after day, trying to figure out what had happened, what had gone wrong. There was nothing specific Catherine could think of, no single moment of revelation that she could point to and say, *That was it, that was when Larry stopped loving me.* Possibly it had started when Larry came back after three weeks in Africa where he had flown Constantin Demiris on a safari. Catherine had missed Larry more than she had thought possible. *He's away all the time,* she thought. *It's like during the war, only this time there's no enemy.*

But she was wrong. There was an enemy.

"I haven't told you the good news," Larry said. "I got a raise. Seven hundred a month. How about that?"

"That's wonderful," she replied. "We can go back home that much sooner." She saw his face tighten. "What's the matter?"

"*This* is home," Larry said, curtly.

She stared at him uncomprehendingly. "Well, for now," she agreed weakly, "but I mean—you wouldn't want to live here forever."

"You've never had it so good," Larry retorted. "It's like living at a vacation resort."

"But it's not like living in America, is it?"

"Fuck America," Larry said. "I risked my ass for it for four years and what did it get me? A handful of two-bit medals. They wouldn't even give me a job after the war."

"That's not true," she said. "You . . ."

"I what?"

Catherine did not want to provoke an argument, particularly on his first night back. "Nothing, darling," she said. "You're tired. Let's go to bed early."

"Let's not." He went to the bar to pour himself a drink. "A new act's opening at the Argentina Night Club. I told Paul Metaxas that we'd join him and a few friends."

Catherine looked at him. "Larry—" She had to fight to keep her voice steady. "Larry, we haven't seen each other for almost a month. We never get a chance to—to just sit and talk."

"I can't help it if my work takes me away," he replied. "Don't you think I'd like to be with you?"

She shook her head and said, "I don't know. I'll have to ask the Ouija board."

He put his arms around her then and grinned that innocent, boyish grin. "To hell with Metaxas and the whole crowd. We'll stay in tonight, just the two of us. Okay?"

Catherine looked into his face and knew that she was being unreasonable. Of course he couldn't help it if his job took him away from her. And when he got home, it was natural that he would want to see other people. "We'll go out if you like," she decided.

"Uhn-uhn." He held her close. "Just the two of us."

They did not leave the apartment all weekend. Catherine cooked and they made love and sat in front of the fire and talked and played gin rummy and read, and it was everything that Catherine could have asked.

Sunday night after a delicious dinner that Catherine prepared, they went to bed and made love again. She lay in bed watching Larry as he walked toward the bathroom, naked, and she thought what a beautiful man he is and how lucky I am that he belongs to me, and the smile was still on her face when Larry turned at the bathroom door and said casually, "Make a lot of dates next week, will you, so we won't have to be stuck with each other like this again with nothing to do." And he went into the bathroom leaving Catherine with the smile still frozen on her face.

OR PERHAPS THE trouble had started with Helena, the beautiful Greek stewardess. One hot summer afternoon, Catherine had been out shopping. Larry was out of town. She was expecting him home the following day and had decided to surprise him with his favorite dishes. As Catherine was leaving the market with her arms full of groceries, a taxi passed her. In the back seat was Larry, his arms around a girl in a stewardess' uniform. Catherine had one brief glimpse of their faces laughing together, and then the taxi turned a corner and was out of sight.

Catherine stood there numb, and it was not until some small boys came running up to her that she realized the grocery bags had slipped from her nerveless fingers. They had helped Catherine pick up everything and she had stumbled home, her mind refusing to think. She had tried to tell herself that it had not been Larry she had seen in the taxi, it had been someone who resembled him. But the truth was that no one in the world resembled Larry. He was unique, an original work of God, a priceless creation of nature. And he was all hers. Hers and the brunette's in the taxi, and how many others?

Catherine sat up all that night waiting for Larry to walk in, and when he did not come home, she knew that there was no excuse that he could give her that could hold their marriage together, and no excuse that she could give herself. He was a liar and a cheat, and she could not stay married to him any longer.

Larry did not return home until late the following afternoon.

"Hi," he said, cheerfully, as he walked into the apartment. He put down his flight bag and saw her face. "What's wrong?"

"When did you get back to town?" Catherine asked stiffly.

Larry looked at her, puzzled. "About an hour ago. Why?"

"I saw you in a taxi yesterday with a girl." *It was as simple as that,* Catherine thought. *Those are the words that ended my marriage. He's going to deny it, and I'm going to call him a liar and leave him and never see him again.*

Larry was standing there staring at her.

"Go ahead," she said. "Tell me it wasn't you."

Larry looked at her, nodding. "Of course it was me." The sudden sharp pain Catherine felt at the pit of her stomach made her realize how much she had wanted him to deny it.

"Christ," he said, "what have you been thinking?"

She started to speak and her voice trembled with anger. "I—"

Larry held up a hand. "Don't say anything you'll be sorry for."

Catherine looked at him incredulously. "*I'll* be sorry for?"

"I flew back to Athens yesterday for fifteen minutes to pick up a girl named Helena Merelis to fly her to Crete for Demiris. Helena works for him as a stewardess."

"But . . ." It was possible. Larry could have been telling the truth; or was it *polymechanos,* fertile in devices? "Why didn't you telephone me?" Catherine asked.

"I did," Larry said curtly. "There was no answer. You were out, weren't you?"

Catherine swallowed. "I—I went out shopping for your dinner."

"I'm not hungry," Larry snapped. "Nagging always makes me lose my appetite." He turned and walked out the door, leaving Catherine standing there, her right hand still raised, as though it was silently beseeching him to come back.

IT WAS SHORTLY after that Catherine began to drink. It started in a small, harmless way. She would be expecting Larry home for dinner at seven o'clock, and when nine o'clock came and he had not called, Catherine would have a brandy to help kill the time. By ten o'clock, she would have had several brandies, and by the time he came home, if he did, the dinner would have been long since ruined, and she would be a little tight. It made it much easier to face what was happening to her life.

Catherine could no longer hide from herself the fact that Larry was cheating on her and had probably been cheating from the time they were married. Going through his uniform trousers one day before sending them to the cleaners, she found a lace handkerchief stiff with dried semen. There was lipstick on his shorts.

She thought of Larry in the arms of some other woman.

And she wanted to kill him.

17

NOELLE AND CATHERINE

ATHENS: 1946

A s Time had become Catherine's enemy, so it had become Larry's friend. The night in Amsterdam had been nothing less than a miracle. Larry had courted disaster and in so doing had, incredibly, found the solution to all his problems. *It's the Douglas luck,* he thought with satisfaction.

But he knew that it was more than luck. It was some obscure, perverse instinct in him that needed to challenge the Fates, to brush against the parameters of death and destruction, a testing, a pitting of himself against Fortune for life-and-death stakes.

Larry remembered a morning over the Truk Islands when a squadron of Zeros had zoomed out of a cloud cover. He had been flying point, and they had concentrated their attack on him. Three Zeros had maneuvered him away from the rest of the squadron and opened fire on him. In a kind of supra-clarity that came to him in moments of danger, he was blindingly aware of the island below, the dozens of ships bobbing on the rolling seas, the roaring planes slashing at each other in the bright blue sky. It was one of the happiest moments of Larry's life, the fulfillment of Life and the mocking of Death.

He had put the plane into a spin and had pulled out of it on the tail of one of the Zeros. He had watched it explode as he opened up with his machine guns. The other two planes had closed in on either side. Larry watched them as they raced down to him, and at the last instant he pulled the plane into an Immelmann, and the two Japanese planes collided in midair. It was a moment Larry savored in his mind often.

For some reason it had come back to him that night in Amsterdam. He had made wild, violent love to Noelle, and afterward she had lain in his arms, talking of the two of them in Paris together before the war, and it suddenly brought back a dim memory of an eager young girl, but good God, there had been hundreds of eager young girls since then, and Noelle was no more than an elusive, half-recalled wisp of memory in his past.

How lucky it was, Larry thought, that their paths had crossed again accidentally, after all these years.

"You belong to me," Noelle said. "You're mine now."

Something in her tone made Larry uneasy. *And yet,* he asked himself, *what do I have to lose?*

With Noelle under his control, he could stay on with Demiris forever, if he wanted to.

She was studying him as though reading his mind, and there was an odd expression in her eyes that Larry did not understand.

It was just as well.

ON A RETURN trip from Morocco Larry took Helena out to dinner and spent the night at her apartment.

In the morning he drove to the airport to check out his plane. He had lunch with Paul Metaxas.

"You look like you hit the jackpot," Metaxas said. "Can you spare a piece for me?"

"My boy." Larry grinned. "You couldn't handle them. It takes a master."

They had a pleasant lunch and then Larry drove back into town to pick up Helena, who was to be on his flight.

He knocked at the door of her apartment and after a long while, Helena slowly opened it. She was naked. Larry stared at her, not recognizing her. Her face and body were a mass of ugly bruises and puffy swellings. Her eyes were slits of pain. She had been beaten up by a professional.

"Christ!" Larry exclaimed. "What happened?"

Helena opened her mouth and Larry saw that three of her upper front teeth had been knocked out. "T-two men," she chattered. "They came in as soon as you l-left."

"Didn't you call the police?" Larry demanded, horrified.

"Th-they said they would kill me if I told anyone. They meant it, L-Larry." She stood there in shock, holding onto the door for support.

"Did they rob you?"

"N-no. They f-forced their way in and raped me and then they—they beat me up."

"Get some clothes on," he ordered. "I'm taking you to the hospital."

"I can't g-go out with my face like this," she said.

And of course she was right. Larry telephoned a doctor who was a friend of his and arranged for him to come over.

"I'm sorry I can't stay," Larry told Helena. "I have to fly Demiris out in half an hour. I'll see you as soon as I return."

But he never saw her again. When Larry returned two days later, the apartment was empty, and the landlady told him that the young lady had moved and had left no forwarding address. Even then Larry had no suspicion of the truth. It was not until several nights later when he was making love to Noelle that he had an inkling of what had happened. "You're so goddamn fantastic," he said. "I've never known anybody like you."

"Do I give you everything you want?" she asked.

"Yes," he moaned. "Oh, Christ, yes."

Noelle stopped what she was doing. "Then don't ever sleep with another woman," she said softly. "Next time, I'll kill her."

Larry remembered her words: You belong to me. And they suddenly took on a new and ominous meaning. For the first time he had the premonition that this was not some fly-by-night affair that he could get out of anytime he felt like it. He sensed the cold, deadly, untouchable center that was in Noelle Page, and he was chilled and a little frightened by it. Half a dozen times during the night he started to bring up the subject of Helena, and each time he stopped because he was afraid to know, afraid to have it put into words, as though the words had more power than the deed itself. If Noelle were capable of that . . .

At breakfast the next morning Larry studied Noelle when she was unaware of it, looking for signs of cruelty, of sadism, but all he saw was a loving, beautiful woman, telling him amusing anecdotes, anticipating and catering to his every want. *I have to be wrong about her,* he thought. But after that he was careful not to date any other girls, and in a few short weeks he had lost all desire to do so because Noelle had become a complete obsession with him.

From the beginning Noelle warned Larry that it was essential that they keep their affair from Constantin Demiris.

"There must never be the slightest whisper of suspicion about us," Noelle cautioned.

"Why don't I rent an apartment?" Larry suggested. "A place where we . . ."

Noelle shook her head. "Not in Athens. Someone would recognize me. Let me think about it."

Two days later Demiris sent for Larry. At first Larry was apprehensive, wondering whether the Greek tycoon could have heard about Noelle and him, but Demiris greeted him pleasantly and led him into a discussion of a new plane he was considering buying.

"It's a converted Mitchell Bomber," Demiris told him. "I want you to have a look at it."

Larry's face lit up. "It's a great plane," he said. "For its weight and size, it will give you the best ride you can buy."

"How many passengers will it carry?"

Larry thought a moment. "Nine in luxury, plus a pilot, navigator and flight engineer. It flies at four hundred eighty miles an hour."

"It sounds interesting. Will you check it out for me and give me a report?"

"I can't wait." Larry grinned.

Demiris rose to his feet. "By the way, Douglas, Miss Page is going to Berlin in the morning. I want you to fly her there."

"Yes, sir," Larry said. And then added, innocently, "Did Miss Page tell you that we're getting along better?"

Demiris looked up at him. "No," he said puzzled. "As a matter of fact this morning she complained to me about your insolence."

Larry stared at him in surprise, and then as realization flooded through him, he quickly tried to cover up his blunder. "I'm trying, Mr. Demiris," he said, earnestly. "I'll try harder."

Demiris nodded. "Do that. You're the best pilot I've ever had, Douglas. It would be a shame to . . ." He let his voice trail off, but the message was clear.

On the drive home Larry cursed himself for a fool. He had better remember he was playing in the big leagues now. Noelle had been bright enough to realize that any sudden change in her attitude toward Larry would make Demiris suspicious. The old relationship between them was a perfect cover for what they were doing. Demiris was trying to bring them together. The thought made Larry laugh aloud. It was a good feeling to know that he had something that one of the most powerful men in the world thought belonged to him.

ON THE FLIGHT to Berlin Larry turned the wheel over to Paul Metaxas and told him that he was going back to talk to Noelle Page.

"Aren't you afraid of getting your head bitten off?" Metaxas asked.

Larry hesitated, tempted to brag. But he conquered the impulse. "She's a bitch on wheels," Larry shrugged, "but if I don't find some way to soften her up, I could find myself out on my ass."

"Good luck," Metaxas said soberly.

"Thanks."

Larry carefully closed the cockpit door and went back to the lounge where Noelle was seated. The two stewardesses were at the rear of the plane. Larry started to sit down across from Noelle.

"Be careful," she warned softly. "Everyone who works for Constantin reports back to him."

Larry glanced toward the stewardesses and thought of Helena.

"I've found a place for us," Noelle said. There was pleasure and excitement in her voice.

"An apartment?"

"A house. Do you know where Rafina is?"

Larry shook his head. "No."

"It's a little village on the sea, a hundred kilometers north of Athens. We have a secluded villa there."

He nodded. "Whose name did you rent it in?"

"I bought it," Noelle said, "in someone else's name."

Larry wondered what it must feel like to be able to afford to buy a villa just to get in the hay with someone once in a while. "Great," he said. "I can't wait to see it."

She studied him a moment. "Will you have any trouble getting away from Catherine?"

Larry looked at Noelle in surprise. It was the first time she had ever mentioned his wife. He had certainly made no secret of his marriage, but it was a strange feeling to hear Noelle use Catherine's name. Obviously she had done some checking, and knowing her as well as he was beginning to, it was probably very thorough. She was waiting for an answer. "No," Larry replied. "I come and go as I please."

Noelle nodded, satisfied. "Good. Constantin is going on a business cruise to Dubrovnik. I've told him I can't go with him. We'll have ten lovely days together. You'd better go now."

Larry turned and walked back to the cockpit.

"How did it go?" Metaxas asked. "Loosen her up any?"

"Not much," Larry replied, carefully. "It's going to take time."

Larry owned a car, a Citroen convertible, but at Noelle's insistence, he went to a small rent-a-car agency in Athens and hired an automobile. Noelle had driven up to Rafina alone and Larry was to join her there. The drive was a pleasant one on a winding ribbon of dusty road high above the sea. Two and a half hours out of Athens Larry came to a tiny, charming village nestled along the coastline. Noelle had given him careful directions so that he would not have to stop and inquire at the village. As he reached the outskirts of the village, he turned to the left and drove down a small dirt road that led to the sea. There were several villas, each one secluded behind high stone walls. At the end of the road built on an outcropping of rock on a promontory that jutted out over the water was a large, luxurious-looking villa.

Larry drove up to the gate and rang the bell. A moment later the electric gate swung open. He drove inside and the gate closed behind him. He found himself in a large courtyard with a fountain in the center. The sides of the courtyard were filled with a profusion of flowers. The house itself was a typical Mediterranean villa, as impregnable as a fortress. The front door opened and Noelle appeared, wearing a white cotton dress. They stood there smiling at each other, and then she was in his arms.

"Come and see your new house," she said eagerly, and she took him inside.

The interior of the house was cavernous, large spacious rooms with high domed ceilings. There was an enormous living room downstairs, a library, a formal dining room and an old-fashioned kitchen with a circular cooking range in the center. The bedrooms were upstairs.

"What about the servants?" Larry asked.

"You're looking at them."

Larry regarded her in surprise. "*You're* going to do the cooking and cleaning?"

She nodded. "There will be a couple coming in to clean after we leave here, but they will never see us. I arranged it through an agency."

Larry grinned sardonically.

There was a warning note in Noelle's voice. "Don't ever make the mistake of underestimating Constantin Demiris. If he finds out about us, he will kill both of us."

Larry smiled. "You're exaggerating," he said. "The old man may not like it, but . . ."

Her violet eyes locked on his. "He will kill us both." There was something in her voice that sent a feeling of apprehension through him.

"You're serious, aren't you?"

"I was never more serious in my life. He's ruthless."

"But when you say he'll *kill* us," Larry protested, "he wouldn't . . ."

"He won't use bullets," Noelle said flatly. "He'll find a complicated, ingenious way to do it, and he'll never be punished for it." Her tone lightened. "But he won't find out, darling. Come, let me show you our bedroom." She took his hand and they went up the sweeping stairway. "We have four guest bedrooms," she said and added with a smile, "we can try them all." She took him into the master bedroom, a huge corner suite that overlooked the sea. From the window Larry could see a large terrace and the short path that wound down to the water. There was a dock with a large sailboat and a motor boat moored to it.

"Who do the boats belong to?"

"You," she said. "It's your welcome-home present."

He turned to her and found that she had slipped out of her cotton dress. She was naked. They spent the rest of the afternoon in bed.

THE NEXT TEN days flew by. Noelle was quicksilver, a nymph, a genie, a dozen beautiful servants catering to Larry's every wish before he even knew what he wanted. He found the library in the villa stocked with his favorite books and records. Noelle cooked all his favorite dishes to perfection, sailed with him, swam in the warm blue sea with him, made love to him, gave him massages at night until he fell asleep. In a sense they were prisoners there together, for they dared not see anyone else. Every day Larry found new facets in Noelle. She entertained him with fascinating anecdotes about famous people she knew. She tried to discuss business and politics with him until she found that he was interested in neither.

They played poker and gin rummy, and Larry was furious because he could never win. Noelle taught him chess and backgammon and he could never beat her at either. On their first Sunday at the villa she fixed a delicious picnic lunch, and they sat on the beach in the sun and enjoyed it. While they were eating, Noelle looked up and saw two men in the distance. They were strolling toward them along the beach.

"Let's go inside," Noelle said.

Larry looked up and saw the men. "Jesus, don't be so jumpy. They're just a couple of villagers out for a walk."

"Now," she commanded.

"OK," he said ungraciously, irritated by the incident and by her tone.

"Help me pack up the things."

"Why don't we just leave them?" he asked.

"Because it would look suspicious."

Quickly they stuffed everything into the picnic hamper and started toward the house. Larry was silent for the rest of the afternoon. He sat in the library, his mind preoccupied, while Noelle worked in the kitchen.

Late in the afternoon she came into the library and sat at his feet. With her uncanny knack of reading his mind, she said. "Stop thinking about them."

"They were just a couple of goddamn villagers," Larry snapped. "I hate sneaking around like some kind of criminal." He looked at her and his voice changed. "I don't want to have to hide from anybody. I love you."

And Noelle knew that this time it was true. She thought of the years during which she had planned to destroy Larry and of the fierce pleasure she had taken in imagining his destruction: And yet the moment Noelle had seen Larry again she had known instantly that there was something deeper than hate still alive in her. When she had pushed him to the brink of death, forcing him to risk both their lives on that terrible flight to Amsterdam, it was as though she were testing his love for her in a wild defiance of fate. She had been with Larry in that cockpit, flying the plane with him, suffering with him, knowing that if he died they would die together, and he had saved them both. And when he had come to her room in Amsterdam and made love to her, her hatred and her love had become intermingled with their two bodies, and somehow time had expanded and contracted and they were back in their little hotel room in Paris and Larry was saying to her, "Let's get married; we'll find some little *maire* in the country," and the present and the past had exploded dazzlingly into one and Noelle knew then that they were timeless, had always been timeless, that nothing had really changed and that the depths of her hatred for Larry had come from the heights of her love. If she destroyed him she would be destroying herself, for she had given herself completely to him long ago and nothing could ever change that.

It seemed to Noelle that everything she had achieved in her life had been through her hatred. Her father's betrayal had molded and shaped her, annealed and hardened her, filled her with a hunger for vengeance that could be satisfied with nothing less than a kingdom of her own in which she was all-powerful, in which she could never be betrayed again, never be hurt. She had finally achieved that. And now she was ready to give it up for this man. Because she knew now that what she had always wanted was for Larry to need her, to love her. And, at last, he did. And that, finally, was her real kingdom.

18

NOELLE AND CATHERINE

ATHENS: 1946

For Larry and Noelle the next three months was one of those rare, idyllic periods when everything went right, a magic time of floating from one wonderful day to the next, with not the faintest cloud on the horizon. Larry spent his working hours doing what he loved to do, flying, and whenever he had time off he went to the villa in Rafina and spent a day or a weekend or a week with Noelle. In the beginning Larry had been afraid that the arrangement would become a millstone that would drag him down into the kind of domesticity that he loathed; but each time he saw Noelle, he became more enchanted and he began to look eagerly forward to the hours he would spend with her. When she had to cancel one weekend because of an unexpected trip with Demiris, Larry stayed alone at the villa, and he found himself angry and jealous, thinking about Noelle and Demiris together. When he saw Noelle the following week, she was surprised and pleased by his eagerness.

"You missed me," she said.

He nodded. "A lot."

"Good."

"How's Demiris?"

She hesitated a moment. "All right."

Larry noticed her hesitation. "What is it?"

"I was thinking of something you said."

"What?"

"You said you hated the feeling of sneaking around like a criminal. I hate it too. Every moment I was with Constantin, I wanted to be with you. I once told you, Larry, I want all of you. I meant it. I don't want to share you with anyone. I want you to marry me."

He stared at her in surprise, caught off guard.

Noelle was watching him. "Do you want to marry me?"

"You know I do. But how? You keep telling me what Demiris will do if he finds out about us."

She shook her head. "He won't find out. Not if we're clever and plan it properly. He doesn't own me, Larry. I'll leave him. There's nothing he can do about that. He has too much pride to try to stop me. A month or two later, you'll quit your job. We'll go away somewhere, separately, perhaps to the United States. We can be married there. I have more money than we'll ever need. I'll buy you a charter airline, or a flying school or whatever you like."

He stood there listening to what she was saying, weighing what he would be giving up against what he would be gaining. And what would he be giving up? A lousy job as a pilot. The thought of owning his own planes sent a small thrill coursing through him. He'd have his own converted Mitchell. Or maybe the new DC-6 that had just come out. Four radial engines, eighty-five passengers. And Noelle, yes, he wanted Noelle. Jesus, what was he even hesitating about?

"What about my wife?" he asked.

"Tell her you want a divorce."

"I don't know if she'll give me one."

"Don't ask her," Noelle replied. "Tell her." There was a final implacable note in her voice.

Larry nodded. "All right."

"You won't be sorry, darling. I promise," Noelle said.

· · ·

FOR CATHERINE TIME had lost its circadian rhythm; she had fallen into a tesseract of time, and day and night blended into one. Larry was almost never home, and she had long since stopped seeing any of their friends, because she did not have the energy to make any more excuses or to face people. Count Pappas had made half a dozen attempts to see her, and had finally given up. She found herself only able to cope with people secondhand: by telephone or letter or cable. But face to face, she turned to stone, and conversations flinted off her in hopeless, futile sparks. Time brought pain and people brought pain, and the only surcease Catherine found was in the wonderful forgetfulness of liquor. Oh how it eased the suffering, softened the sharp edge of rebuffs and gentled down the pitiless sun of reality that beat down on everyone else.

When Catherine had first come to Athens, she and William Fraser had written to each other frequently, swapping news and keeping each other up-to-date on the activities of their mutual friends and foes. Since Catherine's problems with Larry had begun, however, she had not had the heart to write to Fraser. His last three letters had gone unanswered, and his last letter had gone unopened. She simply did not have the energy to cope with anything outside the microcosm of self-pity in which she was trapped.

One day a cable arrived for Catherine, and it was still lying on the table unopened a week later, when the doorbell rang and William Fraser appeared. Catherine stared at him, unbelievingly. "Bill!" she said, thickly. "Bill Fraser!"

He started to speak and she saw the excited look in his eyes turn to something else, something startled and shocked.

"Bill, darling," she said. "What are you doing here?"

"I had to come to Athens on business," Fraser explained. "Didn't you get my cable?"

Catherine looked at him, trying to remember. "I don't know," she said finally. She led him into the living room, strewn with old newspapers, filled ashtrays and plates of half-eaten food. "Sorry the place is such a mess," she said, waving a vague hand. "I've been busy."

Fraser was studying her worriedly. "Are you all right, Catherine?"

"Me? Fantastic. How about a little drink?"

"It's only eleven o'clock in the morning."

She nodded. "You're right. You're absolutely right, Bill. It's too early to have a drink, and to tell you the truth I wouldn't have one except to celebrate your coming here. You're the only one in the whole world who could make me have a drink at eleven o'clock in the morning."

Fraser watched with dismay as Catherine staggered to the liquor cabinet and poured a large drink for herself and a smaller one for him.

"Do you like Greek brandy?" she asked as she carried his drink to him. "I used to hate it, but you get used to it."

Fraser took his drink and set it down. "Where's Larry?" he asked quietly.

"Larry? Oh, good old Larry's flying around somewhere. He works for the richest man in the world, you know. Demiris owns everything, even Larry."

He studied her a moment. "Does Larry know you drink?"

Catherine slammed down her glass and stood swaying in front of him. "What do you mean, does Larry know I drink?" she demanded indignantly. "Who says I drink? Just because I want to celebrate seeing an old friend, don't you start attacking me!"

"Catherine," he began, "I'm . . ."

"You think you can come in here and accuse me of being some kind of a drunk?"

"I'm sorry, Catherine," Fraser said painfully, "I think you need help."

"Well you're wrong," she retorted. "I don't need any help. Do you know why? Because I'm—I'm self—I'm self . . ." she groped for the word and finally gave it up. "I don't need any help."

Fraser watched her for a moment. "I have to go to a conference now," he said. "Have dinner with me tonight."

"OK." She nodded.

"Good. I'll pick you up at eight."

Catherine watched Bill Fraser as he walked out the door. Then with unsteady steps, she walked into her bedroom and slowly opened the closet door, staring into the mirror hanging on the back of the door. She stood there frozen, unable to believe what she was seeing, sure that the mirror was playing some dreadful trick on her. Inside she was still the pretty little girl adored by her father, still the young college girl standing in a motel room with Ron Peterson and hearing him say, "My God, Cathy, you're the most beautiful thing I've ever seen," and Bill Fraser holding her in his arms and saying, "You're so beautiful, Catherine," and Larry saying, "Stay this beautiful, Cathy, you're gorgeous," and she looked at the figure in the mirror and croaked aloud, "Who are you?" and the sad, shapeless woman in the mirror began to cry, hopeless, empty tears that coursed down the obscene bloated face. Hours later the doorbell rang. She heard Bill Fraser's voice calling, "Catherine! Catherine, are you there?" And then the bell rang some more, and finally the voice stopped and the ringing stopped and Catherine was left alone with the stranger in the mirror.

At nine o'clock the following morning, Catherine took a taxi to Patission Street. The doctor's name was Nikodes and he was a large, burly man with a white shaggy mane, a wise face with kind eyes, and an easy, informal manner.

A nurse ushered Catherine in to his private office and Doctor Nikodes indicated a chair. "Sit down, Mrs. Douglas."

Catherine took a seat, nervous and tense, trying to stop her body from trembling.

"What seems to be your problem?"

She started to answer and then stopped, helplessly. *Oh, God,* she thought, *where can I begin?* "I need help," she said, finally. Her voice was dry and scratchy, and she ached for a drink.

The doctor was leaning back in his chair watching her. "How old are you?"

"Twenty-eight." She watched his face as she said it. He tried to conceal the look of shock, but she caught it and in some perverse way was pleased by it.

"You're an American?"

"Yes."

"Are you living in Athens?"

She nodded.

"How long have you lived here?"

"A thousand years. We moved here before the Peloponnesian Wars."

The doctor smiled. "I feel that way sometimes too." He offered Catherine a cigarette. She reached for it, trying to control the trembling of her fingers. If Doctor Nikodes noticed, he said nothing. He lit it for her. "What kind of help do you need, Mrs. Douglas?"

Catherine looked at him helplessly. "I don't know," she whispered. "I don't know."

"Do you feel ill?"

"I am ill. I think I must be very ill. I've become so ugly." She knew she was not crying and yet she felt tears running down her cheeks.

"Do you drink, Mrs. Douglas?" the doctor asked gently.

Catherine stared at him in panic, feeling cornered, attacked. "Sometimes."

"How much?"

She took a deep breath. "Not much. It—it depends."

"Have you had a drink today?" he asked.

"No."

He sat there studying her. "You're not really ugly, you know," he said gently. "You're overweight, your body is bloated and you haven't been taking care of your skin or your hair. Underneath that facade there's a very attractive young woman."

She burst into tears, and he sat there letting her cry herself out. Dimly over her racking sobs Catherine heard the buzzer on his desk ring several times, but the doctor ignored it. The spasm of sobbing finally subsided. Catherine pulled out a handkerchief and blew her nose. "I'm sorry," she apologized. "C-can you help me?"

"That depends entirely on you," Doctor Nikodes replied. "We don't really know what your problem is yet."

"Take a look at me," Catherine responded.

He shook his head. "That's not a problem, Mrs. Douglas, that's a symptom. Forgive me for being blunt, but if I am to help you, we must be totally honest with each other. When an attractive young woman lets herself go as you have, there must be a very strong reason. Is your husband alive?"

"Holidays and weekends."

He studied her. "Do you live with him?"

"When he's home."

"What is his work?"

"He's Constantin Demiris' personal pilot." She saw the reaction on the doctor's face, but whether he was reacting to the name of Demiris or whether he knew something about Larry, she could not tell. "Have you heard of my husband?" she asked.

"No." But he could have been lying. "Do you love your husband, Mrs. Douglas?"

Catherine opened her mouth to answer and then stopped. She knew that what she was going to say was very important, not only to the doctor, but to herself. Yes, she loved her husband and yes, she hated him, and yes, at times she felt such a rage toward him that she knew she was capable of killing him, and yes, at times she was so overwhelmed by a tenderness for him that she knew she would gladly die for him and what was the word that could say all that? Perhaps it was love. "Yes," she said.

"Does he love you?"

Catherine thought of the other women in Larry's life and his unfaithfulness and she thought of the awful stranger in the mirror last night and she could not blame Larry for not wanting her. But who was to say which came first? Did the woman in the mirror create his infidelity, or did his infidelity create the woman in the mirror? She became aware that her cheeks were wet with tears again.

Catherine shook her head helplessly. "I—I don't know."

"Have you ever had a nervous breakdown?"

She was watching him now, her eyes wary. "No. Do you think I need one?"

He did not smile. He spoke slowly, choosing his words with care. "The human psyche is a delicate thing, Mrs. Douglas. It can take only so much pain and when the pain becomes unbearable, it escapes into hidden recesses of the mind that we are just beginning to explore. Your emotions are stretched very tight." He looked at her a moment. "I think it is a good thing you came to someone for help."

"I know I'm a little nervous," Catherine said defensively. "That's why I drink. To relax me."

"No," he said bluntly. "You drink to escape." Nikodes got up and walked over to her. "I think there's probably a good deal we can do for you. By 'we,' I mean you and I. It will not be simple."

"Tell me what to do."

"To begin with I am going to send you to a clinic for a thorough physical examination. My feeling is that they will find nothing basically wrong with you. Next, you are going to stop drinking. Then I am going to put you on a diet. All right so far?"

Catherine hesitated, then nodded.

"You are going to enroll in a gymnasium, where you will work out regularly to get your body back in shape. I have an excellent physiotherapist who will give you massages. You will go to a beauty parlor once a week. All this will take time, Mrs. Douglas. You did not get in this condition overnight, and it will not be changed overnight." He smiled at her reassuringly. "But I can promise you that in a few months—even a few weeks—you will begin to look and feel like a different woman. When you look in your mirror, you will feel proud—and when your husband looks at you, he will find you attractive."

Catherine stared at him, her heart lifting. It was as though some unbearable burden had been removed from deep inside her, as though she had suddenly been given a new chance to live.

"You must clearly understand that I can only suggest this program for you," the doctor was saying. "It is you who must do it."

"I will," Catherine said fervently. "I promise."

"To stop drinking will be the most difficult part."

"No, it won't," Catherine said. And as she said it, she knew it was true. The doctor had been right: She had been drinking in order to escape. Now she had a goal, she knew where she was going. She was going to win back Larry. "I won't touch another drop," she said firmly.

The doctor saw the look on her face and nodded, satisfied. "I believe you, Mrs. Douglas."

Catherine rose to her feet. It amazed her how clumsy and awkward her body was, but all that would change now. "I'd better go out and start buying some skinny clothes," she smiled.

The doctor wrote something on a card. "This is the address of the clinic. They will be expecting you. I will see you again after you have had your examination."

On the street Catherine looked for a taxi, then she thought, *To hell with that. I might as well start getting used to exercise.* She began to walk. She passed a shop window and stopped to stare at her reflection.

She had been so quick to blame Larry for the disintegration of their marriage without ever questioning what share of the blame was hers. Why would he want to come home to someone who looked like she did? How slowly and subtly this stranger had crept in without her being aware of it. She wondered how many marriages had died in this same way, not with a bang—*and there certainly hasn't been much of that lately,* Catherine thought, wryly—but with a whimper, just like good old T.S. Eliot said. Well, that was all in the past. From now on she would not look back, she would only look ahead to the wonderful future.

Catherine had reached the fashionable Salonika district. She was walking past a beauty parlor and on a sudden impulse she turned and went inside. The reception room was white marble, large and elegant. A haughty receptionist looked at Catherine disapprovingly and said, "Yes, may I help you?"

"I want to make an appointment for tomorrow morning," Catherine said. "I want everything. The works." The name of their top hair stylist suddenly popped into her head. "I want Aleko."

The woman shook her head. "I can give you an appointment, Madame, but you will have to take someone else."

"Listen," Catherine said firmly, "you tell Aleko that he either takes me or I'll go around Athens telling everyone I'm one of his regular customers."

The woman's eyes opened wide in shocked surprise. "I—I will see what I can do," she said hastily. "Come in at ten in the morning."

"Thanks." Catherine grinned. "I'll be here." And she walked out.

Ahead of her she saw a small taverna with a sign in the window that read "MADAME PIRIS—FORTUNE-TELLING." It seemed vaguely familiar and she suddenly remembered the day that Count Pappas had told her a story about Madame Piris. It was something about a policeman and a lion—but she could not remember the details. Catherine did not believe in fortune-tellers and yet the impulse to go in was irresistible. She needed reassurance, someone to confirm her feeling about her wonderful new future, to tell her that life was going to be beautiful again, worth living again. She opened the door and walked inside.

After the bright sunshine it took Catherine several moments to get used to the cavernous darkness of the room. She made out a bar in the corner and a dozen tables and chairs. A tired-looking waiter walked up to her and addressed her in Greek.

"Nothing to drink, thank you," Catherine said. She enjoyed hearing herself say the words and she repeated them. "Nothing to drink. I want to see Madame Piris. Is she here?"

The waiter gestured toward an empty table in the corner of the room and Catherine walked over and sat down. A few minutes later, she felt someone standing at her side, and looked up.

The woman was incredibly old and thin, dressed in black, with a face that had been washed by time into desiccated angles and planes.

"You asked to see me?" Her English was halting.

"Yes," Catherine said. "I would like a reading, please."

The woman sat down and raised a hand, and the waiter came over to the table bearing a cup of thick black coffee on a small tray. He set it down in front of Catherine.

"Not for me," Catherine said. "I . . ."

"Drink it," Madame Piris said.

Catherine looked at her in surprise, then picked up the cup and took a sip of the coffee. It was strong and bitter. She put down the cup.

"More," the woman said.

Catherine started to protest, then thought, *What the hell. What they lose on the fortune-telling, they make up on the coffee.* She swallowed another mouthful. It was vile.

"Once more," Madame Piris said.

Catherine shrugged and took a final sip. In the bottom of the cup were thick, viscous dregs. Madame Piris nodded, reached over and took the cup from Catherine. She stared into it for a long time, saying nothing. Catherine sat there feeling foolish. *What's a nice, intelligent girl like me doing in a place like this, watching an old Greek nut staring into an empty coffee cup?*

"You come from a faraway place," the woman said suddenly.

"Bull's eye," Catherine said flippantly.

Madame Piris looked up into her eyes and there was something in the look of the old woman that chilled Catherine.

"Go home."

Catherine swallowed. "I—I am home."

"Go back where you came from."

"You mean—America?"

"Anywhere. Get away from this place—quickly!"

"Why?" Catherine said, a sense of horror slowly filling her. "What's wrong?"

The old woman shook her head. Her voice was harsh and she was finding it difficult to get the words out. "It is all around you."

"*What* is?"

"Get out!" There was an urgency in the woman's voice, a high, shrill keening sound like an animal in pain. Catherine could feel the hair on her scalp begin to rise.

"You're frightening me," she moaned. "Please tell me what's wrong."

The old woman shook her head from side to side, her eyes wild. "Go away before it gets you."

Catherine felt a panic rising in her. It was difficult for her to breathe. "Before *what* gets me?"

The old woman's face was contorted with pain and terror. "Death. It is coming for you." And the woman rose and disappeared into the back room.

Catherine sat there, her heart pounding, her hands trembling, and she clasped them tightly together to stop them. She caught the waiter's eye and started to order a drink, but stopped herself. She was not going to let a crazy woman spoil her bright future. She sat there breathing deeply until she had gotten control of herself, and after a long time she rose, picked up her purse and gloves and walked out of the taverna.

Out in the dazzlingly bright sunlight Catherine felt better again. She had been foolish to let an old woman frighten her. A horror like that should be arrested instead of being allowed to terrify people. *From now on,* Catherine told herself, *you'll stick to fortune cookies.*

She stepped into her apartment and looked at the living room, and it was as though she were seeing it for the first time. It was a dismaying sight. Dust was thick everywhere, and articles of clothing were strewn around the room. It was incredible to Catherine that in her drunken haze she had not even been aware of it. Well, the first exercise she was going to get was making this place look spic and span. She was starting toward the kitchen when she heard a drawer close in the bedroom. Her heart leaped in sudden alarm, and she moved cautiously toward the bedroom door.

Larry was in the bedroom. A closed suitcase lay on his bed, and he was finishing packing a second suitcase. Catherine stood there a moment, watching him. "If those are for the Red Cross," she said, "I already gave."

Larry glanced up. "I'm leaving."

"Another trip for Demiris?"

"No," he said without stopping, "this one's for me. I'm getting out of here."

"Larry . . ."

"There's nothing to discuss."

She moved into the bedroom, fighting for self-control. "But—but there is. There's a lot to discuss. I went to see a doctor today and he told me I'm going to be fine." The words were coming out in a torrent. "I'm going to stop drinking and . . ."

"Cathy, it's over. I want a divorce."

The words hit her like a series of blows to the stomach. She stood there, clamping her jaw tight so that she would not retch, trying to fight down the bile that rose in her throat. "Larry," she said, speaking slowly to keep her voice from trembling, "I don't blame you for the way you feel. A lot of it is my fault—maybe most of it—but it's going to be different. I'm going to change—I mean *really* change." She held out her hand pleadingly. "All I ask is a chance."

Larry turned to face her and his dark eyes were cold and contemptuous. "I'm in love with someone else. All I want from you is a divorce."

Catherine stood there a long moment, then turned and walked back into the living room and sat on the couch, looking at a Greek fashion magazine while he finished packing. She heard Larry's voice saying, "My attorney will be in touch with you" and then the slam of a door. Catherine sat there carefully turning the pages of the magazine, and when she had come to the end she set it down neatly in the center of the table, went into the bathroom, opened the medicine chest, took out a razor blade and slashed her wrists.

NOELLE AND CATHERINE

ATHENS: 1946

There were ghosts in white and they floated around her and then drifted away into space with soft whispers in a language that Catherine could not understand, but she understood that this was Hell and that she had to pay for her sins. They kept her strapped down on the bed, and she supposed that was part of her punishment, and she was glad of the straps because she could feel the earth spinning around through space and she was afraid she was going to fall off the planet. The most diabolical thing they had done was to put all her nerves on the outside of her body so that she felt everything a thousand-fold, and it was unbearable. Her body was alive with terrifying and unfamiliar noises. She could hear the blood as it ran through her veins, and it was like a roaring red river moving through her. She heard the strokes of her heart, and it sounded like an enormous drum being pounded by giants. She had no eyelids and the white light poured into her brain, dazzling her with its brightness. All the muscles of her body were alive, in constant, restless motion like a nest of snakes under her skin ready to strike.

Five days after Catherine had been admitted to Evangelismos Hospital, she opened her eyes and found herself in a small, white hospital room. A nurse in a starched white uniform was adjusting her bed, and Dr. Nikodes had a stethoscope to her chest.

"Hey, that's cold," she protested weakly.

He looked at her and said, "Well, well, look who's awake."

Catherine moved her eyes slowly around the room. The light seemed normal and she could no longer hear the roaring of her blood or the pounding of her heart or the dying of her body.

"I thought I was in Hell." Her voice was a whisper.

"You have been."

She looked at her wrists. For some reason, they were bandaged. "How long have I been here?"

"Five days."

She suddenly remembered the reason for the bandages. "I guess I did a dumb thing," she said.

"Yes."

She squeezed her eyes shut and said, "I'm sorry," and opened them and it was night and Bill Fraser was sitting in a chair beside her bed, watching her. Flowers and candy were on her bedside table.

"Hi there," he said cheerfully. "You're looking much better."

"Better than what?" she asked weakly.

He put his hand over hers. "You really gave me a scare, Catherine."

"I'm so sorry, Bill." Her voice started to choke up, and she was afraid that she was going to cry.

"I brought you some flowers and candy. When you're feeling stronger, I'll bring you some books."

She looked at him, at his kind strong face, and she thought: *Why don't I love him? Why am I in love with the man I hate? Why did God have to turn out to be Groucho Marx?* "How did I get here?" Catherine asked.

"In an ambulance."

"I mean—who found me?"

Fraser paused. "I did. I tried phoning you several times and when you didn't answer, I got worried and broke in."

"I suppose I should say thanks," she said, "but to tell you the truth, I'm not sure yet."

"Do you want to talk about it?"

Catherine shook her head and the movement caused her head to begin throbbing. "No," she said in a small voice.

Fraser nodded. "I have to fly home in the morning. I'll keep in touch."

She felt a gentle kiss on her forehead and closed her eyes to shut out the world and when she opened them again, she was alone and it was the middle of the night.

Early the next morning Larry came to visit her. Catherine watched him as he walked into the room and sat down in a chair next to her bed. She had expected him to be drawn-looking and unhappy, but the truth was that he looked wonderful, lean and tan and relaxed. Catherine wished desperately that she had had a chance to comb her hair and put on some lipstick.

"How do you feel, Cathy?" he asked.

"Terrific. Suicide always stimulates me."

"They didn't expect you to pull through."

"I'm sorry to have disappointed you."

"That's not a very nice thing to say."

"It's true though, isn't it, Larry? You'd have been rid of me."

"For Christ's sake, I don't want to be rid of you that way, Catherine. All I want is a divorce."

She looked at him, this bronzed, handsome man she had married, his face a little more dissipated now, his mouth a little harder, his boyish charm worn a bit thin. What was she hanging onto? Seven years of dreams? She had given herself to him with such love and high hopes and she could not bear to let them go, could not bear to admit that she had made a mistake that had turned her life into a barren wasteland. She remembered Bill Fraser and their friends in Washington and the fun they had known. She could not remember the last time she had laughed aloud, or even smiled. But none of that really mattered. In the end the reason that she would not let Larry go was that she still loved him. He was standing there waiting for an answer. "No," Catherine said. "I'll never give you a divorce."

LARRY MET NOELLE that night at the deserted monastery of Kaissariani in the mountains and reported his conversation with Catherine.

Noelle listened intently and asked, "Do you think she will change her mind?"

Larry shook his head. "Catherine can be as stubborn as hell."

"You must speak to her again."

AND LARRY DID. For the next three weeks he exhausted every argument he could think of. He pleaded, cajoled, raged at her, offered her money, but nothing moved Catherine. She still loved him, and she was sure that if he gave himself a chance he could love her again.

"You're my husband," she said stubbornly. "You're going to be my husband until I die."

HE REPEATED WHAT she had said to Noelle.

Noelle nodded. "Yes," she said.

Larry looked at her, puzzled. "Yes, what?"

They were lying on the beach at the villa, fluffy white towels spread out beneath them, shielding their bodies from the hot sand. The sky was a deep, blazing blue, dotted with white patches of cirrus clouds.

"You must get rid of her." She rose to her feet and strode back to the villa, her long graceful legs moving smoothly across the sand. Larry lay there, bewildered, thinking that he must have misunderstood her. Surely she had not meant that she wanted him to *kill* Catherine.

And then he remembered Helena.

THEY WERE HAVING supper on the terrace. "Don't you see? She doesn't deserve to live," Noelle said. "She's holding onto you to be vengeful. She's trying to ruin your life, our lives, darling."

THEY LAY IN bed smoking, the glowing embers of the cigarette ends winking into the infinity of the mirrors covering the ceiling.

"You would be doing her a favor. She's already tried to kill herself. She wants to die."

"I could never do it, Noelle."

"Couldn't you?"

She stroked his naked leg, gently moving up toward his belly, making small circles with the tips of her fingernails.

"I'll help you."

He started to open his mouth to protest, but Noelle's two hands had found him, and they began working on him, moving in opposite directions, one softly and slowly, the other one hard and quickly. And Larry moaned and reached for her and put Catherine out of his mind.

SOMETIME DURING THE night Larry awakened in a cold sweat. He had dreamed that Noelle had run away and left him. She was lying in bed next to him, and he took her in his arms and held her close. He lay awake the rest of the night, thinking what it would do to him if he lost her. He was not aware that he had made any decision, but in the morning while Noelle was preparing breakfast, Larry said suddenly, "What if we're caught?"

"If we're clever, we won't be." If she was pleased by his capitulation, she gave no sign of it.

"Noelle," he said earnestly, "every busybody in Athens knows that Catherine and I don't get along. If anything happened to her, the police would be damned suspicious."

"Of course they would be," Noelle agreed calmly. "That is why everything will be planned very carefully."

She served them both and then sat down and began to eat. Larry pushed his plate away from him, his food untasted.

"Isn't it good?" Noelle asked, concerned.

He stared at her, wondering what kind of person she was, able to enjoy a meal while she was planning the murder of another woman.

Later, sailing on the boat, they talked about it further, and the more they talked about it, the more of a reality it became, so that what had begun as a casual idea had been fleshed out with words until it had become a fact.

"It must look like an accident," Noelle said, "so that there will be no police investigation. The police in Athens are very clever."

"What if they *should* investigate?"

"They won't. The accident will not happen here."

"Where, then?"

"Ioannina." She leaned forward and began to talk. He listened to her as she elaborated on her plan, meeting every objection that he raised, improvising brilliantly. At the end when Noelle finished, Larry had to admit that the plan was flawless. They could really get away with it.

PAUL METAXAS WAS nervous. The Greek pilot's usually jovial face was drawn and tense and he could feel a nervous tic pulling at the corner of his mouth. He had had no appointment with Constantin Demiris, and one did not simply barge in on the great man, but Metaxas had told the butler it was urgent, and now Paul Metaxas found himself standing in the enormous hallway of Demiris' villa, staring at him and stammering clumsily, "I—I am terribly sorry to bother you, Mr. Demiris." Metaxas surreptitiously wiped the sweaty palm of his hand against the leg of his flight uniform.

"Has something happened to one of the planes?"

"Oh, no, sir. I—It's—it's a personal matter."

Demiris studied him without interest. He made it a policy never to get involved in the affairs of his underlings. He had secretaries to handle that kind of thing for him. He waited for Metaxas to go on.

Paul Metaxas was becoming more nervous by the second. He had spent a lot of sleepless nights before making the decision that had brought him here. What he was doing now was alien to his character and therefore distasteful, but he was a man of fierce loyalty, and his first allegiance was to Constantin Demiris.

"It's about Miss Page," he said, finally.

There was a moment of silence.

"Come in here," Demiris said. He led the pilot into the paneled library and closed the doors. Demiris took a flat Egyptian cigarette out of a platinum case and lit it. He looked up at the perspiring Metaxas. "What about Miss Page?" he asked, almost absently.

Metaxas swallowed, wondering if he had made a mistake. If he had estimated the situation correctly, his information would be appreciated, but if he was mistaken . . .

He cursed himself for his rashness in having come here, but he had no choice now but to plunge ahead.

"It's—it's about her and Larry Douglas." He watched Demiris' face, trying to read his expression. There was not even the faintest flicker of interest. Christ! Metaxas forced himself to stumble on. "They—they're living in a beach house together in Rafina."

Demiris flicked the ash of the cigarette into a gold, dome-shaped ashtray. Metaxas had the feeling that he was about to be dismissed, that he had made a terrible blunder and that it was going to cost him his job. He had to convince Demiris that he was telling the truth. The words began spilling out of him. "My—my sister is a housekeeper in one of the villas there. She sees the two of them on the beach together all the time. She recognized Miss Page from her pictures in the paper, but she didn't think anything about it until a couple of nights ago when she came down to the airport to have dinner with me. I introduced her to Larry Douglas and—well, she told me he was the man Miss Page is living with."

Demiris' olive black eyes stared at him, completely devoid of expression.

"I—I just thought you would want to know," Metaxas finished lamely.

When Demiris spoke, his voice was toneless. "What Miss Page does with her private life is her own affair. I am sure she would not appreciate anyone's spying on her."

Metaxas' forehead was beaded with sweat. Jesus Christ, he had gotten the whole situation wrong. And he had only wanted to be loyal. "Believe me, Mr. Demiris, I was only trying to . . ."

"I am sure you thought you were serving my best interests. You were mistaken. Is there anything else?"

"No—no, sir." Metaxas turned and fled.

Constantin Demiris leaned back in his chair, his black eyes fixed on the ceiling, staring at nothing.

AT NINE O'CLOCK the following morning Paul Metaxas received a call to report to Demiris' mining company in the Congo, where Metaxas was to spend ten days ferrying equipment from Brazzaville to the mine. On a Wednesday morning on the third flight his plane crashed into the dense, green jungle. No traces of Metaxas' body or the wreckage were ever found.

. . .

TWO WEEKS AFTER Catherine was released from the hospital, Larry came to visit her. It was a Saturday evening, and Catherine was in the kitchen preparing an omelet. The sounds of cooking had prevented her from hearing the front door open, and she was not aware of Larry's presence until she turned and saw him standing in the doorway. She jumped involuntarily, and he said, "Sorry if I scared you. I just dropped in to see how you were getting along."

Catherine felt her heart beating faster and despised herself because he could still affect her that way.

"I'm just fine," she said. She turned and took the omelet out of the pan.

"Smells good," Larry said. "I haven't had time for dinner. If it isn't too much trouble, would you mind fixing me one of those?"

She looked at him a long moment, then shrugged.

She made him dinner but she was so unnerved by his presence that Catherine could not eat a bite. He talked to her, telling her about a flight he had just made and an amusing anecdote about one of Demiris' friends. He was the old Larry, warm and charming and irresistible as though nothing had gone wrong between them, as though he had not smashed their lives together.

When dinner was over, Larry helped Catherine wash and dry the dishes. He stood next to her at the sink, and his nearness gave her a physical ache. How long had it been? It did not bear thinking about.

"I've really enjoyed it," Larry was saying, with that easy, boyish grin of his. "Thanks, Cathy."

And that, Catherine thought, was the end of that.

THREE DAYS LATER, the phone rang and it was Larry phoning from Madrid to say that he was on his way home and to ask whether she would go out to dinner with him that evening. Catherine clutched the phone, listening to his friendly, easy voice, determined not to go. "I'm free for dinner tonight," she said.

THEY DINED AT Tourkolimano at the harbor at Piraeus. Catherine was barely able to touch her food. Being with Larry was far too painful a reminder of other restaurants they had dined in, of too many exciting evenings together in the long-dead past, of the love that was going to last them both a lifetime.

"You're not eating, Cathy. Would you like me to order something else for you?" he asked, concerned.

"I had a late lunch," she lied. *He probably won't ever ask me out again,* Catherine thought, *but if he does I will say no.*

A few days later Larry called and they had lunch at a lovely restaurant in a hidden maze off Syntagma Square. It was called Gerofinikas, the Old Palm Tree, and was reached through a long, cool passageway with a palm tree in front of it. They had an excellent meal, with Hymettus, the light, dry Greek wine. Larry was at his most entertaining.

The following Sunday he asked Catherine to fly to Vienna with him. They had dinner at the Sacher Hotel and flew back the same night. It had been a wonderful evening, filled with wine and music and candle-light, but Catherine had the eerie feeling that somehow it didn't belong to her. It belonged to that other Catherine Douglas who was long since dead and buried. When they got back to the apartment, she said, "Thank you, Larry, it was a lovely day."

He moved toward her and took her in his arms and started to kiss her. Catherine pulled away, her body rigid, her mind filled with a sudden, unexpected panic.

"No," she said.

"Cathy . . ."

"No!"

He nodded. "All right. I understand."

Her body was trembling. "Do you?" she asked.

"I know how badly I've behaved," Larry said softly. "If you'll give me a chance, I'd like to make it up to you, Cathy."

Good God, she thought. She pressed her lips together, willing herself not to cry and shook her head, her eyes bright with unshed tears. "It's too late," she whispered.

And she stood there watching him walk out the door.

Catherine heard from Larry again within the week. He sent flowers with a little note and, after that, miniature birds from the various countries to which he flew. He had obviously gone to a great deal of trouble, for there was an astonishing variety, one in porcelain, one in jade, one in teak, and she was touched that he had remembered.

When the phone rang one day and Catherine heard Larry's voice on the other end saying, "Hey, I found a wonderful Greek restaurant that serves the best Chinese food this side of Peking," she laughed and said, "I can't wait."

And that was when it really began again. Slowly, tentatively, hesitantly, but it was a beginning. Larry did not attempt to kiss her again, nor would she have let him, because Catherine knew that if she let go of her emotions, if she gave herself wholeheartedly to this man she loved, and he betrayed her again, it would destroy her. Finally and forever. And so she dined with him and laughed with him, but all the time the deep secret personal part of her lay back in reserve, carefully aloof, untouched and untouchable.

They were together almost every night. Some evenings Catherine cooked dinner at home, other nights Larry took her out. Once she mentioned the woman that he had said he was in love with, and he replied tersely, "It's over," and Catherine never brought it up again. She watched closely for signs that Larry was seeing other women, but there were none. He was totally attentive to her, never pressing, never demanding. It was as though he were doing penance for the past.

And yet Catherine admitted to herself that it was something more than that. He really seemed interested in her as a woman. At night she would stand in front of the mirror, naked, and examine her reflection and try to figure out why. Her face was not bad, the face of a once-pretty girl who had gone through pain, a sadness in the solemn gray eyes that stared back at her. Her skin was a little puffy and her chin was heavier than it should be, but there was really nothing wrong with the rest of her body that diet and massage could not take care of. She remembered the last time she had thought about this and had wound up with her wrists slashed. A shudder went through her. To hell with Larry, she thought defiantly. If he really wants me, he'll have to take me as I am.

"THEY HAD BEEN to a party and Larry had brought her home at four A.M. It had been a marvelous evening, and Catherine had worn a new dress and looked rather attractive and made people laugh and Larry had been proud of her. When they walked into the apartment, Catherine reached for the light switch and Larry put his hand over hers and said, "Wait. I can say this easier in the dark." His body was close to hers, not even touching her, yet she could feel the physical waves that pulled at her.

"I love you, Cathy," he said. "I've never really loved anyone else. I want another chance."

He switched on the light then to look at her. She was standing there, rigid and frightened, on the brink of panic. "I know you may not be ready yet, but we could start slowly." He grinned. That darling, boyish grin. "We could start out by holding hands."

He reached out and took her hand. And she pulled him to her and they were kissing and his lips were gentle and tender and careful, and hers were demanding and wild with all the pent-up longing that had been stored in her body these long, lonely months. And they were in bed together, making love and it was as though no time had passed, and they were on their honeymoon. But it was more than that. The passion was still there, fresh and wonderful, but with it an appreciation for what they had together, the knowledge that this time it would be all right, this time they would not hurt each other.

"How would you like to go away on a second honeymoon?" Larry was asking.

"Oh, yes, darling. Can we?"

"Sure, I have a vacation coming. We'll leave on Saturday. I know a wonderful little place we can go. It's called Ioannina."

20

NOELLE AND CATHERINE

ATHENS: 1946

The drive to Ioannina took nine hours. To Catherine, the scenery seemed almost Biblical, something out of another age. They drove along the Aegean Sea, past small whitewashed cottages with crosses on the roofs and endless fields of fruit trees, lemon and cherry and apple and orange. Every inch of the land was terraced and farmed and the windows and roofs of the farmhouses were painted with gay blue colors as though in defiance of the hard life being carved out of the rocky soil. Stands of tall, graceful cypress trees grew in wild profusion on the steep mountainsides.

"Look, Larry," Catherine exclaimed, "aren't they beautiful?"

"Not to the Greeks," Larry said.

Catherine looked at him. "What do you mean?"

"They consider them a bad omen. They use them to decorate cemeteries."

They passed field after field of primitive scarecrows, with a scrap of cloth tied to each fence.

"They certainly must have gullible crows around here." Catherine laughed.

They drove through a series of small villages with impossible names: Mesologian and Agelkastron and Etolikon and Amfilhoia.

Late in the afternoon they reached the village of Rion, sloping gently down to the Rio River, where they were to catch the ferryboat to Ioannina. Five minutes later they were sailing toward the island of Epirus where Ioannina lay.

Catherine and Larry sat on a bench outside on the ferry's upper deck where in the distance ahead of them they saw a large island begin to loom out of the afternoon mist. It seemed wild to Catherine and somehow a little ominous. It had a primitive look to it as though it had been created for the Greek gods, and mere mortals were unwelcome intruders. As the boat steamed closer, Catherine could see that the bottom of the island was ringed with sheer rock that dropped off to the sea below. The foreboding mountain had a scarred, gashed look where men had gouged a road out of it. Twenty-five minutes later the ferry was docking at the little harbor of Epirus, and a few moments later Catherine and Larry were driving up the mountain toward Ioannina.

Catherine was reading to Larry from the guidebook.

"Nestled high in the Pindus Mountains, in a steep bowl surrounded by towering Alps, from a distance Ioannina takes on the shape of a double-headed eagle, and at the claw of the eagle is the bottomless Lake Pamvotis, where excursion boats carry passengers across its dark green water to the island in the center of the lake and then on to the distant shores across the lake."

"It sounds perfect," Larry said.

They arrived in the late afternoon and drove directly to their hotel, an old beautifully kept one-story building on a hill high above the town, with a series of guest bungalows scattered about the grounds. An old man in a uniform came out to greet them. He looked at their happy faces.

"Honeymooners," he said.

Catherine glanced at Larry and smiled. "How did you know?"

"You can always tell," the old man declared. He led them into the lobby where they registered and then showed them to their bungalow. It consisted of a living room and bedroom, a bathroom and kitchen and a large terrazzo terrace. Over the tops of the cypresses they had a magnificent view of the village and the lake below, dark and brooding. It had the unreal beauty of a picture postcard.

"It's not much"—Larry smiled—"but it's all yours."

"I'll take it," Catherine exclaimed.

"Happy?"

She nodded. "I don't remember when I've been so happy." She walked over to him and held him tightly. "Don't ever let me go," she whispered.

His strong arms were around her, holding her close. "I won't," he promised.

While Catherine was unpacking, Larry strolled back to the lobby to talk to the room clerk.

"What do people do around here?" Larry asked.

"Everything," the clerk said proudly. "In the hotel we have a health spa. Around the village there is hiking, fishing, swimming, boating."

"How deep is the lake?" Larry inquired casually.

The clerk shrugged. "No one knows, sir. It is a volcanic lake. It is bottomless."

Larry nodded thoughtfully. "What about the caves near here?" he asked.

"Ah! The Caves of Perama. They are only a few miles from here."

"Have they been explored?"

"A few of them. Some are still closed."

"I see," said Larry.

The clerk continued. "If you like mountain climbing, I suggest Mount Tzoumerka. If Mrs. Douglas is not afraid of heights."

"No." Larry smiled. "She's quite an expert climber."

"Then she will enjoy it. You're lucky with the weather. We've been expecting the *meltemi,* but it hasn't come. Now it probably won't."

"What's the *meltemi?*" Larry asked.

"It's a terrible wind that blows down from the north. I suppose it is like your hurricane. When it comes, everyone stays indoors. In Athens, even ocean liners are forbidden to leave the harbor."

"I'm glad we missed it," Larry said.

. . .

WHEN LARRY RETURNED to the bungalow, he suggested to Catherine that they go down to the village for dinner. They took the steep, rocky footpath that led down the slope to the edge of the village. Ioannina consisted of a main street, King George Avenue, with two or three smaller streets on both sides of it. Off of those streets, a warren of tiny dirt roads radiated out to homes and apartments. The buildings were old and weatherbeaten, made of stone carried down by cart from the mountains.

The middle of King George Avenue was sectioned off by ropes, so that cars drove on the left side of the street and pedestrians were free to walk on the right side.

"They should try that on Pennsylvania Avenue," Catherine said.

At the town square was a charming little park with a high tower with a large, lighted clock in it. A street lined with huge Platanus trees ran down to the lake. It appeared to Catherine that all the streets in the village led to the water. It seemed to her that there was something frightening about the lake. It had a strange, brooding quality. All along the shores grew clumps of tall reeds that reached out like greedy fingers, as though waiting for someone.

Catherine and Larry walked down the colorful little shopping center, with shops crowded together on each side. There was a jewelry store and next to it a bakery shop, an open air butcher shop, a tavern, a shoe store. Children stood outside a barber shop, silently watching a customer getting shaved. Catherine thought they were the most beautiful children she had ever seen.

In the past, Catherine had talked to Larry about having a baby, but he had always dismissed the idea, saying that he was not ready to settle down. Now, however, he might feel differently. Catherine glanced at him as he walked at her side, taller than the other men, looking like a Greek god, and she resolved that she would discuss it with him before they left. After all, it was their honeymoon.

They passed a movie theater, the Palladian. Two very old American pictures were playing. They stopped to look at the display posters.

"We're in luck," Catherine joked. "*South of Panama* with Roger Pryor and Virginia Vale, and *Mr. D.A. in The Carter Case.*"

"Never even heard of them," Larry snorted. "This theater must be older than it looks."

They ate *mousaka* in the square, seated outdoors under an unbelievable full moon and then went back to the hotel and made love. It had been a perfect day.

In the morning Catherine and Larry drove around the lovely countryside, exploring the narrow road that wound along the lake, running along the rocky coast for a few miles, then drunkenly weaving its way back up again into the hills. Stone houses were perched on the edge of the steep mountainsides. High above the shore set back in the woods they caught a glimpse of a huge whitewashed building that looked like an ancient castle.

"What's that?" Catherine asked.

"I have no idea," Larry said.

"Let's find out."

"All right."

Larry swung the car onto the dirt track that led to the building, through a meadow, past grazing goats and a shepherd who stared at them as they drove by. They pulled up in front of the deserted entrance to the building. Up close it looked like an old ruined fortress.

"It must be a leftover ogre's castle," Catherine said. "Probably out of the Brothers Grimm."

"Do you really want to find out?" Larry asked.

"Sure. We may be just in time to rescue a maiden in distress."

Larry gave Catherine a quick, strange look.

They got out of the car and walked up to the massive wooden door with a huge iron knocker fastened to the center. Larry hit it several times and they waited. There were no sounds except the buzz of summer insects in the meadow and the whisper of the breeze through the grass.

"I guess no one's home," Larry said.

"They're probably getting rid of the bodies," Catherine whispered.

Suddenly the huge door began to creak open slowly. A nun dressed in black stood facing them.

It caught Catherine off guard. "I—I'm sorry," she said. "We didn't know what this place was. There's no sign or anything."

The nun regarded the two of them for a moment, then gestured for them to enter. They stepped through the doorway and found themselves in a large courtyard that was the center of a compound. There was a strangely still atmosphere, and Catherine suddenly realized what was missing: the sound of human voices.

She turned to the Sister and said, "What place is this?"

The Sister silently shook her head and motioned for them to wait there. They watched as she turned and walked toward an old stone building at the end of the compound.

"She's gone to get Bela Lugosi," Catherine whispered.

Beyond the building toward a promontory that rose above the sea, they could see a cemetery framed by rows of tall Cyprus trees.

"This place gives me the creeps," Larry said.

"It's as though we've stumbled into another century," Catherine replied. Unconsciously they were whispering, as though afraid to disturb the heavy silence. Through the window of the main building they could see inquisitive faces staring out at them, all women, all of them dressed in black.

"It's some kind of religious nuthouse," Larry decided.

A tall, thin woman emerged from the building and started walking briskly toward them. She wore a nun's habit and had a pleasant, friendly face.

"I am Sister Theresa," she said. "May I help you?"

"We were just passing by," Catherine said, "and we were curious about this place." She looked at the faces peering from the windows. "We didn't mean to disturb you."

"We are not honored with many visitors," Sister Theresa said. "We have almost no contact with the outside world. We are an Order of Carmelite nuns. We have taken a vow of silence."

"For how long?" Larry asked.

"*Gia panta*—for the rest of our lives. I am the only one here permitted to speak and then only when necessary."

Catherine gazed around at the large, silent courtyard and repressed a shudder. "Does no one ever leave here?"

Sister Theresa smiled. "No. There is no reason to. Our life is within these walls."

"Forgive us for troubling you," Catherine said.

The Sister nodded. "Not at all. Go with God."

As Catherine and Larry walked out, the huge gate slowly swung closed behind them. Catherine turned to look back at it. It was like a prison. But somehow this seemed worse. Perhaps because it was a voluntary penance, a waste, and Catherine thought of the young women she had seen from the window, walled up here, shut away from the world for the rest of their lives, living in the deep permanent silence of the grave. She knew she would never forget this place.

21

NOELLE AND CATHERINE

ATHENS: 1946

Early the following morning Larry went down to the village. He asked Catherine to join him, but she demurred, telling him that she was going to sleep late. The moment he left, Catherine got out of bed, hurriedly dressed and went over to the hotel gymnasium which she had investigated the day before. The instructress, a Greek Amazon, told her to strip, then examined her body critically.

"You have been lazy, lazy," she scolded Catherine. "That was a good body. If you are willing to work hard, *Theou thellondos*—God willing—it can be good again."

"I'm willing," said Catherine. "Let's see how God shapes up."

Under the tutelage of the Amazon Catherine worked out every day, going through the agonies of body-contouring massage, a Spartan diet and grueling exercises. She kept all this from Larry, but by the end of the fourth day the change in her was noticeable enough for him to comment on it.

"This place really agrees with you," he said. "You look like a different girl."

"I am a different girl," Catherine replied, suddenly shy.

On Sunday morning Catherine went to church. She had never seen a Greek Orthodox mass. In a village as small as Ioannina she had expected to find a little country church, but to her surprise she walked into a large, richly decorated church with beautiful elaborate carvings on the walls and ceiling and a marble floor. In front of the altar were a dozen enormous silver candelabras, and around the room were frescoes of Biblical paintings. The priest was thin and swarthy with a black beard. He wore an elaborate gold and red robe and a tall black hat, and he stood on what looked to Catherine like a sedan chair on a raised platform.

Along the wall were individual wooden benches and next to them a row of wooden chairs. The men sat in the front of the church and the women in the rear. *I guess the men get to Heaven first,* Catherine thought.

A chanting began in Greek, and the priest stepped down from the platform and moved to the altar. A red curtain parted and behind it was a lavishly robed, white-bearded patriarch. On a table in front of him stood a symbolical jeweled hat and a gold cross. The old man lit three candles tied together, representing, Catherine supposed, the Holy Trinity, and handed them to the priest.

The mass lasted for one hour, and Catherine sat there savoring the sights and sounds and thinking about how lucky she was and she bowed her head and gave a prayer of gratitude.

The next morning Catherine and Larry were having breakfast on their bungalow terrace that overlooked the lake. It was a perfect day. The sun was shining down, and a lazy breeze was coming off the water. A pleasant young waiter had brought the food. Catherine was wearing a negligee and when the waiter came in, Larry had put his arms around Catherine and kissed her on the neck. "What a great night," Larry murmured.

The waiter had stifled a smile and discreetly retreated. Catherine had been a little embarrassed. It was unlike Larry to be affectionate in front of strangers. He really has changed, Catherine thought. It seemed that every time a maid or bellboy came into the room, Larry would put his arm around Catherine and show his affection, as though he wanted the whole world to know how much he loved her. Catherine found it very touching.

"I have a great morning planned for us," Larry said. He pointed to the east, where they could see a giant peak towering into the sky. "We're going to climb Mount Tzoumerka."

"I have a rule," Catherine declared. "I never climb anything I can't spell."

"Come on, they say there's a fantastic view from up there."

Catherine saw that Larry was serious. She looked up at the mountain again. It looked as though it went straight up. "Climbing's not what I do best, darling," she said.

"It's an easy hike. Paths all the way up." He hesitated. "If you don't want to go with me, I can go alone." There was sharp disappointment in his voice.

It would be so simple to say no, so simple to just sit here and enjoy the day. The temptation was almost overpowering. But Larry wanted her with him. That was enough for Catherine.

"OK. I'll see if I can find an alpine hat," she said.

A look of such relief came over Larry's face that Catherine was glad she had decided to go. Besides it might be interesting.

She had never climbed a mountain before.

THEY DROVE TO a meadow at the edge of the village where the mountain trail began and parked the car. There was a small food stand at the side of the road, and Larry bought some sandwiches, fruit, candy bars and a large thermos of coffee.

"IF IT'S NICE up there," he told the proprietor, "my bride and I may want to spend the night." He gave Catherine a hug, and the proprietor grinned.

CATHERINE AND LARRY walked up to the beginning of the trail. There were really two trails, branching off in opposite directions. Catherine admitted to herself that it looked like an easy climb. The paths seemed wide and not too steep. When she turned her head to gaze at the top of the mountain, it seemed grim and forbidding, but then they would not be going that high. They would climb a little way up and have a picnic.

"This way," Larry said, and he led Catherine toward the path going to the left. As they started to climb, the Greek proprietor watched them with concern. Should he run after them and tell them they had taken the wrong path? The one they were on was dangerous, for expert climbers only. At that moment some customers came up to the stand and the proprietor put the two Americans out of his mind.

The sun was hot, but as they climbed higher, the breezes grew cooler, and Catherine thought that the combination of the two was delicious. It was a beautiful day and she was with the man she loved. From time to time Catherine glanced down and was amazed at how high they had already climbed. The air seemed to be getting thinner, and breathing was becoming more difficult. She had been walking behind Larry, for the path was now too narrow to permit them to walk side by side. She wondered when they were going to stop and have their picnic.

Larry became aware that Catherine was straggling behind and he stopped to wait for her.

"Sorry," Catherine gasped. "The altitude is beginning to get to me a little." She looked down. "It's going to take a long time to get down."

"No, it won't," Larry replied. He turned and started up the narrow path again. Catherine looked after him, sighed and doggedly started up the trail.

"I should have married a chess player," she called after him. Larry made no response.

He had come to a sudden, sharp turn in the path, and in front of him was a small wooden bridge with a single rope for a handhold that had been built across a deep gorge. The bridge was swaying in the wind and did not look secure enough to carry the weight of a man. Larry put one foot on a rotting wooden plank of the bridge and it started to sink with his weight, then held. He looked down. The gorge was about one thousand feet below. Larry started across, carefully testing each step, and heard Catherine's voice, "Larry!"

He turned. She had reached the foot of the bridge.

"We're not going to cross on *that*, are we?" Catherine asked. "That wouldn't hold a *cat!*"

"We are unless you can fly."

"But it doesn't look safe."

"People cross it every day." Larry turned and started moving across it again, leaving Catherine standing at the foot of the bridge.

Catherine stepped on the bridge, and it began to vibrate. She looked down at the deep gorge, and fear began to fill her. This was no longer fun; it was dangerous. Catherine looked ahead and saw that Larry had almost reached the other side. She gritted her teeth, grabbed the rope and started walking across, the bridge swaying with every step. On the other side Larry had turned to watch her. Catherine was moving slowly, keeping one hand tightly on the rope, trying not to look down at the abyss below. Larry could see the fear written on her face. When Catherine reached Larry's side, she was shivering, either from terror or from the chill wind that was beginning to sweep across the snow-capped mountain tops.

Catherine said, "I don't think I'm cut out to be a mountain climber. Could we go back now, darling?"

Larry looked at her in surprise. "We haven't even seen the view yet, Cathy."

"I've seen enough to last me a lifetime."

He put his arms on hers. "Tell you what," he smiled, "up ahead is a nice quiet place for our picnic. We'll stop there. How's that?"

Catherine nodded reluctantly. "All right."

"That's my girl."

Larry gave her a brief smile, then turned and started up the path again, Catherine following behind him. Catherine had to admit that the view of the village and the valley far below was breathtaking, a peaceful idyllic scene out of a Currier & Ives postcard. She was really glad that she had come. It had been a long time since she had seen Larry so exuberant. He seemed to be possessed by a sense of excitement that kept growing as they climbed higher. His face was flushed, and he chattered on about trivia as though he had to keep talking to release some of his nervous energy. Everything seemed to excite him: the climb, the view, the flowers along the path. Each thing seemed to take on an extraordinary importance as though his senses had somehow been stimulated beyond normal. He was climbing effortlessly, not even out of breath, while the increasingly rarefied air was making Catherine pant.

Her legs were beginning to feel like lead. Her breath was coming in labored gasps now. She had no idea how long they had been climbing, but when she looked down, the village was a tiny miniature far below. It seemed to Catherine that the path was getting steeper and narrower. It wound along the edge of a precipice and Catherine hugged the side of the mountain as closely as she could. Larry had said that it was an easy climb. *For a mountain goat,* Catherine thought. The trail was almost nonexistent, and there was no sign that anyone else had used it. The flowers had thinned out and the only vegetation was moss and a strange-looking, brownish weed that seemed to be growing out of the stones. Catherine was not sure how much longer she could keep climbing. As they rounded a sharp turn, the path suddenly dropped away and a dizzying abyss appeared below her feet.

"Larry!" It was a scream.

He was at Catherine's side instantly. He grabbed her arm and pulled her back, guiding her over the rocks to where the path resumed. Catherine's heart was pounding wildly. *I must be crazy,* she thought. *I'm too old to go on safari.* The altitude and the exertion had made her dizzy and her head was swimming. She turned to speak to Larry, and above him around the next turn, she saw the top of the mountain. They had arrived.

CATHERINE LAY THERE on the flat ground getting her strength back, feeling the cool breeze teasing at her hair. The terror had subsided. There was nothing more to fear now. Larry had said the way down was easy. Larry sat down beside her.

"Feeling better?" he asked.

She nodded. "Yes." Her heart had stopped pounding and she was beginning to breathe normally again. She took a deep breath and smiled up at him.

"The hard part's finished, isn't it?" Catherine asked.

Larry looked at her a long moment. Then he said, "Yes. It's finished, Cathy."

Catherine raised herself up on one elbow. A wooden observation platform had been set up on the small plateau. There was an old railing around the edge, from which there was a spectacular view of the dizzying panorama below. A dozen feet away Catherine could see the path leading down the other side of the mountain.

"Oh, Larry, it *is* beautiful," Catherine said. "I feel like Magellan." She smiled at him, but Larry was looking away and Catherine realized that he wasn't listening to her. He seemed preoccupied—*tense,* as though he were worried about something. Catherine glanced up and said, "Look!" A flurry white cloud was drifting toward them, pushed along by the brisk mountain breezes. "It's coming this way. I've never stood in the clouds before. It must be like being in Heaven."

Larry watched as Catherine scrambled to her feet and moved toward the edge of the cliff to the rickety wooden railing. Larry leaned forward on his elbows, suddenly thoughtful, watching the cloud as it moved toward Catherine. It had almost reached her, was starting to envelope her.

"I'm going to stand in it," she called, "and let it go right through me!"

An instant later Catherine was lost in the swirling gray mist.

Quietly, Larry rose to his feet. He stood there a moment, stock still, then began to move silently toward her. In seconds he was immersed in the fog. He stopped, not sure exactly where she was. Then ahead of him he heard her voice, calling, "Oh, Larry, this is wonderful! Come and join me." He started moving slowly forward toward the sound of her voice, muffled by the cloud. "It's like a soft rain," she cried. "Can you feel it?" Her voice was closer now, only a few feet ahead of him. He took another step forward, his hands outstretched, groping for her.

"Larry! Where are you?"

He could make out her figure now, wraithlike in the mist, just in front of him at the very edge of the cliff. His hands reached out toward her and at that moment the cloud blew past them, and she turned and they were facing each other, no more than three feet apart.

She took a step back in surprise, so that her right foot was at the very edge of the cliff. "Oh! You startled me," she exclaimed.

Larry took another step toward her, smiling reassuringly, and he reached out for her with his two hands, and at that moment a loud voice said, "For Chrissakes, we got bigger mountains than this in Denver!"

Larry swung around in shock, his face white. A group of tourists led by a Greek guide emerged from the far path around the other face of the mountain. The guide stopped as he saw Catherine and Larry.

"Good morning," he said in surprise. "You must have climbed the east slope."

"Yes," Larry said tightly.

The guide shook his head. "They're crazy. They should have told you that that is the dangerous way. The other slope is much easier."

"I'll remember next time," Larry said. His voice was hoarse.

The excitement that Catherine had noticed seemed to have gone out of him, as though a switch had been suddenly turned off.

"Let's get the hell out of here," Larry said.

"But—we just got here. Is anything wrong?"

"No," he snapped. "I just hate mob scenes."

They took the easy path back, and on the way down Larry did not speak at all. It was as though he were filled with an icy rage and Catherine could not imagine why. She was sure she had not said or done anything to offend him. It had been when the other people appeared that his manner had changed so abruptly. Suddenly Catherine thought she guessed the reason for his mood, and smiled. He had wanted to make love to her in the cloud! That was why he had started moving toward her with his arms outstretched. And his plans had been spoiled by the group of tourists. She almost laughed aloud with joy. She watched Larry as he strode down the trail ahead of her, and she was infused with a feeling of warmth. *I'll make it up to him when we get back to the hotel,* she promised herself.

But when they returned to their bungalow, and Catherine put her arms around him and started to kiss him, Larry told her that he was tired.

At three o'clock in the morning Catherine lay in bed, too excited to sleep. It had been a long day and a frightening one. She thought of the mountain path and the shaky bridge and the climb up the face of the rock. And finally she fell asleep.

The following morning Larry went to talk to the reception clerk.

"Those caves you mentioned the other day," Larry began.

"Ah, yes," the clerk replied. "The Caves of Perama. Very colorful. Very interesting. You must not miss them."

"I guess I'll have to see them," Larry said lightly. "I don't care for caves much, but my wife heard about them and she's been after me to take her there. She loves that kind of thing."

"I am certain you will both enjoy it, Mr. Douglas. Just be sure to hire a guide."

"Do I need one?" Larry asked.

The clerk nodded. "It is advisable. There have been several tragedies there, people getting lost." He lowered his voice. "One young couple has not been found to this day."

"If it's so dangerous," Larry asked, "why do they allow people in?"

"It is only the new section that is dangerous," the clerk explained. "It has not been explored yet and there are no lights. But with a guide you will not have to worry."

"What time do they close the caves?"

"At six o'clock."

Larry found Catherine outside, reclining under a giant oxya tree, the beautiful Greek oak, reading.

"How's the book?" he asked.

"Put-downable."

He hunched beside her. "The hotel clerk told me about some caves near here."

Catherine looked up, faintly apprehensive. "Caves?"

"He said it's a must. All the honeymooners go there. You make a wish inside, and it comes true." His voice was boyish and eager. "How about it?"

Catherine hesitated a moment, thinking how like a little boy Larry really was. "If you would like it," she said.

He smiled. "Great. We'll go after lunch. You go ahead and read. I have to drive into town and pick up a few things."

"Would you like me to come with you?"

"No," he said easily, "I'll be right back. You take it easy."

She nodded. "All right."

He turned and left.

IN TOWN LARRY found a small general store that was able to supply him with a pocket flashlight, some fresh batteries and a ball of twine.

"Are you staying up at the hotel?" the shopkeeper asked as he counted out Larry's change.

"No," Larry said. "Just passing through on my way to Athens."

"I'd be careful if I was you," the man advised.

Larry looked up at him sharply. "Of what?"

"There's a storm coming up. You can hear the sheep crying."

Larry returned to the hotel at three o'clock. At four o'clock, Larry and Catherine left for the caves. A troubled wind had sprung up, and to the north large thunderheads were starting to form, erasing the sun from the sky.

THE CAVES OF Perama lie thirty kilometers east of Ioannina. Over the centuries tremendous stalagmites and stalactites have formed into the shapes of animals and palaces and jewels, and the caves have become an important tourist attraction.

When Catherine and Larry arrived at the caves, it was five o'clock, one hour before closing. Larry bought two tickets and a pamphlet at the ticket booth. A shabbily dressed guide came up and offered his services.

"Only fifty drachmas," he intoned, "and I will give you the best guided tour."

"We don't need a guide," Larry said, curtly.

Catherine looked at him, surprised by his sharp tone.

He took Catherine's arm. "Come on."

"Are you sure we shouldn't have a guide?"

"What for? It's a racket. All we do is go inside and look at the cave. The pamphlet will tell us anything we need to know."

"All right," Catherine said agreeably.

The entrance to the cave was larger than she had expected, brightly lit with flood lamps and filled with milling tourists. The walls and roof of the cave seemed to be crammed with heroic figures sculpted out of the rocks: birds and giants and flowers and crowns.

"It's fantastic," Catherine exclaimed. She studied the pamphlet. "No one knows how old it is."

Her voice sounded hollow, reverberating against the rock ceiling. Over their heads, stalactites hung down. A tunnel carved into the rock led to a second smaller room that was lit by naked bulbs wired near the ceiling of the cave. There were more fanciful figures in here, a wild profligate display of nature's art. At the far end of the cave was a printed sign that read: *Danger: Keep Away.*

Beyond the sign was the entrance to a yawning black cavern. Casually Larry walked over to it and looked around. Catherine was studying a carving near the entrance. Larry took the sign and tossed it to one side. He walked back to Catherine.

"It's damp in here," she said. "Shall we leave?"

"No." Larry's tone was firm.

She looked at him in surprise.

"There's more to see," Larry explained. "The hotel clerk told me that the most interesting part is the new section. He said we mustn't miss it."

"Where is it?" Catherine asked.

"Over there." Larry took her arm and they walked toward the rear of the cave and stood in front of the gaping black chasm.

"We can't go in there," Catherine said. "It's dark."

Larry patted her arm. "Not to worry. He told me to bring a flashlight." He produced it from his pocket. "And—*voilà*—see?" He turned it on, and its narrow beam lit up a long dark corridor of ancient rock.

Catherine stood there, staring at the tunnel. "It looks so big," she said uncertainly. "Are you sure it's safe?"

"Of course," Larry replied. "They bring schoolchildren here."

Catherine still hesitated, wishing they could stay with the other tourists. Somehow this seemed dangerous to her.

"All right," she said.

They started into the passage. They had traveled only a few feet when the circle of light from the main cave behind them was swallowed up in the blackness. The passage made an abrupt turn to the left and then curved to the right. They were alone in a cold, timeless primeval world. In the beam of Larry's flashlight Catherine caught a glimpse of his face in the reflection of light and she saw that look of animation again. It was the same way he had looked on the mountain. Catherine tightened her grip on his arm.

Ahead of them the tunnel forked. Catherine could see the rough stone on the low ceiling as it split off in separate directions. She thought of Theseus and the Minotaur in the cave, and she wondered whether they were going to bump into them. She opened her mouth to suggest that they turn back, but before she could speak, Larry said, "We go to the left."

She looked at him and said in what she hoped was a casual voice,

"Darling, don't you think we should start back? It's getting late. The caves will be closing."

"They're open until nine," Larry replied. "There's one particular cave I want to find. They just excavated it. It's supposed to be really fantastic." He started to move forward.

Catherine hesitated, casting about for an excuse not to go farther. After all why *shouldn't* they go exploring? Larry was enjoying it. If that was what it took to make him happy, she would become the world's greatest—what was the word?—spelunker.

Larry had stopped and was waiting for her. "Coming?" he asked impatiently.

She tried to sound enthusiastic. "Yes. Just don't lose me," she said.

Larry did not reply. They took the fork that branched to the left and began walking, careful of the small stones that slipped under their feet. Larry reached into his pocket, and a moment later Catherine heard something fall to the ground. Larry kept walking.

"Did you drop something?" Catherine asked. "I thought I heard—"

"I kicked a stone," he said. "Let's walk faster." And they moved ahead, Catherine unaware that behind them a ball of twine was unwinding.

The ceiling of the cave seemed to be lower here and the walls damper and—Catherine laughed at herself for thinking it—ominous. It was as though the tunnel was beginning to close in on them, threatening and maleficent. "I don't think this place likes us," Catherine said.

"Don't be ridiculous, Cathy; it's just a cave."

"Why do you suppose we're the only ones here?"

Larry hesitated. "Not many people know about this section."

They walked on and on until Catherine began to lose all sense of time and place.

The passage was narrowing again, and the rocks on the sides tore at them with sharp, unexpected protuberances.

"How much farther do you think it is?" Catherine asked. "We must be getting near China."

"It's not far now."

When they spoke, their voices sounded muffled and hollow, like a series of continuous dying echoes.

It was getting cold now, but it was a damp, clammy cold. Catherine shivered. Ahead the beam of the flashlight caught another bifurcation of the passage. They walked up to it and stopped. The tunnel running to the right seemed smaller than the one to the left.

"They should put up neon road signs," Catherine said. "We've probably gone too far."

"No," Larry said. "I'm sure it's the one on the right."

"I'm really getting chilly, darling," she said. "Let's go back now."

He turned to look at her. "We're almost there, Cathy." He squeezed her arm. "I'll warm you up when we get back to our bungalow." He saw the reluctance on her face. "I'll tell you what—if we haven't found the place in the next two minutes, we'll turn around and go home. OK?"

Catherine felt her heart lighten. "Ok," she said thankfully.

"Come on."

They turned down the tunnel to the right, the beam of the flashlight making an eerie, wavering pattern on the gray rock ahead. Catherine glanced back over her shoulder and behind her was complete blackness. It was as though the little flashlight was carving brightness out of the Stygian gloom, moving it forward a few feet at a time, encapsulating them in its tiny womb of light. Larry stopped suddenly.

"Damn!" he said.

"What's the matter?"

"I think we took the wrong turn back there."

Catherine nodded. "All right. Let's go back."

"Let me make sure. You stay here."

She looked at him in surprise. "Where are you going?"

"Just a few feet. Back to that entrance." His voice sounded strained and unnatural.

"I'll come with you."

"I can do it faster alone, Catherine. I just want to check the fork where we made the last turn." He sounded impatient. "I'll be back in ten seconds."

"All right," she said, uneasily.

Catherine stood there watching as Larry turned away from her and walked back into the dark from which they had come, enclosed in a halo of light like a moving angel in the bowels of the earth. A moment later the light disappeared, and she was plunged into the deepest blackness she had ever known. She stood there, shivering, counting off the seconds in her mind. And then the minutes.

Larry did not return.

CATHERINE WAITED, FEELING the blackness lapping around her like malicious invisible waves. She called out, "Larry?" and her voice was hoarse and uncertain, and she cleared her throat and tried again louder. "Larry?" She could hear the sound dying a few feet away from her, murdered by the darkness. It was as though nothing could live in this place, and Catherine began to feel the first tendrils of terror. *Of course Larry will be right back*, she told herself. *All I have to do is stay where I am and remain calm.*

The black minutes dragged by, and she began to face the fact that something had gone terribly wrong. Larry could have had an accident, he could have slipped on the loose stones and hit his head on the sharp sides of the cave. Perhaps at this moment he was lying just a few feet away from her, bleeding to death. Or perhaps he was lost. His flashlight could have gone out and he might be somewhere in the bowels of this cave trapped, as she was trapped.

A feeling of suffocation began to close in on Catherine, choking her, filling her with a mindless panic. She turned and began to walk slowly in the direction from which she had come. The tunnel was narrow, and if Larry was lying on the ground, helpless and hurt, she had a good chance of finding him. Soon she would come to the place where the passage had divided. She moved cautiously, the loose stones rolling beneath her feet. She thought she heard a distant sound and stopped to listen. Larry? It was gone, and she began to move again, and then she heard it once more. It was a whirring sound, as though someone were running a tape recorder. There *was* someone down here!

Catherine yelled aloud and then listened as the sound of her voice drowned in the silence. There it was again! The whirring noise. It was coming this way. It grew louder, racing toward her in a great screaming rush of wind. It was getting closer and closer. Suddenly it leaped on her in the dark; cold and clammy skin brushed against her cheeks and kissed her lips and she felt something crawling on her head and sharp claws in her hair and her face was smothered by the mad beating of wings of some nameless horror attacking her in the blackness.

She fainted.

SHE WAS LYING on a sharp spike of stone and the discomfort of it brought her back to consciousness. Her cheek was warm and sticky, and it was a minute before Catherine realized that it was her blood. She remembered the wings and the claws that had attacked her in the dark and she began to shiver.

There were bats in the cave.

She tried to recall what she knew about bats. She had read somewhere that they were flying rats and that they congregated by the thousands. The only other information she could conjure up from her memory was that there were vampire bats, and she quickly dropped that thought. Reluctantly Catherine sat up, the palms of her hands stinging from being scraped on the sharp stones.

You can't just sit here, she told herself. *You've got to get up and do something.* Painfully she dragged herself to her feet. She had lost a shoe somehow and her dress was torn, but Larry would buy her a new one tomorrow. She pictured the two of them going into a little shop in the village, laughing and happy and buying a white summer dress for her, but somehow the dress became a shroud and her mind began to fill with panic again. She must keep thinking about tomorrow, not the nightmare she was engulfed in now. She must keep walking. But which way? She was turned around. If she walked the wrong way, she would be going deeper into the cave, and yet she knew she could not stay here. Catherine tried to estimate how much time had elapsed since they had entered the cave. It must have been an hour, possibly two. There was no way of knowing how long she had been unconscious. Surely they would be looking for Larry and her. But what if no one missed them? There was no check on who went in or out of the caves. She could be down here forever.

She took off her other shoe and began to walk, taking slow, careful steps, holding her burning hands out to avoid bumping into the rough sides of the tunnel. *The longest journey begins with but a single step,* Catherine told herself. *The Chinese said that and look how smart they are. They invented firecrackers and chop suey, and they were too clever to get caught in some dark hole in the ground where no one could find them. If I keep walking, I'm going to bump into Larry or some tourists and we'll go back to the hotel and have a drink and laugh about all this. All I have to do is keep walking.*

She stopped suddenly. In the distance she could hear the whirring sound again, moving toward her like some ghostly, phantom express train, and her body began to tremble uncontrollably, and she began to scream. An instant later, they were on her, hundreds of them, swarming over her, beating at her with their cold, clammy wings and smothering her with their furry rodent bodies in a nightmare of unspeakable horror.

The last thing she remembered before losing consciousness was calling Larry's name.

SHE WAS LYING on the cold, damp floor of the cave. Her eyes were closed, but her mind had suddenly awakened, and she thought, *Larry wants to kill me.* It was as though her subconscious had put the idea there intact. In a series of kaleidoscopic flashes she heard Larry saying, *I'm in love with someone else . . . I want a divorce . . .* and Larry moving toward her through the cloud on the mountaintop, his hands reaching for her . . . She remembered looking down the steep mountain and saying, *It will take a long time to get down,* and Larry saying, *No, it won't . . .* and Larry saying, *We don't need a guide . . . I think we took the wrong turn. Wait here . . . I'll be back in ten seconds . . .* And then the terrifying blackness.

Larry had never intended to return for her. The reconciliation, the honeymoon . . . it was all pretense, part of a plan to murder her. All the time she had been smugly thanking God for giving her a second chance, Larry was plotting to kill her. And he had succeeded, for Catherine knew she would never get out of here. She was buried alive in a black tomb of horror. The bats had gone, but she could feel and smell the filthy slime they had left all over her face and body, and she knew that they would be back for her. She did not know if she could keep her sanity through another attack. The thought of them made her begin to tremble again, and she forced herself to take slow, deep breaths.

And then Catherine heard it again and knew she could not stand it another time. It started as a low humming, and then a louder wave of sound, moving toward her. There was a sudden, anguished scream, and it rang out into the darkness over and over, and the other sound kept coming louder and louder, and out of the black tunnel a light appeared, and she heard voices calling out and hands began to reach for her and lift her and she wanted to warn them about the bats, but she was unable to stop screaming.

22

NOELLE AND CATHERINE

ATHENS: 1946

S he lay still and rigid so that the bats could not find her, and she listened for the whirr of their wings, her eyes tightly shut.

A man's voice said, "It is a miracle that we found her."

"Is she going to be all right?"

It was Larry's voice.

Terror suddenly flooded through Catherine again. It was as though her body were filled with screaming nerves that warned her to flee. Her killer had come for her. She moaned, "No . . ." and opened her eyes. She was in her bed in the bungalow. Larry stood at the foot of the bed, and next to him was a man she had never seen before. Larry moved toward her. "Catherine . . ."

She flinched as he started toward her. "Don't touch me!" Her voice was weak and hoarse.

"Catherine!" Larry's face was filled with distress.

"Get him away from me," Catherine begged.

"She is still in shock," the stranger said. "Perhaps it would be better if you waited in the other room."

Larry studied Catherine a moment, his face expressionless. "Of course. I want whatever is best for her." He turned and walked out.

The stranger came closer. He was a short, fat man with a pleasant face and a nice smile. He spoke English with a heavy accent. "I am Doctor Kazomides. You have had a most unpleasant time, Mrs. Douglas, but I assure you you are going to be fine. A mild concussion and a severe shock, but in a few days you will be good as new." He sighed. "They should close those damned caves. This is the third accident this year."

Catherine started to shake her head, then stopped, as it began to throb violently. "It was no accident," she said thickly. "He tried to kill me."

He looked down at her. "Who tried to kill you?"

Her mouth was dry and her tongue was thick. It was difficult to get the words out. "M-my husband."

"No," he said.

He did not believe her. Catherine swallowed and tried again. "He l-left me in the cave to die."

He shook his head. "It was an accident. I am going to give you a sedative and when you wake up, you will feel much better."

A surge of fear flowed through her. "No!" she pleaded. "Don't you understand? I'll never wake up. Take me out of here. Please!"

The doctor was smiling reassuringly. "I told you you are going to be fine, Mrs. Douglas. All you need is a nice, long sleep." He reached into a black medical bag and began searching for a hypodermic.

Catherine tried to sit up, but a searing pain shot through her head and she was instantly bathed in perspiration. She fell back on the bed, her head pounding unbearably.

"You must not try to move yet," Dr. Kazomides warned. "You have been through a terrible ordeal." He took out the hypodermic, filled the needle from a vial of amber fluid and turned to her. "Turn over, please. When you waken, you will feel like a new person."

"I won't waken," Catherine whispered. "He'll murder me while I'm asleep."

There was a look of concern on the doctor's face. He walked over to her. "Please turn over, Mrs. Douglas."

She stared at him, her eyes stubborn. Gently he turned Catherine on her side, pulled up her nightgown and she felt a sharp sting in her hip. "There you are."

She rolled on her back and whispered. "You've just killed me." Her eyes filled with helpless tears.

"Mrs. Douglas," the doctor said, quietly, "do you know how we found you?"

She started to shake her head, then remembered the pain. His voice was gentle. "Your husband led us to you."

She stared at him, not comprehending what he was saying.

"He took the wrong turn and got lost in the cave," he explained. "When he could not find you, he became frantic. He summoned the police and we immediately organized a search party."

She looked at him, still not understanding. "Larry . . . sent for help?"

"He was in a terrible state. He blamed himself for what happened."

She lay there trying to take it in, trying to adjust to this new information. If Larry had tried to kill her, he would not have organized a search party to find her, he would not have been frantic about her safety. She was filled with a terrible confusion. The doctor was watching her sympathetically.

"You will sleep now," he told her. "I will come back to see you in the morning."

She had believed that the man she loved was a murderer. She knew she had to tell Larry and ask his forgiveness, but her head was getting heavy and her eyes kept closing. *I'll tell him later,* she thought, *when I wake up. He'll understand and he'll forgive me. And everything will be wonderful again, just the way it was. . . .*

SHE WAS AWAKENED by a sudden, sharp cracking sound, and her eyes flew open, her pulse racing. A torrent of rain was savagely drumming against the bedroom window, and a flash of lightning lit everything in a pale blue light that made the room look like an overexposed photograph. The wind was clawing at the house, trying to scream its way in and the rain beating on the roof and windows sounded like a thousand tiny drums. Every few seconds there was an ominous roll of thunder followed by a flash of lightning.

It was the sound of thunder that had awakened Catherine. She dragged herself up to a sitting position and looked at the small bedside clock. She was groggy from the sedative that the doctor had given her, and she had to squint to make out the figures on the dial. It was three A.M. She was alone. Larry must be in the other room keeping vigil, worried about her. She had to see him, to apologize. Carefully Catherine swung her feet off the edge of the bed and tried to stand up. A wave of dizziness swept over her. She started to fall and held herself against the bedpost until it passed. She walked unsteadily to the door, her muscles feeling stiff and unused, and the pounding in her head a painful, aching throb. She stood there a moment, clinging to the door knob for support, then opened the door and stepped into the living room.

Larry was not there. There was a light on in the kitchen, and she stumbled toward it. Larry was standing in the kitchen, his back to her, and she called out, "Larry!" but her voice was washed away by the loud clap of thunder. Before she could call again, a woman moved into view. Larry said, "It's dangerous for you to—" The screaming wind carried the rest of his words away.

"—had to come. I had to make sure you—"

"—see us together. No one will ever—"

"—I told you I'd take care of—"

"—went wrong. There's nothing they can—"

"—now, while she's asleep."

Catherine stood there paralyzed, unable to move. It was like listening to stroboscopic sounds, quick pulsating phrases of words. The rest of the sentences were lost in the howling wind and crack of thunder.

"—we have to move quickly before she—"

All the old terrors returned, shuddering through her body, engulfing her in a nameless, sickening panic. Her nightmare had been real. He was trying to kill her. She had to get out of here before they found her, before they murdered her. Slowly, her whole body trembling, she started backing away. She brushed against a lamp, and it started to fall, but she caught it before it could hit the floor. The pounding of her heart was so loud that she was afraid they would be able to hear it over the sound of the thunder and the rain. She reached the front door and opened it and the wind almost tore it out of her hands.

Catherine stepped outside into the night and quickly closed the door behind her. She was instantly drenched by the cold, driving rain, and for the first time she became aware that she was wearing nothing but a thin nightgown. It did not matter. All that mattered was that she escape. Through the torrents of rain she could see the lights of the hotel lobby in the distance. She could go there and ask for help. But would they believe her? She remembered the doctor's face when she had told him Larry was trying to kill her. No, they would think she was hysterical, they would turn her over to Larry. She must get away from this place. She headed for the steep rocky path that led down to the village.

The torrential storm had turned the path into a muddy, slippery mire that sucked at her bare feet and slowed her down so that she had the feeling that she was running in a nightmare, vainly trying to escape in slow motion while her pursuers raced after her. She kept slipping and falling to the ground and her feet were bleeding from the sharp stones on the path, but she was not even aware of it. She was in a state of shock, moving like an automaton, falling when a gust of wind hurled her down and picking herself up and moving down the path toward the village again, unaware of where she was running. She was no longer conscious of the rain.

The path suddenly opened out onto a dark, deserted street on the edge of the village. She kept stumbling ahead like a hunted animal, mindlessly putting one foot in front of the other, terrified by the awful sounds that rent the night and the flashes of lightning that turned the sky into an inferno.

She reached the lake and stood there staring at it, the wind whipping the thin nightgown around her body. The calm water had turned into a seething, churning ocean driven by demonic winds that built up high waves that brutally smashed against one another.

Catherine stood there, trying to remember what she was doing here. And suddenly it came to her. She was on her way to meet Bill Fraser. He was waiting for her at his beautiful mansion so they could be married. Across the water Catherine caught a glimpse of a yellow light through the driving rain. Bill was there, waiting. But how was she going to get to him? She looked down and below her she saw the rowboats tied to their moorings, spinning around in the turbulent water, straining to break free.

She knew then what she had to do. She scrambled down to a boat and jumped in. Fighting to keep her balance she untied the rope holding it to the dock. Instantly the boat leaped away from the dock, soaring in its sudden freedom. Catherine was knocked off her feet. She pulled herself onto a seat and picked up the oars, trying to remember how Larry had used them. But there was no Larry. It must have been Bill. Yes, she could remember Bill rowing with her. They were going to meet his mother and father. Now she tried to use the oars, but the giant waves kept pitching the boat from side to side and spinning it around, and the oars were pulled out of her hands and sucked into the water. She sat there watching them disappear from sight. The boat was hurtling toward the center of the lake. Catherine's teeth began to chatter from the cold, and she began to shiver in an uncontrollable spasm. She felt something lap at her feet and she looked down and saw that the boat was filling with water. She started to cry, because her wedding dress was going to get wet. Bill Fraser had bought it for her and now he was going to be angry with her.

She wore a wedding gown because she and Bill were in a church and the minister who looked like Bill's father said *if anyone objects to this marriage speak up now* or . . . and then a woman's voice said, *now, while she's asleep,* and the lights went out and Catherine was back in the cave and Larry was holding her down and the woman was throwing water on her, drowning her. She looked around for the yellow light in Bill's house, but it was gone. He did not want to marry her any more, and now she had no one.

The shore was very far away now, hidden somewhere beyond the beating, driving rain, and Catherine was alone in the stormy night, with the screaming, banshee wind of the *meltemi* in her ears. The boat began to rock treacherously as the huge waves smashed against it. But Catherine was no longer afraid. Her body was slowly filling with a delicious warmth, and the rain felt like soft velvet on her skin. She clasped her hands in front of her like a small child and began to recite the prayer that she had learned as a little girl.

"Now I lay me down to sleep . . . I pray the Lord my soul to keep . . . If I should die before I wake . . . I pray the Lord my soul to take." And she was filled with a wonderful happiness because she knew at last that everything was all right. She was on her way home.

At that moment a large wave caught the stern of the boat, and it slowly began to overturn in the black bottomless lake.

BOOK THREE

23

THE TRIAL

ATHENS: 1947

Five hours before the murder trial of Noelle Page and Larry Douglas was to begin, Room 33 in the Arsakion Courthouse in Athens was overflowing with spectators. The courthouse is an enormous gray building that takes up an entire square block on University Street and Stada. Of the thirty courtrooms in the building, only three rooms are reserved for criminal trials: Rooms 21, 30 and 33. Number 33 had been chosen for this trial because it was the largest. The corridors outside Room 33 were jammed and police in gray uniforms and gray shirts were stationed at the two entrances to control the crowd. The sandwich stand in the corridor was sold out in the first five minutes, and there was a long line in front of the telephone booth.

Georgios Skouri, the Chief of Police, was personally supervising the security arrangements. Newspaper photographers were everywhere and Skouri managed to have his photograph taken with pleasing frequency. Passes to the courtroom were at a premium. For weeks members of the Greek judiciary had been besieged with requests from friends and relatives. Insiders who were able to secure them bartered them in exchange for other favors or sold them to the jackals who were scalping them for as high as five hundred drachmas apiece.

The actual setting of the murder trial was commonplace. Courtroom 33 on the second floor of the courthouse was musty and old, the arena of thousands of legal battles that had taken place over the years. The room was about forty feet wide and three hundred feet long. The seats were divided into three rows, six feet apart, with nine wooden benches to each row.

At the front of the courtroom was a raised dais behind a six-foot polished mahogany partition with high-backed leather chairs for the three presiding judges. The center chair was for the President of the Court and above it hung a square, dirty mirror reflecting a section of the courtroom.

In front of the dais was the witness stand, a small raised platform on which was fixed a reading lectern with a wooden tray to hold papers. On the lectern in gold leaf was the crucifix, Jesus on the cross with two of his disciples by his side. Against the far wall was the jury box, filled now with its ten jurors. On the far left was the box where the accused sat. In front of the defendants' box was the lawyers' table.

The walls of the room were of stucco, and there was linoleum on the floor in contrast to the worn wooden floors in the courtrooms on the first floor. A dozen electric light bulbs hung from the ceiling, covered with glass globes. In a far corner of the room, the airduct of an old-fashioned heater ascended into the ceiling. A section of the room had been reserved for the press, and representatives were there from Reuters, United Press, International News Service, Shsin Hau Agency, French Press Agency and Tass, among others.

The circumstances of the murder trial itself would have been sensational enough, but the personae were so famous that the excited spectators did not know where to look first. It was like a three-ring circus. In the first row of benches was Philippe Sorel, the star, who, it was rumored, was a former lover of Noelle Page. Sorel had smashed a camera on the way into the courtroom and had adamantly refused to speak to the press. He sat in his seat now, withdrawn and silent, an invisible wall around him. One row in back of Sorel sat Armand Gautier. The tall, saturnine director was constantly scanning the courtroom as though mentally making notes for his next picture. Near Gautier sat Israel Katz, the famous French surgeon and resistance hero.

Two seats away from him sat William Fraser, special assistant to the President of the United States. Next to Fraser a seat had been reserved and a rumor swept through the courtroom like wildfire that Constantin Demiris was going to appear.

Everywhere the spectators turned was a familiar face: a politician, a singer, a well-known sculptor, an internationally famous author. But though the audience in the judicial circus was filled with celebrities, the main focus of attention was in the center ring.

At one end of the defendant's box sat Noelle Page, exquisitely beautiful, her honey skin a bit paler than usual, and dressed as though she had just stepped out of Madame Chanèl's. There was a regal quality about Noelle, a noble presence that heightened the drama of what was happening to her. It whetted the excitement of the spectators and sharpened their blood-lust.

As an American newsweekly expressed it: *The emotion that flowed toward Noelle Page from the crowd that had come to witness her trial was so strong that it became an almost physical presence in the courtroom. It was not a feeling of sympathy or of enmity, it was simply a feeling of expectation. The woman being tried for murder by the state was a superwoman, a goddess on a golden pedestal, who was high above them, and they were there to watch their idol being brought down to their level and destroyed. The feeling in the courtroom must have been the same feelings that were in the hearts of the peasants who watched Marie Antoinette riding to her doom in the tumbrel.*

Noelle Page was not the only act in the legal circus. At the other end of the defendant's box sat Larry Douglas, filled with a smoldering anger. His handsome face was pale, and he had lost weight, but those things only served to accentuate his sculptured features, and many of the women in the courtroom had an urge to take him in their arms and console him in one way or another. Since Larry had been arrested, he had received hundreds of letters from women all over the world, dozens of gifts and proposals of marriage.

The third star of the circus was Napoleon Chotas, a man who was as well known in Greece as Noelle Page. Napoleon Chotas was acknowledged to be one of the greatest criminal lawyers in the world. He had defended clients ranging from heads of government who had been found with their fingers in the public coffers, to murderers who had been caught red-handed by the police, and he had never lost a major case. Chotas was thin and emaciated-looking and he sat in the courtroom watching the spectators with large, sad bloodhound eyes in a ruined face. When Chotas addressed a jury, his speech was slow and hesitant, and he had great difficulty expressing himself. Sometimes he was in such an agony of embarrassment that a juror would helpfully blurt out the word that Napoleon Chotas was fumbling for, and when this happened the lawyer's face would fill with such relief and inexpressible gratitude that the entire panel of jurors would feel a wave of affection for the man. Outside the courtroom Chotas was a crisp, incisive speaker with a consummate mastery of language and syntax. He spoke seven languages fluently and when his busy schedule permitted, he gave lectures to jurists all over the world.

Seated on the lawyer's bench a few feet away from Chotas, was Frederick Stavros, the defense attorney for Larry Douglas. The experts agreed that while Stavros might be competent enough to handle routine cases, he was hopelessly out of his depth in this one.

Noelle Page and Larry Douglas had already been tried in the newspapers and in the minds of the populace and had been found guilty. No one doubted their guilt for a moment. Professional gamblers were offering thirty to one that the defendants would be convicted. To the trial, then, was lent the added excitement of watching the greatest criminal lawyer in Europe work his magic against enormous odds.

When it had been announced that Chotas was going to defend Noelle Page, the woman who had betrayed Constantin Demiris and held him up to public ridicule, the news had created a furor. As powerful as Chotas was, Constantin Demiris was a hundred times more powerful and no one could imagine what had possessed Chotas to go against Constantin Demiris. The truth was even more interesting than the bizarre rumors that were flying around.

The lawyer had taken on Noelle Page's defense at the personal request of Demiris.

· · ·

THREE MONTHS BEFORE the trial was scheduled to begin, the warden himself had come to Noelle's cell at the Saint Nikodemous Street Prison to tell her that Constantin Demiris had asked permission to visit her. Noelle had wondered when she would hear from Demiris. There had been no word from him since her arrest, only a deep, foreboding silence.

Noelle had lived with Demiris long enough to know how deep was his sense of *amour-propre* and to what lengths he would go to avenge even the smallest slight. Noelle had humiliated him as no other person ever had before, and he was powerful enough to exact a terrible retribution. The only question was: How would he go about it? Noelle was certain Demiris would disdain anything as simple as the bribing of a jury or judges. He would be satisfied with no less than some complex Machiavellian plot to exact his revenge, and Noelle had lain awake on her cell cot night after night putting herself in Demiris' mind, discarding strategy after strategy, just as he must have done, searching for a perfect plan. It was like playing mental chess with Demiris, except that she and Larry were the pawns, and the stakes were life and death.

It was probable that Demiris would want to destroy her and Larry, but Noelle knew better than anyone the subtlety of Demiris' mind, so it was also possible that he might plan to destroy only one of them and let the other one live and suffer. If Demiris arranged for them both to be executed, he would have his vengeance, but it would be over with too quickly—there would be nothing left for him to savor. Noelle had carefully examined every possibility, each possible variation of the game, and it seemed to her that Constantin Demiris might arrange to let Larry die and let her live, either in prison or under Demiris' control, because that would be the surest way to prolong his vengeance indefinitely. First Noelle would suffer the pain of losing the man she loved, and then she would have to endure whatever exquisite agonies Demiris had planned for her future. Part of the pleasure Demiris would derive from his vengeance would be in telling Noelle in advance, so she could taste the full measure of despair.

It had therefore come as no surprise to Noelle when the warden had appeared at her cell to tell her that Constantin Demiris wished to see her.

· · ·

NOELLE HAD BEEN the first to arrive. She had been ushered into the warden's private office where she had been discreetly left alone with a makeup case brought by her maid, to prepare herself for Demiris' visit.

Noelle ignored the cosmetics and the combs and brushes that lay on the desk and walked over to the window and looked out. It was the first sight she had had of the outside world in three months, other than the quick glimpses when she had been taken from the Saint Nikodemous Street Prison to the Arsakion, the courthouse, on the day of her arraignment. She had been transported to the courthouse in a prison van with bars and escorted to the basement, where a narrow cage elevator had carried her and her warders to the second-floor corridor. The hearing had been held there and she had been remanded for trial and returned to the prison.

Now Noelle stared out the window and watched the traffic below on University Street, men and women and children hurrying home to be united with their families. For the first time in her life Noelle felt frightened. She had no illusions about her chances of acquittal. She had read the newspapers and she knew that this was going to be more than a trial. This was going to be a blood bath in which she and Larry were to be served up as victims to satisfy the conscience of an outraged society. The Greeks hated her because she had mocked the sanctity of marriage, envied her because she was young and beautiful and rich and despised her because they sensed that she was indifferent to their feelings.

In the past Noelle had been careless of life, recklessly squandering time as though it were eternal: but now something in her had changed. The imminent prospect of death had made Noelle realize for the first time how much she wanted to live. There was a fear in her that was like a growing cancer, and if she could, she was ready to make a deal for her life, even though she knew that Demiris would find ways to make it a hell on earth. She would face that when it happened. When the time came, she would find a way to outwit him.

Meanwhile she needed his help to stay alive. She had one advantage. She had always taken the idea of death lightly, so Demiris had no idea how much life meant to her now. If he had, he would surely let her die. Noelle wondered again what webs he had been weaving for her over the past few months, and even as she wondered, she heard the office door open and she turned around and saw Constantin Demiris standing in the doorway and after one shocked look at him, Noelle knew that she had nothing more to fear.

Constantin Demiris had aged ten years in the few months since Noelle had seen him. He looked gaunt and haggard, and his clothes hung loosely on his frame. But it was his eyes that held her attention. They were the eyes of a soul that had been through hell. The essence of power that had been within Demiris, the dynamic, overpowering core of vitality was gone. It was as though a light switch had been turned off, and all that was left was the pale afterglow of a faded, once remembered brilliance. He stood there, staring at her, his eyes filled with pain.

For a split second Noelle wondered whether this could be some kind of trick, part of a plan, but no man on earth could be that good an actor. It was Noelle who broke the long silence. "I'm sorry, Costa," she said.

Demiris nodded slowly, as though the movement cost him an effort. "I wanted to kill you," he said wearily, and it was an old man's voice. "I had everything all worked out."

"Why didn't you?"

He replied quietly, "Because you killed me first. I've never needed anyone before. I suppose I've never really been in pain before."

"Costa—"

"No. Let me finish. I'm not a forgiving man. If I could do without you, believe me I would. But I can't. I can't go through any more. I want you back, Noelle."

She fought to show nothing of what she was feeling inside. "That's really not up to me anymore, is it?"

"If I could have you freed, would you come back to me? To stay?"

To stay. A thousand images flashed through Noelle's mind. She would never see Larry again, never touch him, hold him. Noelle had no choice, but even if she had, life was sweeter. And as long as she was alive, there was always a chance. She looked up at Demiris.

"Yes, Costa."

Demiris stared at her, his face filling with emotion. When he spoke, his voice was husky. "Thank you," he said. "We're going to forget the past. It's gone and nothing will change it." His voice brightened. "It's the future I'm interested in. I'm going to engage an attorney for you."

"Who?"

"Napoleon Chotas."

And that was the moment that Noelle really knew she had won the chess match. Check. Checkmate.

NOW NAPOLEON CHOTAS sat at the long wooden lawyer's table thinking about the battle that was about to take place. Chotas would have much preferred that the trial be held in Ioannina rather than in Athens, but that was impossible, since by Greek law a trial could not take place in the district where the crime had been committed. Chotas had not the slightest doubt about the guilt of Noelle Page, but that was unimportant to him, for like all criminal lawyers he felt that the guilt or innocence of a client was immaterial. Everyone was entitled to a fair trial.

The trial that was about to begin, however, was something different. For the first time in his professional life Napoleon Chotas had allowed himself to become emotionally involved with a client: He was in love with Noelle Page. He had gone to see her at Constantin Demiris' request and though Chotas had been familiar with the public image of Noelle Page, he had been totally unprepared for the reality. She had received him as though he were a guest paying a social call. Noelle had showed neither nervousness nor fear, and at first Chotas had attributed it to her lack of understanding of the desperateness of her situation. The opposite had proved to be true. Noelle was the most intelligent and fascinating woman he had ever encountered and certainly the most beautiful. Chotas, though his appearance belied it, was a connoisseur of women, and he recognized the special qualities that Noelle possessed. It was a joy for Chotas merely to sit and talk with her. They discussed law and art and crime and history, and she was a constant amazement to him. He could fully appreciate Noelle's liaison with a man like Constantin Demiris, but her involvement with Larry Douglas puzzled him. He felt that she was far above Douglas, and yet Chotas supposed that there was some unexplainable chemistry that made people fall in love with the most unlikely partners. Brilliant scientists married empty-headed blondes, great writers married stupid actresses, intelligent statesmen married trollops.

Chotas remembered the meeting with Demiris. They had known each other socially over the years, but Chotas' law firm had never done any work for him. Demiris had asked Chotas to his home at Varkiza. Demiris had plunged into the conversation without preamble. "As you may know," he had said, "I have a deep interest in this trial. Miss Page is the only woman in my life I have ever truly loved." The two men had talked for six hours, discussing every aspect of the case, every possible strategy. It was decided that Noelle's plea would be Not Guilty. When Chotas rose to leave, a deal had been agreed upon. For undertaking Noelle's defense Napoleon Chotas would be given double his usual fee, and his firm would become the major legal counsel to Constantin Demiris' far-flung empire, a plum worth untold millions.

"I don't care how you do it," Demiris had concluded, fiercely. "Just see to it that nothing goes wrong."

Chotas had accepted the bargain. And then, ironically, he had fallen in love with Noelle Page. Chotas had remained a bachelor, though he kept a string of mistresses, and now when he had found the one woman he wanted to marry, she was out of his reach. He looked at Noelle now, sitting in the defendant's box, beautiful and serene. She wore a simple black wool suit with a plain, high-necked white blouse, and she looked like a Princess from a fairy tale.

Noelle turned and saw Chotas staring at her and gave him a warm smile. He smiled back, but his mind was already turning to the difficult task that lay ahead of him. The clerk was calling the Court to order.

The spectators rose as two judges in business suits entered and took their seats on the bench. The third judge, the President of the Court, followed and took the center seat. He intoned, *"I synethriassis archetai."*

The trial had begun.

PETER DEMONIDES, SPECIAL Prosecutor for the State, nervously rose to make his opening address to the jury. Demonides was a skilled and able prosecutor, but he had been up against Napoleon Chotas before—many times, in fact—and the results were invariably the same. The old bastard was unbeatable. Almost all trial lawyers browbeat hostile witnesses, but Chotas coddled them. He nurtured them and loved them and before he was through, they were contradicting themselves all over the place, trying to be helpful to him. He had a knack of turning hard evidence into speculation and speculation into fantasy. Chotas had the most brilliant legal mind Demonides had ever encountered and the greatest knowledge of jurisprudence, but that was not his strength. His strength was his knowledge of people. A reporter had once asked Chotas how he had learned so much about human nature.

"I don't know a damned thing about human nature," Chotas had answered. "I only know about *people,*" and the remark had been widely quoted.

In addition to everything else this was the kind of trial that was tailor-made for Chotas to take before a jury, filled as it was with glamour, passion and murder. Of one thing Demonides was certain: Napoleon Chotas would let nothing stop him from winning this case. But neither would Demonides. He knew that he had a strong evidential case against the defendants, and while Chotas might be able to spellbind the jury into overlooking the evidence, he would not be able to sway the three judges on the bench. So it was with a feeling of determination mixed with apprehension that the Special Prosecutor for the State began his opening address.

In skillful, broad strokes Demonides outlined the State's case against the two defendants. By law the foreman of the ten-man jury was an attorney, so Demonides directed his legal points to him and his general points to the rest of the jury.

"Before this trial has ended," Demonides said, "the State will prove that these two people conspired together to cold-bloodedly murder Catherine Douglas because she stood in the way of their plans. Her only crime was in loving her husband, and for this she was killed. The two defendants have been placed at the scene of the murder. They are the only ones who had the motive and the opportunity. We shall prove beyond a shadow of a doubt . . ."

Demonides kept his address short and to the point, and it was the turn of the Attorney for the Defense.

The spectators in the courtroom watched Napoleon Chotas as he clumsily gathered his papers together and prepared to make his opening speech. Slowly he approached the jury box, his manner hesitant and difficult as though awed by his surroundings.

Watching him William Fraser could not but marvel at his skill. If he had not once spent an evening with Chotas at a party in the British Embassy, Fraser too would have been deceived by the man's manner. He could see the jurors helpfully straining forward to catch the words that fell softly from Napoleon Chotas' lips.

"This woman on trial," Chotas was saying to the jurors, "is not being tried for murder. There has been no murder. If there *had* been a murder, I am sure that my brilliant colleague for the State would have been good enough to have shown us the body of the victim. He has not done so, so we must assume that there is no body. And therefore no murder." He stopped to scratch the crown of his head and looked down at the floor as though trying to remember where he had left off. He nodded to himself, then looked up at the jury. "No, gentlemen, that is not what this trial is about. My client is being tried because she broke *another* law, an unwritten law that says you must not fornicate with another woman's husband. The press has already found her guilty of that charge, and the public has found her guilty, and now they are demanding that she be punished."

Chotas stopped to pull out a large white handkerchief, stared at it a moment as if wondering how it had gotten there, blew his nose and replaced the handkerchief in his pocket. "Very well. If she has broken a law, let us punish her. But not for murder, gentlemen. Not for a murder that was never committed. Noelle Page was guilty of being the mistress of—" he paused delicately "—a most important man. His name is a secret, but if you must know it, you can find it on the front page of any newspaper."

There was appreciative laughter from the spectators.

Auguste Lanchon swung around in his seat and glared at the spectators, his little piggy eyes blazing with rage. How dare they laugh at his Noelle! Demiris meant nothing to her, nothing. It was the man to whom a woman gave up her virginity that she always cherished. The fat little shopkeeper from Marseille had not been able to communicate with Noelle yet, but he had paid four hundred precious drachmas for a courtroom pass, and he would be able to watch his beloved Noelle every day. When she was acquitted, Lanchon would step forward and take over her life. He turned his attention to the lawyer.

"It has been said by the prosecution that the two defendants, Miss Page and Mr. Lawrence Douglas, murdered Mr. Douglas' wife so that the defendants could marry each other. Look at them."

Chotas turned to look at Noelle Page and Larry Douglas and every eye in the courtroom did the same.

"Are they in love with each other? Possibly. But does that make them plotters and schemers and murderers? No. If there are any victims in this trial, you are looking at them now. I have gone into all the evidence very carefully and I have convinced myself, as I will convince you, that these two people are innocent. Please let me make it clear to the jury that I am not representing Lawrence Douglas. He has his own counsel and a very able fellow he is. But it has been alleged by the state that the two people sitting there are fellow conspirators, that they have plotted and committed murder together. So if one is guilty, both are guilty. I tell you now that both are innocent. And nothing less than the corpus delicti will make me change my mind. And there is none."

Chotas' voice was growing angrier. "It is a fiction. My client has no more idea than you do whether Catherine Douglas is dead or alive? How would she know? She has never even met her, let alone harmed her. Imagine the enormity of being accused of killing someone you have never laid eyes on. There are many theories as to what could have happened to Mrs. Douglas. That she was murdered is one of them. But *only* one. The most probable theory is that somehow she discovered that her husband and Miss Page were in love, and out of a feeling of hurt—not fear, gentlemen—*hurt,* she ran away. It is as simple as that, and for that you do not execute an innocent woman and an innocent man."

Frederick Stavros, Larry Douglas' attorney, gave a surreptitious sigh of relief. His constant nightmare had been that Noelle Page would be acquitted, while his client would be convicted. If that happened he would become the laughingstock of the legal profession. Stavros had been looking for a way to hitch onto Napoleon Chotas' star and now Chotas had done it for him. By linking the two defendants together as he had just done, Noelle's defense had become his own client's defense. Winning this trial was going to change Frederick Stavros' entire future, give him everything he had ever wanted. He was filled with a feeling of warm gratitude for the old master.

Stavros noted with satisfaction that the jury was hanging on Chotas' every word.

"This was not a woman who was interested in material things," Chotas was saying with admiration. "She was willing to give everything up without hesitation for the man she loved. Surely, my good friends, that is not the character of a scheming, conniving murderess."

As Chotas went on, the emotions of the jurors shifted like a visible tide, reaching out toward Noelle Page with growing empathy and understanding. Slowly and skillfully the attorney built up a portrait of a beautiful woman who was the mistress of one of the most powerful and richest men in the world, who had every luxury and privilege lavished upon her, but who in the end had succumbed to her love for a penniless young pilot she had only known a short time.

Chotas played on the emotions of the jurors like a master musician, making them laugh, bringing tears to their eyes and always holding their rapt attention. When his opening address was over, Chotas clumsily shuffled back to the long table and awkwardly sat down, and it was all that the spectators could do to keep from applauding.

LARRY DOUGLAS SAT in the witness box listening to Chotas' defense of him, and Larry was furious. He did not need anyone to defend him. He had done nothing wrong, this whole trial was a stupid mistake, and if there was any blame it was Noelle's. It had all been her idea. Larry looked at her now, beautiful and serene. But he felt no stirring of desire, only the memory of a passion, a faint emotional shadow, and he marveled that he had put his life in jeopardy for this woman. Larry's eyes swung toward the press box. An attractive girl reporter in her twenties was staring at him. He gave her a little smile and watched her face light up.

PETER DEMONIDES WAS examining a witness.

"Would you please tell the Court your name?"

"Alexis Minos."

"And your occupation?"

"I am an attorney."

"Would you look at the two defendants seated in the defendant's box, Mr. Minos, and tell the Court if you have ever seen either of them before?"

"Yes, sir. One of them."

"Which one?"

"The man."

"Mr. Lawrence Douglas?"

"That's correct."

"Would you tell us, please, under what circumstances you saw Mr. Douglas?"

"He came to my office six months ago."

"Did he come to consult you in your professional capacity?"

"Yes."

"In other words he required some legal service of you?"

"Yes."

"And would you please tell us what it was that he wanted you to do for him?"

"He asked me to get him a divorce."

"And did he retain you for this purpose?"

"No. When he explained the circumstances to me, I told him it would be impossible for him to get a divorce in Greece."

"And what were the circumstances?"

"First of all he said there must not be any publicity, and secondly he said that his wife refused to give him a divorce."

"In other words he had asked his wife for a divorce and she had refused?"

"That is what he told me."

"And you explained to him that you couldn't help him? That unless his wife was willing to give him a divorce, it would be difficult or impossible for him to obtain one, and that there very well might be publicity?"

"That is correct."

"So, short of taking desperate measures, there was nothing the defendant could—"

"Objection!"

"Sustained."

"Your witness."

. . .

NAPOLEON CHOTAS LIFTED himself out of his chair with a sigh and slowly walked over to the witness. Peter Demonides was not worried. Minos was a lawyer and too experienced to be deceived by Chotas' forensic bag of tricks.

"You're an attorney, Mr. Minos."

"I am."

"And an excellent one, I'm sure. I'm surprised that our professional paths have not crossed sooner. The firm I'm with deals in many branches of law. Perhaps you've run across one of my partners in some corporate litigation?"

"No. I don't do corporate work."

"I beg your pardon. Perhaps in some tax case, then?"

"I am not a tax lawyer."

"Oh." Chotas was beginning to look puzzled and ill-at-ease, as though he was making a fool of himself. "Securities?"

"No." Minos was beginning to enjoy the lawyer's humiliation. His face took on a smug look and Peter Demonides began to worry. How many times had he seen that look on the faces of witnesses that Napoleon Chotas was preparing for the slaughter?

Chotas was scratching his head in bafflement. "I give up," he said ingenuously. "What kind of law do you specialize in?"

"Divorce cases." The answer was a barbed shaft, perfectly delivered.

A rueful look appeared on Chotas' face and he shook his head. "I should have known my good friend Mr. Demonides would have an expert up here."

"Thank you, sir." Alexis Minos made no attempt to conceal his smugness now. Not every witness got a chance to score off Chotas and in Minos' mind he was already embellishing the story to tell at the club that evening.

"I've never even handled a divorce case," Chotas was confiding in an embarrassed voice, "so I'll have to defer to your expertise."

The old lawyer was caving in completely. It would make an even better story than Minos had anticipated.

"I'll bet you keep very busy," Chotas said.

"I have as many cases as I can handle."

"As many as you can handle!" There was open admiration in Napoleon Chotas' voice.

"Sometimes more."

Peter Demonides looked down at the floor, unable to watch what was happening.

Chotas' voice took on an awed tone. "I don't want to pry into your personal business, Mr. Minos, but as a matter of professional curiosity, how many clients would you say walk through your door in a year?"

"Well, that's pretty difficult to say."

"Come on now, Mr. Minos. Don't be modest. Make a guess."

"Oh, I suppose two hundred. That's an approximation, you understand."

"Two hundred divorces a year! The paper work alone must be staggering."

"Well, there aren't actually two hundred divorces."

Chotas rubbed his chin, perplexed. "What?"

"They're not *all* divorces."

A puzzled look came over Chotas' face. "Didn't you say that you only handled divorce cases?"

"Yes, but—" Minos' voice wavered.

"But what?" Chotas asked in bewilderment.

"Well, what I mean is, they don't all get divorced."

"But isn't that why they come to see you?"

"Yes, but some of them—well—change their minds for one reason or another."

Chotas nodded in sudden understanding. "Ah! You mean there's a reconciliation or something of the sort?"

"Exactly," Minos said.

"So that what you're saying is that—what?—ten percent don't bother to go through with the divorce action?"

Minos shifted in his chair uneasily. "The percentage is a bit higher."

"How much higher? Fifteen percent? Twenty?"

"Closer to forty."

Napoleon Chotas stared at him in amazement. "Mr. Minos, are you telling us that almost half the people who come to see you decide not to get a divorce?"

"Yes."

Tiny beads of sweat were popping out on Minos' forehead. He turned to look at Peter Demonides, but Demonides was studiously concentrating on a crack in the floor.

"Well I'm sure it's not a lack of confidence in your ability," said Chotas.

"Certainly not," Minos said defensively. "They very often come to me on a stupid impulse. A husband or wife will have a fight and feel they hate each other and think they want a divorce, but when you come right down to it, in most cases they change their minds."

He stopped abruptly as he realized the full import of his words.

"Thank you," Chotas said gently. "You've been most helpful."

PETER DEMONIDES WAS examining the witness.

"Your name, please?"

"Kasta. Irene Kasta."

"Miss or Mrs.?"

"Mrs. I'm a widow."

"What is your occupation, Mrs. Kasta?"

"I'm a housekeeper."

"Where do you work?"

"For a rich family in Rafina."

"That's a village near the sea, is it not? A hundred kilometers north of Athens?"

"Yes."

"Would you please take a look at the two defendants seated at the table? Have you ever seen them before?"

"Sure. Lots of times."

"Would you tell us under what circumstances?"

"They live in the house next to the villa where I work. I seen them on the beach a lot. They was naked."

There was a gasp from the spectators and then a quick buzz of conversation. Peter Demonides glanced over at Chotas to see if he was going to object, but the old lawyer sat at the table, a dreamy smile on his face. The smile made Demonides more nervous than ever. He turned back to the witness.

"You are certain that these are the two people you saw? You are under oath, you know."

"Them's the two, all right."

"When they were together on the beach, did they seem friendly?"

"Well, they didn't act like brother and sister."

A laugh from the spectators.

"Thank you, Mrs. Kasta." Demonides turned to Chotas. "Your witness."

Napoleon Chotas nodded amiably and rose and ambled over to the formidable-looking woman in the witness box.

"How long have you worked at this villa, Mrs. Kasta?"

"Seven years."

"Seven years! You must be very good at your job."

"You bet I am."

"Perhaps you could recommend a good housekeeper for me. I've been thinking about buying a place on the beach at Rafina. My problem is, I need privacy so I can work. As I remember those villas, they're all bunched together."

"Oh, no, sir. Each villa is separated by a big wall."

"Oh, good. And they're not crowded next to one another?"

"No, sir, not at all. Those villas are at least a hundred yards away from each other. I know one that's up for sale. You'd have all the privacy you need and I can recommend my sister to do the housekeeping for you. She's good and she's tidy and she cooks a bit."

"Well, thank you, Mrs. Kasta, that sounds wonderful. Perhaps I could call her this afternoon."

"She does a bit of day work. She'll be home at six."

"What time is it now?"

"I don't carry a watch."

"Ah. There's a large clock on the wall over there. What does it say?"

"Well, it's hard to make out. It's clear across the room."

"How far away would you say that clock was?"

"About—er—fifty feet."

"Twenty-three feet, Mrs. Kasta. No more questions."

IT WAS THE fifth day of the trial. Doctor Israel Katz's missing leg was paining him again. While he was performing an operation, he could stand on his artificial leg for hours on end, and it never bothered him. But sitting here without the intense concentration to divert his attention, the nerve ends kept sending memory messages to a limb that was no longer there. Katz shifted restlessly in his seat, trying to ease the pressure on his hip. He had tried to see Noelle every day since he had arrived in Athens but with no success. He had spoken to Napoleon Chotas, and the lawyer had explained that Noelle was too upset to see old friends and that it would be best to wait until the trial was over. Israel Katz had asked him to tell Noelle that he was here to help her in every way he could, but he could not be certain that she ever received the message. He had sat in court day after day, hoping Noelle would look his way, but she never even glanced at the spectators.

Israel Katz owed his life to her, and he felt frustrated because there was no way he could help repay that debt. He had no idea how the trial was going or whether Noelle would be convicted or acquitted. Chotas was good. If any man in the world could free Noelle it was he. Yet somehow Israel Katz was filled with unease. The trial was far from over. There could still be some surprises ahead.

A WITNESS FOR the prosecution was being sworn in.

"Your name?"

"Christian Barbet."

"You are a French national, Mr. Barbet?"

"Yes."

"And where is your residence?"

"In Paris."

"Would you tell the Court your occupation?"

"I am the owner of a private detective agency."

"And where is that agency located?"

"The main office is in Paris."

"What kind of cases do you handle?"

"Many kinds . . . commercial pilfering, missing persons, surveillance for jealous husbands or wives. . . ."

"Monsieur Barbet, would you be good enough to look around this courtroom and tell us whether anyone in this room has ever been a client of yours?"

A long, slow look around the room. "Yes, sir."

"Would you tell the Court who this person is, please?"

"The lady sitting over there. Miss Noelle Page."

A murmur of interest from the spectators.

"Are you telling us that Miss Page hired you to do some detective work for her?"

"I am, monsieur."

"And would you tell us exactly what that work consisted of?"

"Yes, sir. She was interested in a man named Larry Douglas. She wanted me to find out everything I could about him."

"That is the same Larry Douglas who is on trial in this courtroom?"

"Yes, sir."

"And Miss Page paid you for this?"

"Yes, sir."

"Would you please look at these exhibits in my hand. Are these the records of the payments that were made to you?"

"That is correct."

"Tell us, Monsieur Barbet, how did you go about obtaining this information on Mr. Douglas?"

"It was very difficult, monsieur. You see I was in France, and Mr. Douglas was in England and later the United States, and with France occupied by the Germans—"

"I beg your pardon?"

"I said, with France occupied—"

"Just a moment. I want to be sure that I understand what you are saying, Monsieur Barbet. We have been told by Miss Page's attorney that she and Larry Douglas met a few short months ago and fell madly in love. Now you are telling this Court that their love affair started—how long ago?"

"At least six years ago."

Pandemonium.

Demonides flashed Chotas a triumphant look. "Your witness."

Napoleon Chotas rubbed his eyes, rose from the long table at which he was sitting and walked over to the witness box.

"I won't detain you long, Mr. Barbet. I know you must be anxious to get back to your family in France."

"You may take your time, monsieur." Smugly.

"Thank you. Forgive me for being personal, but that's certainly a fine-looking suit you're wearing, Mr. Barbet."

"Thank you, monsieur."

"Made in Paris, was it?"

"Yes, sir."

"It fits beautifully. I don't seem to have any luck with my suits. Have you ever tried the English tailors? They're supposed to be excellent, also."

"No, monsieur."

"I'm sure you've been to England many times?"

"Well—no."

"Never?"

"No, sir."

"Have you been to the United States of America?"

"No."

"Never?"

"No, sir."

"Have you ever visited the South Pacific?"

"No, sir."

"Then you must truly be a fantastic detective, Mr. Barbet. My hat is off to you. These reports of yours cover the activities of Larry Douglas in England and the United States and the South Pacific—and yet you tell us that you have never even been to any of these places. I can only assume that you are psychic."

"Permit me to correct you, monsieur. It was not necessary for me to have been in any of those places. I employ what we call correspondent agencies in England and in America."

"Ah, forgive my stupidity. Of course! So it was actually *those* people who covered the activities of Mr. Douglas?"

"*Exactement.*"

"And so the fact is that you yourself have no personal knowledge of Larry Douglas' movements."

"Well . . . no, sir."

"So in reality all your information is secondhand."

"I suppose . . . in a sense, yes."

Chotas turned to the judges. "I move to strike the entire testimony of this witness, Your Honors, on the grounds that it is hearsay."

Peter Demonides leaped to his feet. "Objection, Your Honors! Noelle Page hired Mr. Barbet to get information on Larry Douglas. That is not hearsay—"

"My learned colleague has submitted the records as evidence," Chotas said gently. "I am perfectly willing to accept it—if he wishes to bring the men here who actually conducted the surveillance of Mr. Douglas. Otherwise I must ask the Court to assume that there was no such surveillance and ask that the testimony of this witness be held inadmissible."

The President of the Court turned to Demonides. "Are you prepared to bring your witnesses here?" he asked.

"That's impossible," Peter Demonides spluttered. "Mr. Chotas knows that it would take weeks to locate them!"

The President turned to Chotas. "Motion granted."

PETER DEMONIDES WAS examining.

"Would you state your name, please?"

"George Mousson."

"What is your occupation?"

"I am a reception clerk at the Palace Hotel at Ioannina."

"Would you please take a look at the two defendants sitting at the table. Have you ever seen them before?"

"The man. He was a guest at the hotel last August."

"That would be Mr. Lawrence Douglas?"

"Yes, sir."

"Was he alone when he checked into the hotel?"

"No, sir."

"Would you tell us who he was with?"

"His wife."

"Catherine Douglas?"

"Yes, sir."

"They registered as Mr. and Mrs. Douglas?"

"Yes, sir."

"Did you and Mr. Douglas ever discuss the Caves of Perama?"

"Yes, sir, we did."

"Did you bring up the subject or did Mr. Douglas?"

"As I recall, he did. He asked me about them and said his wife was anxious for him to take her there. That she loved caves. I thought that was unusual."

"Oh? Why was that?"

"Well, women aren't interested in exploring and things like that."

"You didn't happen to discuss the caves with Mrs. Douglas at any time, did you?"

"No, sir. Only with Mr. Douglas."

"And what did you tell him?"

"Well, I remember telling him that the caves could be dangerous."

"Was anything said about a guide?"

The clerk nodded. "Yes, I'm sure I suggested that he use a guide. I recommend one to all our guests."

"No more questions. Your witness, Mr. Chotas."

"HOW LONG HAVE you been in the hotel business, Mr. Mousson?"

"Over twenty years."

"And before that you were a psychiatrist?"

"Me? No, sir."

"A psychologist perhaps?"

"No, sir."

"Oh. Then you're *not* an expert on the behavior of women?"

"Well, I may not be a psychiatrist, but in the hotel business you learn a lot about women."

"Do you know who Osa Johnson is?"

"Osa—? No."

"She's a world famous explorer. Have you ever heard of Amelia Earhart?"

"No, sir."

"Margaret Mead?"

"No, sir."

"Are you married, Mr. Mousson?"

"Not now. But I've been married three times, so I *am* something of an expert on women."

"On the contrary, Mr. Mousson. I suggest that if you were really an expert on women, you would have been able to handle *one* marriage. No further questions."

"YOUR NAME, PLEASE?"

"Christopher Cocyannis."

"Would you tell us your occupation?"

"I am a guide at the Caves of Perama."

"How long have you been a guide there?"

"Ten years."

"Is business good?"

"Very good. Thousands of tourists come to see the caves every year."

"Would you please look at the man sitting over in that box. Have you ever seen Mr. Douglas before?"

"Yes, sir. He came to the caves in August."

"Are you sure?"

"Positive."

"Well now, I'm sure that puzzles all of us, Mr. Cocyannis. Out of all the thousands of people who come to the caves, you can remember one individual?"

"I'm not likely to forget him."

"Why is that, Mr. Cocyannis?"

"First of all he wouldn't take a guide."

"Do all of your visitors take guides?"

"The Germans and the French are too stingy, but all the Americans do."

Laughter.

"I see. Was there any other reason you remembered Mr. Douglas?"

"You bet there was. I wouldn't have noticed him especially except for the guide thing, and the woman with him seemed kind of embarrassed when he said no. Then about an hour later, I saw him hurry out of the entrance, and he was alone and he seemed awfully upset, and I thought maybe the woman had had an accident or something. I went up to him and asked if the lady was all right, and he stared at me kind of funny and said, 'What lady?' and I said, 'The lady you took in the caves with you.' And he turned kind of white and I thought he was going to hit me.

Then he started yelling, 'I've lost her. I need help,' and he began carrying on like a crazy man."

"But he didn't call for help until you asked where the missing woman was?"

"That's right."

"What happened next?"

"Well, I organized the other guides and we began a search. Some damned fool had moved the Danger sign from the new section. That's not open to the public. That's where we finally found her about three hours later. She was in pretty bad shape."

"One last question. And answer this very carefully. When Mr. Douglas first came out of the cave, was he looking around for someone to help him, or did you get the impression that he was leaving?"

"He was leaving."

"Your witness."

NAPOLEON CHOTAS' VOICE was very gentle.

"Mr. Cocyannis, are you a psychiatrist?"

"No, sir. I'm a guide."

"And you're not psychic?"

"No, sir."

"I ask this because over the past week, we've had hotel clerks who are experts on human psychology, eyewitnesses who are nearsighted, and now you tell us that you can look at a man who attracted your attention because he seemed agitated, and you can read his mind. How did you *know* he wasn't looking for help when you went up and spoke to him?"

"He didn't look like it."

"And you can remember his behavior that well?"

"That's right."

"You obviously have a remarkable memory. I want you to look around the courtroom. Have you ever seen anyone in this room before today?"

"The defendant."

"Yes. Aside from him? Take your time."

"No."

"If you had, you would have remembered?"

"Absolutely."

"Have you ever seen me before today?"

"No, sir."

"Would you look at this piece of paper, please. Can you tell me what it is?"

"It's a ticket."

"To what?"

"The Caves of Perama."

"And the date on it?"

"Monday. Three weeks ago."

"Yes. That ticket was purchased and used by me, Mr. Cocyannis. There were five others in my party. You were our guide. No further questions."

"WHAT IS YOUR occupation?"

"I'm a bellboy at the Palace Hotel in Ioannina."

"Would you please look at the defendant seated in the defendant's box. Have you ever seen her before?"

"Yes, sir. In movies."

"Did you ever see her in person before today?"

"Yes, sir. She came into the hotel and asked me what room Mr. Douglas was staying in. I told her she'd have to inquire at the desk and she said she preferred not to bother them, so I gave her the number of his bungalow."

"And this was when?"

"The first day of August. The day of the *meltemi*."

"And are you sure that this is the same woman?"

"How could I forget her? She tipped me two hundred drachmas."

THE TRIAL WAS going into its fourth week. Everyone agreed that Napoleon Chotas was conducting the best defense they had ever witnessed. But in spite of this the web of guilt was being woven tighter and tighter.

Peter Demonides was building up a picture of two lovers, desperate to be together, to be married, with only Catherine Douglas standing in their way. Slowly day by day, Demonides elaborated on the plot to murder her.

Larry Douglas' attorney, Frederick Stavros, had gladly abdicated his position and relied on Napoleon Chotas. But now even Stavros began to feel that it would take a miracle to get an acquittal. Stavros stared at the empty chair in the packed courtroom and wondered if Constantin Demiris was really going to make an appearance. If Noelle Page was convicted, the Greek tycoon would probably not come, for it would mean that he had been defeated. On the other hand, if the tycoon knew there would be an acquittal, he would probably show up. The empty chair was becoming a symbol of which way the trial would go.

The seat remained empty.

IT WAS ON a Friday afternoon that the case finally exploded.

"Would you state your name, please?"

"Doctor Kazomides. John Kazomides."

"Did you ever meet Mr. or Mrs. Douglas, Doctor?"

"Yes, sir. Both of them."

"What was the occasion?"

"I got a call to come to the Caves of Perama. A woman had been lost in there, and when the search party finally found her, she was in a state of shock."

"Had she been hurt physically?"

"Yes. There were multiple contusions. Her hands and arms and cheeks had been badly scraped on the rocks. She had fallen down and hit her head, and I diagnosed a probable concussion. I immediately gave her a shot of morphine for the pain and ordered them to take her to the local hospital."

"And is that where she went?"

"No, sir."

"Would you tell the jury why not?"

"At her husband's insistence she was taken back to their bungalow at the Palace Hotel."

"Did that strike you as peculiar, Doctor?"

"He said he wanted to look after her himself."

"So Mrs. Douglas was taken back to her hotel. Did you accompany her there?"

"Yes. I insisted on going back to her bungalow with her. I wanted to be at her bedside when she awakened."

"And were you there when she awakened?"

"Yes, sir."

"Did Mrs. Douglas say anything to you?"

"She did."

"Would you tell the Court what she said."

"She told me that her husband had tried to murder her."

It was a full five minutes before they could quiet the uproar in the courtroom, and it was not until the President threatened to clear the room that the hubbub finally subsided. Napoleon Chotas had walked over to the defendant's box and was holding a hurried conference with Noelle Page. For the first time she seemed upset. Demonides was going on with the questioning.

"Doctor, you said in your testimony that Mrs. Douglas was in shock. In your professional opinion was she lucid when she told you that her husband tried to murder her?"

"Yes, sir. I had already given her one sedative at the caves, and she was relatively calm. However when I told her I was going to give her another sedative, she became extremely agitated and begged me not to."

The President of the Court leaned down and asked, "Did she explain why?"

"Yes, Your Honor. She said that her husband would kill her while she was asleep."

The President leaned back in his chair thoughtfully and said to Peter Demonides, "You may continue."

"Dr. Kazomides, did you in fact administer a second sedative to Mrs. Douglas?"

"Yes."

"While she was in her bed at the bungalow?"

"Yes."

"How did you administer it?"

"By hypodermic. In the hip."

"And she was asleep when you left?"

"Yes."

"Was there any chance Mrs. Douglas could have awakened any time in the next few hours, gotten out of bed without assistance, dressed herself and walked out of that house unaided?"

"In her condition? No. It would be most unlikely. She was very heavily sedated."

"That is all, thank you, Doctor."

The jurors were staring at Noelle Page and Larry Douglas and their faces had turned cold and unfriendly. A stranger could have walked into the courtroom and known instantly how the case was going.

Bill Fraser's eyes were bright with satisfaction. After Dr. Kazomides' testimony there could no longer be the slightest doubt that Catherine had been murdered by Larry Douglas and Noelle Page. There was nothing Napoleon Chotas would be able to do to eradicate from the minds of the jurors the image of a terrified woman, drugged and defenseless, begging not to be left in the hands of her murderer.

Frederick Stavros was in a panic. He had gladly let Napoleon Chotas run the show, following his lead in blind faith, confident that Chotas would be able to secure an acquittal for his client and therefore for Stavros' client. Now he felt betrayed. Everything was falling apart. The doctor's testimony had been irreparably damaging, both for its evidential and its emotional impact. Stavros looked around the room. Except for the one mysteriously reserved seat the room was filled. The world press was here, waiting to report what happened next.

Stavros had a momentary vision of himself leaping to his feet, confronting the doctor and brilliantly tearing his testimony to shreds. His client would be acquitted and he, Stavros, would be a hero. He knew this would be his last chance. The outcome of this case would mean the difference between fame and obscurity. Stavros could actually feel his thigh muscles bunching up, urging him to get to his feet. But he could not move. He sat there, paralyzed by the overpowering specter of failure. He turned to look at Chotas. The deep, sad eyes in the bloodhound face were studying the doctor on the witness stand, as though trying to come to some decision.

Slowly Napoleon Chotas rose to his feet. But instead of walking over to the witness, he moved toward the bench and quietly addressed the judges.

"Mr. President, Your Honors, I do not wish to cross-examine the witness. With the Court's permission, I would like to ask for a recess in order to confer *in camera* with the Court and the Prosecuting Attorney."

The President of the Court turned to the Prosecutor. "Mr. De-monides?"

"No objection," Demonides said, his voice wary.

The Court was recessed. Not one person moved from his chair.

THIRTY MINUTES LATER Napoleon Chotas returned to the courtroom alone. The instant he walked through the chamber door, everyone in the courtroom sensed that something important had taken place. There was an air of secret self-satisfaction in the lawyer's face, his walk was faster and springier, as though some charade had ended and it was no longer necessary to play games. Chotas walked over to the defendant's box and stared down at Noelle. She looked up into his face, her violet eyes probing, anxious. And suddenly a smile touched the lawyer's lips, and from the light in his eyes Noelle knew that somehow he had done it, he had performed the miracle in spite of all the evidence, in spite of all the odds. Justice had triumphed, but it was the Justice of Constantin Demiris. Larry Douglas was staring at Chotas, too, filled with fear and with hope. Whatever Chotas had done would have been for Noelle. But what about him?

Chotas addressed Noelle in a carefully neutral voice. "The President of the Court has given me permission to speak with you in his chambers." He turned to Frederick Stavros, who was sitting in an agony of uncertainty, not knowing what was going on. "You and your client have permission to join us if you wish."

Stavros nodded. "Of course." He scrambled to his feet, almost knocking over his chair in his eagerness.

Two bailiffs accompanied them to the empty chambers of the President. When the bailiffs had left and they were alone, Chotas turned to Frederick Stavros. "What I am about to say," he said quietly, "is for the benefit of my client. However, because they are co-defendants, I have been able to arrange for your client to be accorded the same privilege as mine."

"Tell me!" Noelle demanded.

Chotas turned to her. He spoke slowly, choosing his words with great care. "I have just had a conference with the judges," he said. "They were impressed with the case the prosecution has made against you. However—" he paused, delicately, "I was able to—er—persuade them that the interests of justice would not be served by punishing you."

"What's going to happen?" Stavros demanded in a fever of impatience.

There was a note of deep satisfaction in Chotas' voice as he continued, "If the defendants are willing to change their pleas to guilty, the judges have agreed to give each of them a five-year sentence." He smiled and added, "Four years of which will be suspended. In reality they will not have to serve more than six months." He turned to Larry. "Because you are an American, Mr. Douglas, you will be deported. You will never be permitted to return to Greece."

Larry nodded, his body flooding with relief.

Chotas turned back to Noelle. "This was not an easy thing to accomplish. I must tell you in all honesty that the primary reason for the leniency of the Court is the interest of your—er—patron. They feel he has already suffered unduly because of all this publicity, and they are anxious to see it ended."

"I understand," Noelle said.

Napoleon Chotas hesitated in embarrassment. "There is one more condition."

She looked at him. "Yes?"

"Your passport will be taken away. You will never be permitted to leave Greece. You will remain here under the protection of your friend."

So it had been done.

Constantin Demiris had kept his bargain. Noelle did not for a moment believe that the judges were being lenient because they were concerned about Demiris' being subjected to unpleasant publicity. No, he had had to pay a price for her freedom, and Noelle knew that it must have been a heavy one. But in return Demiris was getting her back and arranging it so that she could never leave him. Or see Larry again. She turned to Larry and read the relief in his face. He was going to be set free, and that was all he cared about. There was no regret about losing her and about what had happened. But Noelle understood it because she understood Larry, for he was her alter ego, her *Doppelgänger,* and they both had the same reckless zest for life, the same insatiable appetites. They were kindred spirits beyond mortality, beyond laws they had never made and never lived by. In her way Noelle would miss Larry very much, and when he left, a part of her would go with him. But she knew now how precious her life was to her and how terrified she had been of losing it. And so on balance it was a very good bargain, and she accepted it gratefully. She turned to Chotas and said, "That is satisfactory."

Chotas looked at her, and there was a sadness in his eyes as well as the satisfaction. Noelle understood that, too. He was in love with her and had had to use all his skill to save her for another man. Noelle had deliberately encouraged Chotas to fall in love with her because she needed him, needed to make sure that he would stop at nothing to save her. And everything had worked out.

"I think it's absolutely marvelous," Frederick Stavros was babbling. "Absolutely marvelous."

In truth Stavros felt that it was a miracle, nearly as good as an acquittal, and while it was true that Napoleon Chotas would reap most of the benefit from it, the peripheral fallout would still be tremendous. From this moment on Stavros would have his choice of clients, and each time he told the story of the trial, his role in it would get bigger and bigger.

"It sounds like a good deal," Larry was saying. "The only thing is, we're not guilty. We didn't kill Catherine."

Frederick Stavros turned on him in a fury. "Who gives a damn whether you're guilty or not?" he shouted. "We're making you a present of your life." He shot a quick glance at Chotas to see if he had reacted to the "we" but the lawyer was listening, his attitude one of aloof neutrality.

"I want you to understand," Chotas said to Stavros, "that I am only advising *my* client. Your client is free to make his own decision."

"What would have happened to us without this deal?" Larry asked.

"The jury would have—" Frederick Stavros began.

"I want to hear it from *him*," Larry interrupted, curtly. He turned to Chotas.

"In a trial, Mr. Douglas," Chotas replied, "the most important factor is not innocence or guilt, but the *impression* of innocence or guilt. There is no absolute truth, there is only the interpretation of truth. In this case it does not matter whether you are innocent of murder, the jury has the *impression* of guilt. That is what you would have been convicted for, and in the end you would have been just as dead."

Larry looked at him for a long moment, then nodded. "OK," he said. "Let's get it over with."

FIFTEEN MINUTES LATER the two defendants stood before the judges' bench. The President of the Court was seated in the center, flanked by the two justices. Napoleon Chotas stood next to Noelle Page and Frederick Stavros stood at the side of Larry Douglas. The courtroom was charged with an electric tension, for word had flashed about the room that a dramatic development was about to take place. But when it came, it caught everyone completely off guard. In a formal, pedantic voice, as though he had not just made a secret bargain with the three jurists on the bench, Napoleon Chotas said, "Mr. President, Your Honors, my client wishes to change her plea from *not guilty* to *guilty.*"

The President of the Court leaned back in his chair and stared at Chotas in surprise, as though he were hearing the news for the first time.

He's playing it to the hilt, Noelle thought. *He wants to earn his money, or whatever it is Demiris is paying him off with.*

The President leaned forward and consulted with the other justices in a flurry of whispers. They nodded and the President looked down at Noelle and said, "Do you wish to change your plea to guilty?"

Noelle nodded and said firmly, "I do."

Frederick Stavros spoke up quickly, as though afraid of being left out of the procedure. "Your Honors, my client wishes to change his plea from not guilty to guilty."

The President turned to regard Larry. "Do you wish to change your plea to guilty?"

Larry glanced at Chotas and then nodded. "Yes."

The President studied the two prisoners, his face grave. "Have your attorneys advised you that under Greek law the penalty for the crime of premeditated murder is execution?"

"Yes, Your Honor." Noelle's voice was strong and clear.

The President turned to look at Larry.

"Yes, sir," he said.

There was another whispered consultation among the judges. The President of the Court turned to Demonides. "Does the Prosecutor for the State have any objections to the change of plea?"

Demonides looked at Chotas a long moment, then said, "None."

Noelle wondered if he were in on the payoff also, or whether he was simply being used as a pawn.

"Very well," the President said. "This Court has no choice but to accept the change of plea." He turned to the jury. "Gentlemen, in view of this new development, you are herewith released from your duties as jurymen. In effect the trial has come to an end. The Court will pass sentence. Thank you for your services and for your cooperation. The Court will recess for two hours."

In the next moment the reporters began to tumble out of the room, racing to their telephones and teletype machines to report the latest sensational development in the murder trial of Noelle Page and Larry Douglas.

TWO HOURS LATER the courtroom was packed to overflowing as the Court was reconvened. Noelle glanced around the courtroom at the faces of the spectators. They were watching her with expressions of eager expectation, and it was all Noelle could do to keep from laughing aloud at their naïveté. These were the common people, the masses, and they really believed that justice was meted out fairly, that under a democracy all men were created equal, that a poor man had the same rights and privileges as a rich man.

"Will the defendants now rise and approach the bench?"

Gracefully Noelle rose to her feet and moved toward the bench, Chotas at her side. Out of the corner of her eye she saw Larry and Stavros stepping forward.

The President of the Court spoke. "This has been a long and difficult trial," he began. "In capital cases where there is a reasonable doubt of guilt, the Court is always inclined to let the accused have the benefit of the doubt. I must admit that in this case we felt that there existed such a doubt. The fact that the State was unable to produce a *corpus delicti* was a very strong point in favor of the defendants." He turned to look at Napoleon Chotas. "I am sure that the able counsel for the defense is well aware that the Greek Courts have never given the death penalty in a case where a murder has not been definitely proven to have been committed."

A faint sense of unease was beginning to brush Noelle, nothing alarming yet, just the merest whisper, the slightest hint. The President was going on.

"My colleagues and I were, for that reason, frankly surprised when the defendants decided to change their pleas to guilty, in mid-trial."

The feeling was in the pit of Noelle's stomach now, growing, moving upward, beginning to constrict her throat, so that she was suddenly finding it difficult to breathe. Larry was staring at the judge, not fully comprehending yet what was happening.

"We appreciate the agonizing soul-searching that must have taken place before the defendants decided to confess their guilt before this Court and before the world. However, the easing of their consciences cannot be accepted as atonement for the terrible crime they have admitted committing, the cold-blooded murder of a helpless, defenseless woman."

It was at that moment that Noelle knew, with a sudden, mind-smashing certainty that she had been tricked. Demiris had set up a charade to lull her into a feeling of false security so that he could do this to her. This was his game, this was the trap he had baited. He *had* known how terrified she was of dying, so he had held out the hope of life to her and she had accepted it, had believed him, and he had outwitted her. Demiris had wanted his vengeance *now*, not later. Her life could have been saved. Of course Chotas had known that she would not get the death penalty unless a corpse was produced. He had made no deal with the judges. Chotas had rigged this whole defense to lure Noelle to her death. She turned to look at him. He looked up to meet her gaze, and his eyes were filled with a genuine sadness. He loved her and he had murdered her, and if he had it to do over again, he would do the same thing, for in the end he was Demiris' man, just as she was Demiris' woman, and neither of them could fight his power.

The President was speaking. ". . . and so under the powers invested in me by the State, and in accord with its laws, I pronounce that the sentence on the two defendants, Noelle Page and Lawrence Douglas shall be execution by a firing squad. . . . the sentence to be carried out within ninety days from this date."

The Court was in pandemonium, but Noelle neither heard nor saw it. Something had made her turn around. The vacant seat was no longer empty. Constantin Demiris sat in it. He was freshly shaved and barbered. He was dressed in a blue raw-silk suit, flawlessly tailored, a light blue shirt, and a foulard tie. His olive black eyes were bright and alive. There was no sign of the defeated, crumbling man who had come to visit her in prison, because that man had never existed.

Constantin Demiris had come to watch Noelle in the moment of her defeat, savoring the terror in her. His black eyes were locked on hers and for one split instant she saw in them a deep, malevolent satisfaction. And there was something else. Regret, perhaps, but it was gone before she could capture it, and it was all too late now anyway.

The chess game was finally over.

LARRY HAD LISTENED to the President's last words in shocked disbelief, and when a bailiff stepped forward and took him by the arm, Larry shook loose and turned back to the bench.

"Wait a minute!" he yelled. "I didn't kill her! They framed me!"

Another bailiff hurried forward and the two men held Larry. One of them pulled out a pair of handcuffs.

"No!" Larry was screaming. "Listen to me! I didn't kill her!"

He tried to jerk away from the bailiffs, but the handcuffs snapped on his wrists and he was yanked away, out of the room.

NOELLE FELT A pressure on her arm. A matron was waiting there to escort her out of the courtroom.

"They're waiting for you, Miss Page."

It was like a theater call. *They're waiting for you, Miss Page.* Only this time when the curtain went down, it would never rise again. The realization hit Noelle that this was the last time in her life that she would ever be in public, the last time that she would be around other people, uncaged. This was her farewell appearance, this dirty, dreary Greek courtroom, her final theater. *Well,* she thought defiantly, *at least I have a good house.* She looked around the packed courtroom for the last time.

She saw Armand Gautier staring at her in stunned silence, shaken for once out of his cynicism.

There was Philippe Sorel, his rugged face trying hard for an encouraging smile and not quite managing it.

Across the room was Israel Katz, his eyes closed and his lips moving as though in silent prayer. Noelle remembered the night she had smuggled him into the trunk of the General's car, under the nose of the albino Gestapo officer, and the fear that had been in her then. But it was nothing to the terror that was possessing her now.

Noelle's eyes moved across the room and rested on the face of Auguste Lanchon, the shopkeeper. She could not recall his name, but she remembered his porcine face and his gross squat body and the dreary hotel room in Vienne. When he saw her looking at him, he blinked and lowered his eyes.

A tall, attractive, gray-haired American-looking man was standing up staring at her as though wanting to tell her something. Noelle had no idea who he was.

The matron was tugging at her arm now, saying, "Come along, Miss Page. . . ."

FREDERICK STAVROS WAS in a state of shock. He had not only been a witness to a cold-blooded frame-up; he had been a party to it. He could go to the President of the Court and tell him what had happened: what Chotas had promised. But would they believe him? Would they take his word against the word of Napoleon Chotas? It really didn't matter, Stavros thought bitterly. After this he would be finished as a lawyer. No one would ever hire him again. Someone spoke his name and he turned and Chotas was standing there saying, "If you're free tomorrow, why don't you come and have lunch with me, Frederick? I'd like you to meet my partners. I think you have a very promising future."

Over Chotas' shoulder, Frederick Stavros could see the President of the Court exiting through the door that led to his private chambers. Now would be the time to talk to him, to explain what had happened. Stavros turned back to Napoleon Chotas, his mind still filled with the horror of what this man had done, and he heard himself saying, "That's very kind of you, sir. What would be a convenient time . . . ?"

• • •

BY GREEK LAW executions take place on the little island of Ageana, an hour out of the port of Piraeus. A special government boat transports condemned prisoners to the island. A series of small gray cliffs leads to the harbor itself and high on a hill is a lighthouse built on an outcropping of rock. The prison on Ageana is on the north side of the island, out of sight of the little harbor where excursion boats regularly disgorge excited tourists for an hour or two of shopping and sightseeing before sailing on to the next island. The prison is not on the sightseeing schedule, and no one approaches it except on official business.

IT WAS 4:00 A.M. on a Saturday morning. Noelle's execution was scheduled to take place at 6:00 A.M.

They had brought Noelle her favorite dress to wear, a wine-red, brushed-wool Dior, and matching red suede shoes. She had all new silk handstitched lingerie and a white jabot of Venetian lace for her throat. Constantin Demiris had sent Noelle's regular hairdresser to do her hair. It was as though Noelle were preparing to go to a party.

Intellectually Noelle knew that there would be no last-minute reprieve, that in a little while her body was going to be brutally violated and her blood spilled upon the ground. And yet emotionally she could not keep from hoping that Constantin Demiris would make a miracle and spare her life. It would not even have to be a miracle—it only needed a phone call, a word, a wave of his golden hand. If he spared her now, she would make it up to him. She would do anything. If she could only see him, she would tell him she would never look at another man, that she would devote herself to making him happy for the rest of his life. But she knew that it would do no good to beg. If Demiris came to her, yes. If she had to go to him, no.

There were still two hours.

LARRY DOUGLAS WAS in another part of the prison. Since his conviction, his mail had increased tenfold. Letters poured in from women in all parts of the world, and the warden, who considered himself a sophisticated man, was shocked by some of them.

Larry Douglas would probably have enjoyed them if he had known of them. But he was in a drugged world of half-twilight where nothing touched him. During his first few days on the island, he had been in a state of violence, screaming day and night that he was innocent and demanding a new trial. The prison doctor had finally ordered that he be kept on tranquilizers.

At ten minutes before five A.M., when the prison warden and four guards came to Larry Douglas' cell, he was seated on his bunk, quiet and withdrawn. The warden had to speak his name twice before Larry was aware that they had come for him. He rose to his feet, his movements dreamlike and lethargic.

The warden led him out to the corridor, and they walked in a slow procession toward a guarded door at the far end of the corridor. As they reached the door, the guard opened it and they were outside in a walled courtyard. The predawn air was chilly and Larry shivered as he stepped through the door. There was a full moon in the sky and bright stars. It reminded him of the mornings in the South Pacific islands when the pilots left their warm bunks and gathered under the chilly stars for a last minute briefing before takeoff. He could hear the sound of the sea in the distance, and he tried to remember which island he was on and what his mission was. Some men led him to a post in front of a wall and tied his arms behind his back.

There was no anger in him now, only a kind of drowsy wonder about the way the briefing was being handled. He was filled with a deep lassitude but he knew he must not fall asleep because he had to lead the mission. He raised his head and saw men in uniform lined up. They were aiming guns at him. Old, buried instincts began to take over. They would attack from different directions and try to separate him from the rest of his squadron, because they were afraid of him. He saw a movement at three o'clock low and knew they were coming for him. They would expect him to bank out of range, but instead he shoved the stick all the way forward and went into an outside loop that nearly tore the wings off his plane. He pulled out at the bottom of the dive and executed a snap roll to the left. There was no sign of them. He had outmaneuvered them. He began to climb, and below him he saw a Zero. He laughed aloud and gave his plane right stick and rudder until the Zero was centered in his gunsights. Then he swooped down like an avenging angel, closing the distance with dizzying speed. His finger began to tighten on the trigger button when a sudden excruciating pain smashed through his body. And another. And another. He could feel his flesh tearing and his guts spilling out, and he thought, *Oh, my God, where did he come from? . . . There's a better pilot than me . . . I wonder who he is . . .*

And then he began spinning abruptly into space and everything grew dark and silent.

IN HER CELL Noelle's hair was being coifed when she heard a volley of thunder outside.

"Is it going to rain?" she asked.

The hairdresser looked at her strangely for a moment and saw that she really did not know what the sound was. "No," she said quietly, "it is going to be a beautiful day."

And then Noelle knew.

And she was next.

AT FIVE-THIRTY A.M., thirty minutes before her execution was scheduled, Noelle heard footsteps approaching her call. Her heart gave an involuntary leap. She had been sure that Constantin Demiris would want to see her. She knew that she had never looked more beautiful, and perhaps when he saw her. . . . perhaps . . . The prison warden appeared, accompanied by a guard and a nurse carrying a black medical bag. Noelle looked behind them for Demiris. The corridor was empty. The guard opened the cell door, and the warden and nurse entered. Noelle found that her heart was pounding, the wave of fear beginning to lap at her again, drowning out the faint hope that had been stirring.

"It isn't time yet, is it?" Noelle asked.

The warden looked uncomfortable. "No, Miss Page. The nurse is here to give you an enema."

She looked at him, not understanding. "I don't want an enema."

He looked even more uncomfortable. "It will save you being— embarrassed."

And then Noelle understood. And her fear turned into a roaring agony, tearing at her stomach. She nodded her head and the warden turned and left the cell. The guard locked the door and tactfully walked down the corridor out of sight.

"We don't want to spoil that pretty dress," the nurse was cooing. "Why don't we just slip it off and you lie down right there? This will only take a minute."

The nurse began to work on her, but Noelle felt nothing.

She was with her father and he was saying, *Look at her, a stranger could tell she was of royal blood,* and people were fighting to pick her up in their arms and hold her. A priest was in the room and he said, "Would you like to make your confession to God, my child?" but she shook her head impatiently because her father was talking and she wanted to hear what he was saying. *You were born a Princess and this is your Kingdom. When you grow up, you're going to marry a handsome Prince and live in a grand palace.*

She was walking down a long corridor with some men and someone opened a door and she was outside in a cold courtyard. Her father was holding her up to a window and she could see the tall masts of ships bobbing on the water.

The men led her to a post in front of a wall and fastened her hands behind her and tied her waist to the post and her father said, *Do you see those ships, Princess? That's your fleet. One day they'll carry you to all the magic places in the world.* And he held her close and she felt safe. She could not remember why, but he had been angry with her, but now everything was all right, and he loved her again, and she turned to him but his face was a blur, and she could not recall what he looked like. She could not remember her father's face.

She was filled with an overwhelming sadness, as though she had lost something precious, and she knew that she had to remember him or she would die, and she began to concentrate very hard, but before she could see it, there was a sudden roaring sound and a thousand knives of agony tore into her flesh and her mind screamed, *No! Not yet! Let me see my father's face!*

But it was lost forever in the darkness.

EPILOGUE

The man and woman moved through the cemetery, their faces dappled by the shadows of the tall, graceful cypresses that lined the path. They walked slowly in the shimmering heat of the noonday sun.

Sister Theresa said, "I wish to tell you again how grateful we are for your generosity. I do not know what we would have done without you."

Constantin Demiris waved a deprecating hand. *"Arkayto,"* he said. "It is nothing, Sister."

But Sister Theresa knew that without this savior the nunnery would have had to close down years ago. And surely it was a sign from Heaven that now she had been able to repay him in some measure. It was a *thriamvos,* a triumph. She thanked Saint Dionysius again that the Sisters had been permitted to rescue the American friend of Demiris' from the waters of the lake on that terrible night of the storm. True, something had happened to the woman's mind and she was like a child, but she would be cared for. Mr. Demiris had asked Sister Theresa to keep the woman here within these walls, sheltered and protected from the outside world for the rest of her life. He was such a good and kind man.

They had reached the end of the cemetery. A path wound down to a promontory where the woman stood, staring out at the calm, emerald lake below.

"There she is," Sister Theresa said. "I will leave you now. *Hayretay.*"

Demiris watched Sister Theresa start back toward the nunnery, then he walked down the path to where the woman stood.

"Good morning," he said, gently.

She turned around slowly and looked at him. Her eyes were dull and vacant and there was no recognition on her face.

"I brought you something," Constantin Demiris said.

He pulled a small jewelry box out of his pocket and held it out to her. She stared at it like a small child.

"Go on, take it."

Slowly she reached out and took the box. She lifted the lid, and inside, nested in cotton, was a miniature, exquisitely made gold bird with ruby eyes and outstretched wings poised for flight. Demiris watched as the child-woman removed it from the box and held it up. The bright sun caught the gleam of its gold and the sparkle of its ruby eyes and sent tiny rainbows flashing through the air. She turned it from side to side, watching the lights dancing around her head.

"I will not be seeing you again," Demiris said, "but you won't have to worry. No one will harm you now. The wicked people are dead."

As he spoke, her face happened to be turned toward him, and for one frozen instant in time it seemed to him that a gleam of intelligence, a look of joy came into her eyes, but a moment later it was gone and there was only the vacant, mindless stare. It could have been an illusion, a trick of the sunlight reflecting the sparkle of the golden bird across her eyes.

He thought about it as he walked slowly up the hill and out the huge stone gate of the nunnery to where his limousine was waiting to drive him back to Athens.

Chicago
London
Paris
Athens
Ioannina
Los Angeles

RAGE OF ANGELS

"... Tell us of the secret hosts of evil, O Cimon ..."
"Their names may not be spake aloud
lest they profane mortal lips,
for they came out of unholy darknesses
and attacked the heavens,
but they were driven away by the rage of angels ..."

—FROM *Dialogues of Chios*

BOOK ONE

NEW YORK: SEPTEMBER 4, 1969

The hunters were closing in for the kill.

Two thousand years ago in Rome, the contest would have been staged at the Circus Neronis or the Colosseum, where voracious lions would have been stalking the victim in an arena of blood and sand, eager to tear him to pieces. But this was the civilized twentieth century, and the circus was being staged in the Criminal Courts Building of downtown Manhattan, Courtroom Number 16.

In place of Suetonius was a court stenographer, to record the event for posterity, and there were dozens of members of the press and visitors attracted by the daily headlines about the murder trial, who queued up outside the courtroom at seven o'clock in the morning to be assured of a seat.

The quarry, Michael Moretti, sat at the defendant's table, a silent, handsome man in his early thirties. He was tall and lean, with a face formed of converging planes that gave him a rugged, feral look. He had fashionably styled black hair, a prominent chin with an unexpected dimple in it and deeply set olive-black eyes. He wore a tailored gray suit, a light blue shirt with a darker blue silk tie, and polished, custom-made shoes. Except for his eyes, which constantly swept over the courtroom, Michael Moretti was still.

The lion attacking him was Robert Di Silva, the fiery District Attorney for the County of New York, representative of The People. If Michael Moretti radiated stillness, Robert Di Silva radiated dynamic movement; he went through life as though he were five minutes late for an appointment. He was in constant motion, shadowboxing with invisible opponents. He was short and powerfully built, with an unfashionable graying crew cut. Di Silva had been a boxer in his youth and his nose and face bore the scars of it. He had once killed a man in the ring and he had never regretted it. In the years since then, he had yet to learn compassion.

Robert Di Silva was a fiercely ambitious man who had fought his way up to his present position with neither money nor connections to help him. During his climb, he had assumed the veneer of a civilized servant of the people; but underneath, he was a gutter fighter, a man who neither forgot nor forgave.

Under ordinary circumstances, District Attorney Di Silva would not have been in this courtroom on this day. He had a large staff, and any one of his senior assistants was capable of prosecuting this case. But Di Silva had known from the beginning that he was going to handle the Moretti case himself.

Michael Moretti was front-page news, the son-in-law of Antonio Granelli, *capo di capi,* head of the largest of the five eastern Mafia Families. Antonio Granelli was getting old and the street word was that Michael Moretti was being groomed to take his father-in-law's place. Moretti had been involved in dozens of crimes ranging from mayhem to murder, but no district attorney had ever been able to prove anything. There were too many careful layers between Moretti and those who carried out his orders. Di Silva himself had spent three frustrating years trying to get evidence against Moretti. Then, suddenly, Di Silva had gotten lucky.

Camillo Stela, one of Moretti's *soldati,* had been caught in a murder committed during a robbery. In exchange for his life, Stela agreed to sing. It was the most beautiful music Di Silva had ever heard, a song that was going to bring the most powerful Mafia Family in the east to its knees, send Michael Moretti to the electric chair, and elevate Robert Di Silva to the governor's office in Albany. Other New York governors had made it to the White House: Martin Van Buren, Grover Cleveland, Teddy Roosevelt and Franklin Roosevelt. Di Silva intended to be the next.

The timing was perfect. The gubernatorial elections were coming up next year.

Di Silva had been approached by the state's most powerful political boss. "With all the publicity you're getting on this case, you'll be a shoo-in to be nominated and then elected governor, Bobby. Nail Moretti and you're our candidate."

ROBERT DI SILVA had taken no chances. He prepared the case against Michael Moretti with meticulous care. He put his assistants to work assembling evidence, cleaning up every loose end, cutting off each legal avenue of escape that Moretti's attorney might attempt to explore. One by one, every loophole had been closed.

It had taken almost two weeks to select the jury, and the District Attorney had insisted upon selecting six "spare tires"—alternate jurors—as a precaution against a possible mistrial. In cases where important Mafia figures were involved, jurors had been known to disappear or to have unexplained fatal accidents. Di Silva had seen to it that this jury was sequestered from the beginning, locked away every night where no one could get to it.

The key to the case against Michael Moretti was Camillo Stela, and Di Silva's star witness was heavily protected. The District Attorney remembered only too vividly the example of Abe "Kid Twist" Reles, the government witness who had "fallen" out of a sixth-floor window of the Half Moon Hotel in Coney Island while being guarded by half a dozen policemen. Robert Di Silva had selected Camillo Stela's guards personally, and before the trial Stela had been secretly moved to a different location every night. Now, with the trial under way, Stela was kept in an isolated holding cell, guarded by four armed deputies. No one was allowed to get near him, for Stela's willingness to testify rested on his belief that District Attorney Di Silva was capable of protecting him from the vengeance of Michael Moretti.

It was the morning of the fifth day of the trial.

• • •

IT WAS JENNIFER Parker's first day at the trial. She was seated at the prosecutor's table with five other young assistant district attorneys who had been sworn in with her that morning.

Jennifer Parker was a slender, dark-haired girl of twenty-four with a pale skin, an intelligent, mobile face, and green, thoughtful eyes. It was a face that was attractive rather than beautiful, a face that reflected pride and courage and sensitivity, a face that would be hard to forget. She sat ramrod straight, as though bracing herself against unseen ghosts of the past.

JENNIFER PARKER'S DAY had started disastrously. The swearing-in ceremony at the District Attorney's office had been scheduled for eight A.M. Jennifer had carefully laid out her clothes the night before and had set the alarm for six so that she would have time to wash her hair.

The alarm had failed to go off. Jennifer had awakened at seven-thirty and panicked. She had gotten a run in her stocking when she broke the heel of her shoe, and had had to change clothes. She had slammed the door of her tiny apartment at the same instant she remembered she had left her keys inside. She had planned to take a bus to the Criminal Courts Building, but now that was out of the question, and she had raced to get a taxi she could not afford and had been trapped with a cab driver who explained during the entire trip why the world was about to come to an end.

When Jennifer had finally arrived, breathless, at the Criminal Courts Building at 155 Leonard Street, she was fifteen minutes late.

There were twenty-five lawyers gathered in the District Attorney's office, most of them newly out of law school, young and eager and excited about going to work for the District Attorney of the County of New York.

The office was impressive, paneled and decorated in quiet good taste. There was a large desk with three chairs in front of it and a comfortable leather chair behind it, a conference table with a dozen chairs around it, and wall cabinets filled with law books.

On the walls were framed autographed pictures of J. Edgar Hoover, John Lindsay, Richard Nixon and Jack Dempsey.

When Jennifer hurried into the office, full of apologies, Di Silva was in the middle of a speech. He stopped, turned his attention on Jennifer and said, "What the hell do you think this is—a tea party?"

"I'm terribly sorry, I—"

"I don't give a damn whether you're sorry. Don't you ever be late again!"

The others looked at Jennifer, carefully hiding their sympathy.

Di Silva turned to the group and snapped, "I know why you're all here. You'll stick around long enough to pick my brains and learn a few courtroom tricks, and then when you think you're ready, you'll leave to become hotshot criminal lawyers. But there may be one of you—maybe—who will be good enough to take my place one day." Di Silva nodded to his assistant. "Swear them in."

They took the oath, their voices subdued.

When it was over, Di Silva said, "All right. You're sworn officers of the court, God help us. This office is where the action is, but don't get your hopes up. You're going to bury your noses in legal research, and draft documents—subpoenas, warrants—all those wonderful things they taught you in law school. You won't get to handle a trial for the next year or two."

Di Silva stopped to light a short, stubby cigar. "I'm prosecuting a case now. Some of you may have read about it." His voice was edged with sarcasm. "I can use half a dozen of you to run errands for me." Jennifer's hand was the first one up. Di Silva hesitated a moment, then selected her and five others.

"Get down to Courtroom Sixteen."

As they left the room, they were issued identification cards. Jennifer had not been discouraged by the District Attorney's attitude. *He has to be tough,* she thought. *He's in a tough job.* And she was working for him now. She was a member of the staff of the District Attorney of the County of New York! The interminable years of law school drudgery were over. Somehow her professors had managed to make the law seem abstract and ancient, but Jennifer had always managed to glimpse the Promised Land beyond: the real law that dealt with human beings and their follies. Jennifer had been graduated second in her class and had been on Law Review. She had passed the bar examination on the first try, while a third of those who had taken it with her had failed. She felt that she understood Robert Di Silva, and she was sure she would be able to handle any job he gave her.

Jennifer had done her homework. She knew there were four different bureaus under the District Attorney—Trials, Appeals, Rackets and Frauds—and she wondered to which one she would be assigned. There were over two hundred assistant district attorneys in New York City and five district attorneys, one for each borough. But the most important borough, of course, was Manhattan: Robert Di Silva.

Jennifer sat in the courtroom now, at the prosecutor's table, watching Robert Di Silva at work, a powerful, relentless inquisitor.

Jennifer glanced over at the defendant, Michael Moretti. Even with everything Jennifer had read about him, she could not convince herself that Michael Moretti was a murderer. *He looks like a young movie star in a courtroom set,* Jennifer thought. He sat there motionless, only his deep, black eyes giving away whatever inner turmoil he might have felt. They moved ceaselessly, examining every corner of the room as though trying to calculate a means of escape. There was no escape. Di Silva had seen to that.

CAMILLO STELA WAS on the witness stand. If Stela had been an animal, he would have been a weasel. He had a narrow, pinched face, with thin lips and yellow buckteeth. His eyes were darting and furtive and you disbelieved him before he even opened his mouth. Robert Di Silva was aware of his witness's shortcomings, but they did not matter. What mattered was what Stela had to say. He had horror stories to tell that had never been told before, and they had the unmistakable ring of truth.

The District Attorney walked over to the witness box where Camillo Stela had been sworn in.

"Mr. Stela, I want this jury to be aware that you are a reluctant witness and that in order to persuade you to testify, the State has agreed to allow you to plead to the lesser charge of involuntary manslaughter in the murder you are charged with. Is that true?"

"Yes, sir." His right arm was twitching.

"Mr. Stela, are you acquainted with the defendant, Michael Moretti?"

"Yes, sir." He kept his eyes away from the defendant's table where Michael Moretti was sitting.

"What was the nature of your relationship?"

"I worked for Mike."

"How long have you known Michael Moretti?"

"About ten years." His voice was almost inaudible.

"Would you speak up, please?"

"About ten years." His neck was twitching now.

"Would you say you were close to the defendant?"

"Objection!" Thomas Colfax rose to his feet. Michael Moretti's attorney was a tall, silver-haired man in his fifties, the *consigliere* for the Syndicate, and one of the shrewdest criminal lawyers in the country. "The District Attorney is attempting to lead the witness."

Judge Lawrence Waldman said, "Sustained."

"I'll rephrase the question. In what capacity did you work for Mr. Moretti?"

"I was kind of what you might call a troubleshooter."

"Would you be a little more explicit?"

"Yeah. If a problem comes up—someone gets out of line, like—Mike would tell me to go straighten this party out."

"How would you do that?"

"You know—muscle."

"Could you give the jury an example?"

Thomas Colfax was on his feet. "Objection, Your Honor. This line of questioning is immaterial."

"Overruled. The witness may answer."

"Well, Mike's into loan-sharkin', right? A coupla years ago Jimmy Serrano gets behind in his payments, so Mike sends me over to teach Jimmy a lesson."

"What did that lesson consist of?"

"I broke his legs. You see," Stela explained earnestly, "if you let one guy get away with it, they're all gonna try it."

From the corner of his eye, Robert Di Silva could see the shocked reactions on the faces of the jurors.

"What other business was Michael Moretti involved in besides loan-sharking?"

"Jesus! You name it."

"I would like *you* to name it, Mr. Stela."

"Yeah. Well, like on the waterfront, Mike got a pretty good fix in with the union. Likewise the garment industry. Mike's into gamblin', juke boxes, garbage collectin', linen supplies. Like that."

"Mr. Stela, Michael Moretti is on trial for the murders of Eddie and Albert Ramos. Did you know them?"

"Oh, sure."

"Were you present when they were killed?"

"Yeah." His whole body seemed to twitch.

"Who did the actual killing?"

"Mike." For a second, his eyes caught Michael Moretti's eyes and Stela quickly looked away.

"Michael Moretti?"

"That's right."

"Why did the defendant tell you he wanted the Ramos brothers killed?"

"Well, Eddie and Al handled a book for—"

"That's a bookmaking operation? Illegal betting?"

"Yeah. Mike found out they was skimmin'. He had to teach 'em a lesson 'cause they was his boys, you know? He thought—"

"Objection!"

"Sustained. The witness will stick to the facts."

"The facts was that Mike tells me to invite the boys—"

"Eddie and Albert Ramos?"

"Yeah. To a little party down at The Pelican. That's a private beach club." His arm started to twitch again and Stela, suddenly aware of it, pressed against it with his other hand.

Jennifer Parker turned to look at Michael Moretti. He was watching impassively, his face and body immobile.

"What happened then, Mr. Stela?"

"I picked Eddie and Al up and drove 'em to the parkin' lot. Mike was there, waitin'. When the boys got outta the car, I moved outta the way and Mike started blastin'."

"Did you see the Ramos brothers fall to the ground?"

"Yes, sir."

"And they were dead?"

"They sure buried 'em like they was dead."

There was a ripple of sound through the courtroom. Di Silva waited until there was silence.

"Mr. Stela, you are aware that the testimony you have given in this courtroom is self-incriminating?"

"Yes, sir."

"And that you are under oath and that a man's life is at stake?"

"Yes, sir."

"You witnessed the defendant, Michael Moretti, cold-bloodedly shoot to death two men because they had withheld money from him?"

"Objection! He's leading the witness."

"Sustained."

District Attorney Di Silva looked at the faces of the jurors and what he saw there told him he had won the case. He turned to Camillo Stela.

"Mr. Stela, I know that it took a great deal of courage for you to come into this courtroom and testify. On behalf of the people of this state, I want to thank you." Di Silva turned to Thomas Colfax. "Your witness for cross."

Thomas Colfax rose gracefully to his feet. "Thank you, Mr. Di Silva." He glanced at the clock on the wall, then turned to the bench. "If it please Your Honor, it is now almost noon. I would prefer not to have my cross-examination interrupted. Might I request that the court recess for lunch now and I'll cross-examine this afternoon?"

"Very well." Judge Lawrence Waldman rapped his gavel on the bench. "This court stands adjourned until two o'clock."

Everyone in the courtroom rose as the judge stood up and walked through the side door to his chambers. The jurors began to file out of the room. Four armed deputies surrounded Camillo Stela and escorted him through a door near the front of the courtroom that led to the witness room.

At once, Di Silva was engulfed by reporters.

"Will you give us a statement?"

"How do you think the case is going so far, Mr. District Attorney?"

"How are you going to protect Stela when this is over?"

Ordinarily Robert Di Silva would not have tolerated such an intrusion in the courtroom, but he needed now, with his political ambitions, to keep the press on his side, and so he went out of his way to be polite to them.

Jennifer Parker sat there, watching the District Attorney parrying the reporters' questions.

"Are you going to get a conviction?"

"I'm not a fortune teller," Jennifer heard Di Silva say modestly. "That's what we have juries for, ladies and gentlemen. The jurors will have to decide whether Mr. Moretti is innocent or guilty."

Jennifer watched as Michael Moretti rose to his feet. He looked calm and relaxed. *Boyish* was the word that came to Jennifer's mind. It was difficult for her to believe that he was guilty of all the terrible things of which he was accused. *If I had to choose the guilty one,* Jennifer thought, *I'd choose Stela, the Twitcher.*

The reporters had moved off and Di Silva was in conference with members of his staff. Jennifer would have given anything to hear what they were discussing.

Jennifer watched as a man said something to Di Silva, detached himself from the group around the District Attorney, and hurried over toward Jennifer. He was carrying a large manila envelope. "Miss Parker?"

Jennifer looked up in surprise. "Yes."

"The Chief wants you to give this to Stela. Tell him to refresh his memory about these dates. Colfax is going to try to tear his testimony apart this afternoon and the Chief wants to make sure Stela doesn't foul up."

He handed the envelope to Jennifer and she looked over at Di Silva. *He remembered my name,* she thought. *It's a good omen.*

"Better get moving. The D.A. doesn't think Stela's that fast a study."

"Yes, sir." Jennifer hurried to her feet.

She walked over to the door she had seen Stela go through. An armed deputy blocked her way.

"Can I help you, miss?"

"District Attorney's office," Jennifer said crisply. She took out her identification card and showed it. "I have an envelope to deliver to Mr. Stela from Mr. Di Silva."

The guard examined the card carefully, then opened the door, and Jennifer found herself inside the witness room. It was a small, uncomfortable-looking room containing a battered desk, an old sofa and wooden chairs. Stela was seated in one of them, his arm twitching wildly. There were four armed deputies in the room.

As Jennifer entered, one of the guards said, "Hey! Nobody's allowed in here."

The outside guard called, "It's okay, Al. D.A.'s office."

Jennifer handed Stela the envelope. "Mr. Di Silva wants you to refresh your recollection about these dates."

Stela blinked at her and kept twitching.

2

As Jennifer was making her way out of the Criminal Courts Building on her way to lunch, she passed the open door of a deserted courtroom. She could not resist stepping inside the room for a moment.

There were fifteen rows of spectators' benches on each side of the rear area. Facing the judge's bench were two long tables, the one on the left marked *Plaintiff* and the one on the right marked *Defendant*. The jury box contained two rows of eight chairs each. *It's an ordinary courtroom,* Jennifer thought, *plain—even ugly—but it's the heart of freedom.* This room and all the courtrooms like it represented the difference between civilization and savagery. The right to a trial by a jury of one's peers was what lay at the heart of every free nation. Jennifer thought of all the countries in the world that did not have this little room, countries where citizens were taken from their beds in the middle of the night and tortured and murdered by anonymous enemies for undisclosed reasons: Iran, Uganda, Argentina, Peru, Brazil, Romania, Russia, Czechoslovakia . . . the list was depressingly long.

If the American courts were ever stripped of their power, Jennifer thought, *if citizens were ever denied the right to a trial by jury, then America would cease to exist as a free nation.* She was a part of the system now and, standing there, Jennifer was filled with an overwhelming feeling of pride. She would do everything she could to honor it, to help preserve it. She stood there for a long moment, then turned to leave.

From the far end of the hall there was a distant hum that got louder and louder, and became pandemonium. Alarm bells began to ring. Jennifer heard the sound of running feet in the corridor and saw policemen with drawn guns racing toward the front entrance of the courthouse. Jennifer's instant thought was that Michael Moretti had escaped, had somehow gotten past the barrier of guards. She hurried out into the corridor. It was bedlam. People were racing around frantically, shouting orders over the din of the clanging bells. Guards armed with riot guns had taken up positions at the exit doors. Reporters who had been telephoning in their stories were hurrying into the corridor to find out what was happening. Far down the hall, Jennifer saw District Attorney Robert Di Silva wildly issuing instructions to half a dozen policemen, his face drained of color.

My God! He's going to have a heart attack, Jennifer thought.

She pushed her way through the crowd and moved toward him, thinking that perhaps she could be of some use. As she approached, one of the deputies who had been guarding Camillo Stela looked up and saw Jennifer. He raised an arm and pointed to her, and five seconds later Jennifer Parker found herself being grabbed, handcuffed and placed under arrest.

THERE WERE FOUR people in Judge Lawrence Waldman's chambers: Judge Waldman, District Attorney Robert Di Silva, Thomas Colfax, and Jennifer.

"You have the right to have an attorney present before you make any statement," Judge Waldman informed Jennifer, "and you have the right to remain silent. If you—"

"I don't need an attorney, Your Honor! I can explain what happened."

Robert Di Silva was leaning so close to her that Jennifer could see the throbbing of a vein in his temple. "Who paid you to give that package to Camillo Stela?"

"Paid me? Nobody paid me!" Jennifer's voice was quavering with indignation.

Di Silva picked up a familiar looking manila envelope from Judge Waldman's desk. "*No one* paid you? You just walked up to my witness and delivered *this*?" He shook the envelope and the body of a yellow canary fluttered onto the desk. Its neck had been broken.

Jennifer stared at it, horrified. "I—one of your men—gave me—"

"Which one of my men?"

"I—I don't know."

"But you know he was one of my men." His voice rang with disbelief.

"Yes. I saw him talking to you and then he walked over to me and handed me the envelope and said you wanted me to give it to Mr. Stela. He—he even knew my name."

"I'll bet he did. How much did they pay you?"

It's all a nightmare, Jennifer thought. *I'm going to wake up any minute and it's going to be six o'clock in the morning, and I'm going to get dressed and go to be sworn in on the District Attorney's staff.*

"*How much?*" The anger in him was so violent that it forced Jennifer to her feet.

"Are you accusing me of—?"

"Accusing you!" Robert Di Silva clenched his fists. "Lady, I haven't even started on you. By the time you get out of prison you'll be too old to spend that money."

"There is no money." Jennifer stared at him defiantly.

Thomas Colfax had been sitting back, quietly listening to the conversation. He interrupted now to say, "Excuse me, Your Honor, but I'm afraid this isn't getting us anywhere."

"I agree," Judge Waldman replied. He turned to the District Attorney. "Where do you stand, Bobby? Is Stela still willing to be cross-examined?"

"Cross-examined? He's a basket case! Scared out of his wits. He won't take the stand again."

Thomas Colfax said smoothly, "If I can't cross-examine the prosecution's chief witness, Your Honor, I'm going to have to move for a mistrial."

Everyone in the room knew what that would mean: Michael Moretti would walk out of the courtroom a free man.

Judge Waldman looked over at the District Attorney. "Did you tell your witness he can be held in contempt?"

"Yes. Stela's more scared of them than he is of us." He turned to direct a venomous look at Jennifer. "He doesn't think we can protect him anymore."

Judge Waldman said slowly, "Then I'm afraid this court has no alternative but to grant the defense's request and declare a mistrial."

Robert Di Silva stood there, listening to his case being wiped out. Without Stela, he had no case. Michael Moretti was beyond his reach now, but Jennifer Parker was not. He was going to make her pay for what she had done to him.

Judge Waldman was saying, "I'll give instructions for the defendant to be freed and the jury dismissed."

Thomas Colfax said, "Thank you, Your Honor." There was no sign of triumph in his face.

"If there's nothing else . . ." Judge Waldman began.

"There is something else!" Robert Di Silva turned to Jennifer Parker. "I want her held for obstructing justice, for tampering with a witness in a capital case, for conspiracy, for . . ." He was incoherent with rage.

In her anger, Jennifer found her voice. "You can't prove a single one of those charges because they're not true. I—I may be guilty of being stupid, but that's *all* I'm guilty of. No one bribed me to do anything. I thought I was delivering a package for you."

Judge Waldman looked at Jennifer and said, "Whatever the motivation, the consequences have been extremely unfortunate. I am going to request that the Appellate Division undertake an investigation and, if it feels the circumstances warrant it, to begin disbarment proceedings against you."

Jennifer felt suddenly faint. "Your Honor, I—"

"That is all for now, Miss Parker."

Jennifer stood there a moment, staring at their hostile faces. There was nothing more she could say.

The yellow canary on the desk had said it all.

3

Jennifer Parker was not only on the evening news—she *was* the evening news. The story of her delivering a dead canary to the District Attorney's star witness was irresistible. Every television channel had pictures of Jennifer leaving Judge Waldman's chambers, fighting her way out of the courthouse, besieged by the press and the public.

Jennifer could not believe the sudden horrifying publicity that was being showered on her. They were hammering at her from all sides: television reporters, radio reporters and newspaper people. She wanted desperately to flee from them, but her pride would not let her.

"Who gave you the yellow canary, Miss Parker?"

"Have you ever met Michael Moretti?"

"Did you know that Di Silva was planning to use this case to get into the governor's office?"

"The District Attorney says he's going to have you disbarred. Are you going to fight it?"

To each question Jennifer had a tight-lipped "No comment."

On the CBS evening news they called her "Wrong-Way Parker," the girl who had gone off in the wrong direction. An ABC newsman referred to her as the "Yellow Canary." On NBC, a sports commentator compared her to Roy Riegels, the football player who had carried the ball to his own team's one-yard line.

IN TONY'S PLACE, a restaurant that Michael Moretti owned, a celebration was taking place. There were a dozen men in the room, drinking and boisterous.

Michael Moretti sat alone at the bar, in an oasis of silence, watching Jennifer Parker on television. He raised his glass in a salute to her and drank.

LAWYERS EVERYWHERE DISCUSSED the Jennifer Parker episode. Half of them believed she had been bribed by the Mafia, and the other half that she had been an innocent dupe. But no matter which side they were on, they all concurred on one point: Jennifer Parker's short career as an attorney was finished.

She had lasted exactly four hours.

SHE HAD BEEN born in Kelso, Washington, a small timber town founded in 1847 by a homesick Scottish surveyor who named it for his home town in Scotland.

Jennifer's father was an attorney, first for the lumber companies that dominated the town, then later for the workers in the sawmills. Jennifer's earliest memories of growing up were filled with joy. The state of Washington was a storybook place for a child, full of spectacular mountains and glaciers and national parks. There were skiing and canoeing and, when she was older, ice climbing on glaciers and pack trips to places with wonderful names: Ohanapecosh and Nisqually and Lake Cle Elum and Chenuis Falls and Horse Heaven and the Yakima Valley. Jennifer learned to climb on Mount Rainier and to ski at Timberline with her father.

Her father always had time for her, while her mother, beautiful and restless, was mysteriously busy and seldom at home. Jennifer adored her father. Abner Parker was a mixture of English and Irish and Scottish blood. He was of medium height, with black hair and green-blue eyes.

He was a compassionate man with a deep-rooted sense of justice. He was not interested in money, he was interested in people. He would sit and talk to Jennifer by the hour, telling her about the cases he was handling and the problems of the people who came into his unpretentious little office, and it did not occur to Jennifer until years later that he talked to her because he had no one else with whom to share things.

After school Jennifer would hurry over to the courthouse to watch her father at work. If court was not in session she would hang around his office, listening to him discuss his cases and his clients. They never talked about her going to law school; it was simply taken for granted.

When Jennifer was fifteen she began spending her summers working for her father. At an age when other girls were dating boys and going steady, Jennifer was absorbed in lawsuits and wills.

Boys were interested in her, but she seldom went out. When her father would ask her why, she would reply, "They're all so *young*, Papa." She knew that one day she would marry a lawyer like her father.

On Jennifer's sixteenth birthday, her mother left town with the eighteen-year-old son of their next-door neighbor, and Jennifer's father quietly died. It took seven years for his heart to stop beating, but he was dead from the moment he heard the news about his wife. The whole town knew and was sympathetic, and that, of course, made it worse, for Abner Parker was a proud man. That was when he began to drink. Jennifer did everything she could to comfort him but it was no use, and nothing was ever the same again.

The next year, when it came time to go to college, Jennifer wanted to stay home with her father, but he would not hear of it.

"We're going into partnership, Jennie," he told her. "You hurry up and get that law degree."

WHEN SHE WAS graduated she enrolled at the University of Washington in Seattle to study law. During the first year of school, while Jennifer's classmates were flailing about in an impenetrable swamp of contracts, torts, property, civil procedure and criminal law, Jennifer felt as though she had come home. She moved into the university dormitory and got a job at the Law Library.

Jennifer loved Seattle. On Sundays, she and an Indian student named

Ammini Williams and a big, rawboned Irish girl named Josephine Collins would go rowing on Green Lake in the heart of the city, or attend the Gold Cup races on Lake Washington and watch the brightly colored hydroplanes flashing by.

There were great jazz clubs in Seattle, and Jennifer's favorite was Peter's Poop Deck, where they had crates with slabs of wood on top instead of tables.

Afternoons, Jennifer, Ammini and Josephine would meet at The Hasty Tasty, a hangout where they had the best cottage-fried potatoes in the world.

There were two boys who pursued Jennifer: a young, attractive medical student named Noah Larkin and a law student named Ben Munro; and from time to time Jennifer would go out on dates with them, but she was far too busy to think about a serious romance.

THE SEASONS WERE crisp and wet and windy and it seemed to rain all the time. Jennifer wore a green-and-blue-plaid lumber jacket that caught the raindrops in its shaggy wool and made her eyes flash like emeralds. She walked through the rain, lost in her own secret thoughts, never knowing that all those she passed would file away the memory.

In spring the girls blossomed out in their bright cotton dresses. There were six fraternities in a row at the university, and the fraternity brothers would gather on the lawn and watch the girls go by, but there was something about Jennifer that made them feel unexpectedly shy. There was a special quality about her that was difficult for them to define, a feeling that she had already attained something for which they were still searching.

Every summer Jennifer went home to visit her father. He had changed so much. He was never drunk, but neither was he ever sober. He had retreated into an emotional fortress where nothing could touch him again.

He died when Jennifer was in her last term at law school. The town remembered, and there were almost a hundred people at Abner Parker's funeral, people he had helped and advised and befriended over the years. Jennifer did her grieving in private. She had lost more than a father. She had lost a teacher and a mentor.

. . .

AFTER THE FUNERAL Jennifer returned to Seattle to finish school. Her father had left her less than a thousand dollars and she had to make a decision about what to do with her life. She knew that she could not return to Kelso to practice law, for there she would always be the little girl whose mother had run off with a teen-ager.

Because of her high scholastic average, Jennifer had interviews with a dozen top law firms around the country, and received several offers.

Warren Oakes, her criminal law professor, told her: "That's a real tribute, young lady. It's very difficult for a woman to get into a good law firm."

Jennifer's dilemma was that she no longer had a home or roots. She was not certain where she wanted to live.

Shortly before graduation Jennifer's problem was solved for her. Professor Oakes asked her to see him after class.

"I have a letter from the District Attorney's office in Manhattan, asking me to recommend my brightest graduate for his staff. Interested?"

New York. "Yes, sir." Jennifer was so stunned that the answer just popped out.

She flew to New York to take the bar examination, and returned to Kelso to close her father's law office. It was a bittersweet experience, filled with memories of the past and it seemed to Jennifer that she had grown up in that office.

She got a job as an assistant in the law library of the university to tide her over until she heard whether she had passed the New York bar examination.

"It's one of the toughest in the country," Professor Oakes warned her.

But Jennifer *knew.*

She received her notice that she had passed and an offer from the New York District Attorney's office on the same day.

One week later, Jennifer was on her way east.

SHE FOUND A tiny apartment (*Spc W/U fpl gd loc nds sm wk,* the ad said) on lower Third Avenue, with a fake fireplace in a steep fourth-floor walk-up. *The exercise will do me good,* Jennifer told herself. There were no mountains to climb in Manhattan, no rapids to ride. The apartment consisted of a small living room with a couch that turned into a lumpy bed, and a tiny bathroom with a window that someone long ago had painted over with black paint, sealing it shut. The furniture looked like something that could have been donated by the Salvation Army. *Oh, well, I won't be living in this place long.* Jennifer thought. *This is just temporary until I prove myself as a lawyer.*

THAT HAD BEEN the dream. The reality was that she had been in New York less than seventy-two hours, had been thrown off the District Attorney's staff and was facing disbarment.

JENNIFER QUIT READING newspapers and magazines and stopped watching television, because wherever she turned she saw herself. She felt that people were staring at her on the street, on the bus, and at the market. She began to hide out in her tiny apartment, refusing to answer the telephone or the doorbell. She thought about packing her suitcases and returning to Washington. She thought about getting a job in some other field. She thought about suicide. She spent long hours composing letters to District Attorney Robert Di Silva. Half the letters were scathing indictments of his insensitivity and lack of understanding. The other half were abject apologies, with a plea for him to give her another chance. None of the letters was ever sent.

For the first time in her life Jennifer was overwhelmed with a sense of desperation. She had no friends in New York, no one to talk to. She stayed locked in her apartment all day, and late at night she would slip out to walk the deserted streets of the city. The derelicts who peopled the night never accosted her. Perhaps they saw their own loneliness and despair mirrored in her eyes.

Over and over, as she walked, Jennifer would envision the courtroom scene in her mind, always changing the ending.

A man detached himself from the group around Di Silva and hurried toward her. He was carrying a manila envelope.

Miss Parker?

Yes.

The Chief wants you to give this to Stela.

Jennifer looked at him coolly. Let me see your identification, please.

The man panicked and ran.

A MAN DETACHED *himself from the group around Di Silva and hurried toward her. He was carrying a manila envelope.*

Miss Parker?

Yes.

The Chief wants you to give this to Stela. He thrust the envelope into her hands.

Jennifer opened the envelope and saw the dead canary inside. I'm placing you under arrest.

A MAN DETACHED *himself from the group around Di Silva and hurried toward her. He was carrying a manila envelope. He walked past her to another young assistant district attorney and handed him the envelope. The Chief wants you to give this to Stela.*

SHE COULD REWRITE the scene as many times as she liked, but nothing was changed. One foolish mistake had destroyed her. And yet—who said she was destroyed? The press? Di Silva? She had not heard another word about her disbarment, and until she did she was still an attorney. *There are law firms that made me offers,* Jennifer told herself.

Filled with a new sense of resolve, Jennifer pulled out the list of the firms she had talked to and began to make a series of telephone calls. None of the men she asked to speak to was in, and not one of her calls was returned. It took her four days to realize that she was the pariah of the legal profession. The furor over the case had died down, but everyone still remembered.

Jennifer kept telephoning prospective employers, going from despair to indignation to frustration and back to despair again. She wondered what she was going to do with the rest of her life, and each time it came back to the same thing: All she wanted to do, the one thing she really cared about, was to practice law. She was a lawyer and, by God, until they stopped her she was going to find a way to practice her profession.

She began to make the rounds of Manhattan law offices. She would walk in unannounced, give her name to the receptionist and ask to see the head of personnel. Occasionally she was granted an interview, but when she was, Jennifer had the feeling it was out of curiosity. She was a freak and they wanted to see what she looked like in person. Most of the time she was simply informed there were no openings.

AT THE END of six weeks, Jennifer's money was running out. She would have moved to a cheaper apartment, but there *were* no cheaper apartments. She began to skip breakfast and lunch, and to have dinner at one of the little corner dinettes where the food was bad but the prices were good. She discovered the Steak & Brew and Roast-and-Brew, where for a modest sum she was able to get a main course, all the salad she could eat, and all the beer she could drink. Jennifer hated beer, but it was filling.

When Jennifer had gone through her list of large law firms, she armed herself with a list of smaller firms and began to call on them, but her reputation had preceded her even there. She received a lot of propositions from interested males, but no job offers. She was beginning to get desperate. *All right,* she thought defiantly, *if no one wants to hire me, I'll open my own law office.* The catch was that that took money. Ten thousand dollars, at least. She would need enough for rent, telephone, a secretary, law books, a desk and chairs, stationery . . . she could not even afford the stamps.

Jennifer had counted on her salary from the District Attorney's office but that, of course, was gone forever. She could forget about severance pay. She had not been severed; she had been beheaded. No, there was no way she could afford to open her own office, no matter how small. The answer was to find someone with whom to share offices.

Jennifer bought a copy of the *New York Times* and began to search through the want ads. It was not until she was near the bottom of the page that she came across a small advertisement that read: *Wanted:/Prof man sh sm off w/2 oth/prof men. Rs rent.*

The last two words appealed to Jennifer enormously. She was not a professional man, but her sex should not matter. She tore out the ad and took the subway down to the address listed.

It was a dilapidated old building on lower Broadway. The office was on the tenth floor and the flaking sign on the door read:

KENNETH BAILEY
ACE INVEST GA IONS

Beneath it:

ROCKEFELLER C LLECTION AG NCY

Jennifer took a deep breath, opened the door and walked in. She was standing in the middle of a small, windowless office. There were three scarred desks and chairs crowded into the room, two of them occupied.

Seated at one of the desks was a bald, shabbily dressed, middle-aged man working on some papers. Against the opposite wall at another desk was a man in his early thirties. He had brick-red hair and bright blue eyes. His skin was pale and freckled. He was dressed in tight-fitting jeans, a tee shirt, and white canvas shoes without socks. He was talking into the telephone.

"Don't worry, Mrs. Desser, I have two of my best operatives working on your case. We should have news of your husband any day now. I'm afraid I'll have to ask you for a little more expense money . . . No, don't bother mailing it. The mails are terrible. I'll be in your neighborhood this afternoon. I'll stop by and pick it up."

He replaced the receiver and looked up and saw Jennifer.

He rose to his feet, smiled and held out a strong, firm hand. "I'm Kenneth Bailey. And what can I do for you this morning?"

Jennifer looked around the small, airless room and said uncertainly, "I—I came about your ad."

"Oh." There was surprise in his blue eyes.

The bald-headed man was staring at Jennifer.

Kenneth Bailey said, "This is Otto Wenzel. He's the Rockefeller Collection Agency."

Jennifer nodded. "Hello." She turned back to Kenneth Bailey. "And you're Ace Investigations?"

"That's right. What's your scam?"

"My—?" Then, realizing, "I'm an attorney."

Kenneth Bailey studied her skeptically. "And you want to set up an office *here*?"

Jennifer looked around the dreary office again and visualized herself at the empty desk, between these two men.

"Perhaps I'll look a little further," she said. "I'm not sure—"

"Your rent would only be ninety dollars a month."

"I could *buy* this building for ninety dollars a month," Jennifer replied. She turned to leave.

"Hey, wait a minute."

Jennifer paused.

Kenneth Bailey ran a hand over his pale chin. "I'll make a deal with you. Sixty. When your business gets rolling we'll talk about an increase."

It was a bargain. Jennifer knew that she could never find any space elsewhere for that amount. On the other hand, there was no way she could ever attract clients to this hellhole. There was one other thing she had to consider. She did not have the sixty dollars.

"I'll take it," Jennifer said.

"You won't be sorry," Kenneth Bailey promised. "When do you want to move your things in?"

"They're in."

KENNETH BAILEY PAINTED the sign on the door himself. It read:

JENNIFER PARKER
ATTORNEY AT LAW

Jennifer studied the sign with mixed feelings. In her deepest depressions it had never occurred to her that she would have her name under that of a private investigator and a bill collector. Yet, as she looked at the faintly crooked sign, she could not help feeling a sense of pride. She was an attorney. The sign on the door proved it.

NOW THAT JENNIFER had office space, the only thing she lacked was clients.

Jennifer could no longer afford even the Steak & Brew. She made herself a breakfast of toast and coffee on the hot plate she had set up over the radiator in her tiny bathroom. She ate no lunch and had dinner at Chock Full o'Nuts or Zum Zum, where they served large pieces of wurst, slabs of bread and hot potato salad.

She arrived at her desk promptly at nine o'clock every morning, but there was nothing for her to do except listen to Ken Bailey and Otto Wenzel talking on the telephone.

Ken Bailey's cases seemed to consist mostly of finding runaway spouses and children, and at first Jennifer was convinced that he was a con man, making extravagant promises and collecting large advances. But Jennifer quickly learned that Ken Bailey worked hard and delivered often. He was bright and he was clever.

Otto Wenzel was an enigma. His telephone rang constantly. He would pick it up, mutter a few words into it, write something on a piece of paper and disappear for a few hours.

"Oscar does repos," Ken Bailey explained to Jennifer one day.

"Repos?"

"Yeah. Collection companies use him to get back automobiles, television sets, washing machines—you name it." He looked at Jennifer curiously. "You got any clients?"

"I have some things coming up," Jennifer said evasively.

He nodded. "Don't let it get you down. Anyone can make a mistake."

Jennifer felt herself flushing. So *he* knew about her.

Ken Bailey was unwrapping a large, thick roast-beef sandwich. "Like some?"

It looked delicious. "No, thanks," Jennifer said firmly. "I never eat lunch."

"Okay."

She watched him bite into the juicy sandwich. He saw her expression and said, "You sure you—?"

"No, thank you. I—I have an appointment."

Ken Bailey watched Jennifer walk out of the office and his face was thoughtful. He prided himself on his ability to read character, but Jennifer Parker puzzled him. From the television and newspaper accounts he had been sure someone had paid this girl to destroy the case against Michael Moretti. After meeting Jennifer, Ken was less certain. He had been married once and had gone through hell, and he held women in low esteem. But something told him that this one was special. She was beautiful, bright and very proud. *Jesus!* he said to himself. *Don't be a fool! One murder on your conscience is enough.*

EMMA LAZARUS WAS *a sentimental idiot,* Jennifer thought. *"Give me your tired, your poor, your huddled masses yearning to breathe free . . . Send these, the homeless, tempest-tossed, to me."* Indeed! *Anyone manufacturing welcome mats in New York would have gone out of business in an hour. In New York no one cared whether you lived or died. Stop feeling sorry for yourself!* Jennifer told herself. But it was difficult. Her resources had dwindled to eighteen dollars, the rent on her apartment was overdue, and her share of the office rent was due in two days. She did not have enough money to stay in New York any longer, and she did not have enough money to leave.

Jennifer had gone through the Yellow Pages, calling law offices alphabetically, trying to get a job. She made the calls from telephone booths because she was too embarrassed to let Ken Bailey and Otto Wenzel hear her conversations. The results were always the same. No one was interested in hiring her. She would have to return to Kelso and get a job as a legal aide or as a secretary to one of her father's friends. How he would have hated that! It was a bitter defeat, but there were no choices left. She would be returning home a failure. The immediate problem facing her was transportation. She looked through the afternoon *New York Post* and found an ad for someone to share driving expenses to Seattle. There was a telephone number and Jennifer called it. There was no answer. She decided she would try again in the morning.

THE FOLLOWING DAY, Jennifer went to her office for the last time. Otto Wenzel was out, but Ken Bailey was there, on the telephone, as usual. He was wearing blue jeans and a vee-neck cashmere sweater.

"I found your wife," he was saying. "The only problem, pal, is that she doesn't want to go home. . . . I know. Who can figure women out? . . . Okay. I'll tell you where she's staying and you can try to sweet-talk her into coming back." He gave the address of a midtown hotel. "My pleasure." He hung up and swung around to face Jennifer. "You're late this morning."

"Mr. Bailey, I—I'm afraid I'm going to have to be leaving. I'll send you the rent money I owe you as soon as I'm able to."

Ken Bailey leaned back in his chair and studied her. His look made Jennifer uncomfortable.

"Will that be all right?" she asked.

"Going back to Washington?"

Jennifer nodded.

Ken Bailey said, "Before you leave, would you do me a little favor? A lawyer friend's been bugging me to serve some subpoenas for him, and I haven't got time. He pays twelve-fifty for each subpoena plus mileage. Would you help me out?"

ONE HOUR LATER Jennifer Parker found herself in the plush law offices of Peabody & Peabody. This was the kind of firm she had visualized working in one day, a full partner with a beautiful corner suite. She was escorted to a small back room where a harassed secretary handed her a stack of subpoenas.

"Here. Be sure to keep a record of your mileage. You do have a car, don't you?"

"No, I'm afraid I—"

"Well, if you use the subway, keep track of the fares."

"Right."

Jennifer spent the rest of the day delivering subpoenas in the Bronx, Brooklyn and Queens in a downpour. By eight o'clock that evening, she had made fifty dollars. She arrived back at her tiny apartment chilled and exhausted. But at least she had earned some money, her first since coming to New York. And the secretary had told her there were plenty more subpoenas to serve. It was hard work, running all over town, and it was humiliating. She had had doors slammed in her face, had been cursed at, threatened, and propositioned twice. The prospect of facing another day like that was dismaying; and yet, as long as she could remain in New York there was hope, no matter how faint.

Jennifer ran a hot bath and stepped into it, slowly sinking down into the tub, feeling the luxury of the water lapping over her body. She had not realized how exhausted she was. Every muscle seemed to ache. She decided that what she needed was a good dinner to cheer her up. She would splurge. *I'll treat myself to a real restaurant with tablecloths and napkins,* Jennifer thought. *Perhaps they'll have soft music and I'll have a glass of white wine and—*

Jennifer's thoughts were interrupted by the ringing of the doorbell. It was an alien sound. She had not had a single visitor since she had moved in two months earlier. It could only be the surly landlady about the overdue rent. Jennifer lay still, hoping she would go away, too weary to move.

The doorbell rang again. Reluctantly, Jennifer dragged herself from the warm tub. She slipped on a terry-cloth robe and went to the door.

"Who is it?"

A masculine voice on the other side of the door said, "Miss Jennifer Parker?"

"Yes."

"My name is Adam Warner. I'm an attorney."

Puzzled, Jennifer put the chain on the door and opened it a crack. The man standing in the hall was in his middle thirties, tall and blond and broad-shouldered, with gray-blue inquisitive eyes behind horn-rimmed glasses. He was dressed in a tailored suit that must have cost a fortune.

"May I come in?" he asked.

Muggers did not wear tailored suits, Gucci shoes and silk ties. Nor did they have long, sensitive hands with carefully manicured nails.

"Just a moment."

Jennifer unfastened the chain and opened the door. As Adam Warner walked in, Jennifer glanced around the one-room apartment, seeing it through his eyes, and winced. He looked like a man who was used to better things.

"What can I do for you, Mr. Warner?"

Even as she spoke, Jennifer suddenly knew why he was there, and she was filled with a quick sense of excitement. It was about one of the jobs she had applied for! She wished that she had on a nice, dark blue tailored robe, that her hair was combed, that—

Adam Warner said, "I'm a member of the Disciplinary Committee of the New York Bar Association, Miss Parker. District Attorney Robert Di Silva and Judge Lawrence Waldman have requested the Appellate Division to begin disbarment proceedings against you."

4

The law offices of Needham, Finch, Pierce and Warner were located at 30 Wall Street, occupying the entire top floor of the building. There were a hundred and twenty-five lawyers in the firm. The offices smelled of old money and were done in the quiet elegance befitting an organization that represented some of the biggest names in industry.

Adam Warner and Stewart Needham were having their ritual morning tea. Stewart Needham was a dapper, trim man in his late sixties. He had a neat Vandyke beard and wore a tweed suit and vest. He looked as though he belonged to an older era, but as hundreds of opponents had learned to their sorrow through the years, Stewart Needham's mind belonged very much to the twentieth century. He was a titan, but his name was known only in the circles where it mattered. He preferred to remain in the background and use his considerable influence to affect the outcome of legislation, high government appointments and national politics. He was a New Englander, born and reared taciturn.

Adam Warner was married to Needham's niece Mary Beth, and was Needham's protégé. Adam's father had been a respected senator. Adam himself was a brilliant lawyer. When he had been graduated *magna cum laude* from Harvard Law School, he had had offers from prestigious law firms all over the country. He chose Needham, Finch and Pierce, and seven years later became a partner. Adam was physically attractive and charming, and his intelligence seemed to add an extra dimension to him. He had an easy sureness about himself that women found challenging. Adam had long since developed a system for dissuading overamorous female clients. He had been married to Mary Beth for fourteen years and did not approve of extramarital affairs.

"More tea, Adam?" Stewart Needham asked.

"No, thanks." Adam Warner hated tea, and he had been drinking it every morning for the last eight years only because he did not want to hurt his partner's feelings. It was a brew that Needham concocted himself and it was dreadful.

Stewart Needham had two things on his mind and, typically, he began with the pleasant news. "I had a meeting with a few friends last night," Needham said. *A few friends* would be a group of the top power brokers in the country. "They're considering asking you to run for United States senator, Adam."

Adam felt a sense of elation. Knowing Stewart Needham's cautious nature, Adam was certain that the conversation had been more than casual or Needham would not have brought it up now.

"The big question, of course, is whether you're interested. It would mean a lot of changes in your life."

Adam Warner was aware of that. If he won the election, it would mean moving to Washington, D.C., giving up his law practice, starting a whole new life. He was sure that Mary Beth would enjoy it; Adam was not so sure about himself. And yet, he had been reared to assume responsibility. Also, he had to admit to himself that there was a pleasure in power.

"I'd be very interested, Stewart."

Stewart Needham nodded with satisfaction. "Good. They'll be pleased." He poured himself another cup of the dreadful brew and casually broached the other subject that was on his mind. "There's a little job the Disciplinary Committee of the Bar Association would like you to handle, Adam. Shouldn't take you more than an hour or two."

"What is it?"

"It's the Michael Moretti trial. Apparently, someone got to one of Bobby Di Silva's young assistants and paid her off."

"I read about it. The canary."

"Right. Judge Waldman and Bobby would like her name removed from the roster of our honorable profession. So would I. It reeks."

"What do they want me to do?"

"Just make a quick check, verify that this Parker girl behaved illegally or unethically, and then recommend disbarment proceedings. She'll be served with a notice to show cause and they'll handle the rest of it. It's just routine."

Adam was puzzled by something. "Why me, Stewart? We have a couple of dozen young lawyers around here who could handle this."

"Our revered District Attorney specifically asked for you. He wants to make sure nothing goes wrong. As we're both aware," he added dryly, "Bobby's not the most forgiving man in the world. He wants the Parker woman's hide nailed up on his wall."

Adam Warner sat there, thinking about his busy schedule.

"You never know when we might need a favor from the D.A.'s office, Adam. Quid pro quo. It's all cut and dried."

"All right, Stewart." Adam rose to his feet.

"Sure you won't have some more tea?"

"No, thanks. It was as good as always."

WHEN ADAM WARNER returned to his office he rang for one of his paralegal assistants, Lucinda, a bright, young Black woman.

"Cindy, get me all the information you can on an attorney named Jennifer Parker."

She grinned and said, "The yellow canary."

Everybody knew about her.

LATE THAT AFTERNOON Adam Warner was studying the transcript of the court proceedings in the case of *The People of New York* v. *Michael Moretti*. Robert Di Silva had had it delivered by special messenger. It was long past midnight when Adam finished. He had asked Mary Beth to attend a dinner party without him, and had sent out for sandwiches. When Adam was through reading the transcript, there was no doubt in his mind that Michael Moretti would have been found guilty by the jury if fate had not intervened in the form of Jennifer Parker. Di Silva had prosecuted the case flawlessly.

Adam turned to the transcript of the deposition that had been taken in Judge Waldman's chambers afterward.

DI SILVA: *You are a college graduate?*

PARKER: *Yes, sir.*

DI SILVA: *And a law school graduate?*

PARKER: *Yes, sir.*

DI SILVA: *And a stranger hands you a package, tells you to deliver it to a key witness in a murder trial and you just do it? Wouldn't you say that went beyond the bounds of stupidity?*

PARKER: *It didn't happen that way.*

DI SILVA: *You said it did.*

PARKER: *What I mean is, I didn't think he was a stranger. I thought he was on your staff.*

DI SILVA: *What made you think that?*

PARKER: *I've told you. I saw him talking to you and then he came over to me with this envelope and he called me by name, and he said you wanted me to deliver it to the witness. It all happened so fast that—*

DI SILVA: *I don't think it happened that fast. I think it took time to set it up. It took time to arrange for someone to pay you off to deliver it.*

PARKER: *That's not true. I—*

DI SILVA: *What's not true? That you didn't know you were delivering the envelope?*

PARKER: *I didn't know what was in it.*

DI SILVA: *So it's true that someone paid you.*

PARKER: *I'm not going to let you twist my words around. No one paid me anything.*

DI SILVA: *You did it as a favor?*

PARKER: *No. I thought I was acting on your instructions.*

DI SILVA: *You said the man called you by name.*

PARKER: *Yes.*

DI SILVA: *How did he know your name?*

PARKER: *I don't know.*

DI SILVA: *Oh, come on. You must have some idea. Maybe it was a lucky guess. Maybe he just looked around that courtroom and said, There's someone who looks like her name could be Jennifer Parker. Do you think that was it?*

PARKER: *I've told you. I don't know.*

DI SILVA: *How long have you and Michael Moretti been sweethearts?*

PARKER: *Mr. Di Silva, we've gone all over this. You've been questioning me now for five hours. I'm tired. I have nothing more to add. May I be excused?*

DI SILVA: *If you move out of that chair I'll have you placed under arrest. You're in big trouble, Miss Parker. There's only one way you're going to get out of it. Stop lying and start telling the truth.*

PARKER: *I've told you the truth. I've told you everything I know.*

DI SILVA: *Except the name of the man who handed you the envelope. I want his name and I want to know how much he paid you.*

There were thirty more pages of transcript. Robert Di Silva had done everything but beat Jennifer Parker with a rubber hose. She had stuck to her story.

Adam closed the transcript and wearily rubbed his eyes. It was two A.M.

Tomorrow he would dispose of the Jennifer Parker matter.

TO ADAM WARNER'S surprise, the Jennifer Parker case would not be disposed of so easily. Because Adam was a methodical man he ran a check on Jennifer Parker's background. As far as he could determine, she had no crime connections, nor was there anything to link her with Michael Moretti.

There was something about the case that disturbed Adam. Jennifer Parker's defense was too flimsy. If she were working for Moretti, he would have protected her with a reasonably plausible story. As it was, her story was so transparently naïve that it had a ring of truth about it.

At noon Adam received a call from the District Attorney. "How goes it, Adam?"

"Fine, Robert."

"I understand you're handling the hatchet-man job on the Jennifer Parker matter."

Adam Warner winced at the phrase. "I've agreed to make a recommendation, yes."

"I'm going to put her away for a long time." Adam was taken aback by the hatred in the District Attorney's voice.

"Easy, Robert. She's not disbarred yet."

Di Silva chuckled. "I'll leave that to you, my friend." His tone changed. "I hear on the grapevine that you may be moving to Washington soon. I want you to know that you can count on my full support."

Which was considerable, Adam Warner knew. The District Attorney had been around a long time. He knew where the bodies were buried and he knew how to squeeze the most out of that information.

"Thanks, Robert. I appreciate that."

"My pleasure, Adam. I'll wait to hear from you."

Meaning Jennifer Parker. The quid pro quo Stewart Needham had mentioned, with the girl used as a pawn. Adam Warner thought about Robert Di Silva's words: *I'm going to put her away for a long time.* From reading the transcript, Adam judged that there was no real evidence against Jennifer Parker. Unless she confessed, or unless someone came forward with information that proved criminal complicity, Di Silva would not be able to touch the girl. He was counting on Adam to give him his vengeance.

The cold, harsh words of the transcript were clear-cut, and yet Adam wished he could have heard the tone of Jennifer Parker's voice when she denied her guilt.

There were pressing matters claiming Adam's attention, important cases involving major clients. It would have been easy to go ahead and carry out the wishes of Stewart Needham, Judge Lawrence Waldman and Robert Di Silva, but some instinct made Adam Warner hesitate. He picked up Jennifer Parker's file again, scribbled some notes and began to make some long-distance telephone calls.

Adam had been given a responsibility and he intended to carry it through to the best of his ability. He was all too familiar with the long, back-breaking hours of study and hard work it took to become an attorney and to pass the bar. It was a prize that took years to attain, and he was not about to deprive someone of it unless he was certain there was justification.

The following morning Adam Warner was on a plane to Seattle, Washington. He had meetings with Jennifer Parker's law professors, with the head of a law firm where she had clerked for two summers, and with some of Jennifer's former classmates.

Stewart Needham telephoned Adam in Seattle. "What are you doing up there, Adam? You've got a big case load waiting for you back here. That Parker thing should have been a snap."

"A few questions have arisen," Adam said carefully. "I'll be back in a day or so, Stewart."

There was a pause. "I see. Let's not waste any more time on her than we have to."

BY THE TIME Adam Warner left Seattle, he felt he knew Jennifer Parker almost as well as she knew herself. He had built up a portrait of her in his mind, a mental Identi-Kit, with pieces filled in by her law professors, her landlady, members of the law firm where she had served as a clerk, and classmates. The picture that Adam had acquired bore no resemblance to the picture Robert Di Silva had given him. Unless Jennifer Parker was the most consummate actress who ever lived, there was no way she could have been involved in a plot to free a man like Michael Moretti.

NOW, ALMOST TWO weeks after he had had that morning conversation with Stewart Needham, Adam Warner found himself facing the girl whose past he had been exploring. Adam had seen newspaper pictures of Jennifer, but they had not prepared him for the impact she made in person. Even in an old robe, without makeup, and her dark brown hair bath-damp, she was breathtaking.

Adam said, "I've been assigned to investigate your part in the Michael Moretti trial, Miss Parker."

"Have you now!" Jennifer could feel an anger rising in her. It started as a spark and became a flame that exploded inside her. They still were not through with her. They were going to make her pay for the rest of her life. Well, she had had enough.

When Jennifer spoke, her voice was trembling. "I have nothing to say to you! You go back and tell them whatever you please. I did something stupid, but as far as I know, there's no law against stupidity. The District Attorney thinks someone paid me off." She waved a scornful hand in the air. "If I had any money, do you think I'd be living in a place like this?" Her voice was beginning to choke up. "I—I don't care what you do. All I want is to be left alone. Now please go away!"

Jennifer turned and fled into the bathroom, slamming the door behind her.

She stood against the sink, taking deep breaths, wiping the tears from her eyes. She knew she had behaved stupidly. *That's twice,* she thought wryly. She should have handled Adam Warner differently. She should have tried to explain, instead of attacking him. Maybe then she would not be disbarred. But she knew that was wishful thinking. Sending someone to question her was a charade. The next step would be to serve her with an order to show cause, and the formal machinery would be set in motion. There would be a trial panel of three attorneys who would make their recommendation to the Disciplinary Board which would make its report to the Board of Governors. The recommendation was a foregone conclusion: disbarment. She would be forbidden to practice law in the state of New York. Jennifer thought bitterly, *There's one bright side to this. I can get into the* Guinness Book of Records *for the shortest law career in history.*

She stepped into the bath again and lay back, letting the still-warm water lap at her, soothing away her tension. At this moment she was too tired to care what happened to her. She closed her eyes and let her mind drift. She was half asleep when the chill of the water awakened her. She had no idea how long she had lain in the tub. Reluctantly she stepped out and began toweling herself dry. She was no longer hungry. The scene with Adam Warner had taken her appetite away.

Jennifer combed her hair and creamed her face and decided she would go to bed without dinner. In the morning she would telephone about the ride to Seattle. She opened the bathroom door and walked into the living room.

Adam Warner was seated in a chair, leafing through a magazine. He looked up as Jennifer came into the room, naked.

"I'm sorry," Adam said. "I—"

Jennifer gave a small cry of alarm and fled to the bathroom, where she put on her robe. When she stepped out to confront Adam again, Jennifer was furious.

"The inquisition is over. I asked you to leave."

Adam put the magazine down and said quietly, "Miss Parker, do you think we could discuss this calmly for a moment?"

"No!" All the old rage boiled up in Jennifer again. "I have nothing more to say to you or your damned disciplinary committee. I'm tired of being treated like—like I'm some kind of criminal!"

"Have I said you were a criminal?" Adam asked quietly.

"You—isn't that why you're here?"

"I told you why I'm here. I'm empowered to investigate and recommend for or against disbarment proceedings. I want to get your side of the story."

"I see. And how do I buy you off?"

Adam's face tightened. "I'm sorry, Miss Parker." He rose to his feet and started for the door.

"Just a minute!" Adam turned. "Forgive me," she said. "I—everybody seems to be the enemy. I apologize."

"Your apology is accepted."

Jennifer was suddenly aware of the flimsy robe she was wearing. "If you still want to ask me questions, I'll put some clothes on and we can talk."

"Fair enough. Have you had dinner?"

She hesitated. "I—"

"I know a little French restaurant that's just perfect for inquisitions."

IT WAS A quiet, charming bistro on 56th Street on the East Side.

"Not too many people know about this place," Adam Warner said when they had been seated. "It's owned by a young French couple who used to work at Les Pyrénées. The food is excellent."

Jennifer had to take Adam's word for it. She was incapable of tasting anything. She had not eaten all day, but she was so nervous that she was unable to force any food down her throat. She tried to relax, but it was impossible. No matter how much he pretended, the charming man seated opposite her was the enemy. And he *was* charming, Jennifer had to admit. He was amusing and attractive, and under other circumstances Jennifer would have enjoyed the evening enormously; but these were not other circumstances. Her whole future was in the hands of this stranger. The next hour or two would determine in which direction the rest of her life would move.

Adam was going out of his way to try to relax her. He had recently returned from a trip to Japan where he had met with top government officials. A special banquet had been prepared in his honor.

"Have you ever eaten chocolate-covered ants?" Adam asked.

"No."

He grinned. "They're better than the chocolate-covered grasshoppers."

He talked about a hunting trip he had taken the year before in Alaska, where he had been attacked by a bear. He talked about everything but why they were there.

Jennifer had been steeling herself for the moment when Adam would begin to interrogate her, yet when he finally brought up the subject, her whole body went rigid.

He had finished dessert and he said quietly, "I'm going to ask you some questions, and I don't want you to get upset. Okay?"

There was a sudden lump in Jennifer's throat. She was not sure she would be able to speak. She nodded.

"I want you to tell me exactly what happened in the courtroom that day. Everything you remember, everything you felt. Take your time."

Jennifer had been prepared to defy him, to tell him to do whatever he pleased about her. But somehow, sitting across from Adam Warner, listening to his quiet voice, Jennifer's resistance was gone. The whole experience was still so vivid in her mind that it hurt just to think about it. She had spent more than a month trying to forget it. Now he was asking her to go through it again.

She took a deep, shaky breath and said, "All right."

Haltingly, Jennifer began to recount the events in the courtroom, gradually speaking more rapidly as it all came to life again. Adam sat there quietly listening, studying her, saying nothing.

When Jennifer had finished, Adam said, "The man who gave you the envelope—was he in the District Attorney's office earlier that morning when you were sworn in?"

"I've thought about that. I honestly don't remember. There were so many people in the office that day and they were all strangers."

"Had you ever seen the man before, anywhere?"

Jennifer shook her head helplessly. "I can't recall. I don't think so."

"You said you saw him talking to the District Attorney just before he walked over to give you the envelope. Did you see the District Attorney hand him the envelope?"

"I—no."

"Did you actually see this man talking to the District Attorney, or was he just in the group around him?"

Jennifer closed her eyes for a second, trying to bring back that moment. "I'm sorry. Everything was so confused. I—I just don't know."

"Do you have any idea how he could have known your name?"

"No."

"Or why he selected you?"

"That one's easy. He probably knew an idiot when he saw one." She shook her head. "No. I'm sorry, Mr. Warner, I have no idea."

Adam said, "A lot of pressure is being brought to bear on this. District Attorney Di Silva has been after Michael Moretti for a long time. Until you came along, he had an airtight case. The D.A.'s not very happy with you."

"I'm not very happy with me, either." Jennifer could not blame Adam Warner for what he was about to do. He was just carrying out his job. They were out to get her and they had succeeded. Adam Warner was not responsible; he was merely the instrument they were using.

Jennifer felt a sudden, overwhelming urge to be alone. She did not want anyone else to see her misery.

"I'm sorry," she apologized. "I—I'm not feeling very well. I'd like to go home, please."

Adam studied her a moment. "Would it make you feel any better if I told you I'm going to recommend that disbarment proceedings against you be dropped?"

It took several seconds for Adam's words to sink in. Jennifer stared at him, speechless, searching his face, looking into those gray-blue eyes behind the horn-rimmed glasses. "Do—do you really mean that?"

"Being a lawyer is very important to you, isn't it?" Adam asked.

Jennifer thought of her father and his comfortable little law office, and of the conversations they used to have, and the long years of law school, and their hopes and dreams. *We're going into partnership. You hurry up and get that law degree.*

"Yes," Jennifer whispered.

"If you can get over a rough beginning, I have a feeling you'll be a very good one."

Jennifer gave him a grateful smile. "Thank you. I'm going to try."

She said the words over again in her mind, *I'm going to try!* It did not matter that she shared a small and dingy office with a seedy private detective and a man who repossessed cars. It was a *law* office. She was a member of the legal profession, and they were going to allow her to practice law. She was filled with a feeling of exultation. She looked across at Adam and knew she would be forever grateful to this man.

The waiter had begun to clear the dishes from the table. Jennifer tried to speak, but it came out a cross between a laugh and a sob. "Mr. Warner—"

He said gravely, "After all we've been through together, I think it should be Adam."

"Adam—"

"Yes?"

"I hope it won't ruin our relationship, but—" Jennifer moaned, "I'm starved!"

5

The next few weeks raced by. Jennifer found herself busy from early morning until late at night, serving summonses—court orders to appear to answer a legal action—and subpoenas—court orders to appear as a witness. She knew that her chances of getting into a large law firm were nonexistent, for after the fiasco she had been involved in, no one would dream of hiring her. She would just have to find some way to make a reputation for herself, to begin all over.

In the meantime, there was the pile of summonses and subpoenas on her desk from Peabody & Peabody. While it was not exactly practicing law, it was twelve-fifty and expenses.

OCCASIONALLY, WHEN JENNIFER worked late, Ken Bailey would take her out to dinner. On the surface he was a cynical man, but Jennifer felt that it was a facade. She sensed that he was lonely. He had been graduated from Brown University and was bright and well-read. She could not imagine why he was satisfied to spend his life working out of a dreary office, trying to locate stray husbands and wives. It was as though he had resigned himself to being a failure and was afraid to try for success.

Once, when Jennifer brought up the subject of his marriage, he growled at her, "It's none of your business," and Jennifer had never mentioned it again.

Otto Wenzel was completely different. The short, potbellied little man was happily married. He regarded Jennifer as a daughter and he constantly brought her soups and cakes that his wife made. Unfortunately, his wife was a terrible cook, but Jennifer forced herself to eat whatever Otto Wenzel brought in, because she did not want to hurt his feelings. One Friday evening Jennifer was invited to the Wenzel home for dinner. Mrs. Wenzel had prepared stuffed cabbage, her specialty. The cabbage was soggy, the meat inside was hard, and the rice halfcooked. The whole dish swam in a lake of chicken fat. Jennifer attacked it bravely, taking small bites and pushing the food around on her plate to make it seem as though she were eating.

"How do you like it?" Mrs. Wenzel beamed.

"It—it's one of my favorites."

From that time on, Jennifer had dinner at the Wenzel's every Friday night, and Mrs. Wenzel always prepared Jennifer's favorite dish.

EARLY ONE MORNING, Jennifer received a telephone call from the personal secretary of Mr. Peabody, Jr.

"Mr. Peabody would like to see you this morning at eleven o'clock. Be prompt, please."

"Yes, ma'am."

IN THE PAST, Jennifer had only dealt with secretaries and law clerks in the Peabody office. It was a large, prestigious firm, one that young lawyers dreamed of being invited to join. On the way to keep her appointment, Jennifer began to fantasize. If Mr. Peabody himself wanted to see her, it had to be about something important. He probably had seen the light and was going to offer her a job as a lawyer with his firm, to give her a chance to show what she could do. She was going to surprise all of them. Some day it might even be Peabody, Peabody & Parker.

Jennifer killed thirty minutes in the corridor outside the office, and at exactly eleven o'clock, she entered the reception room. She did not want to seem too eager. She was kept waiting for two hours, and was finally ushered into the office of Mr. Peabody, Jr. He was a tall, thin man wearing a vested suit and shoes that had been made for him in London.

He did not invite her to sit down. "Miss Potter—" He had an unpleasant, high-pitched voice.

"Parker."

He picked up a piece of paper from his desk. "This is a summons. I would like you to serve it."

At that instant, Jennifer sensed that she was not going to become a member of the firm.

Mr. Peabody, Jr., handed Jennifer the summons and said, "Your fee will be five hundred dollars."

Jennifer was sure she had misunderstood him. "Did you say five hundred dollars?"

"That is correct. If you are successful, of course."

"There's a problem," Jennifer guessed.

"Well, yes," Mr. Peabody, Jr., admitted. "We've been trying to serve this man for more than a year. His name is William Carlisle. He lives on an estate in Long Island and he never leaves his house. To be quite truthful, a dozen people have tried to serve him. He has a bodyguard-butler who keeps everyone away."

Jennifer said, "I don't see how I—"

Mr. Peabody, Jr., leaned forward. "There's a great deal of money at stake here. But I can't get William Carlisle into court unless I can serve him, Miss Potter." Jennifer did not bother to correct him. "Do you think you can handle it?"

Jennifer thought about what she could do with five hundred dollars. "I'll find a way."

AT TWO O'CLOCK that afternoon, Jennifer was standing outside the imposing estate of William Carlisle. The house itself was Georgian, set in the middle of ten acres of beautiful, carefully tended grounds. A curving driveway led to the front of the house, which was framed by graceful fir trees. Jennifer had given a lot of thought to her problem. Since it was impossible to get into the house, the only solution was to find a way to get Mr. William Carlisle to come out.

Half a block down the street was a gardener's truck. Jennifer studied the truck a moment, then walked over to it, looking for the gardeners. There were three of them at work, and they were Japanese.

Jennifer walked up to the men. "Who's in charge here?"

One of them straightened up. "I am."

"I have a little job for you . . ." Jennifer began.

"Sorry, miss. Too busy."

"This will only take five minutes."

"No. Impossible to—"

"I'll pay you one hundred dollars."

The three men stopped to look at her. The chief gardener said, "You pay us one hundred dollars for five minutes' work?"

"That's right."

"What we have to do . . . ?"

FIVE MINUTES LATER, the gardener's truck pulled into the driveway of William Carlisle's estate and Jennifer and the three gardeners got out. Jennifer looked around, selected a beautiful tree next to the front door and said to the gardeners, "Dig it up."

They took their spades from the truck and began to dig. Before a minute had gone by, the front door burst open and an enormous man in a butler's uniform came storming out.

"What the hell do you think you're doing?"

"Long Island Nursery," Jennifer said crisply. "We're takin' out all these trees."

The butler stared at her. "You're *what*?"

Jennifer held up a piece of paper. "I have an order here to dig up these trees."

"That's impossible! Mr. Carlisle would have a fit!" He turned to the gardeners. "You stop that!"

"Look, mister," Jennifer said, "I'm just doin' my job." She looked at the gardeners. "Keep diggin', fellas."

"No!" the butler shouted. "I'm telling you there's been a mistake! Mr. Carlisle didn't order any trees dug up."

Jennifer shrugged and said, "My boss says he did."

"Where can I get in touch with your boss?"

Jennifer looked at her watch. "He's out on a job in Brooklyn. He should be back in the office around six."

The butler glared at her, furious. "Just a minute! Don't do anything until I return."

"Keep diggin'," Jennifer told the gardeners.

The butler turned and hurried into the house, slamming the door behind him. A few moments later the door opened and the butler returned, accompanied by a tiny middle-aged man.

"Would you mind telling me what the devil is going on here?"

"What business is it of yours?" Jennifer demanded.

"I'll tell you what business it is of mine," he snapped. "I'm William Carlisle and this happens to be my property."

"In that case, Mr. Carlisle," Jennifer said, "I have something for you." She reached in her pocket and put the summons in his hand. She turned to the gardeners. "You can stop digging now."

EARLY THE NEXT morning Adam Warner telephoned. Jennifer recognized his voice instantly.

"I thought you would like to know," Adam said, "that the disbarment proceedings have been officially dropped. You have nothing more to worry about."

Jennifer closed her eyes and said a silent prayer of thanks. "I—I can't tell you how much I appreciate what you've done."

"Justice isn't always blind."

Adam did not mention the scene he had had with Stewart Needham and Robert Di Silva. Needham had been disappointed, but philosophical.

The District Attorney had carried on like a raging bull. "You let that bitch get away with this? Jesus Christ, she's Mafia, Adam! Couldn't you see that? She's conning you!"

And on and on, until Adam had tired of it.

"All the evidence against her was circumstantial, Robert. She was in the wrong place at the wrong time and she got mousetrapped. That doesn't spell Mafia to me."

Finally Robert Di Silva had said, "Okay, so she's still a lawyer. I just hope to God she practices in New York, because the minute she sets foot in any of my courtrooms, I'm going to wipe her out."

Now, talking to Jennifer, Adam said nothing of this. Jennifer had made a deadly enemy, but there was nothing that could be done about it. Robert Di Silva was a vindictive man, and Jennifer was a vulnerable target. She was bright and idealistic and achingly young and lovely.

Adam knew he must never see her again.

THERE WERE DAYS and weeks and months when Jennifer was ready to quit. The sign on the door still read *Jennifer Parker, Attorney at Law*, but it did not deceive anyone, least of all Jennifer. She was not practicing law: Her days were spent running around in rain and sleet and snow, delivering subpoenas and summons to people who hated her for it. Now and then she accepted a *pro bono* case, helping the elderly get food stamps, solving various legal problems of ghetto Blacks and Puerto Ricans and other underprivileged people. But she felt trapped.

The nights were worse than the days. They were endless, for Jennifer had insomnia and when she did sleep, her dreams were filled with demons. It had begun the night her mother had deserted Jennifer and her father, and she had not been able to exorcise whatever it was that was causing her nightmares.

She was consumed by loneliness. She went out on occasional dates with young lawyers, but inevitably she found herself comparing them to Adam Warner, and they all fell short. There would be dinner and a movie or a play, followed by a struggle at her front door. Jennifer was never sure whether they expected her to go to bed with them because they had bought her dinner, or because they had had to climb up and down four steep flights of stairs. There were times when she was strongly tempted to say *Yes,* just to have someone with her for the night, someone to hold, someone to share herself with. But she needed more in her bed than a warm body that talked; she needed someone who cared, someone for whom she could care.

The most interesting men who propositioned Jennifer were all married, and she flatly refused to go out with any of them. She remembered a line from Billy Wilder's wonderful film *The Apartment:* "When you're in love with a married man you shouldn't wear mascara." Jennifer's mother had destroyed a marriage, had killed Jennifer's father. She could never forget that.

CHRISTMAS CAME AND New Year's Eve, and Jennifer spent them alone. There had been a heavy snowfall and the city looked like a gigantic Christmas card. Jennifer walked the streets, watching pedestrians hurrying to the warmth of their homes and families, and she ached with a feeling of emptiness. She missed her father terribly. She was glad when the holidays were over. *Nineteen seventy is going to be a better year,* Jennifer told herself.

On Jennifer's worst days, Ken Bailey would cheer her up. He took her out to Madison Square Garden to watch the Rangers play, to a disco club and to an occasional play or movie. Jennifer knew he was attracted to her, and yet he kept a barrier between them.

IN MARCH, OTTO Wenzel decided to move to Florida with his wife.

"My bones are getting too old for these New York winters," he told Jennifer.

"I'll miss you." Jennifer meant it. She had grown genuinely fond of him.

"Take care of Ken."

Jennifer looked at him quizzically.

"He never told you, did he?"

"Told me what?"

He hesitated, then said, "His wife committed suicide. He blames himself."

Jennifer was shocked. "How terrible! Why—why did she do it?"

"She caught Ken in bed with a young blond man."

"Oh, my God!"

"She shot Ken and then turned the gun on herself. He lived. She didn't."

"How awful! I had no idea that . . . that—"

"I know. He smiles a lot, but he carries his own hell with him."

"Thanks for telling me."

When Jennifer returned to the office, Ken said, "So old Otto's leaving us."

"Yes."

Ken Bailey grinned. "I guess it's you and me against the world."

"I guess so."

And in a way, Jennifer thought, *it is true.*

JENNIFER LOOKED AT Ken with different eyes now. They had lunches and dinners together, and Jennifer could detect no signs of homosexuality about him but she knew that Otto Wenzel had told her the truth: Ken Bailey carried his own private hell with him.

A FEW CLIENTS walked in off the street. They were usually poorly dressed, bewildered and, in some instances, out-and-out nut cases.

Prostitutes came in to ask Jennifer to handle their bail, and Jennifer was amazed at how young and lovely some of them were. They became a small but steady source of income. She could not find out who sent them to her. When she mentioned it to Ken Bailey, he shrugged in a gesture of ignorance and walked away.

Whenever a client came to see Jennifer, Ken Bailey would discreetly leave. He was like a proud father, encouraging Jennifer to succeed.

Jennifer was offered several divorce cases and turned them down. She could not forget what one of her law professors had once said: *Divorce is to the practice of law what proctology is to the practice of medicine.* Most divorce lawyers had bad reputations. The maxim was that when a married couple saw red, lawyers saw green. A high-priced divorce lawyer was known as a *bomber,* for he would use legal high explosives to win a case for a client and, in the process, often destroyed the husband, the wife and the children.

A few of the clients who came into Jennifer's office were different in a way that puzzled her.

They were well dressed, with an air of affluence about them, and the cases they brought to her were not the nickel-and-dime cases Jennifer had been accustomed to handling. There were estates to be settled that amounted to substantial sums of money, and lawsuits that any large firm would have been delighted to represent.

"Where did you hear about me?" Jennifer would ask.

The replies she got were always evasive. From a friend . . . I read about you . . . your name was mentioned at a party . . . It was not until one of her clients, in the course of explaining his problems, mentioned Adam Warner that Jennifer suddenly understood.

"Mr. Warner sent you to me, didn't he?"

The client was embarrassed. "Well, as a matter of fact, he suggested it might be better if I didn't mention his name."

Jennifer decided to telephone Adam. After all, she did owe him a debt of thanks. She would be polite, but formal. Naturally, she would not let him get the impression that she was calling him for any reason other than to express her appreciation. She rehearsed the conversation over and over in her mind. When Jennifer finally got up enough nerve to telephone, a secretary informed her that Mr. Warner was in Europe and was not expected back for several weeks. It was an anticlimax that left Jennifer depressed.

SHE FOUND HERSELF thinking of Adam Warner more and more often. She kept remembering the evening he had come to her apartment and how badly she had behaved. He had been wonderful to put up with her childish behavior when she had taken out her anger on him. Now, in addition to everything else he had done for her, he was sending her clients.

Jennifer waited three weeks and then telephoned Adam again. This time he was in South America.

"Is there any message?" his secretary asked.

Jennifer hesitated. "No message."

Jennifer tried to put Adam out of her mind, but it was impossible. She wondered whether he was married or engaged. She wondered what it would be like to be Mrs. Adam Warner. She wondered if she were insane.

From time to time Jennifer came across the name of Michael Moretti in the newspapers or weekly magazines. There was an in-depth story in the *New Yorker* magazine on Antonio Granelli and the eastern Mafia Families. Antonio Granelli was reported to be in failing health and Michael Moretti, his son-in-law, was preparing to take over his empire. *Life* magazine ran a story about Michael Moretti's lifestyle, and at the end of the story it spoke of Moretti's trial. Camillo Stela was serving time in Leavenworth, while Michael Moretti was free. It reminded its readers how Jennifer Parker had destroyed the case that would have sent him to prison or the electric chair. As Jennifer read the article, her stomach churned. The electric chair? She could cheerfully have pulled the switch on Michael Moretti herself.

MOST OF JENNIFER'S clients were unimportant, but the education was priceless. Over the months, Jennifer came to know every room in the Criminal Courts Building at 100 Centre Street and the people who inhabited them.

When one of her clients was arrested for shoplifting, mugging, prostitution or drugs, Jennifer would head downtown to arrange bail, and bargaining was a way of life.

"Bail is set at five hundred dollars."

"Your Honor, the defendant doesn't have that much money. If the court will reduce bail to two hundred dollars, he can go back to work and keep supporting his family."

"Very well. Two hundred."

"Thank you, Your Honor."

JENNIFER GOT TO know the supervisor of the complaint room, where copies of the arrest reports were sent.

"You again, Parker! For God's sake, don't you ever sleep?"

"Hi, Lieutenant. A client of mine was picked up on a vagrancy charge. May I see the arrest sheet? The name is Connery. Clarence Connery."

"Tell me something, honey. Why would you come down here at three A.M. to defend a vagrant?"

Jennifer grinned. "It keeps me off the streets."

SHE BECAME FAMILIAR with night court, held in Room 218 of the Centre Street courthouse. It was a smelly, overcrowded world, with its own arcane jargon. Jennifer was baffled by it at first.

"Parker, your client is booked on bedpain."

"My client is booked on *what*?"

"Bedpain. Burglary, with a Break, Enter, Dwelling, Person, Armed, Intent to kill, at Night. Get it?"

"Got it."

• • •

"I'M HERE TO represent Miss Luna Tarner."

"Jesus H. Christ!"

"Would you tell me what the charges are?"

"Hold on. I'll find her ticket. Luna Tarner. That's a hot one . . . here we are. Pross. Picked up by CWAC, down below."

"Quack?"

"You're new around here, huh? *CWAC* is the City-Wide Anti-Crime unit. A *pross* is a hooker, and *down below* is south of Forty-Second Street. Capish?"

"Capish."

NIGHT COURT DEPRESSED Jennifer. It was filled with a human tide that ceaselessly surged in and out, washed up on the shores of justice.

There were more than a hundred and fifty cases heard each night. There were whores and transvestites, stinking, battered drunks and drug addicts. There were Puerto Ricans and Mexicans and Jews and Irish and Greeks and Italians, and they were accused of rape and theft and possession of guns or dope or assault or prostitution. And they all had one thing in common: They were poor. They were poor and defeated and lost. They were the dregs, the misfits whom the affluent society had passed by. A large proportion of them came from Central Harlem, and because there was no more room in the prison system, all but the most serious offenders were dismissed or fined. They returned home to St. Nicholas Avenue and Morningside and Manhattan Avenues, where in three and one-half square miles there lived two hundred and thirty-three thousand Blacks, eight thousand Puerto Ricans, and an estimated one million rats.

The majority of clients who came to Jennifer's office were people who had been ground down by poverty, the system, themselves. They were people who had long since surrendered. Jennifer found that their fears fed her self-confidence. She did not feel superior to them. She certainly could not hold herself up as a shining example of success, and yet she knew there was one big difference between her and her clients: She would never give up.

• • •

KEN BAILEY INTRODUCED Jennifer to Father Francis Joseph Ryan. Father Ryan was in his late fifties, a radiant, vital man with crisp gray-and-black hair that curled about his ears. He was always in serious need of a haircut. Jennifer liked him at once.

From time to time, when one of his parishioners would disappear, Father Ryan would come to Ken and enlist his services. Invariably, Ken would find the errant husband, wife, daughter or son. There would never be a charge.

"It's a down payment on heaven," Ken would explain.

One afternoon when Jennifer was alone Father Ryan dropped by the office.

"KEN'S OUT, FATHER Ryan. He won't be back today."

"It's really you I wanted to see, Jennifer," Father Ryan said. He sat down in the uncomfortable old wooden chair in front of Jennifer's desk. "I have a friend who has a bit of a problem."

That was the way he always started out with Ken.

"Yes, Father?"

"She's an elderly parishioner, and the poor dear's having trouble getting her Social Security payments. She moved into my neighborhood a few months ago and some damned computer lost all her records, may it rust in hell."

"I see."

"I knew you would," Father Ryan said, getting to his feet. "I'm afraid there won't be any money in it for you."

Jennifer smiled. "Don't worry about that. I'll try to straighten things out."

She had thought it would be a simple matter, but it had taken her almost three days to get the computer reprogrammed.

ONE MORNING A month later, Father Ryan walked into Jennifer's office and said, "I hate to bother you, my dear, but I have a friend who has a bit of a problem. I'm afraid he has no—" He hesitated.

"—Money," Jennifer guessed.

"Ah! That's it. Exactly. But the poor fellow needs help badly."

"All right. Tell me about him."

"His name is Abraham. Abraham Wilson. He's the son of one of my parishioners. Abraham is serving a life sentence in Sing Sing for killing a liquor store owner during a holdup."

"If he was convicted and is serving his sentence, I don't see how I can help, Father."

Father Ryan looked at Jennifer and sighed. "That's not his problem."

"It isn't?"

"No. A few weeks ago Abraham killed another man—a fellow prisoner named Raymond Thorpe. They're going to try him for murder, and go for the death penalty."

Jennifer had read something about the case. "If I remember correctly, he beat the man to death."

"So they say."

Jennifer picked up a pad and a pen. "Do you know if there were any witnesses?"

"I'm afraid so."

"How many?"

"Oh, a hundred or so. It happened in the prison yard, you see."

"Terrific. What is it you want me to do?"

Father Ryan said simply, "Help Abraham."

Jennifer put down her pen. "Father, it's going to take your Boss to help him." She sat back in her chair. "He's going in with three strikes against him. He's Black, he's a convicted murderer, and he killed another man in front of a hundred witnesses. Assuming he did it, there just aren't any grounds for defense. If another prisoner was threatening him, there were guards he could have asked to help him. Instead, he took the law into his own hands. There isn't a jury in the world that wouldn't convict him."

"He's still a fellow human being. Would you just talk to him?"

Jennifer sighed. "I'll talk to him if you want me to, but I won't make any commitment."

Father Ryan nodded. "I understand. It would probably mean a great deal of publicity."

They were both thinking the same thing. Abraham Wilson was not the only one who had strikes against him.

. . .

SING SING PRISON is situated at the town of Ossining, thirty miles up-state of Manhattan on the east bank of the Hudson River, overlooking the Tappan Zee and Haverstraw Bay.

Jennifer went up by bus. She had telephoned the assistant warden and he had made arrangements for her to see Abraham Wilson, who was being held in solitary confinement.

During the bus ride, Jennifer was filled with a sense of purpose she had not felt in a long time. She was on her way to Sing Sing to meet a possible client charged with murder. This was the kind of case she had studied for, prepared herself for. She felt like a lawyer for the first time in a year, and yet she knew she was being unrealistic. She was not on her way to see a client. She was on her way to tell a man she could not represent him. She could not afford to become involved in a highly publicized case that she had no chance of winning.

Abraham Wilson would have to find someone else to defend him.

A DILAPIDATED TAXI took Jennifer from the bus station to the penitentiary, situated on seventy acres of land near the river. Jennifer rang the bell at the side entrance and a guard opened the door, checked off her name against his list, and directed her to the assistant warden's office.

The assistant warden was a large, square man with an old-fashioned military haircut and an acne-pitted face. His name was Howard Patterson.

"I would appreciate anything you can tell me about Abraham Wilson," Jennifer began.

"If you're looking for comfort, you're not going to get it here." Patterson glanced at the dossier on the desk in front of him. "Wilson's been in and out of prisons all his life. He was caught stealing cars when he was eleven, arrested on a mugging charge when he was thirteen, picked up for rape when he was fifteen, became a pimp at eighteen, served a sentence for putting one of his girls in the hospital . . ."

He leafed through the dossier. "You name it—stabbings, armed robbery and finally the big time—murder."

It was a depressing recital.

Jennifer asked, "Is there any chance that Abraham Wilson *didn't* kill Raymond Thorpe?"

"Forget it. Wilson's the first to admit it, but it wouldn't make any difference even if he denied it. We've got a hundred and twenty witnesses."

"May I see Mr. Wilson?"

Howard Patterson rose to his feet. "Sure, but you're wasting your time."

ABRAHAM WILSON WAS the ugliest human being Jennifer Parker had ever seen. He was coal-black, with a nose that had been broken in several places, missing front teeth and tiny, shifty eyes set in a knife-scarred face. He was about six feet four inches and powerfully built. He had huge flat feet which made him lumber. If Jennifer had searched for one word to describe Abraham Wilson, it would have been *menacing*. She could imagine the effect this man would have on a jury.

Abraham Wilson and Jennifer were seated in a high-security visiting room, a thick wire mesh between them, a guard standing at the door. Wilson had just been taken out of solitary confinement and his beady eyes kept blinking against the light. If Jennifer had come to this meeting feeling she would probably not want to handle this case, after seeing Abraham Wilson she was positive. Merely sitting opposite him she could feel the hatred spewing out of the man.

Jennifer opened the conversation by saying, "My name is Jennifer Parker. I'm an attorney. Father Ryan asked me to see you."

Abraham Wilson spat through the screen, spraying Jennifer with saliva. "That mothafuckin' do-gooder."

It's a wonderful beginning, Jennifer thought. She carefully refrained from wiping the saliva from her face. "Is there anything you need here, Mr. Wilson?"

He gave her a toothless smile. "A piece of ass, baby. You innersted?"

She ignored that. "Do you want to tell me what happened?"

"Hey, you lookin' for my life story, you gotta pay me for it. I gonna sell it for da movin' pitchurs. Maybe I'll star in it mysef."

The anger coming out of him was frightening. All Jennifer wanted was to get out of there. The assistant warden had been right. She was wasting her time.

"I'm afraid there's really nothing I can do to help you unless you help me, Mr. Wilson. I promised Father Ryan I would at least come and talk to you."

Abraham Wilson gave her a toothless grin again. "That's mighty white of ya, sweetheart. Ya sure ya don't wanna change your mind 'bout that piece of ass?"

Jennifer rose to her feet. She had had enough. "Do you hate everybody?"

"Tell ya what, doll, you crawl inta my skin and I'll crawl inta yours, and then you'n me'll rap 'bout hate."

Jennifer stood there, looking into that ugly black face, digesting what he had said, and then she slowly sat down. "Do you want to tell me your side of the story, Abraham?"

He stared into her eyes, saying nothing. Jennifer waited, watching him, wondering what it must be like to wear that scarred black skin. She wondered how many scars were hidden inside the man.

The two of them sat there in a long silence. Finally, Abraham Wilson said, "I killed the somabitch."

"Why did you kill him?"

He shrugged. "The motha' was comin' at me with this great big butcher knife, and—"

"Don't con me. Prisoners don't walk around carrying butcher knives."

Wilson's face tightened and he said, "Get the fuck outa here, lady. I din't sen' for ya." He rose to his feet. "An' don't come round heah botherin' me no more, you heah? I'm a busy man."

He turned and walked over to the guard. A moment later they were both gone. That was that. Jennifer could at least tell Father Ryan that she had talked to the man. There was nothing further she could do.

A guard let Jennifer out of the building. She started across the courtyard toward the main gate, thinking about Abraham Wilson and her reaction to him. She disliked the man and, because of that, she was doing something she had no right to do: She was judging him. She had already pronounced him guilty and he had not yet had a trial. Perhaps someone *had* attacked him, not with a knife, of course, but with a rock or a brick. Jennifer stopped and stood there indecisively. Every instinct told her to go back to Manhattan and forget about Abraham Wilson.

Jennifer turned and walked back to the assistant warden's office.

• • •

"HE'S A HARD case," Howard Patterson said. "When we can, we try re-habilitation instead of punishment, but Abraham Wilson's too far gone. The only thing that will calm him down is the electric chair."

What a weird piece of logic, Jennifer thought. "He told me the man he killed attacked him with a butcher knife."

"I guess that's possible."

The answer startled her. "What do you mean, 'that's possible'? Are you saying a convict in here could get possession of a knife? A butcher knife?"

Howard Patterson shrugged. "Miss Parker, we have twelve hundred and forty convicts in this place, and some of them are men of great inge-nuity. Come on. I'll show you something."

Patterson led Jennifer down a long corridor to a locked door. He selected a key from a large key ring, opened the door and turned on the light. Jennifer followed him into a small, bare room with built-in shelves.

"This is where we keep the prisoners' box of goodies." He walked over to a large box and lifted the lid.

Jennifer stared down into the box unbelievingly.

She looked up at Howard Patterson and said, "I want to see my client again."

6

Jennifer prepared for Abraham Wilson's trial as she had never prepared for anything before in her life. She spent endless hours in the law library checking for procedures and defenses, and with her client, drawing from him every scrap of information she could. It was no easy task. From the beginning, Wilson was truculent and sarcastic.

"You wanna know about me, honey? I got my first fuck when I was ten. How ole was you?"

Jennifer forced herself to ignore his hatred and his contempt, for she was aware that they covered up a deep fear. And so Jennifer persisted, demanding to know what Wilson's early life was like, what his parents were like, what had shaped the boy into the man. Over a period of weeks, Abraham Wilson's reluctance gave way to interest, and his interest finally gave way to fascination. He had never before had reason to think of himself in terms of what kind of person he was, or why.

Jennifer's prodding questions began to arouse memories, some merely unpleasant, others unbearably painful. Several times during the sessions when Jennifer was questioning Abraham Wilson about his father, who had regularly given him savage beatings, Wilson would order Jennifer to leave him alone. She left, but she always returned.

If Jennifer had had little personal life before, she now had none. When she was not with Abraham Wilson, she was at her office, seven days a week, from early morning until long after midnight, reading everything she could find about the crimes of murder and manslaughter, voluntary and involuntary. She studied hundreds of appellate court decisions, briefs, affidavits, exhibits, motions, transcripts. She pored over files on intent and premeditation, self-defense, double jeopardy, and temporary insanity.

She studied ways to get the charge reduced to manslaughter.

Abraham had not planned to kill the man. But would a jury believe that? Particularly a local jury. The townspeople hated the prisoners in their midst. Jennifer moved for a change of venue, and it was granted. The trial would be held in Manhattan.

Jennifer had an important decision to make: Should she allow Abraham Wilson to testify? He presented a forbidding figure, but if the jurors were able to hear his side of the story from his own lips, they might have some sympathy for him. The problem was that putting Abraham Wilson on the stand would allow the prosecution to reveal Wilson's background and past record, including the previous murder he had committed.

Jennifer wondered which one of the assistant district attorneys Di Silva would assign to be her adversary. There were half a dozen very good ones who prosecuted murder trials, and Jennifer familiarized herself with their techniques.

She spent as much time as possible at Sing Sing, looking over the scene of the killing in the recreation yard, talking to guards and Abraham, and she interviewed dozens of convicts who had witnessed the killing.

"Raymond Thorpe attacked Abraham Wilson with a knife," Jennifer said. "A large butcher knife. You must have seen it."

"Me? I didn't see no knife."

"You *must* have. You were right there."

"Lady, I didn't see nothin'."

Not one of them was willing to get involved.

. . .

OCCASIONALLY JENNIFER WOULD take time out to have a regular meal, but usually she grabbed a quick sandwich at the coffee shop on the main floor of the courthouse. She was beginning to lose weight and she had dizzy spells.

Ken Bailey was becoming concerned about her. He took her to Forlini's across from the courthouse, and ordered a large lunch for her.

"Are you trying to kill yourself?" he demanded.

"Of course not."

"Have you looked in a mirror lately?"

"No."

He studied her and said, "If you have any sense, you'll drop this case."

"Why?"

"Because you're setting yourself up as a clay pigeon. Jennifer, I hear things on the street. The press is peeing in its collective pants, they're so eager to start taking potshots at you again."

"I'm an attorney," Jennifer said stubbornly. "Abraham Wilson is entitled to a fair trial. I'm going to try to see that he gets one." She saw the look of concern on Ken Bailey's face. "Don't worry about it. The case isn't going to get *that* much publicity."

"It isn't, huh? Do you know who's prosecuting?"

"No."

"Robert Di Silva."

JENNIFER ARRIVED AT the Leonard Street entrance of the Criminal Courts Building and pushed her way past the people churning through the lobby, past the uniformed policemen, the detectives dressed like hippies, the lawyers identified by the briefcases they carried. Jennifer walked toward the large circular information desk, where no attendant had ever been posted, and took the elevator to the sixth floor. She was on her way to see the District Attorney. It had been almost a year since her last encounter with Robert Di Silva, and Jennifer was not looking forward to this one. She was going to inform him that she was resigning from Abraham Wilson's defense.

. . .

IT HAD TAKEN Jennifer three sleepless nights to make her decision. What it came down to finally was that the primary consideration had to be the best interests of her client. The Wilson case was not important enough for Di Silva to handle himself. The only reason, therefore, for the District Attorney's giving it his personal attention was because of Jennifer's involvement. Di Silva wanted vengeance. He was planning to teach Jennifer a lesson. And so she had finally decided she had no choice but to withdraw from Wilson's defense. She could not let him be executed because of a mistake she had once made. With her off the case, Robert Di Silva would probably deal with Wilson more leniently. Jennifer was on her way to save Abraham Wilson's life.

There was an odd feeling of reliving the past as she got off at the sixth floor and walked toward the familiar door marked *District Attorney, County of New York.* Inside, the same secretary was seated at the same desk.

"I'm Jennifer Parker. I have an appointment with—"

"Go right in," the secretary said. "The District Attorney is expecting you."

Robert Di Silva was standing behind his desk, chewing on a wet cigar, giving orders to two assistants. He stopped as Jennifer entered.

"I was betting you wouldn't show up."

"I'm here."

"I thought you would have turned tail and run out of town by now. What do you want?"

There were two chairs opposite Robert Di Silva's desk, but he did not invite Jennifer to sit.

"I came here to talk about my client, Abraham Wilson."

Robert Di Silva sat down, leaned back in his chair and pretended to think. "Abraham Wilson . . . oh, yes. That's the nigger murderer who beat a man to death in prison. You shouldn't have any trouble defending him." He glanced at his two assistants and they left the room.

"Well, counselor?"

"I'd like to talk about a plea."

Robert Di Silva looked at her with exaggerated surprise. "You mean you came in to make a deal? You amaze me. I would have thought that someone with your great legal talent would be able to get him off scot-free."

"Mr. Di Silva, I know this looks like an open-and-shut case," Jennifer began, "but there are extenuating circumstances. Abraham Wilson was—"

District Attorney Di Silva interrupted. "Let me put it in legal language you can understand, counselor. You can take your extenuating circumstances and shove them up your ass!" He got to his feet and when he spoke his voice was trembling with rage. "Make a deal with you, lady? You fucked up my life! There's a dead body and your boy's going to burn for it. Do you hear me? I'm making it my personal business to see that he's sent to the chair."

"I came up here to withdraw from the case. You could reduce this to a manslaughter charge. Wilson's already in for life. You could—"

"No way! He's guilty of murder plain and simple!"

Jennifer tried to control her anger. "I thought the jury was supposed to decide that."

Robert Di Silva smiled at her without mirth. "You don't know how heartwarming it is to have an expert like you walk into my office and explain the law to me."

"Can't we forget our personal problems? I—"

"Not as long as I live. Say hello to your pal Michael Moretti for me."

HALF AN HOUR later, Jennifer was having coffee with Ken Bailey.

"I don't know what to do," Jennifer confessed. "I thought if I got off the case Abraham Wilson would stand a better chance. But Di Silva won't make a deal. He's not after Wilson—he's after me."

Ken Bailey looked at her thoughtfully. "Maybe he's trying to psych you out. He wants you running scared."

"I *am* running scared." She took a sip of her coffee. It tasted bitter. "It's a bad case. You should see Abraham Wilson. All the jury will have to do is *look* at him and they'll vote to convict."

"When does the trial come up?"

"In four weeks."

"Anything I can do to help?"

"Uh-huh. Put out a contract on Di Silva."

"Do you think there's any chance you can get Wilson an acquittal?"

"Looking at it from the pessimist's point of view, I'm trying my first case against the smartest District Attorney in the country, who has a vendetta against me, and my client is a convicted Black killer who killed again in front of a hundred and twenty witnesses."

"Terrific. What's the optimist's point of view?"

"I could get hit by a truck this afternoon."

THE TRIAL DATE was only three weeks away now. Jennifer arranged for Abraham Wilson to be transferred to the prison at Riker's Island. He was put in the House of Detention for Men, the largest and oldest jail on the island. Ninety-five percent of his prison mates were there awaiting trial for felonies: murder, arson, rape, armed robbery and sodomy.

No private cars were allowed on the island, and Jennifer was transported in a small green bus to the gray brick control building where she showed her identification. There were two armed guards in a green booth to the left of the building, and beyond that a gate where all unauthorized visitors were stopped. From the control building, Jennifer was driven down Hazen Street, the little road that went through the prison grounds, to the Anna M. Kross Center Building, where Abraham Wilson was brought to see her in the counsel room, with its eight cubicles reserved for attorney-client meetings.

Walking down the long corridor on her way to meet with Abraham Wilson, Jennifer thought: *This must be like the waiting room to hell.* There was an incredible cacophony. The prison was made of brick and steel and stone and tile. Steel gates were constantly opening and clanging shut. There were more than one hundred men in each cellblock, talking and yelling at the same time, with two television sets tuned to different channels and a music system playing country rock. Three hundred guards were assigned to the building, and their bellowing could be heard over the prison symphony.

A guard had told Jennifer, "Prison society is the politest society in the world. If a prisoner ever brushes up against another one, he immediately says, 'Excuse me.' Prisoners have a lot on their minds and the least little thing . . ."

. . .

JENNIFER SAT ACROSS from Abraham Wilson and she thought: *This man's life is in my hands. If he dies, it will be because I failed him.* She looked into his eyes and saw the despair there.

"I'm going to do everything I can," Jennifer promised.

THREE DAYS BEFORE the Abraham Wilson trial was to begin, Jennifer learned that the presiding judge was to be the Honorable Lawrence Waldman, who had presided over the Michael Moretti trial and had tried to get Jennifer disbarred.

7

At four o'clock on a Monday morning in late September of 1970, the day the trial of Abraham Wilson was to begin, Jennifer awakened feeling tired and heavy-eyed. She had slept badly, her mind filled with dreams of the trial. In one of the dreams, Robert Di Silva had put her in the witness box and asked her about Michael Moretti. Each time Jennifer tried to answer the questions, the jurors interrupted her with a chant: *Liar! Liar! Liar!*

Each dream was different, but they were all similar. In the last one, Abraham Wilson was strapped in the electric chair. As Jennifer leaned over to console him, he spit in her face. Jennifer awoke trembling, and it was impossible for her to go back to sleep. She sat up in a chair until dawn and watched the sun come up. She was too nervous to eat. She wished she could have slept the night before. She wished that she were not so tense. She wished that this day was over.

As she bathed and dressed she had a premonition of doom. She felt like wearing black, but she chose a green Chanel copy she had bought on sale at Loehmann's.

. . .

AT EIGHT-THIRTY, JENNIFER Parker arrived at the Criminal Courts Building to begin the defense in the case of The People of the State of New York against Abraham Wilson. There was a crowd outside the entrance and Jennifer's first thought was that there had been an accident. She saw a battery of television cameras and microphones, and before Jennifer realized what was happening, she was surrounded by reporters.

A reporter said, "Miss Parker, this is your first time in court, isn't it, since you fouled up the Michael Moretti case for the District Attorney?"

Ken Bailey had warned her. *She* was the central attraction, not her client. The reporters were not there as objective observers; they were there as birds of prey and she was to be their carrion.

A young woman in jeans pushed a microphone up to Jennifer's face. "Is it true that District Attorney Di Silva is out to get you?"

"No comment." Jennifer began to fight her way toward the entrance of the building.

"The District Attorney issued a statement last night that he thinks you shouldn't be allowed to practice law in the New York courts. Would you like to say anything about that?"

"No comment." Jennifer had almost reached the entrance.

"Last year Judge Waldman tried to get you disbarred. Are you going to ask him to disqualify himself from—?"

Jennifer was inside the courthouse.

THE TRIAL WAS scheduled to take place in Room 37. The corridor outside was crowded with people trying to get in, but the courtroom was already full. It was buzzing with noise and there was a carnival atmosphere in the air. There were extra rows reserved for members of the press. *Di Silva saw to that,* Jennifer thought.

ABRAHAM WILSON WAS seated at the defense table, towering over everyone around him like an evil mountain. He was dressed in a dark blue suit that was too small for him, and a white shirt and blue tie that Jennifer had bought him. They did not help. Abraham Wilson looked like an ugly killer in a dark blue suit. *He might just as well have worn his prison clothes,* Jennifer thought, discouraged.

Wilson was staring defiantly around the courtroom, glowering at everyone who met his look. Jennifer knew her client well enough now to understand that his belligerence was a cover-up for his fright; but what would come over to everyone—including the judge and the jury—was an impression of hostility and hatred. The huge man was a threat. They would regard him as someone to be feared, to be destroyed.

There was not a trace in Abraham Wilson's personality that was loveable. There was nothing about his appearance that could evoke sympathy. There was only that ugly, scarred face with its broken nose and missing teeth, that enormous body that would inspire fear.

Jennifer walked over to the defense table where Abraham Wilson was sitting and took the seat next to him. "Good morning, Abraham."

He glanced over at her and said, "I didn't think you was comin'."

Jennifer remembered her dream. She looked into his small, slitted eyes. "You knew I'd be here."

He shrugged indifferently. "It don't matter one way or another. They's gonna get me, baby. They's gonna convict me of murder and then they's gonna pass a law makin' it legal to boil me in oil, then they's gonna boil me in oil. This ain't gonna be no trial. This is gonna be a show. I hope you brung your popcorn."

There was a stir around the prosecutor's table and Jennifer looked up to see District Attorney Di Silva taking his place at the table next to a battery of assistants. He looked at Jennifer and smiled. Jennifer felt a growing sense of panic.

A court officer said, "All rise," and Judge Lawrence Waldman entered from the judge's robing room.

"Hear ye, Hear ye. All people having business with Part Thirty-seven of this Court, draw near, give your attention and you shall be heard. The Honorable Justice Lawrence Waldman presiding."

The only one who refused to stand was Abraham Wilson. Jennifer whispered out of the corner of her mouth, "Stand up!"

"Fuck 'em, baby. They gonna have to come and drag me up."

Jennifer took his giant hand in hers. "On your feet, Abraham. We're going to beat them."

He looked at her for a long moment, then slowly got to his feet, towering over her.

Judge Waldman took his place on the bench. The spectators resumed their seats. The court clerk handed a court calendar to the judge.

"The People of the State of New York versus Abraham Wilson, charged with the murder of Raymond Thorpe."

JENNIFER'S INSTINCT NORMALLY would have been to fill the jury box with Blacks, but because of Abraham Wilson she was not so sure. Wilson was not one of them. He was a renegade, a killer, "a disgrace to their race." They might convict him more readily than would whites. All Jennifer could do was try to keep the more obvious bigots off the jury. But bigots did not go around advertising. They would keep quiet about their prejudices, waiting to get their vengeance.

By late afternoon of the second day, Jennifer had used up her ten peremptory challenges. She felt that her *voir dire*—the questioning of the jurors—was clumsy and awkward, while Di Silva's was smooth and skillful. He had the knack of putting the jurors at ease, drawing them into his confidence, making friends of them.

How could I have forgotten what a good actor Di Silva is? Jennifer wondered.

DI SILVA DID not exercise his peremptory challenges until Jennifer had exhausted hers, and she could not understand why. When she discovered the reason, it was too late. Di Silva had outsmarted her. Among the final prospective jurors questioned were a private detective, a bank manager and the mother of a doctor—all of them *Establishment*—and there was nothing now that Jennifer could do to keep them off the jury. The District Attorney had sandbagged her.

ROBERT DI SILVA rose to his feet and began his opening statement.

"If it please the court"—he turned to the jury—"and you ladies and gentlemen of the jury, first of all I would like to thank you for giving up your valuable time to sit in this case." He smiled sympathetically. "I know what a disruption jury service can be. You all have jobs to get back to, families needing your attention."

It's as though he's one of them, Jennifer thought, *the thirteenth juror.*

"I promise to take up as little of your time as possible. This is really a very simple case. That's the defendant sitting over there—Abraham Wilson. The defendant is accused by the State of New York of murdering a fellow inmate at Sing Sing Prison, Raymond Thorpe. There's no doubt that he did. He's admitted it. Mr. Wilson's attorney is going to plead self-defense."

The District Attorney turned to look at the huge figure of Abraham Wilson, and the eyes of the jurors automatically followed him. Jennifer could see the reactions on their faces. She forced herself to concentrate on what District Attorney Di Silva was saying.

"A number of years ago twelve citizens, very much like yourselves, I am sure, voted to put Abraham Wilson away in a penitentiary. Because of certain legal technicalities, I am not permitted to discuss with you the crime that Abraham Wilson committed. I *can* tell you that that jury sincerely believed that locking Abraham Wilson up would prevent him from committing any further crimes. Tragically, they were wrong. For even locked away, Abraham Wilson was able to strike, to kill, to satisfy the blood lust in him. We know now, finally, that there is only one way to prevent Abraham Wilson from killing again. And that is to execute him. It won't bring back the life of Raymond Thorpe, but it can save the lives of other men who might otherwise become the defendant's next victims."

Di Silva walked along the jury box, looking each juror in the eye. "I told you that this case won't take up much of your time. I'll tell you why I said that. The defendant sitting over there—Abraham Wilson—murdered a man in cold blood. He has confessed to the killing. But even if he had not confessed, we have witnesses who saw Abraham Wilson commit that murder in cold blood. More than a hundred witnesses, in fact.

"Let us examine the phrase, 'in cold blood.' Murder for *any* reason is as distasteful to me as I know it is to you. But sometimes murders are committed for reasons we can at least understand. Let's say that someone with a weapon is threatening your loved one—a child, or a husband or a wife. Well, if you had a gun you might pull that trigger in order to save your loved one's life. You and I might not *condone* that kind of thing, but I'm sure we can at least understand it. Or, let's take another example. If you were suddenly awakened in the middle of the night by an intruder threatening your life and you had a chance to kill him to save yourself, and you killed him—well, I think we can all understand how *that* might happen. And that wouldn't make us desperate criminals or evil people, would it? It was something we did in the heat of the moment." Di Silva's voice hardened. "But *cold-blooded murder* is something else again. To take the life of another human being, without the excuse of any feelings or passions, to do it for money or drugs or the sheer pleasure of killing—"

He was deliberately prejudicing the jury, yet not overstepping the bounds, so that there could be no error calling for mistrial or reversal.

Jennifer watched the faces of the jurors, and there was no question but that Robert Di Silva had them. They were agreeing with every word he said. They shook their heads and nodded and frowned. They did everything but applaud him. He was an orchestra leader and the jury was his orchestra. Jennifer had never seen anything like it. Every time the District Attorney mentioned Abraham Wilson's name—and he mentioned it with almost every sentence—the jury automatically looked over at the defendant. Jennifer had cautioned Wilson not to look at the jury. She had drilled it into him over and over again that he was to look anywhere in the courtroom except at the jury box, because the air of defiance he exuded was enraging. To her horror now, Jennifer found that Abraham Wilson's eyes were fastened on the jury box, locking eyes with the jurors. Aggression seemed to be pouring out of him.

Jennifer said in a low voice, "Abraham . . ."

He did not turn.

The District Attorney was finishing his opening address. "The Bible says, 'An eye for an eye, a tooth for a tooth.' That is vengeance. The State is not asking for vengeance. It is asking for justice. Justice for the poor man whom Abraham Wilson cold-bloodedly—*cold-bloodedly*—murdered. Thank you."

The District Attorney took his seat.

As Jennifer rose to address the jury, she could feel their hostility and impatience. She had read books about how lawyers were able to read juries' minds, and she had been skeptical. But no longer. The message from the jury was coming at her loudly and clearly. They had already decided her client was guilty, and they were impatient because Jennifer was wasting their time, keeping them in court when they could be out doing more important things, as their friend the District Attorney had pointed out. Jennifer and Abraham Wilson were the enemy.

Jennifer took a deep breath and said, "If Your Honor please," and then she turned back to the jurors. "Ladies and gentlemen, the reason we have courtrooms, the reason we are all here today, is because the law, in its wisdom, knows that there are always two sides to every case. Listening to the District Attorney's attack on my client, listening to him pronounce my client guilty without benefit of a jury's verdict—*your* verdict—one would not think so."

She looked into their faces for a sign of sympathy or support. There was none. She forced herself to go on. "District Attorney Di Silva used the phrase over and over, *'Abraham Wilson is guilty.'* That is a lie. Judge Waldman will tell you that no defendant is guilty until a judge or jury declares that he is guilty. That is what we are all here to find out, isn't it? Abraham Wilson has been charged with murdering a fellow inmate at Sing Sing. But Abraham Wilson did not kill for money or for dope. He killed to save his own life. You remember those clever examples that the District Attorney gave you when he explained the difference between killing in cold blood and in hot blood. Killing in hot blood is when you're protecting someone you love, or when you're defending yourself. Abraham Wilson killed in self-defense, and I tell you now that any of us in this courtroom, under identical circumstances, would have done exactly the same thing.

"The District Attorney and I agree on one point: Every man has the right to protect his own life. If Abraham Wilson had not acted exactly as he did, he would be dead." Jennifer's voice was ringing with sincerity. She had forgotten her nervousness in the passion of her conviction. "I ask each of you to remember one thing: Under the law of this state, the prosecution must prove beyond any reasonable doubt that the act of killing was not committed in self-defense. And before this trial is over we will present solid evidence to show you that Raymond Thorpe was killed in order to prevent his murdering my client. Thank you."

THE PARADE OF witnesses for the State began. Robert Di Silva had not missed a single opportunity. His character witnesses for the deceased, Raymond Thorpe, included a minister, prison guards and fellow convicts. One by one they took the stand and testified to the sterling character and pacific disposition of the deceased.

Each time the District Attorney was finished with a witness, he turned to Jennifer and said, "Your witness."

And each time Jennifer replied, "No cross-examination."

She knew that there was no point in trying to discredit the character witnesses. By the time they were finished, one would have thought that Raymond Thorpe had been wrongfully deprived of sainthood. The guards, who had been carefully coached by Robert Di Silva, testified that Thorpe had been a model prisoner who went around Sing Sing doing good works, intent only on helping his fellow man. The fact that Raymond Thorpe was a convicted bank robber and rapist was a tiny flaw in an otherwise perfect character.

What badly damaged Jennifer's already weak defense was the physical description of Raymond Thorpe. He had been a slightly built man, only five feet nine inches tall. Robert Di Silva dwelt on that, and he never let the jurors forget it. He painted a graphic picture of how Abraham Wilson had viciously attacked the smaller man and had smashed Thorpe's head against a concrete building in the exercise yard, instantly killing him. As Di Silva spoke, the jurors' eyes were fastened on the giant figure of the defendant sitting at the table, dwarfing everyone near him.

THE DISTRICT ATTORNEY was saying, "We'll probably never know what caused Abraham Wilson to attack this harmless, defenseless little man—"

And Jennifer's heart suddenly leaped. One word that Di Silva had said had given her the chance she needed.

"—We may never know the reason for the defendant's vicious attack, but one thing we *do* know, ladies and gentlemen—it wasn't because the murdered man was a threat to Abraham Wilson."

"Self-defense?" He turned to Judge Waldman. "Your Honor, would you please direct the defendant to rise?"

Judge Waldman looked at Jennifer. "Does counsel for the defense have any objection?"

Jennifer had an idea what was coming, but she knew that any objection on her part could only be damaging. "No, Your Honor."

Judge Waldman said, "Will the defendant rise, please?"

Abraham Wilson sat there a moment, his face defiant; then he slowly rose to his full height of six feet four inches.

Di Silva said, "There is a court clerk here, Mr. Galin, who is five feet nine inches tall, the exact height of the murdered man, Raymond Thorpe. Mr. Galin, would you please go over and stand next to the defendant?"

The court clerk walked over to Abraham Wilson and stood next to him. The contrast between the two men was ludicrous. Jennifer knew she had been outmaneuvered again, but there was nothing she could do about it. The visual impression could never be erased. The District Attorney stood there looking at the two men for a moment, and then said to the jury, his voice almost a whisper, *"Self-defense?"*

THE TRIAL WAS going worse than Jennifer had dreamed in her wildest nightmares. She could feel the jury's eagerness to get the trial over with so they could deliver a verdict of guilty.

Ken Bailey was seated among the spectators and, during a recess, Jennifer had a chance to exchange a few words with him.

"It's not an easy case," Ken said sympathetically. "I wish you didn't have King Kong for a client. Christ, just looking at him is enough to scare the hell out of anybody."

"He can't help that."

"As the old joke goes, he could have stayed home. How are you and our esteemed District Attorney getting along?"

Jennifer gave him a mirthless smile. "Mr. Di Silva sent me a message this morning. He intends to remove me from the law business."

WHEN THE PARADE of prosecution witnesses was over and Di Silva had rested his case, Jennifer rose and said, "I would like to call Howard Patterson to the stand."

The assistant warden of Sing Sing Prison reluctantly rose and moved toward the witness box, all eyes fixed on him. Robert Di Silva watched intently as Patterson took the oath. Di Silva's mind was racing, computing all the probabilities. He knew he had won the case. He had his victory speech all prepared.

Jennifer was addressing the witness. "Would you fill the jury in on your background, please, Mr. Patterson?"

District Attorney Di Silva was on his feet. "The State will waive the witness's background in order to save time, and we will stipulate that Mr. Patterson is the assistant warden at Sing Sing Prison."

"Thank you," Jennifer said. "I think the jury should be informed that Mr. Patterson had to be subpoenaed to come here today. He is here as a hostile witness." Jennifer turned to Patterson. "When I asked you to come here voluntarily and testify on behalf of my client, you refused. Is that true?"

"Yes."

"Would you tell the jury *why* you had to be subpoenaed to get you here?"

"I'll be glad to. I've been dealing with men like Abraham Wilson all my life. They're born troublemakers."

Robert Di Silva was leaning forward in his chair, grinning, his eyes locked on the faces of the jurors. He whispered to an assistant, "Watch her hang herself."

Jennifer said, "Mr. Patterson, Abraham Wilson is not on trial here for being a troublemaker. He's on trial for his life. Wouldn't you be willing to help a fellow human being who was unjustly accused of a capital crime?"

"If he were unjustly accused, yes." The emphasis on *unjustly* brought a knowing look to the faces of the jurors.

"There have been killings in prison before this case, have there not?"

"When you lock up hundreds of violent men together in an artificial environment, they're bound to generate an enormous amount of hostility, and there's—"

"Just yes or no, please, Mr. Patterson."

"Yes."

"Of those killings that have occurred in your experience, would you say that there have been a variety of motives?"

"Well, I suppose so. Sometimes—"

"Yes or no, please."

"Yes."

"Has self-defense ever been a motive in any of those prison killings?"

"Well, sometimes—" He saw the expression on Jennifer's face. "Yes."

"So, based on your vast experience, it is entirely possible, is it not, that Abraham Wilson was actually defending his own life when he killed Raymond Thorpe?"

"I don't think it—"

"I asked if it is possible. Yes or no."

"It is highly unlikely," Patterson said stubbornly.

Jennifer turned to Judge Waldman. "Your Honor, would you please direct the witness to answer the question?"

Judge Waldman looked down at Howard Patterson. "The witness will answer the question."

"Yes."

But the fact that his whole attitude said *no* had registered on the jury.

Jennifer said, "If the court please, I have subpoenaed from the witness some material I would like to submit now in evidence."

District Attorney Di Silva rose. "What kind of material?"

"Evidence that will prove our contention of self-defense."

"Objection, Your Honor."

"What are you objecting to?" Jennifer asked. "You haven't seen it yet."

Judge Waldman said, "The court will withhold a ruling until it sees the evidence. A man's life is at stake here. The defendant is entitled to every possible consideration."

"Thank you, Your Honor." Jennifer turned to Howard Patterson. "Did you bring it with you?" she asked.

He nodded, tight-lipped. "Yes. But I'm doing this under protest."

"I think you've already made that very clear, Mr. Patterson. May we have it, please?"

Howard Patterson looked over to the spectator area where a man in a prison guard uniform was seated. Patterson nodded to him. The guard rose and came forward, carrying a covered wooden box.

Jennifer took it from him. "The defense would like to place this in evidence as Exhibit A, Your Honor."

"What is it?" District Attorney Di Silva demanded.

"It's called a *goodie box*."

There was a titter from the spectators.

Judge Waldman looked down at Jennifer and said slowly, "Did you say a *goodie box*? What is in the box, Miss Parker?"

"Weapons. Weapons that were made in Sing Sing by the prisoners for the purpose of—"

"Objection!" The District Attorney was on his feet, his voice a roar. He hurried toward the bench. "I'm willing to make allowances for my colleague's inexperience, Your Honor, but if she intends to practice criminal law, then I would suggest she study the basic rules of evidence. There is no evidence linking anything in this so-called *goodie box* with the case that is being tried in this court."

"This box proves—"

"This box proves nothing." The District Attorney's voice was withering. He turned to Judge Waldman. "The State objects to the introduction of this exhibit as being immaterial and irrelevant."

"Objection sustained."

And Jennifer stood there, watching her case collapse. Everything was against her: the judge, the jury, Di Silva, the evidence. Her client was going to the electric chair unless . . .

Jennifer took a deep breath. "Your Honor, this exhibit is absolutely vital to our defense. I feel—"

Judge Waldman interrupted. "Miss Parker, this court does not have the time or the inclination to give you instructions in the law, but the District Attorney is quite right. Before coming into this courtroom you should have acquainted yourself with the basic rules of evidence. The first rule is that you cannot introduce evidence that has not been properly prepared for. Nothing has been put into the record about the deceased being armed or not armed. Therefore, the question of these weapons becomes extraneous. You are overruled."

Jennifer stood there, the blood rushing to her cheeks. "I'm sorry," she said stubbornly, "but it is *not* extraneous."

"That is enough! You may file an exception."

"I don't want to file an exception, Your Honor. You're denying my client his rights."

"Miss Parker, if you go any further I will hold you in contempt of court."

"I don't care what you do to me," Jennifer said. "The ground *has* been prepared for introducing this evidence. The District Attorney prepared it himself."

Di Silva said, "What? I never—"

Jennifer turned to the court stenographer. "Would you please read Mr. Di Silva's statement, beginning with the line, 'We'll probably never know what caused Abraham Wilson to attack . . . '?"

The District Attorney looked up at Judge Waldman. "Your Honor, are you going to allow—?"

Judge Waldman held up a hand. He turned to Jennifer. "This court does not need you to explain the law to it, Miss Parker. When this trial is ended, you will be held in contempt of court. Because this is a capital case, I am going to hear you out." He turned to the court stenographer. "You may proceed."

The court stenographer turned some pages and began reading. "We'll probably never know what caused Abraham Wilson to attack this harmless, defenseless little man—"

"That's enough," Jennifer interrupted. "Thank you." She looked at Robert Di Silva and said slowly, "Those are your words, Mr. Di Silva. *We'll probably never know what caused Abraham Wilson to attack this harmless, defenseless little man . . .*" She turned to Judge Waldman. "The key word, Your Honor, is *defenseless*. Since the District Attorney himself told this jury that the victim was defenseless, he left an open door for us to pursue the fact that the victim might *not* have been defenseless, that he might, in fact, have had a weapon. Whatever is brought up in the direct is admissible in the cross."

There was a long silence.

Judge Waldman turned to Robert Di Silva. "Miss Parker has a valid point. You did leave the door open."

Robert Di Silva was looking at him unbelievingly. "But I only—"

"The court will allow the evidence to be entered as Exhibit A."

Jennifer took a deep, grateful breath. "Thank you, Your Honor." She picked up the covered box, held it up in her hands and turned to face the jury. "Ladies and gentlemen, in his final summation the District Attorney is going to tell you that what you are about to see in this box is not direct evidence. He will be correct. He is going to tell you that there is nothing to link any of these weapons to the deceased. He will be correct. I am introducing this exhibit for another reason. For days now, you have been hearing how the ruthless, trouble-making defendant, who stands six feet four inches tall, wantonly attacked Raymond Thorpe, who stood only five feet nine inches tall. The picture that has been so carefully, and falsely, painted for you by the prosecution is that of a sadistic, murdering bully who killed another inmate for no reason. But ask yourselves this: Isn't there always *some* motive? Greed, hate, lust, *something*? I believe—and I'm staking my client's life on that belief—that there *was* a motive for that killing. The *only* motive, as the District Attorney himself told you, that justifies killing someone: self-defense. A man fighting to protect his own life. You have heard Howard Patterson testify that in his experience murders *have* occurred in prison, that convicts *do* fashion deadly weapons. What that means is that it was possible that Raymond Thorpe was armed with such a weapon, that indeed it was *he* who was attacking the defendant, and the defendant, trying to protect himself, was forced to kill him—*in self-defense.* If you decide that Abraham Wilson ruthlessly—and without any motivation at all—killed Raymond Thorpe, then you must bring in a verdict of guilty as charged. If, however, after seeing this evidence, you have a reasonable doubt in your minds, then it is your duty to return a verdict of not guilty." The covered box was becoming heavy in her hands, "When I first looked into this box I could not believe what I saw. You, too, may find it hard to believe—but I ask you to remember that it was brought here under protest by the assistant warden of Sing Sing Prison. This, ladies and gentlemen, is a collection of confiscated weapons secretly made by the convicts at Sing Sing."

As Jennifer moved toward the jury box, she seemed to stumble and lose her balance. The box fell out of her grasp, the top flew off, and the contents spilled out over the courtroom floor. There was a gasp. The jurors began to get to their feet so they could have a better look. They were staring at the hideous collection of weapons that had tumbled from the box. There were almost one hundred of them, of every size, shape and description. Homemade hatchets and butcher knives, stilettos and deadly looking scissors with the ends honed, pellet guns, and a large, vicious-looking cleaver. There were thin wires with wooden handles, used for strangling, a leather sap, a sharpened ice pick, a machete.

Spectators and reporters were on their feet now, craning to get a better look at the arsenal that lay scattered on the floor. Judge Waldman was angrily pounding his gavel for order.

Judge Waldman looked at Jennifer with an expression she could not fathom. A bailiff hurried forward to pick up the spilled contents of the box. Jennifer waved him away.

"Thank you," she said, "I'll do it."

As the jurors and spectators watched, Jennifer got down on her knees and began picking up the weapons and putting them back in the box. She worked slowly, handling the weapons gingerly, looking at each one without expression before she replaced it. The jurors had taken their seats again, but they were watching every move she made. It took Jennifer a full five minutes to return the weapons to the box, while District Attorney Di Silva sat there, fuming.

When Jennifer had put the last weapon in the deadly arsenal back in the box, she rose, looked at Patterson, then turned and said to Di Silva, "Your witness."

It was too late to repair the damage that had been done. "No cross," the District Attorney said.

"Then I would like to call Abraham Wilson to the stand."

8

Your name?"

"Abraham Wilson."

"Would you speak up, please?"

"Abraham Wilson."

"Mr. Wilson, did you kill Raymond Thorpe?"

"Yes, ma'am."

"Would you tell the court why?"

"He was gonna kill me."

"Raymond Thorpe was a much smaller man than you. Did you really believe that he would be able to kill you?"

"He was comin' at me with a knife that made him purty tall."

Jennifer had kept out two objects from the goodie box. One was a finely honed butcher knife; the other was a large pair of metal tongs. She held up the knife. "Was this the knife that Raymond Thorpe threatened you with?"

"Objection! The defendant has no way of knowing—"

"I'll rephrase the question. Was this similar to the knife that Raymond Thorpe threatened you with?"

"Yes, ma'am."

"And these tongs?"

"Yes, ma'am."

"Had you had trouble with Thorpe before?"

"Yes, ma'am."

"And when he came at you armed with these two weapons, you were forced to kill him in order to save your own life?"

"Yes, ma'am."

"Thank you."

Jennifer turned to Di Silva. "Your witness."

Robert Di Silva rose to his feet and moved slowly toward the witness box.

"Mr. Wilson, you've killed before, haven't you? I mean, this wasn't your first murder?"

"I made a mistake and I'm payin' for it. I—"

"Spare us your sermon. Just answer yes or no."

"Yes."

"So a human life doesn't have much value to you."

"That ain't true. I—"

"Do you call committing two murders valuing human life? How many people would you have killed if you *didn't* value human life? Five? Ten? Twenty?"

He was baiting Abraham Wilson and Wilson was falling for it. His jaw was clenched and his face was filling with anger. *Be careful!*

"I only kilt two people."

"Only! You *only* killed two people!" The District Attorney shook his head in mock dismay. He stepped close to the witness box and looked up at the defendant. "I'll bet it gives you a feeling of power to be so big. It must make you feel a little bit like God. Any time you want to, you can take a life here, take a life there . . ."

Abraham Wilson was on his feet, rising to his full height "You somabitch!"

No! Jennifer prayed. *Don't!*

"Sit down!" Di Silva thundered. "Is that the way you lost your temper when you killed Raymond Thorpe?"

"Thorpe was tryin' ta kill me."

"With these?" Di Silva held up the butcher knife and the pair of tongs. "I'm sure you could have taken that knife away from him." He waved the tongs around. "And you were afraid of this?" He turned back to the jury and held up the tongs deprecatingly. "This doesn't look so terribly lethal. If the deceased had been able to hit you over the head with it, it might have caused a small bump. What exactly is this pair of tongs, Mr. Wilson?"

Abraham Wilson said softly, "They're testicle crushers."

THE JURY WAS out for eight hours.

Robert Di Silva and his assistants left the courtroom to take a break, but Jennifer stayed in her seat, unable to tear herself away.

When the jury filed out of the room, Ken Bailey came up to Jennifer. "How about a cup of coffee?"

"I couldn't swallow anything."

She sat in the courtroom, afraid to move, only dimly aware of the people around her. It was over. She had done her best. She closed her eyes and tried to pray, but the fear in her was too strong. She felt as though she, along with Abraham Wilson, was about to be sentenced to death.

THE JURY WAS filing back into the room, their faces grim and foreboding, and Jennifer's heart began to beat faster. She could see by their faces that they were going to convict. She thought she would faint. Because of her, a man was going to be executed. She should never have taken the case in the first place. What right had she to put a man's life in her hands? She must have been insane to think she could win over someone as experienced as Robert Di Silva. She wanted to run up to the jurors before they could give their verdict and say, *Wait! Abraham Wilson hasn't had a fair trial. Please let another attorney defend him. Someone better than I am.*

But it was too late. Jennifer stole a look at Abraham Wilson's face. He sat there as immobile as a statue. She could feel no hatred coming from him now, only a deep despair. She wanted to say something to comfort him, but there were no words.

Judge Waldman was speaking. "Has the jury reached a verdict?"

"It has, Your Honor."

The judge nodded and his clerk walked over to the foreman of the jury, took a slip of paper from him and handed it to the judge. Jennifer felt as though her heart were going to come out of her chest. She could not breathe. She wanted to hold back this moment, to freeze it forever before the verdict was read.

Judge Waldman studied the slip of paper in his hands; then he slowly looked around the courtroom. His eyes rested on the members of the jury, on Robert Di Silva, on Jennifer and finally on Abraham Wilson.

"The defendant will please rise."

Abraham Wilson got to his feet, his movements slow and tired, as though all the energy had been drained out of him.

Judge Waldman read from the slip of paper. "This jury finds the defendant, Abraham Wilson, not guilty as charged."

There was a momentary hush and the judge's further words were drowned out in a roar from the spectators. Jennifer stood there, stunned, unable to believe what she was hearing. She turned toward Abraham Wilson, speechless. He stared at her for an instant with those small, mean eyes. And then that ugly face broke into the broadest grin that Jennifer had ever seen. He reached down and hugged her and Jennifer tried to fight back her tears.

The press was crowding around Jennifer, asking for a statement, barraging her with questions.

"How does it feel to beat the District Attorney?"

"Did you think you were going to win this case?"

"What would you have done if they had sent Wilson to the electric chair?"

Jennifer shook her head to all questions. She could not bring herself to talk to them. They had come here to watch a spectacle, to see a man being hounded to his death. If the verdict had gone the other way . . . she could not bear to think about it. Jennifer began to collect her papers and stuff them into a briefcase.

A bailiff approached her. "Judge Waldman wants to see you in his chambers, Miss Parker."

She had forgotten that there was a contempt of court citation waiting for her but it no longer seemed important. The only thing that mattered was that she had saved Abraham Wilson's life.

Jennifer glanced over at the prosecutor's table. District Attorney Silva was savagely stuffing papers into a briefcase, berating one of his assistants. He caught Jennifer's look. His eyes met hers and he needed no words.

JUDGE LAWRENCE WALDMAN was seated at his desk when Jennifer walked in. He said curtly, "Sit down, Miss Parker." Jennifer took a seat. "I will not allow you or anyone else to turn my courtroom into a sideshow."

Jennifer flushed. "I tripped. I couldn't help what—"

Judge Waldman raised a hand. "Please. Spare me." Jennifer clamped her lips tightly together.

Judge Waldman leaned forward in his chair. "Another thing I will not tolerate in my court is insolence." Jennifer watched him warily, saying nothing. "You overstepped the bounds this afternoon. I realize that your excessive zeal was in defense of a man's life. Because of that, I have decided not to cite you for contempt."

"Thank you, Your Honor." Jennifer had to force the words out.

The judge's face was unreadable as he continued: "Almost invariably, when a case is finished I have a sense of whether justice has been served or not. In this instance, quite frankly, I'm not sure." Jennifer waited for him to go on.

"That's all, Miss Parker."

IN THE EVENING editions of the newspapers and on the television news that night, Jennifer Parker was back in the headlines, but this time she was the heroine. She was the legal David who had slain Goliath. Pictures of her and Abraham Wilson and District Attorney Di Silva were plastered all over the front pages. Jennifer hungrily devoured every word of the stories, savoring them. It was such a sweet victory after all the disgrace she had suffered earlier.

Ken Bailey took her to dinner at Luchow's to celebrate, and Jennifer was recognized by the captain and several of the customers. Strangers called Jennifer by name and congratulated her. It was a heady experience.

"How does it feel to be a celebrity?" Ken grinned.

"I'm numb."

Someone sent a bottle of wine to the table.

"I don't need anything to drink," Jennifer said. "I feel as though I'm already drunk."

But she was thirsty and she drank three glasses of wine while she re-hashed the trial with Ken.

"I was scared. Do you know what it's like to hold someone else's life in your hands? It's like playing God. Can you think of anything scarier than that? I mean, I come from *Kelso* . . . could we have another bottle of wine, Ken?"

"Anything you want."

Ken ordered a feast for them both, but Jennifer was too excited to eat.

"Do you know what Abraham Wilson said to me the first time I met him? He said, 'You crawl into my skin and I'll crawl into yours and then you and me will rap about hate.' Ken, I was *in* his skin today, and do you know something? I thought the jury was going to convict *me*. I felt as though I was going to be executed. I love Abraham Wilson. Could we have some more wine?"

"You haven't eaten a bite."

"I'm thirsty."

Ken watched, concerned, as Jennifer kept filling and emptying her glass. "Take it easy."

She waved a hand in airy dismissal. "It's California wine. It's like drinking water." She took another swallow. "You're my best friend. Do you know who's not my best friend? The great Robert Di Sliva. Di Sivla."

"Di Silva."

"Him, too. He hates me. D'ja see his face today? O-o-oh, he was mad! He said he was gonna run me out of court. But he didn't, did he?"

"No, he—"

"You know what I think? You know what I *really* think?"

"I—"

"Di Sliva thinks I'm Ahab and he's the white whale."

"I think you have that backwards."

"Thank you, Ken. I can always count on you. Let's have 'nother bottle of wine."

"Don't you think you've had enough?"

"Whales get thirsty." Jennifer giggled. "Tha's me. The big old white whale. Did I tell you I love Abraham Wilson? He's the most beautiful man I ever met. I looked in his eyes, Ken, my frien', 'n' he's beautiful! Y'ever look in Di Sivla's eyes? O-o-oh! They're cold! I mean, he's 'n iceberg. But he's not a bad man. Did I tell you 'bout Ahab 'n' the big white whale?"

"Yes."

"I love old Ahab. I love everybody. 'N' you know why, Ken? 'Cause Abraham Wilson is alive tonight. He's alive. Le's have 'nother bottle a wine to celebrate . . ."

IT WAS TWO A.M. when Ken Bailey took Jennifer home. He helped her up the four flights of stairs and into her little apartment. He was breathing hard from the climb.

"You know," Ken said, "I can feel the effects of all that wine."

Jennifer looked at him pityingly. "People who can't handle it shoudn' drink."

And she passed out cold.

SHE WAS AWAKENED by the shrill screaming of the telephone. She carefully reached for the instrument, and the slight movement sent rockets of pain through every nerve ending in her body.

"'Lo . . ."

"Jennifer? This is Ken."

"'Lo, Ken."

"You sound terrible. Are you all right?"

She thought about it. "I don't think so. What time is it?"

"It's almost noon. You'd better get down here. All hell is breaking loose."

"Ken—I think I'm dying."

"Listen to me. Get out of bed—slowly—take two aspirin and a cold shower, drink a cup of hot black coffee, and you'll probably live."

WHEN JENNIFER ARRIVED at the office one hour later, she was feeling better. *Not good,* Jennifer thought, *but better.*

Both telephones were ringing when she walked into the office.

"They're for you." Ken grinned. "They haven't stopped! You need a switchboard."

There were calls from newspapers and national magazines and television and radio stations wanting to do in-depth stories on Jennifer. Overnight, she had become big news. There were other calls, the kind of which she had dreamed. Law firms that had snubbed her before were telephoning to ask when it would be convenient for her to meet with them.

IN HIS OFFICE downtown, Robert Di Silva was screaming at his first assistant. "I want you to start a confidential file on Jennifer Parker. I want to be informed of every client she takes on. Got it?"

"Yes, sir."

"Move!"

9

H e ain't no button guy anymore'n I'm a fuckin' virgin. He's been workin' on the arm all his life."

"The asshole came suckin' up to me askin' me to put in the word with Mike. I said, 'Hey, paesano, I'm only a soldier, ya know?' If Mike needs another shooter he don't have to go lookin' in shit alley."

"He was tryin' to run a game on you, Sal."

"Well, I clocked him pretty good. He ain't connected and in this business, if you ain't connected, you're nothin'."

They were talking in the kitchen of a three-hundred-year-old Dutch farmhouse in upstate New Jersey.

There were three of them in the room: Nick Vito, Joseph Colella and Salvatore "Little Flower" Fiore.

Nick Vito was a cadaverous-looking man with thin lips that were almost invisible, and deep green eyes that were dead. He wore two hundred dollar shoes and white socks.

Joseph "Big Joe" Colella was a huge slab of a man, a granite monolith, and when he walked he looked like a building moving. Someone had once called him a vegetable garden. "Colella's got a potato nose, cauliflower ears and a pea brain."

Colella had a soft, high-pitched voice and a deceptively gentle manner. He owned a race horse and had an uncanny knack for picking winners. He was a family man with a wife and six children. His specialties were guns, acid and chains. Joe's wife, Carmelina, was a strict Catholic, and on Sundays when Colella was not working, he always took his family to church.

The third man, Salvatore Fiore, was almost a midget. He stood five feet three inches and weighed a hundred and fifteen pounds. He had the innocent face of a choirboy and was equally adept with a gun or a knife. Women were greatly attracted to the little man, and he boasted a wife, half a dozen girl friends, and a beautiful mistress. Fiore had once been a jockey, working the tracks from Pimlico to Tijuana. When the racing commissioner at Hollywood Park banned Fiore for doping a horse, the commissioner's body was found floating in Lake Tahoe a week later.

The three men were *soldati* in Antonio Granelli's Family, but it was Michael Moretti who had brought them in, and they belonged to him, body and soul.

IN THE DINING room, a Family meeting was taking place. Seated at the head of the table was Antonio Granelli, *capo* of the most powerful Mafia Family on the east coast. Seventy-two years old, he was still a powerful-looking man with the shoulders and broad chest of a laborer, and a shock of white hair. Born in Palermo, Sicily, Antonio Granelli came to America when he was fifteen and went to work on the waterfront on the west side of lower Manhattan. By the time he was twenty-one, he was lieutenant to the dock boss. The two men had an argument, and when the boss mysteriously disappeared, Antonio Granelli had taken over. Anyone who wanted to work on the docks had to pay him. He had used the money to begin his climb to power, and had expanded rapidly, branching out into loan-sharking and the numbers racket, prostitution and gambling and drugs and murder. Over the years he had been indicted thirty-two times and had only been convicted once, on a minor assault charge. Granelli was a ruthless man with the down-to-earth cunning of a peasant, and a total amorality.

To Granelli's left sat Thomas Colfax, the Family *consigliere*. Twenty-five years earlier, Colfax had had a brilliant future as a corporation lawyer, but he had defended a small olive-oil company which turned out to be Mafia-controlled and, step by step, had been lured into handling other cases for the Mafia until finally, through the years, the Granelli Family had become his sole client. It was a very lucrative client and Thomas Colfax became a wealthy man, with extensive real estate holdings and bank accounts all over the world.

To the right of Antonio Granelli sat Michael Moretti, his son-in-law. Michael was ambitious, a trait that made Granelli nervous. Michael did not fit into the pattern of the Family. His father, Giovanni, a distant cousin of Antonio Granelli, had been born not in Sicily but in Florence. That alone made the Moretti family suspect—everybody knew that Florentines were not to be trusted.

Giovanni Moretti had come to America and opened a shop as a shoemaker, running it honestly, without even a back room for gambling or loan-sharking or girls. Which made him stupid.

Giovanni's son, Michael, was entirely different. He had put himself through Yale and the Wharton School of Business. When Michael had finished school, he had gone to his father with one request: He wanted to meet his distant relative, Antonio Granelli. The old shoemaker had gone to see his cousin and the meeting had been arranged. Granelli was sure that Michael was going to ask for a loan so that he could go into some kind of business, maybe open a shoe shop like his dumb father. But the meeting had been a surprise.

"I know how to make you rich," Michael Moretti had begun.

Antonio Granelli had looked at the impudent young man and had smiled tolerantly. "I am rich."

"No. You just *think* you're rich."

The smile had died away. "What the hell you talkin' about, kid?"

And Michael Moretti had told him.

ANTONIO GRANELLI HAD moved cautiously at first, testing each piece of Michael's advice. Everything had succeeded brilliantly. Where before, the Granelli Family had been involved in profitable illegal activities, under Michael Moretti's supervision it branched out. Within five years the Family was into dozens of legitimate businesses, including meat-packing, linen supplies, restaurants, trucking companies and pharmaceuticals. Michael found ailing companies that needed financing and the Family went in as a minor partner and gradually took over, stripping away whatever assets there were. Old companies with impeccable reputations suddenly found themselves bankrupt. The businesses that showed a satisfactory profit, Michael hung on to and he increased the profits tremendously, for the workers in those businesses were controlled by his unions, and the company took their insurance through one of the Family-owned insurance companies, and they bought their automobiles from one of the Family's automobile dealers. Michael created a symbiotic giant, a series of businesses through which the consumer was constantly being milked—and the milk flowed to the Family.

In spite of his successes, Michael Moretti was aware that he had a problem. Once he had shown Antonio Granelli the rich, ripe horizons of legitimate enterprise, Granelli no longer needed him. He was expensive, because in the beginning he had persuaded Antonio Granelli to give him a percentage of what everyone was sure would be a small pot. But as Michael's ideas began to bear fruit and the profits poured in, Granelli had second thoughts. By chance, Michael learned that Granelli had held a meeting to discuss what the Family should do with him.

"I don't like to see all this money goin' to the kid," Granelli had said. "We get rid of him."

Michael had circumvented that scheme by marrying into the Family. Rosa, Antonio Granelli's only daughter, was nineteen years old. Her mother had died giving birth to her, and Rosa had been brought up in a convent and was allowed to come home only during the holidays. Her father adored her, and he saw to it that she was protected and sheltered. It was on a school holiday, an Easter, that Rosa met Michael Moretti. By the time she returned to the convent, she was madly in love with him. The memory of his dark good looks drove her to do things when she was alone that the nuns told her were sins against God.

Antonio Granelli was under the delusion that his daughter thought he was merely a successful businessman, but over the years, Rosa's classmates had shown her newspaper and magazine articles about her father and his real business, and whenever the government made an attempt to indict and convict one of the Granelli Family, Rosa was always aware of it. She never discussed it with her father, and so he remained happy in his belief that his daughter was an innocent and that she was spared the shock of knowing the truth.

The truth, if he had know it, would have surprised Granelli for Rosa found her father's business terribly exciting. She hated the discipline of the nuns at the convent and that, in turn, led her to hate all authority. She daydreamed about her father as a kind of Robin Hood, challenging authority, defying the government. The fact that Michael Moretti was an important man in her father's organization made him that much more exciting to her.

FROM THE BEGINNING, Michael was very careful how he handled Rosa. When he managed to be alone with her they exchanged ardent kisses and embraces, but Michael never let it go too far. Rosa was a virgin and she was willing—eager—to give herself to the man she loved. It was Michael who held back.

"I respect you too much, Rosa, to go to bed with you before we're married."

In reality, it was Antonio Granelli he respected too much. *He'd chop my balls off,* Michael thought.

And so it happened that at the time Antonio Granelli was discussing the best way to get rid of Michael Moretti, Michael and Rosa came to him and announced that they were in love and intended to get married. The old man screamed and raged and gave a hundred reasons why it would happen only over someone's dead body. But in the end, true love prevailed and Michael and Rosa were married in an elaborate ceremony.

After the wedding the old man had called Michael aside. "Rosa's all I got, Michael. You take good care of her, huh?"

"I will, Tony."

"I'm gonna be watchin' you. You better make her happy. You know what I mean, Mike?"

"I know what you mean."

"No whores or chippies. Understand? Rosa likes to cook. You see that you're home for dinner every night. You're gonna be a son-in-law to be proud of."

"I'm going to try very hard, Tony."

Antonio Granelli had said casually, "Oh, by the way, Mike, now that you're a member of the Family, that royalty deal I gave you—maybe we oughta change it."

Michael had clapped him on the arm. "Thanks, Papa, but it's enough for us. I'll be able to buy Rosa everything she wants."

And he had walked away, leaving the old man staring after him.

THAT HAD BEEN seven years earlier, and the years that followed had been wonderful for Michael. Rosa was pleasant and easy to live with and she adored him, but Michael knew that if she died or went away, he would get along without her. He would simply find someone else to do the things she did for him. He was not in love with Rosa. Michael did not think he was capable of loving another human being; it was as though something was missing in him.

He had no feelings for people, only for animals. Michael had been given a collie puppy for his tenth birthday. The two of them were insepa-rable. Six weeks later the dog had been killed in a hit-and-run accident, and when Michael's father offered to buy him another dog, Michael had refused. He had never owned another dog after that.

Michael had grown up watching his father slaving his life away for pennies, and Michael had resolved that would never happen to him. He had known what he wanted from the time he had first heard talk about his famous distant cousin Antonio Granelli. There were twenty-six Mafia Families in the United States, five of them in New York City, and his cousin Antonio's was the strongest. From his earliest childhood, Mi-chael thrived on tales of the Mafia. His father told him about the night of the Sicilian Vespers, September 10, 1931, when the balance of power had changed hands. In that single night, the *Young Turks* in the Mafia staged a bloody coup that wiped out more than forty *Mustache Petes,* the old guard who had come over from Italy and Sicily.

Michael was of the new generation. He had gotten rid of the old thinking and had brought in fresh ideas. A nine-man national commis-sion controlled all the Families now, and Michael knew that one day he would run that commission.

• • •

MICHAEL TURNED NOW to study the two men seated at the dining room table of the New Jersey farmhouse. Antonio Granelli still had a few years left but, with luck, not too many.

Thomas Colfax was the enemy. The lawyer had been against Michael from the beginning. As Michael's influence with the old man had increased, Colfax's had decreased.

Michael had brought more and more of his own men into the Organization, men like Nick Vito and Salvatore Fiore and Joseph Colella, who were fiercely loyal to him. Thomas Colfax had not liked that.

When Michael had been indicted for the murders of the Ramos brothers, and Camillo Stela had agreed to testify against him in court, the old lawyer had believed that he was finally going to be rid of Michael, for the District Attorney had an airtight case.

Michael had thought of a way out in the middle of the night. At four in the morning, he had gone out to a telephone booth and called Joseph Colella.

"Next week some new lawyers are going to be sworn in on the District Attorney's staff. Can you get me their names?"

"Sure, Mike. Easy."

"One more thing. Call Detroit and have them fly in a cherry—one of their boys who's never been tagged." And Michael had hung up.

TWO WEEKS LATER, Michael Moretti had sat in the courtroom studying the new assistant district attorneys. He had looked them over carefully, his eyes traveling from face to face, searching and judging. What he planned to do was dangerous, but its very daring could make it work. He was dealing with young beginners who would be too nervous to ask a lot of questions, and anxious to be helpful and make their mark. Well, someone was certainly going to make his mark.

Michael had finally selected Jennifer Parker. He liked the fact that she was inexperienced and that she was tense and trying to hide it. He liked the fact that she was female and would feel under more pressure than the men. When Michael was satisfied with his decision, he turned to a man in a gray suit sitting among the spectators and nodded toward Jennifer. That was all.

Michael had watched as the District Attorney had finished his examination of that son-of-a-bitch, Camillo Stela. He had turned to Thomas Colfax and said, *Your witness for cross.* Thomas Colfax had risen to his feet. *If it please Your Honor, it is now almost noon. I would prefer not to have my cross-examination interrupted. Might I request that the court recess for lunch now and I'll cross-examine this afternoon?*

And a recess had been declared. Now was the moment!

Michael saw his man casually drift up to join the men who were crowded around the District Attorney. The man made himself a part of the group. A few moments later, he walked over to Jennifer and handed her a large envelope. Michael sat there, holding his breath, willing Jennifer to take the envelope and move toward the witness room. She did. It was not until he saw her return without it that Michael Moretti relaxed.

THAT HAD BEEN a year ago. The newspapers had crucified the girl, but that was *her* problem. Michael had not given any further thought to Jennifer Parker until the newspapers had begun recently to feature the Abraham Wilson trial. They had dragged up the old Michael Moretti case and Jennifer Parker's part in it. They had run her picture. She was a stunning-looking girl, but there was something more—there was a sense of independence about her that stirred something in him. He stared at the picture for a long time.

Michael began to follow the Abraham Wilson trial with increasing interest. When the boys had celebrated with a victory dinner after Michael's mistrial was declared, Salvatore Fiore had proposed a toast. "The world got rid of one more fuckin' lawyer."

But the world had not gotten rid of her, Michael thought. Jennifer Parker had bounced back and was still in there, fighting. Michael liked that.

He had seen her on television the night before, discussing her victory over Robert Di Silva, and Michael had been oddly pleased.

Antonio Granelli had asked, "Ain't she the mouthpiece you set up, Mike?"

"Uh-huh. She's got a brain, Tony. Maybe we can use her one of these days."

10

The day after the Abraham Wilson verdict, Adam Warner telephoned. "I just called to congratulate you."

Jennifer recognized his voice instantly and it affected her more than she would have believed possible.

"This is—"

"I know." *Oh, God,* Jennifer thought. *Why did I say that?* There was no reason to let Adam know how often she had thought about him in the past few months.

"I wanted to tell you I thought you handled the Abraham Wilson case brilliantly. You deserved to win it."

"Thank you." *He's going to hang up,* Jennifer thought. *I'll never see him again. He's probably too busy with his harem.*

And Adam Warner was saying, "I was wondering if you'd care to have dinner with me one evening?"

Men hate overeager girls. "What about tonight?"

Jennifer heard the smile in his voice. "I'm afraid my first free night is Friday. Are you busy?"

"No." She had almost said, *Of course not.*

"Shall I pick you up at your place?"

Jennifer thought about her dreary little apartment with its lumpy sofa, the ironing board set up in a corner. "It might he easier if we met somewhere."

"Do you like the food at Lutèce?"

"May I tell you after I've eaten there?"

He laughed. "How's eight o'clock?"

"Eight o'clock is lovely."

Lovely. Jennifer replaced the receiver and sat there in a glow of euphoria. *This is ridiculous,* she thought. *He's probably married and has two dozen children.* Almost the first thing Jennifer had noticed about Adam when they had had dinner was that he was not wearing a wedding ring. *Inconclusive evidence,* she thought wryly. There definitely should be a law forcing all husbands to wear wedding rings.

Ken Bailey walked into the office. "How's the master attorney?" He looked at her more closely. "You look like you just swallowed a client."

Jennifer hesitated, then said, "Ken, would you run a check on someone for me?"

He walked over to her desk, picked up a pad and pencil. "Shoot. Who is it?"

She started to say Adam's name, then stopped, feeling like a fool. What business had she prying into Adam Warner's private life? *For God's sake,* she told herself, *all he did is ask you to have dinner with him, not marry him.* "Never mind."

Ken put the pencil down. "Whatever you say."

"Ken—"

"Yes?"

"Adam Warner. His name is Adam Warner."

Ken looked at her in surprise. "Hell, you don't need me to run a check on him. Just read the newspapers."

"What do you know about him?"

Ken Bailey flopped into a chair across from Jennifer and steepled his fingers together. "Let me see. He's a partner in Needham, Finch, Pierce and Warner; Harvard Law School; comes from a rich socialite family; in his middle thirties—"

Jennifer looked at him curiously. "How do you know so much about him?"

He winked. "I have friends in high places. There's a rumor they're going to run Mr. Warner for the United States Senate. There's even a little presidential ground swell going on. He's got what they call charisma."

He certainly has, Jennifer thought. She tried to make her next question sound casual. "What about his personal life?"

Ken Bailey looked at her oddly. "He's married to the daughter of an ex–Secretary of the Navy. She's the niece of Stewart Needham, Warner's law partner."

Jennifer's heart sank. So that was that.

Ken was watching her, puzzled. "Why this sudden interest in Adam Warner?"

"Just curious."

Long after Ken Bailey had left, Jennifer sat there thinking about Adam. *He asked me to dinner as a professional courtesy. He wants to congratulate me. But he's already done that over the telephone. Who cares why? I'm going to see him again. I wonder whether he'll remember to mention he has a wife. Of course not. Well, I'll have dinner with Adam on Friday night and that will be the end of that.*

LATE THAT AFTERNOON, Jennifer received a telephone call from Peabody & Peabody. It was from the senior partner himself.

"I've been meaning to get around to this for some time," he said. "I wondered if you and I might have lunch soon."

His casual tone did not deceive Jennifer. She was sure the idea of having lunch with her had not occurred to him until after he had read about the Abraham Wilson decision. He certainly did not want to meet with her to discuss serving subpoenas.

"What about tomorrow?" he suggested. "My club."

THEY MET FOR lunch the following day. The senior Peabody was a pale, prissy man, an older version of his son. His vest failed to conceal a slight paunch. Jennifer liked the father just as little as she had liked the son.

"We have an opening for a bright young trial attorney in our firm,

Miss Parker. We can offer you fifteen thousand dollars a year to start with."

Jennifer sat there listening to him, thinking how much that offer would have meant to her a year earlier when she had desperately needed a job, needed someone who believed in her.

He was saying, "I'm sure that within a few years there would be room for a partnership for you in our firm."

Fifteen thousand dollars a year and a partnership. Jennifer thought about the little office she shared with Ken, and her tiny, shabby four-flight walk-up apartment with its fake fireplace.

Mr. Peabody was taking her silence for acquiescence. "Good. We'd like you to begin as soon as possible. Perhaps you could start Monday. I—"

"No."

"Oh. Well, if Monday's not convenient for you—"

"I mean, no, I can't take your offer, Mr. Peabody," Jennifer said, and amazed herself.

"I see." There was a pause. "Perhaps we could start you at twenty thousand dollars a year." He saw the expression on her face. "Or twenty-five thousand. Why don't you think it over?"

"I've thought it over. I'm going to stay in business for myself."

THE CLIENTS WERE beginning to come. Not a great many and not very affluent, but they were clients. The office was becoming too small for her.

One morning after Jennifer had kept two clients waiting outside in the hallway while she was dealing with a third, Ken said, "This isn't going to work. You're going to have to move out of here and get yourself a decent office uptown."

Jennifer nodded. "I know. I've been thinking about it."

Ken busied himself with some papers so that he did not have to meet her eyes. "I'll miss you."

"What are you talking about? You have to go with me."

It took a moment for the words to sink in. He looked up and a broad grin creased his freckled face.

"Go with you?" He glanced around the cramped, windowless room. "And give up all this?"

. . .

THE FOLLOWING WEEK, Jennifer and Ken Bailey moved into larger offices in the five hundred block on Fifth Avenue. The new quarters were simply furnished and consisted of three small rooms: one for Jennifer, one for Ken and one for a secretary.

The secretary they hired was a young girl named Cynthia Ellman fresh out of New York University.

"There won't be a lot for you to do for a while," Jennifer apologized, "but things will pick up."

"Oh, I know they will, Miss Parker." There was heroine worship in the girl's voice.

She wants to be like me, Jennifer thought. *God forbid!*

Ken Bailey walked in and said, "Hey, I get lonely in that big office all by myself. How about dinner and the theater tonight?"

"I'm afraid I—" She was tired and had some briefs to read, but Ken was her best friend and she could not refuse him.

"I'd love to go."

THEY WENT TO see *Applause,* and Jennifer enjoyed it tremendously. Lauren Bacall was totally captivating. Jennifer and Ken had supper afterward at Sardi's.

When they had ordered, Ken said, "I have two tickets for the ballet Friday night. I thought we might—"

Jennifer said, "I'm sorry, Ken. I'm busy Friday night."

"Oh." His voice was curiously flat.

From time to time, Jennifer would find Ken staring at her when he thought he was unobserved, and there was an expression on his face that Jennifer found hard to define. She knew Ken was lonely, although he never talked about any of his friends and never discussed his personal life. She could not forget what Otto had told her, and she wondered whether Ken himself knew what he wanted out of life. She wished that there were some way she could help him.

IT SEEMED TO Jennifer that Friday was never going to arrive. As her dinner date with Adam Warner drew closer, Jennifer found it more and more difficult to concentrate on business. She found herself thinking about Adam constantly. She knew she was being ridiculous. She had seen the man only once in her life, and yet she was unable to get him out of her mind. She tried to rationalize by telling herself that it was because he had saved her when she was facing disbarment proceedings, and then had sent her clients. That was true, but Jennifer knew it was more than that. It was something she could not explain, even to herself. It was a feeling she had never had before, an attraction she had never felt for any other man. She wondered what Adam Warner's wife was like. She was undoubtedly one of the chosen women who, every Wednesday, walked through the red door at Elizabeth Arden's for a day of head-to-toe pampering. She would be sleek and sophisticated, with the polished aura of the wealthy socialite.

ON THE MAGIC Friday morning at ten o'clock, Jennifer made an appointment with a new Italian hairdresser Cynthia had told her all the models were going to. At ten-thirty, Jennifer called to cancel it. At eleven, she rescheduled the appointment.

Ken Bailey invited Jennifer to lunch, but she was too nervous to eat anything. Instead, she went shopping at Bendel's, where she bought a short, dark green chiffon dress that matched her eyes, a pair of slender brown pumps and a matching purse. She knew she was far over her budget, but she could not seem to stop herself.

She passed the perfume department on the way out, and on an insane impulse bought a bottle of Joy perfume. It was insane because the man was married.

Jennifer left the office at five o'clock and went home to change. She spent two hours bathing and dressing for Adam, and when she was finished she studied herself critically in the mirror. Then she defiantly combed out her carefully coiffured hair and tied it back with a green ribbon. *That's better,* she thought. *I'm a lawyer going to have dinner with another lawyer.* But when she closed the door she left behind a faint fragrance of rose and jasmine.

LUTÈCE WAS NOTHING like what Jennifer had expected. A French tricolor flew above the entrance of the small town house. Inside, a narrow hall led to a small bar and beyond was a sunroom, bright and gay, with porch wicker and plaid tablecloths. Jennifer was met at the door by the owner, André Soltner.

"May I help you?"

"I'm meeting Mr. Adam Warner. I think I'm a little early."

He waved Jennifer toward the small bar. "Would you care for a drink while you are waiting, Miss Parker?"

"That would be nice," Jennifer said. "Thank you."

"I'll send a waiter over."

Jennifer took a seat and amused herself watching the bejeweled and mink-draped women arriving with their escorts. Jennifer had read and heard about Lutèce. It was reputed to be Jacqueline Kennedy's favorite restaurant and to have excellent food.

A distinguished-looking gray-haired man walked up to Jennifer and said, "Mind if I join you for a moment?"

Jennifer stiffened. "I'm waiting for someone," she began. "He should be here—"

He smiled and sat down. "This isn't a pickup, Miss Parker." Jennifer looked at him in surprise, unable to place him. "I'm Lee Browning, of Holland and Browning." It was one of the most prestigious law firms in New York. "I just wanted to congratulate you on the way you handled the Wilson trial."

"Thank you, Mr. Browning."

"You took a big chance. It was a no-win case." He studied her a moment. "The rule is, when you're on the wrong side of a no-win case, make sure it's one where there's no publicity involved. The trick is to spotlight the winners and kick the losers under the rug. You fooled a lot of us. Have you ordered a drink yet?"

"No—"

"May I—?" He beckoned to a waiter. "Victor, bring us a bottle of champagne, would you? Dom Perignon."

"Right away, Mr. Browning."

Jennifer smiled. "Are you trying to impress me?"

He laughed aloud. "I'm trying to hire you. I imagine you've been getting a lot of offers."

"A few."

"Our firm deals mostly in corporate work, Miss Parker, but some of our more affluent clients frequently get carried away and have need of a criminal defense attorney. I think we could make you a very attractive proposal. Would you care to stop by my office and discuss it?"

"Thank you, Mr. Browning. I'm really flattered, but I just moved into my own offices. I'm hoping it will work out."

He gave her a long look. "It will work out." He raised his eyes as someone approached and got to his feet and held out his hand. "Adam, how are you?"

Jennifer looked up and Adam Warner was standing there shaking hands with Lee Browning. Jennifer's heart began to beat faster and she could feel her face flush. *Idiot schoolgirl!*

Adam Warner looked at Jennifer and Browning and said, "You two know each other?"

"We were just beginning to get acquainted," Lee Browning said easily. "You arrived a little too soon."

"Or just in time." He took Jennifer's arm. "Better luck next time, Lee."

The captain came up to Adam. "Would you like your table now, Mr. Warner, or would you like to have a drink at the bar first?"

"We'll take a table, Henri."

WHEN THEY HAD been seated, Jennifer looked around the room and recognized half a dozen celebrities.

"This place is like a *Who's Who*," she said.

Adam looked at her. "It is now."

Jennifer felt herself blush again. *Stop it, you fool.* She wondered how many other girls Adam Warner had brought here while his wife was sitting at home, waiting for him. She wondered if any of them ever learned that he was married, or whether he always managed to keep that a secret from them. Well, she had an advantage. *You're going to be in for a surprise, Mr. Warner,* Jennifer thought.

They ordered drinks and dinner and busied themselves making small talk. Jennifer let Adam do most of the talking. He was witty and charming, but she was armored against his charm. It was not easy. She found herself smiling at his anecdotes, laughing at his stories.

It won't do him any good, Jennifer told herself. She was not looking for a fling. The specter of her mother haunted her. There was a deep passion within Jennifer that she was afraid to explore, afraid to release.

THEY WERE HAVING dessert and Adam still had not said one word that could be misconstrued. Jennifer had been building up her defenses for nothing, fending off an attack that had never materialized, and she felt like a fool. She wondered what Adam would have said if he knew what she had been thinking all evening. Jennifer smiled at her own vanity.

"I never got a chance to thank you for the clients you sent me," Jennifer said. "I did telephone you a few times, but—"

"I know." Adam hesitated, then added awkwardly, "I didn't want to return your phone calls." Jennifer looked at him in surprise. "I was afraid to," he said simply.

And there it was. He had taken her by surprise, caught her off guard, but his meaning was unmistakable. Jennifer knew what was coming next. And she did not want him to say it. She did not want him to be like all the others, the married men who pretended they were single. She despised them and she did not want to despise this man.

Adam said, quietly, "Jennifer, I want you to know I'm married." She sat there staring at him, her mouth open.

"I'm sorry. I should have told you sooner." He smiled wryly. "Well, there really was no sooner was there?"

Jennifer was filled with a strange confusion. "Why—why did you ask me to dinner, Adam?"

"Because I had to see you again."

Everything began to seem unreal to Jennifer. It was as though she were being pulled under by some giant tidal wave. She sat there listening to Adam saying all the things he felt, and she knew that every word was true. She knew because she felt the same way. She wanted him to stop before he said too much. She wanted him to go on and say more.

"I hope I'm not offending you," Adam said.

There was a sudden shyness about him that shook Jennifer.

"Adam, I—I—"

He looked at her and even though they had not touched, it was as if she were in his arms.

Jennifer said shakily, "Tell me about your wife."

"Mary Beth and I have been married fifteen years. We have no children."

"I see."

"She—we decided not to have any. We were both very young when we got married. I had known her a long time. Our families were neighbors at a summer place we had in Maine. When she was eighteen, her parents were killed in a plane crash. Mary Beth was almost insane with grief. She was all alone. I—we got married."

He married her out of pity and he's too much of a gentleman to say so, Jennifer thought.

"She's a wonderful woman. We've always had a very good relationship."

He was telling Jennifer more than she wanted to know, more than she could handle. Every instinct in her warned her to get away, to flee. In the past she had easily been able to cope with the married men who had tried to become involved with her, but Jennifer knew instinctively that this was different. If she ever let herself fall in love with this man, there would be no way out. She would have to be insane ever to begin anything with him.

Jennifer spoke carefully. "Adam, I like you very much. I don't get involved with married men."

He smiled, and his eyes behind the glasses held honesty and warmth. "I'm not looking for a backstreet affair. I enjoy being with you. I'm very proud of you. I'd like us to see each other once in a while."

Jennifer started to say, *What good would that do?* but the words came out, "That would be good."

So we'll have lunch once a month, Jennifer thought. *It can't hurt anything.*

11

One of Jennifer's first visitors to her new office was Father Ryan. He wandered around the three small rooms and said, "Very nice, indeed. We're getting up in the world, Jennifer."

Jennifer laughed. "This isn't exactly getting up in the world, Father. I have a long way to go."

He eyed her keenly. "You'll make it. By the way, I went to visit Abraham Wilson last week."

"How is he getting along?"

"Fine. They have him working in the prison machine shop. He asked me to give you his regards."

"I'll have to visit him myself one day soon."

Father Ryan sat in his chair, staring at her, until Jennifer said, "Is there something I can do for you, Father?"

He brightened. "Ah, well, I know you must be busy, but now that you've brought it up, a friend of mine has a bit of a problem. She was in an accident. I think you're just the one to help her."

Automatically Jennifer replied, "Have her come in and see me, Father."

"I think you'll have to go to her. She's a quadruple amputee."

. . .

CONNIE GARRETT LIVED in a small, neat apartment on Houston Street. The door was opened for Jennifer by an elderly white-haired woman wearing an apron.

"I'm Martha Steele, Connie's aunt. I live with Connie. Please come in. She's expecting you."

Jennifer walked into a meagerly furnished living room. Connie Garrett was propped up with pillows in a large armchair. Jennifer was shocked by her youth. For some reason, she had expected an older woman. Connie Garrett was about twenty-four, Jennifer's age. There was a wonderful radiance in her face, and Jennifer found it obscene that there was only a torso with no arms or legs attached to it. She repressed a shudder.

Connie Garrett gave her a warm smile and said, "Please sit down, Jennifer. May I call you Jennifer? Father Ryan has told me so much about you. And, of course, I've seen you on television. I'm so glad you could come."

Jennifer started to reply, "My pleasure," and realized how inane it would have sounded. She sat down in a soft comfortable chair opposite the young woman.

"Father Ryan said you were in an accident a few years ago. Do you want to tell me what happened?"

"It was my fault, I'm afraid. I was crossing an intersection and I stepped off the sidewalk and slipped and fell in front of a truck."

"How long ago was this?"

"Three years ago last December. I was on my way to Bloomingdale's to do some Christmas shopping."

"What happened after the truck hit you?"

"I don't remember anything. I woke up in the hospital. They told me that an ambulance brought me there. There was an injury to my spine. Then they found bone damage and it kept spreading until—" She stopped and tried to shrug. It was a pitiful gesture. "They tried to fit me with artificial limbs, but they don't work on me."

"Did you bring suit?"

She looked at Jennifer, puzzled. "Father Ryan didn't tell you?"

"Tell me what?"

"My lawyer sued the utility company whose truck hit me, and we lost the case. We appealed and lost the appeal."

Jennifer said, "He should have mentioned that. If the appellate court turned you down, I'm afraid there's nothing that can be done."

Connie Garrett nodded. "I didn't really believe there was. I just thought—well, Father Ryan said you could work miracles."

"That's *his* territory. I'm only a lawyer."

She was angry with Father Ryan for having given Connie Garrett false hope. Grimly, Jennifer decided she would have a talk with him.

The older woman was hovering in the background. "Can I offer you something, Miss Parker? Some tea and cake, perhaps?"

Jennifer suddenly realized she was hungry, for she had had no time for lunch. But she visualized sitting opposite Connie Garrett while she was being fed by hand, and she could not bear the thought.

"No, thanks," Jennifer lied. "I just had lunch."

All Jennifer wanted to do was get out of there as quickly as possible. She tried to think of some cheering note she could leave on, but there was nothing. *Damn Father Ryan!*

"I—I'm really sorry. I wish I—"

Connie Garrett smiled and said, "Please don't worry about it."

It was the smile that did it. Jennifer was sure if she had been in Connie Garrett's place she would never have been able to smile.

"Who was your lawyer?" Jennifer heard herself asking.

"Melvin Hutcherson. Do you know him?"

"No, but I'll look him up." She went on, without meaning to, "I'll have a talk with him."

"That would be so nice of you." There was warm appreciation in Connie Garrett's voice.

Jennifer thought of what the girl's life must be like, sitting there totally helpless, day after day, month after month, year after year, unable to do anything for herself.

"I can't promise anything, I'm afraid."

"Of course not. But do you know something, Jennifer? I feel better just because you came."

Jennifer rose to her feet. It was a moment to shake hands, but there was no hand to shake.

She said awkwardly, "It was nice meeting you, Connie. You'll hear from me."

On the way back to her office, Jennifer thought about Father Ryan and resolved that she would never succumb to his blandishments again. There was nothing anyone could do for that poor crippled girl, and to offer her any kind of hope was indecent. But she would keep her promise. She would talk to Melvin Hutcherson.

When Jennifer returned to her office there was a long list of messages for her. She looked through them quickly, looking for a message from Adam Warner. There was none.

12

Melvin Hutcherson was a short, balding man with a tiny button nose and washed-out pale blue eyes. He had a shabby suite of offices on the West Side that reeked of poverty. The receptionist's desk was empty.

"Gone to lunch," Melvin Hutcherson explained.

Jennifer wondered if he had a secretary. He ushered her into his private office, which was no larger than the reception office.

"You told me over the phone you wanted to talk about Connie Garrett."

"That's right."

He shrugged. "There's not that much to talk about. We sued and we lost. Believe me, I did a bang-up job for her."

"Did you handle the appeal?"

"Yep. We lost that, too. I'm afraid you're spinning your wheels." He regarded her a moment. "Why do you want to waste your time on something like this? You're hot. You could be working on big money cases."

"I'm doing a friend a favor. Would you mind if I looked at the tran-scripts?"

"Help yourself." Hutcherson shrugged. "They're public property."

JENNIFER SPENT THE evening going over the transcripts of Connie Garrett's lawsuit. To Jennifer's surprise, Melvin Hutcherson had told the truth: He had done a good job. He had named both the city and the Nationwide Motors Corporation as co-defendants, and had demanded a trial by jury. The jury had exonerated both defendants.

The Department of Sanitation had done its best to cope with the snowstorm that had swept the city that December; all its equipment had been in use. The city had argued that the storm was an act of God, and that if there was any negligence, it was on the part of Connie Garrett.

Jennifer turned to the charges against the truck company. Three eye-witnesses had testified that the driver had tried to stop the truck to avoid hitting the victim, but that he had been unable to brake in time, and the truck had gone into an unavoidable spin and had hit her. The verdict in favor of the defendant had been upheld by the Appellate Division and the case had been closed.

Jennifer finished reading the transcripts at three o'clock in the morn-ing. She turned off the lights, unable to sleep. On paper, justice had been done. But the image of Connie Garrett kept coming into her mind. A girl in her twenties, without arms or legs. Jennifer visualized the truck hitting the young girl, the awful agony she must have suffered, the series of terrible operations that had been performed, each one cutting away parts of her limbs. Jennifer turned on the light and sat up in bed. She dialed Melvin Hutcherson's home number.

"There's nothing in the transcripts about the doctors," Jennifer said into the telephone. "Did you look into the possibility of malpractice?"

A groggy voice said, "Who the fuck is this?"

"Jennifer Parker. Did you—"

"For Christ's sake! It's—it's four o'clock in the morning! Don't you have a watch?"

"This is important. The hospital wasn't named in the suit. What about those operations that were performed on Connie Garrett? Did you check into them?"

There was a pause while Melvin Hutcherson tried to gather his thoughts. "I talked to the heads of neurology and orthopedics at the hospital that took care of her. The operations were necessary to save her life. They were performed by the top men there and were done properly. That's why the hospital wasn't named in the suit."

Jennifer felt a sharp sense of frustration. "I see."

"Look, I told you before, you're wasting your time on this one. Now why don't we both get some sleep?"

And the receiver clicked in Jennifer's ear. She turned out the light and lay back again. But sleep was farther away than ever. After a while, Jennifer gave up the struggle, arose and made herself a pot of coffee. She sat on her sofa drinking it, watching the rising sun paint the Manhattan skyline, the faint pink gradually turning into a bright, explosive red.

Jennifer was disturbed. For every injustice there was supposed to be a remedy at law. Had justice been done in Connie Garrett's case? She glanced at the clock on the wall. It was six-thirty. Jennifer picked up the telephone again and dialed Melvin Hutcherson's number.

"Did you check out the record of the truck driver?" Jennifer asked.

A sleepy voice said, "Jesus Christ! Are you some kind of crazy? When do you sleep?"

"The driver of the utility truck. Did you check out his record?"

"Lady, you're beginning to insult me."

"I'm sorry," Jennifer insisted, "but I have to know."

"The answer is yes. He had a perfect record. This was his first accident."

So that avenue was closed. "I see." Jennifer was thinking hard.

"Miss Parker," Melvin Hutcherson said, "do me a big favor, will you? If you have any more questions, call me during office hours."

"Sorry," Jennifer said absently. "Go back to sleep."

"Thanks a lot!"

Jennifer replaced the receiver. It was time to get dressed and go to work.

13

It had been three weeks since Jennifer had had dinner with Adam at Lutèce. She tried to put him out of her mind, but everything reminded her of Adam: A chance phrase, the back of a stranger's head, a tie similar to the one he had worn. There were many men who tried to date her. She was propositioned by clients, by attorneys she had opposed in court and by a night-court judge, but Jennifer wanted none of them. Lawyers invited her out for what was cynically referred to as "funch," but she was not interested. There was an independence about her that was a challenge to men.

Ken Bailey was always there, but that fact did nothing to assuage Jennifer's loneliness. There was only one person who could do that, damn him!

He telephoned on a Monday morning. "I thought I'd take a chance and see if you happened to be free for lunch today."

She was not. She said, "Of course I am."

Jennifer had sworn to herself that if Adam ever called her again she would be friendly yet distant, and courteous but definitely not available.

The moment she heard Adam's voice she forgot all those things and said, *Of course I am.*

The last thing in the world she should have said.

THEY HAD LUNCH at a small restaurant in Chinatown, and they talked steadily for two hours that seemed like two minutes. They talked about law and politics and the theater, and solved all the complex problems of the world. Adam was brilliant and incisive and fascinating. He was genuinely interested in what Jennifer was doing, and took a joyous pride in her successes. *He has a right to,* Jennifer thought. *If not for him, I'd be back in Kelso, Washington.*

WHEN JENNIFER RETURNED to the office, Ken Bailey was waiting for her.

"Have a good lunch?"

"Yes, thank you."

"Is Adam Warner going to become a client?" His tone was too casual.

"No, Ken. We're just friends."

And it was true.

THE FOLLOWING WEEK, Adam invited Jennifer to have lunch in the private dining room of his law firm. Jennifer was impressed with the huge, modern complex of offices. Adam introduced her to various members of the firm, and Jennifer felt like a minor celebrity, for they seemed to know all about her. She met Stewart Needham, the senior partner. He was distantly polite to Jennifer, and she remembered that Adam was married to his niece.

Adam and Jennifer had lunch in the walnut-paneled dining room run by a chef and two waiters.

"This is where the partners bring their problems."

Jennifer wondered whether he was referring to her.

It was hard for her to concentrate on the meal.

JENNIFER THOUGHT ABOUT Adam all that afternoon. She knew she had to forget about him, had to stop seeing him. He belonged to another woman.

• • •

THAT NIGHT, JENNIFER went with Ken Bailey to see *Two by Two*, the new Richard Rodgers show.

As they stepped into the lobby there was an excited buzz from the crowd, and Jennifer turned to see what was happening. A long, black limousine had pulled up to the curb and a man and woman were stepping out of the car.

"It's him!" a woman exclaimed, and people began to gather around the car. The burly chauffeur stepped aside and Jennifer saw Michael Moretti and his wife. It was Michael that the crowd focused on. He was a folk hero, handsome enough to be a movie star, daring enough to have captured everyone's imagination. Jennifer stood in the lobby watching as Michael Moretti and his wife made their way through the crowd. Michael passed within three feet of Jennifer, and for an instant their eyes met. Jennifer noticed that his eyes were so black that she could not see his pupils. A moment later he disappeared into the theater.

Jennifer was unable to enjoy the show. The sight of Michael Moretti had brought back a flood of fiercely humiliating memories. Jennifer asked Ken to take her home after the first act.

ADAM TELEPHONED JENNIFER the next day and Jennifer steeled herself to refuse his invitation. *Thank you, Adam, but I'm really very busy.*

But all Adam said was, "I have to go out of the country for a while."

It was like a blow to the stomach. "How—how long will you be gone?"

"Just a few weeks. I'll give you a call when I get back."

"Fine," Jennifer said brightly. "Have a nice trip."

She felt as though someone had died. She visualized Adam on a beach in Rio, surrounded by half-naked girls, or in a penthouse in Mexico City, drinking margaritas with a nubile, dark-eyed beauty, or in a Swiss chalet making love to—*Stop it!* Jennifer told herself. She should have asked him where he was going. It was probably a business trip to some dreary place where he would have no time for women, perhaps the middle of some desert where he would be working twenty-four hours a day.

She should have broached the subject, very casually, of course. *Will you be taking a long plane trip? Do you speak any foreign languages? If you get to Paris, bring me back some Vervaine tea. I suppose the shots must be painful. Are you taking your wife with you? Am I losing my mind?*

Ken had come into her office and was staring at her. "You're talking to yourself. Are you okay?"

No! Jennifer wanted to shout. *I need a doctor. I need a cold shower. I need Adam Warner.*

She said, "I'm fine. Just a little tired."

"Why don't you get to bed early tonight?"

She wondered whether Adam would be going to bed early.

FATHER RYAN CALLED. "I went to see Connie Garrett. She told me you've dropped by a few times."

"Yes." The visits were to assuage her feeling of guilt because she was unable to be of any help. It was frustrating.

JENNIFER PLUNGED HERSELF into work, and still the weeks seemed to drag by. She was in court nearly every day and worked on briefs almost every night.

"Slow down. You're going to kill yourself," Ken advised her.

But Jennifer needed to exhaust herself physically and mentally. She did not want to have time to think. *I'm a fool,* she thought. *An unadulterated fool.*

It was four weeks before Adam called.

"I JUST GOT back," he said. The sound of his voice thrilled her. "Can we meet for lunch somewhere?"

"Yes. I'd enjoy that, Adam." She thought she had carried that off well. A simple *Yes, I'd enjoy that, Adam.*

"The Oak Room in the Plaza?"

"Fine."

It was the most businesslike, unromantic dining room in the world, filled with affluent middle-aged wheelers and dealers, stockbrokers and bankers. It had long been one of the few remaining bastions of privacy for men, and its doors had only recently been opened to women.

Jennifer arrived early and was seated. A few minutes later, Adam appeared. Jennifer watched the tall, lean figure moving toward her and her mouth suddenly went dry. He looked tanned, and Jennifer wondered if her fantasies about Adam on some girl-ridden beach had been true. He smiled at her and took her hand, and Jennifer knew in that moment that it did not matter what logic she used about Adam Warner or married men. She had no control over herself. It was as though someone else were guiding her, telling her what she should do, telling her what she must do. She could not explain what was happening to her, for she had never experienced anything like it. *Call it chemistry,* she thought. *Call it karma, call it heaven.* All Jennifer knew was that she wanted to be in Adam Warner's arms more than she had ever wanted anything in her life. Looking at him, she visualized his making love to her, holding her, his hard body on top of her, inside her, and she felt her face becoming red.

Adam said apologetically, "Sorry about the short notice. A client canceled a luncheon date."

Jennifer silently blessed the client.

"I brought you something," Adam said. It was a lovely green and gold silk scarf. "It's from Milán."

So *that's* where he had been. *Italian girls.* "It's beautiful, Adam. Thank you."

"Have you ever been to Milan?"

"No. I've seen pictures of the cathedral there. It's lovely."

"I'm not much of a sightseer. My theory is that if you've seen one church, you've seen them all."

Later, when Jennifer thought about that luncheon, she tried to remember what they had talked about, what they had eaten, who had stopped by the table to say hello to Adam, but all she could remember was the nearness of Adam, his touch, his looks. It was as though he had her in some kind of spell and she was mesmerized, helpless to break it.

At one point Jennifer thought, *I know what to do. I'll make love with him. Once. It can't be as wonderful as my fantasies. Then I'll be able to get over him.*

When their hands touched accidentally, it was like an electric charge between them. They sat there talking of everything and nothing, and their words had no meaning. They sat at the table, locked in an invisible embrace, caressing each other, making fierce love, naked and wanton. Neither of them had any idea what they were eating or what they were saying. There was a different, more demanding hunger in them and it kept mounting and mounting, until neither of them could stand it any longer.

In the middle of their luncheon, Adam put his hand over Jennifer's and said huskily, "Jennifer—"

She whispered, "Yes. Let's get out of here."

Jennifer waited in the busy, crowded lobby while Adam registered at the desk. They were given a room in the old section of the Plaza Hotel, overlooking 58th Street. They used the back bank of elevators, and it seemed to Jennifer that it took forever to reach their floor.

If Jennifer was unable to remember anything about the luncheon, she remembered everything about their room. Years later, she could recall the view, the color of the drapes and carpets, and each picture and piece of furniture. She could remember the sounds of the city, far below, that drifted into the room. The images of that afternoon were to stay with her the rest of her life. It was a magic, multicolored explosion in slow motion. It was having Adam undress her, it was Adam's strong, lean body in bed, his roughness and his gentleness. It was laughter and passion. Their hunger had built to a greed that had to be satisfied. The moment Adam began to make love to her, the words that flashed into Jennifer's mind were, *I'm lost.*

They made love again and again, and each time was an ecstasy that was almost unbearable.

HOURS LATER, AS they lay there quietly, Adam said, "I feel as though I'm alive for the first time in my life."

Jennifer gently stroked his chest and laughed aloud.

Adam looked at her quizzically. "What's so funny?"

"Do you know what I told myself? That if I went to bed with you once, I could get you out of my system."

He twisted around and looked down at her. "And—?"

"I was wrong. I feel as though you're a part of me. At least"—she hesitated—"*part* of you is a part of me."

He knew what she was thinking.

"We'll work something out," Adam said. "Mary Beth is leaving Monday for Europe with her aunt for a month."

14

Jennifer and Adam Warner were together almost every night.

He spent the first night at her uncomfortable little apartment and in the morning he declared, "We're taking the day off to find you a decent place to live."

They went apartment hunting together, and late that afternoon Jennifer signed a lease in a new high-rise building off Sutton Place, called The Belmont Towers. The sign in front of the building had read *Sold Out*.

"Why are we going in?" Jennifer asked.

"You'll see."

The apartment they looked at was a lovely five-room duplex, beautifully furnished. It was the most luxurious apartment Jennifer had ever seen. There was a master bedroom and bath upstairs, and downstairs a guest bedroom with its own bath and a living room that had a spectacular view of the East River and the city. There was a large terrace, a kitchen and a dining room.

"How do you like it?" Adam asked.

"Like it? I love it," Jennifer exclaimed, "but there are two problems, darling. First of all, I couldn't possibly afford it. And secondly, even if I could, it belongs to someone else."

"It belongs to our law firm. We leased it for visiting VIP's. I'll have them find another place."

"What about the rent?"

"I'll take care of that. I—"

"No."

"That's crazy, darling. I can easily afford it and—"

She shook her head. "You don't understand, Adam. I have nothing to give you except me. I want that to be a gift."

He took her in his arms and Jennifer snuggled against him and said, "I know what—I'll work nights."

SATURDAY THEY WENT on a shopping spree. Adam bought Jennifer a beautiful silk nightgown and robe at Bonwit Teller, and Jennifer bought Adam a Turnbull & Asser shirt. They purchased a chess game at Gimbel's and cheesecake in Junior's near Abraham & Straus. They bought a Fortnum & Mason plum pudding at Altman's, and books at Doubleday. They visited the Gammon Shop and Caswell-Massey, where Adam bought Jennifer enough potpourri to last for ten years. They had dinner around the corner from the apartment.

THEY WOULD MEET at the apartment in the evening after work and discuss the day's events, and Jennifer would cook dinner while Adam set the table. Afterward, they read or watched television or played gin rummy or chess. Jennifer prepared Adam's favorite dishes.

"I'm shameless," she told him. "I won't stop at anything."

He held her close. "Please don't."

IT WAS STRANGE, Jennifer thought. Before they began their affair they saw each other openly. But now that they were lovers, they dared not appear in public together, so they went to places where they were not apt to ran into friends: small family restaurants downtown, a chamber music concert at the Third Street Music School Settlement. They went to see a new play at the Omni Theatre Club on 18th Street and had dinner at the Grotta Azzurra on Broome Street, and ate so much that they swore off Italian food for a month. *Only we don't have a month,* Jennifer thought. Mary Beth was returning in fourteen days.

They went to The Half Note to hear avant-garde jazz in the Village, and peeked into the windows of the small art galleries.

Adam loved sports. He took Jennifer to watch the Knicks play, and Jennifer got so caught up in the game she cheered until she was hoarse.

On Sunday they lazed around, having breakfast in their robes, trading sections of the *Times,* listening to the church bells ring across Manhattan, each offering up its own prayer.

Jennifer looked over at Adam absorbed in the crossword puzzle and thought: *Say a prayer for me.* She knew what she was doing was wrong. She knew it could not last. And yet, she had never known such happiness, such euphoria. Lovers lived in a special world, where every sense was hightened, and the joy Jennifer felt now with Adam was worth the price she would have to pay later. And she knew she was going to have to pay.

TIME TOOK ON a different dimension. Before, Jennifer's life had been measured out in hours and meetings with clients. Now her time was counted by the minutes she could spend with Adam. She thought about him when she was with him, and she thought about him when she was away from him.

Jennifer had read of men having heart attacks in the arms of their mistresses, and so she put the number of Adam's personal physician in her private telephone book by her bedside so that if anything ever happened it could be handled discreetly and Adam would not be embarrassed.

Jennifer was filled with emotions that she had not known existed in her. She had never thought of herself as being domestic, but she wanted to do everything for Adam. She wanted to cook for him, to clean for him, to lay out his clothes in the morning. To take care of him.

Adam kept a set of clothes at the apartment, and he would spend most nights with Jennifer. She would lie next to him, watching him fall asleep, and she would try to stay awake as long as possible, terrified of losing a moment of their precious time together. Finally, when Jennifer could keep her eyes open no longer, she would snuggle in Adam's arms and fall asleep, contented and safe. The insomnia that had plagued Jennifer for so long had vanished. Whatever night devils had tormented her had disappeared. When she curled up in Adam's arms, she was instantly at peace.

She enjoyed walking around the apartment in Adam's shirts, and at night she would wear his pajama top. If she was still in bed in the morning when he left, Jennifer would roll over to his side of the bed. She loved the warm smell of him.

It seemed that all the popular love songs she heard had been written for Adam and her, and Jennifer thought, *Noel Coward was right. It's amazing how potent cheap music can be.*

In the beginning, Jennifer had thought that the overwhelming physical feeling they had for each other would diminish in time, but instead it grew stronger.

She told Adam things about herself that she had never told another human being. With Adam, there were no masks. She was Jennifer Parker, stripped naked, and still he loved her. It was a miracle. And they shared another miracle together: laughter.

Impossibly, she loved Adam more each day. She wished that what they had would never end. But she knew it would. For the first time in her life, she became superstitious. There was a special blend of Kenya coffee that Adam liked. Jennifer bought some every few days.

But she bought only one small can at a time.

ONE OF JENNIFER'S terrors was that something would happen to Adam when he was away from her and that she would not know it until she read about it, or heard about it on a news program. She never told Adam of her fears.

Whenever Adam was going to be late he would leave notes for Jennifer around the apartment where she would come upon them unexpectedly. She would find them in the breadbox or in the refrigerator, or in her shoe; they delighted her, and she saved each one.

THEIR LAST REMAINING days together raced by in a blur of joyous activity. Finally, it was the night before Mary Beth was to return. Jennifer and Adam had dinner in the apartment, listened to music and made love.

Jennifer lay awake all night, holding Adam in her arms. Her thoughts were of the happiness they had shared.

The pain would come later.

At breakfast, Adam said, "Whatever happens, I want you to know this—you're the only woman I've ever truly loved."

The pain came then.

15

The anodyne was work, and Jennifer immersed herself in it totally so that she had no time to think.

She had become the darling of the press, and her courtroom successes were highly publicized. More clients came to her than she could handle, and while Jennifer's chief interest was in criminal law, at Ken's urging she began to accept a variety of other cases.

Ken Bailey had become more important than ever to Jennifer. He handled the investigations on her cases, and he was brilliant. She was able to discuss other problems with him and she valued his advice.

Jennifer and Ken moved again, this time into a large suite of offices on Park Avenue. Jennifer hired two bright young attorneys, Dan Martin and Ted Harris, both from Robert Di Silva's staff, and two more secretaries.

Dan Martin was a former football player from Northwestern University and he had the appearance of an athlete and the mind of a scholar.

Ted Harris was a slight, diffident young man who wore thick milk-bottle spectacles and was a genius.

Martin and Harris took care of the legwork and Jennifer handled the appearances at trials.

The sign on the door read: *JENNIFER PARKER & ASSOCIATES.*

THE CASES THAT came into the office ranged from defending a large industrial corporation on a pollution charge to representing a drunk who had suffered whiplash when he was bounced from a tavern. The drunk, of course, was a gift from Father Ryan.

"He has a bit of a problem," Father Ryan told Jennifer. "He's really a decent family man, but the poor fellow has such pressures that he sometimes takes a drop too much."

Jennifer could not help but smile. As far as Father Ryan was concerned, none of his parishioners was guilty and his only desire was to help them get out of the difficulty they had carelessly gotten themselves into. One reason Jennifer understood the priest so well was that basically she felt the same as he did. They were dealing with people in trouble who had no one to help them, with neither the money nor the power to fight the Establishment, and in the end they were crushed by it.

The word *justice* was honored mostly in the breach. In the courtroom, neither prosecuting attorney nor the defense attorney sought justice: The name of the game was to win.

FROM TIME TO time, Jennifer and Father Ryan talked about Connie Garrett, but the subject always left Jennifer depressed. There was an injustice there and it rankled her.

IN HIS OFFICE in the back room of Tony's Place, Michael Moretti watched as Nick Vito carefully swept the office with an electronic device, looking for gypsy taps. Through his police connections, Michael knew that no electronic surveillance had been authorized by the authorities, but once in a while an overzealous tin hotdog, a young detective, would set up a gypsy—or illegal—tap, hoping to pick up information. Michael was a careful man. His office and home were swept every morning and every evening. He was aware that he was the number one target for half a dozen different law agencies, but he was not concerned. He knew what they were doing, but they did not know what he was doing; and if they did, they could not prove it.

Sometimes late at night Michael would look through the peephole of the restaurant's back door and watch the FBI agents pick up his garbage for analysis, and substitute other garbage for it.

One night Nick Vito said, "Jesus, boss, what if the jokers dig up something?"

Michael laughed. "I hope they do. Before they get here we switch our garbage with the restaurant next door."

No, the federal agents were not going to touch him. The Family's activities were expanding, and Michael had plans that he had not even revealed yet. The only stumbling block was Thomas Colfax. Michael knew he had to get rid of the old lawyer. He needed a fresh young mind. And again and again, his thoughts turned to Jennifer Parker.

ADAM AND JENNIFER met for lunch once a week, and it was torture for both of them, for they had no time to be alone together, no privacy. They talked on the telephone every day, using code names. He was Mr. Adams and she was Mrs. Jay.

"I hate sneaking around like this," Adam said.

"I do too." But the thought of losing him terrified her.

THE COURTROOM WAS where Jennifer escaped from her own private pain. The courtroom was a stage, an area where she matched wits against the best that the opposition could offer. Her school was the courtroom and she learned well. A trial was a game played within certain rigid rules, where the better player won, and Jennifer was determined to be the better player.

Jennifer's cross-examinations became theatrical events, with a skilled speed and rhythm and timing. She learned to recognize the leader of a jury and to concentrate on him, knowing he could swing the others into line.

A man's shoes said something about his character. Jennifer looked for jurors who wore comfortable shoes, because they were inclined to be easygoing.

She learned about strategy, the overall plan of a trial, and about tactics, the day-by-day maneuvers. She became an expert at shopping for friendly judges.

Jennifer spent endless hours preparing each case, heeding the adage, *Most cases are won or lost before the trial begins.* She became adept at mnemonics so that she could remember jurors' names: Smith—a muscular man who could handle an anvil; Helm—a man steering a boat; Newman—a newborn baby.

The court usually recessed at four o'clock, and when Jennifer was cross-examining a witness in the late afternoon, she would stall until a few minutes before four and then hit the witness with a verbal blow that would leave a strong overnight impression on the jury.

She learned to read body language. When a witness on the stand was lying, there would be telltale gestures: stroking the chin, pressing the lips together, covering the mouth, pulling the earlobes or grooming the hair. Jennifer became an expert at reading those signs, and she would zero in for the kill.

Jennifer discovered that being a woman was a disadvantage when it came to practicing criminal law. She was in macho territory. There were still very few women criminal attorneys and some of the male lawyers resented Jennifer. On her briefcase one day Jennifer found a sticker that read: *Women Lawyers Make the Best Motions.* In retaliation, Cynthia put a sign on her desk that read: *A Woman's Place is in the House . . . and in the Senate.*

MOST JURIES STARTED out by being prejudiced against Jennifer, for many of the cases she handled were sordid, and there was a tendency to make an association between her and her client. She was expected to dress like Jane Eyre and she refused, but she was careful to dress in such a fashion that she would not arouse the envy of the women jurors, and at the same time appear feminine enough so as not to antagonize the men who might feel she was a lesbian. At one time, Jennifer would have laughed at any of these considerations. But in the courtroom she found them to be stern realities. Because she had entered a man's world she had to work twice as hard and be twice as good as the competition. Jennifer learned to prepare thoroughly not only her own cases, but the cases of her opposition as well. She would lie in bed at night or sit at the desk in her office and plot her opponent's strategy. What would she do if she were on the other side? What surprises would she try to pull? She was a general, planning both sides of a lethal battle.

CYNTHIA BUZZED ON the intercom. "There's a man on line three who wants to talk to you, but he won't give his name or tell me what it's about."

Six months earlier, Cynthia would simply have hung up on the man. Jennifer had taught her never to turn anyone away.

"Put him through," Jennifer said.

A moment later she heard a man's voice ask cautiously, "Is this Jennifer Parker?"

"Yes."

He hesitated. "Is this a safe line?"

"Yes. What can I do for you?"

"It's not for me. It's for—for a friend of mine."

"I see. What's your friend's problem?"

"This has to be in confidence, you understand."

"I understand."

Cynthia walked in and handed Jennifer the mail. "Wait," Jennifer mouthed.

"My friend's family locked her up in an insane asylum. She's sane. It's a conspiracy. The authorities are in on it."

Jennifer was only half-listening now. She braced the telephone against her shoulder while she went through the morning's mail.

The man was saying, "She's rich and her family's after her money."

Jennifer said, "Go on," and continued examining the mail.

"They'd probably have me put away, too, if they found I was trying to help her. It could be dangerous for me, Miss Parker."

A nut case, Jennifer decided. She said, "I'm afraid I can't do anything, but I'd suggest you get hold of a good psychiatrist to help your friend."

"You don't understand. They're all in on it."

"I do understand," Jennifer said soothingly. "I—"

"Will you help her?"

"There's nothing I can—I'll tell you what. Why don't you give me your friend's name and address and if I get a chance, I'll look into it."

There was a long silence. Finally the man spoke. "This is confidential, remember."

Jennifer wished he would get off the telephone. Her first appointment was waiting in the reception room. "I'll remember."

"Cooper. Helen Cooper. She had a big estate on Long Island, but they took it away from her."

Obediently, Jennifer made a note on a pad in front of her. "Fine. What sanatorium did you say she was in?" There was a click and the line went dead. Jennifer threw the note into the waste basket.

Jennifer and Cynthia exchanged a look. "It's a weird world out there," Cynthia said. "Miss Marshall is waiting to see you."

JENNIFER HAD TALKED to Loretta Marshall on the telephone a week earlier. Miss Marshall had asked Jennifer to represent her in a paternity suit against Curtis Randall III, a wealthy socialite.

Jennifer had spoken to Ken Bailey. "We need information on Curtis Randall III. He lives in New York, but I understand he spends a lot of time in Palm Beach. I want to know what his background is, and if he's been sleeping with a girl named Loretta Marshall."

She had told Ken the names of the Palm Beach hotels that the woman had given her. Two days later, Ken Bailey had reported back.

"It checks out. They spent two weeks together at hotels in Palm Beach, Miami and Atlantic City. Loretta Marshall gave birth to a daughter eight months ago."

Jennifer sat back in her chair and looked at him thoughtfully. "It sounds as though we might have a case."

"I don't think so."

"What's the problem?"

"The problem is our client. She's slept with everybody including the Yankees."

"You're saying that the father of the baby could be any number of men."

"I'm saying it could be half the world."

"Are any of the others wealthy enough to give child support?"

"Well, the Yankees are pretty rich, but the big league moneyman is Curtis Randall III."

He handed her a long list of names.

. . .

LORETTA MARSHALL WALKED into the office. Jennifer had not been sure what to expect. A pretty, empty-headed prostitute, in all probability. But Loretta Marshall was a complete surprise. Not only was she not pretty, she was almost homely. Her figure was ordinary. From the number of Miss Marshall's romantic conquests, Jennifer had expected nothing less than a sexy raving beauty. Loretta Marshall was the stereotype of an elementary grade schoolteacher. She was clad in a plaid wool skirt, a button-down-collar shirt, a dark blue cardigan and sensible shoes. At first, Jennifer had been sure that Loretta Marshall was planning to use her to force Curtis Randall to pay for the privilege of raising a baby that was not his. After an hour's conversation with the girl, Jennifer found that her opinion had changed. Loretta Marshall was transparently honest.

"Of course, I have no proof that Curtis is Melanie's father." She smiled shyly. "Curtis isn't the only man I've slept with."

"Then what makes you think he's the father of your child, Miss Marshall?"

"I don't *think*. I'm sure of it. It's hard to explain, but I even know the night Melanie was conceived. Sometimes a woman can feel those things."

Jennifer studied her, trying to find any sign of guile or deceit. There was none. The girl was totally without pretense. Perhaps, Jennifer thought, men found that part of her charm.

"Are you in love with Curtis Randall?"

"Oh, yes. And Curtis said he loved me. Of course, I'm not sure he still does, after what's happened."

If you loved him, Jennifer wondered, *how could you have slept with all those other men?* The answer might have lain in that sad, homely face and plain figure.

"Can you help me, Miss Parker?"

Jennifer said cautiously, "Paternity cases are always difficult. I have a list of more than a dozen men you've slept with in the past year. There are probably others. If I have such a list, you can be sure that Curtis Randall's attorney will have one."

Loretta Marshall frowned. "What about blood samples, that kind of thing . . . ?"

"Blood tests are admissible in evidence only if they prove that the defendant could not be the father. They're legally inconclusive."

"I don't really care about me. It's Melanie I want protected. It's only right that Curtis should take care of his daughter."

Jennifer hesitated, weighing her decision. She had told Loretta Marshall the truth. Paternity cases were difficult. To say nothing about being messy and unpleasant. The attorneys for the defense would have a field day when they got this woman on the stand. They would bring up a parade of her lovers and, before they were through, they would make her look like a whore. It was not the type of case that Jennifer wanted to become involved in. On the other hand, she believed Loretta Marshall. This was no ordinary gold digger out to gouge an ex-lover. The girl was convinced that Curtis Randall was the father of her child. Jennifer made her decision.

"All right," she said, "we'll take a crack at it."

JENNIFER SET UP a meeting with Roger Davis, the lawyer representing Curtis Randall. Davis was a partner in a large Wall Street firm and the importance of his position was indicated by the spacious corner suite he occupied. He was pompous and arrogant, and Jennifer disliked him on sight.

"What can I do for you?" Roger Davis asked.

"As I explained on the telephone, I'm here on behalf of Loretta Marshall."

He looked at her and said impatiently, "So?"

"She's asked me to institute a paternity suit against Mr. Curtis Randall III. I would prefer not to do that."

"You'd be a damned fool if you did."

Jennifer held her temper in check. "We don't wish to drag your client's name through the courts. As I'm sure you know, this kind of case always gets nasty. Therefore, we're prepared to accept a reasonable out-of-court settlement."

Roger Davis gave Jennifer a wintry smile. "I'm sure you are. Because you have no case. None at all."

"I think we have."

"Miss Parker, I haven't time to mince words. Your client is a whore.

She'll have intercourse with anything that moves. I have a list of men she's slept with. It's as long as my arm. You think *my* client is going to get hurt? Your client will be *destroyed*. She's a schoolteacher, I believe. Well, when I get through with her she'll never teach anywhere again as long as she lives. And I'll tell you something else. Randall believes he's the father of that baby. But you'll never prove it in a million years."

Jennifer sat back, listening, her face expressionless.

"Our position is that your client could have become impregnated by anyone in the Third Army. You want to make a deal? Fine. I'll tell you what we'll do. We'll buy your client birth-control pills so that it doesn't happen again."

Jennifer stood up, her cheeks burning. "Mr. Davis," she said, "that little speech of yours is going to cost your client half a million dollars."

And Jennifer was out the door.

KEN BAILEY AND three assistants could turn up nothing against Curtis Randall III. He was a widower, a pillar of society, and he had had very few sexual flings.

"The son of a bitch is a born-again puritan," Ken Bailey complained.

They were seated in the conference room at midnight, the night before the paternity trial was to begin. "I've talked to one of the attorneys in Davis's office, Jennifer. They're going to destroy our client. They're not bluffing."

"Why are you sticking your neck out for this girl?" Dan Martin asked.

"I'm not here to judge her sex life, Dan. She believes that Curtis Randall is the father of her baby. I mean, she really *believes* it. All she wants is money for her daughter—nothing for herself. I think she deserves her day in court."

"We're not thinking about her," Ken replied. "We're thinking about you. You're on a hot roll. Everybody's watching you. I think this is a no-win case. It's going to be a black mark against you."

"Let's all get some sleep," Jennifer said. "I'll see you in court."

THE TRIAL WENT even worse than Ken Bailey had predicted. Jennifer had had Loretta Marshall bring her baby into the courtroom, but now

Jennifer wondered if she had not made a tactical error. She sat there, helpless, as Roger Davis brought witness after witness to the stand and forced each of them to admit they had slept with Loretta Marshall. Jennifer did not dare cross-examine them. They were victims, and they were testifying in public only because they had been forced to. All Jennifer could do was sit by while her client's name was besmirched. She watched the faces of the jurors, and she could read the growing hostility there. Roger Davis was too clever to characterize Loretta Marshall as a whore. He did not have to. The people on the stand did it for him.

Jennifer had brought in her own character witnesses to testify to the good work that Loretta Marshall had done as a teacher, to the fact that she attended church regularly and was a good mother, but all this made no impression in the face of the horrifying array of Loretta Marshall's lovers. Jennifer had hoped to play on the sympathy of the jury by dramatizing the plight of a young woman who had been betrayed by a wealthy playboy and then abandoned when she had become pregnant. The trial was not working out that way.

CURTIS RANDALL III was seated at the defendant's table. He could have been chosen by a casting director. He was an elegant-looking man in his late fifties, with striking gray hair and tanned, regular features. He came from a social background, belonged to all the right clubs and was wealthy and successful. Jennifer could feel the women on the jury mentally undressing him.

Sure, Jennifer thought. *They're thinking that they're worthy to go to bed with Mr. Charming, but not that what-does-he-see-in-her slut sitting in the courtroom with a ten-month old baby in her arms.*

Unfortunately for Loretta Marshall, the child looked nothing like its father. Or its mother, for that matter. It could have belonged to anybody.

As though reading Jennifer's thoughts, Roger Davis said to the jury, "There they sit, ladies and gentlemen, mother and child. Ah! But *whose* child? You've seen the defendant. I defy anyone in this courtroom to point out *one single point of resemblance* between the defendant and this infant. Surely, if my client were the father of this child, there would be *some* sign of it. Something in the eyes, the nose, the chin. Where is that resemblance? It doesn't exist, and for a very simple reason. The defendant is not the father of this child. No, I'm very much afraid that what we have here is the classic example of a loose woman who was careless, got pregnant, and then looked around to see which lover could best afford to pay the bills."

His voice softened. "Now, none of us is here to judge her. What Loretta Marshall chooses to do with her personal life is her own business. The fact that she is a teacher and can influence the minds of small children, well, that is not in my purview, either. I am not here to moralize; I'm simply here to protect the interests of an innocent man."

Jennifer studied the jury and she had the sinking feeling that every one of them was on the side of Curtis Randall. Jennifer still believed Loretta Marshall. If only the baby looked like its father! Roger Davis was right. There was no resemblance at all. And he had made sure the jury was aware of that.

JENNIFER CALLED CURTIS Randall to the stand. She knew that this was her only chance to try to repair the damage that had been done, her final opportunity to turn the case around. She studied the man in the witness chair for a moment.

"Have you ever been married, Mr. Randall?"

"Yes. My wife died in a fire." There was an instinctive reaction of sympathy from the jury.

Damn! Jennifer moved on quickly. "You never remarried?"

"No. I loved my wife very much, and I—"

"Did you and your wife have any children?"

"No. Unfortunately, she was not able to."

Jennifer gestured toward the baby. "Then Melanie is your only—"

"Objection!"

"Sustained. Counsel for the plaintiff knows better than that."

"I'm sorry, Your Honor. It slipped out." Jennifer turned back to Curtis Randall. "Do you like children?"

"Yes, very much."

"You're the chairman of the board of your own corporation, are you not, Mr. Randall?"

"Yes."

"Haven't you ever wished for a son to carry on your name?"

"I suppose every man wants that."

"So if Melanie had been born a boy instead of—"

"Objection!"

"Sustained." The judge turned to Jennifer. "Miss Parker, I will ask you again to stop doing that."

"Sorry, Your Honor." Jennifer turned back to Curtis Randall. "Mr. Randall, are you in the habit of picking up strange women and taking them to hotels?"

Curtis Randall ran his tongue nervously over his lower lip. "No, I am not."

"Isn't it true that you first met Loretta Marshall in a bar and took her to a hotel room?"

His tongue was working at his lips again. "Yes, ma'am, but that was just—that was just sex."

Jennifer stared at him. "You say 'that was just sex' as though you feel sex is something dirty."

"No, ma'am." His tongue flicked out again.

Jennifer was watching it, fascinated, as it moved across his lips. She was filled with a sudden, wild sense of hope. She knew now what she had to do. She had to keep pushing him. And yet she could not push him so hard that the jury would become antagonistic toward her.

"How many women have you picked up in bars?"

Roger Davis was on his feet. "Irrelevant, Your Honor. And I object to this line of questioning. The only woman involved in this case is Loretta Marshall. We have already stipulated that the defendant had sexual intercourse with her. Aside from that, his personal life has no relevance in this courtroom."

"I disagree, Your Honor. If the defendant is the kind of man who—"

"Sustained. Please discontinue that line of questioning, Miss Parker."

Jennifer shrugged. "Yes, Your Honor." She turned back to Curtis Randall. "Let's get back to the night you picked up Loretta Marshall in a bar. What kind of bar was it?"

"I—I really don't know. I'd never been there before."

"It was a singles bar, wasn't it?"

"I have no idea."

"Well, for your information, the *Play Pen* was and is a singles bar. It has the reputation of being a pickup place, a rendezvous where men and women go to meet partners they can take to bed. Isn't that why you went there, Mr. Randall?"

Curtis Randall began to lick his lips again. "It—it may have been. I don't remember."

"You don't remember?" Jennifer's voice was weighted with sarcasm. "Do you happen to remember the date on which you first met Loretta Marshall in that bar?"

"No, I don't. Not exactly."

"Then let me refresh your memory."

Jennifer walked over to the plaintiffs table and began looking through some papers. She scribbled a note as though she were copying a date and handed it to Ken Bailey. He studied it, a puzzled expression on his face.

Jennifer moved back toward the witness box. "It was on January eighteenth, Mr. Randall."

Out of the corner of her eye, Jennifer saw Ken Bailey leaving the courtroom.

"It could have been, I suppose. As I said, I don't remember."

For the next fifteen minutes, Jennifer went on questioning Curtis Randall. It was a rambling, gentle cross-examination, and Roger Davis did not interrupt, because he saw that Jennifer was making no points with the jurors, who were beginning to look bored.

Jennifer kept talking, keeping an eye out for Ken Bailey. In the middle of a question, Jennifer saw him hurry into the courtroom, carrying a small package.

Jennifer turned to the judge. "Your Honor, may I ask for a fifteen-minute recess?"

The judge looked at the clock on the wall. "Since it's almost time for lunch, the court will adjourn until one-thirty."

AT ONE-THIRTY THE court was in session again. Jennifer had moved Loretta Marshall to a seat closer to the jury box, with the baby on her lap.

The judge said, "Mr. Randall, you are still under oath. You will not have to be sworn in again. Take the stand, please."

Jennifer watched as Curtis Randall sat down in the witness box. She walked up to him and said, "Mr. Randall, how many illegitimate children have you sired?"

Roger Davis was on his feet. "Objection! This is outrageous, Your Honor. I will not have my client subjected to this kind of humiliation."

The judge said, "Objection sustained." He turned to Jennifer. "Miss Parker, I have warned you—"

Jennifer said contritely, "I'm sorry, Your Honor."

She looked at Curtis Randall and saw that she had accomplished what she had wanted. He was nervously licking his lips. Jennifer turned toward Loretta Marshall and her baby. The baby was busily licking its lips. Jennifer slowly walked over to the baby and stood in front of her a long moment, focusing the attention of the jury.

"Look at that child," Jennifer said softly.

They were all staring at little Melanie, her pink tongue licking her underlip.

Jennifer turned and walked back to the witness box. "And look at this man."

Twelve pairs of eyes turned to focus on Curtis Randall. He sat there nervously licking his underlip, and suddenly the resemblance was unmistakable. Forgotten was the fact that Loretta Marshall had slept with dozens of other men. Forgotten was the fact that Curtis Randall was a pillar of the community.

"This is a man," Jennifer said mournfully, "of position and means. A man everyone looks up to. I want to ask you only one question: What kind of man is it who would deny his own child?"

THE JURY WAS out less than one hour, returning with a judgment for the plaintiff. Loretta Marshall would receive two hundred thousand dollars in cash and two thousand dollars a month for child support.

When the verdict came in, Roger Davis strode up to Jennifer, his face flushed with anger. "Did you do something with that baby?"

"What do you mean?"

Roger Davis hesitated, unsure of himself. "That lip thing. That's what won the jury over, the baby licking her lips like that. Can you explain it?"

"As a matter of fact," Jennifer said loftily, "I can. It's called heredity." And she walked away.

JENNIFER AND KEN Bailey disposed of the bottle of corn syrup on the way back to the office.

16

Adam Warner had known from almost the beginning that his marriage to Mary Beth had been a mistake. He had been impulsive and idealistic, trying to protect a young girl who seemed lost and vulnerable to the world.

He would give anything not to hurt Mary Beth, but Adam was deeply in love with Jennifer. He needed someone to talk to, and he decided on Stewart Needham. Stewart had always been sympathetic. He would understand Adam's position.

The meeting turned out to be quite different from what Adam had planned. As Adam walked into Stewart Needham's office, Needham said, "Perfect timing. I've just been on the phone with the election committee. They're formally asking you to run for the United States Senate. You'll have the full backing of the party."

"I—that's wonderful," Adam said.

"We have a lot to do, my boy. We have to start organizing things. I'll set up a fund-raising committee. Here's where I think we should begin . . ."

For the next two hours, they discussed plans for the campaign.

When they had finished, Adam said, "Stewart, there's something personal I'd like to talk to you about."

"I'm afraid I'm late for a client now, Adam."

And Adam had the sudden feeling that Stewart Needham had known what was on Adam's mind all the while.

ADAM HAD A date to meet Jennifer for lunch at a dairy restaurant on the West Side. She was waiting for him in a rear booth.

Adam walked in, charged with energy, and from his expression Jennifer knew that something had happened.

"I have some news for you," Adam told her. "I've been asked to run for the United States Senate."

"Oh, Adam!" Jennifer was filled with a sudden excitement. "That's wonderful! You'll make such a great senator!"

"The competition's going to be fierce. New York's a tough state."

"It doesn't matter. No one can stop you." And Jennifer knew it was true. Adam was intelligent and courageous, willing to fight the battles he believed in. As he had once fought her battle.

Jennifer took his hand and said warmly, "I'm so proud of you, darling."

"Easy, I haven't been elected yet. You've heard about cups, lips and slips."

"That has nothing to do with my being proud of you. I love you so much, Adam."

"I love you, too."

Adam thought about telling Jennifer of the discussion he had almost had with Stewart Needham, but he decided not to. It could wait until he had straightened things out.

"When will you start campaigning?"

"They want me to announce that I'm running right away. I'll have unanimous party backing."

"That's wonderful!"

There was something that was *not* wonderful tugging at the back of Jennifer's mind. It was something she did not want to put into words, but she knew that sooner or later she was going to have to face it. She wanted Adam to win, but the Senate race would be a sword of Damocles hanging over her head. If Adam won, Jennifer would lose him. He would be running on a reform ticket and there would be no margin in his life for any scandal. He was a married man and if it was learned he had a mistress, it would be political suicide.

That night, for the first time since she had fallen in love with Adam, Jennifer had insomnia. She was awake until dawn battling the demons of the night.

CYNTHIA SAID, "THERE'S a call waiting for you. It's the Martian again."

Jennifer looked at her blankly.

"You know, the one with the story about the insane asylum."

Jennifer had put the man completely out of her mind. He obviously was someone in need of psychiatric help.

"Tell him to—" She sighed. "Never mind. I'll tell him myself."

She picked up the telephone. "Jennifer Parker."

The familiar voice said, "Did you check the information I gave you?"

"I haven't had a chance." She remembered she had thrown away the notes she had made. "I'd like to help you. Will you give me your name?"

"I can't," he whispered. "They'll come after me, too. You just check it out. Helen Cooper. Long Island."

"I can recommend a doctor who—" The line went dead.

Jennifer sat there a moment, thinking, and then asked Ken Bailey to come into the office.

"What's up, Chief?"

"Nothing—I think. I've had a couple of crank calls from someone who won't leave his name. Would you please see it you can find out anything about a woman named Helen Cooper. She's supposed to have had a large estate on Long Island."

"Where is she now?"

"Either in some insane asylum or on Mars."

TWO HOURS LATER, Ken Bailey walked in and surprised Jennifer by saying, "Your Martian has landed. There's a Helen Cooper committed at The Heathers Asylum in Westchester."

"Are you sure?" Ken Bailey looked hurt. "I didn't mean that," Jennifer said. Ken was the best investigator she had ever known. He never said anything unless he was positive of it, and he never got his facts wrong.

"What's our interest in the lady?" Ken asked.

"Someone thinks she's been framed into the asylum. I'd like you to check out her background. I want to know about her family."

THE INFORMATION WAS on Jennifer's desk the following morning. Helen Cooper was a dowager who had been left a fortune of four million dollars by her late husband. Her daughter had married the super-intendent of the building where they lived and, six months after the marriage, the bride and groom had gone to court to ask that the mother be declared incompetent, and that the estate be put under their control. They had found three psychiatrists who had testified to Helen Cooper's incompetency and the court had committed her to the asylum.

Jennifer finished reading the report and looked up at Ken Bailey. "The whole thing sounds a little fishy, doesn't it?"

"Fishy? You could wrap it up in a newspaper and serve it with chips. What are you going to do about it?"

It was a difficult question. Jennifer had no client. If Mrs. Cooper's family had had her locked away, they certainly would not welcome Jennifer's interference, and since the woman herself had been declared insane, she was not competent to hire Jennifer. It was an interesting problem. One thing Jennifer knew: Client or not, she was not going to stand by and see someone railroaded into an insane asylum.

"I'm going to pay a visit to Mrs. Cooper," Jennifer decided.

THE HEATHERS ASYLUM was located in Westchester in a large, wooded area. The grounds were fenced in and the only access was through a guarded gate. Jennifer was not yet ready to let the family know what she was doing, so she had telephoned around until she had found an ac-quaintance with a connection to the sanatorium. He had made arrange-ments for her to pay a visit to Mrs. Cooper.

The head of the asylum, Mrs. Franklin, was a dour, hard-faced woman who reminded Jennifer of Mrs. Danvers in *Rebecca*.

"Strictly speaking," Mrs. Franklin sniffed, "I should not be letting you talk to Mrs. Cooper. However, we'll call this an unofficial visit. It won't go in the records."

"Thank you."

"I'll have her brought in."

HELEN COOPER WAS a slim, attractive-looking woman in her late sixties. She had vivid blue eyes that blazed with intelligence, and she was as gracious as though she were receiving Jennifer in her own home.

"It was good of you to come and visit me," Mrs. Cooper said, "but I'm afraid I'm not quite sure why you're here."

"I'm an attorney, Mrs. Cooper. I received two anonymous telephone calls telling me you were in here and that you didn't belong here."

Mrs. Cooper smiled gently. "That must have been Albert."

"Albert?"

"He was my butler for twenty-five years. When my daughter, Dorothy, married, she fired him." She sighed. "Poor Albert. He really belongs to the past, to another world. I suppose, in a sense, I do too. You're very young, my dear, so perhaps you're not aware of how much things have changed. Do you know what's missing today? Graciousness. It's been replaced, I'm afraid, by greed."

Jennifer asked quietly, "Your daughter?"

Mrs. Cooper's eyes saddened. "I don't blame Dorothy. It's her husband. He's not a very attractive man, not morally, at least. I'm afraid my daughter is not very attractive physically. Herbert married Dorothy for her money and found out that the estate was entirely in my hands. He didn't like that."

"Did he say that to you?"

"Oh, yes indeed. My son-in-law was quite open about it. He thought I should give my daughter the estate then, instead of making her wait until I died. I would have, except that I didn't trust him. I knew what would happen if he ever got his hands on all that money."

"Have you ever had any history of mental illness, Mrs. Cooper?"

Helen Cooper looked at Jennifer and said wryly, "According to the doctors, I'm suffering from schizophrenia and paranoia."

Jennifer had the feeling that she had never spoken to a more sane person in her life.

"You are aware that three doctors testified that you were incompetent?"

"The Cooper estate is valued at four million dollars, Miss Parker. You can influence a lot of doctors for that kind of money. I'm afraid you're wasting your time. My son-in-law controls the estate now. He'll never let me leave here."

"I'd like to meet your son-in-law."

THE PLAZA TOWERS was on East 72nd Street, in one of the most beautiful residential areas of New York. Helen Cooper had her own penthouse there. Now the name plate on the door read *Mr. and Mrs. Herbert Hawthorne.*

Jennifer had telephoned ahead to the daughter, Dorothy, and when Jennifer arrived at the apartment, both Dorothy and her husband were waiting for her. Helen Cooper had been right about her daughter. She was not attractive. She was thin and mousy-looking, with no chin, and her right eye had a cast in it. Her husband, Herbert, looked like a clone of Archie Bunker. He was at least twenty years older than Dorothy.

"Come on in," he grunted.

He escorted Jennifer from the reception hall into an enormous living room, the walls of which were covered with paintings by French and Dutch masters.

Hawthorne said to Jennifer bluntly, "Now, suppose you tell me what the hell this is all about."

Jennifer turned to the girl. "It's about your mother."

"What about her?"

"When did she first start showing signs of insanity?"

"She—"

Herbert Hawthorne interrupted. "Right after Dorothy and me got married. The old lady couldn't stand me."

That's certainly one proof of sanity, Jennifer thought.

"I read the doctors' reports," Jennifer said. "They seemed biased."

"What do you mean, biased?" His tone was truculent.

"What I mean is that the reports indicated that they were dealing in gray areas where there were no clear-cut criteria for establishing what society calls sanity. Their decision was shaped, in part, by what you and your wife told them about Mrs. Cooper's behavior."

"What are you tryin' to say?"

"I'm saying that the evidence is not clear-cut. Three other doctors could have come up with an entirely different conclusion."

"Hey, look," Herbert Hawthorne said, "I dunno what you think you're tryin' to pull, but the old lady's a looney. The doctors said so and the court said so."

"I read the court transcript," Jennifer replied. "The court also suggested that her case be periodically reviewed."

There was consternation on Herbert Hawthorne's face. "You mean they might let her out?"

"They're *going* to let her out," Jennifer promised. "I'm going to see to it."

"Wait a minute! What the hell is goin' on here?"

"That's what I intend to find out." Jennifer turned to the girl. "I checked out your mother's previous medical history. There has never been anything wrong with her, mentally or emotionally. She—"

Herbert Hawthorne interrupted. "That don't mean a damn thing! These things can come on fast. She—"

"In addition," Jennifer continued to Dorothy, "I checked on your mother's social activities before you had her put away. She lived a completely normal life."

"I don't care what you or anybody else says. She's crazy!" Herbert Hawthorne shouted.

Jennifer turned to him and studied him a moment. "Did you ask Mrs. Cooper to give the estate to you?"

"That's none of your goddamned business!"

"I'm making it my business. I think that's all for now." Jennifer moved toward the door.

Herbert Hawthorne stepped in front of her, blocking her way. "Wait a minute. You're buttin' in where you're not wanted. You're lookin' to make a little cash for yourself, right? Okay, I understand that, honey. Tell you what I'll do. Why don't I give you a check right now for a thousand dollars for services rendered and you just drop this whole thing. Huh?"

"Sorry," Jennifer replied. "No deal."

"You think you're gonna get more from the old lady?"

"No," Jennifer said. She looked him in the eye. "Only one of us is in this for the money."

IT TOOK SIX weeks of hearings and psychiatric consultations and conferences with four different state agencies. Jennifer brought in her own psychiatrists and when they were finished with their examinations and Jennifer had laid out all the facts at her disposal, the judge reversed his earlier decision and Helen Cooper was released and her estate restored to her control.

THE MORNING OF Mrs. Cooper's release she telephoned Jennifer.

"I want to take you to lunch at Twenty-One."

Jennifer looked at her calendar. She had a crowded morning, a luncheon date and a busy afternoon in court, but she knew how much this meant to the elderly woman. "I'll be there," Jennifer said.

Helen Cooper's voice was pleased. "We'll have a little celebration."

THE LUNCHEON WENT beautifully. Mrs. Cooper was a thoughtful hostess, and obviously they knew her well at 21.

Jerry Berns escorted them to a table upstairs, where they were surrounded by beautiful antiques and Georgian silver. The food and service were superb.

Helen Cooper waited until they were having their coffee. Then she said to Jennifer, "I'm very grateful to you, my dear. I don't know how large a fee you were planning to charge, but I want to give you something more."

"My fees are high enough."

Mrs. Cooper shook her head. "It doesn't matter." She leaned forward, took Jennifer's hands in hers and dropped her voice to a whisper.

"I'm going to give you Wyoming."

17

The front page of the *New York Times* carried two stories of interest, side by side. One was an announcement that Jennifer Parker had obtained an acquittal for a woman accused of slaying her husband. The other was an article about Adam Warner running for the United States Senate.

Jennifer read the story about Adam again and again. It gave his background, told about his service as a pilot in the Viet Nam War, and gave an account of his receiving the Distinguished Flying Cross for bravery. It was highly laudatory, and a number of prominent people were quoted as saying that Adam Warner would be a credit to the United States Senate and to the nation. At the end of the article, there was a strong hint that if Adam were successful in his campaign, it could easily be a stepping-stone to his running for the presidency of the United States.

IN NEW JERSEY, at Antonio Granelli's farmhouse, Michael Moretti and Antonio Granelli were finishing breakfast. Michael was reading the article about Jennifer Parker.

He looked up at his father-in-law and said, "She's done it again, Tony."

Antonio Granelli spooned up a piece of poached egg. "Who done what again?"

"That lawyer. Jennifer Parker. She's a natural."

Antonio Granelli grunted. "I don' like the idea of no woman lawyer workin' for us. Women are weak. You never know what the hell they gonna do."

Michael said cautiously, "You're right, a lot of them are, Tony."

It would not pay for him to antagonize his father-in-law. As long as Antonio Granelli was alive, he was dangerous; but watching him now, Michael knew he would not have to wait much longer. The old man had had a series of small strokes and his hands trembled. It was difficult for him to talk, and he walked with a cane. His skin was like dry, yellowed parchment. All the juices had been sucked out of him. This man, who was at the head of the federal crime list, was a toothless tiger. His name had struck terror into the hearts of countless *mafiosi* and hatred in the hearts of their widows. Now, very few people got to see Antonio Granelli. He hid behind Michael, Thomas Colfax, and a few others he trusted.

Michael had not been *raised*—made the head of the Family—yet, but it was just a question of time. "Three-Finger Brown" Lucchese had been the strongest of the five eastern Mafia chieftains, then Antonio Granelli, and soon . . . Michael could afford to be patient. He had come a long, long way from the time when, as a cocky, fresh-faced kid, he had stood in front of the major dons in New York and held a flaming scrap of paper in his hand and sworn: "This is the way I will burn if I betray the secrets of Cosa Nostra."

Now, sitting at breakfast with the old man, Michael said, "Maybe we could use the Parker woman for small stuff. Just to see how she does."

Granelli shrugged. "Just be careful, Mike. I don' wan' no strangers in on Family secrets."

"Let me handle her."

Michael made the telephone call that afternoon.

WHEN CYNTHIA ANNOUNCED that Michael Moretti was calling, it brought an instant spate of memories, all of them unpleasant. Jennifer could not imagine why Michael Moretti would be calling her.

Out of curiosity, she picked up the telephone. "What is it you want?"

The sharpness of her tone took Michael Moretti aback. "I want to see you. I think you and I should have a little talk."

"What about, Mr. Moretti?"

"It's nothing I'd care to discuss on the telephone. I can tell you this, Miss Parker—it's something that would be very much in your interest."

Jennifer said evenly, "I can tell you this, Mr. Moretti. Nothing you could ever do or say could be of the slightest interest to me," and she slammed down the receiver.

MICHAEL MORETTI SAT at his desk staring at the dead phone in his hand. He felt a stirring within him, but it was not anger. He was not sure what it was, and he was not sure he liked it. He had used women all his life and his dark good looks and innate ruthlessness had gotten him more eager bed partners than he could remember.

Basically, Michael Moretti despised women. They were too soft. They had no spirit. *Rosa, for example. She's like a little pet dog who does everything she's told,* Michael thought. *She keeps my house, cooks for me, fucks me when I want to be fucked, shuts up when I tell her to shut up.*

Michael had never known a woman of spirit, a woman who had the courage to defy him. Jennifer Parker had had the nerve to hang up on him. What was it she had said? *Nothing you could ever do or say could be of the slightest interest to me.* Michael Moretti thought about that and smiled to himself. She was wrong. He was going to show her how wrong she was.

He sat back, remembering what she had looked like in court, remembering her face and her body. He suddenly wondered what she would be like in bed. A wildcat, probably. He started thinking about her nude body under his, fighting him. He picked up the telephone and dialed a number.

When a girl's voice answered he said, "Get naked. I'm on my way over."

ON HER WAY back to the office after lunch, as Jennifer was crossing Third Avenue she was almost run down by a truck. The driver slammed on his brakes and the rear end of the truck skidded sideways, barely missing her.

"Jesus Christ, lady!" the driver yelled. "Why don't you watch where the hell you're goin'!"

Jennifer was not listening to him. She was staring at the name on the back of the truck. It read *Nationwide Motors Corporation*. She stood there watching, long after the truck had disappeared from sight. Then she turned and hurried back to the office.

"IS KEN HERE?" she asked Cynthia.

"Yes. He's in his office."

She went in to see him. "Ken, can you check out Nationwide Motors Corporation? We need a list of all the accident cases their trucks have been involved in for the past five years."

"That's going to take a while."

"Use LEXIS." That was the national legal computer.

"You want to tell me what's going on?"

"I'm not sure yet, Ken. It's just a hunch. I'll let you know if anything comes of it."

She had overlooked something in the case of Connie Garrett, that lovely quadruple amputee who was destined to spend the rest of her life as a freak. The driver may have had a good record, but what about the *trucks*? Maybe somebody was liable, after all.

The next morning Ken Bailey laid a report in front of Jennifer. "Whatever the hell you're after, looks like you've hit the jackpot. Nationwide Motors Corporation has had fifteen accidents in the last five years, and some of their trucks have been recalled."

Jennifer felt an excitement begin to build in her. "What was the problem?"

"A deficiency in the braking system that causes the rear end of the truck to swing around when the brakes are hit hard."

It was the rear end of the truck that had hit Connie Garrett.

Jennifer called a staff meeting with Dan Martin, Ted Harris and Ken Bailey. "We're going into court on the Connie Garrett case," Jennifer announced.

Ted Harris stared at her through his milk-bottle glasses. "Wait a minute, Jennifer, I checked that out. She lost on appeal. We're going to get hit with *res judicata*."

"What's *res judicata*?" Ken Bailey asked.

Jennifer explained, "It means for civil cases what double jeopardy means for criminal cases. 'There must be an end to litigation.'"

Ted Harris added, "Once a final judgment has been made on the merits of a case, it can only be opened again under very special circumstances. We have no grounds to reopen."

"Yes, we have. We're going after them on *discovery*."

The principle of discovery read: *Mutual knowledge of all relevant facts gathered by both parties is essential to proper litigation.*

"The deep-pocket defendant is Nationwide Motors. They held back information from Connie Garrett's attorney. There's a deficiency in the braking system of their trucks and they kept it out of the record."

She looked at the two lawyers. "Here's what I think we should do . . ."

TWO HOURS LATER, Jennifer was seated in Connie Garrett's living room.

"I want to move for a new trial. I believe we have a case."

"No. I couldn't go through another trial."

"Connie—"

"Look at me, Jennifer. I'm a freak. Every time I look in the mirror I want to kill myself. Do you know why I don't?" Her voice sank to a whisper. "Because I can't. I *can't*!"

Jennifer sat there, shaken. How could she have been so insensitive?

"Suppose I try for an out-of-court settlement? I think that when they hear the evidence they'll be willing to settle without going to trial."

THE OFFICES OF Maguire and Guthrie, the attorneys who represented the Nationwide Motors Corporation, were located on upper Fifth Avenue in a modern glass and chrome building with a splashing fountain in front. Jennifer announced herself at the reception desk. The receptionist asked her to be seated, and fifteen minutes later Jennifer was escorted into the offices of Patrick Maguire. He was the senior partner in the firm, a tough, hard-bitten Irishman with sharp eyes that missed nothing.

He motioned Jennifer to a chair. "It's nice to meet you, Miss Parker. You've gotten yourself quite a reputation around town."

"Not all bad, I hope."

"They say you're tough. You don't look it."

"I hope not."

"Coffee? Or some good Irish whiskey?"

"Coffee, please."

Patrick Maguire rang and a secretary brought in two cups of coffee on a sterling silver tray.

Maguire said, "Now what is it I can do for you?"

"It's about the Connie Garrett case."

"Ah, yes. As I recall, she lost the case and the appeal."

As I recall. Jennifer would have bet her life that Patrick Maguire could have recited every statistic in the case.

"I'm going to file for a new trial."

"Really? On what grounds?" Maguire asked politely.

Jennifer opened her attaché case and took out the brief she had prepared. She handed it to him.

"I'm requesting a reopening on failure to disclose."

Maguire leafed through the papers, unperturbed. "Oh, yes," he said. "That brake business."

"You knew about it?"

"Of course." He tapped the file with a stubby finger. "Miss Parker, this won't get you anywhere. You would have to prove that the same truck involved in the accident had a faulty brake system. It's probably been overhauled a dozen times since the accident, so there would be no way of proving what its condition was then." He pushed the file back toward her. "You have no case."

Jennifer took a sip of her coffee. "All I have to do is prove what a bad safety record those trucks have. Ordinary diligence should have made your client know that they were defective."

Maguire said casually, "What is it you're proposing?"

"I have a client in her early twenties who's sitting in a room she'll never leave for the rest of her life because she has no arms or legs. I'd like to get a settlement that would make up a little bit for the anguish she's going through."

Patrick Maguire took a sip of his coffee. "What kind of settlement did you have in mind?"

"Two million dollars."

He smiled. "That's a great deal of money for someone with no case."

"If I go to court, Mr. Maguire, I promise you I'll have a case. And I'll win a lot more than that. If you force us to sue, we're going to sue for five million dollars."

He smiled again. "You're scaring the bejeezus out of me. More coffee?"

"No, thanks." Jennifer arose.

"Wait a minute! Sit down, please. I haven't said no."

"You haven't said yes."

"Have some more coffee. We brew it ourselves."

Jennifer thought of Adam and the Kenya coffee.

"Two million dollars is a lot of money, Miss Parker."

Jennifer said nothing.

"Now, if we were talking about a lesser amount, I might be able to—" He waved his hands expressively.

Jennifer remained silent.

Finally Patrick Maguire said, "You really want two million, don't you?"

"I really want five million, Mr. Maguire."

"All right. I suppose we might be able to arrange something."

It had been easy!

"I have to leave for London in the morning, but I'll be back next week."

"I want to wrap this up. I'd appreciate it if you would talk to your client as soon as possible. I'd like to give my client a check next week."

Patrick Maguire nodded. "That can probably be worked out."

All the way back to the office, Jennifer was filled with a sense of unease. It had been too simple.

That night on her way home, Jennifer stopped at a drugstore. When she came out and started across the street, she saw Ken Bailey walking with a handsome young blond man. Jennifer hesitated, then turned into a side street so that she would not be seen. Ken's private life was his own business.

ON THE DAY that Jennifer was scheduled to meet with Patrick Maguire, she received a call from his secretary.

"Mr. Maguire asked me to give you his apologies, Miss Parker. He's going to be tied up in meetings all day. He'll be happy to meet with you at your convenience tomorrow."

"Fine," Jennifer said. "Thank you."

The call sounded an alarm in Jennifer's mind. Her instincts had been right. Patrick Maguire was up to something.

"Hold all my calls," she told Cynthia.

She locked herself in her office, pacing back and forth, trying to think of every possible angle. Patrick Maguire had first told Jennifer she had no case. With almost no persuasion, he had then agreed to pay Connie Garrett two million dollars. Jennifer remembered how uneasy she had been at the time. Since then, Patrick Maguire had been unavailable. First London—if he had really gone to London—and then the conferences that had kept him from returning Jennifer's telephone calls all week. And now another delay.

But why? The only reason would be if— Jennifer stopped pacing and picked up the interoffice telephone and called Dan Martin.

"Check on the date of Connie Garrett's accident, would you, Dan? I want to know when the statute of limitations is up."

Twenty minutes later, Dan Martin walked into Jennifer's office, his face white.

"We blew it," he said. "Your hunch was right. The statute of limitations ran out today."

She felt suddenly sick. "There's no chance of a mistake?"

"None. I'm sorry, Jennifer. One of us should have checked it out before. It—it just never occurred to me."

"Or me." Jennifer picked up the telephone and dialed a number. "Patrick Maguire, please. Jennifer Parker."

She waited for what seemed an eternity, and then she said brightly into the telephone, "Hello there, Mr. Maguire. How was London?" She listened. "No, I've never been there . . . Ah, well, one of these days . . . The reason I'm calling," she said casually, "is that I just talked to Connie Garrett. As I told you before, she really doesn't want to go to court unless she has to. So if we could settle this today—"

Patrick Maguire's laugh boomed through the receiver. "Nice try, Miss Parker. The statute of limitations is up today. No one is going to sue anybody. If you'd like to settle for a lunch sometime we can talk about the fickle finger of fate."

Jennifer tried to keep the anger out of her voice. "That's a pretty rotten trick, friend."

"It's a pretty rotten world, friend." Patrick Maguire chuckled.

"It's not how you play the game, it's whether you win or not, right?"

"You're pretty good, honey, but I've been at it a lot longer than you. Tell your client I said better luck next time."

And he rang off.

Jennifer sat there holding the telephone in her hand. She thought of Connie Garrett sitting at home, waiting for the news. Jennifer's head began to pound and a film of perspiration popped out on her forehead. She reached in her desk drawer for an aspirin and looked at the clock on the wall. It was four o'clock. They had until five o'clock to file with the Clerk of the Superior Court.

"How long would it take you to prepare the filing?" Jennifer asked Dan Martin, who stood there suffering with her.

He followed her glance. "At least three hours. Maybe four. There's no way."

There has to be a way, Jennifer thought.

Jennifer said, "Doesn't Nationwide have branches all over the United States?"

"Yes."

"It's only one o'clock in San Francisco. We'll file against them there and ask for a change of venue later."

Dan Martin shook his head. "Jennifer, all the papers are here. If we got a firm in San Francisco and briefed them on what we need and they drew up new papers, there's no way they could make the five o'clock deadline."

Something in her refused to give up. "What time is it in Hawaii?"

"Eleven in the morning."

Jennifer's headache disappeared as if by magic, and she leapt from her chair in excitement. "That's it, then! Find out if Nationwide does business there. They must have a factory, sales office, garage—anything. If they do, we file there."

Dan Martin stared at her for a moment and then his face lit up. "Gotcha!" He was already hurrying toward the door.

Jennifer could still hear Patrick Maguire's smug tone on the telephone. *Tell your client, better luck next time.* There would never be a next time for Connie Garrett. It had to be *now*.

Thirty minutes later Jennifer's intercom buzzed and Dan Martin said excitedly, "Nationwide Motors manufactures their drive shafts on the island of Oahu."

"We've got them! Get hold of a law firm there and have them file the papers immediately."

"Did you have any special firm in mind?"

"No. Pick someone out of Martindale-Hubbell. Just make sure they serve the papers on the local attorney for National. Have them call us back the minute those papers are filed. I'll be waiting here in the office."

"Anything else I can do?"

"Pray."

THE CALL FROM Hawaii came at ten o'clock that evening. Jennifer grabbed the phone and a soft voice said, "Miss Jennifer Parker, please."

"Speaking."

"This is Miss Sung of the law firm of Gregg and Hoy in Oahu. We wanted to let you know that fifteen minutes ago we served the papers you requested on the attorney for Nationwide Motors Corporation."

Jennifer exhaled slowly. "Thank you. Thank you very much."

CYNTHIA SENT IN Joey La Guardia. Jennifer had never seen the man before. He had telephoned, asking her to represent him in an assault case. He was short, compactly built and wore an expensive suit that looked as though it had been carefully tailored for someone else. He had an enormous diamond ring on his little finger.

La Guardia smiled with yellowed teeth and said, "I come to you 'cause I need some help. Anybody can make a mistake, right, Miss Parker? The cops picked me up 'cause I did a little number on a coupla guys, but I thought they was out to get me, you know? The alley was dark and when

I seen them comin' at me—well, it's a rough neighborhood down there. I jumped them before they could jump me."

There was something about his manner that Jennifer found distasteful and false. He was trying too hard to be ingratiating.

He pulled out a large wad of money.

"Here. A grand down an' another grand when we go to court. Okay?"

"My calendar is full for the next few months. I'll be glad to recommend some other attorneys to you."

His manner became insistent. "No. I don't want nobody else. You're the best."

"For a simple assault charge you don't need the best."

"Hey, listen," he said, "I'll give you more money." There was a desperation in his voice. "*Two* grand down and—"

Jennifer pressed the buzzer under her desk and Cynthia walked in. "Mr. La Guardia's leaving, Cynthia."

Joey La Guardia glared at Jennifer for a long moment, scooped up his money and thrust it back in his pocket. He walked out of the office without a word. Jennifer pressed the intercom button.

"Ken, could you please come in here a minute?"

It took Ken Bailey less than thirty minutes to get a complete report on Joey La Guardia.

"He's got a rap sheet a mile long," he told Jennifer. "He's been in and out of the pen since he was sixteen." He glanced at the piece of paper in his hand. "He's out on bail. He was picked up last week for assault and battery. He beat up two old men who owed the Organization money."

Everything suddenly clicked into place. "Joey La Guardia works for the Organization?"

"He's one of Michael Moretti's enforcers."

Jennifer was filled with a cold fury. "Can you get me the telephone number of Michael Moretti?"

Five minutes later, Jennifer was speaking to Moretti.

"Well, this is an unexpected pleasure, Miss Parker. I—"

"Mr. Moretti, I don't like being set up."

"What are you talking about?"

"Listen to me. And listen well. I'm not for sale. Not now, not ever. I won't represent you or anyone who works for you. All I want is for you to leave me alone. Is that clear?"

"Can I ask you a question?"

"Go ahead."

"Will you have lunch with me?"

Jennifer hung up on him.

CYNTHIA'S VOICE CAME over the intercom. "A Mr. Patrick Maguire is here to see you, Miss Parker. He has no appointment, but he said—"

Jennifer smiled to herself. "Have Mr. Maguire wait."

She remembered their conversation on the telephone. *It's not how you play the game, it's whether you win or not, right? You're pretty good, honey, but I've been at it a lot longer than you. Tell your client I said better luck next time.*

Jennifer kept Patrick Maguire waiting for forty-five minutes, and then buzzed Cynthia.

"Send Mr. Maguire in, please."

Patrick Maguire's genial manner was gone. He had been outwitted, and he was angry and did not bother to conceal it.

He walked over to Jennifer's desk and snapped, "You're causing me a lot of problems, friend."

"Am I, friend?"

He sat down, uninvited. "Let's stop playing games. I had a call from the general counsel of Nationwide Motors. I underestimated you. My client is willing to make a settlement." He reached into his pocket, pulled out an envelope and handed it to Jennifer. She opened it. Inside was a certified check made out to Connie Garrett. It was for one hundred thousand dollars.

Jennifer slipped the check back in the envelope and returned it to Patrick Maguire.

"It's not enough. We're suing for five million dollars."

Maguire grinned. "No, you're not. Because your client's not going into court. I just paid her a visit. There's no way you can ever get that girl into a courtroom. She's terrified and, without her, you haven't got a chance."

Jennifer said angrily, "You had no right to talk to Connie Garrett without my being present."

"I was only trying to do everybody a favor. Take the money and run, friend."

Jennifer got to her feet. "Get out of here. You turn my stomach."

Patrick Maguire rose. "I didn't know your stomach *could* be turned."

And he walked out, taking the check with him.

Watching him go, Jennifer wondered whether she had made a terrible mistake. She thought of what a hundred thousand dollars could do for Connie Garrett. But it was not enough. Not for what that girl would have to endure every day for the rest of her life.

Jennifer knew that Patrick Maguire was right about one thing. Without Connie Garrett in the courtroom, there was no chance that a jury would return a verdict for five million dollars. Words could never persuade them of the horror of her life. Jennifer needed the impact of Connie Garrett's presence in the courtroom, with the jury looking at her day after day; but there was no way Jennifer could persuade the young woman to go into court. She had to find another solution.

ADAM TELEPHONED.

"I'm sorry I couldn't call you before," he apologized. "I've been having meetings on the Senate race and—"

"It's all right, darling. I understand." *I've got to understand,* she thought.

"I miss you so much."

"I miss you, too, Adam." *You'll never know how much.*

"I want to see you."

Jennifer wanted to say, *When?* but she waited.

Adam went on. "I have to go to Albany this afternoon. I'll call you when I get back."

"All right." There was nothing else she could say. There was nothing she could do.

AT FOUR O'CLOCK in the morning, Jennifer awakened from a terrible dream and knew how she was going to win five million dollars for Connie Garrett.

We've set up a series of fund-raising dinners across the state. We'll hit the larger towns only. We'll get to the whistle-stops through a few national television shows like *Face the Nation*, the *Today* show and *Meet the Press*. We figure that we can pick up—Adam, are you listening?"

Adam turned to Stewart Needham and the other three men in the conference room—top media experts, Needham had assured him—and said, "Yes, of course, Stewart."

He had been thinking of something else entirely. Jennifer. He wanted her here at his side, sharing the excitement of the campaign, sharing this moment, sharing his life.

Adam had tried several times to discuss his situation with Stewart Needham, but each time his partner had managed to change the subject.

Adam sat there thinking about Jennifer and Mary Beth. He knew that it was unfair to compare them, but it was impossible not to.

Jennifer is stimulating to be with. She's interested in everything and makes me feel alive. Mary Beth lives in her own private little world . . .

Jennifer and I have a thousand things in common. Mary Beth and I have nothing in common but our marriage . . .

I love Jennifer's sense of humor. She knows how to laugh at herself. Mary Beth takes everything seriously . . .

Jennifer makes me feel young. Mary Beth seems older than her years . . .

Jennifer is self-reliant. Mary Beth depends on me to tell her what to do . . .

Five important differences between the woman I'm in love with and my wife.

Five reasons why I can never leave Mary Beth.

On a Wednesday morning in early August the trial of *Connie Garrett v. Nationwide Motors Corporation* began. Ordinarily, the trial would only have been worth a paragraph or two in the newspapers, but because Jennifer Parker was representing the plaintiff, the media were out in full force.

Patrick Maguire sat at the defense table, surrounded by a battery of assistants dressed in conservative gray suits.

The process of selecting a jury began. Maguire was casual, almost to the point of indifference, for he knew that Connie Garrett was not going to appear in court. The sight of a beautiful young quadruple amputee would have been a powerful emotional lever with which to pry a large sum of money out of a jury—but there would be no girl and no lever.

This time, Maguire thought, *Jennifer Parker has outsmarted herself.*

The jury was impaneled and the trial got underway. Patrick Maguire made his opening statement and Jennifer had to admit to herself that he was very good indeed. He dwelt at length on the plight of poor young Connie Garrett, saying all the things that Jennifer had planned to say, stealing her emotional thunder. He spoke of the accident, stressing the fact that Connie Garrett had slipped on ice and that the truck driver had not been at fault.

"The plaintiff is asking you ladies and gentlemen to award her five million dollars." Maguire shook his head incredulously. "*Five million dollars!* Have you ever seen that much money? I haven't. My firm handles some affluent clients, but I want to tell you that in all my years of practicing law, I have never even seen *one* million dollars—or *half* a million dollars."

He could see by the looks on the faces of the jurors that neither had they.

"The defense is going to bring witnesses in here who will tell you how the accident happened. And it *was* an accident. Before we're through, we'll show you that Nationwide Motors had no culpability in this matter. You will have noticed that the person bringing the suit, Connie Garrett, is not in court today. Her attorney has informed Judge Silverman that she will not make an appearance at all. Connie Garrett is not in this courtroom today where she belongs, but I can tell you where she is. Right now, as I'm standing here talking to you, Connie Garrett is sitting at home counting the money she thinks you're going to give her. She's waiting for her telephone to ring and for her attorney to tell her how many millions of dollars she suckered out of you.

"You and I know that any time there's an accident where a big corporation is involved—no matter how indirectly—there are people who are immediately going to say, 'Why, that company is rich. It can afford it. Let's take it for all we can.'"

Patrick Maguire paused.

"Connie Garrett's not in this courtroom today because she couldn't face you. She knows that what she's trying to do is immoral. Well, we're going to send her away empty-handed as a lesson to other people who might be tempted to try the same thing in the future. A person has to take responsibility for his or her own actions. If you slip on a piece of ice on the street, you can't blame big brother for it. And you shouldn't try to swindle five million dollars out of him. Thank you."

He turned to bow to Jennifer, and then walked over to the defense table and sat down.

Jennifer rose to her feet and approached the jury. She studied their faces, trying to evaluate the impression that Patrick Maguire had made.

"My esteemed colleague has told you that Connie Garrett will not be in this courtroom during the trial. That is correct." Jennifer pointed to an empty space at the plaintiffs table. "That is where Connie Garrett would be sitting if she were here. Not in that chair. In a special wheelchair. The chair she lives in. Connie Garrett won't be in this courtroom, but before this trial is over you will all have an opportunity to meet her and get to know her as I have gotten to know her."

There was a puzzled frown on Patrick Maguire's face. He leaned over and whispered to one of his assistants.

Jennifer was going on. "I listened as Mr. Maguire spoke so eloquently, and I want to tell you I was touched. I found my heart bleeding for this multibillion-dollar corporation that's being mercilessly attacked by this twenty-four-year-old woman who has no arms or legs. This woman who, at this very moment is sitting at home, greedily awaiting that telephone call that will tell her she's rich." Jennifer's voice dropped.

"Rich to do what? Go out and buy diamonds for the hands she doesn't have? Buy dancing shoes for the feet she doesn't have? Buy beautiful dresses that she can never wear? A Rolls Royce to take her to parties she's not invited to? Just think of all the fun she's going to have with that money."

Jennifer spoke very quietly and sincerely as her eyes moved slowly across the faces of the jurors. "Mr. Maguire has never seen five million dollars at one time. Neither have I. But I'll tell you this. If I were to offer any one of you five million dollars in cash right now, and all I wanted in exchange was to cut off both your arms and both your legs, I don't think five million dollars would seem like very much money. . . .

"The law in this case is very clear," Jennifer explained. "In an earlier trial, which the plaintiff lost, the defendants were aware of a defect in the braking system in their trucks, and they withheld that knowledge from the defendant and from the court. In doing so, they acted illegally. That is the basis for this new trial. According to a recent government survey, the biggest contributors to truck accidents involve wheels and tires, brakes and steering systems. If you will just examine these figures for a moment . . ."

Patrick Maguire was appraising the jury and he was an expert at it. As Jennifer droned on about the statistics, Maguire could tell that the jurors were getting bored with this trial. It was becoming too technical. The trial was no longer about a crippled girl. It was about trucks and braking distances and faulty brake drums. The jurors were losing interest.

Maguire glanced over at Jennifer and thought, *She's not as clever as she's reputed to be.* Maguire knew that if he had been on the other side defending Connie Garrett, he would have ignored the statistics and mechanical problems and played on the jury's emotions. Jennifer Parker had done exactly the opposite.

Patrick Maguire leaned back in his chair now and relaxed.

Jennifer was approaching the bench. "Your Honor, with the court's permission, I have an exhibit I would like to introduce."

"What kind of exhibit?" Judge Silverman asked.

"When this trial began I promised the jury that they would get to know Connie Garrett. Since she is unable to be here in person, I would like permission to show some pictures of her."

Judge Silverman said, "I see no objection to that." He turned to Patrick Maguire. "Does the attorney for the defense have any objection?"

Patrick Maguire got to his feet, moving slowly, thinking fast. "What kind of pictures?"

Jennifer said, "A few pictures taken of Connie Garrett at home."

Patrick Maguire would have preferred not to have the pictures, but on the other hand, photographs of a crippled girl sitting in a wheelchair were certainly a lot less dramatic than the actual appearance of the girl herself would have been. And there was another factor to consider: If he objected, it would make him look unsympathetic in the eyes of the jury.

He said generously, "By all means, show the pictures."

"Thank you."

Jennifer turned to Dan Martin and nodded. Two men in the back row moved forward with a portable screen and a motion picture projector and began to set them up.

Patrick Maguire stood up, surprised. "Wait a minute! What is this?"

Jennifer replied innocently, "The pictures you just agreed to let me show."

Patrick Maguire stood there, silently fuming. Jennifer had said nothing about motion pictures. But it was too late to object. He nodded curtly and sat down again.

Jennifer had the screen positioned so the jury and Judge Silverman could see it clearly.

"May we have the room darkened, Your Honor?"

The judge signaled the bailiff and the shades were lowered. Jennifer walked over to the 16mm projector and turned it on, and the screen came to life.

For the next thirty minutes there was not a sound to be heard in the courtroom. Jennifer had hired a professional cameraman and a young director of commercials to make the film. They had photographed a day in the life of Connie Garrett, and it was a stark, realistic horror story. Nothing had been left to the imagination. The film showed the beautiful young amputee being taken out of bed in the morning, being carried to the toilet, being cleaned like a small, helpless baby . . . being bathed . . . being fed and dressed. . . . Jennifer had seen the film over and over and now, as she watched it again, she felt the same lump in her throat and her eyes filled with tears, and she knew that it must be having the same effect on the judge and the jury and the spectators in the courtroom.

When the film was ended, Jennifer turned to Judge Silverman. "The plaintiff rests."

THE JURY HAD been out for more than ten hours, and with each passing hour Jennifer's spirits sank lower. She had been sure of an immediate verdict. If they had been as affected by the film as she had been, a verdict should not have taken more than an hour or two.

WHEN THE JURY had filed out, Patrick Maguire had been frantic, certain that he had lost his case, that he had underestimated Jennifer Parker once again. But as the hours passed and the jury still did not return, Maguire's hopes began to rise. It would not have taken the jury this long to make an emotional decision. "We're going to be all right. The longer they're in there arguing, the more their emotions are going to cool off."

. . .

A FEW MINUTES before midnight, the foreman sent a note to Judge Silverman for a legal ruling. The judge studied the request, then looked up. "Will both attorneys approach the bench, please?"

When Jennifer and Patrick Maguire were standing in front of him, Judge Silverman said, "I want to apprise you of a note I have just received from the foreman. The jury is asking whether they are legally permitted to award Connie Garrett more than the five million dollars her attorney is suing for."

Jennifer felt suddenly giddy. Her heart began to soar. She turned to look at Patrick Maguire. His face was drained of color.

"I'm informing them," Judge Silverman said, "that it is within their province to set any amount they feel is justified."

Thirty minutes later the jury filed back into the courtroom. The foreman announced they had found in favor of the plaintiff. The amount of damages she was entitled to was six million dollars.

It was the largest personal injury award in the history of the State of New York.

20

When Jennifer walked into her office the following morning she found an array of newspapers spread across her desk. She was on the front page of every one of them. There were four dozen beautiful red roses in a vase. Jennifer smiled. Adam had found time to send her flowers.

She opened the card. It read: *Congratulations. Michael Moretti.*

The intercom buzzed and Cynthia said, "Mr. Adams is on the line."

Jennifer grabbed the telephone. She tried to keep her voice calm. "Hello, darling."

"You've done it again."

"I got lucky."

"Your client got lucky. Lucky to have you as an attorney. You must be feeling wonderful."

Winning cases made her feel good. Being with Adam made her feel wonderful. "Yes."

"I have something important to tell you," Adam said. "Can you meet me for a drink this afternoon?"

Jennifer's heart sank. There was only one thing Adam could have to tell her: He was never going to see her again.

"Yes. Yes, of course . . ."

"Mario's? Six o'clock?"

"Fine."

She gave the roses to Cynthia.

ADAM WAS WAITING in the restaurant, seated at a back table. *So he won't be embarrassed if I get hysterical,* Jennifer thought. Well, she was determined not to cry. Not in front of Adam.

She could tell from his gaunt, haggard face what he had been going through, and she intended to make this as easy as possible for him. Jennifer sat down and Adam took her hand in his.

"Mary Beth is giving me a divorce," Adam said, and Jennifer stared at him, speechless.

IT WAS MARY BETH who had begun the conversation. They had returned from a fund-raising dinner where Adam had been the main speaker. The evening had been an enormous success. Mary Beth had been quiet during the ride home, a curious tension about her.

Adam said, "I thought the evening went well, didn't you?"

"Yes, Adam."

Nothing more was said until they reached the house.

"Would you like a nightcap?" Adam asked.

"No, thank you. I think we should have a talk."

"Oh? About what?"

She looked at him and said, "About you and Jennifer Parker."

It was like a physical blow. Adam hesitated for a moment, wondering whether to deny it or—

"I've known it for some time. I haven't said anything because I wanted to make up my mind about what to do."

"Mary Beth, I—"

"Please let me finish. I know that our relationship hasn't been— well—all we hoped it would be. In some ways, perhaps I haven't been as good a wife as I should have been."

"Nothing that's happened is your fault. I—"

"Please, Adam. This is very difficult for me. I've made a decision. I'm not going to stand in your way."

He looked at her unbelievingly. "I don't—"

"I love you too much to hurt you. You have a brilliant political future ahead of you. I don't want anything to spoil that. Obviously, I'm not making you completely happy. If Jennifer Parker can make you happy, I want you to have her."

He had a feeling of unreality, as though the whole conversation were taking place underwater. "What will happen to you?"

Mary Beth smiled. "I'll be fine, Adam. Don't worry about me. I have my own plans."

"I—I don't know what to say."

"There's no need to say anything. I've said it all for both of us. If I held on to you and made you miserable, it wouldn't do either of us any good, would it? I'm sure Jennifer's lovely or you wouldn't feel about her the way you do." Mary Beth walked over to him and took him in her arms. "Don't look so stricken, Adam. What I'm doing is the best thing for everyone."

"You're remarkable."

"Thank you." She gently traced his face with her fingertips and smiled. "My dearest Adam. I'll always be your best friend. Always." Then she came closer and put her head on his shoulder. He could hardly hear her soft voice. "It's been such a long time since you held me in your arms, Adam. You wouldn't have to tell me you love me, but would you—would you like to—hold me in your arms once more and make love to me? Our last time together?"

ADAM WAS THINKING of this now as he said to Jennifer, "The divorce was Mary Beth's idea."

Adam went on talking, but Jennifer was no longer listening to the words; she was only hearing the music. She felt as though she were floating, soaring. She had steeled herself for Adam to tell her he could never see her again—and now this! It was too much to absorb. She knew how painful the scene with Mary Beth must have been for Adam, and Jennifer had never loved Adam more than she did at this moment. She felt as though a crushing load had been lifted from her chest, as though she could breathe again.

Adam was saying, "Mary Beth was wonderful about it. She's an incredible woman. She's genuinely happy for both of us."

"That's hard to believe."

"You don't understand. For some time now we've behaved more like . . . brother and sister. I've never discussed it with you, but—" He hesitated and said carefully, "Mary Beth doesn't have strong . . . drives."

"I see."

"She'd like to meet you."

The thought of it disturbed Jennifer. "I don't think I could, Adam. I'd feel—uncomfortable."

"Trust me."

"If—if you want me to, Adam, of course."

"Good, darling. We'll go for tea. I'll drive you out."

Jennifer thought for a moment. "Wouldn't it be better if I went alone?"

THE FOLLOWING MORNING, Jennifer drove out the Saw Mill River Parkway, headed upstate. It was a crisp, clear morning, a lovely day for a drive. Jennifer turned on the car radio and tried to forget her nervousness about the meeting facing her.

The Warner house was a magnificently preserved house of Dutch origin, overlooking the river at Croton-on-Hudson, set on a large estate of rolling green acres. Jennifer drove up the driveway to the imposing front entrance. She rang the bell and a moment later the door was opened by an attractive woman in her middle thirties. The last thing Jennifer had expected was this shy southern woman who took her hand, gave her a warm smile and said, "I'm Mary Beth. Adam didn't do you justice. Please come in."

Adam's wife was wearing a beige wool skirt that was softly full, and a silk blouse opened just enough to reveal a mature but still lovely breast. Her beige-blond hair was worn long and slightly curling about her face, and was flattering to her blue eyes. The pearls around her neck could never be mistaken as cultured. There was an air of old-world dignity about Mary Beth Warner.

The interior of the house was lovely, with wide, spacious rooms filled with antiques and beautiful paintings.

A butler served tea in the drawing room from a Georgian silver tea service.

When he had left the room, Mary Beth said, "I'm sure you must love Adam very much."

Jennifer said awkwardly, "I want you to know, Mrs. Warner, that neither of us planned—"

Mary Beth Warner put a hand on Jennifer's arm. "You don't have to tell me that. I don't know whether Adam told you, but our marriage has turned into a marriage of politeness. Adam and I have known each other since we were children. I think I fell in love with Adam the first time I saw him. We went to the same parties and had the same friends, and I suppose it was inevitable that one day we would get married. Don't misunderstand. I still adore Adam and I'm sure he adores me. But people do change, don't they?"

"Yes."

Jennifer looked at Mary Beth and she was filled with a deep feeling of gratitude. What could have been an ugly and sordid scene had turned into something friendly and wonderful.

Adam had been right. Mary Beth was a lovely lady.

"I'm very grateful to you," Jennifer said.

"And I'm grateful to you," Mary Beth confided. She smiled shyly and said, "You see, I'm very much in love, too. I was going to get the divorce immediately but I thought, for Adam's sake, we'd best wait until after the election."

Jennifer had been so busy with her own emotions that she had forgotten about the election.

Mary Beth went on: "Everyone seems sure that Adam is going to be our next senator, and a divorce now would gravely hurt his chances. It's only six months away, so I decided it would be better for him if I delayed it." She looked at Jennifer. "But forgive me—is that agreeable with you?"

"Of course it is," Jennifer said.

She would have to completely readjust her thinking. Her future would now be tied to Adam. If he became senator, she would live with him in Washington, D.C. It would mean giving up her law practice here, but that did not matter. Nothing mattered except that they could be together.

Jennifer said, "Adam will make a wonderful senator."

Mary Beth raised her head and smiled. "My dear, one day Adam Warner is going to make a wonderful *President.*"

THE TELEPHONE WAS ringing when Jennifer arrived back at the apartment. It was Adam. "How did you get along with Mary Beth?"

"Adam, she was wonderful!"

"She said the same thing about you."

"You read about old southern charm, but you don't come across it very often. Mary Beth has it. She's quite a lady."

"So are you, darling. Where would you like to be married?"

Jennifer said, "Times Square, for all I care. But I think we should wait, Adam."

"Wait for what?"

"Until after the election. Your career is important. A divorce could hurt you right now."

"My private life is—"

"—going to become your public life. We mustn't do anything that might spoil your chances. We can wait six months."

"I don't want to wait."

"I don't either, darling." Jennifer smiled. "We won't really be waiting, will we?"

21

Jennifer and Adam had lunch together almost every day, and once or twice a week Adam spent the night at their apartment. They had to be more discreet than ever, for Adam's campaign had actively begun, and he was becoming a nationally prominent figure. He gave speeches at political rallies and fund-raising dinners, and his opinions on national issues were quoted more and more frequently in the press.

ADAM AND STEWART Needham were having their ritual morning tea.

"Saw you on the *Today* show this morning," Needham said. "Fine job, Adam. You got every single point across. I understand they've invited you back again."

"Stewart, I hate doing those shows. I feel like some goddamned actor up there, performing."

Stewart nodded, unperturbed. "That's what politicians are, Adam—actors. Playing a part, being what the public wants them to be. Hell, if politicians acted like themselves in public—what expression do the kids use?—letting it all hang out?—this country'd be a damned monarchy."

"I don't like the fact that running for public office has become a personality contest."

Stewart Needham smiled. "Be grateful you've got the personality, my boy. Your ratings in the polls keep going up every week." He stopped to pour more tea. "Believe me, this is only the beginning. First the Senate, then the number one target. Nothing can stop you." He paused to take a sip of his tea. "Unless you do something foolish, that is."

Adam looked up at him, "What do you mean?"

Stewart Needham delicately wiped his lips with a damask napkin.

"Your opponent is a gutter fighter. I'll bet you that right now he's examining your life under a microscope. He won't find any ammunition, will he?"

"No." The word came to Adam's lips automatically.

"Good," Stewart Needham said. "How's Mary Beth?"

JENNIFER AND ADAM were spending a lazy weekend at a country house in Vermont that a friend of Adam's had loaned him. The air was crisp and fresh, hinting at the winter to come. It was a perfect weekend, comfortable and relaxed, with long hikes during the day and games and easy conversation before a blazing fire at night.

They had carefully gone through all the Sunday papers. Adam was moving up in every poll. With a few exceptions, the media were for Adam. They liked his style, his honesty, his intelligence and his frankness. They kept comparing him to John Kennedy.

Adam sprawled in front of the fireplace, watching flame shadows dancing across Jennifer's face. "How would you like to be the wife of the President?"

"Sorry. I'm already in love with a senator."

"Will you be disappointed if I don't win, Jennifer?"

"No. The only reason I want it is because you want it, darling."

"If I do win, it will mean living in Washington."

"If we're together, nothing else matters."

"What about your law practice?"

Jennifer smiled. "The last time I heard, they had lawyers in Washington."

"What if I asked you to give it up?"

"I'd give it up."

"I don't want you to. You're too damned good at it."

"All I care about is being with you. I love you so much, Adam."

He stroked her soft dark brown hair and said, "I love you, too. So much."

They went to bed, and later, they slept.

On Sunday night they drove back to New York. They picked up Jennifer's car at the garage where she had parked it, and Adam returned to his home. Jennifer went back to their apartment in New York.

JENNIFER'S DAYS WERE unbelievably full. If she had thought she was busy before, now she was besieged. She was representing international corporations that had bent a few laws and been caught, senators with their fingers in the till, movie stars who had gotten into trouble. She represented bank presidents and bank robbers, politicians and heads of unions.

Money was pouring in, but that was not important to Jennifer. She gave large bonuses to the office staff, and lavish gifts.

CORPORATIONS THAT CAME up against Jennifer no longer sent in their second string of lawyers, so Jennifer found herself pitted against some of the top legal talent of the world.

She was admitted into the American College of Trial Lawyers, and even Ken Bailey was impressed.

"Jesus," he said, "you know, only one percent of the lawyers in this country can get in?"

"I'm their token woman," Jennifer laughed.

WHEN JENNIFER REPRESENTED a defendant in Manhattan, she could be certain that Robert Di Silva would either prosecute the case personally or mastermind it. His hatred of Jennifer had grown with every victory she had.

During one trial in which Jennifer was pitted against the District Attorney, Di Silva put a dozen top experts on the stand as witnesses for the prosecution.

Jennifer called no experts. She said to the jury: "If we want a space-ship built or the distance of a star measured, we call in the experts. But when we want something really important done, we collect twelve ordinary folks to do it. As I recall, the founder of Christianity did the same thing."

Jennifer won the case.

ONE OF THE techniques Jennifer found effective with a jury was to say, "I know that the words 'law' and 'courtroom' sound a little frightening and remote from your lives, but when you stop to think about it, all we're doing here is dealing with the rights and wrongs done to human beings like ourselves. Let's forget we're in a courtroom, my friends. Let's just imagine we're sitting around in my living room, talking about what's happened to this poor defendant, this fellow human being."

And, in their minds, the jurors *were* sitting in Jennifer's living room, carried away by her spell.

This ploy worked beautifully for Jennifer until one day when she was defending a client against Robert Di Silva. The District Attorney rose to his feet and made the opening address to the jury.

"Ladies and gentlemen," Di Silva said, "I'd like for you to forget you're in a court of law. I want you to imagine that you're sitting at home in my living room and we're just sitting around informally chatting about the terrible things the defendant has done."

Ken Bailey leaned over and whispered to Jennifer, "Do you hear what that bastard's doing? He's stealing your stuff!"

"Don't worry about it," Jennifer replied coolly.

When Jennifer got up to address the jury, she said:

"Ladies and gentlemen, I've never heard anything as outrageous as the remarks of the District Attorney." Her voice rang with righteous indignation. "For a minute, I couldn't believe I had heard him correctly. How dare he tell you to *forget* you're sitting in a court of law! This courtroom is one of the most precious possessions our nation has! It is the foundation of our freedom. Yours and mine and the defendant's. And for the District Attorney to suggest that you forget where you are, that you forget your sworn duty, I find both shocking and contemptible. I'm asking you, ladies and gentlemen, to *remember* where you are, to remember that all of us are here to see that justice is done and that the defendant is vindicated."

The jurors were nodding approvingly.

Jennifer glanced toward the table where Robert Di Silva was sitting. He was staring straight ahead, a glazed look in his eyes.

Jennifer's client was acquitted.

AFTER EACH COURT victory, there would be four dozen red roses on Jennifer's desk, with a card from Michael Moretti. Each time, Jennifer would tear up the cards and have Cynthia take away the flowers. Somehow they seemed obscene coming from him. Finally Jennifer sent Michael Moretti a note, asking him to stop sending her flowers.

When Jennifer returned from the courtroom after winning her next case, there were five dozen red roses waiting for her.

22

The Rainy Day Robber case brought Jennifer new headlines. The accused man had been called to her attention by Father Ryan.

"A friend of mine has a bit of a problem—" he began, and they both burst out laughing.

The friend turned out to be Paul Richards, a transient, accused of robbing a bank of a hundred and fifty thousand dollars. A robber had walked into the bank wearing a long black raincoat, under which was hidden a sawed-off shotgun. The collar of the raincoat was raised so that his face was partially hidden. Once inside the bank, the man had brandished the shotgun and forced a teller to hand over all his available cash. The robber had then fled in a waiting automobile. Several witnesses had seen the getaway car, a green sedan, but the license number had been covered with mud.

Since bank robberies were a federal offense, the FBI had entered the case. They had put the *modus operandi* into a central computer and it had come up with the name of Paul Richards.

• • •

JENNIFER WENT TO visit him at Riker's Island.

"I swear to God I didn't do it," Paul Richards said. He was in his fifties, a red-faced man with cherubic blue eyes, too old to be running around pulling bank robberies.

"I don't care whether you're innocent or guilty," Jennifer explained, "but I have one rule. I won't represent a client who lies to me."

"I swear on my mother's life I didn't do it."

Oaths had ceased to impress Jennifer long ago. Clients had sworn their innocence to her on the lives of their mothers, wives, sweethearts and children. If God had taken those oaths seriously, there would have been a serious decline in the population.

Jennifer asked, "Why do you think the FBI arrested you?"

Paul Richards answered without hesitation. "Because about ten years ago I pulled a bank job and was dumb enough to get caught."

"You used a sawed-off shotgun under a raincoat?"

"That's right. I waited until it was raining, and then hit a bank."

"But you didn't do this last job?"

"No. Some smart bastard copied my act."

THE PRELIMINARY HEARING was before Judge Fred Stevens, a strict disciplinarian. It was rumored that he was in favor of shipping all criminals off to some inaccessible island where they would stay for the rest of their lives. Judge Stevens believed that anyone caught stealing for the first time should have his right hand chopped off, and if caught again, should have his left hand chopped off, in ancient Islamic tradition. He was the worst judge Jennifer could have asked for. She sent for Ken Bailey.

"Ken, I want you to dig up everything you can on Judge Stevens."

"Judge Stevens? He's as straight as an arrow. He—"

"I know he is. Do it, please."

THE FEDERAL PROSECUTOR who was handling the case was an old pro named Carter Gifford.

"How are you going to plead him?" Gifford asked.

Jennifer gave him a look of innocent surprise. "Not guilty, of course."

He laughed sardonically. "Judge Stevens will get a kick out of that. I suppose you're going to move for a jury trial."

"No."

Gifford studied Jennifer suspiciously. "You mean you're going to put your client in the hands of the hanging judge?"

"That's right."

Gifford grinned. "I knew you'd go around the bend one day, Jennifer. I can't wait to see this."

"THE UNITED STATES of America versus Paul Richards. Is the defendant present?"

The court clerk said, "Yes, Your Honor."

"Would the attorneys please approach the bench and identify themselves?"

Jennifer and Carter Gifford moved toward Judge Stevens.

"Jennifer Parker representing the defendant."

"Carter Gifford representing the United States Government."

Judge Stevens turned to Jennifer and said brusquely, "I'm aware of your reputation, Miss Parker. So I'm going to tell you right now that I do not intend to waste this court's time. I will brook no delays in this case. I want to get on with this preliminary hearing and get the arraignment over with. I intend to set a trial date as speedily as possible. I presume you will want a jury trial and—"

"No, Your Honor."

Judge Stevens looked at her in surprise. "You're not asking for a jury trial?"

"I am not. Because I don't think there's going to be an arraignment."

Carter Gifford was staring at her. *"What?"*

"In my opinion, you don't have enough evidence to bring my client to trial."

Carter Gifford snapped, "You need another opinion!" He turned to Judge Stevens. "Your Honor, the government has a very strong case. The defendant has already been convicted of committing exactly the same crime in exactly the same manner. Our computer picked him out of over two thousand possible suspects. We have the guilty man right here in this courtroom, and the prosecution has no intention of dropping the case against him."

Judge Stevens turned to Jennifer. "It seems to the court that there is enough *prima facie* evidence here to have an arraignment and a trial. Do you have anything more to say?"

"I do, Your Honor. There is not one single witness who can positively identify Paul Richards. The FBI has been unable to find any of the stolen money. In fact, the only thing that links the defendant to this crime is the imagination of the prosecutor."

The judge stared down at Jennifer and said with ominous softness, "What about the computer that picked him out?"

Jennifer sighed. "That brings us to a problem, Your Honor."

Judge Stevens said grimly, "I imagine it does. It is easy to confuse a live witness, but it is difficult to confuse a computer."

Carter Gifford nodded smugly, "Exactly, Your Honor."

Jennifer turned to face Gifford. "The FBI used the IBM 370/168, didn't it?"

"That's right. It's the most sophisticated equipment in the world."

Judge Stevens asked Jennifer, "Does the defense intend to challenge the efficiency of that computer?"

"On the contrary, Your Honor. I have a computer expert here in court today who works for the company that manufactures the 370/168. He programmed the information that turned up the name of my client."

"Where is he?"

Jennifer turned and motioned to a tall, thin man seated on a bench. He nervously came forward.

Jennifer said, "This is Mr. Edward Monroe."

"If you've been tampering with my witness," the prosecuting attorney exploded, "I'll—"

"All I did was to request Mr. Monroe to ask the computer if there were other possible suspects. I selected ten people who had certain general characteristics similar to my client. For purposes of identification, Mr. Monroe programmed in statistics on age, height, weight, color of eyes, birthplace—the same kind of data that produced the name of my client."

Judge Stevens asked impatiently, "What is the point of all this, Miss Parker?"

"The point is that the computer identified one of the ten people as a prime suspect in the bank robbery."

Judge Stevens turned to Edward Monroe. "Is this true?"

"Yes, Your Honor." Edward Monroe opened his briefcase and pulled out a computer readout.

The bailiff took it from Monroe and handed it to the judge. Judge Stevens glanced at it and his face became red.

He looked at Edward Monroe. "Is this some kind of joke?"

"No, sir."

"The computer picked *me* as a possible suspect?" Judge Stevens asked.

"Yes, sir, it did."

Jennifer explained, "The computer has no reasoning power, Your Honor. It can only respond to the information it is given. You and my client happen to be the same weight, height and age. You both drive green sedans, and you both come from the same state. That's really as much evidence as the prosecuting attorney has. The only other factor is the way in which the crime was done. When Paul Richards committed that bank robbery ten years ago, millions of people read about it. Any one of them could have imitated his *modus operandi*. Someone did." Jennifer indicated the piece of paper in Judge Stevens' hand. "That shows you how flimsy the State's case really is."

Carter Gifford sputtered, "Your Honor—" and stopped. He did not know what to say.

Judge Stevens looked again at the computer readout in his hand and then at Jennifer.

"What would you have done," he asked, "if the court had been a younger man, thinner than I, who drove a *blue* car?"

"The computer gave me ten other possible suspects," Jennifer said. "My next choice would have been New York District Attorney Robert Di Silva."

JENNIFER WAS SITTING in her office, reading the headlines, when Cynthia announced, "Mr. Paul Richards is here."

"Send him in, Cynthia."

He came into the office wearing a black raincoat and carrying a candy box tied with a red ribbon.

"I just wanted to tell you thanks."

"You see? Sometimes justice *does* triumph."

"I'm leaving town. I decided I need a little vacation." He handed Jennifer the candy box. "A little token of my appreciation."

"Thank you, Paul."

He looked at her admiringly. "I think you're terrific."

And he was gone.

Jennifer looked at the box of candy on her desk and smiled. She had received less for handling most of Father Ryan's friends. If she got fat, it would be Father Ryan's fault.

Jennifer untied the ribbon and opened the box. Inside was ten thousand dollars in used currency.

ONE AFTERNOON AS Jennifer was leaving the courthouse, she noticed a large, black, chauffeured Cadillac limousine at the curb. As she started to walk past it, Michael Moretti stepped out. "I've been waiting for you."

Close up, there was an electric vitality to the man that was almost overpowering.

"Get out of my way," Jennifer said. Her face was flushed and angry, and she was even more beautiful than Michael Moretti had remembered.

"Hey," he laughed, "cool down. All I want to do is talk to you. All you have to do is listen. I'll pay you for your time."

"You'll never have enough money."

She started to move past him. Michael Moretti put a conciliatory hand on her arm. Just touching her increased his excitement.

He turned on all of his charm. "Be reasonable. You won't know what you're turning down until you hear what I have to say. Ten minutes. That's all I want. I'll drop you off at your office. We can talk on the way."

Jennifer studied him a moment and said, "I'll go with you on one condition. I want the answer to a question."

Michael nodded. "Sure. Go ahead."

"Whose idea was it to frame me with the dead canary?"

He answered without hesitation. "Mine."

So now she knew. And she could have killed him. Grimly she stepped into the limousine and Michael Moretti moved in beside her. Jennifer noted that he gave the driver the address of her office building without asking.

As the limousine drove off, Michael Moretti said, "I'm glad about all the great things that are happening to you."

Jennifer did not bother to reply.

"I really mean that."

"You haven't told me what it is you want."

"I want to make you rich."

"Thanks. I'm rich enough." Her voice was filled with the contempt she felt toward him.

Michael Moretti's face flushed. "I'm trying to do you a favor and you keep fighting me."

Jennifer turned to look at him. "I don't want any favors from you."

He made his voice conciliatory. "Okay. Maybe I'm trying to make up a little for what I did to you. Look, I can send you a lot of clients. Important clients. Big money. You have no idea—"

Jennifer interrupted. "Mr. Moretti, do us both a favor. Don't say another word."

"But I can—"

"I don't want to represent you or any of your friends."

"Why not?"

"Because if I represented one of you, from then on you'd own me."

"You've got it all wrong," Michael protested. "My friends are in legitimate businesses. I mean banks, insurance companies—"

"Save your breath. My services aren't available to the Mafia."

"Who said anything about the Mafia?"

"Call it whatever you like. No one owns me but me. I intend to keep it that way."

The limousine stopped for a red light.

Jennifer said, "This is close enough. Thank you for the lift." She opened the door and stepped out.

Michael said, "When can I see you again?"

"Not ever, Mr. Moretti."

Michael watched her walk away.

My God, he thought, *that's a woman!* He suddenly became aware that he had an erection and smiled, because he knew that one way or another, he was going to have her.

23

I t was the end of October, two weeks before the election, and the senatorial race was in full swing. Adam was running against the incumbent Senator John Trowbridge, a veteran politician, and the experts agreed it was going to be a close battle.

Jennifer sat at home one night, watching Adam and his opponent in a television debate. Mary Beth had been right. A divorce now could easily have wrecked Adam's growing chances for victory.

WHEN JENNIFER WALKED into the office after a long business lunch, there was an urgent message for her to call Rick Arlen.

"He's called three times in the last half-hour," Cynthia said.

Rick Arlen was a rock star who had, almost overnight, become the hottest singer in the world. Jennifer had heard about the enormous incomes of rock stars, but until she got involved with Rick Arlen's affairs, she had had no idea what that really meant. From records, personal appearances, merchandising and now motion pictures, Rick Arlen's income was more than fifteen million dollars a year. Rick was twenty-five years old, an Alabama farm boy who had been born with a gold mine in his throat.

"Get him for me," Jennifer said.

Five minutes later he was on the line. "Hey, man, I've been tryin' to reach you for hours."

"Sorry, Rick. I was in a meeting."

"Problem. Gotta see you."

"Can you come in to the office this afternoon?"

"I don't think so. I'm in Monte Carlo, doin' a benefit for Grace and the Prince. How soon can you get here?"

"I couldn't possibly get away now," Jennifer protested. "I have a desk piled up—"

"Baby, I *need* you. You've got to get on a bird this afternoon."

And he hung up.

Jennifer thought about the phone call. Rick Arlen had not wanted to discuss his problem over the telephone. It could be anything from drugs to girls to boys. She thought about sending Ted Harris or Dan Martin to solve whatever the problem was, but she liked Rick Arlen. In the end, Jennifer decided to go herself.

She tried to reach Adam before she left, but he was out of the office.

She said to Cynthia, "Get me reservations on an Air France flight to Nice. I'll want a car to meet me and drive me to Monte Carlo."

Twenty minutes later she had a reservation on a seven o'clock flight that evening.

"There's a helicopter service from Nice directly to Monte Carlo," Cynthia said. "I've booked you on that."

"Wonderful. Thank you."

WHEN KEN BAILEY heard why Jennifer was leaving, he said, "Who does that punk think he is?"

"He *knows* who he is, Ken. He's one of our biggest clients."

"When will you be back?"

"I shouldn't be gone more than three or four days."

"Things aren't the same when you're not here. I'll miss you."

Jennifer wondered whether he was still seeing the young blond man.

"Hold down the fort until I get back."

. . .

AS A RULE, Jennifer enjoyed flying. She regarded her time in the air as freedom from pressures, a temporary escape from all the problems that beset her on the ground, a quiet oasis in space away from her endlessly demanding clients. This flight across the Atlantic, however, was unpleasant. It seemed unusually bumpy, and Jennifer's stomach became queasy and upset.

She was feeling a bit better by the time the plane landed in Nice the next morning. There was a helicopter waiting to fly her to Monte Carlo. Jennifer had never ridden in a helicopter before and she had looked forward to it. But the sudden lift and the swooping motions made her ill again, and she was unable to enjoy the majestic sights of the Alps below and the Grande Corniche, with miniature automobiles winding up the steep mountainside.

The buildings of Monte Carlo appeared, and a few minutes later the helicopter was landing in front of the modern white summer casino on the beach.

Cynthia had telephoned ahead and Rick Arlen was there to meet Jennifer.

He gave her a big hug. "How was the trip?"

"A little rough."

He took a closer look at her and said, "You don't look so hot. I'll take you up to my pad and you can rest up for the big do tonight."

"What big do?"

"The gala. That's why you're here."

"What?"

"Yeah. Grace asked me to invite anyone I liked. I like you."

"Oh, Rick!"

Jennifer could cheerfully have strangled him. He had no idea how much he had disrupted her life. She was three thousand miles away from Adam, she had clients who needed her, court cases to try—and she had been lured to Monte Carlo to attend a party!

Jennifer said, "Rick, how could—?"

She looked at his beaming face and started to laugh.

Oh, well, she was here. Besides, the gala might turn out to be fun.

• • •

THE GALA WAS spectacular. It was a milk fund concert for orphans, sponsored by Their Serene Highnesses, Grace and Rainier Grimaldi, and it was held outdoors at the summer casino. It was a lovely evening. The night was balmy and the slight breeze coming off the Mediterranean stirred the tall palm trees. Jennifer wished Adam could have been here to share it with her. There were fifteen hundred seats occupied by a cheering audience.

Half a dozen international stars performed, but Rick Arlen was the headliner. He was backed up by a raucous three-piece band and flashing psychedelic lights that stained the velvet sky. When he finished, he received a standing ovation.

THERE WAS A private party afterward at the *piscine,* below the Hotel de Paris. Cocktails and a buffet supper were served around the enormous pool, in which dozens of lighted candles floated on lily pads.

Jennifer estimated that there were more than three hundred people there. Jennifer had not brought an evening gown, and just looking at the splendidly dressed women made her feel like the poor little match girl. Rick introduced her to dukes and duchesses and princesses. It seemed to Jennifer that half the royalty of Europe was there. She met heads of cartels and famous opera singers. There were fashion designers and heiresses and the great soccer player, Pele. Jennifer was in the midst of a conversation with two Swiss bankers when a wave of dizziness engulfed her.

"Excuse me," Jennifer said.

She went to find Rick Arlen. "Rick, I—"

He took one look at her and said, "You're white as a sheet, baby. Let's split."

Thirty minutes later, Jennifer was in bed in the villa that Rick Arlen had rented.

"A doctor's on his way," Rick told her.

"I don't need a doctor. It's just a virus or something."

"Right. It's the 'or something' he's gonna check out."

DR. ANDRÉ MONTEUX was an elderly wisp of a man somewhere in his eighties. He wore a neatly trimmed full beard and carried a black medical case.

The doctor turned to Rick Arlen. "If you would leave us alone, please."

"Sure. I'll wait outside."

The doctor moved closer to the bed. "Alors. What have we here?"

"If I knew that," Jennifer said weakly, "I'd be making this house call and you'd be lying here."

He sat down on the edge of the bed. "How are you feeling?"

"Like I've come down with the bubonic plague."

"Put out your tongue, please."

Jennifer put out her tongue and began to gag. Dr. Monteux checked her pulse and took her temperature.

When he had finished, Jennifer asked, "What do you think it is, Doctor?"

"It could be any one of a number of things, beautiful lady. If you are feeling well enough tomorrow, I would like you to come to my office where I can do a thorough examination."

Jennifer felt too ill to argue. "All right," she said. "I'll be there."

IN THE MORNING Rick Arlen drove Jennifer into Monte Carlo where Dr. Monteux gave her a complete examination.

"It's a bug of some kind, isn't it?" Jennifer asked.

"If you wish a prediction," the elderly doctor replied, "I will send out for fortune cookies. If you wish to know what is wrong with you, we will have to be patient until the laboratory reports come back."

"When will that be?"

"It usually takes two or three days."

Jennifer knew there was no way she was going to stay there for two or three days. Adam might need her. She knew she needed him.

"In the meantime, I would like you to stay in bed and rest." He handed her a bottle of pills. "These will relax you."

"Thank you." Jennifer scribbled something on a piece of paper. "You can call me here."

It was not until Jennifer had gone that Dr. Monteux looked at the piece of paper. On it was written a New York telephone number.

AT THE CHARLES de Gaulle Airport in Paris, where she changed planes, Jennifer took two of the pills Dr. Monteaux had given her and a sleeping pill. She slept fitfully during most of the trip back to New York, but when she disembarked from the plane she was feeling no better. She had not arranged for anyone to meet her and she took a taxi to her apartment.

In the late afternoon, the telephone rang. It was Adam.

"Jennifer! Where have you—"

She tried to put energy into her voice. "I'm sorry, darling. I had to go to Monte Carlo to see a client and I couldn't reach you."

"I've been worried sick. Are you all right?"

"I'm fine. I—I've just been running around a lot."

"My God! I was imagining all kinds of terrible things."

"There's nothing to worry about," Jennifer assured him. "How's everything going with the campaign?"

"Fine. When am I going to see you? I was supposed to leave for Washington, but I can postpone—"

"No, you go ahead," Jennifer said. She did not want Adam to see her like this. "I'll be busy. We'll spend the weekend together."

"All right." His tone was reluctant. "If you're not doing anything at eleven, I'm on the CBS news."

"I'll watch, darling."

Jennifer was asleep five minutes after she had replaced the receiver.

IN THE MORNING Jennifer telephoned Cynthia to tell her she was not coming into the office. Jennifer had slept restlessly, and when she awakened she felt no better. She tried to eat breakfast but could not keep anything down. She felt weak and realized she had had nothing to eat for almost three days.

Her mind unwillingly went over the frightening litany of things that could be wrong with her. Cancer first, naturally. She felt for lumps in her breast, but she could not feel anything amiss. Of course, cancer could strike anywhere. It could be a virus of some kind, but the doctor surely would have known that immediately. The trouble was that it could be almost anything. Jennifer felt lost and helpless. She was not a hypochondriac, she had always been in wonderful health, and now she felt as though her body had somehow betrayed her. She could not bear it if anything happened to her. Not when everything was so wonderful.

She was going to be fine. Of course she was.

Another wave of nausea swept through her.

• • •

AT ELEVEN O'CLOCK that morning, Dr. André Monteux called from Monte Carlo. A voice said, "Just a moment. I'll put the doctor on."

The moment stretched into a hundred years, and Jennifer clutched the telephone tightly, unable to bear the waiting.

Finally, Dr. Monteux's voice came on and he said, "How are you feeling?"

"About the same," Jennifer replied nervously. "Are the results of the tests in?"

"Good news," Dr. Monteux said. "It is not the bubonic plague."

Jennifer could stand no more. "What is it? What's the matter with me?"

"You are going to have a baby, Mrs. Parker."

Jennifer sat there numbly staring at the telephone. When she found her voice again she asked, "Are—are you sure?"

"Rabbits never lie. I take it this is your first baby."

"Yes."

"I would suggest you see an obstetrician as soon as possible. From the severity of the early symptoms, there may be some difficulties ahead for you."

"I will," Jennifer replied. "Thank you for calling, Dr. Monteux."

She replaced the receiver and sat there, her mind in a turmoil. She was not sure when it could have happened, or what her feelings were. She could not think straight.

She was going to have Adam's baby. And suddenly Jennifer knew how she felt. She felt *wonderful;* she felt as though she had been given some indescribably precious gift.

The timing was perfect, as though the gods were on their side. The election would soon be over and she and Adam would be married as quickly as possible. It would be a boy. Jennifer knew it. She could not wait to tell Adam.

She telephoned him at his office.

"Mr. Warner is not in," his secretary informed her. "You might try his home."

Jennifer was reluctant to call Adam at home, but she was bursting with her news. She dialed his number. Mary Beth answered.

"I'm sorry to bother you," Jennifer apologized. "There's something I have to talk to Adam about. This is Jennifer Parker."

"I'm pleased that you called," Mary Beth said. The warmth in her voice was reassuring. "Adam had some speaking engagements, but he's returning tonight. Why don't you come up to the house? We can all have dinner together. Say, seven o'clock?"

Jennifer hesitated for a moment. "That will be lovely."

IT WAS A miracle that Jennifer did not have an accident driving to Croton-on-Hudson. Her mind was far away, dreaming of the future. She and Adam had often discussed having children. She could remember his words. *I want a couple that look exactly like you.*

As Jennifer drove along the highway, she thought she could feel a slight stirring in her womb, but she told herself that that was nonsense. It was much too early. But it would not be long now. Adam's baby was in her. It was alive and would soon be kicking. It was awesome, overwhelming. She—

Jennifer heard someone honking at her, and she looked up and saw that she had almost forced a truck driver off the road. She gave him an apologetic smile and drove on. Nothing could spoil this day.

IT WAS DUSK when Jennifer pulled up in front of the Warner house. A fine snow was beginning to fall, lightly powdering the trees. Mary Beth, wearing a long blue brocade gown, opened the front door to greet Jennifer, taking her arm and warmly welcoming her into the house, reminding Jennifer of the first time they had met.

Mary Beth looked radiantly happy. She was full of small talk, putting her visitor at ease. They went into the library where there was a cheerful fire crackling in the hearth.

"I haven't heard from Adam yet," Mary Beth said. "He's probably been detained. In the meantime, you and I can have a nice long chat. You sounded excited on the telephone." Mary Beth leaned forward conspiratorially. "What's your big news?"

Jennifer looked at the friendly woman across from her and blurted out, "I'm going to have Adam's baby."

Mary Beth leaned back in her chair and smiled. "Well! Now isn't that something! So am I!"

Jennifer stared at her. "I—I don't understand."

Mary Beth laughed. "It's really quite simple, my dear. Adam and I *are* married, you know."

Jennifer said slowly, "But—but you and Adam are getting a divorce."

"My dear girl, why on earth would I divorce Adam? I adore him."

Jennifer felt her head beginning to spin. The conversation was making no sense. "You're—you're in love with someone else. You said you—"

"I said that I'm in love. And I am. I'm in love with Adam. I told you, I've been in love with Adam since the first time I saw him."

She could not mean what she was saying. She was teasing Jennifer, playing some kind of silly game.

"Stop it!" Jennifer said. "You're like a brother and sister to each other. Adam doesn't make love to—"

Mary Beth's voice tinkled with laughter. "My poor dear! I'm surprised that someone as clever as you are could—" She leaned forward with concern. "You believed him! I'm so sorry. I am. I really am."

Jennifer was fighting to keep control of herself. "Adam is in love with me. We're getting married."

Mary Beth shook her head. Her blue eyes met Jennifer's and the naked hatred in them made Jennifer's heart stop for an instant.

"That would make Adam a bigamist. I'll never give him a divorce. If I had let Adam divorce me and marry you, he would lose the election. As it is, he's going to win it. Then we'll go on to the White House, Adam and I. There's no room in his life for anyone like you. There never was. He only thinks he's in love with you. But he'll get over that when he finds out I'm carrying his baby. Adam's always wanted a child."

Jennifer squeezed her eyes shut, trying to stop the terrible pain in her head.

"Can I get you something?" Mary Beth was asking solicitously.

Jennifer opened her eyes. "Have you told him you're having a baby?"

"Not yet." Mary Beth smiled. "I thought I'd tell him tonight when he gets home and we're in bed."

Jennifer was filled with loathing. "You're a monster . . ."

"It's all in the point of view, isn't it, honey? I'm Adam's wife. You're his whore."

Jennifer rose to her feet, feeling dizzy. Her headache had become an unbearable pounding. There was a roaring in her ears and she was afraid she was going to faint. She was moving toward the entrance, her legs unsteady.

Jennifer stopped at the door, pressing herself against it, trying to think. Adam had said he loved her, but he had slept with this woman, had made her pregnant.

Jennifer turned and walked out into the cold night air.

24

A dam was on a final campaign swing around the state. He telephoned Jennifer several times, but he was always surrounded by his entourage and it was impossible to talk, impossible for Jennifer to tell him her news.

Jennifer knew the explanation for Mary Beth's pregnancy: She had tricked Adam into sleeping with her. But Jennifer wanted to hear it from Adam.

"I'll be back in a few days and we'll talk then," Adam said.

The election was only five days away now. Adam deserved to win it; he was the better man. Jennifer felt that Mary Beth was right when she said it could be the stepping-stone to the presidency of the United States. She would force herself to wait and see what happened.

If Adam was elected senator, Jennifer would lose him. Adam would go to Washington with Mary Beth. There would be no way he could get a divorce. The scandal of a freshman senator divorcing a pregnant wife to marry his pregnant mistress would be too juicy a story for him ever to live down. But if Adam should lose the race, he would be free. Free to go back to his law practice, free to marry Jennifer and not worry or care about what anyone else thought. They would be able to live the rest of their lives together. Have their child.

ELECTION DAY DAWNED cold and rainy. Because of the interest in the senate race, a large voter turnout was expected at the polls despite the weather.

In the morning, Ken Bailey asked, "Are you going to vote today?"

"Yes."

"Looks like a close race, doesn't it?"

"Very close."

SHE WENT TO the polls late that morning, and as she stepped into the voting booth she thought dully, *A vote for Adam Warner is a vote against Jennifer Parker.* She voted for Adam and left the booth. She could not bear to go back to her office. She walked the streets all afternoon, trying not to think, trying not to feel; thinking and feeling, knowing that the next few hours were going to determine the rest of her life.

25

This is one of the closest elections we have had in years," the television announcer was saying.

Jennifer was at home alone watching the returns on NBC. She had made herself a light dinner of scrambled eggs and toast, and then was too nervous to eat anything. She sat in a robe huddled up on the couch, listening to her fate being broadcast to millions of people. Each viewer had his own reason for watching, for wanting one of the candidates to win or to lose, but Jennifer was sure that none of them was as deeply involved in the outcome of this election as she was. If Adam won, it would mean the end of their relationship . . . and the end of the baby in her womb.

There was a quick shot of Adam on the screen, and by his side, Mary Beth. Jennifer prided herself on being able to read people, to understand their motives, but she had been completely taken in by the moonlight-and-magnolias routine of the honey-voiced bitch. She kept pushing back the picture of Adam going to bed with that woman, making her pregnant.

Edwin Newman was saying, "Here are the latest returns in the senate race between the incumbent, John Trowbridge, and challenger Adam Warner. In Manhattan, John Trowbridge has a total of 221,375 votes. Adam Warner has a total of 214,895.

"In the Forty-fifth Election District of the Twenty-ninth Assembly District in Queens, John Trowbridge is two percentage points ahead."

Jennifer's life was being measured in percentage points.

"The totals from The Bronx, Brooklyn, Queens, Richmond and the counties of Nassau, Rockland, Suffolk and Westchester add up to 2,300,000 for John Trowbridge, and 2,120,000 for Adam Warner, with the votes from upstate New York just beginning to come in. Adam Warner has made a surprisingly strong showing against Senator Trowbridge, who is serving his third term. From the beginning, the polls have been almost evenly divided in this race. According to the latest returns, with sixty-two percent of the votes counted, Senator Trowbridge is beginning to pull ahead. When we read the last returns one hour ago, Senator Trowbridge was two percentage points ahead. The returns now indicate that he has increased his lead to two and a half percentage points. If this trend continues, the NBC computer will predict Senator Trowbridge to be the victor in the senatorial race for the United States Senate. Moving on to the contest between . . ."

Jennifer sat there, looking at the set, her heart pounding. It was as though millions of people were casting a vote to decide whether it would be Adam and Jennifer, or Adam and Mary Beth. Jennifer felt light-headed and giddy. She must remember to eat sometime. But not now. Nothing mattered now except what was happening on the screen in front of her. The suspense kept building, minute by minute, hour by hour.

At midnight, Senator John Trowbridge's lead was three percentage points. At two in the morning, with seventy-one percent of the votes counted, Senator Trowbridge was leading by a margin of three and a half percentage points. The computer declared that Senator John Trowbridge had won the election.

Jennifer sat there staring at the television set, drained of all emotion, of all feeling. Adam had lost. Jennifer had won. She had won Adam and their son. She was free to tell Adam now, to tell him about their baby, to plan for their future together.

Jennifer's heart ached for Adam, for she knew how much the election had meant to him. And yet in time, Adam would get over his defeat. One day he would try again, and she would help him. He was still young. The world lay before both of them. Before the three of them.

JENNIFER FELL ASLEEP on the couch, dreaming about Adam and the election and the White House. She and Adam and their son were in the Oval Office. Adam was making his acceptance speech. Mary Beth walked in and began to interrupt. Adam started to yell at her and his voice got louder and louder. Jennifer woke up. The voice was the voice of Edwin Newman. The television set was still on. It was dawn.

Edwin Newman, looking exhausted, was reading the final election returns. Jennifer listened to him, her mind still half asleep.

As she started to rise from the couch she heard him say, "And here are the final results on the New York State senatorial election. In one of the most stunning upsets in years, Adam Warner has defeated the incumbent, Senator John Trowbridge, by a margin of less than one percent."

It was over. Jennifer had lost.

26

When Jennifer walked into the office late that morning, Cynthia said, "Mr. Adams is on the line, Miss Parker. He's been calling all morning."

Jennifer hesitated, then said, "All right, Cynthia, I'll take it." She went into her office and picked up the telephone. "Hello, Adam. Congratulations."

"Thanks. We have to talk. Are you free for lunch?"

Jennifer hesitated. "Yes."

It had to be faced sometime.

IT WAS THE first time Jennifer had seen Adam in three weeks. She studied his face. Adam looked haggard and drawn. He should have been flushed with victory, but instead he seemed oddly nervous and uncomfortable. They ordered a lunch which neither of them ate, and they talked about the election, their words a camouflage to hide their thoughts.

The charade had become almost unbearable when, finally, Adam said, "Jennifer . . ." He took a deep breath and plunged ahead. "Mary Beth is going to have a baby."

Hearing the words from him somehow made it an unbearable reality. "I'm sorry, darling. It—it just happened. It's difficult to explain."

"You don't have to explain." Jennifer could see the scene clearly. Mary Beth in a provocative negligee—or naked—and Adam—

"I feel like such a fool," Adam was saying. There was an uncomfortable silence and he went on. "I got a call this morning from the chairman of the National Committee. There's talk about grooming me as their next presidential candidate." He hesitated. "The problem is that with Mary Beth pregnant, this would be an awkward time for me to get a divorce. I don't know what the hell to do. I haven't slept in three nights." He looked at Jennifer and said, "I hate to ask this of you, but—do you think we could wait a little while until things sort themselves out?"

Jennifer looked across the table at Adam and felt such a deep ache, such an intolerable loss, that she did not think she could stand it.

"We'll see each other as often as possible in the meantime," Adam told her. "We—"

Jennifer forced herself to speak. "No, Adam. It's over."

He stared at her. "You don't mean that. I love you, darling. We'll find a way to—"

"There is no way. Your wife and baby aren't going to disappear. You and I are finished. I've loved it. Every moment of it."

She rose to her feet, knowing that if she did not get out of the restaurant she would start screaming. "We must never see each other again."

She could not bear to look at his pain-filled eyes.

"Oh, God, Jennifer! Don't do this. Please don't do this! We—"

She did not hear the rest. She was hurrying toward the door, running out of Adam's life.

dam's telephone calls were neither accepted nor returned. His letters were sent back unopened. On the last letter Jennifer received,
she wrote the word "deceased" on the envelope and dropped it in
the mail slot. *It's true,* Jennifer thought. *I am dead.*

She had never known that such pain could exist. She had to be alone,
and yet she was not alone. There was another human being inside her, a
part of her and a part of Adam. And she was going to destroy it.

She forced herself to think about where she was going to have the
abortion. A few years earlier an abortion would have meant some quack
doctor in a dirty, sleazy back-alley room, but now that was no longer
necessary. She could go to a hospital and have the operation performed
by a reputable surgeon. Somewhere outside of New York City. Jennifer's
photograph had been in the newspapers too many times, she had been
on television too often. She needed anonymity, someplace where no one
would ask questions. There must never, never be a link between her and
Adam Warner. *United States Senator* Adam Warner. Their baby must die
anonymously.

Jennifer allowed herself to think of what the baby would have been like, and she began to weep so hard that it was difficult to breathe.

It had started to rain. Jennifer looked up at the sky and wondered whether God was crying for her.

KEN BAILEY WAS the only person Jennifer could trust to help her.

"I need an abortion," Jennifer said without preamble. "Do you know of a good doctor?"

He tried to mask his surprise, but Jennifer could see the variety of emotions that flickered across his face.

"Somewhere out of town, Ken. Someplace where they won't know me."

"What about the Fiji Islands?" There was an anger in his voice.

"I'm serious."

"Sorry. I—you caught me off guard." The news had taken him completely by surprise. He worshipped Jennifer. He knew that he loved her, and there were times when he thought he was in love with her; but he could not be sure, and it was torture. He could never do to Jennifer what he had done to his wife. *God,* Ken thought, *why the hell couldn't You make up Your mind about me?*

He ran his hands through his red hair and said, "If you don't want to have it in New York, I'd suggest North Carolina. It's not too far away."

"Can you check it out for me?"

"Yeah. Fine. I—"

"Yes?"

He looked away from her. "Nothing."

KEN BAILEY DISAPPEARED for the next three days. When he walked into Jennifer's office on the third day, he was unshaven and his eyes were hollow and red-rimmed.

Jennifer took one look at him and asked, "Are you all right?"

"I guess so."

"Is there anything I can do to help?"

"No." *If God can't help me, love, there's nothing you can do.*

He handed Jennifer a slip of paper. On it was written, *Dr. Eric Linden, Memorial Hospital, Charlotte, North Carolina.*

"Thank you, Ken."

"*De nada.* When are you going to do it?"

"I'll go down there this weekend."

He said awkwardly, "Would you like me to go with you?"

"No, thanks. I'll be fine."

"What about the return trip?"

"I'll be all right."

He stood there a moment, hesitating. "It's none of my business, but are you sure this is what you want to do?"

"I'm sure."

She had no choice. She wanted nothing more in the world than to keep Adam's baby, but she knew it would be insane to try to bring the baby up by herself.

She looked at Ken and said again, "I'm sure."

THE HOSPITAL WAS a pleasant old two-story brick building on the outskirts of Charlotte.

The woman behind the registration desk was gray-haired, in her late sixties. "May I help you?"

"Yes," Jennifer said. "I'm Mrs. Parker. I have an appointment with Dr. Linden to—to—" She could not bring herself to say the words.

The receptionist nodded understandingly. "The doctor's expecting you, Mrs. Parker. I'll have someone show you the way."

An efficient young nurse led Jennifer to an examining room down the hall and said, "I'll tell Dr. Linden you're here. Would you like to get undressed? There's a hospital gown on the hanger."

Slowly, possessed by a feeling of unreality, Jennifer undressed and put on the white hospital gown. She felt as though she were putting on a butcher's apron. She was about to kill the life inside her. In her mind, the apron became spattered with blood, the blood of her baby. Jennifer found herself trembling.

A voice said, "Here, now. Relax."

Jennifer looked up to see a burly bald-headed man wearing horn-rimmed glasses that gave his face an owlish appearance.

"I'm Dr. Linden." He looked at the chart in his hand. "You're Mrs. Parker."

Jennifer nodded.

The doctor touched her arm and said soothingly, "Sit down." He went to the sink and filled a paper cup with water. "Drink this."

Jennifer obeyed. Dr. Linden sat in a chair, watching her until the trembling had subsided.

"So. You want to have an abortion."

"Yes."

"Have you discussed this with your husband, Mrs. Parker?"

"Yes. We—we both want it."

He studied her. "You appear to be in good health."

"I feel—I feel fine."

"Is it an economic problem?"

"No," Jennifer said sharply. Why was he bothering her with questions? "We—we just can't have the baby."

Dr. Linden took out a pipe. "This bother you?"

"No."

Dr. Linden lit the pipe and said, "Nasty habit." He leaned back and blew out a puff of smoke.

"Could we get this over with?" Jennifer asked.

Her nerves were stretched to the breaking point. She felt that at any moment she was going to scream.

Dr. Linden took another long, slow puff from his pipe. "I think we should talk for a few minutes."

By an enormous effort of will, Jennifer controlled her agitation. "All right."

"The thing about abortions," Dr. Linden said, "is that they're so final. You can change your mind now, but you can't change it after the baby's gone."

"I'm not going to change my mind."

He nodded and took another slow puff of the pipe. "That's good."

The sweet smell of the tobacco was making Jennifer nauseous. She wished he would put away his pipe. "Doctor Linden—"

He rose to his feet reluctantly and said, "All right, young lady, let's have a look at you."

Jennifer lay back on the examining table, her feet in the cold metal stirrups. She felt his fingers probing inside her body. They were gentle, and skilled, and she felt no embarrassment, only an ineffable sense of loss, a deep sorrow. Unbidden visions came into her mind of her young son, because she knew with certainty it would have been a boy, running and playing and laughing. Growing up in the image of his father.

Dr. Linden had finished his examination. "You can get dressed now, Mrs. Parker. You may stay here overnight, if you like, and we'll perform the operation in the morning."

"No!" Jennifer's voice was sharper than she had intended. "I'd like it done now, please."

Dr. Linden was studying her again, a quizzical expression on his face.

"I have two patients ahead of you. I'll have the nurse come in and get a lab work-up and then put you in your room. We'll go ahead with surgery in about four hours. All right?"

Jennifer whispered, "All right."

SHE LAY ON the narrow hospital bed, her eyes closed, waiting for Dr. Linden to return. There was an old-fashioned clock on the wall and its ticking seemed to fill the room. The tick-tock became words: *Young Adam, Young Adam, Young Adam, our son, our son, our son.*

Jennifer could not shut the vision of the baby out of her mind. At this moment it was inside her body, comfortable and warm and alive, protected against the world in its amniotic womb. She wondered whether it had any primeval fear of what was about to happen to it. She wondered whether it would feel pain when the knife killed it. She put her hands over her ears to shut out the ticking of the clock. She found she was beginning to breathe hard, and her body was covered with perspiration. She heard a sound and opened her eyes.

Dr. Linden was standing over her, a look of concern on his face. "Are you all right, Mrs. Parker?"

"Yes," Jennifer whispered. "I just want it finished."

Dr. Linden nodded. "That's what we're going to do." He took a syringe from the table next to her bed and moved toward her.

"What's in that?"

"Demerol and Phenergan to relax you. We'll be going into the operating room in a few minutes." He gave Jennifer the injection. "I take it that this is your first abortion?"

"Yes."

"Then let me explain the procedure to you. It's painless and relatively simple. In the operating room you'll be given nitrous oxide, a general anesthesia, and oxygen by mask. When you're unconscious, a speculum will be inserted into the vagina, so that we can see what we're doing. We will then begin dilating the cervix with a series of metal dilators, in increasing sizes, and scraping out the uterus with a curette. Any questions so far?"

"No."

A warm, sleepy feeling was stealing over her. She could feel her tension vanishing as though by magic, and the walls of the room began to blur. She wanted to ask the doctor something, but she could not remember what it was . . . something about the baby . . . it no longer seemed important. The important thing was that she was doing what she had to do. It would all be over in a few minutes, and she could start her life again.

She found herself drifting off into a wonderful, dreamy state . . . she was aware of people coming into the room, lifting her onto a metal table with wheels . . . she could feel the coldness of the metal on her back through her thin hospital gown. She was being rolled down the hallway and she started to count the lights overhead. It seemed important to get the number right, but she was not sure why. She was being wheeled into a white, antiseptic operating room and Jennifer thought, *This is where my baby is going to die. Don't worry, little Adam. I won't let them hurt you.* And without meaning to, she began to cry.

Dr. Linden patted her arm. "It's all right. This won't hurt."

Death without pain, Jennifer thought. *That was nice.* She loved her baby. She did not want him to be hurt.

Someone put a mask over her face and a voice said, "Breathe deeply."

Jennifer felt hands raise the hospital gown and spread her legs apart.

It was going to happen. It was going to happen now. Young Adam, Young Adam, Young Adam.

"I want you to relax," Dr. Linden said.

Jennifer nodded. *Good-bye, my baby.* She felt a cold, steel object begin to move between her thighs and slowly slide up inside her. It was the alien instrument of death that was going to murder Adam's baby.

She heard a strange voice scream out, "Stop it! Stop it! Stop it!"

And Jennifer looked up at the surprised faces staring down at her and realized that the screams were coming from her. The mask pressed down harder against her face. She tried to sit up, but there were straps holding her down. She was being sucked into a vortex that was moving faster and faster, drowning her.

The last thing she remembered was the huge white light in the ceiling whirling above her, spinning down and going deep inside her skull.

WHEN JENNIFER AWAKENED, she was lying in the hospital bed in her room. Through the window she could see that it was dark outside. Her body felt sore and battered, and she wondered how long she had been unconscious. She was alive, but her baby—?

She reached for the bell pinned to her bed and pressed it. She kept pressing it, frantic, unable to stop herself.

A nurse appeared in the doorway, then quickly left. A few moments later Dr. Linden hurried in. He moved to the side of the bed and gently pried Jennifer's fingers away from the bell.

Jennifer grabbed his arm fiercely and said in a hoarse voice, "My baby—he's dead!"

Dr. Linden said, "No, Mrs. Parker. He's alive. I hope it's a boy. You kept calling him Adam."

Christmas came and went, and it was a new year, 1973. The snows of February gave way to the brisk winds of March, and Jennifer knew that it was time to stop working.

She called a meeting of the office staff.

"I'm taking a leave of absence," Jennifer announced. "I'll be gone for the next five months."

There were murmurs of surprise.

Dan Martin asked, "We'll be able to reach you, won't we?"

"No, Dan. I'll be out of touch."

Ted Harris peered at her through his thick spectacles. "Jennifer, you can't just—"

"I'll be leaving at the end of this week."

There was a finality in her tone that brooked no further questions. The rest of the meeting was taken up with a discussion of pending cases.

When everyone else had left, Ken Bailey asked, "Have you really thought this thing through?"

"I have no choice, Ken."

He looked at her. "I don't know who the son of a bitch is, but I hate him."

Jennifer put her hand on his arm. "Thank you. I'll be all right."

"It's going to get rough, you know. Kids grow up. They ask questions. He'll want to know who his father is."

"I'll handle it."

"Okay." His tone softened. "If there's anything I can do—anything— I'll always be around."

She put her arms around him. "Thank you, Ken. I—thank you."

JENNIFER STAYED IN her office long after everyone else had left, sitting alone in the dark, thinking. She would always love Adam. Nothing could ever change that, and she was sure that he still loved her. *Somehow,* Jennifer thought, *it would be easier if he did not.* It was an unbearable irony that they loved each other and could not be together, that their lives were going to move farther and farther apart. Adam's life would be in Washington now with Mary Beth and their child. Perhaps one day Adam would be in the White House. Jennifer thought of her own son growing up, wanting to know who his father was. She could never tell him, nor must Adam ever know that she had borne him a child, for it would destroy him.

And if anyone else ever learned about it, it would destroy Adam in a different way.

JENNIFER HAD DECIDED to buy a house in the country, somewhere outside of Manhattan, where she and her son could live together in their own little world.

She found the house by sheer accident. She had been on her way to see a client on Long Island and had turned off the Long Island Expressway at Exit 36, then had taken a wrong turn and found herself in Sands Point. The streets were quiet and shaded with tall, graceful trees, and the houses were set back from the road, each in its private little domain. There was a *For Sale* sign in front of a white colonial house on Sands Point Road. The grounds were fenced in and there was a lovely wrought-iron gate in front of a sweeping driveway, with lamp posts lighting the way, and a large front lawn with a row of yews sheltering the house. From the outside it looked enchanting. Jennifer wrote down the name of the realtor and made an appointment to see the house the following afternoon.

THE REAL ESTATE agent was a hearty, high-pressure type, the kind of salesman Jennifer hated. But she was not buying his personality, she was buying a house.

He was saying, "It's a real beauty. Yessir, a *real* beauty. About a hundred years old. It's in tip-top condition. Absolutely tip-top."

Tip-top was certainly an exaggeration. The rooms were airy and spacious, but in need of repair. *It would be fun*, Jennifer thought, *to fix up this house and decorate it.*

Upstairs, across from the master suite, was a room that could be converted into a nursery. She would do it in blue and—

"Like to walk around the grounds?"

It was the tree house that decided Jennifer. It was built on a platform high up in a sturdy oak tree. Her son's tree house. There were three acres, with the back lawn gently sloping down to the sound, where there was a dock. It would be a wonderful place for her son to grow up in, with plenty of room for him to run around. Later, he would have a small boat. There would be all the privacy here that they would need, for Jennifer was determined that this was going to be a world that belonged only to her and her child.

She bought the house the following day.

JENNIFER HAD HAD no idea how painful it would be to leave the Manhattan apartment she and Adam had shared. His bathrobe and pajamas were still there, and his slippers and shaving kit. Every room held hundreds of memories of Adam, memories of a lovely, dead past. Jennifer packed her things as quickly as possible and got out of there.

AT THE NEW house, Jennifer kept herself busy from early morning until late at night, so that there would be no time to think about Adam. She went into the shops in Sands Point and Port Washington to order furniture and drapes. She bought Porthault linens, and silver and china.

She hired local workmen to come in and repair the faulty plumbing and leaky roof and worn-out electrical equipment. From early morning until dusk, the house was filled with painters, carpenters, electricians and wallpaper hangers. Jennifer was everywhere, supervising everything. She wore herself out during the day, hoping she would be able to sleep at night, but the demons had returned, torturing her with unspeakable nightmares.

She haunted antique shops, buying lamps and tables and objets d'art. She bought a fountain and statues for the garden, a Lipschitz, a Noguchi and a Miró.

Inside the house, everything was beginning to look beautiful.

Bob Clement was a California client of Jennifer's and the area rugs he had designed for the living room and the nursery made the rooms glow with subdued color.

Jennifer's abdomen was getting bigger, and she went into the village to buy maternity clothes. She had an unlisted telephone installed. It was there only for emergencies, and she gave no one the telephone number and expected no calls. The only person in the office who knew where she lived was Ken Bailey, and he was sworn to secrecy.

He drove out to see Jennifer one afternoon, and she showed him around the house and grounds and took enormous pleasure in his delight.

"It's beautiful, Jennifer. Really beautiful. You've done a hell of a job." He looked at her swollen abdomen. "How long is it going to be?"

"Another two months." She put his hand against her belly and said, "Feel this."

He felt a kick.

"He's getting stronger every day," Jennifer said proudly.

She cooked dinner for Ken. He waited until they were having dessert before he brought up the subject.

"I don't want to pry," he said, "but shouldn't whoever the proud papa is be doing something—?"

"Subject closed."

"Okay. Sorry. The office misses you like hell. We have a new client who—"

Jennifer held up a hand. "I don't want to hear about it."

They talked until it was time for Ken to leave, and Jennifer hated to see him go. He was a dear man and a good friend.

JENNIFER SHUT HERSELF off from the world in every possible way. She stopped reading the newspapers and would not watch television or listen to the radio. Her universe was here within these four walls. This was her nest, her womb, the place where she was going to bring her son into the world.

She read every book she could get her hands on about raising children, from Dr. Spock to Ames and Gesell and back again.

When Jennifer finished decorating the nursery, she filled it with toys. She visited a sporting goods shop and looked at footballs and baseball bats and a catcher's mitt. And she laughed at herself. *This is ridiculous. He hasn't even been born yet.* And she bought the baseball bat and the catcher's mitt. The football tempted her, but she thought, *That can wait.*

IT WAS MAY, and then June.

The workmen finished and the house became quiet and serene. Twice a week Jennifer would drive into the village and shop at the supermarket, and every two weeks she would visit Dr. Harvey, her obstetrician. Jennifer obediently drank more milk than she wanted, took vitamins and ate all the proper, healthy foods. She was getting large now and clumsy, and it was becoming difficult for her to move about.

She had always been active, and she had thought she would loathe getting heavy and awkward, having to move slowly; but somehow, she did not mind it. There was no reason to hurry anymore. The days became long and dreamy and peaceful. Some diurnal clock within her had slowed its tempo. It was as though she were reserving her energy, pouring it into the other body living inside her.

ONE MORNING, DR. HARVEY examined her and said, "Another two weeks, Mrs. Parker."

It was so close now. Jennifer had thought she might be afraid. She had heard all the old wives' tales of the pain, the accidents, the malformed babies, but she felt no fear, only a longing to see her child, an impatience to get his birth over with so she could hold him in her arms.

Ken Bailey drove out to the house almost every day now, bringing with him *The Little Engine That Could, Little Red Hen, Pat the Bunny,* and a dozen Dr. Seuss books.

"He'll love these," Ken said.

And Jennifer smiled, because he had said "he." *An omen.*

They strolled through the grounds and had a picnic lunch at the water's edge and sat in the sun. Jennifer was self-conscious about her looks. She thought, *Why would he want to waste his time with the ugly fat lady from the circus?*

And Ken was looking at Jennifer and thinking: *She's the most beautiful woman I've ever seen.*

THE FIRST PAINS came at three o'clock in the morning. They were so sharp that Jennifer was left breathless. A few moments later they were repeated and Jennifer thought exultantly, *It's happening!*

She began to count the time between the pains, and when they were ten minutes apart she telephoned her obstetrician. Jennifer drove to the hospital, pulling over to the side of the road every time a contraction came. An attendant was standing outside waiting for her when she arrived, and a few minutes later Dr. Harvey was examining her.

When he finished, he said reassuringly, "Well, this is going to be an easy delivery, Mrs. Parker. Just relax and we'll let nature take its course."

It was not easy, but neither was it unbearable. Jennifer could stand the pain because out of it something wonderful was happening. She was in labor for almost eight hours, and at the end of that time, when her body was wracked and contorted with spasms and she thought that it was never going to stop, she felt a quick easing and then a rushing emptiness, and a sudden blessed peace.

She heard a thin squeal and Dr. Harvey was holding up her baby, saying, "Would you like to take a look at your son, Mrs. Parker?"

Jennifer's smile lit the room.

29

His name was Joshua Adam Parker and he weighed in at eight pounds, six ounces, a perfectly formed baby. Jennifer knew that babies were supposed to be ugly at birth, wrinkled and red and resembling little apes. Not Joshua Adam. He was beautiful. The nurses at the hospital kept telling Jennifer what a handsome boy Joshua was, and Jennifer could not hear it often enough. The resemblance to Adam was striking. Joshua Adam had his father's gray-blue eyes and beautifully shaped head. When Jennifer looked at him, she was looking at Adam. It was a strange feeling, a poignant mixture of joy and sadness. How Adam would have loved to see his handsome son!

WHEN JOSHUA WAS two days old he smiled up at Jennifer and she excitedly rang for the nurse.

"Look! He's smiling!"

"It's gas, Mrs. Parker."

"With other babies it might be gas," Jennifer said stubbornly. "My son is smiling."

Jennifer had wondered how she would feel about her baby, had worried whether she would be a good mother. Babies were surely boring to be around. They messed their diapers, demanded to be fed constantly, cried and slept. There was no communication with them.

I won't really feel anything about him until he's four or five years old, Jennifer had thought. How wrong, how wrong. From the moment of Joshua's birth, Jennifer loved her son with a love she had never known existed in her. It was a fiercely protective love. Joshua was so small, and the world so large.

When Jennifer brought Joshua home from the hospital, she was given a long list of instructions, but they only served to panic her. For the first two weeks a practical nurse stayed at the house. After that, Jennifer was on her own, and she was terrified she might do something wrong that would kill the baby. She was afraid he might stop breathing at any moment.

The first time Jennifer made Joshua's formula, she realized she had forgotten to sterilize the nipple. She threw the formula in the sink and started all over again. When she had finished she remembered she had forgotten to sterilize the bottle. She began again. By the time Joshua's meal was ready, he was screaming with rage.

THERE WERE TIMES when Jennifer did not think she would be able to cope. At unexpected moments she was overwhelmed with feelings of unexplained depression. She told herself that it was the normal postpartum blues, but the explanation did not make her feel any better. She was constantly exhausted. It seemed to her that she was up all night giving Joshua his feedings and when she did finally manage to drop off to sleep, Joshua's cries would awaken her and Jennifer would stumble back into the nursery.

SHE CALLED THE doctor constantly, at all hours of the day and night.

"Joshua's breathing too fast" . . . "He's breathing too slowly" . . . "Joshua's coughing" . . . "He didn't eat his dinner" . . . "Joshua vomited."

In self-defense, the doctor finally drove to the house and gave Jennifer a lecture.

"Mrs. Parker, I've never seen a healthier baby than your son. He may *look* fragile, but he's as strong as an ox. Stop worrying about him and enjoy him. Just remember one thing—he's going to outlive both of us!"

And so Jennifer began to relax. She had decorated Joshua's bedroom with print curtains and a bedspread with a blue background sprigged with white flowers and yellow butterflies. There was a crib, a play pen, a miniature matching chest and desk and chair, a rocking horse, and the chest full of toys.

Jennifer loved holding Joshua, bathing and diapering him, taking him for airings in his shiny new perambulator. She talked to him constantly, and when Joshua was four weeks old he rewarded her with a smile. *Not gas,* Jennifer thought happily. *A smile!*

THE FIRST TIME Ken Bailey saw the baby, he stared at it for a long time. With a feeling of sudden panic, Jennifer thought, *He's going to recognize it. He's going to know it's Adam's baby.*

But all Ken said was, "He's a real beauty. He takes after his mother."

She let Ken hold Joshua in his arms and she laughed at Ken's awkwardness. But she could not help thinking, *Joshua will never have a father to hold him.*

SIX WEEKS HAD passed and it was time to go back to work. Jennifer hated the idea of being away from her son, even for a few hours a day, but the thought of returning to the office filled her with excitement. She had completely cut herself off from everything for so long. It was time to re-enter her other world.

She looked in the mirror and decided the first thing she had to do was get her body back in shape. She had been dieting and exercising since shortly after Joshua's birth, but now she went at it even more strenuously, and soon she began to look like her old self.

Jennifer started to interview housekeepers. She examined them as though each one was a juror: she probed, looking for weaknesses, lies, incompetence. She interviewed more than twenty potential candidates before she found one she liked and trusted, a middle-aged Scotswoman named Mrs. Mackey, who had worked for one family for fifteen years and had left when the children had grown up and gone away to school.

Jennifer had Ken check her out, and when Ken assured her that Mrs. Mackey was legitimate, Jennifer hired her.

A week later Jennifer returned to the office.

30

Jennifer Parker's sudden disappearance had created a spate of rumors around Manhattan law offices.

When word got out on the grapevine that Jennifer was back, the interest was enormous. The reception that Jennifer received on the morning she returned kept swelling, as attorneys from other offices dropped by to visit her.

Cynthia, Dan and Ted had hung streamers across the room and a huge *Welcome Back* sign. There was champagne and cake.

"At nine o'clock in the morning?" Jennifer protested.

But they insisted.

"It's been a madhouse here without you," Dan Martin told her. "You're not planning to do this again, are you?"

Jennifer looked at him and said, "No. I'm not planning to do this again."

Unexpected visitors kept dropping in to make sure Jennifer was all right and to wish her well.

She parried questions about where she had been with a smile and "We're not allowed to tell."

She held conferences all day with the members of her staff. Hundreds of telephone messages had accumulated.

When Ken Bailey was in Jennifer's office alone with her, he said, "You know who's been driving us nuts trying to reach you?"

Jennifer's heart leaped. "Who?"

"Michael Moretti."

"Oh."

"He's weird. When we wouldn't tell him where you were, he made us swear you were all right."

"Forget about Michael Moretti."

Jennifer went over all the cases that were being handled by the office. Business was excellent. They had acquired a lot of important new clients. Some of the older clients refused to deal with anyone but Jennifer, and were waiting for her return.

"I'll call them as soon as I can," Jennifer promised.

She went through the rest of the telephone messages. There were a dozen calls from Mr. Adams. Perhaps she should have let Adam know that she was all right, that nothing had happened to her. But she knew she could not bear hearing his voice, knowing he was close and that she would not be able to see him, touch him, hold him. Tell him about Joshua.

Cynthia had clipped news stories she thought would be of interest to Jennifer. There was a syndicated series on Michael Moretti, calling him the most important Mafia leader in the country. There was a photograph of him and under it the caption, *I'm just an insurance salesman.*

IT TOOK JENNIFER three months to catch up on her backlog of cases. She could have handled it more rapidly, but she insisted on leaving the office at four o'clock every day, no matter what she was involved in. Joshua was waiting.

Mornings, before Jennifer went to the office, she made Joshua's breakfast herself and spent as much time as possible playing with him before she left.

When Jennifer came home in the afternoon, she devoted all of her time to Joshua. She forced herself to leave her business problems at the office, and turned down any cases that would take her away from her son. She stopped working weekends. She would let nothing intrude on her private world.

She loved reading aloud to Joshua.

Mrs. Mackey protested, "He's an infant, Mrs. Parker. He doesn't understand a word you're saying."

Jennifer would reply confidently, "Joshua understands."

And she would go on reading.

JOSHUA WAS A series of unending miracles. When he was three months old he began cooing and trying to talk to Jennifer. He amused himself in his crib with a large, tinkling ball and a toy bunny that Ken had brought him. When he was six months old, he was already trying to climb out of his crib, restless to explore the world. Jennifer held him in her arms and he grabbed her fingers with his tiny hands and they carried on long and serious conversations.

JENNIFER'S DAYS AT the office were full. One morning she received a call from Philip Redding, president of a large oil corporation.

"I wonder if we could meet," he said. "I have a problem."

Jennifer did not have to ask him what it was. His company had been accused of paying bribes in order to do business in the Middle East. There would be a large fee for handling the case, but Jennifer simply did not have the time.

"I'm sorry," she said. "I'm not available, but I can recommend someone who's very good."

"I was told not to take no for an answer," Philip Redding replied.

"By whom?"

"A friend of mine. Judge Lawrence Waldman."

Jennifer heard the name with disbelief. "Judge Waldman asked you to call me?"

"He said you're the best there is, but I already knew that."

Jennifer held the receiver in her hand, thinking of her previous experiences with Judge Waldman, how sure she had been that he hated her and was out to destroy her.

"All right. Let's have breakfast tomorrow morning," Jennifer said.

When she had hung up, she placed a call to Judge Waldman.

The familiar voice came on the telephone. "Well. I haven't talked to you in some time, young lady."

"I wanted to thank you for having Philip Redding call me."

"I wanted to make certain he was in good hands."

"I appreciate that, Your Honor."

"How would you like to have dinner with an old man one evening?"

Jennifer was taken by surprise. "I'd love having dinner with you."

"Fine. I'll take you to my club. They're a bunch of old fogies and they're not used to beautiful young women. It'll shake them up a bit."

JUDGE LAWRENCE WALDMAN belonged to the Century Association on West 43rd Street, and when he and Jennifer met there for dinner she saw that he had been teasing about old fogies. The dining room was filled with authors, artists, lawyers and actors.

"It is the custom not to make introductions here," Judge Waldman explained to Jennifer. "It's assumed that every person is immediately recognizable."

Seated at various tables, Jennifer recognized Louis Auchincloss, George Plimpton and John Lindsay, among others.

Socially, Lawrence Waldman was totally different from what Jennifer had expected. Over cocktails he said to Jennifer, "I once wanted to see you disbarred because I thought you had disgraced our profession. I'm convinced that I was wrong. I've been watching you closely. I think you're a credit to the profession."

Jennifer was pleased. She had encountered judges who were venal, stupid or incompetent. She respected Lawrence Waldman. He was both a brilliant jurist and a man of integrity.

"Thank you, Your Honor."

"Off the bench, why don't we make it Lawrence and Jennie?"

Her father was the only one who had ever called her Jennie.

"I'd like that, Lawrence."

The food was excellent and that dinner was the beginning of a monthly ritual they both enjoyed tremendously.

t was the summer of 1974. Incredibly, a year had flown by since Joshua Adam Parker had been born. He had taken his first tottering steps and he understood the words for nose and mouth and head.

"He's a genius," Jennifer flatly informed Mrs. Mackey.

Jennifer planned Joshua's first birthday party as though it were being given at the White House. On Saturday she shopped for gifts. She bought Joshua clothes and books and toys, and a tricycle he would not be able to use for another year or two. She bought favors for the neighbors' children she had invited to the party, and she spent the afternoon putting up streamers and balloons. She baked the birthday cake herself and left it on the kitchen table. Somehow, Joshua got hold of the cake and grabbed handfuls of it and crammed it into his mouth, ruining it before the other guests arrived.

Jennifer had invited a dozen children from the neighborhood, and their mothers. The only adult male guest was Ken Bailey. He brought Joshua a tricycle, a duplicate of the one Jennifer had bought.

Jennifer laughed and said, "That's ridiculous, Ken. Joshua's not old enough for that."

The party only lasted two hours, but it was splendid. The children ate too much and were sick on the rug, and fought over the toys and cried when their balloons burst, but all in all, Jennifer decided, it was a triumph. Joshua had been a perfect host, handling himself, with the exception of a few minor incidents, with dignity and aplomb.

That night, after all the guests had left and Joshua had been put to bed, Jennifer sat at his bedside watching her sleeping son, marveling at this wonderful creature that had come from her body and the loins of Adam Warner. Adam would have been so proud to have seen how Joshua had behaved. Somehow, the joy was diminished because it was hers alone.

Jennifer thought of all the birthdays to come. Joshua would be two years old, then five, then ten and twenty. And he would be a man and he would leave her. He would make his own life for himself.

Stop it! Jennifer scolded herself. *You're feeling sorry for yourself.* She lay in bed that night, wide awake, reliving every detail of the party, remembering it all.

One day, perhaps, she could tell Adam about it.

32

In the months that followed, Senator Adam Warner was becoming a household word. His background, ability and charisma had made him a presence in the Senate from the beginning. He won a place on several important committees and he sponsored a piece of major labor legislation that passed quickly and easily. Adam Warner had powerful friends in Congress. Many had known and respected his father. The consensus was that Adam was going to be a presidential contender one day. Jennifer felt a bittersweet pride.

JENNIFER RECEIVED CONSTANT invitations from clients, associates and friends to dinner and the theater and various charity affairs, but she refused almost all of them. From time to time she would spend an evening with Ken. She enjoyed his company immensely. He was funny and self-deprecating, but beneath the facade of lightness, Jennifer knew, there was a sensitive, tormented man. He would sometimes come to the house for lunch or dinner on weekends, and he would play with Joshua for hours. They loved each other.

Once, when Joshua had been put to bed and Jennifer and Ken were having dinner in the kitchen, Ken kept staring at Jennifer until she asked, "Is anything wrong?"

"Christ, yes," Ken groaned. "I'm sorry. What a bitch of a world this is."

And he would say nothing further.

ADAM HAD NOT tried to get in touch with Jennifer in almost nine months now, but she avidly read every newspaper and magazine article about him, and watched him whenever he appeared on television. She thought about him constantly. How could she not? Her son was a living reminder of Adam's presence. Joshua was two years old now and incredibly like his father. He had the same serious blue eyes and the identical mannerisms. Joshua was a tiny, dear replica, warm and loving and full of eager questions.

To Jennifer's surprise, Joshua's first words had been *car-car,* when she took him for a drive one day.

He was speaking in sentences now and he said *please* and *thank you.* Once, when Jennifer was trying to feed him in his high chair, he said impatiently, "Mama, go play with your toys."

Ken had bought Joshua a paint set, and Joshua industriously set about painting the walls of the living room.

When Mrs. Mackey wanted to spank him, Jennifer said, "Don't. It will wash off. Joshua's just expressing himself."

"That's all *I* wanted to do," Mrs. Mackey sniffed. "Express myself. You'll spoil that boy rotten."

But Joshua was not spoiled. He was mischievous and demanding, but that was normal for a two-year-old. He was afraid of the vacuum cleaner, wild animals, trains and the dark.

Joshua was a natural athlete. Once, watching him at play with some of his friends, Jennifer turned to Mrs. Mackey and said, "Even though I'm Joshua's mother, I'm able to look at him objectively, Mrs. Mackey. I think he may be the Second Coming."

JENNIFER HAD MADE it a policy to avoid any cases that would take her out of town and away from Joshua, but one morning she received an urgent call from Peter Fenton, a client who owned a large manufacturing firm.

"I'm buying a factory in Las Vegas and I'd like you to fly down there and meet with their lawyers."

"Let me send Dan Martin," Jennifer suggested. "You know I don't like to go out of town, Peter."

"Jennifer, you can wrap the whole thing up in twenty-four hours. I'll fly you down in the company plane and you'll be back the next day."

Jennifer hesitated. "All right."

She had been to Las Vegas and was indifferent to it. It was impossible to hate Las Vegas or to like it. One had to look upon it as a phenomenon, an alien civilization with its own language, laws and morals. It was like no other city in the world. Huge neon lights blazed all night long, proclaiming the glories of the magnificent palaces that had been built to deplete the purses of tourists who flocked in like lemmings and lined up to have their carefully hoarded savings taken away from them.

Jennifer gave Mrs. Mackey a long and detailed list of instructions about taking care of Joshua.

"How long are you going to be away, Mrs. Parker?"

"I'll be back tomorrow."

"Mothers!"

PETER FENTON'S LEAR jet picked Jennifer up early the next morning and flew her to Las Vegas. Jennifer spent the afternoon and evening working out the details of the contract. When they finished, Peter Fenton asked Jennifer to have dinner with him.

"Thank you, Peter, but I think I'll stay in my room and get to bed early. I'm returning to New York in the morning."

Jennifer had talked to Mrs. Mackey three times during the day and had been reassured each time that little Joshua was fine. He had eaten his meals, he had no fever and he seemed happy.

"Does he miss me?" Jennifer asked.

"He didn't say." Mrs. Mackey sighed.

Jennifer knew that Mrs. Mackey thought she was a fool, but Jennifer did not care.

"Tell him I'll be home tomorrow."

"I'll give him the message, Mrs. Parker."

Jennifer had intended to have a quiet dinner in her suite, but for some reason, the rooms suddenly became oppressive, the walls seemed to be closing in on her. She could not stop thinking about Adam.

How could he have made love to Mary Beth and made her pregnant when . . .

The game Jennifer always played, that her Adam was just away on a business trip and would soon return to her, did not work this time. Jennifer's mind kept returning to a picture of Mary Beth in her lace negligee and Adam . . .

She had to get out, to be somewhere where there were noisy crowds of people. *Perhaps,* Jennifer thought, *I might even see a show.* She quickly showered, dressed and went downstairs.

Marty Allen was starring in the main show room. There was a long line at the entrance to the room for the late show, and Jennifer regretted that she had not asked Peter Fenton to make a reservation for her.

She went up to the captain at the head of the line and said, "How long a wait will there be for a table?"

"How many in your party?"

"I'm alone."

"I'm sorry, miss, but I'm afraid—"

A voice beside her said, "My booth, Abe."

The captain beamed and said, "Certainly, Mr. Moretti. This way, please."

Jennifer turned and found herself looking into the deep black eyes of Michael Moretti.

"No, thank you," Jennifer said. "I'm afraid I—"

"You have to eat." Michael Moretti took Jennifer's arm and she found herself walking beside him, following the captain to a choice banquette in the center of the large room. Jennifer loathed the idea of dining with Michael Moretti, but she did not know how to get out of it now without creating a scene. She wished fervently that she had agreed to have dinner with Peter Fenton.

They were seated at a banquette facing the stage and the captain said, "Enjoy your dinner, Mr. Moretti, miss."

Jennifer could feel Michael Moretti's eyes on her and it made her uncomfortable. He sat there, saying nothing. Michael Moretti was a man of deep silences, a man who distrusted words, as though they were a trap rather than a form of communication. There was something riveting about his silence. Michael Moretti used silence the way other men used speech.

When he finally spoke, Jennifer was caught off guard.

"I hate dogs," Michael Moretti said. "They die."

And it was as though he was revealing a private part of himself that came from some deep wellspring. Jennifer did not know what to reply.

Their drinks arrived and they sat there drinking quietly, and Jennifer listened to the conversation they were not having.

She thought about what he had said: *I hate dogs. They die.* She wondered what Michael Moretti's early life had been like. She found herself studying him. He was attractive in a dangerous, exciting way. There was a feeling of violence about him, ready to explode.

Jennifer could not say why, but being with this man made her feel like a woman. Perhaps it was the way his ebony black eyes looked at her, then looked away from her, as though fearful of revealing too much. Jennifer realized it had been a long time since she had thought of herself as a woman. From the day she had lost Adam. *It takes a man to make a woman feel female,* Jennifer thought, *to make her feel beautiful, to make her feel wanted.*

Jennifer was grateful he could not read her mind.

Various people approached their booth to pay their respects to Michael Moretti: business executives, actors, a judge, a United States senator. It was power paying tribute to power, and Jennifer began to feel a sense of how much influence he wielded.

"I'll order for us," Michael Moretti said. "They prepare this menu for eight hundred people. It's like eating on an airline."

He raised his hand and the captain was at his side instantly. "Yes, Mr. Moretti. What would you like tonight, sir?"

"We'll have a *Chateaubriand,* pink and charred."

"Of course, Mr. Moretti."

"*Pommes soufflées* and an endive salad."

"Certainly, Mr. Moretti."

"We'll order dessert later."

A bottle of champagne was sent to the table, compliments of the management.

Jennifer found herself beginning to relax, enjoying herself almost against her will. It had been a long while since she had spent an evening with an attractive man. And even as the phrase came into Jennifer's mind, she thought, *How can I think of Michael Moretti as attractive? He's a killer, an amoral animal with no feelings.*

Jennifer had known and defended dozens of men who had committed terrible crimes, but she had the feeling that none of them was as dangerous as this man. He had risen to the top of the Syndicate and it had taken more than a marriage to Antonio Granelli's daughter to accomplish that.

"I telephoned you once or twice while you were away," Michael said. According to Ken Bailey, he had called almost every day. "Where were you?" He made the question sound casual.

"Away."

A long silence. "Remember that offer I made you?"

Jennifer took a sip of her champagne. "Don't start that again, please."

"You can have any—"

"I told you, I'm not interested. There's no such thing as an offer you can't refuse. That's only in books, Mr. Moretti. I'm refusing."

MICHAEL MORETTI THOUGHT of the scene that had taken place in his father-in-law's home a few weeks earlier. There had been a meeting of the Family and it had not gone well. Thomas Colfax had argued against everything that Michael had proposed.

When Colfax had left, Michael had said to his father-in-law, "Colfax is turning into an old woman. I think it's time to put him out to pasture, Papa."

"Tommy's a good man. He's saved us a lot of trouble over the years."

"That's history. He doesn't have it anymore."

"Who would we get to take his place?"

"Jennifer Parker."

Antonio Granelli had shaken his head. "I told you, Michael. It ain't good to have a woman know our business."

"This isn't just a woman. She's the best lawyer around."

"We'll see," Antonio Granelli had said. "We'll see."

MICHAEL MORETTI WAS a man who was used to getting what he wanted, and the more Jennifer stood up to him, the more he was determined to have her. Now, sitting next to her, Michael looked at Jennifer and thought, *One day you're going to belong to me, baby—all the way.*

"What are you thinking about?"

Michael Moretti gave Jennifer a slow, easy smile, and she instantly regretted the question. It was time to leave.

"Thank you for a wonderful dinner, Mr. Moretti. I have to get up early, so—"

The lights began to dim and the orchestra started an overture.

"You can't leave now. The show is starting. You'll love Marty Allen."

IT WAS THE kind of entertainment that only Las Vegas could afford to put on, and Jennifer thoroughly enjoyed it. She told herself she would leave immediately after the show, but when it was over and Michael Moretti asked Jennifer to dance, she decided it would be ungracious to refuse. Besides, she had to admit to herself that she was having a good time. Michael Moretti was a skillful dancer, and Jennifer found herself relaxing in his arms. Once, when another couple collided with them, Michael was pushed against Jennifer and for an instant she felt his male hardness, and then he immediately pulled away, careful to hold her at a discreet distance.

AFTERWARD, THEY WALKED into the casino, a vast terrain of bright lights and noise, packed with gamblers engrossed in various games of chance, playing as though their lives depended on their winning. Michael took Jennifer to one of the dice tables and handed her a dozen chips.

"For luck," he said.

The pit boss and dealers treated Michael with deference, calling him *Mr. M.* and giving him large piles of hundred-dollar chips, taking his markers instead of cash. Michael played for large stakes and lost heavily, but he seemed unperturbed. Using Michael's chips, Jennifer won three hundred dollars, which she insisted on giving to Michael. She had no intention of being under any obligation to him.

From time to time during the course of the evening, various women came up to greet Michael. All of them were young and attractive, Jennifer noticed. Michael was polite to them, but it was obvious that he was only interested in Jennifer. In spite of herself, she could not help feeling flattered.

Jennifer had been tired and depressed at the beginning of the evening, but there was such a vitality about Michael Moretti that it seemed to spill over, charging the air, enveloping Jennifer.

Michael took her to a small bar where a jazz group was playing, and afterward they went on to the lounge of another hotel to hear a new singing group. Everywhere they went Michael was treated like royalty. Everyone tried to get his attention, to say hello to him, to touch him, to let him know they were there.

During the time they were together, Michael did not say one word at which Jennifer could take offense. And yet, Jennifer felt such a strong sexuality coming from him that it was like a series of waves beating at her. Her body felt bruised, violated. She had never experienced anything like it. It was a disquieting feeling and, at the same time, exhilarating. There was a wild, animal vitality about him that Jennifer had never encountered before.

IT WAS FOUR o'clock in the morning when Michael finally walked Jennifer back to her suite. When they reached Jennifer's door, Michael took her hand and said, "Good night. I just want you to know this has been the greatest night of my life."

His words frightened Jennifer.

n Washington, Adam Warner's popularity was growing. He was written up in the newspapers and magazines with increasing frequency.
Adam started an investigation of ghetto schools, and headed a Senate
committee that went to Moscow to meet with dissidents. There were
newspaper photographs of his arrival at Sheremetyevo Airport, being
greeted by unsmiling Russian officials. When Adam returned ten days
later, the newspapers gave warm praise to the results of his trip.

The coverage kept expanding. The public wanted to read about
Adam Warner and the media fed their appetite. Adam became the spear-
head for reform in the Senate. He headed a committee to investigate
conditions in federal penitentiaries, and he visited prisons around the
country. He talked to the inmates and guards and wardens, and when his
committee's report was turned in, extensive reforms were begun.

In addition to the news magazines, women's magazines ran articles
about him. In *Cosmopolitan*, Jennifer saw a picture of Adam, Mary Beth
and their little daughter, Samantha. Jennifer sat by the fireplace in her
bedroom and looked at the picture for a long, long time. Mary Beth

was smiling into the camera, exuding sweet, warm southern charm. The daughter was a miniature of her mother. Jennifer turned to the picture of Adam. He looked tired. There were small lines around his eyes that had not been there before, and his sideburns were beginning to be tinged with gray. For a moment, Jennifer had the illusion that she was seeing the face of Joshua, grown up. The resemblance was uncanny. The photographer had had Adam turn directly into the camera, and it seemed to Jennifer that he was looking at her. She tried to read the expression in his eyes, and she wondered whether he ever thought about her.

Jennifer turned to look again at the photograph of Mary Beth and her daughter. Then she threw the magazine into the fireplace and watched it burn.

ADAM WARNER SAT at the head of his dinner table, entertaining Stewart Needham and half a dozen other guests. Mary Beth sat at the other end of the table, making small talk with a senator from Oklahoma and his bejeweled wife. Washington had been like a stimulant to Mary Beth. She was in her element here. Because of Adam's increasing importance, Mary Beth had become one of Washington's top hostesses and she reveled in that position. The social side of Washington bored Adam, and he was glad to leave it to Mary Beth. She handled it well and he was grateful to her.

"In Washington," Stewart Needham was saying, "more deals get made over dinner tables than in the hallowed halls of Congress."

Adam looked around the table and wished that this evening were over. On the surface, everything was wonderful. Inside, everything was wrong. He was married to one woman and in love with another. He was locked into a marriage from which there was no escape. If Mary Beth had not become pregnant, Adam knew he would have gone ahead with the divorce. It was too late now; he was committed. Mary Beth had given him a beautiful little daughter and he loved her, but it was impossible to get Jennifer out of his mind.

The wife of the governor was speaking to him.

"You're so lucky, Adam. You have everything in the world a man could want, don't you?"

Adam could not bring himself to answer.

34

The seasons came and went and they revolved around Joshua. He was the center of Jennifer's world. She watched him grow and develop, day by day, and it was a never-ending wonder as he began to walk and talk and reason. His moods changed constantly and he was, in turn, wild and aggressive and shy and loving. He became upset when Jennifer had to leave him at night, and he was still afraid of the dark, so Jennifer always left a night light on for him.

When Joshua was two years old he was impossible, a typical "Terrible Two." He was destructive and stubborn and violent. He loved to "fix" things. He broke Mrs. Mackey's sewing machine, ruined the two television sets in the house and took Jennifer's wristwatch apart. He mixed the salt with the sugar and fondled himself when he thought he was alone. Ken Bailey brought Jennifer a German shepherd puppy, Max, and Joshua bit it.

When Ken came to the house to visit, Joshua greeted him with, "Hi! Do you have a ding-dong? Can I see it?"

That year, Jennifer would gladly have given Joshua away to the first passing stranger.

At three, Joshua suddenly became an angel, gentle, affectionate and loving. He had the physical coordination of his father, and he loved doing things with his hands. He no longer broke things. He enjoyed playing outdoors, climbing and running and riding his tricycle.

Jennifer took him to the Bronx Zoo and to marionette plays. They walked along the beach and saw a festival of Marx Brothers movies in Manhattan, and had ice cream sodas afterward at Old Fashioned Mr. Jennings on the ninth floor of Bonwit Teller.

Joshua had become a companion. As a Mother's Day gift, Joshua learned a favorite song of Jennifer's father—*Shine On, Harvest Moon*—and sang it to Jennifer. It was the most touching moment of her life.

It's true, Jennifer thought, *that we do not inherit the world from our parents; we borrow it from our children.*

JOSHUA HAD STARTED nursery school and was enjoying it. At night when Jennifer came home, they would sit in front of the fireplace and read together. Jennifer would read *Trial Magazine* and *The Barrister* and Joshua would read his picture books. Jennifer would watch Joshua as he sprawled out on the floor, his brow knit in concentration, and she would suddenly be reminded of Adam. It was still like an open wound. She wondered where Adam was and what he was doing.

What he and Mary Beth and Samantha were doing.

JENNIFER MANAGED TO keep her private and professional life separate, and the only link between the two was Ken Bailey.

He brought Joshua toys and books and played games with him and was, in a sense, a surrogate father.

One Sunday afternoon Jennifer and Ken stood near the tree house, watching Joshua climb up to it.

"Do you know what he needs?" Ken asked.

"No."

"A father." He turned to Jennifer. "His real father must be one prize shit."

"Please don't, Ken."

"Sorry. It's none of my business. That's the past. It's the future I'm concerned about. It isn't natural for you to be living alone like—"

"I'm not alone. I have Joshua."

"That's not what I'm talking about." He took Jennifer in his arms and kissed her gently. "Oh, God damn it, Jennifer. I'm sorry . . ."

MICHAEL MORETTI HAD telephoned Jennifer a dozen times. She returned none of his calls. Once she thought she caught a glimpse of him sitting in the back of a courtroom where she was defending a case, but when she looked again he was gone.

35

Late one afternoon as Jennifer was getting ready to leave the office, Cynthia said, "There's a Mr. Clark Holman on the phone."

Jennifer hesitated, then said, "I'll take it."

Clark Holman was an attorney with the Legal Aid Society.

"Sorry to bother you, Jennifer," he said, "but we have a case downtown that no one wants to touch, and I'd really appreciate it if you could help us out. I know how busy you are, but—"

"Who's the defendant?"

"Jack Scanlon."

The name registered instantly. It had been on the front pages of the newspapers for the past two days. Jack Scanlon had been arrested for kidnapping a four-year-old girl and holding her for ransom. He had been identified from a composite drawing the police had obtained from witnesses to the abduction.

"Why me, Clark?"

"Scanlon asked for you."

Jennifer looked at the clock on the wall. She was going to be late for Joshua. "Where is he now?"

"At the Metropolitan Correctional Center."

Jennifer made a quick decision. "I'll go down and talk to him. Make the arrangements, will you?"

"Right. Thanks a million. I owe you one."

Jennifer telephoned Mrs. Mackey. "I'm going to be a little late. Give Joshua his dinner and tell him to wait up for me."

Ten minutes later, Jennifer was on her way downtown.

TO JENNIFER, KIDNAPPING was the most vicious of all crimes, particularly the kidnapping of a helpless young child; but every accused person was entitled to a hearing no matter how terrible the crime. That was the foundation of the law: justice for the lowliest as well as the highest.

Jennifer identified herself to the guard at the reception desk and was taken to the Lawyers' Visiting Room.

The guard said, "I'll get Scanlon for you."

A few minutes later a thin, aesthetic-looking man in his late thirties, with a blond beard and light blond hair was brought into the room. He looked almost Christlike.

He said, "Thank you for coming, Miss Parker." His voice was soft and gentle. "Thank you for caring."

"Sit down."

He took a chair opposite Jennifer.

"You asked to see me?"

"Yes. Even though I think only God can help me. I've done a very foolish thing."

She regarded him distastefully. "You call kidnapping a helpless little girl for ransom a 'foolish thing'?"

"I didn't kidnap Tammy for ransom."

"Oh? Why *did* you kidnap her?"

There was a long silence before Jack Scanlon spoke. "My wife, Evelyn, died in childbirth. I loved her more than anything in the world. If ever there was a saint on earth, it was that woman. Evelyn wasn't a strong person. Our doctor advised her not to have a baby, but she didn't listen." He looked down at the floor in embarrassment. "It—it may be hard for you to understand, but she said she wanted it anyway, because it would be like having another part of me."

How well Jennifer understood that.

Jack Scanlon had stopped speaking, his thoughts far away.

"So she had the baby?"

Jack Scanlon nodded. "They both died." It was difficult for him to go on. "For a while, I—I thought I would . . . I didn't want to go on living without her. I kept wondering what our child would have been like. I kept dreaming about how it would have been if they had lived. I kept trying to turn the clock back to the moment before Evelyn—" He stopped, his voice choked with pain. "I turned to the Bible and it saved my sanity. *Behold, I have set before you an open door which no one is able to shut.* Then, a few days ago, I saw a little girl playing on the street, and it was as though Evelyn had been reincarnated. She had her eyes, her hair. She looked up at me and smiled and I—I know it sounds crazy, but it was Evelyn smiling at me. I must have been out of my head. I thought to myself, *This is the daughter Evelyn would have had. This is our child.*"

Jennifer could see his fingernails digging into his flesh.

"I know it was wrong, but I took her." He looked up into Jennifer's eyes. "I wouldn't have harmed that child for anything in the world."

Jennifer was studying him closely, listening for a false note. There was none. He was a man in agony.

"What about the ransom note?" Jennifer asked.

"I didn't send a ransom note. The last thing in the world I cared about was money. I just wanted little Tammy."

"*Someone* sent the family a ransom note."

"The police keep saying I sent it, but I didn't."

Jennifer sat there, trying to fit the pieces together. "Did the story of the kidnapping appear in the newspapers before or after you were picked up by the police?"

"Before. I remember wishing they'd stop writing about it. I wanted to go away with Tammy and I was afraid someone would stop us."

"So anyone could have read about the kidnapping and tried to collect a ransom?"

Jack Scanlon twisted his hands helplessly. "I don't know. All I know is I want to die."

His pain was so obvious that Jennifer found herself moved by it. If he was telling the truth—and it was naked in his face—then he did not deserve to die for what he had done. He should be punished, yes, but not executed.

Jennifer made her decision. "I'm going to try to help you."

He said quietly, "Thank you. I really don't care anymore what happens to me."

"I do."

Jack Scanlon said, "I'm afraid I—I have no money to give you."

"Don't worry about it. I want you to tell me about yourself."

"What do you want to know?"

"Start from the beginning. Where were you born?"

"In North Dakota, thirty-five years ago. I was born on a farm. I guess you could call it a farm. It was a poor piece of land that nothing much wanted to grow on. We were poor. I left home when I was fifteen. I loved my mother, but I hated my father. I know the Bible says it's wrong to speak evil of your parents, but he was a wicked man. He enjoyed whipping me."

Jennifer could see his body tighten as he went on.

"I mean, he really enjoyed it. If I did the smallest thing he thought was wrong, he would whip me with a leather belt that had a big brass buckle on it. Then he'd make me get down on my knees and pray to God for forgiveness. For a long time I hated God as much as I hated my father." He stopped, too filled with memories to speak.

"So you ran away from home?"

"Yes. I hitchhiked to Chicago. I didn't have much schooling, but at home I used to read a lot. Whenever my father caught me, that was an excuse for another whipping. In Chicago, I got a job working in a factory. That's where I met Evelyn. I cut my hand on a milling machine and they took me to the dispensary, and there she was. She was a practical nurse." He smiled at Jennifer. "She was the most beautiful woman I'd ever seen. It took about two weeks before my hand was healed, and I went to her for a treatment every day. After that, we just kind of started going together. We talked about getting married, but the company lost a big order and I was laid off with the rest of the people in my department. That didn't matter to Evelyn. We got married and she took care of me. That was the only thing we ever argued about. I was brought up to believe that a man should take care of a woman. I got a job driving a truck and the money was good. The only part I hated was that we were separated, sometimes for a week at a time. Outside of that, I was awfully happy. We were both happy. And then Evelyn got pregnant."

A shudder ran through him. His hands began to tremble.

"Evelyn and our baby girl died." Tears were running down his cheeks. "I don't know why God did that. He must have had a reason, but I don't know why." He was rocking back and forth in his chair, unaware of what he was doing, his arms clasped in front of his chest, holding in his grief. *"I will instruct you and teach you the way you should go; I will counsel you."*

Jennifer thought, *This one the electric chair is not going to get!*

"I'll be back to see you tomorrow," Jennifer promised him.

BAIL HAD BEEN set at two hundred thousand dollars. Jack Scanlon did not have the bond money and Jennifer had it put up for him. Scanlon was released from the Correctional Center and Jennifer found a small motel on the West Side for him to move into. She gave him a hundred dollars to tide him over.

"I don't know how," Jack Scanlon said, "but I'll pay you back every cent. I'll start looking for a job. I don't care what it is. I'll do anything."

When Jennifer left him, he was searching through the want ads.

THE FEDERAL PROSECUTOR, Earl Osborne, was a large, heavy-set man with a smooth round face and a deceptively bland manner. To Jennifer's surprise, Robert Di Silva was in Osborne's office.

"I heard you were taking on this case," Di Silva said. "Nothing's too dirty for you to handle, is it?"

Jennifer turned to Earl Osborne. "What's he doing here? This is a federal case."

Osborne replied, "Jack Scanlon took the girl away in her family's car."

"Auto theft, grand larceny," Di Silva said.

Jennifer wondered if Di Silva would have been there if she were not involved. She turned back to Earl Osborne.

"I'd like to make a deal," Jennifer said. "My client—"

Earl Osborne held up a hand. "Not a chance. We're going all the way on this one."

"There are circumstances—"

"You can tell us all about it at the preliminary."

Di Silva was grinning at her.

"All right," Jennifer said. "I'll see you in court."

JACK SCANLON FOUND a job working at a service station on the West Side near his motel, and Jennifer stopped by to see him.

"The preliminary hearing is the day after tomorrow," Jennifer informed him. "I'm going to try to get the government to agree to a plea bargain and plead you guilty to a lesser charge. You'll have to serve some time, Jack, but I'll try to see that it's as short as possible."

The gratitude in his face was reward enough.

AT JENNIFER'S SUGGESTION, Jack Scanlon had bought a respectable suit to wear at the preliminary hearing. He had had his hair cut and his beard trimmed, and Jennifer was pleased with his appearance.

They went through the court formalities. District Attorney Di Silva was present. When Earl Osbome had presented his evidence and asked for an indictment, Judge Barnard turned to Jennifer.

"Is there anything you would like to say, Miss Parker?"

"There is, Your Honor. I'd like to save the government the cost of a trial. There are mitigating circumstances here that have not been brought out. I would like to plead my client guilty to a lesser charge."

"No way," Earl Osborne said. "The government will not agree to it."

Jennifer turned to Judge Barnard. "Could we discuss this in Your Honor's chambers?"

"Very well. I'll set a date for the trial after I've heard what counsel has to say."

Jennifer turned to Jack Scanlon, who was standing there, bewildered.

"You can go back to work," Jennifer told him. "I'll drop by and let you know what happened."

He nodded and said quietly, "Thank you, Miss Parker."

Jennifer watched him turn and leave the courtroom.

JENNIFER, EARL OSBORNE, Robert Di Silva and Judge Barnard were seated in the judge's chambers.

Osborne was saying to Jennifer, "I don't know how you could even ask me to plea-bargain. Kidnapping for ransom is a capital offense. Your client is guilty and he's going to pay for what he did."

"Don't believe everything you read in the newspapers, Earl. Jack Scanlon had nothing to do with that ransom note."

"Who you trying to kid? If it wasn't for ransom, what the hell *was* it for?"

"I'll tell you," Jennifer said.

And she told them. She told them about the farm and the beatings and about Jack Scanlon falling in love with Evelyn and marrying her, and losing his wife and daughter in childbirth.

They listened in silence, and when Jennifer was finished, Robert Di Silva said, "So Jack Scanlon kidnapped the girl because it reminded him of the kid he would have had? And Jack Scanlon's wife died in childbirth?"

"That's right." Jennifer turned to Judge Barnard. "Your Honor, I don't think that's the kind of man you execute."

Di Silva said unexpectedly, "I agree with you."

Jennifer looked at him in surprise.

Di Silva was pulling some papers out of a briefcase. "Let me ask you something," he said. "How would you feel about executing *this* kind of man?" He began to read from a dossier. "Frank Jackson, age thirty-eight. Born in Nob Hill, San Francisco. Father was a doctor, mother a prominent socialite. At fourteen, Jackson got into drugs, ran away from home, picked up in Haight-Ashbury and returned to his parents. Three months later Jackson broke into his father's dispensary, stole all the drugs he could get his hands on and ran away. Picked up in Seattle for possession and selling, sent to a reformatory, released when he was eighteen, picked up one month later on a charge of armed robbery with intent to kill . . ."

Jennifer could feel her stomach tightening. "What does this have to do with Jack Scanlon?"

Earl Osborne gave her a frosty smile. "Jack Scanlon is Frank Jackson."

"I don't believe it!"

Di Silva said, "This yellow sheet came in from the FBI an hour ago.

Jackson's a con artist and a psychopathic liar. Over the last ten years he's been arrested on charges ranging from pimping to arson to armed robbery. He did a stretch in Joliet. He's never held a steady job and he's never been married. Five years ago he was picked up by the FBI on a kidnapping charge. He kidnapped a three-year-old girl and sent a ransom note. The body of the little girl was found in a wooded area two months later. According to the coroner's report, the body was partially decomposed, but there were visible signs of small knife cuts all over her body. She had been raped and sodomized."

Jennifer felt suddenly ill.

"Jackson was acquitted on a technicality that some hotshot lawyer cooked up." When Di Silva spoke again his voice was filled with contempt. "That the man you want walking around the streets?"

"May I see that dossier, please?"

Silently, Di Silva handed it to Jennifer and she began reading it. It was Jack Scanlon. There was no question about it. There was a police mug shot of him stapled to the yellow sheet. He had looked younger then and he had no beard, but there was no mistaking him. Jack Scanlon—Frank Jackson—had lied to her about everything. He had made up his life story and Jennifer had believed every word. He had been so convincing that she had not even taken the trouble to have Ken Bailey check him out.

Judge Barnard said, "May I see that?"

Jennifer handed the dossier to him. The judge glanced through it and then looked at Jennifer. "Well?"

"I won't represent him."

Di Silva raised his eyebrows in mock surprise. "You shock me, Miss Parker. You're always saying that everyone is entitled to a lawyer."

"Everyone is," Jennifer replied evenly, "but I have a hard and fast rule: I won't represent anyone who lies to me. Mr. Jackson will have to get himself another lawyer."

Judge Barnard nodded. "The court will arrange that."

Osborne said, "I'd like his bail revoked immediately, Your Honor. I think he's too dangerous to be walking the streets."

Judge Barnard turned to Jennifer. "As of this moment you're still the attorney of record, Miss Parker. Do you have any objection to that?"

"No," Jennifer said tightly. "None."

Judge Barnard said, "I'll order his bail revoked."

JUDGE LAWRENCE WALDMAN had invited Jennifer to a charity dinner that evening. She had felt drained after the events of the afternoon and would have preferred to go home and have a quiet evening with Joshua, but she did not want to disappoint the judge. She changed clothes at the office and met Judge Waldman at the Waldorf-Astoria, where the party was taking place.

It was a gala event, with half a dozen Hollywood stars entertaining, but Jennifer was unable to enjoy it. Her mind was elsewhere. Judge Waldman had been watching her.

"Is anything wrong, Jennie?"

She managed a smile. "No, just a business problem, Lawrence."

And what kind of business am I really in, Jennifer wondered, *dealing with the dregs of humanity, the rapists and killers and kidnappers?* She decided it would be a wonderful night to get drunk.

The captain came over to the table and whispered in Jennifer's ear. "Excuse me, Miss Parker, there's a telephone call for you."

Jennifer felt an instant sense of alarm. The only one who knew where to reach her was Mrs. Mackey. She could only be calling because something was wrong.

"Excuse me," Jennifer said.

She followed the captain to a small office off the lobby.

Jennifer picked up the receiver and a man's voice whispered, "You bitch! You double-crossed me."

Jennifer felt her body begin to tremble. "Who is this?" she asked.

But she knew.

"You told the cops to come and get me."

"That's not true! I—"

"You promised to help me."

"I will help you. Where are—?"

"You lying cunt!" His voice dropped so low she could hardly make out his words. "You're going to pay for this. Oh, you're going to pay for this!"

"Wait a min—"

The telephone was dead. Jennifer stood there, chilled. Something had gone terribly wrong. Frank Jackson, alias Jack Scanlon, had somehow escaped and he was blaming Jennifer for what had happened. How had he known where she was? He must have followed her here. He could be waiting outside for her now.

Jennifer was trying to control the trembling of her body, trying to think, to reason out what had happened. He had seen the police coming to arrest him, or perhaps they had picked him up and he had gotten away from them. *How* did not matter. The important thing was that he was blaming her for what had happened.

Frank Jackson had killed before and he could kill again. Jennifer went into the ladies' room and stayed there until she was calm again. When she had regained control of herself, she returned to the table.

Judge Waldman took one look at her face. "What on earth's happened?"

Jennifer told him briefly. He was aghast.

"Good God! Would you like me to drive you home?"

"I'll be all right, Lawrence. If you could just make sure I get to my car safely, I'll be fine."

They quietly slipped out of the large ballroom and Judge Waldman stayed with Jennifer until the attendant brought her car.

"You're certain you don't want me to come with you?"

"Thanks. I'm sure the police will pick him up before morning. There aren't many people walking around who look like him. Good night."

Jennifer drove off, making sure no one was following her. When she was certain she was alone, she turned onto the Long Island Expressway and headed for home.

She kept looking in her rearview mirror, checking the cars behind her. Once she pulled off the road to let all the traffic pass her, and when the road behind her was clear, she drove on. She felt safer now. It could not be many hours before the police picked up Frank Jackson. There would be a general alert out for him by this time.

JENNIFER TURNED INTO her driveway. The grounds and the house, which should have been brightly lighted, were dark. She sat in the car staring at the house unbelievingly, her mind beginning to shriek with alarm. Frantically, she tore the car door open and raced to the front door. It was ajar. Jennifer stood there for an instant, filled with terror, then stepped into the reception hall. Her foot kicked something warm and soft and she let out an involuntary gasp. She turned on the lights. Max lay on the blood-soaked rug. The dog's throat had been cut from ear to ear.

"Joshua!" It was a scream. "Mrs. Mackey!"

Jennifer ran from room to room, switching on all the lights and calling out their names, her heart pounding so hard that it was difficult for her to breathe. She raced up the stairs to Joshua's bedroom. His bed had been slept in, but it was empty.

Jennifer searched every room in the house, then raced downstairs, her mind numb. Frank Jackson must have known all along where she lived. He had followed her home one night from her office or after she left the service station. He had taken Joshua and he was going to kill him to punish her.

She was passing the laundry room when she heard a faint scrabbling sound coming from the closet. Jennifer moved toward the closed door slowly and pulled it open. It was black inside.

A voice whimpered, "Please don't hurt me any more."

Jennifer turned on the light. Mrs. Mackey was lying on the floor, her hands and feet tightly bound with wire. She was only half-conscious.

Jennifer quickly knelt beside her. "Mrs. Mackey!"

The older woman looked up at Jennifer and her eyes began to focus. "He took Joshua." She began to sob.

As gently as she could, Jennifer untwisted the wire that was cutting into Mrs. Mackey's arms and legs. They were raw and bleeding. Jennifer helped the housekeeper to her feet.

Mrs. Mackey cried hysterically. "I c-couldn't stop him. I t-tried. I—"

The sound of the telephone cut into the room. The two women were instantly silenced. The telephone rang again and again, and somehow it had an evil sound. Jennifer walked over to it and picked it up.

The voice said, "I just wanted to make sure you got home all right."

"Where is my son?"

"He is a beautiful boy, isn't he?" the voice asked.

"Please! I'll do anything. Anything you like!"

"You've already done everything, Mrs. Parker."

"No, please!" She was sobbing helplessly.

"I like to hear you cry," the voice whispered. "You'll get your son back, Mrs. Parker. Read tomorrow's papers."

And the line went dead.

Jennifer stood there, fighting against the faintness, trying to think. Frank Jackson had said, "He *is* a beautiful boy, isn't he?" That could mean Joshua was still alive. Otherwise, wouldn't he have said *was* beautiful? She knew she was simply playing games with words, trying to keep her sanity. She had to do something quickly.

Her first impulse was to telephone Adam, ask him to help. It was his son who had been kidnapped, his son who was going to be killed. But she knew there was nothing Adam could do. He was two hundred and thirty-five miles away. She had only two choices: One was to call Robert Di Silva, tell him what had happened and ask him to throw out a dragnet to try to catch Frank Jackson. *Oh, God, that will take too long!*

The second choice was the FBI. They were trained to handle kidnappings. The problem was that this was not like other kidnapping. There would be no ransom note for them to trace, no chance to try to trap Frank Jackson and save Joshua's life. The FBI moved according to its own strict ritual. It would not be of any help in this instance. She had to decide quickly . . . while Joshua was still alive. Robert Di Silva or the FBI. It was difficult to think.

She took a deep breath and made her decision. She looked up a telephone number. Her fingers were trembling so badly she had to dial the number three times before she got it right.

When a man answered, Jennifer said, "I want to speak to Michael Moretti."

orry, lady. This is Tony's Place. I don't know no Mike Moretti."

"Wait!" Jennifer screamed. "Don't hang up!" She forced a calmness into her voice. "This is urgent. I'm a—a friend of his. My name is Jennifer Parker. I need to talk to him right away."

"Look, lady, I said—"

"Give him my name and this telephone number."

She gave him the number. Jennifer was beginning to stutter so badly she could hardly speak. "T-t-tell him—"

The line went dead.

Numbly, Jennifer replaced the receiver. She was back to one of her first two choices. Or both of them. There was no reason why Robert Di Silva and the FBI could not join forces to try to find Joshua. The thing that was driving her mad was that she knew how little chance they would have of finding Frank Jackson. There was no time. *Read tomorrow's papers.* There was a finality about his last words that made Jennifer certain he would not telephone her again, would not give anyone a chance to trace him. But she had to do *something*. She would try

Di Silva. She reached for the telephone again. It rang as she touched it, startling her.

"This is Michael Moretti."

"Michael! Oh, Michael, help me, please! I—" She began to sob uncontrollably. She dropped the telephone, then picked it up again quickly, terrified he had hung up. *"Michael?"*

"I'm here." His voice was calm. "Get hold of yourself and tell me what's wrong."

"I—I'll—" She took in quick, deep breaths, trying to stop the trembling. "It's my son, Joshua. He's—he's been kidnapped. They're going to—kill him."

"Do you know who took him?"

"Y-yes. His name is F-Frank Jackson." Her heart was pounding.

"Tell me what happened." His voice was quiet and confident.

Jennifer forced herself to talk slowly, recounting the sequence of events.

"Can you describe what Jackson looks like?"

Jennifer conjured up a picture of him in her mind. She put the picture into words, and Michael said, "You're doing fine. Do you know where he served time?"

"At Joliet. He told me he's going to kill—"

"Where was the gas station he worked at?"

She gave Michael the address.

"Do you know the name of the motel he was staying at?"

"Yes. No." She could not remember. She dug her fingernails into her forehead until it began to bleed, forcing herself to think. He waited patiently.

It came to her suddenly. "It's the Travel Well Motel. It's on Tenth Avenue. But I'm sure he isn't there now."

"We'll see."

"I want my son back alive."

Michael Moretti did not reply and Jennifer understood why.

"If we find Jackson—?"

Jennifer took a deep, shuddering breath. *"Kill him!"*

"Stay by your telephone."

The connection was broken. Jennifer replaced the receiver. She felt strangely calmer, as though something had been accomplished. There was no reason to feel the confidence she did in Michael Moretti. From a logical point of view, it was a wild, insane thing to have done; but logic had nothing to do with this. Her son's life was at stake. She had deliberately sent a killer to catch a killer. If it did not work . . . She thought of the little girl whose body had been raped and sodomized.

JENNIFER WENT TO tend to Mrs. Mackey. She took care of her cuts and bruises and put her to bed. Jennifer offered her a sedative, but Mrs. Mackey pushed it away.

"I couldn't sleep," she cried. "Oh, Mrs. Parker! He gave that baby sleeping pills."

Jennifer stared at her in horror.

MICHAEL MORETTI SAT at his desk, facing the seven men he had summoned. He had already given instructions to the first three.

He turned to Thomas Colfax. "Tom, I want you to use your connections. Go down and see Captain Notaras and have him pull the package on Frank Jackson. I want everything they've got on him."

"We're wasting a good connection, Mike. I don't think—"

"Don't argue! Just do it."

Colfax said stiffly, "Very well."

Michael turned to Nick Vito. "Check out the gas station where Jackson worked. Find out if he hung around any of the bars there, if he had any friends."

To Salvatore Fiore and Joseph Colella: "Get over to Jackson's motel. He's probably gone by now, but find out if he palled around with anyone. I want to know who his buddies were." He looked at his watch. "It's midnight. I'm giving you eight hours to find Jackson."

The men started out the door.

Michael called after them, "I don't want anything to happen to the kid. Keep calling in. I'll be waiting."

Michael Moretti watched them leave, then picked up one of the telephones on his desk and began to dial.

1:00 A.M.

THE MOTEL ROOM was not large, but it was very neat. Frank Jackson liked things neat. He felt it was part of being brought up properly. The Venetian blinds were rolled down and slanted so that no one could see into the room. The door was locked and chained, and he had pressed a chair against it. He walked over to the bed where Joshua lay. Frank Jackson had forced three sleeping pills down the boy's throat, and he was still sleeping soundly. Still, Jackson prided himself on being a man who took no chances, so Joshua's hands and feet were tightly bound together with the same kind of wire that had been used to tie up the old lady in the house. Jackson looked down at the sleeping boy and he was filled with a sense of sadness.

Why in God's name did people keep forcing him to do these terrible things? He was a gentle, peaceful man, but when everyone was against you, when everyone attacked you, you had to defend yourself. The trouble with everybody was that they always underestimated him. They failed to realize until too late that he was smarter than all of them.

HE HAD KNOWN the police were coming for him half an hour before they arrived. He had been filling the tank of a Chevrolet Camaro and had seen his boss go inside the office to answer the telephone. Jackson had not been able to hear the conversation, but it was not necessary. He saw the covert looks his boss gave him as he whispered into the telephone. Frank Jackson knew immediately what was happening. The police were coming for him. The Parker bitch had double-crossed him, had told the police to lock him up. She was like all the rest of them. His boss was still talking on the telephone when Frank Jackson grabbed his jacket and disappeared. It had taken him less than three minutes to find an unlocked car on the street and hot-wire it, and moments later he was headed for Jennifer Parker's house.

Jackson really had to admire his own intelligence. Who else would have thought of following her to find out where she lived? He had done that the day she had gotten him out on bail. He had parked across the street from her house and had been surprised when Jennifer had been met at the gate by a little boy. He had watched them together and sensed even then that the kid might come in handy. He was an unexpected bonus, what the poets called a hostage to fate.

Jackson smiled to himself at how terrified the old bitch of a housekeeper had been. He had enjoyed twisting the wire into her wrists and ankles. No, not enjoyed, really. He was being too hard on himself. It had been *necessary.* The housekeeper had thought he was going to rape her. She disgusted him. All women did, except for his sainted mother. Women were dirty, unclean, even his whore of a sister. It was only the children who were pure. He thought of the last little girl he had taken. She had been beautiful, with long blond curls, but she had had to pay for her mother's sins. Her mother had had Jackson fired from his job. People tried to keep you from earning an honest living and then punished you when you broke their stupid laws. The men were bad enough, but the women were worse. Pigs who wanted to soil the temple of your body. Like the waitress, Clara, he was going to take to Canada. She was in love with him. She thought he was such a gentleman because he had never touched her. If she only knew! The idea of making love to her sickened him. But he was going to take her out of the country with him because the police would be looking for a man alone. He would shave off his beard and trim his hair, and when he crossed the border he would get rid of Clara. That would give him great pleasure.

Frank Jackson walked over to a battered cardboard suitcase on a luggage rack, opened it and took out a tool kit. From it he removed nails and a hammer. He laid them on the bedside table next to the sleeping boy. Then he went into the bathroom and lifted a two-gallon gasoline can from the bathtub. He carried it into the bedroom and set the can on the floor. Joshua was going to go up in flames. But that would be *after* the crucifixion.

2:00 A.M.

THROUGHOUT NEW YORK and around the country, the word was spreading. It started in bars and flophouses. A cautious word here and there, dropped into a willing ear. It began as a trickle and spread to cheap restaurants and noisy discotheques and all-night newsstands. It was picked up by taxi drivers and truckers and girls working the midnight streets. It was like a pebble dropped into a deep, dark lake, with the ripples beginning to widen and spread. Within a couple of hours everyone on the street knew that Michael Moretti wanted some information and wanted it fast. Not many people were given a chance to do a favor for Michael Moretti. This was a golden opportunity for somebody, because Moretti was a man who knew how to show his appreciation. The word was that he was looking for a thin blond guy who looked like Jesus. People began searching their memories.

2:15 A.M.

JOSHUA ADAM PARKER stirred in his sleep and Frank Jackson moved to his side. He had not yet removed the boy's pajamas. Jackson checked to make sure that the hammer and nails were in place and ready. It was important to be meticulous about these things. He was going to nail the boy's hands and feet to the floor before he set the room on fire. He could have done it while the boy was asleep, but that would have been wrong. It was important that the boy be awake to see what was happening, to know he was being punished for the sins of his mother. Frank Jackson looked at his watch. Clara was coming to the motel to pick him up at seven-thirty. Five hours and fifteen minutes left. Plenty of time.

Frank Jackson sat down and studied Joshua, and once he tenderly fondled an errant lock of the small boy's hair.

3:00 A.M.

THE FIRST OF the telephone calls began coming in.

There were two telephones on Michael Moretti's desk and it seemed that the moment he picked up one, the other started ringing.

"I got a line on the guy, Mike. A couple years ago he was workin' a scam in Kansas City with Big Joe Ziegler and Mel Cohen."

"Fuck what he was doing a couple of years ago. Where is he *now*?"

"Big Joe says he ain't heard from him in about six months. I'm tryin' to get hold of Mel Cohen."

"Do it!"

• • •

THE NEXT PHONE call was no more productive.

"I went over to Jackson's motel room. He checked out. He was carryin' a brown suitcase and a two-gallon can that coulda had gasoline in it. The clerk has no idea where he went."

"What about the neighborhood bars?"

"One of the bartenders recognized his description, but he says he wasn't a regular. He went in two or three times after work."

"Alone?"

"Accordin' to the bartender, yeah. He didn't seem interested in the girls there."

"Check out the gay bars."

THE TELEPHONE RANG again almost as soon as Michael had hung up. It was Salvatore Fiore.

"Colfax talked to Captain Notaras. The police property clerk got a record of a pawn ticket in Frank Jackson's personal effects. I got the number of the ticket and the name of the pawn shop. It's owned by a Greek, Gus Stavros, who fences hot rocks."

"Did you check it out?"

"We can't check it out until mornin', Mike. The place is closed. I—"

Michael Moretti exploded. "We can't *wait* until morning! Get your ass down there!"

THERE WAS A telephone call from Joliet. It was hard for Michael to follow the conversation because his caller had had a laryngectomy and his voice sounded as if it was coming from the bottom of a box.

"Jackson's cellmate was a man named Mickey Nicola. They were pretty tight."

"Any idea where Nicola is now?"

"Last I heard he was back east somewhere. He's a friend of Jackson's sister. We have no address on her."

"What was Nicola sent up for?"

"They nailed him on a jewelry heist."

3:30 A.M.

THE PAWNSHOP WAS located in Spanish Harlem at Second Avenue and 124th Street. It was in an unloved two-story building, with the shop downstairs and living quarters upstairs.

Gus Stavros was awakened by a flashlight shining in his face. He instinctively started to reach for the alarm button at the side of his bed.

"I wouldn't," a voice said.

The flashlight moved away and Gus Stavros sat up in bed. He looked at the two men standing on either side of him and knew he had been given good advice. A giant and a midget. Stavros could feel an asthma attack coming on.

"Go downstairs and take whatever you want," he wheezed. "I won't make a move."

The giant, Joseph Colella said, "Get up. Slow."

Gus Stavros rose from his bed, cautious not to make any sudden movements.

The small man, Salvatore Fiore, shoved a piece of paper under his nose. "This is the number of a pawn ticket. We want to see the merchandise."

"Yes, sir."

Gus Stavros walked downstairs, followed by the two men. Stavros had installed an elaborate alarm system only six months earlier. There were bells he could have pushed and secret places on the floor he could have stepped on and help would be on its way. He did none of those things because his instincts told him he would be dead before anyone could reach him. He knew that his only chance lay in giving the two men what they wanted. He only prayed he would not die from a goddamned asthma attack before he got rid of them.

He turned on the downstairs lights and they all moved toward the front of the shop. Gus Stavros had no idea what was going on, but he knew it could have been a great deal worse. If these men had come merely to rob him, they could have cleaned out the pawn shop and been gone by now. It seemed they were only interested in one piece of merchandise. He wondered how they had circumvented the elaborate new alarms on the doors and windows, but he decided not to ask.

"Move your ass," Joseph Colella said.

Gus looked at the pawn ticket number again and began to sort through his files. He found what he was looking for, nodded in satisfaction, and went to the large walk-in strong room and opened it, the two men close behind him. Stavros searched along a shelf until he found a small envelope. Turning to the two men, he opened the envelope and took out a large diamond ring that sparkled in the overhead lights.

"This is it," Gus Stavros said. "I gave him five hundred for it." The ring was worth at least twenty thousand dollars.

"You gave five hundred to who?" little Salvatore Fiore asked.

Gus Stavros shrugged. "A hundred customers a day come in here. The name on the envelope is John Doe."

Fiore pulled a piece of lead pipe out of nowhere and smashed it savagely against Gus Stavros' nose. He fell to the floor screaming with pain, drowning in his own blood.

Fiore asked quietly, "Who did you say brought it in?"

Fighting for breath, Gus Stavros gasped, "I don't know his name. He didn't tell me. I swear to God!"

"What did he look like?"

The blood was flowing into Gus Stavros' throat so fast he could hardly speak. He was beginning to faint, but he knew if he passed out before he talked he would never wake up.

"Let me think," he pleaded.

Stavros tried to focus, but he was so dizzy from the pain that it was difficult. He forced himself to remember the customer walking in, taking the ring out of a box and showing it to him. It was coming back to him.

"He—he was kind of blond and skinny—" He choked on some blood. "Help me up."

Salvatore Fiore kicked him in the ribs. "Keep talkin'."

"He had a beard, a blond beard . . ."

"Tell us about the rock. Where did it come from?"

Even in his extreme pain, Gus Stavros hesitated. If he talked, he would be a dead man later. If he did not, he would die now. He decided to postpone his death as long as possible.

"It came from the Tiffany job."

"Who was in on the job with the blond guy?"

Gus Stavros was finding it harder to breathe. "Mickey Nicola."

"Where can we find Nicola?"

"I don't know. He—he shacks up with some girl in Brooklyn."

Fiore lifted a foot and nudged Stavros' nose. Gus Stavros screamed with pain.

Joseph Colella asked, "What's the broad's name?"

"Jackson. Blanche Jackson."

4:30 A.M.

THE HOUSE WAS set back from the street, surrounded by a small white picket fence with a carefully tended garden in front. Salvatore Fiore and Joseph Colella tramped through the flowers and made their way to the back door. It took them less than five seconds to open it. They stepped inside and moved toward the stairs. From a bedroom above they could hear the sounds of a bed creaking and the voices of a man and a woman. The two men pulled out their guns and started to move quietly up the stairs.

The woman's voice was saying, "Oh, Christ! You're wonderful, Mickey! Give it to me harder, baby."

"It's all for you, honey, every bit of it. Don't come yet."

"Oh, I won't," the woman moaned. "Let's come to—"

She looked up and screamed. The man whirled around. He started to reach under the pillow but decided against it.

"Okay," he said. "My wallet's in my pants on the chair. Take it and get the hell out of here. I'm busy."

Salvatore Fiore said, "We don't want your wallet, Mickey."

The anger on Mickey Nicola's face turned to something else. He sat up in bed, moving cautiously, trying to figure out the situation. The woman had pulled the sheets up over her breasts, her face a combination of anger and fright.

Nicola carefully swung his feet over the side of the bed, sitting on the edge, ready to spring. His penis had gone limp. He was watching both men, waiting for an opportunity.

"What do you want?"

"Do you work with Frank Jackson?"

"Go fuck yourselves."

Joseph Colella turned to his companion. "Shoot his balls off."

Salvatore Fiore raised his gun and aimed.

Mickey Nicola screamed, "Wait a minute! You guys must be crazy!" He looked into the little man's eyes and said quickly, "Yeah. I've worked with Jackson."

The woman cried out angrily, "Mickey!"

He turned on her savagely. "Shut up! You think I want to be a fuckin' eunuch?"

Salvatore Fiore turned to the woman and said, "You're Jackson's sister, ain't you?"

Her face was filled with fury. "I never heard of him."

Fiore raised his gun and moved closer to the bed. "You got two seconds to talk to me or you two are gonna be splashed all over the wall."

There was something in his voice that chilled her. He raised his gun and the blood began to drain from the woman's face.

"Tell them what they want to know," Mickey Nicola cried.

The gun moved up to press against the woman's breast.

"Don't! Yes! Frank Jackson's my brother."

"Where can we find him?"

"I don't know. I don't see him. I swear to God I don't know! I—"

His hand tightened on the trigger.

She screamed, "*Clara!* Clara would know! Ask Clara!"

Joseph Colella said, "Who's Clara?"

"She's—she's a waitress Frank knows."

"Where can we find her?"

This time there was no hesitation. The words spilled out. "She works at a bar called The Shakers in Queens." Her body began to tremble.

Salvatore Fiore looked at the two of them and said politely, "You can go back to your fuckin' now. Have a nice day."

And the two men departed.

5:30 A.M.

CLARA THOMAS (NEE THOMACHEVSKY) was about to fulfill her life-long dream. She hummed happily to herself as she packed her cardboard suitcase with the clothes she would need in Canada. She had taken trips with gentlemen friends before, but this was different. This was going to be her honeymoon trip. Frank Jackson was like no other man she had known. The men who came into the bar, pawing her and pinching her buttocks, were nothing but animals. Frank Jackson was different. He was a real gentleman. Clara paused in her packing to think about that word: *gentle man.* She had never thought of it that way before, but that was Frank Jackson. She had seen him only four times in her life, but she knew she was in love with him. She could tell he had been attracted to her from the very beginning, because he always sat at her booth. And after the second time he had walked her home when the bar had closed.

I must still have it, Clara thought smugly, *if I can get a handsome young guy like that.* She stopped her packing to walk over to the closet mirror to study herself. Maybe she was a little too heavy and her hair was a couple of shades too red, but dieting would take care of the extra pounds and she would be more careful the next time she dyed her hair. All in all, she wasn't too dissatisfied with what she saw. *The old broad's still pretty good-lookin',* she told herself. She knew that Frank Jackson wanted to take her to bed, even though he had never touched her. He was really special. There was an almost—Clara furrowed her forehead, trying to think of the word—*spiritual* quality about him. Clara had been brought up a good Catholic and she knew it was sacrilegious to even think such a thought, but Frank Jackson reminded her a little bit of Jesus. She wondered what Frank would be like in bed. Well, if he was shy, she would show him a trick or two. He had talked about their getting married as soon as they got to Canada. Her dream come true. Clara looked at her watch and decided she had better hurry. She had promised to pick Frank up at his motel at seven-thirty.

SHE SAW THEM in the mirror as they walked into her bedroom. They had come out of nowhere. A giant and a little fellow. Clara watched as the two of them moved toward her.

The small man looked at the suitcase. "Where you goin', Clara?"

"None of your business. Just take what you want and get out of here. If there's anything in this joint worth more than ten bucks, I'll eat it."

"I got something you can eat," the big man Colella said.

"Up yours, buster," Clara snapped. "If this is gonna be a rape job, I want you to know the doctor's treatin' me for gonorrhea."

Salvatore Fiore said, "We ain't gonna hurt you. We just wanna know where Frank Jackson is."

They could see the change that came over her. Her body suddenly stiffened and her face became a mask.

"Frank Jackson?" There was a note of deep puzzlement in her voice. "I don't know any Frank Jackson."

Salvatore Fiore pulled a lead pipe out of his pocket and took a step toward her.

"You don't scare me," Clara said, "I—"

His arm lashed out across her face, and in the midst of the blinding pain she could feel her teeth crumbling inside her mouth like tiny pieces of grit. She opened her mouth to speak and blood began pouring out. The big man raised his pipe again.

"No, please don't!" She gagged.

Joseph Colella said politely, "Where can we find this Frank Jackson?"

"Frank is—is—"

Clara thought of her sweet, gentle man in the hands of these two monsters. They were going to hurt him and, instinctively, she knew that Frank would not be able to stand the pain. He was too sensitive. If she could only find a way to save him, he would be grateful to her forever.

"I don't know."

Salvatore Fiore moved forward and Clara heard the sound of her leg breaking at the same instant she felt the excruciating pain. She fell to the floor, unable to scream because of all the blood in her mouth.

Joseph Colella stood over her and said pleasantly, "Maybe you don't unnerstan. We ain't gonna kill you. We're just gonna keep breakin' things. When we're through with you, you'll look like a piece of garbage the cat threw away. Do you believe me?"

Clara believed him. Frank Jackson would never want to look at her again. She had lost him to these two bastards. No dream come true, no marriage. The little man was moving forward with the lead pipe again.

Clara moaned, "Don't. Please don't. Frank's at the—the Brookside Motel on Prospect Avenue. He—"

She fainted.

Joseph Colella walked over to the telephone and dialed a number.

Michael Moretti answered. "Yes?"

"Brookside Motel on Prospect Avenue. Want us to take him?"

"No. I'll meet you there. Make sure he doesn't leave."

"He won't go anywhere."

6:30 A.M.

THE BOY WAS beginning to stir again. The man watched as Joshua opened his eyes. The boy looked down at the wire on his wrists and legs, and then looked up and saw Frank Jackson, and the memories came flooding back.

This was the man who had pushed those pills down his throat and kidnapped him. Joshua knew all about kidnappings from television. The police would come and save him and put the man in jail. Joshua was determined not to show his fear, because he wanted to be able to tell his mother how brave he had been.

"My mother will be here with the money," Joshua assured the man, "so you don't have to hurt me."

Frank Jackson walked over to the bed and smiled down at the boy. He really was a beautiful child. He wished he could take the boy to Canada instead of Clara. Reluctantly, Frank Jackson looked at his watch. It was time to get things ready.

The boy held up his bound wrists. The blood had caked dry.

"Would you mind taking this off, please?" he asked politely. "I won't run away."

Frank Jackson liked it that the boy had said "please." It showed good manners. These days, most kids had no manners at all. They ran around the streets like wild animals.

Frank Jackson went into the bathroom where he had put the can of gasoline back in the tub so that it would not stain the rug in the living room. He prided himself on details like that. He carried the can into the bedroom and set it down. He moved to the boy's side, lifted up the bound figure and placed him on the floor. Then he picked up the hammer and two large nails and knelt next to the boy.

Joshua Parker was watching him, wide-eyed. "What are you going to do with that?"

"Something that will make you very happy. Have you ever heard of Jesus Christ?" Joshua nodded. "Do you know how he died?"

"On the cross."

"That's very good. You're a bright boy. We don't have a cross here, so we'll have to do the best we can."

The boy's eyes were beginning to fill with fear.

Frank Jackson said, "There's nothing to be afraid of. Jesus wasn't afraid. You mustn't be afraid."

"I don't want to be Jesus," Joshua whispered. "I want to go home."

"I'm going to send you home," Frank Jackson promised. "I'm going to send you home to Jesus."

Frank Jackson took a handkerchief out of his back pocket and moved it toward the boy's mouth. Joshua gritted his teeth together.

"Don't make me angry."

Frank Jackson pressed his thumb and forefinger against Joshua's cheeks and forced his mouth open. He shoved the handkerchief into Joshua's mouth and slapped a piece of tape across it to hold the handkerchief in place. Joshua was straining against the wires that bound his wrists and hands, and they began to bleed again. Frank Jackson ran his hands over the fresh cuts.

"The blood of Christ," he said softly.

He picked up one of the boy's hands, turned it over and held it down against the floor. Then he picked up a nail. Holding it against Joshua's palm with one hand, Frank Jackson picked up the hammer with his other. He drove the nail through the boy's hand into the floor.

7:15 A.M.

MICHAEL MORETTI'S BLACK limousine was stalled on the Brooklyn-Queens Expressway in early morning traffic, held up by a vegetable truck that had overturned and spilled its cargo across the road. Traffic had come to a standstill.

"Pull over to the other side of the road and get past him," Michael Moretti ordered Nick Vito.

"There's a police car up ahead, Mike."

"Go up and tell whoever's in charge that I want to talk to him."

"Right, boss."

Nick Vito got out of the car and hurried toward the squad car. A few moments later he returned with a police sergeant. Michael Moretti opened the window of the car and held out his hand. There were five one hundred dollar bills in it.

"I'm in a hurry, officer."

Two minutes later the police car, red light flashing, was guiding the limousine past the wreckage on the road. When they were clear of the traffic, the sergeant got out of the police car and walked back to the limousine.

"Can I give you an escort somewhere, Mr. Moretti?"

"No, thank you," Michael said. "Come and see me Monday." To Nick Vito: "Move it!"

7:30 A.M.

THE NEON SIGN in front read:

BROOKSIDE MOTEL

SINGLES—DOUBLES

DAILY AND WEEKLY RATES

INDIVIDUALES—DOBLES

PRECIOS ESPECIALES

Joseph Colella and Salvatore Fiore sat in their car across from Bungalow 7. A few minutes earlier they had heard a thump from inside, so they knew that Frank Jackson was still there.

We oughta jump in and cool him, Fiore thought. But Michael Moretti had given instructions.

They settled back to wait.

7:45 A.M.

INSIDE BUNGALOW 7, Frank Jackson was making his final preparations. The boy was a disappointment. He had fainted. Jackson had wanted to wait until Joshua regained consciousness before the other nails were driven in, but it was getting late. He picked up the can of gasoline and sprinkled it across the boy's body, careful not to let it touch that beautiful face. He visualized the body under the pajamas and wished that he had time to—but, no, that would be foolish. Clara would be here any moment. He must be ready to leave when she arrived. He reached in his pockets, pulled out a box of matches, and set them neatly beside the can of gasoline, the hammer and the nails. People simply did not appreciate how important neatness was.

Frank Jackson looked at his watch again and wondered what was keeping Clara.

7:50 A.M.

OUTSIDE BUNGALOW 7, the limousine skidded to a stop and Michael Moretti jumped out of the car. The two men in the sedan hurried over to join him.

Joseph Colella pointed to Bungalow 7. "He's in there."

"What about the kid?"

The big man shrugged. "Dunno. Jackson's got the curtains drawn."

"Should we go in now and take him?" Salvatore Fiore asked.

"Stay here."

The two men looked at him in surprise. He was a *capo-regime*. He had soldiers to make hits for him while he sat back in safety. And yet he was going in himself. It was not right.

Joseph Colella said, "Boss, Sal and I can—"

But Michael Moretti was already moving to the door of Bungalow 7, a gun fitted with a silencer in his hand. He paused for a second to listen, then stepped back and smashed the door open with one powerful kick.

Moretti took in the scene in a single frozen moment: the bearded man kneeling on the floor beside the small boy; the boy's hand nailed to the floor, the room reeking of gasoline.

The bearded man had turned toward the door and was staring at Michael. The last sounds he ever uttered were, "You're not Cl—"

Michael's first bullet took him in the center of his forehead. The second bullet shattered his pharynx, and the third bullet took him in the heart. But by that time he no longer felt anything.

Michael Moretti stepped to the door and waved to the two men outside. They hurried into the cabin. Michael Moretti knelt beside the boy and felt his pulse. It was thin and thready, but he was still alive. He turned to Joseph Colella.

"Call Doc Petrone. Tell him we're on our way over."

9:30 A.M.

THE INSTANT THE telephone rang, Jennifer snatched it up, squeezing it tightly. "Hello!"

Michael Moretti's voice said, "I'm bringing your son home."

JOSHUA WAS WHIMPERING in his sleep. Jennifer leaned over and put her arms around him, holding him gently. He had been asleep when Michael had carried him into the house. When Jennifer had seen Joshua's unconscious body, his wrists and ankles heavily bandaged, his body swathed in gauze, she had nearly gone out of her mind. Michael had brought the doctor with him and it had taken him half an hour to reassure Jennifer that Joshua was going to be all right.

"His hand will heal," the doctor assured her. "There will be a small scar there, but fortunately no nerves or tendons were damaged. The gasoline burns are superficial. I bathed his body in mineral oil. I'll look in on him for the next few days. Believe me, he's going to be fine."

Before the doctor left, Jennifer had him attend to Mrs. Mackey.

Joshua had been put to bed and Jennifer stayed at his side, waiting to reassure him when he awakened. He stirred now and his eyes opened.

When he saw his mother, he said tiredly, "I knew you'd come, Mom. Did you give the man the ransom money?"

Jennifer nodded, not trusting her voice.

Joshua smiled. "I hope he buys too much candy with the money and gets a stomachache. Wouldn't that be funny?"

She whispered, "Very funny, darling. Do you know what you and I are going to do next week? I'm going to take you to—"

Joshua was asleep again.

• • •

IT WAS HOURS later when Jennifer walked back into the living room. She was surprised to see that Michael Moretti was still there. Somehow it reminded her of the first time she had met Adam Warner, when he had waited for her in her little apartment.

"Michael—" It was impossible to find the words. "I—I can't tell you how—how grateful I am."

He looked at her and nodded.

She forced herself to ask the question. "And—and Frank Jackson?"

"He won't bother anyone again."

So it was over. Joshua was safe. Nothing else mattered.

Jennifer looked at Michael Moretti and thought, *I owe him so much. How can I ever repay him?*

Michael was watching her, wrapped in silence.

BOOK TWO

37

Jennifer Parker stood naked, staring out of the large picture window that overlooked the Bay of Tangier. It was a beautiful, crisp autumn day and the bay was filled with skimming white sails and deep-throated power boats. Half a dozen large yachts bobbed at anchor in the harbor. Jennifer felt his presence and turned.

"Like the view?"

"Love it."

He looked at her naked body. "So do I." His hands were on her breasts, caressing them. "Let's go back to bed."

His touch made Jennifer shiver. He demanded things that no man had ever dared ask of her, and he did things to her that had never been done to her before.

"Yes, Michael."

They walked back into the bedroom and there, for one fleeting moment, Jennifer thought of Adam Warner, and then she forgot everything except what was happening to her.

Jennifer had never known anyone like Michael Moretti. He was insatiable. His body was athletic, lean and hard, and it became a part of Jennifer's body, catching her up in its own frenzy, carrying her along on a rising wave of pounding excitement that went on and on until she wanted to scream with a wild joy. When they had finished making love and Jennifer lay there, spent, Michael began once more, and Jennifer was caught up with him again and again in an ecstasy that became almost too much to bear.

Now he lay on top of her, staring into her flushed, happy face. "You love it, don't you, baby?"

"Yes."

There was a shame in it, a shame at how much she needed him, needed his lovemaking.

Jennifer remembered the first time.

IT WAS THE morning Michael Moretti had brought Joshua safely back home. Jennifer had known that Frank Jackson was dead and that Michael Moretti had killed him. The man standing in front of her had saved her son for her, had killed for her. It filled Jennifer with some deep, primordial feeling.

"How can I thank you?" Jennifer had asked.

And Michael Moretti had walked over to her, taken her in his arms and kissed her. Out of some old loyalty to Adam, Jennifer had pretended to herself that it would end with that kiss; but instead, it became a beginning. She knew what Michael Moretti was, and yet all that counted as nothing against what he had done. She stopped thinking and let her emotions take over.

They went upstairs to her bedroom, and Jennifer told herself that she was repaying Michael for what he had done for her, and then they were in bed and it was an experience beyond anything that Jennifer had ever dreamed.

Adam Warner had made love to her, but Michael Moretti possessed her. He filled every inch of her body with exquisite sensations. It was as though he were making love in bright, flashing colors, and the colors kept changing from one moment to the next, like some wonderful kaleidoscope. One moment he made love gently and sensitively, and the next moment he was cruel and pounding and demanding, and the changes made Jennifer frantic. He withdrew from her, teasing her, making her want more, and when she was on the verge of fulfillment he pulled away.

When she could stand it no longer, she begged, "Please take me! Take me!"

And his hard organ began to pound into her again until she screamed with pleasure. She was no longer a woman paying back a debt. She was a slave to something she had never known before. Michael stayed with her for four hours, and when he left, Jennifer knew that her life had changed.

She lay in her bed thinking about what had happened, trying to understand it. How could she be so much in love with Adam and still have been so overwhelmed by Michael Moretti? Thomas Aquinas had said that when you got to the heart of evil, there was nothing there. Jennifer wondered if it was also true of love. She was aware that part of what she had done was out of a deep loneliness. She had lived too long with a phantom, a man she could neither see nor have, yet she knew she would always love Adam. Or was it just a memory of that love?

Jennifer was not sure what she felt about Michael. Gratitude, yes. But that was a small part of it. It was more. Much more. She knew who and what Michael Moretti was. He had killed for her, but he had killed for others, too. He had murdered men for money, for power, for vengeance. How could she feel as she did about a man like that? How could she have let him make love to her and have been so excited by him? She was filled with a sense of shame and she thought, *What kind of person am I?*

She had no answer.

THE AFTERNOON NEWSPAPERS reported the story of a fire in a Queens motel. The remains of an unidentified man were found in the ruins. Arson was suspected.

AFTER JOSHUA'S RETURN, Jennifer had tried to make everything as normal for him as possible, fearful of the trauma the preceding night might have inflicted upon him. When Joshua woke up, Jennifer prepared a meal and brought it to him in bed. It was a ridiculous meal, consisting of all the junk foods he loved: a hot dog and a peanut butter sandwich and Fritos and Hostess Twinkies and root beer.

"You should have seen him, Mom," Joshua said between bites. "He was crazy!" He held up his bandaged hand. "Do you think he really thought I was Jesus Christ?"

Jennifer repressed a shudder. "I—I don't know, darling."

"Why do people want to kill other people?"

"Well—" and Jennifer's thoughts suddenly went back to Michael Moretti. Did she have the right to judge him? She did not know the terrible forces that had shaped his life, that had turned him into what he had become. She had to learn more about him, to get to know and understand him.

Joshua was saying, "Do I have to go to school tomorrow?"

Jennifer put her arms around him. "No, darling. We're both going to stay home and play hooky all week. We— "

The telephone rang.

It was Michael. "How's Joshua?"

"He's wonderful—thank you."

"And how are you feeling?"

Jennifer felt her throat thickening with embarrassment. "I'm—I—I feel fine."

He chuckled. "Good. I'll see you for lunch tomorrow. Donato's on Mulberry Street. Twelve-thirty."

"All right, Michael. Twelve-thirty."

Jennifer spoke those words and there was no turning back.

THE CAPTAIN AT Donato's knew Michael, and the best table in the restaurant had been reserved for him. People kept stopping by to say hello, and Jennifer was again amazed at the way everyone kowtowed to him. It was strange how much Michael Moretti reminded her of Adam Warner, for each, in his own way, was a man of power.

Jennifer started to question Michael about his background, wanting to learn how and why he had gotten trapped into the life he led.

He interrupted her. "You think I'm in this because of my family or because someone put pressure on me?"

"Well—yes, Michael. Of course."

He laughed. "I worked my butt off to get where I am. I love it. I love the money. I love the power. I'm a king, baby, and I love being king."

Jennifer looked at him, trying to understand. "But you can't enjoy—"

"Listen!" His silence had suddenly turned into words and sentences and confidences, pouring out as though they had been stored inside him for years, waiting for someone to come along to share them with. "My old man was a Coca-Cola bottle."

"A Coca-Cola bottle?"

"Right. There are billions of them in the world and you can't tell one from another. He was a shoemaker. He worked his fingers to the bone, trying to put food on the table. We had nothing. Being poor is only romantic in books. In real life, it's smelly rooms with rats and cockroaches and bad food that you can never get enough of. When I was a young punk, I did anything I could to make a buck. I ran errands for the big shots, I brought them coffee and cigars, I found them girls—anything to stay alive. Well, one summer I went down to Mexico City. I had no money, nothing. My ass was hanging out. One night a girl I met invited me to a large dinner party at a fancy restaurant. For dessert they served a special Mexican cake with a little clay doll baked inside it. Someone at the table explained that the custom was that whoever got the clay doll had to pay for the dinner. I got the clay doll." He paused. "I swallowed it."

Jennifer put her hand over his. "Michael, other people have grown up poor and—"

"Don't confuse me with other people." His tone was hard and uncompromising. "I'm me. I know who I am, baby. I wonder if you know who you are."

"I think I do."

"Why did you go to bed with me?"

Jennifer hesitated. "Well, I—I was grateful and—"

"Bullshit! You wanted me."

"Michael, I—"

"I don't have to buy my women. Not with money and not with gratitude."

Jennifer admitted to herself that he was right. She *had* wanted him, just as he had wanted her. *And yet*, Jennifer thought, *this man deliberately tried to destroy me once. How can I forget that?*

Michael leaned forward and took Jennifer's hand, palm up. Slowly, he caressed each finger, each mound, never taking his eyes from her.

"Don't play games with me. Not ever, Jennifer."

She felt powerless. Whatever there was between them transcended the past.

IT WAS WHEN they were having dessert that Michael said, "By the way, I have a case for you."

It was as though he had slapped her in the face.

Jennifer stared at him. "What kind of case?"

"One of my boys, Vasco Gambutti, has been arrested for killing a cop. I want you to defend him."

Jennifer sat there filled with hurt and anger that he was still trying to use her.

She said evenly, "I'm sorry, Michael. I told you before. I can't get involved with—with your . . . friends."

He gave her a lazy grin. "Did you ever hear the story about the little lion cub in Africa? He leaves his mother for the first time to go down to the river to get a drink, and a gorilla knocks him down. While he's picking himself up, a big leopard shoves him out of the way. A herd of elephants comes along and almost tramples him to death. The little cub returns home all shaken up and he says, 'You know something, Ma—it's a jungle out there!'"

There was a long silence between them. It *was* a jungle out there, Jennifer thought, but she had always stood at the edge of it, outside it, free to flee whenever she wanted to. She had made the rules and her clients had had to live by them. But now, Michael Moretti had changed all that. This was *his* jungle. Jennifer was afraid of it, afraid to get caught up in it. Yet, when she thought about what Michael had done for her, she decided it was a small thing he was asking.

She would do Michael this one favor.

38

W e're going to handle the Vasco Gambutti case," Jennifer informed Ken Bailey.

Ken looked at Jennifer in disbelief. "He's Mafia! One of Michael Moretti's hit men. That's not the kind of client we take."

"We're taking this one."

"Jennifer, we can't afford to get mixed up with the mob."

"Gambutti's entitled to a fair trial, just like anyone else." The words sounded hollow, even to her.

"I can't let you—"

"As long as this is my office, I'll make the decisions." She could see the surprise and hurt that came into his eyes.

Ken nodded, turned and walked out of the office. Jennifer was tempted to call him back and try to explain. But how could she? She was not sure she could even explain it to herself.

WHEN JENNIFER HAD her first meeting with Vasco Gambutti, she tried to regard him as just another client. She had handled clients before who were accused of murder, but somehow, this was different. This man was a member of a vast network of organized crime, a group that bled the country of untold billions of dollars, an arcane cabal that would kill when necessary to protect itself.

The evidence against Gambutti was overwhelming. He had been caught during the holdup of a fur shop and had killed an off-duty policeman who had tried to stop him. The morning newspapers announced that Jennifer Parker was going to be the defense attorney.

Judge Lawrence Waldman telephoned. "Is it true, Jennie?"

Jennifer knew instantly what he meant. "Yes, Lawrence."

A pause. "I'm surprised. You know who he is, of course."

"Yes, I know."

"You're getting into dangerous territory."

"Not really. I'm just doing a friend a favor."

"I see. Be careful."

"I will," Jennifer promised.

It was only afterward that Jennifer realized he had said nothing about their having dinner together.

AFTER LOOKING OVER the material her staff had assembled, Jennifer decided that she had no case at all.

Vasco Gambutti had been caught red-handed in a robbery-murder, and there were no extenuating circumstances. Furthermore, there was always a strong emotional pull in the minds of the jurors when the victim was a policeman.

She called Ken Bailey in and gave him his instructions.

He said nothing, but Jennifer could feel his disapproval and was saddened. She promised herself that this was the last time she would work for Michael.

Her private phone rang and she picked it up. Michael said, "Hello, baby. I'm hungry for you. Meet me in half an hour."

She sat there, listening, already feeling his arms around her, his body pressing against hers.

"I'll be there," Jennifer said.

The promise to herself was forgotten.

• • •

THE GAMBUTTI TRIAL lasted ten days. The press was there in full force, eager to watch District Attorney Di Silva and Jennifer Parker in open combat again. Di Silva had done his homework thoroughly, and he deliberately understated his case, letting the jurors take the suggestions he dropped and build on them, creating horrors in their minds even greater than the ones he depicted.

Jennifer sat quietly through the testimony, seldom bothering to raise objections.

On the last day of the trial, she made her move.

There is an adage in law that when you have a weak defense, you put your opponent on trial. Because Jennifer had no defense for Vasco Gambutti, she had made a decision to put Scott Norman, the slain policeman, on trial. Ken Bailey had dug up everything there was to know about Scott Norman. His record was not good, but before Jennifer was through she made it seem ten times worse than it was. Norman had been on the police force for twenty years, and in that period had been suspended three times on charges of unnecessary violence. He had shot and almost killed an unarmed suspect, he had beaten up a drunk in a bar and he had sent to the hospital a man involved in a domestic quarrel. Although these incidents had taken place over a period of twenty years, Jennifer made it seem as though the deceased had committed an unbroken series of despicable acts. Jennifer had a parade of witnesses on the stand giving testimony against the dead police officer, and there was not one thing Robert Di Silva could do about it.

In his summation, Di Silva said, "Remember, ladies and gentlemen of the jury, that Officer Scott Norman is not the one on trial here. Officer Scott Norman was the victim. He was killed by"—pointing—"the defendant, Vasco Gambutti."

But even as the District Attorney spoke, he knew it was no use. Jennifer had made Officer Scott Norman appear to be as worthless a human being as Vasco Gambutti. He was no longer the noble policeman who had given his life to apprehend a criminal. Jennifer Parker had distorted the picture so that the victim was no better than the accused slayer.

The jury returned a verdict of not guilty on the charge of murder in the first degree and convicted Vasco Gambutti of manslaughter. It was a stunning defeat for District Attorney Di Silva, and the media were quick to announce another victory for Jennifer Parker.

"WEAR YOUR CHIFFON. It's a celebration," Michael told her.

They had dinner at a seafood restaurant in the Village. The restaurant owner sent over a bottle of rare champagne and Michael and Jennifer drank a toast.

"I'm very pleased."

Coming from Michael, it was an accolade.

He placed a small red-and-white-wrapped box in her hands. "Open it."

He watched as she untied the gold thread and removed the lid. In the box lay a large, square-cut emerald, surrounded by diamonds.

Jennifer stared at it. She started to protest. "Oh, Michael!" And she saw the look of pride and pleasure on his face.

"Michael—what am I going to do with you?"

And she thought: *Oh, Jennifer, what am I going to do with you?*

"You need it for that dress." He placed the ring on the third finger of her left hand.

"I—I don't know what to say. I—thank you. It's really a celebration, isn't it!"

Michael grinned. "The celebration hasn't started yet. This is only the foreplay."

THEY WERE RIDING in the limousine on their way to an apartment that Michael kept uptown. Michael pressed a button and raised the glass that separated the rear of the car from the driver.

We're locked away in our own little world, Jennifer thought. Michael's nearness excited her.

She turned to look into his black eyes and he moved toward her and slid his hand along her thighs, and Jennifer's body was instantly on fire.

Michael's lips found hers and their bodies were pressed together. Jennifer felt the hard maleness of him and she slid down to the floor of the car. She began to make love to him, caressing him and kissing him until Michael began to moan, and Jennifer moaned with him, moving faster and faster until she felt the spasms of his body.

The celebration had begun.

. . .

JENNIFER WAS THINKING of the past now as she lay in bed in the hotel room in Tangier, listening to the sounds of Michael in the shower. She felt satisfied and happy. The only thing missing was her young son. She had thought of taking Joshua with her on some of her trips, but instinctively she wanted to keep him and Michael Moretti far away from each other. Joshua must never be touched by that part of her life. It seemed to Jennifer that her life was a series of compartments: There was Adam, there was her son and there was Michael Moretti. And each had to be kept separate from the others.

Michael walked out of the bathroom wearing only a towel. The hair on his body glistened from the dampness of the shower. He was a beautiful, exciting animal.

"Get dressed. We have work to do."

39

It happened so gradually that it did not seem to be happening at all. It had begun with Vasco Gambutti, and shortly afterward Michael asked Jennifer to handle another case, then another, until soon it became a steady flow of cases.

Michael would call Jennifer and say, "I need your help, baby. One of my boys is having a problem."

And Jennifer was reminded of Father Ryan's words, *A friend of mine has a bit of a problem.* Was there really any difference? America had come to accept the Godfather syndrome. Jennifer told herself that what she was doing now was the same as what she had been doing all along. The truth was that there was a difference—a big difference.

She was at the center of one of the most powerful organizations in the world.

MICHAEL INVITED JENNIFER to the farmhouse in New Jersey, where she met Antonio Granelli for the first time, and some of the other men in the Organization.

At a large table in the old-fashioned kitchen were Nick Vito, Arthur "Fat Artie" Scotto, Salvatore Fiore and Joseph Colella.

As Jennifer and Michael came in and stood in the doorway, listening, Nick Vito was saying, ". . . like the time I did a pound in Atlanta. I had a heavy H book goin'. This popcorn pimp comes up and tries to fuck me over 'cause he wants a piece of the action."

"Did you know the guy?" Fat Artie Scotto asked.

"What's to know? He wants to get his lights turned on. He tried to put the arm on me."

"On *you?*"

"Yeah. His head wasn't wrapped too tight."

"What'd you do?"

"Eddie Fratelli and me got him over in the ghinny corner of the yard and burned him. What the hell, he was doin' bad time, anyway."

"Hey, whatever happened to Little Eddie?"

"He's doin' a dime at Lewisburg."

"What about his bandit? She was some class act."

"Oh, yeah. I'd love to make her drawers."

"She's still got the hots for Eddie. Only the Pope knows why."

"I liked Eddie. He used to be an up-front guy."

"He went ape-shit. Speakin' of that, do you know who turned into a candy man . . . ?"

Shop talk.

Michael grinned at Jennifer's puzzled reaction to the conversation and said, "Come on—I'll introduce you to Papa."

ANTONIO GRANELLI WAS a shock to Jennifer. He was in a wheelchair, a feeble skeleton of a man, and it was hard to imagine him as he once must have been.

An attractive brunette with a full figure walked into the room, and Michael said to Jennifer, "This is Rosa, my wife."

Jennifer had dreaded this moment. Some nights after Michael had left her—fulfilled in every way a woman could be—she had fought with a guilt that almost overpowered her. *I don't want to hurt another woman. I'm stealing. I've got to stop this! I must!* And, always, she lost the battle.

Rosa looked at Jennifer with eyes that were wise. *She knows,* Jennifer thought.

There was a small awkwardness, and then Rosa said softly, "I'm pleased to meet you, Mrs. Parker. Michael tells me you're very intelligent."

Antonio Granelli grunted. "It's not good for a woman to be too smart. It's better to leave the brains to the men."

Michael said with a straight face, "I think of Mrs. Parker as a man, Papa."

THEY HAD DINNER in the large, old-fashioned dining room.

"You sit next to me," Antonio Granelli commanded Jennifer.

Michael sat next to Rosa. Thomas Colfax, the *consigliere,* sat opposite Jennifer and she could feel his animosity.

The dinner was superb. An enormous antipasto was served, and then *pasta fagioli.* There was a salad with garbanzo beans, stuffed mushrooms, veal *piccata,* linguini and baked chicken. It seemed that the dishes never stopped coming.

There were no visible servants in the house, and Rosa was constantly jumping up and clearing the table to bring in new dishes from the kitchen.

"My Rosa's a great cook," Antonio Granelli told Jennifer. "She's almost as good as her mother was. Hey, Mike?"

"Yes," Michael said politely.

"His Rosa's a wonderful wife," Antonio Granelli went on, and Jennifer wondered whether it was a casual remark or a warning.

Michael said, "You're not finishing your veal."

"I've never eaten so much in my life," Jennifer protested.

And it was not over yet.

There was a bowl of fresh fruit and a platter of cheese, and ice cream with a hot fudge sauce, and candy and mints.

Jennifer marveled at how Michael managed to keep his figure.

The conversation was easy and pleasant and could have been taking place in any one of a thousand Italian homes, and it was hard for Jennifer to believe that this family was different from any other family.

Until Antonio Granelli said, "You know anythin' about the *Unione Siciliana?*"

"No," Jennifer said.

"Let me tell you about it, lady."

"Pop—her name is Jennifer."

"That's not no Italian name, Mike. It's too hard for me to remember. I'll call you lady, lady. Okay?"

"Okay," Jennifer replied.

"The *Unione Siciliana* started in Sicily to protect the poor against injustices. See, the people in power, they robbed the poor. The poor had nothin'—no money, no jobs, no justice. So the *Unione* was formed. When there was injustice, people came to the members of the secret brotherhood and they got vengeance. Pretty soon the *Unione* became stronger than the law, because it was the *people's* law. We believe in what the Bible says, lady." He looked Jennifer in the eye. "If anyone betrays us, we get vengeance."

The message was unmistakable.

JENNIFER HAD ALWAYS known instinctively that if she ever worked for the Organization she would be taking a giant step, but like most outsiders, she had a misconception of what the Organization was like. The Mafia was generally depicted as a bunch of mobsters sitting around ordering people murdered and counting the money from loan-sharking and whorehouses. That was only a part of the picture. The meetings Jennifer attended taught her the rest of it: These were businessmen operating on a scale that was staggering. They owned hotels and banks, restaurants and casinos, insurance companies and factories, building companies and chains of hospitals. They controlled unions and shipping. They were in the record business and sold vending machines. They owned funeral parlors, bakeries and construction companies. Their yearly income was in the billions. How they had acquired those interests was none of Jennifer's concern. It was her job to defend those of them who got into trouble with the law.

ROBERT DI SILVA had three of Michael Moretti's men indicted for shaking down a group of lunch wagons. They were charged with conspiracy to interfere with commerce by extortion and seven counts of interference with commerce. The only witness willing to testify against the men was a woman who owned one of the stands.

"She's going to blow us away," Michael told Jennifer. "She's got to be handled."

"You own a piece of a magazine publishing company, don't you?" Jennifer asked.

"Yes. What does that have to do with lunch wagons?"

"You'll see."

Jennifer quietly arranged for the magazine to offer a large sum of money for the witness's story. The woman accepted. In court, Jennifer used that to discredit the woman's motives, and the charges were dismissed.

JENNIFER'S RELATIONSHIP WITH her associates had changed. When the office had begun to take a succession of Mafia cases, Ken Bailey had come into Jennifer's office and said, "What's going on? You can't keep representing these hoodlums. They'll ruin us."

"Don't worry about it, Ken. They'll pay."

"You can't be that naïve, Jennifer. You're the one who's going to pay. They'll have you hooked."

Because she had known he was right, Jennifer said angrily, "Drop it, Ken."

He had looked at her for a long moment, then said, "Right. You're the boss."

THE CRIMINAL COURTS was a small world, and news traveled swiftly. When word got out that Jennifer Parker was defending members of the Organization, well-meaning friends went to her and reiterated the same things that Judge Lawrence Waldman and Ken Bailey had told her.

"If you get involved with these hoodlums, you'll be tarred with the same brush."

Jennifer told them all: "Everyone is entitled to be defended."

She appreciated their warnings, but she felt that they did not apply to her. She was not a part of the Organization; she merely represented some of its members. She was a lawyer, like her father, and she would never do anything that would have made him ashamed of her. The jungle was there, but she was still outside it.

. . .

FATHER RYAN HAD come to see her. This time it was not to ask her to help out a friend.

"I'm concerned about you, Jennifer. I hear reports that you're handling—well—the wrong people."

"Who are the wrong people? Do you judge the people who come to you for help? Do you turn people away from God because they've sinned?"

Father Ryan shook his head. "Of course not. But it's one thing when an individual makes a mistake. It's something else when corruption is organized. If you help those people, you're condoning what they do. You become a part of it."

"No. I'm a lawyer, Father. I help people in trouble."

JENNIFER CAME TO know Michael Moretti better than anyone had ever known him. He exposed feelings to her that he had never revealed to anyone else. He was basically a lonely, solitary man, and Jennifer was the first person who had ever been able to penetrate his shell.

Jennifer felt that Michael *needed* her. She had never felt that with Adam. And Michael had forced her to admit how much she needed him. He had brought out feelings in her that she had kept suppressed—wild, atavistic passions that she had been afraid to let loose. There were no inhibitions with Michael. When they were in bed together, there were no limits, no barriers. Only pleasure, a pleasure Jennifer had never dreamed possible.

Michael confided to Jennifer that he did not love Rosa, but it was obvious that Rosa worshiped Michael. She was always at his service, waiting to take care of his needs.

Jennifer met other Mafia wives, and she found their lives fascinating. Their husbands went out to restaurants and bars and racetracks with their mistresses while their wives stayed home and waited for them.

A Mafia wife always had a generous allowance, but she had to be careful how she spent it, lest she attract the attention of the Internal Revenue Service.

There was a pecking order ranging from the lowly *soldato* to the *capo di tutti capi,* and the wife never owned a more expensive coat or car than the wife of her husband's immediate superior.

The wives gave dinner parties for their husbands' associates, but they were careful not to be more lavish than their position permitted in relation to the others.

At ceremonies such as weddings or baptisms, where gifts were called for, a wife was never allowed to spend more than the wife above her station in the hierarchy.

The protocol was as stringent as that at U.S. Steel, or any other large business corporation.

The Mafia was an incredible moneymaking machine, but Jennifer became aware that there was another element in it that was equally important: power.

"The Organization is bigger than the government of most of the countries of the world," Michael told Jennifer. "We gross more than a half a dozen of the largest companies in America, put together."

"There's a difference," Jennifer pointed out. "They're legitimate and—"

Michael laughed. "You mean the ones that haven't been caught. Dozens of the country's biggest companies have been indicted for violating one law or another. Don't kid yourself about heroes, Jennifer. The average American today can't name two astronauts who have been up in space, but they know the names of Al Capone and Lucky Luciano."

Jennifer realized that in his own way, Michael was equally as dedicated as Adam was. The difference was that their lives had gone in opposite directions.

When it came to business, Michael had a total lack of empathy. It was his strong point. He made decisions based solely on what was expedient for the Organization.

In the past, Michael had been completely dedicated to fulfilling his ambitions. There had been no emotional room for a woman in his life. Neither Rosa nor Michael's girl friends had ever been a part of his real needs.

Jennifer was different. He needed her as he had needed no other woman. He had never known anyone like her. She excited him physically, but so had dozens of others. What made Jennifer special was her intelligence, her independence. Rosa obeyed him; other women feared him; Jennifer challenged him. She was his equal. He could talk to her, discuss things with her. She was more than intelligent. She was smart.

He knew that he was never going to let her go.

OCCASIONALLY JENNIFER TOOK business trips with Michael, but she tried to avoid traveling whenever she could because she wanted to spend as much time as possible with Joshua. He was six years old now and growing unbelievably fast. Jennifer had enrolled him in a private school nearby, and Joshua loved it.

He rode a two-wheel bicycle and had a fleet of toy racing cars and carried on long and earnest conversations with Jennifer and Mrs. Mackey.

Because Jennifer wanted Joshua to grow up to be strong and independent, she tried to walk a carefully balanced line, letting Joshua know how much she loved him, making him aware that she was always there when he needed her and yet giving him a sense of his own independence.

She taught him to love good books and to enjoy music. She took him to the theater, avoiding opening nights because there would be too many people there who might know her and ask questions. On weekends she and Joshua would have a movie binge. On Saturday they would see a movie in the afternoon, have dinner at a restaurant and then see a second movie. On Sunday they would go sailing or bicycling together. Jennifer gave her son all the love that was stored in her, but she was careful to try not to spoil him. She planned her strategy with Joshua more carefully than she had planned any court case, determined not to fall into the traps of a one-parent home.

Jennifer felt no sacrifice in spending so much time with Joshua; he was great fun. They played word games and Impressions and Twenty Questions, and Jennifer was delighted by the quickness of her son's mind. He was at the head of his class and an outstanding athlete, but he did not take himself seriously. He had a marvelous sense of humor.

When it did not interfere with his schoolwork, Jennifer would take Joshua on trips. During Joshua's winter vacation, Jennifer took time off to go skiing with him in the Poconos. In the summer she took him to London on a business trip with her, and they spent two weeks exploring the countryside. Joshua adored England.

"Could I go to school here?" he asked.

Jennifer felt a pang. It would not be long before he left her to go away to school, to seek his fortune, to get married and have his own home and family. Was that not what she wanted for him? Of course it was. When Joshua was ready, she would let him go with open arms, and yet she knew how difficult it was going to be.

Joshua was looking at her, waiting for an answer. "Can I, Mom?" he asked. "Maybe Oxford?"

Jennifer held him close. "Of course. They'll be lucky to get you."

ON A SUNDAY morning when Mrs. Mackey was off, Jennifer had to go into Manhattan to pick up a transcript of a deposition. Joshua was visiting some friends. When Jennifer returned home, she started to prepare dinner for the two of them. She opened the refrigerator—and stopped dead in her tracks. There was a note inside, propped up between two bottles of milk. Adam had left her notes like that. Jennifer stared at it, mesmerized, afraid to touch it. Slowly, she reached for the note and unfolded it. It said, *Surprise! Is it okay if Alan has dinner with us?*

It took half an hour for Jennifer's pulse to return to normal.

FROM TIME TO time, Joshua asked Jennifer about his father.

"He was killed in Viet Nam, Joshua. He was a very brave man."

"Don't we have a picture of him anywhere?"

"No, I'm sorry, darling. We—we weren't married very long before he died."

She hated the lie, but she had no choice.

Michael Moretti had only asked once about Joshua's father.

"I don't care what happened before you belonged to me—I'm just curious."

Jennifer thought about the power that Michael would have over Senator Adam Warner if Michael ever learned the truth.

"He was killed in Viet Nam. His name's not important."

40

In Washington, D.C., a Senate investigating committee headed by Adam Warner was in its final day of an intensive inquiry into the new XK-1 bomber that the Air Force was trying to get the Senate to approve. For weeks, expert witnesses had paraded up to Capitol Hill, half of them testifying that the new bomber would be an expensive albatross that would destroy the defense budget and ruin the country, and the other half testifying that unless the Air Force could get the bomber approved, America's defenses would be so weakened that the Russians would invade the United States the following Sunday.

Adam had volunteered to test-fly a prototype of the new bomber, and his colleagues had eagerly seized on his offer. Adam was one of them, a member of the club, and he would give them the truth.

Adam had taken the bomber up early on a Sunday morning with a skeleton crew and had put the plane through a series of rigorous tests. The flight had been an unqualified success, and he had reported back to the Senate committee that the new XK-1 bomber was an important advance in aviation. He recommended that the airplane go into production immediately. The Senate approved the funds.

The press enthusiastically played up the story. They described Adam as one of the new breed of investigative senators, a lawmaker who went out into the field to study the facts for himself instead of taking the word of lobbyists and others who were concerned with protecting their own interests.

Newsweek and *Time* both did cover stories on Adam, and the *Newsweek* story ended with:

> The Senate has found an honest and capable new guardian to investigate some of the vital problems that plague this country, and to bring to them light instead of heat. There is a growing feeling among the kingmakers that Adam Warner has the qualities that would grace the presidency.

Jennifer devoured the stories about Adam and she was filled with pride. And pain. She still loved Adam and she loved Michael Moretti, and she did not understand how it was possible, or what kind of woman she had become. Adam had created the loneliness in her life. Michael had erased it.

THE SMUGGLING OF drugs from Mexico had increased enormously, and it was obvious that organized crime was behind it. Adam was asked to head an investigating committee. He coordinated the efforts of half a dozen United States law enforcement agencies, and flew to Mexico and obtained the cooperation of the Mexican government. Within three months, the drug traffic had slowed to a trickle.

IN THE FARMHOUSE in New Jersey, Michael Moretti was saying, "We've got a problem."

They were seated in the large, comfortable study. In the room were Jennifer, Antonio Granelli and Thomas Colfax. Antonio Granelli had suffered a stroke and it had aged him twenty years overnight. He looked like a shrunken caricature of a man. The paralysis had affected the right side of his face so that when he spoke, saliva drooled from the corners of his mouth. He was old and almost senile, and he leaned more and more on Michael's judgment. He had even reluctantly come to accept Jennifer.

Not so Thomas Colfax. The conflict between Michael and Colfax had grown stronger. Colfax knew it was Michael's intention to replace him with this woman. Colfax admitted to himself that Jennifer Parker was a clever lawyer, but what could she possibly know of the traditions of the *borgata*? Of what had made the brotherhood work so smoothly all these years? How could Michael bring in a stranger—worse, a woman!—and trust her with their life-and-death secrets? It was an untenable situation. Colfax had talked to the *capo-regimi*—the squad lieutenants—and the *soldati*—the soldiers—one by one, voicing his fears, trying to win them over to his side, but they were afraid to go against Michael. If he trusted this woman, then they felt they must trust her also.

Thomas Colfax decided he would have to bide his time. But he would find a way to get rid of her.

Jennifer was well aware of his feelings. She had replaced him, and his pride would never let him forgive her for that. His loyalty to the Syndicate would keep him in line and protect her, but if his hatred for her should become stronger than that loyalty . . .

Michael turned to Jennifer. "Have you ever heard of Adam Warner?"

Jennifer's heart stopped for an instant. It was suddenly hard for her to breathe. Michael was watching her, waiting for an answer.

"You—you mean the senator?" Jennifer managed to say.

"Uh-huh. We're going to have to cool the son of a bitch."

Jennifer could feel the blood drain from her face. "Why, Michael?"

"He's hurting our operation. Because of him, the Mexican government is closing down factories belonging to friends of ours. Everything's starting to come apart. I want the bastard out of our hair. He's got to go."

Jennifer's mind was racing. "If you touch Senator Warner," she said, choosing her words carefully, "you'll destroy yourself."

"I'm not going to let—"

"Listen to me, Michael. Get rid of him, and they'll send ten men to take his place. A hundred. Every newspaper in the country will be after you. The investigation that's going on now will be nothing compared to what will happen if Senator Warner is harmed."

Michael said angrily, "I'm telling you we're *hurting*!"

Jennifer changed her tone. "Michael, use your head. You've seen these investigations before. How long do they last? Five minutes after the senator is finished, he'll be investigating something else and all this will be over. The factories that are closed down will open up again and you'll be back in business. That way there won't be any repercussions. You try to do it your way and you'll never hear the end of it."

"I disagree," Thomas Colfax said. "In my opinion—"

Michael Moretti growled, "No one asked for your opinion."

Thomas Colfax jerked as though he had been slapped. Michael paid no attention. Colfax turned to Antonio Granelli for support. The old man was asleep.

Michael said to Jennifer, "Okay, counselor, we'll leave Warner alone for now."

Jennifer realized she had been holding her breath. She exhaled slowly. "Is there anything else?"

"Yeah." Michael picked up a heavy gold lighter and lit a cigarette. "A friend of ours, Marco Lorenzo, has been convicted of extortion and robbery."

Jennifer had read about the case. According to the newspapers, Lorenzo was a congenital criminal with a long string of arrests for crimes of violence.

"Do you want me to file an appeal?"

"No, I want you to see that he goes to jail."

Jennifer looked at him in surprise.

Michael put the cigarette lighter back on his desk. "I got word that Di Silva wants to ship him back to Sicily. Marco's got enemies there. If they send him back he won't live twenty-four hours. The safest place for him is Sing Sing. When the heat's off in a year or two we'll get him out. Can you swing it?"

Jennifer hesitated. "If we were in another jurisdiction I could probably do it. But Di Silva won't plea-bargain with me."

Thomas Colfax said quickly, "Perhaps we should let someone else take care of this."

"If I had wanted someone else to take care of it," Michael snapped, "I would have said so." He turned back to Jennifer. "I want you to handle it."

MICHAEL MORETTI AND Nick Vito watched from the window as Thomas Colfax climbed into his sedan and drove off.

Michael said, "Nick, I want you to get rid of him."

"Colfax?"

"I can't trust him anymore. He's living in the past with the old man."

"Whatever you say, Mike. When do you want me to do it?"

"Soon. I'll let you know."

JENNIFER WAS SEATED in Judge Lawrence Waldman's chambers. It was the first time she had seen him in more than a year. The friendly telephone calls and dinner invitations had stopped. Well, that could not be helped, Jennifer thought. She liked Lawrence Waldman and she regretted losing his friendship, but she had made her choice.

They were wailing for Robert Di Silva and they sat there in an uncomfortable silence, neither bothering to make small talk. When the District Attorney walked in and took a seat, the meeting began.

Judge Waldman said to Jennifer, "Bobby says that you want to discuss a plea bargain before I pass sentence on Lorenzo."

"That's right." Jennifer turned to District Attorney Di Silva. "I think it would be a mistake to send Marco Lorenzo to Sing Sing. He doesn't belong here. He's an illegal alien. I feel he should be shipped back to Sicily where he came from."

Di Silva looked at her in surprise. He had been going to recommend deportation, but if that was what Jennifer Parker wanted, then he would have to reevaluate his decision.

"Why do you recommend that?" Di Silva asked.

"For several reasons. First of all, it will keep him from committing any more crimes here, and—"

"So will being in a cell in Sing Sing."

"Lorenzo is an old man. He can't stand being confined. He'll go crazy if you put him in jail. All his friends are in Sicily. He can live there in the sun and die in peace with his family."

Di Silva's mouth tightened with anger. "We're talking about a hoodlum who's spent his life robbing and raping and killing, and you're worried about whether he's with his friends in the sun?" He turned to Judge Waldman. "She's unreal!"

"Marco Lorenzo has a right to—"

Di Silva pounded his fist on the desk. "He has no rights at all! He's been convicted of extortion and armed robbery."

"In Sicily, when a man—"

"He's not in Sicily, goddamn it!" Di Silva yelled. "He's here! He committed the crimes here and he's going to pay for them here." He stood up. "Your Honor, we're wasting your time. The state refuses any plea bargaining in this case. We're asking that Marco Lorenzo be sentenced to Sing Sing."

Judge Waldman turned to Jennifer. "Do you have anything more to say?"

She looked at Robert Di Silva angrily. "No, Your Honor."

Judge Waldman said, "Sentencing will be tomorrow morning. You are both excused."

Di Silva and Jennifer rose and left the office.

In the corridor outside, the District Attorney turned to Jennifer and smiled. "You've lost your touch, counselor."

Jennifer shrugged. "You can't win them all."

Five minutes later, Jennifer was in a telephone booth talking to Michael Moretti.

"You can stop worrying. Marco Lorenzo will be going to Sing Sing."

ime was a swiftly flowing river that had no shores, no boundaries. Its seasons were not winter, spring, fall or summer, but birthdays and joys and troubles and pain. They were court battles won, and cases lost; the reality of Michael, the memories of Adam. But mainly, it was Joshua who was time's calendar, a reminder of how quickly the years were passing.

He was, incredibly, seven years old. Overnight, it seemed, he had gone from crayons and picture books to airplane models and sports. Joshua had grown tall and he resembled his father more every day, and not merely in his physical appearance. He was sensitive and polite, and he had a strong sense of fair play. When Jennifer punished him for something he had done, Joshua said stubbornly, "I'm only four feet tall, but I've got my rights."

He was a miniature Adam. Joshua was athletic, as Adam was. His heroes were the Bebble brothers and Carl Stotz.

"I never heard of them," Jennifer said.

"Where have you *been*, Mom? They invented Little League."

"Oh. *That* Bebble brothers and Carl Stotz."

On weekends, Joshua watched every sports event on television—football, baseball, basketball—it did not matter. In the beginning, Jennifer had let Joshua watch the games alone, but when he tried to discuss the plays with her afterward and Jennifer was completely at sea, she decided she had better watch with him. And so the two of them would sit in front of the television set, munching popcorn and cheering the players.

ONE DAY JOSHUA came in from playing ball, a worried expression on his face, and said, "Mom, can we have a man-to-man talk?"

"Certainly, Joshua."

They sat down at the kitchen table and Jennifer made him a peanut butter sandwich and poured a glass of milk.

"What's the problem?"

His voice was sober and filled with concern. "Well, I heard the guys talkin' and I was just wonderin'—do you think there'll still be sex when I grow up?"

JENNIFER HAD BOUGHT a small Newport sailboat, and on weekends she and Joshua would go out on the sound for a sail. Jennifer liked to watch his face when he was at the helm. He wore an excited little smile, which she called his "Eric the Red" smile. Joshua was a natural sailor, like his father. The thought brought Jennifer up sharply. She wondered whether she was trying to live her life with Adam vicariously through Joshua. All the things she was doing with her son—the sailing, the sporting events—were things she had done with his father. Jennifer told herself she was doing them because Joshua liked doing them, but she was not sure she was being completely honest. She watched Joshua sheet in the jib, his cheeks tanned from the wind and the sun, his face beaming, and Jennifer realized that the reasons did not matter. The important thing was that her son loved his life with her. He was not a surrogate for his father. He was his own person and Jennifer loved him more than anyone on earth.

42

Antonio Granelli died and Michael took over full control of his empire. The funeral was lavish, as befitted a man of the Godfather's stature. The heads and members of Families from all over the country came to pay their respects to their departed friend, and to assure the new *capo* of their loyalty and support. The FBI was there, taking photographs, as well as half a dozen other government agencies.

Rosa was heartbroken, because she had loved her father very much, but she took consolation and pride in the fact that her husband was taking her father's place as head of the Family.

JENNIFER WAS PROVING more valuable to Michael every day. When there was a problem, it was Jennifer whom Michael consulted. Thomas Colfax was becoming an increasingly bothersome appendage.

"Don't worry about him," Michael told Jennifer. "He's going to retire soon."

. . .

THE SOFT CHIMES of the telephone awakened Jennifer. She lay in bed, listening a moment, then sat up and looked at the digital clock on the nightstand. It was three o'clock in the morning.

She lifted the receiver. "Hello."

It was Michael. "Can you get dressed right away?"

Jennifer sat up straighter and tried to blink the sleep from her eyes. "What's happened?"

"Eddie Santini was just picked up on an armed robbery charge. He's a two-time loser. If they convict him, they'll throw the key away."

"Were there any witnesses?"

"Three, and they all got a good look at him."

"Where is he now?"

"The Seventeenth Precinct."

"I'm on my way, Michael."

Jennifer put on a robe and went down to the kitchen and made herself a steaming pot of coffee. She sat drinking it in the breakfast room, staring out at the night, thinking. *Three witnesses. And they all got a good look at him.*

She picked up the telephone and dialed. "Give me the City Desk."

Jennifer spoke rapidly. "I got some information for you. A guy named Eddie Santini's just been picked up on an armed robbery charge. His attorney's Jennifer Parker. She's gonna try to spring him."

She hung up and repeated the call to two other newspapers and a television station. When Jennifer was through telephoning, she looked at her watch and had another leisurely cup of coffee. She wanted to make certain the photographers had time to get to the precinct on 51st Street. She went upstairs and got dressed.

Before Jennifer left, she went into Joshua's bedroom. His night-light was on. He was sound asleep, the blankets twisted around his restless body. Jennifer gently straightened the blankets, kissed him on the forehead and started to tiptoe out of the room.

"Where you goin'?"

She turned and said, "I'm going to work. Go back to sleep."

"What time is it?"

"It's four o'clock in the morning."

Joshua giggled. "You sure work funny hours for a lady."

She came back to his bedside. "And you sure sleep funny hours for a man."

"Are we going to watch the Mets game tonight?"

"You bet we are. Back to Dreamland."

"Okay, Mom. Have a good case."

"Thanks, pal."

A few minutes later, Jennifer was in her car, on her way into Manhattan.

WHEN JENNIFER ARRIVED, a lone photographer from the *Daily News* was waiting. He stared at Jennifer and said, "It's true! You really handling the Santini case?"

"How did you know that?" Jennifer demanded.

"A little birdie, counselor."

"You're wasting your time. No pictures."

She went inside and arranged for Eddie Santini's bail, stalling the proceedings until she was sure the television cameraman and a reporter and photographer had arrived from the *New York Times*. She decided she could not wait for the *Post*.

The police captain on duty said, "There're some reporters and television people out front, Miss Parker. You can go out the back way if you want."

"It's all right," Jennifer said. "I'll handle them."

She led Eddie Santini to the front corridor where the photographers and reporters were waiting.

She said, "Look, gentlemen, no pictures, please."

And Jennifer stepped aside while the photographer and television cameraman took pictures.

A reporter asked, "What makes this case big enough for you to handle?"

"You'll find out tomorrow. Meanwhile, I would advise you not to use those pictures."

One of the reporters called out, "Come on, Jennifer! Haven't you heard of freedom of the press?"

. . .

AT NOON JENNIFER got a call from Michael Moretti. His voice was angry. "Have you seen the newspapers?"

"No."

"Well, Eddie Santini's picture is all over the front pages and on the television news. I didn't tell you to turn this goddamned thing into a circus!"

"I know you didn't. It was my own idea."

"Jesus! What's the point?"

"The point, Michael, is those three witnesses."

"What about them?"

"You said they got a good look at Eddie Santini. Well, when they get up in court to identify him, they're going to have to prove they didn't identify him because they saw his picture all over the newspapers and television."

There was a long silence, and then Michael's voice said admiringly, "I'm a son of a bitch!"

Jennifer had to laugh.

KEN BAILEY WAS waiting in her office that afternoon when Jennifer walked in, and she knew instantly from the look on his face that something was wrong.

"Why didn't you tell me?" Ken demanded.

"Tell you what?"

"About you and Mike Moretti."

Jennifer checked the retort that rose to her lips. Saying *It's none of your business* was too easy. Ken was her friend; he cared. In a way, it was his business. Jennifer remembered it all, the tiny office they had shared, how he had helped her. *I've got a lawyer friend who's been bugging me to serve some subpoenas for him. I haven't got time. He pays twelve-fifty for each subpoena plus mileage. Would you help me out?*

"Ken, let's not discuss this."

His tone was filled with cold fury. "Why not? Everybody else is discussing it. The word is that you're Moretti's girl." His face was pale. "Jesus!"

"My personal life—"

"He lives in a sewer and you brought that sewer into the office! You've got us all working for Moretti and his hoodlums."

"Stop it!"

"I am. That's what I came to tell you. I'm leaving."

His words were a shock. "You can't leave. You're wrong about what you think of Michael. If you'll just meet him, you'll see—"

The moment the words were out, Jennifer knew she had made a mistake.

He looked at her sadly and said, "He's really wrapped you up, hasn't he? I remember you when you knew who you were. That's the girl I want to remember. Say good-bye to Joshua for me."

And Ken Bailey was gone.

Jennifer felt the tears begin to come, and her throat constricted so tightly that she could hardly breathe. She put her head down on the desk and closed her eyes, trying to shut out the hurt.

WHEN SHE OPENED her eyes, night had fallen. The office was in darkness except for the eerie red glow cast by the city lights. She walked over to the window and stared out at the city below. It looked like a jungle at night, with only a dying campfire to keep away the encroaching terrors.

It was Michael's jungle. There was no way out of it.

43

The Cow Palace in San Francisco was a madhouse, filled with noisy, chanting delegates from all over the country. There were three candidates vying for the presidential nomination, and each had done well in the primaries. But the star, the one who outshone them all, was Adam Warner. The nomination was his on the fifth ballot, and it was made unanimous. His party finally had a candidate they could put forward with pride. The incumbent President, the leader of the opposition party, had a low credibility rating and was considered by the majority of people to be inept.

"Unless you take your cock out and pee in front of a camera on the six o'clock news," Stewart Needham told Adam, "you're going to be the next President of the United States."

AFTER HIS NOMINATION, Adam flew to New York for a meeting at the Regency Hotel with Needham and several influential members of the party. Present in the room was Blair Roman, head of the second largest advertising agency in the country.

Stewart Needham said, "Blair will be in charge of running the publicity end of your campaign, Adam."

"Can't tell you how glad I am to be aboard." Blair Roman grinned. "You're going to be my third President."

"Really?" Adam was not impressed with the man.

"Let me fill you in on some of the game plan." Blair Roman started pacing the room, swinging an imaginary golf club as he walked. "We're going to saturate the country with television commercials, build an image of you as the man who can solve America's problems. Big Daddy—only a young, good-looking Big Daddy. You get it, Mr. President?"

"Mr. Roman . . ."

"Yes?"

"Would you mind not calling me 'Mr. President'?"

Blair Roman laughed. "Sorry. Slip of the tongue, A.W. In my mind you're already in the White House. Believe me, I know you're the man for the job or I wouldn't be undertaking this campaign. I'm too rich to have to work for money."

Beware of people who say they're too rich to have to work for money, Adam thought.

"*We* know you're the man for the job—now we have to let the *people* know it. If you'll just take a look at these charts I've prepared, I've broken down different sections of the country into various ethnic groups. We're going to send you to key places where you can press the flesh."

He leaned forward into Adam's face and said earnestly, "Your wife is going to be a big asset. Women's magazines will go crazy for stuff on your family life. We're going to *merchandise* you, A.W."

Adam found himself beginning to get irritated. "Just how do you plan to do that?"

"It's simple. You're a product, A.W. We're going to sell you just like we'd sell any other product. We—"

Adam turned to Stewart Needham. "Stewart, could I see you alone?"

"Certainly." Needham turned to the others and said, "Let's break for dinner and meet back here at nine o'clock. We'll continue the discussion then."

When the two men were alone, Adam said, "Jesus, Stewart! He's planning to turn this thing into a circus! 'You're a product, A.W. We're going to sell you just like we'd sell any other product.' He's disgusting!"

"I know how you feel, Adam," Stewart Needham said soothingly, "but Blair gets results. When he said you're his third President, he wasn't kidding. Every President since Eisenhower has had an advertising agency masterminding his campaign. Whether you like it or not, a campaign needs salesmanship. Blair Roman knows the psychology of the public. As distasteful as it may be, the reality is that if you want to be elected to any public office, you have to be sold—you have to be merchandised."

"I hate it."

"That's part of the price you're going to have to pay." He walked over to Adam and put an arm across his shoulder. "All you have to do is keep the objective in mind. You want the White House? All right. We're going to do everything we can to get you there. But you have to do your part. If being the ringmaster in a three-ring circus is part of it, bear with it."

"Do we really need Blair Roman?"

"We need *a* Blair Roman. Blair's as good as there is. Let me handle him. I'll keep him away from you as much as possible."

"I'd appreciate that."

THE CAMPAIGN BEGAN. It started with a few television spots and personal appearances and gradually grew bigger and bigger until it spanned the nation. Wherever one went, there was Senator Adam Warner in living color. In every part of the country he could be watched on television, heard on radio, seen on billboards. Law and order was one of the key issues of the campaign, and Adam's crime investigation committee was heavily stressed.

Adam taped one-minute television spots, three-minute television spots and five-minute spots, geared for different sections of the country. The television spots that went to West Virginia dealt with unemployment and the vast supply of underground coal that could make the area prosperous; the television segments for Detroit talked about urban blight; in New York City, the subject was the rising crime rate.

Blair Roman confided to Adam, "All you have to do is hit the highlights, A.W. You don't have to discuss key issues in depth. We're selling the product, and that's *you*."

Adam said, "Mr. Roman, I don't care what your goddamned statistics say. I'm not a breakfast food and I don't intend to be sold like one. I *will* talk about issues in depth because I think the American people are intelligent enough to want to know about them."

"I only—"

"I want you to try to set up a debate between me and the President, to discuss the basic issues."

Blair Roman said, "Right. I'll take a meeting with the President's boys right away, A.W."

"One more thing," Adam said.

"Yes? What's that?"

"Stop calling me A.W."

44

In the mail was a notice from the American Bar Association announcing its annual convention in Acapulco. Jennifer was in the midst of handling half a dozen cases, and ordinarily she would have ignored the invitation, but the convention was going to take place during Joshua's school vacation and Jennifer thought about how much Joshua would enjoy Acapulco.

She said to Cynthia, "Accept. I'll want three reservations."

She would take Mrs. Mackey along.

At dinner that evening, Jennifer broke the news to Joshua. "How would you like to go to Acapulco?"

"That's in Mexico," he announced. "On the west coast."

"That's right."

"Can we go to a topless beach?"

"Joshua!"

"Well, they have them there. Being naked is only natural."

"I'll think about it."

"And can we go deep-sea fishing?"

Jennifer visualized Joshua trying to pull in a large marlin and she contained her smile. "We'll see. Some of those fish get pretty big."

"That's what makes it exciting," Joshua explained seriously. "If it's easy, it's no fun. There's no sport to it."

It could have been Adam talking.

"I agree."

"What else can we do there?"

"Well, there's horseback riding, hiking, sightseeing—"

"Let's not go to a bunch of old churches, okay? They all look alike."

Adam saying, *If you've seen one church, you've seen them all.*

THE CONVENTION BEGAN on a Monday. Jennifer, Joshua and Mrs. Mackey flew to Acapulco on Friday morning on a Braniff jet. Joshua had flown many times before, but he was still excited by the idea of airplanes. Mrs. Mackey was petrified with fear.

Joshua consoled her. "Look at it this way. Even if we crash, it'll only hurt for a second."

Mrs. Mackey turned pale.

THE PLANE LANDED at Benito Juarez Airport at four o'clock in the afternoon, and an hour later the three of them arrived at Las Brisas. The hotel was eight miles outside of Acapulco, and consisted of a series of beautiful pink bungalows built on a hill, each with its private patio. Jennifer's bungalow, like several of the others, had its own swimming pool. Reservations had been difficult to get, for there were half a dozen other conventions and Acapulco was overcrowded, but Jennifer had made a telephone call to one of her corporate clients, and an hour later she had been informed that Las Brisas was eagerly expecting her.

WHEN THEY HAD unpacked, Joshua said, "Can we go into town and hear them talk? I've never been to a country where nobody speaks English." He thought a moment and added, "Unless you count England."

They went into the city and wandered along the Zocalo, the frenetic center of downtown, but to Joshua's disappointment the only language to be heard was English. Acapulco was crowded with American tourists.

They strolled along the colorful market on the main pier opposite Sanborn's in the old part of town, where there were hundreds of stalls selling a bewildering variety of merchandise.

In the late afternoon, they took a *calandria,* a horse-drawn carriage, to Pie de la Cuesta, the sunset beach, and then returned to town.

THEY HAD DINNER at Armando's Le Club, and it was excellent.

"I *love* Mexican food," Joshua declared.

"I'm glad," Jennifer said. "Only this is French."

"Well, it has a Mexican flavor."

SATURDAY WAS A full day. They went shopping in the morning at the Quebrada, where the nicer stores were, and then stopped for a Mexican lunch at Coyuca 22. Joshua said "I suppose you're going to tell me this is French, too."

"No, this is the real thing, gringo."

"What's a gringo?"

"You are, amigo."

They walked by the *fronton* building near the Plaza Caleta, and Joshua saw the billboards advertising jai alai inside.

He stood there, wide-eyed, and Jennifer asked, "Would you like to see the jai alai games?"

Joshua nodded. "If it's not too expensive. If we run out of money we won't be able to get home."

"I think we can manage."

They went inside and watched the furious play of the teams. Jennifer placed a bet for Joshua and his team won.

When Jennifer suggested returning to the hotel, Joshua said, "Gosh, Mom, can't we see the divers first?"

The hotel manager had mentioned them that morning.

"Are you sure you wouldn't like to rest, Joshua?"

"Oh, if you're too tired, sure. I keep forgettin' about your age."

That did it. "Never mind my age." Jennifer turned to Mrs. Mackey. "Are you up to it?"

"Certainly," Mrs. Mackey groaned.

THE DIVING ACT was at La Quebrada cliffs. Jennifer, Joshua and Mrs. Mackey stood on a public viewing platform while divers carrying lighted torches plunged one hundred and fifty feet into a narrow, rock-lined cove, timing their descent to coincide with the arrival of incoming breakers. The slightest miscalculation would have meant instant death.

When the exhibition was over, a boy came around to collect a donation for the divers.

"*Uno peso, por favor.*"

Jennifer gave him five pesos.

She dreamed about the divers that night.

LAS BRISAS HAD its own beach, La Concha, and early Sunday morning Jennifer, Joshua and Mrs. Mackey drove down in one of the pink canopied jeeps that the hotel supplied to its guests. The weather was perfect. The harbor was a sparkling blue canvas dotted with speedboats and sailboats.

Joshua stood at the edge of the terrace, watching the water skiers race by.

"Did you know water skiing was invented in Acapulco, Mom?"

"No. Where did you hear that?"

"I either read it in a book or I made it up."

"I vote for 'made it up.'"

"Does that mean I can't go water skiing?"

"Those speedboats are pretty fast. Aren't you afraid?"

Joshua looked out at the skiers skimming over the water. "That man said, 'I'm going to send you home to Jesus.' And then he put a nail in my hand."

It was the first reference he had made to the terrible ordeal he had gone through.

Jennifer knelt and put her arms around her son. "What made you think of that, Joshua?"

He shrugged. "I don't know. I guess because Jesus walked on water and everyone out there is walking on water." He saw the stricken look on his mother's face. "I'm sorry, Mom. I don't think about it much, honest."

She hugged him tightly and said, "It's all right, darling. Of course you can go water skiing. Let's have lunch first."

• • •

THE OUTDOOR RESTAURANT at La Concha had wrought-iron tables set with pink linen, shaded by pink-and-white-striped umbrellas. Lunch was a buffet and the long serving table was crowded with an incredible assortment of dishes. There were fresh lobster and crab and salmon, selections of cold and hot meats, salads, a variety of raw and cooked vegetables, cheeses and fruits. There was a separate table for an array of freshly baked desserts. The two women watched Joshua fill and empty his plate three times before he sat back, satisfied.

"It's a very good restaurant," he pronounced. "I don't care *what* kind of food it is." He stood up. "I'll go check on the water skiing."

Mrs. Mackey had barely picked at her food.

"Are you feeling all right?" Jennifer asked. "You haven't eaten anything since we arrived."

Mrs. Mackey leaned forward and whispered darkly, "I don't want Montezuma's Revenge!"

"I don't think you have to worry about that in a place like this."

"I don't hold with foreign food," Mrs. Mackey sniffed.

Joshua ran back to the table and said, "I got a boat. Is it okay if I go now, Mom?"

"Don't you want to wait a while?"

"What for?"

"Joshua, you'll sink with all you've eaten."

"Test me!" he begged.

While Mrs. Mackey watched on shore, Jennifer and Joshua got into the speedboat and Joshua had his first water-skiing lesson. He spent the first five minutes falling down, and after that, performed as though born to water skiing. Before the afternoon was over, Joshua was doing tricks on one ski, and finally skiing on his heels with no skis.

They spent the rest of the afternoon lazing on the sand and swimming.

On the way back to Las Brisas in the jeep, Joshua snuggled up against Jennifer and said, "You know something, Mom? I think this was probably the best day of my whole life."

Michael's words flashed through her mind: *I just want you to know this has been the greatest night of my life.*

• • •

EARLY MONDAY MORNING Jennifer arose and got dressed to attend the convention. She put on a full-flowing dark green skirt and an off-the-shoulder blouse embroidered in giant red roses, that revealed her patina of suntan. She studied herself in the mirror and was pleased. Despite the fact that her son thought she was over the hill, Jennifer was aware that she looked like Joshua's beautiful thirty-four-year-old sister. She laughed to herself and thought that this vacation was one of her better ideas.

Jennifer said to Mrs. Mackey, "I have to go to work now. Take good care of Joshua. Don't let him get too much sun."

THE HUGE CONVENTION center was a cluster of five buildings joined by roofed circulation terraces, sprawled over thirty-five acres of lush greenery. The carefully tended lawns were studded with pre-Columbian statues.

The Bar Association Convention was being held in *Teotihuacan,* the main hall, holding an audience of seventy-five hundred people.

Jennifer went to the registration desk, signed in and entered the large hall. It was packed. In the crowd she spotted dozens of friends and acquaintances. Nearly all of them had changed from conservative business suits and dresses to brightly colored sport shirts and pants. It was as though everyone was on vacation. *There is a good reason,* Jennifer thought, *for holding the convention in a place like Acapulco instead of in Chicago or Detroit.* They could take off their stiff collars and somber ties and let themselves go under a tropical sun.

Jennifer had been given a program at the door but, deep in conversation with some friends, had paid no attention to it.

A deep voice boomed over the loudspeaker, "Attention, please! Would you all please take your seats? Attention, please! We would like to get the meeting started. Would you sit down, please!"

Reluctantly the small groups began to break up as people started to find seats. Jennifer looked up to see that half a dozen men had mounted the dais.

In the center was Adam Warner.

Jennifer stood there, frozen, as Adam walked to the chair next to the microphone and took a seat. She felt her heart begin to pound. The last time she had seen Adam had been when they had had lunch at the little Italian restaurant, the day he had told her that Mary Beth was pregnant.

Jennifer's immediate impulse was to flee. She had had no idea Adam would be there and she could not bear the thought of facing him. Adam and his son being in the same city filled her with panic. Jennifer knew she had to get out of there quickly.

She turned to leave as the chairman announced over the loudspeaker, "If the rest of you ladies and gentlemen will take your seats, we will begin."

As people around her began sitting down, Jennifer found herself conspicuous by standing. Jennifer slid into a seat, determined to slip away at the first opportunity.

The chairman said, "We are honored this morning to have us our guest speaker a nominee for the presidency of the United States. He is a member of the New York Bar Association and one of the most distinguished members of the United States Senate. It is with great pride that I introduce *Senator Adam Warner*."

Jennifer watched as Adam rose, accepting the warm applause. He stepped to the microphone and looked out across the room. "Thank you, Mr. Chairman, ladies and gentlemen."

Adam's voice was rich and resonant, and he had an air of authority that was mesmerizing. The silence in the room was total.

"There are many reasons why we are gathered here today." He paused. "Some of us like to swim and some of us like to snorkel. . . ." There was a swell of appreciative laughter. "But the main reason we are here is to exchange ideas and knowledge and discuss new concepts. Today, lawyers are under greater attack than at any time in my memory. Even the Chief Justice of the Supreme Court has been sharply critical of our profession."

Jennifer loved the way he used *our*, making him one with the rest of them. She let his words wash over her, content just to look at him, to watch the way he moved, to hear his voice. At one point he stopped to run his fingers through his hair, and it gave Jennifer a sharp pang. It was a gesture of Joshua's. Adam's son was only a few miles away and Adam would never know.

Adam's voice grew stronger, more forceful. "Some of you in this room are criminal lawyers. I must admit I have always considered that to be the most exciting branch of our profession. Criminal lawyers often deal in life and death. It is a very honorable profession and one of which we can all be proud. However"—his voice grew hard—"there are some of them"—and now Jennifer noticed that Adam was disassociating himself by his choice of the pronoun—"who are a disgrace to the oath they have taken. The American system of jurisprudence is based on the inalienable right of every citizen to have a fair trial. But when the law is made a mockery of, when lawyers spend their time and energy, imagination and skill, finding ways to defy that law, finding ways to subvert justice, then I think it is time something must be done." Every eye in the room was fastened on Adam as he stood there, eyes blazing. "I am speaking, ladies and gentlemen, out of personal experience and a deep anger for some of the things I see happening. I am currently heading a Senate committee conducting an investigation of organized crime in the United States. My committee has found itself thwarted and frustrated time after time by men who hold themselves to be more powerful than the highest enforcement agencies of our nation. I have seen judges suborned, the families of witnesses threatened, key witnesses disappear. Organized crime in our country is like a deadly python that is squeezing our economy, swallowing up our courts, threatening our very lives. The great majority of lawyers are honorable men and women doing honorable jobs, but I want to give warning to that small minority who think their law is above our law: You're making a grave mistake and you're going to pay for that mistake. Thank you."

Adam sat down to a tumultuous burst of applause that became a standing ovation. Jennifer found herself on her feet applauding with the others, but her thoughts were on Adam's last words. It was as though he had been speaking directly to her. Jennifer turned and headed toward the exit, pushing her way through the crowd.

As Jennifer approached the door she was hailed by a Mexican lawyer with whom she had worked a year earlier.

He kissed her hand gallantly and said, "What an honor to have you in our country again, Jennifer. I insist you have dinner with me this evening."

Jennifer and Joshua had planned to go to The Maria Elena that night to watch the native dancers. "I'm sorry, Luis. I have an engagement."

His large, liquid eyes showed his disappointment. "Tomorrow then?"

Before Jennifer could answer, an assistant district attorney from New York was at her side.

"Hello, there," he said. "What are you doing slumming with the common folk? How about having dinner with me tonight? There's a Mexican disco called Nepentha, where they have a glass floor lit from underneath and a mirror overhead."

"It sounds fascinating, thanks, but I'm busy tonight."

A few moments later Jennifer found herself surrounded by lawyers she had worked for and against all over the country. She was a celebrity and they all wanted to talk to her. It was half an hour before Jennifer could break free. She hurried toward the lobby, and as she moved to the exit, Adam was walking toward her, surrounded by the press and secret service men. Jennifer tried to retreat, but it was too late. Adam had seen her.

"Jennifer!"

For an instant she thought of pretending she had not heard him, but she could not embarrass him in front of the others. She would say hello quickly and be on her way.

She watched as Adam moved toward her, saying to the press, "I have no more statements to make now, ladies and gentlemen."

A moment later Adam was touching her hand, looking into her eyes, and it was as though they had never been apart. They stood there in the lobby, surrounded by people, and yet they might have been completely alone. Jennifer had no idea how long they stood there looking at each other.

Finally, Adam said, "I—I think we'd better have a drink."

"It would be wiser if we didn't." She had to get out of this place.

Adam shook his head. "Overruled."

He took her arm and led her into the crowded bar. They found a table at the rear of the room.

"I've called you and I've written to you," Adam said. "You never called me back and my letters were returned."

He was watching her, his eyes filled with questions. "There isn't a day that's gone by that I haven't thought about you. Why did you disappear?"

"It's part of my magic act," Jennifer said lightly.

A waiter came to take their order. Adam turned to Jennifer. "What would you like?"

"Nothing. I really have to leave, Adam."

"You can't go now. This is a celebration. The anniversary of the revolution."

"Theirs or ours?"

"What's the difference?" He turned to the waiter. "Two margaritas."

"No. I—" *All right,* she thought, *one drink.* "Make mine a double," Jennifer said recklessly.

The waiter nodded and left.

"I read about you all the time," Jennifer said. "I'm very proud of you, Adam."

"Thank you." Adam hesitated. "I've been reading about you, too."

She responded to the tone in his voice. "But you're not proud of me."

"You seem to have a lot of Syndicate clients."

Jennifer found her defenses going up. "I thought your lecture was over."

"This isn't a lecture, Jennifer. I'm concerned about you. My committee is after Mike Moretti, and we're going to get him."

Jennifer looked around the bar filled with lawyers. "For God's sake, Adam, we shouldn't be having this discussion, especially in here."

"Where, then?"

"Nowhere. Michael Moretti is my client. I can't discuss him with you."

"I want to talk to you. Where?"

She shook her head. "I told you I—"

"I have to talk about us."

"There is no us." Jennifer started to rise.

Adam put his hand on her arm. "Please, don't go. I can't let you go. Not yet."

Reluctantly, Jennifer sat down.

Adam's eyes were fastened on her face. "Do you ever think of me?"

Jennifer looked up at him and did not know whether to laugh or cry.

Did she ever think of him! He lived in her house. She kissed him good morning every day, made his breakfast, went sailing with him, loved him. "Yes," Jennifer said finally, "I think of you."

"I'm glad. Are you happy?"

"Of course." She knew she had said it too quickly. She made her voice more casual. "I have a successful practice, I'm well off financially, I travel a great deal, I see a lot of attractive men. How is your wife?"

"She's fine." His voice was low.

"And your daughter?"

He nodded, and there was pride in his face. "Samantha's wonderful. She's just growing up too fast."

She would be Joshua's age.

"You've never married?"

"No."

There was a long moment, and then Jennifer tried to continue, but she had hesitated too long. It was too late. Adam had looked into her eyes and he had known instantly.

He clasped her hand in his. "Oh, Jennifer. Oh, my darling!"

Jennifer could feel the blood rushing to her face. She had known all along that this would be a terrible mistake.

"I have to go, Adam. I have an appointment."

"Break it," he urged.

"I'm sorry. I can't." All she wanted to do was get out of there, to get her son away from there, to flee back home.

Adam was saying, "I'm supposed to fly back to Washington on an afternoon plane. I can arrange to stay over if you'll see me tonight."

"No. No!"

"Jennifer, I can't let you go again. Not like this. We have to talk. Just have dinner with me."

He was pressing her hand tighter. She looked at him and fought with all her strength and found herself weakening.

"Please, Adam," she begged. "We shouldn't be seen together. If you're after Michael Moretti—"

"This has nothing to do with Moretti. A friend of mine has offered me the use of his boat. It's called the *Paloma Blanca*. It's docked at the Yacht Club. Eight o'clock."

"I won't be there."

"I will. I'll be waiting for you."

ACROSS THE ROOM, at the crowded bar, Nick Vito was sitting with two Mexican *puttanas* a friend had delivered to him. Both were pretty and coarse and underage, the way Nick Vito liked them. His friend had promised they would be special, and he had been right. They were rubbing up against him, whispering exciting promises in his ear, but Nick Vito was not listening. He was staring across the room at the booth where Jennifer Parker and Adam Warner were seated.

"Why don't we go up to your room now, *querido*?" one of the girls suggested to Nick.

Nick Vito was tempted to walk over to Jennifer and the stranger she was with and say hello, but both girls had their hands between his legs and were stroking him. He was going to make one hell of a sandwich.

"Yeah, let's go upstairs," Nick Vito said.

45

The *Paloma Blanca* was a motor sailer and it shone proud and white and gleaming in the moonlight. Jennifer approached it slowly, looking around to make sure that no one had observed her. Adam had told her he would elude the secret service men and apparently he had succeeded. After Jennifer had seated Joshua and Mrs. Mackey at Maria Elena, she had taken a taxi and had had the driver drop her off two blocks before the pier.

Jennifer had picked up the phone half a dozen times to call Adam to say she would not meet him. She had started to write a note, then had torn it up. From the moment she had left Adam at the bar, Jennifer had been in an agony of indecision. She thought of all the reasons why she should not see Adam. Nothing good could possibly come of it, and it could lead to a tremendous amount of harm. Adam's career could be at stake. He was riding on a crest of public popularity, an idealist in a time of cynicism, the country's hope for the future. He was the darling of the media, but the same press that had helped to create him would be out there waiting to push him into the abyss if he betrayed their image of him.

And so Jennifer had made up her mind not to see him. She was another woman, living a different life, and she belonged to Michael now. . . .

ADAM WAS WAITING for her at the top of the gangplank.

"I was so afraid you weren't coming," he said.

And she was in his arms and they were kissing.

"What about the crew, Adam?" Jennifer finally asked.

"I sent them away. Do you still remember how to sail?"

"I still remember."

They hoisted the sail and sheeted in for a starboard tack, and ten minutes later the *Paloma Blanco* was heading through the harbor toward the open sea. For the first half hour they were busy navigating, but there was not a moment when they were not acutely aware of each other. The tension kept mounting, and they both knew that what was going to happen was inevitable.

When they finally cleared the harbor and were sailing into the moonlit Pacific, Adam moved to Jennifer's side and put his arms around her.

They made love on the deck under the stars, with the soft, fragrant breeze cooling their naked bodies.

The past and the future were swept away and there was only the present holding the two of them together in its swiftly fleeting moments. For Jennifer knew that this night in Adam's arms was not a beginning; it was an ending. There was no way to bridge the worlds that separated them. They had traveled too far from each other and there was no road back. Not now, not ever. She would always have a part of Adam in Joshua, and that would be enough for her, would have to be enough for her.

This night would have to last her the rest of her life.

They lay there together, listening to the gentle susurration of the sea against the boat.

Adam said, "Tomorrow—"

"Don't talk," Jennifer whispered. "Just love me, Adam." She covered his lips with small kisses and fluttered her fingers delicately along the strong, lean lines of his body. She moved her hands down in slow circles until she found him, and her fingers began to stroke him.

"Oh God, Jennifer," Adam whispered, and his mouth began to move slowly down her naked body.

46

The cocksucker kept givin' me the *malocchio*," little Salvator Fiore was complaining, "so I finally hadda burn 'im."

Nick Vito laughed, for anyone who was stupid enough to fool around with the Little Flower had to be out to lunch. Nick Vito was enjoying himself in the farmhouse kitchen with Salvatore Fiore and Joseph Colella, talking over old times, waiting for the conference in the living room to end. The midget and the giant were his best friends. They had gone through the fire together. Nick Vito looked at the two men and thought happily, *They're like my brothers.*

"How's your cousin Pete?" Nick asked the giant Colella.

"He did cancer and he's under the hammer, but he's gonna be okay."

"He's beautiful."

"Yeah. Pete's good people; he's just had a little bad luck. He was back-up man on a bank job, but it wasn't his stick, and the fuckin' cops tagged him and put him away. He did hard time. The hacks tried to turn him around but they was spinnin' their wheels."

"Hell, yes. Pete's got class."

"Yeah. He always went for big bucks, big broads and big cars."

From the living room there came the sound of raised, angry voices. They listened a moment.

"Sounds like Colfax has a bug up his ass."

THOMAS COLFAX AND Michael Moretti were alone in the room, discussing a large gambling operation that the Family was about to start in the Bahamas. Michael had put Jennifer in charge of making the business arrangements.

"You can't do it, Mike," Colfax protested. "I know all the boys down there. She doesn't. You must let me handle it." He knew he was talking too loudly, but he was unable to control himself.

"Too late," Michael said.

"I don't trust the girl. Neither did Tony."

"Tony's not with us anymore." Michael's voice was dangerously quiet.

Thomas Colfax knew that this was the moment to back down. "Sure, Mike. All I'm saying is that I think the girl's a mistake. I grant you she's smart, but I'm warning you, before she's through she could send us all away."

It was Thomas Colfax whom Michael was concerned about. The Warner Crime Commission investigation was in full swing. When they reached Colfax, how long would the old man stand up to them before he cracked? He knew more about the Family than Jennifer Parker could ever know. Colfax was the one who could destroy them all, and Michael did not trust him.

Thomas Colfax was saying, "Send her away for awhile. Just until this investigation cools down. She's a woman. If they start putting pressure on her, she'll talk."

Michael studied him and made his decision. "All right, Tom. Maybe you've got a point there. Jennifer may not be dangerous, but on the other hand, if she's not with us a hundred percent, why take unnecessary chances?"

"That's all I'm suggesting, Mike." Thomas Colfax rose from his chair, relieved. "You're doing the wise thing."

"I know." Michael turned toward the kitchen and yelled out, "Nick!"

A moment later Nick Vito appeared.

"Drive the *consigliere* back to New York, will you, Nick?"

"Sure thing, boss."

"Oh. On the way I want you to stop and deliver a package for me." He turned to Thomas Colfax. "You don't mind?"

"Of course not, Mike." He was flushed with his victory.

Michael Moretti said to Nick Vito, "Come on. It's upstairs."

Nick followed Michael up to his bedroom. When they were inside, Michael closed the door.

"I'd like you to make a stop before you get out of New Jersey."

"Sure, boss."

"I want you to drop off some garbage." Nick Vito looked puzzled. "The *consigliere*," Michael explained.

"Oh. Okay. Whatever you say."

"Take him out to the dump. There won't be anyone around at this time of night."

FIFTEEN MINUTES LATER the limousine was headed for New York. Nick Vito was at the wheel, with Thomas Colfax in the passenger seat beside him.

"I'm glad Mike decided to sideline that bitch," Thomas Colfax said.

Nick glanced sideways at the unsuspecting lawyer seated beside him. "Uh-huh."

Thomas Colfax looked at the gold Baume & Mercier watch on his wrist. It was three o'clock in the morning, long past his bedtime. It had been a long day and he was tired. *I'm getting too old for these battles,* he thought.

"How far out are we driving?"

"Not far," Nick mumbled.

Nick Vito's mind was in a turmoil. Killing was a part of his job and it was a part he enjoyed, because of the sense of power it gave him. Nick felt like a god when he killed; he was omnipotent. But tonight, he was bothered. He could not understand why he had been ordered to blow away Thomas Colfax. Colfax was the *consigliere,* the man everyone turned to when they were in trouble. Next to the Godfather, the *consigliere* was the most important man in the Organization. He had kept Nick out of the slammer a dozen times.

Shit! Nick thought. *Colfax was right. Mike should never have let a woman come into the business. Men thought with their brains. Women thought with their pussies. Oh, how he'd love to get his hands on Jennifer Parker! He'd fuck her until she cried 'Uncle' and then—*

"Watch it! You're going off the road!"

"Sorry." Nick quickly steered the car back into his lane.

The dump was a short distance ahead. Nick could feel the perspiration popping out under his arms. He glanced over again at Thomas Colfax.

Snuffing him out would be a cinch. It would be like putting a baby to sleep but, goddamn it! it was the wrong baby! Someone was giving Mike a hand job. This was a sin. It was like murdering his old man.

He wished he could have talked it over with Salvatore and Joe. They could have told him what to do.

Nick could see the dump ahead to the right of the highway. His nerves began to tighten, just as they always did before a hit. He pressed his left arm against his side and felt the reassuring bulk of the short-barreled .38 Smith & Wesson nestling there.

"I could use a good night's sleep," Thomas Colfax yawned.

"Yeah." He was going to get a long, long sleep.

The car was nearing the dump now. Nick checked the rear-view mirror and scanned the road ahead. There were no cars in sight.

He put his foot on the brake suddenly and said, "Goddamn it, it feels like I'm getting a flat."

He brought the car to a stop, opened the door and stepped out onto the road. He slipped the gun out of its holster and held it at his side. Then he moved around to the passenger side of the car and said, "Could you give me a hand?"

Thomas Colfax opened the door and stepped out. "I'm not very good at—" He saw the raised gun in Nick's hand and stopped. He tried to swallow. "W-What's the matter, Nick?" His voice cracked. "What have I done?"

That was the question that had been burning inside Nick Vito's mind all evening. Someone was running a game on Mike. Colfax was on *their* side, he was one of them. When Nick's younger brother had gotten in trouble with the Feds, it had been Colfax who had stepped in and saved the boy. He had even gotten him a job. *I owe him, goddamn it,* Nick thought.

He let his gun hand drop. "Honest to God, I don't know, Mr. Colfax. It ain't right."

Thomas Colfax looked at him a moment and sighed. "Do what you have to do, Nick."

"Jesus, I can't do this. You're my *consigliere.*"

"Mike will kill you if you let me go."

Nick knew that Colfax was telling the truth. Michael Moretti was not a man to tolerate disobedience. Nick thought of Tommy Angelo. Angelo had been the wheel man on a fur heist. Michael had ordered him to take the car they had used and have it crushed in a compactor in a New Jersey junkyard the Family owned. Tommy Angelo had been in a hurry to keep a date, so he had dumped the car on an East Side street, where investigators had found it. Angelo had disappeared the next day, and the story was that his body had been put in the trunk of an old Chevy and compacted. No one crossed Michael Moretti and lived. *But there is a way,* Nick thought.

"Mike don't have to know it," Nick said. His usually slow brain was working rapidly, with an unnatural clarity. "Look," he said, "all you gotta do is blow the country. I'll tell Mike I buried you under the garbage so they'll never find you. You can hide out in South America or somewhere. You must have a little dough stashed away."

Thomas Colfax tried to keep the sudden hope out of his voice. "I have plenty, Nick. I'll give you whatever—"

Nick shook his head fiercely. "I ain't doin' this for money. I'm doin' it because"—*How could he put it into words?*—"I got *respect* for you. The only thing is, you gotta protect me. Can you catch a mornin' plane to South America?"

Thomas Colfax said, "No problem, Nick. Just drop me off at my house. My passport's there."

TWO HOURS LATER, Thomas Colfax was on an Eastern Airlines jet. It was bound for Washington, D.C.

t was their last day in Acapulco, a perfect morning with warm, soft breezes playing melodies through the palm trees. The beach at La Concha was crowded with tourists greedily soaking up the sun before returning to the routine of their everyday lives.

Joshua came running up to the breakfast table wearing a bathing suit, his athletic little body fit and tan. Mrs. Mackey lumbered along behind him.

Joshua said, "I've had plenty of sufficient time to digest my food, Mom. Can I go water skiing now?"

"Joshua, you just finished eating."

"I have a very high metabolism rate," he explained earnestly. "I digest food fast."

Jennifer laughed. "All right. Have a good time."

"I will. Watch me, huh?"

Jennifer watched as Joshua raced along the pier to a waiting speedboat. She saw him engage the driver in earnest conversation, and then they both turned to look at Jennifer. She signaled an okay, and the driver nodded and Joshua began to put on water skis.

The motor boat roared into life and Jennifer looked up to see Joshua beginning to rise on his water skis.

Mrs. Mackey said proudly, "He's a natural athlete, isn't he?"

At that moment, Joshua turned to wave at Jennifer and lost his balance, falling against the pilings. Jennifer leaped to her feet and began racing toward the pier. An instant later, she saw Joshua's head appear above the surface of the water and he looked at her, grinning.

Jennifer stood there, her heart beating fast, and watched as Joshua put the water skis back on. As the boat circled and began to move forward again, it gained enough momentum to pull Joshua to his feet. He turned once to wave at Jennifer and then was racing away on top of the waves. She stood there watching, her heart still pounding from fright. If anything happened to him . . . She wondered whether other mothers loved their children as much as she loved her son, but it did not seem possible. She would have died for Joshua, killed for him. *I have killed for him,* she thought, *with the hand of Michael Moretti.*

Mrs. Mackey was saying, "That could have been a nasty fall."

"Thank God it wasn't."

Joshua was out on the water for an hour. When the boat pulled back into the slip, he let go of the tow rope and gracefully skied up onto the sand.

He ran over to Jennifer, filled with excitement. "You should have seen the accident, Mom. It was incredible! A big sailboat tipped over and we stopped and saved their lives."

"That's wonderful, son. How many lives did you save?"

"There were six of them."

"And you pulled them out of the water?"

Joshua hesitated. "Well, we didn't exactly pull them out of the water. They were kinda sittin' on the side of their boat. But they probably would have starved to death if we hadn't come along."

Jennifer bit her lip to keep from smiling. "I see. They were very lucky you came along, weren't they?"

"I'll say."

"Did you hurt yourself when you fell, darling?"

"'Course not." He felt the back of his head. "I got a little bump."

"Let me feel it."

"What for? You know what a bump feels like."

Jennifer reached down and gently ran her hand along the back of Joshua's head.

Her fingers found a large lump. "It's as big as an egg, Joshua."

"It's nothing."

Jennifer rose to her feet. "I think we'd better get started back to the hotel."

"Can't we stay a little while longer?"

"I'm afraid not. We have to pack. You don't want to miss your ball game Saturday, do you?"

He sighed. "No. Old Terry Waters is just waitin' to take my place."

"No chance. He pitches like a girl."

Joshua nodded smugly. "He does, doesn't he?"

WHEN THEY RETURNED to Las Brisas, Jennifer telephoned the manager and asked him to send a doctor to the room. The doctor arrived thirty minutes later, a portly, middle-aged Mexican dressed in an old-fashioned white suit. Jennifer admitted him into the bungalow.

"How may I serve you?" Dr. Raul Mendoza asked.

"My son had a fall this morning. He has a nasty bump on his head. I want to make sure he's all right."

Jennifer led him into Joshua's bedroom, where he was packing a suitcase.

"Joshua, this is Doctor Mendoza."

Joshua looked up and asked, "Is somebody sick?"

"No. No one's sick, my lad. I just wanted the doctor to take a look at your head."

"Oh, for Pete's sake, Mom! What's the matter with my head?"

"Nothing. I would just feel better if Doctor Mendoza checked it over. Humor me, will you?"

"Women!" Joshua said. He looked at the doctor suspiciously. "You're not going to stick any needles in me or anything, are you?"

"No, senor, I am a very painless doctor."

"That's the kind I like."

"Please sit down."

Joshua sat on the edge of the bed and Dr. Mendoza ran his fingers over the back of Joshua's head. Joshua winced with pain but he did not cry out. The doctor opened his medical bag and took out an ophthalmo-scope. "Open your eyes wide, please."

Joshua obeyed. Dr. Mendoza stared through the instrument.

"You see any naked dancin' girls in there?"

"Joshua!"

"I was just askin'."

Dr. Mendoza examined Joshua's other eye. "You are fit as a fiddle. That is the American slang expression, no?" He rose to his feet and closed his medical bag. "I would put some ice on that," he told Jennifer. "Tomorrow the boy will be fine."

It was as though a heavy load had been lifted from Jennifer's heart. "Thank you," she said.

"I will arrange the bill with the hotel cashier, senora. Good bye, young man."

"Good-bye, Doctor Mendoza."

When the doctor had gone, Joshua turned to his mother. "You sure like to throw your money away, Mom."

"I know. I like to waste it on things like food, your health—"

"I'm the healthiest man on the whole team."

"Stay that way."

He grinned. "I promise."

They boarded the six o'clock plane to New York and were back in Sands Point late that night. Joshua slept all the way home.

48

The room was crowded with ghosts. Adam Warner was in his study, preparing a major television campaign speech, but it was impossible to concentrate. His mind was filled with Jennifer. He had been able to think of nothing else since he had returned from Acapulco. Seeing her had only confirmed what Adam had known from the beginning. He had made the wrong choice. He should never have given up Jennifer. Being with her again was a reminder of all that he had had, and thrown away, and he could not bear the thought of it.

He was in an impossible situation. A *no-win* situation, Blair Roman would have called it.

There was a knock on the door and Chuck Morrison, Adam's chief assistant, came in carrying a cassette. "Can I talk to you a minute, Adam?"

"Can it wait, Chuck? I'm in the middle of—"

"I don't think so." There was excitement in Chuck Morrison's voice.

"All right. What's so urgent?"

Chuck Morrison moved closer to the desk. "I just got a telephone

call. It could be some crazy, but if it's not, then Christmas came early this
year. Listen to this."

He placed a cassette in the machine on Adam's desk, pressed a switch
and the tape began to play.

What did you say your name was?

It doesn't matter. I won't talk to anyone except Senator Warner.

*The Senator is busy just now. Why don't you drop him a note and I'll
see to—*

*No! Listen to me. This is very important. Tell Senator Warner I can de-
liver Michael Moretti to him. I'm taking my life in my hands making this
phone call. Just give Senator Warner the message.*

All right. Where are you?

*I'm at the Capitol Motel on Thirty-second Street. Room Fourteen. Tell
him not to come until after dark and to make sure he's not followed. I know
you're taping this. If you play the tape for anyone but him, I'm a dead man.*

There was a click and the tape ended.

Chuck Morrison said, "What do you think?"

Adam frowned. "The town is full of cranks. On the other hand,
our boy sure knows what bait to use, doesn't he? Michael—by God—
Moretti!"

AT TEN O'CLOCK that night, Adam Warner, accompanied by four secret
service men, cautiously knocked at the door of Room 14 of the Capitol
Motel. The door was opened a crack.

The moment Adam saw the face of the man inside, he turned to
the men with him and said, "Stay outside. Don't let anyone near this
place."

The door opened wider and Adam stepped into the room.

"Good evening, Senator Warner."

"Good evening, Mr. Colfax."

The two men stood there appraising each other.

Thomas Colfax looked older than when Adam had last seen him, but
there was another difference, almost indefinable. And then Adam realized what it was. Fear. Thomas Colfax was frightened. He had always
been a self-assured, almost arrogant man, and now that self-assurance
had disappeared.

"Thank you for coming, Senator." Colfax's voice sounded strained and nervous.

"I understand you want to talk to me about Michael Moretti."

"I can lay him in your lap."

"You're Moretti's attorney. Why would you want to do that?"

"I have my reasons."

"Let's say I decided to go along with you. What would you expect in return?"

"First, complete immunity. Second, I want to get out of the country. I'll need a passport and papers—a new identity."

So Michael Moretti had put out a contract on Thomas Colfax. It was the only explanation for what was happening. Adam could hardly believe his good fortune. It was the best possible break he could have had.

"If I get immunity for you," Adam said, "—and I'm not promising you anything yet—you understand that I would expect you to go into court and testify fully. I would want everything you've got."

"You'll have it."

"Does Moretti know where you are now?"

"He thinks I'm dead." Thomas Colfax smiled nervously. "If he finds me, I will be."

"He won't find you. Not if we make a deal."

"I'm putting my life in your hands, Senator."

"Frankly," Adam informed him, "I don't give a damn about you. I want Moretti. Let's lay down the ground rules. If we come to an agreement, you'll get all the protection the government can give you. If I'm satisfied with your testimony, we'll provide you with enough money to live in any country you choose under an assumed identity. In return for that, you'll have to agree to the following: I'll want full testimony from you regarding Moretti's activities. You'll have to testify before a grand jury, and when we bring Moretti to trial, I'll expect you to be a witness for the government. Agreed?"

Thomas Colfax looked away. Finally he said, "Tony Granelli must be turning over in his grave. What happens to people? Whatever happened to honor?"

Adam had no answer. This was a man who had cheated the law a hundred times, who had gotten paid killers off scot-free, who had helped mastermind the activities of the most vicious crime organization the civilized world had ever known. And he was asking what had happened to honor.

Thomas Colfax turned to Adam. "We have a deal. I want it in writing, and I want it signed by the Attorney General."

"You'll have it." Adam looked around the shabby motel room. "Let's get out of this place."

"I won't go to a hotel. Moretti's got ears everywhere."

"Not where you're going."

AT TEN MINUTES past midnight a military truck and two jeeps, manned by armed marines, rolled up in front of Room 14. Four military police went into the room and came out a few moments later, closely escorting Thomas Colfax into the back of the truck. The procession pulled away from the motel with one jeep in front of the truck and the second jeep following in the rear, headed for Quantico, Virginia, thirty-five miles south of Washington. The three-car caravan proceeded at high speed, and forty minutes later arrived at the United States Marine Corps base at Quantico.

The commandant of the base, Major General Roy Wallace, and a detail of armed marines were waiting at the gate. As the caravan came to a stop, General Wallace said to the captain in charge of the detail, "The prisoner is to be taken directly to the stockade. There is to be no conversation with him."

Major General Wallace watched as the procession entered the compound. He would have given a month's pay to know the identity of the man in the truck. The general's command consisted of a 310-acre Marine Corps air station and part of the FBI's Academy, and was the principal center for training officers of the United States Marine Corps. He had never before been asked to house a civilian prisoner. It was totally outside regulations.

Two hours earlier, he had received a telephone call from the commandant of the Marine Corps himself. "There's a man on his way to your base, Roy. I want you to clear out the stockade and keep him in there until further orders."

General Wallace thought he had heard wrong. "Did you say *clear out the stockade,* sir?"

"That's right. I want this man in there by himself. No one is to be allowed near him. I want you to double the stockade guard. Understood?"

"Yes, General."

"One more thing, Roy. If anything happens to that man while he's in your custody, I'm going to have roasted ass for breakfast."

And the commandant had hung up.

General Wallace watched the truck lumber toward the stockade, then returned to his office and rang for his aide, Captain Alvin Giles.

"About the man we're putting in the stockade—" General Wallace said.

"Yes, General?"

"Our primary objective is his safety. I want you to hand-pick the guards yourself. No one else is to go near him. No visitors, no mail, no packages. Understood?"

"Yes, sir."

"I want you personally to be in the kitchen when his food is being prepared."

"Yes, General."

"If anyone shows any undue curiosity about him, I want that reported to me immediately. Any questions?"

"No, sir."

"Very good, Al. Stay on top of it. If anything goes wrong, I'll have roasted ass for breakfast."

49

Jennifer was awakened by the soft drumming of the early morning ram, and she lay in bed listening to it gently hammering against the house.

She glanced at the alarm clock. It was time to begin her day.

Half an hour later, Jennifer walked downstairs into the dining room to join Joshua for breakfast. He was not there.

Mrs. Mackey came in from the kitchen. "Good morning, Mrs. Parker."

"Good morning. Where's Joshua?"

"He seemed so tired that I thought I'd let him sleep a little longer. He doesn't have to start back to school until tomorrow."

Jennifer nodded. "Good idea."

She ate her breakfast and went upstairs to say good-bye to Joshua. He was lying in his bed, sound asleep.

Jennifer sat on the edge of the bed and said softly, "Hey, sleepyhead, do you want to say good-bye?"

He slowly opened one eye. "Sure, friend. 'Bye." His voice was heavy with sleep. "Do I have to get up?"

"No. Tell you what. Why don't you laze around today? You can stay inside and have fun. It's raining too hard to go outdoors."

He nodded drowsily. "Okay, Mom."

His eyes closed again and he was asleep.

JENNIFER SPENT THE afternoon in court, and by the time she finished and arrived home it was after seven o'clock. The rain, which had been a drizzle all day, was coming down in torrents, and as Jennifer drove up the driveway, the house looked like a besieged castle surrounded by a gray, churning moat.

Mrs. Mackey opened the front door and helped Jennifer out of her dripping raincoat.

Jennifer shook the damp out of her hair and said, "Where's Joshua?"

"He's asleep."

Jennifer looked at Mrs. Mackey with concern. "Has he been sleeping all day?"

"Heavens, no. He's been up and around. I fixed his dinner, but when I went upstairs to get him he had dozed off again, so I just thought I'd let him be."

"I see."

Jennifer went upstairs into Joshua's room and quietly entered. Joshua was asleep. Jennifer leaned over and touched his forehead. He had no fever; his color was normal. She felt his pulse. There was nothing wrong except her imagination. She was letting it run away with her. Joshua had probably been playing too hard all day and it was natural that he was tired. Jennifer slipped out of the room and returned downstairs.

"Why don't you make some sandwiches for him, Mrs. Mackey? Leave them at the side of the bed. He can have them when he wakes up."

Jennifer had dinner at her desk, working on briefs, preparing a trial deposition for the next day. She thought about calling Michael to tell him she was back, but she was hesitant about speaking to him so soon after the night with Adam . . . He was too perceptive. It was after midnight when she finished reading. She stood up and stretched, trying to relieve the tension in her back and neck. She put her papers in her attaché case, turned out the lights and went upstairs. She passed by Joshua's room and looked in. He was still asleep.

The sandwiches on the stand beside the bed were untouched.

· · ·

THE FOLLOWING MORNING when Jennifer went down to breakfast, Joshua was there, dressed and ready for school.

"Morning, Mom."

"Good morning, darling. How are you feeling?"

"Great. I was really tired. Must have been that Mexican sun."

"Must have been."

"Acapulco's really neat. Can we go back there on my next vacation?"

"I don't know why not. You glad to be getting back to school?"

"I refuse to answer on the grounds that it might incriminate me."

IN THE MIDDLE of the afternoon, Jennifer was taking a deposition when Cynthia buzzed.

"I'm sorry to disturb you, but there's a Mrs. Stout on the line and—"

Joshua's homeroom teacher. "I'll take it."

Jennifer picked up the telephone. "Hello, Mrs. Stout. Is anything wrong?"

"Oh no, everything's fine, Mrs. Parker. I didn't mean to alarm you. I just thought I might suggest to you that it would be a good idea if Joshua got more sleep."

"What do you mean?"

"He slept through most of his classes today. Miss Williams and Mrs. Toboco both mentioned it. Perhaps you could see to it that he gets to bed a bit earlier."

Jennifer stared at the telephone. "I—yes, I'll do that."

Slowly, she replaced the receiver and turned to the people in the room watching her.

"I—I'm sorry," she said. "Excuse me."

She hurried out to the reception room. "Cynthia, find Dan. Ask him to finish the deposition for me. Something has come up."

"All—" Jennifer was already out the door.

She drove home like a madwoman, exceeding the speed limit, going through red lights, her mind filled with visions of something terrible having happened to Joshua. The drive seemed interminable and when her house appeared in the distance, Jennifer half expected to see the driveway filled with ambulances and police cars. The driveway was deserted. Jennifer pulled up beside the front door and hurried into the house.

"Joshua!"

He was in the den watching a baseball game on television.

"Hi, Mom. You're home early. Did you get fired?"

Jennifer stood in the doorway staring at him, her body flooding with relief. She felt like an idiot.

"You should have seen the last inning. Craig Swan was fantastic!"

"How do you feel, son?"

"Great."

Jennifer put her hand on his forehead. He had no fever.

"You sure you're all right?"

"Of course I am. Why do you look so funny? You worried about something? You want to have a man-to-man talk?"

She smiled. "No, darling, I just—does anything hurt you?"

He groaned. "I'll say. The Mets are losing six to five. You know what happened in the first inning?"

He began an excited replay of his favorite team's exploits. Jennifer stood there looking at him, adoring him, thinking, *Damn my imagination! Of course he's all right.*

"You go on and watch the rest of the game. I'll see about dinner."

Jennifer went into the kitchen, lighthearted. She decided to make a banana cake, one of Joshua's favorite desserts.

Thirty minutes later, when Jennifer returned to the study, Joshua was lying on the floor, unconscious.

THE RIDE TO Blinderman Memorial Hospital seemed to take forever. Jennifer sat in the back of the ambulance clutching Joshua's hand. An attendant was holding an oxygen mask over Joshua's face. He had not regained consciousness. The ambulance's siren was keening, but the traffic was heavy and the ambulance went slowly while curious people gaped through the windows, staring at the white-faced woman and the unconscious boy. It seemed to Jennifer a sickening violation of privacy.

"Why can't they use one-way glass in ambulances?" Jennifer demanded.

The attendant looked up, startled. "Ma'am?"

"Nothing . . . nothing."

After what seemed an eternity, the ambulance pulled up at the emergency entrance at the back of the hospital. Two interns were waiting at the door. Jennifer stood there helpless, watching as Joshua was removed from the ambulance and transferred to a gurney.

An attendant asked, "Are you the boy's mother?"

"Yes."

"This way, please."

What followed was a blurred kaleidoscope of sound and light and movement. Jennifer watched Joshua being wheeled down a long, white corridor to an X-ray room.

She started to follow, but the attendant said, "You'll have to check him in first."

A thin woman at the front desk was saying to Jennifer, "How do you plan to pay for this? Do you have Blue Cross or some other form of insurance?"

Jennifer wanted to scream at the woman, wanted to get back to Joshua's side, but she forced herself to answer the questions, and when they were over and Jennifer had filled out several forms, the woman allowed Jennifer to leave.

She hurried down to the X-ray room and went inside. The room was empty. Joshua was gone. Jennifer ran back to the hallway, looking around frantically. A nurse passed by.

Jennifer clutched her arm. "Where's my son?"

The nurse said, "I don't know. What's his name?"

"Joshua. Joshua Parker."

"Where did you leave him?"

"He—he was having X rays—he—" Jennifer was beginning to be incoherent. "What have they done with him! Tell me!"

The nurse took a closer look at Jennifer and said, "Wait here, Mrs. Parker. I'll see if I can find out."

She came back a few minutes later. "Dr. Morris would like to see you. Come this way, please."

Jennifer found that her legs were trembling. It was difficult to walk.

"Are you all right?" The nurse was staring at her.

Her mouth was dry with fear. "I want my son."

They came to a room filled with strange-looking equipment. "Wait here, please."

Dr. Morris came in a few moments later. He was a very fat man with a red face and nicotine stains on his fingers. "Mrs. Parker?"

"Where's Joshua?"

"Step in here a moment, please." He led Jennifer into a small office across from the room with the strange-looking equipment. "Please sit down."

Jennifer took a seat. "Joshua is—it's—it's nothing serious, is it, Doctor?"

"We don't know yet." His voice was surprisingly soft for a man of his size. "I need some information. How old is your son?"

"He's only seven."

The *only* had slipped out, a reprimand to God.

"Was he in an accident recently?"

A vision flashed through Jennifer's mind of Joshua turning to wave and losing his balance and hitting the pilings. "He—he had a water skiing accident. He bumped his head."

The doctor was making notes. "How long ago was that?"

"I—a few—a few days ago. In Acapulco." It was difficult to think straight.

"Did he seem all right after the accident?"

"Yes. He had a lump on the back of his head, but otherwise he—he seemed fine."

"Did you notice any lapse of memory?"

"No."

"Any personality changes?"

"No."

"No convulsions or stiff neck or headache?"

"No."

The doctor stopped writing and looked up at Jennifer. "I've had an X ray done, but it's not enough. I want to do a CAT scan."

"A—?"

"It's a new computerized machine from England that takes pictures of the inside of the brain. I may want to make some additional tests afterward. Is that all right with you?"

"If—if—if"—she was stammering—"it's necessary. It—it won't hurt him, will it?"

"No. I may also need to do a spinal puncture."

He was frightening her.

She forced the question out of her mouth. "What do you think it is? What's the matter with my son?" She did not recognize the sound of her own voice.

"I'd prefer not to make any guesses, Mrs. Parker. We'll know in an hour or two. He's awake now, if you'd like to see him."

"Oh, please!"

A NURSE LED her to Joshua's room. He was lying in bed, a pale small figure. He looked up as Jennifer entered.

"Hi, Mom."

"Hi there." She sat at the edge of his bed. "How do you feel?"

"Kind of funny. It's like I'm not here."

Jennifer reached out and took his hand. "You're here, darling. And I'm with you."

"I can see two of everything."

"Did—did you tell the doctor that?"

"Uh-huh. I saw two of him. I hope he doesn't send you two bills."

Jennifer gently put her arms around Joshua and hugged him. His body seemed frail and shrunken.

"Mom?"

"Yes, darling?"

"You won't let me die, will you?"

Her eyes were suddenly stinging. "No, Joshua, I won't let you die. The doctors are going to make you well and then I'm going to take you home."

"Okay. And you promised we can go back to Acapulco sometime."

"Yes. As soon as—"

He was asleep.

. . .

DR. MORRIS CAME into the room with two men wearing white jackets.

"We'd like to begin the tests now, Mrs. Parker. They won't take long. Why don't you wait in here and make yourself comfortable?"

Jennifer watched them take Joshua out of the room. She sat on the edge of the bed, feeling as though she had been physically beaten. All the energy had drained out of her. She sat there, staring at the white wall, in a trance.

A moment later a voice said, "Mrs. Parker—"

Jennifer looked up and Dr. Morris was there.

"Please go ahead and do the tests," Jennifer said.

He looked at her oddly. "We've finished."

Jennifer looked at the clock on the wall. She had been sitting there for two hours. Where had the time gone? She looked into the doctor's face, reading it, searching for the small, telltale signs that would reveal whether he had good news or bad news for her. How many times had she done this before, reading the faces of jurors, knowing in advance from their expressions what the verdict would be? A hundred times? Five hundred? Now, because of the panic raging within her, Jennifer could tell nothing. Her body began to shake uncontrollably.

Dr. Morris said, "Your son is suffering from a subdural hematoma. In layman's terms, there has been a massive trauma to his brain."

Her throat was suddenly so dry that no words could come out.

"Wh—" She swallowed and tried again. "What does that—?" She could not finish the sentence.

"I want to operate immediately. I'll need your permission."

He was playing some kind of cruel prank on her. In a moment he was going to smile and tell her that Joshua was fine. I was just punishing you, Mrs. Parker, for wasting my time. There's nothing wrong with your son except that he needs sleep. He's a growing boy. You mustn't take up our time when we have patients to look after who are really ill. He was going to smile at her and say, "You can take your son home now."

Dr. Morris was going on. "He's young and his body seems strong. There's every reason to hope the operation will be a success."

He was going to cut open her baby's brain, tear into it with his sharp instruments, perhaps destroy whatever it was that made Joshua, Joshua. Perhaps—kill him.

"No!" It was an angry cry.

"You won't give us permission to operate?"

"I—" Her mind was so confused she could not think. "Wh-what will happen if you don't operate?"

Dr. Morris said simply, "Your son will die. Is the boy's father here?"

Adam! Oh, how she wanted Adam, how she wanted to feel his arms around her, comforting her. She wanted him to tell her that everything was going to be all right, that Joshua was going to be fine.

"No," Jennifer replied finally, "he's not. I—I give you my permission. Go ahead with the operation."

Dr. Morris filled out a form and handed it to her. "Would you sign this, please?"

Jennifer signed the paper without looking at it. "How long will it take?"

"I won't know until I open—" He saw the look on her face. "Until I begin the operation. Would you like to wait here?"

"No!" The walls were closing in on her, choking her. She could not breathe. "Is there a place where I can pray?"

IT WAS A small chapel with a painting of Jesus over the altar. The room was deserted except for Jennifer. She knelt, but she was unable to pray. She was not a religious person; why would God listen to her now? She tried to quiet her mind so that she could talk to God, but her fear was too strong; it had taken complete possession of her. She kept berating herself mercilessly. *If only hadn't taken Joshua to Acapulco,* she thought . . . *If I hadn't let him go water skiing . . . If I hadn't trusted that Mexican doctor . . .* If. If. If. She made bargains with God. *Make him well again and I'll do anything you ask of me.*

She denied God. *If there was a God, would he do this to a child who had never harmed anyone? What kind of God lets innocent children die?*

Finally, out of sheer exhaustion, Jennifer's thoughts slowed and she remembered what Dr. Morris had said. *He's young and his body seems strong. There's every reason to hope the operation will be a success.*

Everything was going to be all right. Of course it was. When this was over, she would take Joshua away someplace where he could rest. Acapulco, if he liked. They would read and play games and talk . . .

When finally Jennifer was too exhausted to think any longer, she slumped into a seat, her mind a dazed blank, empty. Someone was touching her arm and she looked up and Dr. Morris was standing over her. Jennifer looked into his face and had no need to ask any questions.

She lost consciousness.

50

Joshua lay on a narrow metal table, his body eternally still. He looked as though he were peacefully asleep, his handsome young face filled with secret, far-off dreams. Jennifer had seen that expression a thousand times as Joshua had snuggled into his warm bed while Jennifer had sat at his side, studying the face of her young son, filled with a love that was so strong it choked her. And how many times had she gently tucked his blanket around him to protect him from the cold of the night?

Now the cold was deep inside Joshua's body. He would never be warm again. Those bright eyes would never open again and look at her, and she would never see the smile on his lips, or hear his voice, or feel his small, strong arms around her. He was naked beneath the sheet.

Jennifer said to the doctor, "I want you to cover him with a blanket. He'll be cold."

"He can't—" and Dr. Morris looked into Jennifer's eyes and what he saw there made him say, "Yes, of course, Mrs. Parker," and he turned to the nurse and said, "Get a blanket."

There were half a dozen people in the room, most of them in white uniforms and they all seemed to be talking to Jennifer, but she could not hear what they were saying. It was as though she were in a bell jar, shut off from the rest of them. She could see their lips moving, but there was no sound. She wanted to yell at them to go away, but she was afraid of frightening Joshua. Someone was shaking her arm and the spell was broken and the room was suddenly filled with a roar of sound, and everyone seemed to be talking at once.

Dr. Morris was saying, ". . . necessary to perform an autopsy."

Jennifer said quietly, "If you touch my son again, I'll kill you."

And she smiled at everyone around her because she did not want them to become angry with Joshua.

A nurse was trying to persuade Jennifer to leave the room, but she shook her head. "I can't leave him alone. Someone might turn out the lights. Joshua is afraid of the dark."

Someone squeezed her arm and Jennifer felt the prick of a needle, and a moment later a feeling of great warmth and peace engulfed her, and she slept.

When Jennifer awakened, it was late afternoon. She was in a small room in the hospital and someone had undressed her and clothed her in a hospital gown. She rose to her feet and dressed and went looking for Dr. Morris. She was supernaturally calm.

Dr. Morris said, "We'll make all the funeral arrangements for you, Mrs. Parker. You won't have to—"

"I'll take care of it."

"Very well." He hesitated, embarrassed. "About the autopsy, I know you didn't mean what you said this morning."

"You're wrong."

DURING THE NEXT two days, Jennifer went through all the rituals of death. She went to a local undertaker and made the funeral arrangements. She selected a white casket with a satin lining. She was self-possessed and dry-eyed and, later, when she tried to think about it, she had no recollection of any of it. It was as though someone else had taken over her body and mind and was acting for her. She was in a state of deep shock, hiding behind its protective shell to keep from going insane.

As Jennifer was leaving the undertaker's office, he said, "If there are any special clothes you would like your son buried in, Mrs. Parker, you can have them brought in and we'll dress him."

"I'll dress Joshua myself."

He looked at her in surprise. "If you wish, of course, but—" He watched her leave, wondering if she knew what it was like to dress a corpse.

JENNIFER DROVE HOME, pulled the car into the driveway and entered the house.

Mrs. Mackey was in the kitchen, her eyes red, her face twisted with grief. "Oh, Mrs. Parker! I can't believe—"

Jennifer neither saw nor heard her. She moved past Mrs. Mackey and walked upstairs into Joshua's room. It was exactly the same. Nothing had changed, except that the room was empty. Joshua's books and games and baseball and skiing equipment were all there, waiting for him. Jennifer stood in the doorway, staring at the room, trying to remember why she had come there. *Oh, yes. Clothes for Joshua.* She walked over to the closet. There was a dark blue suit she had bought for him on his last birthday. Joshua had worn it the evening she had taken him to dinner at Lutèce. She remembered that evening vividly. Joshua had looked so grown up and Jennifer had thought with a pang, *One day he'll be sitting here with the girl he's going to marry.* That day would never come now. There would be no growing up. No girl. No life.

Next to the blue suit were several pairs of blue jeans and slacks and tee shirts, one with the name of Joshua's baseball team on it. Jennifer stood there running her hands aimlessly over the clothes, losing all track of time.

Mrs. Mackey appeared at her side. "Are you all right, Mrs. Parker?"

Jennifer said politely, "I'm fine, thank you, Mrs. Mackey."

"Can I help you with something?"

"No, thank you. I'm going to dress Joshua. What do you think he would like to wear?" Her voice was bright and cheerful, but her eyes were dead.

Mrs. Mackey looked into them and was frightened. "Why don't you lie down a bit, dear? I'm going to call the doctor."

Jennifer's hands moved across the clothes hanging in the closet. She pulled the baseball uniform from the hanger. "I think Joshua would like this. Now, what else will he need?"

Mrs. Mackey watched helplessly as Jennifer went over to the dresser and took out underwear, socks and a shirt. *Joshua needed these things because he was going away on a holiday. A long holiday.*

"Do you think he'll be warm enough in this?"

Mrs. Mackey burst into tears. "Please, don't," she begged. "Leave those things. I'll take care of it."

But Jennifer was already on her way downstairs with them.

THE BODY WAS in the mortuary's slumber room. They had placed Joshua on a long table that dwarfed the small figure.

When Jennifer returned with Joshua's clothes, the mortician tried once again. "I spoke to Doctor Morris. We both agree that it would be much better, Mrs. Parker, if you would let us handle this. We're quite used to it and—"

Jennifer smiled at him. "Get out."

He swallowed and said, "Yes, Mrs. Parker."

Jennifer waited until he had left the room and then she turned to her son.

She looked into his sleeping face and said, "Your mother is going to take care of you, my darling. You're going to wear your baseball uniform. You'll like that, won't you?"

She pulled the sheet away and looked at his naked, shrunken body, and then she began to dress him. She started to slip his shorts on him and she recoiled from the icy cold of his flesh. It was as hard and stiff as marble. Jennifer tried to tell herself that this piece of chill, lifeless flesh was not her son, that Joshua was away somewhere, warm and happy, but she was unable to make herself believe it. It was Joshua on this table. Jennifer's body began to shake. It was as though the cold inside Joshua had gotten inside her, chilling her to the marrow. She said fiercely to herself, *Stop it! Stop it! Stop it! Stop it! Stop it!*

She took deep, shuddering breaths, and when she was finally calmer she resumed dressing her son, talking to him all the while. She pulled his shorts on, then his trousers, and when she lifted him up to put his shirt on, his head slipped and fell against the table and Jennifer cried out, "I'm sorry, Joshua, forgive me!" and she began to weep.

IT TOOK JENNIFER almost three hours to dress Joshua. He was wearing his baseball uniform and favorite tee shirt, white socks and sneakers. The baseball cap shadowed his face, so Jennifer finally laid it on his chest. "You can carry it with you, my darling."

When the undertaker came and looked into the room, Jennifer was standing over the dressed body, holding Joshua's hand and talking to him.

The man walked over and said gently, "We'll take care of him now."

Jennifer took one last look at her son. "Please be careful with him. He hurt his head, you know."

THE FUNERAL WAS simple. Jennifer and Mrs. Mackey were the only ones there to watch the small white coffin being lowered into the freshly dug grave. Jennifer had thought of telling Ken Bailey, for Ken and Joshua had loved each other, but Ken was no longer in their lives.

When the first shovelful of dirt had been thrown on the coffin, Mrs. Mackey said, "Come along, dear. I'll take you home."

Jennifer said politely, "I'm fine. Joshua and I won't be needing you any more, Mrs. Mackey. I'll see that you get a year's wages and I'll give you a reference. Joshua and I thank you for everything."

Mrs. Mackey stood there staring as Jennifer turned and walked away. She walked carefully, standing very straight, as though she were going down an eternal corridor wide enough for only one person.

THE HOUSE WAS still and peaceful. She went up to Joshua's room and closed the door behind her and lay on his bed, looking at all the things that belonged to him, all the things he had loved. Her whole world was in this room. There was nothing for her to do now, nowhere for her to go. There was only Joshua. Jennifer started with the day he was born and relived all her memories of him.

Joshua taking his first steps . . . Joshua saying *car-car* and *Mama, go play with your toys* . . . Joshua going off to school alone for the first time, a tiny, brave figure . . . Joshua lying in bed with the measles, his body racked with misery . . . Joshua hitting a home run and winning the game for his team . . . Joshua sailing . . . Joshua feeding an elephant at the zoo . . . Joshua singing *Shine On, Harvest Moon* on Mother's Day . . . The memories flowed on, home movies in her mind. They stopped on the day Jennifer and Joshua were to leave for Acapulco.

Acapulco . . . where she had seen Adam and made love with him. She was being punished because she had thought only of herself. *Of course,* Jennifer thought. *This is my punishment. This is my hell.*

AND SHE STARTED all over again, beginning with the day Joshua was born . . . Joshua taking his first steps . . . Joshua saying *car-car,* and *Mama, go play with your toys . . .*

Time slipped away. Sometimes Jennifer would hear a telephone ring in some distant recess of the house, and once she heard someone knocking at the front door, but those sounds had no meaning for her. She would not allow anything to interrupt her being with her son. She stayed in the room, eating nothing and drinking nothing, lost in her own private world with Joshua. She had no sense of time, no idea how long she lay there.

IT WAS FIVE days later that Jennifer heard the front door bell again and the sound of someone pounding on the door, but she paid no attention. Whoever it was would go away and leave her alone. Dimly she heard the sound of glass breaking, and a few moments later the door to Joshua's room burst open and Michael Moretti loomed in the doorway.

He took one look at the gaunt, hollow-eyed figure staring up at him from the bed and he said, "Jesus Christ!"

It took all of Michael Moretti's strength to get Jennifer out of the room. She fought him hysterically, punching him and clawing at his eyes. Nick Vito was waiting downstairs and it took the two of them to force Jennifer into the car. Jennifer had no idea who they were or why they were there. She only knew that they were taking her away from her son. She tried to tell them that she would die if they did this to her, but she was finally too exhausted to fight any longer. She fell asleep.

· · ·

WHEN JENNIFER AWAKENED, she was in a bright, clean room with a picture window with a view of a mountain and a blue lake in the distance. A uniformed nurse was seated in a chair next to the bed, reading a magazine. She looked up as Jennifer opened her eyes.

"Where am I?" It hurt her throat to speak.

"You're with friends, Miss Parker. Mr. Moretti brought you here. He's been very concerned about you. He'll be so pleased to know you're awake."

The nurse hurried out of the room. Jennifer lay there, her mind blank, willing herself not to think. But the memories began to return, unbidden, and there was nowhere to hide from them, nowhere to escape to. Jennifer realized that she had been trying to commit suicide without actually having the courage to do it. She simply had wanted to die and was willing it to happen. Michael had saved her. It was ironic. Not Adam, but Michael. She supposed it was unfair to blame Adam. She had kept the truth from him, had kept him ignorant of the son who had been born and who was now dead. Joshua was dead. Jennifer could face that now. The pain was deep and agonizing, and she knew it was a pain that would be with her for as long as she lived. But she could bear it. She would have to. It was justice, demanding its payment.

Jennifer heard footsteps and looked up. Michael had come into the room. He stood there, looking at her with wonder. He had been like a wild man when Jennifer had disappeared. He had nearly been out of his mind for fear that something had happened to her.

He walked over to her bed and looked down at her. "Why didn't you tell me?" Michael sat down on the side of the bed. "I'm sorry."

She took his hand. "Thank you for bringing me here. I—think I was a little crazy."

"A little."

"How long have I been here?"

"Four days. The doctor's been feeding you intravenously."

Jennifer nodded, and even that small movement caused great effort. She felt inordinately weary.

"Breakfast is on the way. He gave me orders to fatten you up."

"I'm not hungry. I don't think I ever want to eat again."

"You'll eat."

And to Jennifer's surprise, Michael was right. When the nurse brought her soft-boiled eggs and toast and tea on a tray, Jennifer found she was famished.

Michael stayed there and watched her, and when Jennifer was finished Michael said, "I've got to go back to New York to take care of a few things. I'll return in a couple of days."

He leaned over and kissed her gently. "See you Friday." He slowly traced his fingers across her face. "I want you well, quick. You hear?"

Jennifer looked at him and said, "I hear."

51

The large conference room at the United States Marine Corps base was filled to overflowing. Outside the room, a squad of armed guards was on the alert. Inside was an extraordinary gathering. A special grand jury was seated in chairs against the wall. On one side of a long table sat Adam Warner, Robert Di Silva and the assistant director of the FBI. Across from them sat Thomas Colfax.

Bringing the grand jury to the base had been Adam's idea.

"It's the only way we can be sure of protecting Colfax."

The grand jury had agreed to Adam's suggestions, and the secret session was about to begin.

Adam said to Thomas Colfax, "Would you identify yourself, please?"

"My name is Thomas Colfax."

"What is your occupation, Mr. Colfax?"

"I'm an attorney, licensed to practice in the State of New York, as well as in many other states in this country."

"How long have you been practicing law?"

"For more than thirty-five years."

"Do you have a general practice?"

"No, sir. I have one client."

"Who is your client?"

"For most of those thirty-five years it was Antonio Granelli, now deceased. His place was taken by Michael Moretti. I represent Michael Moretti and his Organization."

"Are you referring to organized crime?"

"I am, sir."

"Because of the position you held for so many years, is it a fair assumption to say that you are in a unique position to know the inner workings of what we shall call the Organization?"

"Very little went on there that I did not know about."

"And criminal activities were involved?"

"Yes, Senator."

"Would you describe the nature of some of those activities?"

FOR THE NEXT two hours, Thomas Colfax spoke. His voice was steady and sure. He named names, places and dates, and at times his recital was so fascinating that the people in the room forgot where they were, caught up in the horror stories Colfax was telling.

He talked of murder contracts given out, of witnesses killed so they could not testify; of arson, mayhem, white slavery—it was a catalogue out of Hieronymus Bosch. For the first time, the innermost operation of the largest crime syndicate in the world was being exposed, laid bare for everyone to see.

Occasionally, Adam or Robert Di Silva would ask a question, prompting Thomas Colfax, having him fill in gaps wherever necessary.

The session was going far better than Adam could have wished when suddenly, near the end, with only a few minutes left, the catastrophe occurred.

One of the men on the grand jury had asked a question about a money-laundering operation.

"That happened about two years ago. Michael kept me away from some of the later stuff. Jennifer Parker handled that."

Adam froze.

Robert Di Silva said, "Jennifer Parker?" There was a bursting eagerness in his question.

"Yes, sir." A vindictive note crept into Thomas Colfax's voice. "She's the Organization's house counsel now."

Adam wanted desperately to quiet him, to keep what he was saying off the record, but it was too late. Di Silva was going for the jugular vein and nothing would stop him.

"Tell us about her," Di Silva said tightly.

Thomas Colfax went on. "Jennifer Parker's involved in setting up dummy corporations, laundering money . . ."

Adam tried to break in. "I don't—"

". . . murder."

The word hung in the room.

Adam broke the silence. "We—we have to stick to the facts, Mr. Colfax. You're not trying to tell us that Jennifer Parker was involved in a killing?"

"That's exactly what I'm telling you. She ordered a hit on a man who kidnapped her son. The man's name was Frank Jackson. She told Moretti to kill him and he did."

There was an excited murmur of voices.

Her son! Adam was thinking: *There has to be some mistake.*

He stammered, "I think—I think we have enough evidence without hearsay. We—"

"It's not hearsay," Thomas Colfax assured him. "I was in the room with Moretti when she called."

Adam's hands under the table were pressing together so hard that they were drained of blood. "The witness looks tired. I think that's enough for this session."

Robert Di Silva said to the special grand jury, "I'd like to make a suggestion about procedure . . ."

Adam was not listening. He was wondering where Jennifer was. She had disappeared again. Adam had repeatedly tried to find her. But now he was desperate. He had to reach her, and quickly.

52

The largest undercover operation in law enforcement in the United States began to move ahead.

The Federal Strike Force Against Organized Crime and Racketeering worked side by side with the FBI, the Postal and Customs Services, the Internal Revenue Service, the Federal Bureau of Narcotics, and half a dozen other agencies.

The scope of the investigation included murder, conspiracy to commit murder, racketeering, extortion, income tax evasion, union frauds, arson, loan-sharking and drugs.

Thomas Colfax had given them the key to a Pandora's box of crime and corruption that was going to help wipe out a major part of organized crime.

Michael Moretti's Family would be hardest hit, but the evidence touched dozens of other Families around the country.

Across the United States and abroad, government agents were quietly questioning friends and business associates of the men on their lists. Agents in Turkey, Mexico, San Salvador, Marseilles and Honduras were liaising with their counterparts, giving them information on illegal activities taking place in those countries. Small-time crooks were pulled into the net, and when they talked they were given their freedom in exchange for evidence against the top crime figures. It was all being handled discreetly, so that the main quarry would have no warning of the storm that was about to break over their heads.

AS CHAIRMAN OF the Senate Investigating Committee, Adam Warner received a steady stream of visitors at his home in Georgetown, and the sessions in his study often lasted until the small hours of the morning. There was little doubt that when this was over and Michael Moretti's Organization was broken, the presidential race would be an easy victory for Adam.

He should have been a happy man. He was miserable, facing the greatest moral crisis of his life. Jennifer Parker was deeply involved, and Adam had to warn her, to tell her to escape while she still had a chance. And yet, he had another obligation: an obligation to the committee that bore his name, an obligation to the United States Senate itself. He was Jennifer's prosecutor. How could he be her protector? If he warned her and it was discovered, it would destroy the credibility of his investigating committee and everything it had accomplished. It would destroy his future, his family.

Adam had been stunned by Colfax's mention of Jennifer having a child.

He knew he had to speak to Jennifer.

Adam dialed her office number and a secretary said, "I'm sorry, Mr. Adams, Miss Parker is not in."

"It's—it's very important. Do you know where I can reach her?"

"No, sir. Can someone else help you?"

No one could help him.

DURING THE NEXT week, Adam tried to reach Jennifer several times each day. Her secretary would only say, "I'm sorry, Mr. Adams, but Miss Parker is away from the office."

Adam was sitting in the study starting to call Jennifer for the third time that day when Mary Beth walked into the room. Adam casually replaced the receiver.

Mary Beth walked up to him and ran her fingers through his hair. "You look tired, darling."

"I'm fine."

She moved over to a suede armchair across from Adam's desk and sat down. "It's all coming together, isn't it, Adam?"

"It looks that way."

"I hope it's over soon, for your sake. The strain must be terrible."

"I'm bearing up under it, Mary Beth. Don't worry about me."

"But I do worry. Jennifer Parker's name is on that list, isn't it?"

Adam looked at her sharply. "How did you know that?"

She laughed. "Angel, you've turned this house into a public meeting place. I can't help but hear a little of what goes on. Everybody seems so terribly excited about catching Michael Moretti and his woman friend." She watched Adam's face, but there was no reaction.

Mary Beth looked at her husband fondly and thought, *How naïve men are.* She knew more about Jennifer Parker than Adam did. It had always amazed Mary Beth how brilliant a man could be in business or politics, and yet be so silly when it came to women. Look how many truly great men had been married to cheap little floozies. Mary Beth understood about her husband having an affair with Jennifer Parker. After all, Adam was a very attractive and desirable man. And like all men, he was susceptible. Her philosophy was to forgive and never forget.

Mary Beth knew what was best for her husband. Everything she did was for Adam's own good. Well, when all this was over, she would take Adam away somewhere. He *did* look tired. They would leave Samantha with the housekeeper and go someplace romantic. Perhaps Tahiti.

Mary Beth glanced out the window and saw two of the secret service men talking. She had mixed feelings about their presence. Mary Beth disliked the intrusion on her privacy, but at the same time, their being there was a reminder that her husband was a candidate for the presidency of the United States. No, how foolish of her. Her husband was going to *be* the next President of the United States. Everyone said so. The idea of living in the White House was so tangible that just thinking about it warmed her. Her favorite occupation, while Adam was busy with all his meetings, was to redecorate the White House. She would sit alone in her room for hours, changing furniture around in her mind, planning all the exciting things she was going to do when she became First Lady.

She had seen the rooms that most visitors were not allowed in: the White House Library with its almost three thousand books, the China Room and the Diplomatic Reception Room, and the family quarters and the seven guest bedrooms on the second floor.

She and Adam would live in that house, become a part of its history. Mary Beth shuddered at the thought of how close Adam had come to throwing away their chances because of that Parker woman. Well, that was all over, thank God.

She watched Adam now as he sat at his desk, looking drawn and haggard.

"Can I fix you a cup of coffee, darling?"

Adam started to say no, then changed his mind. "That would be nice."

"It will just take a jiffy."

The moment Mary Beth left the room, Adam picked up the telephone again and began to dial. It was evening and he knew Jennifer's office was closed, but there should be someone at the answering service. After what seemed an interminable period of time, the operator answered.

"This is urgent," Adam said. "I've been trying to reach Jennifer Parker for several days. This is Mr. Adams."

"One moment, please." The voice came back on the line. "I'm sorry, Mr. Adams. I have no word on where Miss Parker is. Do you want to leave a message?"

"No." Adam slammed down the receiver, filled with frustration, knowing that even if he did leave a message for Jennifer to call him, there was no way she could return that call.

He sat in his den, looking out at the night, thinking about the dozens of arrest warrants that would soon be drawn up. One of them would be for murder.

It would have Jennifer's name on it.

IT WAS FIVE days before Michael Moretti returned to the mountain cabin where Jennifer was staying. She had spent those days resting, eating, taking long walks around the paths. When she heard Michael's car drive up, Jennifer went out to greet him.

Michael looked her over and said, "You look a lot better."

"I feel better. Thank you."

They walked along the path leading to the lake.

Michael said, "I have something for you to do."

"What is it?"

"I want you to leave for Singapore tomorrow."

"Singapore?"

"An airline steward was picked up at the airport there, carrying a load of coke. His name is Stefan Bjork. He's in jail. I want you to bail him out before he starts talking."

"All right."

"Get back as fast as you can. I'll miss you."

He drew her close and kissed her very softly on her lips, then whispered, "I love you, Jennifer."

And she knew that he had never uttered those words to anyone before.

But it was too late. It was finished. Something had died in her forever, and she was left with only the guilt and the loneliness. She had made up her mind to tell Michael that she was leaving. There would be no Adam and no Michael. She had to go away somewhere, alone, and start over. She had a debt to pay. She would do this last thing for Michael and tell him her plans when she returned.

She left for Singapore the next morning.

53

Nick Vito, Tony Santo, Salvatore Fiore and Joseph Colella were having lunch at Tony's Place. They sat at a front booth, and every time the door opened they automatically glanced up to check out the newcomers. Michael Moretti was in the back room, and while there was no current conflict among the Families, it was always better to play it safe.

"What happened to Jimmy?" the giant Joseph Colella was asking.

"Astutatu-morte," Nick Vito told him. "The dumb son of a bitch fell for the sister of a detective. The broad was stacked, I'll give her that. She and her dick brother talked Jimmy into a flip. Jimmy arranged for a sit-down with Mike and he wore a wire hidden in his pants leg."

"So what happened?" Fiore asked.

"What happened was Jimmy got so nervous he had to pee. When he opened up his fly, the fuckin' wire came out."

"Oh, shit!"

"That's what Jimmy did. Mike turned him over to Gino. He used Jimmy's wire to strangle him. He went out *suppilu suppilu*—very slowly."

The door opened and the four men looked up. It was the newspaper boy with the afternoon *New York Post.*

Joseph Colella called out, "Over here, sonny." He turned to the others. "I wanna check the lineup at Hialeah. I got a hot horse runnin' today."

The newspaper boy, a weather-beaten man in his seventies, handed Joseph Colella a paper and Colella gave him a dollar. "Keep the change."

That was what Michael Moretti would have said. Joe Colella started to open the paper and Nick Vito's eye was caught by a photograph on the front page.

"Hey!" he said. "I seen that guy before!"

Tony Santo took a look over Vito's shoulder. "Of course you have, shmuck. That's Adam Warner. He's runnin' for President."

"No," Vito insisted. "I mean I *seen* him." He furrowed his brow, trying to remember. Suddenly it came to him.

"Got it! He was the guy in the bar down in Acapulco with Jennifer Parker."

"What're you talkin' about?"

"Remember when I was down there last month deliverin' a package? I saw this guy with Jennifer. They was havin' a drink together."

Salvatore Fiore was staring at him. "Are you sure?"

"Yeah. Why?"

Fiore said slowly, "I think maybe you better tell Mike."

MICHAEL MORETTI LOOKED at Nick Vito and said, "You're out of your fucking mind. What would Jennifer Parker be doing with Senator Warner?"

"Beats me, boss. All I know is they was sittin' in this bar, havin' a drink."

"Just the two of them?"

"Yeah."

Salvatore Fiore said, "I thought you oughtta hear about it, Mike. This Warner asshole is investigatin' the shit outta us. Why would Jennifer be havin' a drink with him?"

That was exactly what Michael wanted to know. Jennifer had talked about Acapulco and the convention, and she had mentioned half a dozen people she had run into. But she had not said a word about Adam Warner.

He turned to Tony Santo. "Who's the business manager of the janitor's union now?"

"Charlie Corelli."

FIVE MINUTES LATER, Michael was speaking to Charles Corelli on the telephone.

". . . The Belmont Towers," Michael said. "A friend of mine lived there nine years ago. I'd like to talk to the guy who was the janitor there then." Michael listened for a moment. "I appreciate it, pal. I owe you one." He hung up.

Nick Vito, Santo, Fiore and Colella were watching him

"Haven't you bastards got anything to do? Get the fuck out of here." The four men hurriedly left.

Michael sat there, thinking, picturing Jennifer and Adam Warner together. *Why had she never mentioned him? And Joshua's father, who had died in the Viet Nam war. Why hadn't Jennifer ever talked about him?*

Michael Moretti began to pace the office.

THREE HOURS LATER Tony Santo ushered in a timid, badly dressed man in his sixties who was obviously terrified.

"This is Wally Kawolski," Tony said.

Michael rose and shook Kawolski's hand. "Thanks for coming over, Wally. I appreciate it. Sit down. Can I get you anything?"

"No, no thank you, Mr. Moretti. I'm fine, sir. Thank you very much." He was doing everything but bowing.

"Don't be nervous. I just want to ask you a couple of questions, Wally."

"Sure, Mr. Moretti. Anything you want to know. Anything at all."

"Are you still working at the Belmont Towers?"

"Me? No, sir. I left there, oh, about five years ago. My mother-in-law has bad arthritis and—"

"Do you remember the tenants?"

"Yes, sir. Most of 'em, I guess. They was kind of—"

"Do you remember a Jennifer Parker?"

Walter Kawolski's face lit up. "Oh, sure. She was a fine lady. I even remember her apartment number. Nineteen twenty-nine. Like the year the market crashed, you know? I liked her."

"Did Miss Parker have a lot of visitors, Wally?"

Wally slowly scratched his head. "Well, that's hard to say, Mr. Moretti. I only saw her when she was comin' in or goin' out, like."

"Did any men ever spend the night in her apartment?"

Walter Kawolski shook his head. "Oh, no, sir."

So all this had been about nothing. He felt a sharp wave of relief. He had known all along that Jennifer would never—

"Her boyfriend might have come home and caught her."

Michael thought he must have misunderstood. "Her boyfriend?"

"Yeah. The guy Miss Parker was livin' with there."

The words hit Michael in the stomach like a sledgehammer. He lost control of himself. He grabbed Walter Kawolski by the lapels and jerked him to his feet. "You stupid cocksucker! I *asked* you if—what was his name?"

The little man was terrified. "I don't know, Mr. Moretti. I swear to God, I don't know!"

Michael shoved him away. He picked up the newspaper and pushed it under Walter Kawolski's nose.

Kawolski looked at Adam Warner's photograph and said excitedly, "That's him! That's her boyfriend."

And Michael felt the world crashing down around him. Jennifer had lied to him all this time; she had betrayed him with Adam Warner! The two of them had been sneaking behind his back, conspiring against him, making a fool of him. She had put horns on him.

The ancient juices of vengeance stirred strongly within Michael Moretti, and he knew he was going to kill them both.

54

Jennifer flew from New York to London to Singapore, with a two-hour stopover in Bahrain. The almost-new airport at the oil emirate was already a slum, filled with men, women and children in native garb, sleeping on the floors and on benches. In front of the airport liquor store was a printed warning that anyone drinking in a public place was subject to imprisonment. The atmosphere was hostile, and Jennifer was glad when her flight was called.

The 747 jet landed at Changi Airport in Singapore at four-forty in the afternoon. It was a brand new airport, fourteen miles from the center of the city, replacing the old International Airport, and as the plane taxied down the runway Jennifer could see signs of construction still going on.

The Customs building was large and airy and modern, with rows of luggage carts for the convenience of passengers. The Customs officers were efficient and polite, and in fifteen minutes Jennifer was finished and headed for the taxi stand.

Outside the entrance, a heavy middle-aged Chinese man approached her. "Miss Jennifer Parker?"

"Yes."

"I am Chou Ling." Moretti's contact in Singapore. "I have a limousine waiting."

Chou Ling supervised the storing of Jennifer's luggage in the trunk of the limousine, and a few minutes later they were headed toward the city.

"Did you have a pleasant flight?" Chou Ling asked.

"Yes, thank you." But Jennifer's mind was on Stefan Bjork.

As though reading her thoughts, Chou Ling nodded to a building ahead of them. "That is Changi Prison. Bjork is in there."

Jennifer turned to look. Changi Prison was a large building off the highway, surrounded by a green fence and electrified barbed wire. There were watchtowers at each corner, manned by armed guards, and the entrance was blocked by a second barbed wire fence and, beyond that, more guards at the gate.

"During the war," Chou Ling informed Jennifer, "all British personnel on the island were interned there."

"When will I be able to get to see Bjork?"

Chou Ling replied delicately, "It is a very sensitive situation, Miss Parker. The government is most adamant about drug use. Even first offenders are dealt with ruthlessly. People who *deal* in drugs . . ." Chou Ling shrugged expressively. "Singapore is controlled by a few powerful families. The Shaw family, C. K. Tang, Tan Chin Tuan and Lee Kuan Yew, the Prime Minister. These families control the finance and commerce of Singapore. They do not wish drugs here."

"We must have some friends here with influence."

"There is a police inspector, David Touh—a most reasonable man."

Jennifer wondered how much "reasonable" cost, but she did not ask. There would be time enough for that later. She sat back and studied the scenery. They were passing through the suburbs of Singapore now, and the overwhelming impression was of greenery and flowers blooming everywhere. On both sides of MacPherson Road were modern shopping complexes alongside ancient shrines and pagodas. Some of the people walking along the streets wore ancient costumes and turbans, while others were smartly dressed in the latest western styles. The city seemed a colorful mixture of an ancient culture and a modern metropolis. The shopping centers looked new and everything was spotlessly clean. Jennifer commented on that.

Chou Ling smiled. "There is a simple explanation. There is a five-hundred-dollar fine for littering, and it is strictly enforced."

The car turned on to Stevens Road, and on a hill above them Jennifer saw a lovely white building completely surrounded by trees and flowers.

"That is the Shangri-La, your hotel."

The lobby was enormous, white and immaculately clean, with marble pillars and glass everywhere.

While Jennifer was checking in, Chou Ling said, "Inspector Touh will be in touch with you." He handed Jennifer a card. "You can always reach me at this number."

A smiling bellman took Jennifer's luggage and led her through an atrium to the elevator. There was an enormous garden under a waterfall, and a swimming pool. The Shangri-La was the most breathtaking hotel Jennifer had ever seen. Her suite on the second floor consisted of a large living room and bedroom, and a terrace overlooking a colorful sea of white and red anthuriums, purple bougainvillea and coconut palms. *It's like being in the middle of a Gauguin,* Jennifer thought.

A breeze was blowing. It was the kind of day Joshua loved. *Can we go sailing this afternoon, Mom? Stop doing that,* Jennifer told herself.

She walked over to the telephone. "I would like to place a call to the United States. New York City. Person-to-person to Mr. Michael Moretti." She gave the telephone number.

The operator said, "I'm so sorry. All the circuits are busy. Please try again later."

"Thank you."

Downstairs, the operator looked for approval to the man standing next to the switchboard.

He nodded. "Good," he said. "Very good."

THE CALL FROM Inspector Touh came an hour after Jennifer checked into the hotel.

"Miss Jennifer Parker?"

"Speaking."

"This is Inspector David Touh." He had a soft, indefinable accent.

"Yes, Inspector. I've been expecting your call. I'm anxious to arrange—"

The inspector interrupted. "I wonder if I might have the pleasure of your company at dinner this evening."

A warning. He was probably afraid of the phone being bugged.

"I would be delighted."

THE GREAT SHANGHAI was an enormous, noisy restaurant filled, for the most part, with natives who were loudly eating and talking. There was a three-piece band on a platform, and an attractive girl in a *cheongsam* was singing popular American songs.

The maître d' said to Jennifer, "A table for one?"

"I'm meeting someone. Inspector Touh."

The maître d's face broke into a smile. "The inspector is waiting for you. This way, please." He led Jennifer to a table at the front of the room, next to the bandstand.

Inspector David Touh was a tall, thin, attractive man in his early forties, with delicate features and dark, liquid eyes. He was beautifully and almost formally dressed in a dark suit.

He held Jennifer's chair for her, then sat down. The band was playing a deafening rock song.

Inspector Touh leaned across to Jennifer and said, "May I order a drink for you?"

"Yes, thank you."

"You must try a *chendol*."

"A—what?"

"It is made with coconut milk, coconut sugar and little pieces of gelatin. You will like it."

The inspector glanced up and a waitress was at his side instantly. The inspector ordered the two drinks and *dim sum,* Chinese appetizers. "I hope you do not mind if I order your dinner for you?"

"Not at all. I would be pleased."

"I understand that in your country women are used to taking command. Here it is still the man who is in charge."

A sexist, Jennifer thought, but she was in no mood to get into an argument. She needed this man. Because of the incredible din and the music, it was almost impossible to carry on a conversation. Jennifer sat back and looked around the room. Jennifer had been to other Oriental countries, but the people in Singapore seemed extraordinarily beautiful, men and women both.

The waitress put Jennifer's drink in front of her. It resembled a chocolate soda with slippery lumps in it.

Inspector Touh read her expression. "You must stir it."

"I can't hear you."

He shouted, "You must stir it!"

Jennifer dutifully stirred her drink. She tasted it.

It was awful, much too sweet, but Jennifer nodded and said, "It's—it's different."

Half a dozen platters of *dim sum* appeared on the table. Some of them were odd shaped delicacies that Jennifer had never seen before, and she decided not to ask what they were. The food was delicious.

Inspector Touh explained, yelling over the roar of the room, "This restaurant is renowned for the *Nonya* style of food. That is a mixture of Chinese ingredients and Malay spices. No recipes have ever been written down."

"I'd like to talk to you about Stefan Bjork," Jennifer said.

"I can't hear you." The noise of the band was deafening.

Jennifer leaned closer. "I want to know when I can see Stefan Bjork."

Inspector Touh shrugged and pantomimed that he could not hear. Jennifer suddenly wondered whether he had chosen this table so they could talk safely, or whether he had selected it so they could not talk at all.

An endless succession of dishes followed the *dim sum* and it was a superb meal. The only thing that disturbed Jennifer was that she had not once been able to bring up the subject of Stefan Bjork.

WHEN THEY HAD finished eating and were out on the street, Inspector Touh said, "I have my car here." He snapped his fingers and a black Mercedes that had been double-parked pulled up to them. The inspector opened the back door for Jennifer. A large uniformed policeman was behind the wheel. Something was not right. *If Inspector Touh wanted to discuss confidential matters with me,* Jennifer thought, *he would have arranged for us to be alone.*

She got into the back seat of the car and the inspector slid in beside her. "This is your first time in Singapore, is it not?"

"Yes."

"Ah, then, there is much for you to see."

"I didn't come here to sight-see, Inspector. I must return home as quickly as possible."

Inspector Touh sighed. "You Caucasians are always in such a rush. Have you heard of Bugis Street?"

"No."

Jennifer shifted in her seat so that she could study Inspector Touh. He had a face that was highly mobile and his gestures were expressive. He seemed outgoing and communicative, and yet he had spent the entire evening saying exactly nothing.

The car stopped for a *trishaw,* one of the three-wheeled carriages pedaled by natives. Inspector Touh watched with contempt as the *trishaw* carried two tourists down the street.

"We shall outlaw those one day."

JENNIFER AND INSPECTOR Touh got out of the car a block away from Bugis Street.

"No automobiles are allowed in there," Inspector Touh explained.

He took Jennifer's arm and they started walking along the busy sidewalk. In a few minutes, the crowds were so thick it was almost impossible to move. Bugis Street was narrow, with stalls on both sides, fruit stalls and vegetable stands and stalls that sold fish and meat. There were outdoor restaurants with chairs set around small tables. Jennifer stood there, drinking in the sights and the sounds and the smells and the riot of colors. Inspector Touh took her arm and shouldered his way through the crowd, clearing a path. They reached a restaurant with three tables in front of it, all occupied. The inspector gripped the arm of a passing waiter, and a moment later the proprietor was at their side. The inspector said something to him in Chinese. The proprietor walked over to one of the tables, spoke to the guests, and they looked at the inspector and quickly rose and left. The inspector and Jennifer were seated at the table.

"Can I order something for you?"

"No, thank you." Jennifer looked at the teeming sea of people throng-
ing the sidewalks and streets. Under other circumstances she might have
enjoyed this. Singapore was a fascinating city, a city to share with someone you cared about.

Inspector Touh was saying, "Watch. It is almost midnight."

Jennifer looked up. At first she noticed nothing. Then she saw that all
the shopkeepers were simultaneously beginning to close up their stands.
In ten minutes, every stall was closed and locked and their owners had
disappeared.

"What's happening?" Jennifer asked.

"You will see."

There was a murmur from the crowd at the far end of the street, and
the people began to move toward the sidewalk, leaving a cleared place in
the street. A Chinese girl in a long, tight-fitting evening gown was walking down the center of the street. She was the most beautiful woman
Jennifer had ever seen. She walked proudly and slowly, pausing to greet
people at various tables, then moving on.

As the girl neared the table where Jennifer and the inspector were sitting, Jennifer got a better look at her, and up close, she was even lovelier.
Her features were soft and delicate, and her figure was breathtaking. Her
white silk gown was slit at the sides so that one could see the delicately
curved thigh and small, perfectly formed breasts.

As Jennifer turned to speak to the inspector, another girl appeared.
She was, if possible, even lovelier than the first. Two more were walking behind her, and in a moment Bugis Street was filled with beautiful
young girls. They were a mixture of Malaysian, Indian and Chinese.

"They're prostitutes," Jennifer guessed.

"Yes. Transsexuals."

Jennifer stared at him. It was not possible. She turned and looked at
the girls again. She could see absolutely nothing masculine about any of
them.

"You're joking."

"They are known as *Billy Boys*."

Jennifer was bewildered. "But they—"

"They have all had an operation. They think of themselves as
women." He shrugged. "So, why not? They do no harm. You under-

stand," he added, "that prostitution is illegal here. But the *Billy Boys* are good for tourism and as long as they do not disturb the guests, the police close an eye to it."

Jennifer looked again at the exquisite young people moving down the street, stopping at tables to make deals with customers.

"They do well. They charge up to two hundred dollars. When they get too old to work, they become Mamasans."

Most of the girls were seated at tables now with men, dickering for their services. One by one, they began to rise and leave with their clients.

"They handle up to two or three transactions a night," the inspector explained. "They take over Bugis Street at midnight and they must be out by six in the morning so that the stands can open for business again. We can leave whenever you're ready."

"I'm ready."

As they moved along the street, an unbidden image of Ken Bailey flashed through Jennifer's mind and she thought, *I hope you are happy.*

ON THE DRIVE back to the hotel, Jennifer made up her mind that, chauffeur or no chauffeur, she was going to bring up Bjork's name.

As the car turned on to Orchard Road, Jennifer said determinedly, "About Stefan Bjork—"

"Ah, yes. I have arranged for you to visit him at ten o'clock tomorrow morning."

n Washington, D.C., Adam Warner was summoned from a meeting to take an urgent telephone call from New York.

District Attorney Robert Di Silva was on the phone. He was jubilant. "The special grand jury just returned the indictments we asked for. Every one of them! We're all set to move." There was no response. "Are you there, Senator?"

"I'm here." Adam forced enthusiasm into his voice. "That's great news."

"We should be able to start closing in within twenty-four hours. If you can fly up to New York, I think we should have a final meeting tomorrow morning with all the agencies so we can coordinate our moves. Can you do that, Senator?"

"Yes," Adam said.

"I'll make the arrangements. Ten o'clock tomorrow morning."

"I'll be there." Adam replaced the receiver.

The special grand jury just returned the indictments we asked for. Every one of them!

Adam picked up the telephone again and began to dial.

56

The visitors' room at Changi Prison was a small, bare room with whitewashed stucco walls, containing one long table with hard wooden chairs set on either side. Jennifer was seated in one of the chairs, waiting. She looked up as the door opened and Stefan Bjork walked in, accompanied by a uniformed guard.

Bjork was in his thirties, a tall, sullen-faced man with protuberant eyes. *A thyroid condition*, Jennifer thought. There were vivid bruises on his cheeks and forehead. He sat down opposite Jennifer.

"I'm Jennifer Parker, your attorney. I'm going to try to get you out of here."

He looked at her and said, "You better make it soon."

It could have been a threat or a plea. Jennifer remembered Michael's words: *I want you to bail him out before he starts talking.*

"Are they treating you all right?"

He cast a covert look at the guard standing near the door. "Yeah. Okay."

"I've applied for bail for you.

"What are the chances?" Bjork was unable to conceal the hope in his voice.

"I think they're pretty good. It will be two or three days at the most."

"I have to get out of this place."

Jennifer rose to her feet. "I'll see you soon."

"Thanks," Stefan said. He held out his hand.

The guard said sharply, "No!"

They both turned.

"No touching."

Stefan Bjork gave Jennifer a look and then said hoarsely, "Hurry!"

WHEN JENNIFER RETURNED to her hotel, there was a telephone message that Inspector Touh had called. As she was reading it, the phone rang. It was the inspector.

"While you are waiting, Miss Parker, I thought you might enjoy a little tour of our city."

Jennifer's first reaction was to say no, but she realized there was nothing she could do until she had Bjork safely on a plane out of here. Until then, it was important to keep Inspector Touh's goodwill.

Jennifer said, "Thank you. I would enjoy that."

THEY STOPPED TO have lunch at Kampachi, and then headed for the countryside, driving north on Bukit Timah Road to Malaysia, going through a series of colorful little villages with a variety of food stands and shops. The people seemed well-dressed and prosperous looking. Jennifer and Inspector Touh stopped at the Kranji Cemetery and War Memorial, walking up the steps and through the open blue gates. In front of them was a large marble cross, and in the background an enormous column. The cemetery was a sea of white crosses.

"The war was very bad for us," Inspector Touh said. "We all lost many friends and family members."

Jennifer said nothing. Her mind could see a grave in Sands Point. But she could not let herself think about what lay beneath the small mound.

IN MANHATTAN, A meeting of law enforcement agencies was in progress at the Police Intelligence Unit on Hudson Street. There was an air of jubilation in the crowded room. Many of the men had gone into the investigation with cynicism, for they had been through this kind of exercise before. Over the past years they had managed to accumulate overwhelming evidence against mobsters and murderers and blackmailers, and in case after case, high-priced legal talent had won acquittals for the criminals they represented. This time it was going to be different. They had the testimony of the *Consigliere* Thomas Colfax, and no one would be able to shake him. For more than twenty-five years he had been the linchpin of the mob. He would go into court, give names, dates, facts and figures. And now they were being given the go-ahead to move.

Adam had worked harder than anyone in the room to make this moment happen. It was to have been the triumphal carriage that would take him to the White House. Now that the moment was here, it had turned to ashes. In front of Adam was a list of people who had been indicted by the special grand jury. The fourth name on the list was Jennifer Parker, and the charges opposite her name were murder and conspiracy to commit half a dozen different federal crimes.

Adam Warner looked around the room and forced himself to speak. "You're—you're all to be congratulated."

He tried to say more, but the words would not come out. He was filled with such self-loathing that it was a physical pain.

THE SPANISH ARE *right,* Michael Moretti thought. *Vengeance is a dish best eaten cold.* The only reason Jennifer Parker was still alive was because she was out of his reach. But she would be returning soon. And in the meantime, Michael could savor what was going to happen to her. She had betrayed him in every way a woman could betray a man. For that he was going to see that she received special attention.

IN SINGAPORE, JENNIFER tried again to put a call through to Michael.

"I'm sorry," the switchboard operator told her, "the circuits to the United States are busy."

"Will you keep trying, please?"

"Of course, Miss Parker."

The operator looked up at the man standing guard beside the switchboard, and he gave her a conspiratorial smile.

. . .

AT HIS DOWNTOWN headquarters, Robert Di Silva was looking at a warrant that had just been delivered. It had Jennifer Parker's name on it.

I've finally got her, he thought. And he felt a savage satisfaction.

THE TELEPHONE OPERATOR announced, "Inspector Touh is in the lobby to see you."

Jennifer was surprised, for she had not been expecting him. He must have some news about Stefan Bjork.

Jennifer took the elevator down to the lobby.

"Forgive me for not telephoning," Inspector Touh apologized. "I thought it best to speak to you personally."

"You have some news?"

"We can talk in the car. I want to show you something."

THEY DROVE ALONG Yio Chu Kang Road.

"Is there a problem?" Jennifer asked.

"None at all. Bail will be set for the day after tomorrow."

Then where was he taking her?

They were passing a group of buildings on Jalan Goatopah Road, and the driver brought the car to a stop.

Inspector Touh turned to Jennifer. "I'm sure this will interest you."

"What is it?"

"Come along. You will see."

The interior of the building was old and dilapidated-looking, but the overpowering impression was of the smell, wild and primitive and musky. It was like nothing Jennifer had ever smelled before.

A young girl hurried forward and said, "Would you like an escort? I—"

Inspector Touh waved her aside. "We won't need you."

He took Jennifer's arm and they walked outside into the grounds. There were half a dozen large sunken tanks and from them came a series of strange slithering sounds. Jennifer and Inspector Touh reached the first pen. There was a sign: *Keep Your Hands Off the Pool. Danger.* Jennifer looked down. The tank was filled with alligators and crocodiles, dozens of them, all in continuous movement, sliding over and under one another.

Jennifer shuddered. "What is this?"

"It is a crocodile farm." He looked down at the reptiles. "When they are between three and six years old they are skinned and turned into wallets and belts and shoes. You see that most of them have their mouths open. That is the way they relax. It is when they close their mouths that you must be careful."

They moved on to a tank with two enormous alligators in it.

"These are fifteen years old. They are used only for breeding purposes."

Jennifer shivered. "They're so ugly. I don't know how they can stand each other."

Inspector Touh said, "They can't. As a matter of fact, they do not often mate."

"They're prehistoric."

"Precisely. They go back millions of years, with the same primitive mechanisms they had at the beginning of time."

Jennifer wondered why he had brought her here. If the inspector thought that these horrible-looking beasts would interest her, he was mistaken. "May we go now?" Jennifer asked.

"In a moment." The inspector looked up toward the young girl who had met them inside. She was carrying a tray toward the first tank.

"Today is feeding day," the inspector said. "Watch."

He moved with Jennifer toward the first tank. "They feed them fish and pigs' lungs once every three days."

The girl began throwing food into the pen, and instantly it erupted into a churning, swirling mass of activity. The alligators and crocodiles lunged for the raw, bloody food, tearing into it with their saurian fangs. As Jennifer watched, two of them went for the same piece of meat, and instantly they turned on each other, savagely attacking, biting and slashing until the pen started to fill with blood. The eyeball of one was torn loose, but its teeth were sunk into the jaws of its attacker and it would not let go. As the blood began pouring out more heavily, staining the water, the other crocodiles joined in, savaging their two wounded mates, ripping at their heads until the raw skin was exposed. They began to devour them alive.

Jennifer felt faint. "Please, let's get out of here."

Inspector Touh put his hand on her arm. "One moment."

He stood there watching, and after a while he led Jennifer away.

That night, Jennifer dreamt of the crocodiles clawing and tearing each other to pieces. Two of them suddenly turned into Michael and Adam, and in the middle of her nightmare Jennifer woke up, trembling. She was unable to go back to sleep.

THE RAIDS BEGAN. Federal and local law-enforcement agents struck in a dozen different states and in half a dozen foreign countries, and the raids were orchestrated to take place simultaneously.

In Ohio, a senator was arrested while making a speech to a women's club on honesty in government.

In New Orleans, an illegal national bookmaking operation was shut down.

In Amsterdam, a diamond smuggling operation was halted.

A bank manager in Gary, Indiana, was arrested on charges of laundering Organization money.

In Kansas City, a large discount house filled with stolen goods was raided.

In Phoenix, Arizona, half a dozen detectives on the vice squad were placed under arrest.

In Naples, a cocaine factory was seized.

In Detroit, a nationwide automobile theft ring was broken up.

UNABLE TO REACH Jennifer by telephone, Adam Warner went to her office.

Cynthia recognized him instantly.

"I'm sorry, Senator Warner, Miss Parker is out of the country."

"Where is she?"

"The Shangri-La Hotel in Singapore."

Adam's spirits rose. He could telephone her and warn her not to return.

• • •

THE HOTEL HOUSEKEEPER walked in as Jennifer was getting out of the shower.

"Excuse me. What time will you be checking out today?"

"I'm not checking out today. I'm leaving tomorrow."

The housekeeper looked puzzled. "I was told to get this suite ready for a party coming in late tonight."

"Who told you to do that?"

"The manager."

DOWNSTAIRS, AN OVERSEAS call was coming in at the switchboard. There was a different operator on duty and a different man was standing over her.

The operator spoke into her mouthpiece. "New York City calling Miss Jennifer Parker?"

She looked at the man standing next to her. He shook his head.

"I'm sorry. Miss Parker has checked out."

THE SWEEPING RAIDS continued. Arrests were made in Honduras, San Salvador, Turkey and Mexico. The net swept up dealers and killers and bank robbers and arsonists. There were crackdowns in Fort Lauderdale and Atlantic City and Palm Springs.

And they continued.

IN NEW YORK, Robert Di Silva was keeping close track of the progress being made. His heart beat faster as he thought about the net that was closing in on Jennifer Parker and Michael Moretti.

MICHAEL MORETTI ESCAPED the police dragnet by sheer chance. It was the anniversary of his father-in-law's death, and Michael and Rosa had gone to the cemetery to pay homage to her father.

Five minutes after they left, a carload of FBI agents arrived at Michael Moretti's house and another carload at his office. When they learned he was not in either place, the agents settled down to wait.

JENNIFER REALIZED THAT she had neglected to make a plane reservation for Stefan Bjork back to the States. She called Singapore Airlines.

"This is Jennifer Parker. I'm booked on your Flight One-Twelve leaving tomorrow afternoon for London. I'd like to make an additional reservation."

"Thank you. Would you hold the line, please?"

Jennifer waited and after a few minutes the voice came back on the line. "Was that Parker? P-A-R-K-E-R?"

"Yes."

"Your reservation has been canceled, Miss Parker."

Jennifer felt a small shock. "Canceled? By whom?"

"I do not know. You have been taken off our passenger list."

"There's been some mistake. I'd like you to put me back on that list."

"I'm sorry, Miss Parker. Flight One-Twelve is full."

INSPECTOR TOUH WAS the one to straighten everything out, Jennifer decided. She had agreed to have dinner with him. She would find out what was happening then.

HE PICKED HER up early.

Jennifer told the inspector about the mix-up in her hotel and plane reservations.

He shrugged. "Our famous inefficiency, I am afraid. I will look into it."

"What about Stefan Bjork?"

"Everything is arranged. He will be released tomorrow morning."

Inspector Touh said something to the driver in Chinese and the car made a U-turn.

"You have not seen Kallang Road. You will find it most interesting."

The car made a left turn on to Lavender Street, then one block later a right turn to Kallang Bahru. There were large signs advertising florists and casket companies. A few blocks later the car made another turn.

"Where are we?"

Inspector Touh turned to Jennifer and said quietly, "We are on the Street With No Name."

The car began to move very slowly. There were only undertakers on both sides of the street, row after row of them: Tan Kee Seng, Clin Noh,

Ang Yung Long, Goh Soon. Ahead, a funeral was in progress. All the mourners were dressed in white and a three-piece band was playing: a tuba, a sax and drums. A body was laid out on a table with wreaths of flowers around it and a large photograph of the deceased sat on an easel facing the front. Mourners were sitting around, eating.

Jennifer turned to the inspector. "What is this?"

"These are the houses of death. The natives call them the *die houses*. The word death is difficult for them to pronounce." He looked at Jennifer and said, "But death is only a part of life, is it not?"

Jennifer looked into his cold eyes and was suddenly frightened.

THEY WENT TO the Golden Phoenix, and it was not until they were seated that Jennifer had a chance to question him.

"Inspector Touh, did you have a reason for taking me to the crocodile farm and the die houses?"

He looked at her and said evenly, "Of course. I thought they would interest you. Especially since you came here to free your client, Mr. Bjork. Many of our young people are dying because of the drugs that are brought into our country, Miss Parker. I could have taken you to the hospital where we try to treat them, but I felt it might be more informative for you to see where they end up."

"All that has nothing to do with me."

"That is a matter of opinion." All the friendliness had gone out of his voice.

Jennifer said, "Look, Inspector Touh, I'm sure you're being well paid to—"

"There is not enough money in the world for anyone to pay me."

He stood up and nodded to someone, and Jennifer turned. Two men in gray suits were approaching the table.

"Miss Jennifer Parker?"

"Yes."

There was no need for them to pull out their FBI credentials. She knew before they spoke. "FBI. We have extradition papers and a warrant for your arrest. We're taking you back to New York on the midnight plane."

57

When Michael Moretti left his father-in-law's grave, he was already late for an appointment. He decided to call the office and reschedule it. He stopped at a telephone booth along the highway and dialed the number. The phone rang once and a voice answered, "Acme Builders."

Michael said, "This is Mike. Tell—"

"Mr. Moretti isn't here. Call back later."

Michael felt his body tightening. All he said was "Tony's Place."

He hung up and hurried back to the car. Rosa looked at his face and asked, "Is everything all right, Michael?"

"I don't know. I'm going to drop you off at your cousin's. Stay there until you hear from me."

TONY FOLLOWED MICHAEL into the office in the rear of the restaurant.

"I got word that the Feds are crawlin' all over your house and the downtown office, Mike."

"Thanks," Michael said. "I don't want to be disturbed."

"You won't be."

Michael waited until Tony walked out of the room and closed the door behind him. Then Michael picked up the telephone and furiously began to dial.

IT TOOK MICHAEL Moretti less than twenty minutes to learn that a major disaster was taking place. As the reports of the raids and arrests began to filter in, Michael received them with mounting disbelief. All his soldiers and lieutenants were being picked up. Drops were being raided; gambling operations were being seized; confidential ledgers and records were being impounded. What was happening was a nightmare. The police had to be obtaining information from someone in his Organization.

Michael placed telephone calls to other Families around the country, and all of them demanded to know what was going on. They were being badly hurt and no one knew where the leak was coming from. They all suspected it was coming from the Moretti Family.

Jimmy Guardino, in Las Vegas, gave him an ultimatum. "I'm calling on behalf of the Commission, Michael." The National Commission was the supreme power that superseded the power of any individual Family when there was trouble. "The police are rounding up all the Families. Someone big is singing. The word we get is that it's one of your boys. We're giving you twenty-fours to find him and take care of him."

In the past, police raids had always netted the small fry, the expendables. Now, for the first time, the men at the top were being pulled in. *Someone big is singing. The word we get is that it's one of your boys.* They had to be right. Michael's Family had been the hardest hit, and the police were looking for him. Someone had given them solid evidence, or they never would have mounted a campaign this big. But who could it be? Michael sat back, thinking.

Whoever was tipping off the authorities had inside information that was known only to Michael and his two top lieutenants, Salvatore Fiore and Joseph Colella. Only the three of them knew where the ledgers were hidden, and the FBI had found them. The only other person who would have had the information was Thomas Colfax, but Colfax was buried under a garbage dump in New Jersey.

Michael sat there and thought about Salvatore Fiore and Joseph Colella. It was difficult to believe that either one of them could have broken *omertà* and talked. They had been with him from the beginning; he had handpicked them. He had allowed them to have their own loan-sharking operation on the side and to run a small prostitution ring. Why would they betray him? The answer, of course, was simple: the chair he was sitting in. They wanted his chair. Once he was out, they could move in and take over. They were a team; they had to be in it together.

Michael was filled with a murderous rage. The stupid bastards were trying to pull him down, but they would not live long enough to enjoy it. The first thing he had to do was arrange bail for his men who had been arrested. He needed a lawyer he could trust—Colfax was dead, and Jennifer—Jennifer! Michael could feel the coldness creeping around his heart again. In his head he could hear himself saying, *Get back as fast as you can. I'll miss you. I love you, Jennifer.* He had said that and she had betrayed him. She would pay for that.

MICHAEL MADE A telephone call and sat back to wait, and fifteen minutes later Nick Vito hurried into the office.

"What's happening?" Michael asked.

"The place is still buzzin' with Feds, Mike. I drove around the block a couple of times, but I did like you said. I stayed away."

"I've got a job for you, Nick."

"Sure, boss. What can I do for you?"

"Take care of Salvatore and Joe."

Nick Vito stared at him, "I—I don't understand. When you say, *take care of them,* you don't mean—"

Michael shouted, "I mean blow their fucking brains out! Do you need a blueprint?"

"N-no," Nick Vito stammered. "It's just that I—I—I mean—Sal and Joe are your top men!"

Michael Moretti moved to his feet, his eyes dangerous. "You want to tell me how to run my business, Nick?"

"No, Mike. I—sure. I'll take care of them for you. When—?"

"Now. Right away. I don't want them to live to see the moon tonight. Do you understand?"

"Yeah. I understand."

Michael's hands tightened into fists. "If I had time, I'd take care of them myself. I want them to hurt, Nick. Make it slow, you hear? *Suppilu suppilu.*"

"Sure. Okay."

The door opened and Tony hurried in, his face gray. "There's two FBI agents out there with a warrant for your arrest. I swear to God I don't know how they knew you was here. They—"

Michael Moretti turned to Nick Vito and snapped, "Out the back way. Move!" He turned to Tony. "Tell them I'm in the can. I'll be right with them."

Michael picked up the telephone and dialed a number. One minute later he was talking to a judge of the Superior Court of New York.

"There are two Feds out here with a warrant for my arrest."

"What are the charges, Mike?"

"I don't know and I don't give a shit. I'm calling you to set things up so that I'm bailed out. I can't sit around in the slammer. I've got things to do."

There was a silence and the judge's voice said carefully, "I'm afraid I won't be able to help you this time, Michael. The heat's on all over and if I try to interfere—"

When Michael Moretti spoke, there was an ominous note in his voice. "Listen to me, you asshole, and listen good. If I spend one hour in jail, I'll see to it that you're behind bars for the rest of your life. I've been taking good care of you for a long time. You want me to tell the D.A. how many cases you fixed for me? Would you like me to give the IRS the number of your Swiss bank account? Would you—"

"For God's sake, Michael!"

"Then move!"

"I'll see what I can do," Judge Lawrence Waldman said. "I'll try to—"

"Try to, shit! Do it! Do you hear me, Larry? Do it!" Michael slammed down the receiver.

His mind was working swiftly and coolly. He was not concerned about being taken to jail. He knew that Judge Waldman would do as he was told, and he could trust Nick Vito to attend to Fiore and Colella.

Without their testimony, the government could not prove a thing against him.

Michael looked in the small mirror on the wall, combed back his hair, straightened his tie, and went out to meet the two FBI agents.

JUDGE LAWRENCE WALDMAN came through, as Michael had known he would. At the preliminary hearing, an attorney selected by Judge Waldman requested bail, and it was set at five hundred thousand dollars.

Di Silva stood there, angry and frustrated, as Michael Moretti walked out of the courtroom.

58

Nick Vito was a man of limited intelligence. His value to the Organization lay in the fact that he followed orders without question and that he carried them out efficiently. Nick Vito had been up against guns and knives dozens of times, but he had never known fear. He knew it now. Something was happening that was beyond his understanding, and he had a feeling that somehow he was responsible for it.

All day he had been hearing about the raids that were taking place, the sweeping arrests that were being made. The street talk was that there was a traitor loose, someone high up in the Organization. Even with his limited intellect, Nick Vito was able to connect the fact that he had let Thomas Colfax live and that, shortly afterward, someone had started betraying the Family to the authorities. Nick Vito knew that it could not be Salvatore Fiore or Joseph Colella. The two men were like brothers to him and they were both as fanatically loyal to Michael Moretti as he was. But there was no way he could ever explain that to Michael, not without getting himself chopped into small pieces; because the only other one who could be responsible was Thomas Colfax, and Colfax was supposed to be dead.

Nick Vito was in a dilemma. He loved the Little Flower and the giant. Fiore and Colella had done him dozens of favors in the past, just as Thomas Colfax had; but he had helped Colfax out of a jam, and look what it had gotten him. So Nick Vito decided he was not going to be softhearted again. It was his own life he had to protect now. Once he killed Fiore and Colella, he would be in the clear. But because they were like brothers to him, he would see that they died quickly.

IT WAS SIMPLE for Nick Vito to determine their whereabouts, for they always had to be available in case Michael needed them. Little Salvatore Fiore was visiting his mistress's apartment on 83rd Street near the Museum of Natural History. Nick knew that Salvatore always left there at five o'clock to go home to his wife. It was now three. Nick debated with himself. He could either hang around the front of the apartment building or go upstairs and take Salvatore inside the apartment. He decided he was too nervous to wait. The fact that he was nervous made Nick Vito more nervous. The whole thing was beginning to get to him. *When this is over,* he thought, *I'm gonna ask Mike for a vacation. Maybe I'll take a couple of young girls and go down to the Bahamas.* Just thinking about that made him feel better.

Nick Vito parked his car around the corner from the apartment house and walked up to the building. He let himself in the front door with a piece of celluloid, ignored the elevator and walked up the stairs to the third floor. He moved toward the door at the end of the corridor, and when he reached it he pounded on it.

"Open up! Police!"

He heard quick sounds from behind the door and a few moments later it opened on a heavy chain and he could see the face and part of the naked figure of Marina, Salvatore Fiore's mistress.

"Nick!" she said. "You crazy idiot. You scared the hell out of me."

She took the chain off the door and opened it. "Sal, it's Nick!"

Little Salvatore Fiore walked in from the bedroom, naked. "Hey, Nicky boy! What the fuck you doin' here?"

"Sal, I got a message for you from Mike."

Nick Vito raised a .22 automatic with a silencer and squeezed the trigger. The firing pin slammed into the .22 caliber cartridge, sending the bullet out of the muzzle at a thousand feet a second. The first bullet shattered the bridge of Salvatore Fiore's nose. The second bullet put out his left eye. As Marina opened her mouth to scream, Nick Vito turned and put a bullet in her head. As she fell to the floor, he put one more bullet in her chest, to make certain. *It's a waste of a beautiful piece of ass,* Nick thought, *but Mike wouldn't like it if I left any witnesses around.*

BIG JOSEPH COLELLA owned a horse that was running in the eighth race at Belmont Park in Long Island. Belmont was a one-and-one-half-mile track, the perfect length for the filly that the giant was running. He had advised Nick to bet on it. In the past, Nick had won a lot on Colella's tips. Colella always put a little money on for Nick when his horses ran. As Nick Vito walked toward Colella's box, he thought regretfully about the fact that there would be no more tips. The eighth race had just started. Colella was standing up in his box, cheering his horse on. It was a large-purse race and the crowd was screaming and yelling as the horses rounded the first turn.

Nick Vito stepped into the box behind Colella and said, "How you doin', pal?"

"Hey, Nick! You got here just in time. Beauty Queen's gonna win this one. I put a little bet on it for you."

"That's great, Joe."

Nick Vito pressed the .22 caliber gun against Joseph Colella's spine and fired three times through his coat. The muffled noise went unnoticed in the cheering crowd. Nick watched Joseph Colella slump to the ground. He debated for an instant whether to take the pari-mutuel tickets out of Colella's pocket, then decided against it. After all, the horse could lose.

Nick Vito turned and unhurriedly walked toward the exit, one anonymous figure among thousands.

MICHAEL MORETTI'S PRIVATE line rang.

"Mr. Moretti?"

"Who wants him?"

"This is Captain Tanner."

It took Michael a second to place the name. A police captain. Queens precinct. On the payroll.

"This is Moretti."

"I just received some information I think might interest you."

"Where are you calling from?"

"A public telephone booth."

"Go ahead."

"I found out where all the heat's coming from."

"You're too late. They've been taken care of already."

"*They?* Oh. I only heard about Thomas Colfax."

"You don't know what the hell you're talking about. Colfax is dead."

It was Captain Tanner's turn to be confused. "What are *you* talking about? Thomas Colfax is sitting at the Marine Base in Quantico right now, spilling his guts to everybody who'll listen."

"You're out of your mind," Michael snapped. "I happen to know—" He stopped. What *did* he know? He had told Nick Vito to kill Thomas Colfax, and Vito had said that he had. Michael sat there thinking. "How sure are you about this, Tanner?"

"Mr. Moretti, would I be calling you if I wasn't sure?"

"I'll check it out. If you're right, I owe you one."

"Thank you, Mr. Moretti."

Captain Tanner replaced the receiver, pleased with himself. In the past he had found Michael Moretti to be a very appreciative man. This could be the *big* one, the one that could enable him to retire. He stepped out of the telephone booth into the cold October air.

There were two men standing outside the booth, and as the captain started to step around them, one of them blocked his way. He held up an identification card.

"Captain Tanner? I'm Lieutenant West, Internal Security Division. The Police Commissioner would like to have a word with you."

MICHAEL MORETTI HUNG up the receiver slowly. He knew with a sure animal instinct that Nick Vito had lied to him. Thomas Colfax was still alive. That would explain everything that was happening. *He* was the one who had turned traitor. And Michael had sent Nick Vito out to kill Fiore and Colella. Jesus, he had been stupid! Outsmarted by a dumb hired gunman into wasting his two top men! He was filled with an icy rage.

He dialed a number and spoke briefly into the telephone. After he made a second telephone call, he sat back and waited.

When he heard Nick Vito on the phone, Michael forced himself to keep the fury he felt out of his voice. "How did it go, Nick?"

"Okay, boss. Just like you said. They both suffered a lot."

"I can always count on you, Nick, can't I?"

"You know you can, boss."

"Nick, I want you to do me one last favor. One of the boys left a car at the corner of York and Ninety-fifth Street. It's a tan Camaro. The keys are behind the sun visor. We're going to use it for a job tonight. Drive it over here, will you?"

"Sure, boss. How soon do you need it? I was going to—"

"I need it now. Right away, Nick."

"I'm on my way."

"Good-bye, Nick."

Michael replaced the receiver. He wished he could be there to watch Nick Vito blow himself to hell, but he had one more urgent thing to do.

Jennifer Parker would be on her way back soon, and he wanted to get everything ready for her.

59

It's like some kind of goddamned Hollywood movie production, Major General Roy Wallace thought, *with my prisoner as the star.*

The large conference room at the United States Marine Corps base was filled with technicians from the Signal Corps, scurrying around setting up cameras and sound and lighting equipment, using an arcane jargon.

"Kill the brute and hit the inkies. Bring a baby over here . . ."

They were getting ready to put Thomas Colfax's testimony on film.

"It's extra insurance," District Attorney Di Silva had argued. "We know that no one can get to him, but it will be good to have it on the record, anyway." And the others had gone along with him.

The only person absent was Thomas Colfax. He would be brought in at the last minute, when everything was in readiness for him.

Just like a goddamn movie star.

THOMAS COLFAX WAS having a meeting in his cell with David Terry of the Justice Department, the man in charge of creating new identities for witnesses who wished to disappear.

"Let me explain a bit about the Federal Witness Security Program," Terry said. "When the trial is over, we'll send you to whichever country you choose. Your furniture and other belongings will be shipped to a warehouse in Washington, with a coded number. We'll forward it to you later. There won't be any way for anyone to trace you. We'll supply you with a new identity and background and, if you wish, a new appearance."

"I'll take care of that." He trusted no one to know what he was going to do with his appearance.

"Ordinarily when we set people up with a new identity, we find jobs for them in whatever field they're suited for, and we supply them with some money. In your case, Mr. Colfax, I understand that money is no problem."

Thomas Colfax wondered what David Terry would say if he knew how much money was salted away in his bank accounts in Germany, Switzerland and Hong Kong. Even Thomas Colfax had not been able to keep track of it all, but a modest estimate, he would guess, would be nine or ten million dollars.

"No," Colfax said, "I don't think money will be a problem."

"All right, then. The first thing to decide is where you would like to go. Do you have any particular area in mind?"

It was such a simple question, yet so much lay behind it. What the man was really saying was, *Where do you want to spend the rest of your life?* For Colfax knew that when he got to wherever he was going, he would never be able to leave. It would become his new habitat, his protective cover, and he would not be safe anywhere else in the world.

"Brazil."

It was the logical choice. He already owned a two-hundred-thousand-acre plantation there in the name of a Panamanian corporation that could not be traced back to him. The plantation itself was like a fortress. He could afford to buy himself enough protection so that even if Michael Moretti did finally learn where he was, no one would be able to touch him. He could buy anything, including all the women he wanted. Thomas Colfax liked Latin women. People thought that when a man reached the age of sixty-five he was finished sexually, that he no longer had any interest, but Colfax had found that his appetite had grown as he had gotten older. His favorite sport was to have two or three beautiful young women in bed with him at the same time, working him over. The younger the better.

"Brazil will be easy to arrange," David Terry was saying. "Our government will buy you a small house there, and—"

"That won't be necessary." Colfax almost laughed aloud at the thought of his having to live in a small house. "All I will require of you is that you provide me with the new identification and safe transportation. I'll take care of everything else."

"As you wish, Mr. Colfax." David Terry rose to his feet. "I think we've covered just about everything." He smiled reassuringly. "This is going to be one of the easy ones. I'll begin setting things in motion. As soon as you're finished testifying, you'll be on an airplane to South America."

"Thank you." Thomas Colfax watched his visitor leave and he was filled with a sense of elation. He had done it! Michael Moretti had made the mistake of underestimating him, and it was going to be Moretti's final mistake. Colfax was going to bury him so deep that he would never rise again.

And his testimony was going to be filmed. That would be interesting. He wondered whether they would use makeup on him. He studied himself in the small mirror on the wall. *Not bad,* he thought, *for a man my age. I still have my looks. Those young South American girls love older men with gray hair.*

He heard the sound of the cell door opening, and he turned. A marine sergeant was bringing in Colfax's lunch. There would be plenty of time to eat before the filming began.

The first day, Thomas Colfax had complained about the food that was served to him, and from then on General Wallace had arranged for all of Colfax's meals to be catered. In the weeks that Colfax had been confined at the fort, his slightest suggestion had become their command. They wanted to do everything they could to please him, and Colfax took full advantage of it. He had had comfortable furniture moved in, and a television set, and he received a daily supply of newspapers and current magazines.

THE SERGEANT PLACED the tray of food on a table set for two, and he made the same comment he made every day.

"Looks good enough to eat, sir."

Colfax smiled politely and sat down at the table. Roast beef rare, the way he liked it, mashed potatoes and Yorkshire pudding. He waited as the marine pulled up a chair and sat down across from him. The sergeant picked up a knife and fork, cut off a piece of the meat and began to eat. Another of General Wallace's ideas. Thomas Colfax had his own taster. *Like the kings of ancient times,* he thought. He watched as the marine sampled the roast beef, the potatoes and the Yorkshire pudding.

"How is it?"

"To tell you the truth, sir, I prefer my beef on the well-done side."

Colfax picked up his own knife and fork and began to eat. The sergeant was mistaken. The meat was cooked perfectly, the potatoes were creamy and hot and the Yorkshire pudding was done to a turn.

Colfax reached for the horseradish and spread it lightly over the beef. It was with the second bite that Colfax knew something was terribly wrong. There was a sudden burning sensation in his mouth that seemed to shoot through his whole body. He felt as though he were on fire. His throat was closing, paralyzed, and he began gasping for air. The marine sergeant sitting across from him was staring at him. Thomas Colfax clutched his throat and tried to tell the sergeant what was happening, but no words would come out. The fire in him was spreading more swiftly now, filling him with an unbearable agony. His body stiffened in a terrible spasm and he toppled over backwards to the floor.

The sergeant watched him for a moment, then bent over the body and lifted Thomas Colfax's eyelid to make sure he was dead.

Then he called for help.

60

Singapore Airlines Flight 246 landed at Heathrow Airport in London at seven-thirty A.M. The other passengers were detained in their seats until Jennifer and the two FBI agents were out of the plane and in the airport's security office.

Jennifer was desperately anxious to see a newspaper to find out what was happening at home, but her two silent escorts denied her request and refused to be drawn into conversation.

Two hours later, the three of them boarded a TWA plane bound for New York.

IN THE UNITED States Court House at Foley Square an emergency meeting was taking place. Present were Adam Warner, Robert Di Silva, Major General Roy Wallace, and half a dozen representatives from the FBI, the Justice Department and the Treasury Department.

"How the hell could this have happened?" Robert Di Silva's voice was trembling with rage. He turned to the general. "You were told how important Thomas Colfax was to us."

The general spread his hands helplessly. "We took every precaution we could, sir. We're checking now to see how they could have smuggled prussic acid into—"

"I don't give a shit how they did it! Colfax is dead!"

The man from the Treasury Department spoke up. "How much does Colfax's death hurt us?"

"A hell of a lot," Di Silva replied. "Putting a man on a witness stand is one thing. Showing a lot of ledgers and accounts is something else. You can bet your ass that some smart attorney's going to start talking about how those books could have been faked."

"Where do we go from here?" a man from the Treasury Department asked.

The District Attorney replied, "We keep doing what we're doing. Jennifer Parker's on her way back from Singapore. We have enough to put her away forever. While she's going down, we're going to get her to pull Michael Moretti down with her." He turned to Adam. "Don't you agree, Senator?"

Adam felt ill. "Excuse me."

He quickly left the room.

61

The signalman on the ground, wearing oversized earmuffs, waved his two semaphores, guiding the jumbo 747 toward the waiting ramp. The plane pulled up to a fixed circle and, at a signal, the pilot cut the four Pratt & Whitney turbofan engines.

Inside the giant plane a steward's voice came over the loudspeaker, "Ladies and gentlemen, we have just landed at New York's Kennedy Airport. We thank you for flying TWA. Will all passengers please remain in their seats until a further announcement. Thank you."

There were general murmurs of protest. A moment later the doors were opened by the ramp crew. The two FBI agents seated with Jennifer in the front of the plane rose to their feet.

One of them turned to Jennifer and said, "Let's go."

The passengers watched with curiosity as the three people left the plane. A few minutes later the steward's voice came over the loudspeaker again. "Thank you for your patience, ladies and gentlemen. You may now disembark."

A government limousine was waiting at a side entrance to the airport. The first stop was the Metropolitan Correctional Center at 150 Park Row, that connected into the United States Court House at Foley Square.

After Jennifer had been booked, one of the FBI men said, "Sorry, we can't keep you here. We have orders to take you out to Riker's Island."

THE RIDE TO Riker's Island was made in silence. Jennifer sat in the back seat between the two FBI men, saying nothing, but her mind was busy. The two men had been uncommunicative during the entire trip across the ocean, so Jennifer had no way of knowing how much trouble she was in. She knew that it was serious, for it was not easy to obtain a warrant of extradition.

She could do nothing to help herself while she was in jail. Her first priority was to get out on bail.

THEY WERE CROSSING the bridge to Riker's Island now, and Jennifer looked out at the familiar view, a view she had seen a hundred times on the way to talk to clients. And now *she* was a prisoner.

But not for long, Jennifer thought. *Michael will get me out.*

The two FBI men escorted Jennifer into the reception building and one of the men handed the guard the extradition warrant.

"Jennifer Parker."

The guard glanced at it. "We've been expecting you, Miss Parker. You have a reservation in Detention Cell Three."

"I have the right to one phone call."

The guard nodded toward the telephone on his desk. "Sure."

Jennifer picked it up, silently praying that Michael Moretti was in. She began to dial.

MICHAEL MORETTI HAD been waiting for Jennifer's call. For the last twenty-four hours he had been able to think of nothing else. He had been informed when Jennifer had landed in London, when her plane had left Heathrow, and when she had arrived back in New York. He had sat at his desk, mentally tracking Jennifer on her way to Riker's Island. He had visualized her entering the prison. She would demand to make a phone call before they put her in a cell. She would call him. That was all he asked. He would have her out of there in an hour, and then she would be on her way to him. Michael Moretti was living for the moment when Jennifer Parker walked through the door.

Jennifer had done the unforgivable. She had given her body to the man who was trying to destroy him. And what else had she given him? What secrets had she told him?

Adam Warner was the father of Jennifer's son. Michael was certain of that now. Jennifer had lied to him from the beginning, had told him that Joshua's father was dead. *Well, that was a prophecy that will soon be fulfilled,* Michael told himself. He was caught in an ironic conflict. On the one hand, he had a powerful weapon he could use to discredit and destroy Adam Warner. He could blackmail Warner with the threat of exposing his relationship with Jennifer; but if he did that, he would be exposing himself. When the Families learned—and they would learn—that Michael's woman was the mistress of the head of the Senate Investigating Committee, Michael would become a laughingstock. He would no longer be able to hold up his head or command his men. A cuckold was not fit to be a *don.* So the blackmail threat was a double-edged sword and, as tempting as it was, Michael knew that he dare not use it. He would have to destroy his enemies in another way.

Michael looked at the small, crudely drawn map on the desk in front of him. It was Adam Warner's route to where he was going to attend a private fund-raising dinner party that evening. The map had cost Michael Moretti five thousand dollars. It was going to cost Adam Warner his life.

The telephone rang on Michael's desk and he involuntarily started. He picked it up and heard Jennifer's voice on the other end. That voice that had whispered endearments into his ear, that had begged him to make love to her, that—

"Michael—are you there?"

"I'm here. Where are you?"

"They've got me at Riker's Island. They're holding me on a murder charge. Bail hasn't been set yet. When can you—?"

"I'll have you out of there in no time. Just sit tight. Okay?"

"Yes, Michael." He could hear the relief in her voice.

"I'll have Gino pick you up."

A few moments later Michael reached for the telephone and dialed a number. He spoke into the phone for several minutes.

"I don't care how high the bail is. I want her out *now*."

He replaced the receiver and pressed a button on his desk. Gino Gallo came in.

"Jennifer Parker's at Riker's Island. She should be sprung in an hour or two. Pick her up and bring her here."

"Right, boss."

Michael leaned back in his chair. "Tell her we won't have to worry about Adam Warner after today."

Gino Gallo's face brightened. "No?"

"No. He's on his way to deliver a speech, but he'll never get there. He's going to have an accident at the bridge at New Canaan."

Gino Gallo smiled. "That's great, boss."

Michael gestured toward the door. "Move."

DISTRICT ATTORNEY DI Silva fought Jennifer's bail with every stratagem at his command. They were appearing before William Bennett, a judge of the Supreme Court of New York.

"Your Honor," Robert Di Silva said, "the defendant is charged with a dozen counts of felony. We had to extradite her from Singapore. If she's granted bail, she'll flee to someplace where there is no extradition. I ask that Your Honor deny bail."

John Lester, a former judge who was representing Jennifer, said, "The District Attorney is guilty of gross distortion, Your Honor. My client did not flee anywhere. She was in Singapore on business. If the government had asked her to return she would have done so voluntarily. She's a reputable attorney with a large practice here. It would be inconceivable that she would run away."

The arguments went on for more than thirty minutes.

At the end of that time, Judge Bennett said, "Bail is granted in the sum of five hundred thousand dollars."

"Thank you, Your Honor," Jennifer's attorney said. "We'll pay the bail."

FIFTEEN MINUTES LATER, Gino Gallo was helping Jennifer into the back of a Mercedes limousine.

"That didn't take long," he said.

Jennifer did not reply. Her mind was on what was happening. She had been completely isolated in Singapore. She had no idea of what had been going on in the United States, but she was certain that her arrest was not an unrelated incident. They would not be after her alone. She badly needed to talk to Michael and find out what had been happening. Di Silva had to be very sure of himself to have had her brought back on a murder charge. He—

Gino Gallo said two words that caught Jennifer's attention.

". . . Adam Warner . . ."

Jennifer had not been listening.

"What did you say?"

"I said we won't have to worry about Adam Warner no more. Mike is havin' him took care of."

Jennifer could feel her heart begin to pound. "He is? When?"

Gino Gallo raised his hand from the wheel to glance at his watch. "In about fifteen minutes. It's set up to look like an accident."

Jennifer's mouth was suddenly dry. "Where—" She could not get the words out. "Where—where is it going to happen?"

"New Canaan. The bridge."

They were passing through Queens. Ahead was a shopping center with a pharmacy.

"Gino, will you pull up in front of that drugstore? I have to get something."

"Sure." He skillfully turned the wheel and swung into the entrance to the shopping center. "Can I help you?"

"No, no. I'll—I'll only be a minute."

Jennifer got out of the car and hurried inside, nerves screaming. There was a telephone booth at the back of the store. Jennifer reached into her purse. She had no change except for some Singapore coins. She hurried over to the cashier and pulled out a dollar.

"Could I have change, please?"

The bored cashier took Jennifer's money and gave her a handful of silver. Jennifer dashed back to the telephone. A stout woman was picking up the receiver and dialing.

Jennifer said, "I have an emergency. I wonder if I could—"

The woman glared at her and kept dialing.

"Hello, Hazel," the woman whooped. "My horoscope was right. I've had the worst day! You know the shoes I was going to pick up at Delman's? Would you believe they sold the only pair they had in my size?"

Jennifer touched the woman's arm and begged, "Please!"

"Get your own phone," the woman hissed. She turned back to the receiver. "Remember the suede ones we saw? Gone! So you know what I did? I said to that clerk . . ."

Jennifer closed her eyes and stood there, oblivious to everything but the torment inside her. Michael must not kill Adam. She had to do whatever she could to save him.

The woman hung up and turned to Jennifer. "I should make another call, just to teach you a lesson," she said.

As she walked away, smiling at her little victory, Jennifer made a grab for the phone. She called Adam's office.

"I'm sorry," his secretary said, "but Senator Warner is not in. Do you wish to leave a message?"

"It's urgent," Jennifer said. "Do you know where he can be reached?"

"No, I'm sorry. If you would like to—"

Jennifer hung up. She stood there a moment, thinking, then quickly dialed another number. "Robert Di Silva."

There was an interminable wait and then: "The District Attorney's office."

"I have to speak to Mr. Di Silva. This is Jennifer Parker."

"I'm sorry. Mr. Di Silva is in a conference. He can't be dis—"

"You get him on this telephone. This is an emergency. Hurry!" Jennifer's voice was trembling.

Di Silva's secretary hesitated. "Just a moment."

A minute later, Robert Di Silva was on the telephone. "Yes?" His voice was unfriendly.

"Listen, and listen carefully," Jennifer said. "Adam Warner's going to be killed. It's going to happen in the next ten or fifteen minutes. They're planning to do it at the New Canaan bridge."

She hung up. There was nothing more she could do. A brief vision of Adam's torn body came into her mind and she shuddered. She looked at her watch and silently prayed that Di Silva would be able to get help there in time.

ROBERT DI SILVA replaced the receiver and looked at the half-dozen men in his office. "That was a weird call."

"Who was it?"

"Jennifer Parker. She said they're going to assassinate Senator Warner."

"Why did she call you?"

"Who knows?"

"Do you think it's on the level?"

District Attorney Di Silva said, "Hell, no,"

JENNIFER WALKED THROUGH the office door and, in spite of himself, Michael could not help reacting to her beauty. It was the same way he felt every time he saw her. Outside, she was the loveliest woman he had ever seen. But inside she was treacherous, deadly. He looked at the lips that had kissed Adam Warner and at the body that had lain in Adam Warner's arms.

She was walking in saying, "Michael, I'm so glad to see you. Thank you for arranging everything so quickly."

"No problem. I've been waiting for you, Jennifer." She would never know how much he meant that.

She sank into an armchair. "Michael, what in God's name is going on? What's happening?"

He studied her, half admiring her. She was responsible for helping to bring his empire crashing down, and she was sitting there innocently asking what was going on!

"Do you know why they brought me back?"

Sure, he thought. *So you can sing some more for them.* He remembered the little yellow canary with its broken neck. That would be Jennifer soon.

Jennifer looked into his black eyes. "Are you all right?"

"I've never been better." He leaned back in his chair. "In a few minutes, all our problems are going to be over."

"What do you mean?"

"Senator Warner is going to have an accident. That'll cool off the committee pretty good." He looked at the clock on the wall. "I should be getting a phone call any minute."

There was something odd in Michael's manner, something forbidding. Jennifer was filled with a sudden premonition of danger. She knew she had to get out of there.

She stood up. "I haven't had a chance to unpack. I'll go—"

"Sit down." The undertone in Michael's voice sent a chill down her back.

"Michael—"

"Sit down."

She glanced toward the door. Gino Gallo was standing there, his back against it, watching Jennifer with no expression on his face.

"You're not going anywhere," Michael told her.

"I don't under—"

"Don't talk. Don't say another word."

They sat there waiting, staring at each other, and the only sound in the room was the loud ticking of the clock on the wall. Jennifer tried to read Michael's eyes, but they were blank, filled with nothing, giving away nothing.

The sudden ringing of the telephone jarred the stillness of the room. Michael picked up the receiver. "Hello? . . . Are you sure? . . . All right. Get out of there." He replaced the receiver and looked up at Jennifer. "The bridge at New Canaan is swarming with cops."

Jennifer could feel the relief flooding through her body. It became a sense of exhilaration. Michael was watching her and she made an effort not to let her emotions show.

Jennifer asked, "What does that mean?"

Michael said slowly, "Nothing. Because that's not where Adam Warner is going to die."

62

The twin bridges of the Garden State Parkway were not named on the map. The Garden State Parkway crossed the Raritan River between the Amboys, splitting into the two bridges, one northbound and the other southbound.

The limousine was just west of Perth Amboy, heading toward the southbound bridge. Adam Warner was seated in back, with a secret service man beside him, and two secret service men in front.

Agent Clay Reddin had been assigned to the senator's guard detail six months earlier, and he had come to know Adam Warner well. He had always thought of him as an open, accessible man, but all day the senator had been strangely silent and withdrawn. *Deeply troubled* were the words that came to Agent Reddin. There was no question in his mind but that Senator Warner was going to be the next President of the United States, and it was Reddin's responsibility to see that nothing happened to him. He reviewed again the precautions that had been taken to safeguard the senator, and he was satisfied that nothing could go wrong.

Agent Reddin glanced again at the probable President-to-be, and wondered what he was thinking.

Adam Warner's mind was on the ordeal that was confronting him. He had been informed by Di Silva that Jennifer Parker had been arrested. The thought of her being locked away like an animal was anathema to him. His mind kept returning to the wonderful moments they had shared together. He had loved Jennifer as he had never loved another woman.

One of the secret service men in the front seat was saying, "We should be arriving in Atlantic City right on schedule, Mr. President."

Mr. President. That phrase again. According to all the latest polls, he was far ahead. He was the country's new folk hero, and Adam knew it was due in no small measure to the crime investigation he had headed, the investigation that would destroy Jennifer Parker.

Adam glanced up and saw that they were approaching the twin bridges. There was a side road just before the bridge and a huge semi-trailer truck was stopped at the entrance on the opposite side of the road. As the limousine neared the bridge, the truck started to pull out, so that the two vehicles arrived at the bridge at the same time.

The secret service driver applied his brakes and slowed down. "Look at that idiot."

The shortwave radio crackled into life. "Beacon One! Come in, Beacon One!"

The agent in the front seat next to the driver picked up the transmitter. "This is Beacon One."

The large truck was abreast of the limousine now as it started across the span. It was a behemoth, completely blocking out the view on the driver's side of the car. The limousine driver started to speed up to get ahead of it, but the truck simultaneously increased its speed.

"What the hell does he think he's doing?" the driver muttered,

"We've had an urgent call from the District Attorney's office. Fox One is in danger! Do you read me?"

Without warning, the truck veered to the right, hitting the side of the limousine, forcing it against the bridge railing. In seconds, the three secret service men in the car had their guns out.

"Get down!"

Adam found himself pushed down onto the floor, while Agent Reddin shielded Adam's body. The secret service agents rolled down the

windows on the left side of the limousine, guns pointed. There was
nothing at which to shoot. The side of the huge semitrailer blotted out
everything. The driver was up ahead, out of sight. There was another
jolt and a grinding crash as the limousine was knocked into the railing
again. The driver swung the wheel to the left, fighting to keep the car on
the bridge, but the truck kept forcing him back. The cold Raritan River
swirled two hundred feet below them.

The secret service agent next to the driver had grabbed his radio microphone and was calling wildly into it, "This is Beacon One! Mayday!
Mayday! Come in all units!"

But everyone in the limousine knew that it was too late for anyone to
save them. The driver tried to stop the car, but the truck's huge fenders
were locked into it, sweeping the limousine along. It was only a matter
of seconds before the huge truck would edge them over the side of the
bridge. The agent driving the car tried evasive tactics, alternately using
the brake and the accelerator to slow down and speed up, but the truck
had the car cruelly pinned against the bridge railing. There was no room
for the car to maneuver. The truck blocked off any escape on the left
side, and on the right side the limousine was being pushed against the
iron railing of the bridge. The agent fought the wheel desperately as the
truck pressed hard into the limousine once again, and everyone in the car
could feel the bridge railing start to give way.

The truck was jamming harder now, forcing the limousine over the
side. Those in the car could feel the sudden list as the front wheels broke
through the railing and went over the edge of the bridge. The car was
teetering on the brink and each man, in his own way, prepared to die.

Adam felt no fear, only an ineffable sadness at the loss, the waste. It
was Jennifer he should have shared his life with, had children with—and
suddenly Adam knew, from somewhere deep within himself, that they
had had a child.

The limousine gave another lurch and Adam cried out once aloud at
the injustice of what had happened, what was happening.

From overhead came the roar of two police helicopters as they
swooped down out of the sky, and a moment later there was the sound of
machine guns. The semitrailer lurched and all motion suddenly stopped.
Adam and the others could hear the helicopters circling overhead. The

men remained motionless, knowing that the slightest movement could send the car over the bridge, into the waters below.

There was the distant scream of police sirens drawing nearer, and a few minutes later the sound of voices barking out commands. The engine of the truck roared into life again. Slowly, carefully, the truck moved, inching away from the trapped car, removing the pressure against it. The limousine tilted for one terrible instant, and then was still. A moment later, the truck had been backed out of the way and Adam and the others could see out of the left-hand windows.

There were half a dozen squad cars and uniformed policemen with drawn guns swarming over the bridge.

A police captain was at the side of the battered car.

"We'll never get the doors open," he said. "We're going to bring you out through the windows—real easy."

Adam was lifted out of the window first, slowly and carefully, so as not to upset the balance of the car and send it over the side. The three secret service men were next.

When all the men had been removed from the car, the police captain turned to Adam and asked, "Are you all right, sir?"

Adam turned to look at the car hanging over the edge of the bridge, and then at the dark water of the river far below.

"Yes," he said. "I'm all right."

MICHAEL MORETTI GLANCED up at the clock on the wall. "It's all over." He turned to face Jennifer. "Your boyfriend's in the river by now."

She was watching him, her face pale. "You can't—"

"Don't worry. You're going to have a fair trial." He turned to Gino Gallo. "Did you tell her that Adam Warner was going to be blown away in New Canaan?"

"Just like you told me, boss."

Michael looked at Jennifer. "The trial's over."

He rose to his feet and walked over to where Jennifer was sitting. He grabbed her blouse and pulled her to her feet.

"I loved you," he whispered. He hit her hard across the face. Jennifer did not flinch. He hit her again, harder, then a third time, and she fell to the floor.

"Get up. We're taking a trip."

Jennifer lay there, dizzy from the blows, trying to clear her head. Michael hauled her roughly to her feet.

"You want me to take care of her?" Gino Gallo asked.

"No. Bring the car around the back."

"Right, boss." He hurried out of the room.

Jennifer and Michael were alone.

"Why?" he asked. "We owned the world, and you threw it away. *Why?*"

She did not answer.

"You want me to fuck you once more for old times' sake?" Michael moved toward her and grabbed her arm. "Would you like that?" Jennifer did not respond. "You're never going to fuck anyone again, you hear? I'm going to put you in the river with your lover! You can keep each other company."

Gino Gallo came back into the room, his face white. "Boss! There's a—"

There was a crashing sound from outside the room. Michael dived for the gun in his desk drawer. He had it in his hand when the door burst open. Two federal agents came through the door, guns drawn.

"Freeze!"

In that split second, Michael made his decision. He raised the gun and turned and fired at Jennifer. He saw the bullets go into her a second before the agents started shooting. He watched the blood spurt out of her chest, then he felt a bullet tear into him, and then another. He saw Jennifer lying on the floor, and Michael did not know which was the greater agony, her death or his. He felt the hammer blow of another bullet, and then he felt nothing.

63

T wo interns were wheeling Jennifer out of the operating room and into Intensive Care. A uniformed policeman followed at Jennifer's side. The hospital corridor was a bedlam of policemen, detectives and reporters.

A man walked up to the reception desk and said, "I want to see Jennifer Parker."

"Are you a member of her family?"

"No. I'm a friend."

"I'm sorry. No visitors. She's in Intensive Care."

"I'll wait."

"It could be a long time."

"That doesn't matter," Ken Bailey said.

A SIDE DOOR opened and Adam Warner, gaunt and haggard, entered, flanked by a team of secret service men.

A doctor was waiting to greet him. "This way, Senator Warner." He led Adam into a small office.

"How is she?" Adam asked.

"I'm not optimistic. We removed three bullets from her."

The door opened and District Attorney Robert Di Silva hurried in. He looked at Adam Warner and said, "I'm sure glad you're okay."

Adam said, "I understand I owe my thanks to you. How did you know?"

"Jennifer Parker called me. She told me they were setting you up in New Canaan. I figured it was probably some kind of diversionary ploy, but I couldn't take a chance, so I covered it. Meanwhile, I got hold of the route you were taking and we sent some choppers after you to protect you. My hunch is that Parker tried to set you up."

"No," Adam said. "No."

Robert Di Silva shrugged. "Have it your way, Senator. The important thing is that you're alive." As an afterthought he turned to the doctor. "Is she going to live?"

"Her chances are not very good."

The District Attorney saw the look on Adam Warner's face and misinterpreted it. "Don't worry. If she makes it, we've got her nailed down tight."

He looked at Adam more closely. "You look like hell. Why don't you go home and get some rest?"

"I want to see Jennifer Parker first."

The doctor said, "She's in a coma. She may not come out of it."

"I would like to see her, please."

"Of course, Senator. This way."

The doctor led the way out of the room, with Adam following and Di Silva behind him. They walked a few feet down the corridor to a sign that said INTENSIVE CARE UNIT—KEEP OUT.

The doctor opened the door and held it for the two men. "She's in the first room."

There was a policeman in front of the door, guarding it. He came to attention as he saw the District Attorney.

"No one gets near that room without written authorization from me. You understand?" Di Silva asked.

"Yes, sir."

Adam and Di Silva walked into the room. There were three beds, two of them empty. Jennifer lay in the third, tubes running into her nostrils and wrists. Adam moved close to the bed and stared down at her. Jennifer's face was very pale against the white pillows, and her eyes were closed. In repose, her face seemed younger and softer. Adam was looking at the innocent girl he had met years ago, the girl who had said angrily to him, *If anyone had paid me off, do you think I'd be living in a place like this? I don't care what you do. All I want is to be left alone.* He remembered her courage and idealism and her vulnerability. She had been on the side of the angels, believing in justice and willing to fight for it. What had gone wrong? He had loved her and he loved her still, and he had made one wrong choice that had poisoned all their lives, and he knew he would never feel free of guilt for as long as he lived.

He turned to the doctor. "Let me know when she—" He could not say the words. "—what happens."

"Of course," the doctor said.

Adam Warner took one long last look at Jennifer and said a silent good-bye. Then he turned and walked out to face the waiting reporters.

THROUGH A DIM, misty haze of semiconsciousness, Jennifer heard the men leave. She had not understood what they were saying, for their words were blurred by the pain that gripped her. She thought she had heard Adam's voice, but she knew that could not be. He was dead. She tried to open her eyes, but the effort was too great.

Jennifer's thoughts began to drift . . . Abraham Wilson came running into the room carrying a box. He stumbled and the box opened and a yellow canary flew out of it . . . Robert Di Silva was screaming, *Catch it! Don't let it get away!* . . . and Michael Moretti was holding it and laughing, and Father Ryan said, *Look, everybody! It's a miracle!* and Connie Garrett was dancing around the room and everyone applauded . . . Mrs. Cooper said, *I'm going to give you Wyoming . . . Wyoming . . . Wyoming . . .* and Adam came in with dozens of red roses and Michael said, *They're from me,* and Jennifer said, *I'll put them in a vase in water,* and they shriveled and died and the water spilled onto the floor and became a lake, and she and Adam were sailing, and Michael was chasing them on water skis and he became Joshua and he smiled at Jennifer and waved and started to lose his balance, and she screamed,

Don't fall . . . Don't fall . . . Don't fall . . . and an enormous wave swept Joshua into the air and he held out his arms like Jesus and disappeared.

For an instant, Jennifer's mind cleared.

Joshua was gone.

Adam was gone.

Michael was gone.

She was alone. In the end, everyone was alone. Each person had to die his own death. It would be easy to die now.

A feeling of blessed peace began to steal over her. Soon there was no more pain.

64

It was a cold January day in the Capitol when Adam Warner was sworn in as the fortieth President of the United States. His wife wore a sable hat and a dark sable coat that did wonderful things for her pale complexion and almost concealed her pregnancy. She stood next to her daughter and they both watched proudly as Adam took the oath of office, and the country rejoiced for the three of them. They were the best of America: decent and honest and good, and they belonged in the White House.

IN A SMALL law office in Kelso, Washington, Jennifer Parker sat alone looking at the inauguration on television. She watched until the last of the ceremony was over and Adam and Mary Beth and Samantha had left the podium, surrounded by secret service men. Then Jennifer turned off the television set and watched the images fade into nothingness. And it was like turning off the past: shutting out all that had happened to her, the love and the death and the joy and the pain. Nothing had been able to destroy her. She was a survivor.

She put on her hat and coat and walked outside, pausing for a moment to look at the sign that said: *Jennifer Parker, Attorney at Law.* She thought for an instant of the jury that had acquitted her. She was still a lawyer, as her father had been a lawyer. And she would go on, searching for the elusive thing called justice. She turned and headed in the direction of the courthouse.

Jennifer walked slowly down the deserted, windswept street. A light snow had begun to fall, casting a chiffon veil over the world. From an apartment building nearby there came a sudden burst of merriment, and it was such an alien sound that she stopped for a moment to listen. She pulled her coat tighter about her and moved on down the street, peering into the curtain of snow ahead, as though she were trying to see into the future,

But she was looking into the past, trying to understand when it was that all the laughter died.

BLOODLINE

"The physician will carefully prepare a mixture of crocodile dung, lizard flesh, bat's blood and camel's spit . . ."

—FROM A PAPYRUS LISTING
811 PRESCRIPTIONS USED
BY THE EGYPTIANS IN 1550 B.C.

BOOK ONE

I

ISTANBUL.
SATURDAY, SEPTEMBER 5.
TEN P.M.

He was seated in the dark, alone, behind the desk of Hajib Kafir, staring unseeingly out of the dusty office window at the timeless minarets of Istanbul. He was a man who was at home in a dozen capitals of the world, but Istanbul was one of his favorite cities. Not the tourist Istanbul of Beyoglu Street, or the gaudy Lalezab Bar of the Hilton, but the out-of-the-way places that only the Moslems knew: the *yalis,* and the small markets beyond the *souks,* and the Telli Baba, the cemetery where only one person was buried, and the people came to pray to him.

His waiting had the patience of a hunter, the quiet stillness of a man in control of his body and his emotions. He was Welsh, with the dark, stormy good looks of his ancestors. He had black hair and a strong face, and quick intelligent eyes that were a deep blue. He was over six feet tall, with the lean muscular body of a man who kept himself in good physical condition. The office was filled with the odors of Hajib Kafir, his sickly sweet tobacco, his acrid Turkish coffee, his fat, oily body. Rhys Williams was unaware of them. He was thinking about the telephone call he had received from Chamonix an hour earlier.

". . . A terrible accident! Believe me, Mr. Williams, we are all devastated. It happened so quickly that there was no chance to save him. Mr. Roffe was killed instantly . . ."

Sam Roffe, president of Roffe and Sons, the second largest pharmaceutical company in the world, a multibillion-dollar dynasty that girdled the globe. It was impossible to think of Sam Roffe as being dead. He had always been so vital, so full of life and energy, a man on the move, living in airplanes that raced him to company factories and offices all over the world, where he solved problems others could not deal with, created new concepts, pushed everyone to do more, to do better. Even though he had married, and fathered a child, his only real interest had been the business. Sam Roffe had been a brilliant and extraordinary man. Who could replace him? Who was capable of running the enormous empire he had left? Sam Roffe had not chosen an heir apparent. But then, he had not planned to die at fifty-two. He had thought there would be plenty of time.

And now his time had run out.

The lights in the office suddenly flashed on and Rhys Williams looked toward the doorway, momentarily blinded.

"Mr. Williams! I did not know anyone was here."

It was Sophie, one of the company secretaries, who was assigned to Rhys Williams whenever he was in Istanbul. She was Turkish, in her middle twenties, with an attractive face and a lithe, sensuous body, rich with promise. She had let Rhys know in subtle, ancient ways that she was available to bring him whatever pleasures he wished, whenever he desired them, but Rhys was not interested.

Now she said, "I returned to finish some letters for Mr. Kafir." She added softly, "Perhaps there is something I can do for you?"

As she moved closer to the desk, Rhys could sense the musky smell of a wild animal in season.

"Where is Mr. Kafir?"

Sophie shook her head regretfully. "He has left for the day." She smoothed the front of her dress with the palms of soft, clever hands. "Can I help you in some way?" Her eyes were dark and moist.

"Yes," Rhys said. "Find him."

She frowned. "I have no idea where he could—"

"Try the Kervansaray, or the Mermara." It would probably be the former, where one of Hajib Kafir's mistresses worked as a belly dancer. Although you never knew with Kafir, Rhys thought. He might even be with his wife.

Sophie was apologetic. "I will try, but I am afraid I—"

"Explain to him that if he's not here in one hour, he no longer has a job."

The expression on her face changed. "I will see what I can do, Mr. Williams." She started toward the door.

"Turn out the lights."

SOMEHOW, IT WAS easier to sit in the dark with his thoughts. The image of Sam Roffe kept intruding. Mont Blanc should have been an easy climb this time of the year, early September. Sam had tried the climb before, but storms had kept him from reaching the peak.

"I'll plant the company flag up there this time," he had promised Rhys, jokingly.

And then the telephone call a short while ago as Rhys was checking out of the Pera Palace. He could hear the agitated voice on the telephone. ". . . .They were doing a traverse over a glacier. . . . Mr. Roffe lost his footing and his rope broke. . . . He fell into a bottomless crevasse . . ."

Rhys could visualize Sam's body smashing against the unforgiving ice, hurtling downward into the crevasse. He forced his mind away from the scene. That was the past. There was the present to worry about now. The members of Sam Roffe's family had to be notified of his death, and they were scattered in various parts of the world. A press announcement had to be prepared. The news was going to travel through international financial circles like a shock wave. With the company in the midst of a financial crisis, it was vital that the impact of Sam Roffe's death be minimized as much as possible. That would be Rhys's job.

Rhys Williams had first met Sam Roffe nine years earlier. Rhys, then twenty-five, had been sales manager for a small drug firm. He was brilliant and innovative, and as the company had expanded, Rhys's reputation had quickly spread. He was offered a job at Roffe and Sons and when he turned it down, Sam Roffe bought the company Rhys worked for and sent for him. Even now he could recall the overwhelming power of Sam Roffe's presence at their first meeting.

"You belong here at Roffe and Sons," Sam Roffe had informed him. "That's why I bought that horse-and-buggy outfit you were with."

Rhys had found himself flattered and irritated at the same time. "Suppose I don't want to stay?"

Sam Roffe had smiled and said confidently, "You'll want to stay. You and I have something in common, Rhys. We're both ambitious. We want to own the world. I'm going to show you how."

The words were magic, a promised feast for the fierce hunger that burned in the young man, for he knew something that Sam Roffe did not: There was no Rhys Williams. He was a myth that had been created out of desperation and poverty and despair.

HE HAD BEEN born near the coalfields of Gwent and Carmarthen, the red scarred valleys of Wales where layers of sandstone and saucer-shaped beds of limestone and coal puckered the green earth. He grew up in a fabled land where the very names were poetry: Brecon and Pen-y Fan and Penderyn and Glyncorrwg and Maesteg. It was a land of legend, where the coal buried deep in the ground had been created 280 million years before, where the landscape was once covered with so many trees that a squirrel could travel from Brecon Beacons to the sea without ever touching the ground. But the industrial revolution had come along and the beautiful green trees were chopped down by the charcoal burners to feed the insatiable fires of the iron industry.

The young boy grew up with the heroes of another time and another world. Robert Farrer, burned at the stake by the Roman Catholic Church because he would not take a vow of celibacy and abandon his wife; King Hywel the Good, who brought the law to Wales in the tenth century; the fierce warrior Brychen, who sired twelve sons and twenty-four daughters and savagely put down all attacks on his kingdom. It was a land of glorious histories in which the lad had been raised. But it was not all glory. Rhys's ancestors were miners, every one of them, and the young boy used to listen to the tales of hell that his father and his uncles recounted. They talked of the terrible times when there was no work, when the rich coalfields of Gwent and Carmarthen had been closed in a bitter fight between the companies and the miners, and the miners were debased by a poverty that eroded ambition and pride, that sapped a man's spirit and strength and finally made him surrender.

When the mines were open, it was another kind of hell. Most of Rhys's family had died in the mines. Some had perished in the bowels of the earth, others had coughed their blackened lungs away. Few had lived past the age of thirty.

Rhys used to listen to his father and his aging young uncles discussing the past, the cave-ins and the cripplings and the strikes; talking of the good times and the bad, and to the young boy they seemed the same. All bad. The thought of spending his years in the darkness of the earth appalled Rhys. He knew he had to escape.

He ran away from home when he was twelve. He left the valleys of coal and went to the coast, to Sully Ranny Bay and Lavernock, where the rich tourists flocked, and the young boy fetched and carried and made himself useful, helping ladies down the steep cliffs to the beach, lugging heavy picnic baskets, driving a pony cart at Penarth, and working at the amusement park at Whitmore Bay.

He was only a few hours away from home, but the distance could not be measured. The people here were from another world. Rhys Williams had never imagined such beautiful people or such glorious finery. Each woman looked like a queen to him and the men were all elegant and splendid. This was the world where he belonged, and there was nothing he would not do to make it his.

By the time Rhys Williams was fourteen, he had saved enough money to pay for his passage to London. He spent the first three days simply walking around the huge city, staring at everything, hungrily drinking in the incredible sights and the sounds and the smells.

His first job was as a delivery boy at a draper's shop. There were two male clerks, superior beings both, and a female clerk, who made the young Welsh boy's heart sing every time he looked at her. The men treated Rhys as he was meant to be treated, like dirt. He was a curiosity. He dressed peculiarly, had abominable manners and spoke with an incomprehensible accent. They could not even pronounce his name. They called him Rice, and Rye, and Rise. "It's pronounced Reese," Rhys kept telling them.

The girl took pity on him. Her name was Gladys Simpkins and she shared a tiny flat in Tooting with three other girls. One day she allowed the young boy to walk her home after work and invited him in for a cup of tea. Young Rhys was overcome with nervousness. He had thought this was going to be his first sexual experience, but when he began to put his arm around Gladys, she stared at him a moment, then laughed. "I'm not giving none of that to you," she said. "But I'll give you some advice. If you want to make somethin' of yourself, get yourself some proper clothes and a bit of education and learn yourself some manners." She studied the thin, passionate young face and looked into Rhys's deep blue eyes, and said softly, "You're gonna be a bit of all right when you grow up."

IF YOU WANT *to make somethin' of yourself*. . . That was the moment when the fictitious Rhys Williams was born. The real Rhys Williams was an uneducated, ignorant boy with no background, no breeding, no past, no future. But he had imagination, intelligence and a fiery ambition. It was enough. He started with the image of what he wanted to be, who he intended to be. When he looked in his mirror, he did not see the clumsy, grubby little boy with a funny accent; his mirror image was polished and suave and successful. Little by little, Rhys began to match himself to the image in his mind. He attended night school, and he spent his weekends in art galleries. He haunted public libraries and went to the theater, sitting in the gallery, studying the fine clothes of the men seated in the stalls. He scrimped on food, so that once a month he could go to a good restaurant, where he carefully copied the table manners of others. He observed and learned and remembered. He was like a sponge, erasing the past, soaking up the future.

In one short year Rhys had learned enough to realize that Gladys Simpkins, his princess, was a cheap Cockney girl who was already beneath his tastes. He quit the draper's shop and went to work as a clerk at a chemist's shop that was part of a large chain. He was almost sixteen now, but he looked older. He had filled out and was taller. Women were beginning to pay attention to his dark Welsh good looks and his quick, flattering tongue. He was an instant success in the shop. Female customers would wait until Rhys was available to take care of them. He dressed well and spoke correctly, and he knew he had come a long way from

Gwent and Carmarthen, but when he looked in the mirror, he was still not satisfied. The journey he intended to make was still ahead of him.

Within two years Rhys Williams was made manager of the shop where he worked. The district manager of the chain said to Rhys, "This is just the beginning, Williams. Work hard and one day you'll be the superintendent of half a dozen stores."

Rhys almost laughed aloud. To think that that could be the height of anyone's ambition! Rhys had never stopped going to school. He was studying business administration and marketing and commercial law. He wanted more. His image in the mirror was at the top of the ladder; Rhys felt he was still at the bottom. His opportunity to move up came when a drug salesman walked in one day, watched Rhys charm several ladies into buying products they had no use for, and said, "You're wasting your time here, lad. You should be working in a bigger pond."

"What did you have in mind?" Rhys asked.

"Let me talk to my boss about you."

Two weeks later Rhys was working as a salesman at the small drug firm. He was one of fifty salesmen, but when Rhys looked in his special mirror, he knew that that was not true. His only competition was himself. He was getting closer to his image now, closer to the fictitious character he was creating. A man who was intelligent, cultured, sophisticated and charming. What he was trying to do was impossible. Everyone knew that one had to be born with those qualities; they could not be created. But Rhys did it. He became the image he had envisioned.

He traveled around the country, selling the firm's products, talking and listening. He would return to London full of practical suggestions, and he quickly began to move up the ladder.

Three years after he had joined the company, Rhys was made general sales manager. Under his skillful guidance the company began to expand.

AND FOUR YEARS later, Sam Roffe had come into his life. He had recognized the hunger in Rhys.

"You're like me," Sam Roffe had said. "We want to own the world. I'm going to show you how." And he had.

Sam Roffe had been a brilliant mentor. Over the next nine years under Sam Roffe's tutelage, Rhys Williams had become invaluable to the company. As time went on, he was given more and more responsibility, reorganizing various divisions, troubleshooting in whatever part of the world he was needed, coordinating the different branches of Roffe and Sons, creating new concepts. In the end Rhys knew more about running the company than anyone except Sam Roffe himself. Rhys Williams was the logical successor to the presidency. One morning, when Rhys and Sam Roffe were returning from Caracas in a company jet, a luxurious converted Boeing 707-320, one of a fleet of eight planes, Sam Roffe had complimented Rhys on a lucrative deal that he had concluded with the Venezuelan government.

"There'll be a fat bonus in this for you, Rhys."

Rhys had replied quietly, "I don't want a bonus, Sam. I'd prefer some stock and a place on your board of directors."

He had earned it, and both men were aware of it. But Sam had said, "I'm sorry. I can't change the rules, even for you. Roffe and Sons is a privately held company. No one outside of the family can sit on the board or hold stock."

Rhys had known that, of course. He attended all board meetings, but not as a member. He was an outsider. Sam Roffe was the last male in the Roffe bloodline. The other Roffes, Sam's cousins, were females. The men they had married sat on the board of the company. Walther Gassner, who had married Anna Roffe; Ivo Palazzi, married to Simonetta Roffe; Charles Martel, married to Hélène Roffe. And Sir Alec Nichols, whose mother had been a Roffe.

So Rhys had been forced to make a decision. He knew that he deserved to be on the board, that one day he should be running the company. Present circumstances prevented it, but circumstances had a way of changing. Rhys had decided to stay, to wait and see what happened. Sam had taught him patience. And now Sam was dead.

THE OFFICE LIGHTS blazed on again, and Hajib Kafir stood in the doorway. Kafir was the Turkish sales manager for Roffe and Sons. He was a shorty, swarthy man who wore diamonds and his fat belly like proud ornaments. He had the disheveled air of a man who had dressed hastily. So Sophie had not found him in a nightclub. Ah, well, Rhys thought. A side effect of Sam Roffe's death. Coitus interruptus.

"Rhys!" Kafir was exclaiming. "My dear fellow, forgive me! I had no idea you were still in Istanbul! You were on your way to catch a plane, and I had some urgent business to—"

"Sit down, Hajib. Listen carefully. I want you to send four cables in company code. They're going to different countries. I want them hand-delivered by our own messengers. Do you understand?"

"Of course," Kafir said, bewildered. "Perfectly."

Rhys glanced at the thin, gold Baume & Mercier watch on his wrist. "The New City Post Office will be closed. Send the cables from Yeni Posthane Cad. I want them on their way within thirty minutes." He handed Kafir a copy of the cable he had written out. "Anyone who discusses this will be instantly discharged."

Kafir glanced at the cable and his eyes widened. "My God!" he said. "Oh, my God!" He looked up at Rhys's dark face. "How—how did this terrible thing happen?"

"Sam Roffe died in an accident," Rhys said.

Now, for the first time, Rhys allowed his thoughts to go to what he had been pushing away from his consciousness, what he had been try-ing to avoid thinking about: Elizabeth Roffe, Sam's daughter. She was twenty-four now. When Rhys had first met her, she had been a fifteen-year-old girl with braces on her teeth, fiercely shy and overweight, a lonely rebel. Over the years Rhys had watched Elizabeth develop into a very special young woman, with her mother's beauty and her father's intelligence and spirit. She had become close to Sam. Rhys knew how deeply the news would affect her. He would have to tell her himself.

Two hours later, Rhys Williams was over the Mediterranean on a company jet, headed for New York.

2

BERLIN.
MONDAY, SEPTEMBER 7.
TEN A.M.

Anna Roffe Gassner knew that she must not let herself scream again or Walther would return and kill her. She crouched in a corner of her bedroom, her body trembling uncontrollably, waiting for death. What had started out as a beautiful fairy tale had ended in terror, unspeakable horror. It had taken her too long to face the truth: the man she had married was a homicidal maniac.

ANNA ROFFE HAD never loved anyone before she met Walther Gassner, including her mother, her father and herself. Anna had been a frail, sickly child who suffered from fainting spells. She could not remember a time when she had been free of hospitals or nurses or specialists flown in from far-off places. Because her father was Anton Roffe, of Roffe and Sons, the top medical experts flew to Anna's bedside in Berlin. But when they had examined her and tested her and finally departed, they knew no more than they had known before. They could not diagnose her condition.

Anna was unable to go to school like other children, and in time she had become withdrawn, creating a world of her own, full of dreams and fantasies, where no one else was allowed to enter. She painted her own pictures of life, because the colors of reality were too harsh for her to accept. When Anna was eighteen, her dizziness and fainting spells disappeared as mysteriously as they had started. But they had marred her life. At an age when most girls were getting engaged or married, Anna had never even been kissed by a boy. She insisted to herself that she did not mind. She was content to live her own dream life, apart from everything and everyone. In her middle twenties suitors came calling, for Anna Roffe was an heiress who bore one of the most prestigious names in the world, and many men were eager to share her fortune. She received proposals from a Swedish count, an Italian poet and half a dozen princes from indigent countries. Anna refused them all. On his daughter's thirtieth birthday, Anton Roffe moaned, "I'm going to die without leaving any grandchildren."

On her thirty-fifth birthday Anna had gone to Kitzbühel, in Austria, and there she had met Walther Gassner, a ski instructor thirteen years younger than she.

The first time Anna had seen Walther, the sight of him had literally taken her breath away. He was skiing down the *Hahnenkamm,* the steep racing slope, and it was the most beautiful sight Anna had ever seen. She had moved closer to the bottom of the ski run to get a better look at him. He was like a young god, and Anna had been satisfied to do nothing but watch him. He had caught her staring at him.

"Aren't you skiing, *gnädiges Fräulein?*"

She had shaken her head, not trusting her voice, and he had smiled and said, "Then let me buy you lunch."

Anna had fled in a panic, like a schoolgirl. From then on, Walther Gassner had pursued her. Anna Roffe was not a fool. She was aware that she was neither pretty nor brilliant, that she was a plain woman, and that, aside from her name, she had seemingly very little to offer a man. But Anna knew that trapped within that ordinary facade was a beautiful, sensitive girl filled with love and poetry and music.

Perhaps because Anna was not beautiful, she had a deep reverence for beauty. She would go to the great museums and spend hours staring at the paintings and the statues. When she had seen Walther Gassner it was as though all the gods had come alive for her.

Anna was having breakfast on the terrace of the Tennerhof Hotel on the second day when Walther Gassner joined her. He did look like a young god. He had a regular, clean-cut profile, and his features were delicate, sensitive, strong. His face was deeply tanned and his teeth were white and even. He had blond hair and his eyes were a slate gray. Beneath his ski clothes Anna could see the movement of his biceps and thigh muscles, and she felt tremors going through her loins. She hid her hands in her lap so that he could not see the keratosis.

"I looked for you on the slopes yesterday afternoon," Walther said. Anna could not speak. "If you don't ski, I'd like to teach you." He smiled, and added, "No charge."

He had taken her to the *Hausberg,* the beginner's slope, for her first lesson. It was immediately apparent to them both that Anna had no talent for skiing. She kept losing her balance and falling down, but she insisted on trying again and again because she was afraid that Walther would despise her if she failed. Instead, he had picked her up after her tenth fall and had said gently, "You were meant to do better things than this."

"What things?" Anna had asked, miserable.

"I'll tell you at dinner tonight."

They had dined that evening and breakfasted the next morning, and then had lunch and dinner again. Walther neglected his clients. He skipped skiing lessons in order to go into the village with Anna. He took her to the casino in Der Goldene Greif, and they went sleigh riding and shopping and hiking, and sat on the terrace of the hotel hour after hour, talking. For Anna, it was a time of magic.

Five days after they had met, Walther took her hands in his and said, "Anna, *liebchen,* I want to marry you."

He had spoiled it. He had taken her out of her wonderful fairyland and brought her back to the cruel reality of who and what she was. An unattractive, thirty-five-year-old virginal prize for fortune hunters.

She had tried to leave but Walther had stopped her. "We love each other, Anna. You can't run away from that."

She listened to him lying, listened to him saying, "I've never loved anyone before," and she made it easy for him because she wanted so desperately to believe him. She took him back to her room, and they sat there, talking, and as Walther told Anna the story of his life, she suddenly began to believe, thinking with wonder, It is really the story of my own life.

Like her, Walther had never had anyone to love. He had been alienated from the world by his birth as a bastard, as Anna had been alienated by her illness. Like her, Walther had been filled with the need to give love. He had been brought up in an orphanage, and when he was thirteen and his extraordinary good looks were already apparent, the women in the orphanage had begun to use him, bringing him to their rooms at night, taking him to bed with them, teaching him how to please them. As a reward the young boy was given extra food and pieces of meat, and desserts made with real sugar. He received everything but love.

When Walther was old enough to run away from the orphanage, he found that the world outside was no different. Women wanted to use his good looks, to wear him as a badge; but it never went any deeper than that. They gave him gifts of money and clothes and jewelry, but never of themselves.

Walther was her soul mate, Anna realized, her doppelgänger. They were married in a quiet ceremony at the town hall.

ANNA HAD EXPECTED her father to be overjoyed. Instead, he had flown into a rage. "You're a silly, vain fool," Anton Roffe screamed at her. "You've married a no-good fortune hunter. I've had him checked out. All his life he's lived off women, but he's never found anyone stupid enough to marry him before."

"Stop it!" Anna cried. "You don't understand him."

But Anton Roffe knew that he understood Walther Gassner only too well. He asked his new son-in-law to come to his office.

Walther looked around approvingly at the dark paneling and the old paintings hanging on the walls. "I like this place," Walther said.

"Yes. I'm sure it's better than the orphanage."

Walther looked up at him sharply, his eyes suddenly wary. "I beg your pardon?"

Anton said, "Let's cut out the *Scheiss*. You've made a mistake. My daughter has no money."

Walther's gray eyes seemed to turn to stone. "What are you trying to tell me?"

"I'm not trying to tell you anything. I'm telling you. You won't get anything from Anna because she hasn't got anything. If you had done your homework more thoroughly, you would have learned that Roffe and Sons is a close-held corporation. That means that none of its stock can be sold. We live comfortably, but that's it. There is no big fortune to be milked here." He rumbled in his pocket, drew out an envelope and threw it on the desk in front of Walther. "This will reimburse you for your trouble. I will expect you to be out of Berlin by six o'clock. I don't want Anna ever to hear from you again."

Walther said quietly, "Did it ever cross your mind that I might have married Anna because I fell in love with her?"

"No," Anton said acidly. "Did it ever cross yours?"

Walther looked at him a moment. "Let's see what my market price is." He tore open the envelope and counted the money. He looked up at Anton Roffe again. "I value myself at much higher than twenty thousand marks."

"It's all you're getting. Count yourself lucky."

"I do," Walther said. "If you want to know the truth, I think I am very lucky. Thank you." He put the money in his pocket with a careless gesture and a moment later was walking out the door.

Anton Roffe was relieved. He experienced a slight sense of guilt and distaste for what he had done and yet he knew it had been the only solution. Anna would be unhappy at being deserted by her groom, but it was better to have it happen now than later. He would try to see to it that she met some eligible men her own age, who would at least respect her if not love her. Someone who would be interested in her and not her money or her name. Someone who would not be bought for twenty thousand marks.

When Anton Roffe arrived home, Anna ran up to greet him, tears in her eyes. He took her in his arms and hugged her, and said, "Anna, *liebchen,* it's going to be all right. You'll get over him—"

And Anton looked over her shoulder, and standing in the doorway was Walther Gassner. Anna was holding up her finger, saying, "Look what Walther bought me! Isn't it the most beautiful ring you've ever seen? It cost twenty thousand marks."

In the end, Anna's parents were forced to accept Walther Gassner. As a wedding gift they bought them a lovely Schinkel manor house in Wann-see, with French furniture, mixed with antiques, comfortable couches and easy chairs, a Roentgen desk in the library, and bookcases lining the walls. The upstairs was furnished with elegant eighteenth century pieces from Denmark and Sweden.

"It's too much," Walther told Anna. "I don't want anything from them or from you. I want to be able to buy you beautiful things, *lieb-chen.*" He gave her that boyish grin and said, "But I have no money."

"Of course you do," Anna replied. "Everything I have belongs to you."

Walther smiled at her sweetly and said, "Does it?"

At Anna's insistence—for Walther seemed reluctant to discuss money—she explained her financial situation to him. She had a trust fund that was enough for her to live on comfortably, but the bulk of her fortune was in shares of Roffe and Sons. The shares could not be sold without the unanimous approval of the board of directors.

"How much is your stock worth?" Walther asked.

Anna told him. Walther could not believe it. He made her repeat the sum.

"And you can't sell the stock?"

"No. My cousin Sam won't let it be sold. He holds the controlling shares. One day . . ."

Walther expressed an interest in working in the family business. Anton Roffe was against it.

"What can a ski bum contribute to Roffe and Sons?" he asked.

But in the end he gave in to his daughter, and Walther was given a job with the company in administration. He proved to be excellent at it and advanced rapidly. When Anna's father died two years later, Walther Gassner was made a member of the board. Anna was so proud of him. He was the perfect husband and lover. He was always bringing her flow-ers and little gifts, and he seemed content to stay at home with her in the evening, just the two of them. Anna's happiness was almost too much for her to bear. *Ach, danke, lieber Gott,* she would say silently.

Anna learned to cook, so that she could make Walther's favorite dishes. She made *choucroute,* a bed of crunchy sauerkraut and creamy mashed potatoes heaped with a smoked pork chop, a frankfurter and a Nuremberg sausage. She prepared fillet of pork cooked in beer and flavored with cumin, and served it with a fat baked apple, cored and peeled, the center filled with *airelles,* the little red berries.

"You're the best cook in the world, *liebchen,*" Walther would say, and Anna would blush with pride.

In the third year of their marriage, Anna became pregnant.

There was a great deal of pain during the first eight months of her pregnancy, but Anna bore that happily. It was something else that worried her.

It started one day after lunch. She had been knitting a sweater for Walther, daydreaming, and suddenly she heard Walther's voice, saying, "My God, Anna, what are you doing, sitting here in the dark?"

The afternoon had turned to dusk, and she looked down at the sweater in her lap and she had not touched it. Where had the day gone? Where had her mind been? After that, Anna had other similar experiences, and she began to wonder whether this sliding away into nothingness was a portent, an omen that she was going to die. She did not think she was afraid of death, but she could not bear the thought of leaving Walther.

Four weeks before the baby was due, Anna lapsed into one of her daydreams, missed a step and fell down an entire flight of stairs.

She awakened in the hospital.

Walther was seated on the edge of the bed, holding her hand. "You gave me a terrible scare."

In a sudden panic she thought, The baby! I can't feel the baby. She reached down. Her stomach was flat. "Where is my baby?"

And Walther held her close and hugged her.

The doctor said, "You had twins, Mrs. Gassner."

Anna turned to Walther, and his eyes were filled with tears. "A boy and girl, *liebchen.*"

And she could have died right then of happiness. She felt a sudden, irresistible longing to have them in her arms. She had to see them, feel them, hold them.

"We'll talk about that when you're stronger," the doctor said. "Not until you're stronger."

. . .

THEY ASSURED ANNA that she was getting better every day, but she was becoming frightened. Something was happening to her that she did not understand. Walther would arrive and take her hand and say good-bye, and she would look at him in surprise and start to say, "But you just got here . . ." And then she would see the clock, and three or four hours would have passed.

She had no idea where they had gone.

She had a vague recollection that they had brought the children to her in the night and that she had fallen asleep. She could not remember too clearly, and she was afraid to ask. It did not matter. She would have them to herself when Walther took her home.

THE WONDERFUL DAY finally arrived. Anna left her hospital room in a wheelchair, even though she insisted she was strong enough to walk. She actually felt very weak, but she was so excited that nothing mattered except the fact that she was going to see her babies. Walther carried her into the house, and he started to take her upstairs to their bedroom.

"No, no!" she said. "Take me to the nursery."

"You must rest now, darling. You're not strong enough to—"

She did not listen to the rest of what he was saying. She slipped out of his arms and ran into the nursery.

The blinds were drawn and the room was dark and it took Anna's eyes a moment to adjust. She was filled with such excitement that it made her dizzy. She was afraid she was going to faint.

Walther had come in behind her. He was talking to her, trying to explain something, but whatever it was was unimportant.

For there they were. They were both asleep in their cribs, and Anna moved toward them softly, so as not to disturb them, and stood there, staring down at them. They were the most beautiful children she had ever seen. Even now, she could see that the boy would have Walther's handsome features and his thick blond hair. The girl was like an exquisite doll, with soft, golden hair and a small, triangular face.

Anna turned to Walther and said, her voice choked, "They're beautiful. I—I'm so happy."

"Come, Anna," Walther whispered. He put his arms around Anna, and held her close, and there was a fierce hunger in him, and she began to feel a stirring within her. They had not made love for such a long time. Walther was right. There would be plenty of time for the children later.

THE BOY SHE named Peter and the girl Birgitta. They were two beautiful miracles that she and Walther had made, and Anna would spend hour after hour in the nursery, playing with them, talking to them. Even though they could not understand her yet, she knew they could feel her love. Sometimes, in the middle of play, she would turn and Walther would be standing in the doorway, home from the office, and Anna would realize that somehow the whole day had slipped by.

"Come and join us," she would say. "We're playing a game."

"Have you fixed dinner yet?" Walther would ask, and she would suddenly feel guilty. She would resolve to pay more attention to Walther, and less to the children, but the next day the same thing would happen. The twins were like an irresistible magnet that drew her to them. Anna still loved Walther very much, and she tried to assuage her guilt by telling herself that the children were a part of him. Every night, as soon as Walther was asleep, Anna would slip out of bed and creep into the nursery, and sit and stare at the children until dawn started filtering into the room. Then she would turn and hurry back to bed before Walther awoke.

Once, in the middle of the night, Walther walked into the nursery and caught her. "What in God's name do you think you're doing?" he said.

"Nothing, darling. I was just—"

"Go back to bed!"

He had never spoken to her like that before.

At breakfast Walther said, "I think we should take a vacation. It will be good for us to get away."

"But, Walther, the children are too young to travel."

"I'm talking about the two of us."

She shook her head. "I couldn't leave them."

He took her hand and said, "I want you to forget about the children."

"Forget about the children?" There was shock in her voice.

He looked into her eyes and said, "Anna, remember how wonderful it was between us before you were pregnant? What good times we had? How much joy it was to be together, just the two of us, with no one else around to interfere?"

It was then that she understood. Walther was jealous of the children.

THE WEEKS AND months passed swiftly. Walther never went near the children now. On their birthdays Anna bought them lovely presents. Walther always managed to be out of town on business. Anna could not go on deceiving herself forever. The truth was that Walther had no interest in the children at all. Anna felt that perhaps it was her fault, because she was *too* interested in them. *Obsessed* was the word Walther had used. He had asked her to consult a doctor about it, and she had gone only to please Walther. But the doctor was a fool. The moment he had started talking to her, Anna had shut him out, letting her mind drift, until she heard him say, "Our time is up, Mrs. Gassner. Will I see you next week?"

"Of course."

She never returned.

Anna felt that the problem was as much Walther's as hers. If her fault lay in loving the children too much, then his fault lay in not loving them enough.

Anna learned not to mention the children in Walther's presence, but she could hardly wait for him to leave for the office, so she could hurry into the nursery to be with her babies. Except that they were no longer babies. They had had their third birthday, and already Anna could see what they would look like as adults. Peter was tall for his age and his body was strong and athletic, like his father's. Anna would hold him on her lap and croon, "Ah, Peter, what are you going to do to the poor fräuleins? Be gentle with them, my darling son. They won't have a chance."

And Peter would smile shyly and hug her.

Then Anna would turn to Birgitta. Birgitta grew prettier each day. She looked like neither Anna nor Walther. She had spun-golden hair and skin as delicate as porcelain. Peter had his father's fiery temper and sometimes it would be necessary for Anna to spank him gently, but Birgitta had the disposition of an angel. When Walther was not around, Anna played records or read to them. Their favorite book was *101 Märchens*. They would insist that Anna read them the tales of ogres and goblins and witches over and over again, and at night, Anna would put them to bed, singing them a lullaby:

Schlaf, Kindlein, schlaf,
Der Vater hüt't die Schaf . . .

Anna had prayed that time would soften Walther's attitude, that he would change. He did change, but for the worse. He hated the children. In the beginning Anna had told herself that it was because Walther wanted all of her love for himself, that he was unwilling to share it with anyone else. But slowly she became aware that it had nothing to do with loving her. It had to do with hating her. Her father had been right. Walther had married her for her money. The children were a threat to him. He wanted to get rid of them. More and more he talked to Anna about selling the stock. "Sam has no right to stop us! We could take all that money and go away somewhere. Just the two of us."

She stared at him. "What about the children?"

His eyes were feverish. "No. Listen to me. For both our sakes we've got to get rid of them. We must."

It was then that Anna began to realize that he was insane. She was terrified. Walther had fired all the domestic help, and except for a cleaning woman who came in once a week, Anna and the children were alone with him, at his mercy. He needed help. Perhaps it was not too late to cure him. In the fifteenth century they gathered the insane and imprisoned them forever on houseboats, *Narrenschiffe,* the ships of fools, but today, with modern medicine, she felt there must be something they could do to help Walther.

NOW, ON THIS day in September, Anna sat huddled on the floor in her bedroom, where Walther had locked her, waiting for him to return. She knew what she had to do. For his sake, as well as hers and the children's. Anna rose unsteadily and walked over to the telephone. She hesitated for only an instant, then picked it up and began to dial 110, the police emergency number.

An alien voice in her ear said, *"Hallo. Hier ist der Notruf der Polizei. Kann ich ihnen helfen?"*

"Ja, bitte!" Her voice was choked. *"Ich—"*

A hand came out of nowhere and tore the receiver from her, and slammed it down into the cradle.

Anna backed away. "Oh, please," she whimpered, "don't hurt me."

Walther was moving toward her, his eyes bright, his voice so soft that she could hardly make out the words. *"Liebchen,* I'm not going to hurt you. I love you, don't you know that?" He touched her, and she could feel her flesh crawl. "It's just that we don't want the police coming here, do we?" She shook her head from side to side, too filled with terror to speak. "It's the children that are causing the trouble, Anna. We're going to get rid of them. I—"

Downstairs the front doorbell rang. Walther stood there, hesitating. It rang again.

"Stay here," he ordered. "I'll be back."

Anna watched, petrified, as he walked out the bedroom door. He slammed it behind him and she could hear the click of the key as he locked it.

I'll be back, he had said.

Walther Gassner hurried down the stairs, walked to the front door and opened it. A man in a gray messenger's uniform stood there, holding a sealed manila envelope.

"I have a special delivery for Mr. and Mrs. Walther Gassner."

"Yes," Walther said. "I will take it."

He closed the door, looked at the envelope in his hand, then ripped it open. Slowly, he read the message inside.

Deeply regret to inform you that Sam Roffe was killed in a climbing accident. Please be in Zurich Friday noon for an emergency meeting of the Board of Directors.

It was signed "Rhys Williams."

3

ROME.

MONDAY, SEPTEMBER 7.

SIX P.M.

vo Palazzi stood in the middle of his bedroom, the blood streaming down his face. *"Mamma mia! Mi hai rovinato!"*

"I haven't begun to ruin you, you miserable *figlio di putana!*" Donatella screamed at him.

They were both naked in the large bedroom of their apartment in Via Montemignaio. Donatella had the most sensuous, exciting body Ivo Palazzi had ever seen, and even now, as his life's blood poured from his face, from the terrible scratches she had inflicted on him, he felt a familiar stirring in his loins. *Dio,* she was beautiful. There was an innocent decadence about her that drove him wild. She had the face of a leopard, high cheekbones and slant eyes, full ripe lips, lips that nibbled him and sucked him and—but he must not think of that now. He picked up a white cloth from a chair to stanch the flow of blood, and too late he realized that it was his shirt. Donatella was standing in the middle of their huge double bed, yelling at him. "I hope you bleed to death! When I've finished with you, you filthy whoremonger, there won't be enough left for a *gattino* to shit on!"

For the hundredth time Ivo Palazzi wondered how he had gotten himself into this impossible situation. He had always prided himself on being the happiest of men, and all his friends had agreed with him. His *friends? Everybody!* Because Ivo had no enemies. In his bachelor days he had been a happy-go-lucky Roman without a care in the world, a Don Giovanni who was the envy of half the males in Italy. His philosophy was summed up in the phrase *Farsi onore con una donna*—"Honor oneself with a woman." It kept Ivo very busy. He was a true romantic. He kept falling in love, and each time he used his new love to help him forget his old love. Ivo adored women, and to him they were all beautiful, from the *putane* who plied their ancient trade along the Via Appia, to the high-fashion models strutting along the Via Condotti. The only girls Ivo did not care for were the Americans. They were too independent for his taste. Besides, what could one expect of a nation whose language was so unromantic that they would translate the name of Giuseppe Verdi to Joe Green?

Ivo always managed to have a dozen girls in various states of preparation. There were five stages. In stage one were the girls he had just met. They received daily phone calls, flowers, slim volumes of erotic poetry. In stage two were those to whom he sent little gifts of Gucci scarves and porcelain boxes filled with Perugina chocolates. Those in stage three received jewelry and clothes and were taken to dinner at El Toula, or Taverna Flavia. Those in stage four shared Ivo's bed and enjoyed his formidable skills as a lover. An assignation with Ivo was a production. His beautifully decorated little apartment on the Via Margutta would be filled with flowers, *garofani* or *papaveri,* the music would be opera, classical or rock, according to the chosen girl's taste. Ivo was a superb cook, and one of his specialties, appropriately enough, was *pollo alla cacciatora,* chicken of the hunter. After dinner, a bottle of chilled champagne to drink in bed . . . Ah, yes, Ivo loved stage four.

But stage five was probably the most delicate of them all. It consisted of a heartbreaking farewell speech, a generous parting gift and a tearful *arrivederci.*

BUT ALL THAT was in the past. Now Ivo Palazzi took a quick glance at his bleeding, scratched face in the mirror over his bed and was horrified.

He looked as though he had been attacked by a mad threshing machine.

"Look at what you've done to me!" he cried. "*Cara,* I know you didn't mean it."

He moved over to the bed to take Donatella in his arms. Her soft arms flew around him and as he started to hug her, she buried her long fingernails in his naked back and clawed him like a wild animal. Ivo yelled with pain.

"Scream!" Donatella shouted. "If I had a knife, I'd cut your *cazzo* and ram it down your miserable throat."

"Please!" Ivo begged. "The children will hear you."

"Let them!" she shrieked. "It's time they found out what kind of monster their father is."

He took a step toward her. "*Carissima—*"

"Don't you touch me! I'd give my body to the first drunken syphilitic sailor I met on the streets before I'd ever let you come near me again."

Ivo drew himself up, his pride offended. "That is not the way I expect the mother of my children to talk to me."

"You want me to talk nice to you? You want me to stop treating you like the vermin you are?" Donatella's voice rose to a scream. "*Then give me what I want!*"

Ivo looked nervously toward the door. "*Carissima*—I can't. I don't have it."

"Then get it for me!" she cried. "You promised!"

She was beginning to get hysterical again, and Ivo decided the best thing for him to do was to get out of there quickly before the neighbors called the carabinieri again.

"It will take time to get a million dollars," he said soothingly. "But I'll—I'll find a way."

He hastily donned his undershorts and pants, and socks and shoes, while Donatella stormed around the room, her magnificent, firm breasts waving in the air, and Ivo thought to himself, My God, what a woman! How I adore her! He reached for his bloodstained shirt. There was no help for it. He put it on, feeling the cold stickiness against his back and chest. He took a last look in the mirror. Small pools of blood were still oozing from the deep gashes where Donatella had raked her fingernails across his face.

"Carissima," Ivo moaned, "how am I ever going to explain this to my wife?"

IVO PALAZZI'S WIFE was Simonetta Roffe, an heiress of the Italian branch of the Roffe family. Ivo had been a young architect when he had met Simonetta. His firm had sent him to supervise some changes in the Roffe villa at Porto Ercole. The instant Simonetta had set eyes on Ivo, his bachelor days were numbered. Ivo had gotten to the fourth stage with her on the first night, and found himself married to her a short time later. Simonetta was as determined as she was lovely, and she knew what she wanted: she wanted Ivo Palazzi. Thus it was that Ivo found himself transformed from a carefree bachelor to the husband of a beautiful young heiress. He gave up his architectural aspirations with no regrets and joined Roffe and Sons, with a magnificent office in EUR, the section of Rome started with such high hopes by the late, ill-fated Duce.

Ivo was a success with the firm from the beginning. He was intelligent, learned quickly, and everyone adored him. It was impossible not to adore Ivo. He was always smiling, always charming. His friends envied him his wonderful disposition and wondered how he did it. The answer was simple. Ivo kept the dark side of his nature buried. In fact, he was a deeply emotional man, capable of great volatile hatreds, capable of killing.

Ivo's marriage with Simonetta thrived. At first, be had feared that marriage would prove to be a bondage that would strangle his manhood to death, but his fears proved to be unfounded. He simply put himself on an austerity program, reducing the number of his girl friends, and everything went on as before.

Simonetta's father bought them a beautiful home in Olgiata, a large private estate twenty-five kilometers north of Rome, guarded by closed gates and manned by uniformed guards.

Simonetta was a wonderful wife. She loved Ivo and treated him like a king, which was no more than he felt he deserved. There was just one tiny flaw in Simonetta. When she became jealous, she turned into a savage. She had once suspected Ivo of taking a female buyer on a trip to

Brazil. He was righteously indignant at the accusation. Before the argument was over, their entire house was a shambles. Not one dish or piece of furniture was left intact, and much of it had been broken over Ivo's head. Simonetta had gone after him with a butcher knife, threatening to kill him and then herself, and it had taken all of Ivo's strength to wrest the knife from her. They had wound up fighting on the floor, and Ivo had finally torn off her clothes and made her forget her anger. But after that incident Ivo became very discreet. He had told the buyer he could not take any more trips with her, and he was careful never to let the faintest breath of suspicion touch him. He knew that he was the luckiest man in the world. Simonetta was young and beautiful and intelligent and rich. They enjoyed the same things and the same people. It was a perfect marriage, and Ivo sometimes found himself wondering, as he transferred a girl from stage two to stage three, and another from stage four to stage five, why he kept on being unfaithful. Then he would shrug philosophically and say to himself, Someone has to make these women happy.

IVO AND SIMONETTA had been married for three years when Ivo met Donatella Spolini on a business trip to Sicily. It was more of an explosion than a meeting, two planets coming together and colliding. Where Simonetta had the slender, sweet body of a young woman sculpted by Manzù, Donatella had the sensuous, ripe body of a Rubens. Her face was exquisite and her green, smoldering eyes set Ivo aflame. They were in bed one hour after they had met, and Ivo, who had always prided himself on his prowess as a lover, found that he was the pupil and Donatella the teacher. She made him rise to heights he had never achieved before, and her body did things to his that he had never dreamed possible. She was an endless cornucopia of pleasure, and as Ivo lay in bed, his eyes closed, savoring incredible sensations, he knew he would be a fool to let Donatella go.

And so Donatella had become Ivo's mistress. The only condition she imposed was that he had to get rid of all the other women in his life, except his wife. Ivo had happily agreed. That had been eight years ago, and in all that time Ivo had never been unfaithful to either his wife or his mistress. Satisfying two hungry women would have been enough to exhaust an ordinary man, but in Ivo's case it was exactly the opposite. When he made love to Simonetta he thought about Donatella and her ripe full body, and he was filled with lust. And when he made love to Donatella, he thought of Simonetta's sweet young breasts and tiny *culo* and he performed like a wild man. No matter which woman he was with, he felt that he was cheating on the other. It added enormously to his pleasure.

Ivo bought Donatella a beautiful apartment in Via Montemignaio, and he was with her every moment that he could manage. He would arrange to be away on a sudden business trip and, instead of leaving, he would spend the time in bed with Donatella. He would stop by to see her on his way to the office, and he would spend his afternoon siestas with her. Once, when Ivo sailed to New York on the *QE 2* with Simonetta, he installed Donatella in a cabin one deck below. They were the five most stimulating days of Ivo's life.

ON THE EVENING that Simonetta announced to Ivo that she was pregnant, Ivo was filled with an indescribable joy. A week later Donatella informed Ivo that *she* was pregnant, and Ivo's cup ranneth over. Why, he asked himself, are the gods so good to me? In all humility, Ivo sometimes felt that he did not deserve all the great pleasures that were being bestowed upon him.

In due course Simonetta gave birth to a girl and a week later Donatella gave birth to a boy. What more could any man ask? But the gods were not finished with Ivo. A short time later, Donatella informed Ivo that she was pregnant again, and the following week Simonetta also became pregnant. Nine months later, Donatella gave Ivo another son and Simonetta presented her husband with another daughter. Four months later, both women were pregnant again and this time they gave birth on the same day. Ivo frantically raced from the Salvator Mundi, where Simonetta was encouched, to the Clinica Santa Chiara, where Ivo had taken Donatella. He sped from hospital to hospital, driving on the Raccordo Anulare, waving to the girls sitting in front of their little tents along the sides of the road, under pink umbrellas, waiting for customers. Ivo was driving too fast to see their faces, but he loved them all and wished them well.

Donatella gave birth to another boy and Simonetta to another girl.

Sometimes Ivo wished it had been the other way around. It was ironical that his wife had borne him daughters and his mistress had borne him sons, for he would have liked male heirs to carry on his name. Still, he was a contented man. He had three children with outdoor plumbing, and three children with indoor plumbing. He adored them and he was wonderful to them, remembering their birthdays, their saints' days, and their names. The girls were called Isabella and Benedetta and Camilla. The boys were Francesco and Carlo and Luca.

As the children grew older, life began to get more complicated for Ivo. Including his wife, his mistress and his six children, Ivo had to cope with eight birthdays, eight saints' days, and two of every holiday. He made sure that the children's schools were well separated. The girls were sent to Saint Dominique, the French convent on the Via Cassia, and the boys to Massimo, the Jesuit school in EUR. Ivo met and charmed all their teachers, helped the children with their homework, played with them, fixed their broken toys. It taxed all of Ivo's ingenuity to handle two families and keep them apart, but he managed. He was truly an exemplary father, husband and lover. On Christmas Day he stayed home with Simonetta, Isabella, Benedetta and Camilla. On *Befana,* the sixth of January, Ivo dressed up as the *Befana,* the witch, and handed out presents and *carbone,* the black rock candy prized by children, to Francesco, Carlo and Luca.

Ivo's wife and his mistress were lovely, and his children were bright and beautiful, and he was proud of them all. Life was wonderful.

And then the gods shat in Ivo Palazzi's face.

AS IN THE case of most major disasters, this one struck without any warning.

Ivo had made love to Simonetta that morning before breakfast, and then had gone directly to his office, where he did a profitable morning's work. At one o'clock he told his secretary—male, at Simonetta's insistence—that he would be at a meeting the rest of the afternoon.

Smiling at the thought of the pleasures that lay ahead of him, Ivo circled the construction that blocked the street along the Lungo Tevere, where they had been building a subway for the past seventeen years, crossed the bridge to the Corso Francia, and thirty minutes later was driving into his garage at Via Montemignaio. The instant Ivo opened the door of the apartment, he knew something was terribly wrong. Francesco, Carlo and Luca were clustered around Donatella, sobbing, and as Ivo walked toward Donatella, she looked at him with an expression of such hatred on her face that for a moment Ivo thought he must have entered the wrong apartment.

"*Stronzo!*" she screamed at him.

Ivo looked around him, bewildered. "*Carissima*—children—what's wrong? What have I done?"

Donatella rose to her feet. "Here's what you've done!" She threw a copy of the magazine *Oggi* in his face. "Look at it!"

Bewildered, Ivo reached down and picked up the magazine. Staring out from the cover was a photograph of himself, Simonetta and their three daughters. The caption read: "*Padre di Famiglia.*"

Dio! He had forgotten all about it. Months before, the magazine had asked permission to do a story about him and he had foolishly agreed. But Ivo had never dreamed that it would be given this prominence. He looked over at his sobbing mistress and children, and said, "I can explain this . . ."

"Their schoolmates have already explained it," Donatella shrieked. "My children came home crying because everybody at school is calling them bastards!"

"*Cara,* I—"

"My landlord and the neighbors treated us like we were lepers. We can't hold up our heads anymore. I have to get them out of here."

Ivo stared at her, shocked. "What are you talking about?"

"I'm leaving Rome, and I'm taking my sons with me."

"They're mine, too," he shouted. "You can't do it."

"Try to stop me and I'll kill you!"

It was a nightmare. Ivo stood there, watching his three sons and his beloved mistress in hysterics, and he thought, This can't be happening to me.

But Donatella was not finished with him. "Before we go," she announced, "I want one million dollars. In cash."

It was so ridiculous that Ivo started to laugh. "A million—"

"Either that, or I telephone your wife."

. . .

THAT HAD HAPPENED six months earlier. Donatella had not carried out her threat—not yet—but Ivo knew she would. Each week she had increased the pressure. She would telephone him at his office and say, "I don't care how you get the money. Do it!"

There was only one way that Ivo could possibly obtain such a huge sum. He had to be able to sell the stock in Roffe and Sons. It was Sam Roffe who was blocking the sale. Sam who was jeopardizing Ivo's marriage, his future. He had to be stopped. If one knew the right people, anything could be done.

What hurt Ivo more than anything was that Donatella—his darling, passionate mistress—would not let him touch her. Ivo was permitted to visit the children every day, but the bedroom was off limits.

"After you give me the money," Donatella promised, "then I will let you make love to me."

It was out of desperation that Ivo telephoned Donatella one afternoon and said, "I'm coming right over. The money is arranged."

He would make love to her first and placate her later. It had not worked out that way. He had managed to undress her, and when they were both naked, he had told her the truth. "I don't have the money yet, *cara*, but one day soon—"

It was then that she had attacked him like a wild animal.

IVO WAS THINKING of these things now, as he drove away from Donatella's apartment (as he now thought of it) and turned north onto the crowded Via Cassia, toward his home at Olgiata. He glanced at his face in the rearview mirror. The bleeding had lessened, but the scratches were raw-looking and discolored. He looked down at his shirt, stained with blood. How was he going to explain to Simonetta the scratches on his face and his back? For one reckless moment Ivo actually considered telling her the truth, but dismissed the thought as quickly as it came into his head. He might—he just might—have been able to confess to Simonetta that in a moment of mental aberration he had gone to bed with a girl and gotten her pregnant, and he might—he just *might*—have gotten away with a whole skin. But *three children?* Over a period of *three years?* His life would not be worth a five-lire piece. There was no way he could avoid going home now, for they were expecting guests for dinner, and Simonetta would be waiting for him. Ivo was trapped. His marriage was finished. Only San Gennaro, the patron saint of miracles, could help him. Ivo's eye was caught by a sign at the side of the Via Cassia. He suddenly slammed on the brakes, turned off the highway and brought the car to a stop.

Thirty minutes later, Ivo drove through the gates of Olgiata. Ignoring the stares of the guards as they saw his torn-up face and bloodstained shirt, Ivo drove along the winding roads, came to the turn that led to his driveway, and pulled up in front of his house. He parked the car, opened the front door of the house and walked into the living room. Simonetta and Isabella, their eldest daughter, were in the room. A look of shock came over Simonetta's face as she saw her husband.

"Ivo! What happened?"

Ivo smiled awkwardly, trying to ignore the pain it cost, and admitted sheepishly, "I'm afraid I did something stupid, *cara*—"

Simonetta was moving closer, studying the scratches on his face, and Ivo could see her eyes begin to narrow. When she spoke, her voice was frosty. "Who scratched your face?"

"Tiberio," Ivo announced. From behind his back he produced a large, spitting, ugly gray cat that leaped out of his arms and raced off. "I bought it for Isabella, but the damned thing attacked me while I was trying to put it in its case."

"*Povero amore mio!*" Instantly, Simonetta was at his side. "*Angelo mio!* Come upstairs and lie down. I'll get the doctor. I'll get some iodine. I'll—"

"No, no! I'm fine," Ivo said bravely. He winced as she put her arms around him. "Careful! I'm afraid he's clawed my back, too."

"*Amore!* How you must be suffering!"

"No, really," Ivo said. "I feel good." And he meant it.

The front doorbell rang.

"I'll get it," Simonetta said.

"No, I'll get it," Ivo said quickly. "I—I'm expecting some important papers from the office."

He hurried to the front door and opened it.

"Signor Palazzi?"

"*Sì.*"

A messenger, dressed in a gray uniform, handed him an envelope. Inside was a teletype from Rhys Williams. Ivo read the message rapidly. He stood there for a long, long time.

Then he took a deep breath and went upstairs to get ready for his guests.

4

BUENOS AIRES.

MONDAY, SEPTEMBER 7.

THREE P.M.

The Buenos Aires autodrome on the dusty outskirts of Argentina's capital city was crammed with fifty thousand spectators who had come to watch the championship classic. It was a 115-lap race over the almost four-mile circuit. The race had been running for nearly five hours, under a hot, punishing sun, and out of a starting field of thirty cars only a handful remained. The crowd was seeing history being made. There had never been such a race before, and perhaps never would be again. All the names that had become legend were on the track this day: Chris Amon from New Zealand, and Brian Redman from Lancashire. There was the Italian Andrea di Adamici, in an Alfa Romeo Tipo 33, and Carlos Maco of Brazil, in a Mach Formula 1. The prize-winning Belgian Jacky Ickx was there, and Sweden's Reine Wisell in a BRM.

The track looked like a rainbow gone mad, filled with the swirling reds and greens and blacks and whites and golds of the Ferraris and Brabhams and McLaren M19-A's and Lotus Formula 3's.

As lap after grueling lap went by, the giants began to fall. Chris Amon was in fourth place when his throttles jammed open. He sideswiped

Brian Redman's Cooper before he brought his own car under control by cutting the ignition, but both cars were finished. Reine Wisell was in first position, with Jacky Ickx close behind the BRM. On the far turn, the BRM gearbox disintegrated and the battery and electrical equipment caught fire. The car started spinning, and Jacky Ickx's Ferrari was caught in the vortex.

The crowd was in a frenzy.

Three cars were outpacing the rest of the field. Jorje Amandaris from Argentina, driving a Surtees; Nils Nilsson from Sweden in a Matra; and a Ferrari 312 B-2, driven by Martel of France. They were driving brilliantly, daring the straight track, challenging the curves, moving up.

Jorje Amandaris was in the lead, and because he was one of them, the Argentinians cheered him madly. Close behind Amandaris was Nils Nilsson, at the wheel of a red-and-white Matra, and behind him the black-and-gold Ferrari, driven by Martel of France.

The French car had gone almost unnoticed until the last five minutes, when it had started gaining on the field. It had reached tenth position, then seventh, then fifth. And was coming on strong. The crowd was watching it now as the French driver started moving up on number two, driven by Nilsson. The three cars were travelling at speeds in excess of 180 miles an hour. That was dangerous enough at carefully contoured racetracks like Brands Hatch or Watkins Glen, but on the cruder Argentine track it was suicide. A red-coated referee stood at the side of the track, holding up a sign: FIVE LAPS.

The French black-and-gold Ferrari attempted to pass Nilsson's Matra on the outside, and Nilsson inched over, blocking the French car's way. They were lapping a German car on the inside track, moving up on it fast. Now it was opposite Nilsson's car. The French car dropped back and edged over so that it was positioned in the tight space behind the German car and Nilsson's Matra. With a quick burst of acceleration the French driver made for the narrow slot, forcing the two cars out of its way and shooting ahead into the number-two spot. The crowd, which had been holding its breath, roared its approval. It had been a brilliant, dangerous maneuver.

It was Amandaris in the lead now, Martel second and Nilsson in third position, with three laps remaining. Amandaris had seen the move. The

French driver is good, Amandaris told himself, but not good enough to beat me. Amandaris intended to win this race. Ahead of him he saw the sign being flashed—TWO LAPS. The race was almost over, and it was his. Out of the corner of his eye he could see the black-and-gold Ferrari trying to pull up alongside him. He got a glimpse of the driver's goggled, dirt-streaked face, tight and determined. Amandaris gave an inward sigh. He regretted what he was about to do, but he had no choice. Racing was not a game for sportsmen, it was a game for winners.

The two cars were approaching the north end of the oval, where there was a high banking turn, the most dangerous in the track, the scene of a dozen crashes. Amandaris shot another quick look at the French driver of the Ferrari and then tightened his grip on the wheel. As the two cars started to approach the curve, Amandaris imperceptibly lifted his foot from the accelerator, so that the Ferrari began to pull ahead. He saw the driver give him a quick, speculative look. Then the driver was abreast of him, falling into his trap. The crowd was screaming. Jorje Amandaris waited until the black-and-gold Ferrari was fully committed to pass him on the outside. At that moment Amandaris opened his throttles wide and started to move toward the right, cutting off the French driver's path to the straightaway, so that the only choice was to head up the embankment.

Amandaris saw the sudden, dismayed expression on the French driver's face and silently said, *¡Salud!* At that instant the driver of the French car turned the wheel directly into Amandaris's Surtees. Amandaris could not believe it. The Ferrari was on a crash course with him. They were only three feet apart and at that speed Amandaris had to make a split-second decision. *How could anyone have known that the French driver was completely loco?* In a swift, reflex action, Amandaris swung the wheel sharply to the left, trying to avoid the thousand pounds of metal hurtling at him, and braked hard, so that the French car missed him by a fraction of an inch, and shot past him toward the finish line. For a moment Jorje Amandaris's car fishtailed, then went out of control into a spin, flinging itself wildly across the track, rolling over and over until it burst into a tower of red and black flames.

But the crowd's attention was riveted on the French Ferrari, roaring across the finish line to victory. There were wild screams from the spectators as they ran toward the car, surrounding it, cheering. The driver slowly stood up and took off the racing goggles and helmet.

She had wheat-colored hair, cut short, and her face was sculpted with strong, firm features. There was a classic cold beauty about her. Her body was trembling, not with exhaustion, but with excitement, the memory of the moment when she had looked into Jorje Amandaris's eyes as she sent him to his death. Over the loudspeaker the announcer was excitedly yelling, "The winner is Hélène Roffe-Martel, from France, driving a Ferrari."

TWO HOURS LATER, Hélène and her husband, Charles, were in their suite in the Ritz Hotel in downtown Buenos Aires, lying on the rug in front of the fireplace, and Hélène was naked on top of him in the classic position of *la Diligence de Lyon,* and Charles was saying, "Oh, Christ! Please don't do that to me! Please!"

And his begging increased her excitement and she began to put on more pressure, hurting him, watching the tears come to his eyes. I'm being punished for no reason, Charles thought. He dreaded to think what Hélène would do to him if she ever found out about the crime he had committed.

CHARLES MARTEL HAD married Hélène Roffe for her name and for her money. After the ceremony she had kept her name, along with his, and she had kept her money. By the time Charles found out he had made a bad bargain, it was too late.

Charles Martel was a junior attorney in a large Paris law firm when he first met Hélène Roffe. He had been asked to bring some documents into the conference room, where a meeting was taking place. In the room were the four senior partners in the firm and Hélène Roffe. Charles had heard of her. Everyone in Europe had. She was an heiress to the Roffe pharmaceutical fortune. She was wild and unconventional, and the newspapers and magazines adored her. She was a champion skier, flew her own Learjet, had led a mountain-climbing expedition in Nepal, raced cars and horses, and changed men as casually as she changed her wardrobe. Her photograph was constantly appearing in *Paris-Match* and *Jours de France.* She was in the law office now because the firm was handling her divorce. Her fourth or fifth—Charles Martel was not sure which, nor was he interested. The Roffes of the world were out of his reach.

Charles handed the papers to his superior, nervous, not because Hélène Roffe was in the room—he hardly glanced at her—but because of the presence of the four senior partners. They represented Authority, and Charles Martel respected Authority. He was basically a retiring man, content to make a modest living, reside in a little apartment in Passy and tend to his small stamp collection.

Charles Martel was not a brilliant attorney, but he was a competent one, thorough and reliable. He had a stiff *petsec* dignity about him. He was in his early forties and his physical appearance, while not unattractive, was certainly far from prepossessing. Someone had once said that he had the personality of wet sand, and the description was not an unjust one. It was with a good deal of surprise, therefore, that the day after he had met Hélène Roffe, Charles Martel received a summons to go to the office of M. Michel Sachard, the senior partner, where he was told, "Hélène Roffe wishes you to assume personal charge of her divorce case. You will take over at once."

Charles Martel was stunned. He asked, "Why me, Monsieur Sachard?"

Sachard looked him in the eye and replied, "I can't imagine. See that you service her well."

Being in charge of Hélène's divorce action made it necessary for Charles to see her frequently. Too frequently, he felt. She would telephone him and invite him to dinner at her villa in Le Vésinet to discuss the case, and to the opera and to her house in Deauville. Charles kept trying to explain to her that it was a very simple case, that there would be no problem in obtaining the divorce, but Hélène—she insisted that he call her Hélène, to his acute embarrassment—told him she needed his constant reassurance. Later he was to think back on that with bitter amusement.

During the weeks that followed their first meeting, Charles began to suspect that Hélène Roffe was interested in him romantically. He could not believe it. He was a nobody, and she was a member of one of the great families, but Hélène left him in no doubt as to her intentions. "I'm going to marry you, Charles."

He had never thought of getting married. He was not comfortable with women. Besides, he did not love Hélène. He was not even certain he liked her. The fuss and attention that attended her wherever they went discomfited him. He was caught in the limelight of her celebrity and it was a role he was not accustomed to. He was also painfully aware of the contrast between them. Her flamboyance was an irritant to his conservative nature. She set fashion styles and was the epitome of glamour, while he—well, he was a simple, ordinary, middle-aged lawyer. He could not understand what Hélène Roffe saw in him. Nor could anyone else. Because of her well-publicized participation in dangerous sports that were normally the exclusive province of men, there were rumors that Hélène Roffe was an advocate of the women's liberation movement. In fact, she despised the movement, and had only contempt for its concept of equality. She saw no reason why men should be allowed to become the equal of women. Men were handy to have around, when required. They were not particularly intelligent, but they could be taught to fetch and light cigarettes, run errands, open doors and give satisfaction in bed. They made excellent pets, dressed and bathed themselves and were toilet-trained. An amusing species.

Hélène Roffe had had the playboys, the daredevils, the tycoons, the glamour boys. She had never had a Charles Martel. She knew exactly what he was: *Nothing.* A piece of blank clay. And that was precisely the challenge. She intended to take him over, mold him, see what she could make of him. Once Hélène Roffe made up her mind, Charles Martel never had a chance.

They were married in Neuilly and they honeymooned in Monte Carlo, where Charles lost his virginity and his illusions. He had planned on returning to the law firm.

"Don't be a fool," his bride said. "Do you think I want to be married to a law clerk? You'll go into the family business. One day you'll be running it. *We'll* be running it."

Hélène arranged for Charles to work in the Paris branch of Roffe and Sons. He reported to her on everything that went on and she guided him, helped him, gave him suggestions to make. Charles's advancement was rapid. He was soon in charge of the French operation, and a member of the board of directors. Hélène Roffe had changed him from an obscure lawyer to an executive of one of the largest corporations in the world. He should have been ecstatic. He was miserable. From the first moment of their marriage Charles found himself totally dominated by his wife. She chose his tailor, his shoemaker and his shirtmaker. She got him into the exclusive Jockey Club. Hélène treated Charles like a gigolo. His salary went directly to her, and she gave him an embarrassingly small allowance. If Charles needed any extra money, he had to ask Hélène for it. She made him account for every moment of his time, and he was at her constant beck and call. She seemed to enjoy humiliating him. She would telephone him at the office and order him to come home immediately with a jar of massage cream, or something equally stupid. When he arrived, she would be in the bedroom, naked, waiting for him. She was insatiable, an animal. Charles had lived with his mother until he was thirty-two, when she had died of cancer. She had been an invalid for as long as Charles could remember, and he had taken care of her. There had been no time to think about going out with girls or getting married. His mother had been a burden and when she died, Charles thought he would feel a sense of freedom. Instead, he felt a sense of loss. He had no interest in women or sex. He had, in a naive burst of candor, explained his feelings to Hélène when she had first mentioned marriage. "My—libido is not very strong," he had said.

Hélène had smiled. "Poor Charles. Don't worry about sex. I promise you, you'll like it."

He hated it. That only seemed to add to Hélène's pleasure. She would laugh at him for his weakness, and force him to do disgusting things that made Charles feel degraded and sick. The sex act itself was debasing enough. But Hélène was interested in experimenting. Charles never knew what to expect. Once, at the moment he was having an orgasm, she had put crushed ice on his testicles, and another time she had shoved an electric prod up his anus. Charles was terrified of Hélène. She made him feel that she was the male and he was the female. He tried to salvage his pride but, alas, he could find no area in which Hélène was not superior to him. She had a brilliant mind. She knew as much about the law as he did, and much more about business. She spent hour after hour discussing the company with him. She never tired of it. "Think of all that power, Charles! Roffe and Sons can make or break more than half the countries in the world. *I* should be running the company. My great-grandfather founded it. It's part of me."

After one of these outbursts Hélène would be sexually insatiable, and Charles was forced to satisfy her in ways that did not bear thinking about. He came to despise her. His one dream was to get away from her, to escape. But for that he needed money.

One day, over lunch, a friend of his, René Duchamps, told Charles about an opportunity to make a fortune.

"An uncle of mine who owned a large vineyard in Burgundy has just died. The vineyard is going to be put up for sale—ten thousand acres of first-class *Appellation d'origine contrôllée*. I have the inside track," René Duchamps continued, "because it's my family. I don't have enough to swing the deal by myself, but if you came in with me, we could double our money in one year. At least, come and look at it."

Because Charles could not bear to admit to his friend that he was penniless, he went to the rolling red slopes of Burgundy to view the land. He was deeply impressed.

René Duchamps said, "We'll each put in two million francs. In a year we'll each have four million."

Four million francs! It would mean freedom, escape. He could go away to some place where Hélène could never find him.

"I'll think about it," Charles promised his friend.

And he did. Day and night. It was the chance of a lifetime. But *how?* Charles knew that it would be impossible for him to try to borrow money without Hélène immediately learning about it. Everything was in her name, the houses, the paintings, the cars, the jewelry. The jewelry . . . those beautiful, useless ornaments she kept locked up in the safe in the bedroom. Gradually, the idea was born. If he could get hold of her jewelry, a little at a time, he could replace the pieces with copies and borrow money on the real jewelry. After he had made his killing in the vineyard, he would simply return her jewels. And have enough money to disappear forever.

Charles telephoned René Duchamps and said, his heart pounding with excitement, "I've decided to go in with you."

The first part of the plan filled Charles with terror. He had to get into the safe and steal Hélène's jewelry.

The anticipation of the terrible thing he was about to do made Charles so nervous that he was barely able to function. He went through each day like an automaton, neither seeing nor hearing what was happening around him. Every time Charles saw Hélène he began to sweat. His hands would tremble at odd times. Hélène was concerned about him, as she would have been concerned about any pet. She had the doctor examine Charles, but the doctor could find nothing wrong. "He seems a bit tense. A day or two in bed perhaps."

Hélène looked long at Charles, lying in bed, naked, and smiled. "Thank you, Doctor."

The moment the doctor left, Hélène began getting undressed. "I—I'm not feeling very strong," Charles protested.

"I am," Hélène replied.

He had never hated her more.

CHARLES'S OPPORTUNITY CAME the following week. Hélène was going to Garmisch-Partenkirchen to ski with some friends. She decided to leave Charles in Paris.

"I want you home every night," Hélène told him. "I'll telephone you."

Charles watched her speed away, at the wheel of her red Jensen, and the moment she was out of sight he hurried to the wall safe. He had watched her open it often, and he knew most of the combination. It took him an hour to figure out the rest of it. With trembling fingers he pulled the safe open. There, in velvet-lined boxes, sparkling like miniature stars, lay his freedom. He had already located a jeweler, one Pierre Richaud, who was a master at duplicating jewelry. Charles had begun a long, nervous explanation about why he wanted the jewels copied, but Richaud said, matter-of-factly, "Monsieur, I am making copies for everyone. No one with any sense wears real jewelry on the streets these days."

Charles gave him one piece at a time to work on, and when the copy was ready, he substituted it for the real piece. He borrowed money on the real jewelry from the Crédit Municipal, the state-owned pawnshop.

The operation took longer than Charles had anticipated. He could only get into the safe when Hélène was out of the house, and there were unforeseen delays in copying the pieces. But finally the day came when

Charles was able to say to René Duchamps, "I'll have all the money for you tomorrow."

He had accomplished it. He was half-owner of a great vineyard. And Hélène had not the slightest suspicion of what he had done.

Charles had secretly begun to read up on the growing of vines. And why not? Was he not a vintner now? He learned about the different vines: *cabernet sauvignon* was the principal vine used, but others were planted alongside it: *gros cabernet, merlot, malbec, petit verdot.* The desk drawers of Charles's office were filled with pamphlets on soil and vine pressing. He learned about fermentation and pruning and grafting. And that the worldwide demand for wine kept growing.

He met regularly with his partner. "It's going to be even better than I thought," René told Charles. "Prices for wine are skyrocketing. We should get three hundred thousand francs a *tonneau* for the first pressings."

More than Charles had dreamed! The grapes were red gold. Charles began to buy travel pamphlets on the South Sea Islands and Venezuela and Brazil. The very names had a magic about them. The only problem was that there were few places in the world where Roffe and Sons did not have offices, where Hélène could not find him. And if she found him, she would kill him. He knew that with an absolute certainty. Unless he killed her first. It was one of his favorite fantasies. He murdered Hélène over and over again, in a thousand delicious ways.

Perversely, Charles now began to enjoy Hélène's abuse. All the time she was forcing him to do unspeakable things to her, he was thinking, I'll be gone soon, you *convasse.* I'll be rich on your money and there's nothing you can do about it.

And she would command, "Faster now," or "Harder," or "Don't stop!" and he would meekly obey her.

And smile inside.

IN WINE GROWING, Charles knew the crucial months were in the spring and summer, for the grapes were picked in September and they had to have a carefully balanced season of sun and rain. Too much sun would burn the flavor, just as too much rain would drown it. The month of June began splendidly. Charles checked the weather in Burgundy once, then twice a day. He was in a fever of impatience, only weeks away from the fulfillment of his dream. He had decided on Montego Bay. Roffe and Sons had no office in Jamaica. It would be easy to lose himself there. He would not go near Round Hill or Ocho Rios, where any of Hélène's friends might see him. He would buy a small house in the hills. Life was cheap on the island. He could afford servants, and fine food, and in his own small way live in luxury.

And so in those first days of June, Charles Martel was a very happy man. His present life was an ignominy, but he was not living in the present: he was living in the future, on a tropical, sun-bathed, wind-caressed island in the Caribbean.

The June weather seemed to get better each day. There was sun, and there was rain. Perfect for the tender little grapes. And as the grapes grew, so did Charles's fortune.

On the fifteenth day of June it began to drizzle in the Burgundy region. Then it began to rain harder. It rained day after day, and week after week, until Charles could no longer bring himself to check the weather reports.

René Duchamps telephoned. "If it stops by the middle of July, the crop can still be saved."

July turned out to be the rainiest month in the history of the French weather bureau. By the first of August, Charles Martel had lost every centime of the money he had stolen. He was filled with a fear such as he had never known.

"WE'RE FLYING TO Argentina next month," Hélène had informed Charles. "I've entered a car race there."

He had watched her speeding round the track in the Ferrari, and he could not help thinking: *If she crashes, I'm free.*

But she was Hélène Roffe-Martel. Life had cast her in the role of a winner, just as it had cast him in the role of a loser.

Winning the race had excited Hélène even more than usual. They had returned to their hotel suite in Buenos Aires, and she had made Charles get undressed and lie on the rug, on his stomach. When he saw what she had in her hand as she straddled him, he said, "Please, no!"

There was a knock on the door.

"Merde!" Hélène said. She waited, silent, but the knocking was repeated.

A voice called, "Señor Martel?"

"Stay here!" Hélène commanded. She got up, whipped a heavy silk robe around her slim, firm body, walked over to the door and pulled it open. A man in a gray messenger's uniform stood there, holding a sealed manila envelope.

"I have a special delivery for Señor and Señora Martel."

She took the envelope and closed the door.

She tore the envelope open and read the message inside, then slowly read it again.

"What is it?" Charles asked.

"Sam Roffe is dead," she said. She was smiling.

5

LONDON.

MONDAY, SEPTEMBER 7.

TWO P.M.

White's Club was situated at the top of St. James's Street, near Piccadilly. Built as a gambling club in the eighteenth century, White's was one of the oldest clubs in England, and the most exclusive. Members put their sons' names in for membership at birth, for there was a thirty-year waiting list.

The facade of White's was the epitome of discretion. The wide bow windows looking out on St. James's Street were meant to accommodate those within rather than to satisfy the curiosity of the outsiders passing by. A short flight of steps led to the entrance but, aside from members and their guests, few people ever got past the door. The rooms in the club were large and impressive, burnished with the dark rich patina of time. The furniture was old and comfortable—leather couches, newspaper racks, priceless antique tables and deep stuffed armchairs that had held the posteriors of half a dozen prime ministers. There was a backgammon room with a large, open fireplace behind a bronze-covered rail, and a formal curved staircase led to the dining room upstairs. The dining room ran across the entire breadth of the house, and contained one huge mahogany table which seated thirty persons, and five side tables. At any luncheon or dinner the room contained some of the most influential men in the world.

Sir Alec Nichols, Member of Parliament, was seated at one of the small corner tables, having lunch with a guest, Jon Swinton. Sir Alec's father had been a baronet, and his father and grandfather before him. They had all belonged to White's. Sir Alec was a thin, pale man in his late forties, with a sensitive, aristocratic face and an engaging smile. He had just motored in from his country estate in Gloucestershire, and was dressed in a tweed sports jacket and slacks, with loafers. His guest wore a pinstripe suit with a loud checked shirt and a red tie, and seemed out of place in this quiet, rich atmosphere.

"They really do you proud here," Jon Swinton said, his mouth full, as he chewed the remains of a large veal chop on his plate.

Sir Alec nodded. "Yes. Things have changed since Voltaire said, 'The British have a hundred religions and only one sauce.'"

Jon Swinton looked up. "Who's Voltaire?"

Sir Alec said, embarrassed, "A—a French chap."

"Oh." Jon Swinton washed his food down with a swallow of wine. He laid down his knife and fork and wiped a napkin across his mouth. "Well, now, Sir Alec. Time for you and I to talk a little business."

Alec Nichols said softly, "I told you two weeks ago I'm working everything out, Mr. Swinton. I need a bit more time."

A waiter walked over to the table, balancing a high stack of wooden cigar boxes. He skillfully set them down on the table.

"Don't mind if I do," Jon Swinton said. He examined the labels on the boxes, whistled in admiration, pulled out several cigars which he put in his breast pocket, then lit one. Neither the waiter nor Sir Alec showed any reaction to this breach of manners. The waiter nodded to Sir Alec, and carried the cigars to another table.

"My employers have been very lenient with you, Sir Alec. Now, I'm afraid, they've got impatient." He picked up the burned match, leaned forward and dropped it into Sir Alec's glass of wine. "Between you and I, they're not nice people when they're upset You don't want to get them down on you, you know what I mean?"

"I simply don't have the money right now."

Jon Swinton laughed loudly. "Come of it, chum. Your mom was a Roffe, right? You got a hundred-acre farm, a posh town house in Knightsbridge, a Rolls-Royce and a bloody Bentley. You're not exactly on the dole then, are you?"

Sir Alec looked around, pained, and said quietly, "None of them is a liquid asset. I can't—"

Swinton winked and said, "I'll bet that sweet little wife of yours, Vivian, is a liquid asset, eh? She's got a great pair of Bristols."

Sir Alec flushed. Vivian's name on this man's lips was a sacrilege. Alec thought of Vivian as he had left her that morning, still sweetly asleep. They had separate bedrooms, and one of Alec Nichols's great joys was to go into Vivian's room for one of his "visits." Sometimes, when Alec awakened early, he would walk into Vivian's bedroom while she was asleep and simply stare at her. Awake or asleep, she was the most beautiful girl he had ever seen. She slept in the nude, and her soft, curved body would be half exposed as she curled into the sheets. She was blond, with wide, pale-blue eyes and skin like cream. Vivian had been a minor actress when Sir Alec had first met her at a charity ball. He had been enchanted by her looks, but what had drawn him to her was her easy, outgoing personality. She was twenty years younger than Alec, and filled with a zest for living. Where Alec was shy and introverted, Vivian was gregarious and vivacious. Alec had been unable to get her out of his mind, but it had taken him two weeks to summon up nerve enough to telephone her. To his surprise and delight Vivian had accepted his invitation. Alec had taken her to a play at the Old Vic, and then to dinner at the Mirabelle. Vivian lived in a dreary little basement flat in Notting Hill, and when Alec had brought her home, she had said, "Would you like to come in then?" He had stayed the night, and it had changed his whole life. It was the first time that any woman had been able to bring him to a climax. He had never experienced anything like Vivian. She was velvet tongue and trailing golden hair and moist pulsing demanding depths that Alec explored until he was drained. He could become aroused simply thinking about her.

There was something else. She made him laugh, she made him come alive. She poked fun at Alec because he was shy and a bit stodgy, and he adored it. He was with her as often as Vivian would permit it. When

Alec took Vivian to a party, she was always the center of attention. Alec was proud of that, but jealous of the young men gathered around her, and he could not help wondering how many of them she had been to bed with.

On the nights when Vivian could not see him because she had another engagement, Alec was frantic with jealousy. He would drive to her flat and park down the block to see what time she came home, and whom she was with. Alec knew that he was behaving like a fool, and yet he could not help himself. He was in the grip of something too strong to break.

He realized that Vivian was wrong for him, that it was out of the question for him to marry her. He was a baronet, a respected Member of Parliament, with a brilliant future. He was part of the Roffe dynasty, on the board of directors of the company. Vivian had no background to help her cope with Alec's world. Her mother and father had been second-rate music-hall artists, playing the provincial circuit. Vivian had had no education except for what she had picked up in the streets, or backstage. Alec knew that she was promiscuous and superficial. She was shrewd but not particularly intelligent. And yet Alec was obsessed with her. He fought it. He tried to stop seeing her, but it was no use. He was happy when he was with her, and he was miserable when he was without her. In the end he proposed to her because he had to, and when Vivian accepted, Sir Alec Nichols was ecstatic.

His new bride moved into the family house, a beautiful old Robert Adam house in Gloucestershire, a Georgian mansion with Delphic columns and a long sweeping driveway. It was set amid the green of a hundred acres of lush farmland, with its own private hunting, and running streams to fish. At the back of the house was a park that had been laid out by "Capability" Brown.

The interior of the house was stunning. The large front hall had a stone floor and walls of painted wood. There were pairs of old lanterns and marble-topped Adam giltwood tables and mahogany chairs. The library had original eighteenth-century built-in bookcases, and a pair of pedestal tables by Henry Holland, and chairs designed by Thomas Hope. The drawing room was a mixture of Hepplewhite and Chippendale, with a Wilton carpet, and a pair of Waterford glass chandeliers.

There was a huge dining room that would seat forty guests, and a smoking room. On the second floor were six bedrooms, each with an Adam fireplace, and on the third floor were the servants' quarters.

Six weeks after she had moved into the house, Vivian said, "Let's get out of this place, Alec."

He looked at her, puzzled. "You mean you'd like to go up to London for a few days?"

"I mean I want to *move* back to London."

Alec looked out the window at the emerald-green meadows, where he had played as a child, and at the giant sycamore and oak trees, and he said hesitantly, "Vivian, it's so peaceful here. I—"

And she said, "I know, luv. That's what I can't stand—the fucking pcace!"

They moved to London the following week.

ALEC HAD AN elegant four-story town house in Wilton Crescent, off Knightsbridge, with a lovely drawing room, a study, a large dining room, and at the back of the house, a picture window that overlooked a grotto, with a waterfall and statues and white benches set amid a beautiful formal garden. Upstairs were a magnificent master suite and four smaller bedrooms.

Vivian and Alec shared the master suite for two weeks, until one morning Vivian said, "I love you, Alec, but you do snore, you know." Alec had not known. "I really must sleep alone, luv. You don't mind, do you?"

Alec minded deeply. He loved the feel of her soft body in bed, warm against him. But deep inside, Alec knew that he did not excite Vivian sexually the way other men excited her. That was why she did not want him in her bed. So now he said, "Of course I understand, darling."

At Alec's insistence, Vivian kept the master suite, and he moved into one of the small guest bedrooms.

In the beginning, Vivian had gone to the House of Commons and sat in the Visitors' Gallery on days when Alec was to speak. He would look up at her and be filled with a deep, ineffable pride. She was undoubtedly the most beautiful woman there. And then came the day when Alec finished his speech and looked up for Vivian's approval, and saw only an empty seat.

Alec blamed himself for the fact that Vivian was restless. His friends were older than Vivian, too conservative for her. He encouraged her to invite her young companions to the house, and brought them together with his friends. The results were disastrous.

Alec kept telling himself that when Vivian had a child, she would settle down and change. But one day, somehow—and Alec could not bear to know how—she picked up a vaginal infection and had to have a hysterectomy. Alec had longed for a son. The news had shattered him, but Vivian was unperturbed.

"Don't worry, luv," she said, smiling. "They took out the nursery, but they left in the playpen."

He looked at her for a long moment, then turned and walked away.

VIVIAN LOVED TO go on buying sprees. She spent money indiscriminately, recklessly, on clothes and jewelry and cars, and Alec did not have the heart to stop her. He told himself that she had grown up in poverty, hungry for beautiful things. He wanted to buy them for her. Unfortunately, he could not afford it. His salary was consumed by taxes. His fortune lay in his shares of stock in Roffe and Sons but those shares were restricted. He tried to explain that to Vivian but she was not interested. Business discussions bored her. And so Alec let her carry on.

He had first learned of her gambling when Tod Michaels, the owner of Tod's Club, a disreputable gambling place in Soho, had dropped in to see him.

"I have your wife's IOUs here for a thousand pounds, Sir Alec. She had a rotten run at roulette."

Alec had been shocked. He had paid off the IOUs and had had a confrontation with Vivian that evening. "We simply can't afford it," he had told her. "You're spending more than I'm making."

She had been very contrite. "I'm sorry, angel. Baby's been bad."

And she had walked over to him and put her arms around him and pressed her body against his, and he had forgotten his anger.

Alec had spent a memorable night in her bed. He was sure now that there would be no more problems.

Two weeks later Tod Michaels had come to visit Alec again. This time

Vivian's IOUs were five thousand pounds. Alec was furious. "Why did you let her have credit?" he demanded.

"She's your wife, Sir Alec," Michaels had replied blandly. "How would it look if we refused her?"

"I'll—I'll have to get the money," Alec had said. I don't have that much cash at the moment."

"Please! Consider it a loan. Pay it back when you can."

Alec had been greatly relieved. "That's very generous of you, Mr. Michaels."

It was not until a month later that Alec learned that Vivian had gambled away another twenty-five thousand pounds, and that Alec was being charged interest at the rate of 10 percent a week. He was horrified. There was no way he could raise that much cash. There was nothing that he could even sell. The houses, the beautiful antiques, the cars, all belonged to Roffe and Sons. His anger frightened Vivian enough so that she promised not to gamble anymore. But it was too late. Alec found himself in the hands of loan sharks. No matter how much Alec gave them, he could not manage to pay off the debt. It kept mounting each month, instead of getting smaller, and it had been going on for almost a year.

When Tod Michaels's hoodlums first began to press him for the money, Alec had threatened to go to the police commissioner. "I have connections in the highest quarters," Alec had said.

The man had grinned. "I got connections in the lowest."

NOW SIR ALEC found himself sitting here at White's with this dreadful man, having to contain his pride, and beg for a little more time.

"I've already paid them back more than the money I borrowed. They can't—"

Swinton replied, "That was just on the interest, Sir Alec. You still haven't paid the principal."

"It's extortion," Alec said.

Swinton's eyes darkened. "I'll give the boss your message." He started to rise.

Alec said quickly, "No! Sit down. Please."

Slowly Swinton sat down again. "Don't use words like that," he warned. "The last chap who talked like that had both his knees nailed to the floor."

Alec had read about it. The Kray brothers had invented the punishment for their victims. And the people Alec was dealing with were just as bad, just as ruthless. He could feel the bile rising in his throat. "I didn't mean that," Alec said. "It's just that I—I don't have any more cash."

Swinton flicked the ash from his cigar into Alec's glass of wine, and said, "You have a big bundle of stock in Roffe and Sons, don't you, Alec baby?"

"Yes," Alec replied, "but it's nonsalable and nontransferable. It's no good to anyone unless Roffe and Sons goes public."

Swinton took a puff on his cigar. "And is it going public?"

"That's up to Sam Roffe. I've—I've been trying to persuade him."

"Try harder."

"Tell Mr. Michaels he'll get his money," Alec said. "But please stop hounding me."

Swinton stared. "Hounding you? Why, Sir Alec, you little cocksucker, you'll know when we start hounding you. Your fucking stables will burn down, and you'll be eating roast horsemeat. Then your house will burn. And maybe your wife." He smiled, and Alec wished he had not. "Have you ever eaten cooked pussy?"

Alec had turned pale. "For God's sake—"

Swinton said soothingly, "I'm kidding. Tod Michaels's your friend. And friends help each other, right? We were talking about you at our meeting this morning. And do you know what the boss said? He said, 'Sir Alec's a good sort. If he hasn't got the money, I'm sure he'll think of some other way to take care of us.'"

Alec frowned. "What other way?"

"Well, now, it's not all that hard for a bright chap like you to work out, is it? You're running a big drug company, right? You make things like cocaine, for example. Just between you and I, who'd ever know if you happened to accidentally misplace a few shipments here and there?"

Alec stared at him. "You're insane," he said. "I—I couldn't do that."

"It's amazing what people can do when they have to," Swinton said genially. He rose to his feet. "You either have our money for us, or we'll tell you where to deliver the merchandise."

He ground his cigar out in Alec's butter plate. "Give my regards to Vivian, Sir Alec. Ta."

And Jon Swinton was gone.

Sir Alec sat there alone, unseeing, surrounded by all the familiar, comfortable things that were so much a part of his past life, that were now threatened. The only alien thing was the obscene wet cigar butt in the plate. How had he ever allowed them to come into his life? He had permitted himself to be maneuvered into a position where he was in the hands of the underworld. And now he knew that they wanted more than money from him. The money was merely the bait with which they had trapped him. They were after his connections with the drug company. They were going to try to force him to work with them. If it became known he was in their power, the Opposition would not hesitate to make capital of it. His own party would probably ask him to resign. It would be done tactfully and quietly. They would probably exert pressure on him to apply for the Chiltern Hundreds, a post that paid a nominal salary of a hundred pounds a year from the Crown. The one barrier to being an M.P. was that you could not be in receipt of pay from the Crown or the Government. So Alec would no longer be allowed to serve in Parliament. The reason could not be kept secret, of course. He would be in disgrace. Unless he could come up with a large sum of money. He had talked to Sam Roffe again and again, asking him to let the company go public, to let the shares of stock be marketed.

"Forget it," Sam had told him. "The minute we let outsiders in, we have a lot of strangers telling us how to run our business. Before you know it, they'll take over the board, and then the company. What's the difference to you, Alec? You have a big salary, an unlimited expense account. You don't *need* the money."

For a moment Alec had been tempted to tell Sam how desperately he needed it. But he knew it would do no good. Sam Roffe was a company man, a man without compassion. If he knew that Alec had in any way compromised Roffe and Sons, he would have dismissed him without a moment's hesitation. No, Sam Roffe was the last person to whom he could turn.

Alec was facing ruin.

. . .

THE RECEPTION PORTER at White's walked toward Sir Alec's table with a man dressed in a messenger's uniform, carrying a sealed manila envelope.

"Excuse me, Sir Alec," the porter apologized, "but this man insists that he has instructions to deliver something to you personally."

"Thank you," Sir Alec said. The messenger handed him the envelope, and the porter led him back to the door.

Alec sat there a long time before he reached for the envelope and opened it. He read the message through three times, then he slowly crumpled the paper in his fist, and his eyes began to fill with tears.

6

NEW YORK.
MONDAY, SEPTEMBER 7.
ELEVEN A.M.

The private Boeing 707-320 was making its final approach to Kennedy Airport, gliding out of the stacked-up traffic pattern. It had been a long, tedious flight and Rhys Williams was exhausted, but he had been unable to sleep during the night. He had ridden in this plane too often with Sam Roffe. His presence still filled it.

Elizabeth Roffe was expecting him. Rhys had sent her a cable from Istanbul, merely announcing that he would arrive the following day. He could have broken the news of her father's death over the telephone but she deserved more than that.

The plane was on the ground now, taxiing toward the terminal. Rhys carried very little luggage, and he was quickly ushered through Customs. Outside, the sky was gray and bleak, a foretaste of the winter to come. A limousine was waiting at the side entrance to drive him to Sam Roffe's Long Island estate, where Elizabeth would be waiting.

During the drive Rhys tried to rehearse the words that he would say to her, to try to soften the blow, but the moment Elizabeth opened the front door to greet him, the words flew out of his head. Each time Rhys saw Elizabeth, her beauty caught him by surprise. She had inherited her mother's looks, the same patrician features, midnight-black eyes framed by long heavy lashes. Her skin was white and soft, her hair a shiny black. Her figure was rich and firm. She was wearing an open-necked creamy silk blouse and a pleated gray-flannel skirt and fawn-colored pumps. There was no sign of the awkward little girl Rhys had first met nine years earlier. She had become a woman, intelligent and warm and completely unselfconscious about her beauty. She was smiling at him now, pleased to see him. She took his hand and said, "Come in, Rhys," and led him into the large oak-paneled library. "Did Sam fly in with you?"

There was no way to break it gently. Rhys took a deep breath and said, "Sam had a bad accident, Liz." He watched the color drain from her face. She waited for him to go on. "He was killed."

She stood there frozen. When she finally spoke, Rhys could barely hear her. "What—what happened?"

"We don't have any of the details yet. He was climbing Mont Blanc. A rope broke. He fell into a crevasse."

"Did they find—?"

She closed her eyes for a moment, then opened them.

"A bottomless crevasse."

Her face had turned white. Rhys felt a quick sense of alarm. "Are you all right?"

She smiled brightly, and said, "Of course. I'm fine, thank you. Would you like some tea or something to eat?"

He looked at her in surprise, and started to speak, and then he understood. She was in shock. She was rattling on, making no sense, her eyes unnaturally bright, her smile fixed.

"Sam was such a great athlete," Elizabeth was saying. "You've seen his trophies. He always won, didn't he? Did you know he climbed Mont Blanc before?"

"Liz—"

"Of course you did. You went with him once, didn't you, Rhys?"

Rhys let her talk, anesthetizing herself against the pain, trying to build an armor of words to ward off the moment when she would have to face her own anguish. For an instant, as he listened to her, he was reminded of the vulnerable little girl he had first known, too sensitive and shy to have any protection against brutal reality. She was dangerously wound up now, tense and brittle, and there was a fragility about her that worried Rhys.

"Let me call a doctor," he said. "He can give you something to—"

"Oh, no. I'm really quite all right. If you don't mind, I think I'll lie down for a while. I'm feeling a bit tired."

"Would you like me to stay?"

"Thank you. That won't be necessary."

She walked him to the door, and as he started to get into the car Elizabeth called, "Rhys!"

He turned.

"Thank you for coming."

Jesus Christ.

LONG HOURS AFTER Rhys Williams had gone, Elizabeth Roffe lay in her bed, staring at the ceiling, watching the shifting patterns painted by the pale September sun.

And the pain came. She had not taken a sedative, because she wanted the pain. She owed that to Sam. She would be able to bear it, because she was his daughter. And so she lay there, all day and all night, thinking of nothing, thinking of everything, remembering, feeling. She laughed, and she cried, and she supposed that she was in a state of hysteria. It did not matter. There was no one to hear her. In the middle of the night, she suddenly became ravenously hungry and went down into the kitchen and devoured a large sandwich and then threw it up. She felt no better. Nothing could ease the pain that filled her. She felt as though all her nerve ends were on fire. Her mind kept going back, back over the years with her father. Through her bedroom window she watched the sun rise. Sometime later, one of the servants knocked at the door, and Elizabeth sent her away. Once the phone rang, and her heart leaped and she reached for it, thinking, It's Sam! Then she remembered, and snatched her hand away.

He would never call her again. She would never hear his voice again. She would never see him again.

A bottomless crevasse.

Bottomless.

Elizabeth lay there, letting the past wash over her, remembering it all.

7

The birth of Elizabeth Rowane Roffe was a double tragedy. The minor tragedy was that Elizabeth's mother died on the delivery table. The major tragedy was that Elizabeth was born a girl.

For nine months, until she emerged from the darkness of her mother's womb, she was the most eagerly awaited child in the world, heir to a colossal empire, the multibillion-dollar giant, Roffe and Sons.

Sam Roffe's wife, Patricia, was a dark-haired woman of surpassing beauty. Many women had tried to marry Sam Roffe, for his position, his prestige, his wealth. Patricia had married him because she had fallen in love with him. It had proved to be the worst of reasons. Sam Roffe had been looking for a business arrangement, and Patricia had suited his requirements ideally. Sam had neither the time nor the temperament to be a family man. There was no room in his life for anything but Roffe and Sons. He was fanatically dedicated to the company, and he expected no less from those around him. Patricia's importance to him lay solely in the contribution she could make to the image of the company. By the time Patricia came to a realization of what kind of marriage she had made, it was too late. Sam gave her a role to play, and she played it beautifully. She was the perfect hostess, the perfect Mrs. Sam Roffe. She received no love from her husband and in time Patricia learned to give none. She served Sam, and was as much an employee of Roffe and Sons as the lowliest secretary. She was on call twenty-four hours a day, ready to fly wherever Sam needed her, capable of entertaining a small company of world leaders or serving a gourmet dinner to a hundred guests, on a day's notice, with crisp, heavily embroidered tablecloths, gleaming Baccarat crystal, heavy Georgian silverware. Patricia was one of Roffe and Sons' unlisted assets. She worked at keeping herself beautiful, and exercised and dieted like a Spartan. Her figure was perfect, and her clothes were designed for her by Norell in New York, Chanel in Paris, Hartnell in London, and young Sybil Connolly in Dublin. The jewelry Patricia wore was created for her by Jean Schlumberger in Bulgaria. Her life was busy and full and joyless and empty. Becoming pregnant had changed all that.

Sam Roffe was the last male heir of the Roffe dynasty, and Patricia knew how desperately he wanted a son. He was depending on her. And now she was the queen mother, busy with the baby within her, the young prince, who would one day inherit the kingdom. When they wheeled Patricia into the delivery room, Sam clasped her hand and said, "Thank you."

She was dead of an embolism thirty minutes later, and the only blessing about Patricia's death was that she died without knowing that she had failed her husband.

Sam Roffe took time off from his grueling schedule to bury his wife, and then turned his attention to the problem of what he should do with his infant daughter.

One week after Elizabeth was born, she was taken home and turned over to a nanny, the beginning of a long series of nannies. During the first five years of her life, Elizabeth saw very little of her father. He was barely more than a blur, a stranger who was always arriving or leaving. He traveled constantly and Elizabeth was a nuisance who had to be carted along, like a piece of extra luggage. One month Elizabeth would find herself living at their Long Island estate, with its bowling alley, tennis court, swimming pool and squash court. A few weeks later, her nanny would pack Elizabeth's clothes and she would be flown to their villa in Biarritz. It had fifty rooms and thirty acres of grounds and Elizabeth kept getting lost.

In addition, Sam Roffe owned a large duplex penthouse apartment on Beekman Place, and a villa on the Costa Smeralda in Sardinia. Elizabeth traveled to all these places, shunted from house to apartment to villa, and grew up amid all the lavish elegance. But always she felt like an outsider who had wandered by mistake into a beautiful birthday party given by unloving strangers.

As Elizabeth grew older, she came to know what it meant to be the daughter of Sam Roffe. Just as her mother had been an emotional victim of the company, so was Elizabeth. If she had no family life, it was because there was no family, only the paid surrogates and the distant figure of the man who had fathered her, who seemed to have no interest in her, only in the company. Patricia had been able to accept her situation, but for the child it was torment. Elizabeth felt unwanted and unloved, and did not know how to cope with her despair, and in the end she blamed herself for being unlovable. She tried desperately to win the affection of her father. When Elizabeth was old enough to go to school, she made things for him in class, childish drawings and watercolor paintings and lopsided ashtrays, and she would guard them fiercely, waiting for him to return from one of his trips, so that she could surprise him, please him, hear him say, *It's beautiful, Elizabeth. You're very talented.*

When he returned, Elizabeth would present her love offering, and her father would glance at it absently and nod, or shake his head. "You'll never be an artist, will you?"

Sometimes Elizabeth would awaken in the middle of the night, and walk down the long winding staircase of the Beekman Place apartment and through the large cavernous hall that led to her father's study. She would step into the empty room as if she were entering a shrine. This was *his* room, where he worked and signed important pieces of paper and ran the world. Elizabeth would walk over to his enormous leather-topped desk and slowly rub her hands across it. Then she would move behind the desk and sit in his leather chair. She felt closer to her father there. It was as though by being where he was, sitting where he sat, she could become a part of him. She would hold imaginary conversations with him, and he would listen, interested and caring as she poured out her problems. One night, as Elizabeth sat at his desk in the dark, the lights in the room suddenly came on. Her father was standing in the doorway. He looked at Elizabeth seated behind his desk, clad in a thin nightgown, and said, "What are you doing here alone in the dark?" And he scooped her up in his arms and carried her upstairs, to her bed, and Elizabeth had lain awake all night, thinking about how her father had held her.

After that, she went downstairs every night and sat in his office waiting for him to come and get her, but it never happened again.

No one discussed Elizabeth's mother with her, but there was a beautiful full-length portrait of Patricia Roffe hanging in the reception hall, and Elizabeth would stare at it by the hour. Then she would turn to her mirror. Ugly. They had put braces on her teeth, and she looked like a gargoyle. No wonder my father isn't interested in me, Elizabeth thought.

Overnight she developed an insatiable appetite, and began to gain weight. For she had arrived at a wonderful truth: if she were fat and ugly, no one would expect her to look like her mother.

When Elizabeth was twelve years old, she attended an exclusive private school on the East Side of Manhattan, in the upper seventies. She would arrive in a chauffeur-driven Rolls-Royce, walk into her classes and sit there, withdrawn and silent, ignoring everyone around her. She never volunteered to answer a question. And when she was called upon, she never seemed to know the answer. Her teachers soon got in the habit of ignoring her. They discussed Elizabeth among themselves and unanimously agreed that she was the most spoiled child they had ever seen. In a confidential year-end report to the headmistress, Elizabeth's homeroom teacher wrote:

We have been able to make no progress with Elizabeth Roffe. She is aloof from her classmates and refuses to participate in any of the group activities. She has made no friends at school. Her grades are unsatisfactory, but it is difficult to tell if this is because she makes no effort, or because she is unable to handle the assignments. She is arrogant and egotistical. Were it not for the fact that her father is a major benefactor of this school, I would strongly recommend expelling her.

The report was light-years from the reality. The simple truth was that Elizabeth Roffe had no protective shield, no armor against the terrible loneliness that engulfed her. She was filled with such a deep sense of her own unworthiness that she was afraid to make friends, for fear they would discover that she was worthless, unlovable. She was not arrogant, she was almost pathologically shy. She felt that she did not belong in the same world that her father inhabited. She did not belong anywhere. She loathed being driven to school in the Rolls-Royce, because she knew she did not deserve it. In her classes she knew the answers to the questions the teachers asked, but she did not dare to speak out, to call attention to herself. She loved to read, and she would lie awake late at night in her bed, devouring books.

She daydreamed, and oh! what lovely fantasies. She was in Paris with her father, and they were driving through the Bois in a horse-drawn carriage, and he took her to his office, an enormous room something like Saint Patrick's cathedral, and people kept walking in with papers for him to sign, and he would wave them away and say, "Can't you see I'm busy now? I'm talking to my daughter, Elizabeth."

She and her father were skiing in Switzerland, moving down a steep slope side by side, with an icy wind whipping past them, and he suddenly fell and cried out with pain, because his leg was broken, and she said, "Don't worry, Papa! I'll take care of you." And she skied down to the hospital and said, "Quickly, my father's hurt," and a dozen men in white jackets brought him there in a shiny ambulance and she was at his bedside, feeding him (it was probably his arm that was broken, then, not his leg), and her mother walked into the room, alive somehow, and her father said, "I can't see you now, Patricia. Elizabeth and I are talking."

Or they would be in their beautiful villa in Sardinia, and the servants would be away, and Elizabeth would cook dinner for her father. He would eat two helpings of everything and say, "You're a much better cook than your mother was, Elizabeth."

The scenes with her father always ended in the same way. The doorbell would ring and a tall man, who towered over her father, would come in and beg Elizabeth to marry him, and her father would plead with her, "Please, Elizabeth, don't leave me. I need you."

And she would agree to stay.

. . .

OF ALL THE homes in which Elizabeth grew up, the villa in Sardinia was her favorite. It was by no means the largest, but it was the most colorful, the friendliest. Sardinia itself delighted Elizabeth. It was a dramatic, rockbound island, some 160 miles southwest of the Italian coast, a stunning panorama of mountains, sea and green farmland. Its enormous volcanic cliffs had been thrown up thousands of years ago from the primal sea, and the shoreline swept in a vast crescent as far as the eye could follow, the Tyrrhenian Sea framing the island in a blue border.

For Elizabeth the island had its own special odors, the smell of sea breezes and forests, the white and yellow *macchia,* the fabled flower that Napoleon had loved. There were the *corbeccola* bushes that grew six feet high and had a red fruit that tasted like strawberries, and the *guarcias,* the giant stone oaks whose bark was exported to the mainland to be used for making cork for wine bottles.

She loved to listen to the singing rocks, the mysterious giant boulders with holes through them. When the winds blew through the holes, the rocks emitted an eerie keening sound, like a dirge of lost souls.

And the winds blew. Elizabeth grew to know them all. The *mistrale* and the *ponente,* the *tramontana* and the *grecate* and the *levante.* Soft winds and fierce winds. And then there was the dreaded scirocco, the warm wind that blew in from the Sahara.

The Roffe villa was on the Costa Smeralda, above Porto Cervo, set high atop a cliff overlooking the sea, secluded by juniper trees and the wild-growing Sardinian olive trees with their bitter fruit. There was a breathtaking view of the harbor far below, and around it, sprinkled over the green hills, a jumble of stucco and stone houses thrown together in a crazy hodgepodge of colors resembling a child's crayon drawing.

The villa was stucco, with huge juniper beans inside. It was built on several levels, with large, comfortable rooms, each with its own fireplace and balcony. The living room and dining room had picture windows that gave a panoramic view of the island. A free-form staircase led to four bedrooms upstairs. The furniture blended perfectly with the surroundings. There were rustic refectory tables and benches, and soft easy chairs. Across the windows were fringed white wool draperies that had been hand-woven on the island, and the floors were laid with colorful *cerasarda* tiles from Sardinia and other tiles from Tuscany. In the bathrooms and bedrooms were native wool carpets, colored with vegetable dyes in the traditional way. The house was ablaze with paintings, a mixture of French Impressionists, Italian masters and Sardo primitives. In the hallway hung portraits of Samuel Roffe and Terenia Roffe, Elizabeth's great-great-grandfather and grandmother.

The feature of the house that Elizabeth loved most was the tower room, under the sloping tile roof. It was reached by a narrow staircase from the second floor, and Sam Roffe used it as his study. It contained a large work desk and a comfortable padded swivel chair. The walls were lined with bookcases and maps, most of them pertaining to the Roffe empire. French doors led to a small balcony built over a sheer cliff, and the view from there was heart-stopping.

It was in this house, when she was thirteen years old, that Elizabeth discovered the origins of her family, and for the first time in her life that she felt she belonged, that she was part of something.

IT BEGAN THE day she found the Book. Elizabeth's father had driven to Olbia, and Elizabeth had wandered upstairs to the tower room. She was not interested in the books on the shelves, for she had long since learned that they were technical volumes on pharmacology and pharmacognosy, and on multinational corporations and international law. Dull and boring. Some of the manuscripts were rare, and these were kept in glass cases. There was a medical volume in Latin called *Circa Instans,* written in the Middle Ages, and another called *De Materia Medica.* It was because Elizabeth was studying Latin and was curious to see one of the old volumes that she opened the glass case to take it out. Behind it, tucked away out of sight, she saw another volume. Elizabeth picked it up. It was thick, bound in red leather, and had no title.

Intrigued, Elizabeth opened it. It was like opening the door to another world. It was a biography of her great-great-grandfather, Samuel Roffe, in English, privately printed on vellum. There was no author given, and no date, but Elizabeth was sure that it was more than one hundred years old, for most of the pages were faded, and others were yellowed and flaking with age. But none of this was important. It was the story that mattered, a story that brought life to the portraits hanging on the wall downstairs. Elizabeth had seen the pictures of her great-great-grandparents a hundred times: paintings of an old-fashioned man and woman, dressed in unfamiliar clothes. The man was not handsome, but there was great strength and intelligence in his face. He had fair hair, high Slavic cheekbones and keen, bright-blue eyes. The woman was a beauty. Dark hair, a flawless complexion and eyes as black as coal. She wore a white-silk dress with a tabard over the top, and a bodice made of brocade. Two strangers who meant nothing to Elizabeth.

But now, alone in the tower room, as Elizabeth opened the Book and began to read, Samuel and Terenia Roffe became alive. Elizabeth felt as though she had been transported back in time, that she was living in the ghetto of Kraków, in the year 1853, with Samuel and Terenia. As she read deeper and deeper into the Book, she learned that her great-great-grandfather Samuel, the founder of Roffe and Sons, was a romantic and an adventurer.

And a murderer.

amuel Roffe's earliest memory, Elizabeth read, was of his mother being killed in a pogrom in 1855 when Samuel was five years old. He had been hidden in the cellar of the small wooden house the Roffes shared with other families in the ghetto of Kraków. When the rioting was finally over, endless hours later, and the only sound left was the weeping of the survivors, Samuel cautiously left his hiding place and went out into the streets of the ghetto to look for his mother. It seemed to the young boy that the whole world was on fire. The entire sky was red from the blazing wooden buildings that burned on every side, and clouds of thick black smoke hung everywhere. Men and women were frantically searching for their families, or trying to save their businesses and homes and meager possessions. Kraków, in the mid-nineteenth century, had a fire department, but it was forbidden to the Jews. Here in the ghetto, at the edge of the city, they were forced to fight the holocaust by hand, with water drawn from their wells, and scores of people formed bucket brigades to drown the flames. Samuel saw death wherever he looked, mutilated bodies of men and women tossed aside like broken dolls; naked, raped women and children, bleeding and moaning for help.

Samuel found his mother lying in the street, half conscious, her face covered with blood. The young boy knelt down at her side, his heart pounding wildly. "Mama!"

She opened her eyes and saw him, and tried to speak, and Samuel knew that she was dying. He desperately wanted to save her, but he did not know how, and even as he gently wiped the blood away, it was already too late.

Later, Samuel stood there watching as the burial party carefully dug up the ground under his mother's body: for it was soaked in her blood, and according to the Scriptures, it had to be buried with her so that she could be returned to God whole.

It was at that moment that Samuel made up his mind that he wanted to become a doctor.

The Roffe family shared a three-story narrow wooden house with eight other families. Young Samuel lived in one small room with his father and his aunt Rachel, and in all his life he had never been in a room by himself or slept or eaten alone. He could not remember a single moment when he could not hear the sound of voices, but Samuel did not crave privacy, for he had no idea that it existed. He had always lived in a crowded maze.

Each evening Samuel and his relatives and friends were locked into the ghetto by the gentiles, as the Jews penned up their goats and cows and chickens.

At sundown the massive double wooden gates of the ghetto were closed and locked with a large iron key. At sunrise the gates were opened again, and the Jewish merchants were permitted to go into the city of Kraków to conduct business with the gentiles, but they were required to be back inside the ghetto walls before sunset.

Samuel's father had come from Russia, where he had fled from a pogrom in Kiev, and he had made his way to Kraków, where he had met his bride. Samuel's father was a stooped, gray-haired man, his face worn and wrinkled, a pushcart peddler who hawked his wares of notions and trinkets and utensils through the narrow winding streets of the ghetto. Young Samuel loved to roam the crowded, bustling, cobblestoned streets.

He enjoyed the smell of fresh-baked bread mingled with the odors of drying fish and cheeses and ripening fruit and sawdust and leather. He liked to listen to the peddlers singing out their wares, and the housewives bargaining with them in outraged, grieved tones. The variety of goods that the peddlers sold was staggering: linens and laces, ticking and yarn, leather and meats and vegetables and needles and soft soap and plucked whole chickens and candies and buttons and syrups and shoes.

On Samuel's twelfth birthday his father took him into the city of Kraków for the first time. The idea of going through the forbidden gates and seeing Kraków itself, the home of the gentiles, filled the boy with an almost unbearable excitement.

At six o'clock in the morning Samuel, wearing his one good suit, stood in the dark next to his father in front of the huge closed gates to the city, surrounded by a noisy crowd of men with crude, homemade pushcarts, wagons or barrows. The air was cold and raw, and Samuel huddled into his threadbare sheep's-wool coat.

After what seemed hours, a bright-orange sun peeped over the eastern horizon and there was an expectant stir from the crowd. Moments later, the huge wooden gates began to swing open and the merchants started to pour through them like a stream of industrious ants, heading toward the city.

As they approached the wonderful, terrible city, Samuel's heart began to beat faster. Ahead he could see the fortifications towering over the Vistula. Samuel clung to his father more tightly. He was actually in Kraków, surrounded by the feared goyim, the people who locked them up every night. He stole quick, frightened glances at the faces of the passers-by and he marveled at how different they looked. They did not wear *payves*, earlocks, and *bekeches*, the long black coats, and many of them were cleanshaven. Samuel and his father walked along the Plante toward the Rynek, the crowded marketplace, where they passed the enormous cloth hall, and the twin-towered Church of Saint Mary. Samuel had never seen such magnificence. The new world was filled with wonders. First of all, there was an exciting feeling of freedom and space that left Samuel breathless. The houses on the streets were all set apart, not jumbled together, and most of them had a small garden in front. Surely, Samuel thought, everyone in Kraków must be a millionaire.

Samuel accompanied his father to half a dozen different suppliers, where his father bought goods which he tossed into the cart. When the cart was filled, he and the boy headed back toward the ghetto.

"Can't we stay longer?" Samuel begged.

"No, son. We have to go home."

Samuel did not want to go home. He had been outside the gates for the first time in his life, and he was filled with an elation that was so strong it almost choked him. That people could live like *this*, free to walk wherever they pleased, free to do whatever they wanted . . . Why could he not have been born outside the gate? Instantly, he was ashamed of himself for having such disloyal thoughts.

That night when Samuel went to bed, he lay awake for a long time, thinking about Kraków and the beautiful houses with their flowers and green gardens. He had to find a way to get free. He wanted to talk to someone about the things he felt, but there was no one who would understand him.

ELIZABETH PUT THE Book down and sat back, closing her eyes, visualizing Samuel's loneliness, his excitement, his frustration.

It was at that moment that Elizabeth began to identify with him, to feel that she was a part of him, as he was a part of her. His blood ran in her veins. She had a wonderful, heady sense of belonging.

Elizabeth heard the sound of her father's car coming up the driveway, and she quickly put the Book away. She had no further chance to read it during her stay there, but when she returned to New York the Book was hidden at the bottom of her suitcase.

fter the warm winter sunshine of Sardinia, New York seemed like
Siberia. The streets were filled with snow and slush, and the wind
blowing off the East River, was frigid; but Elizabeth did not mind.
She was living in Poland, in another century, sharing the adventures
of her great-great-grandfather. Every afternoon after school, Elizabeth
would rush up to her room, lock the door and take out the Book. She
had thought of discussing it with her father, but she was afraid to, for
fear he would take it away from her.

In a wonderful, unexpected way, it was old Samuel who gave Elizabeth encouragement. It seemed to Elizabeth that they were so much
alike. Samuel was a loner. He had no one to talk to. Like me, thought
Elizabeth. And because they were almost the same age—even though a
century apart—she could identify with him.

SAMUEL WANTED TO be a doctor.

Only three physicians were allowed to take care of the thousands of
people crowded into the unsanitary, epidemic-ridden confines of the

ghetto; and of the three, the most prosperous was Dr. Zeno Wal. His house stood among its poorer neighbors like a castle in the midst of a slum. It was three stories high, and through its windows could be seen freshly washed and starched white-lace curtains and glimpses of shining, polished furniture. Samuel could visualize the doctor inside, treating his patients, helping them, curing them: doing what Samuel longed to do. Surely, if someone like Dr. Wal took an interest in him, Samuel thought, he could help him become a doctor. But as far as Samuel was concerned, Dr. Wal was as inaccessible as any of the gentiles living in the city of Kraków, outside the forbidden wall.

From time to time Samuel would catch glimpses of the great Dr. Zeno Wal walking along the street, engaged in earnest conversation with a colleague. One day, as Samuel was passing the Wal house, the front door opened and the doctor came out with his daughter. She was about Samuel's age, and she was the most beautiful creature Samuel had ever seen. The moment Samuel looked at her, he knew she was going to be his wife. He did not know how he was going to manage that miracle, he only knew that he had to.

Every day after that, Samuel found an excuse to be near her house, hoping to get another glimpse of her.

One afternoon, as Samuel was walking by the Wal house on an errand, he heard piano music coming from inside, and he knew that *she* was playing. He had to see her. Looking around to make sure no one was observing him, Samuel walked to the side of the house. The music was coming from upstairs, directly above his head. Samuel stepped back and studied the wall. There were enough handholds for him to climb it, and without a moment's hesitation he started up. The second floor was higher than he had realized, and before he reached the window he was ten feet above the ground. He looked down and felt a momentary sense of dizziness. The music was louder now, and he felt as if she were playing for him. He grabbed another handhold and pulled himself up to the window. Slowly he raised his head so he could peer over the sill. He found himself looking into an exquisitely furnished parlor. The girl was seated before a gold-and-white piano, playing, and behind her in an armchair, reading a book, was Dr. Wal. Samuel had no eyes for him. He could only stare at the beautiful vision, just a few feet away from him.

He loved her! He would do something spectacular and daring so that she would fall in love with him. He would— So engrossed was Samuel in his daydream that he loosened his grip and began to fall into space. He let out a cry and saw two startled faces staring at him just before he plunged to the ground.

He woke up on an operating table in Dr. Wal's office, a spacious room outfitted with medical cabinets and an array of surgical equipment. Dr. Wal was holding an awful-smelling piece of cotton under Samuel's nose. Samuel choked and sat up.

"That's better," Dr. Wal said. "I should remove your brain but I doubt if you have one. What were you planning to steal, boy?"

"Nothing," Samuel replied indignantly.

"What's your name?"

"Samuel Roffe."

The doctor's fingers began to probe Samuel's right wrist, and the boy cried out with pain.

"Hm. You have a broken wrist, Samuel Roffe. Maybe we should let the police fix it."

Samuel groaned aloud. He was thinking about what would happen when the police brought him home in disgrace. His aunt Rachel's heart would be broken; his father would kill him. But, even more important, how could he ever hope to win Dr. Wal's daughter now? He was a criminal, a marked man. Samuel felt a sudden, agonizing jerk on his wrist, and he looked up at the doctor in shocked surprise.

"It's all right," Dr. Wal said. "I've set it." He went to work putting a splint on it. "Do you live around here, Samuel Roffe?"

"No, sir."

"Haven't I seen you hanging about?"

"Yes, sir."

"Why?"

Why? If Samuel told him the truth, Dr. Wal would laugh at him.

"I want to become a doctor," Samuel blurted out, unable to contain himself.

Dr. Wal was staring at him in disbelief. "*That's* why you climbed the wall of my house like a burglar?"

Samuel found himself telling his entire story. He told about his mother dying in the streets, and about his father, about his first visit to Kraków and his frustration at being locked inside the ghetto walls at night like an animal. He told how he felt about Dr. Wal's daughter. He told everything, and the doctor listened in silence. Even to Samuel's ears his story sounded ridiculous; and when he was finished, he whispered, "I—I'm sorry."

Dr. Wal looked at him for a long time, and then said, "I'm sorry, too. For you, and for me, and for all of us. Every man is a prisoner, and the greatest irony of all is to be the prisoner of another man."

Samuel looked up at him, puzzled. "I don't understand, sir."

The doctor sighed. "One day you will." He rose to his feet, walked over to his desk, selected a pipe and slowly and methodically filled it "I'm afraid this is a very bad day for you, Samuel Roffe."

He put a match to the tobacco, blew it out and then turned to the boy. "Not because of your broken wrist. That will heal. But I'm going to have to do something to you that may not heal so quickly." Samuel was watching him, his eyes wide. Dr. Wal walked over to his side, and when he spoke his voice was gentle. "Very few people ever have a dream. You have two dreams. And I'm afraid I am going to have to break both of them."

"I don't—"

"Listen to me carefully, Samuel. You can never be a doctor—not in our world. Only three of us are allowed to practice medicine in the ghetto. There are dozens of skilled doctors here, waiting for one of us to retire or to die, so that they can take our place. There's no chance for you. None. You were born at the wrong time, in the wrong place. Do you understand me, boy?"

Samuel swallowed. "Yes, sir."

The doctor hesitated, then went on. "About your second dream—I'm afraid that one is just as impossible. There is no chance of your ever marrying Terenia."

"Why?" Samuel asked.

Dr. Wal stared at him. "*Why?* For the same reason you can't become a doctor. We live by the rules, by our traditions. My daughter will marry someone of her own class, someone who can afford to keep her in the same style in which she has been raised. She will marry a professional man, a lawyer or a doctor or a rabbi. You—well, you must put her out of your mind."

"But—"

The doctor was ushering him toward the door. "Have someone look at that splint in a few days. See that the bandage is kept clean."

"Yes, sir," Samuel said. "Thank you, Dr. Wal."

Dr. Wal studied the blond, intelligent-looking boy before him. "Good-bye, Samuel Roffe."

EARLY THE NEXT afternoon, Samuel rang the front doorbell of the Wal house. Dr. Wal watched him through the window. He knew that he should send him away.

"Send him in," Dr. Wal said to the maid.

After that, Samuel came to Dr. Wal's house two or three times a week. He ran errands for the doctor, and in exchange Dr. Wal let him watch as he treated patients or worked in his laboratory, concocting medicines. The boy observed and learned and remembered everything. He had a natural talent. Dr. Wal felt a growing sense of guilt, for he knew that in a way he was encouraging Samuel, encouraging him to be something he could never be; and yet he could not bring himself to turn the boy away.

Whether it was by accident or design, Terenia was almost always around when Samuel was there. Occasionally he would get a glimpse of her walking past the laboratory, or leaving the house, and once he bumped into her in the kitchen, and his heart began to pound so hard that he thought he would faint. She studied him for a long moment, a look of speculation in her eyes, then she nodded coolly and was gone. At least she had noticed him! That was the first step. The rest was only a matter of time. There was not the slightest doubt in Samuel's mind. It was fated. Terenia had become a major part of Samuel's dreams about the future. Where once he had dreamed for himself, he now dreamed for the two of them. Somehow he would get them both out of this terrible ghetto, this stinking, overcrowded prison. And he would become a great success. But now his success would not be for him alone, but for both of them.

Even though it was impossible.

. . .

ELIZABETH FELL ASLEEP, reading about old Samuel. In the morning when she awakened, she carefully hid the Book and began to get dressed for school. She could not get Samuel off her mind. How did he marry Terenia? How did he get out of the ghetto? How did he become famous? Elizabeth was consumed by the Book, and she resented the intrusions that tore her away from it and forced her to return to the twentieth century.

One of the classes that Elizabeth had to attend was ballet, and she loathed it. She would stuff herself into her pink tutu, and stare at her image in the mirror and try to tell herself that her figure was voluptuous. But the truth was there for her to see. She was fat. She would never be a ballet dancer.

Shortly after Elizabeth's fourteenth birthday, Mme. Netturova, her dance teacher, announced that in two weeks the class would give its yearly dance recital in the auditorium, and that the students were to invite their parents. Elizabeth was in a state of panic. The mere thought of getting up on a stage in front of an audience filled her with dread. She could not go through with it.

A child was running across a street in front of a car. Elizabeth saw her, raced out and snatched the child from the jaws of death. Unfortunately, ladies and gentlemen, Elizabeth Roffe's toes were crushed by the wheels of the automobile, and she will not be able to dance at the recital this evening.

A careless maid left a bar of soap at the top of the stairs. Elizabeth slipped and fell down the long flight, breaking her hip. Nothing to worry about, the doctor said. It will heal in three weeks.

No such luck. On the day of the performance, Elizabeth was in perfect health, and in a state of hysteria. Again, it was old Samuel who helped her. She remembered how frightened he had been, but he had gone back to face Dr. Wal. She would not do anything to disgrace Samuel. She would face up to her ordeal.

Elizabeth had not even mentioned the recital to her father. In the past she had often asked him to school meetings and parties which parents were requested to attend, but he had always been too busy.

On this evening, as Elizabeth was getting ready to leave for the dance recital, her father returned home. He had been out of town for ten days.

He passed her bedroom, saw her and said, "Good evening, Elizabeth." Then, "You've put on some weight."

She flushed and tried to pull in her stomach. "Yes, Father."

He started to say something, then changed his mind. "How's school coming along?"

"Fine, thank you."

"Any problems?"

"No, Father."

"Good."

It was a dialogue they had had a hundred times over the years, a meaningless litany that seemed to be their only form of communication. How's-school-coming-along-fine-thank-you-any-problems-no-Father-good. Two strangers discussing the weather, neither listening nor caring about the other's opinion. Well, one of us cares, Elizabeth thought.

But this time Sam Roffe stood there, watching his daughter, a thoughtful expression on his face. He was used to dealing with concrete problems and although he sensed that there was a problem here, he had no idea what it was, and if anyone had told him, Sam Roffe's answer would have been, "Don't be a fool. I've given Elizabeth everything."

As her father started to leave, Elizabeth heard herself say, "My—my—ballet class is giving a recital. I'm in it. You don't want to come, do you?"

And even as she said the words, she was filled with a sense of horror. She did not want him there to see her clumsiness. Why had she asked him? But she knew why. Because she was the only girl in the class whose parents would not be in that auditorium. It doesn't matter, anyway, she told herself, because he's going to say no. She shook her head, furious with herself, and turned away. And behind her, incredibly, she heard her father's voice saying, "I'd like that."

THE AUDITORIUM WAS crowded with parents, relatives and friends, watching the students dance to the accompaniment of two grand pianos on either side of the stage. Mme. Netturova stood off to one side, counting the beat aloud as the children danced, calling the attention of the parents to herself.

A few of the children were remarkably graceful, and showed signs of real talent. The others went through their performances determined to substitute enthusiasm for ability. The mimeographed program announced three musical excerpts from *Coppélia, Cinderella* and, inevitably, *Swan Lake*. The *pièce de résistance* was to be the solos, when each child would have her moment of glory, alone.

Backstage, Elizabeth was in an agony of apprehension. She kept peering through the side curtain, and each time she saw her father sitting in the second row center, she thought what a fool she had been to ask him. So far during the show, Elizabeth had been able to lose herself in the background, hidden behind the other dancers. But now her solo was coming up. She felt gross in her tutu, like something in a circus. She was certain they would all laugh at her when she came out on the stage—and she had *invited* her father to watch her humiliation! Elizabeth's only consolation was that her solo lasted for only sixty seconds. Mme. Netturova was no fool. It would all be over so quickly that no one would even notice her. All Elizabeth's father had to do was to glance away for a minute, and her number would be finished.

Elizabeth watched the other girls as they danced, one by one, and they seemed to her like Markova, Maximova, Fonteyn. She was startled by a cold hand on her bare arm, and Mme. Netturova hissed, "On your toes, Elizabeth, you're next."

Elizabeth tried to say, "Yes, madame," but her throat was so dry that no words came out. The two pianists struck up the familiar theme of Elizabeth's solo. She stood there, frozen, incapable of moving, and Mme. Netturova was whispering, "Get out there!" and Elizabeth felt a shove against her back, and she was out on the stage, half naked, in front of a hundred hostile strangers. She did not dare look at her father. All she wanted was to get this ordeal over with as quickly as possible and flee. What she had to do was simple, a few pliés and jetés and leaps. She began to execute the steps, keeping tune to the music, trying to think herself thin and tall and lithe. As she finished, there was a smattering of polite applause from the audience. Elizabeth looked down at the second row, and there was her father, smiling proudly and applauding—applauding *her,* and something inside Elizabeth snapped. The music had stopped. But Elizabeth kept on dancing, doing pliés and jetés and battements and turns, carried away, transported beyond herself. The confused musicians began to pick up her beat, first one pianist, then the other, trying to keep up with her. Backstage, Mme. Netturova was signaling to Elizabeth wildly, her face filled with fury. But Elizabeth was blissfully unaware of her, transported beyond herself. The only thing that mattered to her was that she was onstage, dancing for her father.

"I AM SURE you understand, Mr. Roffe, that this school simply cannot tolerate that type of behavior." Mme. Netturova's voice was trembling with anger. "Your daughter ignored everyone else and took over, as though—as though she were some kind of *star*."

Elizabeth could feel her father turn to look at her, and she was afraid to meet his eyes. She knew that what she had done was unforgivable, but she had been unable to stop herself. For one moment on that stage she had tried to create something beautiful for her father, had tried to impress him, make him notice her, be proud of her. Love her.

Now she heard him say, "You're absolutely right, Madame Netturova. I will see to it that Elizabeth is suitably punished."

Mme. Netturova gave Elizabeth a look of triumph, and said, "Thank you, Mr. Roffe. I will leave it in your hands."

Elizabeth and her father were standing outside the school. He had not said one word to her since leaving Mme. Netturova's office. Elizabeth was trying to compose a speech of apology—but what could she say? How could she ever make her father understand why she had done what she had done? He was a stranger, and she was afraid of him. She had heard him vent his terrible anger on others for making mistakes, or for having disobeyed him. Now she stood there waiting for his wrath to fall upon her.

He turned to her and said, "Elizabeth, why don't we drop in at Rumpelmayer's and get a chocolate soda?"

And Elizabeth burst into tears.

SHE LAY IN her bed that night, wide awake, too stimulated to go to sleep. She kept replaying the evening over and over in her mind. The excitement of it had been almost more than she could bear. Because this was no made-up daydream. It had happened, it was real. She could see herself and her father, seated at the table at Rumpelmayer's, surrounded by the large, colorful stuffed bears and elephants and lions and zebras. Elizabeth had ordered a banana split, which had turned out to be absolutely enormous, and her father had not criticized her. He was talking to her. Not how's-school-coming-along-fine-thank-you-any-problems-no-Father-good. But really *talking*. He told her about his recent trip to Tokyo, and how his host had served chocolate-covered grasshoppers and ants as a special treat for him, and how he had had to eat them in order not to lose face.

When Elizabeth had scooped up the last drop of the ice cream, her father suddenly said, "What made you do it, Liz?"

She knew that everything was going to be spoiled now, that he was going to reprimand her, tell her how disappointed he was in her.

She said, "I wanted to be better than everyone else." She could not bring herself to add, *For you.*

He looked at her for what seemed a long time, and then he laughed. "You certainly surprised the hell out of everybody." There was a note of pride in his voice.

Elizabeth felt the blood rushing to her cheeks, and she said, "You're not angry with me?"

There was a look in his eyes that she had never seen before. "For wanting to be the best? That's what the Roffes are all about." And he reached over and squeezed her hand.

Elizabeth's last thoughts as she drifted off to sleep were: My father likes me, he really likes me. From now on, we'll be together all the time. He'll take me on trips with him. We'll talk about things and we'll become good friends.

THE FOLLOWING AFTERNOON her father's secretary informed her that arrangements had been made to send Elizabeth away to a boarding school in Switzerland.

10

Elizabeth was enrolled in the International Château Lemand, a girls' school situated in the village of Sainte-Blaise, overlooking the Lake of Neuchâtel. The age of the girls ranged from fourteen to eighteen. It was one of the finest schools in the excellent Swiss educational system.

Elizabeth hated every minute of it.

She felt exiled. She had been sent away from home, and it was like some dire punishment for a crime she had not committed. On that one magic evening she had felt that she was on the verge of something wonderful, discovering her father, and her father discovering her, and their becoming friends. But now he was farther away than ever.

Elizabeth was able to keep track of her father in the newspapers and magazines. There were frequent stories and photographs of him meeting with a prime minister or a president, opening a new pharmaceutical plant in Bombay, mountain climbing, dining with the Shah of Iran. Elizabeth pasted all the stories in a scrapbook which she constantly pored over. She hid it next to the book of Samuel.

Elizabeth remained aloof from the other students. Some of the girls shared rooms with two or three others, but Elizabeth had asked for a room by herself. She wrote long letters to her father, then tore up the ones that revealed her feelings. From time to time she received a note from him, and there were gaily wrapped packages from expensive stores on her birthday, sent by his secretary. Elizabeth missed her father terribly.

She was going to join him at the villa in Sardinia for Christmas, and as the time drew nearer, the waiting became almost unbearable. She was sick with excitement. She made a list of resolutions for herself and carefully wrote them down:

Do not be a pest.
Be interesting.
Do not complain about anything, especially school.
Do not let him know you are lonely.
Do not interrupt while he is speaking.
Be well groomed at all times, even at breakfast.
Laugh a lot so that he can see how happy you are.

The notes were a prayer, a litany, her offering to the gods. If she did all these things, maybe—maybe—Elizabeth's resolutions merged into fantasies. She would make profound observations about the Third World and the nineteen developing nations, and her father would say, "I didn't know you were so interesting" (rule number two). "You're a very bright girl, Elizabeth." Then he would turn to his secretary and say, "I don't think Elizabeth needs to go back to school. Why don't I keep her here with me?"

A prayer, a litany.

A COMPANY LEARJET picked Elizabeth up at Zurich and flew her to the airport at Olbia, where she was met by a limousine. Elizabeth sat in the back of the car, silent, forcing her knees together to keep them from trembling. No matter what happens, she thought fiercely, I won't let him see me cry. He mustn't know how much I've missed him.

The car drove up the long, winding mountain highway that led to the Costa Smeralda, then off onto the small road that wound to the top. This road had always frightened Elizabeth. It was very narrow and steep, with the mountain on one side and a terrifying abyss on the other.

The car pulled up in front of the house, and Elizabeth stepped out and began walking toward the house and then running, her legs carrying her as fast as they could. The front door opened and Margherita, the Sardinian housekeeper, stood there smiling. "Hello, Miss Elizabeth."

"Where's my father?" Elizabeth asked.

"He had to go to Australia on some emergency. But he left a lot of pretty presents for you. It's going to be a lovely Christmas."

II

Elizabeth had brought the Book with her. She stood in the hallway of the villa, studying the painting of Samuel Roffe, and next to him, Terenia, feeling their presence, as though they had come to life. After a long time Elizabeth turned and climbed up the ladder to the tower room, taking the Book. She spent hours every day in the tower room, reading and rereading, and each time she felt closer to Samuel and Terenia, the century that separated them disappearing . . .

OVER THE NEXT few years, Elizabeth read, Samuel spent long hours in Dr. Wal's laboratory, helping him mix ointments and medicines, learning how they worked. And always in the background was Terenia, haunting, beautiful. The very sight of her was enough to keep alive Samuel's dream that one day she would belong to him. Samuel got along well with Dr. Wal, but Terenia's mother was another story. She was a sharp-tongued virago, a snob, and she hated Samuel. He tried to keep out of her way.

Samuel was fascinated by the many drugs that could heal people. A papyrus had been found that listed 811 prescriptions used by the Egyptians in 1550 B.C. Life expectancy at birth then was fifteen years and Samuel could understand why when he read some of the prescriptions: crocodile dung, lizard flesh, bat's blood, camel's spit, lion's liver, toe of a frog, unicorn powder. The *Rx* sign on every prescription was the ancient prayer to Horae, the Egyptian god of healing. Even the word "chemistry" derived from the ancient name of Egypt, the land of Kahmi, or Chemi. The priest-physicians were called magi, Samuel learned.

The apothecary shops in the ghetto and in Kraków itself were primitive. Most of the bottles and jars were filled with untested and untried medicinal items, some useless, some harmful. Samuel became familiar with them all. There were castor oil, calomel, and rhubarb, iodine compounds and codeine and ipecac. You could purchase panaceas for whooping cough, colic and typhoid fever. Because no sanitary precautions were taken, it was common to find ointments and gargles filled with dead insects, roaches, rat droppings and bits of feathers and furs. The majority of patients who took the remedies died either of their diseases or from the remedies.

Several magazines were printed that were devoted to apothecary news, and Samuel read them all avidly. He discussed his theories with Dr. Wal.

"It stands to reason," Samuel said, his voice ringing with conviction, "that there must be a cure for every disease. Health is natural, disease is unnatural."

"Perhaps," Dr. Wal said, "but most of my patients won't even let me try the new medications on them." He added dryly, "And I think they're wise."

Samuel devoured Dr. Wal's sparse library on pharmacy. And when he had read and reread those books, he felt frustrated by the unanswered questions that lay between the covers.

Samuel was fired by the revolution that was taking place. Some scientists believed that it was possible to counteract the cause of diseases by building up a resistance that would destroy the illness. Dr. Wal tried it once. He took the blood of a patient with diphtheria and injected it into a horse. When the horse died, Dr. Wal gave up his experiments. But young Samuel was sure that Dr. Wal had been on the right track.

"You can't stop now," Samuel said. "I know it will work."

Dr. Wal shook his head. "That's because you're seventeen, Samuel. When you're my age, you won't be as sure of anything. Forget about it."

But Samuel was not convinced. He wanted to continue his experiments, but for that Samuel needed animals, and there were few available except for the stray cats and rats that he was able to catch. No matter how minute the doses that Samuel gave them, they died. They're too small, Samuel thought. I need a larger animal. A horse or a cow or a sheep. But where was he going to find one?

One late afternoon when Samuel arrived home, an ancient horse and cart stood in front of the house. On the side of the cart a crudely lettered sign read: ROFFE & SON. Samuel stared at it unbelievingly, then raced into the house to find his father. "That—that horse out there," he said. "Where did you get it?"

His father smiled at him proudly. "I made a deal. We can cover more territory with a horse. Maybe in four or five years we can buy another horse. Think of it. We'll have *two* horses."

That was the extent of his father's ambition, owning two broken-down horses pulling carts through the dirty, crowded streets of the Kraków ghetto. It made Samuel want to weep.

That night when everyone was asleep, Samuel went out to the stable and examined the horse, which they had named Ferd. As horses went, this one was without question one of the lowest of the species. She was a very old horse, swaybacked and spavined. It was doubtful whether she could move much faster than Samuel's father. But none of that mattered. What was important was that Samuel now had his laboratory animal. He could do his experiments without having to worry about catching rats and stray cats. Of course, he would have to be careful. His father must never find out what he was doing. Samuel stroked the horse's head. "You're going into the drug business," he informed Ferd.

Samuel improvised his own laboratory, using a corner of the stable in which Ferd was kept.

He grew a culture of diphtheria germs in a dish of rich broth. When the broth turned cloudy, he removed some of it to another container and then weakened it, first by diluting the broth, then by heating it slightly. He filled a hypodermic needle with it and approached Ferd. "Remember what I told you?" Samuel whispered. "Well, this is your big day."

Samuel plunged the contents of the hypodermic into the loose skin of the horse's shoulder, as he had seen Dr. Wal do. Ferd turned to look at him reproachfully, and sprayed him with urine.

Samuel estimated that it would take about seventy-two hours for the culture to develop in Ferd. At the end of that time Samuel would give her a larger dose. Then another. If the antibody theory was right, each dose would build up a stronger blood resistance to the disease. Samuel would have his vaccine. Later, he would have to find a human being to test it on, of course, but that should not be difficult. A victim of the dread disease should be only too happy to try something that might save his life.

For the next two days Samuel spent almost every waking moment with Ferd.

"I've never seen anyone love an animal so much," his father said. "You can't keep away from her, can you?"

Samuel mumbled an inaudible reply. He felt a sense of guilt about what he was doing, but he knew what would happen if he even mentioned it to his father. However, there was no need for his father to know. All Samuel had to do was extract enough blood from Ferd to make up a vial or two of serum, and no one would ever be the wiser.

On the morning of the third and crucial day, Samuel was awakened by the sound of his father's voice from in front of the house. Samuel got out of bed, hurried to the window and looked out. His father was standing in the street with his cart, bellowing at the top of his lungs. There was no sign of Ferd. Samuel threw on some clothes and raced outside.

"Momser!" his father was yelling. "Cheater! Liar! Thief!"

Samuel pushed past the crowd that was beginning to gather around his father.

"Where's Ferd?" Samuel demanded.

"I'm glad you asked me," his father moaned. "She's dead. She died in the streets like a dog."

Samuel's heart sank.

"We're going along as nice as you please. I'm tending to business, not rushing her, you understand, not whipping her, or pushing her like some of the other peddlers I could name. And how does she show her appreciation? She drops dead. When I catch that *gonif* who sold her to me, I'll kill him!"

Samuel turned away, sick at heart. More than Ferd had passed away. Samuel's dreams had died. With Ferd went the escape from the ghetto, the freedom, the beautiful house for Terenia and their children.

But a greater disaster was to befall.

The day after Ferd died, Samuel learned that Dr. Wal and his wife had arranged for Terenia to marry a rabbi. Samuel could not believe it. Terenia belonged to *him!* Samuel raced over to the Wal house. He found Dr. and Mrs. Wal in the parlor. He walked up to them, took a deep breath and announced, "There's been a mistake, Terenia's mistake, Terenia's going to marry *me.*"

They stared at him in astonishment.

"I know I'm not good enough for her," Samuel hurried on, "but she won't be happy married to anyone but me. The rabbi's too old for—"

"*Nebbich!* Out! Out!" Terenia's mother was apoplectic.

Sixty seconds later Samuel found himself standing out in the street, forbidden ever to enter the Wal house again.

In the middle of the night Samuel had a long talk with God.

"What do you want from me? If I can't have Terenia, why did you make me love her? Haven't you any feelings?" He raised his voice in frustration and yelled, "Can you hear me?"

And the others in the crowded little house yelled back, "We can all hear you, Samuel. For God's sake, shut up and let us get some sleep!"

The following afternoon Dr. Wal sent for Samuel. He was ushered into the parlor, where Dr. and Mrs. Wal and Terenia were gathered.

"It seems we have a problem," Dr. Wal began. "Our daughter can be quite a stubborn young lady. For some reason she's taken a fancy to you. I cannot call it love, Samuel, because I don't believe that young girls know what love is. However, she has refused to marry Rabbi Rabinowitz. She thinks she wants to marry you."

Samuel sneaked a glance at Terenia, and she smiled at him and he almost burst with joy. It was short-lived.

Dr. Wal was going on. "You said that you love my daughter."

"Y-y-yes, sir," Samuel stammered. He tried it again, his voice stronger. "Yes, sir."

"Then let me ask you something, Samuel. Would you like Terenia to spend the rest of her life married to a peddler?"

Samuel instantly saw the trap, but there was no way out of it. He looked at Terenia again and said slowly, "No, sir."

"Ah. Then you see the problem. None of us wants Terenia to marry a peddler. And you're a peddler, Samuel."

"I won't always be, Dr. Wal." Samuel's voice was strong and sure.

"And what *will* you be?" Mrs. Wal snapped. "You come from a family of peddlers, you'll remain a family of peddlers. I will not allow my daughter to marry one."

Samuel looked at the three of them, his mind filled with confusion. He had come here with trepidation and despair, had been lifted to the heights of joy, and now he had been plunged into a black abyss again. What did they want from him?

"We've agreed on a compromise," Dr. Wal said. "We're going to give you six months to prove that you're more than just a peddler. If, by the end of that time, you cannot offer Terenia the kind of life she is accustomed to, then she is going to marry Rabbi Rabinowitz."

Samuel stared at him, aghast. "Six months!"

No one could become a success in six months! No one, certainly, who lived in the ghetto of Kraków.

"Do you understand?" Dr. Wal asked.

"Yes, sir." Samuel understood only too well. He felt as if his stomach were filled with lead. He did not need a solution, he needed a miracle. The Wals would only be content with a son-in-law who was a doctor or a rabbi, or who was wealthy. Samuel quickly examined each possibility.

The law forbade him to become a doctor.

A rabbi? One had to start studying for the rabbinate by thirteen, and Samuel was almost eighteen now.

Wealthy? That was out of the question. If he worked twenty-four hours a day peddling his wares in the streets of the ghetto until he was ninety, he would still be a poor man. The Wals had set an impossible task for him. They had seemingly given in to Terenia by allowing her to postpone her marriage to the rabbi, while at the same time setting conditions that they knew would be impossible for Samuel to meet. Terenia was the only one who believed in him. She had confidence that he could find some kind of fame or fortune in six months. She's crazier than I am, Samuel thought in despair.

• • •

THE SIX MONTHS began, and time flew. Samuel's days were spent as a peddler, helping his father. But the moment the shadows of the setting sun began to fall on the walls of the ghetto, Samuel would hurry home, gulp down a bite to eat, and then go to work in his laboratory. He made hundreds of batches of serums, and injected rabbits and cats and dogs and birds, and all the animals died. They're too small, Samuel thought desperately. I need a larger animal.

But he had none, and time was racing by.

Twice a week Samuel would go into Kraków to replenish the merchandise that he and his father sold from the cart. He would stand inside the locked gates at dawn, surrounded by the other peddlers, but he neither saw nor heard them. His mind was in another world.

As Samuel stood there one morning, daydreaming, a voice yelled, "You! Jew! Move on!"

Samuel looked up. The gates had been opened and his cart was blocking the way. One of the guards was angrily motioning for Samuel to move. There were always two guards on duty in front of the gate. They wore green uniforms and special insignia and were armed with pistols and heavy clubs. On a chain around his waist one of the guards carried a large key that opened and locked the gates. Alongside the ghetto ran a small river spanned by an old wooden bridge. Across the bridge was the police garrison where the ghetto guards were stationed. More than once, Samuel had witnessed a hapless Jew being dragged across the bridge. It was always a one-way trip. Jews were required to be back inside the ghetto by sundown, and any Jew caught outside the gates after dark was arrested and deported to a labor camp. It was the nightmare of every Jew that he might be caught outside the ghetto after sunset.

Both guards were supposed to remain on duty, patrolling in front of the gates, all night; but it was common knowledge inside the ghetto that after the Jews were locked in, one of the guards would slip away for a night of pleasure in the city. Just before dawn he would return to help his partner open the gates for the new day.

The two guards that were usually stationed there were named Paul and Aram. Paul was a pleasant man with a genial disposition. Aram was an entirely different matter. He was an animal, swarthy and stockily built, with powerful arms and a body like a beer keg. He was a Jew-baiter, and whenever he was on duty, all the Jews outside the gates made sure that they returned early, because nothing delighted Aram more than to lock a Jew out, club him senseless and drag him across the bridge to the dreaded police barracks.

It was Aram now who stood yelling at Samuel to move his cart. He hurriedly went through the gates and headed for the city, and he could feel Aram's eyes boring into his back.

SAMUEL'S SIX-MONTH GRACE period quickly dwindled to five months and then to four months, then three. There was not a day, not an hour, when Samuel was not thinking about a solution to his problem, or feverishly working in his tiny laboratory. He tried to speak to some of the wealthy merchants of the ghetto, but few had time for him, and those who had time offered him useless advice.

"You want to make money? Save your pennies, boy, and one day you'll have enough to buy a fine business like mine."

That was easy enough for them to say—most of them had been born into wealthy homes.

Samuel thought of taking Terenia and running away. But where? At the end of their journey would lie another ghetto, and he would still be a penniless *nebbich*. No, he loved Terenia too much to do that to her. That was the real trap in which he was caught.

Inexorably the clock ran on, and the three months became two, and then one. Samuel's only consolation during that time was that he was allowed to see his beloved Terenia three times a week, chaperoned, of course, and each time Samuel saw her, he loved her more deeply. It was a bittersweet feeling, for the more often he saw her, the closer he was coming to losing her. "You'll find a way," Terenia kept assuring him.

But now there were only three weeks left, and Samuel was no closer to a solution than when he had started.

Late one night Terenia came to see Samuel at the stable. She put her arms around him and said, "Let's run away, Samuel."

He had never loved her so much as he loved her at that moment. She was willing to disgrace herself, give up her mother and father, the wonderful life she lived, for him.

He held her close and said, "We can't. Wherever we went, I'd still be a peddler."

"I don't mind."

Samuel thought of her beautiful home with the spacious rooms and the servants, and he thought of the tiny squalid room he shared with his father and his aunt, and he said, "*I* would mind, Terenia."

And she turned and left.

The following morning Samuel met Isaac, a former schoolmate, walking down the street, leading a horse. It had one eye, suffered from acute colic, was spavined and deaf.

"Morning, Samuel."

"Morning, Isaac. I don't know where you're going with that poor horse, but you'd better hurry. It doesn't look like it's going to last much longer."

"It doesn't have to. I'm taking Lottie to a glue factory."

Samuel eyed the animal with a sudden, quickened interest. "I shouldn't think they'd give you much for her."

"I know. I just want a couple of florins to buy a cart."

Samuel's heart began to pump faster. "I think I can save you a trip. I'll trade you my cart for your horse."

It took less than five minutes to conclude the bargain.

Now all Samuel had to do was build another cart and explain to his father how he had lost the old one, and how he had come into possession of a horse that was on its last legs.

Samuel led Lottie to the barn where he had kept Ferd. On closer examination the horse was an even more discouraging sight. Samuel patted the animal and said, "Don't worry, Lottie, you're going to make medical history."

A few minutes later Samuel was at work on a new serum.

BECAUSE OF THE crowded and unsanitary conditions of the ghetto, epidemics were frequent. The latest plague was a fever that produced a choking cough, swollen glands and a painful death. The doctors did not know what caused it, or how to treat it. Isaac's father came down with the disease. When Samuel heard the news, he hurried over to see Isaac.

"The doctor has been here," the weeping boy told Samuel. "He said there's nothing to be done."

From upstairs they could hear the terrible sounds of a racking cough that seemed to go on forever.

"I want you to do something for me," Samuel said. "Get me a handkerchief of your father's."

Isaac stared at him. *"What?"*

"One that he's used. And be careful how you handle it. It will be full of germs."

An hour later Samuel was back at the stable, carefully scraping the contents of the handerchief into a dish filled with broth.

He worked all that night and all the next day and the following day, injecting small doses of the substance into the patient Lottie, then larger doses, fighting against time, trying to save the life of Isaac's father.

Trying to save his own life.

IN LATER YEARS Samuel was never sure whether God was looking out for him or for the old horse, but Lottie survived the gradually increased doses, and Samuel had his first batch of antitoxin. His next task was to persuade Isaac's father to let him use it on him.

As it turned out, it needed no persuasion. When Samuel reached Isaac's house, it was filled with relatives, mourning the dying man upstairs.

"He only has a little time left," Isaac told Samuel.

"Can I see him?"

The two boys went upstairs. Isaac's father was in bed, his face flushed with fever. Each racking cough sent his wasted frame into spasms that left him weaker. It was obvious that he was dying.

Samuel took a deep breath and said, "I want to talk to you and your mother."

Neither of them had any confidence in the little glass vial that Samuel had brought, but the alternative was death. They took a chance simply because there was nothing to lose.

Samuel injected Isaac's father with the serum. He waited at the bedside for three hours, and there was no change. The serum had no effect.

If anything, the coughing spells seemed more frequent. Finally Samuel left, avoiding Isaac's eyes.

At dawn the next day Samuel had to go into Kraków to buy goods. He was in a fever of impatience to get back to see whether Isaac's father was still alive.

There were large crowds at all the markets, and it seemed to Samuel that it took forever to make his purchases. It was late afternoon by the time his cart was finally filled and he headed back toward the ghetto.

When Samuel was still two miles away from the gates, disaster struck. One of the wheels of the cart broke in half and the merchandise began to spill onto the sidewalk. Samuel was in a terrible dilemma. He had to find another wheel somewhere, and yet he did not dare leave the cart unguarded. A crowd had begun to gather, eyeing the spilled merchandise with avid eyes. Samuel saw a uniformed policeman approaching—a gentile—and he knew that he was lost. They would take everything away from him. The policeman pushed his way through the crowd and turned to the frightened boy. "Your cart needs a new wheel."

"Y-yes, sir."

"Do you know where to find one?"

"No, sir."

The policeman wrote something on a piece of paper. "Go there. Tell him what you need."

Samuel said, "I can't leave the cart."

"Yes, you can," the policeman said. He cast a stern eye over the crowd. "I'll be right here. Hurry!"

Samuel ran all the way. Following the directions on the piece of paper, he found himself in a blacksmith's shop, and when Samuel explained the situation, the blacksmith found a wheel that was the right size for the wagon. Samuel paid for the wheel out of the small bag of money he carried. He had half a dozen guldens left.

He raced back to his cart, rolling the wheel before him. The policeman was still there, and the crowd had dispersed. The merchandise was safe. With the policeman helping him, it took another half hour to get the wheel on and secure it. Once more he started back home. His thoughts were on Isaac's father. Would Samuel find him dead or alive? He did not think he could stand the suspense of not knowing a moment longer.

He was only a mile from the ghetto now. Samuel could see the high walls rising against the sky. And even as he watched, the sun set on the western horizon, and the unfamiliar streets were bathed in darkness. In the excitement of what had happened, Samuel had forgotten about the time. It was past sundown and he was outside the gates! He began to run, pushing the heavy cart ahead of him, his heart pounding until it felt ready to burst. The ghetto gates would be closed. Samuel recalled all the terrible stories he had heard about Jews who were locked out of the ghetto at night. He began running faster. There would probably be only one guard on duty now. If it were Paul, the friendly one, then Samuel might have a chance. If it were Aram—Samuel could not bear to think about it. The darkness was thickening now, closing in on him like a black fog, and a light rain began to fall. Samuel was nearing the ghetto walls, only two blocks away, and suddenly the huge gates loomed into view. They were locked.

Samuel had never seen them closed from the outside before. It was as though life had suddenly been turned inside out, and he shivered with terror. He was shut away from his family, from his world, from everything that was familiar. He slowed down, approaching the gates warily, looking for the guards. They were not in sight. Samuel was filled with a sudden wild hope. The guards had probably been called away on some emergency. Samuel would find a way to open the gates, or to scale the walls without being seen. As he reached the gates, the figure of a guard stepped out of the shadows.

"Keep coming," the guard commanded.

In the darkness Samuel could not see his face. But he recognized the voice. It was Aram.

"Closer. Come here."

Aram was watching Samuel approach, a thin grin on his face. The boy faltered.

"That's it," Aram called encouragingly. "Keep walking."

Slowly, Samuel moved toward the giant, his stomach churning, his head pounding. "Sir," Samuel said. "Please let me explain. I had an accident. My cart—"

Aram reached out with his hamlike fist, grabbed Samuel by the collar and lifted him into the air. "You dumb son-of-a-bitch of a Jew," he crooned softly. "Do you think I care why you're out? You're on the wrong side of the gates! Do you know what's going to happen to you now?"

The boy shook his head in terror.

"Let me tell you," Aram said. "We got a new edict last week. All Jews caught outside the gates after sundown are to be shipped to Silesia. Ten years at hard labor. How do you like that?"

Samuel could not believe it. "But I—I haven't done anything. I—"

With his right hand Aram hit Samuel hard across the mouth, then let him drop heavily to the ground. "Let's go," Aram said.

"Wh-where?" Samuel asked. His voice was choked with terror.

"To the police barracks. In the morning you'll be shipped out with the rest of the scum. Get up."

Samuel lay there, unable to bring his mind into focus. "I—I have to go inside to say good-bye to my family."

Aram grinned. "They won't miss you."

"Please!" Samuel pleaded. "Let me—let me at least send them a message."

The smile died on Aram's face. He stood over Samuel menacingly. When he spoke his voice was soft. "I said get up, Jew shit. If I have to say it once more, I'll kick your balls in for you."

Slowly, Samuel rose to his feet. Aram took his arm with an iron grip and started walking him toward the police barracks. *Ten years of hard labor in Silesia!* No one ever returned from there. He looked up at the man holding his arm, pulling him toward the bridge that led to the barracks.

"Please don't do this," Samuel pleaded. "Let me go."

Aram squeezed his arm tighter, so that the blood seemed to stop flowing. "Keep begging," Aram said. "I love to hear a Jew beg. Have you heard about Silesia? You'll be just in time for the winter. But don't worry, it's nice and warm underground in the mines. And when your lungs get black with coal and you start coughing them up, they'll leave you out in the snow to die."

Ahead of them across the bridge, barely visible in the rain, was the stark building that served as the police barracks.

"Faster!" Aram said.

And suddenly Samuel knew that he could not let anyone do this to him. He thought of Terenia and his family and Isaac's father. No one would take his life from him. Somehow he had to escape, to save himself. They were crossing the narrow bridge now, the river running noisily below, swollen by the winter rains. There were only thirty yards left to go. Whatever was going to be done had to be done now. But how could he escape? Aram had a gun and even without it the enormous guard could have killed him easily. He was almost twice as big as Samuel and much more powerful. They had reached the other side of the bridge now, and the barracks lay just ahead of them.

"Hurry up," Aram growled, pulling Samuel along. "I've got other things to do."

They were so close to the building now that Samuel could hear the laughter of the guards coming from inside. Aram tightened his grip and started to drag the boy across the cobblestoned yard that led to the police station. There were only seconds left. Samuel reached into his pocket with his right hand and felt the bag with the half-dozen guldens in it. His fingers closed around it, and his blood began to course with excitement. Carefully, he pulled the bag out of his pocket with his free hand, loosened the drawstring and dropped the bag. It landed on the stones with a loud tinkle of coins.

Aram stopped suddenly. "What was that?"

"Nothing," Samuel replied quickly.

Aram looked into the boy's eyes and grinned. Holding Samuel tightly, he took a step back, looked down at the ground and saw the open bag of money.

"You won't need money where you're going," Aram said.

He reached down to pick up the sack, and Samuel reached down at the same time. Aram snatched the sack of money away from him. But it was not the sack that Samuel was after. His hand closed on one of the large cobblestones lying on the ground, and as Samuel straightened up, he smashed it into Aram's right eye with all his strength, turning it into a red jelly, and he kept pounding at him, again and again. He watched the guard's nose cave in, and then his mouth, until the face was nothing but a gout of red blood. And still Aram stood there on his feet, like some blind monster. Samuel looked at him sick with fear, unable to hit him again. Then, slowly, the giant body began to collapse. Samuel stared down at the dead guard, unable to believe what he had done. He heard the voices from the barracks and he became suddenly aware of the terrible danger he was in. If they caught him now, they would not send him to Silesia. They would flay him alive and hang him in the town square. The penalty for even *striking* a policeman was death. And Samuel had killed one of them. He must get away quickly. He could try to flee across the border, but then he would be a hunted fugitive for the rest of his life. There had to be another solution. He stared down at the faceless corpse and suddenly he knew what he had to do. He reached down and searched the guard's body until he found the large key that opened the gates. Then, overcoming his revulsion, Samuel grabbed Aram's boots and began pulling the guard toward the riverbank. The dead man seemed to weigh a ton. Samuel kept pulling, spurred by the sounds coming from the barracks. He reached the riverbank. He stopped a moment to regain his breath, then shoved the body over the edge of the steep embankment and watched it roll into the coursing waters below. One hand clung to the sides of the bank for what seemed an eternity, and then the body was slowly washed downstream, out of sight. Samuel stood there, hypnotized, filled with horror at what he had done. He picked up the rock he had used and threw it into the water. He was still in great danger. He turned and ran back across the bridge toward the huge, locked gates of the ghetto. There was no one around. With trembling fingers Samuel placed the giant key into the lock and turned it. He pulled against the great wooden gates. Nothing happened. They were too heavy for him to move. But on *that* night nothing was impossible to Samuel. He was filled with a strength that came from outside and he pulled the huge gates open. He shoved the cart inside, then closed the gates behind him, and ran toward his house, pushing the cart ahead of him. The tenants of the house were gathered in the living room, and when Samuel walked in, they stared at him as if he were a living ghost.

"They let you come back!"

"I—I don't understand," his father stammered. "We thought you—"

Quickly, Samuel explained what had happened, and their looks of concern turned to expressions of terror.

"Oh, my God!" groaned Samuel's father. "They'll murder us all!"

"Not if you listen to me," Samuel said. He explained his plan.

Fifteen minutes later Samuel and his father and two of their neighbors stood at the gates of the ghetto.

"Suppose the other guard comes back?" Samuel's father whispered.

Samuel said, "We have to take that chance. If he's there, I'll take all the blame."

Samuel pushed open the huge gates and slipped outside alone, expecting to be pounced upon at any moment. He put the huge key in the lock and turned it. The gates of the ghetto were now locked from the outside. Samuel tied the key around his waist, and walked a few yards to the left of the gates. A moment later a rope slithered down the wall like a thick snake. Samuel clung to it while on the other side his father and the others began to haul him up. When Samuel reached the top of the wall, he made a noose of one end of the rope, fastened it to a projecting spike and lowered himself to the ground. When he was safely down, he shook the rope loose.

"Oh, my God!" his father was mumbling. "What's going to happen at sunup?"

Samuel looked at him and replied, "We're going to be pounding on the gates, telling them to let us out."

AT DAWN THE ghetto was swarming with uniformed police and soldiers. They had had to locate a special key to open the gates at sunrise for the merchants who were yelling to be let out. Paul, the second guard, had confessed to leaving his post and spending the night in Kraków, and he had been placed under arrest. But that still did not solve the mystery of Aram. Ordinarily the incident of a guard disappearing so close to the ghetto would have been a perfect excuse to start a pogrom. But the police were baffled by the locked gate. Since the Jews were safely locked up on the *inside,* they obviously could not have harmed him. In the end they decided that Aram must have run off with one of his many girl friends. They thought he might have thrown away the heavy, cumbersome key, and they searched for it everywhere, but they could not find it. Nor would they because it was buried deep in the ground, under Samuel's house.

Exhausted physically and emotionally, Samuel had fallen into his bed and was asleep almost instantly. He was awakened by someone yelling and shaking him. Samuel's first thought was: *They've found Aram's body. They've come to get me.*

He opened his eyes. Isaac was standing there in a state of hysteria. "It's stopped," Isaac was screaming. "The coughing's stopped. It's a *bracha!* Come back to the house."

Isaac's father was sitting up in bed. The fever had miraculously disappeared, and the coughing had stopped.

As Samuel walked up to his bedside, the old man said, "I think I could eat some chicken soup," and Samuel began to cry.

In one day he had taken a life and saved a life.

The news about Isaac's father swept through the ghetto. The families of dying men and women besieged the Roffe house, pleading with Samuel for some of his magic serum. It was impossible for him to keep up with the demand. He went to see Dr. Wal. The doctor had heard about what Samuel had done, but was skeptical.

"I'll have to see it with my own eyes," he said. "Make up a batch and I'll try it out on one of my patients."

There were dozens to choose from, and Dr. Wal selected the one he felt was closest to death. Within twenty-four hours the patient was on his way to recovery.

Dr. Wal went to the stable where Samuel had been working day and night, preparing serum, and said, "It works, Samuel. You've done it. What do you want for your dowry?"

And Samuel looked up at him and replied wearily, "Another horse."

THAT YEAR, 1868, was the beginning of Roffe and Sons.

Samuel and Terenia were married, and Samuel's dowry was six horses and a small, well-equipped laboratory of his own. Samuel expanded his experiments. He began to distill drugs from herbs, and soon his neighbors began coming to the little laboratory to buy remedies for whatever ills bothered them. They were helped, and Samuel's reputation spread. To those who could not afford to pay, Samuel would say, "Don't worry about it. Take it anyway." And to Terenia, "Medicine is for healing, not for profit."

His business kept increasing, and soon he was able to say to Terenia,

"I think it's time to open a small apothecary shop where we can sell ointments and powders and other things besides prescriptions."

The shop was a success from the beginning. The rich men who had refused to help Samuel before came to him now with offers of money.

"We'll be partners," they said. "We'll open a chain of shops."

Samuel discussed it with Terenia. "I'm afraid of partners. It's *our* business. I don't like the idea of strangers owning part of our lives."

Terenia agreed with him.

As the business grew and expanded into additional shops, the offers of money increased. Samuel continued to turn them all down.

When his father-in-law asked him why, Samuel replied, "Never let a friendly fox into your hen house. One day he's going to get hungry."

As the business flourished, so did the marriage of Samuel and Terenia. She bore him five sons—Abraham, Joseph, Anton, Jan and Pitor—and with the birth of each son Samuel opened a new apothecary shop, each one larger than the one before. In the beginning Samuel hired one man to work for him, then two, and soon he had more than two dozen employees.

One day Samuel received a visit from a government official. "We're lifting some of the restrictions on Jews," he told Samuel. "We would like you to open an apothecary shop in Kraków."

And Samuel did. Three years later he had prospered enough to erect his own building in downtown Kraków and to buy Terenia a beautiful house in the city. Samuel had finally achieved his dream of escaping from the ghetto.

But he had dreams far beyond Kraków.

As the boys grew older, Samuel hired tutors for them, and each of the boys learned a different language.

"He's gone crazy," Samuel's mother-in-law said. "He's the laughingstock of the neighborhood, teaching Abraham and Jan English, Joseph German, Anton French and Pitor Italian. Who are they going to speak to? No one here speaks any of those barbaric languages. The boys won't even be able to talk to one another!"

Samuel merely smiled and said patiently, "It's part of their education." He knew to whom his sons would be talking.

By the time the boys reached their middle teens, they had traveled to different countries with their father. On each of his trips Samuel laid the groundwork for his future plans. When Abraham was twenty-one years old, Samuel called the family together and announced, "Abraham is going to America to live."

"America!" Terenia's mother shouted. "It's filled with savages! I will not let you do this to my grandson. The boy is staying here where he will be safe."

Safe. Samuel thought of the pogroms and Aram, and of his mother's murder.

"He's going abroad," Samuel declared. He turned to Abraham. "You'll open a factory in New York and be in charge of the business there."

Abraham said proudly, "Yes, Father."

Samuel turned to Joseph. "On your twenty-first birthday you will go to Berlin." Joseph nodded.

Anton said, "And I will go to France. Paris, I hope."

"Just watch yourself," Samuel growled. "Some of those gentiles are very beautiful."

He turned to Jan. "You will go to England."

Pitor, the youngest son, said eagerly, "And I'm going to Italy, Papa. How soon can I leave?"

Samuel laughed and replied, "Not tonight, Pitor. You'll have to wait until you're twenty-one."

And thus it worked out. Samuel accompanied his sons abroad and helped them establish offices and factories. Within the next seven years, there were branches of the Roffe family in five foreign countries. It was becoming a dynasty, and Samuel had his lawyer set it up so that, while each company was independent, it was at the same time responsible to the parent company.

"No strangers," Samuel kept warning the lawyer. "The stock must never leave the family."

"It won't," the lawyer assured him. "But if your sons can't sell their stock, Samuel, how are they going to get along? I'm sure you'll want them to live in comfort."

Samuel nodded. "We'll arrange for them to live in beautiful homes. They'll have generous salaries and expense accounts, but everything else must go back into the business. If they ever want to sell the stock, it must be unanimous. The majority of the stock will belong to my oldest son, and his heirs. We're going to be big. We're going to be bigger than the Rothschilds."

Over the years Samuel's prophecy became a reality. The business grew and prospered. Though the family was widely scattered, Samuel and Terenia saw to it that they remained as closely knit as possible. Their sons returned home for birthdays and high holidays. Their visits were more than festive occasions, however. The boys would closet themselves with their father and discuss business. They had their own private espionage system. Whenever one son in one country heard about a new drug development, he would dispatch couriers to report it to the others, and they would begin manufacturing it themselves, so that in this way they kept constantly ahead of their competitors.

AS THE WHEEL of the century turned, the boys married and had children and gave Samuel grandchildren. Abraham had gone to America on his twenty-first birthday, in the year 1891. He had married an American girl seven years later and in 1905 she gave birth to Samuel's first grandchild, Woodrow, who sired a son named Sam. Joseph had married a German girl, who bore him a son and a daughter. The son in his turn married a girl, who bore a daughter, Anna. Anna married a German, Walther Gassner. In France, Anton had married a French girl, by whom he had two sons. One son committed suicide. The other married and had one daughter, Hélène. She married several times but had no children. Jan, in London, had married an English girl. Their only daughter had married a baronet named Nichols and had a son whom they christened Alec. In Rome, Pitor had married an Italian girl. They had a son and a daughter. When the son, in his turn, married, his wife gave him a daughter, Simonetta, who fell in love with and married a young architect, Ivo Palazzi.

These then were the descendants of Samuel and Terenia Roffe.

Samuel lived long enough to see the winds of change that swept across the world. Marconi created wireless telegraphy and the Wright brothers launched the first aeroplane at Kitty Hawk. The Dreyfus affair captured the headlines and Admiral Peary reached the North Pole. Ford's Model T's were in mass production; there were electric lights and telephones.

In medicine, the germs that caused tuberculosis and typhoid and malaria were isolated and tamed.

Roffe and Sons, a little less than half a century after it had been founded, was a multinational behemoth that circled the globe.

Samuel and his broken-down horse, Lottie, had created a dynasty.

WHEN ELIZABETH HAD finished reading the Book for perhaps the fifth time, she quietly returned it to its place in the glass case. She no longer needed it. She was a part of it, just as it was a part of her.

For the first time in her life, Elizabeth knew who she was, and where she had come from.

12

I t was on her fifteenth birthday in the second term of her first year at school that Elizabeth first met Rhys Williams. He had dropped in at the school to bring Elizabeth a birthday present from her father.

"He wanted to come himself," Rhys explained, "but he couldn't get away." Elizabeth tried to conceal her disappointment but Rhys was quick to see it. There was something forlorn about the young girl, a naked vulnerability, that touched him. On an impulse he said, "Why don't you and I have dinner together?"

It was a terrible idea, Elizabeth thought. She could visualize the two of them walking into a restaurant together: him, incredibly good-looking and suave, and her, all braces and pudge. "Thank you, no," Elizabeth said stiffly. "I—I have some studying to do."

But Rhys Williams refused to accept no for an answer. He thought of the lonely birthdays he had spent by himself. He got permission from the headmistress to take Elizabeth out for dinner. They got into Rhys's car and started heading toward the airport.

"Neuchâtel is the other way," Elizabeth said.

Rhys looked at her and asked innocently, "Who said we were going to Neuchâtel?"

"Where are we going?"

"Maxim's. It's the *only* place to celebrate a fifteenth birthday."

They flew to Paris in a private jet, and had a superb dinner. It began with pâté de foie gras with truffles, lobster bisque, crisp duck à l'orange and Maxim's special salad, and ended with champagne and a birthday cake. Rhys drove Elizabeth down the Champs-Élysées afterward, and they returned to Switzerland late that night.

It was the loveliest evening of Elizabeth's life. Somehow Rhys managed to make her feel interesting, and beautiful, and it was a heady experience. When Rhys dropped Elizabeth off at school, she said, "I don't know how to thank you. I—it's the nicest time I've ever had."

"Thank your father." Rhys grinned. "It was all his idea."

But Elizabeth knew that that was not true.

She decided that Rhys Williams was the most wonderful man she had ever met. And without doubt the most attractive. She got into her bed that night thinking about him. Then she rose and went to the small desk under the window. She took out a piece of paper and a pen, and wrote, "Mrs. Rhys Williams."

She stared at the words for a long time.

RHYS WAS TWENTY-FOUR hours late for his date with a glamorous French actress, but he was not concerned. They wound up at Maxim's, and somehow Rhys could not help thinking that his evening there with Elizabeth had been more interesting.

She would be someone to reckon with, one day.

ELIZABETH WAS NEVER certain who was more responsible for the change that began in her—Samuel or Rhys Williams—but she began to take a new pride in herself. She lost the compulsion to eat constantly, and her body began to slim down. She began to enjoy sports and started to take an interest in school. She made an effort to socialize with the other girls. They could not believe it. They had often invited Elizabeth to their pajama parties, and she had always declined. Unexpectedly, she appeared at a pajama party one night.

The party was being held in a room shared by four girls, and when Elizabeth arrived, the room was crammed with at least two dozen students, all in pajamas or robes. One of the girls looked up in surprise and said, "Look who's here! We were betting you wouldn't come."

"I—I'm here."

The air was filled with the pungent sweet aroma of cigarette smoke. Elizabeth knew that many of the girls smoked marijuana, but she had never tried any. Her hostess, a French girl named Renée Tocar, walked up to Elizabeth, smoking a stubby brown cigarette. She took a deep puff, then held it out to Elizabeth. "You smoke?"

It was more of a statement than a question.

"Of course," Elizabeth lied. She took the cigarette, hesitated a moment, then put it between her lips and inhaled. She could feel her face going green, and her lungs rebelling, but she managed a smile and gasped, "Neat."

The moment Renée turned away, Elizabeth sank down onto a couch. She experienced a dizziness, but in a moment it passed. Experimentally she took another puff. She began to feel curiously lightheaded. Elizabeth had heard and read about the effects of marijuana. It was supposed to release inhibitions, take you out of yourself. She took another puff, deeper this time, and she began to feel a pleasant floating sensation, as if she were on another planet. She could see the girls in the room and hear them talking, but somehow they were all blurred, and the sounds were muted and far away. The lights seemed very bright, and she closed her eyes. The moment she did, she was floating off into space. It was a lovely feeling. She could watch herself drifting over the roof of the school, up and up, over the snowy Alps into a sea of fluffy white clouds. Someone was calling her name, calling her back to earth. Reluctantly, Elizabeth opened her eyes. Renée was leaning over her, a look of concern on her face.

"Are you all right, Roffe?"

Elizabeth gave her a slow, contented smile, and said fuzzily, "I'm just wonderful." And in her infinite, euphoric state, she confessed, "I've never smoked marijuana before."

Renée was staring at her. "Marijuana? That's a Gauloise."

. . .

ON THE OTHER side of the village of Neuchâtel was a boys' school, and Elizabeth's classmates sneaked away for trysts at every opportunity. The girls talked about the boys constantly. They talked about their bodies and the size of their penises and what they allowed the boys to do to them, and what they did to the boys in turn. At times it seemed to Elizabeth that she was trapped in a school full of raving nymphomaniacs. Sex was an obsession with them. One of the private games at school was *frôlage*. A girl would completely strip, and lie in bed on her back while another girl stroked her from her breasts to her thighs. The payment was a pastry bought in the village. Ten minutes of *frôlage* earned one pastry. By the end of ten minutes the girl usually reached orgasm, but if she had not, the one administering the *frôlage* would continue and earn an additional pastry.

Another favorite sexual *divertissement* was to be found in the bathroom. The school had large, old-fashioned bathtubs, with flexible hand showers that could be removed from the hook on the side of the wall. The girls would sit in a tub, turn on the shower, and then with the warm water gushing out, they would push the head of the shower between their legs and rub it gently back and forth.

Elizabeth indulged in neither *frôlage* nor the shower head, but her sexual urges were beginning to get stronger and stronger. It was at about this time that she made a shattering discovery.

One of Elizabeth's teachers was a small, slim woman named Chantal Harriot. She was in her late twenties, almost a schoolgirl herself. She was attractive-looking, and when she smiled she became beautiful. She was the most sympathetic teacher Elizabeth had, and Elizabeth felt a strong bond with her. Whenever Elizabeth was unhappy, she would go to Mlle. Harriot and tell her her problems. Mlle. Harriot was an understanding listener. She would take Elizabeth's hand and stroke it, and give her soothing advice and a cup of hot chocolate and cookies, and Elizabeth always felt better immediately.

Mlle. Harriot taught French and also taught a class in fashion, in which she emphasized style and harmony of colors, and the proper accessories.

"Remember, girls," she would say, "the smartest clothes in the world will look terrible if you wear the wrong accessories." "Accessories" was Mlle. Harriot's watchword.

Whenever Elizabeth lay in the warm tub, she found that she was thinking of Mlle. Harriot, of the look on her face when they talked together, and of the way Mlle. Harriot caressed her hand, softly and tenderly.

When Elizabeth was in other classes, she would find her mind drifting toward Mlle. Harriot, and she would remember the times that the teacher had put her arms around her, consoling her, and had touched her breasts. At first Elizabeth had believed that the touches were accidental, but they had happened more and more often, and each time Mlle. Harriot would give Elizabeth a soft, questioning look as though waiting for some response. In her mind Elizabeth could see Mlle. Harriot, with her gently swelling breasts, and her long legs, and she would wonder what she looked like naked, in bed. It was then that the full realization stunned Elizabeth.

She was a lesbian.

She was not interested in boys, because she was interested in girls. Not the kind of silly little girls who were her classmates, but someone sensitive and understanding, like Mlle. Harriot. Elizabeth could visualize the two of them in bed together, holding and comforting each other.

Elizabeth had read and heard enough about lesbians to know how difficult life was for them. Society did not approve. Lesbianism was considered a crime against nature. But what was wrong, Elizabeth wondered, in loving someone tenderly and deeply? Did it matter whether it was a man or a woman? Was it not the love itself that was the important thing? Was it better to have a loveless heterosexual marriage than a loving homosexual one?

Elizabeth thought about how horrified her father was going to be when he learned the truth about her. Well, she would just have to face up to it. She would have to readjust her thinking about the future. She could never have a so-called normal life like other girls, with a husband and children. Wherever she went, she would always be an outcast, a rebel, living outside the mainstream of society. She and Mlle. Harriot—Chantal—would find a little apartment somewhere, or perhaps a small house. Elizabeth would decorate it beautifully in soft pastels, with all the proper accessories. There would be graceful French furniture and lovely paintings on the walls. Her father could help—no, she must not expect any help from her father. In all probability he would never even speak to her again.

Elizabeth thought about her wardrobe. She might be a lesbian, but she was determined not to dress like one. No tweeds or slacks, or tailored suits or vulgar mannish hats. They were the lepers' bells of emotionally crippled women. She would try to look as feminine as possible.

Elizabeth decided that she would learn to be a great cook so that she could prepare Mlle. Harriot's—Chantal's—favorite dishes. She visualized the two of them sitting in their apartment, or small house, enjoying a candle-lit dinner that Elizabeth had prepared. First, there would be vichyssoise, followed by a lovely salad, then perhaps shrimp or lobster, or a Chateaubriand, with delicate ices for dessert. After dinner they would sit on the floor before a blazing fire in the hearth, watching the soft snowflakes fall outside. *Snowflakes.* So it would be winter. Elizabeth hastily revised the menu. Instead of a cold vichyssoise she would prepare a nice, hearty onion soup, and perhaps make a fondue. The dessert could be a soufflé. She would have to learn to time it so that it would not fall. *Then* the two of them would sit on the floor before a warming fire, and read poetry to each other. T. S. Eliot, perhaps. Or V. J. Rajadhon.

> *Time is the enemy of love,*
> *The thief that shortens*
> *All our golden hours.*
> *I have never understood then*
> *Why lovers count their happiness*
> *In days and nights and years,*
> *While our love can only be measured*
> *In our joys and sighs and tears.*

Ah, yes, Elizabeth could see the long years stretching out before the two of them, and the passage of time would begin to melt into a golden, warm glow.

She would fall asleep.

• • •

ELIZABETH HAD BEEN expecting it, and yet when it happened it caught her by surprise. She was awakened one night by the sound of someone entering her room and softly closing the door. Elizabeth's eyes flew open. She could see a shadow moving across the moon-dappled room toward her bed, and a ray of moonlight fell across Mlle. Harriot's—Chantal's— face. Elizabeth's heart began to beat wildly.

Chantal whispered, "Elizabeth," and, standing there, slipped off her robe. She was wearing nothing underneath. Elizabeth's mouth went dry. She had thought of this moment so often, and now that it was actually happening, she was in a panic. In truth she was not sure exactly what she was supposed to do, or how. She did not want to make a fool of herself in front of the woman she loved.

"Look at me," Chantal commanded hoarsely. Elizabeth did. She let her eyes roam over the naked body. In the flesh Chantal Harriot was not quite what Elizabeth had envisioned. Her breasts looked a little like puckered apples, and they sagged a bit. She had a tiny potbelly, and her derrière seemed—this was the only word Elizabeth could think of—underslung.

But none of that was important. What mattered was what lay underneath, the soul of the woman, the courage and the daring to be different from everyone else, to defy the whole world and to want to share the rest of her life with Elizabeth.

"Move over, *mon petit ange*," she was whispering.

Elizabeth did as she was told, and the teacher slipped into bed beside her. There was a strong, feral smell about her. She turned toward Elizabeth and put her arms around her, and said, "Oh, *chérie*, I have dreamed of this moment." And she kissed Elizabeth on the lips, forcing her tongue into Elizabeth's mouth, and making quick, groaning noises.

It was without doubt the most unpleasant sensation Elizabeth had ever experienced. She lay there in shock. Chantal's—Mlle. Harriot's— fingers were moving across Elizabeth's body, squeezing her breasts, slowly sliding down her stomach toward her thighs. And all the time her lips were on Elizabeth's, slobbering, like an animal.

This was it. This was the beautiful magic moment. *If we were one, you and I, together we would make a universe to shake the stars and move the heavens.*

Mlle. Harriot's hands were moving downward, caressing Elizabeth's thighs, starting to reach between her legs. Quickly, Elizabeth tried to conjure up the candlelit dinners and the soufflé and the evenings before the fireplace, and all the wonderful years the two of them would share together; but it was no use. Elizabeth's mind and flesh were repelled; she felt as though her body was being violated.

Mlle. Harriot moaned, "Oh, *chérie,* I want to fuck you."

And all Elizabeth could think of to say was, "There's a problem. One of us has the wrong accessories."

And she began to laugh and cry hysterically, weeping for the beautiful candlelit vision that had died, and laughing because she was a healthy, normal girl who had just learned that she was free.

The next day Elizabeth tried the shower nozzle.

13

At Easter vacation, in her final year at school, when she was eighteen, Elizabeth went to the villa in Sardinia to spend ten days. She had learned to drive, and for the first time she was free to explore the island on her own. She took long drives along the beaches and visited tiny fishing villages. She swam at the villa, under the warm Mediterranean sun, and at night lay in her bed listening to the mournful sound of the singing rocks, as the wind gently blew through them. She went to a carnival in Tempio, where the entire village dressed up in national costumes. Hidden behind the anonymity of domino masks, the girls invited the boys to dance, and everyone felt free to do things they would not dare do at any other time. A boy might *think* he knew which girl he made love to that night, but the next morning he could not be certain. It was, Elizabeth thought, like an entire village playing *The Guardsman*.

She drove to Punta Murra and watched the Sardos cook small lambs on open fires. The native islanders gave her *seada*, a goat cheese covered in a dough, with hot honey over it. She drank the delicious *selememont*, the local white wine that could be had nowhere else in the world because it was too delicate to travel.

One of Elizabeth's favorite haunts was the Red Lion Inn at Porto Cervo. It was a little pub in a basement, with ten tables for dining, and an old-fashioned bar.

Elizabeth dubbed that vacation the Time of the Boys. They were the sons of the rich, and they came in swarms, inviting Elizabeth to a constant round of swimming and riding parties. It was the first move in the mating rite.

"They're all highly eligible," Elizabeth's father assured her.

To Elizabeth they were all clods. They drank too much, talked too much and pawed her. She was sure they wanted her not for herself, because she might be an intelligent or worthwhile human being, but because she was a Roffe, heiress to the Roffe dynasty. Elizabeth had no idea that she had grown into a beauty, for it was easier to believe the truth of the past than the reflection in her mirror.

The boys wined and dined her and tried to get her into bed. They sensed that Elizabeth was a virgin, and some aberration in the male ego deluded each boy into the conviction that if he could take away Elizabeth's virginity, she would fall madly in love with him and be his slave forever. They refused to give up. No matter where they took Elizabeth, the evenings always ended up the same. "Let's go to bed." And always she politely refused them.

They did not know what to make of her. They knew she was beautiful, so it followed that she must be stupid. It never occurred to them that she was more intelligent than they. Who ever heard of a girl being both beautiful *and* intelligent?

And so Elizabeth went out with the boys to please her father, but they all bored her.

Rhys Williams came to the villa, and Elizabeth was surprised at how excited and pleased she was to see him again. He was even more attractive than she had remembered.

Rhys seemed glad to see her. "What's happened to you?" he asked.

"What do you mean?"

"Have you looked in your mirror lately?"

She blushed. "No."

He turned to Sam. "Unless the boys are all deaf, dumb and blind, I have a feeling Liz isn't going to be with us much longer."

Us! Elizabeth enjoyed hearing him say that. She hung around the two men as much as she dared, serving them drinks, running errands for them, enjoying just looking at Rhys. Sometimes Elizabeth would sit in the background, listening as they discussed business affairs, and she was fascinated. They spoke of mergers and of new factories, and products that had succeeded and others that had failed, and why. They talked about their competitors, and planned strategies and counter-strategies. To Elizabeth it was all heady stuff.

One day when Sam was up in the tower room, working, Rhys invited Elizabeth to lunch. She took him to the Red Lion and watched him shoot darts with the men at the bar. Elizabeth marveled at how much at home Rhys was. He seemed to fit in anywhere. She had heard a Spanish expression that she had never understood, but she did now as she watched Rhys. *He's a man easy in his skin.*

They sat at a small corner table with a red-and-white tablecloth, and had shepherd's pie and ale, and they talked. Rhys asked her about school.

"It's really not too bad," Elizabeth confessed. "I'm learning how little I know."

Rhys smiled. "Very few people get that far. You finish in June, don't you?"

Elizabeth wondered how he had known. "Yes."

"Do you know what you want to do after that?"

It was the question she had been asking herself. "No. Not really."

"Interested in getting married?"

For one quick instant her heart missed a beat. Then she realized that it was a general question. "I haven't found anyone yet." She thought of Mlle. Harriot and the cozy dinners in front of the fireplace and the snow falling, and she laughed aloud.

"Secret?" Rhys asked.

"Secret." She wished she could share it with him, but she did not know him well enough. The truth was, Elizabeth realized, that she did not know Rhys at all. He was a charming, handsome stranger who had once taken pity on her and flown her to Paris for a birthday dinner. She knew that he was brilliant in business and that her father depended on him. But she knew nothing about his personal life, or what he was really like. Watching him, Elizabeth had the feeling that he was a many-layered man, that the emotions he showed were to conceal the emotions he felt, and Elizabeth wondered if anyone really knew him.

IT WAS RHYS Williams who was responsible for Elizabeth's losing her virginity.

The idea of going to bed with a man had become more and more appealing to Elizabeth. Part of it was the strong physical urge that sometimes caught her unaware and gripped her in waves of frustration, an urgent physical ache that would not leave. But there was also a strong curiosity, the need to know what *it* was like. She could not go to bed with just anyone, of course. He had to be someone special, someone she could cherish, someone who would cherish her.

On a Saturday night Elizabeth's father gave a gala at the villa.

"Put on your most beautiful dress," Rhys told Elizabeth. "I want to show you off to everyone."

Thrilled, Elizabeth had taken it for granted that she would be Rhys's date. When Rhys arrived, he had with him a beautiful blond Italian princess. Elizabeth felt so outraged and betrayed that at midnight she left the party and went to bed with a bearded drunken Russian painter named Vassilov.

The entire, brief affair was a disaster. Elizabeth was so nervous and Vassilov was so drunk that it seemed to Elizabeth that there was no beginning, middle or end. The foreplay consisted of Vassilov pulling down his pants and flopping onto the bed. At that point Elizabeth was tempted to flee but she was determined to punish Rhys for his perfidy. She got undressed and crawled into bed. A moment later, with no warning, Vassilov was entering her. It was a strange sensation. It was not unpleasant, but neither did the earth shake. She felt Vassilov's body give a quick shudder, and a moment later he was snoring. Elizabeth lay there filled with self-disgust. It was hard to believe that all the songs and books and poems were about *this*. She thought of Rhys, and she wanted to weep. Quietly, Elizabeth put on her clothes and went home. When the painter telephoned her the next morning, Elizabeth had the housekeeper tell him that she was not in. The following day Elizabeth returned to school.

She flew back in the company jet with her father and Rhys. The plane, which had been built to carry a hundred passengers, had been converted into a luxury ship. It had two large, beautifully decorated bedrooms in the rear, with full bathrooms, a comfortable office, a sitting room amidship, with paintings, and an elaborately equipped galley up front. Elizabeth thought of it as her father's magic carpet.

The two men talked business most of the time. When Rhys was free, he and Elizabeth played a game of chess. She played him to a draw, and when Rhys said, "I'm impressed," Elizabeth blushed with pleasure.

THE LAST FEW months of school went by swiftly. It was time to begin thinking about her future. Elizabeth thought of Rhys's question, *Do you know what you want to do with your life?* She was not sure yet. But because of old Samuel, Elizabeth had become fascinated by the family business, and knew that she would like to become a part of it. She was not sure what she could do. Perhaps she could start by helping her father. She remembered all the tales of the wonderful hostess her mother had become, how invaluable she had been to Sam. She would try to take her mother's place.

It would be a start.

14

The Swedish Ambassador's free hand was squeezing Elizabeth's bottom, and she tried to ignore it as they danced around the room, her lips smiling, her eyes expertly scanning the elegantly dressed guests, the orchestra, the liveried servants, the buffet heaped with a variety of exotic dishes and fine wines, and she thought to herself with satisfaction, It's a good party.

They were in the ballroom of the Long Island estate. There were two hundred guests, all of them important to Roffe and Sons. Elizabeth became aware that the Ambassador was pressing his body closer to hers, trying to arouse her. He flicked his tongue in her ear and whispered, "You're a beautiful dancer."

"So are you," Elizabeth said with a smile, and she made a sudden misstep and came down hard on his toe with the sharp heel of her shoe. He gave a cry of pain and Elizabeth exclaimed contritely, "I'm so sorry, Ambassador. Let me get you a drink."

She left him and threaded her way toward the bar, making her way easily through the guests, her eyes moving carefully around the room, checking to see that everything was perfect.

Perfection—that was what her father demanded. Elizabeth had been the hostess for a hundred of Sam's parties now, but she had never learned to relax. Each party was an event, an opening night, with dozens of things that could go wrong. Yet she had never known such happiness. Her girlhood dream of being close to her father, of his wanting her, needing her, had come true. She had learned to adjust to the fact that his needs were impersonal, that her value to him was based on how much she could contribute to the company. That was Sam Roffe's only criterion for judging people. Elizabeth had been able to fill the gap that had existed since her mother's death. She had become her father's hostess. But because Elizabeth was a highly intelligent girl, she had become much more than that. She attended business conferences with Sam, in airplanes and in foreign hotel suites and factories and at embassies and palaces. She watched her father wield his power, deploying the billions of dollars at his command to buy and sell, tear down and build. Roffe and Sons was a vast cornucopia, and Elizabeth watched her father bestow its largesse on its friends, and withhold its bounty from its enemies. It was a fascinating world, filled with interesting people, and Sam Roffe was the master of it all.

As Elizabeth looked around the ballroom now, she saw Sam standing at the bar, chatting with Rhys, a prime minister and a senator from California. Her father saw Elizabeth and waved her over. As Elizabeth moved toward him, she thought of the time, three years earlier, when it had all begun.

ELIZABETH HAD FLOWN home the day of her graduation. She was eighteen. Home, at the moment, had been the apartment at Beekman Place in Manhattan. Rhys had been there with her father. She had somehow known that he would be. She carried pictures of him in the secret places of her thoughts, and whenever she was lonely or depressed or discouraged, she would take them out and warm herself with her memories. In the beginning it had seemed hopeless. A fifteen-year-old schoolgirl and a man of twenty-five. Those ten years might as well have been a hundred. But through some wonderful mathematical alchemy, at eighteen the difference in years was less important. It was as though she were growing older faster than Rhys, trying to catch up to him.

Both men rose as she walked into the library, where they were talking business. Her father said casually, "Elizabeth. Just get in?"

"Yes."

"Ah. So school's finished."

"Yes."

"That's fine."

And that was the extent of her welcome home. Rhys was walking toward her, smiling. He seemed genuinely pleased to see her. "You look wonderful, Liz. How was the graduation? Sam wanted to be there but he couldn't get away."

He was saying all the things her father should have been saying.

Elizabeth was angry with herself for being hurt. It was not that her father did not love her, she told herself, it was just that he was dedicated to a world in which she had no part. He would have taken a son into his world; a daughter was alien to him. She did not fit into the Corporate Plan.

"I'm interrupting." She moved toward the door.

"Wait a minute," Rhys said. He turned to Sam. "Liz has come home just in time. She can help with the party Saturday night."

Sam turned to Elizabeth, studying her objectively, as though newly assessing her. She resembled her mother. She had the same beauty, the same natural elegance. A flicker of interest came into Sam's eyes. It had not occurred to him before that his daughter might be a potential asset to Roffe and Sons. "Do you have a formal dress?"

Elizabeth looked at him in surprise. "I—"

"It doesn't matter. Go buy one. Do you know how to give a party?"

Elizabeth swallowed and said, "Certainly." Wasn't that one of the advantages of going to a Swiss finishing school? They taught you all the social graces. "Of course I know how to give a party."

"Good. I've invited a group from Saudi Arabia. There'll be about—" He turned to Rhys.

Rhys smiled at Elizabeth and said, "Forty. Give or take a few."

"Leave everything to me," Elizabeth said confidently.

The dinner was a complete fiasco.

Elizabeth had told the chef to prepare crab cocktails for the first course, followed by individual cassoulets, served with vintage wines. Unfortunately the cassoulet had pork in it, and the Arabs touched neither shellfish nor pork. Nor did they drink alcoholic beverages. The guests stared at the food, eating nothing. Elizabeth sat at the head of the long table, across the room from her father, frozen with embarrassment, dying inside.

It was Rhys Williams who saved the evening. He disappeared into the study for a few moments and spoke into the telephone. Then he came back into the dining room and entertained the guests with amusing stories, while the staff began to clear the table.

In what seemed no time at all, a fleet of catering trucks drove up, and as if by magic a variety of dishes began appearing. Couscous and lamb *en brochette* and rice and platters of roast chicken and fish, followed by sweetmeats and cheese and fresh fruits. Everyone enjoyed the food except Elizabeth. She was so upset that she could not swallow a bite. Each time she looked up at Rhys, he was watching her, a conspiratorial look in his eyes. Elizabeth could not have said why, but she was mortified that Rhys should not only witness her shame but save her from it. When the evening finally ended, and the last of the guests had reluctantly departed in the early hours of the morning, Elizabeth and Sam and Rhys were in the drawing room. Rhys was pouring a brandy.

Elizabeth took a deep breath and turned to her father, "I'm sorry about the dinner. If it hadn't been for Rhys—"

"I'm sure you'll do better next time," Sam said flatly.

Sam was right. From that time on, when Elizabeth gave a party, whether it was for four people or for four hundred, she researched the guests, found out their likes and dislikes, what they ate and drank, and what type of entertainment they enjoyed. She kept a catalog with file cards on each person. The guests were flattered to find that their favorite brand of wine or whiskey or cigars had been stocked for them, and that Elizabeth was able to discuss their work knowledgeably.

Rhys attended most of the parties, and he was always with the most beautiful girl there. Elizabeth hated them all. She tried to copy them. If Rhys brought a girl who wore her hair pinned up in the back, Elizabeth did her hair the same way. She tried to dress the way Rhys's girls dressed, to act the way they acted. But none of it seemed to make any impression on Rhys. He did not even seem to notice. Frustrated, Elizabeth decided that she might as well be herself.

On the morning of her twenty-first birthday, when Elizabeth came down to breakfast, Sam said, "Order some theater tickets for tonight. Supper afterward at 'Twenty-one.'"

Elizabeth thought, He remembered, and she was inordinately pleased.

Then her father added, "There'll be twelve of us. We'll be going over the new Bolivian contracts."

She said nothing about her birthday. She received telegrams from a few former schoolmates, but that was it. Until six o'clock that evening, when an enormous bouquet of flowers arrived for her. Elizabeth was sure it was from her father. But the card read: "What a lovely day for a lovely lady." It was signed "Rhys."

Her father left the house at seven o'clock that evening on his way to the theater. He noticed the flowers and said absently, "Got a beau, huh?"

Elizabeth was tempted to say, "They're a birthday present," but what would have been the point? If you had to remind someone you loved that it was your birthday, then it was futile.

She watched her father leave, and wondered what she would do with her evening. Twenty-one had always seemed such an important milestone. It signified growing up, having freedom, becoming a woman. Well, here was the magic day, and she felt no different from the way she had felt last year, or the year before. Why couldn't he have remembered? Would he have remembered if she were his son?

The butler appeared to ask her about dinner. Elizabeth was not hungry. She felt lonely and deserted. She knew she was feeling sorry for herself, but it was more than this uncelebrated birthday she was regretting. It was all the lonely birthdays of the past, the pain of growing up alone, without a mother or a father or anyone to give a damn.

At ten o'clock that night she dressed in a robe, sitting in the living room in the dark, in front of the fireplace, when a voice said, "Happy birthday."

The lights came on and Rhys Williams stood there. He walked over to her and said reprovingly, "This is no way to celebrate. How many times does a girl have a twenty-first birthday?"

"I—I thought you were supposed to be with my father tonight," Elizabeth said, flustered.

"I was. He mentioned that you were staying home alone tonight. Get dressed. We're going to dinner."

Elizabeth shook her head. She refused to accept his pity, "Thank you, Rhys. I—I'm really not hungry."

"I am, and I hate eating alone. I'm giving you five minutes to get into some clothes, or I'm taking you out like that."

They ate at a diner in Long Island, and they had hamburgers and chili and french-fried onions and root beer, and they talked, and Elizabeth thought it was better than the dinner she had had at Maxim's. All of Rhys's attention was focused on her, and she could understand why he was so damned attractive to women. It was not just his looks. It was the fact that he truly liked women, that he enjoyed being with them. He made Elizabeth feel like someone special, that he wanted to be with her more than with anyone else in the world. No wonder, Elizabeth thought, everyone fell in love with him.

Rhys told her a little about his boyhood in Wales, and he made it sound wonderful and adventurous and gay. "I ran away from home," he said, "because there was a hunger in me to see everything and do everything. I wanted to be everyone I saw. *I* wasn't enough for me. Can you understand that?"

Oh, how well she understood it!

"I worked at the parks and the beaches and one summer I had a job taking tourists down the Rhosili in coracles, and—"

"Wait a minute," Elizabeth interrupted. "What's a Rhosili and what's a—a coracle?"

"The Rhosili is a turbulent, swift-flowing river, full of dangerous rapids and currents. Coracles are ancient canoes, made of wooden lathes and waterproof animal skins, that go back to pre-Roman days. You've never seen Wales, have you?" She shook her head. "Ah, you would love it." She knew she would. "There's a waterfall at the Vale of Neath that's one of the beautiful sights of this world. And the lovely places to see: Aber-Eiddi and Caerbwdi and Porthclais and Kilgetty and Llangwm," and the words rolled off his tongue like the lilt of music. "It's a wild, untamed country, full of magical surprises."

"And yet you left Wales."

Rhys smiled at her and said, "It was the hunger in me. I wanted to own the world."

What he did not tell her was that the hunger was still there.

. . .

OVER THE NEXT three years Elizabeth became indispensable to her father. Her job was to make his life comfortable, so that he could concentrate on the thing that was all-important to him: the Business. The details of running his life were left entirely to Elizabeth. She hired and fired servants, opened and closed the various houses as her father's needs required, and entertained for him.

More than that, she became his eyes and ears. After a business meeting Sam would ask Elizabeth her impression of a man, or explain to her why he had acted in a particular fashion. She watched him make decisions that affected the lives of thousands of people and involved hundreds of millions of dollars. She heard heads of state plead with Sam Roffe to open a factory, or beg him not to close one down.

After one of those meetings Elizabeth said, "It's unbelievable. It's—it's as though you're running a country."

Her father laughed and replied, "Roffe and Sons has a larger income than three quarters of the countries in the world."

In her travels with her father Elizabeth became reacquainted with the other members of the Roffe family, her cousins and their husbands or wives.

As a young girl Elizabeth had seen them during holidays when they had come to one of her father's houses, or when she had gone to visit them during brief school vacations.

Simonetta and Ivo Palazzi, in Rome, had always been the most fun to be with. They were open and friendly, and Ivo had always made Elizabeth feel like a woman. He was in charge of the Italian division of Roffe and Sons, and he had done very well. People enjoyed dealing with Ivo. Elizabeth remembered what a classmate had said when she had met him. "You know what I like about your cousin? He has warmth and charmth."

That was Ivo, warmth and charmth.

Then there was Hélène Roffe-Martel, and her husband, Charles, in Paris. Elizabeth had never really understood Hélène, or felt at ease with her. She had always been nice to Elizabeth, but there was a cool reserve that Elizabeth had never been able to break through. Charles was head of the French branch of Roffe and Sons. He was competent, though from what Elizabeth had overheard her father say, he lacked drive. He could follow orders, but he had no initiative. Sam had never replaced him, because the French branch ran very profitably. Elizabeth suspected that Hélène Roffe-Martel had a great deal to do with its success.

Elizabeth liked her German cousin Anna Roffe Gassner, and her husband, Walther. Elizabeth remembered hearing family gossip that Anna Roffe had married beneath her. Walther Gassner was reputed to be a black sheep, a fortune hunter, who had married an unattractive woman years older than himself, for her money. Elizabeth did not think her cousin was unattractive. She had always found Anna to be a shy, sensitive person, withdrawn, and a little frightened by life. Elizabeth had liked Walther on sight. He had the classic good looks of a movie star, but he seemed to be neither arrogant nor phony. He appeared to be genuinely in love with Anna, and Elizabeth did not believe any of the terrible stories she had heard about him.

Of all her cousins, Alec Nichols was Elizabeth's favorite. His mother had been a Roffe, and she had married Sir George Nichols, the third baronet. It was Alec to whom Elizabeth had always turned when she had a problem. Somehow, perhaps because of Alec's sensitivity and gentleness, he had seemed to the young child to be her peer, and she realized now what a great compliment that was to Alec. He had always treated her as an equal, ready to offer whatever aid and advice he could. Elizabeth remembered that once, in a moment of black despair, she had decided to run away from home. She had packed a suitcase and then, on a sudden impulse, had telephoned Alec in London to say good-bye. He had been in the middle of a conference, but he had come to the phone and talked to Elizabeth for more than an hour. When he had finished, Elizabeth had decided to forgive her father and give him another chance. That was Sir Alec Nichols. His wife, Vivian, was something else. Where Alec was generous and thoughtful, Vivian was selfish and thoughtless. She was the most self-centered woman Elizabeth had ever known.

Years ago, when Elizabeth was spending a weekend in their country home in Gloucestershire, she went on a picnic by herself. It had begun to rain, and she had returned to the house early. She had gone in the back door, and as she had started down the hallway, she had heard voices from the study, raised in a quarrel.

"I'm damned tired of playing nursemaid," Vivian was saying. "You can take your precious little cousin and amuse her yourself tonight. I'm going up to London. I have an engagement."

"Surely you can cancel it, Viv. The child is only going to be with us another day, and she—"

"Sorry, Alec. I feel like a good fuck, and I'm getting one tonight."

"For God's sake, Vivian!"

"Oh, shove it up your ass! Don't try to live my life for me."

At that moment, before Elizabeth could move, Vivian had stormed out of the study. She had taken one quick look at Elizabeth's stricken face, and said cheerily, "Back so soon, pet?" And strode upstairs.

Alec had come to the doorway. He had said gently, "Come in, Elizabeth."

Reluctantly she had walked into the study. Alec's face was aflame with embarrassment. Elizabeth had wanted desperately to comfort him, but she did not know how. Alec had walked over to a large refectory table, picked up a pipe, filled it with tobacco and lit it. It had seemed to Elizabeth that he took forever.

"You must understand Vivian."

Elizabeth had replied, "Alec, it's none of my business. I—"

"But in a sense it is. We're all family. I don't want you to think harshly of her."

Elizabeth could not believe it. After the incredible scene she had just heard, Alec was defending his wife.

"Sometimes in a marriage," Alec had continued, "a husband and a wife have different needs." He had paused awkwardly, searching for the right phrase. "I don't want you to blame Vivian because I—I can't fulfill some of those needs. That's not her fault, you see."

Elizabeth had not been able to stop herself. "Does—does she go out with other men often?"

"I'm rather afraid she does."

Elizabeth had been horrified. "Why don't you leave her?"

He had given her his gentle smile. "I can't leave her, dear child. You see, I love her."

The next day Elizabeth had returned to school. From that time on, she had felt closer to Alec than to any of the others.

. . .

OF LATE, ELIZABETH had become concerned about her father. He seemed preoccupied and worried about something, but Elizabeth had no idea what it was. When she asked him about it, he replied, "Just a little problem I have to clear up. I'll tell you about it later."

He had become secretive, and Elizabeth no longer had access to his private papers. When he had said to her, "I'm leaving tomorrow for Chamonix to do a little mountain climbing," Elizabeth had been pleased. She knew he needed a rest. He had lost weight and had become pale and drawn-looking.

"I'll make the reservations for you," Elizabeth had said.

"Don't bother. They're already made."

That, too, was unlike him. He had left for Chamonix the next morning. That was the last time she had seen him. The last time she would ever see him . . .

ELIZABETH LAY THERE in her darkened bedroom, remembering the past. There was an unreality about her father's death, perhaps because he had been so alive.

He was the last to bear the name of Roffe. Except for her. What would happen to the company now? Her father had held the controlling interest. She wondered to whom he had left the stock.

Elizabeth learned the answer late the next afternoon. Sam's lawyer had appeared at the house. "I brought a copy of your father's will with me. I hate to intrude on your grief at a time like this, but I thought it best that you know at once. You are your father's sole beneficiary. That means that the controlling shares of Roffe and Sons are in your hands."

Elizabeth could not believe it. Surely he did not expect *her* to run the company. "Why?" she asked. "Why me?"

The attorney hesitated, then said, "May I be frank, Miss Roffe? Your father was a comparatively young man. I'm sure he didn't expect to die for many years. In time, I'm confident he would have made another will, designating someone to take over the company. He probably had not made up his mind yet." He struggled. "All that is academic, however. The point is that the control now rests in your hands. You will have to decide what you want to do with it, who you want to give it to." He studied her for a moment then continued, "There has never before been a woman on the board of directors of Roffe and Sons, but—well, for the moment you're taking your father's place. There's a board meeting in Zurich this Friday. Can you be there?"

Sam would have expected it of her.

And so would old Samuel.

"I'll be there," Elizabeth said.

BOOK TWO

15

PORTUGAL.
WEDNESDAY, SEPTEMBER 9.
MIDNIGHT.

In the bedroom of a small rented apartment in Rua dos Bombeiros, one of the winding, dangerous back alleys of Alto Estoril, a motion-picture scene was being filmed. There were four people in the room. A cameraman, and on a bed the two actors in the scene, the man in his thirties and a young blond girl with a stunning figure. She wore nothing except a vivid red ribbon tied around her neck. The man was large, with a wrestler's shoulders and a barrel-shaped, incongruously hairless chest. His phallus, even in detumescence, was huge. The fourth person in the room was a spectator, seated in the background, wearing a black broad-brimmed hat and dark glasses.

The cameraman turned to the spectator, questioningly, and the spectator nodded. The cameraman pressed a switch and the camera began to whir. He said to the actors, "All right. Action."

The man knelt over the girl and she took his penis in her mouth until it began to grow hard. The girl took it out and said, "Jesus, that's big!"

"Shove it in her," the cameraman ordered.

The man slid down over the girl and put his penis between her legs.

"Take it easy, honey." She had a high, querulous voice.

"Look as though you're enjoying it."

"How can I? It's the size of a fucking watermelon."

The spectator was leaning forward, watching every move as the man entered her. The girl said, "Oh, my God, that feels wonderful. Just take it slow, baby."

The spectator was breathing harder now, staring at the scene on the bed. This girl was the third, and she was even prettier than the others. She was writhing from side to side now, making little moaning noises. "Oh, yes," she gasped. "Don't stop!" She grasped the man's hips and began pulling them toward her. The man began to pump harder and faster, in a frantic, pounding motion. Her movements began to quicken, and her nails dug into the man's naked back. "Oh, yes," she moaned. "Yes, yes, yes! I'm coming!"

The cameraman looked toward the spectator, and the spectator nodded, eyes glistening behind the dark glasses.

"Now!" the cameraman called to the man on the bed.

The girl, caught in her own furious frenzy, did not even hear him. As her face filled with a wild ecstasy, and her body began to shudder, the man's huge hands closed around her throat and began to squeeze, closing off the air so that she could not breathe. She stared up at him, bewildered, and then her eyes filled with a sudden, terrified comprehension.

The spectator thought: *This is the moment. Now! Jesus God! Look at her eyes!* They were dilated with terror. She fought to tear away the iron bands around her throat, but it was useless. She was still coming, and the deliciousness of her orgasm and the frantic shudder of her death throes were blending into one.

The spectator's body was soaked with perspiration. The excitement was unbearable. In the middle of life's most exquisite pleasure the girl was dying, her eyes staring into the eyes of death. It was so beautiful.

Suddenly it was over. The spectator sat there, exhausted, shaken with spasms of pleasure, lungs filled with long, deep breaths. The girl had been punished.

The spectator felt like God.

16

ZURICH.

FRIDAY, SEPTEMBER 11.

NOON.

The World Headquarters of Roffe and Sons occupied sixty acres along the Sprettenbach on the western outskirts of Zurich. The administration building was a twelve-story modern glass structure, towering over a nest of research buildings, manufacturing plants, experimental laboratories, planning divisions, and railroad spurs. It was the brain center of the far-flung Roffe and Sons empire.

The reception lobby was starkly modern, decorated in green and white, with Danish furniture. A receptionist sat behind a glass desk, and those who were admitted by her into the recesses of the building had to be accompanied by a guide. To the right rear of the lobby was a bank of elevators, with one private express elevator for the use of the company president.

On this morning the private elevator had been used by the members of the board of directors. They had arrived within the past few hours from various parts of the world by plane, train, helicopter and limousine. They were gathered now in the enormous, high-ceilinged, oak-paneled boardroom; Sir Alec Nichols, Walther Gassner, Ivo Palazzi and Charles Martel. The only nonmember of the board in the room was Rhys Williams.

Refreshments and drinks had been laid out on a sideboard, but no one in the room was interested. They were tense, nervous, each preoccupied with his own thoughts.

Kate Erling, an efficient Swiss woman in her late forties, came into the room. "Miss Roffe's car has arrived."

Her eyes swept around the room to make sure that everything was in order: pens, note pads, a silver carafe of water at each place, cigars and cigarettes, ashtrays, matches. Kate Erling had been Sam Roffe's personal secretary for fifteen years. The fact that he was dead was no reason for her to lower his standards, or hers. She nodded, satisfied, and withdrew.

Downstairs, in front of the administration building, Elizabeth Roffe was stepping out of a limousine. She wore a black tailored suit with a white blouse. She had on no makeup. She looked much younger than her twenty-four years, pale and vulnerable.

The press was waiting for her. As she started into the building, she found herself surrounded by television and radio and newspaper reporters, with cameras and microphones.

"I'm from *L'Europeo*, Miss Roffe. Could we have a statement? Who's going to take over the company now that your father—?"

"Look this way, please, Miss Roffe. Can you give our readers a big smile?"

"Associated Press, Miss Roffe. What about your father's will?"

"New York *Daily News*. Wasn't your father an expert mountain climber? Did they find out how—?"

"*Wall Street Journal.* Can you tell us something about the company's financial—?"

"I'm from the London *Times*. We're planning to do an article on the Roffe—"

Elizabeth was fighting her way into the lobby, escorted by three security guards, pushing through the sea of reporters.

"One more picture, Miss Roffe—"

And Elizabeth was in the elevator, the door closing. She took a deep breath and shuddered. Sam was dead. Why couldn't they leave her alone?

A few moments later, Elizabeth walked into the boardroom. Alec Nichols was the first to greet her. He put his arms around her shyly and said, "I'm so sorry, Elizabeth. It was such a shock to all of us. Vivian and I tried to telephone you but—"

"I know. Thank you, Alec. Thank you for your note."

Ivo Palazzi came up and gave her a kiss on each cheek. "*Cara,* what is there to say? Are you all right?"

"Yes, fine. Thank you, Ivo." She turned. "Hello, Charles."

"Elizabeth, Hélène and I were devastated. If there is anything at all—"

"Thank you."

Walther Gassner walked over to Elizabeth and said awkwardly, "Anna and I wish to express our great sorrow at what has happened to your father."

Elizabeth nodded, her head high. "Thank you, Walther."

She did not want to be here, surrounded by all the reminders of her father. She wanted to flee, to be alone.

Rhys Williams was standing off to one side, watching Elizabeth's face, and he was thinking, If they don't stop, she's going to break down. He deliberately moved through the group, held out his hand and said, "Hello, Liz."

"Hello, Rhys." She had last seen him when he had come to the house to bring her the news of Sam's death. It seemed like years ago. Seconds ago. It had been one week.

Rhys was aware of the effort it was costing Elizabeth to keep her composure. He said, "Now that everyone's here, why don't we begin?" He smiled reassuringly. "This won't take long."

She gave him a grateful smile. The men took their accustomed places at the large rectangular oak table. Rhys led Elizabeth to the head of the table and pulled out a chair for her. My father's chair, Elizabeth thought. Sam sat here, chairing these meetings.

Charles was saying, "Since we do not have a—" He caught himself and turned to Alec. "Why don't you take over?"

Alec glanced around, and the others murmured approval. "Very well."

Alec pressed a button on the table in front of him, and Kate Erling returned, carrying a notebook. She closed the door behind her and pulled up a straight chair, her notebook and pen poised.

Alec said, "I think that under the circumstances we can dispense with the formalities. All of us have suffered a terrible loss. But"—he looked apologetically at Elizabeth—"the essential thing now is that Roffe and Sons show a strong public face."

"*D'accord.* We have been taking enough of a hammering in the press lately," Charles growled.

Elizabeth looked over at him and asked, "Why?"

Rhys explained, "The company is facing a lot of unusual problems just now, Liz. We're involved in heavy lawsuits, we're under government investigation and some of the banks are pressing us. The point is that none of it is good for our image. The public buys pharmaceutical products because they trust the company that makes them. If we lose that trust, we lose our customers."

Ivo said reassuringly, "We have no problems that can't be solved. The important thing is to reorganize the company immediately."

"How?" Elizabeth asked.

Walther replied, "By selling our stock to the public."

Charles added, "In that way we can take care of all our bank loans, and have enough money left—" He let the sentence trail off.

Elizabeth looked at Alec. "Do you agree with that?"

"I think we're all in agreement, Elizabeth."

She leaned back in her chair, thoughtful. Rhys picked up some papers, rose and carried them to Elizabeth. "I've had all the necessary documents prepared. All you have to do is sign."

Elizabeth glanced at the papers lying before her. "If I sign these, what happens?"

Charles spoke up. "We have a dozen international brokerage firms ready to form a consortium to underwrite the stock issue. They will guarantee the sale at a price we mutually agree upon. In an offering as large as this one, there will be several institutional purchases, as well as private ones."

"You mean like banks and insurance companies?" Elizabeth asked.

Charles nodded. "Exactly."

"And they'll put their people on the board of directors?"

"That's usual . . ."

Elizabeth said, "So, in effect, they would control Roffe and Sons."

"We would still remain on the board of directors," Ivo interposed quickly.

Elizabeth turned to Charles. "You said a consortium of stockbrokers is ready to move ahead."

Charles nodded. "Yes."

"Then why haven't they?"

He looked at her, puzzled. "I don't understand."

"If everyone is in agreement that the best thing for the company is to let it get out of the family and into the hands of outsiders, why hasn't it been done before?"

There was an awkward silence. Ivo said, "It has to be by mutual consent, *cara. Everyone* on the board must agree."

"Who didn't agree?" Elizabeth asked.

The silence was longer this time.

Finally Rhys spoke up. "Sam."

And Elizabeth suddenly realized what had disturbed her from the moment she had walked into this room. They had all expressed their condolences and their shock and grief over her father's death, and yet at the same time there had been an atmosphere of charged excitement in the room, a feeling of—strangely, the word that came into her mind was *victory.* They had had the papers all drawn up for her, everything ready. *All you have to do is sign.* But if what they wanted was right, then why had her father objected to it? She asked the question aloud.

"Sam had his own ideas," Walther explained. "Your father could be very stubborn."

Like old Samuel, Elizabeth thought. Never let a friendly fox into your hen house. One day he's going to get hungry. And Sam had not wanted to sell. He must have had good reason.

Ivo was saying, "Believe me, *cara,* it is much better to leave all this to us. You don't understand these things."

Elizabeth said quietly, "I would like to."

"Why bother yourself with this?" Walther objected. "When your stock is sold, you will have an enormous amount of money, more than you'll ever be able to spend. You can go off anywhere you like and enjoy it."

What Walther said made sense. Why *should* she get involved? All she had to do was sign the papers in front of her, and leave.

Charles said impatiently, "Elizabeth, we're simply wasting time. You have no choice."

It was at that instant that Elizabeth knew she did have a choice. Just as her father had had a choice. She could walk away and let them do as they pleased with the company, or she could stay and find out why they were all so eager to sell the stock, why they were pressuring her. For she could feel the pressure. It was so strong it was almost physical. Everyone in that room was *willing* her to sign the papers.

She glanced over at Rhys, wondering what he was thinking. His expression was noncommittal. Elizabeth looked at Kate Erling. She had been Sam's secretary for a long time. Elizabeth wished she could have had a chance to speak to her alone. They were all looking at Elizabeth, waiting for her to agree.

"I'm not going to sign," she said. "Not now."

There was a moment of stunned silence. Then Walther said, "I don't understand, Elizabeth." His face was ashen. "Of course you must! Everything is arranged."

Charles said angrily, "Walther's right. You must sign."

They were all speaking at once, in a confused and angry storm of words that beat at Elizabeth.

"*Why* won't you sign?" Ivo demanded.

She could not say: *Because my father would not sign. Because you're rushing me.* She had a feeling, an instinct that something was wrong, and she was determined to find out what it was. So now she merely said, "I'd like a little more time to think about it."

The men looked at one another.

"How much time, *cara?*" Ivo asked.

"I don't know yet. I'd like to get a better understanding of what's involved here."

Walther exploded. "Damn it, we can't—"

Rhys cut in firmly, "I think Elizabeth is right."

The others turned to look at him. Rhys went on, "She should have a chance to get a clear picture of the problems the company is facing, and then make up her own mind."

They were all digesting what Rhys had said.

"I agree with that," Alec said.

Charles said bitterly, "Gentlemen, it doesn't make any difference whether we agree with it or not. Elizabeth is in control."

Ivo looked at Elizabeth. "*Cara*—we need a decision quickly."

"You'll have it," Elizabeth promised.

They were all watching her, each busy with his own thoughts.

One of them was thinking, Oh, God. *She's going to have to die, too.*

17

Elizabeth was awed.

She had been here in her father's Zurich headquarters often, but always as a visitor. The power belonged to him. And now it belonged to her. She looked around the huge office and felt like an imposter. The room had been magnificently decorated by Ernst Hohl. At one end stood a Roentgen cabinet with a Millet landscape over it. There was a fireplace, and in front of it a chamois leather couch, a large coffee table and four easy chairs. Around the walls were Renoirs, Chagalls, Klees and two early Courbets. The desk was a solid block of black mahogany. Next to it, on a large console table, was a communications complex—a battery of telephones with direct lines to company headquarters around the world. There were two red phones with scramblers, an intricate intercom system, a ticker tape machine, and other equipment. Hanging behind the desk was a portrait of old Samuel Roffe.

A private door led to a large dressing room, with cedar closets and lined drawers. Someone had removed Sam's clothing, and Elizabeth was grateful. She walked through a tiled bathroom that included a marble bathtub and a stall shower. There were fresh Turkish towels hanging on warming racks. The medicine chest was empty. All the daily paraphernalia of her father's life had been taken away. Kate Erling, probably. Elizabeth idly wondered whether Kate had been in love with Sam.

The executive suite included a large sauna, a fully equipped gymnasium, a barbershop and a dining room that could seat a hundred people. When foreign guests were being entertained, a little flag representing their country was placed in the floral centerpiece on the table.

In addition, there was Sam's private dining room, tastefully decorated, with muraled walls.

Kate Erling had explained to Elizabeth, "There are two chefs on duty during the day, and one at night. If you are having more than twelve guests for luncheon or dinner, they need two hours' notice."

Now Elizabeth sat at the desk, piled high with papers, memoranda, and statistics and reports, and she did not know where to begin. She thought of her father sitting here, in this chair, behind this desk, and she was suddenly filled with a sense of unbearable loss. Sam had been so able, so brilliant. How she needed him now!

Elizabeth had managed to see Alec for a few moments before he returned to London.

"Take your time," he had advised her. "Don't let anyone pressure you." So he had sensed her feelings.

"Alec, do you think I should vote to let the company go public?"

He had smiled at her and said awkwardly, "I'm afraid I do, old girl, but then I've got my own ax to grind, haven't I? Our shares are no good to any of us until we can sell them. That's up to you now."

Elizabeth was remembering that conversation as she sat alone in the huge office. The temptation to telephone Alec was overpowering. All she had to say was, "I've changed my mind." And get out. She did not belong here. She felt so inadequate.

She looked at the set of intercom buttons on the console. Opposite one of them was the name RHYS WILLIAMS. Elizabeth debated a moment, then flicked down the switch.

RHYS WAS SEATED across from her, watching her. Elizabeth knew exactly what he must be thinking, what they were all thinking. That she had no business being there.

"That was quite a bomb you dropped at the meeting this morning," Rhys said.

"I'm sorry if I upset everyone."

He grinned. "'Upset' is hardly the word. You put everyone in a state of shock. It was all supposed to have been cut-and-dried. The publicity releases were ready to send out." He studied her a moment. "What made you decide not to sign, Liz?"

How could she explain that it was nothing more than a feeling, an intuition? He would laugh at her. And yet Sam had refused to let Roffe and Sons go public. She had to find out why.

As though reading her thoughts, Rhys said, "Your great-great-grand-father set this up as a family business, to keep away outsiders. But it was a small company then. Things have changed. We're running one of the biggest drugstores in the world. Whoever sits in your father's chair has to make all the final decisions. It's one hell of a responsibility."

She looked at him and wondered whether this was Rhys's way of telling her to get out. "Will you help me?"

"You know I will."

She felt a rush of relief and she realized how much she had been counting on him.

"The first thing we'd better do," Rhys said, "is take you on a tour of the plant here. Do you know about the physical structure of this company?"

"Not much."

That was not true. Elizabeth had been in enough meetings with Sam over the past few years to have picked up a good deal of knowledge about the workings of Roffe and Sons. But she wanted to hear it from Rhys's point of view.

"We manufacture much more than drugs, Liz. We make chemicals and perfumes and vitamins and hair sprays and pesticides. We produce cosmetics and bio-electronic instruments. We have a food division, and a division of animal nitrates." Elizabeth was aware of all that, but she let Rhys go on. "We publish magazines for distribution to doctors. We make adhesives, and building protection agents and plastic explosives."

Elizabeth could sense that he was becoming caught up by what he was saying, she could hear the undertone of pride in his voice, and she was oddly reminded of her father.

"Roffe and Sons owns factories and holding companies in over a hundred countries. Every one of them reports to this office." He paused, as though to make sure that she understood the point. "Old Samuel went into business with a horse and a test tube. It's grown to sixty factories around the world, ten research centers and a network of thousands of salesmen and detail men and women." They were the ones, Elizabeth knew, who called on the doctors and hospitals. "Last year, in the United States alone, they spent over fourteen billion dollars on drugs—and we have a healthy share of that market."

And yet Roffe and Sons was in trouble with the banks. Something was wrong.

RHYS TOOK ELIZABETH on a tour of the company's headquarters' factory. In actuality, the Zurich division was a dozen factories, with seventy-five buildings on the sixty acres of ground. It was a world in microcosm, completely self-sustaining. They visited the manufacturing plants, the research departments, the toxicology laboratories, the storage plants. Rhys brought Elizabeth to a sound stage, where they made motion pictures for research and for their worldwide advertising and products divisions. "We use more film here," Rhys told Elizabeth, "than the major Hollywood studios."

They went through the molecular biology department, and the liquid center, where fifty giant stainless steel, glass-lined tanks hung suspended from the ceiling, filled with liquids ready to be bottled. They saw the tablet-compression rooms, where powders were formed into tablets, sized, stamped with ROFFE AND SONS, packaged and labeled, without anyone ever touching them. Some of the drugs were ethical products, available only on prescription, others were proprietary items, sold over the counter.

Set apart from the other buildings were several small buildings. These were for the scientists: the analytical chemists, biochemists, organic chemists, parasitologists, pathologists.

"More than three hundred scientists work here," Rhys told Elizabeth. "Most of them are Ph.D.'s. Would you like to see our hundred-million-dollar room?"

Elizabeth nodded, intrigued.

It was in an isolated brick building, guarded by a uniformed police-man with a gun. Rhys showed his security pass, and he and Elizabeth were permitted to enter a long corridor with a steel door at the end of it. The guard used two keys to open the door, and Elizabeth and Rhys entered. The room contained no windows. It was lined from floor to ceiling with shelves filled with every variety of bottles, jars and tubes.

"Why do they call this the hundred-million-dollar room?" Elizabeth asked.

"Because that's what it cost to furnish it. See all those compounds on the shelves? None of them have names, only numbers. They're the ones that didn't make it. They're the failures."

"But a hundred million—"

"For every new drug that works, there are about a thousand that end up in this room. Some drugs are worked on for as long as ten years, and then abandoned. A single drug can cost five or ten million dollars in research before we find out that it's no good, or that someone else has beaten us to it. We don't throw any of these things away because now and then one of our bright young men will back into a discovery that can make something in this room valuable."

The amounts of money involved were awesome.

"Come on," Rhys said, "I'll show you the Loss Room."

It was in another building, this one unguarded, containing, like the other rooms, only shelves filled with bottles and jars.

"We lose a fortune here, too," Rhys said. "But we plan it that way."

"I don't understand."

Rhys walked over to a shelf and picked up a bottle. It was labeled "Botulism." "Do you know how many cases of botulism there were in the United States last year? Twenty-five. But it costs us millions of dollars to keep this drug in stock." He picked up another bottle at random. "This is an antidote for rabies. This room is full of drugs that are cures for rare diseases—snakebites, poisonous plants. We furnish them free to the armed forces and to hospitals, as a public service."

"I like that," Elizabeth said. Old Samuel would have liked it, too, she thought.

Rhys took Elizabeth to the capsule rooms, where empty bottles were carried in on a giant conveyor belt. By the time they had crossed the room, the bottles had been sterilized, filled with capsules, labeled, topped with cotton and sealed. All done by automation.

There was a glassblowing factory, an architectural center to plan new buildings, a real estate division to acquire the land for them. In one building there were scores of writers turning out pamphlets in fifty languages, and printing presses to print them.

Some of the departments reminded Elizabeth of George Orwell's *1984*. The Sterile Rooms were bathed in eerie ultraviolet lights. Adjoining rooms were painted in different colors—white, green or blue—and the workers wore uniforms to match. Each time they entered or left the room, they had to go through a special sterilizing chamber. Blue workers were locked in for the entire day. Before they could eat or rest or go to the toilet, they had to undress, enter a neutral green zone, put on other clothes and reverse the process when they returned.

"I think you'll find this interesting," Rhys said.

They were walking down the gray corridor of a research building. They reached a door marked RESTRICTED—DO NOT ENTER. Rhys pushed the door open, and he and Elizabeth walked through. They went through a second door and Elizabeth found herself in a dimly lit room filled with hundreds of cages containing animals. The room was hot and humid, and she felt as if she had suddenly been transported to a jungle. As her eyes grew accustomed to the half-light, she saw that the cages were filled with monkeys and hamsters and cats and white mice. Many of the animals had obscene-looking growths protruding from various parts of their bodies. Some had their heads shaven, and were crowned with electrodes that had been implanted in their brains. Some of the animals were screaming and gibbering, racing around in their cages, while others were comatose and lethargic. The noise and the stench were unbearable. It was like some kind of hell. Elizabeth walked up to a cage that contained a single white kitten. Its brain was exposed, enclosed in a clear plastic covering through which protruded half a dozen wires.

"What—what's going on here?" Elizabeth asked.

A tall, bearded young man making notes in front of a cage explained, "We're testing a new tranquilizer."

"I hope it works," Elizabeth said weakly. "I think I could use it." And she walked out of the room before she could become sick.

Rhys was at her side in the corridor. "Are you all right?"

She took a deep breath. "I—I'm fine. Is all that really necessary?"

Rhys looked at her and replied. "Those experiments save a lot of lives. More than one third of the people born since nineteen fifty are alive only because of modern drugs. Think about that."

Elizabeth thought about it.

IT TOOK SIX full days to tour the key buildings, and when Elizabeth had finished, she was exhausted, her head spinning with the vastness of it. And she realized she was seeing just one Roffe plant. There were dozens of others scattered around the world.

The facts and figures were stunning. "It takes between five and ten years to market a new drug, and out of every two thousand compounds tested, we'll average only three products. . . ."

And ". . . Roffe and Sons has three hundred people working here in quality control alone."

And ". . . Worldwide, Roffe and Sons is responsible for over half a million employees. . . ."

And ". . . our gross income last year was . . ."

Elizabeth listened, trying to digest the incredible figures that Rhys was throwing at her. She had known that the company was large, but "large" was such an anonymous word. Having it actually translated into terms of people and money was staggering.

That night as Elizabeth lay in bed, recalling all the things she had seen and heard, she was filled with an overpowering feeling of inadequacy.

Ivo: *Believe me,* cara, *it is much better to leave all this to us. You don't understand these things.*

Alec: *I think you should sell but I have an ax to grind.*

Walther: *Why bother yourself with this? You can go off anywhere you like and enjoy your money.*

They were right, all of them, Elizabeth thought. I'm going to get out and let them do what they like with the company. I do not belong in this position.

The moment she made the decision, she felt a deep sense of relief. She fell asleep almost immediately.

THE FOLLOWING DAY, Friday, was the beginning of a holiday weekend. When Elizabeth arrived at the office, she sent for Rhys to announce her decision.

"Mr. Williams had to fly to Nairobi last night," Kate Erling informed her. "He said to tell you he would be back on Tuesday. Can anyone else help you?"

Elizabeth hesitated. "Put in a call to Sir Alec, please."

"Yes, Miss Roffe." Kate added, a note of hesitation in her voice, "A package for you was delivered this morning by the police department. It contains the personal belongings your father had with him at Chamonix."

The mention of Sam brought back that sharp sense of loss, of grief.

"The police apologized because they could not give it to your messenger. It was already on its way to you."

Elizabeth frowned. "My messenger?"

"The man you sent to Chamonix to pick it up."

"I didn't send anyone to Chamonix." It was obviously some bureaucratic mix-up. "Where is it?"

"I put it in your closet."

There was a Vuitton suitcase, containing Sam's clothes, and a locked attaché case with a key taped to it. Probably company reports. She would let Rhys handle them. Then she remembered that he was away. Well, she decided, she would go away for the weekend, too. She looked at the attaché case and thought, Perhaps there's something personal belonging to Sam. I'd better look at it first.

Kate Erling buzzed. "I'm sorry, Miss Roffe. Sir Alec's out of the office."

"Leave a message for him to call me, please. I'll be at the villa in Sardinia. Leave the same message for Mr. Palazzi, Mr. Gassner and Mr. Martel."

She would tell them all that she was leaving, that they could sell the stock, do as they pleased with the company.

She was looking forward to the long weekend. The villa was a retreat, a soothing cocoon, where she could be alone to think about herself and her future. Events had been flung at her so rapidly that she had had no chance to put things into any kind of perspective. Sam's accident—Elizabeth's mind tripped over the word "death"; inheriting the controlling stock of Roffe and Sons; the urgent pressure from the family to let the company go public. And the company itself. The awesome heartbeat of a behemoth whose power spanned the world. It was too much to cope with all at once.

When she flew to Sardinia late that afternoon, Elizabeth had the attaché case with her.

She took a taxi from the airport. There was no one at the villa because it had been closed, and Elizabeth had not told anyone she was coming. She let herself in and walked slowly through the large familiar rooms and it was as if she had never been away. She had not realized how much she had missed this place. It seemed to Elizabeth that the few happy memories of her childhood had been here. It felt strange to be alone in this labyrinth where there had always been half a dozen servants bustling around, cooking, cleaning, polishing. Now there was only herself. And the echoes of the past.

She left Sam's attaché case in the downstairs hallway and carried her suitcase upstairs. With the habit of long years, she started to head for her bedroom in the center of the hallway, then stopped. Her father's room was at the far end. Elizabeth turned and walked toward it. She opened the door slowly, because while her mind understood the reality, some deep, atavistic instinct made her half expect to see Sam there, to hear the sound of his voice.

The room was empty, of course, and nothing had changed since

Elizabeth had last seen it. It contained a large double bed, a beautiful highboy, a dressing table, two comfortable overstuffed chairs, and a couch in front of the fireplace. Elizabeth set down her suitcase and walked over to the window. The iron shutters had been closed against the late September sun, and the draperies were drawn. She opened them wide and let the fresh mountain air flow in, soft and cool with the promise of fall. She would sleep in this room.

Elizabeth returned downstairs and went into the library. She sat down in one of the comfortable leather chairs, rubbing her hands along the sides. This was where Rhys always sat when he had a conference with her father.

She thought about Rhys and wished that he were here with her. She remembered the night he had brought her back to school after the dinner in Paris, and how she had gone back to her room and had written "Mrs. Rhys Williams" over and over. On an impulse Elizabeth walked over to the desk, picked up a pen and slowly wrote "Mrs. Rhys Williams." She looked at it and smiled. "I wonder," she mocked herself aloud, "how many other idiots are doing the same thing right now?"

She turned her thoughts away from Rhys, but still he was at the back of her mind, pleasantly comforting. She got up and wandered around the house. She explored the large, old-fashioned kitchen, with its wood-burning stove, and two ovens.

She walked over to the refrigerator and opened it. It was empty. She should have anticipated that, with the house shut down. Because the refrigerator was empty, she became suddenly hungry. She searched the cupboards. There were two small cans of tuna fish, a half-filled jar of Nescafé and an unopened package of crackers. If she was going to be here for a long weekend, Elizabeth decided, she had better do some planning. Rather than drive into town for every meal, she would shop at one of the little markets in Cala di Volpe and stock enough food for several days. A utility Jeep was always kept in the carport and she wondered if it was still there. She went to the back of the kitchen and through the door that led to the carport, and there was the Jeep. Elizabeth walked back into the kitchen, where, on a board behind the cupboard, were hooks with labeled keys on them. She found the key to the Jeep and returned to the carport. Would there be gasoline in it? She turned the key and pressed the starter. Almost immediately the motor sparked into life. So *that* problem was eliminated. In the morning she would drive into town and pick up whatever groceries she needed.

She went back into the house. As she walked across the tiled floor of the reception hall, she could hear the echo of her footsteps, and it was a hollow, lonely sound. She wished that Alec would call, and even as she was thinking it the telephone rang, startling her. She walked to it and picked it up. "Hello."

"Elizabeth. It's Alec here."

Elizabeth laughed aloud.

"What's so funny?"

"You wouldn't believe me if I told you. Where are you?"

"Down in Gloucester." And Elizabeth felt a sudden, urgent impulse to see him, to tell him her decision about the company. But not over the telephone. "Would you do me a favor, Alec?"

"You know I will."

"Could you fly down here for the weekend? I'd like to discuss something with you."

There was only the slightest hesitation, and then Alec said, "Of course."

Not a word about what engagements he would have to break, how inconvenient it might be. Just "Of course." That was Alec.

Elizabeth forced herself to say, "And bring Vivian."

"I'm afraid she won't be able to come. She's—ah—rather involved in London. I can arrive tomorrow morning. Will that do?"

"Perfect. Let me know what time, and I'll pick you up at the airport."

"It will be simpler if I just take a taxi."

"All right. Thank you, Alec. Very much."

When Elizabeth replaced the receiver, she was feeling infinitely better.

She knew she had made the right decision. She was in this position only because Sam had died before he had had the time to name his successor.

Elizabeth wondered who the next president of Roffe and Sons would be. The board could decide that for themselves. She thought about it from Sam's point of view, and the name that sprang instantly to mind was Rhys Williams. The others were competent in their own areas, but Rhys was the only one who had a working knowledge of the company's complete global operation. He was brilliant and effective. The problem, of course, was that Rhys was not eligible to be president. Because he was not a Roffe, or married to a Roffe, he could not even sit on the board.

Elizabeth walked into the hallway and saw her father's attaché case. She hesitated. There was hardly any point in her going through it now. She could give it to Alec when he arrived in the morning. Still, if there *was* something personal in it . . . She carried it into the library, set it on the desk, untaped the key and opened the little locks on each side. In the center of the case lay a large manila envelope. Elizabeth opened it and removed a sheaf of typewritten papers lying loosely in a cardboard cover labeled:

Mr. Sam Roffe

Confidential

No copies

It was obviously a report of some kind, but without anyone's name on it so that Elizabeth could not know who had drawn it. She started to skim through the report, then slowed down, then stopped. She could not believe what she was reading. She carried the papers over to an armchair, kicked off her shoes, curled her legs up underneath her and turned to page one again.

This time she read every word, and she was filled with horror.

IT WAS AN astonishing document, a confidential report of an investigation into a series of events that had occurred over the past year.

In Chile a chemical plant owned by Roffe and Sons had exploded, sending tons of poisonous materials spouting over a ten-square-mile area. A dozen people had been killed, hundreds more had been taken to hospitals. All the livestock had died, the vegetation was poisoned. The entire region had had to be evacuated. The lawsuits filed against Roffe and Sons had run into hundreds of millions of dollars. But the shocking thing was that the explosion had been deliberate. The report read: "The Chilean government's investigation into the accident was cursory. The official attitude seems to be: the Company is rich, the people are poor, let the Company pay. There is no question in the minds of our investigating staff but that it was an act of sabotage, by a person or persons unknown, using plastic explosives. Because of the antagonistic official attitude here, it will be impossible to prove."

Elizabeth remembered the incident only too well. Newspapers and magazines had been full of horror stories complete with photographs of the victims, and the world's press had attacked Roffe and Sons, accusing it of being careless and indifferent to human suffering. It had damaged the image of the company badly.

The next section of the report dealt with major research projects that Roffe and Sons' scientists had been working on for a number of years. There were four projects listed, each of them of inestimable potential value. Combined, they had cost more than fifty million dollars to develop. In each case a rival pharmaceutical firm had applied for a patent to one of the products, just ahead of Roffe and Sons, using the identical formula. The report continued: "One isolated incident might have been put down as coincidence. In a field where dozens of companies are working in related areas, it is inevitable that several companies might be working on the same type of product. But four such incidents in a period of a few months force us to the conclusion that someone in the employ of Roffe and Sons gave or sold the research material to the competitive firms. Because of the secret nature of the experiments, and the fact that they were conducted in widely separated laboratories under conditions of maximum security, our investigation indicates that the person, or persons, behind this would need to have access to top security clearances. We therefore conclude that whoever is responsible is someone in the highest executive echelon of Roffe and Sons."

There was more.

A large batch of toxic drugs had been mislabeled and shipped. Before they could be recalled there were several deaths, and more bad publicity for the company. No one could learn where the wrong labels had come from.

A deadly toxin had disappeared from a heavily guarded laboratory.

Within an hour an unidentified person had leaked the story to the newspapers and started a scare-hunt.

THE AFTERNOON SHADOWS had long since lengthened into evening, and the night air had turned chilly. Elizabeth remained totally absorbed in the document she held in her hand. When the study became dark, she switched on a lamp and continued to read, the horror piled on horror.

Not even the dry, terse tone of the report could conceal the drama in it. One thing was clear. Someone was methodically attempting to damage or destroy Roffe and Sons.

Someone in the highest echelon of the company. On the last page was a marginal note in her father's neat, precise handwriting. "Additional pressure on me to let the company go public? Trap the bastard."

She remembered now how worried Sam had been, and his sudden secrecy. He had not known whom to trust.

Elizabeth looked at the front page of the report again. "No copies."

Elizabeth was sure the report had been done by an outside investigative agency. So in all probability no one had been aware of this report but Sam. And now herself. The guilty person had no idea he was under suspicion. Had Sam known who he was? Had Sam confronted him before his accident? Elizabeth had no way of knowing. All she knew was that there was a traitor.

Someone in the highest echelon of the company.

No one else would have the opportunity or the ability to carry out so much destruction on so many different levels. Was that why Sam had refused to let the company go public? Was he trying to find the guilty person first? Once the company was sold, it would be impossible to conduct a secret investigation, with every move being reported to a group of strangers.

Elizabeth thought about the board meeting, and how they had urged her to sell. All of them.

Elizabeth suddenly felt very alone in the house. The loud ringing of the telephone made her jump. She walked over to it and picked it up. "Hello?"

"Liz? It's Rhys. I just received your message."

She was glad to hear his voice, but she suddenly remembered why she had called him. To tell him that she was going to sign the papers, let the company be sold. In a few short hours everything had completely changed. Elizabeth glanced out into the hallway, at the portrait of old Samuel. He had founded this company and had fought for it. Elizabeth's father had built it up, helped turn it into a giant, had lived for it, dedicated himself to it.

"Rhys," Elizabeth said, "I'd like to have a board meeting Tuesday. Two o'clock. Would you please arrange for everyone to be there?"

"Tuesday at two o'clock," Rhys agreed. "Anything else?"

She hesitated. "No. That's all. Thank you."

Elizabeth slowly replaced the receiver. She was going to fight them.

SHE WAS HIGH on a mountain with her father, climbing at his side. *Don't look down,* Sam kept saying, and Elizabeth disobeyed, and there was nothing below but thousands of feet of empty space. There was a loud rumble of thunder, and a bolt of lightning came hurtling toward them. It hit Sam's rope and set it on fire, and Sam started falling through space. Elizabeth watched her father's body tumble end over end, and she began to scream, but her screams were drowned out by the roar of the thunder.

Elizabeth awakened suddenly, her nightgown drenched with perspiration, her heart pounding wildly. There was a loud clap of thunder, and she looked toward the window and saw that it was pouring outside. The wind was driving the rain into the bedroom through the open French doors. Quickly, Elizabeth got out of bed, crossed over to the doors and pushed them tightly shut. She looked out at the storm clouds that filled the sky, and at the lightning flashes across the horizon, but she was not seeing them.

She was thinking about her dream.

IN THE MORNING the storm had passed over the island, leaving only a light drizzle. Elizabeth hoped that the weather would not delay Alec's arrival. After reading the report she desperately needed someone to talk to. In the meantime she decided it would be a good idea to put it away in a secure place. There was a safe up in the tower room. She would keep it there. Elizabeth bathed, put on a pair of old slacks and a sweater and went down into the library to get the report.

It was gone.

The room looked as though a hurricane had swept through it. The storm had blown open the French doors during the night, and the wind and the rain had wreaked havoc, scattering everything before it. A few loose pages of the report lay on the wet rug, but the rest of the pages had obviously been carried away by the wind.

Elizabeth stepped to the French windows and looked out She could see no papers on the lawn, but the wind could easily have blown them over the cliff. That must have been what happened.

No COPIES. She must find out the name of the investigator Sam had hired. Perhaps Kate Erling would know. But Elizabeth could not be sure now that Sam had trusted Kate. This had become like a terrible game, where no one could trust anybody. She would have to move very carefully.

Elizabeth suddenly remembered that there was no food in the house. She could shop at Cala di Volpe and be back before Alec arrived. She went to the hall closet and got her raincoat and a scarf for her hair. Later, when the rain let up, she would search the grounds for the missing papers. She went into the kitchen and took the key to the Jeep from the key rack. She walked out the back door that led to the carport.

Elizabeth started the engine and carefully backed the Jeep out of the carport. She turned it around and headed out the private driveway, braking to slow down because of the wet surface. At the bottom of the driveway she turned right, onto the narrow mountain road that led to the little village of Cala di Volpe below. There was no traffic on the road at this hour, but there seldom was, for few houses had been built up this high. Elizabeth glanced down to her left and saw that the sea below had become dark and angry, swollen with the night storm.

She drove slowly, for this part of the road became treacherous. It was narrow, with two lanes that had been cut into the side of the mountain, along a sheer precipice. On the inside lane was the solid rock of the mountain, and on the outside, a drop of hundreds of feet to the sea below. Elizabeth kept as close as she could to the inside lane, braking to fight the momentum of the steep mountain gradient.

The car was approaching a sharp curve. Automatically, Elizabeth put her foot on the brakes to slow the Jeep down.

The brakes were dead.

It took a long moment to register. Elizabeth pressed again, harder, pushing down on the pedal with all her strength, and her heart began to pound as the Jeep kept gathering speed. It took the curve and was moving faster now, racing down the steep mountain road, gaining momentum with each second. She pressed down on the brakes again. They were useless.

Another curve lay ahead. Elizabeth was afraid to take her eyes off the road to look at the speedometer, but out of the corner of her eye she could see the needle racing upward and she was filled with an icy terror. She reached the curve and skidded around it, much too fast. The back wheels slid toward the edge of the precipice, then the tires found their traction and the Jeep plunged forward again, hurtling down the steep road ahead. There was nothing to stop it now, no barriers, no controls, only the swift roller-coaster ride down, and the deadly, beckoning curves ahead.

Elizabeth's mind raced frantically, seeking some escape. She thought of jumping. She risked a quick look at the speedometer. She was going seventy miles an hour now, and building up speed every moment, trapped between the solid mountain wall on one side and the deadly drop into space on the other. She was going to die. And in an instant revelation, Elizabeth knew that she was being murdered, and that her father had been murdered. Sam had read the report, and he had been killed. As she was going to be killed. And she had no idea who her murderer was, who hated them enough to do this terrible thing. Somehow she could have borne it better if it had been a stranger. But it was someone she knew, someone who knew her. Faces flashed through her mind. Alec . . . Ivo . . . Walther . . . Charles . . . It had to be one of them. *Someone in the highest echelon of the company.*

Her death would be listed as an accident, as Sam's had been. Elizabeth was crying now, silently, her tears mixing with the fine mist of rain that was falling, but she was not even aware of it. The Jeep was beginning to skid out of control on the wet surface, and Elizabeth fought to keep the wheels on the road. She knew it was only a matter of seconds before she hurtled over the cliff, into oblivion. Her body became rigid, and her hands, were numb from gripping the steering wheel. There was nothing in the universe now but herself, careening down the mountain road, with the roaring wind tugging at her, saying *Come join me,* tearing at the car, trying to push it over the brink of the cliff. The Jeep started into another skid, and Elizabeth fought desperately to straighten it out, remembering what she had been taught. *Steer into the skid, always into the skid,* and the rear wheels straightened out and the car continued racing downhill. Elizabeth stole another quick glance at the speedometer . . . eighty miles an hour. She was catapulting toward a steep hairpin curve ahead, and she knew she was not going to make this one.

Something in her mind seemed to freeze, and it was as if there was a thin veil between her and reality. She heard her father's voice saying, *What are you doing down here alone in the dark?* and he was picking her up and carrying her to bed and she was on stage dancing and turning and turning and turning and she could not stop, and Mme. Netturova was screaming at her (or was it the wind?) and Rhys was there, saying, *How many times does a girl have her twenty-first birthday?* And Elizabeth thought, I'll never see Rhys again, and she screamed his name and the veil disappeared, but the nightmare was still there. The sharp curve was looming closer now, the car speeding toward it like a bullet. She would go over the cliff. *Let it happen quickly,* she prayed silently.

At that moment, to the right, just before the hairpin curve, Elizabeth caught a glimpse of a small firebreak trail that had been cut through the rock, going up the mountainside. She had to make a decision in a split second. She had no idea where the trail led. All she knew was that it went *upward,* that it might slow her momentum, give her a chance. And she took it. At the last instant, as the Jeep reached the trail, Elizabeth swung the wheel hard to the right. The rear wheels started to skid, but the front wheels were on the gravel road and the momentum gave them enough traction to hold. The Jeep was now hurtling upward, and Elizabeth was fighting the wheel, trying to keep the car on the narrow trail. There was a thin line of trees and their branches were slashing at her as she raced by them, tearing at her face and her hands. She looked ahead, and to her horror, she could see the Tyrrhenian Sea below. The path had merely led to the other side of the cliff. There was no safety here at all.

She was getting closer and closer to the brink now, moving too fast to jump from the Jeep. The edge of the cliff was just ahead of her, the sea hundreds of feet below. As the Jeep hurtled toward the edge, it went into a wild skid, and the last thing Elizabeth remembered was a tree looming up in front of her and then an explosion that seemed to fill the universe.

After that the world became still and white and peaceful and silent.

20

She opened her eyes and she was in a hospital bed and the first thing she saw was Alec Nichols.

"There's nothing in the house for you to eat," she whispered, and started to cry.

Alec's eyes filled with pain, and he put his arms around her and held her close. "Elizabeth!"

And she mumbled, "It's all right, Alec. Everything is fine."

And it was. Every inch of her body felt bruised and beaten, but she was alive, and she could not believe it. She remembered the terror of that drive down the mountain, and her body went cold.

"How long have I been here?" Her voice was weak and hoarse.

"They brought you in two days ago. You've been unconscious since then. The doctor says it was a miracle. According to everybody who saw the scene of the accident, you should be dead. A service crew came across you and rushed you in here. You have a concussion and a hell of a lot of bruises, but, thank the Lord, there's nothing broken." He looked at her, puzzled, and said, "What were you doing up there on that firebreak road?"

Elizabeth told him. She could see the horror on his face as he lived through the terrible ride with her. He kept repeating, "Oh, my God," over and over. When Elizabeth had finished, Alec was pale. "What a stupid, terrible accident!"

"It wasn't an accident, Alec."

He looked at her, puzzled. "I don't understand."

How could he? He had not read the report. Elizabeth said, "Someone tampered with the brakes."

He shook his head incredulously. "Why would anyone do that?"

"Because—" She could not tell him. Not yet. She trusted Alec more than she trusted anyone else, but she was not ready to talk. Not until she felt stronger, not until she had had time to think.

"I don't know," she said evasively. "I'm just sure someone did."

She watched him and she could read the changing expressions on his face. They went from disbelief to puzzlement to anger.

"Well, we're certainly going to find out." His voice was grim.

He picked up the telephone, and a few minutes later he was talking to the Chief of Police in Olbia. "This is Alec Nichols," he said. "I—Yes, she's fine, thank you. . . . Thank you. I'll tell her. I'm calling about the Jeep she was driving. Could you tell me where it is? . . . Would you keep it there, please? And I'd like you to get hold of a good mechanic. I'll be there in half an hour." He replaced the receiver. "It's in the police garage. I'm going over."

"I'm coming with you."

He looked at her in surprise. "The doctor said you must stay in bed for at least another day or two. You can't—"

"I'm coming with you," she insisted stubbornly.

Forty-five minutes later Elizabeth checked her bruised and swollen body out of the hospital over a doctor's protests, and was on her way to the police garage with Alec Nichols.

Luigi Ferraro, the Chief of Police of Olbia, was a swarthy, middle-aged Sardo, with a large stomach and bandy legs. Next to him was Detective Bruno Campagna, who towered over his chief. Campagna was a muscularly built man in his fifties, with an air of solid competence. He stood next to Elizabeth and Alec, watching a mechanic examine the underside of a Jeep that was raised on a hydraulic hoist. The left front fender and radiator had been smashed, and they were streaked with the sap of the trees they had crashed into. Elizabeth had felt faint at her first sight of the car, and she had had to lean on Alec for support. He looked at her with concern. "Are you sure you're up to this?"

"I feel fine," Elizabeth lied. She felt weak and terribly tired. But she had to see for herself.

The mechanic wiped his hands on a greasy cloth and walked over to the group. "They don't build them like that no more," he said.

Thank God, Elizabeth thought.

"Any other car woulda been in bits and pieces."

"What about the brakes?" Alec asked.

"The brakes? They're in perfect condition."

Elizabeth felt a sudden sense of unreality engulfing her. "What—what do you mean?"

"They're working fine. The accident didn't hurt them at all. That's what I meant when I said that they don't build—"

"That's impossible," Elizabeth interrupted. "The brakes weren't working on that Jeep."

"Miss Roffe believes that someone tampered with them," Chief Ferraro explained.

The mechanic shook his head. "No, sir." He walked back to the Jeep and pointed to the underside. "There's only two ways you can *fregare*—" He turned to Elizabeth. "Excuse me, signorina—screw up the brakes on a Jeep. You can either cut the brake links or you can loosen this nut"— he indicated a piece of metal on the underside—"and let the brake fluid run out. You can see for yourself that this link is solid, and I checked the brake drum. It's full."

Chief Ferraro said to Elizabeth soothingly, "I can understand how in your condition it could—"

"Just a moment," Alec interrupted. He turned to the mechanic. "Isn't it possible that those links were cut and then replaced or that someone drained the brake fluid and then filled it again?"

The mechanic shook his head stubbornly. "Mister, those links ain't been touched." He took his rag again and carefully wiped off the oil around the nut that held the brake fluid. "See this nut? If anyone had loosened it, there'd be fresh wrench marks on it. I'll guarantee that no one's touched it in the last six months. There's not a thing wrong with these brakes, I'll show you."

He walked over to the wall and pulled a switch. There was a whirring sound and the hydraulic lift began to lower the Jeep to the floor. They watched as the mechanic got in it, started the engine and backed the Jeep up. When it was touching the back wall, he put the Jeep in first gear and pressed down on the accelerator. The car raced toward Detective Campagna. Elizabeth opened her mouth to scream, and at that instant the Jeep jerked to a stop an inch away from him. The mechanic ignored the look the detective gave him and said, "See? These brakes are perfect."

They were all looking at Elizabeth now, and she knew what they were thinking. But that did not change the terror of that ride down the mountain. She could feel her foot pressing on the brakes, and nothing happening. Yet the police mechanic had proved that they worked. Unless he was in on it. And that meant the Chief of Police probably knew, too. I'm becoming paranoiac, Elizabeth thought.

Alec said helplessly, "Elizabeth—"

"When I drove that Jeep, those brakes were not working."

Alec studied her for a moment, then said to the mechanic, "Let's suppose that someone *did* arrange it so that the brakes on this Jeep wouldn't work. How else could it have been done?"

Detective Campagna spoke up. "They could have wet the brake lining."

Elizabeth could feel an excitement stirring in her. "What would happen if they did that?"

Detective Campagna said, "When the brake lining pressed against the drum, it would have no traction."

The mechanic nodded. "He's right. The only thing is—" He turned to Elizabeth. "Were your brakes working when you started driving?"

Elizabeth remembered using the brakes to back out of the carport, and braking again later when she came to the first curves. "Yes," she said, "they were working."

"There's your answer," the mechanic said triumphantly. "Your brakes got wet in the rain."

"Hold on," Alec objected. "Why couldn't someone have wet them *before* she started?"

"Because," the mechanic said patiently, "if anyone had wet them *before* she started, she wouldn'ta had no brakes at all."

The Chief of Police turned to Elizabeth. "Rain can be dangerous, Miss Roffe. Particularly on these narrow mountain roads. This sort of thing happens all too often."

Alec was watching Elizabeth, not knowing what to do next. She felt like a fool. It *had* been an accident after all. She wanted to get out of here. She looked at the Chief of Police. "I—I'm sorry to have put you to all this trouble."

"*Please.* It is a pleasure. I mean—I am distressed about the circumstances, but it is always a pleasure to be of service. Detective Campagna will drive you back to your villa."

ALEC SAID TO her, "If you don't mind my saying so, old girl, you look ghastly. Now, I want you to hop into your bed and stay there for a few days. I'll order some groceries by telephone."

"If I stay in bed, who's going to cook?"

"I am," Alec declared.

That evening he prepared dinner and served it to Elizabeth in bed.

"I'm afraid I'm not a very good cook," he said cheerfully, as he set a tray down in front of Elizabeth.

It was the understatement of the year, Elizabeth thought. Alec was a terrible cook. Every dish was either burned, underdone or oversalted. But she managed to eat, partly because she was starving, and partly because she did not want to hurt Alec's feelings. He sat with her, making cheerful small talk. Not a word about what a fool she had made of herself at the police garage. She loved him for it.

THE TWO OF them spent the next few days at the villa, with Elizabeth remaining in bed, and Alec fussing over her, cooking all the meals, reading to her. During that time it seemed to Elizabeth that the telephone never stopped ringing. Ivo and Simonetta called every day to see how she was, and Hélène and Charles, and Walther. Even Vivian called. They all offered to come and stay with her.

"I'm really all right," she told them. "There's no reason for you to come. I'll be returning to Zurich in a few days."

Rhys Williams called. Elizabeth had not realized how much she had missed him until she heard the sound of his voice.

"I hear you decided to give Hélène some competition," he said. But she could hear the concern in his voice.

"Wrong. I only race on mountains, downhill." It was incredible to her that she could joke about it now.

Rhys said, "I'm glad you're all right, Liz."

His tone, as much as his words, warmed her. She wondered if he was with another woman now, and who she was. It would be someone beautiful, of course.

Damn her.

"Did you know you made the headlines?" Rhys asked.

"No."

" 'Heiress narrowly escapes death in car accident. Only a few weeks after her father, the well-known—' You can write the rest of the story yourself."

They spoke on the phone for half an hour, and when Elizabeth hung up she was feeling much better. Rhys seemed so genuinely interested in her, and concerned. She wondered whether he made every woman he knew feel that way about him. It was part of his charm. She remembered how they had celebrated her birthdays together. *Mrs. Rhys Williams.*

Alec walked into the bedroom. He said, "You look like the Cheshire cat."

"Do I?"

Rhys had always been able to make her feel that way. Perhaps, she thought, I should tell Rhys about the confidential report.

ALEC HAD ARRANGED for one of the company planes to fly them back to Zurich.

"I hate to take you back so soon," he said apologetically, "but there are some rather urgent decisions that have to be made."

The flight to Zurich was uneventful. There were reporters at the airport. Elizabeth made a brief statement about her accident, and then Alec had her safely inside the limousine and they were on their way to the company headquarters.

. . .

SHE WAS IN the conference room with all the members of the board, and Rhys, present. The meeting had been going on for the past three hours, and the air was stale with cigar and cigarette smoke. Elizabeth was still shaken from her experience, and she had a pounding headache—*Nothing to be concerned about, Miss Roffe. When the concussion wears off, the headaches will go away.*

She looked around the room, at the tense, angry faces. "I've decided not to sell," Elizabeth had told them. They thought she was being arbitrary and stubborn. If they only knew how close she had come to giving in. But now it was impossible. Someone in this room was an enemy. If she quit now, it would be his victory.

They had all tried to convince her, each in his own fashion.

Alec said reasonably, "Roffe and Sons needs an experienced president, Elizabeth. Particularly now. For your own sake, as well as everyone else's, I would like to see you walk away from this."

Ivo used his charm. "You're a beautiful young girl, *carissima.* The whole world is yours. Why do you want to become a slave to something as dull as business when you could be out, having a wonderful time, traveling—"

"I've traveled," Elizabeth said.

Charles used Gallic logic. "You happen to hold the controlling stock, through a tragic accident, but it makes no sense for you to try to run the company. We have serious problems. You will only make them worse."

Walther spoke bluntly. "The company is in enough trouble. You have no idea how much trouble. If you do not sell now, it will be too late."

Elizabeth felt as though she were under siege. She listened to them all, studying them, evaluating what they were telling her. Each of them based his argument on the good of the company—yet one of them was working to destroy it.

One thing was clear. They all wanted her to get out, to let them sell their stock, and bring in outsiders to take over Roffe and Sons. Elizabeth knew that the moment she did that, her chances of finding out who was behind this were finished. As long as she stayed here, on the inside, there was the possibility that she could learn who was sabotaging the company. She would stay only as long as she had to. She had not spent the last three years with Sam without learning something about the business. With the help of the experienced staff he had built up, she would continue to carry out her father's policies. The insistence from all the board members that she get out now only made her more stubbornly determined to remain.

She decided it was time to end the meeting.

"I've made my decision," Elizabeth said. "I don't plan to run this company alone. I'm aware of how much I have to learn. I know I can count on all of you to help me. We'll deal with the problems one by one."

She sat at the head of the table, still pale from her accident, looking small and defenseless.

Ivo threw up his hands helplessly. "Can't anyone talk logic into her?"

Rhys turned to Elizabeth and smiled. "I think everyone's going to have to go along with whatever the lady wants to do."

"Thank you, Rhys." Elizabeth looked at the others. "There's one thing more. Since I'm taking my father's place, I think it would be best to make it official."

Charles stared at her. "You mean—you want to become president?"

"In effect," Alec reminded him dryly, "Elizabeth is already president. She's merely showing us the courtesy of letting us handle the situation gracefully."

Charles hesitated then said, "All right. I move that Elizabeth Roffe be nominated president of Roffe and Sons."

"I second the motion," Walther said.

The motion was carried.

IT WAS SUCH *a bad time for presidents, he thought sadly. So many were being assassinated.*

21

No one was more aware than Elizabeth of the enormous responsibility she had assumed. As long as she was running the company, the jobs of thousands of people depended upon her. She needed help, but she had no idea whom she could trust. Alec and Rhys and Ivo were the ones she most wanted to confide in, but she was not ready yet. It was too soon. She sent for Kate Erling.

"Yes, Miss Roffe?"

Elizabeth hesitated, wondering how to begin. Kate Erling had worked for Elizabeth's father for many years. She would have a sense of the undercurrents that flowed beneath the deceptively calm surface. She would know about the inner workings of the company, about Sam Roffe's feelings, his plans. Kate Erling would make a strong ally.

Elizabeth said, "My father was having some kind of confidential report drawn up for him, Kate. Do you know anything about it?"

Kate Erling frowned in concentration, then shook her head. "He never discussed it with me, Miss Roffe."

Elizabeth tried another approach. "If my father had wanted a confidential investigation, to whom would he have gone?"

This time the answer was unhesitating. "Our security division."

The last place Sam would have gone. "Thank you," Elizabeth said.

There was no one she could talk to.

THERE WAS A current financial report on her desk. Elizabeth read it with growing dismay, and then sent for the company comptroller. His name was Wilton Kraus. He was younger than Elizabeth had expected. Bright, eager, an air of faint superiority. The Wharton School, she decided, or perhaps Harvard.

Elizabeth began without preamble. "How can a company like Roffe and Sons be in financial difficulty?"

Kraus looked at her and shrugged. He was obviously not used to reporting to a woman. He said condescendingly, "Well, putting it in words of one syllable—"

"Let's begin with the fact," Elizabeth said curtly, "that up until two years ago Roffe and Sons had always done its own capital financing."

She watched his expression change, trying to adjust. "Well—yes, ma'am."

"Then why are we so heavily indebted to banks now?"

He swallowed and said, "A few years ago, we went through a period of unusually heavy expansion. Your father and the other members of the board felt that it would be wise to raise that money by borrowing from banks on short-term loans. We have current net commitments to various banks for six hundred and fifty million dollars. Some of those loans are now due."

"Overdue," Elizabeth corrected him.

"Yes, ma'am. Overdue."

"We're paying the prime rate, plus one percent plus penalty interest. Why haven't we paid off the overdue loans and reduced the principal on the others?"

He was beyond surprise now. "Because of—er—certain unfortunate recent occurrences, the company's cash-flow position is considerably less than we had anticipated. Under ordinary circumstances we would go to the banks and ask for extensions. However, with our current problems, the various litigation settlements, the write-offs in our experimental laboratory, and . . ." His voice trailed off.

Elizabeth sat there, studying him, wondering whose side he was on. She looked down at the balance sheets again, trying to pinpoint where things had gone wrong. The statement showed a sharp decline over the past three quarters, largely because of the heavy lawsuit payoffs listed under the column "Extraordinary Expenses. (Nonrecurring)." In her mind's eye she saw the explosion in Chile, the cloud of poisonous chemicals spouting into the air. She could hear the screams of the victims. A dozen people dead. Hundreds more taken to hospitals. And in the end all the human pain and misery had been reduced to money, to Extraordinary Expenses (Nonrecurring).

She looked up at Wilton Kraus. "According to your report, Mr. Kraus, our problems are of a temporary nature. We are Roffe and Sons. We're still a first-class risk for any bank in the world."

It was his turn to study her. His supercilious air was gone, but he was wary now.

"You must realize, Miss Roffe," he began cautiously, "that a drug firm's reputation is as important as its products."

Who had said that to her before? Her father? Alec? She remembered. Rhys.

"Go on."

"Our problems are becoming too well-known. The business world is a jungle. If your competitors suspect that you've been wounded, they move in for the kill." He hesitated, then added, "They're moving in for the kill."

"In other words," Elizabeth replied, "our competitors bank with our bankers, too."

He gave her a brief congratulatory smile. "Exactly. The banks have a limited amount of funds to loan out. If they're convinced that A is a better risk than B—"

"And *do* they think that?"

He ran his fingers through his hair, nervously. "Since your father's death I've had several calls from Herr Julius Badrutt. He heads up the banking consortium we're dealing with."

"What did Herr Badrutt want?" She knew what was coming.

"He wanted to know who was going to be the new president of Roffe and Sons."

"Do you know who the new president is?" Elizabeth asked.

"No ma'am."

"I am." She watched him try to conceal his surprise. "What do you think will happen when Herr Badrutt learns the news?"

"He'll pull the plugs on us," Wilton Kraus blurted out.

"I'll talk to him," Elizabeth said. She leaned back in her chair and smiled. "Would you care for some coffee?"

"Why that's—that's very kind of you. Yes, thank you."

Elizabeth watched him relax. He had sensed that she had been testing him, and he felt that he had passed the test.

"I'd like your advice," Elizabeth said. "If you were in my position, Mr. Kraus, what would you do?"

That faintly patronizing air was back. "Well," he said confidently, "that's very simple. Roffe and Sons has enormous assets. If we sold off a substantial block of stock to the public, we could easily raise more than enough money to satisfy all our bank loans."

She knew now whose side he was on.

22

HAMBURG.

FRIDAY, OCTOBER 2.

TWO A.M.

The wind was blowing from the sea, and the early-morning air was chill and damp. In the Reeperbahn section of Hamburg the streets were crowded with visitors eager to experience the forbidden pleasures of the city of sin. The Reeperbahn catered to all tastes impartially. Drinks, drugs, girls or boys—they were all available at a price.

The garishly lighted hostess bars were on the main street, while the Grosse Freiheit featured the lewd strip shows. The Herbertstrasse, one block away, was for pedestrians only, and both sides of the street were lined with prostitutes sitting in the windows of their flats, displaying their wares through flimsy soiled nightgowns that concealed nothing. The Reeperbahn was a vast market, a human butcher shop, where you could select any piece of meat you could afford to pay for. For the strait-laced there was simple sex, missionary style; for those who enjoyed a bit of variety there was cunnilingus and analingus and sodomy. On the Reeperbahn you could buy a twelve-year-old boy or girl, or get into bed with a mother and daughter. If your tastes ran that way, you could watch a woman being serviced by a Great Dane, or get yourself whipped until you achieved orgasm. You could hire a toothless crone to perform fellatio on you in a busy alley or buy yourself an orgy in an elaborately mirrored bedroom with as many girls or boys as your libido required. The Reeperbahn prided itself on having something for everyone. Younger whores in short skirts and tight-fitting blouses cruised the pavements, propositioning men, women and couples impartially.

The cameraman walked down the street slowly, the target for a dozen girls and brightly rouged boys. He ignored them all until he came to a girl who looked to be no more than eighteen. She had blond hair. She was leaning against a wall, talking to a girl friend. She turned as the man approached, and smiled. "Would you like a party, *liebchen?* My friend and I will show you a good time."

The man studied the girl and said, "Just you."

The other girl shrugged and moved off.

"What's your name?"

"Hildy."

"Would you like to be in the movies, Hildy?" the cameraman asked.

The young girl studied him with cold eyes. *"Herr-gott!* You're not going to give me that old Hollywood *Scheiss?"*

He smiled reassuringly. "No, no. This is a genuine offer. It's a porno film. I make them for a friend of mine."

"It will cost you five hundred marks. In advance."

"Gut."

She regretted instantly that she had not asked for more. Well, she would find some way to get a bonus out of him. "What do I have to do?" Hildy asked.

HILDY WAS NERVOUS.

She lay sprawled out naked on the bed in the small, shabbily furnished apartment, watching the three people in the room, and thinking, There's something wrong here. Her instincts had been sharpened on the streets of Berlin and Munich and Hamburg. She had learned to rely on them. There was something about these people she did not trust. She would have liked to have walked out before it started, but they had already paid her five hundred marks, and promised her another five hundred if she did a good job. She would do a good job. She was a professional and she took pride in her work. She turned to the naked man in bed beside her. He was strong and well built; his body was hairless. What bothered Hildy was his face. He was too old for this sort of film. But it was the spectator who sat quietly at the back of the room who disturbed Hildy the most. The spectator wore a long coat, a large hat and dark glasses. Hildy could not even tell if it was a man or a woman. The vibrations were bad. Hildy fingered the red ribbon tied around her neck, wondering why they had asked her to wear it. The cameraman said, "All right. We're ready now. Action."

The camera began whirring. Hildy had been told what to do. The man was lying on his back. Hildy went to work.

She started with a trip around the world, skillfully using her tongue and lips on the man's ears and neck, moving down across his chest and stomach and belly, lightly flicking her tongue in quick butterfly strokes against his groin and penis, then each leg, down to his toes, slowly licking each toe, watching his erection begin. She rolled him over on his stomach, and her tongue began to work its way back up his body, moving slowly, expertly, finding all the erotic crevices and sensitive areas and exploring them. The man was fully aroused now, rock-hard.

"Get inside her," the cameraman said. The man rolled her over and was on top of her, forcing her thighs apart, his penis swollen to an enormous tumescence, and as he entered her, Hildy forgot her earlier fears. It felt wonderful.

"Shove it in me, *liebchen!*" she cried.

The man was deep, deep inside her, rocking back and forth, and Hildy started to move with him, her hips writhing in quickening spasms. In the back of the room the spectator was leaning forward, watching every movement. The girl on the bed closed her eyes.

She was spoiling it!

"Her eyes!" the spectator shouted.

The director called out, *"Öffne die Augen!"*

Startled, Hildy opened her eyes. She watched the man on top of her. He was good. It was the kind of sex she liked. Hard and thrusting. He was moving faster now, and she began to respond to him. Usually she did not have orgasms, except with her girl friend. With customers she always faked it, and they never knew the difference. But the cameraman had warned her that if she did not have an orgasm, she would not be paid the bonus. And so now she relaxed and let herself think about all the beautiful things she was going to buy with the money, and she felt herself beginning to climax.

"*Schneller!*" she cried. "*Schneller!*"

Her body began to shudder. "*Ah, jetzt!*" she screamed. "*Es kommt! Es kommt!*"

The spectator nodded, and the cameraman cried, "Now!"

The man's hands moved up toward the girl's neck. His enormous fingers closed over the windpipe and squeezed. She looked up into his eyes and saw what was there, and she was filled with terror. She tried to scream, but she was unable to breathe. She fought desperately to fight free, her body jerking in great, orgiastic spasms, but he had her pinned down. There was no escape.

The spectator sat there drinking it in, feasting on it, looking into the dying girl's eyes, watching her being punished.

The girl's body shuddered once, and then was still.

23

ZURICH.

MONDAY, OCTOBER 5.

TEN A.M.

When Elizabeth arrived at her office, a sealed envelope marked "confidential," with her name on it, was lying on her desk. She opened it. In it was a report from the chemical laboratory. It was signed "Emil Joeppli." It was full of technical terms, and Elizabeth read it through without understanding it. Then she read it again. And again. Each time more slowly. When finally she had grasped its significance, she said to Kate, "I'll be back in an hour." And she went to find Emil Joeppli.

He was a tall man about thirty-five, with a thin, freckled face, and a scalp that was bald except for a tonsure of bright red hair. He fidgeted uncomfortably, as though unused to having visitors in his little laboratory.

"I read your report," Elizabeth told him. "There's a great deal in it that I don't understand. I wonder if you would mind explaining it to me."

Instantly, Joeppli's nervousness vanished. He leaned forward in his chair, sure and confident, and began to speak rapidly. "I've been experimenting with a method of inhibiting rapid differentiation of the collagens, by using mucopolysaccharides and enzyme blocking techniques. Collagen, of course, is the fundamental protein basis of all connective tissue."

"Of course," Elizabeth said.

She did not even try to understand the technical part of what Joeppli was saying. What Elizabeth did understand was that the project he was working on could retard the aging process. It was a breathtaking concept.

She sat there, silent, listening, thinking about what this could mean in terms of revolutionizing the lives of men and women all over the world. According to Joeppli, there was no reason why everyone should not live to be a hundred, or a hundred and fifty, or even two hundred years old.

"It would not even be necessary to have injections," Joeppli told Elizabeth. "With this formula the ingredients could be taken orally in a pill or a capsule."

The possibilities were staggering. It would mean nothing less than a social revolution. And billions of dollars for Roffe and Sons. They would manufacture it themselves, and license it out to other companies as well. There was no one over fifty years of age who would not take a pill that would keep him or her young. It was difficult for Elizabeth to conceal her excitement.

"How far along are you on this project?"

"As I wrote in my report, I've been doing tests with animals for the last four years. All the recent results have been positive. It's just about ready for testing on human beings." She liked his enthusiasm.

"Who else knows about this?" Elizabeth asked.

"Your father knew. It's a Red Folder project. Top security. That means that I report only to the president of the company and to one member of the board."

Elizabeth suddenly felt chilled. "Which member?"

"Mr. Walther Gassner."

Elizabeth was silent for a moment. "From this time on," she said, "I want you to report directly to me. And only to me."

Joeppli looked at her in surprise. "Yes, Miss Roffe."

"How soon could we have this on the market?"

"If everything goes well, eighteen to twenty-four months from now."

"Fine. If you need anything—money, extra help, equipment—let me know. I want you to move as quickly as possible."

"Yes, ma'am."

Elizabeth rose, and instantly Emil Joeppli jumped to his feet.

"It's a pleasure meeting you." He smiled, and added shyly, "I liked your father."

"Thank you," Elizabeth said. Sam had known about this project. Was that another reason he refused to sell the company?

At the door Emil Joeppli turned to Elizabeth.

"It's going to work on people!"

"Yes," Elizabeth said. "Of course it will."

It had to.

"HOW IS A Red Folder project handled?"

Kate Erling asked, "From the beginning?"

"From the beginning."

"Well. As you know, we have several hundred new products in various experimental stages. They—"

"Who authorizes them?"

"Up to a certain amount of money, the heads of the different departments involved," Kate Erling said.

"What amount of money?"

"Fifty thousand dollars."

"And after that?"

"There must be board approval. Of course, a project does not come into the Red Folder category until it has passed its initial tests."

"You mean until it looks like it has a chance of being successful?" Elizabeth asked.

"That's right."

"How is it protected?"

"If it's an important project, all the work is transferred to one of our high-security laboratories. All the papers are removed from the general files and put into a Red Folder file. Only three people have access to that. The scientist in charge of the project, the president of the company, and one member of the board."

"Who decides who that member will be?" Elizabeth asked.

"Your father selected Walther Gassner."

The moment the words were out of her mouth, Kate realized her mistake.

The two women looked at each other, and Elizabeth said, "Thank you, Kate. That will be all."

Elizabeth had made no mention of Joeppli's project. Yet Kate had known what Elizabeth was talking about. There were two possibilities. Either Sam had trusted her and told her about Joeppli's project, or she had learned about it on her own. For someone else.

This was too important to allow anything to go wrong. She would check on the security herself. And she had to speak to Walther Gassner. She reached for the telephone, then stopped. There was a better way.

Late that afternoon Elizabeth was on a commercial airliner to Berlin.

WALTHER GASSNER WAS nervous.

They were seated at a corner booth in the upstairs dining room of the Papillon on the Kurfürstendamm. Whenever Elizabeth had visited Berlin in the past, Walther had always insisted that Elizabeth have dinner at his home, with Anna and him. This time there had been no mention of that. He had suggested instead that they meet at this restaurant. And he had come without Anna.

Walther Gassner still had the clean-cut, boyish, moviestar handsomeness, but the surface gloss had begun to crack. There were lines of tension in his face, and his hands never stopped moving. He seemed to be under some extraordinary tension. When Elizabeth asked about Anna, Walther was vague. "Anna's not feeling well. She couldn't come."

"Is it anything serious?"

"No, no. She'll be fine. She's at home, resting."

"I'll call her and—"

"Better not to disturb her."

It was a puzzling conversation, totally unlike Walther, whom Elizabeth had always found so open and outgoing.

She brought up the subject of Emil Joeppli. "We need what he's working on very badly," Elizabeth said.

Walther nodded. "It's going to be big."

"I've asked him not to report to you anymore," Elizabeth told him.

Walther's hands suddenly went very still. It was like a shout. He looked at Elizabeth and asked, "Why did you do that?"

"It has nothing to do with you, Walther. I would have done exactly the same thing with any other board member working with him. I simply want to handle this my own way."

He nodded. "I see." But his hands remained motionless on the table. "You have a right, of course." He forced a smile and she could see what it was costing him. "Elizabeth," he said, "Anna has a lot of stock in the company. She can't sell it unless you vote yes. It's—it's very important I—"

"I'm sorry, Walther, I can't let the stock be sold now."

His hands suddenly began to move again.

24

Herr Julius Badrutt was a thin, brittle man who resembled a praying mantis in a black suit. He was like a stick figure drawn by a child, with angular arms and legs, and a dry, unfinished face sketched on top of his body. He was seated stiffly at the conference table of the Roffe and Sons boardroom, facing Elizabeth. There were five other bankers with him. They all wore black suits with waistcoats, white shirts and dark ties. They appeared, Elizabeth thought, not so much *dressed* as in uniform. Looking around at the cold, impassive eyes at the table, Elizabeth was filled with a sense of misgiving. Before the meeting had begun, Kate had brought in a tray of coffee and delicious, freshly baked pastries. The men had all declined. Just as they had declined Elizabeth's invitation to come to lunch. She decided it was a bad sign. They were there to get the money that was owed them.

Elizabeth said, "First of all, I wish to thank all of you for coming here today."

There were polite, meaningless murmurs in response.

She took a deep breath. "I asked you here to discuss an extension on the loans owed to you by Roffe and Sons."

Julius Badrutt shook his head in tiny, jerky movements. "I am sorry, Miss Roffe. We have already informed—"

"I haven't finished," Elizabeth said. She glanced around the room. "If I were you, gentlemen, I would refuse."

They stared at her, then looked at one another in confusion.

Elizabeth continued, "If you were concerned about the loans when my father was running this company—and he was a brilliant business-man—why would you extend them for a woman who is inexperienced in business?"

Julius Badrutt said dryly, "I think you have answered your own ques-tion, Miss Roffe. We have no intention of—"

Elizabeth said, "I haven't finished."

They were eyeing her more warily now. She looked at each of them in turn, making sure she had their full attention. They were Swiss bankers, admired, respected and envied by their lesser colleagues in other parts of the financial world. They were leaning forward now, listening carefully, their attitude of impatience and boredom replaced by curiosity.

"You have all known Roffe and Sons for a long time," Elizabeth went on. "I am sure most of you knew my father and, if you did, you must have respected him."

There were nods of agreement from some of the men.

"I imagine," Elizabeth continued, "that you gentlemen must have choked over your morning coffee when you learned that I was taking his place here."

One of the bankers smiled, then laughed aloud, and said, "You are quite right, Miss Roffe. I do not mean to be ungallant, but I think I am speaking for the rest of my colleagues when I say that—what were your words?—we choked over our morning coffee."

Elizabeth smiled ingenuously. "I don't blame you. I'm sure I would have reacted in exactly the same way."

Another banker spoke up. "I am curious, Miss Roffe. Since we are all in agreement about the outcome of this meeting"—he spread his hands expressively—"why are we here?"

"You're here," Elizabeth said, "because in this room are some of the greatest bankers in the world. I can't believe that you became so success-ful by looking at everything only in terms of dollars and cents. If that were true, then any of your bookkeepers could run your business for you. I am sure that there is much more to banking than that."

"Of course there is," another banker murmured, "but we're businessmen, Miss Roffe, and—"

"And Roffe and Sons is a business. It's a great business. I didn't know how great until I sat behind my father's desk. I had no idea how many lives this company has saved in countries all over the world. Or of the enormous contributions we've made to medicine. Or how many thousands of people depend on this company for their livelihood. If—"

Julius Badrutt interrupted. "That is all very commendable, but we seem to be getting off the point. I understand that it has been suggested to you that if you release the company stock, there will be more than sufficient monies to satisfy our loans."

His first mistake, Elizabeth thought. *I understand that it has been suggested to you.*

The suggestion had been made in the privacy of a board of directors' meeting, where everything was confidential. Someone at that meeting had talked. Someone who was trying to put pressure on her. She intended to find out who, but that would have to come later.

"I want to ask you a question," Elizabeth said. "If your loans are repaid, would it matter to you where the money came from?"

Julius Badrutt studied her, his mind circling the question, looking for a trap. Finally he said, "No. Not as long as we receive the money due us."

Elizabeth leaned forward and said earnestly, "So it doesn't matter whether you're paid from the sale of company stock to outsiders, or from our own financial resources. All of you know that Roffe and Sons isn't going out of business. Not today. Not tomorrow. Not ever. All I'm asking is the courtesy of a little extra time."

Julius Badrutt smacked his dry lips and said, "Believe me, Miss Roffe, we are most sympathetic. We understand the terrible emotional stress you have gone through, but we cannot—"

"Three months," Elizabeth said. "Ninety days. With your getting additional penalty interest, of course."

There was a silence around the table. But it was a negative silence. Elizabeth could see their cold, hostile faces. She decided on one last desperate gamble.

"I—I don't know whether it's proper for me to reveal this," she said with deliberate hesitation, "and I must ask you to keep it confidential." She looked around and saw that she had their interest again. "Roffe and Sons is on the verge of a breakthrough that's going to revolutionize the entire pharmaceutical industry." She paused to heighten the suspense. "This company is about to reveal a new product that our projections show will *far outsell every drug available on the market today.*"

She could feel the change in the atmosphere.

It was Julius Badrutt who rose to the bait first. "What—er—type of—?"

Elizabeth shook her head. "I'm sorry, Herr Badrutt. Perhaps I've already said too much. I can only tell you that it will be the biggest innovation in the history of this business. It will require a tremendous expansion of our facilities. We'll have to double them, perhaps triple them. Of course, we'll be looking for new financing on a large scale."

The bankers were glancing at one another, exchanging silent signals. The silence was broken by Herr Badrutt. "If we *were* to give you a ninety-day extension, we would naturally expect to act as the prime bankers for Roffe and Sons in all future transactions."

"Naturally."

Another exchange of meaningful looks. It's like a form of jungle drums, Elizabeth thought.

"In the meantime," Herr Badrutt said, "we would have your assurance that at the end of ninety days all your outstanding notes will be met in full?"

"Yes."

Herr Badrutt sat there, staring into space. He looked at Elizabeth, then looked around at the others, and received their silent signals. "For my part, I am willing to agree. I do not think a delay—with penalty interest—will do any harm."

One of the other bankers nodded. "If you think we should go along, Julius . . ."

And it was done. Elizabeth leaned back in her chair, trying to conceal the feeling of relief flooding through her. She had gained ninety days.

She would need every minute of that time.

25

I t was like being in the eye of a hurricane.

Everything flowed across Elizabeth's desk from the hundreds of departments at headquarters, from the factories in Zaire, the laboratories in Greenland, the offices in Australia and Thailand, from the four corners of the earth. There were reports on new products, sales, statistical projections, advertising campaigns, experimental programs.

There were decisions to be made on building new factories, selling old ones, acquiring companies, hiring and firing executives. Elizabeth had expert advice on every phase of the business, but all final decisions had to be made by her. As they had once been made by Sam. She was grateful now for the three years she had worked with her father. She knew much more about the company than she had realized, and much less. Its very scope was awesome. Elizabeth had once thought of it as a kingdom, but it was a *series* of kingdoms, run by viceroys, with the president's office as the throne room. Each of her cousins had charge of his own domain, but in addition they supervised other overseas territories, so that they were all traveling constantly.

Elizabeth soon learned that she had a special problem. She was a woman in a man's world, and she discovered that it made a difference. She had never really believed that men subscribed to the myth of the inferiority of women, but she quickly learned better. No one ever put it into words or acted overtly, but Elizabeth was faced with it every day. It was an attitude born of ancient prejudices and it was inescapable. The men did not like taking orders from a woman. They resented the idea of a woman questioning their judgments, trying to improve on their ideas. The fact that Elizabeth was young and attractive made it worse. They tried to make her feel that she should be at home, in a bed or kitchen, and that she should leave serious business matters to the men.

Elizabeth scheduled meetings with different department heads every day. Not all were hostile. Some were predatory. A beautiful girl sitting behind the president's desk was a challenge to the male ego. Their minds were easy to read: If I can fuck her, I can control her.

Like the grown-up version of the boys in Sardinia.

The men went after the wrong part of Elizabeth. They should have gone after her mind, because in the end that was where she controlled them. They underestimated her intelligence, and that was their mistake.

They miscalculated her capacity to assume authority, and that was another error.

And they misjudged her strength, and that was their greatest mistake. She was a Roffe, with the bloodline of old Samuel and her father in her, and she had their determination and spirit.

While the men around her were trying to use Elizabeth, she used them. She tapped the knowledge and the experience and the insights that they had accumulated, and she made them her own. She let the men talk, and she listened. She asked questions, and she remembered the answers.

She learned.

Every night Elizabeth took home two heavy briefcases filled with reports to be studied. Sometimes she worked until four in the morning. One evening a newspaper photographer snapped a picture of Elizabeth walking out of the building with a secretary carrying her two briefcases. The photograph appeared in the newspapers the next day. The caption read: "Working Heiress."

. . .

ELIZABETH HAD BECOME an international celebrity overnight. The story of a beautiful young girl inheriting a multibillion-dollar corporation and then taking command was irresistible. The press jumped at it. Elizabeth was lovely, intelligent, and down-to-earth, a combination they rarely came across in celebrities. She made herself available to them whenever possible, trying to build up the damaged image of the company, and they appreciated it. When she didn't know the answer to a reporter's question, she was not afraid to pick up a telephone and ask someone. Her cousins flew into Zurich once a week for meetings and Elizabeth spent as much time with them as possible. She saw them together, and one at a time. She talked to them and studied them, searching for a clue as to which one of them had allowed innocent people to die in an explosion, had sold secrets to competitors, and which one of them was trying to destroy Roffe and Sons. One of her cousins.

Ivo Palazzi, with his irresistible warmth and charmth.

Alec Nichols, a correct and proper gentleman, and gentle man, always helpful when Elizabeth needed him.

Charles Martel, a dominated, frightened man. And frightened men could be dangerous when cornered.

Walther Gassner. The All-German boy. Beautiful-looking and friendly on the outside. What was he like on the inside? He had married Anna, an heiress, thirteen years his senior. Had he married for love or money?

When Elizabeth was with them, she watched, and listened, and probed. She mentioned the explosion in Chile and studied their reactions, and she talked about the patents that Roffe had lost to other companies, and she discussed the impending government suits.

She learned nothing. Whoever it was, he was too clever to give himself away. He would have to be trapped. Elizabeth recalled Sam's marginal note on the report. *Trap the bastard.* She would have to find a way.

ELIZABETH FOUND HERSELF becoming more and more fascinated by the inside operation of the pharmaceutical business.

Bad news was deliberately spread. If there was a report that a patient had died from a competitor's medication, within half an hour a dozen men were placing telephone calls all around the world. "By the way, did you happen to hear about . . . ?"

Yet on the surface all the companies appeared to be on the best of terms. The heads of some of the large firms held regular informal get-togethers, and Elizabeth was invited to one. She was the only woman present. They talked about their mutual problems.

The president of one of the large companies, a pompous, middle-aged roué, who had been following Elizabeth around all evening, said, "Government restrictions get more unreasonable every Goddamned day. If some genius invented aspirin tomorrow, the government would never okay it." He gave Elizabeth a superior smile. "And do you have any idea, little lady, how long we've had aspirin?"

Little lady replied, "Since four hundred B.C., when Hippocrates discovered salicin in the bark of the willow tree."

He stared at her a moment, and the smile died. "Right." He walked away.

The company heads all agreed that one of their biggest problems was the me-too firms, the copycat houses that stole the formulas of successful products, changed the names and rushed them onto the market. It was costing the reputable drug firms hundreds of millions of dollars a year.

In Italy it was not even necessary to steal it.

"Italy is one of the countries that has no patent regulations protecting new drugs," one of the executives told Elizabeth. "For a bribe of a few hundred thousand lire, anyone can buy the formulas and pirate them under another name. We spend millions of dollars on research—they walk off with the profits."

"Is it just Italy?" Elizabeth asked.

"Italy and Spain are the worst. France and West Germany aren't bad. England and the United States are clean."

Elizabeth looked around at all these indignant, moral men and wondered if any of them was involved in the thefts of the patents of Roffe and Sons.

IT SEEMED TO Elizabeth that she spent most of her time in airplanes. She kept her passport in the top drawer of her desk. At least once a week there was a frantic call from Cairo or Guatemala or Tokyo, and within a few hours Elizabeth would find herself in a plane with half a dozen members of her staff, to cope with some emergency.

She met factory managers and their families in large cities like Bombay, and at remote outposts like Puerto Vallarta, and gradually Roffe and Sons began to take on a new perspective. It was no longer an impersonal mass of reports and statistics. A report headed "Guatemala" now meant Emil Nunoz and his fat, happy wife and their twelve children; "Copenhagen" was Nils Bjorn and the crippled mother with whom he lived; "Rio de Janeiro" was an evening spent with Alessandro Duval and his exquisite mistress.

Elizabeth kept in regular touch with Emil Joeppli. She always telephoned him on her private line, calling him at his little flat in Aussersihl in the evenings.

She was cautious even over the telephone.

"How are things going?"

"A little slower than I hoped, Miss Roffe."

"Do you need anything?"

"No. Just time. I ran into a little problem but I think it's solved now."

"Good. Call me if you need anything—anything at all."

"I will. Thank you, Miss Roffe."

Elizabeth hung up. She had an urge to push him, to tell him to hurry, for she knew that her time with the banks was running out. She desperately needed what Emil Joeppli was working on, but pressing him was not the answer, and so she kept her impatience to herself. Elizabeth knew that the experiments could not possibly be completed by the time the bank notes were due. But she had a plan. She intended to let Julius Badrutt into the secret, take him into the laboratory and let him see for himself what was happening. The banks would give them all the time they needed.

ELIZABETH FOUND HERSELF working with Rhys Williams more and more closely, sometimes late into the night. They often worked alone, just the two of them, having dinner in her private dining room at the office, or at the elegant apartment she had taken. It was a modern condominium in Zurichberg, overlooking the Lake of Zurich, and it was large and airy and bright. Elizabeth was more aware than ever of the strong animal magnetism of Rhys, but if he felt an attraction for her, he was careful not to show it. He was always polite and friendly. *Avuncular* was the word that came into Elizabeth's mind, and somehow it had a pejorative sound. She wanted to lean on him, confide in him, and yet she knew she had to be careful. More than once she had found herself on the verge of telling Rhys about the efforts to sabotage the company, but something held her back. She was not ready to discuss it with anyone yet. Not until she knew more.

ELIZABETH WAS GAINING more confidence in herself. At a sales meeting they were discussing a new hair conditioner that was selling badly. Elizabeth had tried it, and she knew that it was superior to similar products on the market.

"We're getting heavy returns from drugstores," one of the sales executives complained. "It's just not catching on. We need more advertising."

"We're already over our advertising budget," Rhys objected. "We'll have to find a different approach."

Elizabeth said, "Take it out of the drugstores."

They all looked at her. "What?"

"It's too available." She turned to Rhys. "I think we should continue the advertising campaign, but sell it only at beauty salons. Make it exclusive, hard to get. That's the image it should have."

Rhys thought for a moment, then nodded and said, "I like it. Let's try it."

It became a big seller overnight.

Afterward, Rhys had complimented her. "You're not just another pretty face," he had said, grinning.

So he *was* beginning to notice!

26

LONDON.

FRIDAY, NOVEMBER 6.

FIVE P.M.

Alec Nichols was alone in the club sauna when the door opened and a man walked into the steam-filled room, wearing a towel around his waist. He sat down on the wooden bench, next to Alec. "Hot as a witch's tit in here, ain't it, Sir Alec?"

Alec turned. It was Jon Swinton. "How did you get in here?"

Swinton winked. "I said you was expectin' me. He looked into Alec's eyes and asked, "You *was* expectin' me, wasn't you, Sir Alec?"

"No," Alec replied. "I told you I need more time."

"You also told us your little cousin was going to sell the stock, and you'd give us our money."

"She—she changed her mind."

"Ah, then you'd better change it back for her, hadn't you?"

"I'm trying. It's a question of—"

"It's a question of how much more horseshit we're going to take from you." Jon Swinton was moving closer, forcing Alec to slide along the bench. "We don't want to get rough with you 'cause it's nice to have a good friend like you in Parliament. You know what I mean? But there's a limit." He was leaning against Alec now, and Alec slid farther away from him. "We did you a favor. Now it's time to pay us back. You're gonna get hold of a shipment of drugs for us."

"No! That's impossible," Alec said. "I can't. There's no way—"

Alec suddenly found that he had been crowded to the end of the bench, next to the large metal container filled with hot rocks. "Be careful," Alec said. "I—"

Swinton grabbed hold of Alec's arm and twisted it, forcing it toward the bed of rocks. Alec could feel the hair on his arm begin to singe.

"No!"

The next instant his arm was pressed down onto the rocks, and he screamed with pain and fell to the floor in agony. Swinton was standing over him.

"You find a way. We'll be in touch."

27

Anna Roffe Gassner did not know how much longer she would be able to stand it.

She had become a prisoner in her own home. Except for the cleaning woman who came in for a few hours once a week, Anna and the children were alone, completely at Walther's mercy. He no longer bothered to conceal his hatred. Anna had been in the children's room as they listened together to one of their favorite records.

> "Welch ein Singen, Musizieren,
> Pfeifen, Zwitschken, Tiriliern . . ."

Walther had stormed in. "I'm sick of that!" he had yelled.

And he had smashed the record, while the children cowered in terror.

Anna had tried to placate him. "I—I'm sorry, Walther. I—I didn't know you were home. Can I do something for you?"

He had walked up to her, his eyes blazing, and he said, "We're going to get rid of the children, Anna."

In front of them!

He put his hands on her shoulders. "What happens in this house must be our secret." *Our secret. Our secret. Our secret.*

She could feel the words reverberating in her head, and his arms started to crush her until she could not breathe. She fainted.

WHEN ANNA WOKE up, she was lying in her bed. The shades were drawn. She looked at the bedside clock. Six P.M. The house was quiet. Too quiet. Her first thought was of the children, and terror swept through her. She rose from the bed on shaky legs, and stumbled over to the door. It was locked from the outside. She pressed her ear hard against the panel, listening. There should have been the sounds of the children. They should have come up to see her.

If they had been able to. If they were still alive.

Her legs were trembling so hard that she could barely walk to the telephone. She breathed a silent prayer, then picked it up. She heard the familiar dial tone. She hesitated, dreading the thought of what Walther would do to her if he caught her again. Without giving herself a chance to think, Anna began to dial 110. Her hands shook so badly that she dialed a wrong number. And another. She began to sob. There was so little time left. Fighting her growing hysteria, she tried again, willing her fingers to move slowly. She heard a ringing, then miraculously a man's voice said, *"Hier ist der Notruf der Polizei."*

Anna could not find her voice.

"Hier ist der Notruf der Polizei. Kann ich Ihnen helfen?"

"Ja!" It was a high-pitched sob. *"Ja, bitte! Ich bin in grosser Gefahr. Bitte schicken sie jemanden—"*

Walther loomed in front of her, ripping the telephone out of her hand and hurling her against the bed. He slammed down the receiver, breathing hard, tore the cord out of the wall and turned to Anna.

"The children," she whispered. "What have you done with the children?"

Walther did not answer.

THE CENTRAL DIVISION of the Berlin Kriminal Polizei was located at 2832 Keithstrasse in a district of ordinary-looking apartment houses and office buildings. The emergency number of the *Delikt am Mensch* department was equipped with an automatic hold system, so that a caller was unable to disconnect until the line had been electronically released by the switchboard. In this way every number calling in could be traced, no matter how brief the conversation. It was a sophisticated piece of equipment of which the department was proud.

Within five minutes of Anna Gassner's telephone call, Detective Paul Lange walked into the office of his chief, Major Wageman, carrying a cassette player.

"I would like you to listen to this." Detective Lange pressed a button. A metallic male voice said, *"Hier ist der Notruf der Polizei. Kann ich Ihnen helfen?"*

Then a woman's voice, filled with terror. *"Ja! Ja, bitte! Ich bin in grosser Gefahr. Bitte schicken sie jemanden—"*

There was the sound of a thud, a click and the line went dead. Major Wageman looked up at Detective Lange. "You've traced the call?"

"We know whose residence it came from," Detective Lange replied carefully.

"Then what's the problem?" Major Wageman demanded impatiently. "Have Central send a car to investigate."

"I wanted your authority first." Detective Lange placed a slip of paper on the desk in front of the major.

"Scheiss!" Major Wageman stared at him. "Are you sure?"

"Yes, Major."

Major Wageman looked down at the slip of paper again. The telephone was listed in the name of Gassner, Walther. Head of the German division of Roffe and Sons, one of the industrial giants of Germany.

There was no need to discuss the implications. Only an idiot could miss them. One wrong move and they would both be walking the streets, looking for a job. Major Wageman thought for a moment and then said, "All right. Check it out. I want you to go there yourself. And walk on fucking eggs. Do you understand?"

"I understand, Major."

THE GASSNER ESTATE was in Wannsee, an exclusive suburb in southwest Berlin. Detective Lange took the longer Hohenszollerndamm instead of the speedier autobahn, because the traffic was lighter. He went through the Clayalle, past the CIA building, hidden behind half a mile of barbed-wire fences. He passed the American Army Headquarters and turned right on what was once known as Road One, the longest road in Germany, running from East Prussia to the Belgian border. On his right was the Brücke der Einheit, the Bridge of Unity, where the spy Abel had been exchanged for the American U-2 pilot Gary Powers. Detective Lange turned the car off the highway into the wooded hills of Wannsee.

The houses were beautiful, impressive. On Sundays, Detective Lange sometimes took his wife out here, just to look at the outside of the houses and the grounds.

He found the address he was looking for and turned into the long driveway leading to the Gassner estate. The estate represented something more than money: it represented power. The Roffe dynasty was big enough to make governments fall. Major Wageman had been right: he would be very careful.

Detective Lange drove to the front door of the three-story stone house, got out of the car, took off his hat and pressed the doorbell. He waited. There was the heavy hanging silence of a house that has been deserted. He knew that was impossible. He rang again. Nothing but that still, oppressive silence. He was debating whether to go around to the back when the door unexpectedly opened. A woman stood in the doorway. She was middle-aged, plain-looking, wearing a wrinkled dressing gown. Detective Lange took her for the housekeeper. He pulled out his identification. I'd like to see Mrs. Walther Gassner. Please tell her Detective Lange . . ."

"I am Mrs. Gassner," the woman said.

Detective Lange tried to conceal his surprise. She was totally unlike his image of the lady of this house.

"I—we received a telephone call at police headquarters a short time ago," he began.

She watched him, her face blank, disinterested. Detective Lange felt that he was handling this badly, but he did not know why. He had a feeling that he was missing something important.

"Did you make that call, Mrs. Gassner?" he asked.

"Yes," she answered. "It was a mistake."

There was a dead, remote quality to her voice that was disturbing. He remembered the shrill, hysterical voice on the tape recorder half an hour earlier.

"Just for our records, may I ask what kind of mistake?"

Her hesitation was barely perceptible. "There was—I thought that a piece of my jewelry was missing. I found it."

The emergency number was for murder, rape, mayhem. *Walk on fucking eggs.*

"I see." Detective Lange hesitated, wanting to get inside the house, wanting to find out what she was covering up. But there was nothing more he could say or do. "Thank you, Mrs. Gassner. I'm sorry to have troubled you."

He stood there, frustrated, and watched the door close in his face. He slowly got into his car and drove off.

Behind the door Anna turned.

Walther nodded and said softly, "You did very well, Anna. Now we're going back upstairs."

He turned toward the stairway, and Anna pulled out a pair of shears that had been concealed in the folds of her dressing gown and plunged them into his back.

28

ROME.
SUNDAY, NOVEMBER 8.
NOON.

It was a perfect day, Ivo Palazzi thought, for visiting the Villa d'Este with Simonetta and their three beautiful daughters. As Ivo strolled through the fabled Tivoli Gardens arm in arm with his wife, watching the girls race ahead from fountain to splashing fountain, he idly wondered whether Pirro Ligorio, who had built the park for his patrons, the D'Este family, had ever dreamed how much joy he would one day give to millions of sightseers. The Villa d'Este was a short distance northeast of Rome, nestled high in the Sabine Hills. Ivo had been there often, but it always gave him a feeling of special pleasure to stand at the very top level and look down on the dozens of sparkling fountains below, each one cunningly designed, each one different from the others.

In the past Ivo had taken Donatella and his three sons here. How they had adored it! The thought of them made Ivo sad. He had not seen or talked to Donatella since that horrifying afternoon at the apartment. He still remembered vividly the terrible scratches she had inflicted on him. He knew what remorse she must be going through, and how she must be longing for him. Well, it would do her good to suffer for a while, as he had suffered. In his mind he could hear Donatella's voice, and she was saying, "Come along. This way, boys."

It was so clear it seemed almost real. He could hear her say, "Faster, Francesco!" and Ivo turned and Donatella was in back of him, with their three boys, moving determinedly toward him and Simonetta and the three girls. Ivo's first thought was that Donatella had happened to be here at the Tivoli Gardens by coincidence, but the instant he saw the expression on her face, he knew better. The *putana* was trying to bring his two families together, trying to destroy him! Ivo rose to the occasion like a madman.

He shouted to Simonetta, "There's something I must show you. Quickly, everybody."

And he swept his family down the long winding stone steps toward a lower level, pushing tourists aside, casting frantic glances over his shoulder. Above, Donatella and the boys were moving toward the steps. Ivo knew that if the boys saw him, everything was lost. All it needed was for one of them to shout "Papa!" and he might as well drown himself in the fountains. He hurried Simonetta and the girls along, not giving them a chance to pause, not daring to let them stop for an instant.

"Where are we rushing to?" Simonetta gasped. "What's the hurry?"

"It's a surprise," Ivo said gaily. "You'll see."

He risked another quick glance back. Donatella and the three boys were out of sight for the moment. Ahead was a labyrinth, with one set of stairs leading up and another leading down. Ivo chose the stairs going up.

"Come along," he called to the girls. "Whoever gets to the top first gets a prize!"

"Ivo! I'm exhausted!" Simonetta complained. "Can't we rest a minute?"

He looked at her in shock. "*Rest?* That would spoil the surprise. Hurry!"

He took Simonetta's arm and dragged her up the steep steps, his three daughters racing ahead of them. Ivo found himself gasping for breath. It would serve them all right, he thought bitterly, if I have a heart attack and die right here. Goddamn women! You can't trust any of them. How could she do this to me? She adores me. I'll kill the bitch for this.

He could visualize himself strangling Donatella in her bed. She was wearing nothing by a flimsy negligée. He ripped it off and began to mount her, while she screamed for mercy. Ivo could feel himself getting an erection.

"Can we stop now?" Simonetta begged.

"No! We're almost there!"

They had reached the upper level again. Ivo took a hasty look around. Donatella and the boys were nowhere in sight.

"Where are you taking us?" Simonetta demanded.

"You'll see," Ivo said hysterically. "Follow me!" He shoved them toward the exit.

Isabella, the oldest girl, said, "Are we leaving, Papa? We just got here!"

"We're going to a better place," Ivo panted. He glanced back. Coming into sight, climbing the stairs, were Donatella and the boys.

"Faster, girls!"

A moment later Ivo and one of his families were outside the gates of the Villa d'Este, racing toward their car on the large square.

"I've never seen you like this," Simonetta gasped.

"I've never been like this," Ivo said truthfully. He had the motor going before the car doors were closed, and he raced out of the parking lot like the devil was pursuing him.

"Ivo!"

He patted Simonetta's hand. "I want everybody to relax now. As a special treat I'm—I'm taking you to lunch at the Hassler."

THEY SAT AT a picture window overlooking the Spanish Steps, with Saint Peter's looming gloriously in the distance.

Simonetta and the children had a marvelous time. The food was delicious. Ivo could have been eating cardboard. His hands were trembling so badly that he could hardly hold his knife and fork. *I can't stand much more of this*, he thought. *I'm not going to let her ruin my life.*

For he had no doubt now that that was exactly what Donatella intended to do. *Il giuoco è stato fatto.* The game was up. Unless he could find a way to give Donatella the money she was demanding.

He had to get it. It did not matter how.

29

PARIS.

MONDAY, NOVEMBER 9.

SIX P.M.

The instant Charles Martel arrived home he knew he was in trouble. Hélène was waiting for him, and with her was Pierre Richaud, the jeweler who had made the replicas of her stolen jewelry. Charles stood in the doorway, in shock.

"Come in, Charles," Hélène said. There was an undercurrent in her voice that terrified him. "I believe that you and M. Richaud know each other."

Charles stared, knowing that whatever he said would hang him. The jeweler was studying the floor in embarrassment, obviously ill at ease.

"Sit down, Charles." It was a command. Charles sat down.

Hélène said, "What you're facing, *mon cher mari,* is a criminal charge of grand theft. You have been stealing my jewelry and replacing the pieces with clumsy imitation paste, made by M. Richaud."

To his horror Charles found himself wetting his pants, a thing he had not done since he was a small boy. He blushed. He wished desperately that he could leave the room for a moment to clean himself. No, he wanted to flee and never return.

Hélène knew everything. It did not matter how she had found him out. There would be no escape and no mercy. It was terrifying enough that Hélène had discovered he had been stealing from her. Wait until she learned his motive! Wait until she found out that he had been planning to use the money to run away from her! Hell was going to have a new meaning. No one knew Hélène as Charles did. She was *une sauvage,* capable of anything. She would destroy him, without a moment's thought, turn him into a *clochard,* one of those sad bums who sleep on the streets of Paris in rags. His life had suddenly turned into an *emmerdement,* a shower of shit.

"Did you really think you could get away with anything so stupid!" Hélène was asking.

Charles remained miserably silent. He could feel his pants getting wetter, but he did not dare look down.

"I have persuaded M. Richaud to give me all the facts."

Persuaded. Charles dreaded to think how.

"I have photostatic copies of the receipts for the money you stole from me. I can put you in prison for the next twenty years." She paused, and added, "If I choose to."

Her words only served to increase Charles's panic. Experience had taught him that a generous Hélène was a dangerous Hélène. Charles was afraid to meet her glance. He wondered what it was she would demand from him. Something monstrous.

Hélène turned to Pierre Richaud. "You will say nothing of this to anyone until I have made up my mind what I wish to do."

"Of course, Mme. Roffe-Martel, of course, of course." The man was babbling. He looked hopefully toward the door. "May I—?"

Hélène nodded, and Pierre Richaud scurried out.

Hélène watched him go, then swung around to study her husband. She could smell his fear. And something else. Urine. She smiled. Charles had pissed himself out of fear. She had taught him well. Hélène was pleased with Charles. It was a very satisfying marriage. She had broken Charles, then made him her creature. The innovations he had brought to Roffe and Sons were brilliant, for they had all come from Hélène. She ruled a small part of Roffe and Sons through her husband, but now it was not enough. She was a Roffe. She was wealthy in her own right; her earlier marriages had made her even wealthier. But it was not money she was interested in. It was the control of the company. She had planned to use her stock to acquire more stock, to buy up the interest of the others. She had already discussed it with them. They were willing to go along with her, to form a minority group. First, Sam had stood in the way of her plan, and now Elizabeth. But Hélène had no intention of allowing Elizabeth or anyone else to keep her from getting what she wanted. Charles was going to get it for her. If anything went wrong, he would be her scapegoat.

Now, of course, he must be punished for his *petite révolte.* She watched his face and said, "No one steals from me, Charles. No one. You're finished. Unless I decide to save you."

He sat there, silent, wishing her dead, terrified of her. She walked over to where he sat, her thighs brushing against his face.

She said, "Would you like me to save you, Charles?"

"Yes," he said hoarsely. She was stepping out of her skirt, her eyes vicious, and he thought, *Oh, my God! Not now!*

"Then listen to me. Roffe and Sons is my company. I want the controlling interest."

He looked up at her miserably and said, "You know Elizabeth won't sell."

Hélène slipped out of her blouse and pants. She stood there, animal naked, her body lean and magnificent, her nipples hard. "Then you must do something about her. Or spend the next twenty years of your life in prison. Don't worry. I'll tell you what you will do. But first, come here, Charles."

30

The following morning, at ten o'clock, Elizabeth's private phone rang. It was Emil Joeppli. She had given him the number so that no one would be aware of their conversations. "I wonder if I could see you," he said. He sounded excited.

"I'll be there in fifteen minutes."

Kate Erling looked up in surprise as Elizabeth came out of her office wearing a coat. "You have an appointment at—"

"Cancel everything for the next hour," Elizabeth said, and walked out.

In the Development Building an armed guard examined Elizabeth's pass. "Last door to the left, Miss Roffe."

Elizabeth found Joeppli alone in his laboratory. He greeted her with enthusiasm.

"I finished the final tests last night. It works. The enzymes completely inhibit the aging process. Look."

He led her to a cage holding four young rabbits, alert and filled with restless vitality. Next to it was another cage containing four more rabbits, quieter, more mature.

"This is the five hundredth generation to receive the enzyme," Joeppli said.

Elizabeth stood in front of the cage. "They look healthy."

Joeppli smiled. "*That's* part of the control group." He pointed to the cage on the left. "*Those* are the senior citizens."

Elizabeth stared at the energetic rabbits, frisking around in the cage like newborn bunnies, and she could not believe it.

"They'll outlive the others by at least three to one," Joeppli told her.

When you applied that ratio to human beings, the implications were staggering. She could barely contain her excitement.

"When—when will you be ready to start testing it on people?"

"I'm getting my final notes together. After that, another three or four weeks at the most."

"Emil, don't discuss this with anyone," Elizabeth warned.

Emil Joeppli nodded. "I won't, Miss Roffe. I'm working alone. I'm being very careful."

THE ENTIRE AFTERNOON had been taken up with a board meeting, and it had gone well. Walther had not appeared. Charles had again brought up the subject of selling the stock, but Elizabeth had firmly vetoed it. After that, Ivo had been his charming self, as had Alec. Charles seemed unusually tense. Elizabeth wished she knew why.

She invited them all to stay in Zurich and have dinner with her. As casually as possible, Elizabeth brought up the problems that had been mentioned in the report, watching for a reaction of some kind, but she could detect no sign of nervousness or guilt. And everyone who could have been involved, except for Walther, was seated at that table.

RHYS HAD NOT attended the meeting or the dinner. "I have some urgent business to take care of," he had said, and Elizabeth had wondered if it was a girl. Elizabeth was aware that whenever Rhys stayed late at night to work with her, he had had to cancel a date. Once, when he had been unable to reach the girl in time, she had appeared at the office. She was a stunning redhead, with a figure that made Elizabeth feel like a boy. The girl had been furious at being stood up, and she had not bothered to hide her displeasure. Rhys had escorted her to the elevator and returned.

"Sorry about that," he had said.

Elizabeth could not help herself. "She's charming," she said sweetly. "What does she do?"

"She's a brain surgeon," Rhys had replied earnestly, and Elizabeth had laughed. The following day Elizabeth had learned that the girl *was* a brain surgeon.

There were others, and Elizabeth found herself resenting all of them. She wished that she understood Rhys better. She knew the gregarious and public Rhys Williams; she wanted to meet the private Rhys Williams, the self he kept hidden. More than once, Elizabeth had thought, Rhys should be running this company instead of taking orders from me. I wonder how he really feels about it?

THAT EVENING AFTER dinner, when the members of the board had dispersed to catch trains and planes back to their homes, Rhys walked into Elizabeth's office where she was working with Kate. "Thought I ought to give you a hand," Rhys said lightly.

No explanation of where he had been. Why should there be? Elizabeth thought. He doesn't have to account to me.

They all set to work and the time flew. Elizabeth watched Rhys now, bent over some papers, rapidly scanning them, his eyes quick and alert. He had found several flaws in some important contracts that the attorneys had missed. Now Rhys straightened up, stretched and glanced at his watch.

"Oops! It's after midnight. I'm afraid I have an appointment. I'll come in early tomorrow and finish checking these agreements."

Elizabeth wondered if his appointment was with the brain surgeon or with one of his other— She stopped herself. What Rhys Williams did with his private life was his own business.

"I'm sorry," Elizabeth said. "I didn't realize it was so late. You run along. Kate and I will finish reading these papers."

Rhys nodded. "See you in the morning. Good night, Kate."

"Good night, Mr. Williams."

Elizabeth watched Rhys leave, then forced her mind back to the contracts. But a moment later her thoughts were on Rhys again. She had been eager to tell him about the progress that Emil Joeppli was making on the new drug, to share it with him, yet she had held back. Soon, she told herself.

BY ONE O'CLOCK in the morning, they were finished.

Kate Erling said, "Will there be anything else, Miss Roffe?"

"No, I think that's all. Thank you, Kate. Come in late tomorrow."

Elizabeth stood up, and realized how stiff her body felt from sitting so long.

"Thank you. I'll have everything typed up for you tomorrow afternoon."

"That will be fine."

Elizabeth got her coat and purse, waited for Kate, and they walked to the door. They went out into the corridor together and headed toward the private express elevator that stood there, door open, waiting. The two of them stepped inside the elevator. As Elizabeth reached for the lobby button, they heard the sudden ringing of the telephone from the office.

"I'll answer it, Miss Roffe," Kate Erling said. "You go on ahead." She stepped out of the car.

Downstairs the night guard on duty in the lobby looked up at the elevator control board as a red light at the top of the board flashed on and began descending. It was the signal light for the private elevator. That meant Miss Roffe was on her way down. Her chauffeur was sitting in a chair in a corner, drowsing over a newspaper.

"The boss is coming," the guard said.

The chauffeur stretched, and started lazily to his feet.

An alarm bell suddenly shattered the peace of the lobby. The guard's eyes flashed to the control board. The red light was moving in a quick plunging pattern, gathering speed, marking the descent of the elevator.

It was out of control.

"Oh, Jesus!" the guard mumbled.

He hurried to the board, jerked open a panel and pulled the emergency switch to activate the safety brake. The red light continued its downward plunge. The chauffeur had hurried over to the control panel. He saw the look on the guard's face.

"What's going—?"

"Get away!" the guard yelled. "It's going to crash!"

They ran from the bank of elevators toward the farthest wall. The lobby was beginning to vibrate with the speed of the runaway car inside the shaft, and the guard thought, *Don't let her be in it,* and as the plunging elevator shot past the lobby, he heard the terrified screams from inside.

An instant later, there was a loud roar, and the building shuddered as though it had been hit by an earthquake.

31

C hief Inspector Otto Schmied of the Zurich Kriminal Polizei was seated at his desk, eyes closed, taking deep yoga breaths, trying to calm himself, trying to control the fury that filled him.

In police procedure there were rules that were so basic, so obvious, that no one had thought it even necessary to put them in the police manual. They were simply taken for granted, like eating, or sleeping, or breathing. For example, when an accident-related fatality occurred, the first thing the investigating detective did—the *very* first thing a detective did, the simple, obvious, you-don't-have-to-draw-it-on-a-fucking-blackboard thing he did—was to visit the scene of the accident. Nothing could be more elementary than that. Yet staring up at Chief Inspector Otto Schmied from his desk was a report from Detective Max Hornung that violated every element of police procedure. I should have expected it, the inspector told himself bitterly. Why am I even surprised?

Detective Hornung was Inspector Schmied's albatross, his bête noire, his—Inspector Schmied was an ardent admirer of Melville—his Moby Dick. The inspector took another deep breath and slowly exhaled. Then, only slightly less agitated, he picked up Detective Hornung's report and read it again from the beginning.

BRANDTOUR OFFIZIER REPORT

Wednesday, November 11

TIME:	1:15 A.M.
SUBJECT:	Report from central switchboard of accident at Roffe and Sons administration building at Eichenbahn factory
TYPE OF ACCIDENT:	Unknown
CAUSE OF ACCIDENT:	Unknown
NUMBER OF INJURED OR DECEASED:	Unknown
TIME:	1:27 A.M.
SUBJECT:	Second message from central switchboard re accident at Roffe and Sons
TYPE OF ACCIDENT:	Elevator crash
CAUSE OF ACCIDENT:	Unknown
NUMBER OF INJURED OR DECEASED:	One female, deceased

I began an immediate investigation. By 1:35 A.M. I obtained the name of the superintendent of the Roffe and Sons administration building and from him got the name of the chief architect of the building.

2:30 A.M. I located the chief architect. He was celebrating his birthday at La Puce. He gave me the name of the company that had installed the elevators in the building, Rudolf Schatz, A. G.

At 3:15 A.M. I telephoned Mr. Rudolf Schatz at his home and requested him to immediately locate the plans for the elevators. I also requested the master budget sheets along with preliminary estimates, final estimates and final costs;

I also requested a complete inventory of all mechanical and electrical materials used.

At this point Inspector Schmied could feel a familiar twitch starting in his right cheek. He took several deep breaths and read on.

> 6:15 A.M. The requested documents were delivered to me here at police headquarters by Mr. Schatz's wife. After an examination of the preliminary budget and final costs I was satisfied that:
> a) no inferior materials were substituted in building the elevators;
> b) because of the reputation of the builders, inferior workmanship could be ruled out as a cause of the crash;
> c) the safety measures built into the elevators were adequate;
> d) my conclusion therefore was that the cause of the crash was not an accident. [Signed] *Max Hornung, CID*
>
> N.B. Since my phone calls took place during the course of the night and early morning, it is possible that you may receive one or two complaints from some of the people I might have awakened.

Inspector Schmied savagely slammed the report down on his desk. "It is possible!" "Might have awakened!" The chief inspector had been under attack the entire morning by half of the officials of the Swiss government. What did he think he was running—a gestapo? How dare he awaken the president of a respectable building corporation and order him to deliver documents in the middle of the night? How dare he impugn the integrity of a reputable firm like Rudolf Schatz? And on and on and on.

But the thing that was so stunning—that was so incredible—was that Detective Max Hornung had not even *appeared* at the scene of the accident until *fourteen hours* after it was reported! By the time he arrived the victim had been removed, identified and autopsied. Half a dozen other detectives had examined the scene of the accident, had questioned witnesses and had filed their reports.

When Chief Inspector Schmied finished rereading Detective Max Hornung's report, he summoned him to his office.

The very sight of Detective Max Hornung was anathema to the chief inspector. Max Hornung was a dumpy, wistful-looking man, egg-bald, with a face that had been put together by an absentminded prankster. His head was too large, his ears were too small and his mouth was a raisin stuck in the middle of a pudding face. Detective Max Hornung was six inches too short to meet the rigid standards of the Zurich Kriminal Polizei, fifteen pounds too light, and hopelessly nearsighted. To top it all off, he was arrogant. All the men on the force felt unanimously about Detective Hornung: they hated him.

"Why don't you fire him?" the chief inspector's wife had asked, and he had almost struck her.

The reason that Max Hornung was on the Zurich detective force was that he had single-handedly contributed more to the Swiss national income than all the chocolate and watch factories combined. Max Hornung was an accountant, a mathematical genius with an encyclopedic knowledge of fiscal matters, an instinct for the chicanery of man and a patience that would have made Job weep with envy. Max had been a clerk in the Betrug Abteilung, the department set up to investigate financial frauds, irregularities in stock sales and banking transactions, and the ebb and flow of currency in and out of Switzerland. It was Max Hornung who had brought the smuggling of illegal money into Switzerland to a standstill, who had ferreted out billions of dollars' worth of ingenious but illicit financial schemes and who had put half a dozen of the world's most respected business leaders in prison. No matter how cunningly assets were concealed, mingled, remingled, sent to the Seychelles to be laundered, transferred and retransferred through a complex series of dummy corporations, in the end Max Hornung would ferret out the truth. In short, he had made himself the terror of the Swiss financial community.

Above all things that they held sacred and dear, the Swiss valued their privacy. With Max Hornung on the loose, there was no privacy.

Max's salary as a financial watchdog was meager. He had been offered bribes of a million francs in numbered bank accounts, a chalet at Cortina d'Ampezzo, a yacht and in half a dozen instances beautiful, nubile women. In each case the bribe had been rejected and the authorities promptly notified. Max Hornung cared nothing for money. He could have become a millionaire simply by applying his financial skills to the stock market, but the idea never even occurred to him. Max Hornung was interested in but one thing: catching those who strayed from the path of financial probity. Ah, yes, there was one other wish that consumed Max Hornung, and in the end it proved to be a blessing to the business community. For reasons which no one could fathom, Max Hornung wanted to be a police detective. He envisioned himself as a kind of Sherlock Holmes or Maigret, patiently following a labyrinth of clues, relentlessly stalking the criminal to his lair. When one of Switzerland's leading financiers accidentally learned of Max Hornung's ambitions to be a sleuth, he immediately got together with a few powerful friends, and within forty-eight hours Max Hornung was offered a job on the Zurich police force as a detective. Max could not believe his good fortune. He accepted with alacrity, and the entire business community breathed a collective sigh of relief and resumed its arcane activities.

Chief Inspector Schmied had not even been consulted about the matter. He had received a telephone call from the most powerful political leader in Switzerland, had been given his instructions, and there the matter had ended. Or, to be more accurate, there it had begun. For the chief inspector, it was the beginning of a Gethsemane that showed no sign of ending. He had honestly tried to get over his resentment at having a detective—an inexperienced and unqualified one at that—forced upon him. He assumed that there had to be some strong political motivation for such an unheard-of move. Very well, he was determined to cooperate, confident that he could handle the situation easily. His confidence was shaken the moment Max Hornung reported to him. The detective's appearance was ridiculous enough. But what stunned Inspector Schmied as he looked at this lump of humanity was the man's attitude of superiority. He exuded an air that said: Max Hornung is here—now you can all relax and stop worrying.

Inspector Schmied's thoughts of any easy cooperation vanished. Instead he devised another approach. He tried to sweep Max Hornung under the rug, as it were, by transferring him from department to department, assigning him unimportant jobs. Max worked in the Kriminal-Tech Abteilung, the fingerprint-and-identification division, and the Fahn-dungsabteilung, the division for stolen property and missing persons. But always Max Hornung kept returning, like a bad centime.

There was a rule that every detective had to work as *Brandtour Offizier,* on the night emergency desk, one week out of every twelve. Without fail, each time Max was on duty, something important would occur, and while Inspector Schmied's other detectives ran around trying to track down clues, Max would solve the case. It was infuriating.

He knew absolutely nothing about police procedure, criminology, forensics, ballistics or criminal psychology—all the things that the other detectives were experienced in—and yet he kept solving cases that baffled everyone else. Chief Inspector Schmied came to the conclusion that Max Hornung was the luckiest man who ever lived.

In reality, luck had nothing to do with it. Detective Max Hornung solved criminal cases in exactly the same way that accountant Max Hornung had exposed a hundred ingenious schemes to defraud banks and the government. Max Hornung had a single-track mind, and it was a very narrow-gauge track at that. All he needed was one loose thread, one tiny piece that did not fit into the rest of the fabric, and once he had that he would begin to unravel it, until somebody's brilliant, foolproof scheme fell apart at the seams.

The fact that Max had a photographic memory drove his colleagues crazy. Max could instantly recall anything he had ever heard, read or seen.

Another mark against him, if indeed one was needed, was that his expense accounts were an embarrassment to the entire detective squadron. The first time he had turned in an expense sheet, the *Oberleutnant* had summoned him to his office and said genially, "You've obviously made a mistake in your figures here, Max."

The equivalent of informing Capablanca that he had sacrificed his queen through stupidity.

Max blinked. "A mistake in my figures?"

"Yes. Several, in fact." The *Oberleutnant* pointed to the paper in front of him. "Transportation across town, eighty centimes. Return, eighty centimes." He looked up and said, "The maximum taxi fare would be thirty-four francs each way."

"Yes, sir. That's why I used the bus."

The *Oberleutnant* stared at him. "A *bus?*"

None of the detectives was required to ride buses while on a case. It was unheard of. The only reply he could think of was "Well, it's—it's not necessary. I mean—we naturally don't encourage spendthrifts in this department, Hornung, but we do have a decent expense budget. Another thing. You were out in the field on this case for three days. You forgot to include meals."

"No, Herr Oberleutnant. I only take coffee in the morning and I prepare my own lunches and carry a lunch pail. My dinners are listed there."

And so they were. Three dinners, total: sixteen francs. He must have eaten at the Salvation Army kitchen.

The *Oberleutnant* said coldly, "Detective Hornung, this department existed for a hundred years before you joined it, and it will exist for a hundred years after you leave it. There are certain traditions that we observe here." He shoved the expense account back to Max. "You must think about your colleagues, you know. Now take this, revise it, and return it."

"Yes, Herr Oberleutnant. I—I'm sorry if I did it incorrectly."

A generous wave of the hand. "Quite all right. After all, you're new here."

Thirty minutes later Detective Max Hornung turned in his revised account. He had decreased his expenses by another 3 percent.

Now, on this day in November, Chief Inspector Schmied was holding Detective Max Hornung's report in his hand while the author of the report stood before him. Detective Hornung was wearing a bright-blue suit, brown shoes and white socks. In spite of his resolves, and the calming yoga breathing exercises, Inspector Schmied found himself yelling. "You were in charge here when that report came in. It was *your* job to investigate the accident and you arrived on the scene *fourteen hours later!* The whole fucking New Zealand police force could have been flown here and been back home in that time."

"Oh, no, sir. The flying time from New Zealand to Zurich by jet is—"

"Oh, shut up!"

Chief Inspector Schmied ran his hands through his thick, rapidly graying hair, trying to think what to say to this man. You could not insult him, you could not reason with him. He was an idiot, shot with luck.

Chief Inspector Schmied barked, "I will not tolerate incompetence in my department, Hornung. When the other detectives came on duty and saw the report, they immediately went to the scene to inspect the accident. They called an ambulance, had the body taken to the morgue, identified it—" He knew he was talking too fast again, and he forced himself to calm down. "In short, Hornung, they did everything a good detective is supposed to do. While you were sitting in your office waking up half of the most important men in Switzerland, in the middle of the night."

"I thought—"

"Don't! I've been on the phone apologizing the whole damned morning because of you."

"I had to find out—"

"Oh, get out of here, Hornung!"

"Yes, sir. Is it all right if I attend the funeral? It's this morning."

"Yes! Go!"

"Thank you, sir. I—"

"Just go!"

It was thirty minutes before Chief Inspector Schmied was breathing normally again.

32

The funeral parlor at Sihlfeld was crowded. It was an ornate, old-fashioned building of stone and marble, with preparation rooms and a crematorium. Inside the large chapel two dozen executives and employees of Roffe and Sons occupied the front row of seats. Toward the rear were the friends, the community representatives and the press. Detective Hornung was seated in the last row, thinking that death was illogical. Man reached his prime and then, when he had the most to give, the most to live for, he died. It was inefficient.

The casket was mahogany and covered with flowers. More waste, Detective Hornung thought. The casket had been ordered sealed. Max could understand why. The minister was speaking in a doomsday voice, ". . . death in the midst of life, born in sin, ashes to ashes." Max Hornung paid little attention. He was studying those in the chapel.

"The Lord giveth, and the Lord taketh away," and people were beginning to stand and head for the exit. The services were over.

Max stood near the door, and as a man and a woman approached him, he stepped in front of the woman and said, "Miss Elizabeth Roffe? I wonder if I might have a word with you?"

. . .

DETECTIVE MAX HORNUNG was seated with Elizabeth Roffe and Rhys Williams in a booth at a *Konditorei* across from the funeral parlor. Through the window they could see the coffin being loaded into a gray hearse. Elizabeth looked away. Her eyes were haunted.

"What's this all about?" Rhys demanded. "Miss Roffe has already given her statement to the police."

Detective Max Hornung said, "Mr. Williams, isn't it? There are just a few little details I want to check out."

"Can't they wait? Miss Roffe has been through a very trying—"

Elizabeth put her hand on Rhys's. "It's all right. If I can be of any help—" She turned to Max. "What would you like to know, Detective Hornung?"

Max stared at Elizabeth, and for the first time in his life he was at a loss for words. Women were as foreign to Max as creatures from an alien planet. They were illogical and unpredictable, subject to emotional reactions rather than rational ones. They did not compute. Max had few sexual stirrings, for he was mind-oriented, but he could appreciate the precise logic of sex. It was the mechanical construction of moving parts fitting together into a coordinated, functioning whole that excited him. That, for Max, was the poetry of loving. The sheer dynamics of it. Max felt that the poets had all missed the point. Emotions were imprecise and untidy, a waste of energy that could not move the smallest grain of sand one inch, while logic could move the world. What was puzzling Max now was that he felt comfortable with Elizabeth. It made him uneasy. No woman had ever affected him that way before. She did not seem to think he was an ugly, ridiculous little man, the way other women did. He forced himself to look away from her eyes so that he could concentrate.

"Were you in the habit of working late at night, Miss Roffe?"

"Very often," Elizabeth said. "Yes."

"How late?"

"It varied. Sometimes until ten. Sometimes until midnight, or after."

"So it was a kind of pattern? That is, people around you would have known about it?"

She was studying him, puzzled. "I suppose so."

"On the night the elevator crashed, you and Mr. Williams and Kate Erling were all working late?"

"Yes."

"But you didn't leave together?"

Rhys said, "I left early. I had an engagement."

Max regarded him a moment, then turned back to Elizabeth. "How long after Mr. Williams left did you leave?"

"I think it was about an hour."

"Did you and Kate Erling leave together?"

"Yes. We got our coats and went out into the hall." Elizabeth's voice faltered. "The—the elevator was there, waiting for us."

The special express elevator.

"What happened then?"

"We both got in. The telephone in the office rang. Kate—Miss Erling—said, 'I'll get it,' and she started to get out. But I was expecting an overseas call I had placed earlier, so I told her I would answer it." Elizabeth stopped, her eyes suddenly brimming with tears. "I got out of the elevator. She asked if she should wait, and I said, 'No, go ahead.' She pressed the lobby button, I started back to the office, and as I was opening the door, I heard—I heard the screaming, then—" She was unable to go on.

Rhys turned to Max Hornung, his face clouded with anger. "That's enough. Will you tell us what this is all about?"

It was about murder, Max thought. Someone had tried to kill Elizabeth Roffe. Max sat there concentrating, recalling everything he had learned in the past forty-eight hours about Roffe and Sons. It was a deeply plagued company, forced to pay astronomical damages in lawsuits, swamped by bad publicity, losing customers, owing enormous sums of money to banks that had grown impatient. A company ripe for a change. Its president, Sam Roffe, who had held the controlling vote, had died. An expert mountain climber who had been killed in a climbing accident. The controlling stock had gone to his daughter, Elizabeth, who had almost died in a Jeep accident in Sardinia, and had narrowly missed being killed in an elevator that had passed a recent inspection. Someone was playing deadly games.

Detective Max Hornung should have been a happy man. He had

found a loose thread. But now he had met Elizabeth Roffe, and she was no longer simply a name, an equation in a mathematical puzzle. There was something very special about her. Max felt an urge to shield her, to protect her.

Rhys said, "I asked what this—"

Max looked at him and said vaguely, "Er—police procedure, Mr. Williams. Just routine." He rose. "Excuse me."

He had some urgent work to do.

33

Chief Inspector Schmied had had a full morning. There had been a political demonstration in front of Iberia Air Lines, three men detained for questioning. A fire of suspicious origin at a paper factory in Brunau. It was being investigated. A girl had been raped in Platzspitz Park. A smash-and-grab job at Guebelin and another at Grima, next to the Baur-au-Lac. And if that weren't enough, Detective Max Hornung was back, filled with some kind of nonsensical theory. Chief Inspector Schmied found himself starting to hyperventilate again.

"The elevator cable drum was cracked," Max was saying. "When it collapsed, all the safety controls went out. Someone—"

"I saw the reports, Hornung. Normal wear and tear."

"No, Chief Inspector. I examined the specifications for the cable drum. It should have lasted another five or six years."

Chief Inspector Schmied felt the tic in his cheek. "What are you trying to say?"

"Someone tampered with the elevator."

Not, I think someone tampered with the elevator, or, In my opinion someone tampered with the elevator. Oh, no! Someone tampered with the elevator.

"Why would they do that?"

"That's what I would like to find out."

"You want to go back to Roffe and Sons?"

Detective Max Hornung looked at Inspector Schmied in genuine surprise. "No, sir. I want to go to Chamonix."

THE TOWN OF Chamonix lies forty miles southeast of Geneva, 3,400 feet above sea level in the French department of Haute-Savoie, between the Mont Blanc massif and the Aiguille Rouge range, with one of the most breathtaking vistas in the world. ·

Detective Max Hornung was completely unaware of the scenery as he debouched from the train at the Chamonix station, carrying a battered cardboard suitcase. He waved a taxi away and headed on foot for the local police station, a small building situated on the main square in the center of town. Max entered, feeling instantly at home, reveling in the warm camaraderie that he shared with the fraternity of policemen all over the world. He was one of *them*.

The French sergeant behind the desk looked up and asked, *"On vous pourrait aider?"*

"Oui." Max beamed. And he started to talk. Max approached all foreign languages in the same fashion: he slashed his way through the impenetrable thicket of irregular verbs and tenses and participles, using his tongue like a machete. As he spoke, the expression on the desk sergeant's face changed from puzzlement to disbelief. It had taken the French people hundreds of years to develop their tongues and soft palates and larynxes to form the glorious music that was the French language. And now this man standing before him was somehow managing to turn it into a series of horrible, incomprehensible noises.

The desk sergeant could bear no more. He interrupted. "What—what are you trying to *say?*"

Max replied, "What do you mean? I'm speaking French."

The desk sergeant leaned forward and asked with unabashed curiosity, "Are you speaking it *now?*"

The fool doesn't even speak his own language, Max thought. He pulled out his warrant card and handed it to the sergeant. The sergeant read it through twice, looked up to study Max, and then read it again. It was impossible to believe that the man standing before him was a detective.

Reluctantly he handed the identification back to Max. "What can I do for you?"

"I'm investigating a climbing accident that happened here two months ago. The victim's name was Sam Roffe."

The sergeant nodded. "Yes, I remember."

"I would like to talk to someone who can give me some information about what happened."

"That would be the mountain-rescue organization. It is called the Société Chamoniarde de Secours en Montagne. You will find it in Place du Mont Blanc. The telephone number is five-three-one-six-eight-nine. Or they might have some information at the clinic. That's in Rue du Valais. The telephone number there is five-three-zero-one-eight-two. Here. I'll write all this down for you." He reached for a pen.

"That won't be necessary," Max said. "Société Chamoniarde de Secours en Montagne, Place du Mont Blanc, five-three-one-six-eight-nine. Or the clinic in Rue du Valais, five-three-zero-one-eight-two."

The sergeant was still staring, long after Max had disappeared through the door.

THE SOCIÉTÉ CHAMONIARDE de Secours was in the charge of a dark, athletic-looking young man seated behind a battered pine desk. He looked up as Max walked in, and his instant thought was that he hoped this odd-looking visitor did not plan to climb a mountain.

"Can I help you?"

"Detective Max Hornung." He showed his warrant card.

"What can I do for you, Detective Hornung?"

"I am investigating the death of a man named Sam Roffe," Max said.

The man behind the desk sighed. "Ah, yes. I liked Mr. Roffe very much. It was an unfortunate accident."

"Did you see it happen?"

A shake of the head. "No. I took my rescue team up as soon as we received their distress signal, but there was nothing we could do. Mr. Roffe's body had fallen into a crevasse. It will never be found."

"How did it happen?"

"There were four climbers in the party. The guide and Mr. Roffe were last. As I understand it, they were traversing an icy moraine. Mr. Roffe slipped and fell."

"Wasn't he wearing a harness?"

"Of course. His rope broke."

"Does a thing like that happen often?"

"Only once." He smiled at his little joke, then saw the detective's look and added quickly, "Experienced climbers always check their equipment thoroughly, but accidents still happen."

Max stood there a moment, thinking. "I'd like to speak to the guide."

"Mr. Roffe's regular guide didn't make the climb that day."

Max blinked. "Oh? Why not?"

"As I recall, he was ill. Another guide took his place."

"Do you have his name?"

"If you'll wait a minute, I can look it up for you."

The man disappeared into an inner office. In a few minutes he returned with a slip of paper in his hand. "The guide's name was Hans Bergmann."

"Where can I find him?"

"He's not a local." He consulted the piece of paper. "He comes from a village called Lesgets. It's about sixty kilometers from here."

Before Max left Chamonix, he stopped at the desk of the Kleine Scheidegg hotel and talked to the room clerk. "Were you on duty when Mr. Roffe was staying here?"

"Yes," the clerk said. "The accident was a terrible thing, terrible."

"Mr. Roffe was alone here?"

The clerk shook his head. "No. He had a friend with him."

Max stared. "A friend?"

"Yes. Mr. Roffe made the reservation for both of them."

"Could you give me the name of his friend?"

"Certainly," the clerk said. He pulled out a large ledger from beneath the desk and began to turn back the pages. He stopped, ran his fingers down a page and said, "Ah, here we are . . ."

• • •

IT TOOK ALMOST three hours for Max to drive to Lesgets in a Volkswagen, the cheapest rental car he could find, and he almost passed through it. It was not even a village. The place consisted of a few shops, a small Alpine lodge and a general store with a single gas pump in front of it.

Max parked in front of the lodge and walked in.

There were half a dozen men seated in front of an open fireplace, talking. The conversation trailed off as Max entered.

"Excuse me," he said, "I'm looking for Herr Hans Bergmann."

"Who?"

"Hans Bergmann. The guide. He comes from this village."

An elderly man with a face that was a weather map of his years spat into the fireplace and said, "Somebody's been kidding you, mister. I was born in Lesgets. I never heard of any Hans Bergmann."

34

I t was the first day that Elizabeth had gone to the office since the death of Kate Erling a week earlier. Elizabeth entered the downstairs lobby with trepidation, responding mechanically to the greetings of the doorman and guards. At the far end of the lobby she saw workmen replacing the smashed elevator car. She thought about Kate Erling, and Elizabeth could visualize the terror she must have felt as she plunged twelve interminable stories to her death. She knew that she could never ride in that elevator again.

When she walked into her office, her mail had already been opened by Henriette, the second secretary, and neatly placed on her desk. Elizabeth went through it quickly, initialing some memos, writing questions on others, or marking them for various department heads. At the bottom of the pile was a large sealed envelope marked "Elizabeth Roffe—Personal." Elizabeth took a letter opener and slit the envelope across the top. She reached in and took out an 8-by-10 photograph. It was a close-up of a mongoloid child, its bulging eyes staring out of its encephalic head. Attached to the picture was a note printed in crayon: "THIS

IS MY BEAUTIFUL SON JOHN. YOUR DRUGS DID THIS TO HIM. I AM GOING TO KILL YOU."

Elizabeth dropped the note and the picture, and found that her hands were trembling. Henriette walked in with a handful of papers.

"These are ready to be signed, Miss—" She saw the look on Elizabeth's face. "Is something wrong?"

Elizabeth said, "Please—ask Mr. Williams to come in here." Her eyes went back to the picture on her desk.

Roffe and Sons could not be responsible for anything so dreadful.

"IT WAS OUR fault," Rhys said. "A shipment of drugs was mislabeled. We managed to recall most of it, but—" He raised his hands expressively.

"How long ago did this happen?"

"Almost four years ago."

"How many people were affected?"

"About a hundred." He saw the expression on her face and added quickly, "They received compensation. They weren't all like this, Liz. Look, we're damned careful here. We take every safety precaution we can devise, but people are human. Mistakes are sometimes made."

Elizabeth sat staring at the picture of the child. "It's horrible."

"They shouldn't have shown you the letter." Rhys ran his fingers through his thick black hair and said, "This is a hell of a time to bring it up, but we have a few other problems more important than this."

She wondered what could be more important. "Yes?"

"The FDA just gave a decision against us on our aerosol sprays. There's going to be a complete ban on aerosols within two years."

"How will that affect us?"

"It's going to hurt us badly. It means we'll have to close down half a dozen factories around the world and lose one of our most profitable divisions."

Elizabeth thought about Emil Joeppli and the culture he was working on, but she said nothing. "What else?"

"Have you seen the morning papers?"

"No."

"A government minister's wife in Belgium, Mme. van den Logh, took some Benexan."

"That's one of our drugs?"

"Yes. It's an antihistamine. It's contraindicated for anyone with essential hypertension. Our label carries a clear warning. She ignored it."

Elizabeth felt her body beginning to tense. "What happened to her?"

Rhys said, "She's in a coma. She may not live. The newspaper stories mention that it's our product. Cancellations on orders are pouring in from all over the world. The FDA notified us that it's starting an investigation, but that will take at least a year. Until they finish, we can keep selling the drug."

Elizabeth said, "I want it taken off the market."

"There's no reason to do that. It's a damned effective drug for—"

"Have any other people been hurt by it?"

"Hundreds of thousands of people have been helped by it." Rhys's tone was cool. "It's one of our most effective—"

"You haven't answered my question."

"A few isolated cases, I suppose, yes. But—"

"I want it taken off the market. Now."

He sat there, fighting his anger, then he said, "Right. Would you like to know what that will cost the company?"

"No," Elizabeth said.

Rhys nodded. "So far you've only heard the good news. The bad news is that the bankers want a meeting with you. Now. They're calling in their loans."

ELIZABETH SAT IN her office alone, thinking about the mongoloid child, and about the woman who lay in a coma because of a drug that Roffe and Sons had sold her. Elizabeth was well aware that these kinds of tragedies involved other pharmaceutical firms as well as Roffe and Sons. There were almost daily stories in the newspapers about similar cases, but they had not touched her as this had. She felt responsible. She was determined to have a talk with the department heads who were in charge of safety measures to see if they could not be improved.

This is my beautiful son John.

Mme. van den Logh is in a coma. She may not live.

The bankers want a meeting with you. Now. They've decided to call in their loans.

She felt choked, as though everything was beginning to close in on her at once. For the first time Elizabeth wondered if she was going to be able to cope. The burdens were too heavy, and they were piling up too fast. She swung around in her chair, to look up at the portrait of old Samuel hanging on the wall. He looked so competent, so sure. But she knew about his doubts and uncertainties, and his black despairs. Yet he had come through. She would survive somehow, too. She was a Roffe.

She noticed that the portrait was askew. Probably as a result of the elevator crash. Elizabeth got up to straighten it. As she tilted the picture, the hook holding it gave way, and the painting crashed to the floor. Elizabeth did not even look at it. She was staring at the place where the painting had hung. Taped to the wall was a tiny microphone.

IT WAS 4 A.M., and Emil Joeppli was working late again. It had become a habit of his recently. Even though Elizabeth Roffe had not given him a specific deadline, Joeppli knew how important this project was to the company and he was pushing to get it finished as quickly as possible. He had heard disturbing rumors about Roffe and Sons lately. He wanted to do everything he could to help the company. It had been good to him. It gave him a handsome salary and complete freedom. He had liked Sam Roffe, and he liked his daughter, too. Elizabeth Roffe would never know, but these late hours were Joeppli's gift to her. He was hunched over his small desk, checking out the results of his last experiment. They were even better than he had anticipated. He sat there, deep in concentration, unaware of the fetid smell of the caged animals in the laboratory or the cloying humidity of the room or the lateness of the hour. The door opened, and the guard on the graveyard shift, Sepp Nolan, walked in. Nolan hated this shift. There was something eerie about the deserted experimental laboratories at night. The smell of the caged animals made him ill. Nolan wondered whether all the animals they had killed here had souls and came back to haunt these corridors. I ought to put in for spook pay, he thought. Everyone in the building had long since gone home. Except for this fucking mad scientist with his cages full of rabbits and cats and hamsters.

"How long you gonna be, Doc?" Nolan asked.

Joeppli looked up, aware of Nolan for the first time. "What?"

"If you're gonna be here awhile, I can bring you back a sandwich or something. I'm gonna run over to the commissary for a quick bite."

Joeppli said, "Just coffee, please." He turned back to his charts.

Nolan said, "I'll lock the outside door behind me when I leave the building. Be right back."

Joeppli did not even hear him.

Ten minutes later the door to the laboratory opened, and a voice said, "You're working late, Emil."

Joeppli looked up, startled. When he saw who it was, he got to his feet, flustered, and said, "Yes, sir." He felt flattered that this man had dropped in to see him.

"The Fountain of Youth project, top secret, eh?"

Emil hesitated. Miss Roffe had said no one was supposed to know about it. But, of course, that did not include his visitor. It was this man who had brought him into the company. So Emil Joeppli smiled and said, "Yes, sir. Top secret."

"Good. Let's keep it that way. How is it going?"

"Wonderfully, sir."

The visitor wandered over to one of the rabbit cages. Emil Joeppli followed him. "Is there anything I can explain to you?"

The man smiled. "No. I'm pretty familiar with it, Emil." As the visitor started to turn away, he brushed against an empty feeding dish on the ledge and it fell to the floor. "Sorry."

"Don't worry about it, sir. I'll get it." Emil Joeppli reached down to pick it up and the back of his head seemed to explode in a shower of red, and the last thing he saw was the floor racing up to meet him.

THE INSISTENT RINGING of the telephone awakened Elizabeth. She sat up in bed, heavy with sleep, and looked at the digital clock on the little table. Five A.M. She fumbled the telephone off the hook. A frantic voice said, "Miss Roffe? This is the security guard at the plant.

There's been an explosion at one of the laboratories. It was completely destroyed."

Instantly she was wide-awake. "Was anybody hurt?"

"Yes, ma'am. One of the scientists was burned to death."

He did not have to tell Elizabeth the name.

etective Max Hornung was thinking. The detective bureau was filled with the noise of typewriters clattering, voices raised in argument, telephones ringing, but Hornung saw and heard nothing of these things. He had the single-minded concentration of a computer. He was thinking about the charter of Roffe and Sons, as old Samuel had set it up, keeping control within the family. Ingenious, Max thought. And dangerous. It reminded him of the tontine, the Italian insurance plan devised by the banker Lorenzo Tonti in 1695. Every member of the tontine put in an equal amount of money, and as each member died, the survivors inherited his share. It provided a powerful motive to eliminate the other members. Like Roffe and Sons. It was too much of a temptation to let people inherit stock worth millions, and then tell them they could not sell it unless everyone agreed.

Max had learned that Sam Roffe had not agreed. He was dead. Elizabeth Roffe had not agreed. She had narrowly escaped death twice. Too many accidents. Detective Max Hornung did not believe in accidents. He went to see Chief Inspector Schmied.

The chief inspector listened to Max Hornung's report on Sam Roffe's climbing accident and growled, "So there's been a mix-up about the name of a guide. That hardly constitutes a case for murder, Hornung. Not in *my* department, it doesn't."

The little detective said patiently, "I think there's more to it. Roffe and Sons is having big internal problems. Perhaps someone thought that getting rid of Sam Roffe would solve them."

Chief Inspector Schmied sat back and eyed Detective Hornung. He was certain that there was nothing to his theories. But the idea of having Detective Max Hornung out of sight for a while filled Chief Inspector Schmied with a deep pleasure. His absence would be a boost to the morale of the entire department. And there was something else to consider: The people Max Hornung wanted to investigate. No less than the powerful Roffe family. Ordinarily, Schmied would have ordered Max Hornung to keep a million miles away from them. If Detective Hornung irritated them—and how could he not!—they had enough power to have him thrown off the force. And no one could blame Chief Inspector Schmied. Hadn't the little detective been forced on him? And so he said to Max Hornung, "The case is yours. Take your time."

"Thank you," Max said happily.

AS MAX WAS walking through the corridor toward his office, he ran into the coroner. "Hornung! Can I borrow your memory for a minute?"

Max blinked. "I beg your pardon?"

"The river patrol has just fished a girl out of the river. Will you take a look at her?"

Max swallowed and said, "If you wish."

This was not a part of the job that Max enjoyed, but he felt that it was his duty.

She lay in the impersonal metal drawer in the chill of the morgue. She had blond hair and was in her late teens or early twenties. Her body was bloated from the water, and naked, except for a red ribbon knotted around her neck.

"There are signs of sexual intercourse just before death. She was strangled and then dumped into the river," the coroner said. "There's no water in her lungs. We can't get any fingerprints on her. Ever seen her before?"

Detective Max Hornung looked down at the girl's face and said, "No."

He left to catch his bus to the airport.

36

When Detective Max Hornung landed at the Costa Smeralda airport in Sardinia, he rented the cheapest car available, a Fiat 500, and drove into Olbia. Unlike the rest of Sardinia, Olbia was an industrial city, and the outskirts were an ugly sprawl of mills and factories, a city dump and a giant graveyard of once-beautiful automobiles, now useless old hulks, good only for scrap. Every city in the world had its automobile junkyards, Max thought. Monuments to civilization.

Max reached the center of town and drove up in front of a building with a sign that read: QUESTURA DI SASSARI COMMISSARIATO DI POLIZIA OLBIA. The moment Max entered, he felt that familiar sense of identity, of belonging. He showed his warrant card to the desk sergeant, and a few minutes later he was ushered into the office of the Chief of Police, Luigi Ferraro. Ferraro rose to his feet, a welcoming smile on his face. It died as he saw his visitor. There was something about Max that did not spell "detective."

"Could I see your identification?" Chief Ferraro asked politely.

"Certainly," Max said. He pulled out his warrant card and Chief Ferraro examined both sides of it carefully, then returned it. His immediate conclusion was that Switzerland must be very hard up for detectives. He took a seat behind his desk and said, "What can I do for you?"

Max started to explain, in fluent Italian. The problem was that it took Chief Ferraro some moments to figure out what language Max was speaking. When he realized what it was supposed to be, he held up a horrified hand and said, "*Basta!* Do you speak English?"

"Of course," Max replied.

"Then I beg of you! Let us speak in English."

When Max was through talking, Chief Ferraro said, "You are mistaken, signore. I can tell you that you are wasting your time. My mechanics have already examined the Jeep. Everyone is agreed that it was an accident."

Max nodded, unperturbed. "*I* haven't looked at it."

Chief Ferraro said, "Very well. It is in a public garage now, up for sale. I will have one of my men take you there. Would you like to see the scene of the accident?"

Max blinked and said, "What for?"

Detective Bruno Campagna was elected as Max's escort. "We've already checked it out. It was an accident," Campagna said.

"No," Max replied.

The Jeep was in a corner of the garage, its front still dented and splashed with dried green sap.

"I haven't had time to work on it yet," the mechanic explained.

Max walked around the Jeep, examining it. "How were the brakes tampered with?" he asked.

The mechanic said, "*Gesù!* You, too?" A note of irritation crept into his voice. "I been a mechanic for twenty-five years, signore. I examined this Jeep myself. The last time anyone touched these brakes was when this car left the factory."

"Someone tampered with them," Max said.

"How?" The mechanic was spluttering.

"I don't know yet, but I will," Max assured him confidently. He took a last look at the Jeep, then turned and walked out of the garage.

CHIEF OF POLICE Luigi Ferraro looked at Detective Bruno Campagna and demanded, "What did you *do* with him?"

"I didn't do anything. I took him to the garage, he made an ass of himself with the mechanic, then he said he wanted to go for a stroll by himself."

"*Incredible!*"

MAX WAS STANDING on the shore, staring out at the emerald Tyrrhenian waters, seeing nothing. He was concentrating, his mind busily putting pieces together. It was like working a giant jigsaw puzzle. Everything always went neatly into place when you knew where it fitted. The Jeep was a small but important part of the puzzle. Its brakes had been examined by expert mechanics. Max had no reason to doubt either their honesty or competence. He therefore accepted the fact that the brakes of the Jeep had not been tampered with. Because Elizabeth had been driving the Jeep and someone wanted her dead, he also accepted the fact that they *had* been tampered with. There was no way it could have been done. Yet someone had done it. Max was up against someone clever. It made things more interesting.

Max stepped out onto the sandy beach, sat down on a large rock, closed his eyes and began to concentrate again, focusing on the pieces, shifting, dissecting, rearranging the bits of the puzzle.

Twenty minutes later the last piece clicked into place. Max's eyes flew open and he thought admiringly, Bravo! I must meet the man who thought of this.

After that, Detective Max Hornung had two stops to make, the first just outside Olbia and the second in the mountains. He caught the late afternoon plane back to Zurich.

Economy class.

37

The head of the security forces of Roffe and Sons said to Elizabeth, "It all happened too fast, Miss Roffe. There was nothing we could do. By the time the fire-fighting equipment got into action, the whole laboratory was gone."

They had found the remains of Emil Joeppli's charred body. There was no way of knowing whether his formula had been removed from the laboratory before the explosion.

Elizabeth asked, "The Development Building was under twenty-four-hour guard, was it not?"

"Yes, ma'am. We—"

"How long have you been in charge of our security department?"

"Five years. I—"

"You're fired."

He started to say something in protest, then changed his mind. "Yes, ma'am."

"How many men are there on your staff?"

"Sixty-five."

Sixty-five! And they could not save Emil Joeppli. "I'm giving them twenty-four hours' notice," Elizabeth said. "I want them all out of here."

He looked at her a moment. "Miss Roffe, do you think you're being fair?"

She thought of Emil Joeppli, and the priceless formula that had been stolen, and of the bug that had been planted in her office that she had ground under the heel of her shoe.

"Get out," Elizabeth said.

She filled every minute that morning, trying to wipe out the vision of the charred body of Emil Joeppli and his laboratory full of burned animals. She tried not to think about what the loss of that formula was going to cost the company. There was a chance a rival company might patent it and there was nothing Elizabeth could do about it. It *was* a jungle. When your competitors thought you were weak, they moved in for the kill. But this wasn't a competitor doing this. This was a friend. A deadly friend.

Elizabeth arranged for a professional security force to take over immediately. She would feel safer with strangers around her.

She phoned the Hôpital Internationale in Brussels to check on the condition of Mme. van den Logh, the wife of the Belgian minister. They reported that she was still in a coma. They did not know whether she would live.

Elizabeth was thinking about Emil Joeppli and the mongoloid child and the minister's wife when Rhys walked in. He looked at her face and said gently, "As bad as that?"

She nodded, miserable.

Rhys walked over to her and studied her. She looked tired, drained. He wondered how much more she could stand. He took her hands in his and asked gently, "Is there anything I can do to help?"

Everything, Elizabeth thought. She needed Rhys desperately. She needed his strength and his help and his love. Their eyes met and she was ready to go into his arms, to tell him everything that had happened, that was happening.

Rhys said, "There's nothing new on Mme. van den Logh?"

And the moment had passed.

"No," Elizabeth said.

He asked, "Have you had any calls yet on the *Wall Street Journal* story?"

"What story?"

"You haven't seen it?"

"No."

Rhys sent to his office for a copy. The article enumerated all the recent troubles of Roffe and Sons, but the major theme of the story was that the company needed someone experienced to run it. Elizabeth put the newspaper down. "How much damage will this do?"

Rhys shrugged. "The damage has already been done. They're just reporting it. We're beginning to lose a lot of our markets. We—"

The intercom buzzed. Elizabeth pressed the switch. "Yes?"

"Herr Julius Badrutt is on line two, Miss Roffe. He says it's urgent."

Elizabeth looked up at Rhys. She had been postponing the meeting with the bankers. "Put him on." She picked up the phone. "Good morning, Herr Badrutt."

"Good morning." Over the phone, his voice sounded dry and brittle. "Are you free this afternoon?"

"Well, I'm—"

"Fine. Will four o'clock be satisfactory?"

Elizabeth hesitated. "Yes. Four o'clock."

There was a dry, rustling sound over the phone and Elizabeth realized that Herr Badrutt was clearing his throat. "I was sorry to hear about Mr. Joeppli," he said.

Joeppli's name had not been mentioned in the newspaper accounts of the explosion.

She hung up slowly, and found that Rhys was watching her.

"The sharks smell blood," Rhys said.

THE AFTERNOON WAS filled with phone calls. Alec telephoned. "Elizabeth, did you see the story in the newspaper this morning?"

"Yes," Elizabeth said. "The *Wall Street Journal* was exaggerating."

There was a pause, and then Alec said, "I'm not talking about the *Wall Street Journal.* The *Financial Times* has a headline story on Roffe and Sons. It's not good. My phones haven't stopped ringing. We're getting heavy cancellations. What are we going to do?"

"I'll get back to you, Alec," Elizabeth promised.

Ivo called. "*Carissima,* I think you'd better prepare yourself for a shock."

I'm prepared, Elizabeth thought wryly. "What is it?"

Ivo said, "An Italian minister was arrested a few hours ago for accepting bribes."

Elizabeth had a sudden feeling of what was coming. "Go on."

There was a note of apology in Ivo's voice. "It wasn't our fault," Ivo said. "He got greedy and he was careless. They caught him at the airport, trying to smuggle money out of Italy. They've traced the money to us."

Even though Elizabeth was prepared for it, she still felt a shock of disbelief. "Why were we bribing him?"

Ivo said matter of factly, "So that we could do business in Italy. It's a way of life here. Our crime was not in bribing the minister, *cara*—it was in getting caught."

She sat back in her chair, her head beginning to pound.

"What happens now?"

"I would suggest that we meet with the company attorneys as quickly as possible," Ivo said. "Don't worry. Only the poor go to jail in Italy."

Charles called from Paris, his voice frantic with worry. The French press was full of Roffe & Sons. Charles urged Elizabeth to sell the company while it still had a reputation.

"Our customers are losing faith," Charles said. "Without that, there is no company."

Elizabeth thought about the phone calls, the bankers, her cousins, the press. Too much was happening too quickly. Someone was making it happen. She *had* to find out who.

THE NAME WAS still in Elizabeth's private telephone book. Maria Martinelli. It brought back long-ago memories of the tall, leggy Italian girl who had been a classmate of Elizabeth's in Switzerland. They had corresponded from time to time. Maria had become a model and she had written to Elizabeth that she was engaged to marry an Italian newspaper publisher in Milan. It took Elizabeth fifteen minutes to reach Maria. When the social amenities had been disposed of, Elizabeth said into the phone, "Are you still engaged to that newspaper publisher?"

"Of course. The minute Tony gets his divorce, we're going to be married."

"I want you to do me a favor, Maria."

"Name it."

Less than one hour later Maria Martinelli called back. "I got that information you wanted. The banker who was caught trying to smuggle money out of Italy was set up. Tony says a man tipped off the border police."

"Was he able to find out the name of the man?"

"Ivo Palazzi."

DETECTIVE MAX HORNUNG had made an interesting discovery. He had learned that not only was the explosion at the Roffe and Sons laboratory set deliberately, but that it had been caused by an explosive called Rylar X, made exclusively for the military, and not available to anyone else. What intrigued Max was that Rylar X was manufactured at one of the factories of Roffe and Sons. It took Max only one telephone call to learn which one.

The factory outside Paris.

AT EXACTLY 4 P.M. Herr Julius Badrutt lowered his angular figure into a chair and said without preamble, "As much as we would like to accommodate you, Miss Roffe, I am afraid our responsibility toward our stockholders must take precedence."

It was the kind of statement, Elizabeth thought, that bankers made to widows and orphans before they foreclosed their mortgages. But this time she was ready for Herr Badrutt.

". . . My board of directors has therefore instructed me to inform you that our bank is calling in the notes on Roffe and Sons immediately."

"I was told I had ninety days," Elizabeth said.

"Unfortunately, we feel that the circumstances have changed for the worse. I should also inform you that the other banks you are dealing with have reached the same decision."

With the banks refusing to help her, there would be no way to keep the company private.

"I'm sorry to bring you such bad news, Miss Roffe, but I felt that I should tell you personally."

"You know, of course, that Roffe and Sons is still a very strong and healthy company."

Herr Julius Badrutt nodded his head, once. "Of course. It's a great company."

"Yet you won't give us more time."

Herr Badrutt looked at her for a moment, then said, "The bank thinks your problems are manageable, Miss Roffe. But . . ." He hesitated.

"But you don't think there's anyone to manage them?"

"I'm afraid that is correct." He started to rise.

"What if someone else were president of Roffe and Sons?" Elizabeth asked.

He shook his head. "We have discussed that possibility. We don't feel that any of the present members of the board have the overall ability to cope with—"

She said, "I was thinking of Rhys Williams."

38

C onstable Thomas Hiller of the Thames Marine Police Division was in terrible shape. He was sleepy, hungry, horny and wet; and he could not decide which was the greatest of his miseries.

He was sleepy because his fiancée, Flo, had kept him awake all night, fighting; he was hungry because by the time she was through screaming at him, he was late for duty, and he had had no time to pick up a bite; he was horny because she had refused to let him touch her and he was wet because the thirty-foot police boat on which he was traveling had been built for service, not comfort, and a rising wind was driving the rain into the small wheelhouse where he stood. On days like this there was bloody little to see and even bloody less to do. The Thames Division covered fifty-four miles of river from Dartford Creek to Staines Bridge, and ordinarily Constable Hiller enjoyed patrol duty. But not when he was in this shape. Damn all women! He thought about Flo in bed, naked as a pouter pigeon, her large tits waving up and down as she yelled at him. He glanced at his watch. Another half hour and this miserable tour would be finished. The boat had turned and was headed back toward Waterloo Pier. His only problem now was deciding what to do first: sleep, eat or jump in the kip with Flo. Maybe all three at once, he thought. He rubbed his eyes to force the sleep out of them, and turned to look at the muddy, swollen river pimpled by the rain.

It seemed to loom out of nowhere. It looked like a large white fish floating belly up, and Constable Hiller's first thought was: If we haul it aboard, we're going to stink of it. It was about ten yards to starboard and the boat was moving away from it. If he opened his mouth, the bloody fish was going to delay his getting off duty. They would have to stop and grapple it, and either pull it over the side or tow it in. Whichever they did would delay his getting to Flo. Well, he didn't *have* to report it. What if he had not seen it? What if—? They were moving farther away.

Constable Hiller called out, "Sergeant, there's a floating fish twenty degrees off starboard. Looks like a big shark."

The hundred-horsepower diesel engine suddenly changed rhythm, and the boat began to slow. Sergeant Gaskins stepped to his side. "Where is it?" he asked.

The dim shape was gone now, buried in the rain. "It was over there."

Sergeant Gaskins hesitated. He too was anxious to get home. His impulse was to ignore the damned fish.

"Was it big enough to menace navigation?" he asked.

Constable Hiller fought with himself and lost. "Yes," he said.

And so the patrol boat turned and slowly headed toward where the object had last been seen. It materialized again unexpectedly, almost under the bow, and they both stood there, staring down at it. It was the body of a young blond girl.

She was naked, except for a red ribbon tied around her swollen neck.

39

A t the moment when Constable Hiller and Sergeant Gaskins were fishing the body of the murdered girl out of the Thames, ten miles on the other side of London, Detective Max Hornung was entering the gray-and-white marble lobby of New Scotland Yard. Just walking through the storied portals gave him a sense of pride. They were all part of the same great fraternity. He enjoyed the fact that the Yard's cable address was HANDCUFFS. Max was very fond of the English. His only problem concerned their ability to communicate with him. The English spoke their native language so strangely.

The policeman behind the reception desk asked, "Can I help you, sir?"

Max turned. "I have an appointment with Inspector Davidson."

"Name, sir?"

Max said, slowly and distinctly, "Inspector Davidson."

The guard looked at him with interest. "Your name is Inspector Davidson?"

"My name is *not* Inspector Davidson. My name is Max Hornung."

The policeman behind the desk said apologetically, "Excuse me, sir, but do you speak any English?"

Five minutes later Max was seated in the office of Inspector David-son, a large, middle-aged man with a florid face and uneven yellow teeth. Typically British-looking, Max thought happily.

"Over the phone you said you were interested in information on Sir Alec Nichols as a possible suspect in a murder case."

"He's one of half a dozen."

Inspector Davidson stared at him. "His wanted toes are frozen?"

Max sighed. He repeated what he had just said, slowly and carefully.

"Ah." The inspector thought for a moment. "Tell you what I'll do. I'll turn you over to C-Four Criminal Records Department. If they have nothing on him, we'll try C-Eleven and C-Thirteen—Criminal Intelligence."

Sir Alec Nichols's name was not listed in any of the files. But Max knew where he could get the information he wanted.

EARLIER THAT MORNING Max had phoned a number of executives who worked in the City, the financial center of London.

Their reactions were identical. When Max announced his name, they were filled with trepidation, for everyone doing business in the City had *something* to hide, and Max Hornung's reputation as a financial avenging angel was international. The moment that Max informed them that he was seeking information about someone else, they fell over themselves to cooperate with him.

Max spent two days visiting banks and finance companies, credit rating organizations and vital statistics offices. He was not interested in talking to the people at those places: he was interested in talking to their computers.

Max was a genius with computers. He would sit before the console board and play the machines like a virtuoso. It did not matter what language the computer had been taught, for Max spoke all of them. He talked to digital computers and low-level and high-level language computers. He was at ease with FORTRAN and FORTRAN IV, the giant IBM 370's and the PDP 10's and 11's and ALGOL 68.

He was at home with COBOL, programmed for business, and BASIC, used by the police, and the high speed APL, which conversed solely in charts and graphs. Max talked to LISP and APT, and PL-1. He held conversations in the binary code, and questioned the arithmetic units and the CPV units, and the high-speed printer answered his questions at the rate of eleven hundred lines a minute. The giant computers had spent their lives sucking up information like insatiable pumps, storing it, analyzing it, remembering it, and now they were spewing it out in Max's ear, whispering their secrets to him in their secluded air-conditioned crypts.

Nothing was sacred, nothing was safe. Privacy in today's civilization was a delusion, a myth. Every citizen was exposed, his deepest secrets laid bare, waiting to be read. People were on record if they had a Social Security number, an insurance policy, a driver's license or a bank account. They were listed if they had paid taxes or drawn unemployment insurance or welfare funds. Their names were stored in computers if they were covered by a medical plan, had made mortgage payments on a home, owned an automobile or bicycle or had a savings or checking account. The computers knew their names if they had been in a hospital, or in the military service, had a fishing or hunting license, had applied for a passport, or telephone, or electricity, or if they had been married or divorced or born.

If one knew where to look, and if one was patient, all the facts were available.

Max Hornung and the computers had a wonderful rapport. They did not laugh at Max's accent, or the way he looked, or acted or dressed. To the computers Max was a giant. They respected his intelligence, admired him, loved him. They happily gave up their secrets to him, sharing their delicious gossip about the fools that mortals made of themselves. It was like old friends chatting.

"Let's talk about Sir Alec Nichols," Max said.

The computers began. They gave Max a mathematical sketch of Sir Alec, drawn in digits and binary codes and charts. In two hours Max had a composite picture of the man, a financial Identi-Kit.

Copies of bank receipts and canceled checks and bills were all laid out before him. The first puzzling item that caught Max's eye was a series of checks for large amounts, all made out to "Bearer," cashed by Sir Alec Nichols. Where had the money gone? Max looked to see if it had been reported as a business or personal expense, or as a tax deduction. Negative. He went back over the lists of expenditures again; a check to White's Club, a meat-market bill, unpaid . . . an evening gown from John Bates . . . the Guinea . . . a dentist's bill, unpaid Annabelle's . . . one challis robe from Saint Laurent in Paris . . . a bill from the White Elephant, unpaid . . . a rates bill . . . John Wyndham, the hairdresser, unpaid . . . four dresses from Yves Saint Laurent, Rive Gauche . . . household salaries . . .

Max asked a question of the computer at the Vehicle Licensing Center.

Affirmative. *Sir Alec owns a Bentley and a Morris.*

Something was missing. There was no mechanic's bill.

Max had the computers search their memories. In seven years no such bill existed.

Did we forget something? the computers asked.

No, Max replied, *you didn't forget.*

Sir Alec did not use a mechanic. He repaired his own cars. A man with that mechanical ability would have no trouble causing an elevator, or a Jeep, to crash. Max Hornung pored over the arcane figures that his friends set before him, with the eagerness of an Egyptologist translating a set of newly discovered hieroglyphics. He found further mysteries. Sir Alec was spending a great deal more than his income.

Another loose thread.

Max's friends in the City had connections in many quarters. Within two days Max learned that Sir Alec had been borrowing money from Tod Michaels, the owner of a club in Soho.

Max turned to the police computers and asked questions. They listened, and they replied. *Yes, we have Tod Michaels for you. Has been charged with several crimes, but never convicted. Suspected of being involved in blackmail, dope, prostitution and loan-sharking.*

Max went down to Soho and asked more questions. He found out that Sir Alec Nichols did not gamble. But his wife did.

When Max was finished, there was no doubt in his mind that Sir Alec Nichols was being blackmailed. He had unpaid bills, he needed money fast. He had stock that would be worth millions, if he could sell it. Sam Roffe had stood in his way, and now Elizabeth Roffe.

Sir Alec Nichols had a motive for murder.

. . .

MAX CHECKED OUT Rhys Williams. The machines tried, but the information proved too sketchy.

The computers informed Max that Rhys Williams was male, born in Wales, thirty-four years of age, unmarried. An executive of Roffe and Sons. Salary eighty thousand dollars a year, plus bonuses. A London savings account with a balance of twenty-five thousand pounds, a checking account with an average balance of eight hundred pounds. A safety-deposit box in Zurich, contents unknown. All major charge accounts and credit cards. Many of the items purchased with them were for women. Rhys Williams had no criminal record. He had been employed at Roffe and Sons for nine years.

Not enough, Max thought. Not nearly enough. It was as though Rhys Williams was hiding behind the computers. Max remembered how protective the man had been when Max had questioned Elizabeth, after Kate Erling's funeral. Whom had he been protecting? Elizabeth Roffe? Or himself?

AT SIX O'CLOCK that evening Max booked himself on an Alitalia economy flight to Rome.

vo Palazzi had spent almost ten years carefully and skillfully building an intricate double life that not even his closest associates had penetrated.

It took Max Hornung and his computer friends in Rome less than twenty-four hours. Max held discussions with the computer at the Anagrafe Building, where vital statistics and city-administration data were kept, and he visited the computers at SID, and went to call on the bank computers. They all welcomed Max.

Tell me about Ivo Palazzi, Max said.

Happily, they replied.

The conversations began.

A grocery bill from Amici . . . a beauty salon bill from Sergio in the Via Condoitti . . . one blue suit from Angelo . . . flowers from Carducci . . . two evening dresses from Irene Galitzine . . . shoes from Gucci . . . a Pucci purse . . . utility bills . . .

Max kept reading the printouts, examining, analyzing, smelling. Something smelled wrong. There were tuition fees for six children.

Have you made an error? Max asked.

Sorry. What type of error?

The computers at Anagrafe told me that Ivo Palazzi is registered as the father of three children. Do you verify six tuition fees?

We do.

You show Ivo Palazzi's address as being in Olgiata?

That is correct.

But he is paying for an apartment in Via Montemignaio?

Yes.

Are there two Ivo Palazzis?

No. One man. Two families. Three daughters by his wife. Three sons by Donatella Spolini.

Before Max was through, he knew the tastes of Ivo's mistress, her age, the name of her hairdresser and the names of Ivo's illegitimate children. He knew that Simonetta was a blonde, and Donatella a brunette. He knew what size dresses and bras and shoes each wore and how much they cost.

Among the expenses several interesting items caught Max's eye. The amounts were small, but they stood out like beacons. There was a receipted check for a lathe, a plane and a saw. Ivo Palazzi liked to work with his hands. Max thought about the fact that an architect would probably know something about elevators.

Ivo Palazzi applied for a large bank loan recently, the computers informed Max.

Did he receive it?

No. The bank asked him to have his wife cosign. He withdrew the request.

Thank you.

Max took a bus to the Polizia Scientifica center at EUR, where the giant computer was kept in a large round room.

Does Ivo Palazzi have a criminal record? Max asked.

Affirmative. Ivo Palazzi was convicted on an assault-and-battery charge at age twenty-three. His victim went to the hospital. Palazzi went to jail for two months.

Anything else?

Ivo Palazzi keeps a mistress at Via Montemignaio.

Thank you. I know.

There are several police reports of complaints from neighbors.

What sort of complaints?

Disturbing the peace. Fighting, yelling. One night she smashed all the dishes. Is that important?

Very, Max said. *Thank you.*

So Ivo Palazzi had a temper. And Donatella Spolini had a temper. Had something happened between her and Ivo? Was she threatening to expose him? Was that why he had suddenly gone to the bank for a large loan? How far would a man like Ivo Palazzi go to protect his marriage, his family, his way of life?

There was one final item that caught the little detective's attention. A large payment had been made to Ivo Palazzi by the financial section of the Italian security police. It was a reward, a percentage of the money found on the banker whom Ivo had turned in. If Ivo Palazzi was that desperate for money, what else would he do for it?

MAX BADE FAREWELL to his computers and caught a noon flight to Paris on Air France.

41

The taxi fare from Charles de Gaulle Airport to the Notre Dame area is seventy francs, not including a tip. The fare by city bus Number 351, to the same area, is seven and a half francs, no tip required. Detective Max Hornung took the bus. He checked into the inexpensive Hôtel Meublé and began making phone calls.

He talked to the people who held in their hands the secrets of the citizens of France. The French were normally more suspicious than even the Swiss, but they were eager to cooperate with Max Hornung. There were two reasons. The first was that Max Hornung was a virtuoso in his field, greatly admired and it was an honor to cooperate with such a man. The second was that they were terrified of him. There were no secrets from Max. The odd-looking little man with the funny accent stripped everyone naked. "Certainly," they told Max. "You're welcome to use our computers. Everything to be kept confidential, of course."

"Of course."

MAX DROPPED IN at the Inspecteurs des Finances, the Crédit Lyonnais and the Assurance Nationale and chatted with the tax computers. He visited the computers at the *gendarmerie* at Rosny-sous-Bois and the ones at the Préfecture of Police at Île de la Cité.

They started off with the light, easy gossip of old friends. *Who are Charles and Hélène Roffe-Martel?* Max asked.

Charles and Hélène Roffe-Martel, residence Rue François Premier 5, Vésinet, married May 24,1970, at the Mairie in Neuilly, children none, Hélène three times divorced, maiden name Roffe, bank account at the Crédit Lyonnais in Avenue Montaigne in name of Hélène Roffe-Martel, average balance in excess of twenty thousand francs.

Expenditures?

With pleasure. A bill from Librairie Marceau for books . . . a dental bill for root-canal work for Charles Martel . . . hospital bills for Charles Martel . . . doctor's bill for examination of Charles Martel.

Do you have result of diagnosis?

Can you wait? I will have to speak to another computer.

Yes, please. Max waited.

The machine containing the doctor's report began to speak. *I have the diagnosis.*

Go ahead.

A nervous condition.

Anything else?

Severe bruises and contusions on thighs and buttocks.

Any explanation?

None given.

Go on, please.

A bill for a pair of men's shoes from Pinet . . . one hat from Rose Valois . . . foie gras from Fauchon . . . Carita beauty salon . . . Maxim's, dinner party for eight . . . flat silver from Christofle . . . a man's robe from Sulka . . . Max stopped the computer. Something was bothering him. Something about the bills. He realized what it was. Every purchase had been signed by Mme. Roffe-Martel. The bill for men's clothes, the restaurant bills—all the accounts were in her name. Interesting.

And then the first loose thread.

A company named Belle Paix had purchased a land tax stamp. One of the owners of Belle Paix was named Charles Dessain. Charles Dessain's Social Security number was the same as Charles Martel's. Concealment.

Tell me about Belle Paix, Max said.

Belle Paix is owned by René Duchamps and Charles Dessain, also known as Charles Martel.

What does Belle Paix do?

It owns a vineyard.

How much is the company capitalized at?

Four million francs.

Where did Charles Martel get his share of the money?

From Chez ma Tante.

The house of your aunt?

Sorry. A French slang expression. The proper name is Crédit Municipal.

Is the vineyard profitable?

No. It failed.

Max needed more. He kept talking to his friends, probing, cajoling, demanding. It was the insurance computer that confided to Max that there was a warning on file of a possible insurance fraud. Max felt something delicious stir within him.

Tell me about it, he said.

And they talked, like two women gossiping back and forth over the Monday wash.

When Max was through he went to see a jeweler named Pierre Richaud.

In thirty minutes Max knew to a franc how much of Hélène Roffe-Martel's jewelry had been duplicated. It came to just over two million francs, the amount Charles Martel had invested in the vineyard. So Charles Dessain-Martel had been desperate enough to steal his wife's jewelry.

What other acts of desperation had he committed?

There was one other entry that interested Max. It might be of little significance, but Max methodically filed it away in his mind. It was a bill for the purchase of one pair of mountain-climbing boots. It gave Max pause, because mountain climbing did not fit in with his image of Charles Martel-Dessain, a man who was so dominated by his wife that he was allowed no charge accounts of his own, had no bank account in his name and was forced to steal in order to make an investment.

No, Max could not visualize Charles Martel challenging a mountain. Max went back to his computers.

The bill you showed me earlier from Timwear Sports Shop. I would like to see an itemized statement, please.

Certainly.

It flashed on the screen before him. There was the bill for the boots. Size *36A*. A woman's size. It was Hélène Roffe-Martel who was the mountain climber.

Sam Roffe had been killed on a mountain.

42

Rue Armengaud was a quiet Paris street lined with one- and two-story private residences, each with its sloping guttered roof. Towering above its neighbors was Number 26, an eight-story modern structure of glass, steel and stone, the headquarters of Interpol, the clearinghouse for information in international criminal activities.

Detective Max Hornung was talking to a computer in the huge, air-conditioned basement room when one of the staff members walked in and said, "They're running a snuff film upstairs. Want to see it?"

Max looked up and said, "I don't know. What is a snuff film?"

"Come take a look."

Two dozen men and women were seated in the large screening room on the third floor of the building. There were members of the Interpol staff, police inspectors from the Sûreté, plainclothes detectives and a scattering of uniformed policemen.

Standing at the front of the room next to a blank screen, René Almedin, an assistant to the secretary of Interpol, was speaking. Max entered and found a seat in the back row.

René Almedin was saying, ". . . for the last several years we have been hearing increasing rumors of snuff films, pornographic films in which at the end of the sexual act the victim is murdered on camera. There has never been proof that such films actually existed. The reason, of course, is obvious. These films would not have been made for the public. They would have been made to be shown privately to wealthy individuals who got their pleasure in twisted, sadistic ways." René Almedin carefully removed his glasses. "As I have said, everything has been rumor and speculation. That has now changed, however. In a moment you are going to see footage from an actual snuff film." There was an expectant stir from the audience. "Two days ago, a male pedestrian carrying an attaché case was struck down in a hit-and-run accident in Passy. The man died on the way to the hospital. He is still unidentified. The Sûreté found this reel of film in his attaché case and turned it over to the laboratory, where it was developed." He gave a signal and the lights began to dim. The film began.

The blond girl could not have been more than eighteen. There was something unreal about watching that young face and budding woman's body performing fellatio, analingus and a variety of other sexual acts with the large hairless man in bed with her. The camera moved in to a close-up to show his enormous penis driving into her body, then pulled back to show her face. Max Hornung had never seen her face before. But he had seen something else that was familiar. His eyes were fixed on the ribbon that the girl was wearing around her neck. It triggered a memory. A red ribbon. Where? Slowly, the girl on the screen began to build to a peak, and as she started to climax, the man's fingers went around her throat and began to squeeze. The look on the girl's face changed from ecstasy to horror. She fought wildly to escape, but his hands pressed tighter, until at the final moment of orgasm the girl died. The camera moved in for a close-up of her face. The film ended. The lights suddenly came on in the room. Max remembered.

The girl who had been fished out of the river in Zurich.

AT INTERPOL HEADQUARTERS in Paris, replies from urgent inquiry cables were beginning to arrive from all over Europe. Six similar murders had taken place—in Zurich, London, Rome, Portugal, Hamburg and Paris.

René Almedin said to Max, "The descriptions match exactly. The victims were all blond, female, young; they were strangled during sexual intercourse and their bodies were nude except for a red ribbon around their necks. We're dealing with a mass murderer. Someone who has a passport, and is either affluent enough to travel extensively on his own or is on an expense account."

A man in plain clothes walked into the office and said, "We ran into some good luck. The raw stock of the film is manufactured by a small outfit in Brussels. This particular batch had a color-balance problem, which makes it easy for them to identify. We're getting a list of the customers they sold it to."

Max said, "I would like to see that list when you have it."

"Of course," René Almedin said. He studied the little detective. Max Hornung looked like no detective he had ever seen. And yet it was Max Hornung who had tied the snuff murders together.

"We owe you a debt of gratitude," Almedin said.

Max Hornung looked at him and blinked. "What for?" he asked.

43

Alec Nichols had not wanted to attend the banquet, but he had not wished Elizabeth to go alone. They were both scheduled to speak. The banquet was in Glasgow, a city Alec hated. A car was outside the hotel, waiting to take them to the airport as soon as they could decently make their excuses. He had already given his speech but his mind had been elsewhere. He was tense and nervous, and his stomach was upset. Some fool had had the bad judgment to serve haggis. Alec had barely tasted it. Elizabeth was seated next to him. "Are you all right, Alec?"

"Fine." He patted her hand reassuringly.

The speeches were almost finished when a waiter came up to Alec and whispered, "Excuse me, sir. There's a trunk call for you. You can take it in the office."

Alec followed the waiter out of the large dining room into the small office behind the reception desk. He picked up the telephone. "Hello?"

Swinton's voice said, "This is your last warning!" The line went dead.

44

The last city on Detective Max Hornung's agenda was Berlin.

His friends the computers were waiting for him. Max spoke to the exclusive Nixdorf computer, to which one had access only with a specially punched card. He talked to the great computers at Allianz and Schuffa and to the ones at the Bundeskrimalamt at Wiesbaden, the collection point for all criminal activity in Germany.

What can we do for you? they asked.

Tell me about Walther Gassner.

And they told him. When they were through telling Max Hornung their secrets, Walther Gassner's life was spread out before Max in beautiful mathematical symbols. Max could see the man as clearly as if he were looking at a photograph of him. He knew his taste in clothes, wines, food, hotels. A handsome young ski instructor who had lived off women and had married an heiress much older than himself.

There was one item that Max found curious: a canceled check made out to a Dr. Heissen, for two hundred marks. On the check was written "For consultation." What kind of consultation? The check had been cashed at the Dresdner Bank in Dusseldorf. Fifteen minutes later Max was speaking to the branch manager of the bank. Yes, of course the branch manager knew Dr. Heissen. He was a valued client of the bank.

What kind of doctor was he?

A psychiatrist.

When Max had hung up, he sat back, his eyes closed, thinking. A loose thread. He picked up the telephone and placed a call to Dr. Heissen in Dusseldorf.

An officious receptionist told Max that the doctor could not be disturbed. When Max insisted, Dr. Heissen got on the telephone and rudely informed Max that he never revealed any information about his patients, and that he would certainly not dream of discussing such matters over the telephone. He hung up on the detective.

Max went back to the computers. *Tell me about Dr. Heissen,* he said.

Three hours later Max was speaking to Dr. Heissen on the telephone again.

"I told you before," the doctor snapped, "that if you want any information about any of my patients, you will have to come to my office with a court order."

"It is inconvenient for me to come to Dusseldorf just now," the detective explained.

"That's your problem. Anything else? I'm a busy man."

"I know you are. I have in front of me your income tax reports for the past five years."

"So?"

Max said, "Doctor, I don't want to make trouble for you. But you are illegally concealing twenty-five percent of your income. If you prefer, I can just forward your files to the German income tax authorities and tell them where to look. They could start with your safe-deposit box in Munich, or your numbered bank account in Basel."

There was a long silence, and then the doctor's voice asked, "Who did you say you were?"

"Detective Max Hornung of the Swiss Kriminal Polizei."

There was another pause. The doctor said politely, "And what is it exactly you wish to know?"

Max told him.

Once Dr. Heissen began talking, there was no stopping him. Yes, of course he remembered Walther Gassner. The man had barged in without an appointment and had insisted on seeing him. He had refused to give his name. He had used the pretext that he wanted to discuss the problems of a friend.

"Of course, that alerted me instantly," Dr, Heissen confided to Max. "It is a classic syndrome of people unwilling or afraid to face their problems."

"What *was* the problem?" Max asked.

"He said his friend was schizophrenic and homicidal, and would probably kill someone unless he could be stopped. He asked if there was some kind of treatment that could help. He said he could not bear to have his friend locked away in an insane asylum."

"What did you tell him?"

"I told him that first, of course, I would have to examine his *friend,* that some types of mental illness could be helped with modern drugs and other psychiatric and therapeutic treatments, and that other types were incurable. I also mentioned that in a case such as he described, treatment might be necessary for an extended period of time."

"What happened then?" Max asked.

"Nothing. That was really all. I never saw the man again. I would like to have helped him. He was very distraught. His coming to me was obviously a cry for help. It is similar to a killer who writes on the wall of his victim's apartment, 'Stop me before I kill again!' "

There was one thing still puzzling Max. "Doctor, you said he wouldn't give you his name, and yet he gave you a check and signed it."

Dr. Heissen explained, "He had forgotten to bring any money with him. He was very upset about that. In the end he had to write the check. That's how I happened to learn his name. Is there anything else you need to know, sir?"

"No."

Something was disturbing Max, a loose thread dangling tantalizingly out of reach. It would come to him—meanwhile, he had finished with the computers. The rest was up to him now.

. . .

WHEN MAX RETURNED to Zurich the following morning, he found a teletype on his desk from Interpol. It contained a list of customers who had purchased the batch of raw stock used to make the snuff murder film.

There were eight names on the list.

Among them was Roffe and Sons.

CHIEF INSPECTOR SCHMIED was listening to Detective Max Hornung make his report. There was no doubt about it. The lucky little detective had stumbled onto another big case.

"It's one of five people," Max was saying, "They all have a motive and they had the opportunity. They were all in Zurich for a board meeting the day the elevator crashed. Any one of them could have been in Sardinia at the time of the Jeep accident."

Chief Inspector Schmied frowned. "You said there were five suspects. Aside from Elizabeth Roffe, there are only four members of the board. Who's your other suspect?"

Max blinked and said patiently, "The man who was in Chamonix with Sam Roffe, when he was murdered. Rhys Williams."

45

Mrs. *Rhys Williams.*

Elizabeth could not believe it. The whole thing had an air of unreality. It was something out of a blissful girlhood dream. Elizabeth remembered how she had written in her exercise book, over and over, *Mrs. Rhys Williams, Mrs. Rhys Williams.* She glanced down now at the wedding ring on her finger.

Rhys said, "What are you grinning about?" He was seated in an easy chair across from her in the luxurious Boeing 707-320. They were thirty-five thousand feet somewhere above the Atlantic ocean, dining on Iranian caviar and drinking chilled Dom Pérignon, and it was such a cliché of *La Dolce Vita* that Elizabeth had to laugh aloud.

Rhys smiled. "Something I said?"

Elizabeth shook her head. She looked at him and marveled at how attractive he was. Her husband. "I'm just happy."

He would never know how happy. How could she tell him how much this marriage meant to her? He would not understand, because to Rhys it was not a marriage, it was a business proposition. But she loved Rhys.

It seemed to Elizabeth that she had always loved him. She wanted to spend the rest of her life with him, have his children, belong to him, have him belong to her. Elizabeth looked over at Rhys again and thought wryly, But first I have to solve one small problem. I have to find a way to make him fall in love with me.

ELIZABETH HAD PROPOSED to Rhys the day of her meeting with Julius Badrutt. After the banker had left, Elizabeth had carefully brushed her hair, walked into Rhys's office, taken a deep breath and said, "Rhys— would you marry me?"

She had seen the look of surprise on his face, and before he could speak, she had gone hurriedly on, trying to sound efficient and cool. "It would be a purely business arrangement. The banks are willing to extend our loans if you take over as president of Roffe and Sons. The only way you can do that"—to Elizabeth's horror her voice had cracked—"is to marry a member of the family, and I—I seem to be the only one available."

She felt her face flush. She could not look at him.

"It wouldn't be a real marriage, of course," Elizabeth had said, "in the sense that—I mean—you'd be free to—to come and go as you pleased."

He had watched her, not helping her. Elizabeth wished he would say something. Anything.

"Rhys—"

"Sorry. You took me by surprise." He had smiled. "It isn't every day a man gets proposed to by a beautiful girl."

He was smiling, trying to get out of this without hurting her feelings. *I'm sorry, Elizabeth, but—*

"You have a deal," Rhys said.

And Elizabeth had suddenly felt as though a heavy burden had been lifted from her. She had not realized until that moment how important this had been. She had bought time now to learn who the enemy was. Together she and Rhys could stop all the terrible things that had been happening. There was one thing she had to make clear to him.

"You will be president of the company," she had said, "but the voting control of the stock will remain in my hands."

Rhys had frowned. "If I'm running the company—"

"You will be," Elizabeth had assured him.

"But the controlling stock—"

"Stays in my name. I want to make sure that it can't be sold."

"I see."

She could sense his disapproval. She had wanted to tell him that she had reached a decision. She had decided that the company should go public, that the members of the board should be able to sell their shares. With Rhys as president, Elizabeth would no longer have any fears about strangers coming in and taking over. Rhys would be strong enough to handle them. But Elizabeth could not let that happen until she found out who was trying to destroy the company. She had wanted desperately to tell Rhys all these things, but she knew that now was not the time, and so all she said was "Other than that, you'll have complete control."

Rhys had stood there, silently studying her for what seemed a long time. When he spoke, he said, "When would you like to get married?"

"As soon as possible."

EXCEPT FOR ANNA and Walther, who was home, ill, they all came to Zurich for the wedding. Alec and Vivian, Hélène and Charles, Simonetta and Ivo. They seemed delighted for Elizabeth, and their pleasure made her feel like a fraud. She had not made a marriage, she had made a business deal.

Alec hugged her and said, "You know I wish you everything wonderful."

"I know, Alec. Thank you."

Ivo waxed ecstatic. "*Carissima, tanti auguri e figli maschi.* 'To find riches is a beggar's dream, but to find love is the dream of kings.'"

Elizabeth smiled. "Who said that?"

"I did," Ivo declared. "I hope Rhys appreciates what a lucky man he is."

"I keep telling him," she said lightly.

Hélène took Elizabeth aside. "You are full of surprises, *ma chère.* I had no idea that you and Rhys were interested in each other."

"It happened suddenly."

Hélène studied her with cool, calculating eyes. "Yes, I'm sure it did." And she walked away.

After the ceremony there was a wedding reception at the Baur-au-Lac. On the surface it was gay and festive, but Elizabeth felt the undercurrents. There was something evil in the room, a malediction, but she could not tell from whom it was coming. All she knew was that someone in the room hated her. She could feel it, deep down inside her, yet when she looked around, all she saw were smiles and friendly faces. Charles raising his glass in a toast to her . . . Elizabeth had received a report on the laboratory explosion. *The explosive was manufactured by your factory outside Paris.*

Ivo, a happy grin on his face . . . *The banker who was caught trying to smuggle money out of Italy was set up. A man tipped off the border police. Ivo Palazzi.*

Alec? Walther? Which? Elizabeth wondered.

THE FOLLOWING MORNING a board meeting was held, and Rhys Williams was unanimously elected president and chief operating officer of Roffe and Sons. Charles raised the question that was on everyone's mind. "Now that you are running the company, are we going to be allowed to sell our stock?"

Elizabeth could feel the sudden tension in the room.

"The controlling stock is still in Elizabeth's hands," Rhys informed them. "It's her decision."

Every head turned toward Elizabeth.

"We're not selling," she announced.

When Elizabeth and Rhys were alone, he said, "How would you like to honeymoon in Rio?"

Elizabeth looked at him, and her heart soared. He added matter-of-factly, "Our manager there is threatening to quit. We can't afford to lose him. I was planning to fly there tomorrow to straighten things out. It would look a bit strange if I went without my bride."

Elizabeth nodded and said, "Yes, of course." You're a fool, she told herself. This was your idea. It's an arrangement, not a marriage. You have no right to expect anything from Rhys. And still, a small voice, deep inside her, said, Who knows what can happen? . . .

WHEN THEY GOT off the plane at the Galeão airport, the air was surprisingly warm, and Elizabeth realized that in Rio it was summer. A Mercedes 600 was waiting for them. The chauffeur was a thin, dark-skinned man in his late twenties. When they got into the car, Rhys asked the driver, "Where's Luis?"

"Luis is sick, Mr. Williams. I'll be driving you and Mrs. Williams."

"Tell Luis I hope he'll be better soon."

The driver studied them in the rearview mirror and said, "I will."

Half an hour later they were driving along the esplanade, over the colorful tiles of the broad avenue along the Copacabana Beach. They pulled up in front of the modern Princessa Sugarloaf Hotel and a moment later, their luggage was being attended to. They were ushered into an enormous suite with four bedrooms, a beautiful living room, a kitchen and a huge terrace overlooking the bay. The suite had been stocked with flowers in silver vases, champagne, whiskey and boxes of chocolates. The manager himself had escorted them to their suite.

"If there is anything at all we can do for you—anything—I am personally at your service twenty-four hours a day." And he bowed himself out.

"They're certainly friendly," Elizabeth said.

Rhys laughed and replied, "They should be. You own this hotel."

Elizabeth felt herself color. "Oh. I—I didn't know."

"Hungry?"

"I— No, thank you," Elizabeth replied.

"Some wine?"

"Yes, thank you."

In her own ears her voice sounded stilted and unnatural. She was not certain how she was supposed to behave, or what to expect from Rhys. He had suddenly become a stranger, and she felt terribly conscious of the fact that they were alone in the honeymoon suite of a hotel, that it was getting late and that it would soon be time for bed.

She watched Rhys as he deftly opened a bottle of champagne. He did everything so smoothly, with the easy assurance of a man who knows exactly what he wants and how to get it. What did he want?

Rhys carried a glass of champagne to Elizabeth and raised his own glass in a toast. "To beginnings," he said.

"To beginnings," Elizabeth echoed. *And happy endings,* she added silently.

They drank.

We should smash our glasses into a fireplace, Elizabeth thought, to celebrate. She gulped down the rest of her champagne.

They were in Rio on their honeymoon, and she wanted Rhys. Not just for now, but forever.

The phone rang. Rhys picked it up and spoke into it briefly. When he finished he hung up and said to Elizabeth, "It's late. Why don't you get ready for bed?"

It seemed to Elizabeth that the word "bed" hung heavily in the air.

"Right," she said weakly. She turned and went into the bedroom where the bellboys had put their luggage. There was a large double bed in the center of the room. A maid had unpacked their suitcases and prepared the bed. On one side was a sheer silk nightgown of Elizabeth's, and on the other side a pair of men's blue pajamas. She hesitated a moment, then began to undress. When she was naked, she walked into the large mirrored dressing room and carefully removed her makeup. She wrapped a Turkish towel around her head, went into the bathroom and showered, slowly lathering her body and feeling the warm soapy water running between her breasts and down her belly and thighs, like warm wet fingers.

All the time she was trying not to think about Rhys, and she could think of nothing else. She thought of his arms around her and his body on hers. Had she married Rhys to help save the company, or was she using the company as an excuse because she wanted him? She no longer knew. Her desire had turned into one burning, all-consuming need. It was as though the fifteen-year-old child had been waiting for him all these years without being aware of it, and the need had turned into a hunger. She stepped out of the shower, dried herself with a soft warmed towel, put on the sheer silk nightgown, let her hair fall loose and free and climbed into bed. She lay there waiting, thinking about what was going to happen, wondering what he would be like, and she found that her heart was beginning to pound faster. She heard a sound and looked up. Rhys was standing in the doorway. He was fully dressed.

"I'll be going out now," he said.

Elizabeth sat up. "Where—where are you going?"

"It's a business problem I have to take care of." And he was gone.

ELIZABETH LAY AWAKE all that night, tossing and turning, filled with conflicting emotions, telling herself how grateful she was that Rhys had kept to their agreement, feeling like a fool for what she had been anticipating, furious with him for rejecting her.

It was dawn when Elizabeth heard Rhys return. His footsteps moved toward the bedroom, and Elizabeth closed her eyes, pretending to be asleep. She could hear Rhys's breathing as he came over to the bed. He stood there, watching her for a long time. Then he turned and walked into the other room.

A few minutes later Elizabeth was asleep.

In the late morning they had breakfast on the terrace. Rhys was pleasant and chatty, telling her what the city was like at Carnival time. But he volunteered no information about where he had spent the night, and Elizabeth did not ask. One waiter took their order for breakfast. Elizabeth noticed that it was a different waiter who served it. She thought no more about it, nor about the maids who were constantly in and out of the suite.

ELIZABETH AND RHYS were at the Roffe and Sons factory on the outskirts of Rio, seated in the office of the plant manager, Señor Tumas, a middle-aged, frog-faced man who perspired copiously.

He was addressing Rhys. "You must understand how it is; Roffe and Sons is dearer to me than my own life. It is my family. When I leave here, it will be like leaving home. A part of my heart will be torn out. More than anything in the world, I want to stay here." He stopped to wipe his brow. "But I have a better offer from another company, and I have my wife and children and mother-in-law to think of. You understand?"

Rhys was leaning back in his chair, his legs casually stretched out before him. "Of course, Roberto. I know how much this company means to you. You have spent many years here. Still, a man has to think of his family."

"Thank you," Roberto said gratefully. "I knew I could count on you, Rhys."

"What about your contract with us?"

Tumas shrugged. "A piece of paper. We will tear it up, no? What good is a contract if a man is unhappy in his heart?"

Rhys nodded. "That's why we flew down here, Roberto—to make you happy in your heart."

Tumas sighed. "Ah, if only it were not too late. But I have already agreed to go to work for this other company."

"Do they know you're going to prison?" Rhys asked conversationally.

Tumas gasped at him. "Prison?"

Rhys said, "The United States government has ordered every company doing business overseas to turn in a list of all foreign bribes they've paid over the past ten years. Unfortunately, you're heavily involved in that, Roberto. You've broken a few laws here. We had planned to protect you—as a faithful member of the family—but if you're not with us, there's no longer any reason to, is there?"

All the color had drained from Roberto's face. "But—but it was for the company that I did it," he protested. "I was only following orders."

Rhys nodded sympathetically. "Of course. You can explain that to the government at your trial." He rose to his feet and said to Elizabeth, "We'd better be starting back."

"Wait a minute," Roberto yelled. "You can't walk out and leave me like this."

Rhys said, "I think you're confused. *You're* the one who's leaving."

Tumas was mopping his brow again, his lips twitching uncontrollably. He walked over to the window and looked out. A heavy silence hung over the room. Finally, without turning, he said, "If I stay with the company—will I be protected?"

"All the way," Rhys assured him.

THEY WERE IN the Mercedes, the thin dark chauffeur at the wheel, driving back to the city. "You blackmailed him," Elizabeth declared.

Rhys nodded. "We couldn't afford to lose him. He was going over to a competitor. He knows too much about our business. He would have sold us out."

Elizabeth looked at Rhys and thought, I have so much to learn about him.

THAT EVENING THEY went to Mirander for dinner, and Rhys was charming and amusing and impersonal. Elizabeth felt as though he were hiding behind a facade of words, putting up a verbal smoke screen to conceal his feelings. When they finished dinner, it was after midnight. Elizabeth wanted to be alone with Rhys. She had hoped they would return to the hotel. Instead he said, "I'm going to show you some of the nightlife in Rio."

They made the rounds of nightclubs, and everyone seemed to know Rhys. Wherever they went, he was the center of attention, charming everyone. They were invited to join couples at other tables, and groups of people joined them at their table. Elizabeth and Rhys were never alone for a moment. It seemed to Elizabeth that it was intentional, that Rhys was deliberately putting a wall of people between them. They had been friends before, and now they were—what? Elizabeth only knew that there was some unseen barrier between them. What was he afraid of and why?

At the fourth nightclub, where they had joined a table with half a dozen of Rhys's friends, Elizabeth decided she had had enough. She broke into the conversation between Rhys and a lovely looking Spanish girl. "I haven't had a chance to dance with my husband. I'm sure you'll excuse us."

Rhys looked at her in quick surprise, then rose to his feet. "I'm afraid I've been neglecting my bride," he said lightly to the others. He took Elizabeth's arm and led her out to the dance floor. She was holding herself stiffly, and he looked at her face and said, "You're angry."

He was right, but it was an anger directed at herself. She had made the rules, and was upset now because Rhys would not break them. But it was more than that, of course. It was not knowing how Rhys felt. Was he sticking to their agreement because of a sense of honor, or because he was simply not interested in her? She had to know.

Rhys said, "Sorry about all these people, Liz, but they're in the business, and in one way or another they can be helpful to us."

So he was aware of her feelings. She could feel his arms around her, his body against hers. She thought, It feels right. Everything about Rhys was right for her. They belonged together. She knew it. But did he know how much she wanted him? Elizabeth's pride would not let her tell him. And yet he must feel something. She closed her eyes and pressed closer to him. Time had stopped and there was nothing but the two of them and the soft music and the magic of this moment. She could have gone on dancing forever in Rhys's arms. She relaxed and gave herself up to him completely and she began to feel his male hardness pressing against her thighs. She opened her eyes and looked up at him and there was something in his eyes she had never seen there before, an urgency, a wanting, that was a reflection of her own.

When he spoke, his voice was hoarse. He said, "Let's go back to the hotel."

And she could not speak.

When he helped her on with her wrap, his fingers burned her skin. They sat apart in the back of the limousine, afraid to touch. Elizabeth felt as if she were on fire. It seemed to her that it took an eternity for them to reach their suite. She did not think she could wait another moment. As the door closed, they came together in a wonderful wild hunger that swept through both of them. She was in his arms and there was a ferocity in him that she had never known. He picked her up and carried her into the bedroom. They could not get their clothes off quickly enough. We're like eager children, Elizabeth thought, and she wondered why it had taken Rhys all this time. But it did not matter now. Nothing mattered except their nakedness and the wonderful feel of his body against hers. They were in bed, exploring each other, and Elizabeth gently pulled away from his embrace and started kissing him, her tongue moving down his lean, taut body, embracing him with her lips, feeling his velvet hardness inside her mouth. His hands were on her hips, turning her on her side, and his mouth was running down between her thighs, parting them with his tongue and thrusting into the sweetness there, and when neither of them could bear it an instant longer, he moved on top of her and slowly slid inside her, thrusting deep and making gently circling motions and she began to move to his rhythm, their rhythm, the rhythm of the universe, and everything began to move faster and faster, spinning out of control, until there was a vast ecstatic explosion and the earth became still and peaceful again.

They lay there, holding each other close, and Elizabeth thought joyfully, *Mrs. Rhys Williams.*

46

E xcuse me, Mrs. Williams," Henriette's voice said on the inter-com, "there's a Detective Hornung here to see you. He says it's urgent."

Elizabeth turned to look up at Rhys, puzzled. They had just returned from Rio to Zurich the evening before, and they had only been in the office a few minutes. Rhys shrugged. "Tell her to send the man in. Let's find out what's so important."

A few moments later the three of them were seated in Elizabeth's of-fice. "What did you want to see me about?" Elizabeth asked.

Max Hornung had no small talk. He said, "Someone is trying to murder you." As he watched the color drain from Elizabeth's face, Max was genuinely distressed, wondering if there might have been a more tactful way he could have phrased it.

Rhys Williams said, "What the hell are you talking about?"

Max continued to address himself to Elizabeth. "There have already been two attempts on your life. There will probably be more."

Elizabeth stammered, "I—you must be mistaken."

"No, ma'am. That elevator crash was meant to kill you."

She stared at him in silence, her dark eyes filled with bewilderment, and some other emotion buried deeper, that Max could not define. "So was the Jeep."

Elizabeth found her voice again. "You're wrong. That was an accident. There was nothing the matter with the Jeep. The police in Sardinia examined it."

"No."

"I saw them," Elizabeth insisted.

"No, ma'am. You saw them examine *a* Jeep. It wasn't yours."

They were both staring at him now.

Max went on, "Your Jeep was never in that garage. I found it in an auto junkyard at Olbia. The bolt that sealed the master cylinder had been loosened, and the brake fluid had run out. That's why you had no brakes. The left front fender was still bashed in and there were green markings on it from the sap of the trees you ran into. The lab checked it out. It matches."

The nightmare was back. Elizabeth felt it sweep through her, as though the floodgates of her hidden fears had suddenly opened, and she was filled again with the terror of that ride down the mountains.

Rhys was saying, "I don't understand. How could anyone—?"

Max turned to look at Rhys. "All Jeeps look alike. That's what they were counting on. When she crashed instead of going off the mountain, they had to improvise. They couldn't let anyone examine that Jeep because it had to look like an accident. They had expected it to be at the bottom of the sea. They probably would have finished her off there, but a maintenance crew came along, found her and took her to the hospital. They got hold of another Jeep, smashed it up a little and made the switch before the police came."

Rhys said, "You keep saying 'they.'"

"Whoever was behind it had help."

"Who—who would want to kill me?" Elizabeth asked.

"The same person who killed your father."

She had a sudden feeling of unreality, as if none of this was happening. It was all a nightmare that would go away.

"Your father was murdered," Max went on. "He was set up with a phony guide who killed him. Your father didn't go to Chamonix alone. There was someone with him."

When Elizabeth spoke, her voice was a hollow whisper. "Who?"

Max looked at Rhys and said, "Your husband."

The words echoed in her ears. They seemed to come from far away, fading in and out, and she wondered if she was losing her mind.

"Liz," Rhys said, "I wasn't there with Sam when he was killed."

"You were in Chamonix with him, Mr. Williams," Max insisted.

"That's true." Rhys was talking to Elizabeth now. "I left before Sam went on his climb."

She turned to look at him. "Why didn't you tell me?"

He hesitated a moment, then seemed to make a decision. "It's something I couldn't discuss with anyone. For the past year someone has been sabotaging Roffe and Sons. It was done very cleverly so that it seemed to be a series of accidents. But I began to see a pattern. I went to Sam with it, and we decided to hire an outside agency to investigate."

Elizabeth knew then what was coming, and she was simultaneously filled with a deep sense of relief and a feeling of guilt. Rhys had known about the report all along. She should have trusted him enough to tell him about it, instead of keeping her fears to herself.

Rhys turned to Max Hornung. "Sam Roffe got a report that confirmed my suspicions. He asked me to go up to Chamonix to discuss it with him. I went. We decided to keep it just between the two of us until we could find out who was responsible for what was happening." When he continued, there was a note of bitterness in his voice. "Obviously, it wasn't kept quiet enough. Sam was killed because someone knew we were getting on to him. The report is missing."

"I had it," Elizabeth said. Rhys looked at her in surprise. "It was with Sam's personal effects." She said to Max, "The report indicates that it was someone on the board of Roffe and Sons, but they all have stock in the company. Why would they want to destroy it?"

Max explained, "They're not trying to destroy it, Mrs. Williams. They're trying to cause enough trouble to make the banks nervous enough to start calling in their loans. They wanted to force your father to sell the stock and go public. Whoever is behind this hasn't gotten what he wanted yet. Your life is still in danger."

"Then you've got to give her police protection," Rhys demanded.

Max blinked and said tonelessly, "I wouldn't worry about that, Mr. Williams. She hasn't been out of our sight since she married you."

47

BERLIN.

MONDAY, DECEMBER 7.

TEN A.M.

The pain was unbearable and he had lived with it for four weeks.

The doctor had left some pills for him, but Walther Gassner was afraid to take them. He had to stay constantly alert to see that Anna did not try to kill him again, or to escape.

"You should get right to a hospital," the doctor had told him. "You've lost a good deal of blood—"

"No!" That was the last thing Walther wanted. Stab wounds were reported to the police. Walther had sent for the company doctor because he knew he would not report it. Walther could not afford to have the police snooping around. Not now. The doctor had silently stitched up the gaping wound, his eyes filled with curiosity. When he had finished, he had asked, "Would you like me to send a nurse to the house, Mr. Gassner?"

"No. My—my wife will take care of me."

That had been a month ago. Walther had telephoned his secretary and told her that he had had an accident and would be staying home.

He thought about that terrible moment when Anna had tried to kill him with the shears. He had turned just in time to catch the blade in his shoulder instead of through the heart. He had almost fainted from the pain and shock, but he had retained consciousness long enough to drag Anna to her bedroom and lock her in. And all the while she was screaming, "What have you done with the children? What have you done with the children? . . ."

Since then Walther had kept her in the bedroom. He prepared all her meals. He would take a tray up to Anna's room, unlock the door and enter. She would be huddled in a corner, cringing from him and she would whisper, "What have you done with the children?"

Sometimes he would open the bedroom door and find her with her ear pressed against the wall, listening for the sounds of their son and daughter. The house was silent now, except for the two of them. Walther knew there was very little time left. His thoughts were interrupted by a faint noise. He listened. And then he heard it again. *Someone was moving around in the hallway upstairs. There was not supposed to be anyone in the house. He had locked all the doors himself.*

UPSTAIRS, FRAU MENDLER was dusting. She was a dayworker, and this was only her second time in this house. She did not like it. When she had worked here on Wednesday the week before, Herr Gassner had followed her around as though expecting her to steal something. When she had tried to go upstairs to clean, he had angrily stopped her, given her her wages and sent her away. There was something about his manner that frightened her.

Today he was nowhere in sight, *Gott sei Dank.* Frau Mendler had let herself in with the key she had taken the week before, and she had gone upstairs. The house was unnaturally silent, and she decided that no one was at home. She had cleaned one bedroom and had found some loose change lying around, and a gold pillbox. She started down the hallway toward the next bedroom and tried to open the door. It was locked. Strange. She wondered if they kept something valuable inside. She turned the handle again, and a woman's voice from behind the door whispered, "Who is it?"

Frau Mendler jerked her hand away from the knob, startled.

"Who is it? Who's out there?"

"Frau Mendler, the cleaning lady. Do you want me to do your bedroom?"

"You can't. I'm locked in." The voice was louder now, filled with hysteria. "Help me! Please! Call the police. Tell them my husband has killed our children. He's going to kill me. Hurry! Get away from here before he—"

A hand spun Frau Mendler around and she found herself staring up into the face of Herr Gassner. He looked as pale as death.

"What are you sneaking around here for?" he demanded. He was holding her arm, hurting it.

"I—I'm not sneaking," she said. "Today is my day to clean. The agency—"

"I told the agency I didn't want anyone here. I—" He stopped. Had he telephoned the agency? He had meant to, but he was in such pain that he could no longer remember. Frau Mendler looked into his eyes and she was terrified by what she saw there.

"They never told me," she said.

He stood still, listening for sounds from behind the locked door. Silence.

He turned to Frau Mendler. "Get out of here. Don't come back."

She could not leave the house fast enough. He had not paid her, but she had the gold pillbox and the coins she had found on the dresser. She felt sorry for the poor woman behind the door. She wished she could help her, but she could not afford to get involved. She had a police record.

IN ZURICH, DETECTIVE Max Hornung was reading a teletype from Interpol headquarters in Paris.

INVOICE NUMBER ON SNUFF FILM RAW STOCK USED FOR ROFFE AND SONS GENERAL EXECUTIVE ACCOUNT. PURCHASING AGENT NO LONGER WITH COMPANY. TRYING TO TRACE. WILL KEEP YOU INFORMED. END MESSAGE.

· · ·

IN PARIS THE police were fishing a nude body out of the Seine. She was a blonde in her late teens. She wore a red ribbon around her neck.

IN ZURICH, ELIZABETH Williams had been placed under twenty-four-hour police protection.

48

The white light flashed, signaling a call on Rhys's private line. Fewer than half a dozen people had the number. He picked up the telephone. "Hello."

"Good morning, darling." There was no mistaking the husky, distinctive voice.

"You shouldn't be calling me."

She laughed. "You never used to worry about things like that. Don't tell me that Elizabeth has tamed you already."

"What do you want?" Rhys asked.

"I want to see you this afternoon."

"That's impossible."

"Don't make me cross, Rhys. Shall I come to Zurich or—?"

"No. I can't see you here." He hesitated. "I'll come there."

"That's better. Our usual place, *chéri*."

And Hélène Roffe-Martel hung up.

Rhys replaced the receiver slowly and sat thinking. As far as he was concerned, he had had a brief physical affair with an exciting woman, and it had been finished for some time. But Hélène was not a woman who let go easily. She was bored with Charles, and she wanted Rhys. "You and I would make a perfect team," she had said, and Hélène Roffe-Martel could be very determined. And very dangerous. Rhys decided the trip to Paris was necessary. He had to make her understand once and for all that there could be nothing further between them.

A few moments later he walked into Elizabeth's office, and her eyes brightened. She put her arms around him and whispered, "I've been thinking about you. Let's go home and play hooky this afternoon."

He grinned. "You're becoming a sex maniac."

She held him closer. "I know. Isn't it lovely?"

"I'm afraid I have to fly to Paris this afternoon, Liz."

She tried to conceal her disappointment. "Shall I come with you?"

"No point. It's just a minor business problem. I'll be back tonight. We'll have a late supper."

WHEN RHYS WALKED into the familiar small hotel on the Left Bank, Hélène was already there, seated in the dining room, waiting for him. Rhys had never known her to be late. She was organized and efficient, extraordinarily beautiful, intelligent, a wonderful lover; and yet something was missing. Hélène was a woman without compassion. There was a ruthlessness about her, a killer's instinct. Rhys had seen others hurt by it. He had no intention of becoming one of her victims. He sat down at the table.

She said, "You're looking well, darling. Marriage agrees with you. Is Elizabeth taking good care of you in bed?"

He smiled to take the sting out of his words. "That's none of your business."

Hélène leaned forward and took one of his hands. "Ah, but it is, *chéri*. It is *our* business."

She began stroking his hand, and he thought of her in bed. A tiger, wild, skilled and insatiable. He withdrew his hand.

Hélène's eyes dulled. She said, "Tell me, Rhys. How does it feel to be president of Roffe and Sons?"

He had almost forgotten how ambitious she was, how greedy. He remembered the long conversations they had once had. She was obsessed by the idea of taking control of the company. *You and I, Rhys. If Sam were out of the way, we could run it.*

Even in the midst of their lovemaking: *It's my company, darling. Samuel Roffe's blood is in me. It's mine. I want it. Fuck me, Rhys.*

Power was Hélène's aphrodisiac. And danger. "What did you want to see me about?" Rhys asked.

"I think it's time you and I made some plans."

"I don't know what you're talking about."

She said maliciously, "I know you too well, darling. You're as ambitious as I am. Why did you serve as Sam's shadow all those years when you had dozens of offers to run other companies? Because you knew that one day you would be running Roffe and Sons."

"I stayed because I liked Sam."

She grinned. "Of course, *chéri.* And now you've married his charming little daughter." She took a thin black cigar from her purse and lit it with a platinum lighter. "Charles tells me that Elizabeth has arranged to keep control of the stock and that she refuses to sell."

"That's right, Hélène."

"It's occurred to you, of course, that if she had an accident, you would inherit her estate."

Rhys stared at her for a long time.

49

I n his home in Olgiata, Ivo Palazzi was casually looking out the window of his living room when he saw a terrifying sight. Coming up the driveway were Donatella and their three sons. Simonetta was upstairs, taking a nap. Ivo hurried out the front door and went to meet his second family. He was filled with such rage that he could have killed. He had been so wonderful to this woman, so kind, so loving, and now she was deliberately trying to destroy his career, his marriage, his life. He watched Donatella get out of the Lancia Flavia he had so generously given her. Ivo thought she had never looked more beautiful. The boys climbed out of the car, and were hugging and kissing him. Oh, how Ivo loved them. Oh, how he hoped that Simonetta would not wake up from her nap!

"I came to see your wife," Donatella said stiffly. She turned to the boys. "Come on, boys."

"No!" Ivo commanded.

"How are you going to stop me? If I don't see her today, I'll see her tomorrow."

Ivo was cornered. There was no way out. Yet he knew that he could not let her or anyone else ruin everything he had worked so hard for. Ivo thought of himself as a decent man, and he hated what he must do. Not just for himself, but for Simonetta and Donatella and all his children.

"You will have your money," Ivo promised. "Give me five days."

Donatella looked into his eyes. "Five days," she said.

IN LONDON, SIR Alec Nichols was taking part in a floor debate in the House of Commons. He had been chosen to make a major policy speech dealing with the crucial subject of the labor strikes that were crippling the British economy. But it was difficult for him to concentrate. He was thinking about the series of telephone calls he had received over the past few weeks. They had managed to find him wherever he was, at his club, at his barber, restaurants, business meetings. And each time Alec had hung up on them. He knew that what they were asking was only the beginning. Once they controlled him, they would find a way to take over his stock, they would own a piece of a gigantic pharmaceutical company that manufactured drugs of every description. He could not let that happen. They had begun telephoning him four and five times a day until his nerves were stretched to the breaking point. What worried Alec now was that on this day he had *not* heard from them. He had expected a call at breakfast, and then again when he had lunched at White's. But there were no calls and somehow he could not shake off the feeling that the silence was more ominous than the threats. He tried to push these thoughts away now as he addressed the House.

"No man has been a stauncher friend of labor than I. Our labor force is what makes our country great. Workers feed our mills, turn the wheels in our factories. They are the true elite of this country, the backbone that makes England stand tall and strong among nations." He paused. "However, there comes a time in the fortunes of every nation when certain sacrifices must be made . . ."

He spoke by rote. He was wondering whether he had frightened them off by calling their bluff. After all, they were just small-time hoodlums. He was Sir Alec Nichols, Baronet, M.P. What could they do to him? In all probability he would not hear from them again. From now on they would leave him in peace. Sir Alec finished his speech amid vociferous applause from the back benches.

He was on his way out when an attendant came up to him and said, "I have a message for you, Sir Alec."

Alec turned. "Yes?"

"You're to go home as quickly as possible. There has been an accident."

THEY WERE CARRYING Vivian into the ambulance when Alec arrived at the house. The doctor was at her side. Alec slammed the car against the curb and was out running before it had stopped. He took one look at Vivian's white unconscious face and turned to the doctor. "What happened?"

The doctor said helplessly, "I don't know, Sir Alec. I received an anonymous call that there had been an accident. When I got here, I found Lady Nichols on the floor of her bedroom. Her—her kneecaps had been hammered to the floor with spikes."

Alec closed his eyes, fighting off the spasm of nausea that gripped him. He could feel the bile rising in his throat.

"We'll do everything we can, of course, but I think you had better be prepared. It's unlikely that she'll ever walk again."

Alec felt as though he could not breathe. He started toward the ambulance.

"She's under heavy sedation," the doctor said. "I don't think she'll recognize you."

Alec did not even hear him. He climbed into the ambulance and sat in a jump seat, staring down at his wife, obvious to the back doors being closed, the sound of the siren, and the ambulance beginning to move. He took Vivian's cold hands in his. Her eyes opened. "Alec." Her voice was a slurred whisper.

Alec's eyes filled with tears. "Oh, my darling, my darling . . ."

"Two men . . . wore masks . . . they held me down . . . broke my legs. . . . I'll never be able to dance again . . . I'm going to be a cripple, Alec. . . . Will you still want me?"

He buried his head in her shoulder and wept. They were tears of despair and agony, and yet there was something else, something he hardly dared admit to himself. He felt a sense of relief. If Vivian were crippled, he would be able to take care of her, she could never leave him for anyone else.

But Alec knew that this was not over. They were not finished with him. This was only their warning. The only way he would ever get rid of them was to give them what they wanted.

Quickly.

50

t was exactly noon when the call came through the switchboard at the Kriminal Polizei headquarters in Zurich. It was routed through to Chief Inspector Schmied's office, and when the chief inspector had finished talking, he went to find Detective Max Hornung.

"It's all over," he told Max. "The Roffe case has been solved. They've found the killer. Get out to the airport. You've just got time to catch your plane."

Max blinked at him. "Where am I going?"

"To Berlin."

CHIEF INSPECTOR SCHMIED telephoned Elizabeth Williams. "I am calling to bring you some good news," he said. "You will no longer need a bodyguard. The murderer has been caught."

Elizabeth found herself gripping the telephone. At long last she was going to learn the name of her faceless enemy. "Who is it?" she asked.

"Walther Gassner."

. . .

THEY WERE SPEEDING along the autobahn, heading for Wannsee. Max was in the back seat, next to Major Wageman, and two detectives sat in front. They had met Max at Tempelhof Airport, and Major Wageman had briefed Max on the situation as they drove. "The house is surrounded, but we have to be careful how we move in. He's holding his wife hostage."

Max asked, "How did you get on to Walther Gassner?"

"Through you. That's why I thought you would like to be here."

Max was puzzled. "Through me?"

"You told me about the psychiatrist he visited. On a hunch, I sent out Gassner's description to other psychiatrists and found out that he had gone to half a dozen of them, looking for help. Each time he used a different name, then ran away. He knew how ill he was. His wife had phoned us for help a couple of months ago, but when one of our men went out to investigate, she sent him away." They were turning off the autobahn now, only a few minutes from the house. "This morning we received a call from a cleaning woman, a Frau Mendler. She told us she was working at the Gassner house on Monday and that she talked to Mrs. Gassner through the locked door of her bedroom. Mrs. Gassner told her that her husband had killed their two children and was going to kill her."

Max blinked. "This happened on *Monday?* And the woman didn't call you until this morning?"

"Frau Mendler has a long police record. She was afraid to come to us. Last night she told her boyfriend what had happened, and this morning they decided to call us."

They had reached the Wannsee. The car pulled up a block away from the entrance to the Gassner estate, behind an unmarked sedan. A man got out of the sedan and hurried toward Major Wageman and Max. "He's still inside the house, Major. I have men all around the grounds."

"Do you know if the woman is still alive?"

The man hesitated. "No, sir. All the blinds are drawn."

"All right. Let's make it fast and quiet. Get everyone in place. Five minutes."

The man hurried off. Major Wageman reached into the car and pulled out a small walkie-talkie. He began rapidly to issue orders. Max was not listening. He was thinking of something that Major Wageman had said to him a few minutes ago. Something that made no sense. But there was no time to ask him about it now. Men were starting to move toward the house, using trees and shrubs as cover. Major Wageman turned to Max. "Coming, Hornung?"

It seemed to Max that there was an army of men infiltrating the garden. Some of them were supplied with telescopic rifles and armored vests; others carried snubnosed tear gas rifles. The operation was carried out with mathematical precision. At a signal from Captain Wageman, tear gas grenades were simultaneously hurled through the downstairs and upstairs windows of the house and at the same instant the front and rear doors were smashed in by men wearing gas masks. Behind them came more detectives with drawn guns.

When Max and Major Wageman ran through the open front door, the hallway was filled with acrid smoke, but it was rapidly being dispersed by the open windows and doors. Two detectives were bringing Walther Gassner into the hallway in handcuffs. He was wearing a robe and pajamas and he was unshaven and his face looked gaunt and his eyes swollen.

Max stared at him, seeing him for the first time in person. Somehow he seemed unreal to Max. It was the *other* Walther Gassner who was real, the man in the computer, whose life had been spelled out in digits. Which was the shadow and which was the substance?

Major Wageman said, "You're under arrest, Herr Gassner. Where is your wife?"

Walther Gassner said hoarsely, "She's not here. She's gone! I—"

Upstairs there was the sound of a door being forced open, and a moment later a detective called down, "I've found her. She was locked in her room."

The detective appeared on the staircase, supporting a trembling Anna Gassner. Her hair was stringy and her face was streaked and blotchy, and she was sobbing.

"Oh, thank God," she said. "Thank God you've come!"

Gently the detective led her downstairs toward the group standing in the enormous reception hall. When Anna Gassner looked up and saw her husband, she began to scream.

"It's all right, Frau Gassner," Major Wageman said soothingly. "He can't harm you anymore."

"My children," she cried. "He killed my children!"

Max was watching Walther Gassner's face. He was staring at his wife with an expression of utter hopelessness. He looked broken and lifeless.

"Anna," he whispered. "Oh, Anna."

Major Wageman said, "You have the right to remain silent or to ask for a lawyer. For your own sake I hope you will cooperate with us."

Walther was not listening. "Why did you have to call them, Anna?" he pleaded. "Why? Weren't we happy together?"

"The children are dead," Anna Gassner shrieked. "They're dead."

Major Wageman looked at Walther Gassner and asked, "Is that true?"

Walther nodded, and his eyes looked old and defeated. "Yes . . . They're dead."

"Murderer! Murderer!" his wife was shrieking.

Major Wageman said, "We would like you to show us the bodies. Will you do that?"

Walther Gassner was crying now, the tears rolling down his cheeks. He could not speak.

Major Wageman said, "Where are they?"

It was Max who answered. "The children are buried in Saint Paul's graveyard."

Everyone in the room turned to stare at him. "They died at birth five years ago," Max explained.

"Murderer!" Anna Gassner screamed at her husband.

And they turned and saw the madness blazing out of her eyes.

51

ZURICH.

THURSDAY, DECEMBER 10.

EIGHT P.M.

The cold winter night had fallen, snuffing out the brief twilight. It had begun to snow, a soft, windblown powder that dusted the city. In the administration building of Roffe and Sons, the lights of the deserted offices glowed against the darkness like pale yellow moons.

In her office Elizabeth was alone, working late, waiting for Rhys to return from Geneva, where he had gone for a meeting. She wished that he would hurry. Everyone had long since left the building. Elizabeth felt restless, unable to concentrate. She could not get Walther and Anna out of her mind. She remembered Walther as she had first met him, boyish and handsome and madly in love with Anna. Or pretending to be. It was so hard to believe that Walther was responsible for all those terrible acts. Elizabeth's heart went out to Anna. Elizabeth had tried several times to telephone her, but there had been no answer. She would fly to Berlin, to give her whatever comfort she could. The telephone rang, startling her. She picked it up. It was Alec on the other end of the line, and Elizabeth was pleased to hear his voice.

"You've heard about Walther?" Alec asked.

"Yes. It's horrible. I can't believe it."

"Don't, Elizabeth."

She thought she had misunderstood him. "What?"

"Don't believe it. Walther's not guilty."

"The police said—"

"They've made a mistake. Walther was the first person Sam and I checked out. We cleared him. He's not the one we were looking for."

Elizabeth stared at the phone, filled with a sense of confusion. *He's not the one we were looking for.* She said, "I—I don't understand what you're saying."

Alec replied hesitantly, "It's awkward doing this over a telephone, Elizabeth, but I haven't had an opportunity to speak to you alone."

"Speak to me about what?" Elizabeth asked.

"For the past year," Alec said, "someone has been sabotaging the company. There was an explosion in one of our South American factories, patents have been stolen, dangerous drugs have been mislabeled. There isn't time to go into it all now. I went to Sam and suggested that we engage an outside investigating agency to try to find out who was behind it. We agreed not to discuss it with anyone else."

It was as though the earth had suddenly stopped and time was frozen. A dizzying feeling of *déjà vu* swept through Elizabeth. Alec's words were coming through the telephone, but it was Rhys's voice she was hearing. Rhys saying, *Someone has been sabotaging Roffe and Sons. It was done very cleverly, so that it seemed to be a series of accidents. But I began to see a pattern. I went to Sam with it and we decided to hire an outside agency to investigate.*

Alec's voice was going on. "They finished their report and Sam took it with him to Chamonix. We discussed it over the telephone."

Elizabeth could hear Rhys's voice saying, *Sam asked me to come up to Chamonix to discuss it with him. . . . We decided to keep it just between the two of us until we could find out who was responsible for what was happening.*

Elizabeth was suddenly finding it hard to breathe. When she spoke, she tried to make her voice sound normal. "Alec, who—who else knew about the report besides you and Sam?"

"No one. That was the whole point. According to Sam, the report showed that whoever was guilty had to be someone high up in the company."

The highest echelon. And Rhys had not mentioned being in Chamonix until the detective had brought it up.

She asked slowly, the words dragged out of her, "Could Sam have told Rhys about it?"

"No. Why?"

There was only one way Rhys could have known what was in the report. He had stolen it. There was only one reason he could have gone to Chamonix. To kill Sam. Elizabeth did not hear the rest of what Alec was saying. The roaring in her ears drowned out his words. She dropped the receiver, her head spinning, fighting off the horror that was starting to engulf her. Her mind was a series of chaotic, jumbled images. At the time she had had the Jeep accident, she had left a message for Rhys that she would be in Sardinia. The night of the elevator crash, Rhys had not been at the board meeting, but he had appeared later when she and Kate were alone. *Thought I ought to give you a hand.* And soon afterward he had left the building. *Or had he?* Her body was trembling now. It had to be some terrible mistake. Not Rhys. *No!* It was a scream in her mind.

Elizabeth rose from the desk and on unsteady legs walked through the connecting door to Rhys's office. The room was dark. She turned on the lights and stood looking around uncertainly, not sure what she expected to find. She was not searching for evidence of Rhys's guilt, she was looking for evidence of his innocence. It was unbearable to think that the man she loved, the man who had held her in his arms and made love to her, could be a cold-blooded murderer.

There was an engagement book on Rhys's desk. Elizabeth opened it, turning the pages back to September, to the holiday weekend of the Jeep accident. Nairobi was marked on his calendar. She would need to check his passport to see if he had gone there. She started to look through Rhys's desk for the passport, feeling guilty, knowing that somehow there had to be an innocent explanation.

The bottom drawer of Rhys's desk was locked. Elizabeth hesitated. She knew she had no right to break into it. Somehow it was a violation of faith, the crossing of a forbidden boundary, from which there could be no return. Rhys would know that she had done this and she would have to tell him why. And yet Elizabeth had to know. She picked up a letter opener from the desk and broke the lock, splintering the wood.

In the drawer were stacks of notes and memoranda. She lifted them out. There was an envelope addressed to Rhys Williams in a woman's handwriting. It was postmarked a few days earlier, from Paris. Elizabeth hesitated a moment, then opened it. The letter was from Hélène. It began, "*Chéri,* I tried to reach you by phone. It is urgent that we meet again soon to make our plans. . . ." Elizabeth did not finish reading the letter.

She was staring at the stolen report in the drawer.

MR. SAM ROFFE
CONFIDENTIAL
NO COPIES

She felt the room begin to spin and she clutched the edge of the desk for support She stood there forever, eyes closed, waiting for the dizziness to pass. Her killer had a face now. It was the face of her husband.

The silence was broken by the insistent ringing of a distant telephone. It took Elizabeth a long time to realize where the sound was coming from. Slowly she walked back to her office. She picked up the telephone.

It was the attendant in the lobby, his voice cheerful. "Just checkin' that you're still there, Mrs. Williams. Mr. Williams is on his way up to you."

To stage another accident.

Her life was all that stood between Rhys and the control of Roffe and Sons. She could not face him, could not pretend that nothing was wrong. The moment he saw her, he would know. She had to escape. In a blind panic, Elizabeth grabbed her purse and coat and started out of the office. She stopped. She had forgotten something. Her passport! She had to get far away from Rhys, someplace where he could not find her. She hurried back to her desk, found the passport and ran out into the corridor, her heart pounding as though it would burst. The indicator on the private elevator was swinging upward.

Eight . . . nine . . . ten . . .

Elizabeth began racing down the stairs, running for her life.

52

There was a ferryboat that ran between Civitavecchia and Sardinia, carrying passengers and automobiles. Elizabeth drove aboard in a rental car, lost among a dozen other cars. Airports kept records, but the huge boat was anonymous. Elizabeth was one of a hundred passengers crossing over to the island of Sardinia for a holiday. She was sure she could not have been followed, and yet she was filled with an unreasoning fear. Rhys had gone too far to let anything stop him now. She was the only one who could expose him. He would have to get rid of her.

When Elizabeth had fled from the building, she had had no idea where she was going. She knew only that she must get out of Zurich and hide somewhere, that she would not be safe until Rhys was caught. *Sardinia.* It was the first place she thought of. She had rented a small car and had stopped at a phone booth along the auto route to Italy and had tried to call Alec. He was out. She left a message for him to call her in Sardinia. Unable to reach Detective Max Hornung, she left the same message for him.

She would be at the villa in Sardinia. But this time she would not be alone. The police would be there to protect her.

When the ferryboat landed in Olbia, Elizabeth found that it would not be necessary to go to the police. They were waiting for her in the person of Bruno Campagna, the detective she had met with Chief of Police Ferraro. It had been Campagna who had taken her to look at the Jeep following the accident. The detective hurried over to Elizabeth's car and said, "We were beginning to get very worried about you, Mrs. Williams."

Elizabeth looked at him, surprised.

"We received a call from the Swiss police," Campagna explained, "asking us to keep an eye out for you. We've been covering all the boats and airports."

Elizabeth was filled with a feeling of gratitude. Max Hornung! He had gotten her message. Detective Campagna looked at her tired, drawn face. "Would you like me to drive?"

"Please," Elizabeth said gratefully.

She slid over to the passenger seat, and the tall detective got behind the wheel. "Where would you rather wait—the police station or your villa?"

"The villa, if someone could stay with me. I'd—rather not be there alone."

Campagna nodded reassuringly. "Don't worry. We have orders to keep you well guarded. I'll stay there with you tonight, and we'll have a radio car stationed at the driveway leading to your place. No one will be able to get near you."

His confidence was enough to let Elizabeth relax. Detective Campagna drove swiftly and expertly, winding through the little streets of Olbia, heading up the mountain road that led to the Costa Smeralda. Every place they passed reminded her of Rhys.

Elizabeth asked, "Has there been any—any news of my husband?"

Detective Campagna gave her a quick, compassionate glance, then turned his eyes back to the road. "He's on the run, but he won't get far. They expect to have him in custody by morning."

Elizabeth knew that she should feel a sense of relief, and instead the words brought a terrible, aching pain. It was Rhys they were talking about, Rhys who was being hunted like some animal. He had placed her in this terrible nightmare, and now he was caught up in his own nightmare, fighting for his life, as he had made her fight for hers. And how she had trusted him! How she had believed in his kindness and his gentleness and his love! She shuddered. Detective Campagna asked her, "Are you cold?"

"No. I'm fine." She felt feverish. A warm wind seemed to be whistling through the car, setting her nerves on edge. At first she thought it was her imagination until Detective Campagna said, "I'm afraid we're in for a scirocco. It's going to be a busy night."

Elizabeth understood what he meant. The scirocco could drive people and animals crazy. The wind blew in from the Sahara, hot and dry and grainy with sand, with a macabre keening sound that had an eerie, unbalancing effect on the nerves. The crime rate always went up during a scirocco, and the judges treated criminals leniently.

An hour later, out of the dark, the villa loomed ahead of them. Detective Campagna turned into the driveway, drove into the empty carport and turned off the engine. He walked around to the side of the car and opened Elizabeth's door. "I'd like you to stay right behind me, Mrs. Williams," he said. "Just in case."

"All right," Elizabeth replied.

They moved toward the front door of the darkened villa. Detective Campagna said, "I'm sure he's not here but we won't take any chances. May I have your key?"

Elizabeth handed him the key. He gently edged her to one side of the door, inserted the key and opened the door, his other hand hovering near his gun. He reached inside and flicked on the light switch, and the hallway was suddenly flooded with brilliant light.

"I'd like you to show me the house," Detective Campagna said. "Make sure we cover every room. Okay?"

"Yes."

They started walking through the house, and everywhere they went the huge detective turned the lights on. He looked in all the closets and corners and checked to make sure the windows and doors were locked. There was no one else in the house. When they returned to the living room downstairs, Detective Campagna said, "If you don't mind, I'd like to call headquarters."

"Of course," Elizabeth said. She led him into the study.

He picked up the telephone and dialed. A moment later he said, "Detective Campagna. We're at the villa. I'll camp here for the night. You can send a cruiser up to park, at the foot of the driveway." He listened a moment, then said into the phone, "She's fine. Just a little tired. I'll check in later." He replaced the receiver.

Elizabeth sank into a chair. She was feeling tense and nervous, but she knew that it was going to be worse tomorrow. Much worse. She would be safe but Rhys would be either dead or in prison. Somehow, in spite of everything he had done, she could not bear the thought of that.

Detective Campagna was studying her, a look of concern on his face. "I could use a cup of coffee," he said. "How about you?"

She nodded. "I'll make some." She started to rise.

"You stay where you are, Mrs. Williams. My wife says I make the best coffee in the world."

Elizabeth managed a smile. "Thank you." She sank back gratefully. She had not realized how emotionally drained she felt. For the first time now, Elizabeth admitted to herself that even during the telephone conversation with Alec she had felt that there might be some mistake, some explanation, that Rhys must be innocent. Even while she was fleeing, she had held on to the thought that he could not have done all those terrible things, that he could not have killed her father and then made love to her and tried to kill her. It would take a monster to do those things. And so she had kept that tiny ember of hope flickering in her. It had died when Detective Campagna had said, *He's on the run, but he won't get far. They expect to have him in custody by morning.*

She could not bear to think about it anymore, but she could think of nothing else. How long had Rhys been planning to take over the company? Probably from the moment he had met that impressionable fifteen-year-old girl, alone and lonely in a Swiss boarding school. That was when he must have first decided how he was going to outwit Sam—through his daughter. How easy it had been for him. The dinner at Maxim's and the long friendly talks during the years, and the charm—oh, the incredible charm! He had been patient. He had waited until she had become a woman, and the greatest irony of all was that Rhys did not even have to woo her. She had wooed *him*. How he must have laughed at her. He and Hélène. Elizabeth wondered whether they were in it together, and she wondered where Rhys was now, and whether the police would kill him when they caught him. She began to weep uncontrollably.

"Mrs. Williams . . ." Detective Campagna was standing over her, holding out a cup of coffee.

"Drink this," he said "You'll feel better."

"I—I'm sorry," Elizabeth apologized. "I don't usually carry on this way."

He said to her gently, "I think you're doing *molto bene.*"

Elizabeth took a sip of the hot coffee. He had put something in it. She looked up at him, and he grinned. "I decided a shot of Scotch wouldn't do you any harm."

He sat down across from her in a companionable silence. She was grateful for his company. She could never have stayed here alone. Not until she knew what had happened to Rhys, not until she knew whether he was dead or alive. She finished her coffee.

Detective Campagna looked at his watch. "The patrol car should be here any minute. There'll be two men in it on guard duty all night. I'll stay downstairs. I suggest you go up to bed now and try to get some sleep."

Elizabeth shivered. "I couldn't sleep." But even as she said it, her body was filled with an enormous lassitude. The long drive and the tremendous strain she had been under for so long were finally taking their toll.

"Maybe I'll just lie down for a bit," she said. She found it difficult to get the words out.

ELIZABETH LAY IN her bed, fighting against sleep. Somehow it did not seem fair that she should be asleep while Rhys was being hunted. She visualized him being shot down on some cold dark street and she shuddered. She tried to keep her eyes open, but they were heavy weights, and the instant they closed she began to feel herself sinking down, down, into a soft cushion of nothingness.

SOMETIME LATER SHE was awakened by the screams.

53

Elizabeth sat up in bed, her heart beating wildly, not knowing what it was that had awakened her. Then she heard it again. An eerie, high-pitched scream that seemed to come from right outside her window, the sound of someone in the agony of death. Elizabeth arose and stumbled over to the window and looked out into the night. It was a landscape by Daumier, lit by a chill winter moon. The trees were black and stark, their branches whipped by a wild wind. In the distance, far below, the sea was a boiling caldron.

The scream came again. And again. And Elizabeth realized what it was. The singing rocks. The sirocco had risen in intensity and was blowing through them, making that terrible keening sound, over and over. And it became Rhys's voice she was hearing, crying out for her, begging her to help him. She could not stand it. She covered her ears with her hands, but the sound would not go away.

Elizabeth started toward the bedroom door, and she was surprised at how weak she was. Her mind was hazy with exhaustion. She walked out into the hallway and started down the stairs. She felt dazed, as though she had been drugged. She tried to call out to Detective Campagna, but her voice was a hoarse croak. She kept descending the long flight of stairs, fighting to keep her balance. She called aloud, "Detective Campagna."

There was no answer. Elizabeth stumbled into the living room. He was not there. She moved from room to room, holding on to furniture to keep from falling down.

Detective Campagna was not in the house.

She was alone.

ELIZABETH STOOD IN the hallway, her mind confused, trying to force herself to think. The detective had stepped outside to talk to the policemen in the patrol car. Of course that was it. She walked to the front door and opened it and looked outside.

No one was there. Only the black night and the screaming wind. With a growing feeling of fear, Elizabeth turned and made her way back to the study. She would call the police station and find out what had happened. She picked up the telephone, and the line was dead.

It was at that instant that all the lights went out.

n London, at Westminster Hospital, Vivian Nichols regained consciousness as she was being wheeled out of the operating room, down the long bleak corridor. The operation had taken eight hours. In spite of everything the skilled surgeons had been able to do, she would never walk again. She woke in agonizing pain, whispering Alec's name over and over. She needed him, she needed to have him at her side, to have him promise that he would still love her.

The hospital staff was unable to locate Alec.

IN ZURICH, IN the communications room of the Kriminal Polizei, an Interpol message was received from Australia. The former film purchasing agent for Roffe and Sons had been located in Sydney. He had died of a heart attack three days earlier. His ashes were being shipped home. Interpol had been unable to obtain any information regarding the purchase of the film. They were awaiting further instructions.

IN BERLIN, WALTHER Gassner was seated in the discreet waiting room of an exclusive private sanatorium in a pleasant suburb outside the city.

He had been there, motionless for almost ten hours. From time to time a nurse or an attendant would stop by to speak to him and offer him something to eat or drink. Walther paid no attention to them. He was waiting for his Anna.

It would be a long wait.

IN OLGIATA, SIMONETTA Palazzi was listening to a woman's voice on the telephone. "My name is Donatella Spolini," the voice said. "We've never met, Mrs. Palazzi, but we have a great deal in common. I suggest we meet for luncheon at the Bolognese in the Piazza del Popolo. Shall we say one o'clock tomorrow?"

Simonetta had a conflicting appointment at the beauty parlor the next day but she adored mysteries. "I'll be there," she said. "How will I know you?"

"I'll have my three sons with me."

IN HER VILLA in Le Vésinet, Hélène Roffe-Martel was reading a note she had found waiting for her on the mantelpiece in the drawing room. It was from Charles. He had left her, run away. "You will never see me again," the note said. "Don't try to find me." Hélène tore the note into small pieces. She would see him again. She would find him.

IN ROME, MAX Hornung was at Leonardo da Vinci Airport. For the past two hours he had been trying to get a message through to Sardinia, but because of the storm all communications were down. Max went back to the flight operations office to talk to the airport manager again. "You've *got* to get me on a plane to Sardinia," Max said. "Believe me, it's a matter of life and death."

The airport manager said, "I believe you, signore, but there is nothing I can do about it. Sardinia is shut up tight. The airports are closed. Even the boats have stopped running. Nothing is going in or out of that island until the scirocco is over."

"When will that be?" Max asked.

The airport manager turned to study the large weather map on the wall. "It looks like it's good for at least another twelve hours."

Elizabeth Williams would not be alive in twelve hours.

55

The dark was hostile, filled with invisible enemies waiting to strike at her. And Elizabeth realized now that she was completely at their mercy. Detective Campagna had brought her here to be murdered. He was Rhys's man. Elizabeth remembered Max Hornung explaining about switching the Jeeps. *Whoever did it had help. Someone who knew the island.* How convincing Detective Campagna had been. *We've been covering all the boats and airports.* Because Rhys had known she would come here to hide. *Where would you like to wait—at the police station or your villa?* Detective Campagna had had no intention of letting her go to the police. It had not been headquarters he had phoned. It had been Rhys. *We're at the villa.*

Elizabeth knew she had to flee, but she no longer had the strength. She was fighting to keep her eyes open, and her arms and legs felt heavy. She suddenly realized why. He had drugged her coffee. Elizabeth turned and made her way into the dark kitchen. She opened a cabinet and fumbled around until she found what she wanted. She took down a bottle of vinegar and splashed some into a glass with water and forced herself to drink it. Immediately she began to retch into the sink. In a few minutes she felt a little better, but she was still weak. Her brain refused to function. It was as if all the circuits inside her had already closed down, were preparing for the darkness of death.

"No," she told herself fiercely. "You're not going to die like that. You're going to fight. They're going to have to kill you." She raised her voice and said, "Rhys, come and kill me," but her voice was barely a whisper. She turned and headed for the hallway, feeling her way by instinct. She stopped under the portrait of old Samuel, while outside the moaning, alien wind tore against the house, screaming at her, taunting her, warning her. She stood there in the blackness, alone, facing a choice of terrors. She could go outside, into the unknown, and try to escape from Rhys, or she could stay here and try to fight him. But how?

Her mind was trying to tell her something but she was still dazed by the drug. She could not concentrate. Something about an accident.

She remembered then and said aloud, "He has to make it look like an accident."

You must stop him, Elizabeth. Had Samuel spoken? Or was it in her mind?

"I can't. It's too late." Her eyes were closing, and her face was pressed against the coolness of the portrait. It would be so wonderful to go to sleep. But there was something she had to do. She tried to remember what it was, but it kept slipping away.

Don't let it look like an accident. Make it look like murder. Then the company will never belong to him.

Elizabeth knew what she had to do. She walked into the study. She stood there a moment, then reached for a table lamp and hurled it against a mirror. She could hear them both smash. She lifted a small chair and pounded it against the wall until the chair began to splinter. She moved over to the bookcase and began ripping pages out of the books, scattering them around the room. She tore the useless telephone cord out of the wall. Let Rhys explain this to the police, she thought. Do not go gentle into that good night. Well, she would not go gentle. They would have to take her by force.

A sudden gale swept through the room, swirling the papers through the air, then died away. It took Elizabeth a moment to realize what had happened.

She was no longer alone in the house.

. . .

AT LEONARDO DA Vinci Airport, near the *merci* area where freight was handled, Detective Max Hornung was watching a helicopter land. By the time the pilot had his door open Max was at his side. "Can you fly me to Sardinia?" he asked.

The pilot stared at him. "What's going on? I just flew somebody there. There's a bad storm blowing."

"Will you take me?"

"It'll cost you triple."

Max did not even hesitate. He climbed into the helicopter. As they took off, Max turned to the pilot and asked, "Who was the passenger you took to Sardinia?"

"His name was Williams."

THE DARK WAS Elizabeth's ally now, concealing her from her killer. It was too late to get away. She had to try to find a place to hide somewhere in the house. She went upstairs, putting distance between herself and Rhys. At the top of the stairs she hesitated, then turned toward Sam's bedroom. Something leaped at her out of the dark, and she started to scream, but it was only the shadow of a wind-whipped tree through the window. Her heart was pounding so hard that she was sure that Rhys would be able to hear it downstairs.

Delay him, her mind said. *But how?* Her head felt heavy. Everything was fuzzy. Think! she told herself. What would old Samuel have done? She walked to the bedroom at the end of the hall, took the key from the inside and locked the door from the outside. Then she locked the other doors and they were the doors of the gates of the ghetto in Kraków, and Elizabeth was not sure why she was doing it, and then she remembered that she had killed Aram and that they must not catch her. She saw the beam of a flashlight below, starting to move up the stairs, and her heart leaped. Rhys was coming for her. Elizabeth began to climb the tower stairs, and halfway up, her knees began, to buckle. She slid to the floor and crawled the rest of the way on her hands and knees. She reached the top of the stairs and dragged herself upright. She opened the door to the tower room and went in. *The door,* Samuel said. *Lock the door.*

Elizabeth locked the door, but she knew that that would not keep

Rhys out. At least, she thought, he will have to break it down. More violence to explain. Her death was going to look like murder. She pushed furniture against the door, moving slowly, as though the darkness were a heavy sea dragging her down. She pushed a table against the door, then an armchair and another table, working like an automaton, fighting for time, building her pitiable fortress against death. From the floor below she heard a crash and a moment later another and then a third. Rhys was breaking down the bedroom doors, looking for her. Signs of an attack, a trail for the police to follow. She had tricked him, as he had tricked her. Yet something was vaguely bothering her. If Rhys had to make her death look like an accident, why was he breaking down doors? She moved to the French doors and looked outside, listening to the mad wind singing a dirge to her. Beyond the balcony there was a sheer drop to the sea below. There was no escape from this room. This was where Rhys would have to come to get her. Elizabeth felt around for a weapon, but there was nothing that could help her.

She waited in the dark for her killer.

What was Rhys waiting for? Why didn't he break the door down and get it over with? *Break the door down.* Something was wrong. Even if he took her body away from here and disposed of it somewhere else, Rhys would still not be able to explain the violence of the house, the smashed mirror, the broken doors. Elizabeth tried to put herself into Rhys's mind, to figure out what plan he could have that would explain all those things without the police suspecting him of her death. There was only one way.

And even as Elizabeth thought of it, she could smell the smoke.

From the helicopter Max could see the coast of Sardinia, thickly blanketed by a cloud of swirling red dust. The pilot shouted above the din of the rotor blades, "It's gotten worse. I don't know if I can land."

"You've got to!" Max yelled. "Head for Porto Cervo."

The pilot turned to look at Max. "That's at the top of a fucking mountain."

"I know," Max said. "Can you do it?"

"Our chances are about seventy-thirty."

"Which way?"

"Against."

THE SMOKE WAS seeping in under the door, coming up from below through the floorboards, and a new sound had been added to the shrieking of the wind. The roar of flames. Elizabeth knew now, she had the answer, but it was too late to save her life. She was trapped here. Of course it did not matter whether doors and mirrors and furniture had been smashed, because in a few minutes nothing would be left of this house or of her. Everything would be ruined by the fire, as the laboratory and Emil Joeppli had been destroyed, and Rhys would have an alibi in some other place, so that he could not be blamed. He had beaten her. He had beaten them all.

The smoke was beginning to billow into the room now—yellow, acrid fumes that made Elizabeth choke. She could see the edges of flame start to lick at the cracks of the door, and she began to feel the heat.

It was her anger that gave Elizabeth the strength to move.

Through the blinding haze of smoke she felt her way toward the French doors. She pushed them open and stepped onto the balcony. The instant the doors opened, the flames from the hallway leaped into the room, licking at the walls. Elizabeth stood on the balcony, gratefully gulping in deep breaths of fresh air as the wind tore at her clothes. She looked down. The balcony protruded from the side of the building, a tiny island hanging over an abyss. There was no hope, no escape.

Unless . . . Elizabeth looked up at the sloping slate roof above her head. If there was some way for her to reach the roof and get to the other side of the house that was not burning yet, she might get away. She stretched her arms as high as she could, but the eave of the roof was beyond her reach. The flames were beginning to move closer now, enveloping the room. There was one slender chance. Elizabeth took it. She forced herself to go back into the blazing, smoke-filled room, choking from the acrid fumes. She grabbed the chair behind her father's desk and dragged it onto the balcony. Fighting to keep her balance, she positioned the chair and stood on top of it. Her fingers could reach the roof now, but they could not find a grip. She fumbled blindly, vainly, searching to get a purchase.

Inside, the flames had reached the curtains and were dancing all around the room, attacking the books and the carpet and the furniture, moving toward the balcony. Elizabeth's fingers suddenly found a grip on a protruding slate. Her arms were leaden; she was not sure she could hold on. She started to pull herself up, and the chair began to slip away from her. With her last remaining strength she pulled herself up and held on. She was climbing the walls of the ghetto now, fighting for her life. She kept pulling and straining and suddenly she found herself lying on the sloping roof, gasping for breath. She forced herself to move, inching her way upward, pressing her body hard against the steep pitch of the roof, aware that one slip would hurtle her into the black abyss below. She reached the peak of the roof and paused to catch her breath and take her bearings. The balcony she had just escaped from was blazing. There could be no turning back.

Looking down on the far side of the house, Elizabeth could see the balcony of one of the guest bedrooms. There were no flames there yet. But Elizabeth did not know whether she would be able to reach it. The roof slanted sharply downward, the slates were loose, the wind was pulling madly at her. If she slipped, there would be nothing to stop her fall. She stayed where she was, frozen, afraid to try it. And then like a sudden miracle, a figure appeared on the guest balcony, and it was Alec, and he was looking up and calling out calmly, "You can make it, old girl. Nice and easy."

And Elizabeth's heart soared within her.

"Take it slow," Alec counseled. "One step at a time. It's a piece of cake."

And Elizabeth began to let herself move toward him, carefully, sliding down inch by inch, not letting go of one slate until she had found a firm grip on another. It seemed to take forever. And all the while she heard Alec's encouraging voice, urging her on. She was almost there now, sliding toward the balcony. A slate loosened, and she started to fall.

"Hold on!" Alec called.

Elizabeth found another hold, grabbing it fiercely. She had reached the edge of the roof now, with nothing below her but endless space. She would have to drop down onto the balcony where Alec stood waiting. If she missed . . .

Alec was looking up at her, his face filled with quiet confidence. "Don't look down," he said. "Close your eyes, and let yourself go. I'll catch you."

She tried. She took a deep breath, and then another. She knew she had to let go and yet she could not bring herself to do it. Her fingers were frozen to the tiles.

"Now!" Alec called, and Elizabeth let herself drop and she was falling into space, and suddenly she was caught in Alec's arms as he pulled her to safety. She closed her eyes in relief.

"Well done," Alec said.

And she felt the muzzle of the gun against her head.

57

The helicopter pilot was flying as low as he dared over the island, skimming the treetops, trying to avoid the punishing winds. Even at that altitude the air was filled with turbulence. In the distance ahead the pilot saw the mountain peak of Porto Cervo. Max saw it at the same moment. "There it is!" Max shouted. "I can see the villa." And then he saw something else that made his heart jump. "It's on fire!"

ON THE BALCONY Elizabeth heard the sound of the approaching helicopter over the wind, and she looked up. Alec paid no attention. He was watching Elizabeth, his eyes filled with pain. "It was for Vivian. I had to do it for Vivian. You see that, don't you? They have to find you in the fire."

Elizabeth was not listening. She could only think, *It wasn't Rhys. It wasn't Rhys.* All the time it had been Alec. Alec had killed her father and had tried to kill her. He had stolen the report and then tried to frame Rhys with it. He had terrified her into running away from Rhys because Alec had known that she would come here.

The helicopter had disappeared from sight now, beyond some nearby trees.

Alec said, "Close your eyes, Elizabeth."

She said fiercely, "No!"

And Rhys's voice suddenly called, "Drop the gun, Alec!"

They both looked down, and on the lawn below, in the light of the flickering flames, they saw Rhys and Chief of Police Luigi Ferraro and half a dozen detectives, armed with rifles.

"It's finished, Alec," Rhys shouted. "Let her go."

One of the detectives with a telescopic rifle said, "I can't shoot at him unless she moves out of the way."

Move, Rhys prayed. *Move!*

From behind the trees across the lawn Max Hornung came hurrying up to Rhys. He stopped as he saw the tableau above. Rhys said, "I got your message. I was too late."

They were both staring up at the two figures on the balcony, puppets, backlit by the rising flames coming from the far side of the villa. The wind was whipping the house into a gigantic torch, lighting the surrounding mountains, turning the night into an inferno, a blazing Valhalla.

Elizabeth turned and looked into Alec's face, and it was a mask of death, his eyes unseeing. He moved away from her toward the balcony door.

On the ground the detective said, "I've got him," and raised his rifle. He fired once. Alec staggered, then disappeared through the door into the house.

One moment there were two figures on the balcony, and then only one.

Elizabeth screamed, "Rhys!"

But he was already racing toward her.

Everything after that happened in a quick, confused kaleidoscope of motion. Rhys was picking her up and carrying her down to safety and she clung tightly to him and could not hold him close enough.

She was lying on the grass, with her eyes closed, and Rhys was holding her in his arms, saying, "I love you, Liz. I love you, my darling."

She listened to his voice washing over her, caressing her. She could not speak. She looked into his eyes and saw all the love and anguish, and there was so much she wanted to tell him. She was filled with guilt for all of her terrible suspicions. She would spend the rest of her life making it up to him.

She was too weary to think about it now, too weary to think about any of it. It was as though it had all happened to someone else in some other place, at some other time.

The only important thing was that she and Rhys were together. She felt his strong arms holding her close, forever, and it was enough.

58

I t was like stepping into a blazing corner of hell. The smoke was getting thicker, filling the room with dancing chimeras that kept vanishing. The fire leaped down at Alec, fondling his hair, and the crackle of the flames became Vivian's voice calling to him in an irresistible siren song.

In a sudden flare of brightness, he saw her. She was stretched out on the bed, her beautiful body naked except for the scarlet ribbon tied around her neck, the same red ribbon she had worn the first time he had made love to her. She called his name again, her voice filled with longing. And this time she wanted *him,* not the others. He moved closer, and she whispered, "You're the only one I ever loved."

And Alec believed it. He had had to punish her because of the things she had done. But he had been clever—he had made those others pay for her sins. The terrible things he had done had been for her. As he moved toward her, Vivian whispered again, "You're the only one I ever loved, Alec," and he knew that it was true.

She was holding out her beckoning arms to him, and he sank down beside her. He embraced her, and they became one. He was inside her, and he *was* her. And this time he was able to satisfy her. And he felt such pleasure that it became an exquisite pain beyond bearing. He could feel the heat from her body consuming him, and even as he watched in wonder, the ribbon around Vivian's neck turned into a vivid tongue of flame caressing him, licking at him. In the next instant, a blazing beam from the ceiling crashed on top of him in a fiery pyre.

Alec died as the others had. In ecstasy.